D0019621

Peru

Carolina A Miranda

Aimée Dowl, Katy Shorthouse, Luke Waterson

Beth Williams

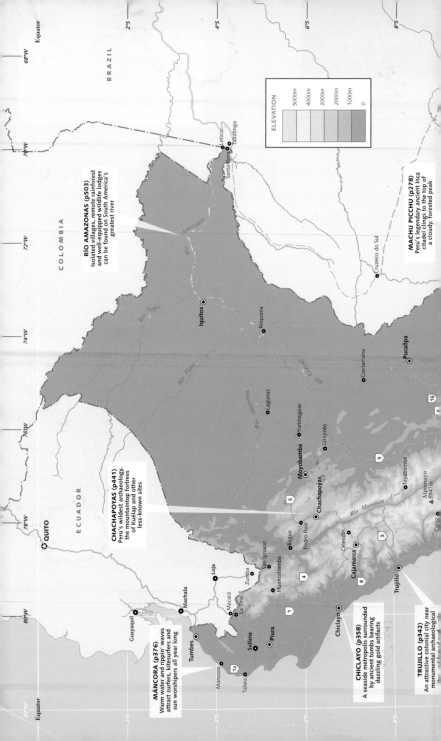

Equator

68°W

BRAZIL

70°W

Leticia

Tabatinga

2°S

RÍO AMAZONAS (p503)
Isolated villages, remote rainforest and well-equipped wildlife lodges can be found on South America's greatest river

COLOMBIA

72°W

Santa Rosa

Río Amazonas

4°S

MACHU PICCHU (p278)
Peru's legendary ancient Inca citadel clings to the top of a cloudy, forested peak

Cruzeiro do Sul

74°W

Río Napo

Iquitos

Requena

6°S

ELEVATION

5000m
4000m
3000m
2000m
1000m
0

Pucallpa

Contamana

76°W

Río Tigre

Río Ucayali

8°S

Río Marañón

Río Huallaga

Lagunas

CHACHAPOYAS (p441)
Peru's wildest archaeology, the mountaintop fortress of Kuélap and other less-known sites

Yurimaguas

Moyobamba

Tarapoto

78°W

QUITO

ECUADOR

Loja

5

Chachapoyas

Tayabamba

Alpamayo
▲5947m

Bagua

Pedro Ruiz

San Ignacio

Huancabamba

Zumba

Macará

La Tina

80°W

Machala

Guayaquil

4

1

Celendín

Cajamarca

Río Marañón

3

8

Trujillo

Caraz

16

5

TRUJILLO (p342)
An attractive colonial city near monumental archaeological

MÁNCORA (p376)
Warm water and rippin' waves attract surfers, kitesurfers and sun worshipers all year long

Tumbes

Máncora

Talara

1a

Sullana

Piura

Chiclayo

82°W

CHICLAYO (p358)
A seaside metropolis surrounded by ancient tombs bearing dazzling gold artifacts

Equator

2°S

4°S

6°S

8°S

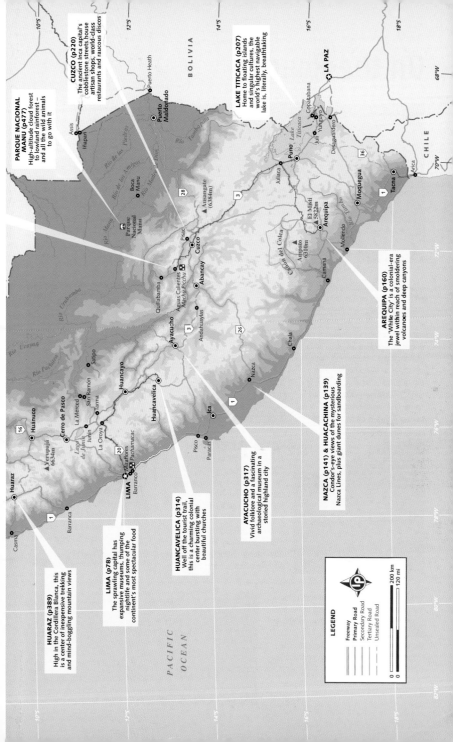

PARQUE NACIONAL
MANU (p477)
High-altitude cloud forest –
to lowland rainforest –
and all the wild animals
to go with it

CUZCO (p220)
The ancient Inca capital's
cobblestone streets house
artisan shops, world-class
restaurants and raucous discos

LAKE TITICACA (p207)
Home to floating islands
and singular cultures, the
world's highest navigable
lake is, literally, breathtaking

AREQUIPA (p160)
The 'White City' is a colonial-era
jewel within reach of smoldering
volcanoes and deep canyons

NAZCA (p141) & HUACACHINA (p139)
Condor's-eye views of the mysterious
Nazca Lines, plus giant dunes for sandboarding

AYACUCHO (p317)
Vivid folklore and a fascinating
archaeological museum in a
storied highland city

HUANCAVELICA (p314)
Well off the tourist trail,
this is a charming colonial
center bursting with
beautiful churches

LIMA (p78)
The sprawling capital has
expansive museums, thumping
nightlife and some of the
continent's most spectacular food

HUARAZ (p389)
High in the Cordillera Blanca, this
is a center of inexpensive trekking
and mind-boggling mountain views

LEGEND

Freeway
Primary Road
Secondary Road
Tertiary Road
Unsealed Road

0   200 km
0   120 mi

On the Road

CAROLINA A MIRANDA
Coordinating Author

On this assignment, I literally ate my way through Lima. This gobble-fest was with a friend at a popular *chifa* (Chinese restaurant) in Barranco (p115). After carbo-loading on wontons, langostino fried rice and steamy piles of noodles, we were ready to destroy our livers at the neighborhood's many – and I mean *many* – bars.

AIMÉE DOWL Southern Peru's archaeological riches get top billing, but northern Peru's mysterious ruins – mist-shrouded temples, haunting hilltop sarcophagi and mummies, mummies everywhere! turned on the amateur archaeologist in me. My guide at Chavín de Huántar (p422) explained details about spine-chilling carvings that brought this ancient world to life.

KATY SHORTHOUSE Some bears and me in a village between Cuzco and Puno (p288). My intrepid traveling companion Steve Wilson and I hit the area as the sun went down, stumbling straight into a huge fiesta. The only gringos for miles around, we ended up with places of honor at the postparade festivities.

BETH WILLIAMS That claw protruding from the bottom of this photo belongs to the enormous *chupe de camarones* (shrimp chowder) I devoured after a trek in the Cañón del Colca (p187). It was well earned after a night spent in a leaky thatched hut at the base of the canyon – and they said rainy season was over!

LUKE WATERSON I'd been stranded for two days in the remote town of Pevas (p507), located on an Amazon tributary. No boats were headed back to civilization, so I hitched a lift on this raft. The 'captain' intended to sail on it all the way to the Atlantic Ocean!

For full author biographies see p560.

BEST OF PERU

Clinging to the Andes, between the parched coastal desert and the drippy expanse of the Amazon rainforest, Peru offers such a wide range of experiences that it can be difficult to choose between them. Solemn pilgrimages honor gods both Christian and indigenous. Neon-lit discos get jam-packed with reveling youth. Ancient ruins regularly divulge bits of prehistory. And then, of course, there is the food – a bounty of sublime concoctions made from ingredients native and contemporary. Welcome to Peru – it's going to be one tasty trip.

RICHARD I'ANSON

Essential Peru

There's north, there's south, desert and jungle. There are museums to visit, lakes to ogle, waves to surf, labyrinthine cities to explore – and enough ancient ruins to keep archaeologists employed for centuries. Where to start? This is our guide to a few essentials.

1 Lake Titicaca

Less a lake than a highland ocean, the Titicaca area is home to fantastical sights: floating islands made of totora reeds (p207), pre-Columbian funerary towers (p206) and fertility temples full of stone phalluses (p212). Far out.

2 Parque Nacional Manu

Covering an area the size of Wales, this vast Amazon reserve (p474) protects cloud forest and rainforest ecosystems – making for maximum wildlife-spotting. Not to be missed: the clay licks that draw hundreds of squawking macaws.

3 Monasterio de Santa Catalina

The eternally graceful city of Arequipa is home to this dazzling, citadel-sized monastery (p164), which dates back to the 16th century. It even has its own cafe, serving pastries and espresso.

4 Lima Nightlife

Tourism in Peru is devoted to the past, but Lima is all about the present. Here, discos spin international beats (p117), lounges serve frothy fusion cocktails (p115) and restaurants draw late-night crowds with a bevy of inventive dishes (p109).

5 Máncora

This internationally famous surf spot (p376) has something for everyone – even folks who don't hang ten. There's horse riding, hot springs and beach combing to fill the days, while street parties and beachside bonfires light up the nights.

6 Nazca Lines

The meaning behind these mysterious glyphs (p142) continues to elude scholars. Not that it matters. Their magnificence and breathtaking scale – which can only be appreciated from the air – make them a wonder to behold.

7 Kuélap

Archaeology buffs refer to the Chachapoyas people's mountaintop fortress (p448) as the 'other Machu Picchu,' but its unique stonework and proud position overlooking the Utcubamba valley make it a special – and incomparable – place to visit.

8 The Streets of Cuzco

Once the capital of the Inca empire, tourist-thronged Cuzco (p220) – the gateway to the mountaintop refuge of Machu Picchu (p267) – is lined with extraordinary cobblestone passageways and indigenous structures that have been inhabited continuously since pre-Hispanic times.

Natural Wonders

Get ready to send your vision into overdrive. Peru is home to snow-capped mountains, giant sand dunes, flocks of brightly hued tropical birds, postcard-perfect volcanoes and rocky Pacific outcroppings inhabited by argumentative sea lions. Here's a rundown of some of the most extraordinary.

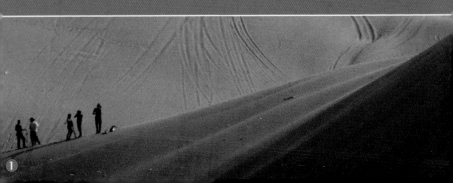

❶ Huacachina

Towering, undulating dunes the size of small office towers hug the coastal desert oasis of Huacachina (p139). The craziest part? You can strap on a board and glide down the face of these monstrous, sandy waves.

❷ El Misti

The snow-covered, pointy-peaked volcano that presides over Arequipa, El Misti (p169) can give Japan's Mt Fuji a run for its money when it comes to perfect form. It was venerated by the Incas, who sacrificed humans at its summit.

❸ Islas Ballestas

Off Peru's arid southern shore, these rocky islands (p130) are home to colonies of sea lions, masses of endangered Humboldt penguins and lots and lots of boobies – brown boobies, that is.

❹ Amazon Wildlife

Gaggles of cackling macaws, slinky jaguars, languid sloths, mighty anacondas, army ants and iridescent morpho butterflies – the Amazon is home to an astonishing array of extraordinary fauna. See prime examples at the Reserva Nacional Pacaya-Samiria (p493).

❺ Puya Raimondii

If Dr Seuss designed a plant, this would be it: a 10m-tall behemoth (p72) that takes a century to burst into thousands of lily-white flowers, only to die shortly thereafter. Find forests of these in the central highlands (p326) and near Huaraz (p418).

❻ Cordillera Blanca

Camping in these high-altitude valleys (p404) can make for the coldest nights of your life, but your first step into daylight is rewarded with soul-warming views of the jagged spine of glaciated peaks against an impossibly blue sky.

❼ Marvelous Spatuletail Hummingbird

Few birds can compete with this species' extravagantly plumed male (p452), now much easier to see thanks to conservation efforts in the highlands. He's a small bird, but with a tail like that, he might as well be king of the jungle.

❽ Puerto Pizarro

The sound of nothing but a crocodile moving through dark water adds to the magic of these ghostly endangered mangroves (p386). Visit this eerie world of swamp-rooted trees at dusk, when thousands of seabirds come home to roost.

Culture & Tradition

This is a country where practices run deep – 5000 years, to be exact. Yet, it is a place continuously energized by fresh influences. In Peru, you can groove to African beats, attend solemn Catholic processions and examine indigenous textiles inspired by pre-Columbian tradition. Take your pick.

① Arts & Crafts

Regal ceramics, detailed dioramas, elaborate reproductions of Cuzco School paintings and handwoven indigenous textiles with intricate designs are evidence of Peru's artful soul. Find the best in Lima (p118), Ayacucho (p324), Huancayo (p312) and Cuzco (p252).

② Inti Raymi

An annual ceremony in honor of the Inca sun god, Inti Raymi (p240) was prohibited by the Spanish for centuries. Visitors to Cuzco, however, can see an interpretation of this pomp-filled ceremony (sans animal sacrifice) every June.

③ Lima

Narrow streets cluttered with baroque churches. Rambling colonial structures clad with elaborate balconies. Atmospheric eateries and museums stuffed with pre-Columbian treasures. The web of streets (p87) laid out by Francisco Pizarro in 1532 are still full of life.

④ Verano Negro

Celebrating Afro-Peruvian culture, this festival in the district of El Carmen in Chincha (p128) features food, music and lots of dance – much of it set to the distinct thump of the *cajón*, a wooden box used as a drum.

⑤ Holy Week in Ayacucho

Catholic rites in Peru don't get more extravagant or brilliantly illuminated than in the central-highland settlement of Ayacucho (p321), where parades and processions mark the week before Easter.

⑥ Asháninka Culture

An Amazon tribe known for fiercely resisting acculturation (even from Sendero Luminoso's terrorists) and for their delicate, geometric textiles, the Asháninka people welcome visitors to villages outside of Puerto Bermúdez (p484).

CAROLINA MIRANDA

Taste of Peru

To begin to savor the vast selection of delicacies could take weeks – even months. Every little bend in the Andes produces a divine local dish, featuring everything from rare strains of potato to guinea pig to succulent ocean mollusks. Here's our list of the flavors not to miss.

❶ Causas

Potato dishes come in all manner of scrumptious forms in Peru, but none as sculptural as these incredible potato salads (p58), constructed in a rainbow of colors and stuffed full of vegetables, seafood and chicken.

❷ Cuy

The Andes' most famous contribution to the world of animal protein: the guinea pig. Small, flavorful, with just the right amount of fatty crispness. Cuzco (p246) is the spot to nibble on these.

❸ Pisco Sour

The national cocktail (p60), crafted from the local grape brandy with fresh lime juice, sugar and a splash of bitters, is lip-smackingly good. They taste innocuous but pack a punch.

❹ Ceviche

Fish or seafood marinated in lime juice, with onion, chilies and a dash of cilantro – it is divinely delicious. The best place to taste this lunchtime staple is Lima (p109), whose busy port assures fresh treats plucked straight from the sea.

Contents

Regional Map Contents

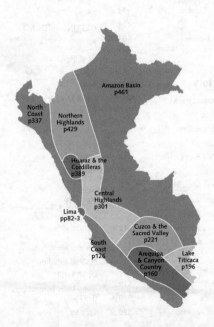

North Coast
p337

Northern
Highlands
p429

Amazon Basin
p461

Huaraz & the
Cordilleras
p389

Central
Highlands
p301

Lima
pp82-3

Cuzco & the
Sacred Valley
p221

South
Coast
p126

Arequipa
& Canyon
Country
p160

Lake
Titicaca
p196

Destination Peru

For a country born of a tumultuous history, Peru has its moments of incredible grace. There is the award-winning literature, the baroque-style architecture, the soulful music and, of course, the food – a sublime combination of ethnic and regional specialties that have spent the last 500 years on a slow simmer and are now ready to be served. Peru, in case you haven't heard, is in the midst of a buzzing culinary renaissance.

Led by a charismatic young chef named Gastón Acurio, the country's native cuisine is the subject of write-ups in international food magazines. Once regarded as a charmless capital city, Lima is now a bastion of excellent dining. And Peruvian gastronomic festivals – once the purview of a few dedicated food-service types – attract tens of thousands of visitors. La Mistura, a culinary gathering organized by Acurio, drew more than 150,000 people from all over Peru and the world to its second annual convocation in Lima in September of 2009. Thousands more were unable to get in.

The relentless focus on food – and it is *relentless* – has not only generated a great deal of pride among every layer of Peruvian society, it has had a ripple effect on other aspects of the culture. Young fashion designers produce avant-garde clothing lines with alpaca knits. Cutting-edge musical groups fuse elements of regional folk music into mainstream electronica. In the world of architecture, builders are starting to create contemporary structures that pay tribute to pre-Columbian design. In other words, Peru is experiencing a remarkable cultural boom.

The country has also experienced a period of unparalleled economic expansion, linked to significant growth in the mining and agricultural sectors. Since 2004, Peru's gross domestic product has grown steadily, year after year – even in 2008 and 2009, when the global economy was shrinking. The influx of wealth has helped alleviate some of the most extreme cases of poverty and has allowed the administration to improve infrastructure and expand social services. By 2011, the government expects to complete a US$1 billion electrification project, which will improve energy delivery to the southern part of Peru.

This represents an incredible turnaround for a nation that was torn apart by a period of protracted internal conflict between the military and various guerrilla groups in the 1980s and '90s – an episode that left thousands of civilians dead and countless others displaced. Peru has yet to completely emerge from the shadow of that era. For two years beginning in 2007, the nation was riveted by the legal trials of former President Alberto Fujimori.

Elected in 1990, in the midst of the conflict, Fujimori, the Lima-born son of Japanese immigrants, cracked down on guerrilla groups, but also tightened his grip on power. Among other things, he staged a coup that filled the legislature with his cronies, reworked the constitution and ran all manner of shady financial and political operations while in office. His presidency ended in 2001, when his security chief was caught on camera bribing just about any official willing to accept a suitcase full of money. The disgraced former president is now serving almost three decades of prison terms for an array of convictions, ranging from embezzlement to bribery to wiretapping to the ordering of extrajudicial killings. But that isn't the end of Fujimori. It is widely expected that his daughter, Keiko, a congresswomen, will run for the presidency in 2011. She has hinted that if she wins, she will pardon her father.

Peru faces other challenges as well. A prolonged global recession could put a quick end to this period of growth. (Economic figures already

FAST FACTS

Population: 28.2 million

Median age: 26 years

Poverty rate: 54%

Gross Domestic Product (GDP): US$131.4 billion

Estimated hectares of coca production: 56,000

Rate of inflation: 5.8%

Navigable tributaries in the Amazon Basin: 8600km

Average daily visitors to Machu Picchu: 2500

Loss of forest area in 2005: 150,000 hectares

Native varieties of potato: almost 4000

indicated a slow-down in the export market by the end of 2009 and inflation tripled – to 6% – from 2008 to 2009.) Equally fragile is the political situation. President Alan García, who served a disastrous first term as president in the '80s (see p42), has seen his approval rating steadily sink since he took office in 2006. In 2008, his entire cabinet was forced to resign due to allegations of corruption. And, in 2009, a clash between various indigenous tribes and the national police – over development rights to extensive tracts of rainforest lands – left almost three dozen dead in the remote northern region of Bagua.

These events have left the president with a weakened mandate at a potentially fractious time. Members of the Sendero Luminoso (Shining Path) guerrillas have shown renewed (if limited) signs of life in the central highlands around Ayacucho. In the Amazon, the imminent opening of the Interoceanic Highway, connecting Peru to Brazil and running straight through the southern Amazon, could have a negative impact on delicate rainforest ecosystems. And there is still plenty of poverty to contend with: despite the years of growth, one in five Peruvians still lives on less than US$2 a day.

To some, the country's problems might seem insurmountable. But living in Peru – and being Peruvian – has always required just a little bit of defiance. In the 1950s, Peruvian journalist Jorge Donayre Belaúnde penned a lengthy poem to his homeland called '*Viva el Perú...¡Carajo!*' (Long Live Peru...Damn It!). The verse is an epic, warts-and-all tribute to Peru, depicting life in Andean villages as well as sprawling urban shantytowns. Peruvians, wrote Donayre, aren't scared off by difficult circumstances – not by cataclysmic earthquakes, nor difficult geography, nor the bad habits of their wily politicians. In the face of adversity, there is an intractable optimism. In the 50-plus years since Donayre first wrote those words, that hasn't changed one bit.

Viva el Perú...¡Carajo!

Getting Started

Luminous archaeological sites? Check. Lush Amazon rainforest? Check. An arid coast lapped by a highly surfable Pacific swell? Check.

Peru, it seems, has it all. Every cranny of this part of the Andes offers a unique glimpse into singular cultures, incredible foods and enough natural wonders to keep a *National Geographic* cameraman employed for decades.

Visit for a week and you can take in a main site or two. Got two? Then join a trekking party, or add another destination to your itinerary. And if you have plenty of time on your hands, strap on a pack and hit the road for months – there's that much to do. Best of all, transportation is plentiful and generally inexpensive, and accommodations are available to suit every budget, from cheap backpacker hostels to atmospheric colonial mansions.

This chapter will help you figure out when to go, what to pack, how much to spend and which places you won't want to miss.

WHEN TO GO

Peru's climate has two main seasons – wet and dry – though the weather varies greatly depending on the region. Temperature is mostly influenced by elevation: the higher you climb, the cooler it becomes.

The peak tourist season is from June to August, which coincides with the cooler dry season in the Andean highlands and summer vacation in North America and Europe. This is the best (and busiest) time to go trekking – on the Inca Trail to Machu Picchu, or anywhere else. It's also the best time for climbing, hiking and mountain biking.

People can and do visit the highlands year-round, though the wettest months of December to March make this a cold and muddy proposition. Plus, during February the Inca Trail is closed for cleanup. Many of the major fiestas (see p517), such as La Virgen de la Candelaria, Carnaval and

A Peruvian weather site (in Spanish) is www .senamhi.gob.pe.

DON'T LEAVE HOME WITHOUT...

- A passport valid for six months beyond your trip and, if necessary, a visa (p526).
- All recommended immunizations (p544) – make sure any prior vaccinations are up-to-date before setting off.
- A copy of your travel insurance policy (p520).
- An ATM or traveler's-check card with a four-digit PIN (p521).
- Reservations for trekking the Inca Trail (p283) or, better yet, an alternative route (see boxed text, p285).
- A lightweight, wind-resistant waterproof jacket to shield you from the sun and keep you dry.
- Earplugs – long-distance buses and many hotels enjoy ear-splitting entertainment at all hours.
- A Swiss Army–style knife – remember to place it in your checked luggage when flying or it will be confiscated.
- Duct tape – make a mini-roll around a pencil, then use it to repair backpacks, seal shut leaky bottles etc.
- Toilet paper – essential as public toilets (p525) and most restaurants don't supply it.
- Your sense of adventure.

See Climate Charts (p513) for more information.

Semana Santa, occur in the wettest months and continue undiminished even during heavy rainstorms.

On the arid coast, Peruvians visit the beaches during summer, from December through March, when the Pacific's chilly waters warm up. In central and southern Peru, the coast is cloaked in *garúa* (coastal fog) for much of the rest of the year and temperatures are cool. As a result, southern beaches tend to be deserted during this period. In the far north, the coast usually sees more sun (and the water is warmer), so beach lovers can be found there year-round.

In the eastern rainforest, of course, it rains – a lot. The wettest months are December through May. And while it is still possible to travel through the Amazon at this time, it will be slow going, and wildlife-viewing opportunities will be reduced. The best times to go are the drier months of July and August, followed by September, October and November.

COSTS & MONEY

HOW MUCH?

Local phone call S1.50

Internet café per hour S1-2

Short taxi ride (not in Lima)S3

Double room with bathroom and TV S100

Round-trip flight between most cities from US$150

See also the Lonely Planet Index, inside front cover.

Shoestring travelers watching their *céntimos* – by sleeping in dormitory rooms, traveling on economy buses, eating set menus – can get by on a minimum of US$25 a day. Visitors who prefer private hot showers, à la carte meals in moderately priced restaurants, comfortable buses and occasional flights will find that at least US$60 to US$100 a day should meet their needs. Staying at luxury hotels and dining at top-end restaurants will cost several hundred dollars a day. Prices are always higher if you're doing your trip by organized tour (see p534). The most expensive cities are Cuzco and Lima.

You can stretch your budget by traveling with a partner as double rooms are usually less expensive than two singles (see p508). Hone your bargaining skills – taxi cabs don't have meters, and drivers routinely overcharge gringos. Hotels often give discounts if you simply ask for their 'best price' (*el mejor precio*) or if you inquire about promotional rates. For top-end places, check the website for special offers.

Many restaurants offer filling three-course set lunches for around S7; eating à la carte will triple your bill. Pay with cash rather than credit cards, in order to avoid hefty surcharges. Many Peruvian ATMs dispense local currency (*nuevos soles*) and US dollars. Above all, keep your money safely stashed – an economical trip can get expensive if you're pickpocketed! For tips on avoiding theft, see p514.

Note to adventurers on a tight budget: hiking the Inca Trail to Machu Picchu is expensive. Unguided trips are now illegal (this is strictly enforced) and the cheapest four-day trips start at around US$300 per person, not including equipment rental, tips for the guides and porters, or any incidental expenses, such as bottled water. Plan on spending US$400 if you're going with a reputable outfitter, p286. A day trip to Machu Picchu isn't always cheap either (see p255).

For exchange rates, see the inside front cover of this book. For more information on money issues, see p521.

TRAVEL LITERATURE

Inca Land: Explorations in the Highlands of Peru, by Hiram Bingham, is the classic traveler's tale. The book was first published in 1922, a little more than a decade after the American author 'discovered' the ancient Inca citadel of Machu Picchu.

The White Rock: An Exploration of the Inca Heartland, by Hugh Thomson, describes a filmmaker's search for hidden archaeological sites throughout the Peruvian Andes and Bolivia. It includes a lot of background on earlier travelers and explorers.

TOP PICKS

THE BEST FIESTAS

Hallowed religious processions and resuscitated Inca ceremonies – Peru's hallucinatory festivals go off year-round (see p517 for the full list). Our favorites:

- Virgen de la Candelaria (February 2) – Puno's festive, multi-day tribute to the Virgin offers plenty of highland music and dance (p198)

- Carnaval (before the start of Lent) – elaborate costumes and crazy water fights are at their most boisterous in Cajamarca (see boxed text, p433)

- Semana Santa (Holy Week) – an important event around the country, but no town beats Ayacucho for its spectacular religious processions (p321)

- Q'oyoriti (May/June) – a Christian pilgrimage with animist overtones held on a chilly mountain in the Cuzco region (see boxed text, p295)

- Inti Raymi (June 24) – Cuzco's 'Festival of the Sun' is a tradition with Inca roots (p240)

- Fiestas Patrias (July 28–29) – Peru's National Independence Days can be enjoyed anywhere and everywhere (p517)

- Feast of Santa Rosa de Lima (August 30) – the continent's first saint is heralded around the country, but colorful processions abound in Lima (p103)

- El Señor de los Milagros (October 18) – all the pomp and circumstance of a religious procession with everyone and everything decked out in purple (p103)

FOR A RAGING ADRENALINE RUSH

From Andean highlands to Amazon rainforests to arid coastal deserts, Peru is an all-seasons playground. You will find the complete guide to outdoor activities on p173 and a directory of the top parks and wilderness areas in the boxed text, p74. Try these for some of the most thrilling activities:

- Scale Peru's highest peak Huascarán, which stands at a gasping 6768m, outside Huaraz (p404)

- Sandboard the colossal, high-altitude sand dunes on the south coast at Huacachina (p140)

- Trek into the craggy Cordilleras – Blanca and Huayhuash – where you'll travel through remote indigenous villages and alongside glistening Andean glaciers (p401)

- Run the rapids on the Río Tambopata on a 10- to 12-day trip, which plunges from the Andes straight into Amazon rainforest (p235)

- Surf legendary waves, including one of the world's longest left-hand breaks, on Peru's north coast (p381)

- Trek two of the world's deepest canyons, the Cañóns del Colca and Cotahuasi, near Arequipa (p169)

PERU, THE SURREAL

Seen it? Done it? Been there? Not in Peru, you haven't. A very necessary guide to the country's most unusual experiences:

- Eat dirt in Sillustani, literally (p206)

- Admire the skulls of revered saints at a storied colonial church in Lima (p90)

- Visit an art gallery…in the middle of the Amazon (p507)

- Dine on tasty felines in the mountain town of Huari (see boxed text, p425)

- Gaze upon an Inca maiden – in a freezer – at the Museo Santury in Arequipa (p165)

- Have a shaman cure what ails you in Huancabamba, on Peru's north coast (see boxed text, p374)

- Sashay into a neon-lit, fish-tank-encrusted *Miami Vice*–style dance club in the ancient Inca capital of Cuzco (p251)

- See ancient whistling pots in a well-known archaeological museum…that resides in the basement of a gas station in Trujillo (p345)

At Play in the Fields of the Lord, by Peter Matthiessen, is a classic, superb and true-to-life novel about the conflicts between the forces of 'development' and indigenous peoples in the Amazon jungle.

Trail of Feathers: In Search of the Birdmen of Peru, by Tahir Shah, is an amusing tall tale about what lies behind the 'birdmen' legends of the Peruvian desert, eventually leading the author to a tribe of cannibals in the Amazon.

Cut Stones and Crossroads: A Journey in the Two Worlds of Peru, by Ronald Wright, is a comprehensive journey through some of Peru's ancient cities and archaeological sites, and it comes with helpful guides to Quechua terminology and traditional Andean music.

Eight Feet in the Andes: Travels with a Donkey from Ecuador to Cuzco, by Dervla Murphy, is an insightful, witty travelogue of this peripatetic travel writer's 2000km journey with her daughter through remote regions, ending at Machu Picchu.

INTERNET RESOURCES

For many more websites targeted to specific topics, such as volunteering in Peru or gay and lesbian travel, thumb through the Directory at the back of this book, starting p508.

Andean Travel Web (www.andeantravelweb.com/peru) Independent travel directory with loads of links to hotels, tour companies, volunteer programs etc.

Expat Peru (expatperu.com) Helpful site that details important government and other resources; has a complete listing of immigration offices and customs regulations.

Latin America Network Information Center (www.lanic.utexas.edu) The University of Texas provides hundreds of informative links on all subjects.

Living in Peru (www.livinginperu.com) This English-speaking expats' guide is an excellent source of Lima-centric news; the site has a handy events calendar.

Peru Links (www.perulinks.com) Thousands of links on a range of topics; many are in Spanish, some in English. Editor's picks and top 10 sites are always good.

Peruvian Times (www.peruviantimes.com) The latest news, in English.

PromPerú (www.peru.info) The official government tourism agency, with a good overview of Peru in Spanish, English, French, German, Italian and Portuguese.

The Peru Guide (theperuguide.com) A broad travel overview to the country.

Itineraries
CLASSIC ROUTES

THE GRINGO TRAIL
Two to Four Weeks / Lima to Cuzco

Leaving **Lima** (p78), journey south to **Pisco** and **Paracas** (p129), where you can catch a boat tour to the wildlife-rich **Islas Ballestas** (p130). Then it's on to **Ica** (p136), Peru's wine and pisco (grape brandy) capital, and the palm-fringed, dune-lined oasis of **Huacachina** (p139), famous for sandboarding. Next is **Nazca** (p141), for a flight over the mysterious Nazca Lines.

Turn inland for the 'White City' of **Arequipa** (p160), with its colonial architecture and stylish nightlife. Go trekking in **Cañón del Colca** (p187) or **Cañón del Cotahuasi** (p193) – perhaps the world's deepest canyon – or climb **El Misti** (p169), a postcard-perfect 5822m volcano. Then it's upwards to **Puno** (p198), Peru's port on **Lake Titicaca** (p207), one of the world's highest navigable lakes. From here you can visit traditional islands and the *chullpas* (ancient funerary towers) at **Sillustani** and **Cutimbo** (p206).

Wind through the Andes to **Cuzco** (p220), South America's oldest continuously inhabited city. Browse colorful markets and explore archaeological sites in the **Sacred Valley** (p258), then trek to **Machu Picchu** (p267) via an adventurous **alternative route** (p285).

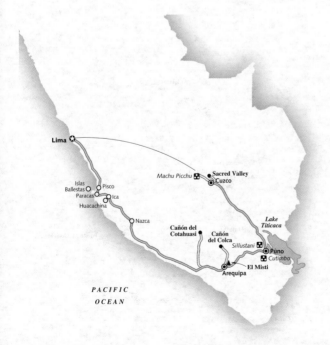

This loop starts in Lima, zips down along the coastal desert, climbs to Arequipa and Lake Titicaca and ends at Machu Picchu. It is one of the most popular routes on the continent. You could do much of this in two weeks, but a meandering month is ideal.

ONLY THE BEST OF PERU   Four Weeks / Lima to Máncora

Get over your jet lag with some fine cuisine in **Lima** (p109), then head south through the coastal desert for a flyover of the **Nazca Lines** (p142) before arriving in stylish, cosmopolitan **Arequipa** (p160), with its mysterious monasteries, deep canyons and smoking volcanoes. Fly high into the Andes to reach the ancient Inca capital of **Cuzco** (p220) for a few days of acclimatization before boarding the train to **Machu Picchu** (p267), the most visited archaeological site in South America.

From Cuzco, fly to **Puerto Maldonado** (p460) to stay at a wildlife lodge along one of the mighty rivers in the Amazon Basin. Alternatively, take an overland tour from Cuzco to the **Manu area** (p474), where a Unesco-listed haven protects the priceless rainforest. Another option for exploring the Amazonian *selva* (jungle) is to first fly back to Lima, then onward to **Iquitos** (p494).

Back in Lima, take a bus or fly north to the adventurers' base camp of **Huaraz** (p389), where a short trek will take you to the precipitous peaks of the **Cordillera Blanca** (p404). A day trip to **Chavín de Huántar** (p422) will lead you to one of Peru's oldest ancient sites. Rumble back down to the coast at **Chimbote** (p340), then dash north to historic **Trujillo** (p342), which is surrounded by a cornucopia of archaeological sites. These include the ruins of the largest pre-Columbian city in the Americas, **Chan Chan** (p349), and the fascinating **Huacas del Sol y de la Luna** (p351). Finish up the journey with a seaside break at the bustling surf town of **Máncora** (p376).

If you want to get a taste of everything, this whirlwind tour hits Peru's top must-see attractions. Give yourself a full month if you want to brag that you've really seen it all.

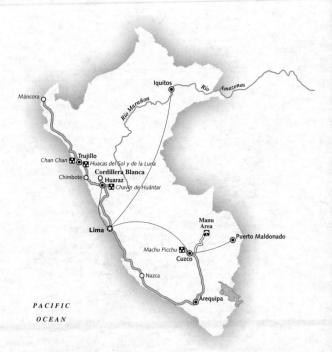

ROADS LESS TRAVELED

NORTH COASTIN'   Three Weeks / Lima to Tumbes

The first stop north of **Lima** (p78) could be **Caral** (p338), where the oldest known civilization in South America arose about 5000 years ago. Further north is the gruesome ancient site of **Sechín** (p339), although many travelers prefer to continue to **Trujillo** (p342). Nearby attractions include the well-preserved Moche pyramids of **Huacas del Sol y de la Luna** (p351) and the ruins of the once-mighty **Chan Chan** (p349).

Off the sleepy beaches at **Huanchaco** (p352), modern surfers paddle out to the breakers alongside local fishers in traditional reed canoes. En route to Chiclayo is the surf spot of **Puerto Chicama** (p357), which boasts one of the world's longest left-hand breaks. Then it's **Chiclayo** (p358), with several nearby towns that contain world-class museums showcasing riches from the important archaeological site of **Sipán** (p364).

Piura (p367) is a hub for visiting the craft markets and *picanterías* (local restaurants) of dusty **Catacaos** (p371), or the witch doctors of **Huancabamba** (p373), hidden away in the Andes. Peru's best beaches lie along the Pacific shoreline heading further north, and resorts such as **Máncora** (p376) offer lots of places to munch on great seafood and dance the balmy nights away.

The journey ends at **Tumbes** (p382), a gateway to Ecuador. It's the jumping-off point for visiting Peru's endangered mangrove swamps, which are teeming with wildlife (watch out for the crocodiles!).

Straight as an arrow, the Panamericana Norte passes archaeological sites, renowned surf spots, colonial cities and museums with fascinating artifacts. Hemingway liked it – you will too. Unless you're in a hurry to reach Ecuador, you'll want to spend a minimum of two weeks on your journey.

Tumbes

Máncora

Piura

Catacaos   Huancabamba

Río Marañón

Chiclayo   Sipán

Puerto Chicama
Huanchaco   Trujillo
Chan Chan   Huacas del Sol y de la Luna

Sechín

*PACIFIC
OCEAN*

Caral

Lima

BACK DOOR INTO THE AMAZON   Two Weeks / Chiclayo to Iquitos

Leaving **Chiclayo** (p358), with its nearby ancient ruins and witches' market, take a bus over the Andean continental divide to **Chachapoyas** (p441), a base for visiting the isolated, untouristed fortress of **Kuélap** (p448), dating from AD 800, and many other remote, barely known archaeological sites. Chachapoyas can easily be reached in 10 hours from Chiclayo, traveling along the quicker paved road via the highland jungle town of **Jaén** (p441), a remote border crossing to Ecuador.

Hardier travelers can take the wild, unpaved, longer route to **Cajamarca** (p429), a lovely highland provincial town where the Inca Atahualpa was imprisoned by Spanish conquistadors. Outside of the wet season, continue on the slow, spectacular route to friendly **Celendín** (p439) and on to **Leimebamba** (p449) to see the Marvelous Spatuletail hummingbird (p450). Then, continue on the scenic but kidney-busting drive to Chachapoyas (p441).

From Chachapoyas, take the unpaved road to **Pedro Ruíz** (p451), where transportation is readily available to **Tarapoto** (p453). Break your journey here to hike to high jungle waterfalls. The last road section travels to **Yurimaguas** (p491), where on most days you can find cargo boats that make the two-day trip to **Iquitos** (p494) via the village of **Lagunas** (p492), the best entry point to the **Reserva Nacional Pacaya-Samiria** (p493). Hammock or cabin space is readily available. Don't expect much comfort, but the trip will provide an unforgettable glimpse of the world's greatest river basin. At Iquitos, you can arrange boat trips that go even deeper – and on into Brazil.

This route crosses the little-traveled northern highlands by road and ends at the Amazonian port of Iquitos – the largest city in the world that cannot be reached by road. Hurrying locals get from Chiclayo to Iquitos in less than a week; curious travelers might take a month.

JUNGLE BOOGIE   Four Weeks / Cuzco to Iquitos

More than half of Peru is made up of jungle, which dramatically drops away from the eastern slopes of the Andes and deep into the Amazon Basin – stretching all the way to the Atlantic.

The most popular excursion starts from **Cuzco** (p220 and p289) and heads to the **Manu area** (p474), itself the size of a small country and full of jungle lodges and wildlife-watching opportunities. Or you can fly from Cuzco to **Puerto Maldonado** (p460) and rent a thatch-roofed bungalow with a view either along the **Río Madre de Dios** (p467), the gateway to lovely **Lago Sandoval** (p470), or along the **Río Tambopata** (p471), where a national reserve protects one of the country's largest clay licks. During the dry season (July and August), it's possible for hard-core types to travel overland back to Cuzco.

With the south out of the way, you can turn your attention to the north. The easiest way to get there is to fly to Lima, then onward to **Pucallpa** (p484), near **Yarinacocha** (p489). The lake in this area is ringed by tribal villages, including those of the matriarchal Shipibo people, renowned for their pottery. A more challenging bus journey reaches Pucallpa from Lima via the coffee-growing settlement of **San Ramón** (p480) and the miniscule village of **Puerto Bermúdez** (p484), the stronghold of Peru's largest Amazon tribe, the Asháninka.

From Pucallpa, begin the classic slow riverboat journey north along the **Río Ucayali** (p488) to **Iquitos** (p494). This northern jungle capital has a floating market and a bustling port, where you can catch a more comfortable cruise into Peru's largest national park, **Reserva Nacional Pacaya-Samiria** (p493), via **Lagunas** (p492). It's also tempting to float over into Brazil via the unique **tri-border zone** (p506).

Expect to fly if your time is limited, or spend weeks on epic river and road journeys through the unforgettable Amazon Basin, populated by spectacular wildlife and tribal peoples. Bring bucket loads of patience and self-reliance – and a lot of luck never hurts.

TAILORED TRIPS

ANCIENT TREASURES

Peru's main attractions are the Inca ruins at **Machu Picchu** (p267) and the **Sacred Valley** (p258). Near Puno, the funerary towers of the Colla, Lupaca and Inca cultures can be found at **Sillustani** and **Cutimbo** (p206), near Lake Titicaca.

Trujillo is an excellent base for seeing **Chan Chan** (p349), as well as ongoing excavations of the Moche temple mounds of **Huacas del Sol y de la Luna** (p351). If you have time in Huaraz, the 3000-year-old ruins and on-site museum at **Chavín de Huántar** (p422) are worth a trip. Or keep going north to **Chiclayo** (p358), another treasure-house of ancient sites. Nearby, gold and other riches from the excavated site of **Sipán** (p364) are found in the museum at **Lambayeque** (p365). Chiclayo is also the springboard for side trips into the northern highlands, where archaeological sites lie hidden in the cloud forest outside **Chachapoyas** (p441) – such as **Kuélap** (p448), a monolithic monument that gives Machu Picchu a run for its money – and it's blissfully crowd free.

The wonderfully woven artifacts of the Paracas are best seen in museums – Lima's **Museo de la Nación** (p94) and the **Museo Larco** (p95) in particular. To the south, the **Nazca Lines** (p142) can only be appreciated properly from the air. Lima is also a convenient base for a quick jaunt to **Caral** (p338), where you'll see the remnants of America's oldest civilization.

TASTE SENSATIONS

In between all those hikes to Inca ruins and treks around Andean peaks, you're going to build up one heck of an appetite – and what better to sate it with than Peru's myriad regional dishes.

Start in **Lima** (p109), home to hole-in-the-wall joints serving succulent ceviches (seafood marinated in lime juice), as well as trendy *novoandina* (Peruvian nouvelle cuisine) spots. Fill your belly with *picantes* (spicy stews) in **Arequipa** (p182). To the interior, warm up with a cup of steaming *api* (a sweet corn drink) in **Puno** (p204) and subsist on highland staples such as seared *cuy* (guinea pig) and *choclo con queso* (white Andean corn with cheese) in **Cuzco** (p246). **Huancayo** (p311), in the central highlands, is the home of *papas a la huancaína* (potatoes with a creamy cheese sauce), as well as mouth-watering *trucha* (river trout).

To the north, you can slurp *chupes* (seafood chowders) in **Trujillo** (p347) and gobble up manta-ray omelets and duck stewed in cilantro in **Chiclayo** (p361) – till the seams of your pants groan. **Cajamarca** (p436), to the interior, is another fine spot to eat *cuy*. While in the Amazon cities of **Iquitos** (p494) and **Puerto Maldonado** (p460), never pass up an opportunity to feast on *juanes* – banana leaves stuffed with chicken or pork and rice.

History

In 1532, when Francisco Pizarro and his men landed on the north coast of Peru with the intention of conquering the area in the name of God and the Spanish crown, the Andes had already been witness to the epic rise and fall of various civilizations. There had been the Chavín, dating back to 1000 BC – not so much a culture, or a civilization, but a unifying cultural ethos that brought together the northern and central highlands. There were the militaristic Wari, who starting at about AD 600 took over an area that stretched from Chiclayo to Cuzco, building a network of arterial roadways in the process. And, of course, there were the Incas who administered a sprawling kingdom that began somewhere in southern Colombia and ended in the middle of present-day Chile.

The arrival of Pizarro in the early 16th century, however, would see the beginning of one of Peru's most protracted shifts. The Spanish conquest changed everything about life in the Andes: the economics, the political systems, the language and even the food – not to mention the power structure, which was uprooted from Cuzco and taken to foggy Lima, the heart of the new empire. It was the port from which tons of Inca gold were dispatched off to Europe. It was where liberator José de San Martín declared the country independent from Spain in 1821. And it's played host to palace coups and dictatorial regimes – where the wealthy, fair-skinned *criollo* ruling class has exerted its influence over the entire nation.

To some degree, Peru's modern history has been a series of aftershocks from that seismic clash between the Inca and the Spanish. It is a conflict that remains deeply embedded in the Peruvian psyche. Yet, its circumstances have produced incredible things: new cultures, new races, new voices, new cuisine – one could even say, a new civilization.

Though out of date, Jane Holligan's Peru in Focus: A Guide to the People, Politics and Culture *offers a worthwhile overview of the country's economy, history and traditions.*

EARLY SETTLERS: THE PRECERAMIC PERIOD

Humans are relatively recent arrivals in the New World, probably spreading throughout the Americas after migrating across the Bering Strait about 20,000 years ago. Peru's first inhabitants were nomadic hunter-gatherers who roamed the country in loose-knit bands, living in caves and hunting fearsome (now extinct) animals such as giant sloths, saber-toothed tigers and mastodons. There is some debate about how long, exactly, there has been a human presence in Peru. Based on radio carbon dating of artifacts found in caves in the Ayacucho Basin, some scholars have suggested that humans occupied Peru as far back as 14,000 BC (with at least one academic reporting that it could precede even that early date). Certainly, there is archaeological evidence that puts humans in the region at 8000 BC: caves in Lauricocha, near Huánuco, and Toquepala, near Tacna, bear paintings that record hunting

Spanning several millennia worth of finds, Andean Archeology, *by Helaine Silverman, is a concise guide to the most noteworthy archaeological discoveries of the region.*

TIMELINE

8000 BC	c 3000 BC	3000 BC
Hunting scenes are painted in caves by hunter-gatherers near Huánuco in the central highlands and in Toquepala in the south – early evidence of humans in Peru.	Settlement of Peru's coastal oases begins; some of the first structures are built at the ceremonial center of Caral.	Potatoes, squash, cotton, corn, *lúcuma* (a type of fruit) and quinoa begin to be domesticated; at this point, llamas, alpacas and guinea pigs had likely been tamed for about 1000 years.

scenes. The latter site shows a group of hunters cornering and killing what appears to be a group of camelid animals.

Domestication of the llama, alpaca and guinea pig began in the highlands by about 4000 BC. Around the same time, people began planting seeds and learning how to improve crops by simple horticultural techniques such as weeding. By 3000 BC, potatoes, gourds, squash, cotton, *lúcuma* (a type of fruit), quinoa and amaranth were being cultivated. By the next millennium, corn and beans had been added as crops. By 2500 BC, various cultures began to flourish on the coast. Nomadic hunters and gatherers clustered into settlements along the Pacific, which was then wetter than today's desert. The inhabitants of these early communities survived by practicing agriculture and fishing – using nets or bone hooks (and sometimes rafts), and collecting foods such as shellfish, sea urchins, seabird eggs and sea lions. They cooked with hot stones, and cotton was used to make clothing, mainly by using simple twining techniques.

Even as groups settled into pockets of the Andes and along the ocean, there was nonetheless mobility among these populations. Plants from more temperate climates, such as manioc (also called cassava or yuca) and sweet potatoes, appeared on the coast early on, indicating trade links with the Amazon. Other signs of an exchange are evidenced by the use of coca – a tropical plant – for ritual and analgesic purposes, as well as rainforest bird feathers. Ceramics and metalwork were still unknown in both coastal and highland cultures during this period, although jewelry made of bone and shell has been found.

Coastal peoples generally lived in simple one-room dwellings lined with stone or made from branches and reeds. These early Peruvians also built many structures for ceremonial or ritual purposes. Some of the oldest – raised temple platforms facing the ocean and containing human burials – date from the 3rd millennium BC, indicating a prosperity based on the rich marine life of the coast. Some of these platforms were decorated with painted mud friezes.

In recent years, studies at archaeological sites have revealed that these early cultures were far more developed than previously imagined. Ongoing excavations at Caral (p338), roughly 200km north of Lima, have uncovered evidence of the oldest civilization in the Americas – existing at roughly the same time as the more famous ancient cultures of Egypt, India and China. The 626-hectare site was a city that once housed about 3000 people, with structures that are estimated to be up to 5000 years old. It contains irrigation systems, sunken circular courts and pyramidal structures, all indications of a society that had a powerful central government and established religious beliefs. In June of 2009, Caral was declared a Unesco World Heritage Site.

Roughly contemporary with the coastal settlements of this period is the enigmatic Temple of Kotosh (p329) near Huánuco, whose structures are roughly 4000 years old. The site features two temple mounds with wall niches and decorative friezes – some of the most sophisticated architecture produced in the highlands during the period.

Prior to the Incas, there were scores of different cultures and civilizations dating back at least to 2500 BC – and *The Ancient Kingdoms of Peru*, by Nigel Davies, covers almost all of them.

The erratic climate system of El Niño has likely been responsible for the rise and fall of various pre-Columbian civilizations. For more on this phenomenon, turn to p364.

1000 BC	200 BC	AD 1
The Chavín Horizon begins, in which various highland and coastal communities are united by uniform religious deities.	The Nazca culture on the southern coast starts construction on a series of giant glyphs that adorn the desert to this day.	The southern coast sees the rise of the Paracas Necropolis culture, known for its highly intricate textiles that depict stylized images of warriors, animals and gods.

CLAY & CLOTH

The period from 1800 BC to about 900 BC – referred to as the Initial Period by some scholars and the Formative Period by others – was when ceramics and a more sophisticated textile production came into being. Some of the earliest pottery comes from coastal archaeological sites at Las Haldas in the Casma Valley, south of Chimbote, and the Huaca La Florida, an unmapped temple structure in Lima. During this time, ceramics developed from basic undecorated bowls to sculpted, incised vessels of high quality. In the highlands, the people of Kotosh (which had remained continuously inhabited since the late Preceramic Period) produced similarly straightforward ceramics fashioned from black, red or brown clay – though a few rare examples of more complex double-spout bottles do exist from this era.

This period also saw the introduction of looms, used to produce plain cotton cloths, as well as improvements in fishing and agriculture (such as early experimentation with the terrace system).

It is illegal to buy pre-Columbian antiquities and take them out of the country.

THE CHAVÍN HORIZON

Named after the site of Chavín de Huántar (p422), east of Huaraz, this was a rich period of development for Andean culture – when artistic and religious phenomena appeared, perhaps independently, over a broad swath of the central and northern highlands, as well as the coast. Lasting roughly from 1000 BC to 300 BC – Chavín was a period when more efficient agricultural methods led to greater urbanization, and therefore a greater cultural complexity.

The salient feature of the Chavín influence is the repeated representation of a stylized feline (jaguar or puma) with prominently religious overtones, perhaps symbolizing spiritual transformations experienced under the influence of hallucinogenic plants. One of the most famous depictions of this deity resides at the Museo Nacional de Antropología, Arqueología e Historia del Perú in Lima (p97): a bas-relief carving from Chavín de Huántar of a many-headed god. (The piece is known as the Raimondi Stela after the Italian-born explorer who found it.) The feline deity also figures prominently in some ceramics of the era – particularly the finely crafted, black-clay specimens referred to as Cupisnique, a style that flourished in the Virú and Chicama valleys on the north coast. Methods of working with gold, silver and copper were also developed. In short, it was a period of great development in the areas of weaving, pottery, religion and architecture – in a word, culture.

For more on the Chavín culture, see p424.

Tejidos Milenarios del Perú: Ancient Peruvian Textiles is a weighty, beautifully illustrated bilingual encyclopedia of the magnificent textiles produced by every Peruvian culture from Chavín to the Incas.

THE BIRTH OF LOCAL CULTURES

After 300 BC, Chavín lost its unifying influence and several local cultures became regionally important. South of Lima, in the area surrounding the Paracas Peninsula, lived a coastal community whose most significant phase is referred to as Paracas Necropolis (AD 1–400), after a large burial site.

Chavín: Art, Architecture and Culture, by William Conklin and Jeffrey Quilter, provides an excellent, accessible overview of Peru's first widespread culture.

200	500	600
The Tiwanaku begin their 400-year domination of the area around Lake Titicaca, into what is today Bolivia and northern Chile.	The Moche culture, in the north, begins work on Huaca del Sol y de la Luna, adobe temples situated outside of present-day Trujillo.	The Wari culture emerges from the Ayacucho area and consolidates an empire that covers a territory from Cuzco to Chiclayo.

It is here that some of the finest pre-Columbian textiles in the Americas have been unearthed: colorful, intricate fabrics that depict oceanic creatures, feline warriors and highly stylized anthropomorphic figures. (Some absolutely stunning examples of these are on view at the Museo Larco in Lima, p95; for more on Paracas culture, turn to p133.)

To the south, in the area of Nazca, the local culture (200 BC–AD 600) carved giant, enigmatic designs into the desert landscape that can only be seen from the air. Known as the Nazca Lines (p143), these were mapped early in the 20th century – though their ultimate purpose remains up for debate. (Everything from alien landing strip to astronomical calendar has been posited.) The culture was best documented by German-born archaeologist Max Uhle, who cataloged a lot of the fine textile and pottery works, the latter of which utilized, for the first time in Peruvian history, a polychrome (multicolored) paint technique. Visitors today can view Nazca mummies at the Chauchilla Cemetery (p144), and also visit the pyramids of Cahuachi (p145), which are still being excavated.

During this period, another distinct culture noted for its exceptional pottery blossomed in the north: the Moche, which settled the area around Trujillo from about AD 100 to 800. Using press molds, this coastal society created some of the most remarkable portrait art in history – astonishing, highly individualistic ceramic heads, no two of which are exactly alike, each bearing signs of human asymmetry and imperfection. (Once again, Lima's Museo Larco best displays some of this absolutely sublime work, p95.) In addition, the Moche left behind temple mounds – popularly called 'pyramids' – such as the Huacas del Sol y de la Luna (Temples of the Sun and Moon; p351), located near Trujillo, as well as the impressive burial site of Sipán (p364), near Chiclayo. The latter contains a series of tombs that have been under excavation since 1987 – one of the most important archaeological discoveries in South America since Machu Picchu. In 2006, archaeologists in the vicinity of Trujillo made another important find when they unearthed an elaborately tattooed mummy of a woman who was likely a significant leader. A catastrophic drought in the latter half of the 6th century may have contributed to the demise of the Moche as a culture. (For more information, see p354.)

Ultimately, however, all of these cultures recorded many aspects of their daily existence on their ceramics, metalwork and textiles, leaving archaeologists a rich archive about life and culture during this period.

WARI EXPANSION

As the influence of regional states waned, the Wari – an ethnic group from the Ayacucho Basin – emerged as a force to be reckoned with for 500 years beginning in AD 600. (They are closely linked, stylistically, to the Tiwanaku culture of Bolivia, which was at its height from AD 200 to 600.) Unlike Chavín, however,

1491: New Revelations of the Americas Before Columbus by Charles C Mann is an engaging look at what daily life was like in the Americas before the arrival of the Spanish.

Sex, Death and Sacrifice in Moche Religion and Visual Culture by Steve Bourget is an intriguing look at life and death in this pre-Columbian north-coast society.

c 800	c 850	1100–1200
The fiercely independent Chachapoyas build Kuélap, a citadel in the northern highlands composed of 400 constructions.	The Chimú begin development of Chan Chan, outside of present-day Trujillo, a sprawling adobe urban center.	The Incas emerge as a presence in Cuzco – according to legend, they were led to the area by a divine figure known as Manco Cápac and his sister, Mama Ocllo.

the Wari were not limited to the diffusion of artistic and religious influence. They were vigorous military conquerors who built and maintained important outposts throughout a vast territory that covered an area from Chiclayo to Cuzco. Though their ancient capital lay outside of present-day Ayacucho – the ruins of which can still be visited (p325) – they also operated the major lowland ceremonial center of Pachacamac, just outside of Lima (p122), where people from all over the region came to pay tribute.

As with many conquering cultures, the Wari attempted to subdue other groups by emphasizing their own traditions over local belief. Thus from about AD 700 to 1100, Wari influence is noted in the art, technology and architecture of most areas in Peru. These include elaborate tie-dyed tunics and delicate and finely woven textiles featuring stylized designs of human figures and geometric patterns – some of which contained a record-breaking 398 threads per linear inch. (A fragment of one of these can be seen at the Museo Larco, p95.) In addition, they produced monumental sculpture, painted ceramics and ornamental jewelry. They are most significant, however, for investing in an extensive network of roadways and for greatly expanding the terrace agriculture system – an infrastructure that would serve the Incas well when they came into power just a few centuries later. For more on the culture, see p326.

Ferdinand Anton's highly readable *The Art of Ancient Peru* – with almost 300 photographic images – is a good (if out-of-date) primer to pre-Hispanic art, from Chavín through the Incas.

REGIONAL KINGDOMS

The Wari were replaced by a gaggle of small nation-states that thrived from about 1000 to the Inca conquest in the early 1400s. One of the biggest and best studied of these are the Chimú, of the Trujillo area, whose capital was the famed Chan Chan (p349), the largest adobe city in the world. Their economy was based on agriculture and they had a heavily stratified society with a healthy craftsman class, which produced painted textiles and beautifully fashioned pottery that is distinctive for its black stain.

Closely connected to the Chimú are the Sicán from the Lambayeque area, renowned metallurgists who produced, among other artifacts, the *tumi* – a ceremonial knife with a rounded blade used in sacrifices or for the purposes of skull trepanation – otherwise known as brain surgery. (The *tumi* has since become a national symbol in Peru and replicas of these can be found in crafts markets everywhere.) In 2006, archaeologists excavating under an adobe pyramid near Lambayeque found 12 of these ceremonial knives – the first time scholars had found *tumis* undisturbed at a burial site. All previous specimens had come entirely from the hands of looters.

Further down the coast were the Chancay people (1000–1500), who inhabited the area north of Lima, and are known for producing a fine geometrically patterned lace and a crude-if-humorous (just about every figure seems to be drinking) sand-colored pottery. The best collections of these can be found at the Museo Andrés del Castillo (p93) and the Fundación Museo Amano (p97), both of which are in Lima. Further south were the Ica and Chincha cultures, whose artifacts can be seen in the Museo Regional de Ica (p136).

The must-have book for all things Tiwanaku (the pre-Inca culture based around Lake Titicaca) is Margaret Young-Sanchez' beautifully illustrated *Tiwanaku: Ancestors of the Inca.*

The Chimú city of Chan Chan, outside of modern-day Trujillo was the largest city in pre-Hispanic America.

1438–71	**1492**	**1493**
The reign of Inca Yupanqui – also known as Pachacutec – represents a period of aggressive empire-building for the Incas; during this time, Machu Picchu and Saqsaywamán are built.	Funded by the Spanish crown, Genoa-born explorer Christopher Columbus arrives in the Americas.	Inca Huayna Cápac begins his reign, pushing the empire north to Colombia; his untimely death in 1525 – probably from small pox – would leave the kingdom fatally divided.

An absolutely indispensable collection of articles covering every historical era, with rare translations of key works, can be found in *The Peru Reader* by Orin Starn, Carlos Iván Degregori and Robin Kirk.

In the highlands, several other cultures were significant during this time. In a relatively isolated and inaccessible patch of the Utcubamba Valley, in the northern Andes, the cloud-forest-dwelling Chachapoyas culture (p448) erected the expansive mountain settlement of Kuélap (p448). It is one of the most intriguing and significant highland ruins – and one that is reasonably accessible to travelers, in addition to being blissfully crowd-free. Further south, several small altiplano (Andean plateau) kingdoms situated near Lake Titicaca left impressive *chullpas* (funerary towers) dotting the bleak landscape – the best remaining examples are at Sillustani (p206) and Cutimbo (p207). The formation of chiefdoms in the Amazon began during this period, too.

ENTER THE INCAS

Secrets of Lost Empires: Inca is an informative DVD produced by the US public-TV program *Nova* which thoughtfully explores Inca history and architecture.

Even though dozens of fascinating and highly developed civilizations had existed prior to the establishment of the Inca empire, Peruvian pre-Columbian history is often equated to just Inca history. This omission has occurred largely because none of the area's pre-Columbian cultures had a written language, leaving contemporary archaeologists to piece together the history of pre-Inca Peru through the examination of artifacts found at grave sites and ceremonial centers. When the Spanish showed up, in the 1500s, with their many chroniclers in tow, the Incas had little interest in recounting the long and complex history that had preceded them. They gave the Europeans an image-burnishing account of their civilization, in which the Andes was described as a place of naked savagery until the Incas showed up and started running the show. For all its glory, however, the truth is that the empire really only existed for barely a century before the arrival of the Spanish.

According to Inca lore, their civilization was born when Manco Cápac and his sister Mama Ocllo, children of the sun, emerged from Lake Titicaca to establish a civilization in the Cuzco Valley. Whether Manco Cápac was a historical figure is up for debate, but what is certain is that the Inca civilization was established in the area of Cuzco at some point in the 12th century. The reign of the first several *incas* (kings) is largely unremarkable – and for a couple of centuries, they remained a small, regional state.

At its acme, the Inca empire was larger than imperial Rome and boasted 40,000km of roadways.

Growth began in earnest in the 1300s under Mayta Cápac, who began attacking neighboring villages in the Cuzco area, putting them under his control. But Inca expansion would really pick up under the ninth king, Inca Yupanqui, who in 1438, defended Cuzco – against incredible odds – from the invading Chanka people to the north. After the victory he took on the new name of Pachacutec, which means 'Transformer of the Earth.'

Buoyed by his victory, Pachacutec spent the next 25 years bagging much of the Andes, as well as the area around Lake Titicaca, into Bolivia. He allegedly gave Cuzco its layout in the form of a puma and built fabulous stone monuments in honor of Inca victories, including Sacsaywamán

1532	**1569**	**1572**
Atahualpa wins a protracted struggle for control over Inca territories; at virtually the same time, the Spanish land in Peru – in less than a year, Atahualpa is dead.	Spaniard Francisco de Toledo, one of the more able administrators in the history of the colony, assumes the position of viceroy.	Túpac Amaru, the last reigning leader of the Incas, is beheaded in Cuzco's town square.

(p256), the temple-fortress at Ollantaytambo (p264) and possibly, Machu Picchu (p278). He also improved the network of roads that connected the empire, further developed terrace agricultural systems and made Quechua the lingua franca. Under his reign, the Incas grew from a regional fiefdom in the Cuzco Valley into a broad empire of about 10 million people known as Tawantinsuyo (Land of Four Quarters), covering most of modern Peru, in addition to pieces of Ecuador, Bolivia and Chile. All of this was made more remarkable by the fact that the Incas, as an ethnicity, never numbered more than about 100,000.

The Inca empire was connected by a network of chasquis *(runners) that could relay fresh-caught fish from the coast to Cuzco in 24 hours.*

ATAHUALPA'S BRIEF REIGN

After Christopher Columbus' historic journey to the New World in 1492, life for people in the Andes would continue much as it always had for another four decades. A succession of leaders followed in the wake of Pachacutec. His son, Túpac Yupanqui expanded the empire's northern limits, establishing the city of Tumipampa (now Cuenca, within Ecuador). His son, Huayna Cápac, who began his rule in 1493, would continue the push north, taking over Ecuador all the way to the border with Colombia. Consequently, he spent much of his life living, governing and commanding his armies from Ecuador, rather than Cuzco.

History of the Inca Realm, by celebrated Peruvian historian María Rostworawski, examines every aspect of Inca society – from trading systems to the role of women.

By the 1520s, small pox and other epidemics, transmitted by European soldiers, were starting to sweep through the indigenous populations of the entire American continent. The epidemics were so swift, in fact, that they arrived in the Andes long before the Spanish ever did, claiming thousands of indigenous lives – including, in all likelihood, that of Huayna Cápac, who unexpectedly succumbed to some sort of plague in 1525.

Without a clear plan of succession, the emperor's untimely death left a power vacuum. The contest turned into a face-off between two of the deceased emperor's many children: the Quito-born Atahualpa, who commanded his father's army in the north, and Huáscar, who was based in the capital of Cuzco. The ensuing struggle plunged the empire into a bloody civil war, reducing entire cities to rubble, with Atahualpa emerging as the victor in April of 1532. The vicious nature of the conflict left the Incas with a lot of enemies throughout the Andes – which is why some tribes were so willing to cooperate with the Spanish when they arrived just five months later.

The Angry Aztecs and the Incredible Incas is one of a series of kids' books that delivers spine-shivering facts (hello, human sacrifice!) on various cultures – perfect for tykes who love being grossed-out.

THE SPANISH INVADE

After conquering the Caribbean islands and the Aztec and Mayan cultures of Mexico and Central America, the Spanish were ready to turn their attention to South America. In 1522 Pascual de Andagoya sailed as far as the Río San Juan in Ecuador. Two years later, Pizarro headed south but was unable to make much headway. Skirmishes with natives – one of which

A classic of the genre, John Hemming's *The Conquest of the Incas*, first published in 1970, is a wonderfully written, highly regarded tome on the demise of the Inca civilization.

left Pizarro's right-hand man, Diego del Almagro, missing an eye – forced them to turn back. In November 1526, he sailed again, this time with more success: in 1528 he landed in Tumbes (in what is today the north coast of Peru), a rich coastal settlement that served as one of the many far-flung outposts of the Inca empire. There, he was greeted by natives who offered him meat, fruit, fish and *chicha* (fermented corn beer). More significantly for the Spanish, a cursory examination of the city revealed an abundance of objects crafted in silver and gold.

Pizarro quickly made his way back to Spain to court royal support for his impending conquest and returned to the area in September of 1532 with a shipload of arms, horses and slaves – as well as a battalion of 168 men. Tumbes, the rich town he had visited just four years earlier had been devastated by epidemics, as well as the recent Inca civil war. Atahualpa, in the meantime, was in the process of making his way down from Quito to Cuzco to claim his hard-won throne. When the Spanish arrived, he was in the northern Peruvian highland settlement of Cajamarca, enjoying some rest at the area's mineral baths.

Pizarro quickly deduced that the empire was in a fractious state. He and his men charted a course to Cajamarca and approached Atahualpa with promises of brotherhood and offering greetings from distant kings. But soon enough, the Spaniards had launched a surprise attack that left thousands of indigenous people dead and Atahualpa as a prisoner of war. (Between their horses, their protective armor and the steel of their blades, the vastly outnumbered Spanish were practically invincible against Inca warriors armed only with clubs, slings and wicker helmets.) In an attempt to regain his freedom, Atahualpa offered the Spanish gold and silver – and thus began one of the

Guns, Germs & Steel, the Pulitzer Prize–winning book by Jared Diamond, is a thoughtful biological examination of why some European societies triumphed over so many others; Latin America figures prominently.

most famous ransoms in history, with the Incas attempting to fill an entire room with the precious stuff in order to placate the unrelenting appetites of the Spanish. (During this time, the conquistadors also stripped bare the walls of Cuzco's Qorikancha, p232.) But a roomful of gold was not enough, and the Spanish held Atahualpa prisoner for eight months before sentencing him to death. He died of strangulation at the garrote at the age of 31.

Despite sporadic rebellions led by his followers and children – some of which would even lay siege to the Spanish capital of Lima – the Inca empire would never recover from this fateful encounter.

THE TUMULTUOUS COLONY

Following the death of Atahualpa, the Spanish quickly got to work organizing their new colony. The Inca capital of Cuzco was of little use to them, since they would need a port from which to ship the spoils of their conquest back to Spain. So, on January 6, 1535, Pizarro sketched out his new administrative center in the sands that bordered the Río Rímac on the central coast. This would be Lima, the so-called 'City of Kings' (named in honor of the Feast of

1781	1810	1821
Inca noble Túpac Amaru II is brutally executed by the Spanish after leading an unsuccessful indigenous rebellion.	Painter Pancho Fierro, a watercolorist known for recording daily life, is born in Lima.	José de San Martín rides into Lima and declares Peru independent; true sovereignty, however, doesn't come for another three years, when Simón Bolivar's forces vanquish the Spanish in battles at Junín and Ayacucho.

EL INCA GARCILASO DE LA VEGA: THE FIRST MESTIZO INTELLECTUAL

Of all the chronicles documenting the particulars of Inca culture and its subjugation by the Spanish, none has received as much widespread literary acclaim as the seminal work produced by El Inca Garcilaso de la Vega (1539–1616), the illegitimate son of a Spanish conquistador and an Inca princess. His book *Comentarios Reales de los Incas* (Royal Commentaries of the Incas) records the ways and history of the Inca people prior to the conquest – and to this day remains required reading for all students of Latin American colonial history.

As with all first-person narratives, *Comentarios* is not without political expediency. Garcilaso portrays the Incas as a great people who brought civilization to the Andes – avoiding any reference to other well-established cultures. He also describes the empire as a kingdom where every citizen was well cared for and contented (not the case for the many regional ethnicities who had been brutally conquered by the Incas). Most significantly, he was gratefully admiring of the Christian religion – which had spent its early decades in Peru violently extirpating any evidence of indigenous faith. (Garcilaso may not have had much choice in this regard, since to do otherwise would have brought the wrath of the Church upon him.) Even so, his celebrated chronicle remains a rich and insightful record of Inca life – and one of the most masterful works ever produced in the Spanish language.

the Epiphany or Three Kings' Day), the new capital of the viceroyalty of Peru, an empire that for more than 200 years would cover much of South America and serve as the crown jewel in the Spanish colonial system.

The following three decades, however, would be a period of great turmoil. For the indigenous people, the arrival of the Spanish brought on a cataclysmic collapse of their society. One scholar estimates that the indigenous population – around 10 million when Pizarro arrived – was reduced to a mere 600,000 within a century. As elsewhere in the Americas, the Spanish ruled by terror. (In 1613, in fact, an Inca noble named Guamán Poma de Ayala wrote a lengthy report on the abuses, which he sent to King Philip III in Spain – to no avail. His chronicle was likely never read by the Spanish royal.)

Rebellions erupted regularly. Atahualpa's half-brother Manco Inca (who had originally sided with the Spanish and served as a puppet emperor under Pizarro) tried to regain control of the highlands in 1536 – laying siege to the city of Cuzco for almost a year – but was ultimately forced to retreat to the jungle, to the site of the fabled Vilcabama, the Incas last settlement. He was stabbed to death by a contingent of Spanish soldiers in 1544. A couple of other indigenous figures would serve as de facto heads of the Inca state, until 1572, when the Spanish viceroy put a bounty on the head of the last Inca leader, Túpac Amaru (a son of Manco Inca). He was captured and, after a short trial, publicly decapitated before a crowd of thousands in Cuzco's main square.

Throughout all of this, the Spanish were doing plenty of fighting among themselves, splitting up into a complicated series of rival factions, each of

Kim MacQuarrie's gripping 2007 book, *The Last Days of the Incas*, is a page-turning, can't-put-it-down narrative of the history-making clash between two civilizations.

In addition to taxes and tributes, indigenous peoples during the viceroyalty were forced to participate in *repartos* – forced purchases of articles produced by the colony.

1826	**1845**	**1854**
The last of the Spanish military forces depart from Callao, after which the country descends into a period of anarchy.	Ramón Castilla begins the first of four nonconsecutive presidential terms and brings some degree of stability to Peru.	Peru abolishes slavery.

which wanted control of the new empire. In 1538, Diego de Almagro was sentenced to death by strangulation for an attempt to take over Cuzco. Three years later, Francisco Pizarro was assassinated in Lima by a band of disgruntled De Almagro supporters. Other conquistadors met equally violent fates.

Things grew relatively more stable after the arrival of Francisco de Toledo as viceroy, an able administrator who brought some order to the emergent Spanish province. Lima solidified its position as the main political, social and economic center, while Cuzco was relegated to backwater status. (The city nonetheless made its mark on the era for its role in the development of an ornate style of religious painting known as the *escuela cusqueña,* or Cuzco School, in the 17th and 18th centuries.)

Until independence, the country was ruled by a series of Spanish-born viceroys appointed by the crown. Immigrants from Spain held the most prestigious positions, while *criollos* (Spaniards born in the colony) were generally confined to middle management. (This is how Spain controlled its colonies – and bred resentment.) *Mestizos* – people who were of mixed blood were placed even further down the social scale. Full-blooded *indígenas* resided at the bottom, exploited as *peones* (expendable laborers) in *encomiendas,* a feudal system that granted Spanish colonists land titles that included the property all of the indigenous people living in that area.

Tensions between *indígenas* and Spaniards reached a boiling point in the late 18th century, when the Spanish crown levied a series of new taxes on the colony, which, naturally, hit indigenous people the hardest. In 1780, José Gabriel Condorcanqui – a descendant of Túpac Amaru who resided in the southern region of Tinta – arrested and executed a Spanish administrator on charges of cruelty. His act unleashed an indigenous rebellion that spread throughout southern Peru and into Bolivia and Argentina. Condorcanqui, regarded as Inca royalty by many peasants, adopted the name Túpac Amaru II, in honor of his slain great-grandfather, and traveled the region fomenting revolution. The Spanish reprisal was swift – and brutal. In 1781, the captured indigenous leader was dragged to the main plaza in Cuzco, where he would watch his followers, his wife and his sons killed in a day-long orgy of violence, before being drawn and quartered himself. Pieces of his remains were displayed in towns around the Andes as a way of discouraging further insurrection.

INDEPENDENCE

By the early 19th century, *criollos* in many of Spain's Latin American colonies had grown increasingly dissatisfied with their lack of administrative power and the crown's heavy taxes. In many colonies, the time was ripe for revolt and independence. Yet, in Peru, this wasn't so much the case. For one, the area was South America's oldest viceroyalty and its society was dominated, to an overwhelming degree, by the Spanish. Moreover, Lima's powerful elite

1872	1879–83	1892
Scholar Ricardo Palma publishes the first of a series of books – known as the *Tradiciones Peruanas* – that chronicle *criollo* folklore.	Chile wages war against Peru and Bolivia over nitrate-rich lands in the Atacama Desert; Peru loses the conflict – in addition to its southernmost region of Tarapacá.	Poet César Vallejo is born in a highland town; he lived for only 46 years, but nonetheless became one of the continent's finest literary figures.

THE MAKING OF PERU'S SAINTS

The first century of the Peruvian colony produced an unusual number of Catholic saints – five in all. There was the highly venerated Santa Rosa of Lima (1556–1617), a devout *criolla* (Spaniard born in Peru) who, though never a nun, nonetheless took a vow of chastity before withdrawing into a secluded life of prayer and mortification, wearing a cilice and sleeping on a bed of broken glass and pottery. (She was particularly renowned for having all manner of visions.) In addition, there was San Juan Macías (1585–1645), who counseled the needy, and San Martín de Porres (1579–1639), the New World's first black saint, who reportedly cured illness with the touch of his hand. (You can view relics from all these saints at the Iglesia de Santo Domingo in Lima, p90.) Other lesser-known figures from this period have also been canonized.

Why so many? Miracles aside, a lot of it had to do with the Spanish program to systematically replace the old indigenous order with its own traditions. Catholic authorities, through a process known as the Extirpation, worked to exterminate indigenous religious beliefs by prohibiting idolatry and ancestor worship – and by producing catechisms in Aymara and Quechua. To get this message across, the Church held ceremonies in which pre-Columbian religious idols were burned and natives were whipped. The most famous of these took place in December of 1609, in Lima's main plaza, when Church officials immolated a pile of figurines confiscated from indigenous parishes and then administered 200 lashes to an indigenous man accused of having ties to the devil.

The whole process, ultimately, gave rise to a crop of local holy figures that Catholic officials could hold up as praiseworthy examples of religious piousness. Priests preached the wonders of everyday people (especially those of mixed race) who helped care for the sick, rejected worldly possessions, practiced chastity and displayed extreme humility – qualities that the Church was eager to cultivate in its flock of newfound converts. A lot of the figures touted during these times would never attain full sainthood – but those that did have remained an integral part of Peruvian spiritual culture to this day.

were continually nervous about any sort of political shift that might lead to another rebellion.

The winds of change, however, arrived – inevitably – from two directions. Argentine revolutionary José de San Martín led independence campaigns in Argentina and Chile, before entering Peru by sea, at the port of Pisco, in 1820. With San Martín's arrival, royalist forces retreated into the highlands, allowing him to ride into Lima unobstructed. On July 28, 1821, independence was declared. But real independence wouldn't materialize for another three years: with Spanish forces still at large in the interior, San Martín would need more men to fully defeat the Spanish.

Enter Simón Bolívar, the venerated Venezuelan revolutionary, who had been leading independence fights in Venezuela, Colombia and Ecuador. San Martín met with Bolívar privately in Ecuador, in 1822, to seek help on the Peruvian campaign. Bolívar, however, was not interested in sharing

Women in 19th-century Lima took to donning head scarves that obscured everything but one eye. This unusual fashion led people to dub them *'las tapadas'* ('the covered ones').

1895	1911	1924
Nicolás de Piérola is elected president, beginning a period of relative stability buoyed by a booming world economy.	US historian Hiram Bingham arrives at the ruins of Machu Picchu.	Northern political leader Victor Raúl Haya de la Torre founds APRA, a populist, anti-imperialist political party that is immediately declared illegal.

command, so San Martín withdrew. In 1823, the Peruvians gave Bolívar dictatorial powers (an honor that had been bestowed upon him in other countries as well). By the latter half of 1824, he and his lieutenant, Antonio José de Sucre, had routed the Spanish in decisive battles in Junín, as well as in Ayacucho – where the revolutionaries faced staggering odds, but nonetheless managed to capture the viceroy and negotiate a surrender. As part of the deal, the Spanish would retire all of their forces from Peru and Bolivia. In January of 1826, the last detachment of royal soldiers left from the port of Callao.

THE NEW REPUBLIC

The lofty idealism of the revolution was followed by the harsh reality of having to govern. Peru, the young nation, proved to be just as anarchic as Peru, the young viceroyalty. Between 1825 and 1841, there was a revolving door of regime changes (two dozen!) as regional *caudillos* (chieftains) scrambled for power. The situation improved in the 1840s with the mining of vast deposits of guano off the Peruvian coast, the nitrate-rich bird droppings that reaped unheard-of profits on international markets as fertilizer. (Nineteenth-century Peruvian history is – literally – rife with poop jokes.)

The country would also find some measure of stability under the governance of Ramón Castilla (a *mestizo*), who would be elected to his first term in 1845. The income from the guano boom – which he had been key in exploiting – helped Castilla make needed economic improvements. He abolished slavery, paid off some of Peru's debt and established a public school system. Castilla served as president three more times over the course of two decades – at times, by force; at others, in an interim capacity – at one point, for less than a week. Following his final term, he was exiled by competitors who wanted to neutralize him politically. He died in 1867, in northern Chile, attempting to make his way back to Peru. (Visitors can see his impressive crypt at the Panteón de los Proceres in Central Lima, p93.)

THE WAR OF THE PACIFIC

With Castilla's passing, the country once again descended into chaos. A succession of *caudillos* squandered the enormous profits of the guano boom and, in general, managed the economy in a deplorable fashion. Moreover, military skirmishes would ensue with Ecuador (over border issues) and Spain (which was trying to dominate its former South American colonies). The conflicts left the nation's coffers empty. By 1874, Peru was bankrupt.

This left the country in a weak position to deal with the expanding clash between Chile and Bolivia over nitrate-rich lands in the Atacama Desert. Borders in this area had never been clearly defined and escalating tensions eventually led to outright military engagement. To make matters worse for the Peruvians, their president, Mariano Prado, abandoned the country for

Peru's exports of guano fertilizer in the mid-1800s totaled more than US$20 million a year; that's more than US$500 million a year by today's standards.

It was Chinese migrants who staffed many of the guano operations on the country's south coast during the 19th century.

1928	1932	1936
Journalist and thinker José Carlos Mariátegui publishes the *Seven Interpretive Essays on Peruvian Reality,* which heavily critiques the feudal nature of Peruvian society.	More than a thousand APRA party followers are killed by the military at the ancient ruins of Chan Chan following an uprising in Trujillo.	Acclaimed novelist, journalist and future presidential candidate Mario Vargas Llosa is born in Arequipa.

Europe on the eve of the conflict. The war was a disaster for Peru at every level (not to mention Bolivia, which lost its entire coastline). Despite the very brave actions of numerous military figures – such as Navy Admiral Miguel Grau – the Chileans were simply better organized and had more resources, including the support of the British. In 1881, they led a land campaign deep into Peru, occupying the capital of Lima, during which time they ransacked the city, making off with the priceless contents of the National Library. By the time the conflict came to a close in 1883, Peru had permanently lost its southernmost region of Tarapacá – and it wouldn't regain the area around Tacna until 1929.

As the 20th century loomed, however, things would look up for Peru. A buoyant world economy helped fuel an economic recovery through the export of sugar, cotton, rubber, wool and silver. And, in 1895, Nicolás de Piérola was elected President – beginning an era known as the 'Aristocratic Republic.' Hospitals and schools were constructed and de Piérola undertook a campaign to build highways and railroads.

A NEW INTELLECTUAL ERA

The dawn of the 20th century would witness a sea change in Peruvian intellectual thought. The late 1800s had been an era in which many thinkers (primarily in Lima) had tried to carve out the notion of an inherently Peruvian identity – one largely based on *criollo* experience. Key among them was Ricardo Palma, a scholar and writer renowned for rebuilding Lima's ransacked National Library. Beginning in 1872, he published a series of books on *criollo* folk tradition known as the *Tradiciones Peruanas* (Peruvian Traditions) – now required reading for every Peruvian schoolchild.

But as one century gave way to the next, intellectual circles saw the rise of *indigenismo* (Indianism), a continent-wide movement that advocated for a dominant social and political role for indigenous people. In Peru, this translated into a wide-ranging (if fragmented) cultural movement. Historian Luis Valcárcel attacked his society's degradation of the indigenous class. Poet César Vallejo wrote critically acclaimed novels and verse that took on indigenous oppression as themes. And painter José Sabogal led a generation of visual artists who explored these ideas in their work. In 1928, journalist and thinker José Carlos Mariátegui penned a seminal Marxist work – *Seven Interpretive Essays on Peruvian Reality* – in which he criticized the feudal nature of Peruvian society and celebrated the communal aspects of the Inca social order. (The book remains a vital treatise to Latin American leftists and historical scholars.)

In this climate, in 1924, Trujillo-born political leader Victor Raúl Haya de la Torre founded the Alianza Popular Revolucionaria Americana (American Popular Revolutionary Alliance) – otherwise known as APRA. The party espoused populist values, celebrated 'Indo-America' and rallied against US

The arrival of Peru's sizeable Japanese population began at the turn of the 20th century, with most migrants working in agriculture before settling into cities.

Peruvian Traditions, by Merlin Compton, provides a worthwhile selection – in English – of 19th-century scholar Ricardo Palma's celebrated folk tales.

A 1920 law passed by the Peruvian legislature protected communal indigenous lands, but was rarely enforced – which ultimately helped give rise to *indigenismo* (Indianism), a social movement.

1948	**1968**	**1970**
General Manuel Odría assumes power for eight years, encouraging a high degree of foreign investment.	Juan Velasco Alvarado takes power; in his seven years in office, he promulgates a populist agenda that involves 'Peruvianization' of all industry.	A 7.7-magnitude earthquake in northern Peru kills almost 80,000 people, leaves 140,000 injured and another 500,000 homeless.

Celebrated poet César Vallejo was a close associate of leftist thinker José Carlos Mariátegui and regularly contributed stories to his avant-garde cultural publication *Amauta*.

imperialism. It appealed overwhelmingly to the lower and middle classes, but it was abhorred by the ruling oligarchy. Augusto Leguía, who was in the midst of an 11-year dictatorship, made the party illegal – and it would remain so for long periods of the 20th century. Haya de la Torre, at various points in his life, lived in hiding and in exile, and endured a 15-month stint as a political prisoner.

DICTATORSHIPS & REVOLUTIONARIES

Following the beginning of the Great Depression in 1929 (which hit the Peruvian economy very hard), the country's history becomes a blur of military dictatorships punctuated by periods of democracy. Leguía was overthrown by Colonel Luis Sánchez Cerro, who came down hard on APRA – when the military gunned down and killed more than a thousand people at the ancient Chimú city of Chan Chan, following an uprising in Trujillo in 1932. By 1948 another dictator had taken power: Manuel Odría, who held APRA in high disdain, and spent his time in office encouraging US foreign investment in Peru. Haya de la Torre, in the meantime, spent five straight years hiding out at the Colombian embassy in Lima.

APRA founder Raúl Haya de la Torre would never see his party take executive power. He died in 1979 – six years before Alan García became the party's first president.

The most fascinating of Peru's 20th-century dictators, however, is Juan Velasco Alvarado, the former commander-in-chief of the army who took control of Peru in 1968. Though the expectation was that he would lead a conservative regime, Velasco turned out to be an inveterate populist (to the point that some APRA members complained that he had stolen their party platform away from them). He established a nationalist agenda that included 'Peruvianizing' (securing Peruvian majority ownership) various industries and in his rhetoric he celebrated the indigenous peasantry, championed a radical program of agrarian reform and made Quechua an official language. He also severely restricted press freedoms, which drew the wrath of the power structure in Lima. Ultimately, his economic policies were failures – and in 1975, in declining health, he was replaced by another, more conservative military regime.

THE INTERNAL CONFLICT

Mid-20th-century dictator Manuel Odría was known as the 'Happy General' because he liked to throw extravagant parties.

Peru returned to civilian rule in 1980, when President Fernando Belaúnde Terry was elected into office – the first election in which leftist parties (including APRA) were allowed to participate. But with Velasco's promised agrarian reform a thing of the past, and Belaúnde mired in trying to jump-start the moribund economy, the inequities facing indigenous *campesinos* (peasants) once again fell off the political radar.

At this time, a radical Maoist group from the poor region of Ayacucho began its unprecedented rise. Founded by philosophy professor Abimael Guzmán, Sendero Luminoso (Shining Path) wanted nothing less than an overthrow of the social order via violent armed struggle. Over the next two

1980	1983	1985
Fernando Belaúnde Terry becomes the first democratically elected president after a 12-year military dictatorship, but his term is plagued by economic instability and a growing highland guerrilla war.	In one of the more high-profile massacres of the Internal Conflict, eight journalists are murdered in the Andean town of Uchuraccay under suspicious circumstances.	APRA leader Alan García becomes president, but his term is marked by hyperinflation and increased attacks by terrorist groups; he flees the country in 1992, clouded by allegations of embezzlement.

decades, the situation escalated into a phantasmagoria of violence, with Sendero Luminoso assassinating political leaders and community activists, carrying out attacks on police stations and universities and, at one point, stringing up dead dogs all over downtown Lima. During this time, another leftist guerilla group also sprung into action – the Movimiento Revolucionario Túpac Amaru (MRTA) – attacking police stations and military outposts. The government response was fierce: Belaúnde and his successor, APRA candidate Alan García, who took over as president in 1985, sent in the military – a heavy-handed outfit that knew little about how to handle a guerrilla insurgency. There was torture, rape, disappearances and massacres – none of which did anything to quell Sendero Luminoso. Caught in the middle were tens of thousands of poor *campesinos* who bore the brunt of the casualties.

The name Sendero Luminoso – 'Shining Path' – is taken from a piece of text by José Carlos Mariátegui: 'Marxism-Leninism will open the shining path to revolution.'

In the early days, García's presidency generated a great deal of hope. He was young, he was a gifted public speaker, he was popular – and he was the first member of the storied APRA party to win a presidential election. But his economic program was catastrophic (his decision to nationalize the banks and suspend foreign-debt payments led to economic ruin), and, by the late 1980s, Peru faced a staggering hyperinflation rate of 7500%. Thousands of people were plunged into poverty. There were food shortages and riots. Throughout all of this, Sendero Luminoso and MRTA stepped up attacks. The government was forced to declare a state of emergency. Two years after completing his term, García fled the country after being accused of embezzling millions of dollars (though he would return to Peru in 2001, when the statute of limitations on his case ran out). It was a disappointing, ignominious end for a political party that had struggled for decades – against crackdowns and illegality – to get into power.

The Monkey's Paw: New Chronicles from Peru, by Robin Kirk, covers the violent history of the Internal Conflict, and is an excellent examination of how individuals manage to survive terror.

FUJISHOCK

With the country in a state of chaos, the 1990 presidential elections took on more importance than ever. The contest was between famed novelist Mario Vargas Llosa and Alberto Fujimori, an agronomist of Japanese descent. During the campaign, Vargas Llosa promoted an economic 'shock treatment' program that many feared would send more Peruvians into poverty, while Fujimori positioned himself as an alternative to the Peruvian status quo. Fujimori won handily. But as soon as he got into office, he implemented an even more austere economic plan that, among other things, drove up the price of gasoline by 3000%. The measures, known as 'Fujishock,' ultimately succeeded in reducing inflation and stabilizing the economy – but not without costing the average Peruvian dearly.

Mario Vargas Llosa's son Álvaro has become a famous political commentator in his own right, producing more than a dozen books on various aspects of Peruvian and Latin American history.

Fujimori followed this, in April of 1992, with an *autogolpe* (coup from within). He dissolved the legislature and generated an entirely new congress, one stocked with his allies. Peruvians, not unused to *caudillos*, tolerated the

1987	1990	1992
Archaeologists working near Lambayeque uncover a rare, undisturbed tomb of a Moche warrior-priest known as *El Señor de Sipán*.	Alberto Fujimori is elected president; his authoritarian rule leads to improvements in the economy, but charges of corruption plague his administration.	Sendero Luminoso detonates truck bombs in Miraflores, killing 25 and wounding scores more; following this act, public opinion turns decisively against the guerrillas.

power grab, hoping that Fujimori might help stabilize the economic and political situation – which he did. The economy grew. And by the end of the year, leaders of both Sendero Luminoso and MRTA had been apprehended (though, sadly, not before Sendero Luminoso had brutally assassinated beloved community activist María Elena Moyano and detonated lethal truck bombs in the Lima neighborhood of Miraflores).

Despite the arrests, the Internal Conflict wasn't over. In December of 1996, during Fujimori's second term as president, 14 members of MRTA stormed the Japanese ambassador's residence and hundreds of prominent people were taken hostage. The guerrillas demanded, among other things, the release of imprisoned MRTA members, a rollback of the government's free-market reforms and improvements in prison conditions. Most of the hostages were released, although 72 men were held until the following April, when Peruvian commandos stormed the embassy, killing the captors and releasing all of the hostages except one, who died along with two soldiers. This action later came under intense criticism as it was claimed that members of MRTA were repeatedly shot – despite attempts to surrender.

By the end of his second term, Fujimori's administration was plagued by allegations of corruption. He ran for a third term in 2000 (which is technically unconstitutional) and remained in power despite the fact that he didn't have the simple majority necessary to claim the election. Within the year, however, he was forced to flee the country after it was revealed that his security chief Vladimiro Montesinos had been embezzling government funds and bribing elected officials and the media. (Many of these acts were caught on film: the 'Vladivideos' – all 2700 of them – riveted the nation when they first aired in 2001.) Fujimori formally resigned the presidency from abroad, but the legislature rejected the gesture, voting him out of office and declaring him 'morally unfit' to govern.

Peru, however, hadn't heard the last of Fujimori. In 2005, he returned to South America, only to be arrested in Chile on an extradition warrant to face long-standing charges of corruption, kidnapping and human-rights violations. He was extradited to Peru in 2007 and, that same year, was convicted of ordering an illegal search. Two years later, he was convicted of ordering extrajudicial killings, and three months after that, was convicted of channeling millions of dollars in state funds to Montesinos. In 2009, he also pleaded guilty to wiretapping and bribery. Altogether, he faces almost three decades in state prison. (Montesinos, in the meantime, is serving a prison term of 20 years, for bribery and selling arms to Colombian rebels.)

Fujimori has shown little remorse for his actions. At his embezzlement trial, he simply said, 'The true judgment for me is that of the people, who have long absolved me in their hearts.'

The life of activist María Elena Moyano – assassinated by Sendero Luminoso in 1992 – is wonderfully chronicled in *The Autobiography of María Elena Moyano*, by Patricia Taylor Edmisten.

The hard-hitting documentary *State of Fear: The Truth About Terrorism* (2005), directed by Pamela Yates, examines Sendero Luminoso's devastating effect on Peru and the erosion of democracy under Alberto Fujimori.

1992	**1993**	**1996**
Abimael Guzmán, the founder of Sendero Luminoso, is captured in Lima after he is found hiding out above a dance studio in the well-to-do neighborhood of Surco.	Mario Vargas Llosa publishes *Death in Andes*, a novel based on his experience leading the commission that investigated the murder of the journalists killed in Uchuraccay.	Guerrillas from the Movimiento Revolucionario Túpac Amaru (MRTA) storm the Japanese ambassador's residence in Lima and hold 72 people hostage for four months; all of the guerrillas are killed in the ensuing raid.

THE 21ST CENTURY

The new millennium, thus far, has been better to Peru than the previous two, and the country has been enjoying a decade of relative stability. In 2001, shoeshine-boy-turned-Stanford-economist Alejandro Toledo became the first person of Quechua ethnicity to ever be elected to the presidency. (Until then, Peru had had *mestizo* presidents, but never a full-blooded *indígena*.) However, along with his new title Toledo inherited some very difficult economic and political situations: he lacked a majority in congress, which hampered his effectiveness, and the country was in the midst of an economic recession. By 2003, his popularity had reached an all-time low of less than 10%.

Following the conclusion of Toledo's term in 2006, the election turned into a three-way contest between right-wing candidate Lourdes Flores, populist Ollanta Humala and – of all people – the APRA's Alan García, the very man who had put Peru on a path to financial ruin during the late 1980s. After a run-off election, voters eventually settled on García. His second term – thus far – has been relatively stable. The economy has performed well, due to a strong market in mining and agricultural exports, and strong local governance in Lima has left the capital renewed and its port facilities upgraded after decades of decay.

Forgotten Continent: The Battle for Latin America's Soul (2009) is an acclaimed political tome by *Economist* contributor Michael Reid that examines the continent's strained relations with the US and Europe.

IN THE WAKE OF THE INTERNAL CONFLICT: TRUTH & RECONCILIATION

One of the most remarkable things to come out of Alejandro Toledo's presidency (2001–2006) was the establishment of the country's Comisión de la Verdad y Reconciliación (Truth & Reconciliation Commission). Chaired by Salomón Lerner, a philosopher at Lima's Catholic University, the commission thoroughly examined the innumerable acts of mass violence that plagued Peru throughout the Internal Conflict (1980–2000). Though the panel wasn't endowed with prosecutorial powers, its public hearings nonetheless proved to be an emotional – and tremendously cathartic act. Men and women of all ages and races came forward to testify to the massacres, rapes and disappearances that had occurred at the hands of the military and the various guerrilla groups during those 20 years.

In August of 2003, the commission issued its final report, revealing that the death toll from that era was more than twice what anyone had ever estimated: almost 70,000 people had been killed or disappeared. Moreover, children had been left orphaned, villages had been abandoned and thousands of lives left in tatters. Along with the final report, the commission also staged an extraordinarily moving exhibit of photography called *Yuyanapaq* ('to remember' in Quechua) that is now housed at Lima's Museo de la Nación (p94). A permanent museum to house this archive – to be called the Museo de la Memoria (Museum of Memory), spearheaded by Mario Vargas Llosa – was in the early planning stages in 2009.

Learn more about the commission's work (and download their final report) by visiting their website at www.cverdad.org.pe.

2000	2001	2003
Fujimori flees to Japan after videos surface showing his intelligence chief bribing officials and the media; the Peruvian legislature votes him out of office.	Alejandro Toledo becomes the first indigenous person to govern an Andean country; Alan García returns to Peru after the statute of limitations expires on the corruption charges against him.	The country's Truth & Reconciliation Commission releases its final report on Peru's Internal Conflict; estimates of the dead reach 70,000.

García's term, however, has not been without outrage. His entire cabinet was forced to resign in 2008, after widespread allegations of bribery and corruption surfaced. And, that same year, he signed a law that allowed foreign companies to exploit natural resources in the Amazon. The legislation caused a backlash among various Amazon tribes, who blocked roads in the area in protest. In June of 2009, a confrontation between police and natives outside of Bagua left 33 people dead (most of them officers) and hundreds of civilians injured. The Peruvian congress revoked the law and, for now, the situation has cooled off. But the president nonetheless faces untold challenges: the development (or not) of the Amazon; how to deal with the resurgence of Sendero Luminoso around Ayacucho; and the continuing chasm that exists between rich and poor, indigenous and white in Peru. For the meantime, however, the country is enjoying a rare moment of prosperity and hope. One can only hope it will last.

2005	**2006**	**2009**
Construction of the Interoceanic Hwy, which opens an overland trade route between Peru and Brazil, begins in the Amazon Basin.	APRA candidate Alan García is elected to a second, nonconsecutive term as president after a run-off contest.	Fujimori is convicted of embezzling; this is in addition to prior convictions for authorizing an illegal search and ordering military death squads to carry out extrajudicial killings.

The Culture

THE NATIONAL PSYCHE

National identity is a tricky thing in Peru, which is less a nation than an agglomeration of cultures thrown together by historical circumstance. There is the culture of the coast: a boisterous blend of Spanish tradition infused with African and indigenous ways. There is the culture of the Andes, more timid in its aspect, where Catholic belief is honored with indigenous rite. There is the culture of the Amazon Basin – not a single culture, but an only-in-the-jungle mix of enterprising frontier settlers and an abundance of local ethnicities, from Asháninkas to Shipibos. Each of these regional identities is as unique as the singular geographies they emerge from, yet each is also dynamic and elastic, continually digesting a bounty of influences from outside. Dance bands from Chiclayo play *cumbias* (salsa-like music) imported from Colombia. Lima's designers incorporate traditional alpaca weaving styles into avant-garde fashion. And Cuzco restaurants serve Andean specialties prepared using Mediterranean techniques. So what is Peruvian? And what does it mean to be Peruvian? The answer all depends on who you ask – and when. Peru is still trying to figure it out.

This bubbling social tension has produced a rich legacy of art, literature, music and cuisine – but it hasn't come without conflict. In the Andes, the area surrounding the department of Ayacucho is still recovering from hostilities in the 1980s and '90s that left almost 70,000 dead and hundreds of thousands of civilians trapped in a spin cycle of violence between Sendero Luminoso (Shining Path) guerrillas and the Peruvian military. In 2009, in the northern province of Bagua, various indigenous groups clashed with police over the development of Amazonian lands without their consent. The confrontation left roads blocked, cities cut off and almost three dozen dead.

Moreover, Peru continues to struggle with issues of race and class. Long dominated by a fair-skinned oligarchy in Lima, the country has, over the years, begun to embrace its indigenous roots. Since the 1970s, Quechua has been listed as an official language. In 2001, Alejandro Toledo became the first indigenous Peruvian to be elected to the presidency. And, more recently, a culinary renaissance has popularized dishes that incorporate traditionally indigenous foodstuffs such as *cuy* (guinea pig) and quinoa (a native grain). Despite the gains, racism persists – and while official acts of discrimination are prohibited, they are not uncommon.

Also significant are the economic issues. While the boom of recent years has helped reduce the poverty rate by about 15%, there is still an extraordinary disparity between the wealthy few and everyone else, with about half of Peru living under the poverty line. In some segments of society, highly traditional notions of gender roles – men at work, women at home – remain firmly in place (though there is a burgeoning generation of professional women). Attitudes towards homosexuality remain retrograde.

But even as the meaning of 'Peruvian' varies from one individual to another, from one region to the next, there are unifying elements. Peruvians share a fervor for robust cuisine, soulful music and the thrill of a neck-and-neck soccer match. At any time, a small gathering can turn into an impromptu party. Peru is a country that takes family and friendship seriously, treating its guests with warmth and consideration. It is a culture, ultimately, that faces its setbacks with stoicism and plenty of dark humor – and also lots of hope.

Based on the real-life search for the elusive leader of Sendero Luminoso, *The Dancer Upstairs* is a gripping novel by Nicholas Shakespeare that was made into a movie of the same name starring Javier Bardem.

LIFESTYLE

With a geography that encompasses desert, Andean plateau and lowland jungle, Peru is relentlessly touted as a land of contrasts. This metaphor couldn't be more appropriate in describing its society: a mixture of rich and poor, indigenous and white, black and Asian, young and old. Nowhere is this more obvious than in Lima, where wealthy neighborhoods, full of sprawling modernist mansions, abut shantytowns built with salvaged tin.

The recent economic boom has been good to the country. Roads have been paved, trash has been picked up and urban infrastructure – even in poor neighborhoods – has been improved. However, there is still a yawning disparity between rich and poor. The richest 10th of the country receives 41% of the income, while the poorest fifth makes do with less than 4%. The poverty is grinding: the minimum monthly wage stands at about US$200, and according to one UN report from 2008, 54% of the population lives below the poverty line, with almost 20% of the people surviving on less than US$2 per day. Approximately one in four children under the age of five is malnourished, and more than a quarter of the population does not have access to electricity. Naturally, it is rural, indigenous people who make up the majority of the country's poor and represent an outsized share of the extreme poverty cases. In rural areas, the poor survive largely from subsistence agriculture, living in traditional adobe or tin houses that often lack electricity and indoor plumbing.

In cities, the extreme poor live in shantytowns, while the lower and middle classes live in concrete, apartment-style housing or small stand-alone homes, much of which was produced throughout the 20th century. Units have a shared living area, a kitchen and one or more bedrooms – these are generally shared by more than one generation. More affluent urban homes consist of stand-alone houses, many built in a modernist or Spanish style and bordered by gardens and high walls.

The national life expectancy has reached an all-time high of 71 years – a vast improvement from 1960, when it stood at a meager 48. (As a comparison: life expectancy in the USA is 78 years.) However, this statistic can vary dramatically with geography: someone living in the Andes, for example, has a life expectancy of only 57 years. Though big cities feature all the amenities of modern life, access to technology remains uneven. Peru has 81 telephone main lines per 1000 people, compared to 588 in the US and 221 in neighboring Chile. However, the increased availability of cell-phone technology means that 55 out of 100 people in Peru have access to telephone systems of one sort or another.

Family remains the nucleus of social and cultural life, and groups of the same clan will often live near each other. Couples have an average of 2.4 children, though rural families tend to be bigger and poor extended families are more likely to live together. However, like everywhere else in the world, Peru has a high degree of internal migration: according to the Peruvian census bureau, almost 76% of the country's total population is now urban. This means that the villager born in Alca might one day find himself working in Arequipa. But most likely, he will go to Lima, which continues to serve as the center of industry, business and government life in Peru.

SOCIAL GRACES

Peruvians are polite, indeed formal, in their interactions. Even a brief interchange, such as giving a taxi driver your destination, is preceded by *'buenos días'* (good morning). A hearty handshake is normally given at the beginning and end of even the briefest meeting. Among friends, an *abrazo* (back-slapping hug) is in order. Women will often greet each

---

For a well-written, well-reported overview of the capital's social and cultural past, pick up James Higgins' *Lima: A Cultural History*.

Death in the Andes by Mario Vargas Llosa is a fictional examination of the violence that gripped the country in the 1980s. Its characterization of Peruvian society is, as always, revealing.

other with a kiss, as will men and women – except in business settings, where a handshake is appropriate. Indigenous people don't kiss and their handshakes, when offered, tend to have a light touch. If invited to visit a Peruvian home, it is considered good manners to take a gift such as flowers or candy.

As in the rest of Latin America, the concept of time is elastic; the concept of 'on time' (especially outside big cities) is purely relative. Moreover, locals are used to less personal space than some Western travelers may be accustomed to: expect seating in public areas, such as buses and trains, to be thisclose.

POPULATION

Peru is essentially a bicultural society, comprised of two roughly same-sized parts: indigenous people and *criollos*. It's a division that breaks out roughly along class lines. The more affluent urban class is made up of whites and fair-skinned *mestizos* (people of mixed indigenous and Spanish descent) – all of whom generally refer to themselves as *criollos* (natives of Peru). Within this segment, a wealthy upper class has historically taken the top roles in politics and business, while the middle class has filled midlevel white-collar positions, such as clerks, teachers and entrepreneurs.

The other half of the population is made up primarily of indigenous *campesinos* (peasants). About 45% of Peru's population is pure *indígena* (people of indigenous descent), making it one of three countries in Latin America to have such high indigenous representation. (Note: in Spanish, *indígena* is the appropriate term; *indios* can be considered insulting, depending on how it is used.) Most *indígenas* are Quechua-speaking and live in the highlands, while a smaller percentage around the Lake Titicaca region speak Aymara. In the Amazon, which contains about 6% of the country's total population, various indigenous ethnic groups speak a plethora of other languages.

Afro-Peruvians, Asians and other immigrant groups are also represented, but cumulatively make up only 3% of the population. Among the elite, retrograde ideas about race persist. Nonwhite people are often discriminated against, especially in Lima's upmarket bars, nightclubs and discos.

More than a quarter of all Peruvians – mostly *indígenas* – live in rural settings, surviving from subsistence farming or working as laborers. This statistic represents a shift from the 1960s, when more than half of the population lived in the countryside. The turmoil of the 1980s helped fuel an exodus from the highlands to the cities, which taxed overburdened municipal infrastructures, particularly in the capital. Issues of effective sanitation and electrification remain challenges for some informal squatter settlements known as *pueblos jovenes* (young towns). Moreover, life doesn't always get better for people who move to the cities. Though the national unemployment rate is officially 8.4%, underemployment is rampant – especially in Lima, with some experts estimating that more than half of the city's residents are underemployed.

MEDIA

The situation for the working press has improved greatly since the 1980s, when civil strife resulted in the deaths of both foreign and domestic journalists. But Alberto Fujimori's regime still casts a shadow over the industry: his administration was renowned for spying on opposition journalists and bribing broadcasters for favorable coverage. Though things have improved, first under Toledo, and then under Alan García, free expression has its limits. Television and radio stations critical of government policy are often

Daniel Alarcón's often heart-breaking short stories cover the gamut of contemporary Peruvian culture. The best of these can be found in the 2007 collection *War by Candlelight*.

Puno-born Martin Chambi (1891–1973) was a celebrated photographer who spent the early 20th century assiduously documenting life in the Andes. See a gallery of his starkly beautiful black-and-white images at www.martinchambi .com.

One of the few works by Julio Ramón Ribeyro available in translation, *Chronicle of San Gabriel* is a poignant tale of a young man from Lima who goes to live with his frayed, extended family at a highland ranch.

shut down for procedural reasons, such as expired licenses. In June 2009, for example, a broadcaster in Bagua was shut down on a technicality following the area's violent protests against the development of Amazonian lands. (The government accused the station of inciting riots. The station's management responded that they simply aired interviews with individuals who had witnessed the clashes.) In addition, the government owns two TV networks, a radio station and a print news agency (Andina) – which means that it has a strong role in shaping the news.

Working conditions are most difficult for journalists who work in the provinces, with physical aggression and death threats (from private interests, government officials and drug traffickers) being the most common problems, according to Freedom House, an international nonprofit that monitors press freedoms.

RELIGION

It was a Peruvian priest, Gustavo Gutiérrez, who first articulated the principles of liberation theology – the theory that links Christian thought to social justice – in 1971. He now teaches in the United States.

Though there is widespread freedom of religion, Peru remains largely Roman Catholic. More than 81% of the population identifies as such (though only 15% of them attend services on a weekly basis). The Church enjoys support from the state: it has a largely tax-exempt status and Catholicism is the official religion of the military. Moreover, all of the Church's bishops, and up to an eighth of its overall clergy, receive monthly government stipends. This has generated outcries from some evangelical groups that do not receive the same generous treatment. Even so, evangelicals and other Protestants are a growing force, representing up to 13% of the nation's population.

Indigenous people have largely adapted Catholic deities to their own beliefs. Viracocha (the creator) is symbolized by the Christian God, while Pachamama (the earth mother) is represented by the Virgin Mary. Indigenous festivities that are purportedly Catholic have many layers of meaning. In Puno, for example, the locals host a festival in honor of La Virgen de la Candelaria every February 2 (Candlemas). The Virgin, however, is closely identified with Pachamama, as well as natural elements such as lightning. Moreover, she is often referred to as Mamacha Candelaria and is upheld as a symbol of fertility. The feast can last for up to two weeks, during which time local dancers – dressed in bright outfits and large animal masks – take to the streets in her honor. (See p201 for more on Puno's religious fiestas.)

WOMEN IN PERU

Award-winning Peruvian filmmaker Claudia Llosa directed the drama *Madeinusa* – an official selection at the Sundance Film Festival in 2006 – about an Andean girl's tragic coming-of-age. It is available internationally on DVD.

Women can vote and own property, but the situation remains challenging in a country where the unwritten laws of machismo are widely accepted. For starters, the female illiteracy rate of more than 16% is almost three times that of men. In addition, women, on average, make only 56 cents to every dollar a man earns. Access to health care is limited, especially in the Andes: Peru has one of the highest maternal mortality rates in Latin America. In addition, the leading cause of death among women of child-bearing age is breast or gynecological cancer. In the mid '90s, under Fujimori, a number of civil organizations, including Amnesty International, reported that the government forcibly sterilized tens of thousands of women in poor, rural areas. As a result, a law was passed in 1999 requiring informed consent for any sterilization procedure.

In recent decades, the overall situation has improved. A number of laws barring domestic violence and sexual assault have been passed, and women now make up 28% of the country's professional class (senior officials, managers and legislators) and almost 30% of congress. In 2006, right-of-center candidate Lourdes Flores ran for the presidency, losing a chance at the final run-off by only 1% of the vote. And, interestingly, Peruvian women have been making great strides in sports (see p57).

ARTS
Literature

Mario Vargas Llosa (b 1936) is Peru's most famous writer, hailed alongside 20th-century Latin American luminaries such as Gabriel García Márquez, Julio Cortázar and Carlos Fuentes. His novels evoke James Joyce in their complexity, meandering through time and shifting perspectives, demanding alertness through each turn of the page. Beyond his artistry, Vargas Llosa is also a keen social observer, casting a spotlight on the naked corruption of the ruling class and the peculiarities of Peruvian society. (This instinct is what led him to make his failed bid for the presidency in 1989.) Luckily for English-language readers, his more than two dozen novels are available in translation. The best place to start is *La ciudad y los perros* (The Time of the Hero), based on his experience at a Peruvian military academy. (The soldiers at his old academy responded to the novel by burning it.) Other standouts include *La fiesta del chivo* (The Feast of the Goat), which takes place in the Dominican Republic, and *Historia de Mayta* (The Real Life of Alejandro Mayta), a bleak, multifaceted look at the life of a fictional revolutionary.

Alfredo Bryce Echenique (b 1939) is another keen observer, particularly of the upper class. His most well known book, *Un mundo para Julius* (A World for Julius), published in 1972, tracks a bourgeois child's relationship to a distant mother and his loyalty to the servants with whom he spends much of his time. In 2002, Echenique won the Planeta literary award, Spain's most lucrative literary prize, for *El huerto de mi amada* (My Beloved's Garden), which recounts an affair between a 33-year-old woman and a teenage boy in 1950s Lima.

Demonstrating a distinct Peruvian penchant for dark humor is Julio Ramón Ribeyro (1929–94). Though never a bestselling author, he is critically acclaimed for his insightful stories and essays, which focus on the vagaries of lower-middle-class life. His work is available in English in *Marginal Voices: Selected Stories* (1993). If you are just learning to read Spanish, his concisely written pieces are an ideal place to start exploring Peruvian literature.

Also significant is rising literary star Daniel Alarcón (b 1977), a Peruvian-American writer whose award-winning short stories have appeared in the *New Yorker* magazine. His debut novel, *Lost City Radio*, about a country recovering from civil war, was published to wide acclaim in 2007.

Two Peruvian writers are noted for their portrayals of indigenous reality. José María Arguedas (1911–69), who was born in the Andes, introduced a Quechua syntax to Spanish fiction in novels such as *Los ríos profundos* (Deep Rivers) and *Yawar fiesta*, among others. Ciro Alegría (1909–67) covered the repression of Andean communities in *El mundo es ancho y ajeno* (Broad and Alien is the World). For a worthwhile compilation of women writers, pick up *Fire From the Andes: Short Fiction by Women from Bolivia, Ecuador and Peru* (1998), which includes stories by Peruvian authors such as Catalina Lohmann and Pilar Dughi.

If Vargas Llosa is the country's greatest novelist, then César Vallejo (1892–1938) is its greatest poet. A protégé of renowned Peruvian essayist Abraham Valdelomar (1888–1919), he published only three slim books –

Students of Latin American literature can log on to www.peru.info to find free, downloadable brochures (in Spanish) that detail important sites in the lives of Peruvian literary figures. Click on 'Publicaciones y Folletos.'

Mario Vargas Llosa's reigning literary masterpiece is *The War of the End of the World* (1981), which examines the disaffected sides of a bloody uprising in Brazil in rich, psychological detail.

César Vallejo's complete works – in English and Spanish – are now available in a single volume, *The Complete Poetry of César Vallejo: A Bilingual Edition*, with translations by Clayton Eshleman.

Los heraldos negros (The Black Heralds), *Trilce* and *Poemas humanos* (Human Poems) – but has long been regarded as one of the most innovative Latin American poets of the 20th century. Vallejo frequently touched on existential themes and was known for pushing the language to its limits, inventing words when real ones no longer suited him.

Cinema & Television

Prominent German film director Werner Herzog has had a long-running love–hate affair with the Peruvian Amazon, best appreciated in his movies *Aguirre, the Wrath of God* and *Fitzcarraldo*.

Once in a state of perpetual anemia, Peruvian cinema has rebounded in recent years. In 2008, historically underfunded CONACINE, the government institute devoted to film production, invested US$500,000 in four projects by young Peruvian filmmakers. These include *Tarata* (2009) by Fabrizio Aguilar, about the Sendero Luminoso bombing of a Miraflores street in 1992.

Claudia Llosa is perhaps the most noteworthy contemporary director of the moment: in 2009, she received a Golden Bear at the Berlin International Film Festival for *La teta asustada* (The Milk of Sorrow), a drama about the fears plaguing an abused woman. Also very well known is Francisco Lombardi, who produced a film version of Vargas Llosa's *La ciudad y los perros* (The Time of the Hero) in 1985, as well as the prize-winning *Caídos del Cielo* (Fallen From Heaven), based on a story by Ribeyro. He has overseen almost a dozen other productions.

Peruvian TV can't be said to be doing quite as well. Entire networks are controlled by the government, and the bulk of programming consists largely of *telenovelas* (Spanish-language soaps) and low-budget talk and news shows (the most intriguing of which is hosted by journalist Jaime Bayly). The medium is regaining some credibility after it was revealed in 2001 that executives from the major networks took money from Fujimori's intelligence-agency chief Vladimiro Montesinos in exchange for positive coverage. Many deals were captured on film and showed Montesinos giving network heads cash payoffs of hundreds of thousands of dollars. The 'Vladivideos,' as they were known, riveted the country when they began surfacing at the beginning of Toledo's presidency. He is currently in jail, having been found guilty of embezzlement, influence peddling and bribery.

Music

Groove to Peru's Amazon-meets-the-Andes-meets-Colombian-*cumbias* dance music with *The Roots of Chicha*, the first *chicha* compilation album to be released outside Peru.

Like Peru's food, its traditional music is an intercontinental fusion of elements. Pre-Columbian cultures contributed bamboo flutes, the Spaniards brought stringed instruments and the Africans gave it a backbone of fluid, percussive rhythm. By and large, music tends to be a regional affair: African-influenced *landós* are predominant on the coast, indigenous *huaynos* are heard in the Andes and *criollo* waltzes are danced to in the coastal urban centers.

In the mountains, *huayno* is the purest expression of pre-Columbian music. (The most famous *huayno* is certainly 'El Cóndor Pasa', which was made over as a pop standard in the 1970s by the US duo Simon & Garfunkel – and which has been beaten to death by 'lite' music enthusiasts ever since.) Stylistically, it's heavy on bamboo wind instruments such as *quenas* (bamboo flutes of varying lengths) and *zampoñas* (panpipes). Also seen are *ocarinas,* small, oval, clay instruments with up to 12 holes. For percussion, drums are typically made from a hollowed tree trunk covered with a stretched goatskin. *Huaynos,* typically referred to as *música folklórica* (folkloric music), are musical arrangements that include the use of string instruments, the most typical being the *charango,* a tiny 10-stringed mandolin made out of an armadillo shell. Many contemporary *huaynos* also include the use of harps, and even brass instruments can generally be seen being used by the cacophonous strolling bands that parade through small Peruvian towns on fiesta days. For a worthwhile roundup of good *música folklórica,* pick up *Andean Legacy* by Narada, a label specializing in global sounds.

Over the last several decades, the *huayno* has blended with surf guitars and Colombian *cumbia* to produce *chicha* – a danceable sound closely identified with the Amazon region. It is what you will likely hear if holed up in a working-class bar, though it does turn up regularly on dance floors at upscale discos in Lima. Well-known *chicha* bands include Los Shapis, Los Mirlos and Grupo Belen de Tarma. *Cumbia,* as a result, is also very popular. Grupo 5, which hails from the Chiclayo area, is currently one of the favorite bands in this genre.

On the coast, *música criolla* (*criollo* music) has its roots in both Spain and Africa. The main instrumentation is guitars and a *cajón,* a wooden box on which the player sits and drums out a rhythm with his hands. The most famous of *criollo* styles is the *vals peruano* (Peruvian waltz), a 3/4-time waltz that in no way resembles anything coming out of Vienna. It is fast moving, rhythmic and full of complex Spanish-guitar melodies. The most legendary *criolla* singer and composer is Chabuca Granda (1920–1983), whose breathy vocals and expressive lyrics are full of longing and nostalgia. Also well regarded is Lucha Reyes (1936–1973), who in addition to her powerful voice was renowned for her extravagant wigs. Arturo 'Zambo' Cavero (1940–2009) was another revered crooner, known for his gravelly vocals and soulful interpretation of Peruvian classics. (His death, in 2009, generated wall to wall coverage on Peruvian television and drew thousands of mourners, including President Alan García.)

Sharing the African-Spanish roots is *landó,* on the bluesier end of the *criolla* scale. These include elements of call-and-response backed up by guitar and percussion. The lyrics focus on slavery, violence and other social issues. Standout performers in the genre include contemporary singers Susana Baca (b 1944) and Eva Ayllón (b 1956). One of the best ways to enjoy *música criolla* is to see it performed live at one of the many *peñas* (small clubs) in Lima (p117) or by traveling to Chincha (p128), on the south coast, for Verano Negro, an Afro-Peruvian cultural festival that takes place every February. (For more on Afro-Peruvian music, see the boxed text, p129.)

Contemporary popular music in Peru includes a selection of rock, pop, ska, hip-hop and punk. The home-grown Peruvian rock scene is limited, but, as a genre it has made significant strides since the 1970s, when it was cast out as 'alienating and Yankee' by Juan Velasco's military regime. In the '80s an underground scene emerged, led by bands such as Autopsia, Leusemia and Narcosis – the latter two are still playing today. Other newer groups have met with more international success. The pop-rock band Libido, for example, has sold millions of albums and received a number of Video Music Awards from MTV Latin America. In early 2009, the band released its fifth album, *Un nuevo día.* In recent years, as different genres such as electronica have become increasingly popular, a growing number of musicians, such as Miki González, Novalima and Jaime Cuadra, have started sampling traditional *criolla* and *huayno* sounds and fusing them with digital beats.

Architecture

From Inca monumentalism to Spanish baroque to boxy modernism, an extraordinarily varied assortment of architectural styles can be found in Peru. The most renowned example of pre-Columbian architecture is the impressive mountaintop retreat built by the Incas at Machu Picchu, a site that dates back to 1440. Built in the imperial style, it is composed of roughly 140

If you're going to buy only one piece of *criollo* music to take home, consider Arturo 'Zambo' Cavero's achingly beautiful eponymous album from 1993. A downloadable version can be purchased online.

For an excellent primer on black Peruvian music, pick up – or download – the David Byrne–produced compilation *Afro-Peruvian Classics: The Soul of Black Peru.*

A comprehensive listing of concerts, as well as links and information on just about every known Peruvian rock band, can be found online at www .rockperu.com.

PERUVIAN PLAYLIST

Interested in picking up a little traditional Peruvian music without having to drag home a stack of albums? No problem. We've compiled a playlist of essential songs for download. All you need is the pisco.

'Cada Domingo a las 12 después de la misa,' Arturo 'Zambo' Cavero The lyric pays tribute to a love lost; Cavero at his best.

'La flor de la canela,' Chabuca Granda A paean to Lima by Peru's most venerated songwriter.

'Azucar de caña,' Eva Ayllón A *landó* by Peru's premiere Afro-Peruvian songstress.

'El huerto de mi amada,' Los Morochucos This celebrated 20th-century trio produced incredible harmonies. The title of this song (My Beloved's Garden) inspired a novel of the same name by Alfredo Bryce Echenique.

'Machete,' Novalima Grooving *landó* beats are given a contemporary makeover by a band that fuses traditional sounds with electronica.

'La danza de Los Mirlos,' Los Mirlos The grooviest of the Amazon's psychedelic *chicha* tunes.

'Zamba Malató,' Perú Negro A percussion-driven piece by one of the country's longest-running Afro-Peruvian bands.

'Cuando llora mi guitarra,' Oscar Áviles A traditional waltz performed by one of the most prolific composers of traditional 20th-century music.

'Toro mata,' Susana Baca Another hip-shaking *landó* by a singer renowned for repopularizing Afro-Peruvian music.

A buzzing visual tribute to the capital, Mario Testino's book *Lima* features the renowned fashion photographer's pictures of the city alongside works by emerging Peruvian artists.

structures connected by more than 100 flights of stone steps. It epitomizes the grand scale of Inca architecture, with engineering that is just as impressive: trapezoidal window frames are earthquake resistant, and intricate stone walls are constructed without mortar. Other period structures can be found at Cuzco and its environs (p232) and Pisac (p259).

Far more horizontal in its lines is the pre-Columbian architecture of the coast. A good example of this is Chan Chan (p349), north of Trujillo, erected by the Chimú civilization between AD 1000 and 1400. Built entirely of adobe brick, the ancient city's temples and houses are flat, blending seamlessly into the broad desert horizon – the sort of lines that would do Frank Lloyd Wright proud.

Juxtaposed against the austerity of indigenous architecture are the hundreds of ornate Spanish churches and colonial houses that serve as the center of so many cities and towns. The 16th century saw a veritable building boom of structures constructed in what is referred to as 'Andean baroque' – a baroque style with indigenous flourishes. Prime examples are the grand Iglesia de la Compañía de Jesús (p230) in Cuzco and the fabulously ornate Jesuit church in Andahuaylillas (p288), known as the 'Sistine Chapel of Latin America.' Less flamboyant – but still equally intriguing – are the colonial and colonial-style structures found in Arequipa. The city's gleaming buildings are made primarily from a white volcanic rock called *sillar*. Particularly worthwhile is the Monasterio de Santa Catalina (p164) – even if you think you've already been to every church worth seeing in Peru, this is one not to miss.

During the 19th century, the influence of Western European architecture was seen in neoclassical, beaux arts and Victorian structures, which popped up in major cities. The 20th century saw buildings constructed in various idioms, from art deco to space-age modern. In the 1960s and '70s, cities such as Lima produced more concrete-heavy brutalism than you can shake a cement mixer at. In recent years, some Peruvian design offices – such as Longhi Architects – have begun to incorporate pre-Columbian design elements into contemporary architecture, but these projects have been primarily residential.

Painting & Sculpture

The country's most famous art movement dates from the 17th and 18th centuries, when the artists of the Cuzco School produced thousands of religious paintings, the vast majority of which remain unattributed. Created by native and *mestizo* artists, the pieces frequently feature holy figures laced in gold paint and rendered in a style inspired by mannerist and late Gothic art, but also bear traces of an indigenous color palette and iconography. Today, these hang in museums and churches throughout Peru – and reproductions are sold in many crafts markets.

One of the most well-known artistic figures of the 19th century is Pancho Fierro (1807–1879), the illegitimate son of a priest and a slave, who painted highly evocative watercolors of the everyday figures that occupied Lima's streets: fishmongers, teachers and Catholic religious figures clothed in lush robes.

In the early 20th century, an indigenous movement led by painter José Sabogal (1888–1956) achieved national prominence. Like his contemporaries in Mexico (Diego Rivera and Rufino Tamayo), Sabogal was interested in integrating pre-Columbian design with Peruvian fine art. He painted *indígena* women and incorporated textile patterns into his work. As director of the National School of Arts in Lima, he influenced a whole generation of painters, including Julia Codesido (1892–1979), Mario Urteaga (1875–1957) and Enrique Camino Brent (1909–1960). By the 1960s, abstract art took hold, led by artists such as Fernando de Szyszlo (b 1925), who incorporated pre-Columbian myth into his imagery. Other well-known 20th-century artists are Alberto Quintanilla (b 1934), and Victor Delfín (b 1927), whose sculpture of a couple kissing sits prominently on a Miraflores cliff top. Two contemporary artists whose work is worth seeking out are photographer Natalia Iguíñiz (b 1973) and the award-winning painter Fernando Gutiérrez (b 1978). Iguíñiz' oversized portraits starkly illustrate issues of race and class; Gutiérrez produces manga-influenced canvases that illustrate the hapless adventures of invented Peruvian superheroes.

Crafts

Peru has a long tradition of producing extraordinarily rendered crafts and folk art. Intricate textiles have an extensive history among both Andean and coastal indigenous cultures, who have long woven rugs, ponchos and wall hangings decorated with elaborate anthropomorphic designs and graphic elements. On the coast, Paracas is historically famous for its weaving: a stellar textile featuring felines, serpents and birds, held in the Museo Larco in Lima (p95), is more than 1000 years old.

Pottery is also well developed. The most stunning designs are those made in the tradition of the Moche people of the northern coast, who thrived for six centuries from AD 100. Vases and other vessels are made to depict humans in a realist style. The most famous of these – the *huacos eróticos* – depict a variety of sexual acts. Increasingly popular is pottery made in the Chancay style: cartoonish figures crafted with sand-colored clay and painted with brown ink. In the north, the contemporary, rounded black-and-white pottery made in the village of Chulucanas (p373) is also popular.

Religious crafts are bountiful in most regions, with the *retablos* (three-dimensional dioramas) of Ayacucho being particularly renowned. Other popular items include hand-tooled leather, filigree jewelry in gold and

Art of the Andes: From Chavín to Inca by Rebecca Stone-Miller provides a broad overview of Andean art and architecture, with more than 180 images to accompany and explain the text.

For a visual overview of some of the most stunning works of pre-Columbian ceramic portraiture, pick up *Moche Portraits from Ancient Peru* by Christopher Donnan.

THE MACHU PICCHU ARTIFACTS: PERU VERSUS YALE UNIVERSITY

When Hiram Bingham – the American explorer who told the world about Machu Picchu – left Peru after his final expedition in 1915, he could have never imagined that the pottery, bones and utensils (not to mention several mummies) he carted back to the USA would become the source of diplomatic friction between the United States and Peru almost a hundred years later.

When Bingham made his discoveries, in excursions that were financed by the National Geographic Society and Yale University, Peruvian law explicitly forbade the export of archaeological artifacts. Bingham, however, got a special one-time exemption so that he could study his Machu Picchu finds – under the condition that he return them to Peru by 1918. As part of the agreement, it was acknowledged that ultimate ownership of the artifacts resided with Peru.

Almost a century later, Yale still holds a vast majority of the pieces (which apparently number in the thousands), much to the dismay of the Peruvian government. With the university unwilling to return the objects, Peru threatened a lawsuit in 2005, but pulled back after both parties entered into negotiations. In 2007, a tentative settlement was announced: Yale would recognize Peru's title to the artifacts – but as part of the agreement, most of the pieces would remain in the USA for another century for the purpose of study. Eventually, the deal collapsed, and in late 2008 Peru officially filed suit against the university in US federal court. At the time of research, Yale had moved to dismiss the case. (The university's spokespeople have said that it is not clear whether the agreement Bingham had with the Peruvian government covered artifacts discovered on all three of his Machu Picchu expeditions or just the last one.) National Geographic's board of trustees, in the meantime, announced its unanimous position that the pieces should be returned to Peru. The response from Yale on that count has been silence.

silver, woven baskets and religious icons. Contemporary indigenous textiles, pottery and crafts, as well as replicas of historical pieces, can easily be found in crafts markets in Lima (p118), Ayacucho (p324), Cuzco (p253), Arequipa (p185) and Chulucanas (p373).

Dance

The national dance is the *marinera,* which has its roots in Peruvian colonial history. Performed to *música criolla,* the dance is a flirtation between a man and a woman, who circle each other in a rhythmic courtship. The man uses a straw hat to make way for a woman while she coyly hides her face behind a white handkerchief. Other dances include the *zamacueca,* which is closely related to the *marinera,* and the *vals peruano* (Peruvian waltz), both of which are danced by couples. *Zapateo* (literally, foot-stomping) is a popular Afro-Peruvian dance.

SPORTS

Everything you ever need to know about every regional Peruvian soccer team – large and small – is available at www.peru.com/futbol (in Spanish).

Fútbol (soccer) is the most sanctified spectator sport, followed with a fervor that borders on religious piety. The soccer season is from late March to November. Though there are many teams, their abilities are not exceptional: Peru hasn't qualified for the World Cup since 1982, and has not won a Copa América trophy (a competition among South American nations) since 1975. The best teams are from Lima, and the traditional *clásico* is the match between Alianza Lima and the Universitario de Deportes (La U).

Bullfighting is also well attended, particularly in Lima, where it is most popular. The traditional season runs from October to early December, when Lima's Plaza de Acho attracts internationally famous matadors. Outside of Lima, small bullfights occur at fiestas, but are rarely of a high standard. Travelers should be aware that the bulls are killed in Peruvian fights – so be prepared for gory spectacle.

Interestingly enough, the pieces appear to be of little aesthetic value. Bingham, in a 1920 letter in which he discussed returning the artifacts, wrote: 'There is nothing here that they will not be disappointed in. In fact when they see the material they will probably accuse us of having sent them a lot of rubbish instead of the original material.' Yale has reported that of the thousands of pieces, only 329 of the objects are 'museum-quality.'

For Peruvians, however, the case is about getting back what they feel is rightfully theirs. (Former Peruvian first lady Eliane Karp-Toledo has written opinion pieces on the matter in various US publications.) But the spat is also part of a larger issue facing the world of antiquities, in which renewed national pride is butting up against the acquisition practices of some global institutions. In recent years, countries such as Italy and Greece have begun demanding that museums return artifacts that may have been acquired through looting or theft. In 2008, the Metropolitan Museum of Art in New York City was forced to return an ancient terracotta vessel to Italy after it was reported that the piece had been looted. Greece is currently prodding the British Museum in Londo to return the Elgin marbles, part of a series of sculptures that once decorated the Parthenon.

Yale has argued that the case should be dismissed on the grounds that Peru's claims are without justification and that it has waited too long to file suit. (In addition, one of Bingham's descendants alleged in the press that the objects are better cared for at Yale than they would have been in Peru.) But, in this case, Peru has the paperwork in its favor. The European precedent, however, suggests that the case could drag on for years or even decades – in which case, the main group to benefit will be the lawyers.

Other sports, though not necessarily popular in Peru, have been well represented by Peruvian athletes, in particular, women. In 1988, the Peruvian women's volleyball team won the silver medal at the Seoul Olympics, and they still play competitively at an international level. Surfer Sofía Mulanovich became the first Peruvian – and Latin American – to win the Association of Professional Surfers world championship in 2004. And, in 2009, female professional boxer Kina Malpartida defeated a Brazilian opponent to retain her title as the World Boxing Association Champion in the super featherweight class.

Food & Drink

There is a revolution going on in Peru – and it has everything to do with food.

The country has long been a place where the concept of 'fusion' was a part of everyday cooking. Over the course of the last 400 years, nutty Andean stews mingled with Asian stir-fry techniques and Spanish rice dishes absorbed flavors from the Amazon, producing the country's famed *criollo* (creole) cooking. In the past decade, however, a generation of experimental young innovators has pushed this local fare forward by leaps and bounds. Led by charismatic Peruvian chef Gastón Acurio, this nouvelle cuisine movement, dubbed *novoandina*, has taken traditional cooking to unheard-of gastronomic heights.

Peru, once a country where important guests were treated to French meals and Scotch whisky, is now a place where high-end restaurants spotlight local flavors, serving up deft interpretations of Andean favorites such as seared *cuy* (guinea pig) and quinoa. The dining scene has blossomed. And tourism outfits have swept in to incorporate a culinary something as part of every tour. In 2000, the country became the site of the first Cordon Bleu academy in Latin America, and in 2009, *Bon Appétit* magazine named Lima the 'next great food city.'

The foodie fever has infected Peruvians at every level, with even the most humble *chicharrón* (fried pork) vendor hyperattentive to the vagaries of preparation and presentation. No small part of this is due to the media-friendly Acurio, whose culinary skill (his food is *that good*) and business acumen (at press time, he owned more than 20 restaurants around the globe) have given him rock-star status: children want to grow up to be chefs and his photograph seems to hang in more restaurants than the venerated local saints.

The short of it is that you will never go hungry in Peru: from humble spots in Moyobamba to trendy boîtes in Miraflores, this is a country devoted to keeping the human palate entertained.

STAPLES & SPECIALTIES

Peruvians typically begin their day with bread and coffee or tea, and in some cases, corn tamales or a pork sandwich, although American-style egg breakfasts are available in most restaurants. Lunch is the main meal of the day and generally includes three courses: an appetizer, main and dessert. Dinner tends to be smaller – often consisting of just one dish and a dessert.

Given the country's craggy topography, there are an infinite number of regional cuisines. But at a national level much of the country's cooking begins and ends with the humble potato. The tuber is from Peru, where hundreds of local varieties are transformed into a mind-boggling number of incredible dishes. Standouts include *ocopa* (potatoes with a spicy peanut sauce), *papa a la huancaína* (potato bathed in a creamy cheese sauce) and *causa* (an architectural potato salad stuffed with seafood, vegetables or chicken). Also popular is *papa rellena*, a mashed potato filled with ground beef and then deep-fried. Potatoes are also found in the chowderlike soups known as *chupe* and in *lomo saltado*, the simple beef stir-fries that headline every Peruvian menu.

Along the coast, ceviche plays a starring role. A chilled concoction of fish, shrimp or other seafood marinated in lime juice, onions, cilantro and chili peppers, it is typically served with a wedge of boiled corn and sweet potato.

Peruvian food is so popular among global chefs that even famed Spanish chef Ferran Adrià incorporates Andean ingredients into the cutting-edge molecular gastronomy at El Bulli, his Michelin-starred restaurant on Spain's Costa Brava.

Revolución Gastronómica, by noted Peruvian journalist Mirko Lauer and his daughter, Vera Lauer, examines (in Spanish) the complex set of social and political circumstances that gave rise to the country's current culinary boom.

Inka Kola, the neon-yellow soft drink, outsells global behemoths Coke and Pepsi in Peru.

THE COUNTRY'S TOP EATS

Collectively, the writers on this guidebook spent months on the road and ate hundreds of meals. Herewith, a list of the places so good they brought tears to our eyes and unbridled joy to our palates:

Arequipa: La Nueva Palomino serves melt-in-your-mouth roast pork and monstrous jars of *chicha* (fermented corn beer) in a packed, informal setting (see boxed text, p183).

Cuzco: Gastón Acurio's latest chic eat, Chicha (p248), serves an achingly tender *estofado de res* (beef stew). Look for a second outpost of this restaurant in Arequipa (p184).

Huancayo: Dip into the creamiest *papas a la huancaína* (steamed potatoes served with a spicy, creamy cheese sauce) in a flower-filled courtyard at Huancahuasi (p311).

Iquitos: A vintage rubber boom eatery, Gran Maloka produces an exquisite *chupín de pollo,* a thick, beautiful soup of chicken, egg and rice (p500).

Lima: El Verídico de Fidel has ceviches so deliciously aphrodisiacal you might find yourself making out with a waiter after your meal (p110).

Tarapoto: At La Patarashca don't miss the namesake dish, traditional platters of fresh-grilled Amazon giant shrimp and fish doused in garlic and cilantro (p457).

Trujillo: Restaurant Demarco is a small bistro that ladles out the butteriest, most lip-smacking *chupe de camarones* (shrimp chowder) in the land (p348).

Tiradito is a Japanese-influenced version: thin slices of fish served without onions, and sometimes bathed in a creamy hot pepper sauce. Seafood in general is a major facet of Peruvian cuisine – even in the mountains, where river trout is popular. Fish is prepared dozens of ways: *al ajo* (bathed in garlic), *frito* (fried) or *a la chorrillana* (cooked in white wine, tomatoes and onions). Shellfish appear regularly in soups, stews and Spanish omelets. *Choros a la chalaca* (chilled mussels with fresh corn salsa), *conchitas a la parmesana* (scallops baked with cheese) and *pulpo al olivo* (octopus in a smashed olive sauce) are favorites.

Soups are extraordinarily popular, especially in the chilly highlands, where these tend to be a generous, gut-warming experience. *Chupe de camarones* (shrimp chowder) is a mainstay, along with *sopa a la criolla* (a mild, creamy noodle soup with beef and vegetables) and *caldo de gallina* (a nourishing chicken soup with potatoes and vegetables).

Other common main dishes include *ají de gallina* (shredded chicken in spicy walnut sauce), *picante de pollo* (stewed chicken with yellow chilies and cilantro) and, in the highlands, *cuy chactado* (seared, pressed guinea pig). In the north, a favorite is *arroz con pato a la chiclayana* (a dish of duck and rice simmered in beer and cilantro, typical of the northern city of Chiclayo). *Aguaditos* are soupy risottos made with chicken, seafood or beef. In recent years, Amazonian dishes, such as *juanes* (a banana leaf stuffed with rice and chicken or pork), have also grown in popularity around the country.

Desserts tend to be hypersweet diabetes-inducing concoctions. *Suspiro limeña* is the most famous, consisting of *manjar blanco* (caramel) topped with sweet meringue. Also popular are *alfajores* (cookie sandwiches with caramel) and *crema volteada* (flan). Lighter and fruitier is *mazamorra morada,* a purple-corn pudding (of Afro-Peruvian origin) stocked with chunks of fresh pineapple.

In addition to Gastón Acurio, Peru's most celebrated *novoandina* chefs (all based in Lima) include Pedro Miguel Schiaffino (Malabar), Rafael Osterling (Rafael) and Rafael Piqueras (Fusión).

Conchas negras (literally, black shells) are a mangrove mollusk resembling a mussel that are popular in ceviche. They are alleged, by some, to have unmatched aphrodisiac qualities.

DRINKS

The main soft drink brands are available here, though the locals have a passion for the bubble-gum-flavored Inca Kola, the nuclear-yellow national favorite. Fresh fruit juices are also popular, as are traditional drinks such as

The Exotic Kitchens of Peru by noted food writer Copeland Marks is not only a comprehensive cookbook, but an excellent guide to understanding the origins of many Peruvian dishes.

Cuy was an important source of protein for pre-Columbian native people in an area that ranged from Venezuela to central Chile.

President Alejandro Toledo designated the first Saturday of every February 'Pisco Sour Day' in 2003 as a way to promote the Peruvian liquor.

chicha morada, a sweet, refreshing, nonalcoholic beverage made from purple corn. *Agua con/sin gas* (carbonated/noncarbonated water) is available in restaurants, corner shops and supermarkets. (Don't drink unpurified tap water – it will make you sick.)

Though Peru exports coffee to the world, the locals tend to drink it instant. Many restaurants provide hot water and a packet of Nescafé. In more cosmopolitan cities, however, cafes serving espresso and cappuccino have proliferated. Tea and *mates* (herbal teas) are also widely available. The latter includes *manzanilla* (chamomile), *menta* (mint) and *mate de coca*, a coca-leaf tea. The last will not get you high, but it can soothe stomach ailments and help with high-altitude acclimatization.

Local beers are good and generally inexpensive. The best-known brands are Pilsen Callao, Brahma, Cristal and Cusqueña, all of which are light lagers. Arequipeña and Trujillana are regional brews served in and around those cities. Some brands, such as Pilsen, offer *cerveza negra* (dark beer) as well.

In the Andes, homemade *chicha* (corn beer) is very popular. It tastes slightly bitter, is low in alcoholic content and is found almost exclusively at small markets and private homes (though some high-end restaurants now sell it as well). In the Andes, a red flag posted near a door indicates that *chicha* is available.

Local wines have improved greatly over the years (though they are generally not as good as vintages from Chile and Argentina). The best local labels are Tabernero, Tacama, Ocucaje and Vista Alegre. Also very popular is pisco (see boxed text, below).

CELEBRATIONS

Every Peruvian town has some celebratory day in which everyone pours into the streets to drink, dance and eat – and then drink some more. These events are usually centered on religious holidays, such as Carnaval (Shrove

---

A PISCO PRIMER

It is the national beverage: pisco, the omnipresent grape brandy served at events from the insignificant to the momentous. Production dates back to the early days of the Spanish colony in Ica, where it was distilled on private haciendas and then sold to sailors making their way through the port of Pisco. In its early years, pisco was the local firewater: a great way to get ripped – and wake up the following morning feeling as if you had been hammered over the head.

By the early 20th century, the pisco sour (pisco with lime juice and sugar) arrived on the scene, and with the assistance of a few skilled bartenders at the Gran Hotel Bolívar (p104) and the Hotel Maury (p104) in Lima it became the national drink.

In recent decades, production of pisco has become increasingly sophisticated. The result is excellent piscos that are nuanced and flavorful (without the morning-after effects). The three principal types of Peruvian pisco are *Quebranta*, *Italia* and *acholado*. *Quebranta* (a pure-smelling pisco) and *Italia* (slightly aromatic) are each named for the varieties of grape from which they are crafted, while *acholado* is a blend of varietals that has more of an alcohol top-note (best for mixed drinks). There are also many aromatic small-batch specialty piscos made from grape must (pressed juice with skins), known as *mosto verde* or *mosto yema*. These have a flowery, fragrant smell and are best sipped straight.

The most common brands include Tres Generaciones, Ocucaje, Ferreyros and La Botija, while Viñas de Oro, Viejo Tonel, Estirpe Peruano, LaBlanco and Gran Cruz are among the finest. Any pisco purchased in a bottle that resembles the head of an Inca will make for an unusual piece of home decor – and not much else.

If you're interested in picking up a few bottles before flying home, find an extensive selection of duty-free brands at **El Rincón del Pisco** (Gate 17, Aeropuerto Internacional Jorge Chávez), a well-organized pisco boutique inside Lima's international airport. See p119 for more information.

Tuesday), or civil ones, such as Fiestas Patrias (National Independence Days). For these occasions, entire marketplaces spring up in town squares selling *chicharrones, lechón* (suckling pig), boiled corn with cheese and plenty of beer. During October, bakeries (mainly along the coast) are stocked with *turrón de Doña Pepa,* a sticky, molasses-drenched cake eaten in honor of *El Señor de los Milagros.* Pastelería San Martín in Lima has the finest *turrón* around; see p109.

In the Andes, festivals are infused with indigenous foodstuffs such as *chicha* and roasted *cuy* (for a history of the guinea pig, see boxed text, p440). For special occasions and weddings, families will gather to make *pachamanca:* a mix of marinated meats, vegetables, cheese, chilies and fragrant herbs buried in the ground and baked on hot rocks. This pre-Columbian tradition has its roots in nature worship: by using the earth – or Pachamama – to cook, it is being honored as well.

WHERE TO EAT & DRINK

For the most part, restaurants in Peru are a community affair, and local places will cater to a combination of families, tourists, teenagers and packs of chatty businessmen. *Almuerzo* (lunch), served at around 1pm, is the main meal of the day. This is when many eateries serve a *menú,* the set meal of the day, consisting of an *entrada* (appetizer), *segundo* or *plato fuerte* (main course) and *postre* (dessert). This is generally a good value. (Note: if you request the *menú,* you'll get the special. If you want the menu, ask for *la carta.*)

The coast is home to an endless number of Chinese eateries known as *chifas,* which generally serve simple, Cantonese-style food. At lunch, they offer a variety of *menús* for all tastes and budgets. Appetizers will consist of *wantan frito* (fried wontons) or *enrollado con verduras* (spring rolls), followed by a main course of stir-fried chicken, beef or seafood with rice or noodles.

Cevicherías, places where ceviche is sold, are also popular along the coast – though they pop up in the highlands, too, where they serve river trout. In the countryside, small, informal restaurants known as *picanterías* are a staple, and in some cases are operated right out of a person's home, serving a few generously apportioned daily specials.

Outside of the tourist areas, an early *desayuno* (breakfast) can be problematic since most restaurants don't open until at least 8am. If you need to eat early, high-end hotel restaurants often have more flexible hours.

Cena (dinner) is eaten late, and restaurants, which may be dead at 7pm, come alive at 9pm. This is not generally the case in tiny, remote towns, where everything is usually closed by 9pm.

Quick Eats

Peruvians love to eat on the street and the most popular items are *anticuchos* (beef heart skewers), ceviche, boiled quail eggs and *choclo con queso* (boiled corn with cheese). Also popular, and quite delicious, are *picarones* (fritters). Street stands can be extraordinarily cheap and efficient; they can also be spectacularly unhygienic. Examine closely before eating.

Also quick, cheap and tasty are the many *pollerías* (spit-roasted chicken joints) that can be found just about everywhere. Bakeries are also an excellent way to eat well and maintain a tight budget. Most sell empanadas (meat or cheese turnovers), cakes, cookies and bread, and some sell coffee and simple meals to take away as well.

The coca sour – a pisco cocktail laced with crushed, macerated coca leaves – is growing in popularity as an aperitif in Peru.

The dessert *turrón de Doña Pepa* was first made by a slave woman, in 1800, to honor the Christ of Miracles after she regained the use of her paralyzed arms.

Rafael Palomino's pan–Latin American cookbook *Fiesta Latina* features almost a dozen ceviche recipes.

VEGETARIANS & VEGANS

Big Papa: All of the
potatoes in the world can
be traced back to a single
progenitor from Peru.

In a country where most people survive on potatoes, there can be a general befuddlement over why anyone would choose to be vegetarian. This attitude has started to change, however, and many large cities and especially tourist-heavy towns have restaurants that are strictly veggie. Among other things, these places serve popular national dishes that use soy substitutes in place of meat. Vegetarian restaurants are found primarily in Lima and cities such as Cuzco and Arequipa.

It is possible, however, for vegetarians to find dishes at the average restaurant. Many of the potato salads, such as *papas a la huancaína, ocopa* and *causa* are made without meat, as is *palta a la jardinera*, an avocado stuffed with vegetable salad. *Sopa de verduras* (vegetable soup), *tortilla* (Spanish omelet) and *tacu tacu* (beans and rice mixed together) are other options. If there aren't any vegetarian dishes on the menu, just ask for *un plato vegetariano* (a vegetarian dish): most restaurants will readily accommodate the request. Be aware that the term *sin carne* (without meat) refers only to red meat or pork, so you could end up with chicken or seafood instead. *Chifas* are always a good bet since they generally feature at least one meat-free *menú*.

Eat Smart in Peru by
Joan Peterson and Brook
Soltvedt is a well-
illustrated food, menu
and market guide to the
country that also offers a
smattering of recipes.

Vegans will have a much harder time. Peruvian cuisine is based on eggs, cheese and milk, and infinite combinations thereof. Self-catering is the best option; markets have wide selections of grains, legumes, fruits and vegetables.

EATING WITH KIDS

'Kids' meals' (small portions at small prices) are not normally offered in Peruvian restaurants. However, most establishments are quite family-friendly and can produce simple foods, such as *bistec a la plancha* (grilled steak) or *pollo a la plancha* (grilled chicken) on request. Other basic items include cheese and ham sandwiches, pasta and hamburgers. Among Peruvian kids, a perennial dinnertime favorite is *arroz con huevo frito* (rice with a fried egg).

The culinary website
Yanuq (www.yanuq.com)
has an extensive online
database of Peruvian
recipes in Spanish and
English.

If traveling with an infant, stock up on formula and baby food before heading into rural areas. Avocados are safe and nutritious, and can be served to children as young as six months old. Bananas are found just about everywhere and make a great snack, mashed or whole. Young children should avoid water and ice as they are more susceptible to stomach illnesses.

For other tips on traveling with children, see p512.

TRAVEL YOUR TASTE BUDS

In the Andes, potato dishes and spicy soups are de rigueur but it is the roasted *cuy* (guinea pig) that grabs every traveler's attention (see boxed text, p440). On the coast, where seafood reigns supreme, ceviche attracts the most inspection, especially in Lima, where it is a lunchtime staple. (Though most people assume it is raw – it isn't. The fish is 'cooked' by lime juice through a process of oxidation.)

The area around Arequipa, in the south, is renowned for its *picantes* (spicy, bubbling stews served with chunks of white cheese) and *rocoto relleno* (hot peppers stuffed with meat and cheese). Huancayo, to the north, is home to *papas a la huancaína*, steamed potatoes served with a spicy, creamy cheese sauce; while on the far north coast, locals dig into omelets made of manta ray and heaping plates of duck stewed with rice in cilantro. The Amazon region adds tropical notes to the national menu. Keep an eye peeled for *juanes,* banana-leaf tamales made of rice, chicken and garlic.

HABITS & CUSTOMS

Meals in Peru are a conversational, leisurely affair. Other than the bustling business-district restaurants in downtown Lima, don't expect anyone to be in much of a hurry – including your server.

When sitting down, it is polite to say *buenos días* or *buenas tardes* to the server. And when dining with locals, wish them *buen provecho* (bon appétit) before eating. Tips of 10% or more are customary at finer restaurants, but not expected at casual dining establishments such as *pollerías*. More upscale places will also include the *propina* (tip) in the bill – along with a 19% tax.

Do note that if you invite locals out to eat, the expectation is that you will pay. Likewise, if you are invited to someone's home, it is considered good manners to bring a gift. Flowers, sweets or pisco are customary items.

EAT YOUR WORDS

The following is a list of foods and drinks, with their English translations and pronunciations. These should provide a good start to your comprehension of Peruvian menus. For further pronunciation guidelines and useful phrases, see the Language chapter, p551.

Food Glossary

agua con/sin gas	*a*·gwa kon/seen gas	water (carbonated/noncarbonated)
agua mineral	*a*·gwa mee·ne·*ral*	water (mineral)
agua potable	*a*·gwa po·*ta*·ble	water (drinking)
aguardiente	a·gwar·*dyen*·te	cane alcohol
aguaymanto	a·*gway*·man·to	a citrus-y Amazon berry
ají	a·*hee*	chili
ají de gallina	a·*hee* de ga·*lee*·na	a spicy stew of shredded chicken with walnuts served over potatoes and rice
alfajor	al·*fa*·khor	a cookie sandwich of thick, sweet caramel
almejas	al·*me*·khas	clams
anticucho	an·tee·*koo*·cho	generally a beef heart skewer
arroz	a·*ros*	rice
atún	a·*toon*	tuna fish
azúcar	a·*soo*·kar	sugar
bistec	*bee*·stek	steak
cabro, cabrito	*ka*·bro, ka·*bree*·to	goat
calamares	ka·la·*ma*·res	squid
caldo	*kal*·do	broth
camarones	ka·ma·*ro*·nes	shrimp
camote	ka·*mo*·te	sweet potato
cancha	*kan*·cha	roasted, dried corn kernels eaten like nuts
cangrejo	kan·*gre*·kho	crab
carne	*kar*·ne	meat
carne de res	*kar*·ne de res	beef
cau cau	kow kow	a tripe stew served with beans and potatoes over rice
causa	*kaw*·sa	a cold potato salad stuffed with vegetables or seafood
cecina	se·*see*·na	jungle dish of dehydrated pork
cerdo, chancho	*ser*·do, *chan*·cho	pork

Sumptuous photographs and recipes of local specialties are available in Tony Custer and Miguel Etchepare's hardback tome *The Art of Peruvian Cuisine*. Log on to www .artperucuisine.com for a delicious preview.

Alpaca meat tastes like beef but has only half the fat.

Noted American chef Douglas Rodríguez has compiled an extensive list of recipes in his comprehensive seafood guide *The Great Ceviche Book*.

cerveza	ser·ve·sa	beer
ceviche	se·vee·che	raw seafood marinated in lime juice
charqui	char·kee	beef jerky; biltong
chaufa, chaulafan	chow·fa, chow·la·fan	fried rice (Chinese style)
chicha	chee·cha	fermented corn beer
chicha morada	chee·cha mo·ra·da	a sweet, nonalcoholic purple-corn drink
chicharrones	chee·cha·ro·nes	cracklings made with chicken, pork or fish
chirimoya	chee·ree·mo·ya	a white-fleshed highland fruit served on its own or in orange juice
chita	chee·tah	red snapper
choclo	cho·klo	corn on the cob
choclo con queso	cho·klo kon ke·so	boiled corn with cheese
choros	cho·ros	mussels
choros a la chalaca	cho·ros a la cha·la·ka	steamed, fresh mussels served in a omato and corn salsa
chupe	choo·pe	a hearty chowder-style soup generally made with seafood
conchitas	kon·chee·tas	scallops
cordero	kor·de·ro	mutton
cuy	kooy	guinea pig
empanadas	em·pa·na·das	meat and/or cheese turnovers
ensalada	en·sa·la·da	salad
estofado	es·to·ta·dó	stew
farína	fa·ree·na	muesli-like yucca concoction eaten toasted or in lemonade
frejoles	fre·ho·les	beans
frutas	froo·tas	fruit
galleta de soda	ga·ye·ta de so·da	soda cracker
gallinaga·yee·na		chicken, specifically hen
helado	e·la·do	ice cream
huacatay	wa·ka·tay	a mintlike herb frequently used in sauces
huevos	we·vos	eggs
huevos fritos/revueltos	we·vos free·tos/re·vwel·tos	fried/scrambled eggs
jamón	kha·mon	ham
juane	khwa·ne	jungle dish of steamed rice with fish or chicken, wrapped in a banana leaf
jugo	hoo·go	juice
langosta	lan·gos·ta	lobster
leche	le·che	milk
lechón	le·chon	suckling pig
lenguado	len·gwa·do	flounder
licór	lee·kor	liquor
locro	lo·kro	meat and vegetable stew
lomo	lo·mo	beef
lomo saltado	lo·mo sal·ta·do	strips of beef stir-fried with onions, tomatoes, potatoes and chili
manjar blanco	man·khar blan·ko	caramel

mantequilla	man·te·*kee*·ya	butter
manzana	man·*sa*·na	apple
maracuyá	ma·ra·koo·*ya*	passion fruit
mariscos	ma·*rees*·kos	seafood
mate	*ma*·te	herbal tea
mazamorra morada	ma·sa·*mo*·ra mo·*ra*·da	a sweet, purple-corn pudding served for dessert
mora	*mo*·ra	blackberry
naranja	na·*ran*·kha	orange
ocopa	o·*ko*·pa	potatoes served with a spicy, creamy peanut sauce
pachamanca	pa·cha·*man*·ka	meat, potatoes and vegetables cooked in an earthen 'oven' of hot rocks
palta	*pal*·ta	avocado
pan	pan	bread
papa a la huancaína	*pa*·pa a la hwan·*kay*·na	boiled potato topped with a creamy cheese sauce
papa rellena	*pa*·pa re·*ye*·na	a deep-fried, mashed potato filled with ground beef
papas fritas	*pa*·pas *free*·tas	french fries
parrillada	pa·ree·*ya*·da	grilled meats
pastel	pas·*tel*	cake
pescado	pes·*ka*·do	fish
pescado a la chorrillana	pes·*ka*·do a la *cho*·ree·ya·na	a fish fillet served with a sauté of onions, garlic and tomatoes
picante de pollo	pee·*kan*·te de *po*·yo	spicy chicken stew made with turmeric and cilantro
picarones	pee·ka·*ro*·nes	a sweet fritter often served with molasses syrup
piña	*pee*·nya	pineapple
plátano	*plu*·la·no	plantain or banana
pollo	*po*·yo	chicken
postre	*pos*·tre	dessert
queso	*ke*·so	cheese
quinua	kee·*no*·a	a highly nutritious, protein-rich grain of the high Andes
rocoto	ro·*ko*·to	a spicy hot pepper resembling a red bell pepper
rocoto relleno	ro·*ko*·to re·*ye*·no	a *rocoto* stuffed with rice and meat
sandía	san·*dee*·a	watermelon
seco de cabrito	*se*·ko de ka·*bree*·to	roasted kid goat
solterito arequipeño	sol·te·*ree*·to a·re·kee·*pe*·nyo	a fava bean salad typical of Arequipa
sopa, chupe	*so*·pa, *choo*·pe	soup
sopa a la criolla	*so*·pa a la kree·*ol*·ya	a mildly spiced, creamy noodle soup with beef and peppers
sudado	soo·*da*·do	fish (or seafood) soup or stew
suprema de pollo	soo·*pre*·ma de *po*·yo	breaded chicken fillet
suspiro limeña	soos·*pee*·ro lee·*me*·nya	a caramel meringue dessert
tacu tacu	*ta*·koo *ta*·koo	pan-fried rice and beans served with steak, seafood or fried eggs

tallarines	ta·ya·*ree*·nes	noodles
tamal	ta·*mal*	corn-meal cake stuffed with meat, beans or chilies
tiradito	*tee*·ra·dee·to	Japanese-style ceviche, without onions
toronja	to·*ron*·kha	grapefruit
torta	*tor*·ta	cake
tortilla	tor·*tee*·ya	Spanish omelet
trucha	*troo*·cha	trout
verduras	ver·*doo*·ras	vegetables
vino	*vee*·no	wine

Environment

THE LAND

Few countries have topographies as rugged, as forbidding and as wildly diverse as Peru. The third-largest country in South America – at 1,285,220 sq km – it is five times larger than the UK, almost twice the size of Texas and one-sixth the size of Australia. It lies in the tropics, south of the equator, straddling three strikingly different geographic zones: the arid Pacific coast, the craggy Andes mountain range and a good portion of the Amazon basin.

On the coast, a narrow strip of land, which lies below 1000m in elevation, hugs the country's 3000km-long shoreline. Consisting primarily of scrubland and desert, it eventually merges, in the south, with Chile's Atacama Desert, one of the driest places on earth. The coast includes Lima, the capital, and several major cities – oases watered by dozens of rivers that cascade down from the Andes. These settlements emerged as agricultural centers over the centuries when irrigation canals deposited fertile silt all along these desert valleys. They make for strange sights: sandy, rocky desert can give way to bursts of green fields within the course of a few meters. The coast contains some of Peru's flattest terrain, so it's no surprise that the country's best road, the Carretera Panamericana (Pan-American Hwy), borders much of the Pacific from Ecuador to Chile.

The Andes, the world's second-greatest mountain chain, form the spine of the country. Rising steeply from the coast, and growing sharply in height and gradient from north to south, they reach spectacular heights of more than 6000m just 100km inland. Peru's highest peak, Huascarán (6768m), located northeast of Huaraz (p389), is the world's highest tropical summit and the sixth-tallest mountain in the Americas (the highest peak in the Andes being Mt Aconcagua, 6960m, in Chile). Though the portion of the Andes that lies in Peru resides in the tropics, the mountains are laced with a web of glaciers above elevations of 5000m. Between 3000m and 4000m lie the agricultural Andean highlands, which support more than a third of Peru's population. Overall, it is a landscape that brims with jagged ranges separated by deep valleys and rewards resilient travelers with plenty of spectacular scenery.

The eastern Andean slopes receive much more rainfall than the dry western slopes and are draped in lush cloud forests as they descend into the lowland rainforests of the Amazon. In the low-lying Amazon basin, the undulating landscape rarely rises more than 500m above sea level as various tributary systems feed into the mighty Río Amazonas (Amazon River), the largest river in the world. Weather conditions are hot and humid year-round, with most precipitation falling between December and

The origin of the word 'Andes' is uncertain. Some historians believe it comes from the Quechua *anti*, meaning 'east,' or *anta*, an Aymara-derived term that signifies 'copper-colored.'

The Amazonian drainage system covers a surface area equivalent to continental USA.

The Andes don't stop at the Pacific coast; 100km offshore there is a trench that's as deep as the Andes are high.

THE DEEPEST CANYON

Not far outside of Arequipa, in southern Peru, the Cañón del Colca (p187), at 3191m deep, was once considered to be the deepest canyon in the world. That honor has since been taken by the Cañón del Cotahuasi (p193), beyond Nevado Coropuna to the west, which has a floor that lies 3345m below its adjacent snowy peaks. Both of these canyons are more than twice as deep as Arizona's Grand Canyon (which has a depth of about 1500m), making them the deepest canyons in the western hemisphere.

There is some debate, however, as to whether Cotahuasi can claim the title of deepest canyon *in the world*. Nepal's Kali Gandaki valley floor lies some 6000m below the neighboring 8000m-plus summits of Dhaulagiri and Annapurna, but this, apparently, is considered a gorge by some, and not a canyon. Regardless of the outcome of these internecine debates, southern Peru's canyons remain an awe-inspiring sight.

May. Roads into and within the Peruvian Amazon region are few, and people typically get around by boat or airplane.

WILDLIFE

One of the most engagingly written books on rainforest life is Adrian Forsyth and Ken Miyata's *Tropical Nature: Life and Death in the Rain Forests of Central and South America*.

With its folds, bends and plunging river valleys, Peru is home to countless kinds of ecosystems, each with its own unique climate, elevation, vegetation and soil type. As a result, it boasts a spectacular diversity of desert, highland and rainforest plant and animal life. Colonies of sea lions occupy rocky, desert outcroppings on the coast, while raucous flocks of brightly colored macaws descend on clay licks encircled by strangler figs in the Amazon. In the Andes, rare vicuñas (endangered relatives of the alpaca) trot about in packs in search of low grasses as fabled condors take to the wind currents. Peru is one of only a dozen or so countries in the world considered to be 'megadiverse.'

Animals

Wildlife enthusiasts come to see Peru to see a rainbow variety of birds, as well as camelids, freshwater dolphins, condors, butterflies, jaguars, anacondas, macaws and spectacled bears, to name just a few of the country's many engrossing species. Naturally, many animals can be difficult to see. But for travelers equipped with plenty of patience, and armed with a skilled local guide, it is certainly not impossible. Just be prepared for plenty of predawn wake-up calls, since many animals are most active in the wee hours of the morning.

BIRDS

Travellers' Wildlife Guides: Peru, by David Pearson and Les Beletsky, helpfully lists the country's most important and frequently seen birds, mammals, amphibians, reptiles and ecosystem habitats.

Peru has more than 1800 bird species. That's more than the number of species found in North America and Europe together, so it's no wonder ornithologists flock to Peru en masse. From the tiniest hummingbirds to the majestic Andean condor, the variety is colorful and seemingly endless, new species are discovered regularly.

Along the Pacific, marine birds of all kinds are most visible, especially in the south, where they can be found clustered on rocky outcroppings along the shore. Here you'll see exuberant Chilean flamingos, oversized Peruvian pelicans, plump Inca terns sporting white-feather mustaches and bright orange

---

WATCHING WILDLIFE IN PERU

Sea lions, vicuñas, condors, scarlet macaws and sloths: a lot of travelers come to Peru specifically to observe the extraordinary animal life. A few tips on making the most of your wildlife-watching:

■ be willing to travel – the coast has limited fauna and some highland areas have been hunted out; remote is the way to go

■ hire a knowledgeable local guide – they know what to look for and where

■ get up *really* early – animals tend to be most active at dawn and dusk

■ bring a pair of lightweight binoculars, they will improve wildlife observation tremendously

■ be very quiet; animals tend to avoid loud packs of chatty humans, so keep chit-chat to a whisper; in the Amazon, opt for canoes instead of motorboats – you'll see much more

■ keep still, hang out for a while – in the Amazon, animals might just come to you

■ have realistic expectations: vegetation can be thick, animals are shy, and others are nocturnal – you're not going to see everything in a single hike

For the top wildlife-watching spots, see boxed text, p178. For tips on what to pack for an Amazon adventure, see boxed text, p472.

FOR THE DOGS: PERUVIAN HAIRLESS

Visit many of the ancient sites around Peru and you'll be greeted by a strangely awesome canine sight: hairless dogs – some with small mohawks on the crown of their heads – bounding about the ruins. A pre-Inca breed whose roots in the Andes date back almost 3000 years, the *perro biringo* or *perro calato* (naked dog), as it is known, has been depicted in Moche, Chimú and Chancay pottery. These funny-looking creatures were once thought to have curative properties: since they have no fur, it was alleged that the proximity of their warm bodies could alleviate symptoms of illnesses such as arthritis.

Over the centuries, as cutesy breeds from abroad have been introduced to Peru, the population of Peruvian hairless has declined. But, in recent years, they've started to make a comeback, with dedicated Lima breeders working to keep the species alive, and the government employing them as staple attractions at pre-Columbian sites. In 2009 they were even awarded with their own commemorative stamp. The dogs may not be pretty, but they are generally very friendly. And they do have one thing going for them: no fur means no fleas.

---

beaks, colonies of brown boobies engaged in elaborate mating dances, cormorants and endangered Humboldt penguins, which can be spotted waddling around the Islas Ballestas (p130). Even in dreary Lima you'll find birds, such as bright vermilion flycatchers, rufous-collared sparrows and Pacific doves – the latter two of which can't be found on any other continent. Bosque El Olivar, in Lima's San Isidro neighborhood (p97), is a good spot to see birds.

In the highlands, the most famous bird of all is the Andean condor. Weighing up to 10kg, with a 3m-plus wingspan, this monarch of the air (a member, incidentally, of the vulture family) once ranged over the entire Andean mountain chain from Venezuela to Tierra del Fuego. Considered the largest flying bird in the world, the Andean condor was put on the endangered species list in the 1970s, due mostly to loss of its natural habitat and environmental pollution. But it was also hunted to the brink of extinction because its body parts were believed to increase male virility, ward off nightmares and cure a variety of physical ailments. (It is most threatened in the northern end of its territory, in Venezuela and Colombia.) Condors usually nest in impossibly high, inaccessible mountain cliffs that prevent predators from snatching their young. Their main food source is carrion and they're most easily spotted riding thermal air currents above their wide-open hunting grounds. The canyons around Arequipa (p190) are a good place to look for them.

Other prominent high altitude birds include the Andean gull (don't call it a seagull!), which is commonly sighted along lakes and rivers as high as 4500m. The mountains are also home to several species of ibis, such as the puna ibis, which inhabits lakeside marshes, as well as roughly a dozen types of cinclodes, a type of ovenbird (their clay nests resemble ovens, hence the name) endemic to the Andes. Area species also include torrent ducks that nest in small waterside caves, gaggles of stocky Andean geese, spotted Andean flickers, black-and-yellow Andean siskins and, of course, a panoply of hummingbirds (see boxed text, p70).

Swoop down toward the Amazon and you'll catch sight of the world's most iconic tropical birds, including boisterous flocks of parrots and macaws festooned in brightly plumed regalia. You'll also see clusters of aracaris, toucans, parakeets, toucanets, ibises, regal gray-winged trumpeters, umbrella birds donning gravity-defying feathered hairdos, crimson-colored cocks of the rock, soaring hawks and harpy eagles. The list goes on. The best way to see many of these is on a quiet river trip at dawn, which is prime avian feeding time. Many lodges know a local salt lick where flocks of macaws and parakeets come to feed on mineral-laden clay.

Peruvian Wildlife: A Visitor's Guide to the High Andes, by Gerard Cheshir, Huw Lloyd and Barry Walker, provides a broad overview of the mountains' many species.

A comprehensive overview of the country's avian life is contained in the 656-page Princeton Field Guide *Birds of Peru*, by Thomas Schulenberg.

Don Stap's *A Parrot Without a Name: The Search for the Last Unknown Birds on Earth* is an engaging narrative that records the discovery of a new parrot species in the Amazon.

FREQUENT FLYERS

For many bird enthusiasts who visit Peru, the diminutive hummingbirds are among the most delightful to observe. More than 100 species have been recorded in the country, and their exquisite beauty is matched by their extravagant names. There's the 'green-tailed goldenthroat,' the 'spangled coquette,' the 'fawn-breasted brilliant' and 'amethyst-throated sunangel.'

Hummingbirds are capable of beating their wings in a figure-eight pattern up to almost 80 times a second, thus producing the typical hum for which they are named. This exceptionally rapid wing-beat enables them to hover in place when feeding on nectar, or even to fly backward. These tiny birds must feed frequently to gain the energy needed to keep them flying.

Species such as the red-headed Andean hillstar, living in the *puna* (high Andean grasslands), have evolved an amazing strategy to survive a cold night. They go into a state of torpor, which is like a nightly hibernation, by lowering their body temperature by up to 30°C, thus drastically slowing their metabolism.

One of the most unusual species of hummingbird is the marvelous spatuletail, found in the Utcubamba Valley in northern Peru. Full-grown adult males are adorned with two extravagant feathery spatules on the tail, which are used during mating displays to attract females. Though endangered by loss of habitat due to logging and wildfires, it is nonetheless possible to see this bird in the wild. See boxed text, p452, for more details.

MAMMALS

The Living Edens: Manu, Peru's Hidden Rain Forest, produced by Kim McQuarrie, is a public TV program about a journey deep into the Peruvian Amazon; check out the informative website at www.pbs.org/edens/manu.

The Amazon is also home to a bounty of exciting mammals. More than two dozen species of monkeys are found here, including howlers, acrobatic spider monkeys and wide-eyed marmosets. With the help of a guide, you may also see sloths, bats, piglike peccaries, anteaters, ambling armadillos and curious coatis (ring-tailed members of the raccoon family). And if you're really lucky, you'll find giant river otters, capybaras (a rodent of unusual size), river dolphins, tapirs and maybe one of half a dozen elusive felines, including the fabled jaguar.

Toward the west, the cloud forests straddling the Amazon and the eastern slopes of the Andean highlands are home to the endangered spectacled bear. South America's only bear is a black, shaggy mammal, known for its white, masklike face markings, that grows up to 1.8m in length. Avid tree climbers, they do not hibernate, though they do hole up in dens during bad weather.

Sloths spend only 10% of their time moving.

The highlands are, most famously, home to roving wool-bearing packs of camelids: llamas and alpacas are the most easily spotted since they are domesticated, and used as pack animals or for their wool; vicuñas and guanacos live exclusively in the wild. You can see llamas, alpacas and vicuñas at the Reserva Nacional Salinas y Aguada Blanca (p187) outside Arequipa. Far inland from Nazca, the Reserva Nacional Pampas Galeras (p145) is a vicuña sanctuary with a biannual roundup and ceremonial shearing in late May or early June. On highland talus slopes, watch out for the viscacha, which looks like the world's most cuddly rabbit. Foxes, deer and domesticated *cuy* (guinea pigs) are also highland dwellers, as is the puma (cougar or mountain lion).

Llamas are domestic animals thought to have been bred from guanacos by pre-Columbian civilizations.

On the coast, huge numbers of sea lions and seals are easily seen on the Islas Ballestas (p130). Dolphins are commonly seen offshore, but whales very rarely. In the coastal desert strip, there are few unique species of land animals. One is the near-threatened Sechuran fox, the smallest of the South American foxes (found in northern Peru), which has a black-tipped tail, pale, sand-colored fur and an omnivorous appetite for small rodents and seed pods.

REPTILES, AMPHIBIANS, INSECTS & MARINE LIFE

The greatest variety of reptiles, amphibians, insects and marine life can be found in the Amazon basin. Here, you'll find hundreds of amphibian species, such as toads, tree frogs and thumbnail-sized, brightly colored poison dart frogs (indigenous peoples once used the frogs' deadly poison on the points of their blow-pipe darts). Rivers teem with schools of piranhas, paiche and doncella (various types of freshwater fish), while the air buzzes with the activity of thousands of insects: thirsty mosquitoes, armies of ants, squadrons of beetles, katydids, stick insects, fuzzy caterpillars, long-legged spiders, praying mantis, transparent moths, and butterflies of all shapes and sizes. A blue morpho butterfly in flight is one of the Amazon's most remarkable sights: with wingspans of up to 10cm, its iridescent-blue coloring can seem downright hallucinogenic when they are fluttering.

Naturally, there are all kinds of reptiles, too, including tortoises and river turtles, lizards, caimans and, of course, that jungle-movie favorite: the anaconda. An aquatic boa snake that can measure more than 10m in length, it will often ambush its prey by the water's edge, constrict its body around it and then drown it in the river. Caimans, tapirs, deer, turtles and peccaries are all tasty meals for this killer snake; human victims are almost unheard of (unless you're Jennifer Lopez and Ice Cube in a low-rent Hollywood production). Far more worrisome to the average human is the bushmaster, a deadly, reddish brown viper that likes to hang out inside rotting logs and among the buttress roots of trees. Thankfully, it's a retiring creature, and is rarely found on well-trodden trails.

On the coast, most life is found in the ocean. The waters of Peru's coast teem with tuna, marlin, swordfish, sea bass and flounder, as well as manta rays, scallops, shrimp, mussels and other mollusks.

Plants

At high elevations in the Andes, especially in the Cordillera Blanca p404 and Huayhuash (p410), outside Huaraz, there is a cornucopia of distinctive alpine flora and fauna. Plants encountered in this region include native lupins, spiky tussocks of ichu grass, striking quenua *(Polylepis)* trees with their distinctive curly, red paperlike bark, in addition to unusual bromeliads (see boxed text, p72). Many alpine wildflowers bloom during the trekking season, between May and September.

Neotropical Rainforest Mammals, by Louise Emmons and Francois Feer, is an illustrated full-color field guide to more than 300 species of rainforest animals, with distribution and range maps.

Rainforest Publications (www.rainforest publications.com) sells handy, laminated foldout guides for quickly identifying common birds, mammals, marine mammals, reef fish and birds in Peru.

LEAF-CUTTER ANTS

One of hundreds of ant species in the Amazon's rainforests, leaf-cutter ants live in colonies numbering in the hundreds of thousands. Their homes are huge nests dug deep into the ground. Foraging ants search the vegetation for particular types of leaves, cut out small sections and, holding the leaf segments above their heads like a small umbrella, bring them back to the nest. Travelers frequently come across long lines of them in the jungle, scurrying along carrying leaf sections back to the nest. Amazingly, they consume more than 10% of all available leaves in the world's neotropical zones each year.

Workers within the nest sort out the leaves that will easily decompose into a type of compost (unsuitable material is ejected from the nest). The leaves are then composted to form a mulch, which quickly grows a fungus. The ants tend these fungal gardens, which serve as the colony's main source of food. Queen ants will genetically secrete an antibiotic strain of bacteria to combat any alien fungi that might try to invade these gardens.

Army ants and other species prey upon this ready and constant supply of foragers. To combat this, leaf-cutter ants are morphologically separated by size and jaw structure into different castes. Some specialize in tending the fungal gardens, others have vibrating jaws designed for cutting leaf segments, and yet others are soldier ants (armed with huge mandibles) which accompany the foragers to protect them from attackers. Close observation reveals yet another caste – a microscopic ant that rides along on the leaf segments without disturbing the foragers. The riders' function is unclear, but biologists suggest that they act as protection against parasitizing insects that try to lay eggs on the leaves before they are carried into the nest.

GIANT FLOWERS OF THE MOUNTAINS

Reaching the staggering height of more than 10m, with an explosive, flower-encrusted cigar shape that looks to be straight out of a Dr Seuss book, the *Puya raimondii* can certainly take the award for most unusual flora. The world's tallest flowering plant is a member of the pineapple family and can take up to a century or more to mature. In full bloom, each plant flaunts up to 8000(!) white flowers, each resembling a lily. It blooms only once in its lifetime, after which the plant dies. Some of the most famous stands of *Puya raimondii* can be found in the Peruvian Andes, in the rocky mountainscape outside Huaraz, near Catac (p421) and Punta Winchus (p418). Both of these sites can easily be visited on organized day tours from Huaraz (see p394).

A good guide to the flora of the Andes is Alwyn Gentry's *Field Guide to the Families and Genera of Woody Plants of North-west South America.*

Monga Bay (www .mongabay.com) is an excellent online resource for news and information related to rainforests around the world.

In the highlands, particularly in the south, you'll find the distinctive *puna* ecosystem. These areas have a fairly limited flora of hard grasses, cushion plants, small herbaceous plants, shrubs and dwarf trees. Many plants in this environment have developed small, thick leaves that are less susceptible to frost, and curved leaves to reflect extreme radiation. In the north of the country there is some *páramo*, which has a harsher climate, is less grassy and has an odd mixture of landscapes, including peat bogs, glacier-formed valleys, alpine lakes, wet grasslands and patches of scrubland and forest.

As the eastern Andean slopes descend into the western Amazon uplands, the scenery once again changes. Here, tropical cloud forests – so named because they trap (and help create) clouds that drench the forest in a fine mist – allow delicate forms of plant life to survive. Cloud forest trees are adapted to steep slopes, rocky soils and a rugged climate. They are characterized by low, gnarled growth, dense small-leafed canopies and moss-covered branches supporting a host of plants such as orchids, ferns and bromeliads. These aerial plants, which gather their moisture and some nutrients from the air, without the benefit of ground roots, are collectively termed epiphytes. The dense vegetation at all levels of the cloud forest gives it a mysterious and delicate, fairy-tale appearance. It is also important as a source of fresh water and for controlling erosion.

At lowland altitudes lies the Amazon rainforest, with its untold wealth of flora and fauna. A short walk into this jungle will reveal that it is vastly different from the temperate forests of North America and Europe. The sheer density is astonishing: tens of thousands of species of plant that can be found living on top of and around each other. There are strangler figs (known as *matapalos*), palms, ferns, epiphytes, bromeliads, flowering orchids, fungi, mosses and lianas, to name a few. Some rainforest trees are supported by strange roots that look like props or stilts. These are most frequently found where periodic floods occur; the stilt roots are thought to play a role in keeping the tree upright during the inundation. Rainforest palms, such as the so-called 'walking palm,' are among the trees that have these kinds of roots.

Andean Botanical Information System (www .sacha.org) is a veritable online encyclopedia of flowering plants in Peru's coastal areas and the Andes.

One thing that often astounds visitors is the sheer immensity of many trees. A good example is the ceiba (also called the 'kapok' or cotton silk tree), which has huge flattened trunk supports, known as buttresses, around its base. The trunk of a ceiba can easily measure 3m across and will grow straight up for 50m before the first branches are reached. These spread out into a huge crown with a slightly flattened appearance. The staggering height of many Amazon trees, some reaching a height of 80-plus meters, creates a whole ecosystem or life at the canopy level, inhabited by creatures that never descend to the forest floor.

In areas that have been cleared (often naturally by a flash flood or when a gap is created by an ancient forest giant falling during a storm) various fast-growing pioneer species appear. These may grow several meters a year in areas where abundant sunlight is suddenly available. Some of the most common and easily recognized of these are in the nettle family of the genus *Cecropia*, often found on riverbanks. Their smooth, hollow trunks are often circled by ridges at intervals of a few centimeters, and their branches form a small canopy at the top. These trees, which attract sloths, birds and bats as occasional residents, are best known for their symbiotic relationship with ant colonies that inhabit the spongy, internal tissue of the trunk and protect the tree from insect attacks on its foliage.

In stark contrast to the Amazon, the coastal desert is generally barren of vegetation, apart from around water sources, which may spring into palm-fringed lagoons. Otherwise, the limited plant life you'll glimpse will consist of cacti and other succulents, as well as *lomas* (a blend of grasses and herbaceous species in mist-prone areas). On the far north coast, in the ecological reserves around Tumbes (p387), is a small cluster of mangrove forest, as well as a tropical dry forest ecosystem, of which there is little in Peru.

NATIONAL PARKS

Peru's vast wealth of wildlife is protected by a system of national parks and reserves with 60 areas covering almost 15% of the country. The newest is the Sierra del Divisor Reserve Zone, created in 2006 to protect 1.5 million hectares of rainforest on the Brazilian border. All of these protected areas are administered by the **Instituto Nacional de Recursos Nacionales** (Inrena; www.inrena .gob.pe), a division of the Ministry of Agriculture.

The idea of conservation, however, often looks better on paper than it does in practice. Unfortunately, resources are lacking to conserve protected areas, which are subject to illegal hunting, fishing, logging and mining. The

Breakfast of Biodiversity: The Truth about Rain Forest Destruction, by John Vandermeer, is a gripping account of the causes of rainforest destruction worldwide, including the Peruvian Amazon.

Natural history buffs may want to pick up *The Journals of Hipólito Ruiz*, the chronicles of an 18th-century Spanish botanist who kept a detailed diary of his 11-year journey through Peru and Chile.

THE COCA LEAF: PAST & PRESENT

Cultivation of the coca plant dates back at least 5000 years and its traditional uses have always included the practical and the divine. In pre-Hispanic times, chewing coca was a traditional treatment for everything from a simple toothache to exhaustion. It was used to help patients withstand the practice of cranial trepanation (in which a slice of the skull is removed, usually to relieve pressure on the brain after an injury). Chewing coca has also historically played a vital role in communal life, having been long used in religious rituals as a sacred offering.

It was the Incas who placed the coca leaf at the pinnacle of sacred ritual. As the Inca empire rapidly expanded, the Incas created a monopoly in coca production. They established large plantations at the edge of the Amazon jungle, not only using the abundant harvests for religious rituals (typically in veneration of the sun god Inti), but also to help fuel its armies and make allies through trade.

When the Spaniards arrived in the 15th century, they attempted to outlaw the 'heathen' practice of cultivating this 'diabolical' plant. However, with coca-chewing an essential part of life for the colony's indigenous labor pool, the Spanish quickly reversed their policies and ultimately encouraged the coca trade. Viceregal authorities, including the Catholic Church, went as far as accepting taxes paid in coca leaves.

Today, there continues to be a struggle surrounding coca, but it has to do with its derivative product, cocaine (in which a paste derived from coca leaves is treated with kerosene and refined into powder). In an attempt to stem the flow of this narcotic, the US has led eradication programs of coca plants in Peru (as well as in Colombia and Bolivia). These programs appear to have done little to curb coca's cultivation – Peru's harvest was up in 2008 – but it has disrupted indigenous communities where the plant continues to be consumed in a time-honored manner. The use of chemical herbicides to eradicate plants has damaged some agricultural lands, and an attempt to encourage traditional agricultural communities to replace coca with other crops has resulted in diminished earnings for those societies.

The traditional way to chew coca is to place a few leaves in the mouth, along with a catalyst, such as wood ash or mineral lime. Some chewers also add a sweet substance (for example, cane sugar or licorice) to alleviate the bitter taste of the leaves. As each leaf is thoroughly chewed, others are added to form a wad in the cheek. The effect: a mild appetite suppressant and stimulant, on par with strong coffee.

PERU'S TOP PROTECTED & NATURAL AREAS

Area	Best time to visit	Sights & Activities
Ausangate	May-Sep, May-Jun for Q'oyoriti, a religious pilgrimage (see boxed text, p295)	trekking
Cañón del Colca	May-Nov	flora, Andean condors, trekking
Cañón del Cotahuasi	May-Nov	hiking, trekking, hot springs
Cordillera Blanca	May-Sep	hiking, trekking, mountain climbing, flora
Cordillera Huayhuash	May-Nov	trekking, hiking
Cordillera Negra	May-Nov	mountain biking, rock climbing, flora
El Misti	Jul-Nov	mountaineering
Islas Ballestas	any	boat tours to view sea lions, rare Humboldt penguins and sea birds
Lake Titicaca	Apr-Oct	boating, island-hopping
Laguna de Salinas	Jan-Apr for flamingos	hiking, birds (flamingos)
Lagunas Llanganuco	May-Sep	hiking, flora
Parque Nacional Bahuaja-Sonene	May-Aug	birds, wildlife, flora, endangered species, hiking
Parque Nacional Huascarán	May-Sep	trekking, mountaineering
Parque Nacional Manu	Jun-Nov	birds, wildlife, endangered species, flora, canopy walks, hiking, canoeing
Parque Nacional Tingo María	any	birding
Reserva de Biosfera del Noroeste	any	hiking, canoeing, wildlife
Reserva Ecológica Chaparrí	any	hiking, wildlife, endangered species, spectacled bears
Reserva Nacional de Paracasdesert	Dec-Apr, Jun-Aug for flamingos	flamingo and sea lion colonies
Reserva Nacional Junín	Apr-Nov	birds, more than 10 species of duck
Reserva Nacional Lomas de Lachay	Jun-Nov	flora, wildlife, including 55 bird species
Reserva Nacional Pacaya-Samiria	Jun-Nov	canoeing, flora, birds and aquatic wildlife such as manatees, pink dolphins, river otters
Reserva Nacional Pampas Galeras	May-Oct	flora, herds of vicuñas
Reserva Nacional Salinas y Aguada Blanca	Apr-Oct, Jan-Apr for flamingos	flora, birds (Chilean flamingos), wildlife, including vicuñas, guanacos and the endangered south Andean deer
Reserva Nacional Tambopata	May-Oct	birds, wildlife, hiking
Santuario Nacional Ampay	May-Sep	flora, wildlife, camping, hiking
Santuario Nacional Huayllay	May-Oct	hiking, wildlife
Santuario Nacional Lagunas de Mejía	Jan-April	more than 200 species of endemic and migratory birds
Yarinacocha	Jun-Nov	canoeing, wildlife

Features	Page
the Cuzco region's highest peak	p233
100km-long canyon near Arequipa	p187
remote canyon that is possibly the deepest in the world	p193
breathtaking snowcapped mountain range that is home to the vertiginous Huascarán	p404
glaciers, summits and lakes outside Huaraz	p410
the arid mountains near Huaraz are home to strands of rare *Puya raimondii* plants	p412
snowcapped volcano looming over Arequipa	p169
rocky outcrops with stone arches	p130
the world's highest navigable lake	p207
a high-altitude salt lake near Arequipa that turns into a salt flat in the dry season	p194
near Yungay, two stunning lakes surrounded by rare *Polylepis* trees	p417
remote southern Amazon rainforest park	p471
located in the Cordillera Blanca, this national park contains Peru's highest peak	p404
famed Amazon park north of Cuzco with rainforest and cloud forest habitats	p477
caves used as nests by bats and oilbirds	p333
various wilderness areas, including tropical dry forest, pre-montane forest, a hunting reserve and mangroves	p387
private hillside reserve 75km east of Chiclayo	p366
park on the south coast	p131
53,000-hectare reserve protects large, highland lake with extensive marshes	p327
mist-fed coastal reserve in the desert foothills 100km north of Lima	p337
the largest of Peru's parks, this northern Amazon spot protects a seasonally flooded lowland forest	p493
scrubby mountain reserve east of Nazca	p145
protected peaks, volcanoes and lagoons northeast of Arequipa	p187
southern Amazon reserve protecting Peru's largest clay lick, popular with macaws	p471
mountain reserve near Cuzco protecting the Intimpa tree	p295
central highland sanctuary full of unusual rock formations	p327
coastal lagoons rife with avian life on the south coast	p150
an oxbow lake in the central Amazon	p489

THROUGH THE AMAZON: THE INTEROCEANIC HIGHWAY

One of the biggest environmental issues facing Peru is the looming completion of the Interoceanic Hwy, which cuts through the southern part of the Amazon. Beginning at the port of Ilo, on the southern Pacific coast of Peru, this transcontinental road will travel up into the Andes, through Cuzco, down into the Amazon basin at Puerto Maldonado, to the border village of Iñapari, and from there over the Integration Bridge into Brazil and onto the capital of Brasilia. Upon its completion (estimated for some time in 2010), it will go through two of the biggest protected rainforests in the area.

The project has conservationists deeply worried about a potential boom in poaching and illegal logging. Certainly, the environment has not fared well along other rainforest roads. In 2008, *The Economist* reported that within a decade of being paved, roads in the Brazilian Amazon typically resulted in 'a halo of deforestation' that extended as far as 50km on either side of a road.

The Peruvian government has voiced its commitment, on paper, to preserving the area. But its enforcement of these ideals on the ground, without adequate resources, will remain a significant challenge.

---

government simply doesn't have the funds to hire enough rangers and provide them with the equipment necessary to patrol the parks. Official infrastructure might consist of little more than a lone ranger overseeing a scanty information center with outdated maps. Nevertheless, the parks do receive some measure of protection, and various international agencies contribute money, staff and resources to help with conservation and education projects.

ENVIRONMENTAL ISSUES

Cocaine: An Unauthorized Biography is an engaging book by Dominic Streatfield about the history of one of the world's most notorious substances.

Peru faces major challenges in the stewardship of its natural resources, with problems compounded by a lack of well-run environmental law enforcement and its impenetrable geography. Deforestation and erosion are major issues, as is industrial pollution, urban sprawl and the continuing attempted eradication (with herbicides) of coca plantations on some Andean slopes. In addition, a soon-to-be-completed roadway through the heart of the Amazon may imperil thousands of square kilometers of rainforest (see boxed text, above).

In the early 1990s, Peru took steps to formulate a national environmental and natural resource code, but the government (occupied with a bloody guerrilla war in the highlands) lacked the funding and political will to enforce it. In 1995 Peru's congress created a National Environmental Council (CONAM) to manage the country's national environmental policy. Though there have been some success stories (eg flagrant polluters being fined for poor practices), enforcement remains weak (see boxed text, p432). In addition, the federal government faces chronic problems related to poverty and public health, making money for enforcement difficult to come by.

The Nature Conservancy (www.nature.org), the World Wildlife Fund (www.wwf.org) and Amazon Watch (www.amazonwatch.org) all keep a keen eye on Peru's environmental and conservation issues.

At the ground level, clear-cutting of the highlands for firewood, of the rainforests for valuable hardwoods, and of both to clear land for agriculture, oil drilling and mining has led to severe erosion. In the highlands, where deforestation and overgrazing of Andean woodlands and *puna* grass is severe, soil quality is rapidly deteriorating. In the Amazon rainforest, deforestation has led to erosion and a decline in bellwether species such as frogs, despite the fact that this long-running environmental cause has attracted all manner of international attention. For the government, balancing the development goals of poor, rural communities with the needs of large-scale multinational companies and the policy plans of an infinite number of nonprofit conservation groups is an ongoing dilemma. (Struggles over development of Amazon lands have even resulted in death: see boxed text, p478, for more on this topic.)

Erosion has also led to decreased water quality, particularly in the Amazon basin, where silt-laden water is unable to support microorganisms at the base of the food chain. Other water-related problems include pollution from mining in the highlands and from industrial waste. Sewage contamination along the coast has led to many beaches around Lima and other coastal cities being declared unfit for swimming. Pollution and overfishing have led to the continued decline of the Humboldt penguin (its numbers have declined by more than a third since the 1980s). As well, the unpredictable climate condition of El Niño (see boxed text, p364), which can wreak havoc on fragile ecosystems.

Continuing controversy surrounds the issue of coca cultivation, with efforts by the US Drug Enforcement Agency to eradicate this thousands-year-old crop, which is used to produce cocaine (see boxed text, p73). *Cocaleros* (coca growers' associations), such as the one led by indigenous activist and congressional representative Nancy Obregón, oppose the eradication of coca, not all of which ends up as cocaine. Some critics of the US-sponsored programs, such as President Evo Morales of Bolivia, have called for regulation of eradication. The problem remains far from resolved; according to one recent UN report, coca production in Peru grew by almost 5% in 2008. For more on coca and drug trafficking in Peru, see boxed text, p334.

Some positive measures are being taken to help protect the country's environment. For example, the Peruvian government and private interests within the tourism industry have come together to develop sustainable travel projects in the Amazon. In September, 2005, Peru became one of 17 Latin American countries, along with Spain, to sign the Amazon River Declaration, which calls for environmental safeguards to ensure biodiversity and for the development of tourism strategies that will fight rural poverty and spur regional development in sustainable ways.

In the southern Andes, Peru has started to act on a US$130 million master plan submitted to Unesco to preserve Machu Picchu, which has become a victim of its own success. It was declared one of the planet's top 100 most endangered sites by the World Monuments Fund in 2009. There are limits on how many people may visit the site in one day (2500 maximum), but issues related to governance, deforestation and illegal access remain, with Unesco's World Heritage Committee also evaluating the site annually to determine whether it has once again become endangered. In the meantime, the government is attempting to steer visitors away from the country's well-trammeled Gringo Trail to its equally Edenic destinations in the north.

Sponsored by the US public TV news program *Frontline,* the online report at www.pbs .org/frontlineworld/ fellows/peru0803/intro .html documents one corporation's search for natural gas reservoirs beneath Peru's Amazon jungle.

A Neotropical Companion, by John Kricher, provides an introduction to the wildlife and ecosystems of the New World tropics, including coastal and highland regions.

LIMA

Lima

On its surface, Lima is no thing of beauty. A sprawling desert city clinging precariously to dusty cliffs, it spends much of the year marinated in a perpetual fog that turns the sky the color of Styrofoam. It is loud, chaotic, and gritty; much of its architecture is bulky and gray. Foreign travelers tend to scuttle through on their way to more pastoral destinations in the Andes.

This is unfortunate. Lima may not wear its treasures on its sleeve, but peel back the foggy layers and you'll find pre-Columbian temples sitting silently amid condominium high-rises. Vestiges of colonial mansions proudly display lavish, Moorish-style balconies. And, here and there, graceful modernist structures channel architecture's most hopeful era.

What Lima lacks in attractiveness, it makes up with a huge array of downright literary experiences. Stately museums display sublime pottery; edgy art spaces host multimedia installations. There are solemn religious processions dating back to the 18th century and crowded nightclubs swaying to tropical beats. You'll find encyclopedic bookstores and cavernous shopping malls, well-heeled private golf clubs and baroque churches ornamented with the skulls of saints. It's a cultural phantasmagoria with a profusion of exceptional eateries, from humble to high-brow, all part of a gastronomic revolution more than 400 years in the making.

This is Lima. Shrouded in history, gloriously messy and full of aesthetic delights. Don't even think of missing it.

HIGHLIGHTS

- Dipping into the continent's most inventive cuisine at the bustling restaurants of **Miraflores** (p112)

- Admiring sublime Moche portrait vessels and naughty erotic pots at the **Museo Larco** (p95)

- Sipping a simple beer or a high-brow fusion cocktail at the vintage bars and chic lounges of always-hopping **Barranco** (p116)

- Walking around the sandy ruins of several civilizations' worth of temples at **Pachacamac** (p122)

- Leaping off the Miraflores clifftops and **paragliding** (p101) past the shoppers and diners at the trendy **LarcoMar shopping mall** (p119)

- Gazing upon the skulls of some of Latin America's most celebrated saints at the **Iglesia de Santo Domingo** (p90) in Central Lima

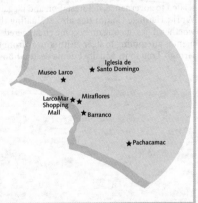

| ■ TELEPHONE CODE: 01 | ■ POPULATION: 8.5 million (Greater Metropolitan Area) | ■ AVERAGE TEMPERATURE: January 17°C to 27°C, July 11°C to 21°C |

HISTORY

Lima has survived endless cycles of destruction and rebirth. Regular apocalyptic earthquakes, warfare and the rise and fall of civilizations have resulted in a city that is as ancient as it is new. In pre-Hispanic times, the area served, at one time or another, as an urban center for the Lima, Wari, Ichsma and even the Inca cultures. When Francisco Pizarro sketched out the boundaries of his 'City of Kings' in January of 1535, there were roughly 200,000 indigenous people living in the area.

By the 18th century, the Spaniards' tumbledown village of adobe and wood had given way to a viceregal capital, where fleets of ships arrived to transport the conquest's golden spoils back to Europe. In 1746, a disastrous earthquake wiped out much of the city, but the rebuilding was rapid and streets were soon lined with baroque churches and ample *casonas* (mansions). The city's importance began to fade after independence in 1821, when other urban centers were crowned capitals of newly independent states.

In 1880, Lima found itself under siege when it was ransacked and occupied by the Chilean military during the War of the Pacific (1879–83). As part of the pillage, the Chileans made off with thousands of tomes from the National Library (though they would eventually return them – in 2007). The war was followed by another period of expansion, and by the 1920s Lima was crisscrossed by a network of broad boulevards inspired by Parisian urban design. Once again, however, a devastating earthquake struck, this time in 1940, and the city again had to be rebuilt.

By the mid-1900s the number of inhabitants began to grow exponentially. An influx of rural poor took the metro area population from 661,000 in 1940 to 8.5 million by 2007. The migration was particularly intense during the 1980s, when the conflict between the military and assorted guerilla groups in the Andes sent victims of the violence flocking to the capital. Shantytowns mushroomed, crime soared and the city fell into a period of steep decay. In 1992, the terrorist group Sendero Luminoso (Shining Path) detonated deadly truck bombs in middle-class Miraflores, marking one of Lima's darkest hours.

But the city has again dusted itself off and rebuilt – to an astonishing degree. A robust economy and a vast array of municipal improvement efforts have led to repaved streets,

refurbished parks, and cleaner and safer public areas, not to mention a thriving cultural and culinary life.

ORIENTATION

Planted on the sandy foothills of the Andes, Lima is a rambling metropolis composed of more than 30 municipalities or districts. The city's historic heart, Lima Centro (Central Lima), lies at a bend on the southern banks of the Río Rímac. Here, around the Plaza de Armas, a grid of crowded streets laid out in the days of Pizarro houses most of the city's surviving colonial architecture. On this neighborhood's southern flank, around the Plaza San Martín, the Plaza Bolognesi and the Parque de la Cultura, the city takes on a 19th-century veneer, where grand boulevards are lined with extravagant (if decayed) structures built in a panoply of architectural styles, from Victorian to beaux arts.

From this point, Av Arequipa, one of the city's principal thoroughfares, plunges southeast, through Santa Beatriz, Jesús María and Lince, before arriving in well-to-do San Isidro. This is Lima's banking center and one of its most affluent settlements. San Isidro quickly gives way to the contiguous, seaside neighbourhood of Miraflores, which serves as Lima's contemporary core, bustling with commerce, restaurants and nightlife. Immediately to the south lies Barranco, a stately turn-of-the-20th-century resort community. Long the city's bohemian center, today it boasts some of the most hopping bars in the city.

The airport resides in the port city of Callao, about 12km west of downtown or 20km northwest of Miraflores. The area is also home to a naval base, an old colonial fort and the pleasant seaside community of La Punta.

The principal bus routes connecting Central Lima with San Isidro and Miraflores run along broad avenues such as Tacna, Garcilaso de la Vega and Arequipa. These neighborhoods are also connected by the short highway Paseo de la República or Vía Expresa, known informally as *el zanjón* (the ditch).

Street Names

The city is generally laid out in a grid with street numbers that are easy to follow, jumping to the next 100 for each *cuadra* (block; ie '*cuadra* 5' will be numbered from 500 to 599). However, street names can be confusing. For one, they change with alarming regularity. Second, the same street can have several names as it traverses Lima. Av Arequipa, for example, turns into Garcilaso de la Vega, which is also known as Wilson. Locals will refer to a given street by the name which most suits them; not necessarily the newest one. In some instances, a street can have a different name on almost every block. To keep things extra confusing, some names are repeated across different districts. (When hiring taxis, be sure to indicate which neighborhood you're going to.) For the purposes of this chapter, the most common and clearly marked names are used.

Maps

A broad map of Lima can be indispensable for cross-town jaunts. The city map produced by Canada-based **ITBM** (www.itbm.com) features much of the city, including downtown and environs, as well as San Isidro and Miraflores. For a far more detailed map that covers almost the entire metropolitan area, opt for *Lima Plan Metro*, produced by the Peruvian company Editorial Lima 2000.

If you're in downtown, the top spot for maps is the **Caseta el Viajero Kiosk** (Map pp88-9; ☎ 423-5436; Jirón Belén 1002), a cluttered stand facing Plaza San Martín that is run by the congenial Federico Quispe. He carries the maps mentioned, as well as smaller ones devoted to individual neighborhoods. Maps are also widely available in bookstores.

INFORMATION
Bookstores

Lima is dotted with well-stocked shops that carry the latest bestsellers, natural-history tomes, fiction classics and lush hardbacks devoted to every aspect of Peruvian cuisine. All of the following stores also sell maps, English-language titles and guidebooks.

Crisol (www.crisol.com.pe; ☿ 10am-11pm) Óvalo Gutiérrez (Map p98; ☎ 221-1010; Av Santa Cruz 816, Miraflores); Jockey Plaza (Map pp82-3; ☎ 436-0004; Av Javier Prado Este 4200)

El Virrey (www.elvirrey.com; ☿ 10am-7pm) Central Lima (Map pp88-9; ☎ 427-5080; Pasaje de los Escribanos 107-115, Lima); San Isidro (Map p96; ☎ 440-0607; Dasso 141, San Isidro) The San Isidro branch is a bibliophile's

---

LIMA IN...

Two Days

Start with the city's colonial heart, at the **Plaza de Armas** (p87), which is bordered by the stately **Cathedral** (p87) and the **Palacio de Gobierno** (p87). From there, head west to the **Iglesia de Santo Domingo** (p90), where Peru's most revered saints are entombed, then east, to the centuries-old catacombs at the **Monasterio de San Francisco** (p91), then south to **Iglesia de la Merced** (p91), home to awe-inducing baroque altars. For lunch, try the historic **El Cordano** (p110) or the lovely **Domus** (p110).

Afterwards, continue on to the **Plaza San Martín** (p93), where you can see Chancay pottery inside a pristine historic mansion at the **Museo Andrés del Castillo** (p93) and end the day with a most important pilgrimage: a pisco sour at **El Bolivarcito** (p115), the renowned bar inside the Gran Hotel Bolivar.

On the second day, you can go pre-Columbian or contemporary: view breathtaking Moche pottery at the **Museo Larco** (p95) or see a gripping exhibit on the Internal Conflict at the **Museo de la Nación** (p94). In the afternoon, savor Lima's tastiest ice cream at the **News Café** (p111) in San Isidro, stroll through the shady **Bosque El Olivar** (p97) and visit **Huaca Pucllana** (p97), the centuries-old adobe temple at the heart of Miraflores. Spend the evening watching the world go by from the outdoor terrace at **Haiti** (p113), in full view of the Parque Kennedy.

For a multitude of dining options, see boxed text, p109.

Three Days

Seeking something colonial? In the morning, visit the exquisite **Museo Pedro de Osma** (p98) in Barranco to view some of the most intriguing Cuzco School canvases and an abundance of relics from the days of the viceroyalty. Otherwise, make the day trip to **Pachacamac** (p122) to stand amid arid ruins dating back almost two millennia. Spend the afternoon haggling for crafts at the **Mercado Indio** (p118) in Miraflores.

dream, with a vintage book room stocked with thousands of rare editions.

Ibero (www.iberolibrerias.com.pe; 10am-8pm) Diagonal (Map p98; ☎ 242-2798; Diagonal 500, Miraflores); Surco (Monterrey 170, Santiago de Surco); Larco (Map p98; ☎ 445-5520; Av José Larco 199, Miraflores); LarcoMar (Map p98; ☎ 242- 6777; Malecón de la Reserva 610, Miraflores)

KSA Tomada (Map p96; ☎ 422-5449; www.ksatomada .com; Conquistadores 1238; 7:30am-11pm Mon-Sat) Great selection. Plus a cafe, free wi-fi and comfy couches.

Cultural Centers

Some of the best events in the city – film screenings, art exhibits, theatre and dance – are put on by the various cultural institutes, some of which have several branches. Check individual websites, newspapers or the web portal *The Peru Guide* (www.theperuguide .com) for listings.

Alianza Francesa (☎ 610-8000; alianzafrancesa.org .pe) Central Lima (Map pp88-9; Av Garcilaso de la Vega 1550); Miraflores (Map p98; Av Arequipa 4598, Miraflores) In addition to French cultural events, the Alianza stages annual runway shows of contemporary Peruvian fashion.

Asociación Cultural Peruano Británica (☎ 615-3434; www.britanico.edu.pe) Miraflores (Map p98; Malecón Balta 740); San Isidro (Map p96; Av Arequipa 3495) The institute has a library with British newspapers, an impressive gallery space, and is host to film and theater productions.

Centro Cultural de España (CCELIMA; Map pp88-9; ☎ 330-0412; www.ccelima.org; Plaza Washington, Natalio Sánchez 181, Santa Beatriz; 9am-9pm) A full range of offerings, including a roomy 1st-floor gallery that puts on some of Lima's most intriguing contemporary art exhibits.

Centro Cultural Inca Garcilaso (Map pp88-9; ☎ 623-2656; www.ccincagarcilaso.gob.pe; Ucayali 391, Central Lima; 10am-7:30pm Tue-Sat, 10am-6pm Sun) Part of the Ministry of Foreign Relations, the Centro hosts concerts and exhibits related to Peruvian culture.

Goethe-Institut (☎ 433-3180; www.goethe.de/ins/pe/ lim/esindex.htm; Jirón Nazca 722, Jesús María) A hub for German speakers; it has a library and a theater program.

Instituto Cultural Peruano Norteamericano (ICPNA; ☎ 706-7000; www.icpna.edu.pe) Central Lima (Map pp88-9; Cuzco 446); Miraflores (Map p98; Av Arequipa 4798) Perhaps the biggest of the foreign cultural institutes, with expansive libraries, a video archive, Spanish courses, art exhibits, and theater and dance performances.

Emergency

Policía Nacional head office (Map pp82-3; ☎ 460-0921; Moore 268, Magdalena del Mar; 24hr)

Tourism Police (Policía de Turismo, Poltur; Map p98; ☎ 460-0844; Colón 246; 24hr) A division of the Policía Nacional (National Police) that usually has English-speaking officers who can provide theft reports for insurance claims or traveler's check refunds. In heavily touristed areas, it is easy to identify members of Poltur by their white shirts.

Immigration

For general information about visas and stay extensions, see p526. See p517 for a list of embassies in Lima.

Arrive first thing in the morning to the **oficina de migraciónes** (immigration office; Map pp88-9; ☎ 417-6900, 417-6950/6951/6952; www.migraciones .gob.pe; Prolongación España 734, Breña; 8am-1pm Mon-Fri) if you want to get your tourist-card extension (US$50) on the same day. The specially stamped paperwork can be bought beforehand at the nearby Banco de la Nación (S40.47). You will need a copy of form F-007 (available for download on the website, in the section titled *Prórroga de Residencia*), along with your passport and the immigration slip you received upon entry into Peru. Make an extra photocopy of each to make the process faster. If you've lost the immigration slip, it will take longer and be more expensive. You may be asked to show a ticket out of the country, or prove that you have sufficient funds – the more affluent you look, the less hassle you'll have. Process your paperwork only with officials inside the office; do not accept offers of help from people on the street.

Internet & Fax

There are internet cafes (many of which can send faxes) on practically every block in the city. In addition, most hotels offer internet access – many through wi-fi. The following places provide high-speed access for S1 to S2 an hour.

Cabina Internet (Map p98; ☎ 446-6814; Pasaje Tarata 230, Miraflores; 24hr)

Internet cafes (Map p100; cnr Av Grau & Sáenz Peña, Barranco; 8am-11pm)

Internet Mundonet (Map pp88-9; Ancash 412, Central Lima) Access is through the main lobby of the Hotel España, via Calle Azángaro.

ZonaNet (Map p96; ☎ 221-5463; Av 2 de Mayo 615; 9am-10pm Mon-Sat)

Laundry

Hotels can have your laundry done for you or direct you to the closest *lavandería* (laundry), of which there is an abundance. Some

LIMA

METROPOLITAN LIMA

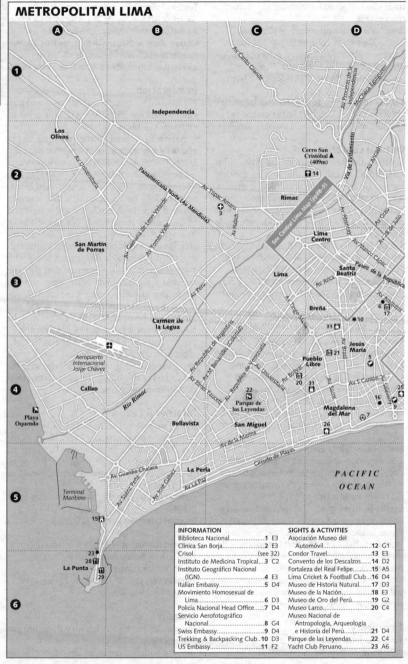

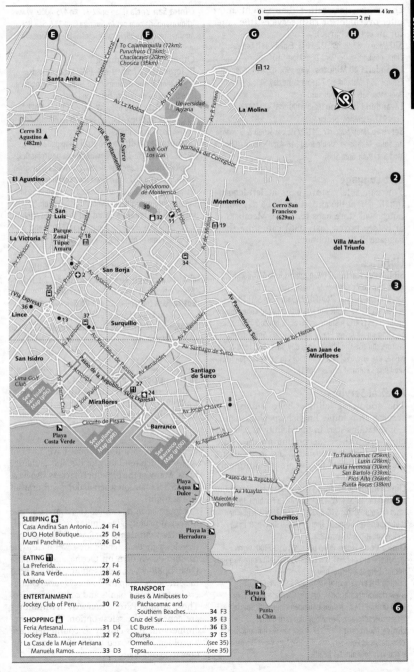

charge per item rather than weight; most offer overnight or rush services (the latter for an extra charge).

KIO (Map pp88-9; ☎ 332-9035; España 481, Central Lima; per kg S3; ☽ 9am-8pm Mon-Sat)

Lavandería 40 Minutos (Map p98; ☎ 446-5928; Av Espinar 154, Miraflores; 2 items same day S11; ☽ 8am-8pm Mon-Sat, 9am-1pm Sun)

Lavandería Neptuno (Map p100; ☎ 477-4472; Av Grau 912, Barranco; per kg S3)

Servirap (Map p98; ☎ 241-0759; cnr Schell & Grimaldo del Solar, Miraflores; single load S16-43; ☽ 8am-10pm Mon-Sat, 9am-6pm Sun)

Left-Luggage

You can safely store bags at **left-luggage** (☎ 517-3217) at the airport for S14 a day. Many hotels will store bags for a fee. Members of SAE (see boxed text, p86) can store their baggage at the clubhouse.

Libraries

Biblioteca Nacional (Map pp82-3; ☎ 513-6900; www.bnp.gob.pe; Av de la Poesía 160, San Borja; ☽ 9:15am-7:30pm Mon-Fri, 9:15am-2pm Sat) The nation's biggest public library, with a broad collection of Spanish texts and historic archives, is housed in a corner building on Av Javier Prado and Aviación. Short-term visitors can use the library on a day pass (S8); long-term passes are also available. For books in other languages, see Lima's cultural centers (p81).

Medical Services

The following clinics have emergency service and some English-speaking staff. Consultations start in the vicinity of S80 and climb from there, depending on the clinic and the doctor. Treatments and medications are an additional fee, as are appointments with specialists.

Clínica Anglo-Americana (www.clinangloamericana .com.pe) La Molina (☎ 436 9933; Av La Fontana 362); San Isidro (Map p96; ☎ 616-8900; Salazar 350) A renowned (but expensive) hospital. There's a walk-in center in La Molina, near the US embassy.

Clínica Good Hope (Map p98; ☎ 610-7300; www .goodhope.org.pe; Malecón Balta 956) Quality care at good prices; there is a dental unit.

Clínica Internacional (Map pp88-9; ☎ 619-6161; www.clinicainternacional.com.pe; Garcilaso de la Vega 1420 Central Lima) A well-equipped clinic with specialties in gastroenterology, neurology and cardiology.

Clínica Montesur (☎ 317-4000; www.clinicamontesur .com.pe; Av El Polo 505, Monterrico; fees vary) Devoted exclusively to women's health.

Clínica San Borja (Map pp82-3; ☎ 475-4000; www .clinicasanborja.com.pe; Av Guardia Civil 337, San Borja) Another reputable clinic, with cardiology services.

Other medical options:

Dr Jorge Bazan (☎ 99-735-2668; backpackersdr@ yahoo.com) A well-recommended English-speaking medic who makes house calls to hotels and hostels.

Dr Victor Aste (Map p96; ☎ 421-9169, 441-7502; No 101, Antero Aspillaga 415, San Isidro) A recommended, English-speaking dentist.

Instituto de Medicina Tropical (Map pp82-3; ☎ 482-3903, 482-3910; www.upch.edu.pe/tropicales; Hospital Nacional Cayetano Heredia, Av Honorio Delgado 430, San Martín de Porras) Good for treating tropical diseases. The immediate area around the hospital is safe, but the surrounding neighborhood can be rough.

Instituto Nacional de Salud del Niño (Map pp88-9; ☎ 330-0066; www.isn.gob.pe; Brasil 600, Breña) A pediatric hospital; gives tetanus and yellow-fever jabs.

Pharmacies abound in Lima. The following chains are well stocked and open 24 hours. They often deliver free of charge.

Botica Fasa (Map p98; ☎ 619-0000; www.boticafasa .com.pe; cnr Av José Larco 129-35, Miraflores)

InkaFarma (Map p98; ☎ 315-9000; deliveries 314-2020; www.inkafarma.com.pe; Alfredo Benavides 425, Miraflores)

You can have eyeglasses made cheaply by one of the opticians along Miró Quesada in the vicinity of Camaná in Central Lima (Map pp88–9) or around Schell and Av José Larco in Miraflores (p98).

Money

Banks are plentiful and most have 24-hour ATMs, which tend to offer the best exchange rates. Many of the big supermarkets also have ATMS. Use caution when making withdrawals late at night.

Lima's *casas de cambio* (foreign-exchange bureaus) usually give similar or slightly better rates than banks for cash (although not traveler's checks). There are several *casas de cambio* downtown on Ocoña and Camaná (Map pp88–9), as well as along Av José Larco in Miraflores (Map p98). Street moneychangers hang around banks and *casas de cambio*. Those around Parque Kennedy in Miraflores are generally the safest option. Even so, examine your bills closely as counterfeits are a problem. See boxed text, p523, for tips on how to avoid fakes.

The following are some of the most useful options:

American Express/Travex (Map p98; ☎ 710-3900; www.amextravelresources.com/offices/806; Av Santa Cruz 621, Miraflores; ☥ 8:30am-6pm Mon-Fri, 9am-1pm Sat) Buy traveler's checks or replace lost ones.

Banco Continental (www.bbvabancocontinental .com; ☥ 9am-6pm Mon-Fri, 9:30am-12:30pm Sat) Central Lima (Map pp88-9; ☎ 311-0231; Cuzco 286-290); Miraflores (Map p98; ☎ 241-5645; Av José Larco 631) A representative of Visa; its ATMs also take Cirrus, Plus and MasterCard.

Banco de Crédito del Perú (BCP; www.viabcp.com; ☥ 9am-6:30pm Mon-Fri, 9:30am-1pm Sat) Central Lima (Map pp88-9; ☎ 427-5600; cnr Lampa & Ucayali, Central Lima); José Gonzales (Map p98; cnr Av José Larco & José Gonzales, Miraflores); José Pardo (Map p98; ☎ 242-5900; Av José Pardo 425, Miraflores) With 24-hour Visa and Plus ATMs, also gives cash advances on Visa, and changes Amex, Citicorp and Visa traveler's checks. The Central Lima branch has incredible stained-glass ceilings.

Citibank (☎ 221-7000; www.citibank.com.pe; ☥ 10am 7pm Mon-Fri, 10am-1pm Sat) San Isidro (Map p96; Av 2 de Mayo 1547); Miraflores (Map p98; Av José Pardo 127, Miraflores) These locations have 24-hour ATMS operating on the Cirrus, Maestro, MasterCard and Visa systems; they cash Citicorp traveler's checks.

LAC Dólar (☥ 9:30am-6pm Mon-Fri, 9am-2pm Sat) Central Lima (Map pp88-9; ☎ 428-8127; Camaná 779); Miraflores (Map p98; ☎ 242-4069; Av La Paz 211) A reliable exchange house; can also deliver cash to your hotel in exchange for traveler's checks.

Moneygram (Map p98; ☎ 444-3381; www.money gram.com; Pasaje Tarata 299, Miraflores; ☥ 9am-9pm Mon-Sat) Money transfers.

Scotiabank (☎ 311-6000; www.scotiabank.com.pe; ☥ 9:15am-6pm Mon-Fri, 9:15am-12:30pm Sat) San Isidro (Map p96; Av 2 de Mayo 1510-1550); Miraflores Larco (Map p98; Av José Larco 1119); Miraflores Pardo (Map p98; cnr Av José Pardo & Bolognesi, Miraflores) ATMs (24-hour) operate on the MasterCard, Maestro, Cirrus, Visa and Plus networks and dispense soles and US dollars.

Photography

The city is dotted with photo processing shops. Slide and print-film developing tends to be mediocre, but most places can transfer digital images onto a disc.

Taller de Fotografía Profesional (Map p98; ☎ 628-5195; Av Alfredo Benavides 1171, Miraflores; ☥ 9am-7pm Mon-Fri, 9:30am-1pm Sat) One of the best photo shops in the city, with processing, camera repairs and sales.

Post

Serpost, the national postal service, has outlets throughout Lima. Mail sent to you at Lista de Correos (Poste Restante), Correo Central, Lima, can be collected at the main post office in Central Lima. Take identification.

Serpost (www.serpost.com.pe; ☎ 511-2001) Central Lima (Main post office; Map pp88-9; Pasaje Piura s/n, Central Lima; ☥ 8am-9pm Mon-Sat); San Isidro (Map p96; ☎ 422-0985; Las Palmeras 205; ☥ 9am-1pm & 2-5:40pm Mon-Fri, 9-11:40am Sat); Miraflores (Map p98; Av Petit Thouars 5201; ☥ 8am-8:45pm Mon-Sat, 9am-1:30pm Sat, 9am-2pm Sun); Larco (Map p98; Av José Larco 868; ☥ 8am-7:30pm Mon-Sat)

Other shipping services:

DHL (Map p96; ☎ 517-2500; www.dhl.com.pe; Los Castaños 225, San Isidro; ☥ 9:30am-8:30pm Mon-Fri)

Federal Express (FedEx; Map p98; ☎ 242-2280; www .fedex.com.pe; BSC Miraflores, Pasaje Olaya 260, Miraflores; ☥ 9am-7pm Mon-Fri, 10am-3pm Sat)

Telephone

Telefónica-Perú has pay phones on almost every street corner. Most accept phone cards, which can be purchased at supermarkets and groceries. Call ☎ 103 (no charge) for directory inquiries within Lima and ☎ 109 for assistance with provincial numbers.

For fax, see p81.

Tourist Information

iPerú (http://peru.info/iperu) Aeropuerto Internacional Jorge Chávez (Map pp82-3; ☎ 574-8000; Main Hall; ☥ 24hr); Miraflores LarcoMar (Map p98; ☎ 445-9400; Module 14, by movie theater box office, LarcoMar, Malecón de la Reserva 610; ☥ noon-8pm); San Isidro (Map p96; ☎ 421-1627; Jorge Basadre 610; ☥ 9am-6pm Mon-Fri) The government's reputable tourist bureau dispenses maps, offers good advice and can help handle complaints. The Miraflores office is tiny but is highly useful on weekends.

Municipal tourist office (Map pp88-9; ☎ 315-1542; munlima.gob.pe; Pasaje de los Escribanos 145, Central Lima; ☥ 9am-5pm Mon-Fri, 11am-3pm Sat & Sun) A not-very-useful office that keeps a limited listing of local events; find these on its website by clicking on the link labeled 'Actividades del mes.'

South American Explorers Club See boxed text, p86.

Trekking & Backpacking Club (Map pp82-3; ☎ 423-2515; www.angelfire.com/mi2/tebac; Huascar 1152, Jesús María) Provides information, maps, brochures, equipment rental and guide information for independent trekkers.

Travel Agencies

For companies in Lima offering local and regional tours, see p102. For travel agencies to organize airline bookings and other arrangements try the following:

Fertur Peru Travel (www.fertur-travel; ☺ 9am-7pm Mon-Fri, 9am-noon Sat) Central Lima (Map pp88-9; ☎ 427-2626, 427-1958; Jirón Junín 211, Central Lima); Miraflores (Map p98; ☎ 242-1900; Calle Schell 485, Miraflores) A highly recommended agency that can book local, regional and international travel, as well as create custom group itineraries. Discounts available for students and SAE members.

InfoPerú (Map pp88-9; ☎ 431-0117; http://infoperu .com.pe; Jirón Belén 1066, Central Lima; ☺ 9:30am-6pm Mon-Fri, 10am-2pm Sat) Books bus and plane tickets and dispenses reliable information on hotels and sightseeing.

Intej (Map p100; ☎ 247-3230; www.intej.org; San Martín 240, Barranco) The official International Student Identity Card (ISIC) office, Intej can arrange discounted air, train and bus fares, among other services.

Lima Tours (Map pp88-9; ☎ 619-6901; www.lima tours.com.pe; Jirón Belén 1040, Central Lima; ☺ 9:30am-6pm Mon-Fri, 9:30am-1pm Sat) A well-known agency that handles all manner of travel arrangements. Also organizes gay-friendly trips and basic gastronomic tours of Lima.

Romao Tours (Map pp88-9; ☎ 627-4578, 627-4579, Nicolás de Piérola 994, Central Lima; ☺ 9:30am-7pm Mon-Sat) From plane tickets to train tickets.

Victor Travel Services (Map pp88-9; ☎ 433-5547; www.victortravelservice.com; Jirón de la Unión 1068, Central Lima) Helpful for local information, as well as travel all over Peru.

DANGERS & ANNOYANCES

Like any large Latin American city, Lima is a land of haves and have-nots, something that has made stories about crime here the stuff of legend. To some degree, the city's dangers have been overblown. Lima has improved greatly since the 1980s, when pickpockets, muggers and carjackers plied their trade with impunity. Even so, this is a big city, in which one in five people live in poverty, so crime is to be expected. The most common offense is theft and readers have reported regular muggings. You are unlikely to be physically hurt, but it is nonetheless best to keep a streetwise attitude.

Do not wear flashy jewelry and keep your camera in your bag when you are not using it. It is best to keep your cash in your pocket and take only as much as you'll need for the day. And, unless you think you'll need your passport for official purposes, leave it at the hotel; a photocopy will do. Blending in helps, too: *limeños* favor a muted wardrobe of jeans and sweaters. Hitting the streets in designer sneakers or brand-new trekking gear will get you noticed.

Be wary at crowded events and the areas around bus stops and terminals. These bring out pickpockets – even in upscale districts. Late at night, it is preferable to take taxis, especially in downtown, or if you've been partying until late in Barranco. The areas of Rímac, Callao, Surquillo and La Victoria can get quite

---

SOUTH AMERICAN EXPLORERS

Now more than three decades old, the venerable **South American Explorers Club** (SAE; Map p98; ☎ 445-3306; Piura 135, Miraflores; ☺ 9:30am-5pm Mon-Fri, 9:30am-8pm Wed, 9:30am-1pm Sat) is an indispensable resource for long-term travelers, journalists and scientists spending long periods in Peru, Ecuador, Bolivia and Argentina. It has an extensive library as well as a vast array of guides and maps for sale, from topographic plans to trail maps for the Inca Trail, Mt Ausangate, the Cordillera Blanca and Cordillera Huayhuash. You can also get useful information on travel conditions in remote areas, research volunteer opportunities and pick up a copy of the *Lima Survival Kit* (US$35), a handy guide for new long-term residents that details how to find health care and good schools for kids.

The club is a member-supported, nonprofit organization (it helped launch the first cleanup of the Inca Trail and has supported local medicine drives). Annual dues are US$60 per person (US$90 per couple); special discounts are available for ISIC holders and volunteers. Members receive full use of the clubhouse and its facilities, including luggage storage, poste restante, a book exchange, access to the online magazine *South American Explorer,* and discounts on items sold on-site. Members are also eligible for discounts at participating businesses throughout Peru. There are additional clubhouses in Cuzco, Quito and Buenos Aires. (Find contact information for these online.) You can sign up in person at one of the offices or via the website.

Nonmembers are welcome to browse some of the information and purchase guides or maps.

rough so approach with caution (taxis are best). The most dangerous neighborhoods are San Juan de Lurigancho, Los Olivos, Comas, Vitarte and El Agustino.

In addition, be skeptical of unaffiliated touts and taxi drivers who try to sell you on tours or tell you that the hotel you've booked is a crime-infested bordello. Many of these are scam artists who will say and do anything to steer you to places that pay them a commission. For more tips on safe travel in Peru, see p514.

SIGHTS

Museums filled with millennia worth of artifacts and artistic treasures. Baroque churches that have their roots in the early days of the Spanish colony. Historic houses painted shades of yellow, pink and blue. And, to top it all off, water shows that put Las Vegas to shame. You could spend weeks in Lima and still not see it all.

Central Lima

Bustling narrow streets are lined with ornate baroque churches in the city's historic and commercial center, located on the south bank of the Río Rímac.

PLAZA DE ARMAS

It is here that Lima was born. The 140-sq-meter **Plaza de Armas** (Map pp88–9), also called the Plaza Mayor, was not only the heart of the 16th-century settlement established by Francisco Pizarro, it was a center of a continent-wide empire ruled by the Spanish. Sadly, not one original building remains. But, at the center of the plaza you will find one of the area's oldest features: an impressive bronze fountain erected in 1650.

Surrounding the plaza are a number of significant public buildings: to the east resides the **Palacio Arzobispal** (Archbishop's Palace) built in 1924 in a colonial style and boasting some of the most exquisite Moorish-style balconies in the city. To the northeast is the block-long **Palacio de Gobierno**, a grandiose baroque-style building from 1937 that serves as the residence of Peru's president. Out front stands a handsomely uniformed presidential guard (think French Foreign legion, c 1900) that conducts a changing of the guard every day at noon – a ceremonious affair that involves slow-motion goose-stepping and the sublime

sounds of a brass band playing *El Cóndor Pasa* as a military march.

Unfortunately, the palace is no longer regularly open to visitors. However, there are occasional exhibits to which the public is admitted, provided you make an appointment at least 48 hours in advance. Check the website for a schedule of exhibits; if one is happening, make an appointment through the **Office of Public Relations** (☎ 311-4200, 311-3900, ext 378; www .presidencia.gob.pe; ⌚ 8:30am-1pm & 2:30-5:30pm Mon-Fri). Otherwise, the web page offers a virtual tour (click on *Visita Virtual*) in which you can see the building's lavish interiors.

La Catedral de Lima

Next to the Archbishop's palace resides the **cathedral** (Map pp88–9; ☎ 427-9647; admission S10; ⌚ 9am-5pm Mon-Fri, 10am-1pm Sat), on the same plot of land that Pizarro designated for the city's first church in 1535. Though it retains a baroque facade, the building you see today has been built and rebuilt numerous times: in 1551, in 1622 and after the earthquakes of 1687 and 1746. The last major restoration was completed in 1940.

Unfortunately, a craze for all things neoclassical in the late 18th century left much of the interior (and the interiors of many Lima churches) stripped of its elaborate baroque decor. Even so, there is plenty to see. The various chapels along the nave display more than a dozen altars carved in every imaginable style and the ornate wood **choir**, produced by Pedro de Noguera in the early 17th century, is a masterpiece of rococo sculpture. A **religious museum**, in the rear, features paintings, vestments and an intricate sacristy.

By the cathedral's main door is the **mosaic-covered chapel** where the battered remains of Pizarro have long lain. The authenticity of these came into question in 1977, after workers cleaning out a crypt discovered several bodies and a sealed lead box containing a skull that bore the inscription, 'Here is the head of the gentleman Marquis Don Francisco Pizarro, who found and conquered the kingdom of Peru…' After a battery of tests in the 1980s, a US forensic scientist concluded that the body previously on display was of an unknown official and that the brutally stabbed and headless body from the crypt was Pizarro's. Head and body were reunited

LIMA

CENTRAL LIMA

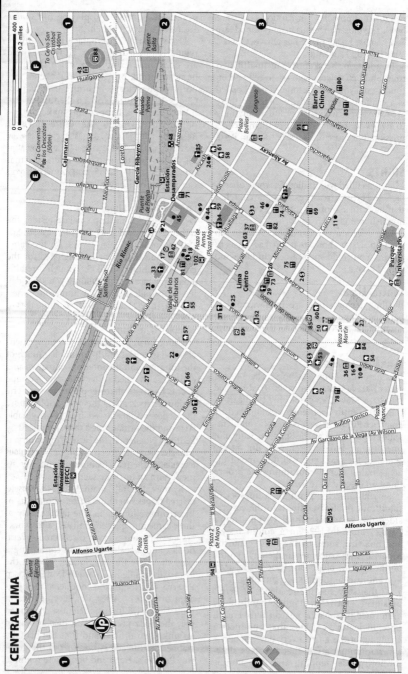

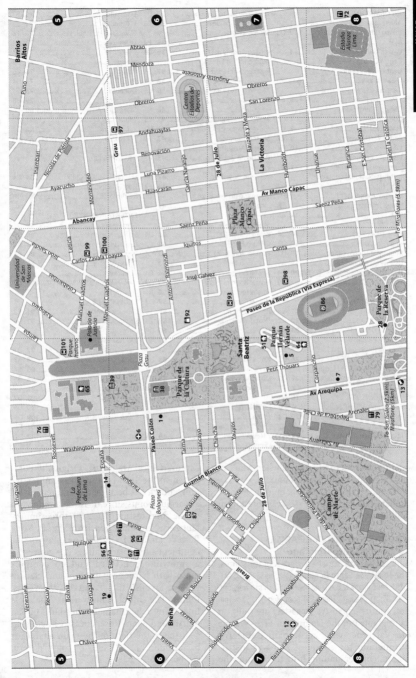

and transferred to the chapel, where you can also view the inscribed lead box.

Guide services in Spanish, English, French, Italian and Portuguese are available for an additional fee.

AROUND THE PLAZA DE ARMAS
Iglesia de Santo Domingo

One of Lima's most storied religious sites, the **Iglesia de Santo Domingo** (Map pp88-9; ☎ 427-6793; cnr Camaná & Conde de Superunda; convent S5; ⏰ 9am-12:30pm & 3-6pm Mon-Sat, 9am-1pm Sun) and its expansive **monastery** are built on land granted to the Dominican Friar Vicente de Valverde, who accompanied Pizarro throughout the conquest and was instrumental in persuading him to execute the captured Inca Atahualpa. Originally completed in the 16th century, this impressive pink church has been rebuilt and remodeled at various points since. It is most renowned as the final resting place for three important Peruvian saints: San Juan Macías, Santa Rosa de Lima and San Martín de Porres (the continent's first black saint). The convent – a sprawling courtyard-studded complex lined with baroque paintings and clad in vintage Spanish tile – contains the saints' tombs. The church, however, has the most interesting relics: namely, the skulls of San Martín and Santa Rosa, encased in glass, in a shrine to the right of the main altar. (For background on the saints of colonial Peru, see boxed text, p39.)

Monasterio de San Francisco

This bright yellow Franciscan **monastery and church** (Map pp88-9; ☎ 426-7377; www.museocatacumbas .com; cnr Lampa & Ancash; adult/child under 15 S5/1; ☻ 9:30am-5:30pm) is most famous for its bone-lined catacombs (containing an estimated 70,000 burials) and its remarkable library, where you can take in the sight of 25,000 antique texts, some of them predating the conquest. But this baroque structure has many other things worth seeing: the most spectacular is a geometric Moorish-style cupola, over the main staircase, which was carved in 1625 (restored 1969) out of Nicaraguan cedar. In addition, the refectory contains 13 paintings, of the biblical patriarch Jacob and his 12 sons, attributed to the studio of Spanish master Francisco de Zurbarán.

Admission includes a 30-minute guided tour in English or in Spanish. Tours leave as groups gather.

Iglesia de la Merced

The first Latin mass in Lima was held in 1534, on a small patch of land now marked by the **Iglesia de la Merced** (Map pp88-9; ☎ 427-8199; cnr Jirón de la Unión & Miró Quesada; admission free; ☻ 10am-noon & 5-7pm). It was originally built in 1541 and then rebuilt several times over the course of the next two centuries. Most of today's structure dates to the 18th century, with its most striking feature being the imposing granite facade, carved in the *churrigueresque* manner (a highly ornate style popular during the late Spanish baroque). Inside, the nave is lined by more than two-dozen jaw-droppingly magnificent baroque and Renaissance-style altars, some of which are carved entirely out of mahogany.

To the right as you enter is a large silver cross that once belonged to Father Pedro Urraca (1583–1657), a priest renowned for having had a vision of the Virgin. This is a place of pilgrimage for Peruvians, attracting worshipers who come to place a hand on the cross and beg for needed miracles.

Other Colonial Religious Sites

Santuario de Santa Rosa de Lima (Map pp88-9; ☎ 425-1279; cnr Tacna & Callao; admission free; ☻ 7:30am-noon & 5-8pm) honors the first saint of the Americas in a plain, terra-cotta-hued church on a congested avenue located roughly at the site of her birth. You can find a modest adobe sanctuary in the gardens, built in the 17th century for Santa Rosa's prayers and meditation. Right across the street, the **Casa-Capilla de San Martín de Porres** (Map pp88-9; ☎ 423-0707; Callao 535; admission free; ☻ 9am-1pm & 3-6pm Mon-Fri, 9am-1pm Sat) commemorates the birthplace of San Martín (now a center of religious study). Visitors are welcome to view the bright interior patios and the diminutive chapel.

Two blocks south lies **Iglesia de las Nazarenas** (Map pp88-9; ☎ 423-5718; cnr Tacna & Huancavelica; admission free; ☻ 7am-1pm & 5-9pm), one of Lima's most storied churches. In the 17th century, the area was a shantytown inhabited by former slaves, and it was here that one of them painted an image of the Crucifixion on a wall that survived the devastating earthquake of 1655. In the 1700s, a church was built around this wall (which serves as the centerpiece of the main altar), and has been rebuilt many times since. But the wall endures, and on October 18 each year a representation of the mural, known as *El Señor de los Milagros* (Christ of Miracles), is carried around in a tens-of-thousands-strong procession that lasts for days.

Iglesia de San Pedro (Map pp88-9; ☎ 428-3010; www .sanpedrodelima.org; cnr Azángaro & Ucayali; admission free; ☻ 8:30am-1pm & 2-4pm Mon-Fri) is a small 17th-century church considered to be one of the finest examples of baroque colonial-era architecture in Lima. It was consecrated by the Jesuits in 1638 and has changed little since. The interior is sumptuously decorated with gilded altars, Moorish-style carvings and an abundance of glazed tile.

Iglesia de San Agustín (Map pp88-9; ☎ 427-7548; cnr Ica & Camaná; admission free; ☻ 8-9am & 4:30-7:30pm Mon-Fri) has an elaborate *churrigueresque* facade (completed in 1720), replete with stone carvings of angels, flowers, fruit (and, of course, Saint Augustine). Limited operating hours can make it a challenge to visit. The interiors are drab, but the church is home to a curious woodcarving called *La Muerte* (Death) by 18th-century sculptor Baltazar Gavilán. As one (probably fictional) story goes, Gavilán died in a state of madness after viewing his own chilling sculpture in the middle of the night. The piece sometimes travels, so call ahead.

Colonial Mansions

There are few remaining colonial mansions in Lima since many of them have been lost to expansion, earthquakes and the perennially moist weather. Many now operate as private offices or educational centers, which can make seeing interiors difficult. The most immaculate of these *casonas* is the famous **Palacio Torre Tagle** (Map pp88-9; Ucayali 363; ☺ closed Sat & Sun), completed in 1735, with its ornate baroque portico (the best one in Lima) and striking Moorish-style balconies. Unfortunately, it is now home to Peru's Foreign Ministry, so entry is restricted. Groups and educational organizations, however, can request a tour in advance via the **oficina cultural** (☎ 311-2400).

Innocuously tucked on a side street by the post office is **Casa Aliaga** (Map pp88-9; http://casadealiaga.com; Jirón de la Unión 224), which stands on land given in 1535 to Jerónimo de Aliaga, one of Pizarro's followers, and which has been occupied by 16 generations of his descendants. It may not look like much from the outside, but the interiors are lovely, with vintage furnishings and tilework. It can only be visited via organized excursions with Lima Tours (p86).

Other historic (if less pristine) *casonas* include the **Casa de la Riva** (Map pp88-9; Ica 426; admission S5; ☺ 10am-1pm & 2-4pm Mon-Fri), a handsome, 18th-century mansion with beautiful wooden balconies, an elegant patio and period furnishings. Two blocks to the north, the cornflower blue **Casa de Oquendo** (Casa Osambela; Map pp88-9; ☎ 427-7987; Conde de Superunda 298; ☺ 9am-5pm Mon-Fri, 9am-noon Sat) is a ramshackle turn-of-the-19th-century house (in its time, the tallest in Lima) with a creaky lookout tower that, on a clear day, has views of Callao. Tours for small groups can be arranged ahead of time with the helpful manager, Juan Manuel Ugarte, but walk-ins can be accommodated provided he isn't busy. Donations are welcomed in exchange for this service. Toward the center of downtown, another *casona,* the **Casa de Riva-Aguero** (Map pp88-9; ☎ 626-6600; Camaná 459; admission S2; ☺ 10am-7pm Mon-Fri) houses a small, insipid folk-art collection.

East of the plaza, the lovely red **Casa de Pilatos** (Map pp88-9; ☎ 427-5814; Ancash 390; admission free; ☺ 8am-1pm & 2-5pm Mon-Fri) is home to offices for the Tribunal Constitucional (Supreme Court). Access is a challenge: visitors are only allowed into the courtyard provided there aren't official meetings going on. Enter through the side door on Azángaro.

OTHER CENTRAL LIMA SIGHTS

Museo Banco Central de Reserva del Perú

Housed in a graceful bank building, the **Museo Banco Central de Reserva del Perú** (Map pp88-9; ☎ 613-2000, ext 2655; http://museobcr.perucultural.org.pe; cnr Lampa & Ucayali; admission free; ☺ 10am-4:30pm Tue-Fri, 10am-1pm Sat & Sun) is a well-presented overview of several millennia of Peruvian art, from pre-Columbian gold and pottery to a selection of 19th- and 20th-century Peruvian canvases. Don't miss the dozen watercolors by Pancho Fierro, on the top floor, which provide an unparalleled view of dress and class in 19th-century Lima. Identification is required for admittance.

Museo Postal y Filatélico

Everything you've ever wanted to know about the Peruvian mail system can be found at the **Museo Postal y Filatélico** (Postal & Philatelic Museum; Map pp88-9; ☎ 428-0400; Conde de Superunda 170; admission free; ☺ 9am-5pm Tue-Fri, 9am-1pm Sat & Sun), next to the main post office.

Museo de la Inquisición

A graceful neoclassical structure facing the Plaza Bolívar houses this diminutive **museum** (Map pp88-9; ☎ 311-7777, ext 5160; www.congreso.gob.pe/museo.htm; Jirón Junín 548; admission free; ☺ 9am-5pm Mon-Fri), where the Spanish Inquisition once plied its trade. In the 1800s, the building was expanded and rebuilt into the Peruvian senate. Today, guests can tour the basement, where morbidly hilarious wax figures are stretched on racks and flogged – to the delight of visiting eight-year-old boys. The old 1st-floor library retains a remarkable baroque wood ceiling. Entry is by half-hour guided tours, conducted in Spanish and English, after which you are free to wander.

Parque de la Muralla

During the 17th century, the heart of Lima was ringed by a *muralla* (city wall), much of which was torn down in the 1870s, as the city expanded. However, you can view a set of excavated remains at the **Parque de la Muralla** (Map pp88-9; ☎ 427-4125; Amazonas, btwn Lampa & Av Abancay; admission S1, Wed free; ☺ 9am-9pm), where, in addition to the wall, a small on-site **museum** (with erratic hours) details the development of the city and a few objects.

More interestingly, the park is home to a bronze statue of Francisco Pizarro, created by American sculptor Ramsey MacDonald in the early 20th century. The figure once commanded center stage at the Plaza de Armas, but over the years has been moved around various locations as attitudes toward Pizarro have grown critical. The best part: the figure isn't even Pizarro – it's of an anonymous conquistador of the sculptor's invention. MacDonald made three copies of the statue. One was erected in the US; the other, Spain. The third was donated to the city of Lima after the artist's death in 1934 (and only after Mexico rejected it). So now, Pizarro – or, more accurately, his proxy – sits at the edge of this park, a silent witness to a daily parade of amorous Peruvian teens.

Jirón de la Unión

In the late 19th and early 20th centuries, the five pedestrian blocks on **Jirón de la Unión** (Map pp88–9), from the Plaza de Armas to Plaza San Martín, was *the* place to see and be seen. The street has long since lost its aristocratic luster, but the shells of neocolonial and art-deco buildings survive. Watch out for pickpockets who like to work the crowds during street performances.

PLAZA SAN MARTÍN

Built in the early 20th century, **Plaza San Martín** (Map pp88–9) has come to life in recent years as the city has set about restoring its park and giving the surrounding beaux arts architecture a needed scrubbing. (It is especially lovely in the evenings, when it is illuminated.) The plaza is named for the liberator of Peru, José de San Martín, who sits astride a horse at the center of the plaza. At the base, don't miss the bronze rendering of Madre Patria, the symbolic mother of Peru. Commissioned in Spain under instruction to give the good lady a crown of flames, nobody thought to iron out the double meaning of the word flame in Spanish *(llama)*, so the hapless craftsmen duly placed a delightful little llama on her head.

The stately **Gran Hotel Bolívar** (p104), built in the 1920s, presides over the square from the northwest.

MUSEO ANDRÉS DEL CASTILLO

Housed in a pristine 19th-century mansion with Spanish-tile floors, this worthwhile new private **museum** (Map pp88–9; ☎ 433-2831; www.madc.com.pe; Jirón de la Unión 1030; admission S10; ⊙ 9am-6pm, closed Tue) showcases a vast collection of minerals, as well as breathtakingly displayed Nazca textiles and Chancay pottery, including some remarkable representations of Peruvian hairless dogs.

PANTEÓN DE LOS PRÓCERES

Located inside a little-visited 18th-century Jesuit church, this **monument** (Map pp88–9; ☎ 427-8157; Parque Universitario; admission S1; ⊙ 9am-5pm Tue-Sun) pays tribute to a bevy of Peruvian battle heroes, from Túpac Amaru II, the 18th-century Quechua leader who led an indigenous uprising, to José de San Martín, who led the country to independence in the 1820s. The mosaic-lined crypt holds the remains of Ramón Castilla, the four-time Peruvian president who saw the country through a good piece of the 19th century. The building retains an impressive baroque altar, carved out of Ecuadorean mahogany, which dates to the 1500s.

MUSEO DE LA CULTURA PERUANA

About half a dozen blocks west of the Plaza San Martín, on a traffic-choked thoroughfare, resides the **Museo de la Cultura Peruana** (Museum of Peruvian Culture; Map pp88–9; ☎ 423-5892; http://museo delacultura.perucultural.org.pe; Alfonso Ugarte 650; admission S3.60; ⊙ 10am-5pm Tue-Fri, 10am-2pm Sat), a repository of Peruvian folk art. The collection, consisting of elaborate *retablos* (religious dioramas) from Ayacucho, historic pottery from Puno and works in feather from the Amazon, is displayed in a building whose exterior facade is inspired by pre-Columbian architecture.

PARQUE DE LA CULTURA

Originally known as Parque de la Exposición, this newly revamped **park** (Map pp88–9) has gardens and a small amphitheater for outdoor performances. In 2009, major roadway renovation projects in the vicinity turned the area into a symphony of jackhammers, but the work should be completed by 2010. Two of Lima's major art museums reside here.

Museo de Arte de Lima

Known locally as **MALI** (Map pp88–9; ☎ 423-6332; http://museoarte.perucultural.org.pe; Paseo Colón 125; ⊙ 10am-5pm, closed Wed), Lima's principal fine art museum is housed in a striking beaux arts building that, in 2009, underwent an extensive interior renovation. (The museum is scheduled to reopen sometime in 2010.) Until the reopening, small exhibits of objects from the excellent permanent collection – which includes pre-Columbian artifacts, colonial furniture and cutting-edge installation art by contemporary artists – can be found at **Casa Wiese** (Map pp88–9; Carabaya 501; ⊙ 10am-8pm Tue-Sun), a temporary exhibit space in Central Lima run by a local cultural foundation.

Museo de Arte Italiano

Just north of MALI, the **Museo de Arte Italiano** (Italian Art Museum; Map pp88-9; ☎ 423-9932; Paseo de la República 250; adult/child US$1/0.30; ☒ 10am-5pm Mon-Fri) exhibits a tepid collection of 19th- and 20th-century Italian academic art. Its best attribute is the glittering Venetian mosaics on the exterior walls.

EL CIRCUITO MÁGICO DEL AGUA

This indulgent series of **illuminated fountains** (Map pp88-9; Parque de la Reserva, Av Petit Thouars, Cuadra 5; admission $4; ☒ 4-10pm) is so over-the-top it can't help but induce stupefaction among even the most hardened traveling cynic. A dozen different fountains – all splendiferously illuminated – are capped, at the end, by a laser light show at the 120m-long Fuente de la Fantasía (Fantasy Fountain). The whole display is set to a medley of tunes comprised of everything from Peruvian waltzes to ABBA. Has to be seen to be believed.

MUSEO DE HISTORIA NATURAL

One block west of *cuadra* 12 of Av Arequipa, south of the Parque de la Reserva, the **Museo de Historia Natural** (Natural History Museum; Map pp82-3; ☎ 471-0117; http://museohn.unmsm.edu .pe; Arenales 1256, Jesús María; admission $7; ☒ 9am-3pm Mon-Fri, 9am-5pm Sat, 10am-1:30pm Sun), run by the Universidád de San Marcos, has a modest taxidermy collection that's a useful overview of Peruvian fauna.

Rímac

Rímac can be a rough neighborhood. Taxis or organized tours are the best options for the following sights.

MUSEO TAURINO

The Plaza de Acho, Lima's bullring, has been located on the same site north of the Río Rímac since 1766. Here, some of the world's most famous toreadors have taken on the bulls, among them the renowned Manolete from Spain. The **Museo Taurino** (Bullfight Museum; Map pp88-9; ☎ 481-1467; Hualgayoc 332; admission $6; ☒ 9:30am-4:30pm Mon-Fri) documents this history with cluttered displays of weapons, paintings, photographs and the gilded outfits worn by a succession of bullfighters – one of which includes gore holes and blood.

CERRO SAN CRISTÓBAL

This 409m-high **hill** (Map pp82–3) to the northeast of Central Lima has a **mirador** (lookout) at its crown, with views of Lima stretching off to the Pacific (in winter, expect to see nothing but fog). A huge **cross**, built in 1928 and illuminated at night, is a Lima landmark and the object of pilgrimages during Semana Santa (Easter week) and the first Sunday in May. There is a small **museum** (admission $1). From the Plaza Mayor, taxis can take you to the summit (from $15) or you can wait for the **Urbanito bus** (Map pp88-9; ☎ 428-5841; www.urbanito .com.pe; Callao 144; per person $5; ☒ 10am-7pm), on the southwest corner of the plaza, which does a one-hour round-trip tour to the summit. Buses run every 30 minutes.

CONVENTO DE LOS DESCALZOS

At the end of Alameda de los Descalzos, an attractive, if forgotten, avenue, is this 16th-century **convent and museum** (Map pp82-3; ☎ 481-0441; Alameda de los Descalzos s/n; admission $6; ☒ 10am-1pm & 3-6pm, closed Tue), run by the Descalzos ('the Barefooted,' a reference to Franciscan friars). Visitors can see old wine-making equipment in the kitchen, a refectory, an infirmary and the monastic cells. There are also some 300 colonial paintings, including noteworthy canvases by renowned Cuzco School artist Diego Quispe Tito. Spanish-speaking guides will show you around (for a tip); tours last 45 minutes. Taxis from the Plaza Mayor start at about $10.

East Lima

The city begins to rise into the foothills of the Andes as you turn east, an area carpeted with government buildings and teeming residential districts.

MUSEO DE LA NACIÓN

A brutalist concrete tower houses the catch-all **Museo de la Nación** (Museum of the Nation; Map pp82-3; ☎ 476-9878; www.inc.gob.pe/expo1.shtml; Av Javier Prado Este 2466, San Borja; admission $7; ☒ 9am-5pm Tue-Sun), which provides a cursory overview of Peru's civilizations, from Chavín stone carvings and the knotted rope *quipus* of the Incas to artifacts from the colony. Large traveling international exhibits are also shown here (often for an extra fee), but if there is a single reason to visit this museum, it is to view a permanent installation on the 6th floor called **Yuyanapaq** (www.pnud.org.pe/yuyanapaq/yuyanapaq.html). The ex-

---

THE STRANGEST SADDEST CITY

Visit Lima in winter (April through October) and you will likely find it steeped – day after day – in the fog known as *garúa*. It is relentless, a mist that turns the sky an alabaster white and leaves the city draped in a melancholy pall. Interestingly, this otherworldly microclimate has been the source of much literary inspiration. The most famous citation is in none other than *Moby Dick* by Herman Melville, who visited Lima in the 1800s. It is 'the strangest saddest city thou can'st see,' he wrote. 'For Lima has taken the white veil; and there is a higher horror in this whiteness of her woe.'

Countless Peruvian writers have also chronicled this homely aspect. Internationally renowned author Mario Vargas Llosa cites the fog no less than half a dozen times in his 1963 novel *The Time of the Hero*, describing the sky as 'ashen,' 'damp gray' and 'leaden.' Likewise, Peruvian essayist Sebastián Salazar Bondy, in his 1964 treatise, *Lima la horrible* (Lima, the Horrible), describes the mist as a 'tenacious *garúa*, a floating powder, a cold fog.' Novelist Alfredo Bryce Echenique has compared it to 'the belly of a dead whale,' while Daniel Alarcón has depicted it as 'heavy, flat and dim, a dirty cotton ceiling.'

So why would the Spanish build the capital of their Andean empire at the one point on the coast regularly blanketed by this ghostly fog? Well, they likely wouldn't have known. Francisco Pizarro established the city on January 18 – right in the middle of summer – when the skies are blue every day.

---

hibit, named after the Quechua word meaning 'to remember,' was created by Peru's Truth & Reconciliation Commission in 2003 and is a moving and beautifully installed photographic tribute to the Internal Conflict (1980–2000). Students of contemporary Latin American history: consider this an absolute must-see. (For more on the Commission, see boxed text, p45.)

Taxis from Miraflores start at about S8 or, from San Isidro, you can catch one of the many buses or *combis* (minivans) heading east along Av Javier Prado Oeste toward La Molina.

MUSEO DE ORO DEL PERÚ

The now notorious **Museo de Oro del Perú** (Gold Museum of Peru; Map pp82-3; ☎ 345-1292; www.museo roperu.com.pe; Alonso de Molina 1100, Monterrico; adult/child under 11 S33/16; ☼ 11:30am-7pm), a private museum, was a Lima must-see until 2001, when a study revealed that 85% of the museum's metallurgical pieces were fakes. It reopened with an assurance that works on display are bona fide – and some vitrines bear cards that classify certain pieces as 'reproductions' – but the cluttered, poorly signed exhibits leave something to be desired. Better presented and more convenient is the new **annex** (Map p98; ☎ 620-6222; www.larcomar.com/salamuseo; LarcoMar, Malecón de la Reserva 610, Miraflores; admission S25; ☼ 10am-10pm), in the seaside shopping mall of LarcoMar.

Of greater interest (and, in all likelihood, of greater authenticity) are the thousands of weapons presented in the **Arms Museum**, on the museum's ground floor. Here, in various jumbled rooms, you'll find rifles, swords and guns from every century imaginable, including a firearm that once belonged to Fidel Castro.

Taxis from Miraflores start at about S10. Likewise, you can take a *combi* heading northeast on Angamos toward Monterrico and get off at the Puente Primavera. From there, it's a 15-minute stroll north to the museum.

ASOCIACIÓN MUSEO DEL AUTOMÓVIL

The **Asociación Museo del Automóvil** (Automobile Museum; Map pp82-3; ☎ 368-0373; www.museodel automovilnicolini.com; Av La Molina, Cuadra 37, cnr Totoritas, La Molina; adult S20; ☼ 9:30am-7pm) has an impressive array of classic cars dating back to 1901, from a Ford Model T to a Cadillac Fleetwood that was used by no fewer than four Peruvian presidents.

San Isidro & Points West

A combination of middle- and upper-class residential neighborhoods offer some important sights of note.

MUSEO LARCO

An 18th-century viceroy's mansion houses this **museum** (Map pp82-3; ☎ 461-1825; http://museo larco.org; Bolívar 1515, Pueblo Libre; adult/child under 15 S30/15; ☼ 9am-6pm), which has one of the largest,

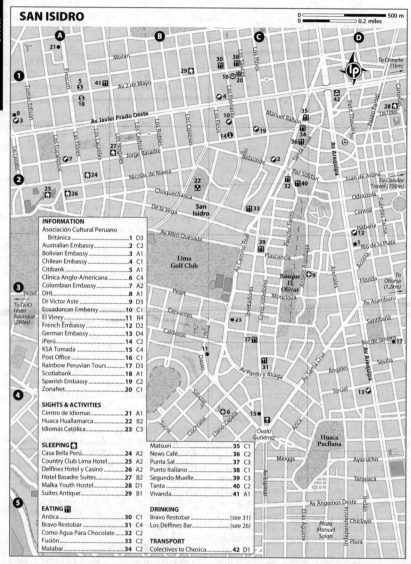

SAN ISIDRO

best-presented displays of ceramics in Lima. Founded by Rafael Larco Hoyle in 1926, a dedicated collector and cataloguer of all things pre-Columbian, the collection is said to include, among other things, more than 50,000 pots (with thousands of extras housed in glass storerooms, which visitors can also see). The museum showcases ceramic works from the Cupisnique, Chimú, Chancay, Nazca and Inca cultures, but the highlight is the sublime Moche portrait vessels, presented in simple, dramatically lit cases. Equally astonishing: a Wari weaving in one of the rear galleries that contains 398 threads to the linear inch – a record. What lures many visitors here, however, is a separately housed collection of pre-Columbian erotic pots that illustrate, with comical explicitness, all manner of sexual activity. Not to be missed is the vitrine that depicts sexually transmitted diseases.

The well-recommended on-site **restaurant** (mains S28-40) faces a private garden draped in bougainvillea and is a perfect spot for ceviche (raw seafood marinated in lime juice).

Catch a bus from Av Arequipa in Miraflores marked 'Todo Bolívar' to Bolívar's 15th block. Taxis start at about S7. A painted blue line on the sidewalk links this building to the Museo Nacional de Antropología, Arqueología e Historía del Perú, about a 15-minute walk away.

MUSEO NACIONAL DE ANTROPOLOGÍA, ARQUEOLOGÍA E HISTORÍA DEL PERÚ

The **Museo Nacional de Antropología, Arqueología e Historía del Perú** (National Anthropology, Archeology and History Museum; Map pp82-3; ☎ 463-5070; http://museo nacional.perucultural.org.pe; cnr San Martín & Vivanco, Pueblo Libre; adult US$3.20; ☀ 9am-5pm Tue-Sat, 9am-4pm Sun) traces the history of Peru from the Preceramic Period to the early republic. Displays include the famous Raimondi Stela, a 2.1m rock carving from the Chavín culture, one of the first Andean cultures to have a widespread, recognizable artistic style. The building was once the home of revolutionary heroes San Martín (from 1821 to 1822) and Bolívar (from 1823 to 1826) and the museum contains late-colonial and early republic paintings, including an 18th-century rendering of the *Last Supper* in which Christ and his disciples feast on *cuy* (guinea pig).

From Miraflores, take a 'Todo Brasil' *combi* from Av Arequipa (just north from Óvalo) to *cuadra* 22 on the corner of Vivanco, then walk seven blocks up that street. A blue line connects this museum with Museo Larco.

HUACA HUALLAMARCA

Nestled among condominium towers and sprawling high-end homes, the simple **Huaca Huallamarca** (Map p96; ☎ 222-4124; Nicolás de Rivera 201, San Isidro; adult/child S5.50/1; ☀ 9am-5pm Tue-Sun) is a highly restored adobe pyramid, produced by the Lima culture, that dates to AD 200 to 500. A small on-site museum, complete with mummy, details its excavation.

BOSQUE EL OLIVAR

This tranquil **park** (Map p96), a veritable oasis in the middle of San Isidro, consists of the remnants of an old olive grove, part of which was planted by the venerated San Martín de Porres in the 17th century.

Miraflores

The city's bustling, modern hub – full of restaurants, shops and nightspots – overlooks the Pacific from a set of ragged cliffs.

FUNDACIÓN MUSEO AMANO

The well-designed **Fundación Museo Amano** (Map p98; ☎ 441-2909; www.museoamano.org; Retiro 160; admission free; ☀ 3-5pm Mon-Fri, by appointment only) features a fine private collection of ceramics, with a strong representation of wares from the Chimú and Nazca cultures. It also has a remarkable assortment of lace and other textiles produced by the coastal Chancay culture. Museum visits are allowed by a one-hour guided tour only, in Spanish or Japanese.

MUSEO ENRICO POLI BIANCHI

The pricey, private **Museo Enrico Poli Bianchi** (Map p98; ☎ 422-2437; Cochrane 400; admission S50; ☀ 4-6pm Tue-Fri, by appointment only) holds a lavish collection of gold textiles, colonial silver and paintings featured in *National Geographic*, and is only available by prearranged tours in Spanish.

CASA DE RICARDO PALMA

This **house** (Map p98; ☎ 445-5836; Gral Suarez 189; adult S6; ☀ 9:15am-12:45pm & 2:30-4:45pm Mon-Fri) was the home of the Peruvian author Ricardo Palma from 1913 until his death in 1919. A listless tour is included in the price.

HUACA PUCLLANA

Located near the Óvalo Gutiérrez, this **huaca** (Map p98; ☎ 617-7138; cnr Borgoño & Tarapacá, Miraflores; admission S7; ☀ 9am-4:30pm Wed-Mon) is a restored adobe ceremonial center from the Lima culture that dates back to AD 400. Though vigorous excavations continue, the site is accessible by regular guided tours in Spanish (for a tip). In addition to a tiny on-site museum, there's a celebrated restaurant (p114) that offers incredible views of the illuminated ruins at night.

Barranco

A tony resort back at the turn of the 20th century, Barranco is lined with grand old *casonas,* many of which have been turned

MIRAFLORES

into eateries and hotels. A block west of the main plaza, look for the **Puente de los Suspiros** (Bridge of Sighs; Map p100), a narrow, wooden bridge over an old stone stairway that leads to the beach. The bridge – which is especially popular with couples on first dates – has inspired many a Peruvian folk song.

MUSEO PEDRO DE OSMA

Housed in a lovely beaux arts mansion surrounded by gardens, this undervisited **museum** (Map p100; ☎ 467-0141; www.museopedrodeosma .org; Av Pedro de Osma 423; admission S10; ☺ 10am-6pm Tue-Sun) has an exquisite collection of colonial furniture, silverwork and art, some of which dates back to the 1500s. Among the many fine pieces, standouts include a 2m-wide canvas that depicts a Corpus Christi procession in turn-of-the-17th-century Cuzco.

GALERÍA LUCÍA DE LA PUENTE

A magnificent two-story *casona* is home to Lima's most prestigious **contemporary art gallery** (Map p100; ☎ 477-9740; www.glucia delapuente.com; Sáenz Peña 206; ⏱ 10:30am-8pm Mon-Fri, 11am-8pm Sat). Look for works by cutting-edge painters such as Fernando Gutiérrez, whose bold canvases often skewer Peruvian culture.

West Lima & Callao

To the west of downtown, cluttered lower-middle-class and poor neighborhoods eventually give way to the port city of Callao, where the Spanish once shipped their gold. Travelers should approach Callao with

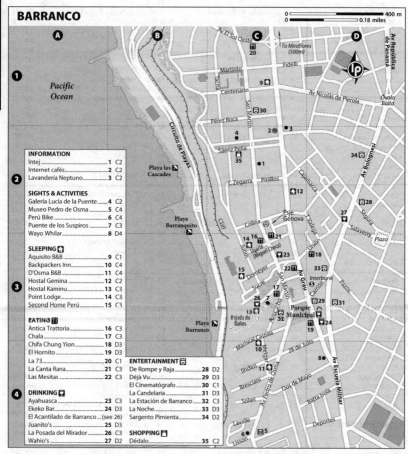

caution, since some areas are dangerous, even during the day.

PARQUE DE LAS LEYENDAS

Located between Central Lima and Callao, the **zoo** (Map pp82-3; ☎ 464-4282; www.patpal.gob.pe; Av Las Leyendas 580-86, San Miguel; adult/child under 11 S9/4.50; ☯ 9am-6pm) covers Peru's major geographical divisions: coast, mountains and jungle. There are up to 210 native animals, with a few imports (such as hippos). The conditions are OK, and the zoo is well maintained.

In Central Lima, catch buses and *colectivos* (shared taxis) that travel past the park at Av Abancay and Garcilaso de la Vega in Central Lima. These run roughly every 30 minutes. Taxis from Miraflores start at S10.

FORTALEZA DEL REAL FELIPE

In the 1820s, the Spanish royalists made their last stand during the battle for independence at this historic **fort** (Map pp82-3; ☎ 429-0532; Plaza Independencia, Callao; admission US$2; ☯ 9am-2pm), which was built in 1747 to guard against pirates. It still houses a small military contingent. Visits are by guided tours in Spanish only.

On the western flank of the fort, don't miss an opportunity to stroll through the truly bizarre **Parque Tématico de la Policía** (Police Park), a nicely landscaped garden that is dotted with police tanks and life-size statues of policemen in riot gear – a perfect place for those surreal family vacation photos.

Note that the nearby dock area is quite a rough neighborhood; taxis are best.

LA PUNTA

A narrow peninsula that extends west into the Pacific Ocean, **La Punta** was once a fishing hamlet, and later, in the 19th century, an upscale summer beach resort. Today this pleasant upper-middle-class neighborhood (Peru's vice president lives here), graced with neocolonial and art-deco homes, is a great spot to stroll by the ocean and enjoy a seafood lunch.

You can take a taxi from Miraflores (about S40). In Central Lima, *combis* traveling to Callao run west along Av Colonial from the Plaza 2 de Mayo (Map pp88–9). Take the ones labeled 'La Punta.' A good spot to get out is Plaza Gálvez; from here, you can head west all along the waterside Malecón Figueredo, which offers magnificent views of craggy Isla San Lorenzo, just off the coast.

ACTIVITIES
Cycling

Popular excursions from Lima include the 31km ride to Pachacamac, where there are good local trails open between April and December. Expert riders can inquire about the stellar downhill circuit from Olleros to San Bartolo south of Lima. For general information (in Spanish) on cycling, try **Federación Deportiva Peruana de Ciclismo** (☎ 346-3493; www.fedepeci.org; Av San Luis 1308, San Luis) or the online portal **Ciclismo Perú** (www.ciclismoperu.com). For organized cycling tours from abroad, see international tour companies, p534.

Dozens of bike shops are listed in Lima's yellow pages under 'Bicicletas.' Check out the following places:

Bike Tours of Lima (Map p98; ☎ 445-3172; www.biketoursoflima.com; Bolívar 150, Miraflores; 🕙 9am-7pm Mon-Sat) Rentals are available (from S27 for a half-day) and there are organized day tours around Miraflores and San Isidro, as well as Sunday excursions into downtown (from S55).

Perú Bike (Map p100; ☎ 467-0757; Av Pedro de Osma 560, Barranco; 🕙 9am-1pm & 4-8pm Mon-Sat) A recommended shop that does repairs.

Paragliding

For paragliding off the Miraflores clifftops, contact **Peru Fly** (☎ 99-591-9928; www.perufly.com) or **Andean Trail Peru** (☎ 99-836-4930, 99-836-3436; http://andeantrailperu.com). Flights take off from

the clifftop 'paraport' at the Parque Raimondi (Map p98) and start at about US$50 for a 15-minute tandem flight. Paragliding companies do not have offices on-site, so if you want to fly, make a reservation in advance – then wave at the bemused shoppers at the cliffside LarcoMar mall as you glide past.

Swimming & Surfing

Despite the newspaper warnings about pollution, *limeños* hit the beaches in droves in summer (January through March). **Playa Costa Verde** in Miraflores (nicknamed Waikiki) is a favorite of local surfers and has good breaks year-round. Barranco's beaches have waves that are better for long boards. There are seven other beaches in Miraflores and four more in Barranco. Serious surfers can also try **Playa La Herradura** in Chorrillos, which has waves up to 5m high during good swells. Do not leave your belongings unattended as theft is a problem. For good surfing to the south of Lima, see p123.

The following stores carry surf equipment:

Big Head (Map p98; ☎ 818-4156; www.bighead.com.pe; LarcoMar, Malecón de la Reserva 610, Miraflores; 🕙 11am-10pm) A popular mall chain that sells fashion and gear.

Focus (☎ 475-8459; Leonardo da Vinci 208, Surquillo; 🕙 8am-8pm Mon-Fri, 9am-1pm Sat) An established board fabrication outlet.

Wayo Whilar (Map p100; ☎ 247-6343; www.wayowhilar.com.pe; Av Grau 111, Barranco; 🕙 9am-7pm Mon-Thu, 9am-4pm Fri & Sat) The shop of a longtime Peruvian surfer who sells his own line of hand-shaped boards.

Scuba Diving

There's reasonable deep-sea diving off Peru's southern coast. Contact **Perú Divers** (☎ 251-6231; www.perudivers.com; Santa Teresa 486, Chorrillos), an excellent dive shop owned by Luis Rodríguez, a PADI-certified instructor who sells gear and arranges certification and diving trips, including regular excursions to Islas Palomino, off the coast of Callao, to see a year-round sea-lion colony (per person US$68, not including gear).

Other Activities

You can go bowling at **LarcoMar Bowling** (Map p98; ☎ 445-7776; LarcoMar, Malecón de la Reserva 610, Miraflores; per hr S55-62; 🕙 11am-1am), in the clifftop mall of the same name. Prices vary depending on time of day; shoe rental is extra (S4.50).

LIMA

Lima has several very expensive tennis and golf clubs (most of them private or by invitation only), but concierges at top-end hotels (such as the Country Club Lima Hotel; see p105) can help organize matches or reserve tee-times for guests. The **Lima Cricket & Football Club** (Map pp82-3; ☎ 264-0027; Justo Vigil 200, Magdalena del Mar) is popular with expats and allows visitors with passports to participate in their activities. It even has an English pub on-site.

Sailors can contact the **Yacht Club Peruano** (Map pp82-3; ☎ 429-0775; www.yachtclubperuano.com; Bolognesi 761, La Punta, Callao), which has a Travelift equipped to move crafts of up to 18 tons, dock security and numerous other services.

COURSES
Language
Lima has plenty of language schools. The following places are recommended:

Centro de Idiomas (Map p96; ☎ 421-2969; Prescott 333, San Isidro) Overseen by the Universidad del Pacífico, it costs US$250 for three months with three 90-minute group classes per week.

El Sol (Map p98; ☎ 242 7763; elsol.idiomasperu.com; Grimaldo del Solar 469, Miraflores) Private classes are US$20 per hour; one-week courses start at US$137.

Idiomas Católica (Map p96; ☎ 626-6500; www.idiomas.pucp.edu.pe; Cam Real 1037, San Isidro) Managed by the prestigious Catholic University, this program charges S360 per month for five two-hour group classes per week.

Instituto Cultural Peruano Norteamericano (ICPNA; ☎ 706-7000; www.icpna.edu.pe) The institute's various branches (see p81 for a full listing) offer Spanish courses for US$95 per month for five two-hour group classes per week.

You can also try a private teacher from about US$7 to US$9 per hour:

Lourdes Gálvez (☎ 435-3910; lourdesgalvezm@hotmail.com) Also teaches Quechua.

Sonia (☎ 251-6168, 99-889-9110; soniacb2002@hotmail.com)

Music & Dance
The **Museo de la Cultura Peruana** (Map pp88-9; ☎ 423-5892; http://museodelacultura.perucultural.org.pe; Alfonso Ugarte 650, Central Lima) runs limited classes on some Peruvian instruments and folk dances such as the *marinera* (from S50 for a month).

TOURS & GUIDES
For guided tours of Lima and nearby archaeological sites such as Pachacamac, as well as trips around Peru, try the following compa-nies. In addition, travel agencies (see p86) organize local, regional and national tours.

Aero Condor Perú (☎ 421-3105, 421-7014; www.aerocondor.com.pe; Av Aramburu 858, Surquillo) Day-long tours to the Nazca lines start at US$391. The company also offers overview flights from Nazca and Ica, which are cheaper.

Aventours (Map p98; ☎ 444-9060; www.aventours.com; Av Arequipa 4799, Miraflores) Private tours, guided trips and treks throughout the country.

Condor Travel (Map pp82-3; ☎ 615-3000; www.condortravel.com; Blondet 249, San Isidro) Recommended for top-end touring and custom itineraries throughout the Andes.

Ecoaventura Vida (☎ 461-2555; www.ecoaventuravida.com) Focused on sustainable travel throughout the country, Ecoaventura organizes a number of trips that include homestays with Peruvian families.

Explorandes (Map p98; ☎ 715-2323; www.explorandes.com; Aristides Aljovín 484, Miraflores) Outdoors travel is the focus, with a specialty in trekking, biking and adventure sports.

Lima Vision (Map p98; ☎ 447-7710; www.limavision.com; Chiclayo 444, Miraflores) Lima Vision has various four-hour city tours (US$28), as well as day-long trips to the ruins at Pachacamac.

Peru Expeditions (Map p98; ☎ 447-2057; www.peru-expeditions.com; Colina 155, Miraflores) Books trips and organized tours around the region and beyond, and also specializes in 4WD excursions.

Peru Hands On (☎ 446-9672; www.peruhandson.com; No 401, Av La Paz 887, Miraflores) A locally run agency specializing in standard and custom itineraries around Peru.

The following guides are registered with **Agotur** (☎ 446-3765), the Peruvian guide organization. Telephone numbers are for Peruvian daytime use only.

Arturo Rojas (☎ 99-738-9276; www.limatastytours.com) In addition to regular guide services, he can arrange gastronomic tours; speaks English.

Mónica Velásquez (☎ 99-943-0796; www.monicatoursperu.com) Reader recommended; speaks English.

Tino Guzman (☎ 420-1723, 99-909-5805) Speaks English; member of SAE.

Toshie Matsumura de Irikura (☎ 225-6518, 99-757-3924) Speaks Japanese.

FESTIVALS & EVENTS
See p517 for major festivals and special events, and p519 for national holidays. For other events, see local newspapers or visit *The Peru Guide* (www.theperuguide.com). Holidays specific to Lima:

Festival of Lima Celebrates the anniversary of Lima's founding on January 18.

Feast of Santa Rosa de Lima Held on August 30, this feast has processions in honor of Santa Rosa, the venerated patron saint of Lima and the Americas.

El Señor de los Milagros (Christ of Miracles) The city drapes itself in purple during this massive religious procession on October 18 in honor of the Christ from the Nazarenas church; smaller processions occur other Sundays in October.

SLEEPING

From diminutive family *pensións* to glassy hotel towers armed with spas, Lima has every type of accommodation imaginable. It is also one of the most expensive destinations in the country (other than the tourist mecca of Cuzco).

The favored traveler neighborhood is Miraflores, where you'll find a bounty of hostels, inns and upscale hotel chains. In recent years, similar spots have started opening up in the burgeoning seaside community of Barranco. More upscale – and generally more tranquil – is San Isidro. The best values can be found in Central Lima, though it is at a remove from the city's hopping restaurants and nightclubs.

If arriving at night, it's worth contacting hotels in advance to arrange for airport pickup; even budget hostels can arrange this – sometimes for a few dollars less than the official airport service.

Central Lima

The city's congested historic heart generally offers the best deals on lodging – and proximity to some of the most storied attractions. The roar of traffic begins early, so select your hotel (and, more significantly, your room) accordingly. Also, note that though the security situation in downtown has improved greatly in recent years, at night it is advisable to take taxis and not to display expensive camera gear or jewelry. The Plaza de Armas and the Plaza San Martín are well policed and are great spots for an evening stroll.

BUDGET

Hostal San Francisco (Map pp88-9; ☎ 426-2735; www .hostalsanfranciscoperu.com; Azángaro 127; dm S14, s/d without bathroom S18/35, s/d S25/45; ☐) It may have all the charm of a government office, complete with bland linoleum floors, but the 16 rooms are big and roomy and the atmosphere is mellow. There is luggage storage, internet

access (S1.50 per hour) and a small on-site cafe for breakfast.

Pensión Ibarra (Map pp88-9; ☎ 427-8603; pension ibarra@gmail.com; 14th fl, No 152, Tacna 359; s/d without bathroom from S20/35) The towering concrete apartment block is scruffy on the outside, but inside the helpful Ibarra sisters keep seven basic guest rooms that are clean and stocked with firm beds. There is a shared kitchen and laundry service. A small balcony has views of the noisy city.

Hostal Wiracocha (Map pp88-9; ☎ 427-1178; Jirón Junín 284; s/d without bathroom S20/35, s/d S30/40) Just steps from the Plaza de Armas, this small, Peruvian-run hotel has 33 basic, dim rooms that are clean and roomy, if a bit noisy. The private showers are hot.

Hostal Belén (Map pp88-9; ☎ 427-8995; patrick@ hotmail.com; Jirón Belén 1049; s/d/tr without bathroom S22/35/50, s/d/tr S30/40/50) Situated in a ramshackle *casona* above a noisy bar, Belén has 20 worn rooms in various configurations, many of which share well-trafficked bathrooms.

Belén Annex (Map pp88-9; Nicolás de Piérola 953; s/d/tr S35/50/70) On the Plaza San Martín, the annex is better. Rooms here are bare-bones, but all come with private showers and TVs and those facing the plaza have incredible nighttime views.

Hotel España (Map pp88-9; ☎ 428-5546, 427-9196; www.hotelespanaperu.com; Azángaro 105; dm S14, s/d/tr without bathroom S28/40/51, s/d/tr S40/50/60; ☐) Forty-six rooms are tucked into every labyrinthine corner of an old mansion stuffed full of Roman-style statuary and baroque art. An established backpacker spot, it can get noisy, but the rooms are clean, the water hot; and the bedspreads, incredibly shiny. A roof deck shrouded in greenery serves as a breakfast cafe (for an extra S4) and a nice spot to check email using free wi-fi.

Familia Rodríguez (Map pp88-9; ☎ 423-6465; jotajot@terra.com.pe; No 201, Nicolás de Piérola 730; dm/d with breakfast US$9/20; ☐) An early-20th-century building west of the Plaza San Martín houses a sprawling old apartment with parquet floors and spotless bathrooms in this tranquil, well-recommended family homestay. All bathrooms are shared.

Hostal Roma (Map pp88-9; ☎ 427-7576; www .hostalroma.8m.com; Ica 326; s/d without bathroom S30/40, s/d S40/60; ☐) The 22 tidy rooms here are dull (some are windowless), but they are quiet and set around a sunny interior courtyard.

Some units are equipped with cable TV. An on-site cafe serves breakfast.

Hostal Iquique (Map pp88-9; ☎ 433-4724; www .hostaliquique.com; Iquique 758; s/d/tr without bathroom S32/50/69, s S50, d S66-79, tr S95; 💻) Recommended Iquique is basic, clean and safe, with small, dark, concrete rooms sporting remodeled bathrooms with hot showers. There is a rooftop terrace with a pool table, an on-site restaurant and shared kitchen facilities. The amiable owner, Fernando, is an excellent cook, and if you're lucky he might provide tips on meal preparation. Credit cards accepted.

MIDRANGE

La Posada del Parque (Map pp88-9; ☎ 433-2412, 99-945-4260; www.incacountry.com; Parque Hernán Velarde 60; s/d/tr/q S108/136/173/210; 💻) Run by the very chatty Mónica and her daughter, Nabila, this graceful, butter yellow Spanish-style house sits on a tranquil, treelined oval that, in the early 20th century, served as Lima's dog-racing track. Small, carpeted rooms have folk-art touches, while the public areas display colonial-style paintings and some astonishing Ayacucho retablos. All rooms have cable TV and luggage storage is available.

Hostal Bonbini (Map pp88-9; ☎ 427-6477; www .hostalbonbini.com; Cailloma 209; s/d/tr with breakfast S110/142/173; 💻) On a street cluttered with print shops is this comfy, 15-room hotel with simple, carpeted rooms, spick-and-span bathrooms and cable TV. It's a nice find in an area short on quality midrange options. Credit cards accepted.

Hotel Continental (Map pp88-9; ☎ 427-5890; www .hotelcontinentallima.com; Puno 196; s/d/tr with breakfast S120/150/180, s/d superior S180/210; 📺 💻) Seventy-seven spacious rooms with spotless restrooms were remodeled in 2009 in modern, muted earth tones. Superior units are much larger and come with sitting areas. All have cable TV and wi-fi. Credit cards accepted.

Hotel Kamana (Map pp88-9; ☎ 426-7204, 427-7106; www.hotelkamana.com; Camaná 547; s/d with breakfast S126/158; 📺 💻) Popular with tour groups and business travelers, this secure and relatively contemporary hotel has 46 tidy, carpeted rooms enlivened by colorful bedspreads. English and French are spoken. Credit cards accepted. An on-site restaurant-cafe is open 24 hours. Overall, very good value.

Clifford Hotel (Map pp88-9; ☎ 433-4249; www .thecliffordhotel.com.pe; Parque Hernán Velarde 27; s/d/tr/ ste with breakfast US$55/65/80/95) Located on the same peaceful oval as Posada del Parque, this smartly decorated hotel is housed in a beautifully maintained *casona* that dates back to the 1930s. Though the decor in the public areas has Spanish baroque touches, the 21 carpeted rooms are modern and equipped with fans, cable TV and telephones. There's a bar, a restaurant and cozy public areas in which to relax, including a nicely manicured garden with a gurgling fountain.

Hotel Maury (Map pp88-9; ☎ 428-8188; hotmaury@ amauta.rep.net.pe; Ucayali 201; s/d with breakfast US$58/69, d with king-size bed US$80; 📺 💻) A longtime Lima outpost renowned for having been one of the first spots to cultivate a new-fangled cocktail known as the pisco sour (grape brandy cocktail) back in the '30s. The public areas at the Maury retain old-world flourishes such as gilded mirrors and Victorian-style furniture. The 76 modern rooms, however, are up-to-date: simple, clean and equipped with Jacuzzi tubs. Credit cards accepted.

TOP END

Central Lima has seen its high-end business slip away as upscale establishments have popped up all over San Isidro and Miraflores. Call ahead or check websites for discounted promotional rates. Both of these places accept credit cards.

Gran Hotel Bolívar (Map pp88-9; ☎ 619-7171; Jirón de la Unión 958; s/d/tr/q US$65/75/85/95; 💻) This venerable 1924 hotel located on the Plaza San Martín was, in its day, one of the most luxurious accommodations in Latin America, where figures like Clark Gable, Mick Jagger and Robert Kennedy all laid their heads. Today, it is frayed at the edges, but, like any grand dame, it possesses a rare finesse. (See the sparkling stained-glass cupola in the lobby for an example.) For anyone chasing the retro atmosphere of a gilded age, the Bolívar is a rare treat.

Lima Sheraton (Map pp88-9; ☎ 619-3300; www .sheraton.com.pe; Paseo de la República 170; d US$139-360; 📺 💻 🏊) Housed in a brutalist high-rise that overlooks the equally dour Palacio de Justicia (Supreme Court), the top hotel in downtown has more than 400 rooms and suites decorated in an array of desert tones. Units are equipped with wi-fi and cable TV and there is 24-hour room service. In addition, there are concierge services, two on-site restaurants, a bar, a gym, a swimming pool and a beauty salon.

West Lima

Mami Panchita (Map pp82-3; ☎ 263-7203; www
.mamipanchita.com; Av Federico Gallesi 198, San Miguel; s/d/tr
US$25/35/45; ☐) A short taxi ride from down-
town, the historic museums of Pueblo Libre
and the nightlife of Miraflores is this Dutch-
Peruvian guesthouse, situated in a charming,
Spanish-style house. It has 14 simple, homey
rooms and a flower-bedecked patio that is
ideal for relaxing.

San Isidro

With a hyper-exclusive golf course at its heart,
San Idro is where many of Lima's elite can be
found: inhabiting expansive modernist homes
and sipping cocktails at members-only social
clubs. (Want to fit in? Carry a tennis racket.)
As is to be expected, accommodations in San
Isidro are unapologetically upscale, though
there are a few other options tucked away
among the treelined streets.

our pick **Malka Youth Hostel** (Map p96; ☎ 222-5589;
www.youthhostelperu.com; Los Lirios 165; dm S25, s & d without bathroom S60, s & d S70; ☐) Near the transit hub
of Av Arequipa and Av Javier Prado, and just
a block from a small park, this wonderful
10-room hostel, run by an amiable mother-
daughter team, has clean rooms that sleep
three to eight people, in addition to a couple of private rooms. There is a large shared
kitchen and laundry facilities, a TV room with
DVD player, luggage storage, free wi-fi and
a small on-site cafe that serves light meals.
There is even a small rock-climbing wall in
the well-manicured garden.

Casa Bella Perú (Map p96; ☎ 421-7354; www
.casabellaperu.net; Las Flores 459; s/d/tr/q with breakfast
US$59/65/79/89; ☐) A great midrange option in
a relentlessly expensive area, this expansive
former 1950s home has contemporary rooms
accented by indigenous textiles. Fourteen
varied units have comfy beds, firm pillows,
cable TV and remodeled bathrooms. There
is a kitchen, an ample garden and a lounge,
and services such as wi-fi are available for an
extra fee. Credit cards accepted.

our pick **DUO Hotel Boutique** (Map pp82-3; ☎ 628-
3245; www.duohotelperu.com; Valle Riesta 576; s S288, d
S352-384, ste S416, all with breakfast; ☒ ☐ ☎) On a
serene, residential street, two blocks west of
the Lima Golf Club, this intimate new boutique hotel offers top-of-the-line amenities.
Twenty elegant, monochromatic rooms are
outfitted with marble baths, minibars, flat-
screen TVs and slippers, while the public areas

are chicly decorated in a contemporary-meets-
pre-Columbian style. An on-site restaurant,
overseen by Chef Javier Paredes, produces
delectable fusion specialties that marry the
best of Peruvian and Italian flavors. Credit
cards accepted; excellent value.

Hotel Basadre Suites (Map p96; ☎ 442-2423; www
.hotelbasadre.com; Av Jorge Basadre 1310; s/d with breakfast
S410/460, extra bed S77; ☒ ☐ ☎) Built around
what was once a private home, this attentive
inn has 20 simple rooms of various sizes and
configurations, decorated in shades of forest
green and bronze. Each unit has a minibar,
hair-dryer, cable TV and lock-box – and the
included breakfast, served in a small room by
the garden, is abundant. Credit cards accepted;
check the website for excellent special offers.

Suites Antique (Map p96; ☎ 222-1094; www.suites
-antique.com; Av 2 de Mayo 954; s/d with breakfast US$100/115;
☒ ☐) A low-key spot with puffy couches and
brightly colored walls. The 23 spotless suites
are very spacious and come with small kitchenettes equipped with microwave ovens and
a minifridge. Breakfast is served at the cozy
in-house cafe.

Country Club Lima Hotel (Map p96; ☎ 611-9000;
www.hotelcountry.com; Los Eucaliptos 590; d from US$200;
☒ ☐ ☎) Built in 1927, this regal hotel is
housed in one of Lima's finest buildings, a
sprawling Spanish-style structure with wood-
beam ceilings that is clad in colorful tile and
dotted with replica Cuzco School paintings.
The lovely lobby cafe, where breakfast is
served, is covered by a stained-glass dome.
The 83 rooms – chock-full of amenities –
range from the simply luxurious Master Room
to the downright opulent Presidential Suite.
Credit cards accepted.

Delfines Hotel y Casino (Map p96; ☎ 215-7000; www
.losdelfineshotel.com; Los Eucaliptos 555; d with breakfast from
US$200; ☒ ☐ ☎) This tall glass tower overlook-
ing the golf course, with 206 spacious, elegant
rooms and suites decorated in warm earth
tones, is one of the top spots in town, having
accommodated all manner of VIPs, from Julio
Iglesias to Kiss. There's a gym, a spa, a salon and
a business center. The Delphos Café, the on-site
restaurant, serves sumptuous seafood meals
within view of a tank that houses two frolicking
bottlenose dolphins. Credit cards accepted.

Miraflores

Overlooking the ocean, this neighborhood's
pedestrian-friendly streets teem with cafes,
restaurants, hotels, high-rises, banks, shops

and nightclubs that pump everything from disco to *cumbia* (Colombian salsa-like dance and musical style). There are many quiet blocks, too.

BUDGET

Friend's House (Map p98; ☎ 446-6248; friends house_peru@yahoo.com.mx; Jirón Manco Cápac 368; dm with breakfast S20, r per person with breakfast S30) This backpacker-friendly hostel has a highly sociable atmosphere – perhaps inescapable given the cramped nature of the dorms. Kitchen privileges are available, as well as a small lounge with cable TV.

Explorer's House (Map p98; ☎ 241-5002; http://geocities.com/explorers_house; Alfredo León 158; dm S21, s/d without bathroom per person S30/24, s/d per person S35/27; 💻) This no-frills eight-room hostel is frayed, but safe (and under new management). There is a shared kitchen, wi-fi and a rooftop terrace with views.

Hitchhikers (Map p98; ☎ 242-3008; www.hhikersperu.com; Bolognesi 400; dm S28, s/d/tr without bathroom S56/62/93, s/d/tr S68/74/112; 💻) Housed in a century-old *casona*, the centrally located Hitchhikers has a good balance of features, security, comfort, cleanliness, sleeper-friendliness and free wi-fi. A lounge comes with cable TV and a DVD library, while a (bare) outdoor patio has barbecue facilities and ping-pong. Overall, a very good choice.

Colibrí Youth Hostel (Map p98; ☎ 444-0954; www.colibriyouthhostel.com; Gral Suárez 543; dm with breakfast US$10; 💻) This tiny but sparkling hostel has three simply furnished rooms, clean bathrooms, lockers, wi-fi and a roomy shared kitchen. Luggage storage is also available. The owner speaks English and German.

Inkawasi (Map p98; ☎ 241-8218; backpacker inkawasi@hotmail.com; Av de la Aviación 210; dm US$10, d US$25-30, all with breakfast) A small budget place that is modern, well furnished and close to the clifftop parks. There's a small interior garden for relaxing. The owner speaks English.

Pensión Yolanda (Map p98; ☎ 445-7565; pension yolanda@hotmail.com; Domingo Elías 230; r per person without bathroom S40, with bathroom S50) The nine rooms here are small, basic, but clean, and proprietor Erwin – who speaks English, French, German, Italian and Portuguese – is helpful. There is a shared kitchen, hot water and laundry service. Fees include breakfast.

Albergue Turístico Juvenil Internacional (Map p98; ☎ 446-5488; www.limahostell.com.pe; Av Casimiro Juan Ulloa 328; dm US$15, s/d US$36/42; 💻 🍴) Tucked away

on a residential street, this modern, well-kept hostel is an excellent choice for its spotless dorms and ample private rooms. A large lounge sports Cuzco School–style paintings, and there are good kitchen facilities, a spacious backyard with an outdoor pool, two friendly pooches, and an on-site cafe that serves breakfast (S5 to S7).

MIDRANGE

Residencial Alfa (Map p98; ☎ 241-1446; residencial_alfa@yahoo.com; Av de la Aviación 565; s/d with breakfast US$25/35; 💻) Close to the relaxing clifftop park on the north side of Miraflores you'll find this quiet option behind a row of international flags (there is no sign). Rooms are airy and well appointed.

Olimpus Hostel (Map p98; ☎ 242-6077; www.olimpus peru.com; Diego Ferre 365; s/d/tr/q US$30/40/50/55; 💻) A gregarious owner manages a variety of tidy rooms at this welcoming spot just a couple of blocks from the LarcoMar shopping mall. There is an on-site cafe, a communal lounge with cable TV and wi-fi.

La Casa Nostra (Map p98; ☎ 241-1718; www.lacasa nostraperu.com; Grimaldo del Solar 265; s/d/tr/q with breakfast US$35/45/55/65; 💻) Seven clean, if uninteresting, rooms inhabit this Spanish-style *casona*, which still retains a vintage wood-beamed ceiling in the lobby. Guests are all greeted with a wag by a sociable canine named Brando.

Hotel Esperanza (Map p98; ☎ 444-2411; www.hotelesperanza-pe.com; Esperanza 350; s/d/tr US$40/50/65) Baroque-style furniture provides an unusual juxtaposition to 39 brick-lined rooms that have the ascetic air of monastic cells. Its advantages: it is clean, functional and has a central location.

our pick **Hostal El Patio** (Map p98; ☎ 444-2107; www.hostalelpatio.net; Ernesto Diez Canseco 341A; s/d/tr with breakfast S120/180/210, ste with breakfast S195-225; 💻) On a quiet side street just steps from the Parque Kennedy is this little gem of a guesthouse with a cheery English- and French-speaking owner. Twenty-four small, spotless rooms with shining wooden floors and colonial-style art surround a plant-filled courtyard with a trickling fountain. A few are equipped with small kitchenettes and minifridges. Check the website for special offers.

Hotel Alemán (Map p98; ☎ 445-6999; www.hotel aleman.com.pe; Av Arequipa 4704; s/d/tr with breakfast US$45/55/65; 💻) A rowdy boulevard gives way to this surprisingly charming 23-room hotel built around a Spanish *casona*. Simple, stuccoed rooms are decorated with Peruvian textiles and colonial-style furnishings and come with wi-fi, cable TV, telephones, desks and minifridges. Credit cards accepted.

Hotel San Antonio Abad (Map p98; ☎ 447-6766; www.hotelsanantonioabad.com; Ramón Ribeyro 301; s/d with breakfast S175/228; 🖳) A bright yellow mansion from the 1940s houses this pleasant, reader-recommended hotel with 24 comfortable rooms (some with air-con), which have carpeted floors, cable TV and soundproofed windows. Breakfast is served in a tiled dining terrace facing the garden. Free airport pickup can be arranged with advance reservation. Credit cards accepted.

Hotel Señorial (Map p98; ☎ 445-7306, 445-1870; www.seniorial.com; José González 567; s/d/tr with breakfast US$52/72/91; 🖳) Sixty-four rooms face the tranquil internal garden at this hospitable spot where a generation's worth of visitors have scribbled their greetings on the walls of the on-site cafe. Units are simple and airy, some with wall-to-wall carpeting; others, with polished wooden floors. (The latter are nicer.) All units have cable TV and access to wi-fi. Credit cards accepted.

Hostal Torreblanca (Map p98; ☎ 447-3363; www.torreblancaperu.com; Av José Pardo 1453; s/d/ste S175/215/264) The lobby may be cramped and the hallways narrow, but the clean, modern rooms in this Spanish-style building are comfortable. A few on the top floor have wood-beamed ceilings, red tilework and fireplaces. Units come with cable TV and telephones; credit cards accepted.

Hotel BayView (Map p98; ☎ 445-7321; www.bayviewhotel.com.pe; Las Dalias 276; s/d/tr/ste with breakfast US$55/65/78/72; 🖳) A simple, pleasant hotel painted in various shades of adobe. It contains 24 carpeted rooms adorned with folksy Peruvian paintings that also come equipped with cable TV and wi-fi.

Casa San Martín (Map p98; ☎ 241-4434, 243-3900; www.casasanmartinperu.com; San Martín 339; s/d/tr with breakfast US$60/84/105; 🖳) A Spanish Revival building houses this relatively new inn that features 20 pleasant, terra-cotta-tiled rooms accented with Andean textiles. Breakfast is served in a bright cafe that faces the outdoor terrace. Credit cards accepted.

Hotel El Doral (Map p98; ☎ 242-7799; www.eldoral.com.pe; Av José Pardo 486; s/d with breakfast S225/255; 🗷 🖳 🕬) It may look businesslike on the outside, but inside you'll find 39 well-appointed suites facing a pleasant, plant-filled interior.

All units have cable TV, minibars and sitting areas – as well as double-glazed windows to block out the noise. Breakfast is served in a rooftop terrace that faces the pool.

Hotel Ariosto (Map p98; ☎ 444-1414; www.hotelariosto.com.pe; Av La Paz 769; s/d/tr with breakfast US$75/75/90; 🗷 🖳) This time-warped, seven-story hotel has a colonial-meets-the-1960s Peruvian formality that is downright charming. A sprawling modernist lobby sports oversized leather couches and lots of baroque art flourishes, while the 96 spacious, carpeted rooms are equipped with king-size beds. There is a small business center, a lounge area and an on-site restaurant. Rates include free airport pickup.

La Castellana (Map p98; ☎ 444-4662; www.castellanahotel.com; Grimaldo del Solar 222; s/d/tr with breakfast S229/279/324) Housed in a refurbished Spanish-style *casona*, this 42-room inn has pleasant, if dark, rooms, all of which face a tiny interior courtyard and terrace, where an à la carte breakfast is served.

TOP END
The following have on-site cafes or restaurants and rooms equipped with telephones, cable TV and internet; all accept credit cards.

Hotel Antigua Miraflores (Map p98; ☎ 241-6116; www.peru-hotels-inns.com; Av Grau 350; s US$79-109, d US$94-129, tr US$129-154; 🗷 🖳) In a converted early-20th-century mansion, this quiet, atmospheric hotel channels colonial charm. The rooms, most of which face an interior courtyard, are equipped with the expected modern amenities, but the furnishings display baroque touches. Units vary in size and style; the more expensive ones have Jacuzzi tubs and kitchenettes.

Casa Andina (☎ 213-9739; www.casa-andina.com) San Antonio (Map pp82-3; ☎ 241-4050; Av 28 de Julio 1088; d with breakfast US$89-129; 🗷 🖳); Miraflores Centro (Map p98; ☎ 447-0263; Av Petit Thouars 5444; d with breakfast US$99-109; 🗷 🖳); Colección Privada (Map p98; ☎ 213-4300; Av La Paz 463; d/ste with breakfast from US$300/419; 🗷 🖳 🕬) This relatively new Peruvian chain has three hotels at various price points scattered around Miraflores. The San Antonio and Miraflores Centro branches are more affordable, each boasting 50-plus rooms decorated in contemporary Andean color schemes. Colección Privada is the company's luxury outpost, situated in a tower that once served as the home of the now-defunct Hotel César (where Frank Sinatra once stayed). In a nod to its history, the elegant lobby lounge is still home to a grand piano played by the same pianist from the César. The hotel's 148 chic, earth-palette rooms are spacious, sporting pre-Columbian flourishes and organic bath products. The best part: the nightly turn-down service; rather than deposit a chocolate on the pillow, the hotel's staff leaves a deliriously stupendous *cocada* (coconut cookie).

La Paz Apart Hotel (Map p98; ☎ 242-9350; www .lapazaparthotel.com; Av La Paz 679; s/d ste with breakfast S365/456, 2-bedroom ste S760; ✖ 🖵) This modern high-rise may have a businesslike demeanor, but the service is attentive and the rooms are comfortable. Twenty-five super-clean suites, all equipped with kitchenettes, minifridges and separate sitting areas, are tastefully decorated. The most spacious of these sleeps up to five people. The hotel also has a minigym and a small conference room.

Miraflores Park Hotel (Map p98; ☎ 242-3000; www .mira-park.com; Malecón de la Reserva 1035; d from US$215; ✖ 🖵 🐾) Surely the best of Lima's smaller luxury hotels, the Miraflores Park has glorious ocean views and all the frills expected of a five-star inn, including a gym, a sauna and a pool overlooking the ocean. Some rooms even come with Roman-style tubs. Want to indulge? For US$50, the bath butler will run an aphrodisiac-salt-infused, petal-strewn, candlelit bath – with champagne and fresh strawberries.

JW Marriott Hotel Lima (Map p98; ☎ 217-7000; www.marriotthotels.com/limdt; Malecón de la Reserva 615; d from US$250; ✖ 🖵 🐾) The most upscale hotel in Lima, the five-star Marriott has a superb seafront location by the LarcoMar shopping mall and sparkling rooms with every amenity imaginable, including minibars and whirlpool baths. There is also an executive lounge, restaurants, a bar, a casino and an open-air tennis court and pool.

Barranco

At the turn of the 20th century, this was a summer resort for the upper-crust. In the 1960s, it was a center of bohemian life. Today, it is cluttered with restaurants and bustling bars, its graceful mansions converted into hotels of every price range.

Hostal Kaminu (Map p100; ☎ 252-8680; www.kaminu .com; Bajada de Baños 342; dm S25-30, d without bathroom S70; 🖵) For travelers who want to be in the thick of it, nothing beats this centrally located crash pad with an easy reggae vibe – and a sleepy pooch named Bingo. If you have your own gear, you can camp on the roof for S15 per night.

Point Lodge (Map p100; ☎ 247-7997; www.thepoint hostels.com; Junín 300; dm S26-34, r per person S34; 🖵) This whitewashed villa is a long-running hostel that is equipped with all the toys that backpackers love: cable TV, a DVD collection, free internet, pool and ping-pong, a garden with hammocks and a convenient in-house bar.

Backpackers Inn (Map p100; ☎ 247-1326; www .barrancobackpackers.com; Mariscal Castilla 260; dm/d with breakfast US$11/30) On a quiet street, this eight-room backpacker hangout is housed in a renovated mansion with ocean views. The dorms have big windows and attached bathrooms with 24-hour hot water. Rates include free wi-fi and there's a kitchen, a TV lounge and convenient access to Bajada de Baños, leading to the beach.

Aquisito B&B (Map p100; ☎ 247-0712; www.aquisito .com.pe; Centenario 114; s/d/tr with breakfast S50/80/110; 🖵) Eight simple, immaculate rooms of various sizes make up this cozy, modern B&B run by the energetic Malisa. There is a teeny patio, an ample shared kitchen and all units have cable TV and private bathrooms. There is no sign. An excellent value.

D'Osma B&B (Map p100; ☎ 251-4178; deosma.com; Av San Pedro de Osma 240; s/d without bathroom US$20/29, s US$26, d US$39-45; 🖵) A tranquil family home on a busy street, this five-room B&B has simple, carpeted rooms that surround a diminutive, interior patio. Guests have access to a small kitchenette with refrigerator and microwave; rates include breakfast. Some English and German are spoken. There is no obvious sign; look for the wooden gate.

Hostal Gemina (Map p100; ☎ 477-0712; hostalgemina@ yahoo.com; Av Grau 620; s/d/tr with breakfast US$33/48/63; 🖵) The building's facade may seem plain, but this smart, well-recommended modern hotel, with 31 spacious units, is very welcoming. Public areas are decorated with vintage radios and TVs and the clean, modern rooms are draped in folky textiles. An on-site cafeteria serves breakfast. Credit cards accepted.

Second Home Perú (Map p100; ☎ 247-5522; www .secondhomeperu.com; Domeyer 366; s/d with breakfast from US$85/95; 🖵 🐾) Run by the children of artist Victor Delfín, this lovely five-room Bavarian-style *casona* has private gardens and breathtaking views of the ocean from Chorrillos to Miraflores. Public areas are dotted with Delfín's sculptures and paintings. Credit cards accepted.

EATING

The gastronomic capital of the continent, it is in Lima that you will find some of the country's most sublime culinary creations: from simple *cevicherías* (ceviche counters) and corner *anticucho* (beef heart skewer) stands to decorous fusion spots where the cuisine is bathed in foam. Lima's prime position on the coast gives it access to a wide variety of staggeringly fresh seafood, while its status as a centralized capital assures the presence of all manner of regional specialties.

You'll find cocktails infused with Amazon berries, nutty chicken stews from Arequipa *(ají de gallina)* and one of the country's most exquisite renderings (outside of Chiclayo) of Chiclayo-style *arroz con pato* (rice and duck), slowly simmered in cilantro, garlic and beer. The city has such a vast assortment of cuisine, in fact, that it's possible to spend weeks in the city without beginning to taste it all.

Pack your appetite. You're going to need it.

Central Lima

Miraflores and San Isidro may have the city's trendiest restaurants, but Central Lima's downtown spots offer deals and history: from functional *comedores* (simple dining rooms) packed with office workers to atmospheric eateries that count Peruvian presidents among the clientele. *Menús* (set meals) in the vicinity of S7 to S10 can be found at many of the cheaper restaurants.

BUDGET

Panko's (Map pp88-9; ☎ 424-9079; Garcilaso de la Vega 1296; items S3-6) A vast array of sweets, sandwiches and potato salads reside in glass counters under a TV blaring Spanish soaps. The flaky palm-leaf pastries are melt-in-your-mouth delicious.

Pastelería San Martín (Map pp88-9; ☎ 428-9091; Nicolás de Piérola 987; serving of turrón S4.50; ⏰ 9am-9pm Mon-Sat) Founded in 1930, this bakery serves what is considered Lima's finest *turrón de Doña Pepa*, a dessert associated with the religious feast of *El Señor de Los Milagros* (see p60): flaky, sticky and achingly sweet, it is best accompanied by a stiff espresso.

Azato (Map pp88-9; ☎ 423-0278; Arica 298; menús S5-8) A cheap and fast spot serving traditional dishes, including a surprisingly well-rendered *lomo saltado* (beef stir-fry with potatoes, onion and tomatoes).

Villa Natura (Map pp88-9; ☎ 426-3944; Ucayali 326; 3-course menús S7-10; ⏰ closed Sun) A no-frills veggie pit stop serving hearty stews, pastas and veggie renditions of the potato salads known as *causas*. There's no sign; look for the street number over the door.

Queirolo (Map pp88-9; ☎ 425-0421; Camaná 900; mains S8-18; ⏰ 9:30am-1am Mon-Sat) Lined with wine bottles, Queirolo is popular with office workers for cheap *menús* (S7) featuring staples such as *papa rellena* (stuffed potatoes). It is also popular for evening gatherings, when locals pop in for *chilcano de pisco* (pisco with ginger ale and lime juice) and chit-chat.

GARDEN OF EARTHLY DELIGHTS: LIMA'S CUISINE SCENE

You're in town for a few days (or, God forbid, a few hours) and are now faced with a life-altering decision: where to eat. In Lima – a city where food is treated with as much reverence as religion – this is no easy task. There is an astonishing number of restaurants catering to every budget and taste. Herewith, an abbreviated guide to some of the best:

Anticuchos: Lima's most tender beef heart skewers can be found in a simple street cart (Anticuchos de la Tía Grima, p112) and a posh Miraflores eatery (Panchita, p113).

Ceviche: Sublime renditions of the country's most seductive dish can be found in places both economical (El Verídico de Fidel, p110) and upscale (Pescados Capitales, p114); for something truly different, however, try it seared (Fiesta, p114).

Criollo cooking: The country's fusion cuisine – a singular blend of Spanish, Andean, Chinese and African influences – is without parallel at neighborhood cheapie Rincón Chami (p112) and the super-chic Huaca Pucllana (p114), both in Miraflores.

Novoandina: First-rate service, encyclopedic wine lists, and sculptural dishes that blend the traditional and the nouveau are at their acme at Astrid y Gastón (p114) and Malabar (p112)

Potatoes: Celebrating the humble tuber, Mi Causa (p112) produces dishes that are as beautiful as they are delectable.

Sandwiches: Mouth-watering slabs of roasted meats heaped on fresh French bread (perfect for hangovers) are tops at El Chinito (p110) in downtown and El Peruanito (p112) in Miraflores.

El Chinito (Map pp88-9; ☎ 423-2197; Chancay 894; sandwiches S10; 🕑 8am-10pm Mon-Sat, 8am-1pm Sun) Nearly half a century old, this venerable downtown outpost, clad in Spanish tile, is *the* spot for heaping sandwiches stuffed with a bevy of fresh-roasted meats: turkey, pork, beef, ham – and the most popular, *chicharrón* (fried pork) – all served with a traditional marinade of red onions, hot peppers and cilantro.

El Cordano (Map pp88-9; ☎ 427-0181; Ancash 202; mains S8-22; 🕑 8am-9pm) A Lima institution since 1905, this old-world dining hall has, at some point or another, counted practically every Peruvian president for the last 100 years as a customer (the presidential palace is right across the street). It is known for its skillfully rendered *tacu tacu* (pan-fried rice and beans) and *butifarra* (French bread stuffed with country ham).

Rovegno (Map pp88-9; ☎ 424-8465; Arenales 456, Jesús María; mains S10-26, 3-course menús S10-15; 🕑 7am-10pm Mon-Sat) This cluttered bakery-deli-restaurant sells an assortment of decent wine, breads, cheeses, ham and olives, plus plenty of pastries in a rainbow of colors. A restaurant dishes out typical Peruvian specialties such as *lomo saltado.*

Domus (Map pp88-9; ☎ 427-0525; Miró Quesada 410; 3-course menús S15; 🕑 8:30am-5pm Mon-Fri) A restored 19th-century mansion houses this modern-yet-intimate two-room restaurant that caters to journalists from the nearby offices of *El Comercio*. There is no à la carte dining, just a rotating daily list of well-executed Peruvian-Italian specialties that always includes a vegetarian option in the mix. Fresh-squeezed juices accompany this well-tended feast. An excellent value; highly recommended.

La Merced (Map pp88-9; ☎ 428-2431; Miró Quesada 158; menús S7-15, mains S10-30; 🕑 9am-8pm Mon-Sat) Bustling with business people at lunchtime, the bland, unsigned exterior gives little clue to the gorgeous baroque wood ceiling inside. The menu is long on traditional dishes; at busy times you may have to wait for a table.

Self-Catering

In Central Lima, the best supermarket is the block-long **Metro** (Map pp88-9; cnr Cuzco & Lampa; 🕑 9am-10pm daily) in downtown, which also stocks prepared foods.

MIDRANGE

Wa Lok (Map pp88-9; ☎ 447-1329, 427-2750; Paruro 878; mains S10-80; 🕑 9am-11pm Mon-Sat, 9am-10pm Sun) One of the best *chifas* (Chinese restaurants) in Chinatown, this longtime Cantonese spot has a 16-page menu that features dumpling, noodles, stir-fries, casseroles and a good selection of vegetarian options (try the braised tofu casserole). Portions are enormous; don't over-order.

Salon Capon (Map pp88-9; ☎ 426-9286; Paruro 819; mains S10-40; 🕑 9am-10pm Mon-Sat, 9am-7pm Sun) Across the street from Wa Lok, the smaller Salon Capon also has a lengthy Cantonese menu, good dim sum and a traditional bakery that sells scrumptious, flaky egg tarts (S1.80).

our pick El Verídico de Fidel (Map pp88-9; www.elveridicodefidel.com; Abtao 935, La Victoria; ceviches S20-32; 🕑 noon-5pm) Not just a *cevichería*, but a place of pilgrimage, this hole-in-the-wall across from the Alianza Lima stadium is renowned for its *leche de tigre* (ceviche broth), served not in the typical shot glass but in a soup bowl, studded with fresh seafood. The ceviches are equally spectacular. This is a rough neighborhood; take a taxi – even in daytime.

Cevichería la Choza Naútica (Map pp88-9; ☎ 423-8087; www.lachozanautica.com.pe; Breña 204; ceviches S20-36, mains S19-32; 🕑 8am-11pm Mon-Sat, 8am-9pm Sun) A surprisingly bright spot for a slightly dingy area, this popular *cevichería*, tended to by bow-tied waiters, offers more than a dozen types of ceviches and *tiraditos* (Japanese-style ceviche, without onions). There is also a long list of soups, seafood and rice dishes. There is live music on busy nights.

TOP END

Tanta (Map pp88-9; ☎ 428-3115; Pasaje de los Escribanos 142, Central Lima; mains S29-38; 🕑 9am-10pm Mon-Sat, 9am-6pm Sun) One of several informal bistros run by celebrity super-chef Gastón Acurio, Tanta serves Peruvian dishes, fusion pastas, heaping salads and sandwiches. Accompanying the encyclopedic menu is a list of house cocktails – such as the 'cholopolitan,' made with pisco, Cointreau, lime and cranberry juices – and a wine list strong on vintages from South America (from S46 per bottle). The food is good (if overpriced), but the desserts are better: don't leave without trying the heavenly passion fruit cheesecake mousse.

L'Eau Vive (Map pp88-9; ☎ 427-5612; Ucayali 370; mains S30-50, 3-course menús S15; 🕑 12:30-3pm & 7:30-9:30pm Mon-Sat) In an 18th-century building with sparkling wood trim is this very simple and somewhat unusual eatery run by French Carmelite nuns. The menu consists largely of French and other continental specialties (think *coquilles St Jacques*) – with various Peruvian influences. Every night, after dinner (at around 9pm), the nuns gather to sing 'Ave Maria.'

San Isidro

Chic dining rooms, frothy cocktails and fusion haute cuisine: San Isidro is a bastion of fine dining – and not much else. Those on a budget may prefer to prepare their own meals, or head to nearby Miraflores, where the eats are generally cheaper.

SELF-CATERING

Vivanda (Map p96; www.vivanda.com.pe; Av 2 de Mayo 1420; ☑ 8am-10pm) Lima's top supermarket has luscious arrays of meats, cheeses, vegetables, baked goods, prepared foods and even a cafe.

MIDRANGE

News Café (Map p96; ☎ 421-6278; Santa Luisa 110; sandwiches S9-26, mains S20-38; ☑ 9am-11pm) Bursting with local office types at lunchtime, this casual cafe serves up bounteous sandwiches, pastas, traditional Peruvian dishes and a wide gamut of international newspapers. The best part: the ice-cream stand located at the entrance, which serves delectable scoops made with Andean fruits such as chirimoya and lúcuma.

Como Agua Para Chocolate (Map p96; ☎ 222-0297; Pancho Fierro 108; mains S20-30) A popular Mexican spot that produces the gamut of Mexican staples, including veggie tacos and, of course, margaritas.

Antica (Map p96; ☎ 222-9488; Av 2 de Mayo 732; mains S20-42; ☑ noon-midnight) On a street littered with European restaurants, this is one of the most reasonable: a woody, candle-bedecked spot serving house-made pastas, gnocchis and pizzas from a wood-fired oven. There is antipasto, as well as a decent wine list strong on South American brands (from S40).

TOP END

Segundo Muelle (Map p96; ☎ 421-1206; www.segundo muelle.com; Conquistadores 490; mains S20-37; ☑ noon-5pm) You'll find no less than a dozen types of ceviches and *tiraditos* at this pleasant, well-tended seafood eatery renowned for its fresh ceviches, some with innovative twists. (Try the *ceviche de mariscos a los tres ajíes*, a stack of mixed fish and shellfish bathed in three

types of hot pepper sauce.) The menu also features heaping rice and other seafood dishes, including a recommended *parrilla marina* (seafood grill).

Punto Sal (Map p96; ☎ 441-7431; Conquistadores 958; mains S22-38; ☑ 11am-5pm) Another great seafood restaurant (it's been around for 20 years), Punta Sal serves at least nine different kinds of ceviche. Try the assassin ceviche – a paradisiacal mix of octopus, squid, crawfish, crab, flounder and mangrove cockles. Reader recommended.

Bravo Restobar (Map p96; ☎ 221-5700; www .bravorestobar.com; Conquistadores 1005; mains S28-54; ☑ 1-11pm Mon-Thu, 1pm-3am Fri & Sat) An inviting restaurant-lounge with a backlit bar and stone and wood interiors, Bravo's able bartenders stir up dozens of spectacular cocktails (try the *aguaymanto* sour, made with pisco and Amazonian berries). There is a lengthy list of Italian-Peruvian fusion dishes, as well as a bar menu with a laundry list of snacks (such as tender seafood grills) in the event that you're just there to sip.

Tanta (Map p96; ☎ 421-9708; Pancho Fierro 115) The San Isidro outpost of Acurio's restaurant-cafe chain (see opposite).

Punto Italiano (Map p96; ☎ 221-3146; Av 2 de Mayo 647; mains S30-45; ☑ lunch & dinner) Italian cuisine with a Sardinian twist is dished up at this homey trattoria. The handmade ravioli are locally renowned while the *carne tagliata* (veal with tagliatelle) with Sardinian cheese is divine.

Matsuei (Map p96; ☎ 422-4323; Manuel Bañon 260; maki S30-45; ☑ 12:30-3:30pm & 7:30-11pm Mon-Sat) None other than the venerated Japanese super-chef Nobu Matsuhisa once co-owned this diminutive sushi bar, now situated on a San Isidro side street. Don't let the modest appearance fool you: Matsuei serves up some of the most spectacular sashimi and *maki* (sushi rolls) in Lima. A must-have: the 'acevichado,' a roll stuffed with shrimp and avocado, and then doused in a house-made mayo infused with ceviche broth. It will make your brain tingle in all the right places.

Fusión (Map p96; ☎ 422-7600; Choquehuanca 714; mains from S35-50; ☑ 1pm-close & 7pm-close) A minimalist dining room in a concrete bunker is home to this cutting-edge – you guessed it – fusion spot by Chef Rafael Piqueras. Expect a run-down of well-rendered international items (think: duck confit), with Peruvian flourishes (tuna *tiradito* drizzled with *rocoto* chilies and soy sauce). An extensive wine list features more than 200 fine vintages from all over the world.

ourpick **Malabar** (Map p96; ☎ 440-5200; www .malabar.com.pe; Cam Real 101; mains S38-55; ⏰ 12:30-4pm & 7:30-11pm Mon-Sat) Rising culinary star Pedro Miguel Schiaffino is the chef at this hot destination restaurant at the heart of San Isidro. Influenced, in particular, by Amazonian produce and cooking techniques, Schiaffino's seasonal menu features deftly prepared delicacies such as crisp, seared *cuy* and Amazonian river snails bathed in a sauce made with spicy chorizo. Do not forego the cocktails (the chef's father, a noted pisco expert, consulted on the menu) or desserts – perhaps the lightest and most refreshing in Lima.

Miraflores

By far the most varied neighborhood for eating, Miraflores carries the breadth and depth of Peruvian cooking at every price range imaginable, from tiny *comedores* with cheap lunchtime *menús* to some of the city's most revered gastronomic outposts. The neighborhood also has the best pavement cafes in Lima, ideal for sipping pisco sours and people-watching.

BUDGET
Casual places with cheap *menús* abound on the tiny streets east of Av José Larco just off the Parque Kennedy.

Bodega Miraflores (Map p98; Diez Canseco 109; coffee S3; ⏰ 9:30am-1pm & 3:30-7:30pm Mon-Sat) A frumpy spot with a grumpy counterman that serves strong, inky *cortados* (espresso with a dollop of steamed milk) made with coffee grown in Chanchamayo (see p480). Bagged, wholebean coffee is available to take home.

Anticuchos de la Tía Grima (Map p98; ☎ 99-849-3137; www.anticuchosdelatiagrima.com; cnr Enrique Palacio & 27 de Noviembre; anticucho S7; ⏰ 7-11pm Mon-Sat) The most venerated *anticuchos* in all of Lima are grilled at this corner cart, which has been tended to by the legendary Doña Grimanesa for more than 30 years. The meat is so tender

---

A LA LIMEÑA

Many restaurants in Lima tone down the spices on some traditional dishes for foreign travelers. If you like your cooking spicy (*picante*), tell them to turn up the heat by asking for your food *a la Limeña* – Lima-style.

---

and the house-made hot sauces so delicious, that it's no wonder the wait is often more than an hour. The best bet: show up at 6:45pm and wait for Doña Grimanesa to roll up or telephone your order in ahead of time.

El Peruanito (Map p98; ☎ 241-2175; Av Angamos Este 391; sandwiches S7; ⏰ 7am-1am) A hopping, informal sandwich spot serving fresh-roasted chicken, ham, turkey and *chicharrón* sandwiches on fresh French bread – each dressed with marinated onions and slim wedges of lightly fried sweet potato. If you've had one too many piscos, these will cure what ails you.

Govinda (Map p98; ☎ 445-8487; Schell 630; 3-course menús from S7; ⏰ noon-8pm Mon-Fri, noon-7pm Sat & Sun) Run by the Hare Krishna, this cheerful cafe serves a Peruvian-Indian fusion of vegetable curries and nonmeat versions of dishes such as *lomo saltado*.

Dove Vai (Map p98; ☎ 241-8763; Diagonal 228; ice cream S6-9) An Italian ice-cream shop serving an array of flavors, including a mighty fine pisco sour sorbet.

San Antonio (Map p98; ☎ 241-3001; Av Vasco Núñez de Balboa 770; sandwiches S8-16; ⏰ 7am-11pm) A cross-section of Miraflores society jams into this 50-year-old institution for an infinite variety of sandwiches, as well as a wide selection of baked goods, including a dreamy chocolate croissant (ask for it warm).

Pardo's Chicken (Map p98; ☎ 446-4790; www.pardos chicken.com; Alfredo Benavides 730; mains S9-21) Lima is littered with rotisserie chicken chains; this one is, hands down, the best.

Café Z (Map p98; ☎ 444-5579; Diagonal 598; sandwiches S10-18; ⏰ 7am-midnight) A gathering spot for Lima hipsters, this lively cafe has live music, delicious sandwiches (try the *Butifarra Z*), a mind-boggling number of coffees and herbal teas – in addition to the world's most uncomfortable chairs.

Rincón Chami (Map p98; ☎ 444-4511; Esperanza 154; mains S10-27; ⏰ 8am-8:30pm Mon-Sat, noon-5pm Sun) A simple, 40-year-old dining hall, with a rotating selection of Peruvian specialties, Chami is renowned for skillfully prepared dishes such as *cau cau* (tripe stew), as well as *milanesa* (breaded steaks) as big as a platter.

ourpick **Mi Causa** (off Map p98; ☎ 222-6258; Av La Mar 814; causas S14-23; ⏰ noon-4:30pm Mon-Fri, noon-5pm Sat & Sun) A temple to the humble potato and the sculptural dishes that can be produced with it, this inventive eatery dishes up more than 50 (including a dozen vegetarian options) varieties of *causa*, a traditional Peruvian potato salad. Expect a rainbow's worth of hot and cold *causas*, layered with mouth-watering combinations of seafood, chicken, beef, cheese and vegetables, some made with uncommon strains of tuber, such as *puca sonqo*, which is pink.

Self-Catering

On Saturdays, a small green market sets up at Parque Reducto, off Alfredo Benavides and Ribeyro. Likewise, try the neighborhood's excellent supermarkets:

Plaza VEA (Map p98; ☎ 625-8000; www.plazavea .com.pe; Av Arequipa 4651; ⏰ 8am-10pm)

Vivanda (☎ 620-3000; www.vivanda.com.pe) Benavides (Map p98; Alfredo Benavides 487; ⏰ 24hr); José Pardo (Map p98; Av José Pardo; ⏰ 8am-10:30pm)

Wong (Map p98; ☎ 625-0000, ext 1130; www.ewong .com; Óvalo Gutiérrez, Av Santa Cruz 771) A massive supermarket built around the courtyard of a vintage home; look for the baroque-style staircase.

MIDRANGE

Helena Chocolatier (Map p98; ☎ 242-8899; http://helena chocolatier.com; Iglesias 498; chocolates from S3; ⏰ 10:30am-7:30pm Mon-Fri) A longtime artisanal chocolate shop that crafts scrumptious 'Chocolates D'Gala', each stuffed with fillings made from pecans, marzipan or raspberries and individually wrapped to resemble small gifts.

Xocolatl (Map p98; ☎ 241-9554, 242-0143; www .xocolatl.pe; Manuel Bonilla 111; chocolates from S3.50; ⏰ 11am-8pm Mon-Sat) Run by pastry chef Giovanna Maggiolo, Xocolatl is a sleek chocolatier specializing in contemporary Peruvian sweets, some sporting designs inspired by pre-Columbian textiles. Expect fillings such as coffee, pisco and *Ranfañote*, a traditional dessert made with coconut, molasses and nuts.

Haiti (Map p98; ☎ 445-0539; Diagonal 160; mains S12-36) This nearly half-century-old cafe is like stepping into 1960s Lima: waiters in green jackets tend to coiffed ladies and chattering businessmen. It's a perfect spot to order a pressed pork sandwich and watch the world go by. Be forewarned: those innocent-looking pisco sours pack a wallop.

La Preferida (Map pp82-3; ☎ 445-5180; Arias Araguez 698; mains S13-20, tapas S1-3; ⏰ 8am-5pm Mon-Sat) Located a couple of blocks north of Av 28 de Julio, just east of the Vía Expresa, this charming take-out place has gorgeous *causas* and fresh seafood specialties such as *pulpo al olivo* (octopus in olive sauce) and *choros a la chalaca* (mussels with a corn and tomato salsa) served in tapas-sized portions. A few stools accommodate diners.

Bircher Benner (Map pp82-3; ☎ 446-5791; 2nd fl, Av José Larco 413; mains S15-22; ⏰ 9am-11pm Mon-Sat) A longtime vegetarian restaurant and shop that produces a lengthy list of dishes, including veg-only versions of Peruvian staples such as *lomo saltado*, as well as a 'ceviche' crafted with marinated mushrooms, onions, cilantro, tomato and ricotta.

Manolo (Map p98; ☎ 444-2244; www.manolochurros .com; Av José Larco 608; mains S15-50, churros S4; ⏰ 7am-1am Sun-Thu, 7am-2am Fri & Sat) Though this popular sidewalk cafe serves a long list of sandwiches, pasta and pizza, it is best known for its piping-hot churros, which go smashingly well with a *chocolate caliente espeso* (a thick hot chocolate) – perfect for dipping.

La Glorietta (Map p98; ☎ 445-0498; Pasaje Juan Figari 181; mains S16-40) Just off the Diagonal, the tiny Pasaje Juan Figari – nicknamed Pizza Street – is cluttered with pizzerias, each of which look and taste much like the other. La Glorietta is one of the better joints, with decent pies laden with fresh garlic.

El Punto Azul (Map p98; ☎ 445-8078; San Martín 595; mains S18-25; ⏰ noon-5pm) This pleasant family eatery dishes up super-fresh ceviches and *tiraditos*, as well as big-enough-to-share rice dishes. Try their risotto with parmesan, shrimp and *ají amarillo* (yellow chili) – and don't miss the line-up of tasty desserts. It gets packed on weekends, so show up before 1pm if you want a table. An excellent value.

Quattro D (Map p98; ☎ 445-4228; Av Angamos Oeste 408; mains S20-31, ice cream from S6; ⏰ 6:30am-11:45pm Mon-Thu, 6:30am-12:30am Fri & Sat, 7-11pm Sun) A bustling cafe that serves hot pressed sandwiches, pasta and other dishes, in addition to a diabetes-inducing assortment of sweets and Italian ice cream (including a few sugar-free flavors).

AlmaZen (Map p98; ☎ 243-0474; Federico Recavarren 298; mains S30; ⏰ 11am-11pm Mon-Fri, 5-11pm Sat) A new vegetarian restaurant and teahouse, this soothing spot features a rotating daily selection of organic dishes such as sweet potato and ginger soup, as well as tarts and risottos. Wheat-free and vegan items are also available.

TOP END

Panchita (Map p98; ☎ 242-5957; Av 2 de Mayo 298; mains S19-54; ⏰ 12:30-9pm Mon-Sat; 12:30-5pm Sun) Gastón Acurio's new restaurant pays homage to

Peruvian street food in a contemporary setting. The *anticuchos* are grilled over an open flame to melt-in-your-mouth perfection. Also worth the cholesterol: the crisp suckling pig with *tacu tacu*. The lengthy wine list (heavily South American) will help wash it all down.

Mangos (Map p98; ☎ 242-8110; www.mangosperu.com; mains S24-43; ☿ 8am-1am Mon-Sat, 8am-10pm Sun) Of all the LarcoMar shopping mall's ocean-view restaurants at the, this one has the most expansive terrace as well as some of the best food – a broad range of Peruvian and international dishes.

La Trattoria di Mambrino (Map p98; ☎ 446-7002; Manuel Bonilla 106; mains S25-40; ☿ 1-3pm & 8-11pm Mon-Sat, 12:30-4pm Sun) One of the top Italian restaurants in town, whose kitchen is overseen by Ugo Plevisani and his wife, Sandra, this white-tablecloth spot has traditional house-made pastas (think: ravioli stuffed with veal and porcini) as well as delectable gnocchi.

Restaurant Huaca Pucllana (Map p98; ☎ 445-4042; www.resthuacapucllana.com; Gral Borgoño cuadra 8; mains S28-60; ☿ 12:30pm-midnight Mon-Sat, 12:30-4pm Sun) This sophisticated establishment overlooks the illuminated ruins at Huaca Pucllana. The menu consists of a skillfully rendered and beautifully presented array of contemporary Peruvian dishes (from grilled *cuy* to seafood chowders), along with a smattering of Italian-fusion specialties. Save room for the pisco and lemon parfait come dessert.

La Mar (off Map p98; ☎ 421-3365; www.lamarcebicheria.com; Av La Mar 770; mains S39-49, ceviches S29-39; ☿ noon-5pm Mon-Fri, 11:45am-5:30pm Sat & Sun) A *cevichería* done Gastón Acurio-style: La Mar is a polished cement patio bursting with VIPs (note the security guards outside) that serves 10 types of ceviche and almost as many varieties of *tiraditos*. Can't make up your mind? Try the *degustación*, with five different kinds. There are grills, rice dishes and soups, but it's the ceviche that is tops. Cocktails here include Lima's best coca-leaf sour.

Tanta (Map p98; ☎ 447-8377; Av 28 de Julio 888) The Miraflores outpost of Gastón Acurio's restaurant-cafe chain (see p110).

Las Brujas de Cachiche (Map p98; ☎ 444-5310; www.brujasdecachiche.com.pe/ibien.html; Bolognesi 460; mains S30-54) A good place for quality Peruvian cooking, the menu has all the popular dishes (such as *ají de gallina*), as well as lesser-known specialties such as *carapulcra*, a dried potato stew. Want to try a bit of everything? Hit the lunch buffet (S75).

Pescados Capitales (off Map p98; ☎ 421-8808; www.pescados-capitales.com; Av La Mar 1337; mains S30-65; ☿ 12:30-5pm) On a street that was once home to nothing but clattering auto shops, this contemporary destination (think: artsy warehouse meets Peruvian rustic) serves some of the finest ceviche around. Try the 'Ceviche Capital,' a mix of flounder, salmon and tuna marinated with red, white and green onions and bathed in a three-chili crème. A nine-page wine list offers a strong selection of Chilean and Argentinean vintages (from S55).

La Tiendecita Blanca (Map p98; ☎ 445-9797; Av José Larco 111; mains S33-46) A Miraflores landmark for more than half a century, fans of Swiss cuisine will find potato *röstis*, fondues and a terrific selection of apple tarts, Napoleons and quiches at this graceful beaux arts bistro.

La Rosa Nautica (Map p98; ☎ 445-0149; Circuito de Playas; mains S36-75, 3-course menús S60) Location, location, location. Though you can get the same (or better) seafood elsewhere for less, the views at this eatery on the historic pier are unparalleled. Go during happy hour (5pm to 7pm), when you can watch the last of the day's surfers skim along the crests of the waves. Take a taxi to the pier and walk the last 100m.

Rafael (Map p98; ☎ 242-4149; http://rafaelosterling.com; San Martín 300; mains S39-65; ☿ 1-3:30pm & 8pm-midnight) Don't let the demure exterior fool you: this is *the* place in Lima to see and be seen. Here, Chef Rafael Osterling produces a panoply of fusion dishes, such as *tiradito* bathed in Japanese citrus or suckling goat stewed in Madeira wine. For those who make it past the generously poured cocktails, there is a lengthy international wine list.

Astrid y Gastón (Map p98; ☎ 444-1496, 242-5387; www.astridygaston.com; Cantuarias 175; mains S39-69; ☿ 12:30-3:30pm & 6:30pm-midnight Mon-Sat) Now one of the older outposts of *novoandina* cooking in Lima, Gastón Acurio's French-influenced standard-bearer nonetheless remains a culinary force to be reckoned with. His seasonal menu is equipped with traditional Peruvian fare, but it's the exquisite fusion specialties – such as the seared filets of *cuy*, served Peking-style, with fluffy purple-corn crêpes – that make this such a sublime fine dining experience. There is a first-rate international wine list (from S46 per bottle).

Fiesta (off Map p98; ☎ 242-9009; www.restaurantfiestagourmet.com; Av Reducto 1278; mains S40-45; ☿ dinner & lunch) Anyone in search of the finest northern Peruvian cuisine in Lima, should make a reservation at this busy establishment on Miraflores' eastern edge. Not only do they cook up an *arroz con pato a la chiclayana* (duck and rice Chiclayo style) that is achingly tender, they also serve *ceviche a la brasa*, traditional ceviche that is given a quick sear before being served, resulting in a fish that is lightly smoky, yet tender. Has to be eaten to be believed. There is a sister restaurant in Chiclayo (p362).

Barranco

Even as Barranco has gone upscale in recent years, with trendy restaurants serving everything fusion, the neighborhood holds on to atmospheric, local spots where life never gets more complicated than ceviche and beer.

BUDGET & MIDRANGE

A number of informal restaurants serving *anticuchos* and cheap *menús* line Av Grau around the intersection with Unión.

Chifa Chung Yion (Map p100; ☎ 477-0550; Calle Unión 126; mains S8-32; ☽ noon-5:30pm & 7pm-midnight) Known locally as the 'Chifa Unión' – and partially owned by the mayor of Barranco's mother – this bustling restaurant serves heaping bowls of wonton soup and well-rendered fried rice with langostinos. There is a list of veggie options as well (from S8).

Las Mesitas (Map p100; ☎ 477-4199; Av Grau 341; menús S9; ☽ noon-2am) A vintage spot with terra-cottatile floors that serves cheap Peruvian classics and an array of recommended desserts. If you've been thinking about dipping into *suspiro limeño* (a caramel-meringue sweet), this would be the place to do it.

El Hornito (Map p100; ☎ 252-8183; Av Grau 209; pizzas S10-37; ☽ 1pm-midnight) Known for their pizzas, this central dining venue also offers up a wide range of *parrilladas* (grilled meats) and pasta dishes. The illuminated vine-covered patio is pleasant at night.

Antica Trattoria (Map p100; ☎ 247-2443; San Martín 201; pastas S20-37; ☽ 12:30-11:30pm) A longtime Italian spot with a nouveau-rustic air serves wood-fired pizza, as well as savory concoctions such as fresh ravioli stuffed with crab and tender osso buco with creamy polenta.

La Canta Rana (Map p100; ☎ 247-7274; Génova 101; mains S20-40; ☽ 8am-11pm Tue-Sat) An unpretentious 25-year-old place, Canta Rana packs in the locals for its more than 17 different types of ceviche. There is no obvious sign: look for the green walls and the expectant-looking cats sitting outside.

TOP END

Chala (Map p100; ☎ 252-8515; www.chala.com.pe; Bajada de Baños 343; mains S26-64, 3-course lunch menú S50; ☽ 1-4pm & 8pm-midnight Mon-Sat, 1-4pm Sun) At the top of the narrow stairway that leads to the beach, a revamped *casona* with a broad terrace is home to this local favorite, which serves modern dishes that blend Peruvian and Japanese flavors. Not to be missed: chicken raviolis bathed in *ají de gallina* and topped with seared langostinos.

La 73 (Map p100; ☎ 247-0780; Av El Sol Oeste 175; mains S34-39; ☽ noon-midnight) This contemporary-yet-cozy neighborhood eatery has an uncomplicated Peruvian-Mediterranean menu strong on Italian specialties such as yellow-potato gnocchi. A pleasant bar serves wine, in addition to eight types of pisco. You may want to start with dessert, however: their crisp, warm churros are orgasmic.

La Punta

A quiet, residential neighborhood with great views of the water, La Punta is perfect for a leisurely lunch.

Manolo (Map pp82-3; ☎ 453-4886; Malecón Pardo s/n, adra 1; ☽ lunch only) This humble-looking fish house draws seafood die hards intent on gobbling up fresh ceviches, grilled fish and hearty soups.

La Rana Verde (Map pp82-3; ☎ 429-5279; Parque Gálvez s/n; mains S29-53; ☽ lunch only) Located on the pier inside the Club Universitario de Regatas, this waterside spot is ideal for Sunday lunch within view of the Isla San Lorenzo. The dishes are all deftly prepared and the *pulpo al olivo* is one of the best in Lima.

DRINKING

Lima is overflowing with establishments of every description, from rowdy beer halls to high-end lounges to atmospheric old bars. In downtown, you can get beer from S6 and pisco sours from S7. But head further south – to San Isidro, Miraflores and Barranco – and the prices steadily climb. Trendier lounges will charge up to S15 to S20 a cocktail.

Central Lima

Nightlife in central Lima is for the nostalgic, composed largely of vintage hotel bars and period halls.

El Bolivarcito (Map pp88-9; ☎ 427-2114; Jirón de la Unión 958) Facing the Plaza San Martín from the Gran Hotel Bolívar, this frayed yet bustling spot is known as 'La Catedral del Pisco' for purveying some of the first pisco sours in Peru. Order the double-sized *pisco catedral* if your liver can take it.

Hotel Maury (Map pp88-9; ☎ 428-8188; Ucayali 201) Another vintage bar renowned for popularizing pisco sours is this intimate, old-world spot lined with stained-glass windows and tended to by a battalion of bow-tie-clad waiters.

Other good evening hangouts include **El Estadio Fútbol Club** (Map pp88-9; ☎ 428-8866; Nicolás de Piérola 934; ☺ noon-11pm Mon-Thu, noon-2am Fri & Sat), a soccer-fanatic hangout-restaurant, and Queirolo (p109), an old-timey spot that stays open until 1am.

San Isidro

Bravo Restobar (Map p96; ☎ 221-5700; www.bravo restobar.com; Conquistadores 1005) An encyclopedic cocktail menu and an excellent selection of small-batch piscos make this mellow San Isidro lounge a good spot to sip and be seen.

Los Delfines Bar (Map p96; Delfines Hotel y Casino, Los Eucaliptos 555) This top hotel's elegant bar marries all the best qualities of a corporate expense account with the dolphin trick show at the local aquarium.

Miraflores

Old-world cafes where suited waiters serve frothy pisco sours, raucous watering holes blaring techno and salsa – Miraflores has a little bit of everything. The area around the Parque Kennedy is particularly suited for sipping and people-watching.

Brenchley Arms (Map p98; ☎ 445-9680; Atahualpa 174; ☺ 6:30pm-close Mon-Sat) A popular hangout with foreign travelers in Lima, this mellow British-style pub has games of darts and a selection of Peruvian draft beers.

Café Bar Habana (Map p98; ☎ 446-3511; www.cafe barhabana.com; Manuel Bonilla 107; ☺ 6pm-close Mon-Sat) Boisterous Cuban proprietor Alexi García and his Peruvian wife, Patssy Higuchi, operate this homey drinking establishment that serves a highly delicious *mojito* (a cocktail of mint, rum and club soda). The couple, both of whom are artists, sometimes display their works in the adjacent gallery.

Huaringas (Map p98; ☎ 447-1883; Bolognesi 460; ☺ 9pm-close Tue-Sat) A popular Miraflores bar and lounge located inside the Brujas de Cachiche restaurant (p114), Huaringas serves a vast array of cocktails, including a well-

recommended passion-fruit sour. On busy weekends, there are DJs.

Old Pub (Map p98; ☎ 242-8155; www.oldpub.com .pe; San Ramón 295; ☺ 4pm-close Mon-Sat) At the far end of 'Pizza Street,' this flag-draped pub has darts, a large-screen cable TV blaring sports, a few British brews (in a tin) and plenty of Cusqueña (a light lager from Cuzco) on tap.

Media Naranja (Map p98; ☎ 446-6946; Schell 130; ☺ 10am-3am Mon-Sat) You can't miss the enormous, brightly colored flags that hang over this boisterous outdoor Brazilian bar-cafe where the cachaça flows like water.

Barranco

Barranco's bars and clubs are concentrated around the Parque Municipal, which is thronged with revelers on Friday and Saturday nights.

Ayahuasca (Map p100; ☎ 247-6751; www.ayahuasca bar.com; San Martín 130; ☺ 8pm-close) Lima's of-the-moment lounge resides in a stunning restored *casona* full of Moorish architectural flourishes. Not that anyone's looking at the architecture – everyone's checking out everyone else, in addition to the hyper-real decor that includes a dangling mobile made with costumes used in Ayacucho folk dances. There's a long list of contemporary pisco cocktails, made with infusions of purple corn and coca leaves.

Ekeko Bar (Map p100; ☎ 247-3148; Av Grau 266; ☺ 10am-midnight Mon-Wed, 10am-3am Thu-Sat) From Monday-night poetry readings to local cover bands, this ragged two-story spot has it all. When popular acts are playing, expect to pay a cover (about $10).

Juanito's (Map p100; Av Grau 274) This worn-in woody bar – it was a leftist hangout in the 1960s – is one of the mellowest haunts in Barranco. Decorated with a lifetime's worth of theater posters, this is where the writerly set arrives to swig *chilcano de pisco* and de-construct the state of humanity. There's no sign; look for the crowded room lined with wine bottles.

La Posada del Mirador (Map p100; ☎ 256-1796; Ermita 104; ☺ 5pm-midnight) A low-key, 2nd-story drinking establishment, the clifftop Posada del Mirador has outdoor tables great for catching the sunset.

Acantilado de Barranco (Map p100; ☎ 247-2145; www.acantiladodebarranco.com; Ermita 102; ☺ 6pm-midnight) Sharing the same good views next door to La Posada del Mirador is this more formal place, where you can still find 1950s cocktails like the Rusty Nail on the menu.

Wahio's (Map p100; ☎ 477-4110; Plaza Espinosa; ✆ Thu-Sat) A large and lively bar with a fair share of dreadlocks and a classic soundtrack of reggae, ska and dub.

ENTERTAINMENT

Cinemas, theaters, traveling art exhibits and concerts are covered in the daily *El Comercio*, with the most detailed listings found in Monday's '*Luces*' section. Likewise, you can log on to the informational portal *Living in Peru* (www.livinginperu.com), which maintains an up-to-date calendar of events. More youth oriented is *Oveja Negra* (www.revistaovejanegra .com), a pocket-sized directory distributed free at restaurants and bars which provides monthly listings of cultural and nightlife happenings.

To purchase tickets for events, see boxed text, below.

Live Music

Many restaurants and bars feature small local acts, while bigger bands tend to play at the casinos or sporting arenas. The following venues are the best-known live-music spots.

Jazz Zone (Map p98; ☎ 241-8139; www.jazzzoneperu .com; Centro Comercial El Suche, Av La Paz 656, Miraflores; admission from S15) A variety of jazz, folk, *cumbia*, flamenco and other acts at this intimate, well-recommended club on the eastern side of Miraflores.

La Estación de Barranco (Map p100; ☎ 247-0344; www.laestaciondebarranco.com; Av Pedro de Osma 112, Barranco; admission from S32) A middling space that hosts a variety of jazz, cabaret, musical and comedy performances.

TELETICKET

A handy place to buy tickets is **Teleticket** (☎ 613-8888; www.teleticket.com.pe), a one-stop-shopping broker that sells tickets to sporting events, concerts, theatre and some *peñas* (bars and clubs featuring live folkloric music), as well as the tourist train to Huancayo (p120). The most convenient Teleticket offices can be found on the 2nd floor of the Wong supermarket at Óvalo Gutiérrez (p113) and inside the Metro supermarket in Central Lima (p110). The website has a full listing of locations all over Lima.

La Noche (Map p100; ☎ 247-1012; www.lanoche .pe; Av Bolognesi 307, Barranco; admission from S15) Get ready to groove! This well-known tri-level bar is *the* spot to see rock, punk and Latin music acts in Lima.

PEÑAS

Peruvian folk music and dance is performed on weekends at *peñas*. There are two main types of Peruvian music performed at these venues: *folklórica* and *criollo*. The first is more typical of the Andean highlands; the other, a coastal music driven by African-influenced beats. Admission varies; dinner is sometimes included in the price.

Las Brisas del Titicaca (Map pp88-9; ☎ 715-6960; www.brisasdeltiticaca.com; Wakuski 168, Central Lima; admission S21-48) The best *folklórica* show in Lima is at this *peña* near Plaza Bolognesi in downtown.

La Candelaria (Map p100; ☎ 247-1314; www .lacandelariaperu.com; Bolognesi 292, Barranco; admission S31-53) In Barranco, a show that incorporates both *folklórica* and *criollo* music and dancing.

De Rompe y Raja (Map p100; ☎ 247-3271; www .derompeyraja.pe; Manuel Segura 127, Barranco; admission S31) Near La Candelaria, a reader-recommended *criollo* performance space.

Nightclubs

The club scene gets started well after midnight and keeps going until the break of dawn. Barranco and Miraflores are the best neighborhoods to go clubbing, but spots come and go, so ask around before heading out. Music styles and cover charges vary depending on the night of the week.

Aura (Map p98; ☎ 242-5516, ext 210; www.aura.com .pe; LarcoMar, Malecón de la Reserva 610, Miraflores; admission S40) Located in the LarcoMar shopping mall, Lima's most exclusive club is minimally decorated and features house and guest DJs who spin a mix of house, hip-hop, electronica and Latin. Dress to the nines or you're not getting in.

Gótica (Map p98; ☎ 628-3033; www.gotica.com .pe; LarcoMar, Malecón de la Reserva 610, Miraflores; admission S40) A fashionable, high-energy dance spot with a churchy interior and a mix of DJs playing electronica, hip-hop and pop. It sometimes serves as a venue for live Latin dance bands.

Sargento Pimienta (Map p100; ☎ 247-3265; www .sargentopimienta.com; Bolognesi 755, Barranco; admission S20) More accessible is this reliable spot in Barranco, whose name means 'Sergeant

Pepper.' The barnlike club hosts various theme nights and occasional live bands.

Déjà Vu (Map p100; ☎ 247-3742; Av Grau 294, Barranco) A bar that also has dancing, this vintage place has two tiers: upstairs, expect thumping international beats; downstairs you'll find traditional Peruvian acts.

For other options, hit 'Pizza Street' (Pasaje Juan Figari) in Miraflores, where a row of raucous clubs regularly spin their wares.

Cinemas

The latest international films are usually screened with the original soundtrack and Spanish subtitles, except children's movies, which are always dubbed. Some cinemas offer reduced admission midweek. Listings can be found online or in the cultural pages of the local newspapers.

Cine Planet (☎ 624-9500; www.cineplanet.com .pe; Central Lima (Map pp88-9; Jirón de la Unión 819; admission S5-9); Miraflores (Map p98; Av Santa Cruz 814; admission S9-17)

Cinerama El Pacífico (☎ 243-0541; cine.peru.com; Av José Pardo 121, Miraflores; admission S11)

El Cinematógrafo (Map p100; ☎ 264-4374; www .elcinematografo.com; Pérez Roca 196, Barranco; admission S6) For esoteric and alternative films.

UVK Multicines (www.uvkmulticines.com); LarcoMar (Map p98; ☎ 446-7336; LarcoMar, Malecón de la Reserva 610, Miraflores; admission S9-17); Plaza San Martín (Map pp88-9; ☎ 428-6042; Ocoña 110, Central Lima; admission S6.50-8.50) The LarcoMar branch has a 'CineBar,' where, for S23, you can sit in a theater with bar tables and have cocktails delivered to your seat.

Theater

Pickings are slim, but the following theaters are worth noting. Built in 1909, the **Teatro Segura** (Map pp88-9; ☎ 426-7189; Huancavelica 265, Central Lima) puts on opera, plays and ballet, while the **Teatro Británico** (Map p98; ☎ 615-3434; www.britanico.edu.pe; Bellavista 527, Miraflores) puts on a variety of works, including plays in English.

Casinos

Many upscale hotels have gaming and there are independent casinos scattered all over Lima, especially Miraflores. High-end spots divvy up their salons between those who bet in US dollars and those who don't.

Some of the trendier options:

Atlantic City (Map p98; ☎ 445-5562; Av José Larco 701, Miraflores) One of the city's newer halls, Atlantic City has enough flashing lights to make Las Vegas blush.

Casino Fiesta (Map p98; ☎ 610-4151; www.fiesta -casino.pe; Alfredo Benavides 509, Miraflores) Another new spot; popular bands often play here.

Sports

Estadio Nacional (Map pp88-9; Central Lima) *Fútbol* is the national obsession, and Peru's Estadio Nacional, off *cuadras* 7 to 9 of Paseo de la República, is the venue for the most important matches and other events. Teleticket (see boxed text, p117) has listings and sales.

Plaza de Acho (Map pp88-9; ☎ 481-1467; Jr Hualgayoc 332, Rímac) Bullfighting remains popular in Lima. The height of the season is in October, during the religious feast of *El Señor de los Milagros*, when Peru's best toreadors arrive to take on the baddest of the bulls. Teleticket has listings (see boxed text, p117).

Jockey Club of Peru (Map pp82-3; ☎ 610-3000; www.jcp.org.pe; Hipódromo de Monterrico) Located at the junction of the Panamericana Sur and Av Javier Prado, the horse track has races three to four days a week.

SHOPPING

Clothing, jewelry and handicrafts from all over Peru can generally be found in Lima. Shop prices tend to be high, but those with less capital can haggle their hearts out at the craft markets. Shopping hours are generally 10am to 8pm Monday to Saturday, with variable lunchtime hours. Credit cards and traveler's checks can be used at some spots, but you'll need photo identification.

Quality pisco can be bought duty-free at the airport just prior to departure (see boxed text, p60).

Handicrafts

Small shops selling crafts dot the major tourist areas around Pasaje de los Escribanos in Central Lima, and near the intersection of Ernesto Diez Canseco and La Paz in Miraflores. To buy crafts directly from artisans, see the Ichimay Wari collective in Lurín (p122).

Mercado Indio (Map p98; Av Petit Thouars 5245, Miraflores) The best place to find everything from pre-Columbian–style clay pottery to alpaca rugs to knock-offs of Cuzco School canvases. Prices vary; shop around.

Feria Artesanal (Map pp82-3; Av de la Marina, Pueblo Libre) Slightly cheaper is this crafts market in Pueblo Libre.

Centro Comercial El Suche (Map p98; Av La Paz, Miraflores) A shady passageway with a jumble of handicrafts, antiques and jewelry stores.

Agua y Tierra (Map p98; ☎ 444-6980; Ernesto Diez Canseco 298, Miraflores; ☺ 10am-2pm & 2:30-6pm Mon-Sat) A tidy shop that specializes in crafts from the Shipibo, Aguaruna and Asháninka cultures from the Amazon.

Dédalo (Map p100; ☎ 477-0562; Sáenz Peña 295, Barranco) A vintage *casona* houses this contemporary crafts store with a lovely cafe.

La Casa de la Mujer Artesana Manuela Ramos (Map pp82-3; ☎ 423-8840; www.casadelamujerartesana.com; Av Juan Pablo Fernandini 1550, Pueblo Libre; ☺ 11am-1pm & 2-6pm Mon-Fri), at *cuadra* 15 of Av Brasil, is a crafts cooperative whose proceeds support women's economic development programs.

A number of Miraflores boutiques sell high-quality, contemporary alpaca knits, among them:

Alpaca 111 (Map p98; ☎ 241-3484; LarcoMar, Malecón de la Reserva 610, Miraflores)

La Casa de la Alpaca (Map p98; ☎ 447-6271; Av La Paz 665, Miraflores)

La Casa de la Llama (Map p98; ☎ 242-1177, ext 113; LarcoMar, Malecón de la Reserva 610, Miraflores)

Local Markets

Both of these places get crowded; watch your wallet.

Mercado Central (Map pp88-9; cnr Ayacucho & Ucayali, Central Lima) From fresh fish to blue jeans, you can buy almost anything at this crowded market close to the Barrio Chino.

Need a socket wrench, a suitcase and a T-shirt of Jesus Christ wearing an Alianza Lima soccer jersey? Then Polvos Azules (Map pp88–9) is the place for you. This multi-level, popular market attracts people of all social strata for a mind-boggling assortment of cheap goods.

Shopping Malls

In San Isidro, Conquistadores street (Map p96) is cluttered with high-end boutiques. For the full-blown Peruvian mall-rat experience, try these two popular spots.

Jockey Plaza (Map pp82-3; Av Javier Prado Este 4200, Monterrico) A huge, relentlessly upscale mall bursting with department stores, boutiques, movie theaters and a food court.

LarcoMar (Map p98; Malecón de la Reserva 610, Miraflores) A well-to-do outdoor mall wedged into the clifftop beneath the Parque Salazar, full of high-end clothing shops, trendy discotheques and a wide range of eateries.

Camping Equipment

These shops sell specialized clothing, backpacks and a variety of other gear:

Alpamayo (Map p98; ☎ 445-1671; 2nd fl, Av José Larco 345, Miraflores)

Tatoo Adventure Gear (Map p98; ☎ 242-1938; www.tatoo.ws; LarcoMar, Malecón de la Reserva 610, Miraflores)

Todo Camping (Map p98; ☎ 242-1318; Angamos Oeste 350, Miraflores) Sells fuel stoves and climbing equipment.

Electronics

You'll find rechargeable and lithium batteries, as well as computer parts, supplies and replacements at **CompuPalace** (Map p98; Av Petit Thouars 5358, Miraflores), a block-long electronics arcade.

GETTING THERE & AWAY

Air

Lima's **Aeropuerto Internacional Jorge Chávez** (code LIM; Map pp82-3; ☎ 517-3100; www.lap.com.pe; Callao) is stocked with the usual facilities: public phones, snack bars, restaurants, sundry stores, a pisco boutique (see boxed text, p60), a post office and a place to store luggage (see p84). Internet access is available on the 2nd floor. For information on international flights, see p530.

The principal domestic destinations from Lima are Arequipa, Ayacucho, Cajamarca, Chiclayo, Cuzco, Iquitos, Juliaca, Piura, Pucallpa, Puerto Maldonado, Tacna, Tarapoto, Trujillo and Tumbes. You can get flight information, buy tickets and reconfirm flights online or via telephone, but for ticket changes or problems, it is best to go to the airline office in person.

For general information on air travel in Peru, see p535. The international departure tax is US$31; the domestic tax is about US$6.

The following are the Lima offices of current domestic operators:

LAN (Map p98; ☎ 213-8200; www.lan.com; Av José Pardo 513, Miraflores) LAN goes to Arequipa, Chiclayo, Cuzco, Iquitos, Juliaca, Piura, Puerto Maldonado, Tacna, Tarapoto and Trujillo. Additionally it offers link services between Arequipa and Cuzco, Arequipa and Juliaca, Arequipa and Tacna, Cuzco and Juliaca, and Cuzco and Puerto Maldonado.

LC Busre (Map pp82-3; ☎ 619-1313; www.lcbusre.com.pe; Los Tulipanes 218, Lince) Flies to Andahuaylas, Ayacucho, Cajamarca, Huancayo, Huánuco, Huaraz, Iquitos, Pucallpa and Tarapoto on smaller turbo-prop aircraft.

Star Perú (Map p98; ☎ 705-9000; www.starperu.com; Espinar 331, Miraflores) Flies to Ayacucho, Cajamarca,

Cuzco, Iquitos, Pucallpa, Puerto Maldonado, Talara and Tarapoto; with link service between Tarapoto and Iquitos.

TACA (Map p98; ☎ 511-8222; www.taca.com; Av José Pardo 811, Miraflores) Flies to Cuzco.

Bus

There is no central bus terminal; each company operates its ticketing and departure points independently. Some companies have several terminals, so always clarify from which point a bus leaves when buying tickets. The busiest times of year are Semana Santa (Easter week) and the weeks surrounding Fiestas Patrias (July 28 to 29), when thousands of *limeños* make a dash out of the city and fares double. At these times, book well ahead.

Some stations are in rough neighborhoods. If possible, buy your tickets in advance and take a taxi when carrying luggage.

There are an infinite number of bus companies. These are the most reliable:

Civa (Map pp88-9; ☎ 418-1111; www.civa.com.pe; cnr 28 de Julio & Paseo de la República 575, Central Lima) For Arequipa, Cajamarca, Chachapoyas, Chiclayo, Cuzco, Ilo, Máncora, Nazca, Piura, Puno, Tacna, Tarapoto, Trujillo and Tumbes. The company also runs a more luxurious sleeper line to various coastal destinations called Excluciva (www.excluciva.com).

Cruz del Sur (☎ 311-5050; www.cruzdelsur.com.pe) Central Lima (Map pp88-9; ☎ 431-5125; Quilca 531); La Victoria (Map pp82-3; ☎ 225-5748, 903-4149; Av Javier Prado Este 1109) One of the biggest companies, serving the coast – as well as inland cities such as Arequipa, Cuzco, Huancayo and Huaraz – with three different classes of service: the cheaper Ideal, and the more luxurious Imperial and Cruzero. The more expensive services usually depart from La Victoria.

Movil Tours (Map pp88-9; ☎ 332-9000, 716-8000; www.moviltours.com.pe; Paseo de la República 749, Central Lima) For Chachapoyas, Chiclayo, Huancayo, Huaraz and Tarapoto.

Oltursa (Map pp82-3; ☎ 708-5000, 225-4495; Av Aramburu 1160, Limatambo) A short distance from San Isidro lies the main terminal for this very reputable company, which travels to Arequipa, Chiclayo, Ica, Máncora, Nazca, Paracas, Piura, Trujillo and Tumbes.

Ormeño (☎ 472-1710; www.grupo-ormeno.com.pe) Central Lima (Map pp88-9; Carlos Zavala Loayza 177); La Victoria (Map pp82-3; Av Javier Prado Este 1059) A huge Lima bus company offering daily service to Arequipa, Ayacucho, Cajamarca, Cañete, Chincha, Cuzco, Huaraz, Ica, Ilo, Nazca, Paracas, Piura, Puno, Tacna, Trujillo and Tumbes, all of which leave from the terminal in La Victoria. It has three classes of service: Econo, Business and Royal. The Central Lima terminal is for buying tickets or arranging transport on

one of the smaller subsidiaries: Expreso Continental (northern Peru), Expreso Chinchano (south coast and Arequipa) and San Cristóbal (Puno and Cuzco).

Soyuz PerúBús (Map pp88-9; ☎ 226-1515; www.perubus.com.pe; Carlos Zavala Loayza 221, Central Lima) Frequent buses to Cañete, Chincha, Ica and Nazca.

Tepsa (☎ 202-3535; www.tepsa.com.pe) Central Lima (Map pp88-9; ☎ 427-5642, 428-4635; Paseo de la República 151-A, Central Lima); Javier Prado (Map pp82-3; ☎ 202-3535; Av Javier Prado Este 1091) Comfortable buses that travel to Arequipa, Cajamarca, Chiclayo, Cuzco, Ica, Lambayeque, Máncora, Nazca, Piura, Tacna, Trujillo and Tumbes.

Destination	Cost* (soles)	Duration (hrs)
Arequipa	46/79	14-16
Ayacucho	50/70	10
Cajamarca	87/117	13
Chiclayo	41/84	12
Cuzco	143/173	30
Huancayo	39/56	7
Huaraz	58/78	8
Ica	46/64	4½
Nazca	66/86	8
Piura	98/138	14
Puno	85	21
Tacna	113/153	18
Trujillo	34/54	9
Tumbes	110/150	18
* prices are general estimates for normal/luxury buses		

Car

Lima has major intersections without stoplights, kamikaze bus drivers, spectacular traffic jams and little to no parking. If you still dare to get behind the wheel, the following companies have 24-hour desks at the airport. Prices range from about US$50 to US$130 per day, not including surcharges, insurance and taxes (of about 19%). Delivery is possible.

Budget (☎ 442-8706; www.budgetperu.com)
Dollar (☎ 444-3050; www.dollar.com)
Hertz (☎ 447-2129; www.hertz.com.pe)
National (☎ 575-1111; www.nationalcar.com.pe)

Train

The **Ferrocarril Central Andino** (☎ 226-6363; www.ferrocarrilcentral.com.pe) railway line runs from Estación Desamparados in Lima inland to Huancayo, climbing from sea level to 4829m – the second-highest point for passenger trains in the world – before descending to Huancayo at 3260m. There is no regular passenger service, but the train makes the journey a couple of times a month as a tourist attraction – a 12-hour odyssey along Andean mountainscapes and vertigo-inducing bridges. The round-trip costs S125 to S300. Check the schedule in advance since the rail lines aren't always operational. Tickets can be purchased through Teleticket (see boxed text, p117).

GETTING AROUND
To/From the Airport

As you come out of customs, inside the airport to the right is the official taxi service: **Taxi Green** (☎ 484-4001; taxigreen.com.pe; Aeropuerto Internacional Jorge Chávez; 1-3 people to Central Lima, San Isidro, Miraflores & Barranco S45). Outside the airport perimeter itself, you will find 'local' taxis. Taking these does not always save you money and safety is an issue – local hustlers use this as an opportunity to pick up foreign travelers and rob them. It is best to use the official airport taxis, or arrange pickup with your hotel.

The cheapest way to get to and from the airport is via the *combi* company known as **'La S'** (per person S2-3) – a giant letter 'S' is pasted to the front windshields – which runs various routes from the port of Callao (where the airport is located) to Miraflores and beyond. From the airport, these can be found heading south along Av Elmer Faucett. For the return trip to the airport, La S *combis* can be found traveling north along Av Petit Thouars and east along Av Angamos in Miraflores. The most central spot to find these is at the *paradero* (bus stop) on Av Petit Thouars, just north of Av Ricardo Palma (Map p98). Expect to be charged additional fares for any seats that your bags may occupy. *Combi* companies change their routes regularly, so ask around before heading out.

In a private taxi, allow at least an hour to the airport from San Isidro, Miraflores or Barranco; by *combi,* expect the journey to take at least two hours – with *plenty* of stops in between. Traffic is lightest before 6:30am.

Bus

Though it is a major urban center, Lima has long functioned without a citywide public transportation system. This should be rectified by 2010, when a trans-Lima electric bus system is supposed to debut. Even so, the system will initially consist of just a single north–south route, which means that the current haphazard network of small private buses (called *combis* and *micros*) will remain vital.

To be sure, the system is mind-boggling: traffic-clogging caravans of minivans hurtle down the avenues with a *cobrador* (ticket taker) hanging out the door and shouting out the stops. Routes change frequently, so go by the destination placards taped to the windshield, rather than the street names painted on the side of the bus. Your best bet is to know the nearest major intersection or landmark close to your stop (eg Parque Kennedy) and tell that to the *cobrador* – he'll let you know whether you've got the right bus. *Combis* are generally slow and crowded, but startlingly cheap: fares run from S1 to S3, depending on the length of your journey.

The most useful routes link Central Lima with Miraflores along Av Arequipa or Paseo de la República. Minibuses along Garcilaso de la Vega (also called Av Wilson) and Av Arequipa are labeled 'Todo Arequipa' or 'Larco/Schell/Miraflores' when heading to Miraflores and, likewise, 'Todo Arequipa' and 'Wilson/Tacna' when leaving Miraflores for central Lima. Catch these buses along Av José Larco or Av Arequipa in Miraflores.

To get to Barranco, look for buses along Av Arequipa labeled 'Chorrillos/Huaylas/Metro' (some will also have signs that say 'Barranco'). You can also find these on the Diagonal, just west of the Parque Kennedy, in Miraflores.

Taxi

Lima's taxis don't have meters, so negotiate a price with the driver before getting in. Fares will vary depending on the length of the journey, traffic conditions, time of day and how well dressed you look. Plan for paying extra for registered taxis and any taxi you hail outside a tourist attraction. As a (very) rough guide, a trip from Central Lima to Miraflores costs around S12, while Central Lima to the airport will run about S20. Fares from Miraflores to the airport generally start at about S40. You can haggle the price – though this is often harder during rush hour. If there are two or more of you be clear on whether the fare is per person or for the car.

The majority of taxis in Lima are unregistered (unofficial); indeed, surveys have indicated that no less than one vehicle in seven here is a taxi. During the day, it is generally not a problem to use either. However, at night it is generally safer to use registered taxis, which have a rectangular authorization sticker with the word SETAME on the upper left corner of the windshield. Registered taxis also usually have a yellow paint job and a license number painted on the sides.

Registered taxis can be called by phone or found at taxi stands, such as the one outside the Sheraton in Central Lima or outside the LarcoMar shopping mall in Miraflores. Registered taxis cost about 30% to 50% more than regular street taxis and can be hired on a per-hour basis.

The following companies all work 24 hours and accept advance reservations:

Moli Taxi (☎ 479-0030)
Taxi América (☎ 165-1960)
Taxi Lima (☎ 271-1763)
Taxi Móvil (☎ 422-6890)
Taxi Real (☎ 470-6263; www.taxireal.com)
Recommended.
Taxi Seguro (☎ 241-9292)

AROUND LIMA

PACHACAMAC
☎ 01

Situated about 31km southeast of the city center, the archaeological complex of **Pachacamac** (☎ 430-0168; http://pachacamac.perucultural .org.pe; admission S6; ☼ 9am-5pm Mon-Fri) is a pre-Columbian citadel made up of adobe and stone palaces and temple pyramids. If you've been to Machu Picchu, it may not look like much, but this was an important Inca site and a major city when the Spanish arrived. It began as a ceremonial center for the Lima culture beginning at about AD 100, and was later expanded by the Waris before being taken over by the Ichsma. The Incas added numerous other structures upon their arrival to the area in 1450. The name Pachacamac, which can be variously translated as 'He who Animated the World' or 'He who Created Land and Time,' comes from the Wari god, whose wooden, two-faced image can be seen in the on-site **museum**.

Most of the buildings are now little more than piles of rubble that dot the desert landscape, but some of the main temples have been excavated and their ramps and stepped sides revealed. You can climb the switchback trail to the top of the **Templo del Sol** (Temple of the Sun), which on clear days offers excellent views of the coast. The most remarkable structure on-site, however, is the Palacio de las Mamacuna (House of the Chosen Women), commonly referred to as the **Acllahuasi**, which boasts a series of Inca-style trapezoidal doorways. Unfortunately, a major earthquake in 2007 has left the structure highly unstable and, as a result, visitors can only admire it from a distance. (Because of the extensive damage – and because there have been no funds available for repair – the World Monuments Fund added Pachacamac to its 2010 Watch List of the planet's most endangered sites.)

There is a visitors center and cafe at the site entrance, which is on the road to Lurín. A simple map can be obtained from the ticket office, and a track leads from here into the complex. Those on foot should allow at least two hours to explore. (In summer, take water and a hat – there is no shade to speak of once you hit the trail.) Those with a vehicle can drive from site to site.

Various agencies in Lima (see p102) offer guided tours (about US$38) that include round-trip transport and a guide. Alternatively, catch a minibus signed 'Pachacamac' from the sunken roadway at the corner of Andahuaylas and Grau in Central Lima (Map pp88–9; S2, 45 minutes); minibuses leave every 15 minutes during daylight hours. From Miraflores, take a taxi to the intersection of Angamos and the Panamericana, also known as the Puente Primavera (Map pp82–3), then take the bus signed 'Pachacamac/Lurín' (S1 to S2, 30 minutes). For both services, tell the driver to let you off near the *ruinas* (ruins) or you'll end up at Pachacamac village, about 1km beyond the entrance. To get back to Lima, flag down any bus outside the gate but expect to stand. You can also hire a taxi per hour (from S20) from Lima.

LURÍN
☎ 01

At the southern edge of Lurín, a working-class enclave that lies 50km south of Central Lima on the Panamericana, are the studios belonging to the crafts collective **Ichimay Wari** (☎ 430-3674; www.ichimaywari.com; Jr Jorge Chávez, Manzana 22, Lote A; ☼ 8am-1pm & 2-5pm Mon-Fri). The group consists of more than a dozen artisans from Ayacucho (p317) who produce traditional *retablos*, pottery, Andean-style Christmas decorations and the colorful clay trees known as *arbolitos de la vida* (trees of life). The central shop is small, but the pieces are well crafted and the prices are a bargain. The best bet, however, is to make an appointment 24 hours in advance to tour individual studios and meet the artisans.

To get here by car, take the Antigua Panamericana (old Pan-American Hwy) south to Km 39 and then turn inland to the Barrio Artesano (the turn-off is marked with a sign). By bus, from the Puente Primavera (Map pp82–3) take any bus headed to Lurín, San Bartolo or San Miguel. Get off at the main stoplight in Lurín. From there, hail a *mototaxi* (motorcycle taxi) and ask them to take you south to the Barrio Artesano. The cost will be S1 to S2. A taxi from Lima will cost S30 to S50.

Parts of Lurín can get rough; take taxis and keep cameras stowed.

SOUTHERN BEACHES
☎ 01

Every summer, *limeños* make a beeline for the beaches clustered along the Panamericana to the south. The exodus peaks on weekends, when, occasionally, the road is so congested that it becomes temporarily one way. The principal beach towns include El Silencio, Señoritas, Caballeros, Punta Hermosa, Punta Negra, San Bartolo, Santa María, Naplo and Pucusana. Don't expect tropical resorts; this stretch of barren, coastal desert is lapped by cold water and strong currents. Inquire locally before swimming as drownings occur annually.

Popular with families is **San Bartolo**, which is cluttered with hostels at budget to midrange rates during the busy summer. Sitting above the bay is **Hostal 110** (☎ 430-7559; www.hostal110.com; Malecón San Martín Nte 110; d S130-180, additional person S30; 🖳), which has 14 simple, yet very spacious, tiled rooms and apartments – some of which sleep up to six – staggered over a swimming pool on the cliffside. On the far southern edge of town (take a *mototaxi*), facing the soccer field, the recommended **Restaurant Rocío** (☎ 430-8184; www.restaurant-rocio.com; Urb Villa Mercedes, Mz A, Lte 5-6; mains S15-35; 🕙 11am-11pm) serves fresh fish grilled, fried and bathed in garlic.

Further south, **Punta Hermosa**, with its relentless waves, is *the* surfer spot. The town has plenty of accommodations. A good choice is the compact **Punta Hermosa Surf Inn** (☎ 230-7732; www.puntahermosasurfinn.com; Bolognesi 407, cnr Pacasmayo; dm/s/d with breakfast US$15/20/40; 🖳) which has six rooms, a cozy hangout area with hammocks and cable TV. The largest wave in Peru is found nearby: **Pico Alto** (at Panamericana Km 43), which can reach a height of 10m.

Punta Rocas, a little further south, is also popular with experienced surfers (annual competitions are held here), who generally crash at the basic **Hostal Hamacas** (☎ 231-5498, 99-985-4766; hamacasperu@gmail.com; Panamericana Km 47; r per person US$10-20), right on the beach. Owner Carlos Zevallos is a surfer and he has 15 rooms and five bungalows (which sleep six), all with private bathrooms, hot water and ocean views. There is an on-site restaurant during the high season (October to April). He also rents boards. Generally, however, surfboard rental is almost nonexistent; best to bring your own.

To get to these beaches, take a bus signed 'San Bartolo' from the Panamericana Sur at the Puente Primavera in Lima (Map pp82–3). You can get off at any of the beach towns along the route, but in many cases it will be a 1km to 2km hike down to the beach. (Local taxis are usually waiting by the road.) A one-way taxi from Lima starts at about S45.

For beaches to the south, such as Pucusana, see p126.

CARRETERA CENTRAL
The Carretera Central (Central Hwy) heads directly east from Lima, following the Rímac valley into the foothills of the Andes and on to La Oroya in Peru's central highlands.

Minibuses to Chosica leave frequently from Arica at the Plaza Bolognesi (Map pp88–9). These can be used to travel to Puruchuco (S1 to S2, 50 minutes), Cajamarquilla (S1 to S2, 1¼ hours) and Chosica (S2 to S3, two hours).

Colectivo taxis also make the journey from the corner of Arequipa and Av Javier Prado in San Isidro for S8 (see Map p96). Recognizing sites from the road can be difficult, so let the driver know where you want to get off.

Puruchuco
☎ 01

The site of **Puruchuco** (☎ 494-2641; http://museo puruchuco.perucultural.org.pe; admission S5; 🕙 9am-4pm Tue-Sun) hit the news in 2002 when about 2000 well-preserved mummy bundles were unearthed from the enormous Inca cemetery. It's one of the biggest finds of its kind, and the multitude of grave goods included a number of well preserved *quipu* (knotted ropes that the Inca used as a system of record-keeping). The site has a highly reconstructed chief's house, with one room identified as a guinea-pig ranch. Situated amid the shantytown of Túpac Amaru, Puruchuco is 13km from Central Lima. (It is best to take a taxi.) A signpost on the highway marks the turn-off, and from here it is several hundred meters along a road to the right.

Cajamarquilla

☎ 01

Another pre-Columbian site, **Cajamarquilla** (admission S5; ⊗ 9am-4pm) is a crumbling adobe city that was built up by the Wari culture (AD 700–1100) on the site of a settlement originally developed by the Lima culture. A road to the left from Lima at about Km 10 (18km from Central Lima) goes to the Cajamarquilla zinc refinery, almost 5km from the highway. The ruins are located about halfway along the refinery road; you take a turn to the right along a short road. There are signs, but ask the locals for the *zona arqueológica* if you have trouble finding them.

Chosica

☎ 01

About 40km from Lima lies the rustic mountain town of Chosica, which sits at 860m above sea level, above the fog line. In the early half of the 20th century, it was a popular weekend getaway spot for *limeños* intent on soaking up sun in winter. Today its popularity has declined, though some visitors still arrive for day trips. The plaza is lined with restaurants and in the evenings *anticucho* vendors gather along some of the fountain-lined promenades. From Chosica, a minor road leads to the ruins of **Marcahuasi** (see p300).

South Coast

Peru's southern coastal desert is refreshed by palm-fringed oases and spanned by a ribbon of pavement, the Carr Panamericana (Pan-American Hwy), which runs along the coast from Ecuador to Chile. It's the best overland route to Arequipa, Lake Titicaca and of course, Cuzco. Yes, you guessed it: this is the start of Peru's well-beaten Gringo Trail.

But the south coast holds far more depth and diversity than the kilometer upon kilometer of arid desert and coastline viewed from a bus window. These lowlands gave birth to some extraordinary pre-Columbian civilizations, especially the Nazca – remembered for their cryptic lines etched across 500 sq km of desolate land – and the Paracas Necropolis culture, whose burial sites still lie in the sands. Spanish haciendas became the birthplace of Afro-Peruvian music and dance, whose untamed protest strains live on, especially around Chincha.

That said, it's also the wildness of the territory that brings travelers here today. Pacific beaches issue a siren's call to surfers, while river runners (white water rafters) get their feet wet in Lunahuaná. Pisco recently endured a disastrous earthquake, but remains a worthwhile destination for its marine wildlife and rugged coast. Ica is surrounded by vineyards and the monstrous sand dunes of Huacachina. Closer to Chile, bird-watchers flock to the coastal lagoons of Mejía.

Peru's south coast is an ideal place to let your wanderlust run wild. Just jump off your bus along Carr Panamericana wherever some dusty track catches your eye; you'll always find something quirky or interesting at the end of these desert roads.

HIGHLIGHTS

- Enjoying the thrill of a swooping flight over the world-famous **Nazca Lines** (p142)
- Paying a visit to flocks of lounging sea lions, Humboldt penguins and Peruvian pelicans on the **Islas Ballestas** (p130)
- Flying down giant dunes on a sandboard or dune buggy at the desert oasis of **Huacachina** (p140)
- Shimmying to Afro-Peruvian beats in **El Carmen** (p128), outside Chincha
- Rafting first-class rapids and stomping wine grapes in **Lunahuaná** (p127)

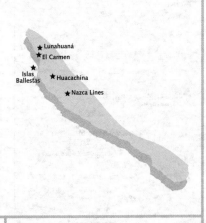

- BIGGEST CITY: TACNA, POPULATION 262,700
- AVERAGE TEMPERATURE: January 23°C to 30°C, July 10°C to 20°C

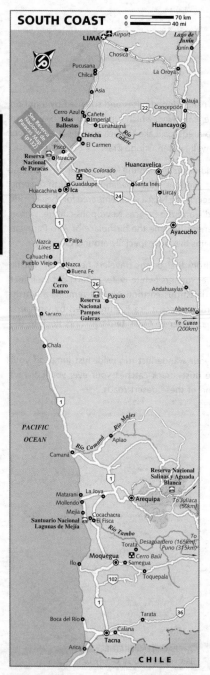

SOUTH COAST

0 ——— 70 km
0 ——— 40 mi

PUCUSANA
☎ 01 / pop 10,000

This small fishing village, 65km south of Lima, is a popular locals' beach resort from January to April. The small Pucusana and Las Ninfas beaches are on the town's seafront and at low tide you can wade to La Isla, an offshore island with a strand of sand. The most exclusive beach in the area is Naplo, 1km away and reached through a tunnel. If you're interested in fishing or bird-watching, boats can be hired (from S30) at the marina, which is two blocks from the main plaza.

South of Pucusana, off Km 64 along Carr Panamericana Sur, is the turnoff to the village of **Chilca**, famed for its muddy and mineral-rich **lagoons** (admission S1; ☽ 24hr), one of which is nicknamed La Milagrosa (the Miracle). The bathing pools allegedly have power to heal everything from infertility to acne – and some believers credit this to intervention by aliens in UFOs. A *mototaxi* (three-wheeled motor-cycle rickshaw taxi) from Carr Panamericana Sur to the pools costs about S5 each way.

The best of the simple hotels in Pucusana, **El Mirador de Pucusana** (☎ 430-9278; s/d/tr S30/40/55) has a breathtaking location atop the bayfront with fantastic views. Rooms are basic, but do have hot water. It's a great place to savor the scenery as you sip on a pisco sour in its **restaurant** (mains S5-10). Try to distinguish the various shapes (including a pig's head) that locals claim can be seen in the surrounding hillsides. If you're hankering for fresh seafood, you'll find it in the *cevicherías* (restaurants serving ceviche) that line the boardwalk below.

From central Lima, *combis* (minibuses) run frequently to Pucusana from Plaza Bolognesi (S5 one-way). Another alternative is to take a taxi from Lima to the Puente Primavera bridge at the intersection of Av Primavera and Carr Panamericana Sur. Most southbound coastal buses along Carr Panamericana Sur can drop you off at Km 57, from where frequent minibuses shuttle during daylight hours to central Pucusana (S1, 10 minutes).

For beaches closer to Lima, see p123.

ASIA
☎ 01 / 4000

During the coastal summer, which lasts from January through March, Km 97 on Car Panamericana Sur is home to a sprawling out-door shopping mall and a dozen electric clubs that make up part of the beach resort called

Asia. Beyond the commercial center lie the resort's private, white-sand beaches where many of Lima's elite have constructed rows upon rows of low-lying, white-washed abodes. This summer escape for the affluent has sprung up, literally, in the middle of nowhere – where DJs can happily crank up the volume with a clear conscience. However, it firmly shuts its doors from April until December, when all the hottest action migrates back to the capital city. For cheap eats in the area, try any of the small stands selling *chicharrón* (deep-fried pork) that line Carr Panamericana Sur; a *chicharrón* and fried sweet-potato sandwich is a surefire cure for that post-*discoteca* hangover.

Almost any bus along Carr Panamericana Sur can drop you here upon request. Most *limeños* (inhabitants of Lima) party all night, then retreat to their private homes or catch a bus back next morning, but there are some basic guesthouses on the main boulevard that are quite expensive due to their central location. Otherwise, you can flag down any southbound bus or hire a taxi to reach the beach at Cerro Azul, which has more appealing lodgings.

CAÑETE & CERRO AZUL
☎ 01 / pop 37,000

The full name of this small market town, about 145km south of Lima, is San Vicente de Cañete. Most Peruvian holidaymakers head north of town to Cerro Azul, a beach that's popular with experienced surfers. It's a 15-minute walk west of Km 131 on Carr Panamericana Sur, about 15km north of town. There's also a small Inca sea fort in the area, known as **Huarco**, but it's in poor state.

In Cerro Azul, the surfer-friendly **Hostal Cerro Azul** (☎ 271-1302, 9-763-1969; www.cerroazulhostal .com; Puerto Viejo 106; d/tr/q/ste S150/185/200/220) is less than 100m from the shoreline. **Hostal Las Palmeras** (☎ 284-6005; Puerto Viejo; d S195; 🖳) has a gorgeous location looking onto the beach and the pier. On the main commercial strip just back from the beach, **Casa Hospedaje Los Delfines** (Comercio 723; d/tr S50/60) is an immaculately kept, family-run guesthouse with cold water only. If you're hungry, beachfront restaurants all serve fresh seafood. **Restaurant Juanito** (☎ 335-3710; Rivera del Mar; mains S20-25; 🕑 8am-9pm) is a popular local pick.

From Lima, buses for Pisco or Ica can drop you at Cañete and sometimes Cerro Azul (S5, 2½ hours). Buses back to Lima are invariably crowded, especially on Sunday from January to April. There are also *combis* between Cañete and Cerro Azul (S1, 30 minutes) or south to Chincha (S2, one hour).

LUNAHUANÁ
☎ 01 / pop 3600 / elev 1700m

Detouring inland from Cañete, a curvy road slopes through the steep-walled Río Cañete Valley and after 38km reaches the pastoral village of Lunahuaná, which offers great opportunities for river running and kayaking. Lunahuaná is also the gateway to one of Peru's coastal wine areas, with several bodegas (wineries, wine shops and cellars) proffering free samples year-round. The best time to show up is during the second week of March for the wine harvest, **Fiesta de la Vendimia**. An **adventure-sports festival** is usually held in late February or early March.

Sights

A rustic bodega producing both wines and piscos, venerable **La Reyna de Lunahuaná** (☎ 99-477-7117; catapalla1@yahoo.es; admission & tours free; 🕑 6am-6pm) presides over the main plaza in **Catapalla**, about 6km east of Lunahuaná. The owners here can teach you the ABCs of pisco (Peruvian grape brandy) and wine production. A one-way taxi ride costs from S6, but you may have to wait until a car shows up for the return. Closer to town, **Bodega Los Reyes** (☎ 284-1206; 🕑 8am-8pm) is also generous in its measures. It still allows visitors to get their feet wet – literally – treading grapes the traditional way during the months of February and March.

Nearby archaeological sites in the Cañete Valley include **Incawasi**, the rough-walled ruins of the military headquarters of the 10th Inca king Túpac Yupanqui, located on the western outskirts of Lunahuaná; and the small pre-Inca fort of **Ungara**, situated closer to Imperial. Either site can be visited by taxi (Incawasi round-trip S10; Ungara round-trip S30), though there's really not much left to see.

Activities

River running can be done year-round, but the best months are from December to April, the rainy months in the Andes when the Río Cañete runs high. Adventure-sport championships, including river running, are held here in late February. River running can be done as part of a day tour from Lima, for which most agencies charge around US$80 per person, but costs considerably less if you organize it in Lunahuaná; **Río Cañete Expediciones** (☎ 284-1271; www.riocanete.com.pe) requires a minimum of four people, and trips that last between 40 minutes and two hours cost between S35 and S80 – most of the year they're suitable for beginners. The tour company is based at **Camping San Jerónimo** (☎ 996-353-921; Km 33 Carr Cañete-Lunahuaná), which also has a rock-climbing wall.

If you'd like to **cycle** out to visit some bodegas, basic mountain bikes can be rented from many storefronts near the plaza and along Av Grau.

Sleeping & Eating

There are several private campgrounds spread out along the river outside town.

Camping San Jerónimo (☎ 284-1271; Km 33 Carr Cañete-Lunahuaná; per person S15) This campground borders the river at the far west of town. Base camp for Río Cañete Expediciones, it has good facilities and a free artificial rock-climbing wall for guests.

Hostal Casuarinas (☎ 284-1045; Av Grau 295; s/d S30/60) A couple of blocks from the plaza in the direction of the main road, this secure budget hotel has tidy rooms with TVs and hot showers.

Hotel Campestre Embassy (☎ 472-2370; www.hotelesembassy.com; Km 39 Carr Cañete-Lunahuaná; s/d/tr from S73/85/122; 🏊) This upscale hotel farther east of town has a restaurant and a disco. The most expensive rooms have breezy balconies overlooking the river. The minimum stay is two nights during the high season.

Hostal Río Alto (☎ 284-1125; www.rioaltohotel.com; Km 39 Carr Cañete-Lunahuaná; s/d S91/147; 🏊) About 1km along the highway east of Lunahuaná, this friendly guesthouse looks down to the river from a shady terrace overrun with plants. Rooms, though plain, are modern and have hot showers.

Refugio de Santiago (☎ 436-2717; www.refugiodesantiago.com; Km 31 Carr Cañete-Lunahuaná; r per person incl breakfast S150) This renovated colonial home a few kilometers west of Lunahuaná is the ultimate relaxing getaway. Rooms are rustic but elegant and the grounds feature a fragrant botanical garden and a restaurant that serves tasty local specialties (mains from S23).

Several local seafood restaurants are found around the main plaza and along Av Grau; the local specialty is crawfish.

Getting There & Away

From Cañete, catch a *combi* to Imperial (S0.80, 10 minutes), from where *combis* also run to Lunahuaná (S3.50, 45 minutes). Faster *colectivos* (shared taxis) wait for passengers on the main road, just downhill from the plaza in Lunahuaná, and then race back to Imperial (S4, 25 minutes).

CHINCHA

☎ 056 / pop 194,000

The sprawling town of Chincha is the next landmark, some 55km south of Cañete, at Km 202 along Carr Panamericana Sur. Once a Spanish colonial stronghold, today it's the beating heart of Afro-Peruvian culture, and it makes an interesting stopover to catch a vibrant music-and-dance performance or visit nearby archaeological sights.

Orientation & Information

The main plaza is a long walk inland from Carr Panamericana Sur, so take a taxi (S5). Banks with international ATMs line Benavides west of the plaza heading toward the market area. Internet cafes are all around the plaza.

Sights

There's not much to see in the city center, but the outlying sites are fascinating.

EL CARMEN DISTRICT

Chincha is famous for the vibrant Afro-Peruvian music heard in the *peñas* (bars and clubs featuring live folkloric music) of the El Carmen district, about 15km outside town. The best times to visit are during the cultural festival of **Verano Negro** (late February/early March), **Fiestas Patrias** (National Independence, in late July) and **La Virgen del Carmen de Chincha** (the festival in honor of the patron Virgin, on December 27). During these times, minibuses run from Chincha to El Carmen all night long, and the *peñas* are full of frenzied *limeños* and locals dancing. One traditional dance not to try at home: 'El Alcatraz,' when a gyrating male dancer with a candle attempts to set fire to a handkerchief attached to the back of his partner's skirt.

ARCHAEOLOGICAL SITES

In ancient times, the small Chincha empire long flourished in this region until it was clobbered by the Incas in the late 15th century. The best surviving archaeological sites in the

SOUTH COAST

AFRO-PERUVIAN MUSIC & DANCE

The mesmerizing beats and lightning-speed movements of this traditional art form are guaranteed to make you want to get up and dance. During the colonial period, when Spanish colonizers banned the use of drums, African slaves working on Peruvian plantations began using hollow wooden crates (now called a *cajón*) and donkey jawbones to create percussion that now forms the base of this distinct musical style. Often music is accompanied by an impressive flamenco-style dance called *zapateo* and impassioned singing.

Over the past few decades, groups such as Perú Negro and the Ballumbrosio family have garnered quite a following both nationally and internationally, making it their mission to preserve Peru's African heritage through the performance of its music and dance. If you're in the right place at the right time, you can catch one of these shows in the community that is famous for it, El Carmen (opposite).

---

area are **Tambo de Mora**, on the coast about 10km from Chincha, and the temple of **La Centinela** northwest of the city, about 8km off Carr Panamericana Sur. Both can be visited by taxi (about S15 one-way).

Sleeping & Eating

Bare-bones cheap hotels and *chifas* (Chinese restaurants) surround Chincha's main plaza. Most fill up and double or triple their prices during festivals, though you can always avoid this problem by dancing all night and taking an early morning bus back to Lima or further south along the coast.

Hostal La Posada (☎ 26-2042; Santo Domingo 200; s/d S32/40) Run by a gregarious Italian-Peruvian couple, this simple guesthouse is one of the most secure choices in the city center, just a stone's throw from the main plaza. The rooms are antique-looking, but decently kept. Ask for one facing away from the street.

El Sausal (☎ 26-2451, in Lima 01-222-0155; www.sausal.com.pe; Carr Panamericana Sur Km 197.5; d/tr S165/230; 🖥 🐘) A surprisingly plush spot to kick back, right on Carr Panamericana Sur, this hotel has a spacious country-club feel with a big swimming pool, sun loungers, lush gardens, a billiards room and alas, a karaoke bar.

In El Carmen, a few local families will take in overnight guests and cook meals for between S10 and S20 per person per night – just ask around. Or you can stay in the town's only hotel, the **Parador Turístico** (☎ 27-4060; Plaza de Armas; s/d S25/40).

Getting There & Around

There are many companies based on Carr Panamericana Sur with buses running through Chincha en route between Lima (S12, 2½ hours) and Ica (S10, two hours). If you're

headed to Pisco, most southbound buses can drop you off at the San Clemente turnoff on Carr Panamericana Sur (S4), from where you can catch frequent *colectivos* and *combis* for the 6km trip into Pisco (S3). From Chincha, *combis* headed north to Cañete (S2, one hour) and south to Paracas (S3, one hour) leave from near Plazuela Bolognesi.

Combis to El Carmen (S2, 30 minutes) leave from Chincha's central market area, a few blocks from the main plaza.

The plaza is a short taxi ride (S4) from Carr Panamericana Sur where the coastal buses stop.

PISCO & PARACAS
☎ 056 / pop 58,200

An important port lying 235km south of Lima, Pisco and the nearby town of Paracas are generally used as bases to see the abundant wildlife of the Islas Ballestas. Pisco also shares its name with the national beverage, a brandy that is made throughout the region. The area is of historical and archaeological interest, having hosted one of the most highly developed pre-Inca civilizations – the Paracas culture from 700 BC until AD 400 (p133). Later it acted as a base for Peru's revolutionary fever in the 1800s.

On August 15, 2007, the region was rocked by a devastating earthquake that lasted for three minutes and registered a whopping 8.0 on the Richter scale. The quake resulted in more than 500 deaths and toppled many of the colonial structures near the city's centre that had long lent the city its charm and beauty – including the grand San Clemente Cathedral that was located right on the Plaza de Armas. Long after the international relief groups have packed up and left, the city is still

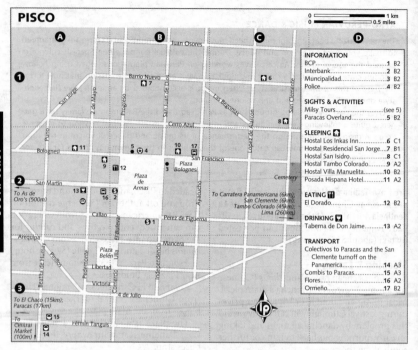

PISCO

struggling to resurrect itself from the rubble. Thousands remain without permanent homes; the murmurs you will hear on street corners and in cafes are that corruption and bureaucracy have prevented international aid money from getting into the hands of those who need it most.

Orientation & Information

Although the Pisco–Paracas area is spread out, it's easy to get around. Public transportation between Pisco and the harbor at Paracas, 15km further south along the coast, leaves from Pisco's market area or the main plaza in the El Chaco beach area of Paracas.

There's no tourist office in Pisco, but travel agencies (see p133), the *municipalidad* (town hall; Map p130) on the main plaza and **police** (Map p130; ☎ 53-2884; San Francisco 132; ⏰ 24hr) help when they can. Everything else you'll need is found around the Plaza de Armas, including internet cafes. **BCP** (Map p130; Perez de Figueroa 162) has a Visa/MasterCard ATM and changes US dollars and traveler's checks. **Interbank** (Map p130; San Martín 101) has a 24-hour global ATM.

Dangers & Annoyances

Never walk alone at night. Central Pisco is fairly safe, but the market and nearby beaches should be avoided after dark and visited only in a group during the day. Muggings at gunpoint are not unheard of, even on busy pedestrian streets, so always take a taxi after sunset. Be wary of taxi drivers at the turnoff on Carr Panamericana Sur who try to sell you on a particular hotel or agency – they are probably working for a commission and as such cannot be trusted to provide accurate information.

Sights & Activities

While the town of Pisco was once a showcase for pretty colonial architecture and monuments to the revolution, after the 2007 earthquake few of these colonial structures were left standing. At the same time, by walking its dusty streets you will witness how a powerful natural disaster can convert a bustling city to a ghost town overnight.

ISLAS BALLESTAS

Although grandiosely nicknamed the 'poor man's Galapagos,' the Islas Ballestas make for a memorable excursion. The only way to get there is on a boat tour, offered by many tour agencies (p133). While the tours do not actually disembark onto the islands, they do get you startlingly close to an impressive variety of wildlife. None of the small boats have a cabin, so dress to protect against the wind, spray and sun. The sea can get rough, so sufferers of motion sickness should take medication before boarding. Wear a hat (cheap ones are sold at the harbor), as it's not unusual to receive a direct hit of guano (droppings) from the seabirds.

On the outward boat journey, which takes about 1½ hours, you can't miss the famous three-pronged **Candelabra geoglyph** (Map p132), a giant figure etched into the sandy hills, which is more than 150m high and 50m wide. No one knows exactly who made the glyph, or when, or what it signifies, but theories abound. Some connect it to the Nazca Lines, while others propound that it served as a navigational guide for ancient sailors and was based on the constellation of the Southern Cross. Some even believe it to have been inspired by a local cactus species with hallucinogenic properties.

An hour is spent cruising around the islands' arches and caves and watching large herds of noisy sea lions sprawl on the rocks. The most common guano-producing birds in this area are the guanay cormorant, the Peruvian booby and the Peruvian pelican, seen in colonies several thousand strong. You'll also see cormorants, Humboldt penguins and, if you're lucky, dolphins. Although you can get close enough to the wildlife for a good look, some species, especially the penguins, are more visible with binoculars.

Back on shore, you can grab a bite to eat at one of the many waterfront restaurants near the dock in El Chaco, or you can continue on a tour of the Reserva Nacional de Paracas. The community of El Chaco is generally a more inviting place to enjoy being oceanside than Pisco; if sleeping in Pisco you can always catch a return *colectivo* later in the day.

RESERVA NACIONAL DE PARACAS

This vast desert reserve occupies most of the Península de Paracas. For tour operators, see p133. Alternatively, taxi drivers who function as guides often wait beyond the dock where passengers disembark in Paracas' beach village of El Chaco, and can take groups into the reserve for around S50 for a three-hour tour. You can also walk from El Chaco – just make sure to allow lots of time, and bring food and plenty of water. To get there, start at the **obelisk** (Map p132) commemorating the landing of the liberator General José de San Martín that lies near the entrance to El Chaco village, and continue on foot along the tarmac road that heads to the south.

About 3km south is a park-entry point, where a S5 entrance fee is charged. Another 2km beyond the entrance is the **park visitor center** (🕘 7am-6pm), which has kid-friendly exhibits on conservation and ecology. The museum next door was closed at the time of research due to earthquake damage; most tours now substitute more time inside the park instead. The bay in front of the complex is the best spot to view Chilean flamingos, and there's now a walkway down to a **mirador** (lookout; Map p132), from where these birds can best be spotted from June through August. Try not to step outside the designated route as this can interfere with the flamingos' food supply.

A few hundred meters behind the visitor complex are the 5000-year-old remains of the **Paracas Necropolis**, a late site of the Paracas

SOUTH COAST

DROPPINGS TO DIE FOR

Layers of sun-baked, nitrogen-rich guano (seabird droppings) have been diligently deposited over millennia on the Islas Ballestas and Península de Paracas by large resident bird colonies – in places, the guano is as much as 50m deep. Guano's recognition as a first-class fertilizer dates back to pre-Inca times, but few would have predicted that these filthy riches were to become Peru's principal export during the mid-19th century, when guano was shipped in vast quantities to Europe and America. In fact, the trade was so lucrative that Spain precipitated the so-called Guano War of 1865–66 over possession of the nearby Chincha Islands. Nowadays, overexploitation and synthetic fertilizers have taken their toll and the birds are largely left to their steady production process in peace, except for licensed extraction every three years – and boatloads of day-trippers, of course.

RESERVA NACIONAL DE PARACAS

SIGHTS & ACTIVITIES	
Candelabra Geoglyph..............**1** B2	
Clifftop Lookout......................**2** B3	
La Mina Beach.......................**3** B3	
Mirador.................................**4** B3	
Obelisk.................................**5** B3	
Paracas Explorer...................(see 11)	
Paracas Necropolis................**6** B3	
Park Visitor Center................**7** B3	

SLEEPING	
Hostal Refugio del Pirata......(see 11)	
Hostal Santa Maria...............(see 11)	
Hotel El Condor.....................**8** B3	
Hotel El Mirador....................**9** C2	
Hotel Libertador Paracas......**10** B3	
Muca House.........................**11** B3	
Posada del Emancipador.......**12** B3	

EATING	
El Chorito.............................(see 11)	
Juan Pablo...........................(see 11)	

TRANSPORT	
Boats to Islas Ballestas..........**13** B3	
Cruz del Sur.........................(see 8)	
Oltursa................................**14** B3	

culture, which predated the Incas by more than a thousand years. A stash of more than 400 funerary bundles was found here, each wrapped in many layers of colorful woven shrouds for which the Paracas culture is famous. There's little to see now though. Lima's Museo Larco (p95) and Ica's Museo Regional de Ica (p136) exhibit some of these exquisite textiles and other finds from the site.

Beyond the visitor complex, the tarmac road continues around the peninsula to Puerto General San Martín, which has a smelly fishmeal plant and a port on the northern tip of the peninsula. Forget this road and head out on the dirt road that branches off a few hundred meters beyond the museum. After about 6km it reaches the tiny village of **Lagunillas**, a fishing outpost that was devastated when a tsunami swept the peninsula after the 2007 earthquake. A few restaurants are back in business cooking up their daily catch for passing tourists. If visiting without a guide, it's sometimes possible to catch a ride back to town, squeezed in alongside the fresh fish. From the village, the road continues a few kilometers to a parking area near a **clifftop lookout** (Map p132), which has grand views of the ocean, with a sea-lion colony on the rocks below and plenty of seabirds gliding by.

Other seashore life around the reserve includes flotillas of jellyfish (swimmers beware!), some of which reach about 70cm in diameter with trailing stinging tentacles of 1m. They are often washed up on the shore, where they quickly dry to form mandala-like patterns on the sand. Beachcombers can also find sea hares, ghost crabs and seashells along the shoreline, and the Andean condor occasionally descends to the coast in search of rich pickings.

Camping is allowed inside the reserve. Recommended spots to pitch tents include the beach near Lagunillas, which lies within reach of public restrooms, or on **La Mina Beach** (Map p132), a short drive or walk south of Lagunillas. Plan to bring all the water you will need, and never camp alone as violent robberies have been reported. To really explore, the entire peninsula is covered by topographic map 28-K, which can be purchased at the South American Explorers Club (p86) or the Instituto Geográfico Nacional (IGN; p521) in Lima.

TAMBO COLORADO

This early Inca lowland **outpost** (off Map p132; admission S8.50; ☺ dawn-dusk), about 45km northeast of Pisco, was named for the red paint that once completely covered its adobe walls. It's one of the best-preserved sites on the south coast and is thought to have served as an administrative base and control point for passing traffic, mostly conquered peoples.

From Pisco, it takes about an hour to get there by car. Hire a taxi for half a day (S50) or take a tour from Pisco (S60, two-person minimum, see right). A *combi* through the village of Humay passes Tambo Colorado 20 minutes beyond the village; it leaves from the Pisco market early in the morning (S8, three hours). Once there, ask the locals about

when to expect a return bus, but you could get really stuck out there, as transportation back to Pisco is infrequent and often full.

Tours & Guides

Prices and service for tours of Islas Ballestas and Reserva Nacional de Paracas are usually very similar. The better tours are escorted by a qualified naturalist who speaks Spanish and English. Most island boat tours leave daily around 8am and cost around S35 per person, but do not include a S1 dock fee. The number of tours and departure times varies, so it is recommended to reserve a day in advance. Less-than-interesting afternoon land tours of the Península de Paracas (S25) briefly stop at the national reserve's visitor center, breeze

---

THE PARACAS CULTURE

Little is known about the early Paracas culture, Paracas Antiguo, except that it was influenced by the Chavín Horizon, an early artistic and religious historical period (see p31). Most of our knowledge is about the middle and later Paracas cultures, which existed from about 700 BC to AD 400. This is divided into two periods known as Paracas Cavernas and Paracas Necropolis, named after the main burial sites discovered.

Paracas Cavernas is the middle period (700 BC to AD 200) and is characterized by communal bottle-shaped tombs dug into the ground at the bottom of a vertical shaft, often to a depth of 6m or more. Several dozen bodies of varying ages and both sexes (possibly family groups) were buried in some of these tombs. They were wrapped in relatively coarse cloth and accompanied by funereal offerings of bone and clay musical instruments, decorated gourds and well-made ceramics.

Paracas Necropolis (AD 1 to 400) is the site that yielded the treasure of exquisite textiles for which the Paracas culture is now known. This burial site can still be seen, despite the cover of drifting sands on the north side of Cerro Colorado, on the isthmus joining the Península de Paracas with the mainland.

The Necropolis consisted of a roughly rectangular walled enclosure in which more than 400 funerary bundles were found. Each contained an older mummified man (who was probably a nobleman or priest) wrapped in many layers of weavings. It is these textiles that are marveled at by visitors now. The textiles consist of a wool or cotton background embroidered with multicolored and exceptionally detailed small figures. These are repeated again and again, until often the entire weaving is covered by a pattern of embroidered designs. Motifs such as fish and seabirds, reflecting the proximity to the ocean, are popular, as are other zoomorphic and geometric designs.

Our knowledge is vague about what happened in the area during the thousand years after the Paracas culture disintegrated. A short distance to the southeast, the Nazca culture became important for several centuries after the disappearance of the Paracas culture. This in turn gave way to Wari influence from the mountains. After the sudden disappearance of the Wari empire, the area became dominated by the Ica culture, which was similar to and perhaps part of the Chincha empire. They in turn were conquered by the Incas.

About this time, a remarkable settlement was built by the expanding Incas, one that is perhaps the best-preserved early Inca site to be found in the desert lowlands today. This is Tambo Colorado (above), a sight filled with hallmarks of Inca architecture including trapezoid-shaped niches, windows and doorways built from adobe bricks. While not as spectacular as the Inca ruins in the Cuzco area, archaeology enthusiasts will find it worth a visit.

by coastal geological formations and spend a long time having lunch in a remote fishing village. Tours of the reserve can be combined with an Islas Ballestas tour to make a full-day excursion (S60).

Established tour operators:

Milsy Tours (Map p130; ☎ 53-5204; www.milsytours .com; San Francisco 113) Milsy has daily tours to the Islas Ballestas and Reserva Nacional de Paracas with guides who speak English and some French and Italian, too. It occasionally takes groups to Tambo Colorado and will arrange customized trips to Nazca.

Paracas Explorer (Map p132; ☎ 53-1487, 54-5089; www.pparacasexplorer.com; Paracas 9) In the El Chaco village of Paracas, this backpacker travel agency offers the usual island and reserve tours, as well as multiday trips that take you to Ica and Nazca (US$48 to US$175 per person).

Paracas Overland (Map p130; ☎ 53-3855; www .paracasoverland.com.pe; San Francisco 111) Popular with backpackers, this agency offers tours of the Islas Ballestas with its own fleet of boats, as well as to the Reserva Nacional de Paracas and Tambo Colorado. It can also arrange sandboarding trips to nearby dunes.

Sleeping

Pisco's hostels generally offer the best deals, whereas Paracas has recently experienced a frenzy of construction of new luxury hotels.

PISCO

Many hostels will pick you up from the San Clemente turnoff on Carr Panamericana Sur.

Hostal Los Inkas Inn (Map p130; ☎ 53-6634, 54-5149; www.losinkasinn.com; Barrio Nuevo 14; dm/s/d/tr S20/35/60/80; 🖳 🖳) This small, family-owned guesthouse has basic but tidy rooms, all with lock-boxes and fans. Dorms have five beds and bathrooms. There is also a mini-swimming pool and a rooftop terrace with games.

Hostal San Isidro (Map p130; ☎ 53-6471; www.san isidrohostal.com; San Clemente 103; dm/s/d/tr S20/40/60/105; 🖳 🖳) This backpacker inn has a free game room complete with all the toys (pool, table tennis etc). Rooms come with fans, cable TV and hot-water showers, and are situated around an outdoor swimming pool. Guests can use the shared kitchen or take advantage of the restaurant that serves up breakfast for S5 extra as well as snacks throughout the day.

Posada Hispana Hotel (Map p130; ☎ 53-6363; www.posadahispana.com; Bolognesi 236; s/d/tr incl breakfast US$15/25/35; 🖳) With legions of fans, this friendly hostel has attractive bamboo and wooden fittings, a full-service restaurant,

and a terrace for kicking back. Some of the well-worn rooms are musty, though all have fans and cable TV.

Hotel Residencial San Jorge (Map p130; ☎ 53-2885; www.hotelsanjorgeresidencial.com; Barrio Nuevo 133; r incl breakfast US$15-48; 🖳) This recently renovated hotel has a breezy, modern entryway, bright cafe, and back garden with lounge chairs and tables for picnicking. Rooms are spotless, with a splash of tropical color and style, though those in the older wing can be dark and cramped.

Hostal Tambo Colorado (Map p130; ☎ 53-1379; www .hostaltambocolorado.com; Bolognesi 159; s/d/tr S50/60/90; 🖳) This hostel is run by a delightful couple who will instill you with true pride for Pisco – both the town and the beverage! Breakfast from S6 is offered in a sunny outdoor sitting area where guests can also use the communal kitchen.

Hostal Villa Manuelita (Map p130; ☎ 53-5218; www .villamanuelitahostal.com; San Francisco 227; s/d/tr incl breakfast S70/95/125; 🖳) Heavily renovated postearthquake, this hotel still achieves the grandeur of its colonial foundations. Plus, it's conveniently located half a block from the plaza.

PARACAS

If arriving directly to Paracas, most hotels and hostels will pick you up from the bus terminal upon request.

Muca House (Map p132; ☎ 54-5141; mucahouse@ hotmail.com; Plaza de Armas; dm per person incl breakfast S15) Digs truly built for backpackers, Muca House offers rooms of four or six beds each. The grounds are dusty and bathrooms not always kept clean, but guests are allowed kitchen privileges.

Hostal Refugio del Pirata (Map p132; ☎ 54-5054; refugiodelpirata@hotmail.com; Av Paracas 6; s/d/tr incl breakfast S60/70/90; 🖳) Rooms are bland but get the job done, and some have ocean views. The upstairs terrace provides a pleasant setting to sip a pisco sour while watching the sunset. Ask to borrow kitchen facilities.

Hostal Santa Maria (Map p132; ☎ 54-5045; www .santamariahostal.com; Av Paracas s/n; s/d/tr incl breakfast S80/100/120; 🖳) Rooms here are functional and squeaky clean, all with cable TV. Staff are knowledgeable and can help arrange tours, though are sometimes preoccupied with looking after the restaurant next door.

Hotel El Mirador (Map p132; ☎ 54-5086; hotel@ elmiradorhotel.com; Km 20 Carr Paracas; s/d/tr incl breakfast S102/138/178; 🖳 🖳) Hidden in the sand dunes before the entrance to Paracas, El Mirador is a peaceful oasis. With a privileged spot above the bay, many rooms afford ocean views, while others look upon the pool and inner courtyard, and out to the dunes beyond.

Posada del Emancipador (Map p132; ☎ 95-667-2163; www.posadadelemancipador.com; Av Paracas 25; s/d/tr/ste incl breakfast US$50/60/70/130; ◙ ⬜) Perfect for families and large groups, this modern complex has a number of well-maintained rooms as well as bungalows with kitchenettes and balconies that overlook the pool, all with charming decoration and some with ocean views.

Hotel El Cóndor (Map p132; ☎ 53-2818; elcondor@hotelcondor.com; Lote 4, Santo Domingo; s/d/tr incl breakfast US$50/80/90; ◙ ⬜) A tranquil spot to lounge right on the bay. Rooms are a bit generic and look out to either the bay or the garden. It also boasts a full-service restaurant with a fireplace and a cozy common room.

Hotel Libertador Paracas (Map p132; ☎ in Lima 01-518-6500; www.libertador.com.pe; Av Paracas 178; r from US$230; ▨ ◙ ⬜) Formerly the Hotel Paracas, after the 2007 earthquake this hotel was gutted and reopened as part of the opulent Libertador chain. This exclusive resort hotel borders the bay and boasts beautiful grounds, an infinity pool, and fast-boat tours of the Islas Ballestas from its private dock.

Eating & Drinking
PISCO
Only a few cafes in Pisco open early enough for breakfast before an Islas Ballestas tour, so many hotels include breakfast in their rates.

El Dorado (Map p130; ☎ 53-4367; Progreso 171; menús from S9, mains S8-35; ◑ 6:30am-11pm) For breakfasts as well as tasty *menús* (set meals) this restaurant is a hit, and it's located smack dab on the Plaza de Armas.

As de Oro's (off Map p130; ☎ 53-2010; San Martín 472; mains from S15; ◑ noon-midnight Tue-Sun) A few blocks west of the Plaza de Armas, this is another popular option for heaping portions of Peruvian fare.

Taberna de Don Jaime (Map p130; ☎ 53-5023; San Martín 203; ◑ 4pm-2am) This smoky tavern is a favorite with locals and tourists alike. It is also a showcase for artisanal wines and piscos. On weekends, the crowds show up to dance to live Latin and rock tunes into the wee hours.

PARACAS
In the waterfront El Chaco village of Paracas there are loads of look-alike beachfront restaurants serving fresh seafood throughout the day. Unfortunately *motelo* (turtle meat) still winds up on some menus, so please don't encourage the catching of this endangered creature by ordering dishes made with its meat.

Juan Pablo (Map p132; ☎ 79,-6806, 79-7240; Blvd Turístico; mains S15-40; ◑ 7am-9pm) Probably the best of the restaurants with a waterfront view, Juan Pablo is a winner for fresh seafood and offers breakfast for those departing early to the Islas Ballestas.

El Chorito (Map p132; ☎ 54-5045; Paracas s/n; mains S20-30; ◑ noon-9pm) This restaurant is located a few blocks back from the waterfront at the back of the Hostal Santa Maria. It offers mostly seafood specialties, and can accommodate large groups.

Getting There & Around
Pisco is 6km west of Carr Panamericana Sur, and only buses with Pisco as the final destination actually go there. Both **Ormeño** (Map p130; ☎ 53-2764; San Francisco) and **Flores** (Map p130; ☎ 79-6643; San Martín) offer multiple daily departures to Lima (S40, 3½ hours) and other places south, such as Nazca (S35, four hours) and Arequipa (S60, 12 to 15 hours). They may also advertise buses to Cuzco or international destinations, but these will most likely not be direct routes.

Since the 2007 earthquake, a number of services have also added multiple daily buses between Lima and the El Chaco beach district of Paracas (S40 to S55, 3½ hours) before continuing to other destinations south. These include **Cruz del Sur** (☎ 53-6336), which stops at a hotel about 2km outside the center of town; Ormeño, which stops in the plaza of El Chaco and sells tickets through **Paracas Explorer** (☎ 53-1487, 54-5089; www.pparacasexplorer.com; Paracas 9); and **Oltursa** (☎ in Lima 01-708-5000; www.oltursa .com.pe), which stops at the Hilton Doubletree Hotel in Paracas.

If you're not on a direct bus to either Pisco or Paracas, ask to be left at the San Clemente turnoff on Carr Panamericana Sur, where fast and frequent *colectivos* wait to shuttle passengers to central Pisco's Plaza de Armas (S3, 10 minutes) or Paracas (S10, 20 minutes). In the reverse direction, *colectivos* for the San Clemente turnoff leave frequently from near Pisco's central market. After dark, avoid the dangerous market area and take a taxi instead (S5). From the San Clemente turnoff, you can flag down buses, which pass frequently heading either north or south.

SOUTH COAST

A short taxi ride around Pisco costs S3. Transportation from Pisco to Paracas is possible via *combi* (Map p130; S1.50, 30 minutes), or *colectivo* (Map p130; S2.50, 20 minutes), which leave frequently from near Pisco's central market.

ICA

☎ 056 / pop 125,200 / elev 420m

The capital of its department, Ica may have a downtrodden air, but it boasts a thriving wine and pisco industry, with grapes irrigated by the river that shares its name, plus an excellent museum, colonial churches and rowdy annual fiestas. Its slightly elevated position means that it sits above the coastal mist and the climate is dry and sunny.

Information

Tour agencies and internet cafes abound in the area around the Plaza de Armas.

BCP (Plaza de Armas) Has a Visa/MasterCard ATM and changes US dollars and traveler's checks.

DIRCETUR (☎ 21-0332; www.dirceturica.gob.pe; Grau 148) Government-sponsored office of tourism.

Hospital (☎ 23-4798, 23-4450; Cutervo 104; ☽ 24hr) For emergency services.

Interbank (Grau cuadra 2) Has a 24-hour global ATM.

Police (☎ 23-5421; Elías cuadra 5; ☽ 24hr) At the city center's edge.

Serpost (☎ 23-3881; San Martín 156) Southwest of the Plaza de Armas.

Telefónica-Perú (☎ 22-2111; Huánuco 289) Open daily for local, long-distance and international calls.

Dangers & Annoyances

Ica has a richly deserved reputation for theft. Stay alert, particularly around the bus terminals and market areas. Sunday is said to be the prime day for petty crimes against tourists, Peruvians and foreigners alike.

Sights & Activities

MUSEO REGIONAL DE ICA

In suburban San Isidro, don't miss this gem of a **museum** (☎ 23-4383; Ayabaca cuadra 8; admission S11.50, cameras S5; ☽ 8am-7pm Mon-Fri, 9am-6pm Sat & Sun). Despite being robbed in 2004, it still has an impressive collection of artifacts from the Paracas, Nazca and Inca cultures, including superb examples of Paracas weavings, as well as textiles made of feathers. There are beautiful Nazca ceramics, scarily well-preserved mummies of everything from children to a small macaw, trepanned skulls and shrunken trophy heads, enormous wigs and tresses of hair. Out back look for a scale model of the Nazca Lines. Word has it that when the JC Tello Museum in Paracas closed due to earthquake damage most of the artifacts were put in storage here, and may be put on display in coming years.

The museum is 2.5km southwest of the city center. Take a taxi from the Plaza de Armas (S3). You could walk, but it's usually not safe to do so alone, and even larger groups may get hassled.

MUSEO CABRERA PIEDRA

On the Plaza de Armas, this unsigned **museum** (☎ 23-1933; Bolívar 174; ☽ hrs vary, closed Sun) has an oddball collection of thousands of carved stones and boulders graphically depicting diverse pre-Columbian themes, from astronomy to surgical techniques and sexual practices. The eccentric collector, Dr Cabrera, claimed the stones were ancient, though there is local speculation as to whether they may be elaborate fakes.

COLONIAL CHURCHES & MANSIONS

The hulking **Iglesia de San Francisco** (cnr Municipalidad & San Martín) has some fine stained-glass windows. Ica's cathedral, **Iglesia de La Merced** (cnr Bolívar & Libertad), was rebuilt in the late 19th century and contains a finely carved wooden altar, though the effects of the 2007 earthquake are clearly visible in its crumpling steeple. The **Santuario de El Señor de Luren** (Cutervo) boasts an image of the patron saint that is venerated by pilgrims during Semana Santa and again in October (p138). The streets surrounding the Plaza de Armas boast a few impressive Spanish colonial mansions, including along the first block of Libertad.

WINERIES

Local wines and piscos can be bought around Ica's Plaza de Armas, but it's more fun to track them down at their source. Bodegas can be visited year-round, but the best time is during the grape harvest from late February until early April.

Some of Peru's finest wine comes from **Bodega Ocucaje** (☎ 40-8011; www.hotelocucaje.com; Av Principal s/n; admission free; ☽ tastings 9am-noon & 2-5pm Mon-Fri, 9am-noon Sat, tours 11am-3pm Mon-Fri), but unfortunately it's fairly isolated, over 30km south of Ica off Carr Panamericana Sur. Hiring a taxi to reach the winery costs around S30 each way, or you can join a local tour leaving from Ica (see p138).

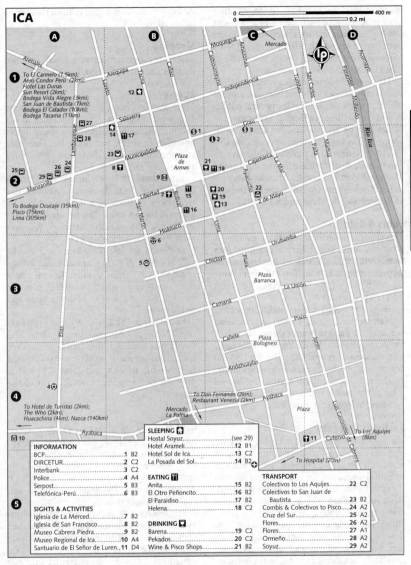

ICA

Another touristy bodega, located less than 10km north of Ica, **Bodega El Catador** (☎ 40-3295; off Carr Panamericana Sur Km 334; ☉ tours & tastings 9:30am-7pm) lets tourists join in a symbolic stomping of the grapes during February and March, and runs free tours and wine and pisco tastings all year. It also has a restaurant that serves local specialties and occasionally has live music. A taxi should cost about S7 each way.

Bodega Vista Alegre (☎ 23-2919; Camino a La Tinguina, Km 2.5; ☉ 8am-noon & 1:45-4:45pm Mon-Fri, 7am-1pm Sat), 3km northeast of Ica in the La Tinguiña district, is the easiest of the large commercial wineries to visit (taxi one-way S5). It's best to go in the morning, as the winery occasionally closes in the afternoon. Another place producing the right stuff is **Bodega Tacama** (☎ 22-8395; www.tacama.com; ☻ 9am-4:30pm), 11km northeast of Ica, which offers interesting tours of its industrial facilities. Again, you'll have to hire a taxi to get here (S15 each way).

The countryside around Ica is also scattered with family-owned artisanal bodegas, most of which welcome visits from the general public. A number of these are located in the suburbs of **San Juan de Bautista** and **Los Aquijes**, both about a 7km taxi (S7 one-way) or *colectivo* (S1.50) ride from Ica's center. *Colectivos* to San Juan de Bautista leave from the corner of Municipalidad and Loreto, whereas *colectivos* to Los Aquijes leave from near the intersection of the streets 2 de Mayo and Ayacucho.

Tours & Guides

Travel agencies around the Plaza de Armas offer city tours and winery excursions. **Aero Condor Perú** (☎ 25-6230; www.aerocondor.com.pe; Hotel Las Dunas Sun Resort, Av La Angostura 400) offers tourist overflights of the Nazca Lines for about US$170 per person.

To gain a unique understanding of secrets hidden in the Ocucaje Desert surrounding Ica, contact **Roberto Penny Cabrera** (☎ 23-7373; http://icaderserttrip.com). A well-known local geologist, Cabrera offers private tours for US$100 per person per day to explore geological formations, discover ancient marine fossils, and take in the desolate desert landscape while camping below the stars.

Festivals & Events

Ica has more than its share of fiestas. February inspires the water-throwing antics typical of any Latin American **carnaval**, plus dancers in beautiful costumes. In early to mid-March, it's time for the famous grape-harvest festival, **Fiesta de la Vendimia**, with all manner of processions, beauty contests, cockfights and horse shows, music and dancing, and of course, free-flowing pisco and wine. Most of the events are reserved for evenings and weekends at the festival site of Campo Feriado, on the outskirts of town, but during the week, the tasting and buying of wine and honey throughout the town dominates. The founding of the city by the Spanish conquistadors on June 17, 1563 is celebrated during **Ica Week**, while **Tourist Week** happens during mid-September. In late October, the religious pilgrimage of **El Señor de Luren** culminates in fireworks and a tra-

ditional procession of the faithful that keeps going all night.

Sleeping

Beware that hotels fill up and double or triple their prices during the many festivals.

BUDGET

Most travelers head for Huacachina, about 4km west of the city. If you get stuck in Ica overnight, dozens of depressing, cheap hotels line the side streets east of the bus terminals and north of the Plaza de Armas, particularly along Calle Tacna.

Hotel Arameli (☎ 23-9107; Tacna 239; s/d/tr S30/40/60) Close to the Plaza de Armas, Arameli has two floors of basic rooms with cable TVs and reliable hot water. But be advised that if you're not a fan of firm mattresses, you may want to hit the sack elsewhere.

La Posada del Sol (☎ 23-8446; Loreto 193-239; s/d/tr S30/60/80; ▯) This newer hotel boasts some smart design details. Rooms meet your needs and service is cordial, plus the location is convenient to both the plaza and bus stations.

Hostal Soyuz (☎ 22-4743; Manzanilla 130; s/d/tr S40/50/70/85; ☒) Sitting directly over the Soyuz bus terminal, this handy option for late arrivals or early departures has carpeted rooms with air-con and cable TV, but is only for heavy sleepers on account of the rumpus below.

MIDRANGE

Hotel Sol de Ica (☎ 23-6168; www.hotelsoldeica.com; Lima 265; s/d/tr incl buffet breakfast S90/120/170; ▯ ☒) This dazzlingly white, three-story central hotel gives personalized service. Remarkably small rooms have unusual wood paneling, TVs and phones. The hotel has a sauna and two swimming pools.

El Carmelo (☎ 23-2191; www.elcarmelohotel hacienda.com; Carr Panamericana Sur Km 301; s/d/tr/q from US$30/50/60/70; ▯ ☒) This romantic roadside hotel on the outskirts of town inhabits a delightful 200-year-old hacienda that has undeniable rustic charm. There's a good restaurant plus a winery on-site. Take a taxi from the city center (S3).

TOP END

Hotel Las Dunas Sun Resort (☎ 25-6224; www .lasdunashotel.com; Av La Angostura 400; s/d/tr from S249/296/615; ▯ ☒) By far the most luxurious hotel in town, the sprawling Las Dunas resort boasts a swimming pool, sauna, tennis courts, mini-golf course, business center, restaurants and bars. Various excursions are offered (for an additional fee), including cycling, horseback riding, sandboarding and winery tours. Service can be haphazard, however. The resort is located off Carr Panamericana Sur Km 300.

Eating

Don Fernando (☎ 21-5792; San Martín 1202; sandwiches & snacks S5-22) Located across from Restaurante Venezia in the suburb of San Isidro, this bakery and cafe offers innovative sandwich and snack options with the freshest ingredients.

El Paraidiso (☎ 22-8303; Loreto 178; menús S6; ⊙ 8am-8pm Sun-Fri) Serves filling vegetarian meals for small change, as well as other plates featuring meat alternatives.

El Otro Peñoncito (☎ 23-3921; Bolívar 225; mains S9-26; ⊙ 8am-midnight Mon-Fri) Ica's most historic and characterful restaurant serves a varied menu of Peruvian and international fare that includes plenty of options for vegetarians. The formal bartenders here shake a mean pisco sour, too.

Anita (☎ 21-8582; Libertad 135; menús from S12, mains S15-36; ⊙ 8am-midnight) Right smack on the Plaza de Armas, this elegant cafe dishes up heaping plates of regional Peruvian specialties, plus lip-smacking desserts.

Restaurant Venezia (☎ 21-0372; San Martín 1229; mains S12-29; ⊙ lunch & dinner Tue-Sun) In a new location about 2.5km south of the town center, Venezia is a popular family-run Italian restaurant. Allow plenty of time, as all plates are made fresh upon ordering.

Several shops in the streets east of the plaza sell *tejas* (caramel-wrapped candies flavored with fruits, nuts etc) including **Helena** (☎ 22-1844; Cajamarca 139).

Drinking

There's not much happening in Ica outside of fiesta times, though nearby Huacachina has some friendly watering holes. On Ica's Plaza de Armas, you'll find several wine and pisco tasting rooms to pop into for a quick tipple. South of the plaza along Lima, local bars and clubs advertise live music, DJs and dancing. Two of the least seedy options include **Pekados** (Lima 225) and **Barena** (Lima s/n). The craziest late-night disco, called the Who, is situated on the north side of the **Hotel de Turistas** (Av de Los Maestros 500), 3km southwest of the plaza; it's a S3 taxi ride.

Getting There & Away

Ica is a main destination for buses along Carr Panamericana Sur, so it's easy to get to/from Lima or Nazca. Most of the bus companies are clustered in a high-crime area at the west end of Salaverry, and also Manzanilla west of Lambayeque.

For Lima (S20 to S55, 4½ hours), **Soyuz** (☎ 23-3312; Manzanilla 130) and **Flores** (☎ 21-2266; Manzanilla s/n) have departures every 15 minutes, while luxury services go a few times daily with **Cruz del Sur** (☎ 22-3333; Lambayeque 140) and **Ormeño** (☎ 21-5600; Lambayeque s/n). Many companies have daytime buses to Nazca (S10 to S35, 2½ hours), while services to Arequipa (S46 to S70, 12 hours) are mostly overnight.

To reach Pisco (S5 to S15, 1½ to two hours), Ormeño is the only major bus company that has direct buses from Ica. Both Cruz del Sur and Ormeño also have services into Paracas. Other bus companies drop passengers at the San Clemente turnoff on Carr Panamericana Sur, about 6km east of Pisco, where a variety of *colectivos* and minivans wait to shuttle passengers into town (S3, 10 minutes). Some faster, but slightly more expensive *colectivos* and *combis* heading for Pisco and Nazca leave when full from near the intersection of Lambayeque and Municipalidad in Ica.

Ormeño as well as some small companies may serve destinations around Peru's central highlands, such as Ayacucho (S40, eight hours) and Huancavelica. Check the ever-changing schedules and fares in person at bus company offices.

HUACACHINA

☎ 056 / pop 200

Just 5km west of Ica, this tiny oasis surrounded by towering sand dunes nestles next to a picturesque (if smelly) lagoon that is featured on the back of Peru's S50 note. Graceful palm trees, exotic flowers and attractive antique buildings testify to the bygone glamour of this resort, which was once a playground for Peruvian elite. These days, it's totally ruled by party-seeking crowds of international backpackers.

Dangers & Annoyances

Though safer than Ica, Huacachina is not a place to be lax about your personal safety or to forget to look after your property. Many guesthouses have well-deserved reputations for ripping off travelers and also harassing

---

TOP FIVE CHILL-OUT SPOTS ALONG PERU'S GRINGO TRAIL

Lunahuaná (p127) Floating by rural vineyards on the Río Cañete, plus eating as much crawfish as you can manage.

Huacachina (below) Sandboarding down gigantic dunes all day long, then partying by the oasis till the break of dawn.

Cabanaconde (p191) Trekking into one of the world's deepest canyons and watching condors soar above.

Isla del Sol y de la Luna (p217) Border-hopping to Bolivia on the shores of aquamarine Lake Titicaca.

Sacred Valley (p258) Leaving behind the Machu Picchu crowds and exploring quaint indigenous towns, lively markets and more untrammeled Inca ruins.

---

young women with sexual advances. Check out all of your options carefully before accepting a room, and never pay for more than a night in advance in case you need to quickly change lodgings. Also, the few small stores around the lake offer plenty of souvenirs but are often out of the basics; come prepared!

Activities

The lagoon's murky waters supposedly have curative properties, though you may find **swimming** in the hotel pools more inviting.

You can rent sandboards for S5 an hour to **slide**, **surf** or **ski** your way down the irresistible dunes, getting sand lodged into bodily nooks and crannies. Though softer, warmer and safer than snowboarding, don't be lulled into a false sense of security – several people have seriously injured themselves losing control of their sandboards. Many hotels offer thrill-rides in **areneros** (dune buggies). They then stop at the top of the soft slopes, from where you can sandboard down and be picked up at the bottom. We've received reports that some drivers take unnecessary risks, so ask around before choosing an operator. Make sure cameras are well protected, as sand can be damaging. The going rate for tours at the time of research was S45, but ask first if sandboard rental is included and how long the tour lasts. Tours do not include a fee of S3.60 that must be paid upon entering the dunes.

It is worth noting that seemingly nobody in Huacachina is worried about the possible effect that hordes of tourists and gas-guzzling

vehicles could be having on the natural environment of the dunes. It is disconcerting to be in the middle of the desert and see plastic bottles and candy wrappers left by careless sandboarders; do your part to not leave waste, and don't hesitate to raise the question of environmental degradation with hotels and tour operators.

Sleeping & Eating

Hostal Rocha (☎ 22-2256; kikerocha@hotmail.com; camping per person S5; 🏊) This hostel next to the chapel Ica allows folks to pitch tents on the grassy back lawn and enjoy bathroom, pool and kitchen access.

Hostal Salvatierra (☎ 23-6132; Malecón de Huacachina s/n; r per person with cold-water shower from S15, per person with hot water S20; 🏊) This budget guesthouse features corridor after corridor of spacious, bare-bones rooms right off the lagoon. The staff are very friendly, and maintain a low-key atmosphere. Guests also have the privilege of a free paddle-boat ride in the lagoon.

Casa de Arena (☎ 21-5274, 23-7398; www.casa-de-arena.com; Balneario de Huacachina; r per person with/without bathroom S40/30; 🏊 💻) The atmosphere at this perennially popular place is that of a constant pool party. The place is recently under new administration after having acquired a bad rap in the past. A bar in back stays open late into the night and options for tours and organized activities abound.

El Huacanicero Hotel (☎ 21-7435; www.elhuacachinero .com; Perotti s/n; dm/s/d/tr incl breakfast S30/100/110/140; 🏊 🏊) A step up from other nearby backpackers' haunts, this hotel has a tranquil outdoor pool area and restaurant that is open all day. Rooms are modern and well outfitted. There is also a 24-hour global ATM here.

Carola del Sur Lodge (☎ 21-5439; Perotti s/n; s/d/tr S45/60/75; 🏊 💻) The Carola del Sur is complete with a poolside bar, and ample green space occupied by hammocks and a roaming turtle. Rooms are simple but secure. The on-premise pizzeria serves varied plates as well as tasty cocktails, and is open late.

Hostería Suiza (☎ 23-8762; www.hostesuiza.5u .com; Balneario de Huacachina; s/d/tr/q incl breakfast S95/155/198/245; 🏊) At the far end of the road beside the oasis, this is a tranquil alternative: no pumping bars here, just an elegant, characterful building and a restful garden. The service is a bit stuffy, but the peace and quiet is priceless. Dutch, French, Italian and English are spoken.

Hotel Mossone (☎ 21-3630; reservas@dematours
hoteles.com; s/d/tr/ste from S186/235/265/292; ✖ ☎ ☐)
The resort's original grand hotel has simple
yet stylish rooms carefully arranged around
an almost Mediterranean-style courtyard. All
rooms have hot showers and TVs. There's
also an upscale restaurant with a convivial
waterfront bar. Walk-in guests can score big
discounts in the low season.

Most hotels have a cafe of sorts and there are a
few touristy restaurants near the waterfront.

Getting There & Away

The only way to get to Huacachina from Ica
is by taxi (S5 one-way).

PALPA

☎ 056 / pop 7200 / elev 300m

From Ica, Carr Panamericana Sur heads
southeast through the small oasis of Palpa,
famous for its orange groves. Like Nazca,
Palpa is surrounded by perplexing **geoglyphs**
in the pampa (large, flat area). The best way
to see these lines is on a combined overflight
from Nazca (p143). Spanish-speaking guides
at the **municipalidad** (☎ 40-4488) may be able to
take you around local archaeological sites with
advance notice.

NAZCA & AROUND

☎ 056 / pop 57,500 / elev 590m

As Carr Panamericana Sur rises through
coastal mountains and stretches across the
arid flats to Nazca, you'd be forgiven for
thinking that this desolate pampa holds little of interest. And indeed this sun-bleached
expanse was largely ignored by the outside
world until 1939, when North American scientist Paul Kosok flew across the desert and
noticed a series of extensive lines and figures
etched below, which he initially took to be an
elaborate pre-Inca irrigation system. In fact,
what he had stumbled across was one of ancient Peru's most impressive and enigmatic
achievements: the world-famous Nazca Lines.
Today the small town of Nazca is continually
inundated by travelers who show up to marvel and scratch their heads over the purpose
of these mysterious lines, which were declared
a Unesco World Heritage Site in 1994.

History

In 1901 archaeologist Max Uhle was the first
to realize that the drifting desert sands hid
remnants of a Nazca culture distinct from

other coastal peoples. Thousands of ceramics
have since been uncovered, mostly by careless *huaqueros* (grave robbers) who plundered
burial sites and sold off their finds to individuals and museums. Archaeologists pieced
together the story of this unique culture from
its highly distinctive ceramics: brightly colored
and naturalistic early pottery (AD 200 to 500),
the stylized and sophisticated designs charac-
terizing the late period (AD 500 to 700), and
also the simpler designs of the terminal period
(AD 700 to 800), influenced by the conquering Wari. Invaluable tools for unraveling
Peru's ancient past, the ceramics depict everything from everyday plants and animals to
fetishes and divinities; some even echo the
Nazca Lines themselves. Even the most heed-
less observer will soon learn to recognize the
strikingly different Nazca ceramics, some of
which can be seen in the local archaeological
museum and at the Museo Regional de Ica
(p136), though the best collections are stashed
away at museums in Lima.

Orientation & Information

All buses arrive and depart near the *óvalo*
(main roundabout) at the west end of town.
From there, it's about a 15-minute walk east
to the Plaza de Armas. Internet cafes are on
every other street. A few international tourist hotels will exchange US dollars or cash
traveler's checks, but it's nearly impossible
to get euros exchanged here.
BCP (Lima 495) Has a Visa/MasterCard ATM and changes
US dollars and traveler's checks.
Casa Andina (Bolognesi 367) Has a global ATM.
DIRCETUR (Parque Bolognesi, 3rd fl) Government-
sponsored tourist information office; can recommend local
tour operators.
Hospital (☎ 52-2586; Callao s/n; ☽ 24hr) For emergency services.
Post office (Castillo 379) Two blocks west of the Plaza
de Armas.
Telefónica-Perú (Lima 525) Stays open late for local,
long-distance and international calls.

Dangers & Annoyances

The town of Nazca is generally safe for travelers, though be wary when walking at night near
either bridge to the south of town. Travelers arriving by bus will be met by persistent *jaladores*
(agents) trying to sell tours or take arriving
passengers to hotels. These touts may use the
names of places listed here but are never to
be trusted. Never hand over any money until

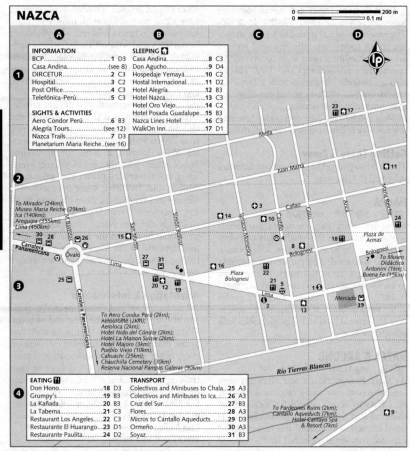

NAZCA

INFORMATION	
BCP	**1** D3
Casa Andina	(see 8)
DIRCETUR	**2** C3
Hospital	**3** C2
Post Office	**4** C3
Telefónica-Perú	**5** C3

SIGHTS & ACTIVITIES	
Aero Condor Perú	**6** B3
Alegría Tours	(see 12)
Nazca Trails	**7** D3
Planetarium Maria Reiche	(see 16)

SLEEPING	
Casa Andina	**8** C3
Don Agucho	**9** D4
Hospedaje Yemayá	**10** C2
Hostal Internacional	**11** D2
Hotel Alegría	**12** B3
Hotel Nazca	**13** C3
Hotel Oro Viejo	**14** C2
Hotel Posada Guadalupe	**15** B3
Nazca Lines Hotel	**16** C3
WalkOn Inn	**17** D1

EATING	
Don Hono	**18** D3
Grumpy's	**19** B3
La Kañada	**20** B3
La Taberna	**21** C3
Restaurant Los Angeles	**22** C3
Restaurante El Huarango	**23** D1
Restaurante Paulita	**24** D2

TRANSPORT	
Colectivos and Minibuses to Chala	**25** A3
Colectivos and Minibuses to Ica	**26** A3
Cruz del Sur	**27** B3
Flores	**28** A3
Micros to Cantallo Aqueducts	**29** D3
Ormeño	**30** A3
Soyaz	**31** B3

To Mirador (24km); Museo Maria Reiche (29km); Ica (140km); Arequipa (355km); Lima (450km)

To Aero Condor Perú (2km); Aeródrome (2km); Aeroloca (2km); Hotel Nido del Cóndor (2km); Hotel La Maison Suisse (2km); Hotel Majoro (3km); Pueblo Viejo (10km); Cahuachi (25km); Chauchilla Cemetery (30km); Reserva Nacional Pampas Galeras (90km)

To Pardeones Ruins (2km); Cantallo Aqueducts (7km); Hotel Cantayo Spa & Resort (7km)

To Museo Didáctico Antonini (1km); Buena Fe (15km)

Río Tierras Blancas

you can personally talk to the hotel or tour-company owner and get a confirmed itinerary in writing. It's best to go with a reliable agency for land tours of the surrounding area, as a few violent assaults and robberies of foreign tourists have been reported recently.

Sights

NAZCA LINES

The best-known lines are found in the desert 20km north of Nazca, and by far the best way to appreciate them is to get a bird's-eye view from a *sobrevuelo* (overflight).

Mirador

You'll get only a sketchy idea of the Lines at the **mirador** (observation tower; admission S1) on Carr Panamericana Sur 20km north of Nazca, which has an oblique view of three figures: the lizard, tree and hands (or frog, depending on your point of view). It's also a lesson in the damage to which the Lines are vulnerable: Carr Panamericana Sur runs smack through the tail of the lizard, which from nearby seems all but obliterated. Signs warning of landmines are a reminder that walking on the Lines is strictly forbidden. It irreparably damages them, and besides, you can't see anything at ground level. To get to the observation tower from Nazca, catch any bus or *colectivo* northbound along Carr Panamericana Sur (S1.50, 30 minutes). Some tours (from S50 per person, p145) also combine a trip to the Mirador with visits to another natural viewpoint and the Maria Reiche Museum.

Museo Maria Reiche

When Maria Reiche, the German mathematician and long-term researcher of the Nazca Lines, died in 1998, her house, which stands another 5km north along Carr Panamericana Sur, was made into a small **museum** (Museo de Sitio; admission S5; ☺ 9am-6pm). Though disappointingly scant on information, you can see where she lived, amid the clutter of her tools and obsessive sketches, and pay your respects to her tomb. Though the sun can be punishing, it's

possible to walk here from the mirador in a sweaty hour or so, or passing *colectivos* can sometimes take you (S1). To return to Nazca, just ask the guard to help you flag down any southbound bus or *colectivo*. A visit to the museum can also be arranged as part of a tour to the nearby *mirador*.

Overflights

Flights over the Lines are taken in light aircraft (three to nine seats) in the morning and early afternoon. The optimal time is usually between 7:30am and 10am, when the sun is low, though flights are at the mercy of the

THE NAZCA LINES: ANCIENT MYSTERIES IN THE SAND

Spread across an incredible 500 sq km of arid, rock-strewn plain in the Pampa Colorada (Red Plain), the Nazca Lines (opposite) remain one of the world's great archaeological mysteries. Consisting of more than 800 straight lines, 300 geometric figures (geoglyphs) and, concentrated in a relatively small area, some 70 spectacular animal and plant drawings (biomorphs), the Lines are almost imperceptible at ground level. It's only when viewed from above that they form their striking network of enormous stylized figures and channels, many of which radiate from a central axis. The figures are mostly etched out in single continuous lines, while the encompassing geoglyphs form perfect triangles, rectangles or straight lines running for several kilometers across the desert.

The lines were made by the simple process of removing the dark sun-baked stones from the surface of the desert and piling them up on either side of the lines, thus exposing the lighter, powdery gypsum-laden soil below. The most elaborate designs represent animals, including a 180m-long lizard, a monkey with an extravagantly curled tail, and a condor with a 130m wingspan. There's also a hummingbird, a spider and an intriguing owl-headed person on a hillside, popularly referred to as an astronaut because of its goldfish-bowl-shaped head, though some are of the opinion that it's a priest with a mystical owl's head.

Endless questions remain. Who constructed the Lines and why? And how did they know what they were doing when the Lines can only be properly appreciated from the air? Maria Reiche (1903–98), a German mathematician and long-time researcher of the Lines, theorized that they were made by the Paracas and Nazca cultures between 900 BC and AD 600, with some additions by the Wari settlers from the highlands in the 7th century. She also claimed that the Lines were an astronomical calendar developed for agricultural purposes, and that they were mapped out through the use of sophisticated mathematics (and a long rope). However, the handful of alignments Reiche discovered between the sun, stars and Lines were not enough to convince scholars.

Later, English documentary-maker Tony Morrison hypothesized that the Lines were walkways linking *huacas* (sites of ceremonial significance). A slightly more surreal suggestion from explorer Jim Woodman was that the Nazca people knew how to construct hot-air balloons and that they did, in fact, observe the Lines from the air. Or, if you believe author George Von Breunig, the Lines formed a giant running track.

A more down-to-earth theory, given the value of water in the sun-baked desert, was suggested by anthropologist Johann Reinhard, who believed that the Lines were involved in mountain worship and a fertility/water cult. Recent work by the **Swiss-Liechtenstein Foundation** (SLSA; www.slsa.ch) agrees that they were dedicated to the worship of water, and it is thus ironic that their theory about the demise of the Nazca culture suggests that it was due not to drought but to destructive rainfall caused by a phenomenon such as El Niño!

About the only thing that is certain is that when the Nazca set about turning their sprawling desert homeland into an elaborate art canvas, they also began a debate that will keep archaeologists busy for many decades, if not centuries to come.

weather. Planes won't take off without good visibility, and there's often a low mist over the desert in the morning. Strong winds in the late afternoon also make flying impractical.

Passengers are usually taken on a first-come, first-served basis, with priority given to tour groups or those who have made reservations in Lima. Because the small aircraft bank left and right, it can be a stomach-churning experience, so motion-sickness sufferers should consider taking medication. Looking at the horizon may help mild nausea.

The standard overflight costs from US$50 for a 30-minute flight. Special discount deals are sometimes available, though prices may climb above US$85 in peak season. In addition, the aerodrome charges a departure tax of S20. Most agencies also offer combination flights that include the Palpa geoglyphs; these cost from US$85 per person and last around 45 minutes. Tour packages include transportation to the aerodrome, about 2km outside town. Make reservations as far in advance as possible. It's cheaper to do this in Nazca, but travel agencies in other major cities, such as Lima, Ica and Arequipa, can also arrange this for a small commission.

Companies that fly over the Lines have ticket offices near the aerodrome. The biggest is **Aero Condor Perú** (☎ 52-2402, in Lima 01-421-3105; www.aerocondor.com.pe; Hotel Nido del Cóndor, Carr Panamericana Sur Km 447), which also offers overflights leaving from Lima and Ica and gives passengers the benefit of waiting at a nearby hotel in Nazca in case of weather delays, followed by **Aerolca** (☎ 52-2434, in Lima 01-445-0859; www.areoica.net; Hotel La Maison Suisse, Carr Panamericana Sur Km 447), which also has an office in Lima. **Alas Peruanas** (☎ 52-2444; www.alasperuanas.com) is affiliated with Alegría Tours (opposite). Flights can also be booked at travel agencies and many of the hotels in town. Going directly to the aerodrome to arrange a flight is not reliable, but you might save a few dollars.

MUSEO DIDÁCTICO ANTONINI
On the east side of town, this excellent **archaeological museum** (☎ 52-3444; http://digilander.libero.it/MDAntonini; Av de la Cultura 600; admission S5, cameras S5; ☼ 9am-7pm) boasts an aqueduct running through the back garden, as well as interesting reproductions of burial tombs, a valuable collection of ceramic pan flutes and a scale model of the Lines. You can get an overview of both the Nazca culture and a glimpse of

most of Nazca's outlying sites here. Though the exhibit labels are in Spanish, the front desk lends foreign-language translation booklets for you to carry around. To get to the museum follow Bolognesi to the east out of town for 1km, or take a taxi (S2).

PLANETARIUM MARIA REICHE
This small **planetarium** (☎ 52-2293; www.concytec.gob.pe/ipa/inicio_ingles.htm; Nazca Lines Hotel, Bolognesi s/n; admission S20) is in the Nazca Lines Hotel and offers scripted evening lectures on the Lines with graphical displays on a domed projection screen that last approximately 45 minutes. Call ahead or check the posted schedules for show times in Spanish or English (French and Italian by reservation only).

OUTLYING SIGHTS
All of the sights listed below can be visited on tours from Nazca (see opposite), although individual travelers or pairs may have to wait a day or two before the agency finds enough people who are also interested in going.

Chauchilla Cemetery
The most popular excursion from Nazca, this **cemetery** (admission S5), 30km south of Nazca, will satisfy any urges you have to see ancient bones, skulls and mummies. Dating back to the Ica-Chinca culture around AD 1000, the mummies were, until recently, scattered haphazardly across the desert, left by ransacking tomb-robbers. Now they are seen carefully rearranged inside a dozen or so tombs, though cloth fragments and pottery and bone shards still litter the ground outside the demarcated trail. Organized tours last three hours and cost US$10 to US$35 per person.

Pardeones Ruins & Cantallo Aqueducts
The **Pardeones ruins**, 2km southeast of town via Arica over the river, are not very well preserved. About 5km further are the underground **Cantallo aqueducts** (admission S10), which are still in working order and essential in irrigating the surrounding fields. Though once possible to enter the aqueducts through the spiraling *ventanas* (windows), which local people use to clean the aqueducts each year, entry is now prohibited; instead, you can take note of the Nazca's exceptional stonework from outside. It's possible, but not necessarily safe, to walk to the aqueducts; at least, don't carry any valuables. It's better to catch

a minibus leaving from the first block of Arica (S0.80, 20 minutes), which will leave you at Cantallo, from where it is a 15-minute walk. Alternatively, take a taxi (around S40 round-trip).Tours from Nazca that take 2½ hours cost from US$5 per person and may be combined with a visit to see **El Telar**, a geoglyph found in the town of **Buena Fe**, and visits to touristy gold and ceramics workshops.

Cahuachi

A dirt road travels 25km west from Nazca to **Cahuachi**, the most important known Nazca center, which is still undergoing excavation. It consists of several pyramids, a graveyard and an enigmatic site called Estaquería, which may have been used as a place of mummification. Tours from Nazca take three hours, cost US$15 to US$50 per person, and may include a side trip to **Pueblo Viejo**, a nearby pre-Nazca residential settlement.

Reserva Nacional Pampas Galeras

This national reserve is a vicuña (threatened wild relatives of alpacas) sanctuary high in the mountains 90km east of Nazca on the road to Cuzco. It is the best place to see these shy animals in Peru, though tourist services are virtually nonexistent. Every year in late May or early June is the **chaccu**, when hundreds of villagers round up the vicuñas for shearing and three festive days of traditional ceremonies, with music and dancing, and of course, drinking. Full-day or overnight tours from Nazca cost US$30 to US$90 per person.

Activities

Need to beat the heat? Go swimming at the **Nazca Lines Hotel** (☎ 52-2993; Bolognesi s/n; admission incl snack & drink S22).

Off-the-beaten-track expeditions offered by several outdoor outfitters include **sandboarding** trips down nearby Cerro Blanco (2078m), the highest-known sand dune in the world, and a real challenge for sandboarders fresh from Huacachina. Half-day **mountain-biking** tours cost about the same (US$25). Ask other travelers to recommend agencies, as some folks report disappointing and even dangerous experiences with unqualified guides and poor equipment.

Tours & Guides

Most people fly over the Lines then leave, but there's more to see around Nazca. If you take one of the many local tours, they typically include a torturously long stop at a potter's and/or gold-miner's workshop for a demonstration of their techniques (tips for those who show you their trade are expected, too).

Hotels and travel agencies tirelessly promote their own tours. Aggressive touts meeting all arriving buses will try to hard-sell you before you've even picked up your bag.

Some established agencies:

Alegría Tours (☎ 52-3775; www.alegriatoursperu.com; Hotel Alegría, Lima 168) Behemoth agency offers all the usual local tours, plus off-the-beaten-track and sandboarding options. The tours are expensive for one person, so ask to join up with other travelers to receive a group discount. Alegría can arrange guides in Spanish, English, French and German in some cases.

Nasca Trails (☎ 52-2858; www.nascatrails.com.pe; Bolognesi 550) Recommended by readers, it's run by the friendly Juan Tohalino Vera, an experienced guide who speaks excellent English, as well as German, French and Italian. Not all the agency's tours have such experienced guides, however. Staff will pick you up at the bus station if you phone ahead.

For more unusual adventure tours, including desert trekking, **Jorge Echeandia** (☎ 52-1134, 971-4038; jorgenasca17@yahoo.com) is a reliable private guide. The well-educated staff at the Museo Didáctico Antonini (opposite) can sometimes be hired on their off-duty time to guide you around local archaeological sites.

Sleeping

Prices drop by up to 50% outside of peak season, which runs from May until August.

BUDGET

WalkOn Inn (☎ 52-2566; www.walkoninn.com; Mejía 108; dm S15, r per person S20; 🖵) This hostel has a social atmosphere and rooms that are small but secure with hot-water showers. A breakfast buffet is offered for S6, and the Dutch owner speaks five languages. Light sleepers should be forewarned about the crowing roosters next door.

Hostal Posada Guadalupe (☎ 52-2249; San Martín 225; s/d without bathroom S15/30, s/d S20/40; 🖵) Hidden on a residential block at the far western edge of town, this relaxed family-run guesthouse is near the bus stations. Some of the rooms have private bathrooms, while others are basically just a bed in a box.

Hotel Nido del Cóndor (☎ 52-3520; www.nidodel condornasca.com; Carr Panamericana Sur Km 447; camping per person S20; 🖳) Out by Nazca's aerodrome, this hotel allows campers to pitch on its grassy front lawn. Campers also have access to bathrooms, pool and a shared kitchen.

Hostal Internacional (☎ 50-6751, 55-2744; Maria Reiche 112; s/d/tr S35/45/50, bungalows from S45) The staff here can be brusque and the bungalows aren't anything to hoot and holler about, but the Hostal International is located just off the plaza and all rooms have cable TV.

Hotel Nasca (☎ 52-2085; marionasca13@hotmail .com; Lima 438; s/d/tr S35/45/65) A friendly, older place, it offers basic courtyard rooms, some with communal tepid showers. Ticket touts often hang around here offering cheap tours – don't pay for anything until you have it in writing.

Hospedaje Yemayá (☎ 52-3146; nascahospedaje yemaya@yahoo.es; Callao 578; s & d/tr incl breakfast S50/70) An indefatigably hospitable family deftly deals with all of the backpackers that stream through their doorway. They offer a few floors of small but well-cared-for rooms with hot showers and cable TV. There's a sociable terrace and cafe.

MIDRANGE

All of the following offer private bathrooms with hot water.

Hotel Oro Viejo (☎ 52-3332, 52-1112; www.hotel oroviejo.net; Callao 483; s/d/tr/ste incl buffet breakfast S100/140/170/315; 🗷 🖳 🖳) This charming hotel retains a familial atmosphere and has airy, well-furnished rooms, a welcoming common lounge, an exquisitely tended garden and even a souvenir shop.

Don Agucho (☎ 52-2048; www.hoteldonagucho .com; Los Maestros 100; s/d/tr incl breakfast US$35/45/50; 🗷 🖳 🖳) The Don Agucho provides chatty service, nice rooms and a great terrace with pool for lounging; the terrace is filled with cacti, wickerwork and wagon wheels. Breakfasts are filling, though hot water is erratic. It's a short walk over the bridge from town.

Hotel Alegría (☎ 52-2702; www.hotelalegria.com; Lima 168; s/d/tr incl breakfast US$40/50/60; 🗷 🖳 🖳) This is a classic travelers' haunt with a restaurant, manicured grounds and pool. It has narrow, carpeted rooms with TVs and fans. English, French, German, Italian and Hebrew are spoken. Rates include a free half-hour of internet access and a pickup from the bus stations, where you should ignore touts from the Hotel Alegría II.

Hotel Majoro (☎ 52-2490; www.hotelmajoro.com; Carr Panamericana Sur Km 452, Vista Alegre; s/d/tr/ste S231/231/316/340; 🗷 🖳 🖳) Housed in a lovely converted hacienda out in the middle of nowhere, this place has simple rooms but tranquil gardens plus a peacock and alpaca. It's 3km out of town beyond the aerodrome (taxi S6).

Also recommended:

Hotel Nido del Cóndor (☎ 52-3520; contanas@terra .com.pe; Carr Panamericana Sur Km 447; s/d/tr/q incl breakfast S81/122/178/213; 🗷 🖳 🖳) Modern place opposite the aerodrome with a small swimming pool. It shows free films on the Nazca Lines. English and German are spoken.

Hotel La Maison Suisse (☎ 52-2434; www.aeroica .net; Carr Panamericana Sur Km 447; s/d/tr/ste incl breakfast US$47/54/74/93; 🗷 🖳 🖳) This place near the aerodrome has a large grassy area with hammocks. Rooms have TVs and phones, while suites have air-con, Jacuzzis and minibars. Check online for discount packages.

TOP END

Catering mostly to tour groups, Nazca's top hotels just aren't that luxurious.

Nazca Lines Hotel (☎ 52-2293; www.peru-hotels .com/nazlines.htm; Bolognesi s/n; s/d/tr/ste incl buffet breakfast US$83/92/95/114; 🗷 🖳 🖳) Overrun nightly by European and Japanese tour groups, the staff here manage to be exceptionally polite and courteous. The hotel boasts rooms with all mod cons, a tennis court, restaurant and nightly lectures on the Lines (see p144).

Casa Andina (☎ 52-3563; www.casa-andina.com; Bolognesi 367; r incl breakfast buffet from S272; 🗷 🖳 🖳) This newly renovated Peruvian chain hotel, poised midway between the bus stations and the Plaza de Armas, offers the best value for money of any of Nazca's upmarket hotels. Rooms have eminently stylish, modern furnishings with bold color schemes, air-con and cable TV.

Hotel Cantayo Spa & Resort (☎ 52-2283; www.hotel cantayo.com; r incl breakfast from US$110; 🗷 🖳 🖳) The ultimate escape from grimy central Nazca, the Hotel Cantayo is run by Italians, and overrun with monkeys, alpacas and a family of peacocks, and has horses for riding. It's just 500m from the Cantallo aqueducts (p144). The rooms are top quality and have varied decor, including four-poster beds and Japanese-style furnishings.

Eating & Drinking

West of the Plaza de Armas, Bolognesi is stuffed full of foreigner-friendly pizzerias, restaurants and bars.

Restaurant Paulita (☎ 52-3854; Tacna 450; menús S6; ☺ 7:30am-8:30pm) With two tiny open-air tables facing the Plaza de Armas, this local fave serves home-style set meals as well as extras such as fruit salads and cakes.

Restaurante El Huarango (☎ 52-2141; Arica 602; mains S7-20; ☺ 8am-10pm) A swish two-story restaurant with a rooftop terrace and top-rated *criollo* coastal fare (a blend of Spanish, African and Asian influences). All meals come with a complimentary pisco sour to boot!

Restaurant Los Angeles (☎ 79-8240; Bolognesi 266; menús from S13, mains S8-24; ☺ noon-11pm) This meticulously run Peruvian and international eatery is known for especially delicious soups and salads, as well as tasty vegetarian options. It's owned by a local tour guide who speaks French and English.

Don Hono (☎ 52-4250; Bolognesi 265; menús from S10; ☺ lunch & dinner) This venerable restaurant doesn't waste effort on atmosphere, but concentrates on serving hearty fare with farm-fresh produce and mean pisco sours. It's a few notches above other touristy eateries around the plaza.

Grumpy's (☎ 95-607-3295; Lima 174; mains S15-25; ☺ 7am-11pm) Close to the bus stations, this thatched-roof eatery gets rave reviews from starving and homesick backpackers. In addition to traditional *criollo* fare, it also offers filling sandwiches and breakfasts.

Also recommended:

La Taberna (☎ 52-3803; Lima 321; menús S6, mains from S15; ☺ lunch & dinner) It's a hole-in-the-wall place: the scribbles covering every inch of wall are a testament to its popularity. Try the spicy fish, challengingly named '*Pescado a lo Macho*' ('macho fish') or chose from a list of vegetarian options.

La Kañada (☎ 52-253; Lima 160; menús S10, mains S12-16; ☺ 8am-11pm) Handy to the bus stations, this old standby still serves tasty Peruvian food. A decent list of cocktails includes *algarrobina*, a cocktail of pisco, milk and syrup from the *huarango* (carob) tree.

Getting There & Around

AIR

People who fly into Nazca normally fly over the Nazca Lines and return the same day. Both **Aero Condor Perú** (☎ 52-1182; www.aerocondor .com.pe; Hotel Nido del Cóndor, Carr Panamericana Sur Km 447) and **Aerodiana** (☎ in Lima 01-447-8540, 01-445-7188; www.aerodiana.com.pe) offer overflight tour packages for small groups departing from Lima with advance reservations.

BUS & TAXI

Nazca is a major destination for buses on Carr Panamericana Sur and is easy to get to from Lima, Ica or Arequipa. Bus companies cluster at the west end of Calle Lima, near the *óvalo* and about a block towards town on the same street. Buses to Arequipa generally originate in Lima, and to get a seat you have to pay the Lima fare.

Almost all services to Lima (S50 to S86, eight hours), Arequipa (S70 to S100, 10 to 12 hours) and for those heading to Chile, Tacna (S70 to S103, 13 to 15 hours), leave in the late afternoon or evening. Those bound for Arequipa will often stop en route upon request at Chala (S15, three hours) and Camaná (S46, seven hours). Located on Av Los Incas, **Cruz del Sur** (☎ 52-3713) and **Ormeño** (☎ 52-2058) have a few luxury buses daily to Lima. Intermediate points such as Ica and Pisco are more speedily served by smaller, *económico* (cheap) bus companies, such as **Flores** and **Soyuz** (☎ 52-1464), which run buses to Ica every half-hour from Av Los Incas. These buses will also drop you at Palpa (S3, one hour).

To go direct to Cuzco (S120 to S180, 14 hours), several companies, including Cruz del Sur, take the paved road east via Abancay. This route climbs over 4000m and gets very cold, so wear your warmest clothes and bring your sleeping bag on board if you have one. Alternatively, some companies also offer direct buses to Cuzco via Arequipa.

For Ica, fast *colectivos* (S15, two hours) and slower minibuses leave when full from near the gas station on the *óvalo*. On the south side of the main roundabout, antiquated *colectivos* wait for enough passengers to make the run down to Chala (S15, 2½ hours).

A taxi from central Nazca to the aerodrome, 2km away, costs about S4.

SACACO

☎ 054

About 100km south of Nazca in the desert is Sacaco, where the sand is made of crushed shells; keep your eyes peeled for fossilized crocodile teeth. There is a small **museum** (admission S5) with a fossilized whale in the middle of nowhere. The 3km road to Sacaco is marked by a sign at Km 539 on Carr Panamericana Sur. You can hire a taxi from Nazca to Chala with a stop at Sacaco (S90 to S100), but the museum's opening hours are erratic and it may be closed when you show up. Operators in Nazca (p145) can arrange tours to Sacaco with advance notice.

CHALA

☎ 054 / pop 2500

The tiny, ramshackle fishing village of Chala, about 170km from Nazca, presents intrepid travelers with an opportunity to break the journey to Arequipa and visit the archaeological site of **Puerto Inca** (admission free; ☽ 24hr), from whence fresh fish was once sent all the way to Cuzco by runners – no mean effort! The well-marked turnoff is 10km north of town, at Km 603 along Carr Panamericana Sur, from where a dirt road leads 3km west to the coastal ruins.

Near the ruins, **Hotel Puerto Inca** (☎ 25-8798; www.puertoinka.com.pe; Carr Panamericana Sur Km 603; s/d/tr/q S96/153/202/242; ☐ ☒) is a large resort set on a pretty bay. It has a campground that costs S13 per person, with a shower complex by the sea. It also offers horseback riding and rents bodyboards, kayaks, and jet skis.

In humble Chala itself are many morebasic guesthouses. The clean, friendly **Hostal Grau** (☎ 55-1009; Comercio 701; s/d S25/40) has only cold-water showers; ask for a room at the back with sea views. Local restaurants along the highway serve set lunches – trout is the special of the day, every day – from S5.

Colectivos to Chala (S15, 2½ hours) leave from the *óvalo* in Nazca when full from the early morning until mid-afternoon. Onward buses to Arequipa (S30, eight hours) via Camaná (S15, 4½ hours) stop in Chala at small ticket offices along Carr Panamericana Sur, with most buses departing in the evening. Major bus companies such as Cruz del Sur and Flores also have daily buses to Lima (S30 to S60, 11 hours) via Nazca (S10, three hours) that stop in Chala.

CAMANÁ

☎ 054 / pop 14,600

After leaving Chala in the dust, Carr Panamericana Sur heads south for 220km, clinging tortuously to sand dunes dropping down to the sea, until it reaches positively urban Camaná. This coastal city has long been a summer resort popular with *arequipeños* (inhabitants of Arequipa) who flock to its beaches, about 5km from the center. An earthquake in June 2001 sparked a tsunami that devastated the beachside community,

but seasonal tourism is now flourishing once again. Camaná is quite bleak during the low season, but is still a possible place to break the journey to Arequipa.

Orientation & Information

The main plaza is about a 15-minute walk toward the coast along the road where all the buses stop. On the plaza, **BCP** (9 de Noviembre 139) changes US dollars and has a 24-hour Visa/MasterCard ATM.

To get to the coast, *colectivos* to La Punta beach (S1, 10 minutes) leave from the intersection where Av Lima turns into a pedestrian walkway.

Sleeping & Eating

At the beach there are a few sparse restaurants and hotels, some bearing scars from the tsunami. Hotels get busy on summer weekends from January to April, even in the city center.

Hostal Montecarlo I (☎ 57-1101; Lima 514; s/d/tr S30/40/60) The main road along which the bus stations are lined up is chock-a-block with cheap, bare-bones hotels. This is one of the flashier ones, with clean rooms, 24-hour hot water, cable TV and phone. It also has a sister location, Hostal Montecarlo II, on the pedestrian walkway towards the main plaza.

Hotel Sun Valley (☎ 79-6108, 934-3969; eridv@hotmail .com; Carr Panamericana Sur Km 850, Cerrillos 2; r from S35; ☒) Outside town and close to the beach, this squeaky-clean hotel has friendly owners that have put comfy beds in every room. It also has its own private patch of beach and a restaurant that comes highly recommended. If arriving late, call for a pickup from the bus station.

Hotel de Turistas (☎ 55-1113; www.hoteldeturistas .net; Lima 138; s/d/tr incl breakfast S90/115/155; ☐ ☒) Housed in a large elegant building set in spacious gardens, this place is a cut above the competition. It has a restaurant and is just a short walk or taxi ride from the bus stations.

Getting There & Away

Frequent bus services to Arequipa (S12 to S42, 3½ hours) are provided by several companies, all of which are found along Lima, including luxurious **Cruz del Sur** (☎ 57-1491; Lima 474), newcomer **Cromotex** (☎ 57-1752; Lima 301) and the always-economical **Flores** (☎ 57-1013; Lima 200). Cruz del Sur and other smaller bus companies also have daily services to Lima (S35 to

S135, 12 hours) that stop at most intermediate coastal points, such as Chala (S15, 4½ hours) and Nazca (S30, seven hours).

MOLLENDO

☎ 054 / pop 22,800

Reached via a desert landscape of delicate pinks, browns and grays, this old-fashioned beach resort is another popular getaway for *arequipeños* during the coastal summer, from January to early April. Beyond the sand dunes the desert becomes very rocky, with brave cacti eking out an existence in the salt-laden soil.

Orientation & Information

Mollendo is a pleasant colonial town, with hilly streets and a long beach. The bus terminal is a quick ride from the town's main plazas, which are just up from the beach. **BCP** (Arequipa 330) has a Visa/MasterCard ATM and changes US dollars. Internet cafes are everywhere; **StarNet** (Arequipa 327; per hr S1) has fast connections. **Telefónica-Perú** (Arequipa 625) is north of the central market. Near the main plaza, **J & R Servicios** (☎ 53-3184; Arequipa 178) is a travel agency that can help with tourist information and the purchase of bus and plane tickets.

Sights & Activities

When temperatures are searing from January through to at least March, **aquatic parks** (admission S4) open alongside the sea, and beachfront discos stay thumping until the wee hours of the morning. But Mollendo can be like a ghost town throughout the rest of the year. Once a bustling port, most ships now dock in the larger port of Matarani, 15km to the northwest.

Sleeping

Reservations are a must during the high season, January through April, when weekend prices may also soar.

La Posada Inn (☎ 53-4610; Arequipa 337; s/d without bathroom S20/40, s & d/tr incl breakfast S60/90) This is an excellent, well-cared-for option run by a welcoming family and scented with honeysuckle in summer. Rooms in the lower area have hot water, and some have local TV. Rates include breakfast.

Hostal La Casona (☎ 53-3160; Arequipa 188-192; s/d S40/60/90) Just as central as El Plaza, La Casona has high-ceilinged, airy rooms with cable TV and hot water. The staff can be stiff necked, but the atmosphere is casual.

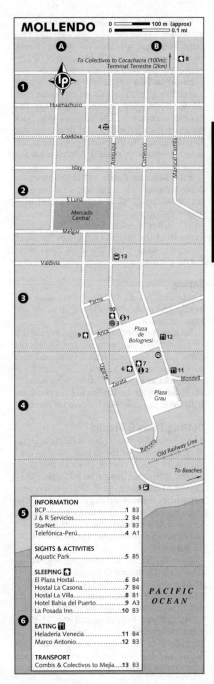

MOLLENDO

To Colectivos to Cocachacra (100m); Terminal Terrestre (2km)

Huamachuco

Cordóva

Islay

S Luna

Mercado Central

Melgar

Valdivia

Tacna

Plaza de Bolognesi

Arica

Zarata

Plaza Grau

Balcony

Old Railway Line

To Beaches

Blondell

PACIFIC OCEAN

INFORMATION	
BCP	1 B3
J & R Servicios	2 B4
StarNet	3 B3
Telefónica-Perú	4 A1

SIGHTS & ACTIVITIES	
Aquatic Park	5 B5

SLEEPING	
El Plaza Hostal	6 B4
Hostal La Casona	7 B4
Hostal La Villa	8 B1
Hotel Bahia del Puerto	9 A3
La Posada Inn	10 B3

EATING	
Heladería Venecia	11 B4
Marco Antonio	12 B3

TRANSPORT	
Combis & Colectivos to Mejía	13 B3

El Plaza Hostal (☎ 53-2460; plazahostalmollendo@hotmail.com; Arequipa 209; s/d/tr S50/70/95; 🖵) This large hotel has spacious yet sparse rooms, hot showers and local TV. It's another flower-bedecked spot with smiling employees.

Hostal La Villa (☎ 53-2317; lavillahotel@speedy.com.pe; Mariscal Castilla 366; s/d/tr incl breakfast S56/73/88; 🖵 ⬛) Bedraggled and showing its age, this historic mansion is a chilled place to lie back on a sun lounger with a cold drink and one foot dangling into the plunge pool. It has carpeted rooms with cable TV, plus a garden terrace and restaurant.

Hotel Bahía del Puerto (☎ 53-2990; hotelbahiadelpuerto@hotmail.com; Ugarte 301; s/d/tr incl breakfast S70/140/150; ⬛ 🖵 ⬛) Set on a cliff high above the ocean, this hotel is light and airy with touches of Asian decor. There are great views from the pool deck, though the smell of frying food from the *chifa* next door is ever-present.

Eating

There are dozens of snack bars near the beach, and *cevicherías* abound in town and near the beach.

Heladería Venecia (Comercio at Blondell; ice cream S2-5; ☾ noon-8pm) For ice cream and snacks, this has some intriguing local fruit flavors and may tempt you with free samples.

Marco Antonio (☎ 53-4258; Comercio 258; mains S15-24; ☾ 8am-8pm Mon-Sat, 8am-7pm Sun) is a good no-frills Peruvian cafe with bargain set meals.

Getting There & Around

The *terminal terrestre* (bus station) is about 2km northwest of the center; there's a S1 departure tax. A couple of small bus companies, including **Transportes del Carpio** (☎ 53-2571) and **Santa Ursula** (☎ 53-2586) have frequent departures throughout the day for Arequipa (S8, two hours). *Colectivos* wait outside the terminal to whisk arriving passengers down to the town's plazas and the beach (S0.50, 10 minutes).

Combis (S1.20, 20 minutes) and *colectivos* (S2, 15 minutes) to the beach resort of Mejía leave from the corner of Valdivia and Arequipa. Unfortunately, there are no direct buses onward to Moquegua or Tacna. *Colectivos* and minivans marked 'El Valle' leave Mollendo from the top end of Mariscal Castilla, by a gas station, and pass through Mejía and the Río Tambo Valley to reach Cocachacra (S4, 1½ hours). There you can immediately jump into a *colectivo* heading for El Fiscal (S3, 15 minutes), a flyblown gas station where buses heading to Moquegua, Tacna, Arequipa and Lima regularly stop. Expect these buses to be standing-room only, and that services to Lima may have no space available.

MEJÍA & RÍO TAMBO VALLEY

A short detour south of Mollendo, the beach resort of Mejía is also a summer beach hangout for *arequipeños*, but it's usually deserted from late April to December. *Colectivos* frequently shuttle between Mejía and Mollendo (S2, 15 minutes).

About 6km southeast of Mejía along an unbroken line of beaches is the **Santuario Nacional Lagunas de Mejía** (☎ 054-83-5001; Carretera Mollendo, Km 32; admission S5; ☾ dawn-dusk), a 690-hectare sanctuary protecting coastal lagoons that are the largest permanent lakes in 1500km of desert coastline. They attract more than 200 species of coastal and migratory birds, best seen in the very early morning. The visitor center has maps of hiking trails leading through the dunes to *miradors*. From Mollendo, *colectivos* pass by the visitor center (S3, 30 minutes) frequently during the daytime. Ask the staff to help you flag down onward transportation, which peters out by the late afternoon.

The road continues along the Río Tambo Valley, which has been transformed by an important irrigation project into fertile rice paddies, sugarcane plantations and fields of potatoes and corn: a striking juxtaposition with the dusty backdrop of sand dunes and desert. The road rejoins the Carr Panamericana Sur at El Fiscal, the only stop in more than 100km of desert road. You can wait here for buses southbound to Moquegua and Tacna or northbound to Arequipa and Lima, but expect them to be standing-room only. Long-distance services to Lima may be completely full.

MOQUEGUA

☎ 053 / pop 56,600 / elev 1420m

This parched, dusty inland town survives in the driest part of the Peruvian coastal desert, which merges into northern Chile's Atacama Desert – the driest in the world. The Río Moquegua delivers enough moisture to the surrounding rural areas to grow avocados and grapes (the latter often used to make Pisco Biondi, one of the nation's better brands), but as you walk away from the river it becomes hard to believe that any agriculture is possible here.

Moquegua means 'quiet place' in Quechua, and the region has long been culturally linked with the Andes. It has peaceful cobblestone streets, a shady central plaza with flower gardens, and some unusual buildings that are roofed with a type of wattle-and-daub mixture mixed from sugarcane thatch and clay, though few are left intact after recent earthquakes.

Orientation & Information

The main plaza is a long walk uphill from where the buses stop. After dark, don't risk being in the dangerous market area; take taxis instead (S3). Cheap but slow internet cafes are near the Plaza de Armas.

BCP (Moquegua 861) Has a 24-hour Visa/MasterCard ATM.

Municipal tourist office (Casa de la Cultura, Calle Moquegua; ⏰ 7am–4pm) Local government-run tourist office located next to BCP.

Serpost (Ayacucho 560; ⏰ 8am–noon & 3-6:30pm Mon-Sat) On the Plaza de Armas.

Sights & Activities

PLAZA DE ARMAS & AROUND

The town's small and shady plaza boasts a 19th-century wrought-iron fountain, thought by some to have been designed in a workshop run by Gustave Eiffel (of eponymous tower fame), and flower gardens that make it a welcome oasis away from the encroaching desert.

The foreign-funded **Museo Contisuyo** (☎ 46-1844; http://bruceowen.com/contisuyo/MuseoE .html; Tacna 294; adult/child S1.50/0.50; ⏰ 8:30am-1pm & 2:30-5:30pm) is an excellent little repository of local archaeological artifacts, including photographs of recent excavations, along with exhibitions of new works by local artists. The labels are in Spanish and English.

Opposite the facade of the town's oldest **church**, which mostly collapsed during a massive earthquake in 1868, is an 18th-century Spanish **colonial jail**, with intimidating iron-grilled windows. At one corner of the Plaza de Armas, visitors can enter the **Casa Posada de Teresa Podesta** (cnr Ancash & Ayacucho; admission S2; ⏰ 10am-3pm Mon-Fri), a stately colonial mansion with its innards still intact.

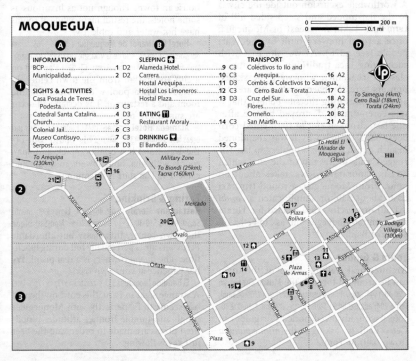

MOQUEGUA

| | 0 ——— 200 m |
| | 0 ——— 0.1 mi |

INFORMATION
BCP....................................1 D2
Municipalidad......................2 D2

SIGHTS & ACTIVITIES
Casa Posada de Teresa
  Podesta.............................3 C3
Catedral Santa Catalina.........4 D3
Church................................5 C3
Colonial Jail........................6 C3
Museo Contisuyo..................7 C3
Serpost...............................8 D3

SLEEPING
Alameda Hotel.......................9 C3
Carrera...............................10 C3
Hostal Arequipa...................11 D3
Hostal Los Limoneros...........12 C3
Hostal Plaza.......................13 D3

EATING
Restaurant Moraly................14 C3

DRINKING
El Bandido..........................15 C3

TRANSPORT
Colectivos to Ilo and
  Arequipa...........................16 A2
Combis & Colectivos to Samegua,
  Cerro Baúl & Torata............17 C2
Cruz del Sur........................18 A2
Flores................................19 A2
Ormeño..............................20 B2
San Martín..........................21 A2

To Samegua (4km);
Cerro Baúl (18km);
Torata (24km)

DETOUR: MOQUEGUA'S WINE COUNTRY

The land around Moquegua is perfect for growing the grapes that go into some of the nation's top-shelf piscos. Eighteen local wineries are open to the public for tasting and tours; these bodegas range from small family-run operations such as **Bodega Villegas** to the industrial exporter **Biondi**. And if you're not a fan of pisco, you'll also find an interesting variety of wines, fruit liqueurs and cognacs. Stop by the municipal tourist office (p151) to pick up a Wine Country map. Most wineries are only accessible by car, so hire a cab (per hour S12).

Walk around the town center to see some of the typical sugarcane thatching, especially along Calle Moquegua, and have a peek inside **Catedral Santa Catalina** (Ayacucho s/n), which houses the body of 18th-century St Fortunata, whose hair and nails are said to be still growing.

CERRO BAÚL

A worthwhile excursion outside the city is to the flat-topped and steep-sided hill of **Cerro Baúl**, 18km northeast of Moquegua, once a royal brewery built by the Wari people (see p326). As was the case with succeeding Inca traditions, it was upper-class Wari women who were the skilled brewers here. Archaeologists who are still at work excavating the site believe that it was ceremonially destroyed by fire after one last, drunken *chicha* (fermented corn beer) bash, though why it was abandoned in such a rush remains a mystery so far. The rugged walk to the top of the site, which boasts panoramic views, takes about an hour. From Moquegua, a round-trip taxi costs about S30, or simply catch a *combi* (S1.50) or *colectivo* (S3) headed for Torata from central Moquegua and ask to be let off at Cerro Baúl.

Tours & Guides

Architectural walking tours of the town can be arranged through the **Museo Contisuyo** (☎ 46-1844; http://bruceowen.com/contisuyo/MuseoE.html; Tacna 294; adult/child S1.50/0.50; ☺ 8:30am-1pm & 2:30-5:30pm) with advanced notice. For guides of Cerro Baúl, try asking at the *municipalidad* (town hall) in Torata.

Sleeping

It's best to pass up the cheap hostels near the bus stations in lieu of a safer option closer to the center of town.

Hospedaje Carrera (☎ 46-2173; Lima 320; s/d without bathroom S15/25, s/d S20/30) Sitting pretty, safe and secure behind its own garden gate, this pastel-colored little hostel has basic rooms and a convivial owner. There may be limited hot water in the communal bathrooms.

Hostal Plaza (☎ 46-1612; Ayacucho 675; s/d/tr S35/45/55) This is a neat spot by the plaza where some of the upstairs rooms have pretty views of the cathedral. The good-value rooms are airy and sport large-screen cable TVs.

Hostal Arequipa (☎ 46-1338; Arequipa 360; s/d/tr S37/48/59) Located on a busy main street not far from the plaza, the Arequipa has clean and cozy rooms with hot showers and cable TV. Service here is reasonably friendly and helpful.

Hostal Los Limoneros (☎ 46-1649; Lima 441; s/d/tr S40/55/70) It's the quiet garden, with its shady patios and delicious smells, that makes this the most attractive and traditional guesthouse in town. Though not as luxurious as some hotels, the restful high-ceilinged rooms have hot water and cable TV.

Hotel El Mirador de Moquegua (☎ 46-1765; hmirador@derrama.org.pe; Alto de la Villa s/n; s/d US$25/40, bungalows from US$54, all incl breakfast; ☐ ☒) Perched on a cliff about 3km from the town center, El Mirador has a pool with a view, a game room and a restaurant. The design and decor are supremely '60s.

Alameda Hotel (☎ 46-3971; Junín 322; s/d/tr incl breakfast S78/108/138; ☐) This bland, out-of-the-way hotel has quality, spick-and-span rooms with sofa, hot showers, minibars and cable TV. The staff is unsmiling.

Eating & Drinking

Restaurant Moraly (☎ 46-3084; Lima 398; menús S8.50, mains S10-30; ☺ 7:30am-9:30pm Mon-Sat) Near the town center, this classy but affordable Peruvian cafe is perennially full during lunchtime. The *dueña* (owner) is a real pistol. Try her patience at your own risk!

El Bandido (Moquegua 333; pizzas from S12; ☺ 7pm-late) A strange sight in Peru, this cowboy-themed bar seems to fit perfectly with Moquegua's rough-and-tumble frontier attitude. Wood-fired pizzas are made to order, and the beer just keeps flowing.

For open-air terrace restaurants serving typical regional food with live *folklórica* (folkloric) music on weekends, catch a taxi to nearby Samegua (S4).

Getting There & Away

Buses leave from several small terminals downhill southwest of the Plaza de Armas. There you'll also find faster, though less safe and more expensive *colectivos* that leave when full for Ilo (S12, 1½ hours) and Arequipa (S30, 3½ hours).

Buses to Lima (S50 to S138, 16 to 20 hours) leave with **Ormeño** (☎ 76-1149; Av La Paz 524), which has one luxury-class service daily; **Cruz del Sur** (☎ 46-2005; Av La Paz 296), which has two luxury services; and **Flores** (☎ 46-2647; Av Ejercito s/n), which has two *económico* services. These buses often make intermediate coastal stops, for example at Nazca and Ica. Other buses to Arequipa (S20 to S40, four hours) leave twice daily with Cruz del Sur and Ormeño and hourly with Flores. These same companies also have buses to Tacna (S10, three hours) and Ilo (S8, 1½ hours); Flores has the cheapest and most frequent departures.

Several smaller companies, including **San Martín** (☎ 95-352-1550; Av La Paz 175), take a mostly paved route to Puno (S25, nine hours) via Desaguadero on the Bolivian border (S18, six hours), usually departing in the evening. This can be a rough, cold overnight journey on *económico* buses that stop infrequently for bathroom breaks at the side of the road. It's wiser to backtrack first to Arequipa, then transfer to a more comfortable bus bound for Puno, from where you can easily cross into Bolivia during daylight hours.

ILO

☎ 053 / pop 58,700

Ilo is the ugly departmental port, about 95km southwest of Moquegua, used mainly to ship copper from the mine at Toquepala further south, and wine and avocados from Moquegua. Ilo does offer a pleasant boardwalk and a few beachside luxury hotels that fill with Peruvian vacationers in the summertime, but though the beach is long and curving, the waters are murky and unappealing for swimming.

Sights

About 15km inland at El Algarrobal is the **Museo Municipal de Sitio** (☎ 83-5000; Centro Mallqui; adult S5; 10am-3pm Mon-Sat, 10am-2pm Sun), which

hosts a surprisingly noteworthy collection of exhibits on the area's archaeology and agriculture, including ceramics, textiles, a collection of feather-topped hats and a mummified llama. A round-trip by taxi costs around S30.

Sleeping & Eating

There's no need to stay overnight, but if you get stuck there are plenty of options.

Hotel San Martín (☎ 48-1082; Matará 325; s/d/tr S35/45/55;) Near the bus companies, this is a good-value hostel with large decent rooms and private hot showers. The staff is extremely eager to rent you a room.

Hostal Plaza (☎ 48-1633; 2 de Mayo 514; s/d/tr S40/55/65) Who says there's no truth in advertising? Just off the plaza, this is a well-kept hotel with good, if bland, rooms with hot showers and cable TV.

Hotel Karina (☎ 48-1397; karinahotel@hotmail.com; Abtao 780; s/d/tr incl breakfast S71/92/123;) This is a well-run hotel with simple decor and amiable service. Some rooms have lovely ocean views, and the bar and restaurant is open to serve all day long.

VIP Hotel (☎ 48-1492; www.viphotelilo.com; 2 de Mayo 608; s/d/tr incl breakfast S128/156/188;) A swish hotel by the plaza, the VIP has a refined restaurant and spacious rooms with all the frills, including cable TV and minibars. The higher the floor, the better the sea views. Rooms with air-con cost slightly more.

Restaurant El Peñon (☎ 79-0964; 2 de Mayo 100; mains S12-24; lunch & dinner) It has a prime shorefront position with tables that afford great views of the fishermen at the port across the way, but you may not be able to enjoy it due to the port's distinctive smell.

Crazy Cow (☎ 48-4367; Moquegua 133; mains S14-27; lunch & dinner Mon-Sat) A short walk from the plaza, this cheerful subterranean *parrillada* (grill house) has a sign (in English) that will make you laugh. It serves all sorts of barbecue-style meats plus pastas and pizzas. It also has a full bar and wine list (bottles from S25).

Getting There & Away

There is an oddly ship-shaped bus terminal 1km northeast of town, but most companies continue to leave from smaller stations in the town center, a short walk from the plaza and the beach.

Cruz del Sur (☎ 48-2071; cnr Moquegua & Matará) and **Ormeño** (☎ 48-4187; cnr Junín & Matará) each have daily buses to Lima (S55 to S138, 16 to 18 hours). Ormeño also has direct services to Moquegua (S7, 1½ hours), and Arequipa (S20, five hours). **Flores** (☎ 48-2512; cnr Ilo & Matará) goes to the same destinations more frequently, with direct services to Tacna (S10, 3½ hours, every 45 minutes) and Arequipa (S18, every two hours).

Faster, slightly pricier *colectivos* to Tacna and sometimes Moquegua leave when full from the side streets near the smaller bus stations. A taxi to anywhere in town should cost S2.

TACNA

☎ 052 / pop 262,700 / elev 460m

At the tail end of Carr Panamericana Sur, almost 1300km southeast of Lima, the hectic border outpost of Tacna is Peru's southernmost city and the capital of its department. It is situated about 40km from the Chilean border and was occupied by Chile in 1880 after the War of the Pacific, until its people voted to return to Peru in 1929. Incidentally, Tacna has some of Peru's best schools and hospitals; whether this is due to its Chilean ties is a matter of hotly debated opinion. The city also shows off British and French influences in its architecture and train system. Yet it remains staunchly, even defiantly, patriotic. You'll never be in doubt as to which side of the border you're actually on.

Information

Internet cafes are everywhere, and most offer inexpensive local, long-distance and international phone calls. Chilean pesos, Peruvian nuevos soles and US dollars can all be easily exchanged in Tacna. There's a global ATM at the *terminal terrestre*.

BCP (San Martín 574) Has a Visa/MasterCard ATM, changes traveler's checks and gives cash advances on Visa cards.

Bolivian consulate (☎ 24-5121; Bolognesi 1721; ☼ 8am-3:30pm Mon-Fri) Some nationalities (American included) will need to solicit a visa one month in advance and pay a US$130 entry fee; there's another Bolivian consulate located in Puno.

Chilean consulate (☎ 42-3063; www.minrel.cl; Presbítero Andía at Saucini; ☼ 8am-1pm Mon-Fri) Most travelers don't need a Chilean visa and head straight for the border instead.

Hospital (☎ 42-2121, 42-3361; Blondell s/n; ☼ 24hr) For emergency services.

Interbank (San Martín 646) Has a 24-hour global ATM.

iPerú (☎ 42-5514; iperutacna@promperu.gob.pe; San Martín 491) National tourist office, provides free information and brochures.

Lavandería Latina (☎ 24-3084; Vizquerra 26B; per kg S5; ☼ 8am-8pm Mon-Sat) Laundry service.

Oficina de Migraciones (immigration office; ☎ 24-3231; Circunvalación s/n, Urb Él Triángulo; ☼ 8am-4pm Mon-Fri)

Police (☎ 41-4141; Calderón de la Barca 353; ☼ 24hr)

Serpost (Bolognesi 361; ☼ 8am-8pm Mon-Sat) South of the Plaza de Armas.

Dangers & Annoyances

Remember that international border traffic attracts thieves and other criminals. Keep a close watch on your belongings at all times, especially in and around the bus terminals, and don't wander around alone after dark. When in doubt, take a taxi instead of walking.

Sights & Activities

You won't need much more than an afternoon to see everything Tacna has to offer. If you're coming from Chile, you may want to continue on immediately to Arequipa instead.

PLAZA DE ARMAS

Tacna's main plaza, which is studded with palm trees and large pergolas topped by bizarre mushroomlike bushes, is a popular meeting place and has a patriotic flag-raising ceremony every Sunday morning. The plaza, famously pictured on the front of Peru's S100 note, features a huge arch – a monument to the heroes of the War of the Pacific. It is flanked by larger-than-life bronze statues of Admiral Grau and Colonel Bolognesi. Nearby, the 6m-high bronze **fountain** was created by the French engineer Gustave Eiffel, who also designed the **cathedral**, noted for its fine stained-glass windows and onyx high altar.

MUSEO FERROVIARIO & EL PARQUE DE LA LOCOMOTORA

This **museum** (☎ 24-5572; admission S5; ☼ 8am-6pm) located inside the train station – just ring the bell at the southern gates – gives the impression of stepping back in time. You can wander amid beautiful though poorly maintained 20th-century steam engines and rolling stock, plus atmospheric salons filled with historic paraphernalia, including a curious collection of international postage stamps, all to the tune of the lonely tap-tapping of the stationmaster's ancient typewriter.

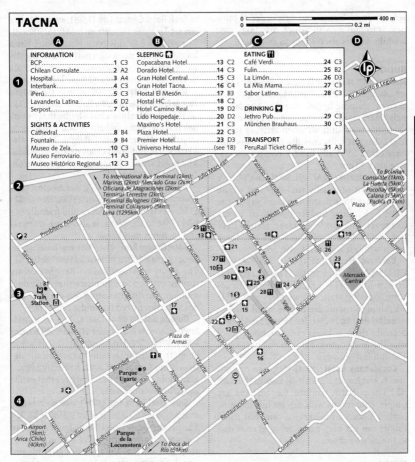

TACNA

0 — 400 m
0 — 0.2 mi

INFORMATION
BCP...................................1 C3
Chilean Consulate...............2 A2
Hospital.............................3 A4
Interbank...........................4 C3
iPerú.................................5 C3
Lavandería Latina...............6 D2
Serpost.............................7 C4

SIGHTS & ACTIVITIES
Cathedral...........................8 B4
Fountain............................9 B4
Museo de Zela..................10 C3
Museo Ferroviario..............11 A3
Museo Histórico Regional...12 C3

SLEEPING
Copacabana Hotel..............13 C2
Dorado Hotel.....................14 C3
Gran Hotel Central.............15 C3
Gran Hotel Tacna..............16 C4
Hostal El Mesón................17 B3
Hostal HC.........................18 C2
Hotel Camino Real............19 D2
Lido Hospedaje.................20 D2
Maximo's Hotel.................21 C3
Plaza Hotel......................22 C3
Premier Hotel...................23 D3
Universo Hostal..............(see 18)

EATING
Café Verdi........................24 C3
Fulin................................25 B2
La Limón..........................26 D3
La Mia Mama...................27 C3
Sabor Latino....................28 C3

DRINKING
Jethro Pub.......................29 C3
München Brauhaus............30 C3

TRANSPORT
PeruRail Ticket Office........31 A3

To International Bus Terminal (2km);
Marinas (2km); Mercado Grau (2km);
Oficiana de Magraciones (2km);
Terminal Terrestre (2km);
Terminal Bolognesi (3km);
Terminal Collasuyo (5km);
Lima (1295km);

To Bolivian
Consulate (1km);
La Huerta (5km);
Pocollay (5km);
Calana (15km);
Pachía (17km)

Train Station

Plaza de Armas

Parque Ugarte

Mercado Central

To Airport (5km);
Arica (Chile) (40km)

Parque de la Locomotora

To Boca del Río (51km)

About a 15-minute walk south of the train station, a British locomotive built in 1859 and used as a troop train in the War of the Pacific is the centerpiece of **El Parque de la Locomotora**, an otherwise empty roadside park.

OTHER MUSEUMS

The small, musty **Museo de Zela** (Zela 542; admission free; 8am-noon & 3-5pm Mon-Sat) provides a look at the interior of one of Tacna's oldest colonial buildings, the Casa de Zela. It houses a motley collection of 19th-century paintings of stately folk.

If the tiny **Museo Histórico Regional** (Casa de la Cultura, Apurímac 202; admission S5; 8am-noon & 1:30-5pm Mon-Fri) is closed, ask someone in the library below to open it. The main

exhibit deals with the War of the Pacific (p40), and features paintings and maps. There's also a small collection of art and archaeological pieces.

BEACHES

Tacna's main seaside resort is **Boca del Río**, about 50km southwest of the city. Minibuses from Terminal Bolognesi go here along a good road (S3.50, one hour).

Sleeping

There's no shortage of hotels catering to Tacna's cross-border traffic. That said, almost all are overpriced and fill up very fast, especially with Chileans who cross the border for weekend shopping trips. No matter what time you arrive in Tacna, your first order of business is to find a room, which may take quite a while, so it is always best to call ahead.

BUDGET

Marinas (☎ 24-6014; Av Circunvalación Sur 40; s without bathroom S20, s/d/tr S30/35/45) One in a line of sketchy-seeming hostels near the bus terminals, Marinas is clean, secure and handy for dropping your stuff off when arriving late at night. Rooms with en-suite bathrooms also have cable TV. Call ahead if you plan to arrive after 11pm.

Lido Hospedaje (☎ 57-7001; San Martín 876A; s/d/tr S20/40/50) An unusually well-run and secure guesthouse that many travelers say is the most welcoming budget option in Tacna. Compact and spotlessly clean rooms have hot water. Penny pinchers can ask for a room without a TV and save S5.

Universo Hostal (☎ 41-5441; Zela 724; s/d/tr S30/40/60) Next door to the Hostal HC, this broken-in hostel is a secure option with accommodating staff, hot showers and cable TV, though rooms are on the small side.

Hostal HC (☎ 24-2042; Zela 734; s/d S35/45/60) A decently clean, if kinda claustrophobic place near the town center. Basic rooms have cable TV and hot showers.

Copacabana Hotel (☎ 42-1721; www.copahotel .com; Av Arias Aragüez 370; s/d/tr incl breakfast S65/75/85; 🖳) The popular, youthful Copacabana has simple, cute rooms with private hot showers, cable TV and a full-service cafe, but some rooms can get very noisy on weekends due to the nearby disco.

MIDRANGE

Many hotels raise their rates just before holidays and on weekends, when international shoppers hit town. All of the following have rooms with private hot-water bathrooms, cable TV and telephones.

Plaza Hotel (☎ 42-2101; www.plazahotel.com.pe; San Martín 421; s/d/tr incl breakfast S65/80/100; 🖳) There's a hospital-like atmosphere to this cool, blocky option by the plaza. Ubiquitous white linoleum lends the corridors a clinical feel. The rooms are worn, but the staff is cheerful.

Premier Hotel (☎ 24-6045; www.hotelpremier.com .pe; Bolognesi 804; s/d/tr incl breakfast S70/85/100; 🖳) Surprisingly popular with travelers, the tired-looking Premier has comfy rooms with a snack bar below. The busy street outside near the central market area can be noisy, though.

Gran Hotel Central (☎ 41-5051; www.hotelcentral peru.net; San Martín 561; s/d/tr incl breakfast S75/105/135) The entrance to this once-plush hotel has a loudly buzzing neon sign that heralds slightly seedy, worn-around-the-edges rooms that are nevertheless spacious and have long sofas.

Maximo's Hotel (☎ 24-2604; www.maximoshotel .com; Av Arias Aragüez 281; s/d/tr incl breakfast S90/115/130; 🖳) Quirky Maximo's has a lobby that's over-laden with plants, balconies and candelabra, all suffused by green-tinted light. There's also a snack bar and good clean rooms with fans. The hotel sauna (S8 for guests) is open from 2pm to 10pm daily.

Hostal El Mesón (☎ 41-4070; www.mesonhotel.com; Hipólito Unánue 175; s/d/tr incl breakfast S100/120/130; 🖳) El Mesón is a clean, modern and friendly option close to the plaza. It also has a cafeteria and in-room minibars.

Hotel Camino Real (☎ 42-1891; creal-hotel@star.com .pe; San Martín 855; s/d/tr incl breakfast S100/130/165; 🖳) The flashy-looking Camino Real has comfy rooms with good amenities that include a minibar, but disappointing '70s decor. It also has a startlingly red bar and a cafeteria.

Dorado Hotel (☎ 41-5/41, 42-1111; www.dorado hoteltacna.com; Av Arias Aragüez 145; s/d/tr incl breakfast S100/130/165; 🖳) Undoubtedly Tacna's top hotel, the elegant Dorado has artistically designed modern rooms with heavenly beds, a grand lobby bar and public spaces that exude an exclusive ambience.

Gran Hotel Tacna (☎ 42-4193; www.granhoteltacna .com; Bolognesi 300; s/d incl breakfast US$56/76; 🖳 🖳) The blocky Gran Hotel Tacna has a choice of suites and many rooms with a balcony. Rooms are plush, and there are pleasant grounds and a pool, a restaurant with 24-hour room service and a bar with dancing.

Eating

Popular local dishes include *patasca a la tacneña,* a thick, spicy vegetable-and-meat soup, and *picante a la tacneña,* hot peppered tripe (it's better than it sounds). A surprising number of hole-in-the-wall cafes serve fresh fruit and yogurt, as well as other healthy, vegetarian snacks.

Café Verdi (☎ 24-5688; Vigil 57; menús S7.50, snacks S3-8; ⏱ 8:30am-9pm Mon-Sat) Serving up tasty baked goods and desserts, as well as affordable fixed lunches, this spot remains chock-a-block with diners throughout the day.

Fulin (☎ 95-233-1369; Av Arias Aragüez 396; menús S4.50; ⏱ 9:30am-4pm Mon-Fri) This is a cheap vegetarian *chifa* in a rickety old building that somehow manages to deny the passing of time, but with a menu that offers gluten-free options. Just look for the sign with Chinese characters outside.

Sabor Latino (☎ 24-2389; Vigil 68; menús S7.50, mains S14-25; ✆ 9am-9pm Mon-Sat) You'll almost always find every table taken at this bustling cafe, which has lazy tropical ceiling fans and a spicy Latin soundtrack. It's especially recommended for filling set lunches and dinners and Andean specialties such as *cuy chactado* (fried guinea pig).

La Mia Mama (☎ 24-2022; Av Arias Aragüez 204; mains S10-18; ✆ 6pm-11pm Mon-Sat) This little Italian joint is a great place to sip a glass of *vino de chacra* (local table wine) over one of the menu's classic pizzas or pastas. Tables fill up quickly.

La Limón (☎ 42-5182; San Martín 843; mains S16-25; ✆ 10am-5pm Sun-Wed, to 11pm Thu-Sat) With its own private entryway guarded by modelesque staff, this courtyard restaurant is vacant at times. On the innovative menu are traditional Peruvian dishes done with fusion flair, accompanied by a top-notch South American wine list.

In the *campiña* (countryside) outside Tacna, several rustic restaurants come alive for weekend lunches, offering traditional fare and live music. In the nearby suburb of Pocollay, **La Huerta** (☎ 41-3080; Zela 132; ✆ 10am-9pm) is a pleasant outdoor place with uproarious birdsong and a terrace with vine-covered trellising and live music some afternoons. Further outside the city, Calana and Pachía also have many open-air restaurants. These destinations can all be reached by catching a *combi* along Bolognesi.

Drinking

The small pedestrian streets of Libertad and Vigil are ground zero for Tacna's limited nightlife. There you'll find a couple of pubs and clubs, some with live music and dancing on weekends. Beer geeks imbibe at the flashy **München Brauhaus** (☎ 24-6125; ✆ 8pm-late) while rockers get down 'n' dirty at **Jethro Pub**; both are on Libertad.

Getting There & Away

AIR

Tacna's **airport** (code TCQ; ☎ 31-4503) is 5km west of town. At the time of research, **LAN** (☎ in Lima 01-213-8200) was the only company offering regularly scheduled passenger services to Lima, as well as thrice-weekly flights to Cuzco.

BUS

There are a few major bus terminals. Most long-distance departures leave from the **terminal terrestre** (☎ 42-7007) on Hipólito Unánue, at the northeast edge of town, with the exception of some buses to Juliaca, Desaguadero and Puno, which leave from **Terminal Collaysuyo** (☎ 31-2538), located in the district of Alta Alianza to the north of town. **Terminal Bolognesi** (Circunavalación), a 1km walk uphill past the Mercado Grau and to the right from the *terminal terrestre*, is for regional buses and *combis* to the beach at Boca del Río (S3.50, one hour) and other villages outside the city limits but within the department of Tacna.

International

Infrequent buses (S10) to Arica, Chile, leave between 6am and 10pm from the international terminal across the street from the *terminal terrestre*.

A few companies, including **Sagitario** (☎ 952-843-439) and **San Martín** (☎ 952-524-252), run overnight *económico* and luxury bus services to Puno (S35 to S45, 10 hours) via Desaguadero on the Bolivian border (S30 to S40, eight hours), finally ending up in Cuzco (S60 to S70, 18 hours). These mostly leave in the evening from Terminal Collaysuyo. When choosing this route, opt for the nicest bus, or you could be in for a cold, bumpy ride with few bathroom breaks – trust us! Alternatively, you can also return to Arequipa and transfer there.

Long-Distance

Buses are frequently stopped and searched by immigration and/or customs officials not far north of Tacna. Have your passport handy, and beware of passengers asking you to hold a package for them while they go to the bathroom or smoke a cigarette.

A S1 terminal-use tax is levied at the *terminal terrestre*. For Lima (S50 to S140, 18 to 22 hours) there are luxury services run by **Cruz del Sur** (☎ 42-5729), **Ormeño** (☎ 42-3292) and at least a half-dozen smaller, cheaper but less-reliable companies. The same services also run periodic buses to Arequipa (S15 to S35, seven hours). Most Lima-bound buses leave in the afternoon or evening and will drop you off at other south-coast towns, including Nazca and Ica. Cruz del Sur also has a daily direct overnight bus to Cuzco (S125, 17 hours) that travels via Arequipa.

SOUTH COAST

BORDER CROSSING: CHILE VIA TACNA

Border-crossing formalities are fairly straightforward, except if you take a public bus, which is not recommended. While trains (below) are the cheapest way of crossing into Chile, *colectivos* (shared taxis; below) are the quickest. Taxi drivers usually help you through the border formalities, making them a safer, more convenient option than the ratty local buses. Allow at least two hours for the 65km trip by road between Tacna and Arica.

The Chilean border post is open 8am to midnight from Sunday to Thursday, and 24 hours on Friday and Saturday. Note that Chile is an hour ahead of Peru, or two hours during daylight-saving time from the last Sunday in October to the first Sunday in April. From Arica, you can continue south into Chile by air or bus, or northeast into Bolivia by air or bus. For more information, consult Lonely Planet's *South America on a Shoestring, Chile & Easter Island* and *Bolivia*.

Flores (☎ 74-1150) has hourly *económico* buses to Moquegua (S10, three hours) and Arequipa (S25, seven hours) from 4:30am until 8:30pm, plus buses every half hour to Ilo (S10, 3½ hours). Some of these departures go directly to their destination, which can cut transit time considerably. Many other bus companies serve these destinations, but not as cheaply or frequently.

TAXI

Numerous *colectivos* (S10 to S15, two hours) to Arica, Chile, leave from the international terminal across the street from the *terminal terrestre* between 6am and 9pm, in order to cross the **Chilean Border** (🕒 8am-midnight Sun-Thu, 24hr Fri & Sat) during operating hours. On Friday and Saturday, taxis may be willing to take you at all hours of the night, but expect to pay over the odds. For border crossing formalities, see above.

Fast, though notoriously unsafe, *colectivos* to Moquegua (S15, 2½ hours) and sometimes Ilo leave when full from Mercado Grau, a short walk uphill from the *terminal terrestre*. Be sure to keep your wits about you in the dangerous market area.

TRAIN

Trains between Tacna's **train station** (☎ 42-4981; Av 2 de Mayo) and Arica, Chile (S7 Monday to Friday, S9 Saturday, 1½ hours) are the cheapest and most charming but also the slowest way to cross the border. Your passport is stamped at the station before boarding the train in Tacna. There is no stop at the actual border and you receive your entry stamp when you arrive in Chile near Arica's Plaza de Armas. Though this historic railway is a must for train buffs, service can be erratic and inconveniently timed. There's usually one train in the early morning before dawn and another in the late afternoon. Tickets may be bought the same day, or reserved the day prior to traveling. Always double check at the station for the latest schedules.

Getting Around

A taxi between the airport and the city center costs about S5, or you can go from the airport to Arica, with stops at the border, for S120. Alternatively, walk out of the airport parking area and get the same cross-border service for half-price. A taxi from the center to the bus terminals costs about S2.50.

Arequipa & Canyon Country

The irresistibly sexy city of Arequipa, known as the Ciudad Blanca (White City), is surrounded by some of the wildest terrain in Peru. This is a land of active, snowy volcanoes, high-altitude deserts, thermal hot springs, salt lakes and, last but not least, the world's deepest canyons.

Whether your heart desires trekking, mountain biking, river running (white-water rafting) or clambering up Andean peaks, Arequipa makes the perfect base camp. No other place in southern Peru delivers the best of both urban and outdoor life – you can slalom down a sandy volcanic summit and still be back in your colonial mansion guesthouse in time for a dinner of spicy *arequipeño* food and all-night dancing in a sizzling-hot nightclub.

Peru's second-largest city is often dismissed as an overland layover en route from Nazca to Lake Titicaca and Cuzco. True, it's an invaluable intermediate stop for acclimatization to high altitudes. But don't leave before exploring the city itself, at least to wander down the hidden passageways of the Monasterio de Santa Catalina and marvel at the icy Inca mummies in the Museo Santury.

Don't miss the spectacular landscape that surrounds the city either, not least the famous Cañón del Colca, shadowed by snow-topped volcanoes and possessing one of the best places to marvel at the flight of the Andean condor. More untrammeled roads, such as those in the Cañón del Cotahuasi, await adventurous souls, passing ancient ruins, waterfalls, hot springs and even dinosaur footprints. What more could you possibly ask for?

AREQUIPA & CANYON COUNTRY

HIGHLIGHTS

- Trekking past waterfalls, towering cacti, rural villages and ruins in the world's deepest canyons, the **Cañón del Colca** (p187) and **Cañón del Cotahuasi** (p193)

- Discovering the hidden secrets that lie behind the high stone walls of the **Monasterio de Santa Catalina** (p164) in Arequipa

- **Dining in style** (p182) and **dancing till dawn** (p185) with fashionable *arequipeños*

- Mountain biking down or march to the summit of the **El Misti volcano** (p169)

- Scratching your head over the meaning of the mysterious **Toro Muerto petroglyphs** (p192)

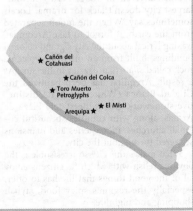

★ Cañón del Cotahuasi

★ Cañón del Colca

★ Toro Muerto Petroglyphs

Arequipa ★ ★ El Misti

- POPULATION: 864,300

- AVERAGE TEMPERATURE: January 9°C to 23°C, July 10°C to 30°C

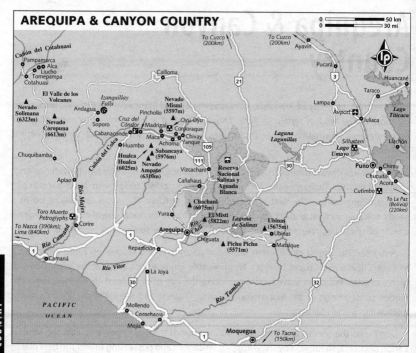

AREQUIPA & CANYON COUNTRY

AREQUIPA

☎ 054 / pop 864,300 / elev 2350m

Rocked by volcanic eruptions and earth-quakes nearly every century since the Spanish arrived in 1532, Peru's second-largest city doesn't lack for drama. Locals sometimes say 'When the moon separated from the earth, it forgot to take Arequipa,' waxing lyrical about the city's grand colonial buildings, built from an off-white volcanic rock called *sillar* that dazzles in the sun. As a result, Arequipa has been baptized the Ciudad Blanca (White City). Its distinctive stonework graces the stately Plaza de Armas, along with countless beautiful colonial churches, monasteries and mansions scattered throughout the city.

What makes this city so irresistible is the obvious relish with which its citizens enjoy all of the good things that life has to offer, especially the region's spicy food, stylish shopping and nightlife.

The pulse of city life is upbeat. The streets are full of jostling vendors, bankers, artists,

students and nuns – in short, a microcosm of modern Peru.

Arequipeños are a proud people fond of intellectual debate, especially about their fervent political beliefs, which find voice through regular demonstrations in the Plaza de Armas. In fact, their stubborn intellectual independence from Lima is so strong that at one time they even designed their own passport and flag. The celebration of the city's founding, every August 15, passionately puts an exclamation point on this regionalist pride.

HISTORY

Evidence of pre-Inca settlement by indigenous peoples from the Lake Titicaca area leads some scholars to think the Aymara people first named the city (*ari* means 'peak' and *quipa* means 'lying behind' in Aymara; hence, Arequipa is 'the place lying behind the peak' of El Misti). However, another oft-heard legend says that the fourth *inca* (king), Mayta Cápac, was traveling through the valley and became enchanted by it. He ordered his retinue to stop, saying, '*Ari, quipay,*' which translates as

'Yes, stay.' The Spaniards refounded the city on August 15, 1540, a date that is remembered with a weeklong fair.

Arequipa is built in an area highly prone to natural disasters; the city was totally destroyed by earthquakes and volcanic eruptions in 1600 and has since been rocked by major earthquakes in 1687, 1868, 1958, 1960 and, most recently, in 2001. For this reason, many of the city's buildings are built low for stability. Despite the disasters, many fetching historic structures survive.

ORIENTATION

The city of Arequipa nestles in a fertile valley under the perfect cone-shaped volcano of El Misti (5822m). Rising majestically behind the cathedral, El Misti can be viewed from the plaza and is flanked to the left by the higher and more ragged Chachani (6075m) and to the right by the peak of Pichu Pichu (5571m).

The city center is based on a checkerboard pattern around the Plaza de Armas. Because streets change names every few blocks, addresses can be confusing. Generally, streets have different names north, south, east and west of the Plaza de Armas, then change names again further out from the center.

Information
Bookstores

Colca Trek (☎ 20-6217; www.colcatrek.com.pe; Jerusalén 401-B) The best place for topographic and DIY trekking maps of the region.
Librería el Lector (☎ 28-8677; San Francisco 221; ☒ 9am-noon Mon-Sat) Two-for-one English book exchange and an excellent selection of new local-interest titles, guidebooks and music CDs.
Librería SBS Internacional (☎ 20-5317; San Francisco 125; ☒ 9am-8pm Mon-Sat) A good selection of books, including titles in English, French, Italian, Portuguese and German.

Cultural Centers

There are a few cultural centers around town that host art shows, music concerts and film screenings, and have libraries and cafes that welcome travelers.
Alianza Francesa (☎ 21-5579; www.afarequipa.org .pe; Santa Catalina 208)
Centro Cultural Peruano Norteamericano (ICPNA; ☎ 39-1020; www.cultural.edu.pe; Melgar 109)
Instituto Cultural Peruano Alemán (ICPA; ☎ 22-8130; www.icpa.org.pe; Ugarte 207)

Emergency

Policía de Turismo (Tourist Police; ☎ 20-1258; Jerusalén 315-317; ☒ 24hr) May be helpful if you need an official theft report for insurance claims.

Immigration

Oficina de migraciónes (Immigration office; ☎ 42-1759; Parque 2, cnr Bustamente & Rivero, Urb Quinta Tristán; ☒ 8am-3:30pm Mon-Fri) Come here for a visa extension.

Internet Access

Most internet cafes charge about S1.50 per hour. Many also offer cheap local and international phone calls.
Ciber Market (☎ 28-4306; Santa Catalina 115B; ☒ 8am-10pm) Private booths, fast computers with printers available, plus Skype, webcams and digital photo CD-burning services.

Laundry

Calle Jerusalén has many spots for having your kit washed.
Magic Laundry (Jerusalén 404; per kg S3; ☒ 8am-8pm Mon-Sat, 8:30am-2pm Sun) Pay S0.50 extra to have clothes washed, dried and folded in three hours.

Left Luggage

Most guesthouses and hotels will store your bags for free for a few days while you explore the surrounding countryside. Always lock your bags securely, keep a list of the contents with you and check over everything carefully when you return.

Medical Services

Clínica Arequipa (☎ 25-3424, 25-3416; Bolognesi at Puente Grau; ☒ 8am-8pm Mon-Fri, 8am-12:30pm Sat) Arequipa's best and most expensive clinic.
Hogar Clínica San Juan de Dios (☎ 25-6844, 27-2740; Av Ejército 1020, Cayma; ☒ 24hr) In the suburb of Cayma, this is also recommended; call ahead for hours.
Hospital Regional Honorio Delgado Espinoza (☎ 21-9702, 23-3812; Av Daniel Alcides Carrión s/n; ☒ 24hr) Emergency 24-hour services.
InkaFarma (☎ 20-1565; Santo Domingo 113; ☒ 24hr) One of Peru's biggest pharmacy chains; it's well stocked.
Paz Holandesa Policlinic (☎ 43-2281; www .pazholandesa.com; Av Jorge Chávez 527; ☒ 8am-8pm Mon-Sat) This appointment-only travel clinic provides vaccinations as well. Doctors here speak English and Dutch. Profits go toward providing free medical services for underprivileged Peruvian children.

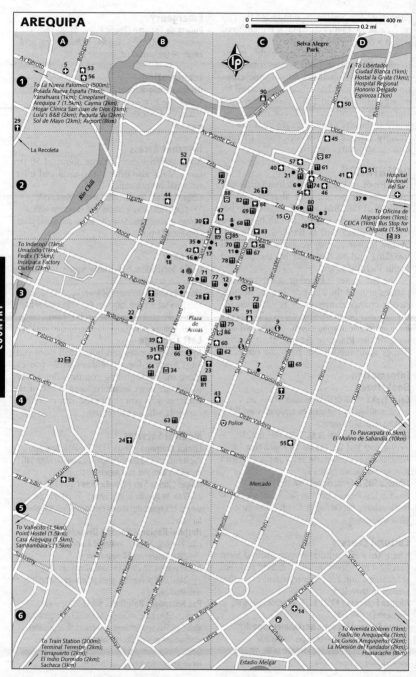

AREQUIPA

0   400 m
0   0.2 mi

To La Nueva Palomino (500m);
Posada Nueva España (1km);
Yanahuara (1km); Cineplanet
Arequipa 7 (1.5km); Cayma (2km);
Hogar Clínica San Juan de Dios (2km);
Lula's B&B (2km); Paquita Siu (2km);
Sol de Mayo (2km); Airport (8km)

La Recoleta

To Libertador
Ciudad Blanca (1km);
Hostal la Gruta (1km);
Hospital Regional
Honorio Delgado
Espinoza (2km)

Hospital
Nacional
del Sur

**To Oficina de
Migraciónes (1km);
CEICA (1km); Bus Stop for
Chiguata (1.5km)**

**To Indecopi (1km);
Umacollo (1km);
FedEx (1.5km);
Incalpaca Factory
Outlet (2km)**

Plaza
de
Armas

Police

**To Paucarpata (6.5km);
El Molino de Sabandía (10km)**

Mercado

**To Vallecito (1.5km);
Point Hostel (1.5km);
Casa Arequipa (1.5km);
Sambambaia's (1.5km)**

**To Train Station (200m);
Terminal Terrestre (2km);
Terrapuerto (2km);
El Indio Dormido (2km);
Sachaca (3km)**

**To Avenida Dolores (1km);
Tradición Arequipeña (1km);
Los Guisos Arequipeños (2km);
La Mansión del Fundador (8km);
Huasacache (8km)**

AREQUIPA & CANYON COUNTRY

AREQUIPA & CANYON COUNTRY

Money

There are moneychangers and ATMs on streets east of the Plaza de Armas. Global ATMs are easy to find in most areas frequented by travelers, including inside the Casona Santa Catalina complex, the bus terminal and the airport.

Both banks listed exchange US traveler's checks.

BCP (San Juan de Dios 125) Has a Visa ATM and changes American dollars.
Interbank (Mercaderes 217) Has a global ATM.

Post

DHL (☎ 22-5332; Santa Catalina 115; ⌚ 8:30am– 7pm Mon-Fri, 9am-1pm Sat)
FedEx (Main office; ☎ 25-6464; Av Belaúnde 121; ⌚ 9am-5pm Mon-Sat) In the suburb of Umacollo.

Main post office (Moral 118; ⌚ 8am-8pm Mon-Sat, 9am-1pm Sun)

Tourist Information

Indecopi (☎ 21-2054; Hipólito Unanue 100A, Urb Victoria; ⌚ 8:30am-4pm Mon-Fri) This is the national tourist-protection agency that deals with complaints against local firms, including tour operators and travel agencies.
iPerú airport (☎ 44-4564; 1st fl, Main Hall, Aeropuerto Rodríguez Ballón; ⌚ 10am-7:30pm); Plaza de Armas (☎ 22-3265; iperuarequipa@promperu.gob.pe; Portal de la Municipalidad 110; ⌚ 8:30am-7:30pm) Government-supported source for objective information on local and regional attractions.

DANGERS & ANNOYANCES

Petty theft is often reported in Arequipa, so travelers are urged to hide their valuables. Most crime is opportunistic, so keep your stuff in sight while in restaurants and internet cafes. While the area south of the Plaza de Armas is reportedly safe after dark, be wary of wandering outside of touristy zones at night. Take great care in Parque Selva Alegre, north of the city center, as muggings have been reported there. Instead of hailing a cab on the street, ask your hostel or tour operator to call you an official one; the extra time and money are worth the added safety. Only pay for tours in a recognized agency and never trust touts in the street – they bamboozle cash out of a surprisingly high number of travelers.

SIGHTS
Monasterio de Santa Catalina

Even if you've already overdosed on colonial edifices, this **convent** (☎ 22-9798; www.santacatalina.org.pe; Santa Catalina 301; admission S30; ☽ 9am-5pm, last entry 4pm, plus 7-9pm Tue & Thu) shouldn't be missed. Occupying a whole block and guarded by imposing high walls, it is one of the most fascinating religious buildings in Peru. Nor is it just a religious building – this 20,000-sq-meter complex is almost a citadel within the city. It is a disorienting place with twisting passageways, ascetic living quarters, period furnishings and religious art – a photographer's paradise. For a brief history of the convent, see boxed text, below.

There are two ways of visiting Santa Catalina. One is to wander around on your own, soaking up the meditative atmosphere and getting slightly lost (there's a finely printed miniature map on the back of your ticket if you're up for an orienteering challenge). Alternatively, informative guides who speak Spanish, English, French, German, Italian and Portuguese are available for S20. The tours last about an hour, after which you're welcome to keep exploring by yourself, until the gates close. The monastery is also open two evenings a week so that visitors can traipse through the shadowy grounds by candlelight as nuns would have done centuries ago.

For visitors who undertake a self-tour of Santa Catalina, a helpful way to begin is to focus a visit on the three main **cloisters**. After passing under the *silencio* (silence) arch you will enter the **Novice Cloister**, marked by a courtyard with a rubber tree at its center. After passing under this arch, novice nuns were required to zip their lips in a vow of solemn silence and resolve to a life of work and prayer. Nuns lived as novices for four years, during which time their families were expected to pay a dowry of 100 gold coins per year. At the end of these four years they could choose between taking their vows and entering into religious service, or leaving the convent – the latter would most likely have brought shame upon their family.

Graduated novices passed onto the **Orange Cloister**, named for the orange trees clustered at its center that represent renewal and eternal life. This cloister allows a peek into the **Profundis Room**, a mortuary where dead nuns were mourned. Paintings of the deceased line the walls. Artists were allotted 24 hours to complete these posthumous paintings,

---

MONASTERIO MISTERIOSO

The Monasterio de Santa Catalina was founded in 1580 by a rich widow, Doña María de Guzmán, who was very selective in choosing her nuns. They came from the best Spanish families, who naturally had to pay a substantial dowry.

Traditionally, the second son or daughter of upper-class Spanish families would enter religious service. For women, this meant going to a nunnery to live in chaste poverty. However, in this particularly privileged convent each nun had between one and four servants or slaves (usually black), and the nuns would invite musicians, have parties and generally live it up in the style to which they had always been accustomed.

After three centuries of these hedonistic goings-on, Pope Pius IX sent Sister Josefa Cadena, a strict Dominican nun, to straighten things out. She arrived like a hurricane in 1871 and set about sending the rich dowries back to Europe and freeing the myriad servants and slaves, some of whom stayed on as nuns. From this point, the convent was shrouded in mystery until it opened to the public in 1970, when the mayor of Arequipa forced the convent to modernize, including opening its doors to tourism.

Today, the three dozen or so remaining nuns continue to live a cloistered life in a far corner of the complex while the rest remains open to the public.

HUMAN SACRIFICE IN THE ANDES

In 1992 local climber Miguel Zárate was guiding an expedition on Nevado Ampato (6.) he found curious wooden remnants, suggestive of a burial site, exposed near the icy s September 1995 he convinced American mountaineer and archaeologist Johan Reinhard the peak, which following recent eruptions of the nearby Sabancaya volcano had been c ed by ash, melting the snow below and exposing the site more fully. Upon arrival, they immediately found a statue and other offerings, but the burial site had collapsed and there was no sign of a body. Ingeniously, the team rolled rocks down the mountainside and, by following them, Zárate was able to spot the bundled mummy of an Inca girl, which had tumbled down the same path when the icy tomb had crumbled.

The girl had been wrapped and almost perfectly preserved by the icy temperatures for about 500 years, and it was immediately apparent from the remote location of her tomb and from the care and ceremony surrounding her death (as well as the crushing blow to her right eyebrow) that this 12- to 14-year-old girl had been sacrificed to the gods at the summit. For the Incas, mountains were gods who could kill by volcanic eruption, avalanche or climatic catastrophes. These violent deities could only be appeased by sacrifices from their subjects, and the ultimate sacrifice was that of a child.

It took the men days to carry the frozen bundle down to the village of Cabanaconde, from where she was transported, on a princely bed of frozen foodstuffs, in Zárate's own domestic freezer to the Universidad Católica (Catholic University) in Arequipa to undergo a battery of scientific examinations. Quickly dubbed 'Juanita, the ice princess,' the mummy was given her own museum in 1998 (Museo Santury; see below). In total, almost two dozen similar Inca sacrifices have been discovered atop various Andean mountains since the 1950s.

since painting the nuns while alive was out of the question.

Leading away from the Orange Cloister, **Córdova Street** is flanked by cells that served as living quarters for the nuns. These dwellings would house one or more nuns, along with a handful of servants, and ranged from austere to lavish depending on the wealth of the inhabitants. Ambling down **Toledo Street** leads you to the cafe, which serves up fresh-baked pastries and espresso drinks, and finally to the communal washing area where servants washed in mountain runoff channeled into huge earthenware jars.

Heading down **Burgos Street** towards the cathedral's sparkling *sillar* tower, visitors may enter the musty darkness of the communal kitchen that was originally used as the church until the reformation of 1871. Just beyond, **Zocodober Square** (the name comes from the Arabic word for 'barter') served as a site where nuns gathered on Sundays to exchange their handicrafts such as soaps and baked goods. Continuing on, to the left you can enter the **cell** of the legendary Sor Ana, a nun renowned for her eerily accurate predictions about the future and the miracles she is said to have performed until her death in 1686.

Finally, the **Great Cloister** is bordered by the **chapel** on one side and the **art gallery**, which used to serve as a communal dormitory, on the other. This building takes on the shape of a cross. Murals along the walls depict scenes from the lives of Jesus and the Virgin Mary.

Museo Santury

Officially the Museo de la Universidad Católica de Santa María, this **museum** (☎ 20-0345; www .ucsm.edu.pe/santury; La Merced 110; admission S15; ⊙ 9am-6pm Mon-Sat, 9am-3pm Sun) exhibits 'Juanita, the ice princess' – the frozen body of an Inca maiden sacrificed on the summit of Nevado Ampato, a snow-covered volcano to the northwest of Arequipa, more than 500 years ago (see boxed text, above). Multilingual tours (available in Spanish, English, French, German and Italian) consist of a video followed by an examination of various burial artifacts, culminating in a respectful viewing of the frozen mummy, preserved in a carefully monitored glass-walled exhibition freezer. Although Juanita is not on display from January to April, another child sacrifice discovered in the mountains around Arequipa is on show. Only guided visits are permitted (expect to tip the guide), and the whole spectacle is done in a respectful, non-ghoulish manner. Allow about an hour for a visit.

Plaza de Armas

Arequipa's main plaza showcases the city's *sillar* architecture and the cathedral. The colonnaded balconies overlooking the plaza are a great place to relax over a snack or a coffee, though it's the views you're paying for, not the bland, overpriced cafe fare.

The history of **La Catedral** (☎ 23-2635; admission free; ☯ 7-11:30am & 5-7:30pm Mon-Sat, 7am-1pm & 5-7pm Sun), the cathedral that dominates Arequipa's main plaza, is filled with doggedness. The original structure, dating from 1656, was gutted by fire in 1844. Consequently rebuilt, it was then promptly flattened by the earthquake of 1868. Most of what you see now has been rebuilt since then. An earthquake in 2001 toppled one enormous tower, and made the other slump precariously, yet by the end of the next year the cathedral looked as good as new once again.

The cathedral is the only one in Peru that stretches the length of a plaza. The interior is simple and airy, with a luminous quality, and the high vaults are uncluttered. It also has a distinctly international flair; it is one of less than 100 basilicas in the world entitled to display the Vatican flag, which is to the right of the altar. Both the altar and the 12 columns (symbolizing the 12 Apostles) are made of Italian marble. The huge Byzantine-style brass lamp hanging in front of the altar is from Spain and the pulpit was carved in France. In 1870, Belgium provided the impressive organ, said to be the largest in South America, though damage during shipping condemned the devout to wince at its distorted notes for more than a century.

Iglesia de la Compañía

Just off the southeast corner of the Plaza de Armas, this **Jesuit church** (☎ 21-2141; admission free; ☯ 9am-12:30pm & 3-6pm Mon-Fri, 11:30am-12:30pm & 3-6pm Sat, 9am-noon & 5-6pm Sun), one of the oldest in Arequipa, is noted for its ornate main facade and main altar, which is carved in the *churrigueresque* style (an intricate decorative motif popular during the late Spanish baroque period) and completely covered in gold leaf. To the left of the altar is the **San Ignacio chapel** (admission S4), with a polychrome cupola smothered in jungle-like murals of tropical flowers, fruit and birds, among which mingle warriors and angels.

Monasterio de la Recoleta

A short cab ride from the city center in a dicey neighborhood, this musty **monastery** (☎ 27-0966; La Recoleta 117; admission S5; ☯ 9am-noon & 3-5pm Mon-Sat) was constructed on the west side of the Río Chili in 1648 by Franciscan friars, though now it has been completely rebuilt. Scholarship was an integral part of the Franciscans' order, and bibliophiles will delight in the huge library, which contains more than 20,000 dusty books and maps; the oldest volume dates back to 1494. The library is open for supervised visits; just ask at the entrance. There is a well-known museum of Amazonian artifacts (including preserved jungle animals) collected by the missionaries, and an extensive collection of pre-Conquest artifacts and religious art of the *escuela cuzqueña* (Cuzco School). Guides who speak Spanish, English, French and Italian are available; a tip is expected.

Museo de Arte Virreinal de Santa Teresa

This gorgeous 17th-century Carmelite **convent** (☎ 28-1188; Melgar 303; admission S10; ☯ 9am-5pm Mon-Sat, 9am-1pm Sun) was only recently opened to the public as a living museum. The colonial-era buildings are justifiably famed for their decoratively painted walls and restored rooms filled with priceless votive *objets d'art*, murals, precious metalworks, colonial-era paintings and other historical artifacts. It is all capably explained by student tour guides who speak Spanish, English, French, German and Portuguese; tips are appreciated. A charming shop at the front of the complex sells baked goods and rose-scented soap made by the nuns.

Colonial Mansions

Some of Arequipa's stately colonial *sillar* mansions can be visited – a real treat.

Built in 1730, **Casa de Moral** (☎ 21-4907; Moral 318; admission S5; ☯ 9am-5pm Mon-Sat) is named after the 200-year-old mulberry tree in its central courtyard. Owned by BCP, the house is now one of the most accessible for snooping, and bilingual guides are available. It has a fascinating little map collection charting South American development.

Another mansion that's easy to visit is **Casa Ricketts** (Casa Tristán del Pozo; ☎ 21-5060; San Francisco 108; admission free; ☯ 9:15am-12:45pm & 4:30-6:30pm Mon-Fri, 9:30am-12:45pm Sat). Built in 1738, it has served as a seminary, archbishop's palace, school, home to well-to-do families, and now as a working bank. Look for the puma-headed fountains in the interior courtyard.

Also worth a peek is the **Casona Iriberry** (Casa Arróspide; ☎ 20-4482; Santa Catalina 101; admission free; ⊙ 8:30am-8:30pm Mon-Fri), housing the Universidad Nacional de San Agustín (UNSA) within its 18th-century colonial halls and patios.

The 17th-century **La Mansión del Fundador** (☎ 44-2460; admission S10; ⊙ 9am-6pm), once owned by Arequipa's founder Garcí Manuel de Carbajal, has been restored with original furnishings and paintings, and even has its own chapel. The mansion is in the village of Huasacache, 9km from Arequipa's city center, most easily reached by taxi (round-trip S20). Local city tours occasionally stop here.

Other Churches

Visiting hours for smaller churches in Arequipa are erratic, but most are open for worship from 7am to 9am and 5pm to 8pm. Originally built in the 16th century, **Iglesia de San Francisco** (☎ 22-3048; Zela cuadra 1; admission S5; ⊙ church & convent 9am-12:30pm & 3-6:30pm Mon-Fri) has been badly damaged by several earthquakes. It still stands, however, and visitors can see a large crack in the cupola – testimony to the power of quakes. Other colonial churches around the city center include San Agustín, La Merced and Santo Domingo.

Other Museums

The university-run **Museo Arqueológico de la Universidad Católica de Santa María** (☎ 22-1083; Cruz Verde 303; voluntary donation; ⊙ 9am-5pm Mon-Fri)

has interesting little displays on local excavation sites, as well as some artifacts, including surprisingly well-preserved ancient ceramics. Guided tours are available in Spanish and English; tips are expected.

Opened in 2008, the **Museo Arqueológico Chiribaya** (☎ 28-6528; www.museochiribaya.org; La Merced 117; admission S15; ⊙ 8:30am-7pm Mon-Fri, 9am-3pm Sun) houses an impressive collection of artifacts from the pre-Incan Chiribaya civilization, including well-preserved textiles and the only pre-Inca gold collection in southern Peru. The museum is housed in a beautiful colonial mansion that features design details by French engineer Gustave Eiffel, of Eiffel Tower fame. University student guides offer 40-minute tours in Spanish, English, Portuguese, French, Italian and German when prearranged.

El Molino de Sabandía

The rural suburb of Paucarpata, about 8km southeast of the city center, makes a pleasant country escape. *Combis* (minibuses) can be caught along Goyeneche, Independencia and Paucarpata, which is the eastern continuation of Mercaderes (S0.70, 25 minutes), or you can take a taxi (round-trip S10). En route you can observe how the ancient Inca terracing that covers the hillsides surrounding Arequipa is slowly being consumed by the city's expansion. Paucarpata itself features an attractive colonial church on the main plaza and several good *picanterías* (local restaurants).

AREQUIPA & CANYON COUNTRY

DETOUR: YANAHUARA & CAYMA

The peaceful neighborhood of Yanahuara makes a diverting excursion from the Arequipa city center. It's within walking distance: go over Av Puente Grau over the Puente Grau (Grau Bridge) and continue on Av Ejército for half a dozen blocks. Turn right on Av Lima and walk five blocks to a small plaza, where you'll find the **Iglesia San Juan Batista** (admission free), which dates from 1750. It housed the highly venerated Virgen de Chapi after the 2001 earthquake brought her church tumbling down about her ears. The popular Fiesta de la Virgen de Chapi is held on May 1. At the side of the plaza there's a *mirador* (lookout) with excellent views of Arequipa and El Misti.

Head back along Av Jerusalén, parallel to Av Lima, and just before reaching Av Ejército you'll see the well-known restaurant Sol de Mayo (see boxed text, p183), where you can stop for a tasty lunch of typical *arequipeño* food. The round-trip walk should take around two hours, but there are also *combis* (minibuses) to Yanahuara from along Av Puente Grau (and returning from Yanahuara's plaza to the city) every few minutes to speed you along (S1, 10 minutes).

Beyond Yanahuara is Cayma, another inner suburb of Arequipa's city center, nicknamed El Balcón (the Balcony) for its privileged views. Here you'll also find the eye-catching **Iglesia de San Miguel Arcángel** (admission free), dating from 1730. For a tip, the church warden may take you up the small tower, which has panoramic views. To reach Cayma from Yanahuara, walk along San Vicente and then take Av León Velarde, or catch one of the regular *combis* marked 'Cayma' from Av Puente Grau (S1, 15 minutes).

A 3km walk from the plaza brings you to **El Molino de Sabandía** (adult/child S5/3; ⊙ 9am-5pm). This mill was built in 1785, fell into disrepair and was restored two centuries later; it now grinds once more for visitors. The neat grounds, shaded with weeping willows and providing great views of El Misti, are a favorite of picnickers. Horseback rides are available outside the restaurant (S20 per hour).

ACTIVITIES

Trekking, mountaineering and rafting trips are offered everywhere in central Arequipa. The most reliable way to find a guide is to go through a reputable agency, as informal tour operators and guides offering less-than-top-notch service abound. Mountain guides should be able to show you their Association of Mountain Guides of Peru certification, as well as a little book with a registry of all the climbs they have led. Because the very best guides are often away on trips, try to make arrangements in advance. Of course, no travel agency or guide can ever be 100% recommended, so check everything exhaustively before shelling out for any trip. The following outdoor outfitters can usually put you in touch with reliable guides:

Carlos Zárate Adventures (☎ 20-2461; www .zarateadventures.com; Santa Catalina 204) This company was founded in 1954 by Carlos Zárate, the great-grand-father of climbing in Arequipa. His son, Carlos Zárate Flores, is also an experienced guide. Guides generally speak Spanish or English, but are available in French when prearranged. The company offers all manner of treks and climbs all the local peaks. Prices vary depending on group size and method of transportation; they charge around S150 per person for a group of four to climb El Misti, and S365 for a three-day trek in the Cañón del Colca with private transport. They also rent all kinds of gear to independent climbers and hikers including ice axes, crampons and hiking boots.

Colca Trek (☎ 20-6217, 9-60-0170; www.colcatrek .com.pe; Jerusalén 401-B) Colca Trek is an ecoconscious adventure-tour agency and shop run by the knowledge-able, English-speaking Vlado Soto. In addition to trekking tours, it organizes mountaineering, mountain-biking and river-running trips; and it is one of the few shops selling decent topographical maps of the area. It is a venerable source of information for those hoping to explore the area on their own. Be careful of copycat travel agencies that use the Colca Trek name and/or web addresses that are similar to the agency's official site.

Naturaleza Activa (☎ 69-5793; naturactiva@yahoo .com; Santa Catalina 211) A favorite of those seeking

adventure tours, and offering a full range of trekking, climbing and mountain-biking options. One popular tour is a three- to four-hour bike trip down El Misti (US$45) including transportation and bike, helmet, guide and snacks. It's also possible to rent mountain bikes for S9 per hour. Guides speak English, French and German.

Pablo Tour (☎ 20-3737; www.pablotour.com; Jerusalén 400 AB-1) Consistently recommended by readers, Pablo Tour's guides are experts in trekking and cultural tours in the region, and can furnish trekkers with all the necessary equipment and topographical maps. They are happy to customize tours depending on clients' needs or offer professional advice to those hoping to go it alone. The owner, Edwin, speaks English and French. Can also help travelers communicate with the Hostal Valle del Fuego in Cabanaconde (p191), or Oasis Bungalows (p191) at the base of the Cañón del Colca.

Mountaineering

Superb mountains for climbing surround Arequipa. Adequate acclimatization for this area is essential and it's best to have spent some time in Cuzco or Puno immediately before a high-altitude expedition. Climbers must carry all the water they will need during climbs for all mountains except for Nevado Coropuna, where freshwater springs can be found along the way. Cold temperatures, which sometimes drop to -29°C at the highest camps, necessitate very warm clothing. The best months for mountain climbing are between April and December.

Though many climbs in the area are not technically difficult, they should never be undertaken lightly. Watch for the symptoms of altitude sickness and if in doubt, go back down. The Association of Mountain Guides of Peru warns that many guides are uncertified and untrained, so climbers are advised to go well informed about medical and wilderness-survival issues.

Maps of the area can be obtained from **Colca Trek** (☎ 20-6217, 9-60-0170; www.colcatrek .pe; Jerusalén 401-B) in Arequipa or the Instituto Geográfico Nacional (see p521) and South American Explorers Club (see boxed text, p86) in Lima. **Carlos Zárate Adventures** (☎ 20-2461; www.zarateadventures.com; Santa Catalina 204) and **Peru Camping Shop** (☎ 22-1658; www.perucampingshop .com; Jerusalén 410) rent tents, ice axes, crampons, stoves and boots. Most agencies sell climbs as packages that include transport, so prices vary widely depending on the size of the group and the mountain, but the current cost for a guide alone is around US$70 per day.

EL MISTI

Looming 5822m above Arequipa, the city's guardian volcano El Misti is the most popular climb in the area. It is technically one of the easiest ascents of any mountain of this size in the world, but it's hard work nonetheless and you normally need an ice ax and, sometimes, crampons. Hiring a guide is highly recommended. A two-day trip will usually cost between US$50 to US$70 per person. The mountain is best climbed from July to November, with the later months being the least cold. Below the summit is a sulfurous yellow crater with volcanic fumaroles hissing gas, and there are spectacular views down to the Laguna de Salinas and back to the city.

The ascent can be approached by many routes, some more worn-in than others, most of which can be done in two days. The Apurímac route is notorious for robberies. One popular route starts from Chiguata, and begins with a hard eight-hour slog uphill to reach base camp (4500m); from there to the summit and back takes eight hours, while the sliding return from base camp to Chiguata takes three hours or less. The Aguada Blanca route is restricted to a handful of official tour operators and allows climbers to arrive at 4100m before beginning to climb.

Determined climbers can reach the Chiguata route via public transport. Buses going to Chiguata leave from Av Sepulveda in Arequipa (S7 one way, one hour) hourly beginning at 5:30am and will drop you off at an unmarked trailhead, from where you can begin the long trek to base camp. On the return trip, you should be able to flag down the same bus heading the opposite way. The more common method to reach the mountain is hiring a 4WD vehicle for around S200 that will take you up to 3300m and pick you up on the return.

OTHER MOUNTAINS

One of the easiest 6000m peaks in the world is **Chachani** (6075m), which is as close to Arequipa as El Misti. You will need crampons, an ice ax and good equipment. There are various routes up the mountain, one of which involves going by 4WD to Campamento de Azufrera at 4950m. From there you can reach the summit in about nine hours and return in under four hours. Alternatively, for a two-day trip, there is a good spot to camp at 5200m. Other routes

take three days but are easier to get to by 4WD (US$110 to US$160).

Sabancaya (5976m) is part of a massif on the south rim of the Cañon del Colca that also includes extinct **Hualca Hualca** (6025m) and **Nevado Ampato** (6310m). Sabancaya has erupted in recent years, and should only be approached with a guide who understands the geologic activity of the area; neighboring Ampato is a fairly straightforward, if strenuous, three-day ascent, and you get safer views of the active Sabancaya from here.

Other mountains of interest near Arequipa include **Ubinas** (5675m), which used to be the easiest mountain to summit but is currently spewing enough toxic ash that it is not recommended for climbing. **Nevado Mismi** (5597m) is a fairly easy three- or four-day climb on the north side of the Cañon del Colca. You can approach it on public transportation and, with a guide, find the lake that is reputedly the source of the Amazon. The highest mountain in southern Peru is the difficult **Nevado Coropuna** (6613m).

Trekking

The spectacular canyons around Arequipa offer many excellent hiking options. Trekking agencies can arrange a whole array of off-the-beaten-track routes to suit your timeline and fitness level. Although you can trek year-round, the best (ie driest) time is from May to November. There is more danger of rockfalls in the canyons during the wet season (between December and April). Easier treks in the Cañon del Colca can be beautifully lush during the wet season, however, while more remote trails, especially those in the Cañon del Cotahuasi, become inaccessible.

Our best advice is that if you're already an experienced trekker and you're trekking in a well-traveled area like the Cañon del Colca, you don't need to go with a guide at all. Hiking from village to village or doing the ever-popular trek from the canyon's rim to **Sangalle** (also popularly called 'the oasis') are the simplest DIY trekking options. In the Cañon del Colca region, the main roads are scenic routes. The roads are a good, easy way to experience village life at a slower pace, although they are dusty and passing traffic can be unnerving.

If you're nervous about hiking solo or want to tackle more untrammeled routes, there are dozens of tour companies based in Arequipa that can arrange guided treks. Expect to pay more when booking a trek before arriving in Arequipa.

For indispensable topographic maps for trekking, as well as top-notch guided trips (including of the Cañón del Cotahuasi), contact **Colca Trek** (☎ 20-6217, 9-60-0170; www.colcatrek .com.pe; Jerusalén 401-B).

River Running

Arequipa is one of Peru's premier bases for river running and kayaking. Many trips are unavailable during the rainy season (between December and March), when water levels can be dangerously high. For more information and advice, surf www.peruwhitewater.com.

The **Río Chili**, about 7km from Arequipa, is the most frequently run local river, with a half-day trip suitable for beginners leaving almost daily from April to November (from US$25). Further afield, you can also do relatively easy trips on the **Río Majes**, into which the Río Colca flows. The most commonly run stretches pass class II and III rapids.

A more off-the-beaten-track possibility is the remote **Río Cotahuasi**, a white-water adventure – not for the fainthearted – that reaches into the deepest sections of what is perhaps the world's deepest known canyon. Expeditions here are infrequent and only for the experienced, usually taking nine days and passing through class IV and V rapids. The **Río Colca** was first run back in 1981, but this is a dangerous, difficult trip, not to be undertaken lightly. A few outfitters will do infrequent and expensive rafting trips, and easier sections can be found upriver from the canyon.

A number of rafting outfitters have been recommended by travelers:

Amazonas Explorer (☎ in Cuzco 084-25-2846; www .amazonas-explorer.com; Collasuyo 910, Urb Marivelle, Cuzco) Located in Cuzco, this company can arrange private trips on the Río Cotahuasi.

Casa de Mauro (☎ 9-59-336-684; raftingguide@ hotmail.com; Ongoro Km 5 s/n) This convenient base camp for rafting the Río Majes is in the village of Ongoro, 190km by road west of Arequipa. The lodge offers one- to three-hour trips for beginner to experienced rafters (S70 to S140 per person). They can also organize multiple-day trips in the upper Río Colca (from S900 per person) and treks to nearby ruins (from S600 per person). The lodge offers camping (S10 per person) or rooms with private bathrooms (S30 per person). It is cheapest to take a Transportes del Carpio bus from Arequipa's *terminal terrestre* to Aplao (S10, three hours, hourly) and then a *combi* (S1.50) or a taxi (S12) to Ongoro.

Cusipata (☎ 20-3966; www.cusipata.com; Jerusalén 408) Cusipata leads recommended white-water and kayaking trips to all major rivers, including the Ríos Colca and Cotahuasi (US$2000, seven days), with the English-speaking Vellutino brothers, Gian Marco and Piero. They also organize introductory three-day kayaking courses (US$150).

Majes River Lodge (☎ 83-0297, 9-59-797-731; www .majesriver.com) Offers easy one-hour rafting trips (S60) or more challenging three-hour trips that pass through class IV rapids (S110) on the Río Majes. Overnight accommodations in bungalows with solar hot-water showers cost S40 per person; camping, meals of fresh river shrimp, and tours to the nearby Toro Muerto petroglyphs are also available. Take a taxi (S10) or a *combi* (S1.50) from Aplao to the Majes River Lodge.

Mountain Biking

The Arequipa area has many mountain-biking possibilities. Many of the same companies that offer trekking or mountain-climbing trips (see p168) also organize downhill volcano mountain-biking trips at Chachani and El Misti or can arrange tailor-made tours. If you have the experience and wherewithal, these agencies can rent you high-end bikes and offer expert trip-planning advice to help get you started on your own. For rentals also try

Peru Camping Shop (☎ 22-1658; www.perucampingshop .com; Jerusalén 410) Mountain bike rentals by the hour (S9) or day (S60) include helmet, gloves and a map of the area. Also rents a variety of other trekking and mountain-climbing gear.

COURSES

For Spanish-language courses, there are literally dozens of schools in Arequipa. Ask around for recent recommendations from other travelers. Also try:

ACI (☎ 22-2595; www.acidelperu.com; Jorge Polar 203) Offers individual courses for US$10 per hour, or group classes starting at US$75 for 10 hours, and can arrange accommodation in a homestay.

CEICA (☎ 22-1165; www.ceica-peru.com/arequipa.htm; Urb Universitaria G-9) It charges S400 for 20 hours of private lessons per week and can arrange family homestays including/excluding meals for S265/173 a week. Call in advance and they'll pick you up from the airport or bus terminal.

CEPESMA (☎ 9-59-961-638; www.cepesmaidiomasceci .com; Puente Grau 108) Charges around S18 per hour for private classes.

EDEAQ (☎ 22-6784, 9-59-342-660; www.edeaq.com; Puente Bolognesi 132, esc Sucre) This is a Peruvian- and Swiss-managed school. It's more expensive, but also more intensive than most, costing from S582 per week for lessons plus homestay or hotel accommodations with breakfast.

Juanjo (www.spanishlanguageperu.com; 2nd epata C-4, Urb Magisterial, Yanahuara) Recommended by travelers, it arranges individual, small-group classes from S72 per week. Homestays and volunteer work can also be arranged.

ROCIO (☎ 22-4568; www.spanish-peru.com; Ayacucho 208) Charges S14 per hour for an individual class, while small group lessons cost S270 per 40-hour week. Classes start every Monday.

TOURS & GUIDES

The streets of Santa Catalina and Jerusalén harbor dozens of travel agencies offering ho-hum city tours and excursions to the canyon country, most with daily departures. While some agencies are professional, there are also plenty of carpetbaggers muscling in on the action, so shop carefully. Never accept tours from street touts and, where possible, tours should be paid for in cash, as occasional credit-card fraud is reported. Most agencies pool their clients into one bus, even though they charge different rates for the tours. Minibuses are the norm for these trips, and the small vehicles are cramped and overcrowded. Guides usually speak some level of English and/or other languages, but some garble a memorized and hard-to-follow script.

The standard two-day tour of the Cañón del Colca (p191) costs S65 to S225 per person, depending on the season, group size and the comfort level of the hotel you choose to stay at in Chivay. All tours leave Arequipa between 7am and 9am, passing through the Reserva Nacional Salinas y Aguada Blanca (p187). A stop is usually made at a teahouse and, later, at the highest point to take in the views before descending to Chivay for lunch. Some agencies then take their groups on a short hike, and the hot springs of Chivay are almost always visited before sunset, so bring a swimsuit and towel. There is usually a visit to a lively, if touristy *peña* (bar or club featuring live folkloric music) in the evening. Be aware that the cost of the tour includes lodging with breakfast in Chivay, but other meals are paid for out of your own pocket, as is the canyon's *boleto turístico* (tourism ticket; S35) and small tips for your guide and driver. On the second morning the group leaves around 6am to reach Cruz del Cóndor by 8:30am for an hour or so of condor-spotting, before returning to Arequipa. Many groups are approached by locals toting captive birds of prey in the hope

that tourists will pay a tip to have their picture taken. Please do not encourage the capture of these endangered wild birds.

Ask Miguel Fernández, owner of **AI Travel Tours** (☎ 22-2052; www.aitraveltours.com; Santa Catalina 203), about unique cultural tours in the Arequipa region.

For agencies offering outdoor activity-based tours, see p168.

FESTIVALS & EVENTS

Semana Santa (Holy Week) *Arequipeños* claim that their Semana Santa celebrations leading up to Easter are similar to the very solemn and traditional Spanish observances from Seville. Maundy Thursday, Good Friday and Holy Saturday processions are particularly colorful and sometimes end with the burning of an effigy of Judas.

Fiesta de la Virgen de Chapi Arequipa also fills up for this festival, celebrated on May 1 in Yanahuara (see boxed text, p167).

August 15 The founding day of the city is celebrated with parades, dancing, beauty pageants, climbing competitions on El Misti and other energetic events over the course of several days. The fireworks show in the Plaza de Armas on the evening of August 14 is definitely worth catching.

SLEEPING

Arequipa has been experiencing a hotel boom for quite some time now, and competition is stiff. It's always worth asking for discounts, especially if you stay put for a few days, though the prices quoted skyrocket around holidays and festivals. Prices listed are for high season (June to August), but fluctuate greatly even during these months.

Budget

Unless otherwise indicated, all accommodations listed here have some hot water.

Hospedaje el Caminante Class (☎ 20-3444; 2nd fl, Santa Catalina 207A; dm/s/d without bathroom S15/20/30, s/d S30/45) This recommended guesthouse near the plaza is a decent budget option. It has basic rooms, kitchen privileges and a rooftop terrace with views. Breakfast is available for S4 extra. Shared bathrooms are dorm style and not always clean.

Le Foyer (☎ 28-6473; hostallefoyer@hotmail.com; Ugarte 114; dm/s/d without bathroom S15/25/35, s/d/tr S35/50/70; 🖳) Though pervaded with hunger-inducing smells from the Mexican restaurant below, this place is a decent-value option if you want to be in the thick of Arequipa's nocturnal action. Rooms have TVs.

Home Sweet Home (☎ 40-5982; www.homesweet home-peru.com; Rivero 509A; dm/s/d without bathroom S18/30/50, s/d S40/60, all with breakfast; 💻) This genuinely friendly homestay has won over countless backpackers with its huge breakfasts and cute, if a bit musty, rooms. It's reliably secure, although some travelers have reported that tours organized through the hostel did not always deliver what they claimed they would.

La Posada del Virrey (☎ 22-4050; laposada delvirrey@yahoo.com; Puente Grau 103; dm/s/d without bathroom S20/20/35, s/d S30/45, all with breakfast; 💻) Popular with readers, this rickety old mansion includes a terrace sitting area and shared kitchen. The decor – ruffled bedspreads and broken-in lazy boys – will remind you of grandma's house.

Los Andes Bed & Breakfast (☎ 33-0015; losandesaqp@ hotmail.com; La Merced 123; s/d/tr without bathroom S22/38/47, s/d S66/86; 💻) Just a stone's throw south of the Plaza de Armas, this airy guesthouse has spacious, if spartan, rooms and sun-drenched common lounges. Justifiably popular with foreign students and volunteers, it's especially comfy for extended stays.

Point Hostel (☎ 28-6920; www.thepointhostels.com; Av Lima 515, Vallecito; dm S24-28, s/d without bathroom from S50/64, all with breakfast; 💻) Located in the verdant suburb of Vallecito, this rambling hostel has a slew of the kind of amenities that backpackers love, including a game room, a library and socializing spaces that make it almost worth the above-average price.

Hostal Núñez (☎ 21-8648; www.hotel_nunez.de; Jerusalén 528; s/d without bathroom S30/45, s/d/tr S45/80/90, all with breakfast; 💻) On a street full of not-so-great guesthouses, this secure, friendly hostel is always stuffed with gringos. The colorful rooms sport frilly decor and cable TV, though the singles are a bit of a squeeze.

La Posada del Cacique (☎ 20-2170; posada delcacique@yahoo.es; Jerusalén 404; s/d/tr S30/50/60; 💻) This 2nd-floor hostel has spacious, sunny rooms, a well-equipped shared kitchen, reliable hot water, and a tranquil rooftop sitting area. The father-son owners are great resources for local info and make guests feel right at home.

La Casa Blanca (☎ 28-2218; informes@yourperu.com; Jerusalén 412; s/d without bathroom S30/60, s/d/q S60/90/140; 💻) This new hostel boasts only a few rooms and is pervaded by tranquil beats from the adjoining coffee shop and bar. The staff is eager to please, but showers must be timed right if they are going to be hot.

La Casa de Sillar (☎ 28-4249; www.thecasadesillar .com; Rivero 504; s/d/tr without bathroom S45/65/85, s/d/tr S55/75/95; 💻) This option is owned by the English-speaking boss of Los Leños pizzeria (p182). Housed in a capacious colonial building tucked down a side alley, the rooms combine rustic style with convenience. There's a huge common kitchen and spacious common spaces.

Casa de Avila (☎ 21-3177; www.casadeavila.com; San Martín 116, Vallecito; s/d/tr/q S70/90/120/150; 💻) A breezy walk southwest of the Plaza de Armas, this family-run guesthouse does everything it can to entice travelers, including providing hot-water showers, a sunny garden ('for taking a beer'), unlimited coffee and taxi pickups. It also has an associated Spanish-language school that gives lessons on the premises.

Casablanca Hostal (☎ 22-1327; www.casablanca hostal.com; Puente Bolognesi 104; s/d/tr with breakfast S70/120/150; 💻) In a beautifully renovated mansion directly off the Plaza de Armas, this hostel adds a touch of luxury at a great value. The stone innards lend it a gothic feel, while the terrace and eating area are sunny and inviting.

Also recommended:

El Indio Dormido (☎ 42-7401; the_sleeping_indian@ yahoo.com; Av Andrés Avelino Cáceres B-9; s/d/tr S25/30/40) Conveniently situated near the bus terminal, this off-the-beaten-path hostel relies on word of mouth from happy guests. It's complete with a pretty (but noisy) terrace with hammocks to laze in. Call ahead for directions.

La Posada del Parque (☎ 21-2275; Deán Valdivia 238A; dm S15, s/d/tr S30/50/70) This low-budget option feels vacant at times, but the gracious hostess and off-the-market location lend it authenticity and charm.

Lula's B&B (☎ 27-2517, 9-34-2660; bbaqpe.com; Cerro San Jacinto, Cayma; s/d US$15/20) A charming apartment-style B&B run by a friendly Spanish teacher in the suburb of Cayma. Big discounts are given for extended stays. Meals (vegetarians OK) and airport and bus terminal pickups also available.

Colonial House Inn (☎ 22-3533; colonialhouseinn@ hotmail.com; Av Puente Grau 114; s/d with breakfast S48/72; 💻) Peaceful, if slightly run-down, colonial house with friendly staff. Rooftop terrace with a garden and striking views of El Misti on clear days.

Hospedaje Familiar Thelma (☎ 28-6357; pension thelma@hotmail.com; Palacio Viejo 107; s/d with breakfast S60/75) Recommended by readers, this quiet homestay's hostess speaks Spanish, French, German, Italian and English.

(Continued on page 181)

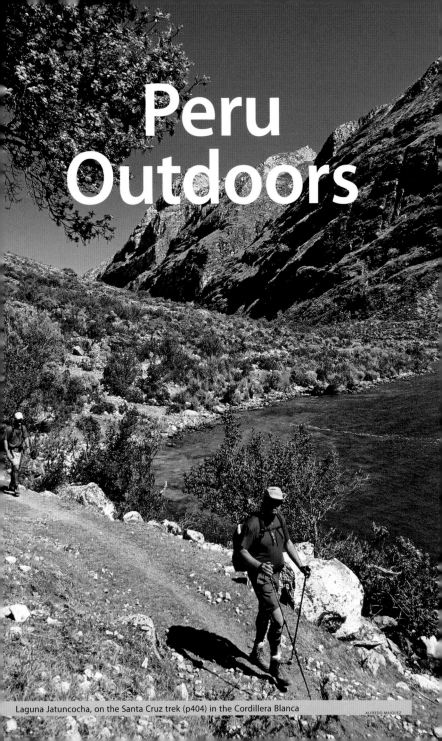

Peru
Outdoors

Laguna Jatuncocha, on the Santa Cruz trek (p404) in the Cordillera Blanca

ALFREDO MAIQUEZ

Scale icy Andean peaks. Raft one of the world's deepest canyons. Walk the flanks of a smoldering volcano where Incas once sacrificed children to appease mountain gods. In Peru, this is just the beginning of a very long menu of activities that can be devoured by devoted adrenaline junkies. There are vertiginous dunes to be sandboarded, pre-Columbian roadways to be hiked, record-breaking waves to be surfed, and labyrinthine mountain descents to be biked. The best part: the fledgling status of some outdoor activities in Peru means that, on some occasions and in some places, you can get a mountain, a wave or a lake to yourself. So gear up – and take the Band-Aids. You're in for one heck of a wild ride.

TREKKING & HIKING

Pack the hiking boots – because the variety of trails in Peru is downright staggering. The main trekking centers are Cuzco (p233) and Arequipa (p169) in the southern Andes, and Huaraz in the north (p402). Hikers will find many easily accessible trails around Peru's archaeological ruins, which are also the final destinations for more challenging trekking routes.

Peru's most famous trek is the Inca Trail to Machu Picchu (p283). Of course, this means it gets crowded, so we highly recommend that you think about taking an alternative route (for ideas, see p285). Other possibilities around Cuzco include the spectacular six-day trek around the venerated Ausangate (6372m; p234), which will take you over 5000m passes, through huge herds of alpacas, and past tiny hamlets unchanged in centuries. Likewise, the Inca site of Choquequirau (p234) is another intriguing and wonderfully isolated spot for a trek.

In nearby Arequipa, you can get down in some of the world's deepest canyons – the world-famous Cañón del Colca (p187) and the Cañón del Cotahuasi (p193). The scenery is

Taking a break on the Inca Trail (p283)
ANTHONY PIDGEON

guaranteed to knock you off your feet, and it's easier going than some higher-altitude destinations. During the wet season, when some Andean trekking routes are impassable, Colca is invitingly lush and green. It's also the best place in Peru for DIY trekking between rural villages. The more-remote and rugged Cañón del Cotahuasi is best visited with an experienced local guide and only during the dry season.

Outside Huaraz, the Cordillera Blanca (p404) can't be beat for vistas of rocky, snowcapped mountaintops, while the remote and rugged Cordillera Huayhuash (p410) is similarly stunning. The classic and favorite trekking route is the four-day journey from Llanganuco to Santa Cruz (p404), where hardy mountaineers climb the 4760m Punta Union pass, surrounded

Nearly there! Atop the summit ridge of Nevado Quitaraju in the Cordillera Blanca (p404)

GRANT DIXON

top five
PERUVIAN PEAKS

Huascarán (p404), 6768m
Contend with ice falls, avalanches and crevasses on Peru's biggest, baddest mountain

Yerupajá (p420), 6634m
Known popularly as 'the Butcher' for its sharp knife edge

Coropuna (p169), 6613m
The highest volcano in the tropics – don't worry, it's extinct

Huandoy (p408), 6395m
Within view of Huascarán lies this pointy, snowcapped massif

Ausangate (p234), 6384m
A snowy peak near Cuzco that is the site of solemn Quechua rituals

by ice-clad peaks. Longer treks include the northern route around the dazzling Alpamayo (p406), which requires at least a week. Shorter overnight trips in the area go to mountain base camps, alpine lakes and even along an old Inca road.

Cuzco and Huaraz (and, to a lesser degree, Arequipa) have outfitters that can provide equipment, guides and even *arrieros* (mule drivers). If you prefer to trek ultralight, you might want to bring your own gear, especially a sleeping bag, as old-generation rental items tend to be heavy. Whether you'll need a guide depends on where you trek. Certain areas of Peru, such as along the Inca Trail, require guides; in other places, such as in the Cordillera Huayhuash, there have been muggings, so it's best to be with a local. Thankfully, scores of other trekking routes are wonderfully DIY. Equip yourself with topographic maps for major routes in the nearest major gateway towns or, better yet, at the Instituto Geográfico Nacional (IGN; p521) or at the South American Explorers Club (p86) in Lima.

Whatever adventure you choose, be prepared to spend a few days acclimating to the dizzying altitudes – or face a heavy-duty bout of altitude sickness (p548).

Trekking is most rewarding during the dry season (May to September) in the Andes. See p394 for tips on responsible trekking.

MOUNTAIN, ROCK & ICE CLIMBING

Peru has the highest tropical mountains in the world, offering some absolutely inspired climbs. The Cordillera Blanca, with its dozens of snowy peaks exceeding 5000m, is one of the top destinations for this in South America. The Andean town of Huaraz (p393) has tour agencies, outfitters, guides, information and climbing equipment for hire (though it's best to bring your own gear for serious ascents). Near Huaraz, Ishinca (5530m) and Pisco (5752m) provide two ascents easy enough for relatively inexperienced climbers. These mountains are also good warm-up climbs for experts acclimating for bigger adventures such as Huascarán (6768m), the highest peak in Peru. Other challenging peaks include the stunning, knife-edged Alpamayo (5947m); to the south, the Cordillera Huayhuash offers Yerupajá (6634m), Peru's second-highest mountain. Rock and ice climbing are also taking off around Huaraz, where a few outfitters have indoor climbing walls, rent out technical equipment and organize group trips.

In southern Peru, there is no shortage of mountain highs. Arequipa (p168) is surrounded by snowy volcanic peaks, some of which can be scaled by beginners (as long as you've got lots of determination and some wilderness experience). The most popular climb around Arequipa is El Misti (5822m), which, despite its height, is basically a very long, tough walk (it was also the site of Inca human sacrifice). Chachani (6075m) is one of the easier 6000m peaks in the world – though it still requires crampons, an ice ax and a good guide. You'll find other tempting climbs in the peaks that tower above the Cañón del Colca (p187).

For beginners looking to bag their first serious mountains, Peru may not be the best place to start. Mountaineering is relatively new and some guides are inexperi-

TOUCHING THE VOID

What inspires a person to endure inhospitable climes, hunger, exhaustion and a lack of oxygen in order to conquer forbidding mountain peaks? It's a question explored at length by Joe Simpson in his celebrated book, *Touching the Void: The True Story of One Man's Miraculous Survival*. This gripping narrative is the story of a climb that Simpson undertook with his climbing partner, Simon Yates. The climb began well enough – with an extremely challenging and, ultimately, successful ascent on the jagged and steep Siula Grande in the Cordillera Huayhuash. But it ended in an accident that almost claimed one man's life. The book examines the thrills and the rewards – and also the agony – that come with journeying through such extraordinary yet dangerous beauty. It was made into an award-winning British documentary in 2003.

Adventures await in the Cañón del Colca (p187)

GRANT D

enced and don't know the basics of first aid or wilderness search and rescue. Check out a prospective guide's credentials carefully and seek out personally recommended guides. When renting equipment, be sure to check it carefully before setting out.

As with trekking, high-elevation climbing is best done during the dry season (mid-June to mid-July). Likewise, acclimatization to altitude is essential.

RIVER RUNNING

Also known as white-water rafting, river running is growing in popularity around Peru. Commercial rafting trips and kayaking are both possible; trips can range from a few hours to more than two weeks.

Cuzco (p234) is undoubtedly the main town for the greatest variety of river-running options. The choices range from a few hours of mild rafting on the Urubamba to adrenaline-pumping rides on the Santa Teresa to several days on the Apurímac, technically the source of the Amazon (and offering world-class rafting between May and November). A river-running trip on the Tambopata, available from June through October, tumbles down the eastern slopes

Enjoy Peru's rivers with a reputable operator
RICHARD I'ANSON

of the Andes, culminating in a couple of days of floating in unspoiled rainforest.

Arequipa (p170) is another rafting center. Here, the Río Chili is the most frequently run local river, with a half-day beginners' trip leaving daily between March and November. Further afield, the expert-level Río Majes passes class II and class III rapids. On the south coast, Lunahuaná (p127), not far from Lima, is a prime spot for beginners and experts alike. Between December and April, rapids here can reach class IV.

Note that rafting is not regulated in Peru. There are deaths every year and some rivers are so remote that rescues can take days. In addition, some companies are not environmentally sensitive, resulting in dirty camping beaches. Book excursions only with reputable, well-recommended agencies and avoid cut-rate trips. A good operator will have insurance, provide you with a document indicating that they are registered, and have highly experienced guides with certified first-aid training who carry a properly stocked medical kit. Choose one that provides top-notch equipment, including self-bailing rafts, US Coast Guard–approved life jackets, first-class helmets and spare paddles. Many good companies raft rivers accompanied by a kayaker experienced in river rescue.

For more on river running in Peru, visit www.peruwhitewater.com.

SURFING

With consistent, uncrowded waves and plenty of remote breaks to explore, Peru has a mixed surfing scene that attracts dedicated locals and international die hards alike.

Waves can be found the moment you land, all along the southern part of Lima (p101) – you'll see surfers riding out popular point and beach breaks at Miraflores (known as Waikiki), Barranquito and La Herradura. (This latter spot has an outstanding left point break, but it gets crowded when there is a strong swell.) In-the-know surfers prefer the smaller crowds further south at Punta Hermosa (p123). Nearby, you'll find Punta Rocas, where annual international and national championships are held, as well as Pico Alto, a 'kamikaze' reef break that boasts one of the largest waves in Peru (seriously, experts only). Isla San Gallán, off the Península de Paracas (p129) also provides a world-class right-hand point break ideal for expert surfers. It's only accessible by boat; ask local fishermen or at hotels.

Peru's north coast has a string of excellent breaks. We've rounded up the top five on p381. The most famous of these is at Puerto Chicama (p357), where rides of more than 2km are possible on a wave considered to be the longest left hand in the world. Also very steady are the waves at Pacasmayo (p357), and Pimentel and Santa Rosa (p363), outside Chiclayo.

top five
WILDLIFE-WATCHING SPOTS

Parque Nacional Manu (p477)
Jaguars, tapirs and monkeys inhabit this expansive rainforest park deep in the Amazon

Cañón del Colca (p187)
Catch the breathtaking sight of Andean condors gliding on wind currents

Islas Ballestas (p130)
Colonies of honking sea lions and penguins make their homes on rocky outcrops in the Pacific

Parque Nacional Huascarán (p404)
See giant *Puya raimondii* plants bursting with flowers and catch sight of vicuñas and viscachas bustling around the Cordillera Blanca

Tumbes (p386)
A rare mangrove forest that's home to crocodiles, seabirds, flamingos and crabs

Peru attracts surfers from around the world
PAUL KENNEDY

The water is cold from April to mid-December (as low as 15°C/60°F), when wet suits are generally needed. Indeed, many surfers wear wet suits year-round, even though the water is a little warmer (around 20°C, or 68°F, in the Lima area) from January to March. The far north coast (north of Talara) stays above 21°C (70°F) most of the year.

Though waves are generally not crowded, surfing can be a challenge – facilities are limited and equipment rental is expensive. The scene on the north coast is the most organized, with surf shops and hostels that offer advice, rent boards and organize surfing day trips. If you're serious about surfing in Peru, however, bring your own board.

For more information check out surfing sites such as www.peruazul.com, www.viva mancora.com and www.wannasurf.com – the last provides a comprehensive, highly detailed list of just about every break in Peru.

SANDBOARDING

For something completely different, hit waves…of sand. Sandboarding down the giant desert dunes is growing in popularity at spots such as Huacachina (p140) and around Nazca (p140), on Peru's south coast. Nazca's Cerro Blanco (2078m) is the highest known sand dune in the world. Some hotels and travel agencies offer tours in *areneros* (dune buggies), where you are hauled to the top of the dunes, then get picked up at the bottom. (Choose your driver carefully; some are notoriously reckless.)

For more information on sandboarding worldwide, check out *Sandboard Magazine* at www.sandboard.com.

Huacachina (p140) offers a new wave to surf
JANE SWEENEY

MOUNTAIN BIKING & CYCLING

In Peru mountain biking is still a fledgling sport. That said, both easy and demanding single-track trails await mountain bikers outside of Huaraz (p393), Arequipa (p170) and even Lima (p101). If you're experienced, there are incredible mountain-biking possibilities around the Sacred Valley and downhill trips to the Amazon jungle, all accessible from Cuzco (p235). Easier cycling routes include the wine country around Lunahuaná (p127) and in the Cañón del Colca, starting from Chivay (p188).

Mountain-bike rental in Peru tends to be basic, so if you are planning on serious

Tour the Sacred Valley on two wheels (p235)
DANNY WARREN / SHUTTERSHOCK

biking it's best to bring your own. (Airline bicycle-carrying policies vary, so shop around.) You'll also need a repair kit and extra parts.

SWIMMING

Swimming is popular along the Peruvian coast from January to March, when the Pacific Ocean waters are warmest. It ain't Ibiza, though. The shoreline is, by and large, composed of desert and not much else. But when the sky is blue and the waves are crashing, it nonetheless becomes quite the scene. Some of the most hopping shore spots are just south of Lima (p123). Far more attractive is the stretch of shore on the north coast, especially at laid-back Huanchaco (p352), around Chiclayo (p363) and the perennially busy jet-set resorts at Máncora (p376).

Only north of Talara does the water stay warm year-round. Watch for dangerous currents and note that beaches near major coastal cities are often polluted.

SCUBA DIVING

Scuba diving in Peru is limited. The water is cold except from mid-December to March. During these months the water is at its cloudiest, due to runoff from mountain rivers. A dive shop in Lima (p101) offers PADI certification classes, rents scuba equipment and offers diving trips to sea-lion colonies along the coast.

A gentler way to explore the countryside
LEANNE WALKER

Drop in to Miraflores (p101), Lima
PAUL KENNEDY

HORSEBACK RIDING

Horse rentals can be arranged in many tourist destinations, but the rental stock is not always treated well, so check your horse carefully before you saddle up. For a real splurge, take a ride on a graceful Peruvian *paso* horse. Supposedly the descendants of horses with royal Spanish and Moorish lineage ridden by the conquistadors, they are reputed to have the world's smoothest gait. Stables around Peru advertise rides for half a day or longer, especially at Urubamba (p261) in the Sacred Valley.

PARAGLIDING

Popular paragliding sites include the coastal clifftops of suburban Miraflores in Lima (p101) and various points along the south coast, including Pisco and Paracas (even, possibly, over the Nazca lines). Because there are few paragliding operators in Peru, book ahead through the agencies in Lima.

(Continued from page 172)

Midrange

All hotels listed here have cable TV, unless otherwise stated.

Hostal Solar (☎ 24-1793; www.hostalsolar.com; Ayacucho 108; s/d with breakfast S90/150; ▣) This snazzy pick is clean and airy, with contemporary decor. Prices include touches like airport pickup and a buffet breakfast served on the rooftop terrace.

Hostal las Torres de Ugarte (☎ 28-3532; www.hotel ista.com; Ugarte 401A; s/d/tr with breakfast S96/128/144; ▣) This is a friendly hostel in a quiet location behind the Monasterio de Santa Catalina. It has immaculate rooms with TVs and colorful wooly bedspreads. You'll just have to ignore the cacophonous echoing hallways. Rates drop considerably in the low season.

our pick **La Casa de Melgar** (☎ 22-2459; www .lacasademelgar.com; Melgar 108; s/d/tr incl buffet breakfast US$43/53/63; ▣) Housed in an 18th-century building, this hotel is nonetheless fitted with all the expected creature comforts. High-domed ceilings and unique decor lend the entire place an old-world feel. Comfy beds and tucked-away inner patios help make this a romantic hideaway within the city limits.

Hostal la Gruta (☎ 22-4631; www.lagrutahotel .com; La Gruta 304, Selva Alegre; s/d/ste with breakfast from US$45/55/65; ▣) Situated over 1km north of the city center, La Gruta (the Grotto) is a beautiful small hotel tucked away on a quiet residential street. Rooms are all tastefully furnished and have large windows or glass walls with views of the garden, as well as a refrigerator and bar; some also have fireplaces. The staff are wonderfully welcoming, too. Rates include airport pickup on request.

La Hostería (☎ 28-9269; lahosteria@terra.com.pe; Bolívar 405; s/d with breakfast US$51/61) Worth every dollar is this picturesque colonial hotel with a flower-bedecked courtyard, light and quiet rooms (with minibar), carefully chosen antiques, a sunny terrace and a lounge. Some rooms suffer from street noise, so request one in the back. Apartment-style suites (US$68) on the upper floors have stellar city views. Prices include airport pickup.

Hotel La Posada del Monasterio (☎ 40-5728; www .posadadelmonasterio.com.pe; Santa Catalina 300; s/d/tr incl buffet breakfast from S160/205/260; ▣ ▣) On a prime pedestrian corner, this hotel gracefully inhabits an architecturally mix-and-match building combining the best of the Old and New Worlds, especially popular with European tour groups. The comfortable modern rooms here have all the expected facilities. From the rooftop terrace there are fine views of the Santa Catalina convent across the street.

La Casa de Mi Abuela (☎ 24-1206; www.lacasade miabuela.com; Jerusalén 606; s/d/tr/q with breakfast US$54/54/70/85; ▣ ▣) The strong points of this hotel, which is often booked by tour groups, are its extensive grounds rattling with birdsong, plus deck chairs, swings, loungers and hammocks for kicking back. There's also a small pool, games area, library and restaurant. The rooms are disappointingly substandard, however, with bizarre floor plans and a hodgepodge of different aged and styled furniture. The front-desk staff can be brusque.

Casa Arequipa (☎ 28-4219; www.arequipacasa.com; Av Lima 409, Vallecito; s/d US$55/65) Inside a cotton-candy pink colonial mansion in the gardens of suburban Vallecito, this gay-friendly B&B offers more than half a dozen guest rooms with fine design touches such as richly painted walls, pedestal sinks, antique handmade furnishings and alpaca wool blankets. A sociable cocktail bar is in the lobby.

Also recommended:

Posada Nueva España (☎ 25-2941; Antiquilla 106, Yanahuara; s/d/tr with breakfast S75/100/125; ▣) This distinguished 19th-century colonial house has just more than a dozen rooms with solar hot showers. It's in the quaint suburb of Yanahuara; call for free pickups. Spanish, French, German and English are spoken.

La Maison d'Elise (☎ 25-6185, 25-3343; www.aqplish .com/hotel/maison; Av Bolognesi 104; s/d/tr US$54/70/86, ste $78-96; ▣) An elegant colonial mansion retreat just north of the Puente Grau bridge. Rooms have telephones, fridges and cable TV.

Top End

There's no shortage of full-service hotels in Peru's second-largest city.

La Posada del Puente (☎ 25-3132; www.posada delpuente.com; Bolognesi 101; s/d US$85/105, ste US$155-190; ▣) Dipping down to the river, the extensive gardens of this high-end hotel make for a tranquil setting that's surprisingly removed from the bustling traffic above. Staying here gives you free access to the sports facilities and swimming pool at the nearby Club Internacional sports complex.

Sonesta Posada del Inca (☎ 21-5530; www.sonesta .com; Portal de Flores 116; s/d/tr with breakfast from US$119/126/140, ste from $140; ▣ ▣ ▣) On the Plaza de Armas, this hotel has some rooms at the front with private terraces and a view of the cathedral through the arches. Other guests can compensate by frequenting the rooftop pool and terrace, which also boasts a fine panorama of the plaza, although the cafe is disappointing.

Libertador Ciudad Blanca (☎ 21-5110; www.libertador .com.pe; Plaza Bolívar s/n, Selva Alegre; r US$150-210, ste US$170-280; ☒ ☐ ☒) This is the grand dame of Arequipa's hotels, situated 1km north of the center. The stylish building is nicely set in gardens with a pool and playground. It has spacious rooms and opulent public areas with wi-fi access, plus its spa boasts a sauna, Jacuzzi and fitness room. The sedate restaurant serves a fine Sunday brunch. Neighboring Selva Alegre park is beautiful, but don't wander too far from the crowds, and avoid it after dark.

EATING

Trendy upscale restaurants line Calle San Francisco north of the Plaza de Armas, while touristy outdoor cafes huddle together on Pasaje Catedral behind the cathedral.

Budget

Café Casa Verde (☎ 22-6376; Jerusalén 406; snacks S2-6; ☼ 8am-6pm) This nonprofit courtyard cafe staffed by underprivileged kids is the perfect spot for a morning or afternoon break. It dishes up yummy German-style pastries and sandwiches, though service can be slow. Attached is a local handicraft store where proceeds also go to helping kids in need.

La Canasta Baguetería (☎ 20-4025; Jerusalén 115; sandwiches & salads S3-10; ☼ 8:30am-8pm Mon-Sat) This French-style bakery serves up flaky pastries, as well as a solid selection of sandwiches, salads and hearty breakfasts. You might have to search a bit as it's situated at the back of a colonial-style courtyard.

Lakshmivan (☎ 22-8768; Jerusalén 400; menús S4-6; ☼ 9am-9pm) Set in a colorful old building with a tiny outdoor courtyard, this place has various menús (set meals) and an extensive à la carte selection, all with a South Asian flair.

Restaurante Gopal (☎ 21-2193; Melgar 101B; menús S5, mains S4-11; ☼ 8am-9pm) This basic, health-conscious vegetarian cafe specializes in traditional Peruvian dishes made with imitation meats, so you can enjoy lomo saltado (strips of beef stir-fried with onions, tomatoes, potatoes and chili) meat-free.

Cusco Coffee Company (☎ 28-1152; La Merced 135; drinks S5-11; ☼ 8am-10pm Mon-Sat, noon-7pm Sun) This Starbucks-style Peruvian coffee shop has the most chatty baristas in town selling sugary baked goods and a full menu of espresso drinks made from beans ground on the spot. There is also a wi-fi hot spot here.

Ribs Cafe (☎ 28-8188; Álvarez Thomas 107; ribs & empanadas S5-18; ☼ 8am-6pm) This surprising storefront cooks up BBQ ribs in a rainbow variety of sauces, ranging from chocolate to honey-mustard to red wine, as well as empanadas (meat or cheese turnovers) and solid American breakfasts.

Fez (☎ 20-5930; San Francisco 229; mains S6-11; ☼ 7:30am-11pm) Have you been craving authentic falafel ever since you landed in South America? Step up to the counter here and order yourself a sandwich dripping with juicy goodness. Crêpes are equally delicious. Garden tables are out back.

El Turko I (☎ 20-3862; www.elturko.com.pe; San Francisco 216; mains S6-14; ☼ 7am-midnight Sun-Wed, 24hr Thu-Sat) Part of an ever-expanding Ottoman empire, this funky little joint serves a hungry crowd late-night kebabs and vegetarian Middle Eastern salads, with excellent coffee and sweet pastries during the day.

Crepisimo (☎ 20-6620; Alianza Francesa, Santa Catalina 208; mains S6-16; ☼ 8am-11pm Mon-Sat, noon-11pm Sun) Yet another cozy place to get your caffeine fix, this cultural cafe has a crackling fireplace, balcony tables, board games and more than 100 kinds of sweet and savory crêpes filled with everything from Chilean smoked trout or wild Swiss mushrooms to exotic South American fruits.

Inkari Pub Pizzeria (Pasaje Catedral; ☼ 8am-midnight) This pizzeria has a delicious happy-hour special of a personal pizza and a copa de vino (glass of wine) for just S13.

Velluto Crepes (☎ 28-7423; Jerusalén 408; sandwiches & crêpes S6-26; ☼ 11am-11pm Mon-Sat) This newcomer to Calle Jerusalén has a twin operation in Cuzco. Sandwiches are substantial, soups are made from fresh ingredients, and crêpes are a twist on the traditional. Additionally, the place boasts a selection of imported beers and wines not available at many places in Peru.

SELF-CATERING

Pick up groceries at **El Super** (☼ 9am-2pm & 4-9pm Mon-Fri, 9am-9pm Sat, 9:30am-1:30pm Sun); Plaza de Armas (Portal de la Municipalidad 130); Piérola (N de Piérola, cuadra 1).

Midrange

Los Leños (☎ 28-9179; Jerusalén 407; pizzas S9-20; ☼ 4:30-11pm Mon-Sat) Pizzas for homesick travelers are baked in a wood-burning oven that adds warmth to the laid-back atmosphere. Rock music is the only soundtrack. If you're more impressed by the food than we were, add your personalized scribble to the already-covered-with-graffiti walls.

Manolo's (☎ 21-9009; Mercaderes 113; mains S10-30; ☯ 7:30am-midnight) With a decidedly retro atmosphere, this mirror-filled cafe looks as if it were established in the early days of the Republic. Its endless menu lists coffees, ice creams, desserts, sandwiches and full Peruvian home-style meals.

Restaurant on the Top (☎ 28-1787; Portal de Flores 102; mains S14-32; ☯ 11am-10pm) It's a hike up the stairs to this rooftop eatery, but well worth the view of the Plaza de Armas and mountains beyond. An enormous menu features everything from sandwiches to Alpaca steaks. The same menu is served at Cafe Restaurant Antojitos de Arequipa (Moran cuadra 1), around the corner from Restaurant at the Top; open 24 hours.

Mixtos (☎ 20-5343; Pasaje Catedral 115; mains S15-36; ☯ 11:30am-9:30pm) Tucked away in the alley behind the cathedral on the Plaza de Armas is this popular and quaint restaurant that serves mainly Italian and *criollo* (spicy Peruvian fare with Spanish and indigenous influences) seafood dishes. Try the enormous and flavorful *sudado de pescado* (fish stew) while enjoying the view from the outdoor balcony.

Paquita Siu (☎ 25-1915; Granada 102, Cayma; mains S18-37; ☯ noon-4pm & 6-11pm Mon-Sat, noon-4pm Sun) Worth going out of your way for, this Asian fusion restaurant specializes in hard-to-find Thai and Japanese favorites like pad thai and sushi. It lies directly behind the department store Saga Falabella on Av Ejército.

El Turko II (☎ 21-5729; www.elturko.com.pe; San Francisco 315; mains S18-38; ☯ 11:30am-midnight) Right in the thick of things on San Francisco, the brother of El Turko I is a highly recommended Middle Eastern restaurant. Sizzling platters of kebabs and other carnivorous and vegetarian specialties are served in elegant surroundings with well-polished service. The drink list includes all the trusted favorites as well as a selection of specialty piscos.

Cevichería Fory Fay (☎ 24-5454; Álvarez Thomas 221; mains S20-25; ☯ lunch) Small and to-the-point, it serves only the best ceviche (seafood marinated in lime juice) and nothing else. Pull up a chair at a rickety table and crack open a beer – limit one per person, though! By the

---

THE SPICE OF LIFE, AREQUIPEÑO STYLE

The best *picanterías* (local restaurants) for traditional regional food are outside Arequipa's city center, and most are open for lunch only. Try tasting the explosively spicy *rocoto relleno* (hot peppers stuffed with meat, rice and vegetables), *ocopa* (potatoes served with a spicy, creamy peanut sauce), *chupe de camarones* (shrimp chowder topped with cheese) or *chancho al horno* (roast suckling pig), and wash it down with *chicha* (fermented corn beer).

Ary Quepay (☎ 20-4583; Jerusalén 502; mains S12-26; ☯ 10:30am-10:30pm) This place offers traditional plates, including alpaca and *cuy* (guinea pig), in a colonial-style building that extends out to a dimly lit rustic area dripping with plants. There's enthusiastic *música folklórica* (Andean folk music) most evenings.

La Nueva Palomino (☎ 25-3500; Leoncio Prado 122; mains S14-29; ☯ lunch only) Definitely the local favourite, the atmosphere at this *picantería* is informal and can turn boisterous even during the week when groups of families and friends file in to eat local specialties and drink copious amounts of *chicha de jora*.

Los Guisos Arequipeños (☎ 46-5151; www.guisosarequipenos.com; Av Pizarro 111; mains S12-36; ☯ noon-6:30pm Mon-Thu, noon-9pm Fri-Sun) This huge, barnlike formal restaurant is in the suburb of Lambramani, 2km southeast of the center. Along with bow-tied waiters, it has bountiful gardens and occasional live music.

Sol de Mayo (☎ 25-4148; www.restaurantsoldemayo.com; Jerusalén 207, Yanahuara; menú S14, mains S18-47; ☯ 11:30am-6pm) Serving good Peruvian food in the Yanahuara district, Sol de Mayo has live *música folklórica* every afternoon from 1pm to 4pm. Book a table in advance. You can combine a visit here with a stop off at the *mirador* (lookout) in Yanahuara (see boxed text, p167).

Tradición Arequipeña (☎ 42-6467; www.tradicionarequipena.com; Av Dolores 111; meals S18-40; ☯ 11:30am-6pm Mon-Fri, 11:30-1am Sat, 8:30am-6pm Sun) This locally famous restaurant has mazelike gardens, live *folklórica* and *criollo* music (upbeat coastal music), and offers a Sunday morning breakfast of *adobo de cerdo*, a traditional slow-cooked pork dish. It's 2km southeast of the center; a taxi ride here should cost S4.

For dinner shows with live traditional music, see p184.

way, the name is a phonetic spelling of how Peruvians say '45' in English.

Nina-Yaku (☎ 28-1432; San Francisco 211; menús S35, mains S25-36; ☻ 3-11pm) This nouveau Peruvian eatery wouldn't look a bit out of place in NYC's Soho or Buenos Aires' Palermo Hollywood. The modern menu includes reinventions of traditional *arequipeño* tastes, with salads, sandwiches and tastebud-tingling desserts, plus coffees and cocktails.

Top End

La Trattoria del Monasterio (☎ 20-4062; Santa Catalina 309; mains S18-33; ☻ lunch from noon daily, dinner from 7pm Mon-Sat) A helping of epicurean delight has descended upon the Monasterio de Santa Catalina. The menu of Italian specialties was created with the help of superstar Peruvian chef Gastón Acurio, and is infused with the flavors of Arequipa. Reservations are essential.

Sambambaia's (☎ 24-1209; www.sambambaias .com.pe; Luna Pizarro 304, Vallecito; mains S19-35; ☻ lunch & dinner Mon-Sat) Located just 2km outside of the city center, this restaurant is an elegant upper-crust alternative with both Italian and Peruvian specialties and live music on the weekends in a tropical garden setting.

El Viñedo (☎ 20-5053; www.vinedogrill.com; San Francisco 319; mains S20-50; ☻ noon-midnight) This intimate spot is one of the best places to knock back a steak or platters of traditional Peruvian food, all in an ornate Victorian atmosphere. The wine list features South American varietals.

our pick **Chicha** (☎ 28-7360; Santa Catalina 210; mains S25-39; ☻ noon-midnight Mon-Sat, to 9pm Sun) Famed chef Gastón Acurio arrived in Arequipa with Chicha. As with the astutely crafted menus he is celebrated for elsewhere in Peru, Chicha's selections turn the freshest local ingredients and regional specialties into noteworthy flavor fusions such as the *cuy laqueado* (guinea-pig appetizer with Arequipan touches of corn and rocoto pepper) and the *rocoto relleno* (in this dessert version red peppers are stuffed with cream cheese and *dulce de leche*). The experience is rounded off with a tantalizing list of cocktails and service that leaves no detail unattended to.

El Gaucho Parrilladas (☎ 22-0301; Portal de Flores 112; mains from S30; ☻ noon-midnight) Not one for vegetarians: these guys are experts in steak and steak alone, and they don't skimp on portions. On a lower level off the Plaza de Armas, the restaurant has a snug atmosphere. It's popular

with locals and tourists staying at nearby hotels alike, so reservations are recommended.

Zig Zag (☎ 20-6020; Zela 210; mains S33-40; ☻ 6pm-midnight) The upscale sister of Crepisimo, this European restaurant inhabits a two-story colonial house with an iron stairway designed by Gustave Eiffel. The expensive menu features decadent fondues, carpaccio, stone-grilled steaks and other South American game dishes.

DRINKING

The nocturnal scene in Arequipa is pretty slow midweek but takes off on weekends. Many of the bars along Calle San Francisco offer happy-hour specials worth taking advantage of.

Al Krajo (☎ 40-2530; San Francisco 300; ☻ 5:30pm-late) Latin music blares through the barred windows of this hole-in-the-wall from opening until closing. It's a decent place to sip a happy-hour pisco sour (grape brandy cocktail) and pester passers-by.

Déjà Vu (☎ 22-1904; San Francisco 319B; ☻ 9am-late) With a rooftop terrace overlooking the church of San Francisco, this eternally popular haunt has a long list of crazy cocktails and a delicious happy hour every evening. After dark, decent DJs keep the scene alive on weekdays and weekends alike.

Farren's Irish Pub (Pasaje Catedral; ☻ noon-11pm) Tucked behind the cathedral, this touristy Irish-themed watering hole is the place to go for deliciously cheap happy-hour pints and sports on satellite TV.

Istanbul (☎ 20-5930; San Francisco 231A; ☻ 10am-3am) Owned by the same folks as El Turko, this Middle Eastern-themed bar with stained-glass windows and overstuffed couches offers exotic liquor concoctions, beers and jet-fuel coffee.

ENTERTAINMENT
Live Music

Be aware that some places advertise a nightly *peña,* but there's rarely anything going on except from Thursday to Saturday nights.

Café Art Montréal (☎ 20-6652; Ugarte 210; ☻ 5pm-1am) This smoky, intimate little bar with live bands playing on a stage at the back would be equally at home as a bohemian student hangout on Paris' Left Bank.

Las Quenas (☎ 28-1115; Santa Catalina 302; ☻ closed Sun) An exception to the rule, this traditional *peña* features performances almost nightly starting around 9pm. The music varies, although *música folklórica* predominates. It also serves decent *arequipeño* food starting at 8pm.

AREQUIPA & CANYON COUNTRY

La Quinta (☎ 20-0964; Jerusalén 522; ✹ 10am-10pm) Another good spot for local food and melodic *folklórica* music. Live bands are featured everyday during the high season (June to August) when the place fills up for lunch, but it's potluck as to whether you get live music on other days.

Retro Bar (☎ 20-4294; San Francisco 317; ✹ 5pm-late) In the same alley as Forum Rock Cafe, this rock 'n' roll bar is a good spot to get the night going. The drink menu offers old favorites to sip on, and the building pulsates with live '80s and '90s music Thursdays through Saturdays.

Nightclubs

For the spiciest nightlife, on the weekends head for the bars and clubs along San Francisco north of the plaza. Beyond the tourist haunts, the hottest local action is to be had at nightclubs strung along Av Dolores, 2km southeast of the center (a taxi costs around S3 one way) where salsa and *cumbia* (Colombian salsa-like dance and musical style) music and dancing predominate.

Dady'o Disco Pub & Karaoke (Portal de Flores 112; admission S10; ✹ 10pm-3am Thu-Sat) On the Plaza de Armas, raucous Dady'o Disco Pub & Karaoke throws open its doors for go-go dancing, live bands and digital karaoke, plus wickedly cheap beers.

Forum Rock Cafe (☎ 20-4294; www.forumrockcafe .com; Casona Forum, San Francisco 317; ✹ 10pm-4am Thu-Sat) It's a gutsy Latin dance club with a thing for bamboo and waterfalls, and is currently the place to be seen on weekend nights. In the same building, Zero Bar & Pool is a busy nightspot with pool tables and spacious booths.

Cinema

A handful of cinemas show English-language movies dubbed or with Spanish subtitles. Local newspapers have listings. It's also worth checking at the various cultural centers (p161) for film festivals and other screenings.

Cineplanet Arequipa 7 (☎ 60-3400; www.cineplanet .com.pe; Los Arces s/n at Av del Ejército) Showing blockbuster movies in a shopping mall just a short taxi ride from the center.

Sports

Conducted *arequipeño* style, *peleas de toros* (bullfights) here are less bloodthirsty than most. They involve pitting two bulls against each other for the favors of a fertile female until one realizes he's beaten. The fights take place on Sundays between April and December. Ask at your hostel for the location of fights – they usually take place at stadiums on the outskirts of town. The three most important fights are in April, mid-August and early December (admission S15).

SHOPPING

Arequipa overflows with antique and artisan shops, especially on the streets around Monasterio de Santa Catalina. High-quality alpaca, vicuña (threatened wild relative of alpacas) and leather goods, and other handmade items, are what you'll see being sold most often.

Casona Santa Catalina (☎ 28-1334; www.santa catalina-sa.com.pe; Santa Catalina 210; ✹ most shops 10am-6pm) Inside this polished tourist complex, you'll find a few shops of major export brands, such as Sol Alpaca and Biondi Piscos.

Incalpaca Factory Outlet (☎ 25-1025; www.incalpaca .com; Juan Bustamante s/n, Tahuayacani; ✹ 9:30am-7pm Mon-Sat, 10:30am-3:30pm Sun) This outlet for the Kuña brand of alpaca woolen goods also has a small petting zoo out back that houses four types of American camelid.

Michell (☎ 20-2525; www.michell.com.pe; Juan de la Torre 101; ✹ 8am-12:30pm & 2:30-6pm) More than just a source for fine alpaca wool goods and raw thread, this complex functions as a tourist center for an international wool export company. It includes a well-presented commercial boutique, a museum detailing the process of wool production, and a small zoo and a cafe.

Patio del Ekeko (☎ 21-5861; www.patiodelekeko .com; Mercaderes 141; ✹ 10am-9pm Mon-Sat, 11am-8pm Sun) This high-end tourist mall has plenty of expensive but good alpaca- and vicuña-wool items, jewelry, ceramics and other arty souvenirs.

GETTING THERE & AWAY
Air

Arequipa's **airport** (code AQP; ☎ 44-3458) is about 8km northwest of the city center.

LAN (☎ 20-1224; Santa Catalina 118C) has daily flights to Lima and Cuzco. **Sky Airline** (☎ 28-2899; La Merced 121) also offers occasional flights to Arica, Chile.

Bus

Night buses provide a convenient means to reach many far-off destinations in a city where options for air travel are limited, although some routes do have histories of accidents, hijackings and robberies. Paying a bit extra for luxury bus services is often worth the added comfort and security. Exercise extreme care with your belongings while on the bus and consider disguising luggage stored beneath the bus with large potato sacks that can be bought cheaply in any market. It is also recommended to carry extra food with you on long bus rides in case of a breakdown or road strike.

INTERNATIONAL

From the Terrapuerto bus terminal, **Ormeño** (☎ 42-7788) has two buses a week to Santiago, Chile (US$130, 2½ days), and three a week to Buenos Aires, Argentina (US$190, three days).

LONG-DISTANCE

Most bus companies have departures from the *terminal terrestre* or the smaller Terrapuerto bus terminal, both of which are together on Av Andrés Avelino Cáceres, less than 3km south of the city center (take a taxi for S4). Check in advance which terminal your bus leaves from and keep a close watch on your belongings while you're waiting there. There's an S1 departure tax from either terminal. Both terminals have shops, restaurants and left-luggage facilities. The more chaotic *terminal terrestre* also has a global ATM and a tourist information office.

For Lima (S42 to S130, 14 to 16 hours), **Cruz del Sur** (☎ 42-7375), **Ormeño** (☎ 42-3855) and several other companies operate daily buses, mostly leaving in the afternoon. Many Lima-bound buses stop en route at other south coast destinations, including Camaná (S15, three hours), Nazca (S42 to S130, 10 to 12 hours) and Ica (S42 to S130, 13 to 15 hours); Pisco is about 6km west of the Panamericana, and few buses go direct (see p135). Many of the same companies also have overnight buses to Cuzco (S50 to S110, nine to 11 hours), either on a direct, mostly paved road or the asphalted highways via Juliaca.

If you're heading toward Lake Titicaca, direct buses to Juliaca (S13 to S53, six hours) and Puno (S13 to S53, six hours) leave every half-hour throughout the day from the *terminal terrestre*. Some continue to Desaguadero (S20, seven to eight hours) on the Bolivian border. Direct services to La Paz, Bolivia, are supposedly offered, but these usually involve a change of buses or at least a stop for a couple of cold predawn hours while you wait for the border posts to open.

Transportes del Carpio (☎ 42-7049) has hourly daytime departures for Mollendo (S8, two to 2½ hours). Cruz del Sur has the most comfortable buses to Tacna (S38, six to seven hours) via Moquegua (S28, four hours). These southern destinations are also served by Ormeño, **Flores** (☎ 42-9905, 43-2228) and several smaller bus companies. For Ilo (S25 to S35, 5½ hours), Flores has nine departures per day from either the *terminal terrestre* or its own **Flores terminal** (☎ 43-1646), diagonally across the roundabout where avenues De Forja and Ibanez intersect, on the north side of the *terminal terrestre*.

REGIONAL SERVICES

Many buses useful for sightseeing in the canyon country also leave from the *terminal terrestre* and Terrapuerto. Travel times and costs can vary depending on road conditions. During the wet season (between December and April), expect significant delays.

Heading for the Cañón del Colca, there are only a few daily buses for Chivay (S12, three hours), some of which continue to Cabanaconde (S15, six hours) at the end of the canyon's main road. It is wise to buy the tickets in advance and know whether you will be expected to switch buses in Chivay. Most buses are run by **Andalucía** (☎ 44-5089), while **Reyna** (☎ 43-0612) and **Transportes Colca** (☎ 42-6357) also provide a few. Try to catch the earliest daylight departure, usually around 5am.

For buses to Corire (S10, three hours) to visit the Toro Muerto petroglyphs, both Transportes del Carpio and Eros Tour run hourly daytime services, from where you can continue on to Aplao in the Valle de Majes (S10, three hours) for river running. **Transportes Trebol** (☎ 42-5936) usually has a service departing around 4pm that continues on to Andagua (S25, 10 to 12 hours) to visit El Valle de los Volcanes. The bus leaves Andagua for the return trip to Arequipa at around 5:30pm.

For the Cañón del Cotahuasi (S30, 12 hours), Reyna has a 4pm departure and **Transportes Alex** (☎ 42-4605) has a 4:30pm departure.

Train

The train station is over 1km south of the Plaza de Armas. Services between Arequipa and Juliaca and Puno on Lake Titicaca have

AREQUIPA & CANYON COUNTRY

been suspended, although **PeruRail** (☎ 21-5350; www.perurail.com) will run private-charter trains for large tourist groups. The Arequipa–Juliaca part of the route is bleak, but the views of the altiplano (Andean plateau) are appealing and you'll see vicuñas, alpacas and llamas along the way, plus flamingos if you're lucky.

GETTING AROUND
To/From the Airport
There are no airport buses. An official taxi from downtown Arequipa to the airport costs around S15. It is possible to take a *combi* marked 'Río Seco' or 'Zamacola' from Av Puente Grau and Ejército that will let you off in a sketchy neighborhood about 700m of the airport entrance. Leaving the airport, *colectivo* (shared) taxis charge around S6 per person to drop you off at your hotel.

Bicycle
You can rent bikes at **Peru Camping Shop** (☎ 22-1658; www.perucampingshop.com; Jerusalén 410) for S9 per hour or S60 per day including helmet, gloves and a map of the area.

Bus
Combis and minibuses go south along Bolívar to the *terminal terrestre* (S2, 20 minutes), next door to the Terrapuerto bus terminal, but it's a slow trip via the market area.

Taxi
You can often hire a taxi with a driver for less than renting a car from a travel agency. Local taxi companies include **Tourismo Arequipa** (☎ 45-8888) and **Taxitel** (☎ 45-2020). A short ride around town costs around S3, while a trip from the Plaza de Armas out to the bus terminals costs about S4. Whenever possible, try to call a recommended company to ask for a pickup as there have been numerous reports of travelers being scammed or assaulted by taxi drivers. If you must hail a taxi off the street, pick a regular size sedan or station wagon over a compact yellow cab.

CANYON COUNTRY

A tour of the Cañón del Colca is the most popular excursion from Arequipa, but climbing the city's guardian volcano El Misti, rafting in the Majes canyon and visiting the petroglyphs at Toro Muerto, exploring El Valle de los Volcanes, and trekking down into the world's deepest canyon at Cotahuasi are more adventurous. Most of these places can be visited by a combination of public bus and hiking. Alternatively, friends can split the cost of hiring a taxi or 4WD vehicle and driver; a two-day trip will set you back more than US$100.

RESERVA NACIONAL SALINAS Y AGUADA BLANCA
The paved road from Arequipa climbs northeast past El Misti and Chachani to this **national reserve** (☎ 054-25-7461; www.inrena .gob.pe/areasprotegidas/rnsalinas/main.html; admission free; ⏱ 24hr), which covers 367,000 hectares at an average elevation of 4300m. Here, vicuñas are often sighted. Later in the trip, domesticated alpacas and llamas are frequently seen, so it is possible to see three of the four members of the South American camelid family in one day. Seeing the fourth member, the guanaco, is very hard, as they have almost disappeared from this area.

Past the reserve, the increasingly bumpy road continues through bleak altiplano and over the highest point of 4800m, from where the snowcaps of Nevado Ampato can be seen. Flamingos may also be seen around here between January and April. From there, you'll drop spectacularly into the Cañón del Colca as the road switchbacks down to the dust-choked village of Chivay.

CAÑÓN DEL COLCA
The 100km-long Cañón del Colca is set among high volcanoes (6613m-high Coropuna and 6310m-high Ampato are the tallest) and ranges from 1000m to more than 3000m in depth. For years there was raging controversy over whether or not this was the world's deepest canyon at 3191m, but recently it ranked a close second to neighboring Cañón del Cotahuasi, which is just over 150m deeper. Amazingly, both canyons are more than twice as deep as the Grand Canyon in the USA (see boxed text, p67).

Despite its depth, the Cañón del Colca is geologically young. The Río Colca has cut into beds of mainly volcanic rocks, which were deposited less than 100 million years ago along the line of a major fault in the earth's crust. Though cool and dry in the hills above, the deep valley and generally sunny weather produce frequent updrafts on which soaring condors often float by at close range. Viscachas (burrowing rodents closely related to chinchillas) are also common around the canyon rim, darting furtively among the rocks. Cacti dot many slopes and, if they're in flower, you may be lucky enough to see tiny nectar-eating birds braving the spines to feed. In the depths of the canyon it can be almost tropical, with palm trees, ferns and even orchids in some isolated areas.

The local people are descendants of two conflicting groups that originally occupied the area, the Cabanas and the Collagua. These two groups used to distinguish themselves by performing cranial deformations, but nowadays use distinctively shaped hats and intricately embroidered traditional clothing to denote their ancestry. In the Chivay area at the east end of the canyon, the white hats worn by women are usually woven from straw and are embellished with lace, sequins and medallions. At the west end of the canyon, the hats have rounded tops and are made of painstakingly embroidered cotton. The women don't particularly enjoy being photographed, so always ask permission. Those who pose for photographs expect a tip.

For more information on outdoor outfitters in Arequipa and activity gear rental, see p169. For guided tours of the canyon leaving from Arequipa, see p168.

Chivay

☎ 054 / pop 6300 / elev 3630m

At the head of the Cañón del Colca, the capital of the province of Caylloma is a small, dusty

---

transportation hub that sees waves of tourists breeze through as part of organized tours from Arequipa. Around the market area and in the main square are good places to catch a glimpse of the decorative clothing worn by local women. The town itself affords enchanting views of snowcapped peaks and terraced hillsides, and serves as a logical base from which to explore smaller towns further up the valley.

INFORMATION

Limited tourist information can be gleaned from semiprofessional travel agencies cropping up around the main plaza. The police station is next to the *municipalidad* (town hall) on the plaza. There is one ATM in town located on Calle Salaverry one block west of the main plaza. Some of the higher-end hotels and a few shops around town exchange US dollars, euros and traveler's checks at unfavorable rates. Internet access is available from a few cybercafes near the plaza.

SIGHTS & ACTIVITIES

At the Casa Andina hotel, a tiny **astronomical observatory** (☎ 53-1070; Huayna Cápac s/n; admission S18) has nightly sky shows in Spanish and English. The price includes a 30-minute explanation and chance to peer into the telescope. It can be hard to catch a night with clear skies between December and April.

Chivay's famous **La Calera hot springs** (admission S10; ⏱ 4:30am-8pm) are 3.5km to the northeast of the village by road. There are large, clean pools, showers, changing rooms, a snack shop and a tiny ethnographic museum. The mineral-laden water leaves the ground at 85°C and is said to have curative properties. There are frequent *colectivos* (S1) from around the main plaza in Chivay to the springs, or you can walk or cycle by following the road downhill past the market and taking a left. *Colectivos* stop running at 6pm.

Several short hikes can easily be made around Chivay. For example, from where the road forks to the hot springs, stay to the left and walk beside the fertile fields to Corporaque, which has an arched colonial-era plaza and church. Head downhill and out of Corporaque past some small ruins and look for the orange bridge across the river. Notice the hanging cliff tombs as you cross the river over to Yanque, from where passing buses or *colectivos* return to Chivay. It's an all-day

---

THE TRUTH ABOUT THE BOLETO TURÍSTICO

While some will say that the *boleto turístico* (tourist ticket; S35) is a scam, it is true that in order to visit most of the points of interest in the Cañón del Colca all foreigners must purchase this ticket. If you are taking an organized tour, the cost of the tour usually does not include this additional fee. If you are traveling alone, tickets can be purchased on most public buses entering or leaving Chivay, or in the town of Cabanaconde. Half of the proceeds from this ticket go to Arequipa for general maintenance and conservation of local tourist attractions, while the other half goes to the national agency of tourism.

walk; alternatively, rent mountain bikes in Chivay (see right).

It's also possible to walk about 27km further up the northern side of the canyon from Corporaque, past **Ichupampa** and **Lari**, to the rarely visited town of **Madrigal**, which is an interesting spot from which to trek into the deepest parts of the canyon. Occasional *combis* also run to these villages from the streets around the main market area in Chivay.

SLEEPING

Though it's a tiny town, Chivay has plenty of budget guesthouses to choose from.

Hostal Municipal (☎ 53-1093; Plaza de Armas; s/d/tr S15/30/45) Though unexciting, this institutional place is fine for an exhausted traveler.

Hostal Estrella de David (☎ 53-1233; Siglo XX 209; s/d/tr S20/20/40) A simple, clean *hospedaje* (small, family-owned inn) with bathrooms and some rooms with cable TV. It's a few blocks from the plaza in the direction of the bus terminal.

Hostal Anita (☎ 53-1114; Plaza de Armas 607; s/d/tr S20/40/50) With a pretty interior courtyard, this friendly hostel smack on the main plaza has hot showers and affable owners. Breakfast is available upon request.

Wasi Kolping Hostel (☎ 53-1076; www.hoteles kolping.net/colcawasi; Siglo XX s/n; s/d/tr with breakfast S30/60/78) An off-the-beaten-path midrange choice, this country inn is set in spacious grounds on the outskirts of town, a minute's walk from the bus terminal. The somewhat bedraggled, but still charming bungalows are also accessible to travelers with disabilities.

Hostal La Pascana (☎ 53-1001; hrlapascana@hotmail .com; Siglo XX 106; s/d/tr with breakfast S54.50/69/86.50) La Pascana is a very good option with carpeted, well-decorated rooms and firm mattresses. It's several notches above the other more modest guesthouses and lies near the plaza.

Casa Andina (☎ 53-1020, 53-1022; www.casa-andina .com; Huayna Cápac s/n; s/d with breakfast S302/354.50) This newly renovated tourist complex recreates a rustic idyll with quaint stone-and-thatch cottages, neatly sculptured bushes and garden views of snowcapped peaks. Every evening the hotel hosts local artisans and a shaman who tells fortunes with coca leaves. Exchange of American dollars is available.

EATING & DRINKING

Innkas (☎ 53-1209; Plaza de Armas 705; snacks S2-8; ☺ 7am-11pm) Built in the oldest house in Chivay, this spot is the perfect place for either a decent morning cup of coffee or an evening beer and pool game.

Lobo's (☎ 53-1081; José Gálvez 101; mains from S6; ☺ 9am-10pm) This place offers a touristy menu and backpacker bar with a cozy interior. It's right on the Plaza de Armas.

Casa Blanca (☎ 9-51-462-944; Plaza de Armas; mains S10-25; ☺ 9am-10pm) A warm subterranean restaurant with a fireplace, friendly Casa Blanca has a pick-and-choose *menú* that includes unusual local specialties. Portions are huge but service can be slow.

GETTING THERE & AROUND

The bus terminal is a 15-minute walk from the plaza. There are nine daily departures to Arequipa (S12, three hours), while buses to Cabanaconde (S5, 2½ hours), stopping at towns along the southern side of the canyon and at Cruz del Cóndor, leave four times daily.

Combis and *colectivo* taxis run to the surrounding villages from street corners in the market area, just north of the main plaza. Mountain bikes in varying condition can be readily hired from travel agencies on the plaza or at **BiciSport** (☎ 9-58-807-652; Zaramilla 112; ☺ 9am-6pm) behind the market for about S5 per day.

Traveling onward to Cuzco from Chivay may be possible, but it's overly complicated and not recommended. Although some travelers have managed to catch *combis* to Puente Callalli and flag down a bus there, it's much safer and probably just as fast to return to Arequipa instead.

Chivay to Cabanaconde

The road following the south bank of the upper Cañón del Colca leads past several villages that still use the Inca terracing that surrounds them. Those on the south side of the canyon are most easily accessible by buses traveling between Chivay and Cabanaconde. Occasional *combis* and *colectivo* taxis also leave from the market area in Chivay for most of the villages in the canyon, so ask around.

YANQUE

☎ 054 / pop 1900

About 7km from Chivay, the peaceful rural village of Yanque has an attractive 18th-century church on the main plaza. Also on the plaza is the excellent **Museo Yanque** (admission S5; ☺ 9am-5pm Mon-Sat), a university-run cultural museum with displays on traditional canyon life. In the central courtyard is an herbal garden of ancient medicinal remedies, some predating Inca times. Brief guided tours are given in Spanish, after which you can borrow foreign-language booklets that explain the main displays. Next door is a small local art gallery and shop.

From the plaza, a 30-minute walk down to the river brings you to a local hot springs called **Baños Chacapi** (admission S5; ⊙ 3am-7pm). In Yanque, a number of simple, family-run guesthouses were started as part of a local development project; they are scattered around town, and offer lodging for S15 per night. Travelers have recommended **Sumaq Huayta Wasi** (☎ 83-2174; Cusco 303), just two blocks from the main plaza. Out on the main road, you'll find the delightful **Tradición Colca Albergue** (☎ 42-4926, 20-5336; www.tradicioncolca.com; Av Colca 119; dm/s/d with breakfast S35/120/140), a European-run country inn designed to help guests relax away from the bustle of the city. It offers a sauna and Jacuzzi, massage services, and a restaurant and cafe and bar with a billiards table. Rates include an afternoon guided hike to the pre-Inca ruins of Oyu Oyu.

CORPORAQUE TO MADRIGAL

Across the river from Yanque, in the village of Corporaque, is the excellent **La Casa de Mamayacchi** (www.lacasademamayacchi.com; d/tr with breakfast from S224/294). Hidden away downhill from the main plaza, this inn is built with traditional materials and boasts awesome canyon views. The cozy rooms have no TVs, but there's a games library, fireplace and bar that make it sociable. Make advance reservations through the **Arequipa office** (☎ 24-1206; Jerusalén 606). Or, for a more authentic barebones option, ask around for the family-run guesthouse **Mumy Kkero** (per night S15), one of many in Corporaque.

Walking or riding from Yanque to Corporaque you will pass a sign marking the ruins of **Oyu Oyu**. Though not visible from the road, the remnants of this pre-Incan settlement are reachable by a half-hour hike up the hill, after which you can continue on to a waterfall whose source is the runoff from Nevado Mismi.

Further up the northern side of the canyon is the upmarket **Colca Lodge** (☎ 53-1191; www.colca-lodge.com; s/d/tr/q with breakfast S596/660/660/724, ste from S937), a large and attractive stone-and-thatch hotel tucked into a bend of the river amid Inca

terracing. Activities including horseback riding, fishing, rafting and mountain biking can be arranged here. The establishment features a new spa and its own private hot springs. For advance reservations, visit the **Arequipa office** (☎ 054-20-2587, 054-20-3604; Benavides 201).

YANQUE TO PINCHOLLO

Further along the main road on the south side of the canyon, the spreading landscape is remarkable for its Inca and pre-Inca terracing, which goes on for many kilometers and is some of the most extensive in Peru. Some tours also stop at a small carved boulder that is supposed to represent a pre-Columbian map of the terracing.

The next big village along the main road is **Pinchollo**, about 30km from Chivay. From here, a trail climbs toward **Hualca Hualca** (a snowcapped volcano of 6025m) to an active geothermal area set amid wild and interesting scenery. Though it's not very clearly marked, there's a four-hour trail up to a bubbling geyser that used to erupt dramatically before a recent earthquake contained it. Ask around for directions, or just head left uphill in the direction of the mountain, then follow the water channel to its end. In Pinchollo, there is the very basic **El Refugio** (dm S10) near the plaza, and the owner is also a local guide. A sleeping bag and flashlight are recommended.

CRUZ DEL CÓNDOR

You can continue on foot from Pinchollo to **Cruz del Cóndor** (admission with boleto turístico) in about two hours or flag down any passing bus headed toward Cabanaconde. This famed viewpoint, also known locally as Chaq'lla, is for many the highlight of their trip to the Cañón del Colca. A large family of Andean condors nests by the rocky outcrop and, with lots of luck, they can occasionally be seen gliding effortlessly on thermal air currents rising from the canyon, swooping low over onlookers' heads. It's a mesmerizing scene, heightened by the spectacular 1200m drop to the river below and the sight of **Nevado Mismi** reaching over 3000m above the canyon floor on the other side of the ravine.

Recently it has become more difficult to see the condors, mostly due to air pollution, including from travelers' campfires and tour buses. Early morning (8am to 10am) or late afternoon (4pm to 6pm) are still the best times to see the birds, though they can appear at various hours during the day. The condors are less likely to appear on rainy days so it's best to visit during the dry season. You can walk from the viewpoint to Cabanaconde, 18km past Pinchollo and almost 50km from Chivay.

Cabanaconde

☎ 054 / pop 2700 / elev 3290m

The quiet rural town of Cabanaconde makes an ideal base for some spectacular hikes into the canyon. It's a very small place, with just a few simple spots to stay and eat. Bring everything you'll need to stay a couple of days, including plenty of Peruvian currency in small bills and any trekking equipment (eg sleeping bags).

ACTIVITIES

The most popular short trek is one that involves a steep two-hour hike down to **Sangalle** (also popularly known as 'the oasis') at the bottom of the canyon, where several sets of basic bungalows and camping grounds have sprung up, all costing from about S10 per person. There are two natural pools for swimming, the larger of which is claimed by Oasis Bungalows, which charges S5 (free if you are staying in its bungalows) to swim. Paraíso Bungalows doesn't charge for the smaller swimming pool, and there is a local dispute over whether travelers should be charged to use the pools at all. Do not light campfires as almost half of the trees in the area have been destroyed in this manner, and cart all trash not just back to the top of the canyon, but all the way back to Arequipa (those garbage cans you see lying about are not emptied properly and many businesses in Cabanaconde throw their trash into the canyon). The return trek to Cabanaconde is a stiff climb and thirsty work; allow about three to four hours.

The charming village of **Tapay** is a destination in itself and is also a base camp for other shorter treks, including to **Bomboya**. Readers have recommended camping or staying overnight at Hostal Isidro, whose owner is a guide and has a shop, satellite phone and rental mules. Another popular trekking route leads into the canyon via a more gradual path (but steep nonetheless!) and crosses the river before arriving in San Juan de Chuccho. Here, accommodation is available at the Casa de Rivelino, where there are bungalows with warm water for S10 per night and a simple restaurant. From here,

trekkers have the option of continuing on to Sangalle to stay a second night before returning to Cabanaconde.

Local guides, guesthouse owners and other travelers can suggest a wealth of other day hikes and longer treks to *miradors,* Inca ruins, waterfalls and geysers. You can buy topographic and trekking maps and rent gear from **Colca Trek** (☎ 054-20-6217, 9-60-0170; www.colcatrek .com.pe; Jerusalén 401-B) in Arequipa. Though it is possible to buy water in the canyon, you are encouraged to bring the water you will need to avoid additional waste from disposable plastic bottles.

TOURS & GUIDES

Local guides can also be hired by consulting with your hostel or the *municipalidad* in Cabanaconde. The going rate for guides is S30 to S60 per day, depending on the type of trek, season and size of the group. Renting a horse or mule, which is an excellent way to carry water into the canyon and waste out, can be arranged easily for about S60 per day.

SLEEPING & EATING

Accommodation options are extremely limited in Cabanaconde. Most people eat where they're sleeping, although there are a couple of cheap local restaurants near the main plaza, too.

Pachamama Backpacker Hostal (☎ 9-59-316-322, 25-3879; www.pachamamahome.com; San Pedro 209; dm S12, r per person without bathroom S20, r per person S30, all with breakfast; 🖳) A relative newcomer to the scene, this cozy backpackers' haunt is owned by a young Peruvian-Belgian couple who have made readers feel right at home by providing a chill atmosphere and simple yet clean rooms. The staff are great sources for info on guides and alternative treks, and can even provide hiking gear such as maps and binoculars. Complimentary breakfasts include yummy crêpes.

Hostal Valle del Fuego (hvalledelfuego@hotmail.com; dm S20, s/d/tr with breakfast S35/50/70; 🖳) This budget hostel is an established travelers' scene, with DVDs, a full bar, solar-powered showers and owners who are knowledgeable about trekking. Ask about free passes to the Sangalle pools. To make a reservation, call Pablo Tours (☎ 054-20-3737) in Arequipa; if you reserve in advance, they will take care of getting you your bus ticket to Cabanaconde the following day for no extra charge.

La Posada del Conde (☎ 40-0408, 83-0033; www
.posadadelconde.com; San Pedro s/n; s/d/tr with breakfast
US$25/30/40) This small modern hotel mostly
has double rooms, but they are well cared-for
with clean bathrooms. The rates often include
a welcome *mate* (herbal tea) or pisco sour in
the downstairs restaurant.

Hotel Kuntur Wassi (☎ 81-2166; www.arequipacolca
.com; Cruz Blanca s/n; s/d/ste with breakfast US$45/55/70;
🖳) This charming upmarket hotel is built
into the hillside above town, with stone
bathrooms, trapezoidal windows overlooking the gardens and a nouveau-rustic feel.
Suites boast enormous bathtubs. There's also
a bar, restaurant, library, laundry and foreign-
currency exchange. In low season prices may
drop significantly.

GETTING THERE & AWAY

Buses for Chivay (S5, 2½ hours) and Arequipa
(S15, six hours) via Cruz del Cóndor leave
Cabanaconde from the main plaza several
times per day. Departure times change frequently though, so check with the bus company office on the main plaza. All buses will
stop upon request at towns along the main
road on the southern side of the canyon.

TORO MUERTO PETROGLYPHS

A fascinating, mystical site in the high desert,
Toro Muerto (meaning 'Dead Bull') is named
for the herds of livestock that commonly died
here from dehydration as they were escorted
from the mountains to the coast. A barren
hillside is scattered with white volcanic boulders carved with stylized people, animals and
birds. Archaeologists have documented more
than 5000 such petroglyphs spread over several square kilometers of desert. Though the
cultural origins of this site remain unknown,
most archaeologists date the mysterious drawings to the period of Wari domination, about
1200 years ago. Interpretations of the drawings vary widely; a guide can fill you in on
some of the most common themes, or you can
wander among the boulders yourself and formulate your own elaborate interpretation of
the message these ancient images aim to tell.

To reach the site by public transport, take
a bus to Corire from Arequipa (S10, three
hours). If you don't want to sleep in Corire,
take an early bus (they start as early as 4am)
and get off at a gas station just past the sign
that denotes the beginning of the town of
Corire. From there, you can walk the hot,

dusty road about 2km uphill to a checkpoint
where visitors must sign in. Otherwise, continue on into Corire, from where you can
catch a taxi to take you to where the petroglyphs start (from S40 round-trip if the taxi
waits). In Corire, **Hostal Willy** (☎ 054-47-2046; r per
person from S35) has basic accommodations and
can provide information on reaching the site.
Bring plenty of water, sunblock and insect
repellent (as there are plenty of mosquitoes
en route).

Buses return from Corire to Arequipa once
an hour, usually leaving at 30 minutes past the
hour. The Toro Muerto petroglyphs can also
be visited more conveniently on expensive
full-day 4WD tours from Arequipa.

EL VALLE DE LOS VOLCANES

El Valle de los Volcanes is a broad valley,
west of the Cañón del Colca and at the foot
of Nevado Coropuna (6613m), famed for its
unusual geological features. The valley floor
is carpeted with lava flows from which rise
many small (up to 200m high) cinder cones,
some 80 in total, aligned along a major fissure,
with each cone formed from a single eruption. Given the lack of erosion of some cones
and minimal vegetation on the associated lava
flows, the volcanic activity occurred no more
than a few thousand years ago, and some was
likely very recent – historical accounts suggest
as recently as the 17th century.

The lava flows have had a major influence
on drainage in the valley, constraining the Río
Challahuire against the east side of the valley
to form the Laguna de Chachas. The outlet of Laguna de Chachas then runs beneath
lava flows for nearly 20km before emerging
at Laguna Mamacocha.

The 65km-long valley surrounds the village of **Andagua**, near the snowy summit of
Coropuna. Visitors seeking a destination full
of natural wonders and virtually untouched
by travelers will rejoice in this remote setting. From Andagua, a number of sites can
be visited by foot or car. It is possible to hike
to the top of the perfectly conical twin volcanoes which lie about 10km from town, though
don't expect a clear-cut trail. Other popular
hikes are to a nearby *mirador* at 3800m and to
the 40m high **Izanquillay** falls which are formed
where the Río Andahua runs through a narrow lava canyon to the northeast of town.
There are some *chullpas* (funerary towers)
at **Soporo**, a two-hour hike or half-hour drive

to the south of Andagua. En route to Soporo are the ruins of a pre-Columbian city named **Antaymarca**. Topographical maps of the area are available at **Colca Trek** (☎ 054-20-6217, 9-60-0170; www.colcatrek.com.pe; Jerusalén 401-B) in Arequipa. An alternative way to enter the valley is by starting from Cabanaconde, crossing the Cañón del Colca, then hiking over a 5500m pass before descending into El Valle de los Volcanes. This trek requires at least five days (plus time for proper acclimatization beforehand), and is best to attempt with an experienced guide and pack mules.

There are several cheap and basic hostels and restaurants in Andagua, including the recommended Casa Blanca. Camping is also possible, though you will need plenty of water and sun protection. To get to the valley from Arequipa, take a **Reyna** (☎ 43-0612) or a **Transportes Trebol** (☎ 42-5936) bus to Andagua (S25, 10 to 12 hours), both of which depart from Arequipa around 4pm. Return buses leave Andagua around 5:30pm. Some tour companies also visit El Valle de los Volcanoes as part of expensive tours in 4WD vehicles that may also include visits to the Cañón del Cotahuasi and Chivay.

CAÑÓN DEL COTAHUASI

While the Cañón del Colca has stolen the limelight for many years, it is actually this remote canyon, 200km northwest of Arequipa as the condor flies, that is the deepest known canyon in the world. It is around twice the depth of the Grand Canyon, with stretches dropping down below 3500m. While the depths of the ravine are only accessible to experienced river runners (p170), the rest of the fertile valley is also rich in striking scenery and trekking opportunities. The canyon also shelters several traditional rural settlements that currently see only a handful of adventurous travelers.

Sights & Activities

The main access town is appropriately named **Cotahuasi** (population 3800) and is at 2620m above sea level on the southeast side of the canyon. Northeast of Cotahuasi and further up the canyon are the villages of **Tomepampa** (10km away; elevation 2500m) and **Alca** (20km away; 2660m), which also have basic accommodations. En route you'll pass a couple of **thermal baths** (admission S2).

Buses to the Sipia bridge (S3, one hour) leave the main plaza of Cotahuasi everyday at 6:30am, from where you can begin a number of interesting hikes into the deepest parts of the canyon. Forty-five minutes up the trail, the **Sipia waterfall** is formed where the Río Cotahuasi takes an impressive 100m tumble. Another 1½ hours on a well-trodden track brings you to **Chaupo**, an oasis of towering cacti and remnants of pre-Incan dwellings. Camping is possible here. From here a dusty path leads either up to **Velinga** and other remote communities where sleeping accommodations are available, or down to **Mallu**, a patch of verdant farmland at the river's edge where the owner, Ignacio, will allow you to pitch tents and borrow his stove for S10 per night. To give advance notice of your arrival, call the satellite phone in Velinga (☎ 054-81-2129). To get back to Cotahuasi, a return bus leaves the Sipia bridge around 11:30am daily.

Another possible day trip from Cotahuasi is to the hillside community of **Pampamarca**. From here, a two-hour hike up a steep switch-backing trail will bring you to an interesting group of rock formations, where locals have likened shapes in the rocks to mystical figures. A short walk from town brings you to a viewpoint with a view of the rushing 80m high **Uscune falls**. To get to Pampamarca, *combis* leave the main square in Cotahuasi twice daily in the early morning and afternoon (S5, two hours), and return shortly after arriving.

Trekking trips of several days' duration can be arranged in Arequipa (p168); some can be combined with the Toro Muerto petroglyphs, and, if you ask, they may return via a collection of dinosaur footprints on the west edge of the canyon.

Sleeping & Eating

Hostal Alcalá (☎ 054-83-0011; Plaza de Armas, Alca; dm/s/d without bathroom S10/15/25, s/d S25/40) In Alca, this guesthouse has a good mix of clean rooms and prices, including some of the most comfortable digs in the whole valley. There is 24-hour hot water here.

Hostal Justito (☎ 054-58-1141; off main plaza, Cotahuasi; s/d without bathroom S15/30, s/d S20/40) Easy to find if arriving in the early morning, rooms here are adequate and the owners are happy to host travelers.

Posada Inti (posada_inti@yahoo.com; near main plaza, Tomepampa; r per person S20) A convenient place to crash in Tomepampa, rooms have private bathrooms with hot water and local TV and are decently clean.

Hostal Hatunhuasi (☎ 054-58-1054, in Lima 01-531-0803; hatunhuasi@gmail.com; Centanario 309, Cotahuasi; s/d S25/50) A notch above the other options in town, this friendly guesthouse has plenty of rooms situated around a sunny inner courtyard and hot water most of the time. Food can be made upon request, and the owners are good sources of hard-to-get information for travelers.

In Pampamarca, ask around for basic family **guesthouses** (S10 per person) that provide travelers with beds and meals.

Getting There & Away

The 420km bus journey from Arequipa, half of which is on unpaved roads, takes 12 hours if the going is good (S25). Over three-quarters of the way there, the road summits a 4500m pass between the huge glacier-capped mountains of Coropuna and Solimana (6323m) before dropping down to Cotahuasi. Wild vicuña can also be spotted here running on the high altiplano. **Reyna** (☎ 43-0612) and **Transportes Alex** (☎ 42-4605) both run buses that leave Arequipa around 4pm. Buses return to Arequipa from Cotahuasi at around 5pm.

There are hourly *combis* from the Cotahuasi plaza up to Alca (S3, one hour) via Tomepampa (S2, 30 minutes). For Pampamarca, there are two daily buses (S5,

two hours) departing in the early morning and again mid-afternoon.

LAGUNA DE SALINAS

This lake (4300m above sea level), east of Arequipa below Pichu Pichu and El Misti, is a salt lake that becomes a white salt flat during the dry months of May to December. Its size and the amount of water in it vary from year to year depending on the weather. During the rainy season it is a good place to see all three flamingo species, as well as myriad other Andean water birds.

Buses to Ubinas (S12, 3½ hours) pass by the lake and can be caught on Av Sepulveda. A small ticket booth on Sepulveda sells tickets, and schedules vary so it is a good idea to inquire a day before you wish to go. You can hike around the lake, which can take about two days, then return on the packed daily afternoon bus at around 3pm (expect to stand) or try to catch a lift with workers from the nearby mine. One-day minibus tours from Arequipa cost about S150 per person; mountain-biking tours are also available (p170). Finally, some mountain-climbing expeditions to Ubinas (p169) stop off at the lake en route to base camp, although few people are now attempting the climb due to Ubinas' constant volcanic activity.

Lake Titicaca

Worlds collide around Lake Titicaca. Here the desolate altiplano (Andean plateau) meets the storied peaks and fertile valleys of the Andes. Green, sun-dazed islands contrast with freezing dirt farms. Ancient agrarian communities live alongside the chaos of the international marketplace.

Campesinas (peasant women) in bowler hats and sandals made from recycled truck tires tend to their llamas as light aircraft full of contraband fly overhead. Coca smugglers count their money in tumbledown towns that rear out of the dust like anthills. On howling cold nights, people huddle together, yet this place parties like nowhere else. In a country known for its riotous religious fiestas, Puno's Candelaria is one of the greatest shows of all.

Lake Titicaca shimmers with a distinctive navy blue, and its gemlike islands and gentle shores are an agricultural paradise. Crumbling cathedrals, rolling hills, checkerboard valleys and Bolivia's highest mountains in the background all conspire to make anyone a pro photographer. According to Andean belief, this lake gave birth to the sun, as well as the father and mother of all the Incas, Manco Cápac and Mama Ocllo. Pre-Inca Pukara, Tiwanaku and Collas all lived here and left monuments scattered across the landscape – from waist-high burial towers for dwarves to comical oversized stone penises. This is the heartland of South America, where priests bless taxis and lawyers sacrifice llamas. Rug up and jump in.

HIGHLIGHTS

- Join mesmerizing celebrations with brass bands and crazy costumes in **Puno** (p198), Peru's *capital folklórico* (folkloric capital)
- Admire towering temples and breathtaking backdrops in Lake Titicaca's tiny **south shore towns** (p212)
- Hike through peaceful farmland to an overgrown ruin, then climb another hill in **Ichu** (p212)
- Visit awe-inspiring funerary towers at **Sillustani** (p206) and **Cutimbo** (p207)
- Recharge your batteries on the sunny, somnolent **Capachica Peninsula** (p210)

- BIGGEST CITY: JULIACA, POPULATION 62,000
- AVERAGE TEMPERATURE: JANUARY 8°C TO 14°C, JULY 4°C TO 10°C

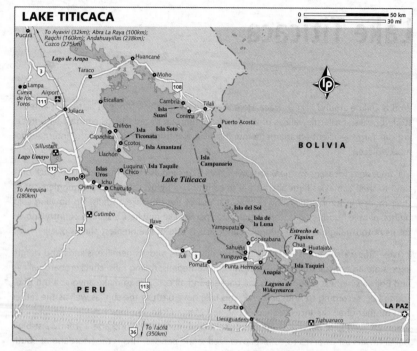

LAKE TITICACA

JULIACA

☎ 051 / pop 62,000 / elev 3826m

As a local wit diplomatically put it: 'If Cuzco is the navel of the world that makes Juliaca the – ahem – *armpit*.' The department's only commercial airport makes Juliaca an unavoidable transit point, but it is ugly, cold, dirty and, outside the central commercial area, dangerous. Stay in Puno or Lampa if you can.

Orientation & Information

Hotels, restaurants, *casas de cambio* (foreign-exchange bureaus), and internet cafes abound along San Román, near Plaza Bolognesi. Buses to the coast leave from within walking distance of this area, on and around San Martín over the railway tracks; *combis* (minibuses) to Puno leave from Plaza Bolognesi.

The **police station** (☎ 32-4795; ☺ 24hr) is on the corner of San Martín and Ramón Castilla. There are several banks with ATMs on Nuñez near Plaza Bolognesi. **Clínica Americana** (☎ 32-1639; Loreto 315; ☺ 24hr) offers emergency medical services. The **post office** (Sandía at Butrón; ☺ 8:15am-7pm Mon-Sat) is a stiff walk northwest of Plaza Bolognesi along San Román.

Dangers & Annoyances

Juliaca's high altitude can cause problems for those arriving from the coast (see p548).

The commercial center is safe for tourists; in other areas, muggings and scary, aggressive drunks are common at all times of day.

Sleeping

There are several bare-bones *hostales* (guesthouses) around Plaza Bolognesi.

Hotel San Antonio (☎ 33-1803; hotel_san_antonio@ hotmail.com; San Martín 347; s/d S32/45, s/d/tr without bathroom from S9.50/15/19.50) San Antonio offers good value with a large array of basic but clean rooms. The better options in the new wing have hot showers and national TV. There's also an attached sauna (entry S9) that's open daily; Friday is ladies only.

Hotel Sakura (☎ 32-2072; San Román 133; s/d/tr S45/70/75, s/d with cable TV US$10.50/12) Just northwest of the plaza, this guesthouse has positive vibrations, and rooms have private bathrooms with hot showers.

La Maison Hotel (☎ 32-1444; www.lamaison hotel.com; 7 de Junio 535; s/d/tr/q with breakfast S60/93/127/147) La Maison has notably comfortable, if low-class, rooms with cable TV and plastic chairs.

Royal Inn Hotel (☎ 32-1561; www.royalinnhoteles .com; San Román 158; s/d/tr S90/120/140) An excellent choice for the price, the towering Royal Inn boasts newly revamped modern rooms with hot showers, heating and cable TV, plus one of Juliaca's best restaurants.

Eating & Drinking

Restaurant Trujillo (San Román 163, mains from S20) and the restaurant at the **Royal Inn Hotel** (☎ 32-1561; San Román 158; mains from S18) over the road are the best in town. **El Oscar Discoteca** (7 de Junio s/n) has the most foreigner-friendly nightlife on offer in Juliaca, with desultory dancing and enthusiastic drinking to a soundtrack of salsa and crunching broken glass underfoot.

Getting There & Away

AIR

The **airport** (☎ 32-8974) is 2km west of town. **LAN** (☎ 32-2228; San Román 125; ☑ 8am-7pm Mon-Fri, to 6pm Sat) has daily flights to/from Lima, Arequipa and Cuzco.

BUS & TAXI

A *terminal terrestre* (bus terminal) has been under construction for years, but long-distance bus companies continue to depart from *cuadra* (block) 12 of San Martín, 2km east of town. Buses leave for Cuzco (S20 to S25, five hours) every hour from 5am to 11pm, and for Arequipa (S13 to S30, four hours), every hour from 2:30am to 11:30pm.

Julsa (☎ 32-6602) has the most frequent departures to Arequipa; **Power** (☎ 32-1952) has the most frequent to Cuzco. **Civa** (☎ 32-6229), **Ormeño** (☎ 32-3101) and **San Cristobal** run to Lima (S50 to S110, 20 hours). Ormeño has the best buses and the highest prices.

Sur Oriente (☎ 32-5947) has a daily bus to Tacna at 7pm (S30, 11 hours). More centrally located, **San Martín** (☎ 32-7501) and other companies along Tumbes between Moquegua and Piérola go to Tacna (S25, seven hours) via Moquegua.

Combis to Puno (S10, 50 minutes) leave from Plaza Bolognesi when full. *Combis* for Lampa (S2, 30 minutes) leave from Jirón Huáscar when full. *Combis* to Huancané (S2, 50 minutes) leave every 15 minutes from Ballón and Sucre, about four blocks east of Apurímac and 1½ blocks north of Lambayeque. *Combis* to Capachica (S3, 1½

hours) leave from Mercado Cerro Colorado in Jirón Cahuide. *Combis* to Escallani (S2.50, 1½ hours), via an incredibly scenic, unpaved back road, leave from the corner of Cahuide and Gonzáles Prada. All of these terminals are a S2 *mototaxi* (three-wheeled motorcycle rickshaw taxi) ride from the center of town.

Getting Around

Mototaxi is the best option for getting around. A ride to local destinations including bus terminals will cost about S2; getting to the airport costs around S8. Bus line 1B cruises around town and down Calle 2 de Mayo before heading to the airport (S0.50). *Colectivos* (shared taxis/minibuses) heading directly to Puno meet each plane, charging around S10 per passenger and taking less than an hour for the trip.

AROUND JULIACA
Lampa
☎ 051 / pop 1655 / elev 3860

This charming little town, 36km northwest of Juliaca, is known as La Ciudad Rosada (the Pink City) for its dusty, pink-colored buildings. A significant commercial center in colonial days, it still shows a strong Spanish influence. It's an excellent place to kill a few hours before flying out of Juliaca, or to spend a quiet night.

SIGHTS & ACTIVITIES

The beautifully constructed church of **Iglesia de Santiago Apostol** is well worth seeing. It contains, among other things, a life-sized sculpture of the Last Supper; a model of Santiago (St James) atop a real stuffed horse, returning from the dead to trample the Moors; creepy catacombs; secret tunnels; and a huge domed tomb topped by a copy of Michelangelo's *Pietà* and lined with hundreds of skeletons arranged in a ghoulishly decorative, skull-and-crossbones pattern. This truly has to be seen to be believed. Excellent guides (Spanish-speaking only) are on hand every day between 9am and 12:30pm and 2pm and 4pm. The tour costs S10.

Staff at the shop opposite **Museo Kampac** (cnr Ugarte & Ayacucho; admission S5; ☎ 951-82-0085; ☑ 7am-6pm), two blocks west of the Plaza de Armas, will give you a Spanish-language guided tour of the museum's small but significant collection of mostly pre-Inca ceramics, monoliths, and one mummy, and may show you a unique vase inscribed with the sacred cosmology of the Incas.

The **Municipalidad** (Town Hall; admission S2; ☿ 8am-12:45pm & 1:30-4pm Mon-Fri; 9am-1pm Sat & Sun), in the small square beside the church, is recognizable by its murals depicting Lampa's history – past, present and future. Inside there's a gorgeous courtyard, another replica of the *Pietà*, and a museum honoring noted Lampa-born painter Víctor Humareda (1920–1986).

Just out of town is a pretty colonial **bridge**, and about 4km west is **Cueva de los Toros**, a bull-shaped cave with prehistoric carvings of llamas and other animals. The cave is on the right-hand side of the road heading west. Its entrance is part of a large, distinctive rock formation. En route you'll see several *chullpas* (funerary towers), not unlike the ones at Sillustani (p206) and Cutimbo (p207).

SLEEPING & EATING

Lampa isn't all that geared up for overnight stays. There are a few basic accommodations, including cozy, quirky, recommended **Casa Romero** (☎ 952-65-1511, 952-71-9073; casaromerolampa@hotmail.com; Aguirre 327; s/d/tr with breakfast S40/60/80), where full board is available with advance booking. There are a couple of restaurants around the Plaza de Armas.

GETTING THERE & AWAY

Combis for Lampa (S2, 30 minutes) leave when full from Jirón Huáscar in Juliaca. If you have time to kill after checking in at Juliaca airport, get a taxi to drop you off in Lampa (about S5); it will wait and bring you back as well for about S40.

Pucará

☎ 051 / pop 675 / elev 3860m

More than 60km northwest of Juliaca, the sleepy village of Pucará is famous for its celebrations of **La Virgen del Carmen** on July 16, and its earth-colored pottery – not least the ceramic *toritos* (bulls) often seen perched on the roofs of Andean houses for good luck. Several local workshops, such as **Maki Pucará** (☎ 951-79-0618), on the highway near bus stop, are open to the public and offer classes where you can make ceramics for yourself from around S30 per hour.

The **Museo Lítico Pucará** (Jirón Lima; ☿ 8:30am-5pm Tue-Sun), by the church, displays a surprisingly good selection of anthropomorphic monoliths from the town's pre-Inca site, **Kalasaya**. The ruins themselves sit above the town, a short walk up Jirón Lima away from the main plaza.

Just S6 gets you into both sites, though there's nobody to check your ticket at the ruin.

If you get stuck, there are some simple accommodations near the bus stop.

Ayaviri

☎ 051 / pop 675 / elev 3928m

Almost 100km northwest of Juliaca is Ayaviri, the first sizable settlement on the road to Cuzco. It's a bustling, chilly market town with a colonial **church**, and the hot springs of **Pojpojquella** (admission S1.50; ☿ 4am-7:45pm Fri-Wed), where you can bathe. Apart from that. there's very little else to do, except eat local specialties: *queso ayavireño* (chewy, salty cheese that's fabulous with bread) and *kankacho*, tender, greasy lamb on the bone. There are several simple hotels in town, the best of which is **Hotel Lumonsa** (☎ 56-3500; cnr Plaza de Armas & Grau; r per person with/without bathroom S35/10).

Abra la Raya

From Ayaviri, the route climbs for almost another 100km to this Andean **mountain pass** (4470m), the highest point on the trip to Cuzco. Buses often stop here to allow passengers to take advantage of the photogenic view of snowcapped mountains and the cluster of handicrafts sellers. The pass also marks the departmental line between Puno and Cuzco; for points of interest north of here, see p288.

PUNO

☎ 051 / pop 120,200 / elev 3830m

Bustling, merrily claustrophobic Puno is known to most as a convenient stop between Cuzco and La Paz and a jumping-off point for Lake Titicaca expeditions, but it may just capture your heart with its own rackety charm.

Crammed together in congested, canyonlike *calles* (streets), cars, trucks, buses, *mototaxis* and *triciclos* (three-wheeled cycles) scream by in jangling waves while pedestrians cower on microscopically narrow pavements. Puno's people are cheerful, cheeky, and ready to drop everything if there's a good time to be had.

A modern city that's a trade nexus between Peru, Bolivia and the two coasts of South America, Puno is overwhelmingly commercial and forward-looking, but a few old buildings, and the many young cadets in the streets, give a sense of its colonial and naval history.

Puno is known as Peru's *capital folklórica* (folkloric capital)– its Virgen de la Candelaria parades are televised across the nation – and the associated drinking is the stuff of legend (see p201). The good times aren't restricted to religious festivals, though – some of Peru's most convivial bars, as well as some of its most innovative restaurants, are in Puno.

Orientation

Puno is handily compact. If you've got energy to spare, you can walk into the center from the port or the bus terminals, otherwise hop into a *mototaxi*. Everything in the town center is within easy walking distance.

Find yourself a coffee and a window seat on Jirón Lima, the main pedestrian street. Abandoned and forlorn in the afternoon, in the early evening it comes alive with *puneños* (inhabitants of Puno) out to promenade. Banks, *centros de llamadas* (call centers) and internet cafes abound on this street.

Information

EMERGENCY
Policía de Turismo (Tourist Police; ☎ 35-3988; Deustua 558; ☼ 24hr) There is also a policeman on duty in the *terminal terrestre* (24 hours) – ask around if you need him.

IMMIGRATION
Bolivian Consulate (☎ 35-1251; Arequipa 136, 2nd fl; ☼ 8am-2pm Mon-Fri)
Oficina de Migraciónes (Immigration Office; ☎ 35-7103; Ayacucho 270-280; ☼ 8am-1pm & 2pm-4:15pm Mon-Fri) May help with student and business visas; doesn't give tourist-card extensions.

MEDICAL SERVICES
Botica Fasa (☎ 36-6862; Arequipa 314; ☼ 24hr) A well-stocked pharmacy that's attended 24 hours, though you may have to pound on the door late at night.
Medicentro Tourist's Health Clinic (☎ 36-5909, 951-62-0937; Moquegua 191; ☼ 24hr) English and French spoken; will also come to your hotel.

MONEY
Bolivianos can be exchanged in Puno or at the border. You'll find an ATM inside the *terminal terrestre* that accepts most bank cards and dispenses US dollars and soles. **BCP** (Jirón Lima 444), **Interbank** (Lima at Libertad) and **Banco Continental** (Lima at Grau) all have branches and ATMs on Jirón Lima; there's another Banco Continental at Libertad. There's a **Moneygram** branch on Jirón Puno, just down from the Plaza.

POST
Serpost (Moquegua 267; ☼ 8am-8pm Mon-Sat)

TOURIST INFORMATION
iPerú (☎ 36-5088; Plaza de Armas, cnr Lima & Deustua; ☼ 8:30am-7:30pm) Puno's helpful and well-informed tourist office; also runs Indecopi, the tourist-protection agency, which registers complaints about travel agencies and hotels.

Dangers & Annoyances

Puno's high altitude gives it extreme weather conditions. Nights get especially cold, particularly during the winter months of June to August (which are also the tourist high season), when temperatures can drop well below freezing. Meanwhile, days are very hot and sunburn is a common problem.

The elevation also means that travelers arriving directly from the coast run a real risk of getting *soroche* (altitude sickness; see p548). Plan on spending some time in Arequipa (2350m) or Cuzco (3326m) first to acclimatize, or take it very easy after arriving in Puno.

Robberies have been reported at the Mirador del Condor and Cerro Huajsapata. Go in the morning and preferably not alone. In addition, serious attacks on travelers have been reported on the outskirts of Puno. Exercise extreme caution there, even during the day.

Sights & Activities

On the western flank of the Plaza de Armas is Puno's baroque **cathedral** (admission free; ☼ 10-11am & 3:30-6pm), which was completed in 1757. The interior is more Spartan than you'd expect from the well-sculpted facade, except for the silver-plated altar, which, following a 1964 visit by Pope Paul VI, has a Vatican flag to its right.

The 17th-century **Casa del Corregidor** (☎ 35-1921; www.casadelcorregidor.pe; Deustua 576; admission free; ☼ 10am-8pm), one of Puno's oldest residences, houses a cultural center where exhibitions, workshops and concerts take place. There's also an art gallery and a bookshop. Its cafe-bar is a great place to hobnob with local expats and artists over a cappuccino and a pastry.

Around the corner, **Museo Carlos Dreyer** (Conde de Lemos 289; admission with English-speaking guide S15; ☼ 9:30am-7pm Mon-Sat) houses a fascinating collection of Puno-related archaeological artifacts and art. Upstairs there are three mummies and a full-scale fiberglass *chullpa*.

Puno's tiny, quirky **Coca Museum** (☎ 36-5087; Deza 301; admission S5; ☼ 9am-1pm & 3-8pm) offers lots of interesting information – historical,

LAKE TITICACA

lonelyplanet.com

PUNO

LAKE TITICACA

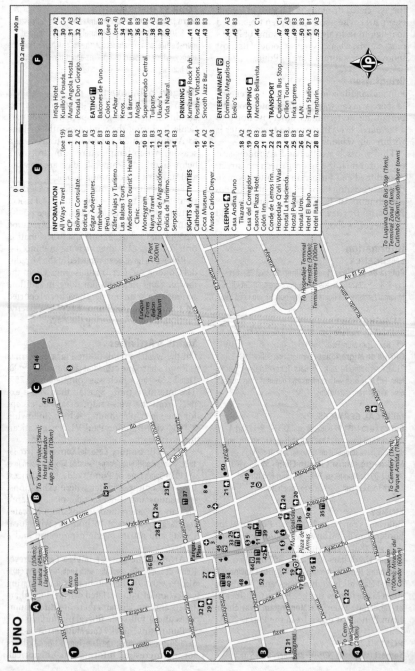

INFORMATION	
All Ways Travel..................	(see 19)
BCP......................................	1 B3
Bolivian Consulate.............	2 A2
Botica Fasa..........................	3 B2
Edgar Adventures...............	4 A3
Interbank............................	5 B3
iPerú....................................	6 B3
Käfer Viajes y Turismo.......	7 B3
Las Balsas Tours..................	8 B2
Medicentro Tourist's Health	
Clinic................................	9 B2
Moneygram.........................	10 B3
Nayra Travel........................	11 B3
Oficina de Migraciones......	12 A3
Policía de Turismo..............	13 A3
Serpost................................	14 B3

SIGHTS & ACTIVITIES	
Cathedral.............................	15 A4
Coca Museum......................	16 A2
Museo Carlos Dreyer..........	17 A3

SLEEPING	
Casa Andina Puno	
Tikarani.............................	18 A2
Casa del Corregidor............	19 A3
Casona Plaza Hotel.............	20 B3
Colón Inn............................	21 B3
Conde de Lemos Inn...........	22 A4
Hospedaje Q'oñi Wasi.........	23 B2
Hostal La Hacienda.............	24 B3
Hostal Pukara......................	25 B3
Hostal Uros.........................	26 B2
Hotel El Buho......................	27 B2
Hotel Italia..........................	28 B2

Intiqa Hotel........................	29 A2
Kusillo's Posada..................	30 C4
María Angola Hostal...........	31 B3
Posada Don Giorgio............	32 A2

EATING	
Balcones de Puno................	33 B3
Colors..................................	(see 4)
IncAbar................................	(see 4)
Keros....................................	34 A3
La Barca..............................	35 B4
Mojsa...................................	36 B3
Supermercado Central.........	37 B2
Tulipans...............................	38 A3
Ukuku's................................	39 B3
Vida Natural........................	40 A3

DRINKING	
Kamizaraky Rock Pub..........	41 B3
Positive Vibrations..............	42 B3
Smooth Jazz Bar..................	43 B3

ENTERTAINMENT	
Dominos Megadisco............	44 A3
Ekeko's................................	45 B3

SHOPPING	
Mercado Bellavista..............	46 C1

TRANSPORT	
Capachica Bus Stop.............	47 C1
Crillon Tours.......................	48 A3
Inka Express........................	49 B3
LAN......................................	50 B3
Train Station.......................	51 B1
Transturin............................	52 A3

FIESTAS & FOLKLORE AROUND LAKE TITICACA

Puno is often said to be the folkloric capital of Peru, boasting as many as 300 traditional dances and celebrating numerous fiestas throughout the year. Although dances often occur during celebrations of Catholic feast days, many have their roots in precolonial celebrations (usually tied in with the agricultural calendar). The dazzlingly ornate and imaginative costumes worn on these occasions are often worth more than an entire household's everyday clothes, and range from strikingly grotesque masks and animal costumes to glittering sequined uniforms.

Accompanying music uses a host of traditional instruments, from Spanish-influenced brass and string instruments to percussion and wind instruments that have changed little since Inca times. These traditional instruments include *tinyas* (wooden hand drums) and *wankaras* (larger drums formerly used in battle), plus a chorus of *zampoñas* (panpipes), which range from tiny, high-pitched instruments to huge bass panpipes almost as tall as the musician. Keep an eye out for *flautas* (flutes): from simple bamboo pennywhistles called *quenas* to large blocks that look as though they've been hollowed out of a tree trunk. The most esoteric is the *piruru*, which is traditionally carved from the wing bone of an Andean condor.

Seeing street fiestas can be planned, or can simply be a matter of luck. Some celebrations are held in one town and not in another; for others, the whole region lets loose. Ask at the tourist office in Puno about any fiestas in the surrounding area while you're in town. The following festivals are particularly important in the Lake Titicaca region, but many countrywide fiestas are celebrated here, too.

La Virgen de la Candelaria is the most spectacular festival. It spreads out for several days around the actual date (February 2), depending upon which day of the week Candlemas falls. If it falls between Sunday and Tuesday, things get under way the previous Saturday; if Candlemas occurs between Wednesday and Friday, celebrations get going the following Saturday. Puno Week (the first week of November), centered on Puno Day (November 5), is also celebrated in style. It marks the legendary birth of Manco Cápac, the first Inca.

No list of regional holidays and fiestas could ever be exhaustive. Most are celebrated for several days before and after the actual day, including Epiphany (January 6); the Feast of St John the Baptist (March 8); Alacitas (May 2), with a miniature handicrafts fair in Puno; Las Cruces (May 3 to 4), with celebrations on Isla Taquile and in Huancané; the Feast of St James (July 25), celebrated mostly on Isla Taquile; and Our Lady of Mercy (September 24). All of these festivals feature traditional music and dancing, as well as merry mayhem of all sorts.

If you plan to visit during any of these festivals, either make reservations in advance or show up a few days early, and expect to pay premium rates for lodgings.

---

medicinal, cultural – about the coca plant and its many uses. Presentation isn't that interesting, though: reams of text (in English only) stuck to the wall interspersed with photographs and old Coca-Cola advertisements. The display of traditional costumes is what makes a visit to this museum worthwhile. Though its relation to coca is unfathomable, it's a boon for making sense of the costumes worn in street parades.

A 10-minute walk west of the Plaza de Armas brings you to the top of **Cerro Huajsapata**, a little hill crowned by a white, larger-than-life statue of the first Inca, Manco Cápac. The view is excellent but robberies have been reported. The same applies to the **Mirador del Condor**, a lookout that rewards a stiff climb with fantastic views of brown, beehive-like

Puno and the endless, shimmering lake beyond. Both can be seen from the plaza, and are helpfully signposted.

Tours

It pays to shop around for a tour operator in Puno. Agencies abound and competition is fierce, leading to touting in streets and bus terminals, undeliverable promises, and prices so low as to negate the possibility of profits for the people at the bottom of the totem pole. Several of the cheaper tour agencies have reputations for ripping off the islanders of Amantaní and Taquile, with whom travelers stay overnight, and whose living culture is one of the main selling points of these tours.

Island-hopping tours, even with the better agencies, are often disappointing: formulaic,

THE YAVARI PROJECT

The much-loved **Yavari** (☎ 36-9329; www.yavari.org; admission by donation; ⏲ 8am-5pm) is the oldest steamship on Lake Titicaca. In 1862 the *Yavari* and its sister ship, the *Yapura*, were built in Birmingham, England, of iron parts – a total of 2766 for the two vessels. These were shipped around Cape Horn to Arica, in what is now northern Chile, from where they were moved by train to Tacna, before being hauled by mule over the Andes to Puno – an incredible undertaking that took six years to complete.

The ships were assembled in Puno and the *Yavari* was launched on Christmas Day 1870. The *Yapura* was later renamed the *BAP Puno* and became a Peruvian Navy medical ship; it can still be seen in Puno. Both had coal-powered steam engines, but due to a shortage of coal, the engines were fuelled with dried llama dung! In 1914 the *Yavari* was further modified with a unique Bolinder four-cylinder, hot-bulb, semidiesel engine.

After long years of service, the ship was decommissioned by the Peruvian Navy and the hull was left to rust on the lakeshore. In 1982, Englishwoman Meriel Larken visited the forgotten boat and decided it was a piece of history that could and should be saved. She formed the Yavari Project to buy and restore the vessel.

Now open as a museum, the *Yavari* is moored behind the Sonesta Posada Hotel del Inca, about 5km from the center of town, on the way out to Isla Esteves and swanky Hotel Libertador (catch the red bus heading northbound along Av El Sol, S0.60). The devoted crew – the shortest serving staff member has worked here for 11 years – happily gives guided tours of the ship. With prior notice, enthusiasts may be able to see the engine fired up. In 1999, to mark the restoration of its engine, the *Yavari* left port under her own power for the first time in nearly half a century, and now test drives across the lake seven times a year. There are even rumors of her being turned into a floating hotel.

lifeless and inflexible, the inevitable result of sheer numbers and repetition. Seeing the islands independently is recommended – you can wander around freely and spend longer in the places you like.

Our research indicates that the following agencies live up to their reputations for equitable treatment of islanders, as well as satisfying customers:

All Ways Travel (☎ 35-3979; www.titicacaperu.com; Deustua 576, 2nd fl)

Edgar Adventures (☎ 35-3444; www.edgaradventures .com; Lima 328)

Käfer Viajes y Turismo (☎ 35-4742; www.kafer -titicaca.com; Arequipa 197)

Las Balsas Tours (☎ 36-4362; www.balsastours.com; Tacna 240)

Nayra Travel (☎ 36-4774, 975-1818; www.nayratravel .com; Lima 419, Office 105)

Sleeping

Travelers arriving by bus at odd hours should know about **Hospedaje Terminal Terrestre** (☎ 36-4737/33; s/d S15/30), inside the very bus station. The views aren't anything to write home about, but it's safe and convenient. And how often do you get to experience opening your bedroom door directly onto a bus terminal concourse? A winning combination of surrealism and practicality.

BUDGET

Duque Inn (☎ 20-5014; Ayaviri 152; r per person with/ without bathroom S20/15) This place is a steal, highly recommended for budget travelers. Archaeologist owner Ricardo Conde takes guests on free tours and at the time of research was in the process of constructing a scale model of an Egyptian pyramid on the hotel's roof. Eccentric gold! Rooms with shared bathrooms enjoy the best view in Puno at a ridiculously low price. To find it, continue along Ilave for three blocks beyond Huancané and turn right into Ayaviri.

Hospedaje Q'oñi Wasi (☎ 36-5784; qoniwasi_puno@ hotmail.com; Av La Torre 135; r per person with/without bathroom S20/15) Tucked up a dark alleyway, Q'oñi Wasi has snug, if run-down, older rooms, and a small common kitchen. French is spoken.

Hostal Uros (☎ 35-2141; www.hostaluros.com; Valcárcel 135; r per person S30) Recently freshened up, close to the action but quiet and serene, Hostal Uros is damn good value. There's plenty of room in the light-filled patio to store bicycles or motorbikes. Ask for a room with a window.

Kusillo's Posada (☎ 36-4579; kusillosposada@yahoo .es; Federico More 162; s/d/tr/q with continental breakfast S40/70/105/140; 🖳) Run by the indefatigable Jenny Juño and her wonderful family, this heart-warming homestay has cozy rooms with electric showers. It's not far from the bus stations, and just a short walk southeast of the Plaza de Armas.

Hotel El Buho (☎ 36-6122; Lambayeque 142; www .hotelbuho.com; s/d with breakfast US$20/23) Don't be put off by the grim exterior. Warm rooms, helpful staff and a groovy patio complete with fountain keep this place full of return guests; reservations are essential. Splurge-worthy for budget travelers.

MIDRANGE

Rates for midrange accommodations include breakfast.

Hostal Pukara (☎ 78-4240/28; www.pukaradeltitikaka .com; Libertad 328; s/d S75/120; 🖳) This quirky, rapidly aging hotel leaves no corner undecorated, with an eye-catching four-story-high relief in the entrance, plus murals, unusual tiling and other touches throughout the hallways. Rooms all have cable TV and phones, and are heated and soundproofed. There's a glass-covered rooftop cafe with a great view.

Posada Don Giorgio (☎ 36-3648; dongiorgio@ titicacalake.com; Tarapacá 238; s/d S79/110; 🖳) With a charming exterior, a mellow interior and exceptionally comfy rooms, Don Giorgio offers very good value for money. It's small enough to provide personal service, and rooms have phones, cable TV and deep armchairs.

Colón Inn (☎ 35-1432; www.titicaca-peru.com/ colon1e.htm; Tacna 290; s/d S108/135; 🖳) Another excellent choice. This is the only hotel in central Puno housed in an unmodernized colonial building – watch your head in the doorways. Rooms are smallish, while shared spaces are sumptuously colonial. Check out the cartoon-style fresco of Puno's history in the tiny, inviting patio.

Hotel Italia (☎ 36-7706; www.hotelitaliaperu.com; Valcárcel 122; s/d/tr S110/150/190; 🖳) Rooms have cable TV, hot showers and heating but vary in quality at this large, well-established midrange hostelry. The long-serving staff is quietly efficient, and the delicious, fairly healthy breakfast includes salty black olives and Puno's own triangular anise bread.

María Angola Hostal (☎ 36-4596; Bolognesi 190; s/d/ tr S122/168/210) Situated away from the hustle of the center, the funky, cozy María Angola has a fixation with intricately carved wood paneling and doors. It's a touch overpriced, but lovers of the South American Bizarre school of hotel design will delight in the contrast between baroque bed heads and fluffy toilet-seat covers.

Conde de Lemos Inn (☎ 36-9898; www.condelemos inn.com; Puno 675-681; s/d S145/190) Housed in a startlingly jagged, glass-fronted ziggurat, bang on the Plaza de Armas, this small hotel has been recommended by many travelers for its personable staff and high standards.

Casona Plaza Hotel (☎ 36-5614; www.casonaplaza hotel.com; Arequipa 655; s/d/tr S165/210/240; 🖳) This well-run, central hotel with 64 rooms is one of the largest in Puno, but is often full. All rooms are good and bathrooms are great, but this one is especially for lovers – most of the *matrimoniales* (matrimonial suites) are big enough to dance the *marinera* (Peru's national dance) between the bed and the lounge suite.

our pick **Intiqa Hotel** (☎ 36-6900; www.intiqahotel .com; Tarapacá 272; s/d/tr S180/210/240; 🖳) Jazzy and bright, Intiqa's refreshingly modern reception area will bring a smile to your face. The superb rooms do not disappoint, with fabulously comfy beds, goose-down quilts, cable TV, indigenous art, and a bathtub in every room. A happy, circus-colored gem of a place.

Hostal La Hacienda (☎ 35-6109; www.lahacienda puno.com; Deustua 297; s/d/tr S210/210/240; 🖳) This colonial-style hotel has lovely, airy common spaces, a mind-bending, *Vertigo*-style spiral staircase, and a 6th-floor dining room with panoramic views on three sides. After all that, rooms are a bit of a generic letdown, but they're warm and comfortable with cable TV and phones. Some have bathtubs.

TOP END

Breakfast is included in the rates of top-end hotels.

Casa Andina Puno Tikarani (☎ 36-7803; www.casa -andina.com; Independencia 185; r from S307; 🖳) A short walk from the center, this Peruvian chain hotel is in sparkling order, with firm beds, quality furnishings and heating. Walls are decked out in bold primary colors, and stone, tiling and modern decor are harmoniously combined. There are also lofty public areas for lounging, a restaurant and free wi-fi access. Casa Andina has two other hotels in Puno; see the website for details.

Hotel Libertador Lago Titicaca (☎ 36-7780, in Lima 01-442 0166; www.libertador.com.pe; Isla Esteves; r/ste S967/1316; 🖳 🖳) This five-star local landmark fills its own private island in the western part of Lake Titicaca, connected to Puno by a causeway. Taxis charge about S8 to get here. All of the 108 luxurious rooms and 16 suites have fabulous views out over the lake, but furniture in the suites feels more board meeting than romantic getaway. There are beautiful gardens on the island's slopes and a collection of pet llamas.

Eating

Tourist haunts huddle together on the glitzy pedestrianized Jirón Lima, and down side passage Calle Grau. Note that many restaurants don't advertise their *menús* (set meals), which are cheaper than ordering à la carte.

Locals eat *pollo a la brasa* (roast chicken) and economical *menús* on Jirón Tacna between Calles Deustua and Libertad. *Api* (hot, sweet corn juice) – one of the best comfort foods in the known world – is found in several places on Calle Oquendo between Parque Pino and the Supermercado. Head into any of several places advertising and ask for the regular deal: a hot, syrupy drink, plus a paper-thin, wickedly delicious envelope of deep-fried dough. It will set you back all of S1.50.

If you're feeling MSG-deprived, head to Calle Arbulú to fill up at a cheap and cheerful *chifa* (Chinese restaurant).

For self-catering, head to **Supermercado Central** (Oquendo s/n; 8am-10pm), but be wary of pickpockets.

Vida Natural (Lambayeque 141; lunch/dinner menú S6/15, mains from S8; closed Sat) The grubby, plastic-heavy ambience doesn't do Vida Natural any favors, but the vegetable-deprived will appreciate its good-value set meals and the long menu, which includes soy versions of Peruvian favorites, from *lomo saltado* (strips of beef stir-fried with onions, tomatoes, potatoes and chili) to *hamburguesas* (hamburgers).

Mojsa (36-3182; Lima 394; sandwiches from S10, mains from S18; 8am-10pm) Mojsa lives up to its name, which is Aymara for 'delicious'. It has a thoughtful range of Peruvian and international food, a design-your-own salad option and a menu full of random and interesting facts. Did you know that astronauts eat *quinua* (quinoa)?

Tulipans (35-1796; Lima 394; sandwiches from S10, mains from S20) Highly recommended for its yummy sandwiches, big plates of meat and steaming piles of vegetables, cozy Tulipans is warmed by the pizza oven in the corner and the hordes of people swarming through the door.

La Barca (36-4210; Arequipa 754; mains from S20; 9am-4pm) Puno's best *cevichería* (ceviche restaurant). The world holds little greater pleasure than swigging down beer in its sunny green courtyard while scoffing piles of delicious marinated fish. The *tiradito de cuatro estaciones* (Japanese-style ceviche without onions) is the house specialty, and is highly recommended if you like your food *picante* (hot).

IncAbar (36-8031; Lima 348; mains from S20; 8:30am–10pm) This stylishly low-slung, cheerily chic restaurant does creative international food with a local twist. The massive Andean platter – bread, chips, to-die-for olives, cheese, ham, avocado and more – is a favorite. A deservedly popular stop on the Gringo Trail, as evidenced by the pinboard full of expat business cards on the front wall.

our pick **Colors** (36-9254; Lima 342; mains from S20; 7am-11pm;) Colors is Puno's best kick-back couch cafe – with free wireless, naturally. The Andean-Greek–Middle East–Asian menu features fusion treats such as Andean cheese fondue and smoked trout ravioli in vodka sauce. There are reasonably priced breakfasts and great coffee too – hmm, you could lose a whole day here.

Balcones de Puno (36-5300, Libertad 354; mains from S20) Offers traditional local food with an emphasis on desserts, but what really sets it apart is its nightly show (7:30pm to 9pm),which stands out for the quality and enthusiasm of its performers, and the lack of cheese – no panpipe butchering of *El Cóndor Pasa* here.

Ukuku's (Grau 172, 2nd fl; mains from S20) Crowds of travelers and locals thaw out in this toasty restaurant, which dishes up good local and Andean food (try alpaca steak with baked apples, or the quinoa omelet), as well as pizzas, pastas, Asian-style vegetarian fare and espresso drinks.

Keros (36-4602; Lambayeque 131; mains from S20) Low-key Keros has a full bar and is heated by a sometimes-stifling open fire. It's a great place to try two Peruvian classics, *sopa a la criolla* (a creamy noodle soup with beef and peppers) and *tiradito*, both of which it prepares to perfection. Its motto is 'Eat like an Inca, pay like a peasant.'

Drinking

Central Puno's nightlife is geared toward tourists, with plenty of lively bars scattered around the bright lights on Jirón Lima, where touts hand out free-drink coupons, and on Jirón Puno, next to the plaza.

Kamizaraky Rock Pub (Grau 158) With our vote for southern Peru's best watering hole, this place feels like your best friend's living room. It has a classic-rock soundtrack, unbelievably cool bartenders and liquor-infused coffee drinks essential for staying warm during Puno's bone-chilling nights. It's a hard place to leave.

Positive Vibrations (Lima 356; 8pm-late) This rock and reggae travelers' haunt is always jumping. The enthusiastic young staff all dream of being DJs someday, and friendly service lives up to the promise of the bar's name. The eye-popping, UV-painted toilet is a little hard on the cortexes by the end of happy hour, but nobody's complaining.

Smooth Jazz Bar (36-4099; Arequipa 454) Absolutely nothing like its name implies, this tiny hole in the wall (holding 25 at a pinch) wins hearts for its phone-book-like list of drinks: three pages of cocktails and five different kinds of alcoholic hot tea are just the beginning. The music videos blasting from the TV in the corner are more likely to be Rod Stewart than Miles Davis, but 34 different piscos later, who cares?

Entertainment

Ekeko's (Lima 355, 2nd fl) Travelers and locals alike gravitate to this tiny, ultraviolet dance floor splashed with psychedelic murals. It moves to a thumping mixture of modern beats and old favorites, from salsa to techno trance, which can be heard several blocks away.

Dóminos Megadisco (Libertad near Lima; 8pm-late) If you want to see how the locals get down, this is the place for you. Multileveled mayhem, a karaoke lounge, a dance floor that explodes to salsa, *reggaetón* (a blend of Puerto Rican *bomba*, dancehall and hip-hop) and rock, and *cuba libre* (rum and cola) by the jug: it all adds up to a great night, but it's not for the fainthearted.

Shopping

Artesanías (handcrafts) – from musical instruments and jewelry to scale models of reed islands – wool and alpaca sweaters and other typical tourist goods are sold in every second shop in the town center. For household goods and clothes, head to **Mercado Bellavista** on Av El Sol (watch out for pickpockets).

Getting There & Away

To get to Bolivia, see p214.

AIR

The nearest airport is in Juliaca, about an hour away. See p197 for more information

on flights. Hotels can book you a shuttle bus for around S15. **LAN** (36-7227; Tacna 299) has an office in Puno.

BOAT

There are no passenger ferries across the lake from Puno to Bolivia, but you can get to La Paz via the lake in one or two days on high-class tours with **Transturin** (35-2771; www.transturin .com; Ayacucho 148) or **Crillon Tours** (35-1052, 35-1884; www.titicaca.com; Libertad 355), visiting Isla del Sol (p217) and other sights along the way.

BUS

The **terminal terrestre** (36-4737; Primero de Mayo 703), three blocks down Ricardo Palma from Av El Sol, houses Puno's long-distance bus companies. **Ormeño** (36-8176; www.grupo -ormeno.com.pe) is the safest and has the newest, fastest buses. **Cruz del Sur** (in Lima 01-311-5050; www.cruzdelsur.com.pe) used to be as good but has slipped in recent times, as the deteriorating fleet fails to be renewed. **Tour Peru** (www.tourperu .com.pe) is the best of the rest.

There's an ATM in the terminal, and hot showers are available for S5 at the station's *hospedaje* (basic hostelry; p202). There's a departure tax of S1.

Buses leave for Cuzco (S20 to S25, six hours) every hour from 4am to 10pm, and for Arequipa (S15 to S20, five hours) every hour from 2am to 10pm.

The most enjoyable way to get to Cuzco is via **Inka Express** (36-5654; www.inkaexpress.com; Tacna 346), whose luxury buses with panoramic windows depart every morning at 8am. Buffet lunch is included, along with an English-speaking tour guide, who talks about the four sites that are briefly visited en route: Andahuaylillas, Raqchi, Abra la Raya and Pucará. The trip takes about eight hours and costs S135 from Inka Express. You may well be able to persuade a travel agency to cut into its commission and sell you a ticket for less.

Getting to Lima takes 18 to 21 hours, depending on how much you pay. Civa will set you back S60, and departs at 12:30pm; all other companies operate luxury buses and cost S110 to S160.

All buses listed above go via Juliaca (S6, one hour).

Local *combis* to Chuquito, Juli, Pomata and the Bolivian border leave from **terminal zonál** (Simón Bolívar s/n), a few blocks northwest of *terminal terrestre*. Head out along Av

El Sol until you see the hospital on your right, then turn left and you'll hit the *terminal zonal* (regional terminal) after two long blocks.

To get to Capachica, catch a *combi* from Jirón Talara, just off El Sol opposite the Mercado Bellavista. They leave once an hour from about 6am to 2pm. The journey takes about 1¼ hours and costs S5.50.

Combis to Luquina leave from opposite the Brahma Beer distributor on Manchero Rossi, about 1.5km south of town, every hour or so in the morning.

TRAIN

The train ride from Puno to Cuzco retains a certain renown from the days – now long gone – when the road wasn't paved and the bus journey was a nightmare. Train fares have skyrocketed in recent years and most travelers now take the bus. The fancy Andean Explorer train, which includes a glass-walled observation car and complimentary lunch, costs S704; there's no cheaper option. The train tracks run next to the road for a lot of the way, so there's not a huge difference in scenery. The train is only marginally more comfortable than the better buses, so unless you're a train buff, there seems little reason to spend the extra S600. Buffs read on.

Trains depart from Puno's **train station** (☎ 36-9179; www.perurail.com; Av La Torre 224; 🕑 7am-12pm & 3pm-6pm Mon-Fri, 7am-3pm Sat) at 8am, arriving at Cuzco around 6pm. Services run on Monday, Wednesday and Saturday from November to March, with an extra departure on Friday from April to October. Tickets can be purchased online.

Getting Around

A short taxi ride anywhere in town (and as far as the transport terminals) costs S3. *Mototaxis* are a bit cheaper at S2, and *triciclos* cheapest of all at S1.50 – but it's an uphill ride, so you may find yourself wanting to tip the driver more than the cost of the fare!

AROUND PUNO

Sillustani

Sitting on rolling hills on the Lake Umayo peninsula, the funerary towers of **Sillustani** (admission S6.50; 🕑 8am-5pm) stand out for miles against the desolate altiplano landscape.

The ancient Colla people who once dominated the Lake Titicaca area were a warlike, Aymara-speaking tribe, who later became the southeastern group of the Incas. They buried their nobility in *chullpas* (funerary towers), which can be seen scattered widely around the hilltops of the region.

The most impressive of these towers are at Sillustani, where the tallest reaches a height of 12m. The cylindrical structures housed the remains of complete family groups, along with plenty of food and belongings for their journey into the next world. Their only opening was a small hole facing east, just large enough for a person to crawl through, which would be sealed immediately after a burial. Nowadays, nothing remains of the burials, but the *chullpas* are well preserved. The afternoon light is the best for photography, though the site can get busy at this time.

The walls of the towers are made from massive coursed blocks reminiscent of Inca stonework, but are considered to be even more complicated. Carved but unplaced blocks and a ramp used to raise them are among the site's points of interest, and you can also see the makeshift quarry. A few of the blocks are decorated, including a well-known carving of a lizard on one of the *chullpas* closest to the parking lot.

Sillustani is partially encircled by the sparkling Lago Umayo (3890m), which is home to a wide variety of plants and Andean waterbirds, plus a small island with vicuñas (threatened, wild relatives of llamas). Birders take note: this is one of the best sites in the area.

Tours to Sillustani leave Puno at around 2:30pm daily and cost from S25. The round-trip takes about 3½ hours and allows you about 1½ hours at the ruins. If you'd prefer more time at the site, hire a private taxi for S60 with waiting time. To save money, catch any bus to Juliaca and ask to be let off where the road splits (S5, 25 minutes). From there, occasional *combis* run to the village of Atun Colla, a 4km walk from the ruins. During high season, *combis* will occasionally continue to the ruins, but don't bank on this.

For longer stays, **Atun Colla** (☎ 951-90-5006, 951-50-2390; www.turismovivencialatuncolla.com) offers *turismo vivencia* (homestays). You can help your host family with farming, hike to lookouts and lesser-known archaeological sites, visit the tiny museum and eat dirt – this area is known for its edible *arcilla* (clay). Served up as a sauce on boiled potato, it goes down surprisingly well.

Cutimbo

Just over 20km from Puno, this dramatic **site** (admission S3; ☺ 8am-5pm) has an extraordinary position atop a table-topped volcanic hill surrounded by a fertile plain. Its modest number of well-preserved *chullpas*, built by the Colla, Lupaca and Inca cultures, come in both square and cylindrical shapes. You can still see the ramps used to build them. Look closely and you'll find several monkeys, pumas and snakes carved into the structures.

This remote place receives few visitors, which makes it both enticing and potentially dangerous for independent travelers, especially women. Go in a group and keep an eye out for those who wait to mug tourists. People are known to hide behind rocks at the top of the 2km trail that leads steeply uphill from the road.

Combis en route to Laraqueri leave the cemetery by Parque Amista, 1km from the center of Puno (S3, 30 minutes). You can't miss the signposted site, which is on the left-hand side of the road – just ask the driver where to get off. A taxi will cost approximately S70 with waiting time.

LAKE TITICACA ISLANDS

Lake Titicaca's islands are world famous for their peaceful beauty and well-preserved traditional agrarian cultures, which you can see up close by staying with families on the islands. A homestay here is a privileged glimpse

---

ETHICAL ISSUES OF COMMUNITY-BASED TOURISM

After Cuzco, Puno is Peru's most touristed town, as it's a base for excursions on and around Lake Titicaca. Archaeology and mythology draw tourists here, sure, but what makes us stay is the chance to spend time in a culture so different from our own. *Turismo vivenciul* (homestay tourism) has taken off around Puno and is now the basis of the tourism industry here.

There are dozens of tour agencies, in many cases offering the same thing at wildly different prices. So what's the difference? Sadly, it's generally the amount of money going to the people who share their lives.

Tour agencies pay host families a set amount per visitor, which is negotiated with islanders separately by each agency. Nearly all of the cheapest agencies (and some of the more expensive ones, too) pay little more than the cost of visitors' meals.

So what can you do? The following tips will help you and your host family to get the most from your community-tourism experience.

- Use one of the agencies listed on p201, or one that's recommended by fellow travelers.
- Check that your guide rotates the houses that visitors stay in and the Uros floating island they visit.
- Insist on handing payment for your lodging to the family yourself.
- Expect to pay well for your homestay. Visitors must pay at least US$50 for a typical two-day island excursion for the host family to make a profit from your stay.
- Travel to the islands independently – it's easy (see p208).
- Carry out your trash – islanders have no way of disposing of it.
- Bring gifts of cooking oil, rice, pasta and fresh fruit – things the islanders can't grow – or school equipment (pens, pencils, notebooks).
- Don't give candy or money to kids, so they don't learn to beg.
- Support communal enterprises, which benefit all. On Taquile, families take turns to run the Restaurante Comunál (p209), which gives many people their only opportunity to benefit from the tidal wave of tourism that hits their island daily. Luquina Chico (p213) and Isla Ticonata (p211) run their tourism communally, through rotation of accommodation, profit sharing, and shared work providing food, transport, guiding and activities.
- Consider visiting one of the communities around the lake. They're harder to get to than the islands but are far more peaceful and less geared to tourism – here you'll see a living, agrarian community, rather than a tourist screen.

LAKE TITICACA

at another way of life that you're unlikely to forget.

That said, the excruciatingly slow chug across the lake (whatever you do, don't forget the sunblock!) is not necessarily more enjoyable than seeing it from the shore, and negative impacts from tourism are being deeply felt in many communities.

Taquile has attracted large numbers of tourists since the 1970s. Tourism income goes mostly to the few families who own restaurants and guesthouses, and resentment towards tourists is increasingly evident in the community. The people of Amantaní tried to avoid this by introducing *turismo vivencial*. Food and lodging were offered at a set price in family homes, not hotels, following a strict rotation system enforced by the community. Yet over time this system broke down, as tour agencies played favorites and some communities began to undercut others. Now, some communities barely profit at all from receiving visitors, and most islanders still live in poverty despite decades of tourism.

All travel agencies in Puno offer one- and two-day tours to Uros, Taquile and Amantaní. Even with the better agencies, island hopping tours tend to have a cookie-cutter, cat-herding vibe, and some are even exploitative. It's easy – and recommended – to travel independently instead. All ferry tickets are valid for 15 days, so you can island hop at will. See the boxed text (p207) for more tips about responsible tourism on Lake Titicaca's islands.

Islas Uros

Just 5km east of Puno, these unique **floating islands** (admission S5) are Lake Titicaca's top tourist attraction. They're built using the buoyant *totora* reeds that grow abundantly in the shallows of the lake. The lives of the Uros people are interwoven with these reeds, which are partially edible (tasting like hearts of palm) and are also used to make their homes, their boats and the crafts they churn out for tourists. The islands are constructed from many layers of the *totora*, which are constantly replenished from the top as they rot from the bottom, so the ground is always soft and springy. (Be careful not to put your foot through any rotten sections!)

Some islands also have elaborately designed versions of traditional tightly bundled reed boats on hand. Be prepared to pay for a ride or to take photographs.

Intermarriage with the Aymara-speaking indigenous people has seen the demise of the pure-blooded Uros, who nowadays all speak Aymara. Always a small tribe, the Uros began their unusual floating existence centuries ago in an effort to isolate themselves from the aggressive Collas and Incas.

The popularity of the islands has led to shocking overcommercialization, and controversy rages over their authenticity, with many *puneños* claiming that islanders sleep on the mainland.

It's worth noting that more authentic reed islands do still exist. These are located further from Puno through a maze of small channels and can only be visited with a private boat. The islanders there continue to live in a relatively traditional fashion, and prefer not to be photographed.

Getting to the Uros is easy – there's no need to go with an organized tour. Ferries leave from the port for Uros (return trip S10) at least once an hour from 6am to 4pm. The community-owned ferry service visits two islands, on a rotation basis. Ferries to Taquile and Amantaní can also drop you off in the Uros.

Nearly the only, and certainly the best, accommodation provider on Uros is **Cristina Suaña** (☎ 951-69-5121, 951-47-2355; uroskhantati@hotmail.com; r per person S120), on Isla Khantati. The tariff is steep but includes top-notch accommodation, three meals, fishing, lots of cultural activity, and the pleasure of the company of the effervescent Cristina. Book in advance so that she can pick you up from Puno in a private boat – if you catch the public ferry you may end up on the wrong island. Highly recommended by readers.

Isla Taquile

Inhabited for thousands of years, **Taquile Island** (admission S5), 35km east of Puno, is a tiny 7-sq-km island with a population of about 2000 people. The Quechua-speaking islanders are distinct from most of the surrounding Aymara-speaking island communities and maintain a strong sense of group identity. They rarely marry non-Taquile people.

Taquile has a fascinating tradition of handicrafts, and the islanders' creations are made according to a system of deeply ingrained social customs. Men wear tightly woven woolen hats that resemble floppy nightcaps, which they knit themselves. These hats are closely bound up with social symbolism: men wear red hats if they are married and red and white hats if they are single, and different colors can denote a man's current or past social position.

Taquile women weave thick, colorful waistbands for their husbands, which are worn with roughly spun white shirts and thick, calf-length black pants. Women wear eye-catching outfits comprising multilayered skirts and delicately embroidered blouses. These fine garments are considered some of the most well-made traditional clothes in Peru, and can be bought in the cooperative store on the island's main plaza.

ORIENTATION & INFORMATION

A stairway of more than 500 steps leads from the dock to the center of the island. The climb takes a breathless 20 minutes if you're acclimatized – more if you're not.

Take in the lay of the land while it's still light – with no roads, streetlights or big buildings to use as landmarks, travelers have been known to get so lost in the dark that they end up roughing it for the night. (A limited electricity supply was introduced to the island in the 1990s but it is not always available, so remember to bring a flashlight.)

Make sure you already have lots of small bills in local currency, because change is limited and there's nowhere to exchange dollars. You may want to bring extra money to buy some of the exquisite crafts sold in the cooperative store.

SIGHTS & ACTIVITIES

Taquile's scenery is beautiful and reminiscent of the Mediterranean. In the strong island sunlight, the deep, red-colored soil contrasts with the intense blue of the lake and the glistening backdrop of Bolivia's snowy Cordillera Real on the far side of the lake. Several hills boast Inca terracing on their sides and small ruins on top. Visitors are free to wander around, explore the ruins and enjoy the tranquility. The island is a wonderful place to catch a sunset and gaze at the moon, which looks twice as bright in the crystalline air, rising over the breathtaking peaks of the Cordillera Real.

FESTIVALS & EVENTS

The **Fiesta de San Diego** (Feast of St James; July 25) is a big feast day on Taquile. Dancing, music and general carousing go on for several days until the start of August, when islanders make traditional offerings to Pachamama (Mother Earth). **Easter** and **New Year's Day** are also festive and rowdy. Many islanders go to Puno for La Virgen de Candelaria and Puno Week (see p201), when the island becomes somewhat deserted.

SLEEPING & EATING

There are many *hospedajes* (small, family-owned inns) on Taquile, offering basic accommodation for around S15 a night. Options range from a room in a family house to small guesthouses. Most offer indoor toilets and showers with electric hot water.

There are plenty of restaurants too, all offering the same fare of *sopa de quinua* (quinoa soup – absolutely delicious everywhere on Lake Titicaca) and lake trout for S18. Consider eating in the **Restaurante Comunál**, Taquile's only community-run food outlet (see p207).

GETTING THERE & AWAY

Ferries (round-trip S20; admission to island S5) leave from the Puno port for Taquile at 6am and 7.45am, and return at 5:30pm. There's a ferry from Amantaní to Taquile every morning at 8am, and it's also possible to get here by ferry from Llachón.

Isla Amantaní

Amantaní Island (admission S5), population 4000, is a few kilometers north of the smaller Taquile. Almost all trips to Amantaní involve an overnight stay with islanders. Helping them cook on open fires in dirt-floored kitchens and meeting small children who walk an hour each way to school every day is humbling and sometimes life changing. Commercial as Amantaní has become, a stay here is unforgettable.

The villagers sometimes organize rousing traditional dances, letting travelers dress in their traditional party gear to dance the night away. Of course, you'll look quite comical in your hiking boots! Don't forget to look up at the incredibly starry night sky as you stagger home.

The island is very quiet (no dogs allowed!), boasts great views and has no roads or vehicles. Several hills are topped by ruins, among the highest and best-known of which are **Pachamama** (Mother Earth) and **Pachatata** (Father Earth). These date to the Tiwanaku culture, a largely Bolivian culture that appeared around Lake Titicaca and expanded rapidly between 200 BC and AD 1000.

As with Taquile, the islanders speak Quechua, but their culture is more heavily influenced by the Aymara.

SLEEPING & EATING

When you arrive, island families will allocate you to your accommodation according to a rotating system. Please respect this system and, if you're with a guide, insist that they do. There's no problem with asking for families or friends to be together. A bed and full board should cost at least S30 per person per night.

GETTING THERE & AWAY

Ferries (round-trip S30; admission to island S5) leave from the Puno port for Amantaní at 8am every day. There are departures from Amantani to Taquile and Puno around 4pm every day – check, though, as times vary – and sometimes from Amantani to Puno around 8am, depending on demand.

CAPACHICA PENINSULA & AROUND

Poking far out into the northwestern part of the lake, midway between Juliaca and Puno, the Capachica Peninsula is as beautiful as the lake islands but without the crowds and commercialism. Each *pueblito* (tiny town) boasts its own glorious scenery, ranging from pastoral and pretty to coweringly majestic. A few days here among the local people –handsome, dignified men in vests and black hats, and shy, smiling women in intricate headgear – with nothing to do but eat well, climb hills and trees, and stare at the lake, is chicken soup for the soul. Homestay is the only accommodation on offer and a major part of the fun.

Strung along the Capachica Peninsula between the towns of Capachica and Llachón, the villages of Ccotos and Chifrón are linked by deserted, eminently walkable dirt roads and lackadaisical bus services (it's generally quicker to walk over the hill than drive around by the road). Escallani is further north, slightly off the peninsula proper, not far from Juliaca. Locals get to the mainland by *lancha* (small motorboat), which they are happy to hire out.

There is no internet reception on the peninsula, but cell phones work. There are no banks or ATMs and, as elsewhere in Peru, breaking big notes can be very difficult. Bring all the money you need, in bills of S20 or smaller if possible.

Travel agencies in Puno (p201) can get you to any of the peninsula's communities. **CEDESOS** (☎ 36-7915; www.cedesos.org; 3rd fl, Moquegua 348, Puno) offers fully guided, standard and tailored trips to these communities and others in the area. This NGO works to improve local income and standards of living through tourism. It offers villagers training and cheap credit to ready themselves to receive tourists. Tours are not cheap, but they're well organized and come highly recommended by readers.

All of the communities listed below offer the same deal on food and accommodation, similar to that encountered on Isla Amantaní. Families have constructed or adapted basic rooms for tourists in their homes, and charge around S20 per person per night for a bed, or about S50 for full board. Full board is recommended – each town has at least one shop, but supplies are limited, and the food provided by the families is healthy and delicious. Apart from trout, the diet is vegetarian, with emphasis on quinoa, potatoes and locally grown *habas* (broad beans).

Llachón and, to a lesser extent, Escallani are set up for travelers just turning up. For other communities, it's very important to arrange accommodation in advance, as hosts need to buy supplies and prepare. It's preferable to call rather than email. Generally, only Spanish is spoken.

Capachica

The peninsula's blisteringly forgettable commercial center has a couple of very basic restaurants and *hospedajes*, as well as a pretty church and an astonishingly oversized sports coliseum, all of which you can see from the bus. There's no reason to stop here unless you need to use the internet or a public telephone (there are a couple around the plaza); you won't find either in any of the other communities on the peninsula.

Llachón

Almost 75km northeast of Puno, this pretty little village community near the peninsula's southern tip offers fantastic views and short hikes to surrounding pre-Inca sites. The most developed of the peninsula's communities, thanks to locally managed tourism, it nevertheless feels far from the bright lights of modern Peru. With few cars and no dogs, it's an incredibly peaceful place to sit and enjoy stunning views of Lake Titicaca, while sheep, cows, pigs, llamas and kids wander by. From January to March, native birds are also a feature.

Some accommodation recommendations are given below, but it's possible to simply turn up in town and ask around.

Community leader **Félix Turpo** (☎ 951-66-4828; hospedajesamary@hotmail.com) has a gorgeous garden and the Capachica Peninsula's most spectacular view, overlooking Isla Taquile. At the time of research Félix was also the proud owner of Llachón's only hot shower, a very high-tech affair consisting of a black rubber pipe on a warm rock. (It worked well during daylight hours.)

Magno Cahui (☎ 951-82-5316; hospedajetikawai@hotmail.com; hospedajetikawai@yahoo.com), his wife and their very cute children have six cozy cabins built around his grandfather's stone altar, and another incredible view of Lake Titicaca.

Local legend **Valentín Quispe** (☎ 951-82-1392; llachon@yahoo.com) and his wife Lucila have a charming guesthouse hidden down a stone path, by an enchanting overgrown cemetery. They also rent out kayaks.

Richard Cahui Flores (☎ 951-63-7382; calixto_cahui@yahoo.es) works with lots of families and is the best point of contact for advance bookings as he will set you up with somebody else if he doesn't have space in his tranquil farmhouse.

Chifrón

If you found Llachón a bit too built-up, tiny somnolent Chifrón (population 24), off the main road in the northeast corner of the peninsula, is for you. Drowsing in rustling eucalypts above a deserted beach, three families offer very basic accommodation for a maximum of 15 people. This is truly a chance to experience another world. Contact **Emiliano** (☎ 951-91-9652) to arrange a stay.

Ccotos & Isla Ticonata

You can't get much further off the beaten track than Ccotos, two-thirds of the way down the peninsula's east coast. Nothing ever happens here except the annual Miss Playa (Miss Beach) competition, in which the wearing of bathing suits stirs much controversy. Stay with the engaging **Alfonso Quispe** (☎ 951-85-6462; incasamanatours@yahoo.es) and his family, right on the edge of the lake. Catch your own fish for breakfast, bird-watch, hike to the lookout and some overgrown ruins, and relax on the beach, which is ar-

guably Capachica's most beautiful (but it's a tough call).

A couple of hundred meters off Ccotos, Isla Ticonata is home to a fiercely united community and some significant mummies, fossils and archaeological sites. Isla Ticonata is only accessible by organized tour, and is a rare example of Lake Titicaca's local communities calling the shots on tour agencies, to the benefit of all. Tours can be booked in Puno at short notice through CEDESOS (see opposite) or the travel agencies listed on p201. Activities include fishing, dancing, cooking and helping till family *chakras* (fields).

Escallani

The settlement of Escallani, off the peninsula itself, on the way to Juliaca, shows the lake from a completely different aspect. Rather than pretty, it's almost stupefyingly majestic. You could spend days staring at the view – of reed beds, cactus thickets, craggy rocks, patchwork fields and Bolivia's highest mountain, the awesome, perennially snowcapped Illimani. There's not much else to do, though there are rumors of rock-climbing possibilities nearby. **Rufino** (☎ 951-64-5325, Spanish only) and his large family have built a rambling complex of more than a dozen rustic, straw-thatched cabins high above the town. Rufino doesn't have telephone service; to reserve a spot, call his relatives in Juliaca well in advance. This area is a little more ready than other communities to receive guests unannounced – ask around at the plaza to find his place.

The trip from Juliaca to Escallani via Pusi by local *micro* is highly recommended for hardy travelers. The scenery on this unpaved, little-traveled road is unparalleled – sit on the left side of the bus if heading from Juliaca to Escallani so that you can see the lake.

Getting There & Around

From Puno, catch a *combi* advertising either Capachica or Llachón. All will stop in Capachica (62km, 80 minutes) and continue to Llachón, 25 minutes further down the road. It costs S5.50 to get from Puno to Capachica, and another S0.50 to S1.50 to destinations beyond.

To get to Ccotos or Escallani, change buses in Capachica. Be patient, as just one *combi* plies the road from here to Ccotos (30 minutes) – if you miss it, it could take up to 1½ hours to arrive.

To get to Chifrón, hike over the hill from Llachón, or walk the 3km from Capachica. It's also possible to talk an off-duty *combi* (often to be found around Capachica's plaza) into driving you for a few soles.

From Juliaca, *combis* run to Capachica (S3, 1½ hours) from Mercado Cerro Colorado in Cahuide. *Combis* to Escallani, which travel on an incredibly scenic, unpaved back road (S2.50, 1½ hours), leave from the corner of Cahuide and Gonzáles Prado. Both terminals are a S2 *mototaxi* ride from the center of Juliaca.

Llachón is also accessible via the Taquile ferry. The easiest way to combine the two is to arrive by road, then have your host family in Llachón show you where to catch the ferry to Taquile.

SOUTH-SHORE TOWNS

The road to Bolivia via Lake Titicaca's southern shore passes through bucolic villages noted for their colonial churches and beautiful views. Traveling this route is an easy way to get a relatively untouristy peek at the region's traditional culture. You can visit all of the following towns in a day and be back in Puno or in Bolivia by nightfall.

For public transport to any south-shore town, go to Puno's Terminal Zonal. *Combis* leave from there as they fill – usually within half an hour – for Ichu (S0.70, 15 minutes), Chucuito (S1, 30 minutes), Juli (S3.50, 1¼ hours), Pomata (S5.50, 1½ hours) and the Bolivian border at Yunguyo (S6, 2¼ hours) or Desaguadero (S7, 2½ hours). Direct transport to the towns closer to Puno are more frequent, but *combis* to most towns leave at least hourly – more often for closer destinations.

Ichu

Ten kilometers out of Puno, this rural community spread across a gorgeous green valley is home to a little-known ruin with superb views, and is a great place for a hike.

Leave the Panamericana at Ichu's second exit (after the service station) and head inland past the house marked 'Villa Lago 1960'. Walk 2km, bearing left at the junction, aiming for the two small, terraced hills you can see in the left of the valley. After bearing left at a second junction (you'll pass the school if you miss it), the road takes you between the two hills.

Turn left again and head straight up the first one. Fifteen minutes of stiff climbing brings you to the top, where you'll be rewarded with the remains of a multilayered temple complex, and breathtaking 360-degree views.

This can be done as an easy half-day trip from Puno. A taxi to take you to the foot of the hill and wait for your return will cost around S25. Take plenty of water and food as there's no store.

Chucuito

☎ 051 / pop 1100

Quiet Chucuito's principal attraction is the outlandish **Templo de la Fertilidad** (Inca Uyu; admission S5; ⊗ 8am-5pm). Its dusty grounds are scattered with large stone phalluses, some up to 1.2m in length. Local guides tell various entertaining stories about the carvings, including tales of maidens sitting atop the stony joysticks to increase their fertility. Further uphill from the main road is the main plaza, which has two attractive colonial churches, **Santo Domingo** and **Nuestra Señora de la Asunción**. You'll have to track down the elusive caretakers to get a glimpse inside.

At time of research there was no public internet access in Chucuito.

SLEEPING & EATING

Albergue Las Cabañas (☎ 36-8494; www.chucuito .com; Tarapacá 153; s/d from S50/94), near the main plaza, has a charming, overgrown garden, rustic stone cabins and familial bungalows complete with wood-burning fires. Prices are flexible (only estimations are given here), so it's worth negotiating. Camping is also allowed for around S10 per person.

The unmissable new-age **Taypikala Hotel** (☎ 79-2252; www.taypikala.com; Km18 Panamericana Sur; s/d/tr S167/220/287) is buried under a confusion of model condors and jagged artificial rocks. Rooms have lake and garden views, and are decorated with copies of local rock art. The main entrance is at the back, near the temple. Across the highway, swanky new sister hotel **Taypikala Lago** (☎ 79-2266; www.taypikala .com; Calle Sandia s/n; s/d/tr S$200/250/320) offers even better views, with understated luxury and less-startling architecture.

There are a couple of very basic places to eat near the plaza. Both Taypikalas have upscale restaurants with touristy menus.

Luquina Chico

This tiny community, 53km east of Puno on the Chucuito peninsula, is stunningly scenic, rurally relaxing and offers the best standard of homestay accommodation of any community around the lake. It boasts a hearteningly united community, which is making economic strides thanks to tourism.

Sweeping views of Puno, Juliaca and all the islands of the lake can be enjoyed from the headland's heights or the fertile flats by the lake. In the wet season, the lagoon that forms here is a haven for migrating wetland birds.

Chullpitas (miniature burial towers) are scattered all around this part of the peninsula. They are said to house the bodies of *gentiles*, little people who lived here in ancient times, before the sun was born and sent them underground.

By the time you read this you may be able to hire kayaks in Luquina Chico.

To get here, catch a *combi* labeled 'Luquina Chico' from Puno, or take the ferry to or from Taquile and ask the driver to drop you off. **Edgar Adventures** (see p201) can also get you here on a mountain bike, a somewhat grueling but extremely scenic three-hour ride along the peninsula.

Juli

☎ 051 / pop 8000

Past Chucuito, the road curves southeast away from the lake and through the commercial center of **Ilave**, best known for its livestock market and a lively sense of community justice, the most famous manifestation of which was the lynching of the town mayor in 2004. Ilave is best avoided in times of civil strife. Sleepy, friendly Juli is a more tourist-friendly stop. It's called Peru's *pequeña Roma* (little Rome) on account of its four colonial churches from the 16th and 17th centuries, which are slowly being restored. Churches are most likely to be open on Sundays, though opening hours here should not be taken as gospel. It's worth hammering on the door if churches seem closed.

Dating from 1570, the adobe baroque church of **San Juan de Letrán** (admission S4; ☼ 10am-3pm Tue-Sun) contains richly framed *escuela cuzqueña* (Cuzco School) paintings that depict the lives of saints. The imposing 1557 church of **Nuestra Señora de la Asunción** (admission S4; ☼ 8am-4:30pm Tue-Sun) has an expansive courtyard approach that may awaken urges to oratory. Its interior is airy, and the pulpit is covered in gold leaf. The church of **Santa Cruz** has lost half its roof and remains closed for the foreseeable future. The 1560 stone church of **San Pedro**, on the main plaza, is in the best condition, with carved ceilings and a marble baptismal font. Mass is celebrated here every Sunday at 8am.

Sunday also the day of Juli's market, the region's largest. Wednesday is a secondary market day.

Micros drop you off near the market, 10 minutes' walk downhill from the center, but leave from Jirón Lima, two blocks up from the plaza. Internet cafes and basic guesthouses can be found around here.

Pomata

☎ 051 / pop 1800

Beyond Juli, the road continues southeast to Pomata, 105km from Puno. As you arrive, you'll see a Dominican **church** – totally out of proportion with the town it dominates, in terms of both size and splendor – dramatically located on top of a small hill. Founded in 1700, it is known for its windows made of translucent alabaster and its intricately carved baroque sandstone facade. Look for the puma carvings – the town's name means 'place of the puma' in Aymara.

Just out of Pomata, the road forks. The main road continues southeast through Zepita to the unsavory border town of Desaguadero (p214). The left fork hugs the shore of Lake Titicaca and leads to another, more pleasant border crossing at Yunguyo (p214). If you're going this way, consider stopping off at the **Mirador Natural de Asiru Patjata** lookout, a few kilometers from Yunguyo. Here, a 5000m-long rock formation resembles a *culebra* (snake), whose head is a viewpoint looking over to Isla del Sol. The area around here is known for its isolated villages and shamans.

BOLIVIAN SHORE

If you find yourself irresistibly drawn to the idea of staying longer in Bolivia, Lonely Planet's *Bolivia* guidebook has more comprehensive information.

Copacabana

☎ 02 / pop 15,900 / elev 3841m

Just across the border from Yunguyo, Copacabana is a restful Bolivian town on Lake Titicaca's south shore. Neither literally nor figuratively 'the hottest place north of Havana,' it's quiet, pretty, and a handy base for visiting the famous Islas del Sol and de la Luna. On the weekend it's full of visitors from La Paz; during the week, it goes to sleep.

In the 16th century the town was presented with an image of the Virgen de la Candelaria (now Bolivia's patron saint), sparking a slew of miracles. Copacabana's Moorish cathedral, where the Virgen is housed in a

---

BORDER CROSSING: BOLIVIA

There are three routes from Puno to Bolivia. The north shore route is very much off the beaten track and rarely used. There are two ways to go via the south shore: through either Yunguyo or Desaguadero. The only reason to go via Desaguadero is if you're pressed for time. The Yunguyo route is safer, prettier and far more popular, and passes through the chilled-out Bolivian lakeshore town of Copacabana, from where Isla del Sol – arguably the most significant site in Andean mythology – can be visited.

There's a Bolivian consulate in Puno (p199). Remember that Bolivian time is one hour ahead of Peruvian time.

US citizens have to pay US$100 cash in US dollars for a tourist visa to enter Bolivia. This can be done at the border.

Via Yunguyo

There are two ways to do this.

The quickest and easiest way is with a cross-border bus company such as Perú Tour or **Ormeño** (☎ 36-8176; www.grupo-ormeno.com.pe). These buses leave from Puno's *terminal terrestre* at 7am and 7:30am respectively. You should buy your tickets at the terminal at least one day in advance. The service stops at a *casa de cambio* (exchange bureau) at the border, shows you where to go for exit and entrance formalities, waits for you to get through, and then drives you to Copacabana (S20, two hours). Here another bus awaits to take you straight to La Paz (B$25, 3½ hours), if you so desire.

The other alternative is catching local transport – *micros* – from the Terminal Zonál. This is the only way to go if you want to stop at some or all of Peru's south-shore towns (see p212), since long-distance buses don't stop between Puno and Yunguyo. Leaving early (say 8am) gives you time to see most or all of the towns listed. When you're ready to move on, just jump on the next *micro* – they come along all the time, especially on Sunday, which is market day in Juli and Yunguyo. This is a great way to get off the beaten track, save a packet and rub shoulders with locals.

Yunguyo is the end of the line. Catch a *triciclo* (three-wheeled cycle) to Kasani for S2, or walk it – it's a pleasant 2km. Continue along Av Ejército – out of town, past a school with the coolest playground equipment in the world, around the bend to the left, and up the hill to Kasani. Change money here; the *casas de cambio* here offer better exchange rates than those on the Bolivian side.

Show your passport to the *policía* (police) in the aqua building, and then to the Control Migratorio (Immigration Office) on the left. Peruvian formalities thus completed, walk up the road and under the arch. To your left, under the 'Welcome to Bolivia' sign, you'll see the Bolivian immigration office – getting your passport stamped here is the final stage in the border-crossing process.

Now catch a *combi* to Copacabana for B$2 – or, if you're so inclined, walk a very pleasant, straightforward 8km around the lake. *Combis* leave more frequently on Sunday; on weekdays you may have to wait up to an hour.

The border is open from 7:30am until 6pm, Peruvian time.

Via Desaguadero

If you're going straight from Puno to La Paz, unsavory Desaguadero is faster, slightly cheaper and more direct than Yunguyo. It's also less scenic and less safe.

Combis leave Puno's *terminal zonal* for Desaguadero (S7, 2½ hours) throughout the day.

From the terminal in Desaguadero, turn left, walk a block, and you'll see the border on your

mystifyingly unsalubrious chapel, is still a pilgrimage site.

Be prepared for heavy rains, especially during December and January, and chilly nights year-round.

ORIENTATION & INFORMATION

Copacabana's main drag is Calle 6 de Agosto, which forms the left flank of the plaza as you face the lake. Tour agencies, bus companies, restaurants, internet cafes, *casas de cambio*

left. (At time of writing, a terminal was under construction on the outskirts of Desaguadero, so in the future you may need to take public transport to the border.) Visit the Peruvian Dirección General de Migraciones y Naturalización to get stamped out of Peru. Then head to the building that says 'Migraciones Desaguadero', to the left of the bridge, to complete Bolivian formalities.

Catch a *triciclo* to the Bolivian-side transport terminal, from where you can get to La Paz in 3½ hours either by *combi* (B$10) or *colectivo* (shared transportation; B$20).

Avoid spending the night in Desaguadero. If you get stuck, the nicest hotels in town (which really isn't saying much) are **Hostal Panamericano** (Panamericana 151; r per person without bathroom B$15, r per person with cable TV B$40) and the similar Hostal San Salvador across the road. They're in the first block on the Bolivian side.

The border is open from 7:30am to 7:30pm Peruvian time.

Note: the Peruvian police have a bad reputation here, sometimes demanding a nonexistent 'exit tax.' Also, there are confirmed reports of a scam in which police search travelers' luggage for 'fake dollars', which are then confiscated – so hide your cash before reaching the border. You are not required to visit the Peruvian police station before leaving the country, so if anyone asks you to go there with them, politely but firmly refuse. There are no ATMs in Desaguadero, so if you need to pay to enter Bolivia (such as US citizens who have to pay $100 for a tourist visa), plan ahead and withdraw money in Puno.

Via the North Shore

This little-traveled route into Bolivia will only really appeal to hardy, off-the-beaten-track travelers with little concern for time or comfort. Speaking at least a little Spanish is essential, as is lots of luck.

Before attempting this, talk to the Peruvian *oficina de migraciónes* (migration office) in Puno (p199). They can help you with information, and this may be the only opportunity you have to get yourself stamped out of Peru. Catch a regular *combi* from Juliaca to the small town of Huancané (p197) to the northeast. There are basic *hostales* (guesthouses) near the bus stop and around Huancané's Plaza de Armas. From here, catch a bus or truck to the friendly little village of Moho (S6, two hours). Nicknamed 'El Jardín del Altiplano' (The Garden of the Altiplano), this is a restful place to break your journey. There are a few basic accommodation options in the town center.

Buses and trucks leave Moho for Tilali most mornings. You may be able to take a direct night bus from Juliaca to Tilali via Huancané, Moho and Conima – ask around. Alternatively, you can walk the 30km or so. It takes about five hours to reach Conima, which has the colonial church of San Miguel Arcangel. From here, follow the lakeshore for another two hours (9km) to Tilali, near the Bolivian border. Local families here may rent rooms – ask around. It's also possible to stay near Conima on Isla Suasi.

However you get there, from Tilali it's about four hours' walk (about 20km) to the nearest Bolivian town of Puerto Acosta. There is a big border market on Wednesday and Saturday mornings, when it becomes easier to find bus and truck transport from Tilali to the market and onward to Puerto Acosta, but you might get stuck otherwise. There are very few private vehicles along this route, so don't count on hitching.

The police on the Bolivian border are unused to dealing with tourists, so it's important to have your documents in order and adopt a respectful, humble approach. Ask them where the Bolivian immigration post is located to get your passport stamped. Transportation out of Puerto Acosta does not leave regularly, so take the first vehicle you can, be it truck or bus, heading toward La Paz.

and banks all abound here. Plaza 2 de Febrero and the cathedral are a couple of blocks up the hill.

The **tourist office** (Calle 6 de Agosto at Plaza Sucre; 9:30am-5pm Tue-Sat) sells good maps and booklets on Copacabana's surroundings, and can hook you up with English-speaking guides.

Banks on Calle 6 de Agosto uphill from the plaza change money and may also give Visa cash advances, but don't count on it. Copacabana has no ATMs, and banks are closed all day Sunday and Monday, as well as Tuesday mornings. At the time of research, one bank, **Prodem**, a block up from Plaza Sucre, was opening on Monday but was under pressure not to. There's a **Moneygram** office in Plaza 2 de Febrero. If you're coming from Peru, change money in Yunguyo for better rates.

The **post office** (Calle 6 de Agosto s/n; 10am-8pm Mon-Fri, 9am-12pm Sat) opens on the same days as the banks.

Outfitter **Spitting Llama** (Plaza Sucre) sells camping gear and technical clothing made by a women's cooperative, and has a large book exchange.

DANGERS & ANNOYANCES

Avoid Copacabana in the first week of August, when thousands of Bolivians and Peruvians bring their cars to be blessed at the cathedral. During this week the town fills with devout drunk drivers and the thieves who prey on them.

SIGHTS & ACTIVITIES

The famous wooden statue of **La Virgen de la Candelaria** lives – behind an unmarked door down a creepy black-wax-caked tunnel – around the side of the sparkling Moorish **cathedral** (admission by donation). Opening hours vary wildly; your best bet is between 2:30pm and 5:30pm.

The hill north of town is **Cerro Calvario** (3966m). The summit can be reached in under an hour and is well worth the climb, especially at sunset. Many pilgrims make this trip, stopping at the Stations of the Cross as they ascend. Far less impressive are the area's minor **Inca sites** a few kilometers outside town.

The Community Tourism Network's tiny new **Centro de Información** (Jáuregui on Plaza Sucre; rtiticaca@gmail.com; admission free; 9am-1pm & 2-6pm) is a brilliant museum about local customs and cultures – see it before you hit the islands.

Head down to the waterfront to rent motorbikes, boats and kayaks. Better still, sit on the beach drinking beer and eating trout, and watch other people exert themselves on the lake.

Yampupata, 17km away on the Sicuani peninsula, is a good destination for a day's hike or bike ride. Various agencies around Plaza Sucre rent bikes for B$15 per hour or B$70 per day, and can show you a map. Take food and water.

FESTIVALS & EVENTS

The blessing of miniature objects, such as cars and houses, happens during **Alasitas** (Festival of Ekeko; January 24) is a prayer that the real thing will be obtained in the coming year. Miniatures are sold in stalls around Copa's main plaza and at the top of Cerro Calvario.

The fiesta of **La Virgen de la Candelaria** is celebrated on the first two days of February. Dancers from Peru and Bolivia perform traditional Aymara dances amid much music, drinking and feasting. On **Good Friday** during Semana Santa (Holy Week), the town fills with pilgrims, who join a solemn procession at dusk.

The biggest fiesta of the year, which is held for a week around Bolivia's **Independence Day** (August 6), features parades, brass bands, fireworks and not much sobriety. This is not a good time to be in Copacabana.

SLEEPING

You can't turn around in Copa without tripping over some kind of accommodation. The cheapest *alojamientos* (guesthouses), around B$15 per person, are uphill from Plaza Sucre, on Calle Pando. Good budget bargains include **Sucre Residencial** (862-2080; Murillo s/n), opposite the cathedral, and **Inca Roca** (862-2215; Potosí 115).

Hotel Ambassador (862-2216; Jáuregui on Plaza Sucre; r per person from B$35) Shabby, gaudy Hotel Ambassador has an altar in the entrance and a playground on the second story. Dark, drafty and echoey, it nevertheless oozes eccentric charm. Pure mad Bolivia.

Hotel Chasqui del Sol (862-2011; www.chasquidelsol .com; Costanera 55; r per person with breakfast B$80) Head-scratching design: 1970s suburban fake-ranch bungalow meets neoclassical dollhouse, right here on Copacabana's lakefront. The untoppable location, dizzying architecture, fabulously hot showers and friendly staff make this place a winner.

Hotel La Cúpula (☎ 862-2029; www.hotelcupula.com; Michel Pérez 1-3; s/d/tr B$80/112/196) This romantic retreat hides away on a shady, hammock-equipped hillside overlooking the lake. There's a restaurant, a TV/video room and shared kitchen and laundry facilities. Charming, comfortable and correspondingly popular – reservations are essential.

Hotel Rosario del Lago (☎ 862-2141; www.hotel rosario.com/lago; cnr Costanera & Rigoberto Paredes; s/d/tr with buffet breakfast B$360/440/600; 💻) Copacabana's finest. Though some of the lovely rooms are smallish, many have French doors looking out onto the lake and all have satellite TV and hot showers. Ask for an upper-floor room for the best views and the quietest night's sleep.

EATING & DRINKING

Tourist-focused restaurants line the bottom block of Calle 6 de Agosto, but varied and exciting food is not a feature of Copacabana. The local specialty is *trucha* (trout) farmed on Lake Titicaca. Competitive stalls along the beachfront serve it in every style imaginable (B$18). On a cold morning, head to the market for a cup of *api* – a hot, sweet, purple-corn drink.

Mankha Uta (Calle 6 de Agosto s/n; menús B$18-25) A cozy, inviting favorite. Offers unbelievably filling set meals, good vegetarian options, board games and a video room.

Sudna Wasi (☎ 862-2271; Jáuregui 127; mains from B$25; 🕑 8am-8pm) A convivial courtyard set back from the hectic market streets. The home-cooked menu includes hearty breakfasts, a dozen different salads and a few Bolivian specialties. The cutest *abuela* (grandmother) in the universe is sometimes sighted here.

Café Bistrot (cnr Zapana & Calle 6 de Agosto; mains from B$25; 🕑 7:30am-9pm) European cool kids hang out here while chain-smoking, drinking espresso and forking into anything from Thai seafood curries to creative vegetarian fare. Service is slow, but nobody seems to mind.

Nemo's (Calle 6 de Agosto s/n; 🕑 from 5pm daily) offers no-frills decor, cool music, a short list of food and a looong list of beer.

GETTING THERE & AWAY

Most buses arrive and depart from Plaza Sucre. Buy tickets at any of the travel agencies around the Sucre.

Buses leave for La Paz (B$25, 3½ hours) at 1:30pm daily. *Micros* leave for La Paz (B$20, 4½ hours) every hour from 7am to 6pm, but leave you in the slightly dodgy cemetery neighborhood there, rather than in the center.

The trip includes a memorable crossing over the 800m-wide Estrecho de Tiquina. You transfer to a passenger boat while your overloaded bus gets shipped across on a rickety barge – loads of fun!

To get to Peru, see p214.

Islas del Sol y de la Luna

The most famous island on Lake Titicaca is Isla del Sol (Island of the Sun), the legendary birthplace of Manco Cápac and his sister-wife Mama Ocllo, and indeed the sun itself. Both Isla del Sol and Isla de la Luna (Island of the Moon) have Inca ruins, reached by delightful walking trails through spectacular scenery dotted with traditional villages – there are no cars on the islands. Sunshine and altitude can take their toll, so bring extra water, food and sunblock. You can visit the main sights in a day, but staying overnight is far more rejuvenating.

SIGHTS & ACTIVITIES

Isla del Sol's **Inca remains** include the **Chincana** labyrinth complex in the north, and fortress-like **Pilkokayna** and the verdant, gorgeous **Inca Stairway** in the south. The Chincana is the site of the sacred Titi Khar'ka (Rock of the Puma), which features in the Inca creation legend and gave the lake its name. The largest villages are Yumani to the south and Ch'allapampa in the north.

Far less touristed, quiet Isla de la Luna boasts the partially rebuilt **ruins** of the convent that housed virgins of the sun – women chosen at a young age to serve as nuns to the sun god Inti.

SLEEPING & EATING

At the time of research there were five basic hostels in restful beachside Ch'allapampa and another three under construction. All charged B$15 to B$20 per person for accommodation. There are a handful of basic restaurants and shops.

Yumani, at the other end of the island, is far more developed, with dozens of accommodations ranging from B$15 to B$90 per person, plus relatively sophisticated dining options – pizza, and even vegetarian food, are on offer.

LAKE TITICACA

On Isla de la Luna, there are five basic *hospedajes* in Coati.

Camping is allowed on both islands. If you're traveling with a tent, this is the perfect place to make use of it.

GETTING THERE & AROUND
There are three ways to 'do' the islands.

Conventional Tours
Common to the point of clichéd, sold by myriad agencies in Copacabana, the 'tour' (B$25; B$45 with Isla de la Luna) most visitors do consists only of boat rides. Admission to the islands (Isla del Sol north B$10, Isla del Sol south B$5, Isla de la Luna B$10) is not included. Competition is fierce and agencies can be dishonest about what you'll get.

Here's the scoop: the one-day tour leaves Copacabana at 8:30am and takes you to Ch'allapampa, to the north of Isla del Sol. Here, a local guide (Spanish-speaking only) meets you at the port and insists on guiding you around the Chincana and the Rock of the Puma, about 40 minutes walk away. It is not obligatory to accept his services, but there is no signposting or interpretive information, so it's advisable to accept. At the end of the tour he will expect a tip of at least B$3.

You'll have time for lunch in Ch'allapampa, where several restaurants offer *sopa de quinua* and trout dishes for around B$20, before the boat takes you to the south side of Isla del Sol. Here, you'll have an hour or so to climb the stunningly beautiful (and stunningly steep) Inca stairway to the township of Yumani.

On the way back to Copacabana, most operators stop at some recently constructed floating islands (B$5) on the Sicuani peninsula – an enterprising attempt to cash in on the popularity of Puno's Uros Islands (p208).

Some operators cut time at Yumani to offer a side trip to Isla de la Luna in the afternoon. This is the only way to get to Isla de la Luna.

The traditional one-day tour is a distressingly rushed and commercial experience. Check out **Transturin** (www.transturin.com) and **Crillon Tours** (www.titicaca.com) in Puno for better, far more expensive tours that are less rushed and include food, luxury boats and English-speaking guides. Neither has an office in Copacabana.

Independent Travel
It's easy to take yourself to the islands, using the same boats the tours use, with the welcome addition of time and flexibility. Buy a one-way ferry ticket to Isla del Sol (Yumani B$10, Ch'allapampa B$15), stay a night or more here or on Isla de la Luna, and return in your own time.

The 11km trail from one end of the island to the other is unmissable once you're on it. A good way to find where it starts is to take the 8:00am boat to Ch'allapampa and join the tour of the **Chincana**, during which the guide will point it out. You can then walk to Yumani in around three hours, enjoying spectacular views on all sides. Take plenty of water and sunblock.

When they run, boats to Isla de la Luna will depart from the north in the early afternoon – ask at the port. See the table below for ferry departure times.

Departure point	Destination	Time
Copacabana	Yumani	8:30am, 1:30pm
Ch'allapampa	Yumani	1:30pm
Copacabana	Ch'allapampa	1:30pm
Yumani	Copacabana	10:30am; 3:30pm

Community Tourism
The **Red de Turismo Comunitario de Lago Titicaca** (Community Tourism Network of Lake Titicaca) is a recent and welcome addition to the scene.

It offers half-day to three-day trips to three communities: Ch'allapampa on Isla del Sol, Coati on Isla de la Luna and Sahuiña on the mainland towards the border.

Programs can include any combination of local food, storytelling, homestay, birdwatching, dances and archaeology. Knowing that your money is going directly to community members is an added bonus.

Community representatives rotate in week-long shifts staffing the network's excellent Centro de Información in Copacabana (p216). This museum is a must-see, even if you don't intend to take a tour, for its fresh and engaging insight into local life.

Cuzco & the Sacred Valley

Cuzco effortlessly enchants, bombarding the senses with a swirl of art, religion, music, architecture, food, and fiestas – every possible manifestation of the syncretic Inca-Spanish culture that makes the Andes so fascinating.

Ladies with llamas walk cobbled streets. Coca-chewing local honchos parade to church in ceremonial regalia for Mass in Quechua. Cuzco's proud pagan past collides with solemn Catholic rituals in parades that stop traffic at the drop of a hat throughout the year, and almost daily for the whole month of June.

The past is ever present. Massive ruins draw tourists in daily droves. Intrepid explorers carve their way through the jungle to genuine lost cities. Colonial churches filled with incomprehensible riches slowly crumble in the drowsy plazas of towns too small to warrant a bus stop. Climb any hill in the Sacred Valley and you'll stumble on piles of rocks – forgotten by all but the locals– that invite you to dream up your own stories.

Cuzco's human history is Peru's biggest tourism drawcard, but there's more on offer. Locals and visitors alike are waking up to the adventure-sport possibilities of a region perched on the eastern edge of the Andes, where you can drop from breathtaking snowy altitudes to the suffocating heat of the Amazon jungle at dizzying speed. While Cuzco's trekking opportunities are already well known, its biking and river routes are now gaining the recognition they deserve. There are extreme sportspeople who have been to Cuzco more than once and never visited Machu Picchu: they're too busy biking, hiking, running rivers and climbing. It's true.

HIGHLIGHTS

- Bike, hike, raft, zip-line and soak your way to **Machu Picchu** via **Santa Teresa** (p285)
- Buy avant-garde clothes and jewelry from hole-in-the-wall shops in Cuzco's artsy **San Blas district** (p252)
- Trek to remote, jungle-clad Inca ruins such as **Choquequirau** (p234) and **Vilcabamba** (p234)
- Soak up the pastoral serenity of the **Sacred Valley** (p258)
- Join locals for an artery-clogging **Sunday lunch** (p248)

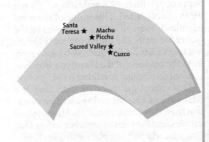

Santa Teresa ★   Machu
★ Picchu
Sacred Valley ★
★Cuzco

- BIGGEST CITY: CUZCO, POPULATION 350,000
- AVERAGE TEMPERATURE: JANUARY 7°C TO 20°C, JULY -1°C TO 21°C

CUZCO

☎ 084 / pop 350,000 / elev 3326m

Legend tells that in the 12th century, the sun god Inti looked down on the earth and decided that the people needed organizing, so he created the first Inca, Manco Cápac, and his sister-wife, Mama Ocllo. They came to life on Isla del Sol (Sun Island), way over in Lake Titicaca, with a long walk ahead of them. Inti gave Manco Cápac a golden rod and told him to settle in the spot where he could plunge it into the ground until it disappeared: this would be the navel of the earth (*qosq'o* in the Quechua language). And so Cuzco got its name. Locals can point out the place where the rod allegedly went in – it's on a hill overlooking the bus terminal.

When Manco discovered the place, he quickly subdued the natives and founded the city that was to become the center of one of the Americas' greatest empires. And people have been here ever since: Cuzco is the oldest continuously inhabited city in South America, and the continent's undisputed archaeological capital.

Despite its wealth of ruins, museums and churches, Cuzco is aptly described by the belly-button analogy: a bit dirty and daunting sometimes, but engagingly, un-self-consciously bursting with life. It's a place that inspires strong feelings. There's a lot of mystical talk in Cuzco, about energy lines and cosmic confluences, and even the most hardened skeptics notice a certain something about the place.

Most South American cities have a merry, hectic street energy; in Cuzco it's overwhelming. Walk through the Plaza de Armas and you'll see people hawking massages, finger puppets, paintings, CDs and tattoos – it's not for the fainthearted. This is one of the most relentlessly tourism-dominated towns on the face of the earth, and unless you make the effort to get a few blocks (that's all it takes) away from the madness of the Plaza, you may find yourself feeling like a walking ATM.

That's about the only downside. Despite a tidal wave of tourism and massive immigration from the provinces over the last couple of decades, and the years of terrorism before that, Cuzco is a relatively safe place with decent infrastructure and a lovable population of dauntless entrepreneurs ranging from singing shoeshine boys to flamboyant nightclub magnates.

Hushed museums and churches. Animal organs on skewers and high-art haute cuisine. Sex, drugs and rock and roll spill out from colonial palaces decked out as nightclubs into cobbled streets built for llama traffic. History forces itself on your attention at every corner. Cuzco is a diverse, gritty, greedy, irresistibly vital madhouse. However long you plan to spend here, it won't be enough.

HISTORY

The Inca empire's main expansion occurred in the hundred years prior to the arrival of the conquistadors in 1532. When the Spanish reached Cuzco, they began keeping chronicles, including Inca history as related by the Incas themselves. The most famous of these accounts was *The Royal Commentaries of the Incas,* written by Garcilaso de la Vega, the son of an Inca princess and a Spanish military captain.

The ninth *inca* (king), Pachacutec, gave the empire its first bloody taste of conquest. Until his time, the Incas had dominated only a modest area close to Cuzco, though they frequently skirmished with other highland tribes. One such tribe was the Chanka, whose growing thirst for expansion led them to Cuzco's doorstep in 1438.

Pachacutec's father, Viracocha Inca, fled in the belief that his small empire was lost. But Pachacutec refused to give up the fight. With the help of some of the older generals, he rallied the Inca army and in a desperate final battle – in which, legend claims, the very boulders transformed themselves into warriors to fight alongside the Incas – he famously managed to vanquish the Chanka. The victorious younger Pachacutec proclaimed himself *inca* and, buoyed by his victory, embarked upon the first wave of expansion that would create the Inca empire. During the next 25 years, he bagged much of the central Andes, including the region between the two great lakes of Titicaca and Junín.

Pachacutec also proved himself a sophisticated urban developer, devising Cuzco's famous puma shape and diverting rivers to cross the city. He also built fine buildings, including the famous Qorikancha temple and a palace on a corner of what is now the Plaza de Armas.

Pachacutec's successor, Túpac Yupanqui, was every bit his father's son. During the 1460s he helped his father subdue a great

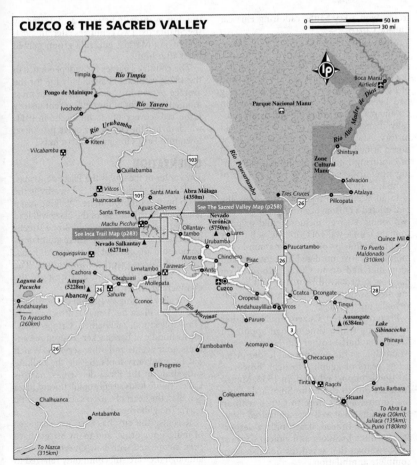

CUZCO & THE SACRED VALLEY

area to the north, including what is today the northern Peruvian and southern Ecuadorian Andes, as well as the northern Peruvian coast. As the 10th *inca*, he expanded the empire dramatically in his lifetime, extending it from Quito, in Ecuador, to the area south of Santiago in Chile.

Huayna Cápac, the 11th *inca*, was the last to rule over a united kingdom, an empire so big that it seemed to have little left to conquer. Nevertheless, Huayna Cápac doggedly expanded the northernmost limits of his empire to the present-day Ecuador–Colombia border, and fought a long series of campaigns during which he sired a son, Atahualpa, whose mother may have been a *quiteña* (inhabitant of Quito, Ecuador).

Then something totally unexpected happened: Europeans discovered the New World, bringing with them various Old World diseases. Epidemics such as smallpox swept down from Central America and the Caribbean. Shortly before dying in 1525 – probably from one of these epidemics – Huayna Cápac divided his empire, giving the northern part to Atahualpa and the southern Cuzco area to another son, Huascar.

Both sons were suited to ruling an empire – so well suited, in fact, that neither wished to share power, and an Inca civil war ensued. As a pure-blooded native *cuzqueño* (inhabitant of Cuzco), Huascar had the people's support, but Atahualpa had the backing of the northern army and early in 1532 his battle-hardened troops won a key battle, capturing Huascar outside Cuzco.

Meanwhile, Francisco Pizarro landed in northern Peru and marched southward. Atahualpa himself had been too busy fighting the civil war to worry about a small band of foreigners, but by 1532 a fateful meeting had been arranged with the Spaniard in Cajamarca. It was a meeting that would radically change the course of South American history: Atahualpa was ambushed by a few dozen armed conquistadors, who succeeded in capturing him, killing thousands of indigenous tribespeople and routing tens of thousands more.

In an attempt to regain his freedom, the *inca* offered a ransom of a roomful of gold and two rooms of silver, including gold stripped from the temple walls of Qorikancha. But after holding Atahualpa prisoner for a number of months, Pizarro murdered him anyway, and soon marched on to Cuzco. Mounted on horseback, protected by armor and swinging steel swords, the Spanish cavalry was virtually unstoppable.

Pizarro entered Cuzco on November 8, 1533, by which time he had appointed Manco, a half-brother of Huascar and Atahualpa, as the new puppet leader. After a few years of keeping to heel, however, the docile puppet rebelled. In 1536, Manco Inca set out to drive the Spaniards from his empire, laying siege to Cuzco with an army estimated at well over a hundred thousand people. Indeed, it was only a desperate last-ditch breakout and violent battle at Sacsaywamán that saved the Spanish from complete annihilation.

Manco Inca was forced to retreat to Ollantaytambo and then into the jungle at Vilcabamba. After Cuzco was safely recaptured, looted and settled, the seafaring Spaniards turned their attentions to the newly founded colonial capital, Lima. Cuzco's importance quickly waned, and it became just another colonial backwater. All the gold and silver was gone, and many Inca buildings were pulled down to accommodate churches and colonial houses.

Few events of historical significance have rocked Cuzco like the Spanish conquest – except for earthquakes in 1650 and 1950, and an infamous Inca uprising led by Túpac Amaru II in 1780. His was the only indigenous revolt that ever came close to succeeding, but eventually he too was defeated by the Spaniards. Two centuries later, in 1984, a Peruvian Marxist guerrilla group named itself after him.

The country's battles for independence in the 1820s wouldn't change daily life for the average person in Cuzco. Perhaps the most momentous event in the city's recent history is the 'rediscovery' of Machu Picchu in 1911, which turned the city from a quiet, provincial town into Peru's foremost tourist hub.

ORIENTATION

The center of the city is the Plaza de Armas, while traffic-choked Av El Sol nearby is the main business thoroughfare. Walking just a few blocks north or east of the plaza will lead you onto steep, twisting cobblestone streets, little changed for centuries, where multifamily homes built around cobbled courtyards house much of Cuzco's working population. The flatter areas to the south and west are the commercial center.

The alley heading away from the northwest side of the Plaza de Armas is Procuradores (Tax Collectors), nicknamed 'Gringo Alley' for its huddle of backpacker-focused restaurants, tour agents and other services. Watch out for predatory touts. Beside the hulking cathedral, on the Plaza de Armas, narrow Calle Triunfo leads steeply uphill toward Plaza San Blas, the heart of Cuzco's eclectic, artistic *barrio* (neighborhood).

Recently the city has seen a resurgence of indigenous pride, and many streets have been signposted with new Quechua names, although they are still commonly referred to by their Spanish names. The most prominent example is Calle Triunfo, which is signposted as Sunturwasi.

Most travelers take a taxi into the city from the airport, bus terminals, or train station – or avail themselves of the free pickup offered by many guesthouses. For public transportation options around the city, see p256.

INFORMATION
Bookstores

Many guesthouses, cafes and pubs have book exchanges. The best source of historical and archaeological information about the city and the surrounding area is the pocket-sized *Exploring Cuzco* by Peter Frost.

Recommended bookstores:

Bookstore Kiosk (Mantas 113; ☻ 9am-2pm & 4-9pm
Mon-Sat) Novels and magazines in English and German.
Located just inside the door of Centro Comercial.
Jerusalén (☎ 23-5428; Heladeros 143; ☻ 10am-2pm
& 4pm-8pm Mon-Sat) Cuzco's most extensive public book
exchange (two used books, or one plus S8, will get you one
book) plus used guidebooks, new titles and music CDs for sale.
SBS Bookshop (☎ 24-8106; Av El Sol 781A; ☻ 9am-
9pm Mon-Sat) Small, but specializes in foreign-language
books, especially in English.
South American Explorers Club (SAE; ☎ 24-5484;
www.saexplorers.org; Atocsaycuchi 670; ☻ 9:30am-5pm
Mon-Fri, to 1pm Sat) Cuzco's biggest book exchange; also
sells foreign-language guidebooks and maps.

Cultural Centers

South American Explorers Club (☎ 24-5484; www
.saexplorers.org; Atocsaycuchi 670; ☻ 9:30am-5pm Mon-
Fri, to 1pm Sat) SAE's Cuzco clubhouse has good-quality
maps, books and brochures for sale, a huge stock of travel
information and recommendations, wi-fi access, a book
exchange and rooms for rent. Weekly events and limited
volunteer information are available to nonmembers. (See
p86 for more on the SAE's many services.)

Embassies & Consulates

Most foreign embassies and consulates are
located in Lima (p517). The following are
honorary consul representatives in Cuzco:
Belgium (☎ 25-1278)
France (☎ 23-3610)
Germany (☎ 23-5459)
Italy (☎ 22-4398)
UK (☎ 23-9974)
USA (☎ 984-62-369)

Emergency

Policía de Turismo (PolTur, Tourist Police; ☎ 23-5123;
Plaza Túpac Amaru s/n; ☻ 24hr) If you have something
stolen, you'll need to see these guys to get an official
police report for insurance claims.

Immigration

Oficina de migraciónes (immigration office; ☎ 22-
2741; www.digemin.com.pe; Av El Sol 612;
☻ 8am-4:30pm Mon-Fri) Will renew your tourist visa for
a cost of US$1 per day. Best to do this before your time runs
out, but still possible a few days after. You also need to
come here if you lose your Tarjeta Andina (tourist card) – be
prepared for a lot of red tape.

Internet Access

Internet cafes are found on almost every
street corner. Many hotels and cafes offer
free wireless.

Internet Resources

Andean Travel Web (www.andeantravelweb.com) More
than 1000 pages of information and recommendations.
Diario del Cusco (www.diariodelcusco.com, in Spanish)
Online edition of the local newspaper.
Municipalidad del Cusco (www.municusco.gob.pe, in
Spanish) The city's official website.

Laundry

Lavanderías (laundries) will wash, dry and
fold your clothes from around S3 per kg.
They're everywhere, but cluster just off the
Plaza de Armas on Suecia, Procuradores and
Plateros, and on Carmen Bajo in San Blas. The
further you get from the Plaza de Armas, the
cheaper they get.

Left Luggage

If you're going trekking for a few days or even
just on an overnight excursion, any hostel will
store your bags for free. Always get a receipt,
and lock your bags. The bags should have
identifying tags showing your name and the
drop-off and expected pickup dates. For soft-
sided bags, we recommend placing them inside a larger plastic bag and sealing them shut
with tape. Then sign your name across the
seal, so that you can tell if your bag has been
opened while you were away. It's best to keep
all valuables (eg passport, credit cards, money)
on your person. Trekkers are required to carry
their passport with them on the Inca Trail.

Medical Services

Pharmacies abound along Av El Sol. Cuzco's
medical facilities are limited; head to Lima for
serious procedures.
Clinica Pardo (☎ 24-0997; Av de la Cultura 710;
☻ 24hr) Well equipped and expensive – perfect if you're
covered by travel insurance.
Clínica Paredes (☎ 22-5265; Lechugal 405; ☻ 24hr)
Consultations S60.
Hospital Regional (☎ 23-9792, emergencies 22-3691;
Av de la Cultura s/n; ☻ 24hr) Public and free, but wait
times can be long and good care is not guaranteed.

Money

ATMs abound in and around the Plaza de
Armas, and are also available at the airport,
Huanchaq train station and the bus terminal.
All accept Visa, most accept MasterCard, and
many will even allow you to withdraw from
a foreign debit account. There are several big
bank branches on Av El Sol; go inside for
cash advances above daily ATM limits. *Casas*

CUZCO

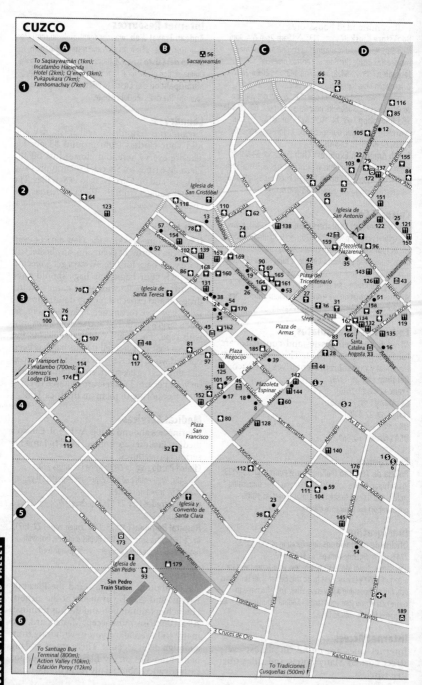

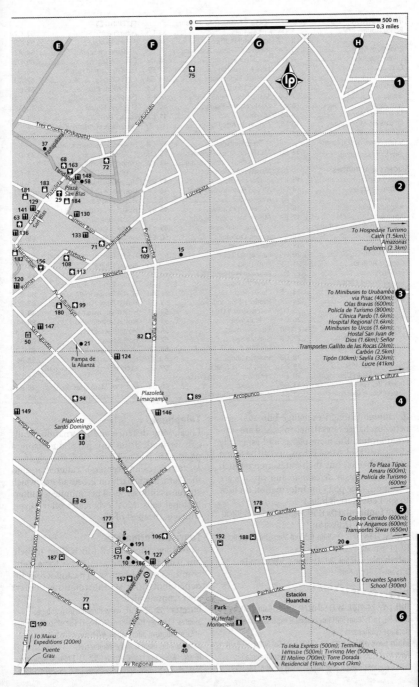

de cambio (foreign-exchange bureaus) give better exchange rates than banks, and are scattered around the main plazas and especially along Av El Sol. Moneychangers can be found outside banks, but their rates aren't much better than *casas de cambio* and rip-offs are common. (See p523 for information on how to spot counterfeit bills.)

Banco Continental (Av El Sol 368; ☉ 9:15am-6:30pm Mon-Fri, 9:30am-12:30pm Sat)

BCP (Av El Sol 189; ☉ 9am-6:30pm Mon-Thu, to 7:30pm Fri, to 1pm Sat)

Interbank (Av El Sol 380; ☉ 9am-6:30pm Mon-Fri, 9:15am-12:30pm Sat)

Post

DHL (☎ 24-4167; Av El Sol 627A; ☉ 8:30am-7:30pm Mon-Fri, to 1:30pm Sat) International express mail and package courier services.

Main post office (☎ 22-4212; Av El Sol 800; ☉ 8am-8pm Mon-Sat) General delivery (poste restante) mail is held here at the main post office; bring proof of identity.

Telephone

Local, long-distance and international calls can be made from any payphone using a phonecard (see p525), or more cheaply from *locutorios* (calling centers) scattered around the Plaza, particularly on Procuradores, which charge as little as S0.50 per minute for international calls. Most cybercafes offer Skype, which is cheapest of all.

Tourist Information

Travel agencies are all too willing to help out with travel arrangements – for a hefty commission, of course. The following independent tourist information centers are recommended:

Dircetur (☎ 22-3701; www.dirceturcusco.gob.pe; Mantas 117; ☉ 10am-8pm Mon-Sat) The official provider of Cuzco tourism information. Well meaning but motley and sporadic; iPerú is more informative.

iPerú (www.peru.info) airport (☎ 23-7364; Aeropuerto, Main Hall; ☉ 6am-4pm); city center (☎ 25-2974; Office

102, Galerías Turísticas, Av El Sol 103; ☽ 8:30am-7:30pm) Apart from providing tourist information about Peru in general, iPerú runs Indecopi (☎ 25-2974), the tourist protection/complaints agency, from its efficient, helpful and knowledgeable city-center office.

South American Explorers Club (☎ 24-5484; www .saexplorers.org; Atocsaycuchi 670; ☽ 9:30am-5pm Mon-Fri, to 1pm Sat) Gives unbiased advice and sells information booklets, including on alternatives to the Inca Trail and Amazon jungle adventures.

DANGERS & ANNOYANCES

Most travelers will experience few problems in Cuzco. Ninety percent of total crime reports received by the tourist police are from two types of easily preventable crime: bags stolen from the backs of chairs in public places, or from overhead shelves in overnight buses. If you keep your bag in your lap, and watch out for pickpockets in crowded streets, transport terminals and markets, you are highly unlikely to be a victim of crime in Cuzco.

Robberies in cabs have been reported. Use only official taxis, especially at night. (Look for the company's lit telephone number on top of the car.) Lock your doors from the inside, and never allow the driver to admit a second passenger.

Avoid walking by yourself late at night or very early in the morning. Revelers returning late from bars or setting off for the Inca Trail before sunrise are particularly vulnerable to 'choke and grab' attacks. For tips on avoiding theft and other common scams, see p514.

Don't buy drugs. Dealers and police often work together, and Procuradores is one of several areas in which you can make a drug deal and get busted all within a couple of minutes. Drink spiking has been reported. Women especially should try not to let go of their glass or accept drinks from strangers.

Take care not to overexert yourself during your first few days if you've flown in from lower elevations, such as Lima. You

CUZCO & THE SACRED VALLEY IN...

Two Days

Spend one day exploring the city of Cuzco, starting with an early *jugo* (fruit juice) in **Mercado San Pedro**, then getting cultural with some of the city's many museums. **Museo Quijote** (p233) and the **Museo Histórico Regional** (p231) are highly recommended for fine art; **El Museo de Arte Popular** (p232) and **Museo Irq'i Yachay** (p230) for folksy art; and the **Museo Inka** (p232) for preconquest Peruvian artifacts. After lunch, gawk at the most imposing relics left by the Incas and the Spanish conquistadors, respectively, at **Qorikancha** (p232) and **La Catedral** (opposite). At 6:45pm check out the nightly music and dance show at the **Centro Qosqo de Arte Nativo** (opposite). The next day, get up early and board a train to **Machu Picchu** (p278), Peru's most renowned ancient site.

Four Days

Follow the Cuzco day of the two-day itinerary. On the second day join a 'backdoor' or 'Inca jungle' alternative tour (p285) to Machu Picchu. Spend the day descending by mountain bike to the cloud forest frontier town of **Santa Teresa** (p290), then soaking in its 24-hour hot springs. On Day 3, get up early and hike to **Machu Picchu** (p278). Spend the night in **Aguas Calientes** (p267), then catch the train to ancient, cobbled **Ollantaytambo** (p264). There's still time to take local buses to the spectacular salt pans of **Salinas** (p263) on the way back to Cuzco.

One Week

Follow the Cuzco day of the two-day itinerary. On the second day, follow the **walking tour** (p237) up through arty San Blas to the impressive fortress of **Sacsaywamán** (p256). Flag down local buses to the nearby ruins of **Tambomachay** (p257), **Q'enqo** (p257) and **Pukapukara** (p257). On the third day, start trekking the spectacular, rugged **Salkantay trail** (p288) to **Machu Picchu** (p278).

may find yourself quickly becoming winded while traipsing up and down Cuzco's narrow streets. Some hotels offer in-room oxygen supplements, which may ease symptoms of altitude. For more advice on altitude sickness, see p548.

SIGHTS

Tourists can't easily buy individual entrance tickets to many of Cuzco's sights. Instead, you are forced to buy a *boleto turístico* (tourist ticket; see opposite). Only a few museums, churches and colonial buildings in and around the city can be visited for free or for a modest admission charge. Almost all have local guides who persistently offer their services. Some speak a varying amount of English or other foreign languages. For more extensive tours at major sites, such as Qorikancha or the cathedral, you should always agree to a fair price in advance. Otherwise, a respectable minimum tip for a short tour is $5 per person in a small group, and a little more for individuals.

Opening hours are erratic and can change for any reason – from Catholic feast days to the caretaker slipping off for

a beer with his mates. A good time to visit Cuzco's well-preserved colonial churches is in the early morning (from 6am to 8am), when they are open for Mass. Officially, they are closed to tourists at these times, but if you go in quietly and respectfully as a member of the congregation, you can see the church as it should be seen: a place of worship, not just a tourist attraction. Flash photography is not allowed inside churches or museums.

Central Cuzco
PLAZA DE ARMAS

In Inca times, the plaza, called Huacaypata or Aucaypata, was the heart of the Inca capital. Today it's the nerve center of the modern city. Two flags usually fly here – the red and white Peruvian flag and the rainbow-colored flag of Tahuantinsuyo, representing the four quarters of the Inca empire. (Foreigners often mistake the latter for an international gay-pride banner, to which it bears a remarkable resemblance. Bringing this up is an excellent way to make normally easygoing *cuzqueños* lose their cool.)

Colonial arcades surround the plaza, which in ancient times was twice as large as it is today, also encompassing the area now called the Plaza Regocijo. On the plaza's northeastern side is the imposing cathedral, fronted by a large flight of stairs and flanked by the churches of Jesús María and El Triunfo. On the southeastern side is the strikingly ornate church of La Compañía de Jesús. The quiet pedestrian alleyway of Loreto, which has Inca walls, is a historic means of access to the plaza.

It's worth visiting the plaza at least twice – by day and by night – as it takes on a strikingly different look after dark, all lit up and even prettier.

LA CATEDRAL

Started in 1559 and taking almost a hundred years to build, the **cathedral** (Plaza de Armas; admission S25 or with boleto religioso; ☾ 10am-5:45pm) squats on the site of Viracocha Inca's palace and was built using blocks pilfered from the nearby Inca site of Sacsaywamán. The cathedral is joined with **Iglesia del Triunfo** (1536) to its right and **Iglesia de Jesús María** (1733) to the left. El Triunfo, Cuzco's oldest church, houses a vault containing the remains of the famous Inca

chronicler Garcilaso de la Vega, who was born in Cuzco in 1539 and died in Córdoba, Spain, in 1616. His remains were returned in 1978 by King Juan Carlos of Spain. (For more on Garcilaso de la Vega, see p37.)

The cathedral is one of the city's greatest repositories of colonial art, especially for works from the *escuela cuzqueña* (Cuzco school), noted for its decorative combination of 17th-century European devotional painting styles with the color palette and iconography of indigenous Andean artists. A classic example is the frequent portrayal of the Virgin Mary wearing a mountain-shaped skirt with a river running around its hem, identifying her with Pachamama (Mother Earth). One of the most famous paintings of the *escuela cuzqueña* is *The Last Supper* by Quechua artist Marcos Zapata, which is found in the northeast corner of the cathedral. It depicts one of the most solemn occasions in the Christian faith, but graces it with a small feast of Andean ceremonial food; look for the plump and juicy-looking roast *cuy* (guinea pig) stealing the show with its feet held plaintively in the air.

Also look for the **oldest surviving painting** in Cuzco, showing the entire city during the great earthquake of 1650. The inhabitants

---

BOLETO TURÍSTICO & BOLETO RELIGIOSO

Cuzco's official **boleto turístico** (tourist ticket; adult/student under 26 with ISIC card S130/70) is exasperating. Apart from the ruins, the nightly show and a couple of the museums, the 17 included sights are eminently miss-able, but you can't visit any of them without it. Since Cuzco's signature attraction, Sacsaywamán, is included, you really can't avoid forking out.

Valid for 10 days, the *boleto turístico* covers entry to the ruins of Sacsaywamán, Q'enqo, Puka-pukara and Tambomachay, right outside Cuzco; Pisac, Ollantaytambo, Chinchero and Moray, in the Sacred Valley; and Tipón and Piquillacta to the south.

It also includes the fascinating Museo de Arte Popular, the eclectic Museo Histórico Regional, and an evening performance of Andean dances and live music at the Centro Qosqo de Arte Nativo. The remaining inclusions are the musty, miss-able archaeological museum at Qorikancha (but not Qorikancha itself), the Museo Municipal de Arte Contemporáneo and the Pachacutec monument near the bus terminal.

There are three different partial *boletos* costing S70 (student S35). One covers the ruins immediately outside Cuzco, one the ruins in the Sacred Valley, and the third the museums in Cuzco. Partial tickets are valid for 10 days.

You can buy *boletos turísticos* from **iPerú** (☎ 25-2974; Office 102, Galerías Turísticas, Av El Sol 103; ☾ 8:30am-7:30pm) or at the sites themselves, except for the Centro Qosqo de Arte Nativo. Students will need to show their ID card along with their *boleto* when entering any site.

There's also a **boleto religioso** (religious tourist ticket; adult/student S50/25), valid for the jaw-dropping Cathedral and Iglesia de la Compañía de Jesús (these are must-sees in the Plaza de Armas), as well as the Iglesia de San Blas, the Museo de Arte Religioso and (strangely) Cuzco's most significant display of contemporary art at Museo Quijote. It's available at any of the sites and is valid for 10 days.

can be seen parading around the plaza with a crucifix, praying for the earthquake to stop, which miraculously it did. This precious crucifix, called **El Señor de los Temblores** (The Lord of the Earthquakes), can still be seen in the alcove to the right of the door leading into El Triunfo. Every year on Holy Monday, the Señor is taken out on parade and devotees throw ñucchu flowers at him – these resemble droplets of blood and represent the wounds of his crucifixion. The flowers leave a sticky residue, to which the smoke of the countless votive candles lit beneath him sticks: this is why he's now black. Legend has it that under his skirt, he's still as lily white as the day he was made.

The **sacristy** of the cathedral is covered with paintings of Cuzco's bishops, starting with Vicente de Valverde, the friar who accompanied Pizarro during the conquest. The crucifixion at the back of the sacristy is attributed to the Flemish painter Anthony van Dyck, though some guides claim it to be the work of the 17th-century Spaniard Alonso Cano. The original wooden **altar** is at the very back of the cathedral, behind the present silver altar, and opposite both is the magnificently carved **choir**, dating from the 17th century. There are also many glitzy silver and gold **side chapels** with elaborate platforms and altars that contrast with the austerity of the cathedral's stonework.

The huge main doors of the cathedral are open to genuine worshippers between 6am and 10am. Religious festivals are a superb time to see the cathedral. During the feast of Corpus Christi (p240), for example, it is filled with pedestals supporting larger-than-life statues of saints, surrounded by thousands of candles and bands of musicians honoring them with mournful Andean tunes.

IGLESIA DE LA COMPAÑÍA DE JESÚS

This **church** (Plaza de Armas; admission S10 or with boleto religioso; 9-11:30am & 1-5:30pm) is built upon the palace of Huayna Cápac, the last Inca to rule an undivided, unconquered empire.

The church was built by the Jesuits in 1571, and was reconstructed after the 1650 earthquake. The Jesuits planned to make it the most magnificent of Cuzco's churches. The archbishop of Cuzco, however, complained that its splendor should not rival that of the cathedral, and the squabble grew to a point where Pope Paul III was called upon to arbitrate. His deci-

sion was in favor of the cathedral, but by the time word had reached Cuzco, La Compañía de Jesús was just about finished, complete with an incredible baroque facade and Peru's biggest altar, all crowned by a soaring dome.

Two large canvases near the main door show early marriages in Cuzco, and are worth examining for their wealth of period detail. Local student guides are available to show you around the church, as well as the grand view from the choir on the 2nd floor, reached via rickety steps. Tips are gratefully accepted.

MUSEO DE HISTORIA NATURAL

The university-run **natural history museum** (Plaza de Armas; admission S2; 9am-5pm Mon-Fri) houses a somewhat motley collection of stuffed local animals and birds and over 150 snakes from the Amazon. The entrance is hidden off the Plaza de Armas, to the right of Iglesia de la Compañía de Jesús.

IGLESIA Y MONASTERIO DE SANTA CATALINA

This **convent** (Arequipa s/n; admission S8; 8.30am-5.30pm Mon-Sat) houses many colonial paintings of the *escuela cuzqueña*, as well as an impressive collection of vestments and other embroidery (definitely a must-see for embroidery fans). It also contains a baroque side chapel with dramatic friezes, and many life-sized (and sometimes startling) models of nuns praying, sewing and going about their lives. The convent also houses 13 real, live contemplative nuns.

MUSEO IRQ'I YACHAY

More an art and craft exhibition than a museum, **Museo Irq'i Yachay** (24-1416; www.aylluyu paychay.org; Teatro 344; admission free; 10am-1pm & 2-5pm Mon-Fri) is the fascinating by-product of an NGO that seeks to give opportunities for cognitive development to kids in remote communities. Of course, the most isolated and neglected communities are the ones in which traditional culture is best preserved, and the result is an engrossing and unique insight into Andean culture. The kids paint what they know – animals, mountains, rivers, people – and incorporate the symbols of the weavings that surround them from birth: north is hope and future, red is love and revenge. Along with the art itself, there's an impressive display of textiles. Accompanying interpretive information in Spanish and English explains this

CUZCO & THE SACRED VALLEY

symbology in detail and makes this museum a must for textile fans.

TEMPLO Y CONVENTO DE LA MERCED

Cuzco's third most important colonial church, **La Merced** (☎ 23-1821; Mantas 121; admission S6; ☯ 8am-noon & 2-5pm Mon-Sat) was destroyed in the 1650 earthquake, but was quickly rebuilt. To the left of the church, at the back of a small courtyard, is the entrance to the monastery and museum. Paintings based on the life of San Pedro Nolasco, who founded the order of La Merced in Barcelona in 1218, hang on the walls of the beautiful colonial cloister. The church on the far side of the **cloister** (☯ 8-11am) contains the tombs of two of the most famous conquistadors: Diego de Almagro and Gonzalo Pizarro (brother of Francisco). Also on the far side of the cloister is a small religious museum that houses vestments rumored to have belonged to conquistador and friar Vicente de Valverde. The museum's most famous possession is a priceless solid-gold monstrance, 1.2m high and covered with rubies, emeralds and no fewer than 1500 diamonds and 600 pearls. Ask to see it if the display room is locked.

MUSEO HISTÓRICO REGIONAL

This eclectic **museum** (Calle Garcilaso at Heladeros; entry with boleto turístico; ☯ 8am-5pm Tue-Sun) is housed in the colonial Casa Garcilaso de la Vega, the house of the Inca-Spanish chronicler who now lies buried in the cathedral. The chronologically arranged collection begins with arrowheads from the Preceramic Period and continues with ceramics and jewelry of the Wari, Pukara and Inca cultures. There is also a Nazca mummy, a few Inca weavings, some small gold ornaments and a strangely sinister scale model of the Plaza de Armas. A big, helpful chart in the courtyard outlines the timeline and characters of the *escuela cuzqueña*.

MUSEO MUNICIPAL DE ARTE CONTEMPORÁNEO

The small collection of contemporary Andean art on display at this **museum** (Plaza Regocijo; entry with boleto turístico; ☯ 9am-6pm Mon-Sat) in the municipality building is really one for the fans. Museo Quijote (p233) has a much better collection, putting a representative range of Peru's contemporary artists on show, with interpretive information that puts art in context with history.

IGLESIA SAN FRANCISCO

More austere than many of Cuzco's other churches, **Iglesia San Francisco** (Plaza San Francisco; admission free; ☯ 6:30-8am & 5:30-8pm Mon-Sat, 6:30am-noon & 6:30-8pm Sun) dates from the 16th and 17th centuries, and is one of the few that didn't need to be completely reconstructed after the 1650 earthquake. It has a large collection of colonial religious paintings and a well-carved cedar choir. The attached **museum** (admission S5; ☯ 9am-noon & 3-5pm Mon-Fri, 9am-noon Sat) houses supposedly the largest painting in South America, which measures 9m by 12m and shows the family tree of St Francis of Assisi, the founder of the order. Also of macabre interest are the two crypts, which are not totally underground. Inside are plenty of human bones, some of which have been carefully arranged in designs meant to remind visitors of the transitory nature of life.

San Blas
IGLESIA DE SAN BLAS

This simple adobe **church** (Plaza San Blas; admission S15 or with boleto religioso; ☯ 10am-6pm Mon-Sat, 2-6pm Sun) is comparatively small, but you can't help but be awed by the baroque, gold-leaf principal altar. The exquisitely carved pulpit, made from a single tree trunk, has been called the finest example of colonial wood carving in the Americas. Legend claims that its creator was an indigenous man who miraculously recovered from a deadly disease and subsequently dedicated his life to carving this pulpit for the church. Supposedly, his skull is nestled in the topmost part of the carving. In reality, no one is certain of the identity of either the skull or the woodcarver.

MUSEO DE ARTE PRECOLOMBINO

Inside a Spanish colonial mansion with an Inca ceremonial courtyard, this dramatically curated **pre-Columbian art museum** (☎ 23-3210; map.perucultural.org.pe; Plazoleta Nazarenas 231; admission S20; ☯ 9am-10pm) showcases a stunningly varied, if selectively small, collection of archaeological artifacts previously buried in the vast storerooms of Lima's Museo Larco (p95). Dating from between 1250 BC to AD 1532, the artifacts show off the artistic and cultural achievements of many of Peru's ancient cultures, with exhibits labeled in Spanish, English and French. Highlights include the Nazca and Moche galleries of multicolored ceramics, *queros* (ceremonial

Inca wooden drinking vessels) and dazzling displays of jewelry made with intricate gold- and silverwork.

MUSEO INKA

The charmingly modest **Museo Inka** (☎ 23-7380; Tucumán at Ataúd; admission S10; ☪ 8am-6pm Mon-Fri, 9am-4pm Sat), a steep block northeast of the Plaza de Armas is the best museum in town for those interested in the Incas. The restored interior is jam-packed with a fine collection of metal- and goldwork, jewelry, pottery, textiles, mummies, models and the world's largest collection of *queros*. There's excellent interpretive information in Spanish, and English-speaking guides are usually available for a small fee.

The museum building, which rests on Inca foundations, is also known as the Admiral's House, after the first owner, Admiral Francisco Aldrete Maldonado. It was badly damaged in the 1650 earthquake and rebuilt by Pedro Peralta de los Ríos, the count of Laguna, whose crest is above the porch. Further damage from the 1950 earthquake has now been fully repaired, restoring the building to its position among Cuzco's finest colonial houses. Look for the massive stairway guarded by sculptures of mythical creatures, and the corner window column that from the inside looks like a statue of a bearded man but from the outside appears to be a naked woman. The ceilings are ornate, and the windows give good views straight out across the Plaza de Armas.

Downstairs in the sunny courtyard, highland Andean weavers demonstrate their craft and sell traditional textiles directly to the public.

MUSEO DE ARTE RELIGIOSO

Originally the palace of Inca Roca, the foundations of this **museum** (cnr Hatunrumiyoc & Herrajes; admission S15 or with boleto religioso; ☪ 8-11am & 3-6pm Mon-Sat) were converted into a grand colonial residence and later became the archbishop's palace. The beautiful mansion is now home to a religious-art collection notable for the accuracy of its period detail, and especially its insight into the interaction of indigenous peoples with the Spanish conquistadors. There are also some impressive ceilings and colonial-style tile work, though this is not original, having been replaced during the 1940s.

Avenida El Sol & Downhill
MUSEO DE ARTE POPULAR

Winning entries in Cuzco's annual Popular Art competition are displayed in this engaging **museum** (basement, Av El Sol 103; admission with boleto turístico; ☪ 9am-6pm Mon-Sat, 8am-1pm Sun). This is where the artisans and artists of San Blas strut their creative stuff in styles ranging from high art to cheeky cute, offering a fascinating, humorous take on ordinary life amid the pomp and circumstance of a once-grandiose culture. Small-scale ceramic models depict drunken debauchery in the *picantería* (local restaurant), torture in the dentist's chair, carnage in the butcher shop, and even a caesarean section.

There's also a display of photographs, many by renowned local photographer Martín Chambi, of Cuzco from the 1900s to the 1950s, including striking images of the aftermath of the 1950 earthquake in familiar streets.

QORIKANCHA

If you visit only one site in Cuzco, make it these **Inca ruins** (Plazoleta Santo Domingo; admission S10; ☪ 8:30am-5:30pm Mon-Sat, 2-5pm Sun), which form the base of the colonial church and convent of Santo Domingo. Qorikancha was once the richest temple in the Inca empire; all that remains today is the masterful stonework.

In Inca times, Qorikancha (Quechua for 'Golden Courtyard') was literally covered with gold. The temple walls were lined with some 700 solid-gold sheets, each weighing about 2kg. There were life-sized gold and silver replicas of corn, which were ceremonially 'planted' in agricultural rituals. Also reported were solid-gold treasures such as altars, llamas and babies, as well as a replica of the sun, which was lost. But within months of the arrival of the first conquistadors, this incredible wealth had all been looted and melted down.

Various other religious rites took place in the temple. It is said that the mummified bodies of several previous *incas* were kept here, brought out into the sunlight each day and offered food and drink, which was then ritually burnt. Qorikancha was also an observatory from which high priests monitored celestial activities. Most of this is left to the imagination of the modern visitor, but the remaining stonework ranks with the finest Inca architecture in Peru. A curved, perfectly fitted 6m-high wall can be seen from both inside and outside the site. This wall has withstood all of the violent earthquakes that leveled most of Cuzco's colonial buildings.

Once inside the site, the visitor enters a courtyard. The octagonal font in the middle was originally covered with 55kg of solid gold. Inca chambers lie to either side of the courtyard. The largest, to the right, were said to be temples to the moon and the stars, and were covered with sheets of solid silver. The walls are perfectly tapered upward and, with their niches and doorways, are excellent examples of Inca trapezoidal architecture. The fitting of the individual blocks is so precise that, in some places, you can't tell where one block ends and the next begins.

Opposite these chambers, on the other side of the courtyard, are smaller temples dedicated to thunder and the rainbow. Three holes have been carved through the walls of this section to the street outside, which scholars think were drains, either for sacrificial *chicha* (fermented corn beer), blood or, more mundanely, rainwater. Alternatively, they may have been speaking tubes connecting the inner temple with the outside. Another feature of this side of the complex is the floor in front of the chambers: it dates from Inca times and is carefully cobbled with pebbles.

The temple was built in the mid-15th century during the reign of the 10th *inca* (king), Túpac Yupanqui. After the conquest, Francisco Pizarro gave it to his brother Juan, but he was not able to enjoy it for long – Juan died in the battle at Sacsaywamán in 1536. In his will, he bequeathed Qorikancha to the Dominicans, in whose possession it has remained ever since. Today's site is a bizarre combination of Inca and colonial architecture, topped with a roof of glass and metal.

Colonial paintings around the outside of the courtyard depict the life of St Dominic, which contain several representations of dogs holding torches in their jaws. These are God's guard dogs (*dominicanus* in Latin), hence the name of this religious order.

IGLESIA DE SANTO DOMINGO

The **church** of Santo Domingo is next door to Qorikancha. Less baroque and ornate than many of Cuzco's churches, it is notable for its charming paintings of archangels depicted as Andean children in jeans and T-shirts. Opening hours are erratic.

MUSEO DEL SITIO DE QORIKANCHA

There are sundry moth-bitten archaeological displays interpreting Inca and pre-Inca cultures at this small, mangy, underground **archaeological museum** (admission with boleto turístico; 9am-6pm Mon-Sat, 8am-1pm Sun), which is entered off Av El Sol.

MUSEO QUIJOTE

This privately owned **museum of contemporary art** (www.museoelquijote.com; San Agustín 275; entry S10 or with boleto religioso; 9am-7:30pm) houses a diverse, thoughtful collection of painting and sculpture ranging from the folksy to the macabre. There's good interpretive information about 20th-century Peruvian art history, some of it translated into English.

ACTIVITIES

Trekking

The department of Cuzco is a hiker's paradise, with huge mountain ranges, winding rivers, isolated villages and ruins, varied ecosystems, and a huge range of altitudes.

The most famous trek in the Cuzco region is the Inca Trail, but it's no longer the only, or even necessarily the best, show in town. It's a stunning walk, but its name is somewhat of a misnomer. What savvy tourism officials and tour operators have christened the Inca Trail is just one of dozens of footpaths that the Incas built to reach Machu Picchu, out of thousands that crisscrossed the Inca empire. Some of these overland routes are even now being dug out of the jungle by archaeologists. Many more have been developed for tourism, and an ever-increasing number of trekkers are choosing these over the Inca Trail. Whatever your pleasure – ruins, mountains, scenery, flora and fauna, cultural encounters – there's a hike to suit you. For more detailed information on the following hikes, purchase an *Alternative Inca Trails Information Packet* from the South American Explorers Club (p227). Closer to Cuzco, imaginative operators such as Chaski Ventura (p240) and Eco Inka (p286) have developed multiday Sacred Valley trekking itineraries that go well off the beaten track to little-visited villages and ruins such as Huchuy Qosqo.

See p283 for full coverage of the Inca Trail and alternative trekking routes to Machu Picchu.

CHOQUEQUIRAU

Remote, spectacular, and still not entirely cleared, the ruins of Choquequirau are often described as a mini–Machu Picchu. This breathtaking site at the junction of three rivers – and the fairly challenging four-day hike required to get there and back – has been firmly positioned as 'the next big thing' for the last few years. It seems inevitable that controls and permits will be introduced in time, but for now it's still easy to organize this walk on your own. A guided version costs US$380 on average. **Apus Peru** (☎ 978-2720; www.apus-peru .com) joins this trek up with the Inca trail, for a total of nine days of spectacular scenery and an ever-more-impressive parade of Inca ruins culminating in Machu Picchu.

Ausangate

Snowcapped Ausangate (6372m), the highest mountain in southern Peru, can be seen from Cuzco on a clear day. Hiking a circuit around its skirts is the most challenging alpine hike in the region. It takes five to six days and crosses four high passes (two over 5000m). The route begins in the rolling brown *puna* (grasslands of the Andean plateau) and features stunningly varied scenery, including fluted icy peaks, tumbling glaciers, turquoise lakes and green marshy valleys. Along the way you'll stumble across huge herds of alpacas and tiny hamlets unchanged in centuries. The walk starts and finishes at Tinqui, where there are warm **mineral springs** and a basic hotel, and mules and *arrieros* (horsemen) are available for about S30 per day each. Average price is US$500 for an organized, tent-based trek with operators such as **Apus Peru** (☎ 978-2720; www .apus-peru.com) or specialist guides such as **Miguel Jove** (☎ 984-79-2227; miguelj24@hotmail.com; contact via South American Explorers Club). For a luxurious, lodge-based experience of Ausangate, check out **Andean Lodges** (☎ 22-4613; www.andeanlodges. com; from US$610).

For more on Q'oyoriti, a ritual festival that takes place on Ausangate every year, see p295.

Vilcabamba

The real 'lost city of the Incas,' Vilcabamba – also known as Espíritu Pampa – is what Hiram Bingham was looking for when he stumbled on Machu Picchu. The beleaguered Manco Inca and his followers fled to this jungle retreat after being defeated by the Spaniards at Ollantaytambo in 1536. The long, low-altitude trek, which takes four to nine days, is very rugged, with many steep ascents and descents before reaching Vilcabamba, 1000m above sea level. You can start at either Huancacalle (p293) or Kiteni.

WHEN TO GO

There are regular departures on these treks from May to September, and private departures can be organized at any time of year. In the wettest months (from December to April), trails can be slippery and campsites muddy, and views are often obscured behind a thick bank of rolling clouds. The best trekking months are June to August; the high jungle Vilcabamba trek is not recommended outside these months. Temperatures can drop below freezing year-round on all the other, higher-altitude treks, and it occasionally rains even during the dry season (late May to early September).

WHAT TO BRING

Modern internal-framed backpacks, tents, sleeping bags and stoves can all be rented in various places in Calle Plateros from around S10 per item per day. Check all equipment carefully before you agree to rent it, as some is pretty shoddy and rarely is it lightweight. For the cheapest deals on new gear, head to El Molino (p253). Other essentials include sturdy shoes, rain gear, insect repellent, sunblock, a flashlight (with fresh batteries), basic first-aid supplies and water-purification tablets. Once you're trekking, there is usually nowhere to buy food, and the small villages where treks begin have very limited supplies, so shop in advance in Cuzco. If you're on a guided trek, take a stash of cash for tipping the guide and the *arrieros*. About US$10 per day per trekker is the minimum decent tip to a guide; a similar amount to divide between group *arrieros* is appropriate.

River Running

Rafting isn't regulated in Peru – literally anyone can start a rafting company. On top of this, discounting wars caused by bargain-hunting travelers working the Plaza de Armas in packs have led to lax safety by many cheaper rafting operators. The degree of risk cannot be stressed enough: there are deaths every year. Rafting companies that take advance bookings online are generally more safety conscious (and more expensive) than those just operating out of storefronts in Cuzco.

RIO URUBAMBA
Rafting the Río Urubamba through the Sacred Valley could offer the best rafting day trip in South America, but Cuzco and all the villages along its course dispose of raw sewage in the river, making for a smelly and polluted trip. Seriously – close your mouth if you fall in.

Despite its unsavory aspects, the **Ollantaytambo to Chilca** (class II to III) section is surprisingly popular, offering 1½ hours of gentle rafting with only two rapids of note. **Huarán** and **Huambutio to Pisac** are other pollution-affected sections.

There are a variety of cleaner sections south of Cuzco on the upper Urubamba (also known as the Vilcanota), including the popular **Chuquicahuana** run (class III to IV+; class V+ in the rainy season). Another less-frenetic section is the fun and scenic **Cusipata to Quiquihana**, (mainly class II to III). In the rainy season, these two sections are often combined. Closer to Cuzco, **Pampa to Huambutio** (class I to II) is a beautiful section, ideal for small children (three years and over) as an introduction to rafting.

SANTA TERESA
Río Santa Teresa offers spectacular rafting in the gorge between the towns of Santa Teresa and Santa María, and downstream as far as Quillabamba. One word of warning: the section from **Cocalmayo Hot Springs to Santa María** consists of almost nonstop class IV to V rapids in a deep, inaccessible canyon. It should only be run with highly reputable operators, such as local experts Cola de Mono (p290). Be very aware, if considering a trip here, that guiding this section safely is beyond the powers of inexperienced (cheaper) rafting guides. This is not the place to economise. Do not underestimate this section of river; raft another section in the area with your chosen operator before even considering it. At the time of research, some cheaper operators were looking at this section, and it seems unlikely they will all resist the temptation to run it.

OTHER RIVERS
For rivers further from Cuzco, you definitely need to book with a top-quality outfit using highly experienced rafting guides who know first aid as well as rafting and swift-water res-

cue techniques, because you will be days away from help in the event of illness or accident.

The **Río Apurímac** offers three- to 10-day trips through deep gorges and protected rainforest, but can only be run from May to November. The rapids are exhilarating (classes IV and V), and the river goes through wild, remote scenery with deep gorges. Rafters camp on sandy beaches (where sandflies can be a nuisance), and sightings of condors and even pumas have been recorded. Four-day trips are the most relaxed, and avoid the busier campsites, but three-day trips are more commonly offered. This section has limited camping places, and those that exist are becoming increasingly overused. Make sure your outfitter cleans up the campsite and leaves nothing behind.

An even wilder expedition is the 10- to 12-day trip along the demanding **Río Tambopata**, which can only be run from May to October. You'll start in the Andes, north of Lake Titicaca, and travel through the heart of the Parque Nacional Bahuaje Sonene deep in the Amazon jungle. It takes two days just to drive from Cuzco to the put-in point! The first days on the river are full of technically demanding rapids (classes III and IV) in wild Andean scenery, and the trip finishes with a couple of gentle floating days in the rainforest. Tapirs, capybara, caiman, giant otters and jaguars have all been seen by keen-eyed boaters.

The following rafting companies have the best reputations for safety:

Amazonas Explorer (☎ 25-2846; www.amazonas -explorer.com) A professional international operator with top-quality equipment and guides, offering rafting trips on the Ríos Apurimac and Tambopata. Private trips on even more remote rivers, such as Río Cotahuasi (p170) near Arequipa, can also be arranged.

Apumayo (☎ 24-6018; www.apumayo.com; Calle Garcilaso 265, Interior 3) Another professional outfitter that takes advance international bookings for Río Tambopata trips. It's also equipped to take travelers with disabilities.

Mayuc (☎ 24-2824; www.mayuc.com; Portal Confiturías 211) This monster operator, very popular with bargain hunters, dwarfs the competition.

River Explorers (☎ 77-9619; www.riverexplorers.com; Calle Garcilaso 210, Interior 128) Runs all sorts of sections, including trips of up to six days on Río Apurímac.

Mountain Biking
Mountain-biking tours are a growing industry in Cuzco, and the local terrain is superb. Rental bikes are poor quality and at time of research only *rígida* (single suspension) models

CUZCO & THE SACRED VALLEY

were available for hire. Good new or second-hand bikes are not easy to buy in Cuzco either, as the ever-growing army of local devotees snap them up as soon as they become available. If you're a serious mountain biker, consider bringing your own bike from home. Selling it in Cuzco is eminently viable.

If you're an experienced rider, some awesome rides are quickly and easily accessible by public transport. Take the Pisac bus (stash your bike on top) and ask to be let off at Abra de Ccorao (S0.70, 30 minutes). From here, you can turn right and make your way back to Cuzco via a series of cart tracks and single track; halfway down is a jump park constructed by local aficionados. This section has many variations and is known as Yuncaypata. Eventually, whichever way you go, you'll end up in Cuzco's southern suburbs, from where you can easily flag down a taxi to get you home.

If you head off the other side of the pass, to the left of the road, you'll find fast-flowing single track through a narrow valley – you won't get lost – which brings you out on the highway in Ccorao. From here, follow the road through a flat section then a series of bends. Just as the valley widens out, turn left past a farmhouse steeply downhill to your left, and into challenging single track through a narrow valley, including a hairy river crossing and some tricky, steep, rocky, loose descents at the end, bringing you down into the village of Taray. From here it's a 10-minute ride along the river to Pisac, where you can catch a bus back to Cuzco.

Many longer trips are possible, but a professionally qualified guide and a support vehicle are necessary. The partly paved road down from Abra Málaga to Santa María, though not at all technical, is a must for any cyclist and is part of the Inca Jungle Trail (see p285), offered by many Cuzco operators. Maras to Salinas is a great little mission. The Lares Valley offers challenging single track, which can be accessed from Cuzco in a long day. If heading to Manu in the Amazon Basin (p474), you can break up the long bus journey by biking from Tres Cruces to La Unión – a beautiful, breathtaking downhill ride – or you could go all the way down by bike. The outfitters of Manu trips can arrange bicycle rental and guides. The descent to the Río Apurímac makes a great burn, as does the journey to Río Tambopata, which boasts a descent of 3500m in five hours. A few bikers attempt the 500km-plus trip all the way to Puerto Maldonado, which gets hot and sweaty near the end but is a great challenge.

The following bike operators are recommended:

Amazonas Explorer (☎ 25-2846; www.amazonas-explorer.com) Offers excellent two- to 10-day mountain-biking adventures; great for families, with kids' bikes available.

Andean Xtreme Adventure (☎ 974-79-0386; www.axaperu.com) Offers a unique two-day Lares trip, as well as all the usual day trips.

Cusco Aventuras (☎ 984-13-7403; cuscoaventura@hotmail.com) Local legend of loconess Luchín will give you the ride of your life.

Gravity Peru (☎ 22-8032; www.gravityperu.com; Santa Catalina Ancha 398) Allied with well-known Gravity Bolivia, this professionally run operator is the only one offering double-suspension bikes for day trips. Highly recommended.

Loreto Tours (☎ 23-6331; www.loretotours.com; Calle del Medio 111) Runs half-day trips to the ruins around Cuzco, full day and overnight trips in the Sacred Valley, and four-day rides down into the Amazon jungle. Rentals available.

Horseback Riding

Most agencies can arrange a morning or afternoon's riding from US$10. Alternatively, you can walk to Sacsaywamán, where many of the ranches are, and negotiate your own terms. Choose carefully, however, as many horses are in a sorry state.

Other horseback-riding options require more legwork. Select agencies will offer multiday trips to the area around Limatambo, and there are some first-rate ranches with highly trained, high-stepping thoroughbred Peruvian *paso* horses in Urubamba (see p261).

Bird-watching

Serious birders should definitely get a hold of *Birds of the High Andes*, by Jon Fjeldså and Niels Krabbe. One of the best birding trips is from Ollantaytambo to Santa Teresa or Quillabamba, over Abra Málaga. This provides a fine cross section of habitats from 4600m to below 1000m. Englishman Barry Walker, owner of the Cross Keys pub (p251), is a self-confessed 'birding bum' and the best resident ornithologist to give serious birders plenty of enthusiastic advice. He has written a field guide, *The Birds of Machu Picchu*, and runs a tour agency, **Birding in Peru** (☎ 22-5990; www.birding-in-peru.com), for bird-watching trips all around Peru, as well as into Bolivia and Chile.

Other Activities

The via ferrata – 'Iron Way' in Italian – is a series of ladders, holds and bridges built into a sheer rockface. First developed in the Italian Alps in WWII, it's a great way for reasonably fit people with no previous experience to experience rock climbing. The **Sacred Valley Via Ferrata** (☎ 984-11-2732; www.naturavive.com; per person S150), located amid stunning scenery in the Sacred Valley, was constructed and operated by rock-climbing and high-mountain professionals. It features a 300m vertical ascent, a heart-hammering hanging bridge 200m above the valley floor, and a 100m rappel. Active, adrenaline-pumping fun. The price includes pickup and drop-off in Cuzco or Urubamba, rock climbing and lunch.

Action Valley (☎ 24-0835; www.actionvalley.com; ☺ 9am-5pm Sun-Fri) is an adventure park with paintball (US$20), a 300m-long zipline ride (US$15), a giant tower swing (US$20), a 122m bungee jump (US$64) and a bungee slingshot (US$64) at the ready. The park is 11km outside Cuzco on the road to Poroy (taxi S12 or Pachacutec combi S0.60 each way). It's closed between January 15 and February 15.

Cusco Planetarium (www.planetariumcusco.com; per person around S30) is a nifty way to learn more about the Inca worldview. It was the only culture in the world to define constellations of darkness as well as light, and studied astronomy seriously: some of Cuzco's main streets are designed to align with the stars at certain times of year. Recommended before you go on a trek – you'll feel clever pointing out the Black Llama to your fellow hikers. Reservations essential; price varies with group size, and includes pickup and drop-off.

US-licensed tandem pilot Richard offers a unique 'condor's view of the Andes' via half-day trips over the Sacred Valley with **Cloudwalker Paragliding** (☎ 984-93-7333; cloudwp@ gmail.com; US$80).

Globos de los Andes (☎ 23-2352; www.globosperu .com) runs hot-air ballooning trips over the Sacred Valley, which can be combined with 4WD tours.

For some pampering or a post-trekking splurge, a blossoming number of spas offer massage services, including the highly professional **Siluet Sauna & Spa** (☎ 23-1504; Quera 253; ☺ 10am-10pm) and the luxurious **Samana Spa** (☎ 23-3721; www.samana-spa.com; lecsecocha 536; ☺ 10am-7pm Mon-Sat). Beware of cheap massages touted in the street; there are reports

of massages getting much more, er, *intimate* than expected.

There is growing interest in **shamanic ceremonies** and the psychedelic properties of the San Pedro and *ayahuasca* plants. These are extremely powerful drugs and can be highly toxic in the wrong hands. While it is hard not to be skeptical about a store-bought spiritual experience, a 'guided ceremony' is a lot safer than scarfing down a powerful narcotic by yourself. The following providers of this service have been recommended:

Lesley Myburgh (☎ 24-1168; Hostal Casa de la Gringa, cnr Tandapata & P'asñapakana)

Shaman Shop (☎ 26-4089; www.shamanshopcusco .com; Triunfo 393)

Victor Peralta (☎ 984-69-1748; vipesoterismo@peru .com)

WALKING TOUR

Start with a leisurely 360-degree survey of your surroundings from the middle of the **Plaza de Armas** (1; p228). Two imposing churches, three charming colonnades – including one that extends across a trafficked street – an elaborate fountain, and a gracefully laid-out square add up to one of the most beautiful (and most photographed) public spaces in South America.

Stroll past more colonnades up pedestrian-only Calle del Medio and head southwest across **Plaza Regocijo** (2). On your left you'll see a beautiful **building** (3), once a hotel and now a tourist precinct that's home to fancy restaurants and hoity-toity clothing stores.

Head up Calle Garcilaso, named for the beloved chronicler of the Incas and conquistadores, Garcilaso de la Vega, whose childhood home on the corner now houses the **Museo Histórico Regional** (4; p231). Most of the buildings in this street are colonial mansions, and many have been converted into hotels with lovely patios. The **Hotel los Marqueses** (5; p243) is particularly stunning.

If it's a Sunday, look out for Quechua-speaking *campesinos* (peasants) hanging out in **Plaza San Francisco** (6). This is where country people who've come to Cuzco for work meet up in their free time. Drop in to the **church and museum of San Francisco** (7; p231) if you're so inclined – one or other is almost bound to be open, although their opening hours never seem to overlap.

Just past the colonial archway of Santa Clara is the **church and convent of Santa Clara** (8), which is very rarely open to the public. Head inside if you get the chance, because this is one of the more bizarre churches in Cuzco. Mirrors cover almost the entire interior; apparently, the colonial clergy used them to entice curious indigenous people into the church for worship. The nuns provide the choir during early morning Mass, sitting at the very back of the church and separated from both the priest and the rest of the congregation by an ominous grille of heavy metal bars stretching from floor to ceiling.

Just beyond the church, the bustle of activity at **Mercado San Pedro** (**9**; p253) spills out onto the pavement. Fuel up with a huge jug of healthy *jugo* (fruit juice) at one of the Mercado's many stalls. When you finish the first glass, don't forget to ask for the *yapa*

WALK FACTS

Start Plaza de Armas
Finish Sacsaywamán
Distance 4km
Duration About three hours, allowing for stops for juice, coffee and shopping

---

WALKING TOUR

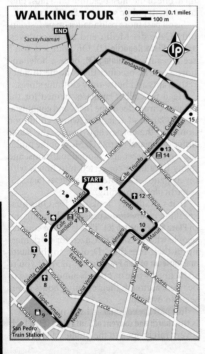

(leftover). It's a good idea to share one juice between two, or you'll be bloated by the sheer bulk of it.

Now, stagger out into Calle Nueva and be swept up in Cuzco's commercial mayhem. Magic spells, electric guitars, pregnancy tests and pirate salsa DVDs jostle for space in the stalls, barrows and blankets that take up every inch of available pavement space and even some of the road.

You'll pop out onto Avenida El Sol opposite the **Palacio de Justicia (10)**, a big white wedding cake of a building whose back garden is home to a pair of lawn-mowing llamas – look out for them as you head up Maruri and take a left into **Loreto (11)**, a pedestrian-only cobbled walkway with Inca walls on both sides. The west wall belongs to Amaruqancha (Courtyard of the Serpents). Its name may be derived from the pair of snakes carved on the lintel of the doorway near the end of the enclosure. Amaruqancha was the site of the palace of the 11th Inca emperor, Huayna Cápac. On the other side of Loreto is one of the best and oldest Inca walls in Cuzco, which belonged to the Acllahuasi (House of the Chosen Women). Following the conquest, the building became part of the **closed convent of Santa Catalina** (**12**; p230) and so went from housing the Inca virgins of the sun to pious Catholic nuns.

Loreto brings you back out into the Plaza de Armas. Turn right up Triunfo (signposted as Sunturwasi) and across Palacio into Hatunrumiyoc, another walled-in pedestrian alley named after the well-known **12-sided stone (13)**. The stone is on the right, and can be recognized by the small children standing loudly pointing it out to tourists, and the dignified, regally clad Inca (rumored to be paid by the municipality) who poses next to it for photos. This excellently fitted stone belongs to a wall of the palace of the sixth *inca*, Inca Roca, which later became the Archbishop's palace and now houses the **Museo de Arte Religioso** (**14**; p232). The fitting of the stone is technically brilliant but is by no means an unusual example of polygonal masonry.

Hatunrumiyoc ends at Choquechaca. Several good cafes are concentrated in the block to your left and this is a good place for a break before the assault on San Blas and Sacsaywamán. You can see what's in store straight ahead on Cuesta San Blas. Charming and cobbled is the good news. Near-vertical is the bad news. Luckily it's only a very short puff up to **Plaza San Blas (15)**, where the un-assuming adobe Iglesia de San Blas and an incomparable view across Cuzco await. Fire twirlers, jugglers and itinerant artisans while away their days around the fountain in the plaza – this is Cuzco's bohemian HQ.

Head left along **Tandapata (16)** for the classic Cuzco cobbled experience. Inca irrigation channels run down ancient stairways, and rock carvings adorn walls and random stones in the path. High walls on either side occasionally part for intriguing glimpses of mansions and tenements. Follow your nose uphill to Sacsaywamán.

COURSES

Cuzco is one of the best places in South America to study Spanish. Shop around – competition is fierce and students benefit with free cultural and social activities. Salsa lessons and cooking nights are more or less ubiquitous.

The standard deal is 20 hours of classes per week, either individual or in groups of up to four people. Most schools will also let you pay by the hour, or study more or less intensively.

Visit your school on a Friday to get tested and assigned to a group for a Monday start, or roll up any time to start individual lessons. All schools can arrange family homestays and volunteer opportunities.

Amauta Spanish School (☎ 26-2345; www.amauta spanishschool.com; Suecia 480; individual/group per hr S28/17.50) Big, professional and popular. Also offers Spanish programs in the Sacred Valley and the Amazon jungle.

Amigos (☎ 24-2292; www.spanishcusco.com; Zaguan del Cielo B-23; individual/group per hr S30/18) A long-established nonprofit school with an admirable public-service record.

Cervantes Spanish School (☎ 50-7051/984-34-8907; cervantesschool@yahoo.es, rocsanac@hotmail.com; Urbanización Fiderando, Camino Real 10; per hr individual/group S21/13.50) Readers rave about lovely Rocsana and her colleagues. Learn to speak Spanish fast from serious, experienced teachers.

Excel Language Center(☎ 23-5298; www.excel -spanishlanguageprograms-peru.org; Cruz Verde 336; per hr individual/group S23/13) Highly recommended for its professionalism.

Fairplay (☎ 984-78-9252; www.fairplay-peru.org; per hr S13.50-21; Choquechaca 188) A unique nonprofit NGO, Fairplay trains Peruvian single mothers to provide Spanish lessons and homestays. Students pay two-thirds of their class fees directly to their teachers. Individual classes only, priced according to the teacher's level of experience.

Proyecto Peru (☎ 984-68-3016; http://proyectoperu centre.org; Tecsecocha 429; per hr individual/group S25/18) A relaxed and funky haven from the madness of downtown.

San Blas Spanish School (☎ 24-7898; www.spanish schoolperu.com; Tandapata 688; per hr individual/group S21/13.50) Students enjoy the informal teaching here, appropriate to the school's location in the heart of bohemian San Blas.

Try **Colegio Andino** (☎ 24-5415; www.cbc.org.pe/colegio andino; Pampa de la Alianza 164) for Quechua courses.

TOURS & GUIDES

There are hundreds of registered travel agencies in Cuzco, but things change quickly, so ask other travelers for recommendations. Be aware that many of the small travel agencies clustered around Procuradores and Plateros earn commissions selling trips run by someone else, and this can lead to organizational mix-ups. If the travel agency also sells ponchos, changes money and has an internet cabin in the corner, chances are it's not operating your tour.

Key questions to ask before handing over your money: Is there an English-speaking guide? What's included? How big will the group be? What kind of transport is used? How long will everything take? Will you explain a special diet to the cook? If going to Machu Picchu via Ollantaytambo, check whether transport back to Cuzco from Ollantaytambo is included. If you're unsure about anything, get any and all guarantees in writing, as some agencies will literally say anything to get your business.

Most of the standard tours offered in Cuzco are rushed and overcrowded, and visit sites that you can get to on your own either by walking or via taxi or public transportation. Classic options include a half-day tour of the city and/or nearby ruins, a half-day trip to the Sunday markets at Pisac or Chinchero and a full-day tour of the Sacred Valley (eg Pisac, Ollantaytambo and Chinchero).

Agents also offer expensive Machu Picchu tours that include transport, admission tickets to the archaeological site, an English-speaking guide and lunch. Since you only get to spend a few hours at the ruins before it's time to return to the train station, it's more enjoyable (not to mention much cheaper) to DIY. You can hire a guide at Machu Picchu (some are great; most are not) or in advance, from Cuzco.

CUZCO & THE SACRED VALLEY

TOUR AGENCIES

These tour agencies are recommended:

Andean Xtreme Adventure (☎ 23-4599/974-79-0386; www.axaperu.com) Knowledgeable, professional tour operator who can make anything happen.

Chaski Ventura (☎ 23-3952; www.chaskiventura.com; Manco Cápac 517) Pioneer of alternative and community tourism, distinguished by the quality of its itineraries and guides, and its thoughtful involvement in community development.

Fertur (☎ 22-1304; www.fertur-travel.com; Procuradores 341) Local office of long-established, very reliable agency for flights and all conventional tours.

Turismo Caith (☎ 23-3595; www.caith.org; Centro Yanapanakusun, Urb Ucchullo Alto, N4, Pasaje Santo Toribio) Offers community visits and the opportunity to participate in educational projects, as well as standard single and multiday trips.

GUIDES

The following guides for Machu Picchu and around Cuzco are recommended:

Leo Garcia (☎ 984-70-2933, 984-75-4022; leogacia@hotmail.com) Personable, passionate and supremely knowledgeable about all things Inca.

Miguel Jove (☎ 984-79-2227; miguelj24@hotmail.com) A highly recommended climbing and alternative-trekking specialist. Can be contacted through South American Explorers Club.

Raul Castelo (☎ 24-3234, 984-31-6345; raulcastelo10@hotmail.com) Has his own transport and equipment for rafting, trekking and mountain biking; specializes in community tourism.

You can also contact guides via the **Asociación de Guías Oficiales de Turismo** (Agotur; ☎ 24-9758; www.agoturcusco.org.pe; Heladeros 157).

FESTIVALS & EVENTS

Cuzco and the surrounding highlands celebrate many lively fiestas and holidays. In addition to national holidays (p519), the following are the most crowded times, when you should book all accommodations well in advance:

El Señor de los Temblores (the Lord of the Earthquakes) This procession on the Monday before Easter dates to the earthquake of 1650 (p229).

Crucifix Vigil On May 2 to 3, a Crucifix Vigil is held on all hillsides with crosses atop them.

Q'oyoriti Less well-known than the spectacular Inti Raymi are the more traditional Andean rites of this festival (see the boxed text, p295), which is held at the foot of Ausangate the Tuesday before Corpus Christi, in late May or early June.

Corpus Christi Held on the nineth Thursday after Easter, Corpus Christi usually occurs in early June and features fantastic religious processions and celebrations in the cathedral.

Inti Raymi Cuzco's most important festival, the 'Festival of the Sun' is held on June 24. It attracts tourists from all over Peru and the world, and the whole city celebrates in the streets. The festival culminates in a re-enactment of the Inca winter-solstice festival at Sacsaywamán. Despite its commercialization, it's still worth seeing the street dances and parades, as well as the pageantry at Sacsaywamán.

Santuranticuy artisan crafts fair A crafts fair held in the Plaza de Armas on December 24 (Christmas Eve).

SLEEPING

Cuzco has hundreds of hotels of all types, and just about the only thing they have in common is that they charge some of the highest room rates in Peru. Cuzco fills to bursting between June and August, especially during the 10 days before Inti Raymi on June 24 and during Fiestas Patrias (Independence Days) on July 28 and 29. You should book in advance for these dates.

Prices are market driven and vary dramatically according to the season and demand. Rates quoted here are for high season and may well be negotiated down in quiet times, particularly in cheaper places.

Though the Plaza de Armas is the most central area, you won't find any bargains there, and accommodations along Av El Sol tend to be bland, expensive and set up for tour groups. As Cuzco is such a compact city, it's just as convenient to stay in another neighborhood nearby. Hilly San Blas has the best views and is deservedly popular. There are also many options west of the Plaza de Armas around Plaza Regocijo, in the commercial area towards the Mercado Central, and downhill from the center in the streets northeast of Av El Sol.

Many of Cuzco's guesthouses and hotels are located in charming colonial buildings with interior courtyards, which can echo resoundingly with noise from other guests or the street outside. Many places that offer breakfast start serving as early as 5am to accommodate Inca Trail trekkers and Machu Picchu day-trippers. For this reason, early check-ins are easier here than in other parts of the world and are often available without prior arrangement.

With advance notice, most midrange and top-end places will pick you up for free at the airport, the train station or the bus terminal.

Inquire insistently about hot water for showers before committing yourself to a hotel. It's often sporadic, even in midrange accommodations, and there's nothing worse after a multiday trek than a lukewarm shower! In some hotels the hot water is more reliable on some floors than others. It helps to avoid showering at peak times of day, and it's always worth telling reception if you're having trouble – they may simply need to flick a switch or hook up a new gas canister.

All places listed claim to offer 24-hour hot-water showers, and unless otherwise noted, midrange and above places include cable TV and internet access. The top hotels all feature rooms with heating and telephone; exceptions are noted in the review. All top-end and some midrange hotels have oxygen tanks available, at a price, for altitude sufferers.

Cuzco's swanky, top-end hotels are usually booked solid during high season. Reserving through a travel agency or via the hotel's website may result in better rates than making reservations yourself by phone or walking in off the street.

Central Cuzco

There are no good-value budget choices on the plaza itself, though you'll find plenty of places within strolling distance. Many of the side streets that climb northwest away from the Plaza towards Sacsaywamán (especially Tigre, Tecsecocha, Suecia, Kiskapata, Resbalosa and 7 Culebras) are bursting with cheap crash pads.

BUDGET

Hostal Andrea (☎ 23-6713; andreahostal@hotmail.com; Cuesta Santa Ana 514; s/d without bathroom S12.50/25, s/d S20/35; ▣) Cuzco's cheapest, and not bad for the price. Rooms are basic and the shared bathrooms are pretty awful, but the kind, unassuming staff make it a reader favorite.

Hostal Suecia II (☎ 23-9757; Tecsecocha 465; s/d/tr S30/50/70, s/d/tr/q without bathroom S20/30/45/60) This long-standing backpacker favorite continues to offer excellent value with central location, friendly owners, a light, bright, flowery patio, decent rooms and a book lending library.

Hospedaje Familiar Munay Wasi (☎ 22-3661; Huaynapata 253; dm & s/d S25/35; ▣) This friendly, homey *hospedaje* (family inn), housed in a ramshackle adobe building without a single right angle to its name, is run by a kindly family. Room 201, which has huge windows, minibalconies and a magic view of downtown Cuzco just a stone's throw away, is understandably popular with families.

Loki Hostel (☎ 24-3705; www.lokihostel.com; Cuesta Santa Ana 601; dm S23-32, d S80; ▣) Expats have rescued this 450-year-old national monument from near ruin and turned it into party central. A great place to eat, drink and be merry – sleeping, not so much. On weekends the on-site bar features local bands and DJs good enough to attract locals and expats for a night out.

ourpick WalkOn Inn (☎ 23-5065; www.walkoninn .com; Suecia 504; dm S25, s & d S60; ▣) Perched on a sunny green corner, this tranquil little place is only a five-minute puff up from the Plaza de Armas but feels almost like the country. Gorgeous views of red-tiled roofs and green hills add to the serenity. Recently refurbished, cozy and family friendly. Excellent value.

Hostal Frankenstein (☎ 23-6999; www.hostal -frankenstein.com; San Juan de Dios 260; s/tr without bathroom S25/65, d/q S65/120; ▣) Advertising 'cold dark gloomy rooms and spiders on request', German-owned Hostal Frankenstein has a sense of humor and a family feel – that would be the Addams family, naturally. A fabulous, freaky, funny crash pad. The double rooms, in particular, are excellent value.

The Point (☎ 25-2266; www.thepointhostels.com; Mesón de la Estrella 172; dm S25-33, d S80; ▣) An industrial-sized party palace, with daily events, on-site bar The Horny Llama, and a grassy backyard with hammocks. Another good choice for the sociably inclined. Hosts electronic music parties of some note.

Qosqo Wasinchis (☎ 23-2132; www.lacasacusco.com; Nueva Alta 424; r per person S30) La Casa de Cultura Solidaria del Comercio Justo – a center for fair trade and community action – offers four big, nice (but dark) rooms to travelers. An awesome place to hook into the local activist scene, drink beer and see music in the sociable restaurant courtyard area, or just enjoy a lively environment where street-kid theater workshops, community choir practice, and indigenous weaving ladies are all part of the scenery. Ask about volunteering opportunities.

Hostal Suecia I (☎ 23-3282; www.hostalsuecia1.com; Suecia 332; s/d S50/75) Most rooms in this pint-sized guesthouse are very basic, but location and staff are fabulous and there's a sociable, stony, indoor courtyard. The two new double rooms on the top floor (311 and 312) are a superb value.

Also recommended:

Albergue Municipal (☎ 25-2506; albergue@ municusco.gob.pe; Kiskapata 240; dm S15-17, d without bathroom S40; ▣) A good choice for the tight of budget, with plenty of space, great views, kitchen access and laundry facilities.

Hostal el Solar (☎ 38-0254; Plaza San Francisco 162; s/d/tr 35/50/70) Run-down exterior, but has colorful rooms and low, arched ceilings. Friendly and family owned.

MIDRANGE

Hostal Residencial Rojas (☎ 22-8184; Tigre 129; s/d/tr/q with breakfast S60/90/120/150; ☐) The vine-covered tree you see as you walk in sets the tone for the rest of this dreamy, undersea-feeling family hostel – fresh green and white is the order of the day. Rooms are nothing special, and some (namely 205 and 206) are much bigger than others. Still, good value for a killer location, a three-minute walk from the Plaza de Armas.

our pick Renacimiento (☎ 22-1596; www.cuscoapart .com/rapart@gmail.com; Ceniza 331; r per person S60-95; ☐) An unsigned treasure, this colonial mansion has been converted into 12 stylish one- and two-bedroom apartments sleeping one to six people, each unique in design and furnishing. Cool and classy but cozy and comfortable, it's fabulous for families and long stays (from S30 per person per night for a monthly stay). Recommended.

Niños Hotel (☎ 23-1424, www.ninoshotel.com; Meloc 442; s/d without bathroom S60/120, d/tr/q with breakfast S132/192/240; ☐) Run by a Dutch-founded nonprofit foundation, this hotel helps underprivileged children in Cuzco by providing food, medical aid and after-school activities. It inhabits a fetching colonial-era house with a sunny courtyard, and rooms somehow manage to embrace coziness and institutional chic at the same time. Long beloved and highly recommended. There's another branch at Fierro 476. Rates include breakfast.

Hospedaje Monte Horeb (☎ 23-6775; montehoreb cusco@yahoo.com; San Juan de Dios 260, 2nd fl; s/d/tr with breakfast S66/102/144) Serene and mint fresh with nice big rooms, an inviting balcony, a be-doilied dining room and a curious mix of furnishings – check out the wood-look couch cover.

Casa Grande (☎ 24-5871; www.casagrandelodging .com.pe; Santa Catalina Ancha 353; s/d/tr with breakfast S75/90/120; ☐) The nice, rickety-balconied colonial building wrapped around a charming patio is the best of this place. Rooms are basic, but all have cable TV and, unusually, separate shower and toilet. Again, you're paying for location rather than quality.

Hotel Wiracocha (☎ 22-1014; www.hotelwiracocha cusco.com; Cruz Verde 364; s/d/tr/q S75/120/180/255) Hotel Wiracocha's inviting patio is a haven

of colonial charm in a frenetic commercial area. Rooms are varied; many have low ceilings and some are a bit poky, but all have phone and cable TV. Three rooms boast mezzanines and can comfortably accommodate up to five. The eccentrically decorated patios and balconies are a good place to be.

Piccola Locanda (☎ 23-6775; www.piccolalocanda .com; Kiskapata 215; s/d without bathroom S80/100, s/d/tr with breakfast S100/130/165) Italian-owned, and founded with the specific purpose of supporting community projects, this place is cool as well as caring, with quixotic, colorful rooms and a cave-like cushioned lounge. Has an in-house responsible-travel operator, and can hook you up with volunteer work. Entrance is on Resbalosa.

Los Aticos (☎ 23-1710; www.losaticos.com; Quera 253, Pasaje Hurtado Álvarez; s/d/apt S90/105/120; ☐) Hidden in an alley, this sleepy, homely place stays under the radar. Rates include a self-service laundry room and a full guest kitchen. The three mini-apartments sleep up to four and are good value for self-catering groups or families. A smaller sister hotel is located on Av Pardo.

Hostal Loreto (☎ 22-6352; www.loretohostal.com; Loreto 115; s/d/tr/q S90/135/165/195) This amiable place has four rooms with Inca walls, which make them rather dark and musty – but then how often do you get to sleep next to an Inca wall? Other rooms are bright, and the location is unbeatable, just steps from the Plaza de Armas. The mirrors and the staircase spiraling like a slide in the center create a bit of a funhouse vibe. Singles and doubles include breakfast.

Teatro Inka B&B (☎ 24-7372, in Lima 01-976-0523; www.teatroinka.com; Teatro 391; s/d/tr & ste with breakfast S97.50/130/180; ☐) Classy, colorful and a bit cosmic, Teatro Inka is a well-located gem, offering simple, tasteful rooms with tribal and colonial touches. All rooms are good value, and the penthouse suite is well worth splashing out on. Recommended.

Los Angeles B&B (☎ 26-1101; www.losangeles cusco.com; Tecsecocha 474; s/d S120/150; ☐) While the public patio is nothing to write home about, rooms are white and bright, with a light colonial touch to make them classy and interesting. The front corner room, furnished with baronial splendor yet spacious and spare, far outshines other rooms.

El Balcón Hostal (☎ 23-6738; www.balconcusco.com; Tambo de Montero 222; s/d/tr with breakfast $120/210/255; ▣) This attractively renovated building dating from 1630 has just 16 guest rooms, all with balconies. It has a beautiful little garden filled with curiosities and some great views over Cuzco. There's also a sauna on the premises.

Hostal Corihuasi (☎ 23-2233; www.corihuasi.com; Suecia 561; s/d/tr with breakfast $126/165/198) A brisk walk uphill from the main plaza, this cozy guesthouse inhabits a mazelike colonial building with postcard views of the Andes. Amply sized rooms are outfitted in a warm, rustic style with alpaca-wool blankets, hand-woven rugs and solid wooden furnishings. Room 1 is the most in demand for its wraparound windows, which are ideal for soaking up panoramic sunsets.

Hotel El Rosal (☎ 23-118; www.hotelcuscoelrosal.com; Cascaparo 116; s/d/tr/q $160/192/224/304) You'll be greeted with smiling faces at this delightful guesthouse over the road from the Mercado San Pedro. The hostel is run by nuns to help fund the neighboring San Pedro home for girls. It feels like a charming hidden world, with manicured rose gardens, long, dreamy hallways, and a soundtrack of children playing. The building has several courtyard gardens, each more inviting than the last, and 29 guestrooms in a spacious modern annex. Highly recommended.

Hotel los Marqueses (☎ 26-4249; www.hotelmarqueses.com; Calle Garcilaso 256; s/d/tr with breakfast from $180/240/300) An air of mystery and romance perfumes this fabulously refurbished colonial villa, built in the 16th century by Spanish conquistadors. Traditional *escuela cuzqueña* paintings, courtyard fountains and balconies with views of the cathedral on the Plaza de Armas will all seduce you. The wood-floored rooms are large and airy; some have split-level sleeping areas and skylights. Most guests here are on package tours.

Also recommended:

Picol Hostal (☎ 24-9191; picolhostal@gmail.com; Quera 253, Pasaje Hurtado Álvarez; s/d/tr with breakfast $60/90/105) New and a bit bland, but spick-and-span and trying hard. It's located amid shops and restaurants in a bustling commercial district, great for travelers who prefer to be in a more 'local' area where there's still plenty of street action.

Andenes de Saphi (☎ 22-7561; www.andenesdesaphi.com; Saphi 848; s/d/tr/q $115/186/216/246) At the far end of Saphi, where the city starts to become more rural, this dependable, modern hotel has a rustic wooden construction with fantastic colorful murals in every room.

TOP END

None of the top-shelf hotels on the plaza can be recommended – they are often overpriced, underwhelmingly serviced and full of noisy package groups. There are some respectable, if unexciting, options nearby.

Hotel Royal Inka (☎ 23-1067; www.royalinkahotel.com; Plaza Regocijo 299; s $235-312 d $287-364) A cheerily eccentric clash between Old World and New greets you in the lobby: 1970s-style furniture and phones, a hip modern bar and modernist sculptures under a somewhat startling mural of naked jungle dwellers, all presided over by a massive golden Inca head. Rooms are good quality – those in the colonial building are a bit dated but comfortable and luxurious, while the modern ones are big, bright and cheery.

Del Prado Inn (☎ 22-442; www.delpradoinn.com; Suecia 310; s/d/tr incl buffet breakfast $263/385/507; ▣) Del Prado is a very welcome addition, located almost on the Plaza de Armas. The all-professional staff gives highly personalized service, and there are just over a dozen snug rooms reached by elevator. Rooms come with lots of extras, including wooden floors, central heating, bathtubs and wi-fi access. Some rooms have tiny balconies with corner views of the plaza, though these can be noisy, especially on weekends. Best of all, the dining room has original Inca walls.

Los Andes de America (☎ 60-6060; www.cuscoandes.com; Calle Garcilaso 150; s/d/tr/q with breakfast $330/390/420/480) A Best Western hotel noted for its buffet breakfast, which includes regional specialties such as *mote con queso* (cheese and corn) and *papa helada* (frozen potato). Rooms are warm and comfortable, bathrooms are big and relatively luxurious, and the atrium boasts an impressive scale model of Machu Picchu.

San Blas
BUDGET
Samay Wasi (☎ 25-3108; www.samaywasiperu.com; Atocsaycuchi 416; dm/d $24/60; ▣) You'll feel like a treehouse-dwelling Ewok in this friendly, rambling hostel clinging precariously to the hillside, hidden up a flight of stairs teetering way above town.

Hospedaje el Artesano de San Blas (☎ 26-3968; hospedajeartesano790@hotmail.com; Suytuccato 790; s/d $25/50) Peaceful and falling-down-charming colonial house with a sunny patio and free use of a large and well-equipped kitchen.

Hospedaje Inka (☎ 23-1995; http://hospedajeinka.weebly.com; Suytuccato 848; r per person with breakfast $25; ▣) This scruffy but charming converted hillside farmhouse high above the Plaza San Blas affords some great views. There's erratic hot water, private bathrooms and a large farm kitchen available for cooking your own meals. Taxis can't climb the final uphill stretch, so be prepared for a stiff walk.

Pak'arincama Casa Hospedaje (☎ 50-1079, 984-37-7275; pakarincama@hotmail.com; Pumapaccha 634; r per person S25) Authentic with a capital A: walk up a chicken- and dog-infested alleyway to get here, and duck under the washing line in the backyard to be introduced to the parrots. Move into one of four basic, clean guest rooms and become part of the Gonzáles family.

Also recommended is **Hospedaje Familiar Kuntur Wasi** (☎ 22-7570; Tandapata 352A; r per person with/without bathroom S35/25), an economical hotel with a star *dueña* (owner), whose concern for traveler well-being is genuine.

MIDRANGE

Amaru Hostal (☎ 22-5933; www.cusco.net/amaru; Cuesta San Blas 541; s/d/tr with breakfast S99/129/165; ☐) In a characterful old building in a prime location, Amaru can't be beat. Flowerpots sit outside relatively peaceful rooms, which have windows to let the sunshine in. Some have rocking chairs from which to admire the rooftop view. Those in the outer courtyard are noisier, and those at the back are newer.

Orquídea Real Hostal (☎ in Lima 01-444-3031; www.orquidea.net; Alabado 520; s/d/t with breakfast S99/132/165) Owned by a package-tour company, this efficiently run small guesthouse has rustic rooms with working fireplaces, exposed wooden beams and skyline views over the city. All rooms have cable TV, phones and safes; matrimonial doubles also have king-sized beds.

Hostal Marani (☎ 24-9462; www.hostalmarani.com; Carmen Alto 194; s/d/tr/q with breakfast S99/153/186/234) This airy oasis has a light-filled courtyard surrounded by humble rooms that vary in size and shape. A few upstairs have vaulted ceilings, skylights and city views.

Madre Tierra (☎ 24-8452; www.hostalmadretierra.com; Atocsaycuchi 647; s & d/tr S135/195, ☐) Warm and supercozy, with plenty of B&B-style luxury comfort touches, farmhouse-like Madre Tierra is a vine-entwined, slightly claustrophobic little jewel box. Good value for money.

Casa de Campo Hostal (☎ 24-4404; www.hotelcasadecampo.com; Tandapata 298; s/d/tr with breakfast S135/165/195; ☐) After climbing steeply to reach this irresistibly charming hillside inn, you may have to persevere for many more

flights of stone steps before reaching your room. But the reward is huge: condor's-eye views over the city and incredibly romantic rooms, some with wood fireplaces. Highly recommended, especially for honeymooning mountain goats.

Eureka Hostal (☎ 23-3505; www.peru-eureka.com; Chihuampata 591; s/d/tr S150/180/250; ☐) A funky blend of old and new, Eureka's styley lobby and sun-soaked cafeteria invite further acquaintance. Rooms don't disappoint, with jolly decor featuring a childlike take on traditional motifs. Orthopedic mattresses and down quilts make them as comfortable as they are cool. Flexible tariffs can make it an even better deal.

Also recommended:

Qori Ñusta Inn (☎ 22-8299; Chihuampata 515; s/d/tr/q S85/120/150/185; ☐) Big rooms, helpful staff and free use of a recently renovated kitchen.

Hostal el Grial (☎ 22-3012; www.hotelelgrial.com; Carmen Alto 112; s/d/tr/q S90/135/152/192) In a rickety old wood-floored building; all rooms have orthopedic mattresses and some have views.

Hostal Pensión Alemana (☎ 22-6861, www.cuzco stay.de; Tandapata 260; s/d/tr with breakfast S120/165/210) With well-kept rooms and a flower garden in the inner courtyard, this rustic Swiss-German lodge wouldn't look out of place in the Alps.

Casona los Pleiades (☎ 22-4713; www.casona-pleiades.com; Tandapata 116; s & d/tr with breakfast S150/200) A sun-drenched B&B with tidy rooms overlooking the city, plus a TV and video lounge.

TOP END

Hostal Rumi Punku (☎ 22-1102; www.rumipunku.com; Choquechaca 339; s/d/tr with breakfast S210/270/345; ☐) A gem of a place, recognizable by the monumental Inca stonework around the entrance, Rumi Punku (Stone Door) sprawls up and down through a stylish complex of old colonial houses, gardens and terraces. The rooftop terraces and other outdoor areas are utterly charming. Rooms ooze comfort and class, with central heating, wooden floors and European bedding. Sauna and Jacuzzi are available for a minimal charge.

Los Apus Hotel & Mirador (☎ 26-4243; www.losapushotel.com; Atocsaycuchi 515; s & d S387; ☒ ☐) Los Apus is a neat, classy little hotel under Swiss management, with an airy courtyard and quality rooms with wooden furnishings. It's so eye-catching that Peruvian feature films have been shot here. Although the place is overpriced, central heating and direct-dial telephones are welcome luxuries. And when it comes to security, this hotel has no equal, with a high-tech alarm system and an emergency water supply. The rooftop terrace is ideal for meeting other travelers. Expect plenty of ambient noise inside your room, however. A wheelchair-accessible room for travelers with disabilities is available.

Hotel Arqueólogo (☎ 23-2569; www.hotel arqueologo.com; Pumacurco 408; s & d/tr/ste with breakfast S435/652.50/630; 🖳) Its name an echo of the Inca stonework in the narrow street running beside it, this antique French-owned guesthouse is renowned for its class. Tastefully done rooms overlook a vast interior courtyard. You can relax in the garden deck chairs, or sip a complimentary pisco sour (grape brandy cocktail) in the fireplace lounge. The hostelry not only supports local artisans, whose weavings are on sale here, but also helps fund public libraries. French, English and German are spoken.

Hotel Monasterio (☎ 60-4000; www.monasterio.orient-express.com; Palacio 136; basic r/luxury r S1690/1901, ste S2150-5952; 🖳) Elegantly arrayed around graceful 16th-century cloisters, the Monasterio has long been Cuzco's top hotel, with majestic public areas and more than 100 exquisitely designed rooms and suites surrounding its genteel courtyards. Although it has been wholly renovated over the years, the accommodations still show their Jesuit roots, with irregular floor plans and varying room sizes. This indubitably five-star hotel boasts two high-class restaurants, along with absolutely everything else expected of an establishment of this sterling caliber.

Casa Cartagena (☎ in Lima 01-242-3147; www.casacartagena.com; Pumacurco 336; basic r/luxury r/ste S1845/1901/5400; 🖳 🔊) Ultramodern and uber-hip, arriviste Casa Cartagena is audaciously pitched at the young rich, with apparently no expense spared. This colonial mansion has been restored and furnished by Italian designers with stunning results. Tinkling water features and oversized installation art, a lap pool, a spa, a sauna and the funkiest multicolored plastic bar furniture this side of Milan all add up to a breathtakingly bold venture. The royal suite, complete with imported Jacuzzi from Italy, sets the benchmark for luxury in Cuzco.

Avenida El Sol & Downhill

BUDGET

Hostal San Juan Masías (☎ 43-1563; Ahuacpinta 600; d/tr/q without bathroom S30/50/75, d/tr/q S40/65/90; 🖳)

An excellent alternative guesthouse run by Dominican nuns on the grounds of the busy Colegio Martín de Porres, this place is clean, safe and friendly, and overlooks frequent games lessons on the courtyard. Breezy, simple, spick-and-span rooms with hot water are arranged off a long, sunny hallway brightened by fresh flowers.

Killa House (☎ 23-4107; killahousehospedaje@gmail.com; Av Tullumayo 279; s/d/tr/with breakfast S40/70/105) Surprisingly light inside, this cozy, impeccably clean little place is hidden behind a forbidding wall.

Mirador Hostal (☎ 24-8986; soldelimperiocusco@yahoo.es; Ahuacpinta s/n; s/d/tr/q with breakfast S48/66/84/102, q without bathroom S80) A cheery, rambling, yellow concrete jungle overlooking a main road. Friendly, helpful staff make it a favorite. Rates include breakfast.

Hostal Señorío Real (☎ 23-6980; senorio_reservas@hotmail.com; Arcopunco 631; s/d/tr/q with breakfast S50/70/75/80; 🖳) Surrounded by *ferreterías* (hardware stores), this hostel is an unexpected treasure in a businesslike part of town. Rooms are comfy but nondescript, with cable TV. The panoramic view from the top-floor dining room is fantastic, and best of all is the charming Inca-walled backyard.

MIDRANGE

Hostal Inkarri (☎ 24-2692; www.inkarrihostal.com; Qolla Calle 204; s/d/tr with breakfast S99/120/165; 🖳) An airy, roomy place with a sunny garden, well-kept colonial terraces and whimsical collections of old sewing machines, phones and typewriters. Staff are friendly and welcoming. Recommended.

Hostal Centenario (☎ 22-4235; www.hostal centenario.com; Centenario 689; d/tr/ste with breakfast S165/210/24) Rambling and varied, with old, somewhat crumbly rooms at the front and a modern annex at the back overlooking a sports ground. Modern rooms have heating and are more comfortable. Staff are young, friendly and professional, and the whole place has a family feel despite its size. Check out the scary art in the dining room.

TOP END

Hotel Libertador Palacio del Inka (☎ 23-1961; www.libertador.com.pe; Plazoleta Santo Domingo 259; s & d/ste S1300/1640; 🔊 🖳) Set in a huge, opulently furnished colonial mansion with a fine interior courtyard, the Libertador boasts Inca foundations. Other parts of the building date back to the 16th century, when Francisco Pizarro was an occupant. It's as luxurious and beautiful as you'd expect at this price. Rooms in the newer section of the gigantic complex have less personality than those of competitor Monasterio; however, at the time of research a major remodeling was about to begin – with the avowed intention of making Libertador Cuzco's undisputed landmark hotel.

Further Afield

Lorenzo's Lodge (☎ 22-3357; www.freehostal.com; Paradero Chosas, Barrio de Callanca, subiendo por Santa Ana; accommodation free; ▢) Local identity Lorenzo Cahuana gives free accommodation – it's basic, with bunk beds, but who's complaining? It's his bold and eccentric way of publicizing his Inka Jungle Trail tour (see p285), but there's no obligation. Mad dreamer or savvy self-promoter? You be the judge. The lodge is a 10-minute, S5 taxi ride from town, with lovely bushy views and space for a couple of tents. Reservations are essential.

Hostal San Juan de Dios (☎ 24-0135; www.san juandedioscusco.com; Manzanares 264, Urb Manuel Prado; s/d/tr/q with breakfast S105/135/165/195; ▢) A truly heart-warming place, this spotless guesthouse with modern decor is part of a nonprofit enterprise that supports a hospital clinic and also provides job opportunities for young people with disabilities. All of the quiet, carpeted rooms have large windows; most have twin beds, though there's one matrimonial double. The wonderful staff can help with everything from laundry services to making international phone calls. Discounts may be available for online reservations. It's a 30-minute walk or S3 taxi ride from the city center, near shops and amenities.

Torre Dorada Residencial (☎ 24-1698; Los Cipreses N-5, Residencial Huancaro; s/d/tr with breakfast S255/315/360; ▢) Torre Dorada is a modern, family-run hotel in a quiet residential district close to the bus terminal. It's recommended for the high quality of service, including free pickup from and drop off to the airport, train stations and the town center. Fluent English is spoken.

EATING

Cuzco's location, nearly dropping off the eastern edge of the Andes, gives it access to an unbelievable range of produce. The Incas had it figured out, working the precipitous altitude changes for all they were worth, to

---

HOSTEL WITH HEART

The heart-warming **Hospedaje Turismo Caith** (☎ 23-3595; www.caith.org; Urb Ucchullo Alto, Pasaje Sto Toribio N4; r per person with breakfast €20; ▢) must be the best deal in Cuzco. Not only does it boast beautiful buildings, gorgeous grounds and one of the best views in town, but it supports and shares a home with **Centro Yanapanakusun**. This girls' home is a real eye-opener about life in Peru.

In many tiny rural communities, poverty means that young girls are sent to work in the city. With no experience away from their families and limited, if any, Spanish, they're extremely vulnerable. Economic abuse is commonplace – some *cama adentro* (live-in) servants receive food and a wage of as little as S90 per month, with half a day off a week. Violence and sexual abuse also occur, and are generally what prompts girls to seek refuge at Centro Yanapanakusun, which houses up to 30 girls aged under 14.

Girls as young as eight have knocked on the door; one current resident was working peeling potatoes in a restaurant at the age of four. Often they lose touch with their families: the centre's Italian founder, Vittoria Savio, stumbled into this world by chance, when a woman told her of her daughter who had gone out to work at the age of eight, 23 years earlier, and not been seen by the family since.

The rambling farmhouse-style hostel shares grounds with the girls' home, and the girls can interact with guests as they please (or not at all). Huge picture windows and various balconies and patios look out over the Plaza de Armas, a 20-minute walk or a five-minute taxi ride away.

This place isn't for everyone: you're asked to be sensitive to the feelings of the girls, most of whom have suffered alcohol-related violence, so it's not the place for late-night riotousness. But it's great for families – big rooms and cots are available, and the rambling, grassy garden is a perfect place for kids to run around. For travelers looking for a restful, family-feeling place, it's an incredible find.

create terraces where stodgy highlanders such as potatoes and quinoa grew practically on top of colorful jungle delicacies such as coca, avocado and *ají picante* (hot chili). Few food stores in the world offer the variety on offer in Cuzco's humblest street market.

The local food scene has taken off over the last decade as incoming influences from all over the world have seen local products, many of them not available outside Peru, combined in ever-fresher ways. Cuzco explodes with taste sensations, from dirt-cheap street snacks to the world-class quality (and prices!) of its top restaurants. If you like to eat and are prepared to try something new, you'll need to loosen your belt a notch after a few days in Cuzco.

Don't waste stomach space on the overpriced, cookie-cutter tourist traps in the Plaza de Armas. The first *cuadra* (block) of Plateros, just off the plaza, is also touristy, but with good possibilities for lounging around drinking coffee and surfing the `net. Trendy eclectic eateries abound in San Blas and towards Limacpampa down the hill, and more and more excellent vegetarian options are emerging.

Many *cuzqueños* eat out every day for lunch and dinner. *Menú* (set meal) is so economical in many places that it's cheaper to eat out than to cook for yourself. You generally have to ask about the *menú* – it's often not advertised, but is available almost everywhere. You'll get soup, a main course, a drink, and sometimes dessert. Some good options are **Che Carlitos** (Av Tullumayo 387; menú S3.50), **Ñucchu** (Choquechaca s/n; menú S4); **Kukuly** (Huaynapata 318; menú S5), **Q'ori Sara** (Calle Garcilaso 290; menú S6), **El Mesón de San Blas** (Carmen Bajo 169; menú S7), and **Urpi** (Tecsecocha 149; menú S8).

If, as has been known to happen, you stumble out of a *discoteca* at 4am with an insatiable hunger, go to **El Rey de Felafel** (Plateros s/n; burgers from S4, falafel from S6; ☉ midnight-5am). Of the many sandwich stalls that serve late-night revelers along Plateros and Saphi, this is by far the best. Not only are the sandwiches clean, safe and tasty, and the felafel itself the best in Cuzco, but Victor is a kindly soul who will let you squeeze behind his hotplate and sit on a bucket to eat.

Self-catering

Small, overpriced grocery shops near the Plaza de Armas include **Gato's Market** (Portal Belén 115; ☉ 7am-10pm) and **Market** (Mantas 119; ☉ 8am-11pm).

For a more serious stock-up head to supermarket **Mega** (cnr Matará & Ayacucho; ☉ 10am-8pm Mon-Sat, to 6pm Sun).

Central

El Ayllu (Marquez 263; snacks from S3.50; ☉ 6:30am-10pm) Beloved by Peruvians for its pastries, especially *lengua de suegra* ('mother-in-law's tongue'; a sweet pastry confection) and *sandwich de cerdo* (pork sandwich), El Ayllu is a slow-paced, old-fashioned, high-ceilinged taste of another time. Most of the solemn, suit-clad staff have worked here for decades. At time of research, to the dismay of the entire population of Cuzco, El Ayllu had just been evicted from its historic home in the Plaza de Armas. Starbucks is said to want the space for its first branch in Cuzco and the Archbishopric, which owns the premises, is inclined to hand it over.

Cafetería Los Reyes (Saphi s/n; breakfast S3.50-12, sandwiches from S3.50; ☉ 7am-7pm Mon-Sat) Cuzco's very own truck stop, complete with photos of overland trucks on the wall, and artery-clogging breakfasts from as early as 5am with prior notice. A big favorite with overland drivers and tour leaders.

ourpick **Los Toldos** (cnr Almagro & San Andrés; mains from S10; ☉ lunch & dinner Mon-Sat) Local favorite with perhaps Cuzco's best salad bar (try the purpley black olive sauce) and an extensive menu of high-class fast food. Most people can't go past the Peruvian classic *cuarto de pollo* (quarter of a chicken cooked on a spit), done here to perfection.

Maikhana (☎ 25-2044; Galerías la Merced, Av El Sol 106, 2nd fl; mains S12-26; ☉ 11am–11pm) A friendly, comfy place to enjoy excellent, good-value renditions of all the Indian classics, including a long list of vegetarian dishes.

Jack's Café (☎ 25-4606; Choquechaca 509; breakfast from S12.50, mains from S14; ☉ 7:30am-11:30pm) The only food outlet in the world this reviewer considers worth standing in line for, and she's clearly not alone in her appreciation – the ever-present crowd of hungry travelers waiting outside Western-style, Australian-run Jack's tells you how popular it is. One breakfast here and you're hooked. You have been warned.

Victor Victoria (☎ 25-2854; Tecsecocha 466; mains from S14; ☉ 7am-10pm) Around the corner from the Plaza is this budget restaurant, providing princely portions of primarily Peruvian food. Backpackers can't recommend it enough, especially for its filling portions.

CUZCO CUISINE

As elsewhere in Peru, Sunday lunch – with friends, family and a few *chelas* (slang for beers; you'll win friends anywhere in Peru with this invaluable piece of vocab) is a major social occasion in Cuzco. Combined with a Sunday drive to the country and a postmeal stroll, it takes up the whole day. If you're prepared to try something new (and particularly if you're a keen carnivore with no family history of coronary problems), it's easy to partake of this slice of local life. Three villages south of town are traditional destinations for this prandial promenade. They're easily accessible by public transport (see p255), or you can hire a taxi and have it wait for you for around S40.

Tipón is *the* place to eat *cuy* (guinea pig), and **Saylla** is the home of *chicharrón* (deep-fried pork). In **Lucre** they've been preparing duck in 1001 ways since ancient times, with the recent welcome addition of the best cake shop in the region.

You'll find the following foods in local restaurants and at festivals in and around Cuzco.

Anticucho The Peruvian answer to the lollipop is beef heart on a stick, with a potato on the end for punctuation. Much more delicious than it sounds – many who try it without realizing it's heart end up addicted.

Caldo de gallina It's impossible to find bad soup in Cuzco, but simple, healthy, hearty *caldo de gallina* (chicken soup) is a standout, and a local favorite hangover breakfast.

Chicharrones Deep-fried chunks of pork, served with corn, mint leaves, fried potato and onion. This one is definitely more than the sum of its parts; get a bit of each ingredient on your fork and experience coronary-inducing heaven. Irresistible – and responsible for the reviewer's spare tire.

Choclo con queso *Choclo* are the huge, pale cobs of corn that are typical of the area. Served with a teeth-squeaking chunk of cheese, it's a great, cheap snack – look out for it in the Sacred Valley.

Cuy Yes, Virginia, they really do eat guinea pig. Nothing to be afraid of (it tastes just like chicken – honestly!), though it's often served complete with head, which can be, er, disconcerting.

Lechón Suckling pig with plenty of crackling, served with tamales (corn cakes). Another shortcut to a heart attack, but what a way to go.

Don't be deterred if you don't like the sounds of these – other meat-, potato- and trout-focused foods are available in the restaurants in each of these towns.

Real McCoy (☎ 26-1111; Plateros 326, 2nd fl; mains from S14; ☷ 7am-late; ▣) Tempts Brits hankering for a taste of home with chips and gravy, PG Tips teabags, real baked beans and roast dinners with Yorkshire pudding. Inviting and chilled out, it offers wi-fi, comfy couches, beanbags and sports on TV for extended relaxation sessions.

Los Perros (Tecsecocha 436; mains S14-20) An Australian-founded godsend, serving Asian/Indian-slanted bar food at stunning prices in an intimate 'couch bar.'

Aldea Yanapay (☎ 25-5134; Ruinas 415, 2nd fl; menú S15, mains from S22; ☷ 9am-11:30pm) With stuffed animals, board games and decor that perfectly evokes the circus you dreamed of running away with as a child, Aldea Yanapay is pitched at families but will appeal to anyone with a taste for the quixotic. Food includes burritos, falafel and tasty little fried things to pick at, and there's a whole separate menu for vegetarians. Profits go to projects helping abandoned children. Highly recommended.

Muse (☎ 25-3631, 984-23-1717; Plateros 316, 2nd fl; mains from S20; ▣) The coolest cafe-bar-restaurant in town, the Muse offers consistently delicious food with lots of vegetarian options, live music every night, an excellent hangover breakfast, very cool staff, great coffee, a good wine list and a rotating display of art – in short, a hard place to leave at any time of day.

Chicha (☎ 24-0520; Regocijo 261, 2nd fl; mains S24-40) Celebrity chef Gastón Acurio's first venture in Cuzco serves up a strangely wide-ranging menu in a too-cool-for-school setting. Burgers, pasta and pizza share space with haute versions of meaty *cuzqueño* classics such as *chicharrones* (deep-fried pork) and *estofado de res* (hearty beef melting off the bone). Naturally, debate rages in Cuzco as to whether it's worth coming here to pay twice what you would elsewhere, but this reviewer's experience was eye-rollingly, plate-lickingly positive.

Al Grano (☎ 22-8032; Santa Catalina Ancha 398; mains from S26; ☷ 10am-9pm Mon-Sat; ▣) Al Grano has a nonspicy menu of varied Asian food, including great vegetarian options, plus big breakfasts and some of Cuzco's best coffee. You're welcome to hang out and enjoy it with cards, games, free wi-fi and a book exchange.

Makayla (☎ 23-4806; cnr Loreto & Plaza de Armas, 2nd fl; mains S30-38) A smart and snappy breath of fresh air in the tourist-trap heavy Plaza, Makayla offers a Peruvian-focused menu with fusion touches, evenly weighted between red meat, white meat and vegetarian dishes. Its *alitas picantes* (spicy chicken wings) and *yuquitas a la huancaína* (fried yucca sticks with peanut sauce) are particularly fabulous for sharing.

Green's Organic (☎ 24-3399; Santa Catalina Angosta 235, 2nd fl; mains S30-38; ☽ 11am-10pm; ▯) With all-organic food and a bright farmhouse feel, Green's Organic oozes health. The salads and wraps are fabulously tasty, telling their own story of pesticide-free, free-range ingredients. The atmosphere is calm and uncluttered, with attentive professional staff. The same consortium owns several of Cuzco's top-end restaurants – Limo, Incanto, MAP Café, Inca Grill and Pacha Papa – all of which have big reputations and receive many recommendations.

ourpick **Cicciolina** (☎ 23-9510; Triunfo 393, 2nd fl; snacks from S16, mains from S36; ☽ 8am-late) Inhabiting a lofty colonial courtyard mansion, Cicciolina has long held its position as Cuzco's best restaurant. The eclectic, sophisticated food is divine, all the way from home-marinated olives through squid-ink pasta to melt-in-the-mouth desserts and biscotti. The service is impeccable, and the ambience will make any laid-back globetrotter feel at home. A huge expat favorite; highly recommended.

Inka Wall (☎ 25-3498; Santa Catalina Ancha 342; dinner buffet & show per person S50) This is the dinner and show locals come to – that pretty much says it all. They're probably inspired by the magnificent buffet, which includes Peruvian and international plates and a staggering array of desserts. The show, which consists of 45 minutes of music followed by six regional dances, runs from 8:15pm to 9:45pm nightly. Good value.

San Blas

ourpick **Govinda Lila's** (Carmen Bajo 225B; menú S5; ☽ breakfast, lunch & dinner) Cuzco's best deal and best-kept secret, Lila's unassuming vegetarian restaurant offers cheap, clean, fresh fare to a devoted following of office workers and San Blas hippies. Her sporadically available chocolate and banana cake is worth flying to South America for. Highly recommended.

Café Punchay (☎ 26-1504; Choquechaca 229; from S7; ☽ 8am-11pm; ▯) A strange mishmash of waffle breakfasts and potato dinners, this vegetarian hole-in-the-wall with a charming terrace area also sells good boxed lunches and a long list of specialty coffees.

Juanito's (Qanchipata 596; from S8; ☽ 8am-8pm) Good sandwiches were hard to find in Cuzco until Juanito's came along. All the traditional favorites are here, plus some fusion treats such as *lechón* (suckling pig) and *lomo saltado* (strips of beef stir-fried with onions, tomatoes, potatoes and chili). The inner room could be San Blas' most inviting lounge hangout.

Picantería María Angola (Choquechaca 292; mains S10-15; ☽ 11am-7pm) A good place to try local foods such as *ubre* (breaded udder), *tripa* (tripe) or *panza apanada* (stomach lining), or more appetizing *chicharrones* and *costillares* (ribs). Turn right and head up the stairs when you walk in.

Muse, Too (☎ 984-76-2602; Tandapata 710; mains S15; ☽ 8am-late) The laid-back San Blas version of the center's iconic cafe-bar, Muse, Too serves up fresh, funky food through the day, big-screen sport and movies in the afternoon, and live music and cocktails at night.

Granja Heidi (☎ 23-8383; Cuesta San Blas 525, 2nd fl; mains from S18) Follow the pictures of cows upstairs to this light Alpine cafe with terrific fresh produce, yogurts, cakes and other snacks on offer. The hot breakfasts are gigantic, and can satisfy any carnivorous cravings you may have.

Café Cultural Ritual (☎ 68-2223; Choquechaca 140; mains from S18; ☽ 7am-10pm) This is a cute little option with a mostly vegetarian menu and yummy desserts. It's run by an NGO that provides training and employment experience to underprivileged youngsters, so service is happy and haphazard.

Marcelo Batata (Palacio 121; mains from S28; ☽ 2-11pm) As if the stunning view from the rooftop terrace, Cuzco's longest coffee list and a daring array of cocktails weren't enough, Marcelo Batata's food is dangerously delicious. Try pasta with *ají de gallina* (spicy chicken and walnut stew) sauce for an exquisite fusion moment.

Av El Sol & Downhill

Pampa de Castillo is the street near Qorikancha where local workers lunch on Cuzco classics (opposite). Expect lots of *caldo de gallina* (chicken soup) and *chicharrones,* deep-fried pork chunks with corn, mint and, of course, potato, in a range of restaurants including **Niko's** (inside Pampa de Castillo 365). Across the street, check out the sandwich windows – if you're feeling especially brave, you could munch out on *queso de chancho* (pig brawn).

Meli Melo (☎ 23-8383; Limacpampa s/n; items from S2.50) A big bakery with meal-sized slabs of reviewer favorite *pastel de acelga* (a savory tart made with Swiss chard) and some of Cuzco's best empanadas too. Cakes here are fabulous too. The trick is to ignore the colorful ones – they're all the same bland sponge. Go for anything beige; you won't go wrong with *tres leches* (a cake made with three types of milk) or *leche asada* (flan).

Don Estéban and Don Pancho (☎ 25-2526; Av El Sol 765A; items from S4.50; ☿ 8am-10pm) The original and still the best. First it was Cuzco's coolest coffee bar. Then it started baking its own bread and created a generation of ciabatta addicts. Now it has specialty empanadas (pastries) – you must try *empanada de ají de gallina* before you die. Service is slow, giving you plenty of time to check out the mesmerizing wall display telling the story of the founders.

Moni (☎ 23-1029; San Agustín 311; mains S9-14; ☿ 8am-9pm) Tiny Moni is much loved for its good-value vegetarian fare, including a mean veg and quinoa curry and other adapted Peruvian dishes. The ambience is fresh and airy. Recommended.

Further Afield

Most popular local restaurants are outside the historic center and focus on lunch; few open for dinner. Don't expect to encounter any language other than Spanish in these places, but the food is worth the effort! The following are all highly recommended.

Tradiciones Cusqueñas (☎ 23-1988; Belén 835; mains S14-25; ☿ 11am-10pm) The home of a good Sunday lunch, Cuzco-style. It features jolly, utilitarian decor, huge piles of meat and potatoes, and delicious homemade *limonada* (lemonade). Come hungry!

Olas Bravas (☎ 43-9328; Mariscal Gamarra 11A; mains from S15; ☿ 9am-5pm) Most *cuzqueños* think Olas Bravas offers the best ceviche in town, so it's often packed. Luckily there's another branch around the corner on Av de la Cultura. Even if ceviche isn't your thing, this is a great place to try other *criollo* (coastal) dishes, such as *causa* (avocado and seafood sandwiched between layers of mashed potato) and *seco a la norteña* (goat stew). Check out the hammocks and the mural of the surfer.

Señor Carbón (☎ 24-4426; Urb Magisterio Segunda Etapa H5; buffet S35; ☿ lunch & dinner) The set deal at Señor Carbón (which translates as 'Lord Coal'!) is a carnivore's dream – all the meat you can eat, cooked to your liking, plus salad bar. If you can still fit it in, there's a scoop of ice cream for dessert.

DRINKING & ENTERTAINMENT

Clubs open early, but crank up a few notches after about 11pm. Happy hour is ubiquitous and generally entails two-for-one on beer or certain mixed drinks.

In popular *discotecas* (beware the word 'nightclub' – it is often used in Peru to indicate a brothel), especially right on the Plaza de Armas, both sexes should beware of drinks being spiked.

Cross Keys, Norton Rats and Paddy Flaherty's are good places to track down those all-important soccer matches, with satellite TVs more or less permanently tuned into sports.

The tried-and-true stops on the big night out in Cuzco are *discotecas* Mythology, Inka Team, Roots, Ukuku's and Mama Africa.

IS THAT A TOAD IN YOUR BEER?

Ever wondered what *cuzqueños* do to relax instead of whiling away the hours over a game of darts or pool in the local bar? Well, next time you're in a *picantería* (local restaurant) or *quinta* (house serving typical Andean food), look out for a strange metal *sapo* (frog or toad) mounted on a large box and surrounded by various holes and slots. Men will often spend the whole afternoon drinking *chicha* (fermented corn beer) and beer while competing at this old test of skill in which players toss metal disks as close to the toad as possible. Top points are scored for landing one smack in the mouth. Legend has it that the game originated with Inca royals, who used to toss gold coins into Lake Titicaca in the hopes of attracting a *sapo,* believed to possess magical healing powers and to have the ability to grant wishes.

Central Cuzco

Indigo (Tecsecocha 2, 2nd fl; 🕙 noon-late) Indigo is the perfect bar to warm up for a big night out, with fresh Thai and Peruvian food (mains from S15), good coffee, games, hookah pipes and famous mojitos. Genuinely friendly staff, comfy couches, an open fire and a seriously cool circus vibe (there are swings!) make it hard to move on. Highly recommended.

Bullfrogs (Huarancalqui 185) This gloriously glamorous new place, run by high-profile hipsters, offers a bit of everything. There's cafe service from breakfast until 11pm, live music every night, billiards, beanbags, fairy lights and hookah pipes. Open early till late.

Paddy Flaherty's (☎ 24-7719; Triunfo 124; 🕙 11am-late) This cramped little Irish pub is packed with random memorabilia, TVs, a working train set and homesick European travelers eating excellent-value hot sandwiches. Happy hours are from 7pm to 8pm and 10pm to 10:30pm.

Cross Keys (Triunfo 350; 🕙 10am-late; 🖳) Cross Keys is the most established expat and traveler watering hole in town. It's smothered in the trappings of a typical British pub, with leather barstools and plenty of dark wood. As well as a huge list of British beer, it offers good-value comfort food. Some say the S15 steak is the best-value meal in town.

Norton Rats (cnr Santa Catalina Angosta & Plaza de Armas, 2nd fl; 🕙 7am-late) Run by a motorcycle enthusiast, this down-to-earth bar overlooking the Plaza de Armas has the best damn burgers in town. It's also got TVs, darts and billiards to help you work up a thirst.

Pepe Zeta (Tecsecocha s/n; 🕙 7pm-late Tue-Sat) The place for *cuzqueños* to see and be seen, Pepe Zeta is a cool and breezy place with bamboo decor and a bewildering array of unusual, uncomfortable yet fascinating seating.

Mythology (Portal de Carnes 300; 🕙 8pm-late) The iconic nightspot in an iconic party town, Mythology advertises itself as 'only for gods'; whether you will feel godlike the morning after is debatable. Early in the night it's dominated by rafting groups watching videos of their exploits on the big screen. After midnight the dance floor dependably goes wild, to the sounds of '80s classics, Latino dance favorites and the guy next to the DJ whose job it is apparently to shout encouragement to the sweating hordes.

Ukuku's (☎ 24-2951; Plateros 316; 🕙 8pm-late) The most consistently popular nightspot in town, Ukuku's plays a winning combina-tion of crowd pleasers – Latin and Western rock, reggae and *reggaetón* (a blend of Puerto Rican *bomba*, dancehall and hip-hop), salsa, hip-hop et al – and often hosts live bands. Usually full to bursting after midnight with as many Peruvians as foreign tourists, it's good, sweaty, dance-a-thon fun. Happy hour is 8pm to 10:30pm.

Inka Team (Portal de Carnes 298; 🕙 8pm-late) Though it may change names, this place usually has the most up-to-the-minute electronic music collection, with trance, house and hip-hop mixed in with mainstream. There are chill-out sofas upstairs but this isn't the place for chat. A good mix of locals and tourists hang out here. Happy hour is 9pm to midnight.

Roots (Tecsecocha s/n; 🕙 8pm-late) This organic-feel club with an underground dance floor is ever-popular with locals and laid-back travelers alike.

Mama Africa (Portal Harinas 191, 2nd fl; 🕙 7pm-late) A favorite with Israelis, Mama Africa is the classic backpackers' hangout, usually packed with people sprawled across cushions or swaying to rock and reggae rhythms. Happy hour is 8:30pm to 11pm.

Kamikase (☎ 23-3865; Plaza Regocijo 274; 🕙 8pm-late) Kamikase is an older, more intimate bar that doesn't offer free drinks, but does have a disarmingly large variety of music that can switch from seductive salsa to live *música folklórica* (folkloric music) in an instant. Happy hour runs from 8pm to 10pm, and there's often a live show beginning at 10:45pm.

Caos (Pasaje Grace s/n; 🕙 8pm-late) At last – a nightclub just as *Miami Vice* tells us a nightclub should be. Make your entrance by sashaying down a neon-illuminated transparent Perspex stairway whose innards are home to some unfortunate, sensorily overstimulated carp. Order a drink at the massive, garish bar while admiring the Inca-styled water feature before hitting the shiny dance floor. The crowd here tends to very young locals, and music is a mixed bag.

San Blas

Many of the *barrio's* eclectic restaurants double as cafes and bars, too.

Km 0 (☎ 23-6009; Tandapata 100; 🕙 11am-late Tue-Sat, 5pm-late Sun & Mon) This convivial bar just off Plaza San Blas has a bit of everything. It serves good Thai food in the evening, and there's live music late every night – local musicians come here to jam after their regular gigs. Happy hour is 9pm to midnight.

7 Angelitos (Siete Angelitos 638; ☽ 6pm-late Mon-Sat) This tiny hillside haunt is the city's unofficial hipster lounge and late-night backup: when everything else has closed and the sun has come up, knock on the door. Happy hours are 7:30pm to 9:30pm and 11pm to 11:30pm.

Fallen Angel (☎ 25-8184; Plazoleta Nazarenas 221; ☽ 6pm-late) This ultrafunky restaurant and lounge is falling all over itself in the rush to cram in as much kitsch as possible, with glitter balls, fake fur and even bathtub-cum-aquarium tables complete with live goldfish. Deservedly popular for many years, Fallen Angel has now become expensive beyond the means of many travelers, but the decor really is worth seeing and the occasional theme parties held here are legendary. The same folks also own jungle-themed restaurant Macondo (☎ 22-9415), at Cuesta San Blas 571.

Other Entertainment

There's no cinema in Cuzco, but there are a few DVD lounges on Procuradores. **Cinema San Blas** (Carmen Alto 111) sometimes shows free art-house movies.

Teatro Kusikay (☎ 25-5414; www.kusikay.com; Unión 117; admission S110) Modern dance, wild costumes and ancient culture collide in Cuzco's own Broadway-style spectacular, which is highly recommended by all who see it.

The **Centro Qosqo de Arte Nativo** (☎ 22-7901; Av El Sol 604; admission with boleto turístico) has live nightly performances of Andean music and dance at 6:45pm.

SHOPPING

San Blas – the plaza itself, Cuesta San Blas, Carmen Alto, and Tandapata east of the plaza – offers Cuzco's best shopping. It's the artisan quarter, packed with the workshops and showrooms of local craftspeople. Some offer the chance to watch artisans at work and see the interiors of colonial buildings while hunting down that perfect souvenir. Prices and quality vary greatly, so shop around and expect to bargain, except in the most expensive stores, where prices are often fixed. Some of the best-known include **Taller Olave** (☎ 23-1835; Plaza San Blas 651), which sells reproductions of colonial sculptures and pre-colonial ceramics. **Taller Mendivil** (☎ 23 3247); San Blas (Cuesta de San Blas, Plaza San Blas); city center (cnr Hatunrumiyoc and Choquechaca) is nationally famous for its giraffe-necked

---

BRICHEROS

The local manifestation of a common tourist-town phenomenon, the *brichero* is a parasite on the gringa (female foreigner). He seduces her as quickly and directly as possible and then shamelessly eats, lives and travels off her for as long as she allows. (We say 'he' and 'her', but they're not all men: there are also female *bricheras* out there hunting men, and gay male Peruvians targeting gay gringos.)

Yes, to put it bluntly, *bricheros* are pretty much prostitutes. If you know this, and still choose to go there, fine – we're all consenting adults, and casual sex while traveling is nothing new. Just don't take the mushy stuff too seriously. In Latin cultures it's common to talk of love far more than in Western cultures; the *brichero* doesn't really expect you to believe his high-flown sentiments, and may genuinely not understand why you get upset when you find out he has two other gringa girlfriends, not to mention a Peruvian wife and kids.

Here are some common identifying features:

- he talks about the mysterious *energía* (energy) of the *apus* (mountain gods) and his Inca ancestor
- he tries to sell you drugs
- he tries to kiss you within half an hour of meeting you
- he buys you a drink within five minutes, then never again spends a cent in your presence
- he works as a musician or jewelry maker

Please don't think that everyone who meets this description, or any man who shows an interest in you, is necessarily trying to make off with your life savings. Just remember, if it seems too good to be true, it probably is.

religious figures and sun-shaped mirrors, and **Taller and Museo Mérida** (☎ 22-1714; Carmen Alto 133) offers striking earthenware statues that straddle the border between craft and art.

The same area is also home to an ever-evolving sprinkling of jewelry stores and quirky, one-off designer-clothes stores – a refreshing reminder that the local aesthetic is not confined to stridently colored ponchos and sheepskin-rug depictions of Machu Picchu. These and other mass-produced tourist tat from textiles to teapots are sold from pretty much every hole-in-the-wall in the historic center, and at the vast **Centro Artesenal Cuzco** (cnr Avs El Sol & Tullumayo; ☉ 9am-10pm).

If you're the type who likes to get your souvenir shopping done fast, **Aymi Wasi** (Nueva Alta s/n) is for you. It's got *everything* – clothes, ornaments, toys, candles, jewelry, art, ceramics, handbags… Your friends and family will never suspect you bought all their gifts in one place! And it's all handmade and fair trade.

Cuzco is not known for its clothes shopping opportunities, though there are a few cool stores hidden away in the **Centro Comercial de Cuzco** (cnr Ayacucho & San Andrés; ☉ 11am-10pm).

Tatoo (☎ 25-4211; Calle del Medio 130; ☉ 9am-9:30pm) has brand-name outdoor clothing and technical gear at high prices. Many shops in Calle Plateros and Mercado El Molino (see right) have a good range of lower-quality, far cheaper gear.

Textiles

Centro de Textiles Tradicionales del Cuzco (☎ 22-8117; www.textilescusco.org; Av El Sol 603A; ☉ 7:30am-8:30pm Mon-Sat, 8:30am-8:30pm Sun) This nonprofit organization, founded in 1996, promotes the survival of traditional weaving. You may be able to catch a shop-floor demonstration illustrating different weaving techniques in all their finger-twisting complexity.

Shop of the Weavers of the Southern Andes (☎ 26-0942; inside CBC, Tullumayo 274; ☉ 9am-noon & 3-6pm Mon-Sat) is a cooperative run by 12 mountain communities from Cuzco and Apurimac.

Casa Ecológica (☎ 25-5646; Triunfo 393; ☉ 9am-9pm Mon-Sun) Handmade textiles from 29 communities as far away as Ausangate, plus homemade jams and essential oils – a little slice of hippie heaven.

Markets

For many travelers, markets are a highlight of South America. If you're one of them, have no fear, Cuzco won't let you down. Keep your wits about you and don't bring valuables; professional pickpockets work them all.

Mercado San Pedro, Cuzco's central market, is a must-see. Pig heads for *caldo* (soup), frogs (to enhance sexual performance), vats of fruit juice, roast *lechón* (suckling pig) and tamales are just a few of the foods on offer. Around the edges are typical clothes, spells, incense and other random products to keep you entertained for hours.

Less touristed, and just as interesting, is the **Mercado Modelo de Huanchac** (cnr Avs Garcilaso & Huascar). It's the local destination of choice for breakfast the morning after, specializing in the two hangover staples – jolting acid ceviche and greasy *chicharrones*.

El Molino, just beyond the *terminal terrestre*, is Cuzco's answer to the department store. Even more congested than San Pedro, it's a bargain hunter's paradise for clothes, housewares, bulk food and alcohol, *electrodomésticos* (electronic goods), camping gear, and pirated CDs and DVDs.

GETTING THERE & AWAY
Air

Most flights from Cuzco's **Aeropuerto Internacional Alejandro Velasco Astete** (CUZ; ☎ 22-2611) are in the morning, because climatic conditions in the afternoon typically make landings and takeoffs more difficult. If you have a tight connection, it's best to reserve the earliest flight available, as later ones are more likely to be delayed or canceled.

Several airlines offer daily flights to and from Lima, Juliaca, Puerto Maldonado and Arequipa. Check in at least two hours before your flight – even people with confirmed seats and boarding passes have been denied boarding because of overbooking errors. During the rainy season, flights in and out of Puerto Maldonado are often seriously delayed.

The only international destination is La Paz, in Bolivia, with AeroSur, on Tuesday, Thursday and Sunday.

Departure tax is $12.77 for domestic flights and $35.50 for international flights.

The following airlines serve Cuzco:

AeroSur (☎ 25-4691; www.aerosur.com; Av El Sol 948, office 120; ☉ 9am-1pm & 3-7pm Mon-Fri, 9am-1pm Sat)
LAN (☎ 25-5555; www.lan.com; Av El Sol 627B; ☉ 8:30am-7pm Mon-Sat, to 1pm Sun)
Star Perú (☎ 01-705-9000; www.starperu.com; Av El Sol 679; ☉ 9am-1pm & 3-6:30pm Mon-Sat, 9am-12:30pm Sun)
TACA (☎ 0800-18-2222; www.taca.com; Av El Sol 602)

Helicusco (☎ in Lima 01-993-52-6251; www.helicusco .com), which has an office in Cuzco's airport, offers scenic helicopter flights between Cuzco, Machu Picchu, Choquequirau and the Sacred Valley.

Bus & Taxi

The journey times given here are only approximate and apply only if road conditions are good. Long delays are likely during the rainy season, particularly going to Puerto Maldonado or, to a lesser extent, towards Lima via Abancay. This road is now all paved, but landslides can block the road in the rainy season.

INTERNATIONAL

All international services depart from the **terminal terrestre** (☎ 22-4471, Vía de Evitamiento 429), about 2km out of town towards the airport. It's a relatively pleasant walk: once Av El Sol turns into Alameda Pachacutec, you can walk in the pedestrian *paseo* in the middle of the road. Straight after you pass the tower and statue of Pachacutec, turn right, following the railway lines into a side street, which brings you to the terminal in five minutes.

To get to Bolivia, catch **Littoral** (☎ 24-8989), **Real Turismo** (☎ 24-3540), or **San Luis** (☎ 22-3647) to La Paz (S60 to S80, 18 hours) via Copacabana (S50 to S70, 13 hours); all depart at 10pm. **Tour Peru** (☎ 24-9977, www.tourperu.com.pe) offers the best value service to Copacabana, departing at 8am daily. **CIAL** (☎ in Lima 01-330-4225) departs at 10:30pm for La Paz via Desaguadero (S70, 12 hours). This is the quickest way to get to La Paz.

Ormeño (☎ 26-1704; www.grupo-ormeno.com.pe) offers fares to most South American capitals.

LONG DISTANCE

Buses to major cities leave from the *terminal terrestre*. Buses for more unusual destinations leave from elsewhere, so check carefully in advance.

Ormeño (☎ 26-1704; www.grupo-ormeno.com.pe) and **Cruz del Sur** (☎ 22-1909; www.cruzdelsur.com.pe) have the safest and most comfortable buses across the board. Of the cheaper companies, **Wari** (☎ 22-2694) and especially Tour Peru have the best buses.

There are departures to Juliaca (five to six hours) and Puno (six to seven hours) every hour from 7am to 10pm, and at random hours through the day. Cheap (S20), slow options include **Power** (☎ 22-7777) and **Libertad** (☎ 43-

2955); these stop to let passengers on and off along the way, so you can use them to access towns along the route. **Littoral** (☎ 24-8989) and **CIAL** (☎ in Lima 01-330-4225) are faster and more comfortable (S30 to S40).

The most enjoyable way to get to Puno is with **Inka Express** (☎ 24-7887; www.inkaexpress.com; Av La Paz C32, El Óvalo) or **Turismo Mer** (☎ 24-5171; www.turismomer.com; Av La Paz A3, El Óvalo), which run luxury buses every morning. The service includes lunch and an English-speaking tour guide, who talks about the four sites that are briefly visited along the way: Andahuaylillas, Raqchi, Abra la Raya and Pucará. The trip takes about eight hours and costs US$35 to US$45 if you buy direct, but you may well be able to persuade a travel agency to cut into its commission and sell you a ticket for less.

Departures to Arequipa (S25 to S30, nine hours) cluster around 6am to 7am and 7pm to 9:30pm. Ormeño has a superexpensive (S70), comfortable service at 9am.

Cruz del Sur, **CIVA** (☎ 24-9961; www.civa.com .pe) and **Celtur** (☎ 23-6075) offer relatively painless services to Lima (S80 to S160 – you pay more for a fully reclining seat, 18 hours). Wari (S60, 22 hours) is the best of the cheaper options. Most buses to Lima stop in Nazca (12 hours) and Ica (14 hours). These buses go via Abancay and can suffer holdups in rainy season. Between January and April, it may be worth going via Arequipa (25 to 27 hours) instead.

Buses depart every couple of hours through the day for Abancay (S15, four hours) and Andahuaylas (S30, 10 hours). Celtur has slightly nicer buses than other companies on this route. Change at Andahuaylas to get to Ayacucho via rough roads that get very cold at night. If you're going to Ayacucho by bus, wear all of your warm clothes and if you have a sleeping bag, bring it onboard the bus.

San Martín (☎ 984-61-2520) and **Expreso Sagitário** (☎ 22-9757) offer direct buses to Tacna (S70, 17 hours). Expreso Sagitário also goes to Arequipa and Lima, and may be more open to bargaining than other companies.

Various companies depart for Puerto Maldonado between 3pm and 4:30pm; CIVA (S60, 17 hours, departs 4pm) is probably the best option. Don't even consider catching the bus to Puerto Maldonado during the rainy season unless you have at least a week to spare.

At time of research, the road was being paved as it will be part of the Interoceánica, a highway that will unite the east and west coasts of South America for the first time. Once this is completed, road access to Puerto Maldonado will become much less taxing.

Buses to Quillabamba (S15, six to seven hours) via Santa María leave from the Santiago terminal, a brisk 20-minute walk from the center. Around the corner in Calle Antonio Lorena, many more companies offer air-conditioned, speedy comfort in the form of modern minivans that cost twice as much and cut a couple of hours off the trip. There are departures of both types of service at 8am, 10am, 1pm and 8pm. Change at Santa María to get to Santa Teresa.

Transportes Siwar (☎ 23-6691; Av Tito Condemayta 1613) has buses to Ocongate and Tinqui (S8, three hours) leaving from behind the Coliseo Cerrado several times a day.

Transportes Gallito de las Rocas (☎ 22-6895; Diagonal Angamos) buses depart to Paucartambo (S7, five hours) daily and to Pilcopata (S18) Monday, Wednesday and Friday. To find the office, look for 'Paucartambo' painted on a lamp post between auto shops. It's on the first block off Av de la Cultura.

REGIONAL SERVICES

Minibuses to Calca (S4, 1½ hours) via Pisac (S3, one hour) leave frequently from the terminal at Tullumayo 207.

Minibuses to Urubamba (S3.50, 1½ hours) via Pisac (S2.40, one hour) leave frequently from the terminal in Puputi, just north of Av de la Cultura.

Minibuses to Urubamba (S3.50, 1½ hrs) and Ollantaytambo (S5, two hours) via Chinchero (one hour) leave from near the Puente Grau. Just around the corner in Pavitos, faster *colectivos* leave when full for Urubamba (S6, one hour) and Ollantaytambo (S10, 1½ hours) via Chinchero.

Colectivos to Urcos (S8) via Tipón (S3), Piquillacta (S5) and Andahuaylillas (S7) leave from the middle of the street outside Tullumayo 207. For S80 they'll drive you into the ruins at Tipón and Piquillacta, wait and bring you back.

You can also get to these places, and Saylla, by catching a minibus headed for Urcos (S8) from a terminal just off Av de la Cultura opposite the regional hospital. Buses to Lucre (S2.50, one hour) depart from Huascar,

between Av Garcilaso and Manco Capac, between 7am and 7pm.

Minibuses for Limatambo (S8, 1½ hrs) and Curahuasi (S11, 2½ hours) leave Arcopata a couple of blocks west of Meloc when they fill, until about 3pm.

Unless otherwise stated, these services run from at least 5am until 7pm.

Car & Motorcycle

Given all the headaches and potential hazards of driving yourself around, consider hiring a taxi for the day – it's cheaper than renting a car. If you must, you'll find a couple of car-rental agencies in the bottom block of Av El Sol. Motorcycle rentals are offered by a couple of agencies in the first block of Saphi heading away from the Plaza de Armas.

Train

Cuzco has two train stations. **Estación Huanchac** (☎ 58-1414; ◷ 7am-5pm Mon-Fri, to midnight Sat & Sun), near the end of Av El Sol, serves Juliaca and Puno on Lake Titicaca. Estación Poroy, east of town, serves Ollantaytambo and Machu Picchu. The two stations are unconnected, so it's impossible to travel directly from Puno to Machu Picchu. (Downtown Estación San Pedro is used only for local trains, which foreigners cannot board.)

A tourist bus to Estación Poroy departs every day at 6:15am from Av Pardo (S6). The bus also meets returning trains, dropping passengers off in Plaza Regocijo. You can also get to Poroy by taxi – S30 for a radio cab, S15 off the street.

You can buy tickets at Huanchac station, and there are ATMs in the station, but the easiest way is directly through **PeruRail** (www.perurail.com).

Over many years of monopolistic bad behavior as the only transport provider on the only route to Machu Picchu, PeruRail earned a bad name. It now seems to be smelling the winds of change, as competing operators get serious about getting started, and the alternative Santa Teresa route gives tourists a different option. Stations have been spruced up, the website is user-friendly and up-to-date, and, yes – the trains run on time.

TO OLLANTAYTAMBO AND MACHU PICCHU

To get to Aguas Calientes from Cuzco by train takes about three hours, and you have two options. The Vistadome service costs S227.20 each way. It leaves Cuzco at 7am each day and returns at 3.25pm. The Hiram

Bingham costs S1881.60 and includes brunch, afternoon tea, entrance to Machu Picchu and a guided tour. It departs Poroy at the civilized hour of 9am and gets you back there at 9pm, and gives you three to four hours at Machu Picchu. It runs daily except Sunday.

The cheapest and quickest way to get from Cuzco to Aguas Calientes is to take a *combi* to Ollantaytambo and catch the train from there (for more details, see p266).

TO PUNO

This train ride retains a certain residual renown from the days, now long gone, when the road wasn't paved and the bus journey was a nightmare.

Train fares have skyrocketed in recent years and most travelers now take the bus. The fancy Andean Explorer train, which includes a glass-walled observation car and complimentary lunch, costs S704 – there's no cheaper option. The train tracks run next to the road for most of the way, so there's not a huge difference in scenery, and the train is only marginally more comfortable than the better buses, so unless you're a train buff, there seems little reason to spend the extra S600. Trains depart from Estación Huanchac at 8am, arriving at Puno around 6pm, on Monday, Wednesday and Saturday from November to March, with an extra departure on Friday from April to October.

GETTING AROUND
To/From the Airport

The airport is about 6km south of the city center. The *combi* lines Imperial and C4M (S0.60, 20 minutes) run from Av El Sol to just outside the airport. A taxi to or from the city center to the airport costs S5. An official radio taxi from within the airport costs S10. With advance reservations, many hotels offer free pickup.

Bus

Local rides on public transportation cost only S0.60, though it's easier to walk or just take a taxi than to figure out where any given *combi* is headed.

Taxi

There are no meters in taxis, but there are set rates. At time of research, trips within the city center cost S2.50, and to destinations further afield, such as El Molino, were S3.

Check with your hotel whether this is still correct, and rather than negotiate, simply hand the correct amount to your driver at the end of your ride; he is unlikely to argue if you seem to know what you're doing. Official taxis, identified by a lit company telephone number on the roof, are more expensive than taxis flagged down on the street, but they are safer. **AloCusco** (☎ 22-2222) is a reliable company to call. Unofficial 'pirate' taxis, which only have a taxi sticker in the window, have been complicit in muggings, violent assaults and kidnappings of tourists. Before getting into any taxi, do as savvy locals do and take conspicuous note of the registration number.

Tram

The Tranvia is a free-rolling tourist tram that conducts a 1½ hour hop-on, hop-off city tour (S15). It leaves at 8:30am, 10am, 11:30am, 2pm, 3:30pm, 5pm and 6:30pm from the Plaza de Armas.

AROUND CUZCO

The four ruins closest to Cuzco are Sacsaywamán, Q'enqo, Pukapukara and Tambomachay. They can all be visited in a day – far less if you're whisked through on a guided tour. If you only have time to visit one site, Sacsaywamán is the most important, and less than a 2km trek uphill from the Plaza de Armas in central Cuzco.

Each site can only be entered with the *boleto turístico* (p229). They're open daily from 7am to 6pm.

The cheapest way to visit the sites is to take a bus bound for Pisac and ask the driver to get off at Tambomachay, the furthest site from Cuzco and, at 3700m, the highest. It's an 8km walk back to Cuzco, visiting all four ruins along the way. Alternatively, a taxi will charge roughly S40 to visit all four sites.

Local guides hang around offering their services, sometimes quite persistently. Agree on a price before beginning any tour.

Robberies at these sites are uncommon but not unheard of. Cuzco's tourist police recommend visiting between 9am and 5pm.

SACSAYWAMÁN

This immense ruin of both religious and military significance is the most impressive in the immediate area around Cuzco.

CUZCO & THE SACRED VALLEY

The long Quechua name means 'Satisfied Falcon,' though tourists will inevitably remember it by the mnemonic 'sexy woman.' Sacsaywamán feels huge, but what today's visitor sees is only about 20% of the original structure. Soon after the conquest, the Spaniards tore down many walls and used the blocks to build their own houses in Cuzco, leaving the largest and most impressive rocks, especially those forming the main battlements.

In 1536 the fort was the site of one of the most bitter battles of the Spanish conquest. More than two years after Pizarro's entry into Cuzco, the rebellious Manco Inca recaptured the lightly guarded Sacsaywamán and used it as a base to lay siege to the conquistadors in Cuzco. Manco was on the brink of defeating the Spaniards when a desperate last-ditch attack by 50 Spanish cavalry led by Juan Pizarro, Francisco's brother, succeeded in retaking Sacsaywamán and putting an end to the rebellion. Manco Inca survived and retreated to the fortress of Ollantaytambo, but most of his forces were killed. Thousands of dead littered the site after the Incas' defeat, attracting swarms of carrion-eating Andean condors. The tragedy was memorialized by the inclusion of eight condors in Cuzco's coat of arms.

The site is composed of three different areas, the most striking being the magnificent three-tiered zigzag fortifications. One stone, incredibly, weighs more than 300 tons. It was the ninth *inca*, Pachacutec, who envisioned Cuzco in the shape of a puma, with Sacsaywamán as the head, and these 22 zigzagged walls as the teeth of the puma. The walls also formed an extremely effective defensive mechanism that forced attackers to expose their flanks when attacking.

Opposite is the hill called **Rodadero**, with retaining walls, polished rocks and a finely carved series of stone benches known as the Inca's Throne. Three towers once stood above these walls. Only the foundations remain, but the 22m diameter of the largest, Muyuc Marca, gives an indication of how big they must have been. With its perfectly fitted stone conduits, this tower was probably used as a huge water tank for the garrison. Other buildings within the ramparts provided food and shelter for an estimated 5000 warriors. Most of these structures were torn down by the Spaniards and later inhabitants of Cuzco.

Between the zigzag ramparts and the hill lies a large, flat parade ground that is used for the colorful tourist spectacle of **Inti Raymi**, held every June 24 (p240).

To walk up to the site from the Plaza de Armas takes 30 to 50 minutes, so make sure you're acclimatized before attempting it. Arriving at dawn will let you have the site almost to yourself, though solo travelers shouldn't come alone at this time of day.

Q'ENQO

The name of this small but fascinating ruin means 'Zigzag.' It's a large limestone rock riddled with niches, steps and extraordinary symbolic carvings, including the zigzagging channels that probably gave the site its name. These channels were likely used for the ritual sacrifice of *chicha* or, perhaps, blood. Scrambling up to the top you'll find a flat surface used for ceremonies and, if you look carefully, some laboriously etched representations of a puma, a condor and a llama. Back below you can explore a mysterious subterranean cave with altars hewn into the rock.

Q'enqo is about 4km northeast of Cuzco, on the left of the road as you descend from Tambomachay.

PUKAPUKARA

Just across the main road from Tambomachay is this commanding structure looking down on the Cuzco valley. In some lights the rock looks pink, and the name literally means 'Red Fort,' though it is more likely to have been a hunting lodge, a guard post and a stopping point for travelers. It is composed of several lower residential chambers, storerooms and an upper esplanade with panoramic views.

TAMBOMACHAY

In a sheltered spot about 300m from the main road, this site consists of a beautifully wrought ceremonial stone bath channeling crystalline spring water through fountains that still function today. It is thus popularly known as El Baño del Inca (The Bath of the Inca), and theories connect the site to an Inca water cult. Pukapukara can be seen from the small signaling post opposite.

THE SACRED VALLEY

The beautiful Río Urubamba valley, popularly known as El Valle Sagrado (The Sacred Valley), is about 15km north of Cuzco as the condor flies. The star attractions are the lofty Inca citadels of Pisac and Ollantaytambo, which preside over its undulating twists and turns, but the valley is also packed with other Inca sites, as well as hectic markets and fetching Andean villages. It's famous for some high-adrenaline activities, from rafting to trekking to rock climbing. Most activities can be organized in Cuzco or at some hotels in Urubamba.

A multitude of travel agencies in Cuzco offer whirlwind tours of the Sacred Valley, stopping at markets and the most significant archaeological sites, but even if you only have a day or two to spare, it's immeasurably rewarding to explore this peaceful, often overlooked corner of the Andes at your own leisure. Visiting the archaeological sites of Pisac, Ollantaytambo and Chinchero requires a *boleto turístico* (p229), which can be bought directly from the guards at the sites.

PISAC

☎ 084 / pop 900 / elev 2715m

Lying 33km northeast of Cuzco by paved road, Pisac is the most convenient starting point for a visit to the Sacred Valley. There are two distinct parts to Pisac (also spelled Pisaq): the colonial village lying beside the river and the Inca fortress perched dramatically on a mountain spur above.

Information

There's an ATM in the Plaza de Armas. There are slow cybercafes around the plaza and a mini-supermarket on Bolognesi.

Sights & Activities

Pisac is known far and wide for its **craft market**, by far the biggest and most touristy in the region. Official market days are Tuesday, Thursday and Sunday, when tourist buses descend on the town in droves. However, the market has taken over Pisac to such an extent that it fills the Plaza de Armas and surrounding streets every day; visit on Monday, Wednesday, Friday or Saturday if you want to avoid the worst of the crowds.

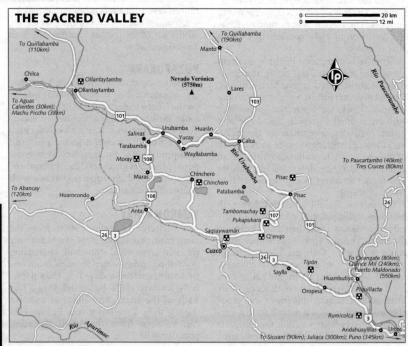

THE SACRED VALLEY

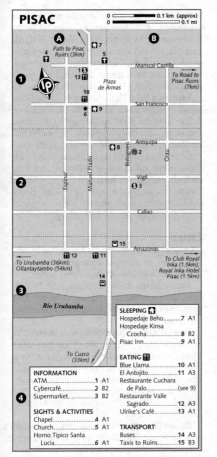

PISAC

Path to Pisac Ruins (3km)

To Road to Pisac Ruins (7km)

Plaza de Armas

Mariscal Castilla

San Francisco

Arequipa

Vigil

Callao

Amazonas

To Urubamba (36km); Ollantaytambo (54km)

To Club Royal Inka (1.5km); Royal Inka Hotel Pisac (1.5km)

Río Urubamba

To Cuzco (33km)

INFORMATION		
ATM	1	A1
Cybercafé	2	B2
Supermarket	3	B2

SIGHTS & ACTIVITIES		
Chapel	4	A1
Church	5	A1
Horno Tipico Santa Lucia	6	A1

SLEEPING		
Hospedaje Beho	7	A1
Hospedaje Kinsa Ccocha	8	B2
Pisac Inn	9	A1

EATING		
Blue Llama	10	A1
El Antojito	11	A3
Restaurante Cuchara de Palo	(see 9)	
Restaurante Valle Sagrado	12	A3
Ulrike's Café	13	A1

TRANSPORT		
Buses	14	A3
Taxis to Ruins	15	B3

Huge clay ovens for baking empanadas and other goodies and *castillos de cuyes* (miniature castles inhabited by guinea pigs) are found in many nooks and crannies, particularly in Mariscál Castilla. **Horno Típico de Santa Lucia** (Manuel Prado s/n) unites both of these with an *artesanía* (crafts) shop. If, for some strange reason, you only have five minutes in Pisac, spend it here – you'll get a pretty good feel for the place.

At time of research, the INC (Instituto Nacional de Cultura), in a characteristically controversial move, had demolished the **church** in the main square in order to reconstruct it in colonial style. Masses have moved to a nearby chapel and are worth tracking down. If you're around on a Sunday, hang around just before 11am, when Mass is celebrated in Quechua. Traditionally dressed locals descend from the hills to attend, including men in traditional highland dress blowing horns and *varayocs* (local authorities) with silver staffs of office.

Club Royal Inka, about 1.5km out of town, is a fabulous place to while away an afternoon. For S10 admission, you get to swim in the be-fountained Olympic-sized indoor pool, lounge around any number of grassy areas, and pose by the ornamental duck pond. There's also a restaurant, a trout pond and facilities for barbecues, billiards, table tennis, volleyball, tennis and *sapo* (see p250).

PISAC RUINS

This hilltop **Inca citadel** (admission with boleto turístico; ☼ dawn-dusk) lies high above the village on a triangular plateau with a plunging gorge on either side. Though it's a truly awesome site, you'll see relatively few tourists here, except midmorning on Sunday, Tuesday and Thursday, when it becomes flooded with tour groups.

To get here, either walk up the steep but spectacular 4km trail from town, or hire a taxi from near the bridge into town to drive you up the 7.5km paved road (S20 one way, or S25 return with two hours' waiting time).

Walking takes about two hours up and 1½ hours back. It's highly worthwhile, but undeniably grueling – steeper than, and recommended training for, the Inca Trail! Taking a taxi up and walking back is a good option.

The footpath to the site starts from above the west side of the church. There are many crisscrossing trails, but if you keep heading upward toward the terracing, you won't get lost. To the west, or the left of the hill as you climb up on the footpath, is the Río Kitamayo gorge; to the east, or right, is the Río Chongo valley.

The most impressive thing about the Pisac ruins is the agricultural **terracing**, which sweeps around the south and east flanks of the mountain in huge and graceful curves, almost entirely unbroken by steps (which require greater maintenance and promote erosion). Instead, the terracing is joined by diagonal flights of stairs made of flagstones set into the terrace walls. Above the terraces are cliff-hugging footpaths, watched over by caracara falcons and well defended by massive stone doorways, steep stairs and a short

CUZCO & THE SACRED VALLEY

tunnel carved out of the rock. Vendors meet you at the top with drinks, and after carrying the bottles this far, they certainly deserve to make a few soles.

This dominating site guards not only the Urubamba valley below, but also a pass leading into the jungle to the northeast. Topping the terraces is the site's **ceremonial center**, with an *intihuatana* (literally 'hitching post of the sun'; an Inca astronomical tool), several working water channels, and some painstakingly neat masonry in the well-preserved **temples**. A path leads up the hillside to a series of ceremonial baths and around to the military area. Looking across the Kitamayo gorge from the back of the site, you'll also see hundreds of holes honeycombing the cliff wall. These are **Inca tombs** that were plundered by *huaqueros* (grave robbers), and are now completely off-limits to tourists.

The site is large and warrants several hours of your time.

Festivals & Events

Pisac is renowned for its celebration of **La Virgen del Carmen** in mid-July. Pisac or Paucartambo (see p293) are the places to be from around July 15 to July 18.

Sleeping

Cheap guesthouses are scattered on and around the main plaza. There are several foreign-run, boutique, mystical/spiritual retreats on the outskirts of town.

Hospedaje Beho (☎ 20-3001; hospedajebeho@yahoo .es; Intihuatana 113; r per person with/without bathroom S30/15) On the path to the ruins, this family-run handicrafts shop offers no-frills lodging with warm showers. The raggedy, rambling garden is a tranquil haven from the madness of the market streets just outside.

Club Royal Inka (☎ 20-3064, 20-3066; camping per person S20) Camping doesn't get any better than this. For S20, you get to pitch a tent in your own designated, fenced-off site with a fireplace, a light and a power plug, and enjoy all the amenities of the club (see p259), including the Olympic-size pool.

Hospedaje Kinsa Ccocha (☎ 20-3110; Arequipa 307A; r per person with/without bathroom S40/30) Rustic and gently colorful, with a fertile fig tree in its stony patio, this laid-back place close to the plaza has a nice vibe and lots of thoughtful touches, such as plenty of power plugs and hot water in sinks, not just showers.

Pisac Inn (☎ 20-3062; www.pisacinn.com; Plaza Constitución; d with/without bathroom S150/120) Recognizable by its funky geometric designs, this plaza hotel has a pretty courtyard and rustic rooms with hand-painted, indigenous-inspired murals. German, English and French are spoken. Rates include breakfast.

Royal Inka Hotel Pisac (☎ 20-3064, 20-3066; www .royalinkahotel.com; s/d with breakfast S187/270; ☒) About 1.5km from the plaza up the road to the ruins, this large converted hacienda is impressive but endearingly un-splendid – more comfy than commanding. Rooms are generous, many with views of the ruins, and it's all surrounded by lovingly kept flower beds and conservatories. Guests can access the facilities of Club Royal Inka across the road, plus the on-site spa and Jacuzzi. A highly worthwhile splurge.

Eating

El Antojito (☎ 79-7525; menú S3.50; Amazonas s/n; ☺ 7am-9pm) Offers an exemplary bargain *menú* – it's one of the best deals in the Sacred Valley.

Restaurante Valle Sagrado (☎ 20-3009; menú S8-15; Amazonas s/n; ☺ lunch & dinner) The *menú* here is somewhat fancier and more foreigner friendly.

Blue Llama (Plaza Constitución; www.bluellamacafe .com; menú S18.50, mains from S10; ☺ 9am-9pm) Blue Llama's surreal, dreamlike interior with a children's-story theme is inviting enough. Happy staff, unusually Western-minded vegetarian dishes (steamed vegetables!), desserts to die for, and some funky jewelry and clothes on sale make it irresistible.

Ulrike's Café (☎ 20-3195; Plaza Constitución; veg/meat menú S17/20, mains from S11; ☺ 9am-9pm) This sunny cafe serves up a great vegetarian *menú*, plus homemade pastas and melt-in-the-mouth cheesecake and brownies. There's a book exchange, DVDs and special events such as yoga classes. English, French and German are spoken.

Restaurante Cuchara de Palo (☎ 20-3062; Plaza Constitución; mains S25; ☺ 7am-9pm) This cozy, classy place inside Pisac Inn offers the finest dining available in downtown Pisac, and very fine it is too. It offers the sorts of interesting combinations – like quinoa in the style of Chinese fried rice – that give *cocina novoandina* (New Andean cuisine) a good name.

Getting There & Away

Buses to Urubamba (S2, one hour) and Cuzco (S2.70, one hour) leave frequently from the downtown bridge between 6am and 8pm. Many travel agencies in Cuzco also operate tour buses to Pisac, especially on market days.

PISAC TO URUBAMBA

Between Pisac and Urubamba is a series of pretty villages (as well as the large-ish, untouristed and fairly uninteresting town of Calca), which can easily be explored in a day. **Yucay** and **Huarán** offer boutique accommodation and food options, and make excellent bases for leisurely exploration of the safe, scenic Sacred Valley and its many intriguing side valleys.

The **Patabamba community tourism association** (☎ 984-78-4368) offers a fascinating participative demonstration of the weaving process, all the way from picking the plants to making dyes, to shearing sheep and setting up a loom – with explanations of the meanings of colors and patterns. Campsites and homestays are available with advance notice. To get here, hire a taxi from Cuzco for about S30 each way. **Chaski Ventura** (☎ 23-3952; www.chaskiventura .com; Manco Cápac 517) also offers a day trip.

URUBAMBA

☎ 084 / pop 2700 / elev 2870m

Urubamba is an unavoidable transport hub whose relatively low altitude and proximity to Machu Picchu has made it popular with package tours. Hotels and restaurants here are mostly geared towards large groups with their own transport. Urubamba offers little of historical interest but it is surrounded by beautiful countryside, enjoys great weather and makes a convenient base from which to explore the extraordinary Salinas and the terracing of Moray.

Orientation & Information

Urubamba is quite spread out, so expect to do a lot of walking or pay for *mototaxis* (three-wheeled motorcycle rickshaw taxis). A standard *mototaxi* ride around town costs S1. The bus terminal is about 1km west of town on the highway. The Plaza de Armas is five blocks east and four blocks north of the terminal, and is bounded by Calle Comercio and Jirón Grau. However, most hotels and restaurants are on or near the highway. **Banco de la Nación** (Mariscal Castilla s/n) changes US dollars. There are ATMs at the *grifo* (gas station) on the corner of the highway and the main street, Mariscal Castilla, and along the highway to its east.

Clínica Pardo (☎ 984-10-8948), on the highway a couple of blocks west of the *grifo*, offers medical attention.

Activities

Many outdoor activities that are organized from Cuzco (see p237) take place near Urubamba, including horseback riding, via-ferrata rock climbing, mountain biking, paragliding and hot-air balloon trips.

Perol Chico (☎ 984-62-4475; www.perolchico .com), run by Dutch-Peruvian Eduard van Brunschot Vega, has an excellent ranch outside Urubamba with Peruvian *paso* horses. Eduard organizes horseback-riding tours that last up to two weeks; a one-day trip to Moray and Salinas costs roughly US$150. Advance bookings are required.

Cusco for you (☎ 79-5301; www.cuscoforyou.com) offers horseback-riding and trekking trips from one to eight days long. A one-day horse trip to Moray and Salinas costs about US$89.

Sleeping

There are very few places to stay in the city center. Most hotels are lined up along the highway, west of town and the bus terminal, on the way to Ollantaytambo.

BUDGET

Los Cedros (☎ 20-1416; www.campingloscedros.com; campsites per person S9, house from S300) This pastoral campground is about 4km above the town on winding country roads. There's also a fully furnished two-story house for hire in the grassy grounds. Sometimes hippies and electronic-music lovers converge here for open-air Full Moon parties.

ourpick Hostal los Perales (☎ 20-1151; Pasaje Arenales 102; s/d/tr S20/35/60) Tucked away up a dusty country lane near the bus terminal, family-run Los Perales is a hidden treasure. Behind its high wall lies a romantic overgrown orchard, where you could lose yourself for days. Rooms are basic but sunny and spotless, the owners are genuinely kind and caring, and English is spoken. Highly recommended.

Quinta los Geranios (☎ 20-1093; geraniosurubamba@ yahoo.com; Conchatupa s/n; s/d/tr/q S45/60/70/105) Los Geranios has airy, spotless rooms and a breathtaking river view from its open-air staircase. Both the hotel and on-site restaurant (mains from S13), open noon to 5pm, are popular and good value.

MIDRANGE

Las Chullpas (☎ 984-68-5713; www.chullpas.uhupi
.com; Pumahuanca Valley; s/d/tr/q S80/130/280/200; 🖳)
Hidden 3km above town, these woodland cottages with fireplaces and private bathrooms
make for the perfect getaway. The site is nestled beneath a mountain and thick eucalyptus
trees. There are hammocks, an open kitchen
where vegetarian food is available, and a sweat
lodge (available on request). Much of the food
served is grown organically at the hotel's own
minifarm, and efforts are made towards com-
posting and recycling. The affable Chilean
owner also guides treks, especially to the Lares
Valley. Highly recommended.

Quinta Patawasi (☎ 20-1386; www.quintapatawasi
.com; s/d/tr/q S115/255/330/405; 🖳) On a small street
right behind Hostal el Maizal, Quinta is a characterful spot recommended for its extremely
cheerful, attentive service. English is spoken.

Hostal el Maizal (☎ 20-1194; maizal@speedy.com
.pe; r from S160; 🖳) West of the bus terminal just
past Km 73, El Maizal is a quiet place with
a large grassy garden, comfortable, slightly
shabby rooms and airy bathrooms. German
and English are spoken.

TOP END

K'uychi Rumi (☎ 20-1169; www.urubamba.com; d/q
S470/810; 🖳) Between Km 74 and Km 75 on
the main highway, more than 2km west of
town, you'll find a half-dozen rustic two-story
private cottages built of colorful clay. Each
comes with its own kitchenette, fireplace, terrace balcony and two bedrooms. Buffet breakfast costs US$5. The name means 'Rainbow
Stone' in Quechua.

Río Sagrado Hotel (☎ 20-1631; www.riosagrado
hotel.com; s/d US$600/800, 3-bedroom villa US$3500; 🖳)
Beverly Hills meets St Tropez meets…some-
thing else incredibly luxurious. This place
has to be seen to be believed. Brand-new and
dripping with designer features, it nestles into
the riverside, its modest, jasmine-smelling,
water-tinkling exterior coyly downplaying
the opulence within. On top of all the luxury you'd expect at this price, rooms boast
showers with picture windows, underfloor
heating, handmade designer furniture, and
high-modern minimalist elegance. Public
facilities include two Jacuzzis, an electric
sauna, a woven marble bar, sculptures by well-
known artists, and – wait for it – breakfast in
a hot-air balloon suspended above the lawn.
Headshakingly fabulous.

Eating & Drinking

Many hotels have buffet-style restaurants
that are filled by tour groups, and there are
a few touristic *quintas* (houses serving typical Andean food) along the highway east of
the *grifo*.

our pick Tres Keros Restaurant Grill & Bar
(☎ 20-1701; cnr hwy & Señor de Torrechayoc; mains from
S26; 🕑 lunch & dinner) Garrulous chef Ricardo
Behar dishes up rich, flavorful *novoandina*
fare to pique any gourmet's interest. He also
smokes his own trout and imports steak from
Argentina – he's serious about his food, and
you will be too after you try it. It's 500m west
of town.

Huacatay (☎ 20-1790; Arica 620; mains from
S30; 🕑 1-9:30pm Mon-Sat) Hidden behind a
grey wall down a side street, Huacatay is
worth hunting down. Peruvian food with
Italian overtones goes down a treat, and
is served by hushed, unctuous waiters
in a cozy dining-room decorated in various shades of brown. An old-fashioned
dining experience with some seriously
good, though extremely heavy, food –
the lightest vegetarian option, for example,
is stir-fried vegetables in creamy mushroom
sauce, served in a phyllo-pastry basket. With
creamy mashed potato. And cheese.

La Alhambra (☎ 20-1200; buffet US$18; 🕑 11:30am-
3:30pm) This *novoandina* buffet place 2km west
of town is the place to be if you're hungry. Set
amid charming gardens where pet alpacas
roam, it serves up a dazzling array of *cuzqueño*
dishes, stylishly done. Saving room for dessert,
though difficult, is worthwhile – the *sauco*
(Andean blackberry) cheesecake deserves
your stomach space.

Shopping

Internationally known local potter Pablo
Seminario creates original work with a pre-
conquest influence. His workshop, **Seminario
Cerámicas** (☎ 20-1002; www.ceramicaseminario.com;
Berriozabal 405; 🕑 8am-7pm) – actually a small
factory – is open to the public and offers
a well-organized tour through the entire
ceramics process.

Getting There & Away

Urubamba serves as the valley's principal
transportation hub. Every 15 minutes buses
leave the terminal on the main highway
about 1km west of town for Cuzco (S3.50,
two hours) via Pisac (S2, one hour) or

Chinchero (S2.50, 50 minutes). Buses (S1.20, 30 minutes) and *colectivos* (S2.50, 30 minutes) to Ollantaytambo leave often from the bus terminal.

SALINAS

This is one of the most spectacular sights in the whole Cuzco area. Thousands of salt pans have been used for salt extraction since Inca times. A hot spring at the top of the valley discharges a small stream of heavily salt-laden water, which is diverted into salt pans and evaporated to produce a salt used for cattle licks. It all sounds very pedestrian but the overall effect is beautiful and surreal.

To get here, cross the Río Urubamba over the bridge in Tarabamba, about 4km down the valley from Urubamba, turn right and follow a footpath along the south bank to a small cemetery, where you turn left and climb up a valley to the **salt pans** (admission S5; ☯ 9am-4:30pm) of Salinas. It's about a 500m uphill hike. A rough dirt road that can be navigated by taxi enters Salinas from above, giving spectacular views. Tour groups visit via this route most days. A taxi from Urubamba to visit Salinas and the nearby Moray costs around S80. You can also walk or bike here from Maras.

CHINCHERO

☎ 084 / pop 900 / elev 3762m

Known to the Incas as the birthplace of the rainbow, this typical Andean village combines Inca ruins with a colonial church, some wonderful mountain views and a colorful Sunday market. Entry to the historic precinct, where the ruins, the church and the museum are all found, requires a *boleto turístico*.

Sights & Activities

The colonial **church** (☯ 8am-5:30pm) is built on Inca foundations and its interior, decked out in merry floral and religious designs, is well worth seeing.

The most extensive **Inca ruins** here consist of terracing. If you start walking away from the village through the terraces on the right-hand side of the valley, you'll also find various rocks carved into seats and staircases.

The small archaeological **museum** (☯ 8am-5pm Tue-Sun) opposite the church, which houses a small collection of unlabeled local archaeological finds – heavy on broken pots – is not worth the extra S7 admission.

On the opposite side of the valley, a clear trail climbs upward before heading north and down to the Río Urubamba valley about four hours away. At the river, the trail turns left and continues to a bridge at **Wayllabamba**, where you can cross. From here, the Sacred Valley road will take you to Calca (turn right, about 13km) or Urubamba (turn left, about 9km). You can flag down any passing bus until midafternoon, or continue walking to **Yucay**, where the trail officially ends. Here there is a colonial church, an Inca ruin, and more than one charming accommodation option.

The Chinchero **markets**, held on Tuesday, Thursday and especially Sunday, are less touristy than those in Pisac and well worth checking out. On Sunday, traditionally dressed locals descend from the hills for the produce market, where the ancient practice of *trueco* (bartering) still takes place; this is a rare opportunity to observe genuine bartering.

There are artisan workshops on every street, the best of which is the **Centro de Textiles Tradicionales** on Manzanares.

Sleeping & Eating

Hospedaje Mi Piuray (☎ 30-6029; Garcilaso 187; s/d/tr/q S30/50/90/120, s without bathroom S25) A helpful, welcoming family hostelry with kitchen access and a sunny courtyard. At time of research a bar was being constructed here, so evenings in Chinchero may be about to get a little more lively.

La Casa de Barro (☎ 30-6031; cnr hwy & Miraflores; s/d/tr/q S105/135/165/195) A romantic or family retreat *par excellence*, with curvy, rambling stairways and nooks, an overgrown garden, and airy, jazzily tasteful rooms with big fluffy quilts. Architect-designed with lots of Italian influence, it's classy at the same time as being playful and colorful. It is also well set up for children, with a playroom and swings.

The restaurants at these two hotels are the only places to eat out in Chinchero.

Getting There & Away

Combis and *colectivos* traveling between Cuzco (S2/S6, one hour) and Urubamba (S2/S6, 30 minutes) stop on the corner of the highway and Calle Manco Capac II; just flag down whatever comes along. They will also drop you off at intermediate points such as the turnoff to Maras.

MORAY AND MARAS

The impressively deep amphitheater-like terracing of **Moray** (admission S10; ☼ dawn to dusk), reached via the small town of **Maras**, is a fascinating spectacle. Different levels of concentric terraces are carved into a huge earthen bowl, each layer of which has its own microclimate, according to how deep into the bowl it is. For this reason, some theorize that the Incas used them as a kind of laboratory to determine the optimal conditions for growing crops of each species. There are three bowls, one of which has been planted with various crops as a kind of living museum.

Though refreshingly off the beaten path, this site is not challenging to reach. Take any transportation bound between Urubamba and Cuzco via Chinchero and ask to be let off at the Maras/Moray turnoff. Taxis usually wait at this turnoff to take tourists to Moray and back for around S30, or both Moray and Salinas and back to the turnoff for around S50. If you're coming in the depths of low season, it's worth calling the **Maras taxi company** (☎ 75-5454, 984-95-6063) to ensure that a taxi is waiting for you at the turnoff. A taxi from Urubamba to visit both Salinas and Moray costs around S80.

You could also tackle the 4km walk to the village of Maras yourself. From there, follow the road another 9km to Moray.

From Maras, you can walk or bike to Salinas, about 6km away. The trail starts behind the church. The Maras taxi company rents out bikes for this purpose – this is a fun, fast, single-track ride.

OLLANTAYTAMBO

☎ 084 / pop 700 / elev 2800m

Dominated by two massive Inca ruins, the quaint village of Ollantaytambo (known to locals and visitors alike as Ollanta) is the best surviving example of Inca city planning, with narrow cobblestone streets that have been continuously inhabited since the 13th century. After the hordes passing through on their way to Machu Picchu die down around late morning, Ollanta is a lovely place to be. It's perfect for wandering the mazy, narrow byways, past stone buildings and babbling irrigation channels, pretending you've stepped back in time. It also offers access to excellent hiking and biking.

There are a couple of internet cafes and ATMs in and around Plaza de Armas.

There are no banks, but several places change money.

Sights & Activities
OLLANTAYTAMBO RUINS

The huge, steep terraces that guard Ollantaytambo's spectacular **Inca ruins** (admission with boleto turístico; ☼ 7am-5pm) mark one of the few places where the Spanish conquistadors lost a major battle. It was to this fortress that the rebellious Manco Inca retreated after his defeat at Sacsaywamán. Then in 1536, Hernando Pizarro (Francisco Pizarro's younger half-brother) led a force of 70 cavalrymen here, supported by large numbers of indigenous and Spanish foot soldiers, in an attempt to capture Manco Inca.

Pizarro's men were showered with arrows, spears and boulders from atop the steep terracing and were unable to climb to the fortress. They were further hampered when Manco Inca, in a brilliant move, flooded the plain below the fortress through previously prepared channels. The Spaniards' horses were bogged down in the water and Pizarro ordered a hasty retreat – which almost became a rout when the conquistadors were followed down the valley by thousands of Manco Inca's victorious soldiers.

The Incas' victory was short lived, however. The Spanish forces soon returned with a quadrupled cavalry force and Manco fled to his jungle stronghold in Vilcabamba.

Though Ollantaytambo was a highly effective fortress, it was as much a temple as a fort. A finely worked **ceremonial center** is at the top of the terracing. Some extremely well-built walls were under construction at the time of the conquest and have never been completed. The stone was quarried from the mountainside 6km away, high above the opposite bank of the Río Urubamba. Transporting the huge stone blocks to the site was a stupendous feat. Their crafty technique to move the massive blocks across the river was to leave the blocks by its side then divert the entire river channel around them!

A good walk from Ollantaytambo is the 6km hike to the **Inca quarry** on the opposite side of the river. The trail starts from the Inca bridge by the entrance to the village and takes a few hours to reach the site, passing several abandoned blocks known as *piedras cansadas* – tired stones. Looking back towards Ollantaytambo, you can see the enigmatic optical illusion of a pyramid in the fields and walls in front of the fortress, which a few scholars believe marks

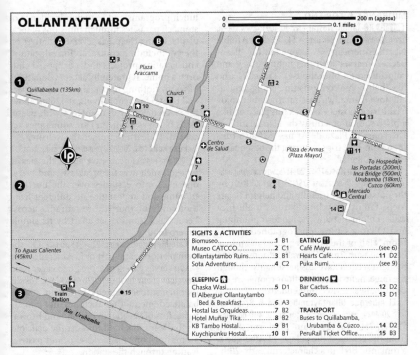

OLLANTAYTAMBO

SIGHTS & ACTIVITIES		
Biomuseo	1	B1
Museo CATCCO	2	C1
Ollantaytambo Ruins	3	B1
Sota Adventures	4	C2

SLEEPING		
Chaska Wasi	5	D1
El Albergue Ollantaytambo Bed & Breakfast	6	A3
Hostal las Orquídeas	7	B2
Hotel Muñay Tika	8	B2
KB Tambo Hostal	9	B1
Kuychipunku Hostal	10	B1

EATING		
Café Mayu	(see 6)	
Hearts Café	11	D2
Puka Rumi	(see 9)	

DRINKING		
Bar Cactus	12	D2
Ganso	13	D1

TRANSPORT		
Buses to Quillabamba, Urubamba & Cuzco	14	D2
PeruRail Ticket Office	15	B3

the legendary place where the original Incas first emerged from the earth.

Sota Adventure (☎ 45-5030; alanelamigo20@hotmail.com; Plaza de Armas s/n) comes highly recommended by readers, particularly for horseback riding. The family-run business also offers mountain biking, multiday hikes and river rafting; however, this area is not recommended for rafting – see p235.

Local community history and ethnography are the main focus of the lovingly tended **Museo CATCCO** (☎ 20-4024; www.ollanta.org; Patacalle s/n; suggested donation S5; ☉ 9am-6pm Mon-Sun). Its displays hold a wealth of fascinating information, all in Spanish, about archaeology, agriculture and religious belief.

The whimsical **Biomuseo** (Convención s/n) explains (only in Spanish, alas!) world biodiversity through the medium of the potato. Opening hours and admission prices are erratic.

Festivals & Events

Epiphany, on January 6, and **Pentecost**, in late May or early June, which commemorates the local miracle of El Señor de Choquechilca (The Christ of Choquechilca), are celebrated with music, dancing and colorful processions.

Sleeping

There are lots of budget and midrange accommodations in the streets east of the Plaza de Armas.

BUDGET

Hospedaje las Portadas (☎ 20-4008; Principal s/n; dm/s/d/tr S15/30/50/60) Although all of the tourist and local buses pass by outside, this family-run place still manages to achieve tranquility. It has a flowery courtyard, a grassy lawn and a rooftop terrace that's excellent for star-gazing. Camping is allowed for S10 per person.

Chaska Wasi (☎ 20-4045; www.hotelchaskawasi.com; katycusco@yahoo.es; Chaupi s/n; r per person with/without bathroom S20/15; ☐) Backpackers flock here to enjoy the company of the lovely, helpful Katy and her tribe of cats. Cheerful basic rooms with electric showers are excellent value, shared spaces are chilled out and perfect for meeting people, and there are bicycles for rent and a DVD library.

CUZCO & THE SACRED VALLEY

MIDRANGE & TOP END

our pick **KB Tambo Hostal** (☎ 20-4091; www.kbperu .com; Ventiderio s/n; per person S45-75; 🖥️) Affable North American KB has nailed the 'flashpacker' market with this light, homey and colorful *hostal* (guesthouse). Travelers who like their home comforts (including, unusually for Ollanta, wireless internet) but enjoy a laid-back, hostel vibe suck this place up like a pisco sour after a dusty day. No relation to KB Tours in Plaza de Armas, KB also runs mountain-bike trips featuring the best quality bikes in Ollanta.

Kuychipunku Hostal (☎ 20-4175; www.kuychipunku .com; s/d/tr/q with breakfast S75/105/135/180) Run by the outstandingly friendly and helpful Bejar-Mejía family, Kuychipunku has it all: Inca walls, colonial archways, modern plumbing and Ollanta's most photographed dining room. Half of the hotel is housed in an Inca building with 2m-thick walls. Rooms in the modern section have less personality, though the huge, light-filled, top-floor rooms are exceptional value. Recommended.

El Albergue Ollantaytambo Bed & Breakfast (☎ 20-4014; www.elalbergue.com; s/d/tr with breakfast S174/222/284) On the train platform, 800m from the center of the village, El Albergue is a romantic B&B in a characterful early-20th-century building with a lovely garden and a tiny sauna. It's captivating – think colonial hacienda meets the age of steam.

Also recommended:

Hostal las Orquídeas (☎ 20-4032; www.hotellas orquideasllantaytambo.com; Av Ferrocarril s/n; s/d/tr/q with breakfast S60/105/150/195) Has a small, grassy courtyard and basic rooms.

Hotel Muñay Tika (☎ 20-4111; www.munaytika.com; Av Ferrocarril s/n; s/d/tr with breakfast S105/120/150) A bit shabby and dated, but cozy and comfortable with a pretty garden.

Eating

our pick **Hearts Café** (☎ 20-4078; www.livingheart peru.org; Plaza de Armas s/n; menú S15, mains from S22 🕑 7:30am-10pm) Hearts Café dishes out delicious, healthy and hearty food and fabulous coffee. The cafe, which endearingly advertises 'mostly whole foods,' was set up to raise money for the Living Heart Association, an NGO founded by English nutritionist Sonia Newhouse, which is doing amazing things in the Sacred Valley. It has measurably improved child health in some villages, mainly by improving nutrition through school lunch programs and reducing incidence of stomach parasites through infusions of local plants. Living Heart has several initiatives on the go, including contraception education, conservation projects and a proposed children's home. It gratefully accepts donations of warm clothing (especially warm jumpers and tights) for people living at 4200m above the Sacred Valley. Volunteers with useful skills (such as medicine) are sometimes accepted. To learn more, see the website.

Puka Rumi (☎ 20-4091; Ventiderio s/n; mains from S17; 🕑 7:30am-10pm) Locals rave about the steaks, travelers melt over the breakfasts, and everyone goes into ecstasies over the burritos. In name and appearance no different from thousands of touristic restaurants across Peru, Puka Rumi is set apart by its simply superb food.

Café Mayu (mains from S22; 🕑 5am-late) On the train platform, and part of El Albergue, Café Mayu serves excellent espresso to eager train travelers from first departure to last. Inside, its open kitchen quietly turns out a well-balanced menu that includes homemade pasta, lots of vegetarian options and brownies to die for. It's hard to resist the delicious aromas of homemade desserts and pastries wafting through the station.

Drinking

Ganso (☎ 984-30-8499; Waqta s/n; 🕑 2pm-late) Treehouse meets circus meets *Batman*! The hallucinatory decor in tiny, friendly Ganso is enough to drive anyone to drink. The firemen's pole and swing seats are the icing on the cake.

Bar Cactus (☎ 79-7162; Principal s/n; 🕑 6pm-late) As well as cheap drinks and plenty of chat, Bar Cactus offers a S10 *menú* till 9pm.

Getting There & Away

BUS & TAXI

Frequent *combis* and *colectivos* shuttle between Urubamba and Ollantaytambo (S1.20/2.50, 30 minutes), from 6am to around 5pm. To get to Cuzco, it's easiest to change in Urubamba, though there are occasional departures direct from Ollantaytambo to Cuzco's Puente Grau (*combis* S5, two hours; *colectivos* S10, 1½ hours).

TRAIN

Ollantaytambo is a transport hub between Cuzco and Machu Picchu, due to the fact that the cheapest and quickest way to travel between Cuzco and Machu Picchu is to catch a *combi* between Cuzco and Ollantaytambo (two hours), and then the train between Ollantaytambo and Aguas Calientes (two hours).

PeruRail (www.perurail.com) has more than a dozen departures each way per day – check the website for exact times and costs, which vary from S38 to S192, depending on departure time and type of train. The Vistadome train costs more, but you can see the spectacular gorge scenery between Ollantaytambo and Aguas Calientes just as well from the cheaper Backpacker train.

Combis meet trains at the station and will get you back to Cuzco in about two hours for S7.

The PeruRail ticket office just outside Ollantaytambo's train station is open from 5am to 8pm every day. Show up at least one day beforehand to buy tickets; during high season, make reservations as far in advance as possible. Buy a return ticket – the vast number of people who hike to Machu Picchu, then catch the train back to Cuzco means that trains out of Aguas Calientes are much fuller than trains into it.

MACHU PICCHU & THE INCA TRAIL

AGUAS CALIENTES

☎ 084 / pop 1000 / elev 2410m

Also known as Machu Picchu Pueblo, this town lies in a deep gorge below the ruins, enclosed by towering walls of stone cliff and cloud forest, and divided by two rushing rivers. The location is eye-poppingly gorgeous – that's the good news. The bad news is that all travelers to and from Machu Picchu must pass through here, so Aguas Calientes is about as touristy a town as you'll ever come across. Come prepared for high prices and a sea of touts, keep your eyes on the hills and reflect on how rare it is to be in a town with no car access, and you'll find a way to love Aguas Calientes. Many choose to overnight here to avoid being engulfed by the hordes of day-trippers arriving from Cuzco by train each morning. Only those who sleep here or walk the Inca Trail get to catch sunrise at Machu Picchu.

Orientation

The footpath from the train station to the Machu Picchu bus stop is stepped. Wheelchairs should be directed across the small bridge to Sinchi Roca and through the center of town.

Information

There's a helpful branch of **iPerú** (☎ 21-1104; Edificio del Instituto Nacional de Cultura, Pachacutec, cuadra 1; ☷ 9am-1pm & 2-8pm) near the **Machu Picchu ticket office** (☷ 5am-10pm). There's currently one ATM, at **BCP** (Av Imperio de los Incas s/n), but it often runs out of money, particularly on weekends. Another ATM, on Av Imperio de los Incas, was planned at the time of research. Currency and traveler's checks can be exchanged in various places at highly unfavorable rates, but it's best to bring plenty of Peruvian currency with you from Cuzco. Pay phones and cybercafes are scattered around the town, and there's a small **post office** (Colla Raymi s/n). There's a **medical center** (☎ 21-1005; Av Imperio de los Incas s/n; ☷ emergencies 24hr) by the train tracks.

Sights & Activities

By Puente Ruinas, at the base of the footpath to Machu Picchu, **Museo de Sitio Manuel Chávez Ballón** (admission S21; ☷ 9am-5pm) has superb information, in Spanish and English, on archaeological excavations of Machu Picchu and Inca building methods. Stop here before or after the ruins to get a sense of context (and to enjoy the air-conditioning and soothing music if you're walking back from the ruins after hours in the sun!) There's a small botanical garden outside, down a nifty, nerve-testing set of Inca stairs.

Weary trekkers soak away their aches and pains in the town's **hot springs** (admission S10; ☷ 5am-8:30pm), 10 minutes' walk up Pachacutec from the train tracks. These tiny, natural thermal springs, from which Aguas Calientes derives its name, are nice enough but far from the best in the area (that would be Santa Teresa's Cocalmayo), and get scungy by late morning. Towels can be rented cheaply outside the entrance. Travelers recommend **Andean Spa** (☎ 21-1355; Plaza Manco Capac s/n) for massages.

For those who still have energy left for trekking, the hike up steep, toothlike minimountain **Putucusi**, directly opposite Machu Picchu, is highly recommended. Follow the

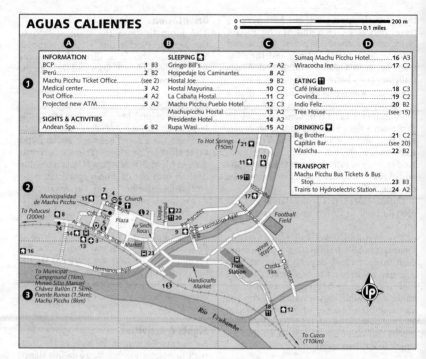

AGUAS CALIENTES

INFORMATION	
BCP	1 B3
iPerú	2 B2
Machu Picchu Ticket Office	(see 2)
Medical center	3 A2
Post Office	4 A2
Projected new ATM	5 A2

SIGHTS & ACTIVITIES	
Andean Spa	6 B2

SLEEPING	
Gringo Bill's	7 A2
Hospedaje los Caminantes	8 A2
Hostal Joe	9 B2
Hostal Mayurina	10 C2
La Cabaña Hostal	11 A2
Machu Picchu Pueblo Hotel	12 C3
Machupicchu Hostal	13 A2
Presidente Hotel	14 A2
Rupa Wasi	15 A2

Sumaq Machu Picchu Hotel	16 A3
Wiracocha Inn	17 C2

EATING	
Café Inkaterra	18 C3
Govinda	19 C2
Indio Feliz	20 B2
Tree House	(see 15)

DRINKING	
Big Brother	21 C2
Capitán Bar	(see 20)
Wasicha	22 B2

TRANSPORT	
Machu Picchu Bus Tickets & Bus Stop	23 B3
Trains to Hydroelectric Station	24 A2

railway tracks about 250m west of town and you'll see a set of stairs; this is the start of a well-marked trail. Parts of the walk are up ladders, which get slippery in the wet season, but the view across to Machu Picchu is worth the trek. Allow three hours.

Sleeping

Bargain *hospedajes* can be found in the area up-hill of the souvenir market; few are cheaper than Hospedaje los Caminantes and Hostal Joe.

BUDGET

Municipal campground (camping per tent S15) This small, charming campground has toilets, showers and kitchen facilities for rent. It's a 20-minute walk downhill from the center of town on the road to Machu Picchu, before the bridge.

Hospedaje los Caminantes (☎ 21-1007; Av Imperio de los Incas 140; per person with/without bathroom S25/15) Well, it ain't much to look at, but this big, multistory guesthouse offers rooms and bathrooms that are big and clean, with comfortable beds and quite reliable hot water. The train hooting directly outside your window at 7am is an unmissable wake-up call.

Hostal Joe (☎ 38-3512; Mayta Cápac 103; per person S20) Uphill from the plaza, friendly Hostal Joe's bare, cell-like rooms are far from fancy but offer unbeatable value in a town where true bargains are harder to find than Inca gold.

MIDRANGE

Hostal Mayurina (☎ 77-7247; www.hostalmayurina.com; Hermanos Ayar s/n; s/d/tr with breakfast S90/120/180) Sparkling new and keen to please, Mayurina is nothing if not airy, with an open-air reception area and spiral staircase. Rooms have phones and televisions.

Machupicchu Hostal (☎ 21-1212; reservas@siahotels.com; Av Imperio de los Incas s/n; s/d with breakfast S122/175) One of the tidy midrange inns right next to the train tracks, this place has a small flower-festooned interior courtyard. The noise from other guests echoes endlessly, and you will certainly hear every train that goes by, but it's still decent value.

Wiracocha Inn (☎ 21-1088; wiracocha-inn@peru.com; Wiracocha s/n; s & d/tr/q S195/240/285) On a side street crowded with midrange hotels, this newer

(Continued on page 277)

Ancient Peru

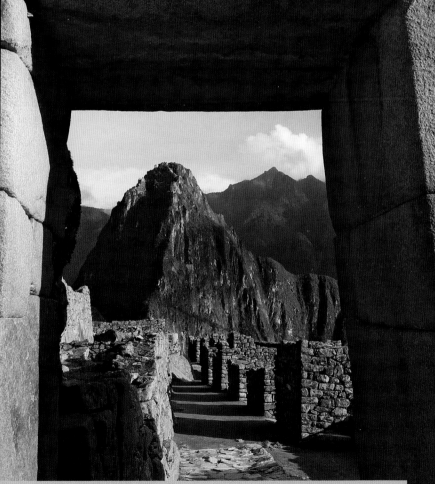

Wayna Picchu, Machu Picchu (p278)

RALPH HOPKINS

A *pachacuti,* according to the Incas, was a cataclysmic event that divided the different ages of history. For the indigenous cultures that inhabited Peru in the 16th century, the arrival of the Spanish was the most earth-shattering *pachacuti* imaginable. As conquerors are wont to do, the Europeans went about obliterating native history: melting gold objects into ingots, immolating religious icons and banning traditions they considered idolatrous.

This has left historians to piece together Peru's vast pre-Columbian history largely by digging up grave goods. (Not a single Andean culture left behind a written language.) Thankfully, the physical legacy is rich. This area has been home to civilizations large and small, each with its own distinctive deities and traditions. Travelers to Peru can see sumptuous textiles, striking ceramics and monumental structures so well engineered that they have not only survived conquest, but centuries of calamitous earthquakes as well.

For the Indiana Jones set, the adventure begins here.

CARAL

About 23km inland from the Pacific, just a couple of hundred kilometers north of Lima, lies one of the most exciting archaeological sites in Peru. It may not look like much – half a dozen dusty temple mounds, a few sunken amphitheaters and remnants of structures crafted from adobe and stone – but it is. This is the oldest known city in the Americas: Caral (p338).

top ten

ARCHAEOLOGICAL MUSEUMS

- Museo Andrés del Castillo (p93), Lima
- Museo Larco (p95), Lima
- Qorikancha (p232), Cuzco
- Museo de Arte Precolombino (p231), Cuzco
- Museo Inka (p232), Cuzco
- Museo Nacional de Chavín (p423), Chavín de Huántar
- Museo Santury (p165), Arequipa
- Museo Tumbas Reales de Sipán (p365), Lambayeque
- Museo Nacional Sicán (p365), Ferreñafe
- Museo Regional de Ica (p136), Ica

Caral (p338): the oldest known city in the Americas
GEORGE STEINMETZ / CORBIS IMAGES

Stone carvings at Chavín de Huántar (p422)

MARIO VERIN / PHOTOLIBRARY

Situated in the Supe Valley, this Preceramic civilization developed almost simultaneously with the ancient cultures of Mesopotamia and Egypt about 5000 years ago, and it predates the earliest civilizations in Mexico by about 1500 years. Little is known about the culture that built this impressive 626-hectare urban center. But archaeologists, led by Ruth Shady Solís, the former director of Lima's Museo Nacional de Antropología, Arqueología e Historia del Perú (p97), have managed to unearth precious details.

Caral was not a militaristic settlement, but a religious one that venerated its holy men and paid tribute to unknown agricultural deities (at times, with human sacrifice). They cultivated crops such as cotton, squashes, beans and chilies, collected area fruits and were knowledgeable fishers. Archaeological finds at the site include pieces of textile, necklaces, ceremonial burials and crude, unbaked clay figurines depicting female forms. The first serious digs began in the area in 1996 and much of the complex has yet to be excavated – expect further discoveries.

CHAVÍN

If Caral is evidence of the earliest sign of functional urban settlement, then Chavín de Huántar (p422), near Huaraz, represents the spread of a unified religious and artistic iconography. In a broad swath of the northern Andes, from roughly 1000 BC to 300 BC, a common culture arose around a feline deity that appears on carvings, friezes, pottery and textiles from the era. As with Caral, there is only patchy information available on the Chavín culture and the structure of its society, but its importance is without question: in Peru, this represents the birth of art. (For more, see p424.)

It is still debated whether the temple at Chavín de Huántar was this culture's capital or merely an important ceremonial site, but what is without doubt is that the setting is extraordinary. With the stunning Cordillera Blanca as a backdrop, the remnants of this elaborate

Detail of Paracas funerary wrapping
MIREILLE VAUTIER / ALAMY

ceremonial complex – built over hundreds of years – include a number of temple structures, as well as a sunken court with stone friezes of jaguars. Here, archaeologists have found pottery from all over the region filled with *ofrendas* (offerings), including shells from as far away as the Ecuadorean coast, and carved bones (some human) featuring supernatural motifs. The site's most remarkable feature is a maze of disorienting galleries beneath the temple complex, one of which boasts a nearly 5m-tall rock carving of a fanged anthropomorphic deity known as the Lanzón – the sort of fierce-looking thing that is bound to turn anyone into a believer.

PARACAS & NAZCA

As the influence of Chavín culture waned, a number of smaller, regional ethnicities rose in its stead. Along the country's south coast, from about 700 BC to AD 400, the culture known as Paracas (p133) – situated around modern-day Ica – produced some of the most renowned textiles ever created. The most impressive of these were woven during the period known as the Paracas Necropolis (AD 1 to 400), so named for a massive gravesite on the Paracas Peninsula uncovered by famed Peruvian archaeologist Julio Tello in 1927. (Tello is considered the father of Peruvian archaeology, one of the first figures to treat sites in a methodical, scientific manner.)

The historical data on this important coastal culture is thin, but the magnificent textiles recovered from the graves – layer upon layer of finely woven fabrics wrapped around mummy bundles – provide important clues about day-to-day life and beliefs. Featured on these colorful, intricate cloths are flowers, fish, birds, knives and cats, with some animals represented as two-headed creatures. Also significant are the human figures, such as warriors carrying shrunken trophy heads, and supernatural anthropomorphic creatures equipped with wings, snake tongues and feline features, as well as *lots* of claws. (You can see some fantastic examples of these at the Museo Regional de Ica, p136, and the Museo Larco in Lima, p95). Many of the mummies found at this site had cranial deformations, most of which showed that the head had been intentionally flattened using two boards.

During roughly the same period, the Nazca culture (200 BC to AD 600), to the south, was producing an array of painted pottery, as well as incredible weavings that featured images both geometric and ornate. These works showcased everyday objects (beans, birds and fish), as well as supernatural cat- and falcon-men in an array of explosive colors. The Nazca were skilled embroiderers: some weavings feature tiny dangling figurines that must have induced blindness in their creators. (Some wonderful Nazca textiles can be seen at the Museo Andrés del Castillo in Lima, p93.) The culture is best known, however, for the Nazca Lines (p143), a series of mysterious geoglyphs carved into a 500-sq-km area in southern Peru.

THE MOCHE

When it comes to ceramics, there is no Andean civilization that compares to the Moche (p354), a culture that inhabited the Peruvian north coast from about AD 100 to AD 800. The Moche were accomplished in many areas. Though not inherently urban, they built sophisticated ceremonial centers, such as the frieze-laden Huacas del Sol y de la Luna (p351), outside of modern-day Trujillo. The Moche created elaborate burial sites for their leaders, such as Sipán (p364), near Chiclayo. They had a well-maintained network of roads and a system of relay runners that carried messages, probably in the form of symbols carved onto beans.

But it's their ceramic portrait pottery that makes the Moche stand out: lifelike depictions of individuals (scars and all) that are so skillfully rendered, some of them seem as if they are about to talk. In some cases, artists created many portraits of a single person over the course of their lifetime; one scholar recorded 45 different pieces depicting the same model. Many ceramics are dedicated to showcasing macho activities: men hunting, running, in combat and about to be sacrificed. This doesn't mean, however, that the Moche didn't know a thing or two about love – they are famous for their encyclopedic, downright acrobatic depictions of human sex. See these saucy pots and other incredible Moche artifacts at the Museo Larco (p95) and the Museo de la Nación (p94), in Lima.

THE WARI

From about AD 600 to 1100, the Andes saw the rise of the first truly expansive kingdom. The Wari (p32) were avid empire builders, expanding from their base around Ayacucho to a territory that occupied an area from Chiclayo to Cuzco. Expert agriculturalists, they improved production by developing the terrace system and creating complex networks of canals for irrigation.

Like many conquering cultures in the region, the Wari built on what was already there, usurping and adding to extant infrastructure created by smaller regional states. Pachacamac (p122), for instance, was originated by the Lima culture, expanded by the Wari and taken over by the Ichsma, before being appropriated and built upon by the Incas.

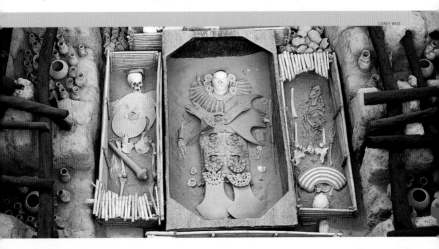
COREY WISE

Roundhouse ruins at Kuélap (p448)
PAUL KENNEDY

Chimú carvings at Huaca Arco Iris (p351)
CHRIS BEALL

Even so, there are definitively Wari sites you can visit. The remains of what was once a 1500-hectare Wari city (p325) is located outside of Ayacucho, and there is a ceremonial center in Piquillacta (p288), near Cuzco. Unfortunately, the Wari's architecture was cruder than that of the Incas, which means that the buildings have not aged gracefully.

In the area of weaving, however, the culture was highly skilled, producing elegant fabrics with elaborate stylized designs. The Wari were masters of color, using as many as 150 distinct shades, which they incorporated into both woven and tie dyed patterns. Many of these textiles feature abstract, geometric designs, as well as supernatural figures; most common is a winged deity holding a staff, which appears on textiles discovered throughout the Wari empire.

CHIMÚ & CHACHAPOYAS

Following the demise of the Wari, a number of small nation-states emerged in different corners of the country. They are too numerous to detail here (for more, see p33), but there are two that merit discussion because of the art and architecture they left behind. The first of these is the Chimú culture (p355), based around present-day Trujillo.

Between about AD 1000 and AD 1400, this incredible north-coast culture built the largest known pre-Columbian city in the Americas. Chan Chan (p349) is a sprawling, 36-sq-km complex, which once housed an estimated 60,000 people. Though over the centuries this adobe city has been worn down by the elements, parts of the complex's geometric friezes have been restored, giving a small inkling of what this incredible metropolis must have been like at its apogee. The Chimú were accomplished artisans and metallurgists – producing, among other things, some absolutely outrageous-looking textiles, some of which were covered top-to-bottom in tassels.

To the interior in the northern highlands is the abandoned cloud-forest citadel of Kuélap (p448), built by the Chachapoyas culture (p448) in the inaccessible Utcubamba Valley beginning around AD 800. It is an incredible structure – or, more accurately, series of structures. The site is composed of more than 400 circular dwellings, in addition to some unusual, gravity-defying pieces of architecture, such as an inverted cone known as El Tintero (The Inkpot). The compound is surrounded by a 6m- to 12m-high wall, which indicates that the site was a fortress – a decidedly impenetrable one at that. (At least one historian has theorized that if the Incas had made their last stand against the Spanish here, rather than outside of Cuzco, history might have been a whole lot different.)

Outside of Machu Picchu, Kuélap is probably the most breathtaking pre-Columbian site in Peru. Unfortunately, almost nothing is known about the people who built it, who are largely remembered for having fiercely resisted the Inca conquest.

THE INCAS

Peru's greatest engineers were also its greatest empire builders. Because the Incas made direct contact with the Spanish, they also happen to be the pre-Columbian Andean culture that is best documented – not only through Spanish chronicle, but also through narratives produced by some of the descendants of the Incas themselves. (The most famous of these is by El Inca Garcilaso de la Vega; see p37.)

The Incas were a Quechua civilization descended from alpaca farmers in the southern Andes. Over several generations, from AD 1100 to the arrival of the Spanish in 1532, they steadfastly grew a small territory around Cuzco (p220) into a highly organized empire that extended over more than 37° latitude from Colombia to Chile. This was an absolutist state with a strong army, where ultimate power resided with the *inca* (emperor). Inca history is ridden with a succession of colorful royals who would make for an excellent TV movie – complete with fratricide, great battles and plenty of beautiful maidens. See p34 and p220 for a more detailed history.

The society was bound by a rigid caste system: there were nobles, an artisan and merchant class, and peasants. The last supplied the manual labor for the Incas' many public-works projects. Citizens were expected to pay tribute to the crown in the form of labor – typically for three months of the year – enabling the civilization to develop and maintain its monuments, canals and roadways. The Incas also kept a highly efficient communications system consisting of a body of *chasquis* (relay runners), which could make the 1600km trip

Travelers flock to world-famous Inca site Machu Picchu (p278)

RALPH HOPKINS

Inca terracing, Pisac (p259)
RALPH HOPKINS

Detail of mortarless Inca stonework
JEFFREY BECOM

between Quito and Cuzco in just seven days. (By comparison, it takes the average traveler three to four days to hike the Inca Trail from Ollantaytambo to Machu Picchu – a mere 43km!) As brutal as the regime was (bloody wars, human sacrifice), the Incas also had a notable social-welfare system, warehousing surplus food for distribution to areas and people in need.

On the cultural front, the Incas had a strong tradition of music, oral literature and textiles. Textiles were generally woven in bold, solid colors and abstract, geometric prints. This civilization, however, is best known for its monumental architecture. Its capital of Cuzco (p220), along with a series of constructions at Sacsaywamán (p256), Pisac (p259), Ollantaytambo (p264) and the fabled Machu Picchu (p267), are all incredible examples of the imperial style of building. Carved pieces of rock, without mortar, are fitted together so tightly that it is impossible to fit a knife between the stones. Most interestingly, walls are built at an angle and windows in a trapezoidal form, so as to resist seismic activity. The Incas kept the exteriors of their buildings austere, opting to put the decoration on the inside, in the form of rich wall hangings made of precious metals.

Nestled into spectacular natural locales, these structures, even in their ruined state, are an unforgettable sight. Their great majesty was something the Spanish acknowledged, even as they pried them apart to raise their own monuments. 'Now that the Inca rulers have lost their power,' wrote Spanish chronicler Pedro Cieza de León in the 16th century, 'all these palaces and gardens, together with their other great works, have fallen, so that only the remains survive. Since they were built of good stone and the masonry is excellent, they will stand as memorials for centuries to come.' León was right. The Inca civilization did not survive the Spanish *pachacuti,* but their architecture did – a reminder of the many grand societies we are just beginning to understand.

(Continued from page 268)

option has well-kept and polished rooms, amiable service and a sheltered patio area near the river. In some rooms you'll be lulled to sleep by the Andean mountain waters rushing by.

Presidente Hotel (☎ 21-1065; reservas@siahotels.com; Av Imperio de los Incas s/n; d S210, d/tr with view S227/262) A solid, professional option. It's worth paying the extra for a room with a view, not just for the outlook over the river but to get as far from the train tracks as possible. Rates include breakfast.

Rupa Wasi (☎ 21-1101; www.rupawasi.net; Huanacaure s/n; d/ste with breakfast S210/300) Hidden away up a steep flight of stairs, Rupa Wasi clings to the hillside like a fairytale castle, all teetering wooden stairways and mysterious stone pathways. Mossy rocks and jungle plants are part of its structure. The atmosphere is dreamy and staff can be, too – it's all part of the hippie-paradise feel. Two-bedroom suites are great for families. Extra beds cost S90.

La Cabaña Hostal (☎ 21-1048; Pachacutec s/n; s & d/tr with breakfast S225/285; 🖳) Further uphill than most of the hotels is this popular, airy spot, which has woody, rustic-feel rooms with phones and heating, and free internet access. Buffet breakfast in the colorful, cushioned restaurant is included.

ourpick Gringo Bill's (☎ 21-1046; www.gringo bills.com; Colla Raymi 104; s & d/jr ste/ste/family ste S225/315/405/450) One of the original places for tourists to stay in Aguas Calientes, multilayered Gringo Bill's continues to charm with its white-walled, flower-bedecked open spaces and comfortable, uniquely decorated rooms. At time of research it was undergoing a major modernization, and may have an on-site restaurant and pisco bar by the time you read this. The two-bedroom family suite sleeps up to five.

TOP END

Machu Picchu Pueblo Hotel (☎ in Lima 01-610-0400; www.inkaterra.com; d US$463-960; 🖳 🖳) For nature lovers who crave creature comforts, this trendy eco-themed hotel is a 100m walk southeast of the train station. Set amid tropical gardens featuring a bamboo-and-eucalyptus sauna, the hotel's hand-hewn cottages are done up in nouveau Andean style and are connected by stone pathways. The whole complex is classy, comfortable and inviting. Recommended.

Sumaq Machu Picchu Hotel (☎ 21-1059; www .sumaqhotelperu.com; Hermanos Ayar s/n; s/d with some meals from S1312/1593; 🖳 🖳) From the outside, Sumac bears an unfortunate resemblance to Fred Flintstone's house, but the inside is a wonderland of hushed, pampering luxury. Light-flooded, white-walled spaces with playful splashes of bold color give this new hotel a modern, stylish look: it's luxurious without being pompous. Rooms boast views of either river and mountains, or a hillside with mini-waterfalls created for your viewing pleasure. There are multiple eating and drinking areas, and a full spa (treatments from S176). Room rates include breakfast, afternoon tea and either lunch or dinner.

Eating

There's a depressing sameness about restaurants in Aguas Calientes. To get away from pizza and overpriced, underspiced *menú turístico* (set meals for tourists), either head to the area around the football stadium for cheap local food, or check out the following.

Café Inkaterra (☎ 21-1122; Machu Picchu Pueblo Hotel; mains from S25; ☻ 11am-9pm) A high-class spot for a filling Peruvian fusion spread, this restaurant is hidden behind the train station. With flickering votive candles and a chilled-out soundtrack to match the tantalizing *novoandina* menu, the atmosphere here is truly an escape from the masses.

Tree House (☎ 21-1101; Huanacaure s/n; mains from S27; ☻ lunch & dinner) Part of the hotel Rupa Wasi, aptly named Tree House's woody ambience provides just the right laid-back setting for its food. Lovingly prepared and locally focused, this is what *novoandina* cuisine is all about – recipes that combine international influences with fresh, distinctive local produce. Alpaca loin with bacon and *chimichurri* (a salty, flavorsome sauce of local herbs), quinoa risotto, and *lúcuma* (an earthy Andean fruit) caramel are some lip-smacking examples.

Indio Feliz (☎ 21-1090; Lloque Yupanqui 4; menú S50, mains from S38; ☻ 11am-10pm) Multi-award-winning Indio Feliz's French cook whips up fantastic meals, which have made this place deservedly popular, and 'world famous' in Aguas Calientes. The S50 *menú* is an extremely good value for a decadent dinner. Indio Feliz has good wheelchair access.

Also recommended:

Govinda (Pachacutec s/n; 3-course menú from S15; h9am-9pm) Trusty Hare Krishna vegetarian standby.

Drinking

There isn't much nightlife in Aguas Calientes. **Big Brother**, at the top of Pachacutec just before the hot springs, is a good spot for a quiet beer, with pool tables and an open-air 2nd-floor terrace. Nearer the plaza, **Wasicha** (☎ 21-1282; Lloque Yupanqui s/n) is a popular *discoteca* with dancing till the wee hours. **Capitán Bar** (Lloque Yupanqui s/n), attached to Indio Feliz restaurant, is for grown-ups. It's a colorful nautical-themed bar – just the place to sip a fine brandy and enlarge on your achievements on the Inca Trail.

Getting There & Away

There are only three options to get to Aguas Calientes, and hence to Machu Picchu: trek it, catch the train via the Sacred Valley, or travel by road and train via Santa Teresa.

TRAIN

To get to Aguas Calientes directly from Cuzco (actually, from Poroy, 20 minutes away by taxi) by **PeruRail** (www.perurail.com) takes about three hours, and you have two options

The Vistadome service (S227.20 each way) leaves Cuzco at 7am each day and returns at 3:25pm.

The fancy Hiram Bingham costs S1881.60 and includes brunch, afternoon tea, entrance to Machu Picchu and a guided tour. It departs Poroy at the civilized hour of 9am and gets you back there at 9pm, and gives you three to four hours at Machu Picchu. It runs daily except Sunday.

It's a lot cheaper, and at least 30 minutes quicker, to catch a *combi* to Ollantaytambo, and take a train from there (see p266) – trains cost as little as S31.

Buy a return ticket to avoid getting stranded in Aguas Calientes – outbound tickets sell out much quicker than tickets in.

Check PeruRail's website for up-to-date schedules and to buy tickets.

BUS

The cheapest way to get to Machu Picchu is via Santa Teresa. Catch a bus headed for Quillabamba, get off in tiny Santa María, and catch frequent local transport to Santa Teresa, where you can buy your train ticket to Aguas Calientes – see p291 for more information.

You can also do this route as a guided multisport tour (see p285).

There is one train daily from Aguas Calientes to the hydroelectric station in Santa Teresa, at 12:30pm. Tickets can only be bought from Aguas Calientes train station on the day of departure, but trains actually leave from the west end of town, outside the police station.

MACHU PICCHU

For many visitors to Peru and even South America, a visit to the Inca city of Machu Picchu is the sweet cherry on the top of their trip. With its spectacular location, it's the best-known archaeological site on the continent. This awe-inspiring ancient city was never revealed to the conquering Spaniards and was virtually forgotten until the early part of the 20th century. In the high season, from late May until early September, 2500 people arrive daily. Despite this great tourist influx, the site manages to retain its air of grandeur and mystery, and is a must for all visitors to Peru.

History

Machu Picchu is not mentioned in any of the chronicles of the Spanish conquistadors. Apart from a couple of German adventurers in the 1860s, who apparently looted the site with the Peruvian government's permission, nobody apart from local Quechua people knew of Machu Picchu's existence until American historian Hiram Bingham was guided to it by locals in 1911. You can read Bingham's own account of his 'discovery' in the classic book *Inca Land: Explorations in the Highlands of Peru*, first published in 1922 and now available as a free download from Project Gutenberg (www.gutenberg.org).

Bingham's search was for the lost city of Vilcabamba, the last stronghold of the Incas, and he thought he had found it at Machu Picchu. We now know that the remote ruins at Espíritu Pampa, much deeper in the jungle, are actually the remains of Vilcabamba. The Machu Picchu site was initially overgrown with thick vegetation, forcing Bingham's team to be content with roughly mapping the site. Bingham returned in 1912 and 1915 to carry out the difficult task of clearing the thick forest, when he also discovered some of the ruins on the so-called Inca Trail. (Over the course of his various journeys, Bingham took thousands of artifacts back to the USA with him; see p56 to learn about the fight for their return to Peru.) Peruvian archaeologist Luis

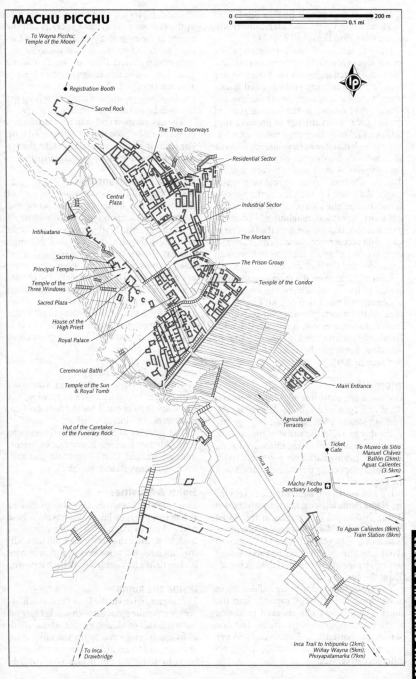

MACHU PICCHU

0   200 m
0   0.1 mi

To Wayna Picchu;
Temple of the Moon

● Registration Booth

● Sacred Rock

The Three Doorways

Residential Sector

Central
Plaza

Industrial Sector

Intihuatana

The Mortars

Sacristy

Principal Temple

The Prison Group

Temple of the
Three Windows

Temple of the Condor

Sacred Plaza

House of the
High Priest

Royal Palace

Ceremonial Baths

Main Entrance

Temple of the Sun
& Royal Tomb

Agricultural
Terraces

Hut of the Caretaker
of the Funerary Rock

● Ticket
Gate

To Museo de Sitio
Manuel Chávez
Ballón (2km);
Aguas Calientes
(3.5km)

Inca Trail

Machu Picchu
Sanctuary Lodge

To Aguas Calientes (8km);
Train Station (8km)

To Inca
Drawbridge

Inca Trail to Intipunku (2km);
Wiñay Wayna (5km);
Phuyapatamarka (7km)

E Valcárcel undertook further studies in 1934, as did a Peruvian-American expedition under Paul Fejos in 1940–41.

Despite scores of more recent studies, knowledge of Machu Picchu remains sketchy. Even today archaeologists are forced to rely heavily on speculation and educated guesswork as to its function. Some believe the citadel was founded in the waning years of the last Incas as an attempt to preserve Inca culture or rekindle their predominance, while others think that it may have already become an uninhabited, forgotten city at the time of the conquest. A more recent theory suggests that the site was a royal retreat or country palace abandoned at the time of the Spanish invasion. The site's director believes that it was a city, a political, religious and administrative center. Its location, and the fact that at least eight access routes have been discovered, suggests that it was a trade nexus between Amazonia and the highlands.

It seems clear from the exceptionally high quality of the stonework and the abundance of ornamental work that Machu Picchu was once vitally important as a ceremonial center. Indeed, to some extent, it still is: Alejandro Toledo, the country's first indigenous Andean president, impressively staged his inauguration here in 2001.

Information

The ruins are most heavily visited between 10am and 2pm, and June to August are the busiest months. Plan your visit early or late in the day to avoid the worst of the crowds. A visit early in the morning midweek during the rainy season guarantees you more room to breathe, especially during February, when the Inca Trail is closed.

It's well worth buying entrance tickets for the **Machu Picchu historical sanctuary** (adult/student S124/62; ☻ 6am-5pm) in advance, at the **Machu Picchu ticket office** (Edificio del Instituto Nacional de Cultura, Pachacutec s/n; ☻ 5am-10pm) in Aguas Calientes, to avoid long line-up times and possible hassles getting change at the overstretched ticket office at the site.

You are not allowed to bring walking sticks or backpacks of over 20L capacity into the ruins – they have to be checked in at one of the two luggage-storage offices. The one outside the entrance gate ruins costs S5 per item and the one inside costs S3; there's no difference in service.

Local guides are readily available for hire at the entrance. They are generally not the cream of the crop and you are better off hiring a guide in Cuzco (see p240 for some recommended guides). If you do decide to hire a guide here, make sure to agree upon a price in advance, clarify whether it's per person or covers the whole group, and agree how long the tour will be and the maximum group size.

The information and map provided in this book should be enough for a self-guided tour. For really in-depth explorations, take along a copy of *Exploring Cuzco* by Peter Frost.

Dangers & Annoyances

Inside the ruins, do not walk on any of the walls – this loosens the stonework and prompts an cacophony of whistle blowing from the guards. Trying to spend the night here is also illegal, and guards do a thorough check of the site before it closes. Food at the cafe just outside the gate is even more overpriced than you'd expect, but eating in the site is forbidden – if you bring your own food, eat it outside the gate. Disposable plastic bottles are also forbidden -the only way to get water in is in camping-type drink bottles. Water is sold at the cafe just outside the entrance, but only in glass bottles.

Use of the only toilet facilities, just below the cafe, will set you back S1.

Tiny sand fly–like bugs abound. You won't notice them biting while it's happening, but you'll know all about it for the next swollen, itchy week. Use insect repellent.

The weather at Machu Picchu seems to have only two settings: heavy rain or bright, burning sunlight. Don't forget rain gear and, even more importantly, sunblock.

Sights & Activities

Don't miss the Museo de Sitio Manuel Chávez Ballón (see p267) by Puente Ruinas at the base of the climb to Machu Picchu. Buses headed back from the ruins to Aguas Calientes will stop upon request at the bridge, and from here it's less than a half-hour's walk back to town.

INSIDE THE RUINS

Unless you arrive via the Inca Trail, you'll officially enter the ruins through a ticket gate on the south side of Machu Picchu. About 100m of footpath brings you to the mazelike main entrance of Machu Picchu proper, where the ruins lie stretched out before you, roughly

CUZCO & THE SACRED VALLEY

divided into two areas separated by a series of plazas.

To get a visual fix of the whole site and snap the classic postcard photograph, climb the zigzagging staircase on the left immediately after entering the complex, which leads to a hut. Known as the **Hut of the Caretaker of the Funerary Rock**, it is one of a few buildings that has been restored with a thatched roof, making it a good shelter in the case of rain. The Inca Trail enters the city just below this hut. The carved rock behind the hut may have been used to mummify the nobility, hence the hut's name.

If you continue straight into the ruins instead of climbing to the hut, you pass through extensive terracing to a beautiful series of 16 connected **ceremonial baths** that cascade across the ruins, accompanied by a flight of stairs.

Just above and to the left of the baths is Machu Picchu's only round building, the **Temple of the Sun**, a curved and tapering tower that contains some of the site's finest stonework. It appears to have been used for astronomical purposes. Inside are an altar and a curiously drilled trapezoidal window that looks onto the site. The Temple of the Sun is cordoned off to visitors, but you can see into it from above, which is how you'll be approaching it if you take the stairs leading down and to the left from the caretaker's hut.

Below the temple is an almost hidden, natural rock cave that has been carefully carved, with a steplike altar and sacred niches, by the Inca stonemasons. It is known as the **Royal Tomb**, though no mummies were actually ever found here.

Climbing the stairs above the ceremonial baths, you reach a flat area of jumbled rocks, once used as a quarry. Turn right at the top of the stairs and walk across the quarry on a short path leading to the four-sided **Sacred Plaza**. The far side contains a small viewing platform with a curved wall, which offers a view of the snowy Cordillera Vilcabamba in the far distance and the Río Urubamba below.

Important buildings flank the remaining three sides of the Sacred Plaza. The **Temple of the Three Windows** commands an impressive view of the plaza below through the huge trapezoidal windows that give the building its name. With this temple behind you, the **Principal Temple** is to your right. Its name derives from the massive solidity and perfection of its construction. The damage to the

rear right corner of the temple is the result of the ground settling below this corner rather than any inherent weakness in the masonry itself. Opposite the Principal Temple is what is known as the **House of the High Priest**.

Behind and connected to the Principal Temple lies a famous small building called the **Sacristy**. It has many well-carved niches, perhaps used for the storage of ceremonial objects, as well as a carved stone bench. The Sacristy is especially known for the two rocks flanking its entrance; each is said to contain 32 angles, but it's easy to come up with a different number whenever you count them.

A staircase behind the Sacristy climbs a small hill to the major shrine in Machu Picchu, the **Intihuatana**. This Quechua word loosely translates as the 'Hitching Post of the Sun' and refers to the carved rock pillar, often mistakenly called a sundial, which stands at the top of the Intihuatana hill. The Inca astronomers were able to predict the solstices using the angles of this pillar. Thus, they were able to claim control over the return of the lengthening summer days. Exactly how the pillar was used for these astronomical purposes remains unclear, but its elegant simplicity and high craftwork make it a highlight of the complex. It is recorded that there were several of these *intihuatanas* in various important Inca sites, but the Spaniards smashed most in an attempt to wipe out the pagan blasphemy of sun worship.

At the back of the Intihuatana is another staircase. It descends to the **Central Plaza**, which separates the ceremonial sector of Machu Picchu from the more mundane residential and industrial sectors, which were not as well constructed. At the lower end of this latter area is the **Prison Group**, a labyrinthine complex of cells, niches and passageways, positioned both under and above the ground. The centerpiece of the group is the **Temple of the Condor**, which contains a carving of the head of a condor, with the natural rocks behind it resembling the Andean bird's outstretched wings. Behind the condor is a well-like hole and, at the bottom of this, the door to a tiny underground cell that can only be entered by bending double.

INTIPUNKU

The Inca Trail ends after its final descent from the notch in the horizon called Intipunku (Sun Gate). Looking at the hill behind you as you enter the ruins, you can see both the trail and Intipunku. This hill, called Machu Picchu (Old Peak) gives the site its name. It takes about an hour to reach Intipunku, and if you can spare at least half a day for the round trip, it may be possible to continue as far as Wiñay Wayna (p284). Expect to pay S15 or more as an unofficial reduced-charge admission fee to the Inca Trail, and be sure to return before 3pm, which is when the checkpoint typically closes.

INCA DRAWBRIDGE

A scenic but level walk from the Hut of the Caretaker of the Funerary Rock takes you right past the top of the terraces and out along a narrow, cliff-clinging trail to the Inca drawbridge. In under a half-hour's walk, the trail gives you a good look at cloud-forest vegetation and an entirely different view of Machu Picchu. This walk is recommended, though you'll have to be content with photographing the bridge from behind a barrier meters above it, as someone crossed the bridge some years ago and tragically fell to their death.

CERRO MACHU PICCHU

A 1½- to two-hour climb brings you to the top of Machu Picchu hill, to be rewarded with the site's most extensive view – along the Inca trail to Wiñay Wayna and Phuyupatamarka, down to the valley floor and the impressive terracing near KM104 (where the two-day Inca Trail begins) and across the site of Machu Picchu itself. This walk is more spectacular than Wayna Picchu, and less crowded. Allow yourself plenty of time to enjoy the scenery (and catch your breath!). Recommended.

WAYNA PICCHU

Wayna Picchu is the small, steep mountain at the back of the ruins. Wayna Picchu is normally translated as 'Young Peak,' but the word *picchu*, with the correct glottal pronunciation, refers to the wad in the cheek of a coca-leaf chewer.

At first glance, it would appear that Wayna Picchu is a difficult climb but, although the ascent is steep, it's not technically difficult. Beyond the central plaza between two open-fronted buildings is a registration booth, where you have to sign in. Note that access to Wayna Picchu is limited to 400 people per day – the first 200 in line are let in at 7am, and another 200 at 10am. Lines are long and competition for places is fierce – get here early

if you're serious about doing this climb. Cerro Machu Picchu is a very good alternative if you miss out (or simply don't feel like lining up to climb a hill).

The 45- to 90-minute scramble up a steep footpath takes you through a short section of Inca tunnel. Take care in wet weather as the steps get dangerously slippery.

Part way up Wayna Picchu, a marked path plunges down to your left, continuing down the rear of Wayna Picchu to the small **Temple of the Moon**. The trail is easy to follow, but involves steep sections, a ladder and an overhanging cave, where you have to bend over to get by. The descent takes about an hour, and the ascent back to the main Wayna Picchu trail longer. The spectacular trail drops and climbs steeply as it hugs the sides of Wayna Picchu before plunging into the cloud forest. Suddenly, you reach a cleared area where the small, very well-made ruins are found. From the Temple of the Moon, another cleared path leads up behind the ruin and steeply onward up the back side of Wayna Picchu.

Sleeping & Eating

Most people either arrive on day trips from Cuzco or stay in Aguas Calientes.

Machu Picchu Sanctuary Lodge (☎ 984-81-6953; www.sanctuarylodgehotel.com; standard/mountain view/ste US$852/1009/1440) is the only place to stay at Machu Picchu itself and is criminally overpriced. There is no earthly reason to stay here – you can catch the bus up from Aguas Calientes in time to be here when the site opens – but it's still often full, so book ahead.

Getting There & Around

From Aguas Calientes, buses for Machu Picchu leave from a ticket office along the main road for the tightly winding 8km trip up the mountain (S21, 25 minutes each way). Departures are frequent, starting at 5:30am and finishing at 2.30pm. Buses return from the ruins when full, with the last departure at 5:45pm.

Otherwise, it's a 20-minute walk from Aguas Calientes to Puente Ruinas, where the road to the ruins crosses the Río Urubamba, near the museum. A breathtakingly steep but well-marked trail climbs another 2km up to Machu Picchu, taking about an hour to hike (less coming down!). At the time of research, an Inca trail from Machu Picchu's eastern flank down to the river was being cleared, and was expected to be operational sometime in 2010. This will be a much nicer walk, featuring waterfalls in the rainy season, and away from buses.

For information about getting to Aguas Calientes, see p278.

THE INCA TRAIL

The most famous hike in South America, the four-day Inca Trail, is walked by thousands every year. Although the total distance is only about 43km, the ancient trail laid by the Incas from the Sacred Valley to Machu Picchu winds its way up and down and around the mountains, snaking over three high Andean passes en route, which have collectively led to the route being dubbed 'the Inca Trial.' The views of snowy mountain peaks, distant rivers and ranges, and cloud forests flush with orchids are stupendous – and walking from one cliff-hugging pre-Columbian ruin to the next is a mystical and unforgettable experience. Except for the sad fact, of course, that you'll never have a moment's peace to really soak it all up, due to the other 499 people walking the trail with you.

Most trekking agencies run buses to the start of the trail near the village of Chilca at Piscacucho, aka Km 82 on the railway to Aguas Calientes.

After crossing the Río Urubamba (2200m) and taking care of registration formalities, you'll climb gently alongside the river to the trail's first archaeological site, **Llactapata** (Town on Hillside), before heading south down a side valley of the Río Cusichaca. (If you start from Km 88, turn west after crossing the river to see the little-visited site of **Q'ente** (Hummingbird), about 1km away, then return east to Llactapata on the main trail.)

The trail leads 7km south to the hamlet of **Wayllabamba** (Grassy Plain; 3100m), near which many tour groups will camp for the first night. You can buy bottled drinks and high-calorie snacks here, and take a breather to look over your shoulder for views of the snowcapped **Nevado Verónica** (5750m).

Wayllabamba is situated near the fork of Ríos Llullucha and Cusichaca. The trail crosses the Río Llullucha, then climbs steeply up along the river. This area is known as **Tres Piedras** (Three White Stones), though these

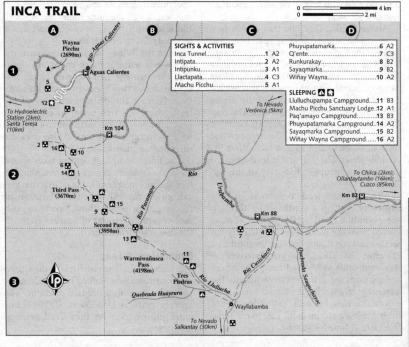

INCA TRAIL

0   4 km
0   2 mi

SIGHTS & ACTIVITIES
Inca Tunnel.................................1 A2
Intipata.....................................2 A2
Intipunku...................................3 A1
Llactapata.................................4 C3
Machu Picchu...........................5 A1
Phuyupatamarka......................6 A2
Q'ente......................................7 C3
Runkurakay..............................8 B2
Sayaqmarka..............................9 B2
Wiñay Wayna..........................10 A2

SLEEPING
Llulluchupampa Campground.....11 B3
Machu Picchu Sanctuary Lodge..12 A1
Paq'amayo Campground............13 B3
Phuyupatamarka Campground....14 A2
Sayaqmarka Campground..........15 B2
Wiñay Wayna Campground......16 A2

boulders are no longer visible. From here it is a long, very steep 3km climb through humid woodlands.

The trail eventually emerges on the high, bare mountainside of **Llulluchupampa**, where water is available and the flats are dotted with campsites, which get very cold at night. This is as far as you can reasonably expect to get on your first day, though many groups will actually spend their second night here.

From Llulluchupampa, a good path up the left-hand side of the valley climbs for a two- to three-hour ascent to the pass of **Warmiwañusca**, also colorfully known as 'Dead Woman's Pass.' At 4198m above sea level, this is the highest point of the trek, and leaves many a seasoned hiker gasping. From Warmiwañusca, you can see the Río Pacamayo (Sunrise River) far below, as well as the ruin of Runkurakay halfway up the next hill, above the river.

The trail continues down a long and knee-jarringly steep descent to the river, where there are large campsites at **Paq'aymayo**. At an altitude of about 3500m, the trail crosses the river over a small footbridge and climbs toward **Runkurakay** (Basket-Shaped Building), a round ruin with superb views. It's about an hour's walk away.

Above Runkurakay, the trail climbs to a false summit before continuing past two small lakes to the top of the second pass at 3950m, which has views of the snow-laden Cordillera Vilcabamba. You'll notice a change in ecology as you descend from this pass – you're now on the eastern, Amazon slope of the Andes and things immediately get lusher. The trail descends to the ruin of **Sayaqmarka** (Dominant Town), a tightly constructed complex perched on a small mountain spur, which offers incredible views. The trail continues downward and crosses an upper tributary of the Río Aobamba (Wavy Plain).

The trail then leads on across an Inca causeway and up a gentle climb through some beautiful cloud forest and an Inca tunnel carved from the rock. This is a relatively flat section and you'll soon arrive at the third pass at almost 3700m, which has grand views of the Río Urubamba valley, and campsites where some groups spend their final night, with the advantage of watching the sun set over a truly spectacular view, but with the disadvantage of having to leave at 3am in the race to reach the Sun Gate in time for sunrise.

Just below the pass is the beautiful and well-restored ruin of **Phuyupatamarka** (Town Above the Clouds), about 3600m above sea level. The site contains a beautiful series of ceremonial baths with water running through them. From Phuyupatamarka, the trail makes a dizzying dive into the cloud forest below, following an incredibly well-engineered flight of many hundreds of Inca steps (which can be nerve-racking in the early hours – take extra batteries for your flashlight). After two or three hours, the trail eventually zigzags its way down to a red-roofed white building that marks the final night's campsite and offers (erratically) hot showers and bottled drinks.

A 500m trail behind the pub leads to the exquisite little Inca site of **Wiñay Wayna** (also spelled Huiñay Huayna), which is variously translated as 'Forever Young,' 'To Plant the Earth Young' and 'Growing Young,' (as opposed to 'growing old'). Peter Frost writes that the Quechua name refers to an orchid that blooms here year-round. The semitropical campsite at Wiñay Wayna boasts one of the most stunning views on the whole trail, especially at sunrise, but many say it's spoiled by the presence of the pub. A few rowdy beers here are traditional with most trail operators, making the obligatory predawn start the next day all the more traumatic. A rough trail leads from this site to another spectacular terraced ruin, called **Intipata**.

From the Wiñay Wayna guard post, the trail winds without much change in elevation through the cliff-hanging cloud forest for about two hours to reach **Intipunku** (Sun Gate) – the penultimate site on the trail, where it's traditional to enjoy your first glimpse of majestic Machu Picchu while waiting for the sun to rise over the surrounding mountains.

The final triumphant descent takes almost an hour. Trekkers generally arrive long before the morning trainloads of tourists, and can enjoy the exhausted exhilaration of reaching their goal without having to push past enormous groups of tourists fresh off the first train from Cuzco.

Regulations & Fees

The Inca Trail is the only trek in the Cuzco area that cannot be walked independently – you must go with a licensed operator. The average price is US$350 to US$500. For more information on Inca Trail pricing, see (p286).

Only 500 people each day (including guides and porters) are allowed to start the trail, and permits are issued (to trail operators only – you can't do it yourself) on a first-come, first-served basis. If you want to walk the trail between May and August, book at least six months in advance. Outside these months, you may get a permit with a few weeks' notice, but it's very hard to predict. To check how many permits are left for a particular date, go to www.nahui.gob.pe, click on 'ingresar como invitado', then 'consultas', then 'Disponibilidad Camino Inca'. Then choose a month and click on 'ver disponibilidad' to see the number of permits left available for each date.

You must go through an approved Inca Trail operator to get a permit. You will need to provide your passport number to get a permit, and carry the passport with you to show at checkpoints along the trail.

When to Go

Organized groups leave year-round except in February, when the Inca trail is closed for maintenance and it rains so much that nobody in their right mind goes trekking. The coldest, driest and most popular months are June to August. Secure your trekking permit before making detailed plans, as they can sell out months in advance for any date.

For more information on when to go trekking in the Cuzco region, see p234.

What to Bring

Trekking poles are highly recommended, as the Inca Trail features a cartilage-crunching number of downhill stone steps. A cheap, effective alternative to expensive trekking poles is to buy a disposable bamboo pole for S5 in the Plaza de Armas in Ollantaytambo.

Take a stash of cash for tipping your guide and porters. You should tip guides at least $US10 per day if you were happy with their work, and give a similar amount to be divided among cooks and group porters. If you had a private porter to carry your personal gear, you should tip him separately – again, around $US10 per day is an appropriate amount.

For more information on packing for treks in the Cuzco region, see p234.

THE INCA JUNGLE TRAIL: BACK DOOR TO MACHU PICCHU

There are outstanding multisport opportunities between Cuzco and Machu Picchu via Santa Teresa, and savvy Cuzco operators have set up all sorts of ways to bike, hike and raft your way here over three to five days. The number of days and activities vary, but the backbone of tours on offer is the same.

The trip starts with a long, four- to five-hour drive from Cuzco to Abra Málaga – the high (4350m) pass between Ollantaytambo and the Amazon Basin. Somewhere on the Amazon side you'll board mountain bikes for the long ride down to Santa María. Descending from the glacial to the tropical, it's an incredibly scenic ride of up to 71km, and almost entirely downhill. It starts on paved road, but after about 20km turns to dirt.

Some operators walk the 23km from Santa María to Santa Teresa; others send you by vehicle (one hour), arguing that it's not a particularly interesting hike, though there is a short section of preconquest *camino de hierro* (iron road) – the Inca version of a superhighway.

Either way you'll arrive in Santa Teresa to the welcome spectacle of the Cocalmayo hot springs – the perfect ending to an active day. (Some companies include rafting near Santa Teresa; see p235 for important information about this.)

From Santa Teresa, you can walk the 20km to Machu Picchu, 12km of it along train tracks. There's nice river scenery but no particular attraction except extreme cheapness. Alternatively, you can catch a bus and a train. You may reverse this route to get back to Cuzco, but it's much quicker to catch the train via the Sacred Valley.

The trip costs between US$160 and US$250, and usually includes a guided tour of Machu Picchu and accommodation in Aguas Calientes. Whether you stay in a tent or a hostel, key factors in the trip price are bike quality and whether you walk or catch the train to Aguas Calientes.

This trip was pioneered by the recommended **Lorenzo Expeditions** (☎ 984-85-1385; www.lorenzo expeditions.com; Plateros 348B). **Gravity Peru** (☎ 22-8032; www.gravityperu.com; Santa Catalina Ancha 398) offers the best-quality bikes. Other respected operators include **Reserv Cusco** (☎ 26-1548; www.reserv-cusco -peru.com; Plateros 326) and **X-treme Tourbulencia** (☎ 22-4362; www.x-tremetourbulencia.com; Plateros 358).

PORTER WELFARE Katy Shorthouse

The substandard treatment of workers is a major issue in Cuzco. It is by no means uncommon for porters to sleep on the ground, with no blankets to keep them warm, after a dinner of your leftovers if they're lucky, or the water your rice was cooked in if they're not. As a guide and tour operator working in the Cuzco region, I have witnessed porters begging for food, carrying packs on infected holes gouged in their backs by impossibly shaped loads, and fainting from hunger and exhaustion on the Inca Trail. Many other travelers have told me similar stories.

Things are a lot better than they used to be, thanks to the recent introduction of laws specifying the following minimum requirements:

- Minimum payment of S170.40 for the Inca trail
- Blankets or sleeping bags must be provided
- Food must be provided specifically for porters, not just leftovers
- Treatment for on-the-job injuries must be covered by the employer
- Some kind of footwear (sandals are acceptable) and something warm must be provided
- Porters must carry no more than 20kg of group gear and 5kg of their own gear

Some of these rules are being obeyed – clothing and bedding are easy to verify, and the authorities do check. Weight, however, is trickier. The law has certainly helped, but abuse still happens. Weight checks also do not distinguish between group gear and porter's gear, so there's a risk that some operators will leave porters little room for their own food and clothing.

Payment is where the most notorious abuses occur. The Peruvian Ministerio de Trabajo (Department of Labor), which monitors working conditions, has received many complaints of operators paying porters as little as S90 – little more than half than the government-mandated minimum. They keep their paperwork in order through discounting for transport, uniform, and

---

Choosing an Inca Trail Operator

The trail is the trail, and all agencies promise great guides, equipment and food, so it's understandable that most people's choice of Inca Trail operator is based largely on price. A cheap trek can be a pretty uncomfortable experience: common complaints include big groups, minimal food, train tickets back to Cuzco failing to materialize, leaking tents and uninterested guiding.

Tour prices include a tent, food, a cook, one-day admission to the ruins and the train fare back to Cuzco.

Porters to carry group gear – tents, food, etc – are also included. You'll be expected to carry your own personal gear, including sleeping bag, unless you pay extra for a personal porter; this usually costs around US$50 for about 10kg.

If you have special dietary requirements, state them clearly and often. If possible, get confirmation in writing that your specific requirements will be met.

For those who do not want to do the hike in a big anonymous group, it's possible to organize private trips with an independent licensed guide. This can be expensive but for groups of six or more it may in fact be cheaper than the standard group treks. Prices vary considerably, so shop around.

Porter welfare is a major issue in the Cuzco region (see the boxed text, above). Porter laws are enforced through fines and license suspensions by Peru's Ministerio de Trabajo (Ministry of Work).

The operators listed below have not been sanctioned in the 12 months prior to time of research, and also got the thumbs-up in discussions with porters. No doubt there are other conscientious operators out there; these are the ones we were able to verify. Do your own research, and let us know what you find out.

These companies offer treks as well as tours around Peru.

Amazonas Explorer (☎ 25-2846; www.amazonas -explorer.com)

Aracari (☎ in Lima 01-651-2424; www.aracari.com)

Eco Inka (☎ 22-4050; www.ecoinka.com)

Explorandes (☎ in Lima 01-715-2323; www.explor andes.com)

GAP (☎ in North America 1-416-260-0999; www .gapadventures.com)

Intrepid Adventures (☎ in Australia 61-3-9473-2626; www.intrepidtravel.com)

anything else they can think of, or by simply having porters sign false declarations that they were paid the full amount.

The best way to improve porter conditions is to vote with your feet. Let operators know that porter treatment is a factor in your buying decision. Be prepared to pay more. Many operators are conscientious, and concerned about these issues, but only a few are confident enough to charge the price that a well-equipped, well-organized, well-guided Inca trail with delicious, plentiful food and good working conditions requires. A quality trip with all these attributes will set you back at least US$400. Paying less than US$250 means that cost cutting is inevitably occurring, and porter welfare is likely to be affected. Be aware, however, that paying more doesn't guarantee that porters are being well treated, so go with a well-recommended company, such as those listed on p286.

So what can you do on the trail?

- Ask to see your porters eat their dinner – not only to see what they're eating, but also what time they get to eat it.

- Ask porters about their treatment, but don't expect to learn much – porters who complain may be sacked, and some porters I talked to even said that agencies explicitly instructed them to lie about working conditions. But asking these questions will let porters know that trekkers support them.

- Don't sit around in the dining tent talking until late; it's where the porters sleep.

- Tip the cooks if you liked the food, and always tip your porters.

- If you have a personal porter, tip him individually – don't assume fair distribution of general tips.

- If you don't like what you see, complain to your guide and to the agency, and register an official complaint with **iPerú** (www.peru.info), either at a branch or online.

Peruvian Odyssey (☎ 22-2105; www.peruvianodyssey.com; Pasaje Pumaqchupan 196)

Tambo Trek (☎ 23-7718; www.tambotreks.net)

These companies are Cuzco-based trekking specialists.

Andina Travel (☎ 25-1892; www.andinatravel.com; Plazoleta Santa Catalina 219)

Eco Trek Peru (☎ 24-7286; www.ecotrekperu.com; Atocsaycuchi 599)

Naty's Travel (☎ 26-1811; www.natystravelcusco.com; Triunfo 342)

Peru Treks (☎ 22-2722; www.perutreks.com; Av Pardo 540)

Peruvian Highland Trek (☎ 24-2480; www.peruvianhighlandtrek.com; Calle del Medio 139)

Alternative Routes to Machu Picchu

For more information on the following hikes, the *Alternative Inca Trails Information Packet* from the South American Explorers Club (p227) is a great resource.

Two-Day Inca Trail

This 16km version of the Inca Trail gives a fairly good indication of what the longer trail is like. It's a real workout, and passes through some of the best scenery and most impressive ruins and terracing of the longer trail.

It's a steep three- or four-hour climb from Km 104 to Wiñay Wayna, then another two hours or so on fairly flat terrain to Machu Picchu.

You then spend the night in a hostel in Aguas Calientes, and the next day visiting Machu Picchu, so it's really only one day of walking. The average price is US$270 to US$370.

Lares Valley Trek

This is not a specific track as such, but a walk along any of a number of different routes to Ollantaytambo through the dramatic Lares Valley. Starting at natural hot springs, the route wanders through rural Andean villages, lesser-known Inca archaeological sites, lush lagoons and river gorges. You'll finish by taking the train from Ollantaytambo to Aguas Calientes. Although this is more of a cultural trek than a technical trip, the mountain scenery is breathtaking, and the highest mountain pass (4450m) is certainly nothing to sneeze at. The average price is US$300 to US$430.

CUZCO & THE SACRED VALLEY

Salkantay Trek

A longer, more spectacular trek, with a slightly more difficult approach to Machu Picchu than the Inca Trail. Its highest point is a high pass of over 4700m near the magnificent glacier-clad peak of Salkantay (6271m; 'Savage Mountain' in Quechua). From here you descend in spectacular fashion to the vertiginous valleys of the subtropics. It takes five to seven days to get to Machu Picchu, and the average price is US$350 to US$500. **Mountain Lodges of Peru** (☎ 23-6069; http://mountainlodgesofperu.com) has pioneered a luxury approach to this trek, offering high-quality guiding and comfortable lodges each night.

CUZCO TO PUNO

The rickety railway and the paved road to Lake Titicaca shadow each other as they both head southeast from Cuzco. En route you can investigate ancient ruins and pastoral Andean towns that are great detours for intrepid travelers who want to leave the Gringo Trail far behind. Most of the following destinations can be reached on day trips from Cuzco; for points of interest closer to Puno, see p206. Inka Express and Turismo Mer run luxury bus tours (see p254) between Cuzco and Puno that visit some but not all of these places. Local and long-distance highway buses run more frequently along this route and are less expensive.

TIPÓN

A demonstration of the Incas' mastery over their environment, this extensive **Inca site** (entry with boleto turístico; ☉ 7am-6pm) about 30km from Cuzco, just before Oropesa, consists of some impressive terracing at the head of a small valley and boasts an ingenious irrigation system. Take any Urcos-bound bus from opposite the hospital in Av de la Cultura in Cuzco, or a *colectivo* from outside Av Tullumayo 207 (S3, 55 minutes), and ask to be let off at the Tipón turnoff (S2, 45 minutes). A steep dirt road from the turnoff (an excellent spot for eating *cuy* to build up your strength) climbs the 4km to the ruins. For S80 (for the whole car), a *colectivo* from outside Av Tullumayo 207 will drive you into the ruins at Tipón and Piquillacta, wait and bring you back.

PIQUILLACTA & RUMICOLCA

Literally translated as 'the Place of the Flea,' **Piquillacta** (entry with boleto turístico; ☉ 7am-6pm) is the only major pre-Inca ruin in the area. It was built around AD 1100 by the Wari culture. It's a large ceremonial center of crumbling two-story buildings, all with entrances that are strategically located on the upper floor. It is surrounded by a defensive wall. The stonework here is much cruder than that of the Incas, and the floors and walls were paved with slabs of white gypsum, of which you can still see traces. On the opposite side of the road about 1km further east is the huge Inca gate of **Rumicolca**, built on Wari foundations. The cruder Wari stonework contrasts with the Inca blocks. It's interesting to see indigenous people working with the mud that surrounds the area's swampy lakes – the manufacture of adobe (mud bricks) is one of the main industries of this area.

Urcos-bound buses from Cuzco pass by both sites.

ANDAHUAYLILLAS

☎ 084 / pop 840 / elev 3123m

Don't confuse this place with Andahuaylas, west of Cuzco. Andahuaylillas is more than 45km southeast of Cuzco, about 7km before the road splits at Urcos. This pretty Andean village is most famous for its lavishly decorated **Jesuit church** (admission S5; ☉ 7am-5:30pm), which is almost oppressive in its baroque embellishments. The church dates from the 17th century and houses many carvings and paintings, including a canvas of the Immaculate Conception attributed to Esteban Murillo. There are reportedly many gold and silver treasures locked in the church, and the villagers are all involved in taking turns guarding it 24 hours a day. Is the rumor true or not? All we can tell you is that the guards take their job *very* seriously.

Near the church are the shop of the **Q'ewar Project**, a women's cooperative that makes distinctive dolls clad in traditional costumes, and the eclectic **Museo Ritos Andinos** (admission by donation; ☉ 7am-6pm), whose somewhat random displays include a mummified child and an impressive number of deformed craniums.

Hospedaje Policlinico El Sol (☎ in Cuzco 084-22-7264; Garcilaso 514; dm S30, d S50-60) has accommodations in a colonial house, and also offers massage and medical treatments. **Chiss**

Hospedaje (Quispicanchi 216, r per person from S15) offers basic accommodation.

To reach Andahuaylillas (S7, one hour), take any Urcos-bound bus from the terminal just off Av de la Cultura in Cuzco.

RAQCHI

☎ 084 / pop 320 / elev 3480m

The little village of **Raqchi**, 125km southeast of Cuzco, is wrapped around an **Inca ruin** (admission S10) that looks from the road like a strange alien aqueduct. These are the remains of the Temple of Viracocha, which was once one of the holiest shrines in the Inca empire. Twenty-two columns made of stone blocks helped support the largest-known Inca roof; most were destroyed by the Spanish, but their foundations are clearly seen. The remains of many houses and storage buildings are also visible, and reconstruction is an ongoing process.

The people of Raqchi are charming, kind and witty. They're also environmentally conscious: at time of research their latest project was trying to become plastic-bag free. And they are famous potters – many of the ceramics on sale in the markets of Pisac and Chinchero come from here.

You can experience life in Raqchi by organizing a **homestay** (☎ 984-82-0598, 984-67-9466; raqchi tuors55@hotmail.com; per person S30). Several families offer accommodation in basic but comfortable guestrooms, with private bathrooms and showers. Meals are available for S20. For another S30 per person, you can have a highly recommended day of **guided activities**. These include a visit to the ruins (admission not included), a heart-pumping hike up to the local *mirador* (lookout) and a ceramics workshop.

On the third Sunday in June, Raqchi is the site of a colorful **fiesta** with much traditional music and dancing.

RAQCHI TO ABRA LA RAYA

About 25km past Raqchi is bustling Sicuani, a market town of 12,000 people, halfway from Cuzco to Puno. There's no real reason to stop here except to break the journey. One economical place to stay is **Hostal Samariy** (☎ 084-35-2518; Centenario 138; s/d/tr without bathroom S10/20/30, s/d/tr S15/30/35), a block to the left of the bus terminal. Another is the trippy, kaleidoscopically colorful **Hospedaje Terminal** (☎ 084-25-3535; s/d S15/25) next door to the terminal, which has nice matrimonial rooms but horrible singles.

Twenty minutes past Sicuani – just before Abra la Raya, the high pass that marks the boundary between the Cuzco and Puno departments – are the **Aguas Calientes de Marangani** (admission S3; ☉ 24hrs). This complex of five fabulously hot thermal pools, linked by rustic bridges over unfenced, boiling tributaries, is quite a sight in itself. The added spectacle of locals washing themselves, their kids and their clothes in the pools makes this an excellent, accessible yet off-the-beaten-track experience.

You can count on local transport to hop between Cuzco, Andahuaylillas, Raqchi, Sicuani and the baths from early morning until at least 3pm. For points of interest south of here, see p197.

CUZCO TO THE JUNGLE

There are three overland routes from Cuzco to the jungle. The least-developed, cheapest and quickest goes northwest from Ollantaytambo over the Abra Málaga pass, to the secondary jungle around Quillabamba and into little-visited Ivochote and Pongo de Mainique beyond.

The other two routes are more popular but are rarely accessed by road. You can get to the area around Parque Nacional Manu through Paucartambo, Tres Cruces and Shintuya, or to Puerto Maldonado via Ocongate and Quince Mil. To get deep into these areas, most people go on organized tours which include light-plane flights in and out, or in some cases, 4WD road transport.

All of these roads are muddy, slow and dangerous. Think twice before deciding to travel overland, and don't even contemplate it in the wettest months (January to April). An invaluable resource for independent travelers is the *Peruvian Jungle Information Packet*, sold by the **South American Explorers Club** (☎ 084-24-5484; www.saexplorers.org; Atocsaycuchi 670, Cuzco; ☉ 9:30am-5pm Mon-Fri, to 1pm Sat).

CUZCO TO IVOCHOTE

Soon after Ollantaytambo, the road leaves the narrowing Sacred Valley and climbs steeply over the 4350m Abra Málaga. From here it's a dizzying, scenic, mostly unpaved descent straight into Amazonia. Dusty **Santa María** has bus company offices and a couple of very basic *hospedajes* and restaurants. It marks the junction where you turn off for Santa Teresa and the backdoor route to Machu Picchu, or continue down to Quillabamba.

Santa Teresa
☎ 084 / pop 460 / elev 1900m

Santa Teresa is an unprepossessing town. Most buildings in its tiny center are emergency-relief prefabricated shells donated after the flood of 1998, which leveled the town. Once you've familiarized yourself with the center (10 minutes at most), listened to chickens clucking in the Plaza de Armas, and marveled at the statue of the strangely ferocious man threatening some flowers, you've pretty much exhausted the entertainment possibilities of Santa Teresa. The real attractions are a few kilometers outside town – the Cocalmayo hot springs and the Cola de Mono zipline are both worth the time and effort required to get to them.

ORIENTATION & INFORMATION

There are no banks or ATMs in Santa Teresa – you must bring all the cash you need. Don't count on being able to change dollars or find internet access, either. The main street, Carrión, runs between the stadium and the Plaza de Armas. Continue east past the plaza to get to Cola de Mono, Lucmabamba and the hydroelectric station; head west past the stadium to get to Baños Termales Cocalmayo. Cusco Medical Assistance in Carrión provides 24-hour medical attention.

SIGHT AND ACTIVITIES

Baños Termales Cocalmayo (admission S10, camping per tent S5; ⏱ 24 hr) is 4km from town. These stunningly landscaped, council-owned natural hot springs are truly a world-class attraction. As if huge, warm pools and a natural shower straight out of a jungle fantasy weren't enough, you can buy beer and snacks and even camp in the gorgeous grassy grounds. The astonishing fact that the baths are open 24 hours has caused many delirious travelers to think they have in fact died and gone to heaven.

You can reliably catch a *colectivo* from Santa Teresa to Cocalmayo at around 3pm, when vehicles head down to collect Inca Jungle Trail walkers arriving from Santa María. Otherwise, you may have to brave the unshaded, dusty walk or pay a taxi up to S10 each way.

ourpick Cola de Mono (☎ 79-2413, 984-70-9878; info@canopyperu.com; US$40) is Peru's only zipline

and South America's highest; a must for thrill seekers. A total of 2500m of zipline in six separate sections whizzes you back and forth high above the Sacsara Valley – it's more about flying through spectacular scenery than learning about the canopy, and all the better for it. Allow about 2½ hours.

To get there, it's a pleasant half-hour stroll east – just follow the road out of town – or a S10 taxi ride.

The owners of Cola de Mono, river guides from way back, also run **rafting** on the spectacular, and so far little-exploited, Santa Teresa river (see p235 for more information) and a three-day **kayak school** (US$150 including food and camping).

You can **hike** to the hydroelectric station via Llactapata, a five-hour walk up and over a hill on well-marked Inca trail, affording views of Machu Picchu and access to a half-cleared ruin. A taxi to drop you off at the start in Lucmabamba and pick you up at the hydroelectric station will set you back S35.

SLEEPING

You can camp at Hugo's Lodge for free, at Baños Termales Cocalmayo for S5 per tent, or at Cola de Mono for S10 per person, including tent and mattress.

A handful of *hospedajes* in the center offer bare-bones accommodation for S10 per person. **Hostal Yacumama** (☎ 77-9980, 984-45-2404; s/d/tr/q S30/40/60/80), downhill from the bus terminal, is a big step-up in quality – still basic but spick-and-span with private bathrooms.

Albergue Municipal (☎ 79-2376; alberguemunicipal_st@hotmail.com; s/d/tr/dm S50/80/90/25), next to the football field, is the best option in town. It has a manicured lawn and cool, spacious rooms. The one dorm holds up to 11 people. Book ahead.

Hugo's Lodge (☎ 77-9956; www.hugoslodge.com; r per person S20) is a bargain, and the Santa Teresa area's finest. Airy bungalows and an expansive bar-restaurant overlook Cocalmayo, a 10-minute hike away. You can camp for free, or hire a fully equipped tent for S10.

EATING & DRINKING

The best food options are Crudo's Club, which offers standard fast food and decent *menús*, and Mama Coca, which serves (at glacial speed) some yummy regional classics. To stock up on self-catering supplies and fresh tropical juice, head to the market above the bus terminal.

CUZCO & THE SACRED VALLEY

Crudo's Club is Santa Teresa's most happening nightspot, with a big bar and a small dance floor. Sentidos, behind the plaza, is the best choice for a quiet beer.

GETTING THERE & AWAY

To get to Santa Teresa from Cuzco, take a bus headed for Quillabamba from the Santiago terminal, get off in Santa María, and catch a local *combi* or *colectivo* (S8, one hour) to Santa Teresa.

To get to Machu Picchu, buy a train ticket to Aguas Calientes (S24) from the **Peru Rail ticket office** (6-8am & 10am-3pm daily, 6-8pm Wed & Sun) in the Santa Teresa bus terminal. Train tickets on this route are sold only at this ticket office, and only on the day of departure. The train leaves 4:30pm daily from the hydroelectric station, about 8km from Santa Teresa. Be at the bus terminal at 3:45pm to catch a *combi* there (S2, 25 minutes). The 13km train ride to Aguas Calientes takes 45 minutes. Some choose to walk by the railway tracks instead, an outstandingly cheap way to get to Machu Picchu in around four sweaty hours.

You can also do this route as part of one of the guided multisport tours on offer (see p285).

Combis going directly to Quillabamba (S20, two hours) depart from Santa María's Plaza de Armas daily at around 4am. There's no need to travel at this unsavory hour, however – *colectivos* to Santa María leave often from the bus terminal. From Santa María you can connect to Quillabamba (S10, one hour) and Cuzco (S15, five to six hours).

Quillabamba

084 / pop 8800 / elev 1050m

Welcome to the jungle! Quillabamba's tropical vibe is almost palpable, in the heat that becomes oppressive by 9am, the music that blares all night, and the ceiling-fanned, fly-spotted, land-that-time-forgot feel to most hotels and restaurants.

Quillabamba itself has few attractions and sees little tourism, but it can be used as a base for trips deeper into the jungle, and there are some outstanding, watery natural attractions nearby.

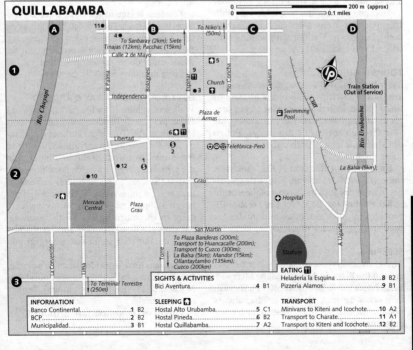

SIGHTS & ACTIVITIES			EATING 🍴		
Bici Aventura	4	B1	Heladería la Esquina	8	B2
			Pizzeria Alamos	9	B1
SLEEPING 🏨					
Hostal Alto Urubamba	5	C1	TRANSPORT		
Hostal Pineda	6	B2	Minivans to Kiteni and Icochote	10	A2
Hostal Quillabamba	7	A2	Transport to Charate	11	A1
			Transport to Kiteni and Icochote	12	B2

INFORMATION		
Banco Continental	1	B2
BCP	2	B2
Municipalidad	3	B1

ORIENTATION

The streets north and south of the Mercado Central, rather than the eternally somnolent Plaza de Armas, are Quillabamba's commercial center.

INFORMATION

BCP (Libertad 549) and Banco Continental on Bolognesi near the corner of Grau have ATMs and change US dollars. There's arm-chewingly slow internet access at a few places around the Plaza de Armas. Limited tourist information is available on the 3rd floor of the Municipalidad.

SIGHTS AND ACTIVITIES

Locals are justifiably proud of **Sanbaray** (admission S0.50; ☺ 8am-late), a delightful complex of swimming pools, lawns, bars and a decent trout restaurant. It's a 10-minute *mototaxi* ride (S3) from the center.

La Balsa, hidden far down a dire dirt track, is a bend in the Río Urubamba that's perfect for swimming and river tubing. Enterprising locals sell beer and food here on weekends.

Mandor, **Siete Tinajas** and **Pacchac** are beautiful waterfalls where you can swim, climb and eat jungle fruit straight off the tree. Siete Tinajas and Pacchac are accessible via public transport for a few soles each to Charate; taxi transport to Mandor with waiting time will set you back S20.

TOURS & GUIDES

Roger Jara (☎ 984-71-2144; rogerjaraalmiron@hotmail .com) offers day trips to all of the attractions listed above, as well as remnant virgin jungle near Quillabamba. He can also guide you through the area's big draws, Pongo de Mainique and Vilcabamba. He speaks some English.

Eco Trek Peru (☎ in Cuzco 24-7286; www.ecotrek peru.com; Atocsaycuchi 599, Cuzco) are passionate specialists in multiday trips in this part of the world.

Bici Aventura (☎ 984-34-0201; Calle 2 de Mayo 423) provides information, bikes and guides for road and single-track missions.

SLEEPING

There are many cheap, cold-water hostels around the Plaza de Armas and the Mercado. **Hostal Pineda** (☎ 28-1447; Libertad 530; s/d/tr S15/30/55, s/d/tr without bathroom S12/24/36) is one, and is notable for the incredible feature of having only single beds.

Hostal Alto Urubamba (☎ 28-1131; altourubamba@ gmail.com; 2 de Mayo 333; s/d/tr S40/60/80, s/d/tr without bathroom S19/26/36) Clean, comfortable-enough rooms with fans encircle a sunny courtyard in this dementedly noisy, long-established traveler favorite.

Hostal Quillabamba (☎ 28-1369; www.hostalquilla bamba.com; Grau 590; s/d/tr/q S50/60/90/110; ☎) Hostal Quillabamba screams cheesy, quasi–*Miami Vice* glam – you wouldn't be surprised to see Roger Moore chatting up a Bond Girl by the swimming pool. Rooms are shabby and dated, but not bad at the price.

EATING & DRINKING

Looking at the *heladerías* (ice-cream shops) on every corner, you could be forgiven for assuming that locals subsist on ice cream. Given the shortage of alternatives, you could be forgiven for doing the same.

Pizzería Alamos (Espinar s/n; mains from S8, pizzas from S11; ☺ 7am-11pm Mon-Sat, 3-11pm Sun) No other place in town is quite so kind to foreign tourists. Staffed by enthusiastic youth, this restaurant fires up pizzas that are big enough to feed an army of Inca warriors, and the open-air courtyard bar is a local hangout after dark.

Heladería la Esquina (cnr Espinar & Libertad; sand-wiches from S2.50; 8am-11pm Mon-Sat) This retro cafe serves up delicious juices, cakes, ice cream and fast-food snacks. Service is grouchy, but the 1950s-diner decor makes up for that.

For a drink, try **Niko's** (Pio Concha s/n).

GETTING THERE & AWAY & AROUND

Walk south along Torre four blocks past Plaza Grau, to Plaza de Banderas, to find transport to Huancacalle. Turn right at the end of Plaza de Banderas to find minivans (S30, four to five hours) to Cuzco in the first block, and the *terminal terrestre* a block later. Buses for Cuzco (S15, six to seven hours) leave from here several times a day before 8am and between 1:30pm and 9:30pm. Minivans leave early in the morning and in the evening. All stop at Ollantaytambo and Urubamba en route, but charge full fare wherever you get off.

Minivans leave from Quillabamba's market area for Kiteni (S15, three to six hours) and Ivochote (S18, five to seven hours), further into the jungle.

The basic *mototaxi* fare around town is S1.

Huancacalle

☎ 084 / pop 300 / elev 3200m

Peaceful, pretty Huancacalle is best known as the jumping-off point for treks to Vilcabamba (see p234), but many more hikes from three to 10 days long are possible from here, including to Puncuyo, Inca Tambo, Choquequirau and Machu Picchu. The town's biggest building is **Hostal Manco Sixpac** (☎ Huancacalle community phone 81-2714, relative in Cuzco 084-27-1358; per person without bathroom S20), run by the Cobos family of local guides. You can organize mules and guides here for around S30 per day each.

Manco Inca's huge palace fortress of **Vitcos** (also known as Rosaspata) is an hour's walk up the hill, and from there you can continue to the amazing, sacred white rock of **Yurac Rumi**. The whole easy-to-follow circuit, which starts just over the bridge at the end of the road, takes a leisurely three hours, including plenty of time for photos and admiration of both scenery and ruins.

Ivochote & Beyond

A long bus journey from Quillabamba takes you through the oil town of Kiteni and on to the more remote **Ivochote**, a small jungle village with a few basic accommodations. From here you can continue into Amazonia by river.

The first major landmark past Ivochote is the **Pongo de Mainique**, a steep-walled canyon carved by cascading waterfalls on the lower Río Urubamba, which marks the border between Amazonia's high and lowland cloud forest. Between June and November, boats can be found in Ivochote to take you there and back – the trip takes the best part of a day. You'll pay anything from S60 to S350 per person; group size is a big factor.

Past the Pongo, at the indigenous Matsiguenka (or Machigengua) community of Timpía, you can find local guides and transport for Santuario Nacional Megantoni. Accommodation is available at **Sabeti Lodge** (www.sabetilodge.com), and you can also camp on the riverside.

CUZCO TO MANU

Paucartambo

pop 1300 / elev 3200m

This small village lies on the eastern slopes of the Andes, about 115km and three hours northeast of Cuzco along a cliff-hanging dirt road (being paved at time of research).

Paucartambo is famous for its riotously colorful celebration in honor of the **Virgen del Carmen**, a festival held annually from July 15 to 18, with hypnotic street dancing, wonderful processions and all manner of weird costumes. The highly symbolic dances are inspired by everything from fever-ridden malaria sufferers to the homosexual practices of the Spanish conquistadors.

Accommodation for the festival needs to be organized in advance; you either have to find a room in one of a few basic hotels or hope a local will give you some floor space. Many tourist agencies in Cuzco run buses specifically for the fiesta and can help arrange accommodations with local families.

Transportes Gallito de las Rocas (☎ 084-22-6895; Diagonal Angamos, 1st block off Av de la Cultura, Cuzco) buses depart to Paucartambo (S7, five hours) daily and to Pilcopata (S18, 12 hours) on Monday, Wednesday and Friday. Look for 'Paucartambo' painted on a lamp post between auto shops to find the office.

Tres Cruces

About two hours beyond Paucartambo is the extraordinary jungle view at Tres Cruces, a lookout off the Paucartambo–Shintuya road. The sight of the mountains dropping away into the Amazon Basin is gorgeous in itself, but is made all the more magical by the sunrise phenomenon that occurs from May to July (other months are cloudy), especially around the time of the winter solstice on June 21. The sunrise here gets optically distorted, causing double images, halos and an incredible multicolored light show. At this time of year, many travel agencies and outdoor adventure outfitters run sunrise-watching trips from Cuzco.

During Paucartambo's Fiesta de la Virgen del Carmen, minibuses run back and forth between Paucartambo and Tres Cruces all night long. You can also take a truck en route to Pillcopata and ask to be let off at the turnoff to Tres Cruces (a further 13km walk). Alternatively, ask around in Paucartambo to hire a truck. Make sure you leave in the middle of the night to catch the dawn, and take plenty of warm clothing. Camping is possible but take all your own supplies.

Tres Cruces is within Parque Nacional Manu and admission costs S10.

For details of the onward trip to Shintuya and the Manu area, see p474.

CUZCO TO PUERTO MALDONADO

This road is vile. It's almost 500km long and takes at least a day to travel in the dry season – much longer in the wet. – and most travelers choose to fly from Cuzco to Puerto Maldonado. At the time of research, the road was being paved, so things may have improved by the time you read this, but don't take this journey lightly: it requires hardiness.

Various companies depart from Cuzco's *terminal terrestre* for Puerto Maldonado between 3pm and 4.30pm daily. CIVA (S60, 17 hours, departs 4pm) is probably the best option. If you want to split up the journey, the best places to stop are Ocongate and Quince Mil, which have basic accommodations. **Transportes Siwar** (☎ 084-23-6691; Av Tito Condemayta 1613, Cuzco) has buses to Ocongate and Tinqui (S8, three hours), leaving from behind the Coliseo Cerrado several times a day.

The route heads toward Puno until soon after Urcos, where the dirt road to Puerto Maldonado begins. About 125km and 2½ hours from Cuzco, you come to the highland town of **Ocongate**, which has a couple of basic hotels around the plaza.

From here, trucks go to the village of **Tinqui**, an hour's drive beyond Ocongate, which is the starting point for the spectacular seven-day trek encircling **Ausangate** (6384m), the highest mountain in southern Peru (see p234).

After Tinqui, the road drops steadily to **Quince Mil**, 240km from Cuzco, less than 1000m above sea level, and the halfway point of the journey. The area is a gold-mining center, and the hotel here is often full. After another 100km, the road into the jungle reaches the flatlands, where it levels out for the last 140km into Puerto Maldonado.

CUZCO TO THE CENTRAL HIGHLANDS

Traveling by bus from Cuzco to Lima via Abancay and Nazca takes you along a remote route closed from the late 1980s until the late 1990s due to guerilla activity and banditry. It now is much safer, and paved, but you should check recent news reports before heading out this way. Going west from Abancay to Andahuaylas and Ayacucho is a tough ride on a rough road rarely used except by the most hard-core travelers.

CUZCO TO ABANCAY

There are several worthwhile stops along this four-hour, 200km ride. To do one or two and bus hop your way to Abancay in a day, start by catching a *colectivo* to Limatambo (S8, 1½ hours) from Arcopata in Cuzco.

Limatambo, 80km west of Cuzco, is named after the Inca site of Rimactambo, also popularly known as **Tarawasi** (admission S10), which is situated beside the road, about 2km west of town. The site was used as a ceremonial center, as well as a resting place for the Inca *chasquis* (Inca runners who delivered messages over long distances). The exceptional polygonal retaining wall, noteworthy for its 28 human-sized niches, is in itself worth the trip from Cuzco. On the wall below it, look for flower shapes and a nine-sided heart amid the patchwork of perfectly interlocking stones. There is basic, hard-to-find accommodation in Limatambo.

The natural thermal baths of **Cconoc** (admission S3) are a 3km walk downhill from a turnoff 10km east of minor transport hub **Corahuasi**, 1½ hours east of Abancay. They have a restaurant, a bar and a basic **hotel** (r per person S15). A taxi from Corahuasi costs S50 with waiting time.

The Inca site of **Saihuite** (admission S20), 45km east of Abancay, has a sizable, intricately carved boulder called the Stone of Saihuite, which is similar to the famous sculpted rock at Q'enqo, near Cuzco, though it's smaller and more elaborate. The carvings of animals are particularly intricate. Ask to be let off at the turnoff to the ruins, from where it is a 1km walk downhill.

Cachora, 15km from the highway from the same turnoff as Saihuite, is the most common starting point for the hike to Choquequirau (see p234). There are a few guesthouses, a campground and local guides and mules for hire.

ABANCAY

☎ 083 / pop 13,800 / elev 2378m

This sleepy rural town is the capital of the department of Apurímac, one of the least-explored regions in the Peruvian Andes. Travelers may opt to use it as a rest stop on the long, tiring bus journey between Cuzco and Ayacucho.

Orientation & Information

Jirón Arequipa and its continuation, Av las Arenas, are the main commercial and entertainment streets, respectively. Av Díaz

APU AUSANGATE

Important geographical features such as rivers and mountains are *apus* (sacred deities) for the Andean people, and are possessed of *kamaq* (vital force). At 6384m, Ausangate is the Cuzco department's highest mountain and the most important *apu* in the area – the subject of countless legends. It is considered the *pakarina* (mythical place of sacred origin) of llamas and alpacas, and controls the health and fertility of these animals. Its freezing heights are also where condemned souls are doomed to wander as punishment for their sins.

Ausangate is the site of the traditional festival of **Q'oyoriti** (Star of the Snow), held in late May or early June between the Christian feasts of the Ascension and Corpus Christi. Despite its overtly Catholic aspect – it's officially all about the icy image of Christ that appeared here in 1783 – the festival remains primarily and obviously a celebration and appeasement of the *apu*, consisting of four or more days of literally nonstop music and dance. Incredibly elaborate costumes and dances – featuring, at the more extreme end, llama fetuses and mutual whipping – repetitive brass-band music, fireworks, and much throwing of holy water all contribute to a dizzy, delirious spectacle. Highly unusual: no alcohol is allowed. Offenders are whipped by anonymous men dressed as *ukukus* (mountain spirits) with white masks that hide their features, who maintain law and order.

It's a belief fervently held by many *cuzqueños* (inhabitants of Cuzco) that if you attend Q'oyoriti three times, you'll get your heart's desire. The traditional way to go about this is to buy an *alacita* (miniature scale model) of your desire. Houses, cars, trucks, petrol stations, university degrees, driver's licenses, money: the usual human desires are on offer for a few soles at stalls lining the pilgrimage pathway. You then line up in the church to have it blessed by a priest. Repeat three years in a row and see what happens.

Q'oyoriti is a pilgrimage – the only way in is by trekking three or more hours up a mountain, traditionally in the wee small hours to arrive around dawn. The sight of a solid, endless line of people quietly wending their way up or down the track and disappearing around a bend in the mountain is unforgettable, as is Q'oyoriti's eerie, other-worldly feel. The fact that everyone's sober at a party gives it an unusual vibe. Then there's the near-total absence of gringos. The author saw a total of perhaps 10 other white faces among a reported 40,000 people in 2009. The majority of attendees are traditionally dressed *campesinos* who feel no compunction about loudly pointing out the unusual sight of a gringo.

Discomfort is another aspect of the pilgrimage. Q'oyoriti takes place at an altitude of 4750m, where glaciers flow down into the Sinakara valley. It's brutally cold, and there's no infrastructure, no town here, just one big elaborate church (complete with flashing lights around the altar) built to house the image of El Señor de Q'oyoriti (The Christ of Q'oyoriti). The temporary toilets are a major ordeal. The blue plastic sea of restaurants, stalls and tents is all carried in, on foot or donkey. The whole thing is monumentally striking: a temporary tent city at the foot of a glacier, created and dismantled yearly to honor two mutually contradictory yet coexisting religions in a festival with dance and costumes whose origins no one can remember. Welcome to Peru – this is the pointy end.

Bárcenas is one block uphill from Jirón Arequipa. **BCP** (Arequipa 218-222) changes US dollars and has an ATM. The post office and a couple of *casas de cambio* are within a stone's throw of the bank. Several cyber-cafes are clustered on Unión just below Arequipa. The bus terminal is a S3 taxi ride from the center.

Sights & Activities

During the dry season (late May to September), hikers and climbers may want to take advantage of the best weather to head for the some-times snowcapped peak of **Ampay** (5228m), about 10km north-northwest of town. The mountain is also the center of the 3635-`hectare **Santuario Nacional Ampay**, where camping and birding are good.

Festivals & Events

Abancay has a particularly colorful **Carnaval** held in the week before Lent, which is a chance to see festival celebrations unaffected by tourism. It includes a nationally acclaimed folk-dancing competition. Book ahead or arrive before the festivities start. **Abancay Day** happens on November 3, the anniversary of the town's founding.

Sleeping

Hostal Victoria (☎ 32-3188; victoriahostal@hotmail.com; Arequipa 305; s/d/tr S28/40/48, s/d without bathroom S15/26) This is an excellent little hostel not far from the BCP. Rooms with private bathrooms come with cable TV.

Saywa Hotel (☎ 32-4876; Arenas 302; www.saywa -hotel.com; s/d/t/q with breakfast S50/85/105/120) What it lacks in personality, Hotel Saywa makes up for in value – comfy beds, excellent showers, and kindly, professional service. Recommended.

HOTURS Hotel Turistas (☎ 32-1017; www.turismo apurimac.com; Díaz Bárcenas 500; s S50-100, d S65-130, ste from S150) Located opposite the Hostal Imperial, the best hotel in town is housed in an imposing, old-fashioned country mansion. An attraction in itself, it provides tasteful, ever so slightly quirky luxury at remarkably low prices.

Eating & Drinking

There are plenty of restaurants and cafes in Arenas. Araujos Rocker Kitchen is a local favorite.

our pick Villa Venecia (☎ 50-4662, Av Bella Abanquina; gigantic mains from S13) Worth the short taxi ride to get to (it's behind the stadium), Villa Venecia is Abancay's most noteworthy restaurant. Serving up every local food imaginable, it's the living embodiment of the Peruvian foodie mantra *'bueno, barato y bastante'* – 'good, cheap and plentiful'. Try *tallarines* (spaghetti), it's an Abancay specialty.

Abancay offers a surprisingly large array of nightlife, centered on Arenas and Pasaje Valdivia just off it. Garabato's Video Pub in Arenas is one spot recommended by locals.

Getting There & Away

Colectivos to Corahuasi via Saihuite (S10, 1½ hours) leave from Jirón Huancavelica, two blocks uphill from Arenas. Vehicles to Cachora leave from one block further uphill. Buses towards Cuzco, Andahuaylas and Lima leave from the *terminal terrestre*.

At least seven companies run buses to Cuzco (S15, five hours), clustered around 6am, 11am and 11pm. Dozens of buses depart to Lima every day, mostly in the afternoon and between 10:30pm and midnight. They cost between S60 and S170 and take from 14 to 18 hours. Departures to Andahuaylas (S10, five hours) cluster around 11:30am and

11:30pm. Faster, more comfortable minibuses to Andahuaylas (S20, four hours) are run by five companies based downstairs in the terminal.

Terminal departure tax is S1.

ANDAHUAYLAS

☎ 083 / pop 6800 / elev 2980m

Andahuaylas, 135km west of Abancay on the way to Ayacucho, is the second-most important town in the department of Apurímac, and a convenient halfway stop on the rough but scenic route between Cuzco and Ayacucho.

Information

BCP (Ramón Castilla s/n) has an ATM and changes US dollars. There's a Western Union office and several *casas de cambio* on Ramón Castilla. There are plenty of internet cafes, some fast – look for the Speedy sign. **Clínica Señor de Huanca** (☎ 42-1418; Andahuaylas 108) provides 24-hour emergency medical attention.

Sights & Activities

Andahuaylas' main attraction, the beautiful **Laguna de Pacucha**, is 17km from town and accessible by bus or taxi. About 15km past the end of the lake is the imposing hilltop site of **Sondor**, built by the Chanka culture. The Chankas were traditional enemies of the Incas, but evidently shared their appreciation of a good view. You can easily access both the lake and the ruin by catching a *combi* from behind the market in Andahuaylas (to Pachuca S2.50, 40 minutes; to Sondor S3, one hour). Go in the morning –transport peters out by 4pm. A taxi will take you to both sites and back for around S40.

Both Andahuaylas and Pacucha have Sunday **markets** that are worth perusing.

Festivals & Events

The annual **Fiesta de Yahuar** (Blood Feast) is on July 28, when traditional dances and music are performed. In the village of Pacucha, the festival includes lashing a condor to the back of a bull and allowing the two to fight in a representation of the highland people's struggle against the Spanish conquistadors.

Sleeping

You can't expect a hot shower in an Andahuaylas hotel, but you can count on cable TV. Go figure.

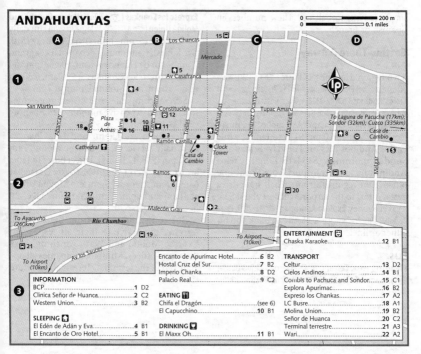

ANDAHUAYLAS

Hostal Cruz del Sur (☎ 42-1571; Andahuaylas 117; s/d/tr without bathroom S10/25/30, d S30) This is the best cheap choice in Andahuaylas, with spacious rooms off outdoor balconies around a flowery patio. Showers S2.

El Edén de Adán y Eva (☎ 42-1746; Palma s/n; s/ d/tr S25/45/60, s/d/tr without bathroom S20/30/50) This friendly, family-run hotel near the Plaza de Armas is good value, with dark but fairly spacious rooms.

Encanto de Apurímac Hotel (☎ 42-3527; hencanto apurimac@yahoo.com; Ramos 401; s without bathroom S25, s/d/tr & ste S35/55/70; 🖳) Nothing fancy, but modern, spacious and bland. The matrimonial suite, with big pink bath, is a great deal. Rates include breakfast.

El Encanto de Oro Hotel (☎ 42-3066; www.hotel andahuaylas.com; Av Casafranca 424; s without bathroom S35, s/d/tr S45/70/90) Friendly and caring, near the market and the Pachuco bus stop. Spotlessly clean rooms are of varying shapes and sizes, and all have frilly curtains and phones. Breakfast is included.

Palacio Real (☎ 20-5361; Andahuaylas 373; s S40, d S50-60; 🖳) This shiny new wireless-enabled hostel offers good doubles and *matrimoniales* (rooms with one large bed). Single rooms are dark but still spacious. Bathrooms are big and blankets are fluffy – a good deal on the whole.

Imperio Chanka (☎ 42-3065; imperiochanka_hotel@ hotmail.com; Vallejo 384; s/d with breakfast S45/70) Has a characterless exterior, but very good, clean rooms. It's Andahuaylas' swankiest hotel, for what that's worth.

Eating, Drinking & Entertainment

El Capucchino (☎ 42-1790; Cáceres Tresierra 321; snacks from S2.50, crepes & salads from S7; ⏰ 9am-11pm Mon-Sat; 🖳) This cheery, breezy, French-run place is a haven of Western home comforts: yummy crepes, waffles and sandwiches, loads of vegetarian options, Andahuaylas' best coffee, plus books, magazines and games. A deservedly popular hangout with both locals and travelers.

Chifa El Dragón (☎ 42-1749; cnr Ramos & Trelles; menú from S7; ⏰ 7am-10pm) El Dragón is a smart restaurant serving Chinese meals with a touch of *criollo* influence.

For a night out, head to *discoteca* **El Maxx Oh** (Cáceres Tresierra s/n; ⏰ Wed-Sun) to bust some moves, or to **Chaska Karaoke** (Constitución

CUZCO & THE SACRED VALLEY

s/n; ☾ 8pm-late) to belt out a few numbers in Spanish or French.

Getting There & Away

AIR

Two regional airlines, **LC Busre** (☎ 42-1591; www .lcbusre.com.pe; Plaza de Armas s/n; ☾ 7:30am-7pm) and **Cielos Andinos** (☎ 42-2328; www.cielosandinos.com.pe; Plaza de Armas s/n; ☾ 8am-1pm & 2-7pm) fly between Andahuaylas, Lima and Ayacucho. LC Busre leaves daily at 10:10am (S119 to Lima), while Cielos Andinos flies on Tuesday, Friday and Sunday mornings (S134 to Lima). Cielos Andinos includes transport from the airline office to the regional airport, a half-hour drive away. A taxi to the airport will cost about S25. Travel agency **Explora Apurímac** (☎ 42-2877; Plaza de Armas s/n; ☾ 8am-1pm & 3-8pm) can book you on either airline.

BUS

Heading east, **Celtur** (☎ 42-2337; cnr Vallejo & Ugarte; ☾), **Señor de Huanca** (☎ 42-1218; Martinelli 170), **Expreso los Chankas** (☎ 42-2441; Malecón Grau s/n) and **Molina Union** (☎ 42-1248; Av los Sauces s/n) run daily to Cuzco (S25, nine hours) via Abancay (S10, five hours). Celtur buses depart at 6:45am and 7pm; Señor de Huanca at 6am, 10am, 1pm and 7pm; Expreso los Chankas at 9:30am, 6:30pm and 7:10pm; and Molina Union at 7pm.

Several companies run faster, more comfortable and expensive minibuses to Abancay (S20, 3½ hours).

Heading west, Celtur and Los Chankas have daily services to Ayacucho around 7am and 7pm (S35, 12 hours). Direct buses to Lima are run by **Wari** (☎ 42-1936; Malecón Grau s/n) at 6am, 11am, 2pm and 5pm, and Molina Union at 10am and 4pm. Getting to Lima takes 20 hours and costs S70.

Bus companies leave from the *terminal terrestre* but arrive to their offices, except Expreso Molino and Wari, which only use their own offices. Minibus companies all operate out of the terminal. Terminal departure tax is S1.

Central Highlands

If it's the breathtaking ruins of ancient civilizations or immersion in uninterrupted wilderness that you seek during your voyage in Peru, take stock for a moment. The rocky, remote central highlands can match the country's better-known tourist destinations for these things and more with one important bonus: the almost total absence of other travelers.

This part of the Central Andes is Peru at its most Peruvian. Travel here is not for the faint-hearted: gone for the most part are the luxury buses, glam restaurants and paved roads. But adventure-spirited travelers will instead discover a better insight into local life than is possible elsewhere. Party at one of the region's myriad fiestas, browse markets teaming with Peru's best handicrafts, bond with the locals on bumpy bus journeys or hike into the high hills to little-known Inca palaces – whatever path you choose in the central highlands, you'll be coming away with authentic experiences. This is the heartland of Andean Peru – its soul, one could say.

Life in this bare, starkly beautiful region is lived largely off the land: llamas and donkeys line the roads more than cars and bright indigenous dress predominates in communities where markets selling produce and handicrafts are the focal points. It often seems as if the rearing, lake-studded mountains here have managed to shield the central highlands from the 21st century. Here, life ticks by much as it has for eons; where festivals, celebrations, ceremonies and traditions thrive. Travelers here are always welcomed and often afforded hospitality beyond the means of the region's modest-living inhabitants. If you want to slip as far from the Gringo Trail as you can get, look no further than Peru's heartland.

HIGHLIGHTS

- Pore over 25,000 colonial-era books in the convent of **Santa Rosa de Ocopa** (p307) at Concepción
- Arrive in the highlands in spectacular style via the world's third-highest railway to **Huancayo** (p312)
- Hunt for handicrafts in the villages of the **Río Mantaro valley** (p313) around Huancayo
- Chill out as the only gringo in forgotten, colonial **Huancavelica** (p314)
- Celebrate the country's top Semana Santa fiesta in **Ayacucho** (p321)
- Hike out to isolated Inca and pre-Inca ruins near **Tantamayo** (p331) and **La Unión** (p330)

- BIGGEST CITY: Huancayo, population 387,700
- AVERAGE TEMPERATURE: January 12°C to 24°C, July 8°C to 24°C

LIMA TO TARMA

SAN PEDRO DE CASTA & MARCAHUASI

Isolated San Pedro de Casta (population 500, elevation 3200m) is the perfect precursor to your Central Andes adventure. The road from Chosica twists spectacularly upward for 40km around a sheer-sided valley before arriving at this mountainside town clustered around a ridge and resounding with the bellows of *burros* (donkeys). A *mirador* (lookout) two blocks up from the plaza offers breathtaking valley views.

People come here principally to visit the little-known archaeological site of Marcahuasi, a nearby 4-sq-km plateau at 4100m. Marcahuasi is famed for its weirdly eroded rocks shaped into animals such as camels, turtles and seals. These have a mystical significance for some people, who claim they are signs of a pre-Inca culture or energy vortices. Locals have fiestas here periodically, but on most occasions it's empty and all yours.

Because of the altitude, it's not advisable to go to Marcahuasi from Lima in one day; acclimatize overnight in San Pedro. It takes two hours to hike the 2km up to the site; you can sometimes catch a bus part of the way if it's not engaged on other municipality business (departing 7:30am from the plaza most days), then hike for 45 minutes. A **Centro de Información** (☎ 01-571-2087; Plaza de Armas; San Pedro) has limited information and maps; staff can arrange guides for S10. Mules and horses can also be hired for similar prices.

You can camp at Marcahuasi but carry water: the few lakes there aren't fit to drink from. In San Pedro, the basic **Gran Hotel Turístico Municipal** (s/d without bathroom S10/20), just off the plaza, has erratic hot water. Local families have beds (ask at the information center). Simple plaza restaurants serve a *menú* (set meal) for about S5.

Getting there entails taking a bus from Lima to Chosica (p124); minibuses to Chosica can be picked up in Central Lima from Arica at Plaza Bolognesi (S3.50, two hours). Then ask for Transportes Municipal San Pedro, which leaves from the bus yard by Parque Echenique on the main drag (the Carretera Central) in Chosica at 9am and 3pm (S6, four hours). The bus back to Choisica leaves at 2pm.

LA OROYA

☎ 064 / pop 35,000 / elev 3731m

Bleak, chilly La Oroya, self-titled 'metallurgical capital of Peru and South America,' is only worthy of a mention for its position on one of the region's main road junctions. (It recently featured in the Blacksmith Institute list of the world's 10 most polluted places). Routes from here lead north towards Cerro de Pasco, Huánuco and Tingo María (and into the northern jungle); east to Tarma (then into the central jungle); south to Huancayo and Ayacucho (and eventually Cuzco) and west to Lima. There are two parts to town: a vast industrial swathe south of the river and the old town (more convenient for onward bus connections) to the northeast. Be wary going out at night here: even locals advise against it.

You'll find a **Banco Continental** (☎ 39-1174; Horacio Zevallos Gomez) with an ATM over the bridge from the old town.

Few travelers stop here: if stranded, basic **Hostal Inti** (☎ 39-1098; Arequipa 117; d without bathroom S18) has hot showers. In the old town, other uninspiring but safe-enough options can be found along Darío León for similar prices. Don't bank on hot water, even if the hotel advertises it.

Huancayo buses pass through the old town. For Cerro de Pasco and Tarma buses and *colectivo* (shared) taxis leave from the other side of the river on Horacio Zevallos Gomez in the west of town.

TARMA

☎ 064 / pop 60,500 / elev 3050m

Tarma, a pleasant, laid-back city surrounded on all sides by scrubby, brown dirt mountains, is easily the best place in this area to stay. From here it's a steep drop down the *ceja de la selva* (eyebrow of the jungle) from the altiplano (highlands) to the Amazon Basin. Lying on the important route linking Lima with its nearest jungle neighborhoods, Tarma sees holiday-makers in the shape of *limeños* (inhabitants of Lima) seeking a tropical change from their desert city but gringos rarely make it here. That said, the city is cottoning on to tourism and facilities are ever-improving. With fascinating excursions on offer in the vicinity, Tarma is a good spot to stop for a couple of days and soak up life in this sector of the central Andes.

The city also has a long history. Hidden in the mountains around town are overgrown

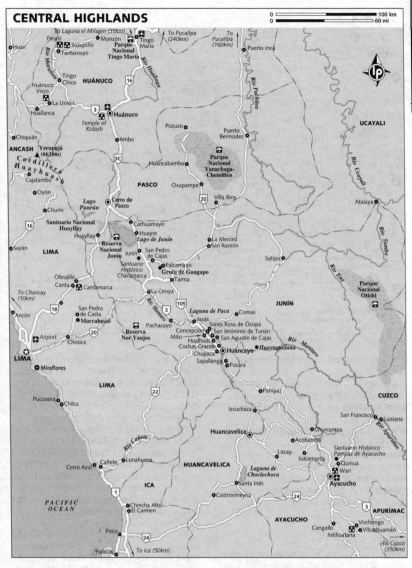

CENTRAL HIGHLANDS

Inca and pre-Inca ruins that have yet to be fully excavated. Tarma was one of the first places to be founded by the Spanish after the conquest (1538 is the generally accepted date). Nothing remains of the early colonial era, but the town has many attractive 19th- and early-20th-century houses with white walls and red-tiled roofs.

Orientation & Information

While the city center is fairly compact, most transport to and from Lima arrives about 800m to the west of the Plaza de Armas, near the *óvalo* (main roundabout) at the arched entrance to central Tarma. Taxis from Huancayo arrive and depart from a rather inconvenient location on the southwest side of town;

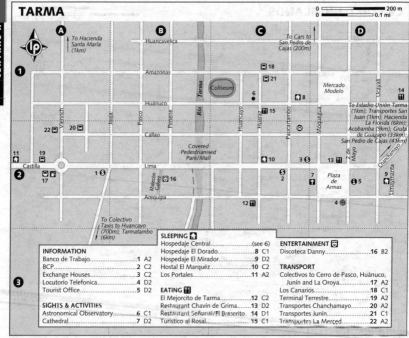

TARMA

0   200 m
0   0.1 mi

Amazon transport leaves from the east side of town.

Casas de cambio (foreign-exchange bureaus) are at the western end of Lima.

Banco de Trabajo (Lima) Has an ATM near the *casas de cambio.*

BCP (☎ 32-2149; Lima at Paucartambo) You can change money here; also has an ATM.

Locutorio Telefónico (Arequipa at Jirón 2 de Mayo) Internet and international telephone *cabinas.*

Tourist office (☎ 32-1010, ext 20; fax 32-3483; Jirón 2 de Mayo 775; ☉ 8am-1pm & 3-6pm Mon-Fri) On the Plaza de Armas, offering information about local tours, in Spanish.

Sights

Tarma is high in the mountains and the clear nights of June, July and August provide ideal opportunities for stargazing, though the surrounding mountains do limit the amount of observable heavens. A small **astronomical observatory** (☎ 32-2625; Huánuco 614; admission S5; ☉ 8-10pm Fri) is run by the owners of Hospedaje Central: admission includes an entertaining talk (in Spanish) on constellations and a peek at some stars.

The town's **cathedral** is modern (1965), and it contains the remains of Tarma's most famous son, Peruvian president Manuel Odría (1897–1974). He organized construction of the cathedral during his presidency. The old clock in the cathedral tower dates from 1862.

Of the myriad archaeological ruins near Tarma, best known is **Tarmatambo** 6km south. Former capital of the Tarama culture and later a major Inca administrative center, the fairly extensive remains include storehouses, palaces and an impressive, still-used aqueduct system. Ask at the tourist office about guides to take you there and to other sites: going solo, these ruins are difficult to find.

Local excursions include visits to the religious shrine of El Señor de Muruhuay (the Christ of Muruhuay) near Acobamba (9km from Tarma; p304), the Gruta de Huagapo (33km away; p305) and San Pedro de Cajas (41km away; p305)

Festivals & Events

The big annual attraction is undoubtedly Easter. For good information on this and other regional festivities (in Spanish) visit www.tarma.info.

Semana Santa (Holy Week) Many processions are held, including several by candlelight after dark. They culminate on the morning of Easter Sunday with a marvelous procession to the cathedral along an 11-block route entirely carpeted with flower petals, attracting thousands of Peruvian visitors. Hotels fill fast and increase prices by up to 50% at these times.

Tarma Tourism Week Another fiesta, held near the end of July, featuring dress-up parades, music, dancing and much raucous merriment.

El Señor de los Milagros (Christ of Miracles) This annual fiesta takes place in late October; the main feast days are the 18th, 28th and 29th. This is another good opportunity to see processions over beautiful, flower-petal carpets.

Sleeping

Choices in Tarma itself are not impressive: just some unspectacular budget options and one expensive resort hotel. A short ride from town, some attractive farmhouse B&Bs provide better accommodation.

BUDGET

The following hotels have hot water, usually in the morning, though they may claim all day.

Hospedaje Central (☎ 32-2625; Huánuco 614; s with/without bathroom S30/15, d S40/25) This old but adequate hotel has an astronomical observatory. Rooms are dark but staff is friendly and bundles of tourist information are available.

Hospedaje El Dorado (☎ 32-1914; fax 32-1634; Huánuco 488; s with/without bathroom S30/15, d S60/25) Sizable, clean, occasionally worn rooms face a leafy internal courtyard and come with cable TV and hot showers. Friendly staff and an in-house cafeteria help make this one of central Tarma's best sleeping options.

Hostal El Marquéz (☎ 32-2731; Huaraz at Lima; s/d/tr S20/35/45) This cavernous place has an aura of faded colonial grandeur and huge rooms, some sporting enough beds to sleep a small army. All have private bathrooms but only larger rooms have hot water.

Hospedaje El Mirador (☎ 32-1988; Limaymanta 205; s/d S30/40) Large, light rooms get prime views over Tarma as well as hot water and cable TV.

MIDRANGE & TOP END

our pick **Hacienda Santa María** (☎ 32-1232; www .haciendasantamaria.com; Vista Alegre 1249; s/d S105/170) Calle Vlenrich becomes Vista Alegre to the northeast of town and after 1km arrives at this charming hacienda (ranch) accommodation:

a white-walled, 18th-century colonial house with wooden balconies perfect for surveying the surrounding lush, flower-abundant grounds. Rustic rooms are full of old furniture and rates include a generous breakfast. There is also a clutch of alternative local tours that the owners can arrange.

Hacienda La Florida (☎ 34-1041, 01-344-1358; www .haciendalaflorida.com; s/d S108/174) Located 6km from Tarma on the Acobamba road, this 250-year-old working hacienda is now a B&B owned by a welcoming Peruvian-German couple, Pepe and Inge. Rooms boast wooden parquet floors and private bathrooms and there is attractive space for campers (per person S14). A filling breakfast is included in the price; homemade dinners are S20 per person. Visitors can partake in farm life or in various two-day workshops (minimum of six people) on relaxation techniques and cooking classes. El Señor de Muruhuay sanctuary is a one-hour hike away.

Los Portales (☎ 32-1411; www.hotelportalestarma .com; Castilla 512; s/d/ste S175/250/480; 🖳) Set in secluded gardens in the west of town, this hotel features a children's playground and 45 standard hotel rooms with cable TV and wi-fi internet access. Rates include continental breakfast and the restaurant provides room service. The two suites have Jacuzzis. This is the best choice for accommodation in Tarma town itself.

Eating

There are disappointingly few good restaurants. Sellers of salted popcorn and other snacks tend to congregate on the west side of the plaza.

Restaurant Chavín de Grima (☎ 32-1892, 32-1341; Lima 270; meals S7-10; ⏰ 7am-7pm) For breakfasts and cheap set lunches on the Plaza de Armas you won't go far wrong by heading to this popular place decorated with San Pedro de Cajas wall hangings. When there are any gringos in town, this is where they hang.

Restaurant Señorial/El Braserito (☎ 32-3334; Huánuco 138/140; mains S5-12; ⏰ 8am-3pm & 6-11pm) Two restaurants rolled into one (just one side is opened if it's slow), this is the local favorite, judging by the nonstop crowds. Sprightly service, huge portions and cheerful surroundings with mirrored walls and neon signs lure diners in. The wholesome menu features the usual Peruvian standards, including traditional dishes like *cuy* (guinea pig).

El Mejorcito de Tarma (☎ 32-1766, 32-3500; Arequipa 501; mains S7-15; ☒ lunch & dinner) From Chiclayo, the owner of this restaurant decided upon arrival in Tarma some years ago that the restaurant food in town wasn't good enough. The positive result is the Mejorcito (the 'bestest'). The modest menu runs the gamut of Peruvian favorites, with grilled trout being a less obvious but excellent choice.

Turistico al Rosal (Huaraz 305; menú S6-8, mains S10-12; ☒ 6am-4pm) The serene flower-filled central courtyard and the excellent fish dishes are the reasons to head here. There are two inside seating areas too. Feeling adventurous? Try the Tarma specialty *mondongo:* a broth made with maize, tripe, minced pork hoof and vegetables.

Drinking

Discoteca Danny (Malecón Galvez 627) Popular with (mostly male) locals and often with a S2 cover charge, Danny has recorded and live Latin music with plenty of space for drinking, too.

Getting There & Around

The forlorn, minuscule (but official) *terminal terrestre* (bus station) has just one bus daily leaving for Lima at 10pm (S20, six hours).

BUS

Bus companies usually have their own terminals here.

Los Canarios (☎ 32-3357; Amazonas 694) Has small buses to Huancayo (S9, three hours) leaving almost hourly from 5am to 6pm.

Transportes Chanchamayo (☎ 32-1882; Callao 1002) Has 9am, 2pm and 11pm departures to Lima (S20). Buses coming through from Lima go to La Merced.

Transportes Junín (☎ 32-1234, 32-3494; Amazonas 669) Has five daily buses to Lima including *bus-camas* (bed buses) at 11:30am and also 11:45pm (S15 to S25). It also has 5:30am and 1pm departures for Cerro de Pasco.

Transportes La Merced (☎ 32-2937; Vlenrich 420) Has buses to Lima at 8:45am, 11:30am, 1:30pm, 10:30pm, 11pm and 11:30pm (S17). The evening services offer *bus-cama* options for S25 (upstairs) or S30 (downstairs). The 12pm service originating in Lima goes on to La Merced and Oxapampa.

Transportes San Juan (☎ 32-2308; Odría 1021) In front of the Estadio Unión Tarma at the northeastern end of town (a *mototaxi* – motorcycle taxi – ride here costs S2). Has big buses to Huancayo (S10, 3½ hours) via Concepción and Jauja, as well as frequent buses to La Merced (S5, two hours).

OTHER TRANSPORT

By the gas station opposite the *terminal terrestre*, *colectivo* taxis take up to four passengers to Lima (S30 each) or local destinations such as Junín (S15) or La Oroya (S15). If you want to go to Cerro de Pasco or Huánuco, you can take *colectivos* from here, too, though you will have to change cars up to three times to get there. Fast *colectivo* taxis to Huancayo (S20) leave from Jauja, about 600m south of the *terminal terrestre*.

Almost opposite Transportes San Juan, *colectivos* to La Merced charge S15. This is a spectacular trip, dropping about 2.5km vertically into the jungle in the space of just over an hour. For destinations beyond La Merced, change at the convenient Transportes San Juan La Merced bus terminal. Ask around the stadium area for other destinations. During the day frequent minibuses for Jauja (S6) leave from the roundabout by the *terminal terrestre* when full. A bus stop next to Transportes San Juan has minibuses to Acobamba and Palcamayo. Cars for San Pedro de Cajas leave from the northern end of Moquegua. The tourist office can help with transport-related queries.

ACOBAMBA
☎ 064

Colorful Acobamba, about 9km from Tarma, has profited substantially from and is famous for the religious sanctuary of **El Señor de Muruhuay**, a white shrine visible on a hill 1.5km away.

The sanctuary, one of Peru's top pilgrimage sites, is built around a rock etching of Christ crucified. The image supposedly appeared to smallpox sufferers during a regional epidemic, healing them when authorities had left them for dead. Historians claim it was carved with a sword by a royalist officer who was one of the few survivors after losing the major independence Battle of Junín (see p327) but this story has less cachet and legends relating to the image's miraculous appearance persist. The first building erected around the image was a roughly thatched hut, which was replaced in 1835 by a small chapel.

The present sanctuary, inaugurated in 1972, is a modern building with an electronically controlled bell tower and is decorated with huge weavings from San Pedro de Cajas.

The feast of El Señor de Muruhuay, held throughout May, has been celebrated annually since 1835. There are religious services, processions, dances, fireworks, ample opportunities to sample local produce and even a few gringos. Stalls sell *chicha* (corn beer) and *cuy*, but be wary unless your stomach is travel-hardened. Visitors usually stay in nearby Tarma, although Acobamba has accommodation possibilities.

PALCAMAYO
☎ 064

From this attractive village, tumbling down a valley-side 28km from Tarma and serviced by regular *colectivo* taxis, you can visit the **Gruta de Huagapo**, a huge limestone cave 4km further up in the hills off the San Pedro de Cajas road. The name means 'cave that cries' in Quechua – testimony to the Tarama people who supposedly hid from and were then massacred by invading Incas here. Various international expeditions have explored the cave, which is one of Peru's largest and is officially protected as a National Speleological Area. Several lesser-known nearby caves like the **Gruta de Rosario** would also be of speleological interest.

A descent into the Gruta de Huagapo requires caving equipment and experience: tourist facilities consist only of a few frayed ropes. The cave contains waterfalls, squeezes and underwater sections (scuba equipment required). It is possible to enter the cave for a short distance but you soon need technical gear. In one of the two houses below the mouth of the cave is a collection of photographs and newspaper clippings describing the exploration of the cave. This is the home of former cave guide Señor Modesto Castro, who has explored the cave on numerous occasions. His son, Ramiro, can still be of assistance. Refreshments are also on offer at the cave.

SAN PEDRO DE CAJAS
☎ 064

Forty kilometers up in the hills from Tarma, peaceful San Pedro is the production center for the country's finest *tapices* (tapestries). Most of the village is involved in making these high-quality woven wall hangings, depicting moving scenes from rural Peruvian life. You can watch locals weaving in workshops round the Plaza de Armas: it's one of Peru's best opportunities for witnessing handicraft production – and purchasing the results.

The **Casa del Artesano** (Plaza de Armas; 🕑 9am-7pm) is one of the largest workshops. On the same street, down from the plaza, two basic *hospedajes* (family inns) offer rooms. *Colectivo* taxis from Tarma (S5, one hour) serve San Pedro regularly. Look out for superbly preserved Inca terraces on the way up.

SOUTHEAST OF TARMA

This section of Peru's central highlands is dominated by the Río Mantaro valley, running between the towns of Jauja and Huancayo and split by the Río Mantaro throughout its length. The valley is a wide, fertile agricultural plain and home to a number of villages renowned for their handicrafts.

Festivals are a way of life in the valley. Valley residents say that there is a festival occurring each day of the year and chancing upon some colorful celebrations is likely. Southwards from Huancayo the road leads through narrow valleys to Huancavelica and further south through a rough but scenic route to Ayacucho.

JAUJA
☎ 064 / pop 25,000 / elev 3250m

Coming from Lima, the first place you pass along this route is Jauja, a small, bustling colonial town of narrow traffic-swamped streets about 60km southeast of Tarma and 40km north of Huancayo. It offers some decent accommodation options, which can be used as a base for sampling attractions including a lakeside resort and several interesting hikes to archaeological ruins.

Orientation & Information

Jauja is a long, spread-out town but is easily explored on foot. Most transportation arrives 500m south of town.

You can change money at **BCP** (☎ 36-2011; Junín 785), which also sports an ATM. Internet *cabinas* dot most central blocks. For good general information, click to www.jauja.info (mostly Spanish; limited English).

Sights & Activities

Jauja was Francisco Pizarro's first capital in Peru, though this honor was short-lived. Some finely carved wooden altars in the main church are all that remain of the early colonial days. Before the Incas, this area was the home of an important Huanca indigenous community, and **Huanca ruins** can be seen on a hill about 3km southeast of town. A brisk walk or *mototaxi* will get you there.

About 4km from Jauja is **Laguna de Paca**, a small lakeside resort offering restaurants, rowboats and fishing. A boat ride around the lake will cost about S3 per passenger (five-person minimum). There are ducks and gulls, and you can stop at **Isla del Amor** – a tiny artificial island. A *mototaxi* here costs S3.

A well-preserved **Camino del Inca** (Inca road) runs from Jauja to Tarma. The most spectacular section is from Tingo (30 minutes from Jauja by taxi) to Inkapatakuna (30 minutes from Tarma), a six- to eight-hour hike.

Straddling the border between the departments of Junín and Lima, half an hour north of Jauja, is **Pachacayo**, gateway to the remote **Reserva Nor Yauyos**, an iconic Andean smorgasbord of glimmering blue-green mountain lakes nestled within towering peaks and home to the **Pariacaca Glacier**. You'll need a 4WD vehicle to get there; Tampu Tours (see below) arranges treks.

There is a colorful **market** in the town center every Wednesday morning.

Tours & Guides

For adventure hiking contact **Tampu Tours** (☎ 36-2314; www.tampu.info, in Spanish; Bolívar 1114), which runs challenging trekking tours in the area.

Sleeping

Many visitors stay in Huancayo and travel to Jauja by minibus or *colectivo* taxi.

Hostal Santa Rosa (☎ 36-2225; Ayacucho 792; s with/without bathroom S25/15, d S35/25) On the corner of the Plaza de Armas, this is the best of the budget bunch (despite its poky entrance). Ask to see several rooms: some are quite dingy. Hot water is provided.

Hostal Manco Cápac (☎ 36-1620; Manco Cápac 575; s/d without bathroom incl breakfast S40/70) By far the best choice in Jauja is this secure, peaceful house with huge rooms abutting two courtyard gardens. Bathrooms are clean and showers hot: each room is allotted its own exclusive bath-

room. It's three blocks north of the Plaza de Armas and rates include a continental breakfast with freshly brewed coffee. The owners are great sources of local information.

Hostal María Nieves (☎ 36-2543; Gálvez 491; s with/without bathroom S30/25, d S40/35) This place also comes recommended: the owner is friendly and the rooms have TVs. Rates include breakfast.

Eating

Out by Laguna de Paca, a string of lakeshore restaurants attempt to entice diners with shrill, piped Andean music. Music aside, the lakeside tables are pleasant enough to sit at. There is little to choose between the bunch, though Las Brisas near the beginning of the strip is considered one of the better ones and does offer a fairly solid plate of *pachamanca* (meat, potatoes and vegetables cooked in an earthen 'oven' of hot rocks). Another specialty here is clay-baked *trucha* (trout) seasoned with chilies, garlic and lemon, wrapped in banana leaves and baked in Laguna mud: delicious. Despite such culinary offerings, several travelers have reported upset stomachs after eating at Laguna de Paca restaurants. Jauja has several simple, central restaurants.

El Paraíso (☎ 36-1599; Ayacucho 917; mains S10-12; ✎ lunch & dinner) The best eatery in town is this vast plant-filled restaurant popular with locals who are attracted by bargain specialties such as *trucha* (from Laguna de Paca) or *picante de cuy* (roast guinea pig in a spicy sauce). It's just south of the main plaza.

Getting There & Away

Jauja has the regional airport, with daily flights to/from Lima courtesy of **LC Busre** (www.lcbusre.com.pe). The airport is south of town on the Huancayo road.

Buses, minibuses and taxis all congregate at the south side of town at the junction of Ricardo Palma and Junín about 500m from the Plaza de Armas. During the day, frequent, inexpensive minibuses (S3) and *colectivos* (S5) leave from here for Huancayo (50 minutes). Minibuses also leave for Tarma (S7, 1½ hours) and La Oroya (two hours). *Colectivos* will also leave to these destinations if there is demand: they normally only leave when they have five passengers (that means two in the front seat).

Getting Around

Mototaxis run anywhere in town for around S1.50. Take a *mototaxi* to get to Laguna de Paca (S3).

Jauja is one of the few towns in the central highlands that sell bicycles. Shops on Junín provide fairly reliable mountain bikes if you plan staying a while.

CONCEPCIÓN

☎ 064 / elev 3283m

South of Jauja, the road branches to follow both the west and east sides of the Río Mantaro valley to Huancayo. Local bus drivers refer to these as *derecha* (right, or west) and *izquierda* (left, or east).

From Concepción, a village halfway between Jauja and Huancayo on the *izquierda* side, you can travel to charming Ocopa village, home to the famous convent of **Santa Rosa de Ocopa** (admission S5; ☺ 9am-noon & 3-6pm Wed-Mon). Admission is by 45-minute guided tour every hour or once groups are large enough (seven person minimum). There is a 50% student discount. The building, set around beautiful gardens and cloistered internal courtyards, was built by the Franciscans in the early 18th century as a center for missionaries heading into the jungle. During the years of missionary work, the friars built up an impressive collection that is displayed in the convent's museum. Exhibits include stuffed jungle wildlife, indigenous artifacts, photographs of early missionary work and a large collection of colonial religious art (mainly in the *escuela cuzqueña* – Cuzco School – style, a combination of Spanish and Andean artistic styles). The highlight, however, is the fantastic 2nd-floor library of some 25,000 volumes – many dating back as far as the 15th century.

Frequent *colectivos* (Monday to Saturday) leave from the plaza in Concepción for Ocopa, about 5km away. *Mototaxis* charge S15 for the return trip, inclusive of an hour's wait. Concepción is easily visited by taking a Huancayo–Jauja *izquierda* bus.

HUANCAYO

☎ 064 / pop 323,050 / elev 3244m

The central altiplano's megametropolis, bustling Huancayo mixes its modern facade with a strong underlying sense of tradition. For many travelers this sophisticated city will be their first experience of the Peruvian high-

lands – it stands within a wide, fertile valley at the start of an exciting overland mountain route to Cuzco – and while its charms are less obvious than those of other Andean locales, Huancayo doesn't disappoint.

Don't let the tumbledown outskirts fool you: this is an arresting city and a gentle introduction to altiplano life. Some of Peru's finest dining outside of Lima and Cuzco lies within the teeming streets, yet once you've sipped your espresso and sampled the region's renowned cuisine in well-appointed restaurants, another ancient side to the city reveals itself. Peru's most interesting handicrafts are sold in Huancayo's markets and in the valley beyond, and colorful fiestas take place almost daily.

Huancayo is, above all, a center of activity for this whole section of the central highlands and on a local level the Río Mantaro valley. When you have had your fill of handicraft-hunting and market-visiting in the fascinating valley villages, there are opportunities to learn Spanish or Quechua at well-organized language courses, learn musical instruments or dabble in Andean cooking. For the adventurous, the dusty nearby hills hide weird rock formations and spectacular lakes while further afield, Andes trekking, extreme mountain biking and jungle tramping await. The city is also the terminus of the world's second-highest railway.

Huancayo might challenge at first: then it will bid you to hang around a while.

Orientation & Information

Huancayo is a sizable town: you'll end up doing a lot of walking. Buses arrive at either to the north or south of the Plaza de la Constitución.

BCP, Interbank, Banco Continental, Banco Wiese and other banks and *casas de cambio* are on Real. Most banks open on Saturday morning and have ATMs. Many places offering internet access are found along Giráldez and other central streets.

Clínica Ortega (☎ 23-2921; Carrín 1124; ☺ 24hr) English is spoken.

Dr Luis Mendoza (☎ 23-9133; Real 968) For a dentist, try here.

Incas del Perú (☎ 22-3303; www.incasdelperu.org; Giráldez 652) A recommended source for information on just about anything in the area.

Lavandería Chic (☎ 23-1107; Breña 154; ☺ 8am-10pm Mon-Sat, 10am-6pm Sun) Offers both self-service (S10 per load, wash and dry, soap included) and drop-off laundry (S12 per load).

Locutorio Telefonica (Puno 200) Internet access and cheap phone calls.

Main post office (Centro Cívico)

Policía de Turismo (☎ 23-4714; Ferrocarril 580) Can help with tourist information, as well as with emergencies.

Tourist office (Casa del Artesano, Real 481; ⏰ 10am-1:30pm & 4-7:30pm Mon-Fri) Located upstairs in the indoor crafts market and has limited information about Río Mantaro valley sightseeing and public transport.

Sights

Museo Salesiano (☎ 24-7763; Arequipa 105; admission S2; ⏰ 9am-1pm & 3-5pm Mon-Fri) can be entered from the Salesian school, and has Amazon fauna, pottery and archaeology exhibits. Hours vary.

Head northeast on Giráldez for a great view of the city. About 2km from the town center is **Cerro de la Libertad**, a popular recreational and dining locale where, apart from the city view, there are artwork stalls and a playground. About 2km further (there is a sign and an obvious path), you will come to the eroded geological formations known as **Torre Torre**. Some of the formations look like towers – hence the name (*torre* means 'tower').

In the city itself, the **Iglesia de La Merced**, on the first block of Real, is where the Peruvian Constitution of 1839 was approved. In the suburb of San Antonio, the **Parque de la Identidad Huanca** is a fanciful park full of stone statues and miniature buildings representing the area's culture.

Activities

The ever-active Lucho Hurtado of **Incas del Perú** (☎ 22-3303; www.incasdelperu.org; Giráldez 652), in the same building as the restaurant La Cabaña,

organizes most activities. Lucho is a local who speaks English and knows the surrounding area well. He arranges demanding, multiday mountain-bike tours and Andean mountain-trekking expeditions to the lake and glacier of Huaytapallana for up to three days; the cost for trekking is around S140 per person day.

Incas del Perú arranges Spanish and even Quechua lessons, including meals and accommodations with a local family (if you wish), from S420 to S840 per week for the interactive course. Lessons can be modified to fit your interests. You can also learn to cook local dishes, make jewelry, engage in gourd carving, practice regional dances or discover how to play the panpipes.

Tours are arranged by Lucho, who guides treks down the eastern slopes of the Andes and into high jungle on foot, horseback or public transport. It isn't luxurious, but it's a good chance to experience something of the real rural Peru: you can stay on Lucho's father's ranch in the middle of nowhere. Trips last anywhere from four to eight days and cost about S120 per person per day including food. Accommodations are rustic and trips can involve camping.

Festivals & Events

There are hundreds of fiestas in Huancayo and surrounding villages – supposedly almost every day somewhere in the Río Mantaro valley. Ask at the tourist office.

Año Nuevo (New Year's Day; see left)

Semana Santa (Holy Week) One of the biggest events in Huancayo, with big religious processions attracting people from all over Peru at Easter.

Fiestas Patrias (28 & 29 July) Peru's Independence Days are celebrated by processions by the military and schools. Hotels fill up and raise their prices during these times.

Sleeping

BUDGET

Hotel Villa Rica (☎ 21-7040; Real 1293; r without bathroom S15, s/d with bathroom S25/35) Conveniently located for the bus stations at the south end of Real, this is a secure hotel and the best of the budget bunch in the vicinity. There is hot water in the evenings and rooms are clean.

La Casa de la Abuela (☎ 22-3303; incasdelperu@gmail .com; Giráldez 691; dm S20, s with/without bathroom S50/40, d S60/50; 🖳) Incas del Perú runs La Casa de la Abuela and makes every effort to welcome tired travelers. This brightly painted, wooden-floored house is clean, friendly and efficient,

---

AÑO NUEVO

Año Nuevo (New Year's Day) is particularly colorful in the Huancayo area, with partygoers wearing yellow (including yellow underwear!) to welcome it in. Festivities continue until January 6. Many local dances are performed, including the *huaconada,* in which revelers dress up to look like quirky old men with big noses, representing village elders who, in times past, would drop by the houses of lazy or mischief-making villagers and whip them into behaving for the coming year. Plenty of butt-whipping takes place. Mito, an hour north of Huancayo, also has vivid celebrations.

HUANCAYO

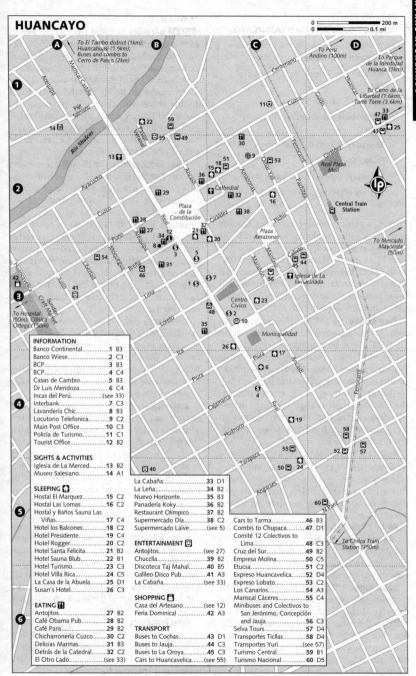

MARKET DAYS AROUND HUANCAYO

Each village and town in the Río Mantaro valley has its own *feria* (market day).

- **Monday** San Agustín de Cajas, Huayucachi
- **Tuesday** Hualhuas, Pucara
- **Wednesday** San Jerónimo de Tunán, Jauja
- **Thursday** El Tambo, Sapallanga
- **Friday** Cochas
- **Saturday** Matahuasi, Chupaca, Marco
- **Sunday** Huancayo, Jauja, Mito, Comas

---

offering a garden, reliable hot water, laundry facilities, a games room, cable TV and DVD. It's popular with backpackers, who are mothered by *la abuela* (Lucho's mom). Ten cozy rooms sleep between two to six people; rates include continental breakfast with homemade bread and jam and real, freshly brewed coffee. Good tourist information is available too.

Peru Andino (☎ 22-3956; www.geocities.com/peru andino_1; Pasaje San Antonio 113; s with/without bathroom S35/30, d S70/60, all incl breakfast) A backpacker favorite, this quiet, secure residential house is near Parque Túpac Amaru a few blocks northeast of the map. You couldn't be in better hands than those of the couple running the place and there is a self-catering kitchen, laundry facilities, hot showers, some tour information and free bus/train station pick-up, given advance notice.

Hostal Las Lomas (☎ 23-7587; laslomashyo@yahoo .es; Giráldez 327; s/d S35/45) Spotless hot-water bathrooms and excellent mattresses make this a fine, central choice. Rooms vary in size; many are quite large, some get lots of street noise.

Hostal y Baños Sauna Las Viñas (☎ 36-5236; Piura 415; s/d S35/45) Rooms are small but squeeze in hot baths, cable TV and phone. Its sauna is open 6am to 9pm. The building offers lovely views from the upper floors.

Hotel Rogger (☎ 23-3488; Ancash 460; s/d S35/50) Around the corner from the plaza, you can stay at this clean, friendly place, which matches the rooms of its plaza-facing neighbors for size, facilities and (almost) ambience – for less money. Expect cable TV and black-and-white-tiled bathrooms dishing out 24-hour hot water.

MIDRANGE

ourpick Hotel los Balcones (☎ 21-1041; www.los balconeshuancayo.com; Puno 282; s/d/tr S/45/55/75; 💻) Next to the El Marquez and sporting plenty of namesake hard-to-miss outside balconies, this is an attractive modern, airy and spacious new-style hotel. Tastefully furnished rooms come with cable TV, phone, alarm clock and reading lights; there's complementary internet access and a busy in-house restaurant too. Look no further for reasonably priced city-center comfort.

Hotel Santa Felicita (☎ 23-5476; irmaleguia@hot mail.com; Giráldez 145; s/d S45/60) Large rooms at this attentive hotel get plaza views, sizable hot showers, cable TV and phone. An attractive cafe lies downstairs.

Susan's Hotel (☎ 20-2251; susans_hotel@yahoo .com; Real 851; s/d S50/70) This spotless, cheerful hotel has rooms with good-sized bathrooms, cable TV, writing desks and firm mattresses. However, rooms are dark and overpriced for what they are; get one at the rear for peace and quiet. The 5th-floor restaurant has cracking views.

Hotel Sauna Blub (☎ 22-1692; www.hotelblubperu .com; Pasaje Verand 187; s/d S85/120) A little west of the center overlooking the river (or its bone-dry bed), the Blub has well-appointed rooms with cable TV, telephones, minifridges and a rather intense maroon color scheme. There is also, as the name implies, a sauna.

Hostal El Marquez (☎ 21-9026; www.elmarquezhuan cayo.com; Puno 294; s/d/ste incl breakfast S100/140/180) This comfortable hotel is better than most, though is somewhat lacking in character. Recently done up, carpeted rooms get the usual direct-dial phones and cable TV, while three suites feature a large bathroom with Jacuzzi tub, king-sized bed and minibar. A small cafe offers room service and continental breakfast is included.

Hotel Turismo (☎ 23-1072; www.hoteles-del-centro .com; Ancash 729; s/d S100/145; 💻) This pleasant-looking old building with wooden balconies and public areas has a certain faded grandeur. Rooms vary in size and quality but all have bathrooms. The hotel has a restaurant and bar and is part of the same organization as the Hotel Presidente.

Hotel Presidente (☎ 23-5419, 23-1736; www.hoteles -del-centro.com; Real 1138; s/d incl breakfast S100/145; 💻) This good modern hotel includes breakfast in the price, and has ample, nicely carpeted rooms and spacious bathrooms.

Eating

Good news for snack lovers: the blocks of Real south of the Plaza abound in cake shops and snack stalls selling strips of grilled *pollo* (chicken) and *lomo* (beef), often in kebab format. Huancayo has some fabulous restaurants: regional specialties include *papas a la huancaína* (boiled potato in a creamy sauce of cheese, oil, hot pepper, lemon and egg yolk, served with boiled egg and olives). The city is also known for its trout, reared in nearby lakes.

Panadería Koky (☎ 23-4707; Puno 298; snacks from S3; ☽ 7am-10.30pm) This modern bakery-coffee shop is a contender for the best breakfast stop in the Central Andes, serving tasty sandwiches, pastries, empanadas, real espresso and other coffees. It's lively from morning until evening and now even does a line in pizzas and other more substantial fare. There's live music sometimes from the upstairs balcony.

Café Paris (Real 370; snacks from S3; ☽ 4-11pm) A hip little joint that favors Nirvana over Andean music and is frequented by trendy young *huancaínos* (Huancayo residents). It does elaborate coffees and cakes, among other snacks.

Nuevo Horizonte (Ica 578; mains S3-8; ☽ 7:30am-10pm Sun-Fri) Inside an atmospheric older house with attractive ceilings, this place has an excellent vegetarian menu using soy to recreate Peruvian plates such as *lomo saltado* (strips of beef stir-fried with onions, tomatoes, potatoes and chili), as well as straightforward veggie meals.

Chicharronería Cuzco (Cuzco 173; mains S5-8) Traditional plates of *chicharrones* (deep-fried pork chunks) at this carnivore-dedicated hole-in-the-wall are about S7.

Café Obama Pub (☎ 76-9618; Puno 598; meals S8-10; ☽ 11am-midnight) New on the eating scene but linked to the president only by name, Obama Pub has Beatles memorabilia as the decor theme and hamburgers, huge sandwiches and cakes as the grub of choice. It does good pisco sours too.

Delicias Marinas (☎ 21-1119; Arequipa 564; menú S12-18; ☽ breakfast, lunch & dinner) They say the highlands can't do ceviche (raw seafood marinated in lime juice): this bright little place is out to prove them wrong.

Restaurant Olímpico (☎ 23-4181; Giráldez 199; mains S12-20) Here for more than six decades, this is Huancayo's oldest (though modernized) restaurant. It features a large open kitchen where you can see the traditional Peruvian dishes prepared and a popular Sunday buffet lunch.

Antojitos (☎ 23-7950; Puno 599; meals S15-25; ☽ 5pm-late Mon-Sat) This restaurant-cum-bar, housed in an antique-filled, wood-beamed, two-story building with the obligatory Lennon and Santana posters, brings in vociferous crowds of upscale locals bent on having roaring conversations over the sounds of anything from *cumbia* (a salsalike Colombian musical style) to Pink Floyd. The well-prepared bar food consists of burgers, pizzas and grills.

La Leña (☎ 20-2096, 22-7813; Breña 146; mains S15-30) This is the most lavish place around (check the waterfall at the entrance) to sample *parrilladas* (grills), as well as the usual chicken dishes in the company of well-heeled, carnivorous locals. Several branches are found city-wide and it does delivery.

La Cabaña (☎ 22-3303; Giráldez 652; mains around S15; ☽ 5-11pm) This haunt is popular with locals and travelers alike for its relaxed ambience, hearty food and tasty pisco sours. When you're suitably mellow order a scrumptious pizza or graze on trout, juicy grills, al dente pastas, among other less-filling appetizers. Live *folklórica* bands play Thursday to Saturday. Next door and part of the same establishment, El Otro Lado is open for lunch from April to October.

Detrás de la Catedral (☎ 21-2969; Ancash 335; mains S12-20; ☽ 11am-11pm) This well-run, attractively presented place exudes a woody, warm feeling and has garnered plenty of regular patrons with its broad menu selection – helped by a user-friendly picture menu decoder. Enjoy filling burgers (veggie or carnie), specials like *asado catedral* (barbecued meats done in house style) and tasty desserts like chocolate-drenched *pionono helado* (pastry with caramel filling). Surrealist paintings grace the walls.

Huancahuasi (☎ 24-4826; Mariscal Castilla 222; mains S12-20; ☽ 8am-7pm Sun-Thu, to 2am Fri & Sat) Northwest of town, Real becomes Mariscal Castilla in El Tambo district. The local eatery of choice for breakfast through to early evening is this classy establishment. A flower-filled courtyard and walls decorated with San Pedro de Cajas tapestries and local poems set the ambience for tucking into regional goodies like *pachamanca*, *papas a la huancaína* and *ceviche de trucha* (river-trout ceviche). It's all well presented and the service comes with a smile. A taxi ride from the center is S3.

Try **Supermercado Dia** (Giráldez) or **Supermercado Laive** (Real at Lima) for self-catering options.

Drinking & Entertainment

There are no stand-out nightclubs: at the time of writing the best were **Galileo Disco-Pub** (Breña 378) and flashier **Discoteca Taj Mahal** (Huancavelica 1052).

Antojitos (☎ 23-7950; Puno 599; ☻ 5pm-late Mon-Sat) Local bands perform at this bar-restaurant most nights from 9pm.

La Cabaña (☎ 22-3303; Giráldez 652; ☻ 5-11pm) This popular eatery has live *folklórica* music and dancing on weekends.

Chucclla (Ayacucho at Ancash; ☻ to late Thu-Sat) The favored spot in town for *folklórica*. A couple of similar places are on the same block.

Shopping

Huancayo has two main markets.

The colorful daily produce market spills out from Mercado Mayorista (which is covered) east along the railway tracks. In the meat section you can buy Andean delicacies such as fresh and dried frogs, guinea pigs and chickens. The most important day is Sunday, coinciding with Huancayo's weekly craft market.

Feria Dominical (Huancavelica), the Sunday craft market, occupies numerous blocks along Huancavelica to the northwest of Piura. There are numerous noncraft items as well as weavings, textiles, embroidered items, ceramics and wood carvings. *Mates burilados* (carved gourds) and many other items from various villages in the Río Mantaro valley (opposite) are also sold here – handy if you don't have time to make the trek out to the villages yourself. Keep an eye on your valuables though.

More handy, **Casa del Artesano** (Plaza de la Constitución), on the south corner of the plaza, has a wide range of art souvenirs for sale in a somewhat more secure environment.

Getting There & Away

BUS

Terminals are in diverse locations, but most are quite central. Bus services change depending on season and demand, as do the location of their offices – particularly for the smaller companies. In this section, we do not list all companies; those listed here are either the better options or the only options.

For Lima, one-way ticket prices range from S30 to S60. For S45 to S60 you get a bed seat on a *bus-cama*; for S30 you get an ordinary seat.

Travel time is seven hours. There are other levels of comfort in between the two. The best company for comfort is **Cruz del Sur** (☎ 23-5650; Ayacucho 281-287), followed by **Etucsa** (☎ 22-6524; Puno 220), which has somewhat more frequent departures. Next is **Mariscal Cáceres** (☎ 21-6633/5; Real 1241). Check each company's buses, or at least brochures, before deciding. If you are in a hurry, **Comité 12** (Loreto 421) has speedy *colectivo* taxis to Lima (S50, five hours).

For Ayacucho (S30, eight to nine hours) the recommended service is **Empresa Molina** (☎ 22-4501; Angaraes 334), with morning and night departures on a mostly rough, unpaved road.

Huancavelica (S10, three to four hours) is served most frequently by **Transportes Ticllas** (☎ 20-1555; Ferrocarril 1590) with six daily buses. **Expreso Lobato** (Omar Yali 148-158) has comfortable overnight buses via Huancayo to Huancavelica. Others include Turismo Nacional, Expreso Huancavelica and Transportes Yuri, all in close proximity on Ferrocarril, with late-night buses only.

Los Canarios (☎ in Tarma 32-3357; Puno 739) serves Tarma almost hourly (S9, three hours) and will stop at Jauja and Concepción.

For Satipo (S18, eight to nine hours) the best service is **Selva Tours** (☎ 21-8427; Ferrocarril 1587) with four daily buses. They take the back route to Satipo via Comas if the road is safe to pass (at research time it was not). **Expreso Lobato** stops at La Merced (seven hours) en route to Satipo.

Turismo Central (☎ 22-3128; Ayacucho 274) has buses north to Huánuco (S20, seven hours), Tingo María (S30, 10 hours) and Pucallpa (S50, 22 hours).

Buses and *combis* for Cerro de Pasco (S15, five hours) leave from Mariategui in El Tambo: a taxi here costs S3.

Inexpensive minibuses (S3) and *colectivos* (S5) for Jauja (about 50 minutes) and Concepción (S2, 30 minutes) leave from Calixto.

TAXI

Colectivo taxis for Huancavelica (S25, 2½ hours) leave when full (four-passenger minimum) from, among other places, from the Mariscal Cáceres terminal.

TRAIN

Huancayo has two unconnected train stations in different parts of town. A special tourist train, the **Ferrocarril Central Andino** (☎ 22-2395), runs up from Lima between mid-April and October for S150/225 one-way/round-trip. The 12-hour trip leaves Lima at 7am Friday and departs Huancayo for the return trip at the rather inconvenient time of 6pm Sunday. For this return night leg bring along warm clothes and perhaps a blanket.

It's a fabulous run, reaching 4829m and passing La Galera which clocks in as one of the world's highest railway stations (the Tibetans are the record holders, followed by the Bolivians). It operates on a single-gauge track and is popular with train enthusiasts the world over. The best ways to book are either to visit the Incas del Perú website (www .incasdelperu.org), where there is an online booking form, or the train's principal booking website, **Teleticket** (www.teletiket.com.pe).

The **Chilca train station** (☎ 21-7724; www.fhh.com .pe) for Huancavelica is at the southern end of town. Disappointingly, following track improvements, the Huancavelica train was not running at the time of research, due to bureaucratic wrangling over who would operate the line and how. The projected date for reopening changes: it was April 2010 at last report. For the latest updates, contact Lucho Hurtado of Incas del Perú (p307) who is passionate (and pretty confident) about getting the line working.

Expreso services used to depart for Huancavelica at 6:30am Monday to Sunday (five hours) and *ordinario* services at 12:30pm Monday to Saturday (five to six hours). Tickets pre-track improvements were about S10/12/15 in 2nd/1st/buffet class. Buffet class on the old train was comfortable, with padded seats and guaranteed seating; 1st class had reserved seats with less padding and 2nd class offered wooden bench-type seats and no seat reservations. The train and its classes are supposed to remain the same.

Once service resumes, it's likely the ticket office will be open from noon to 6pm. The station is a fair hike from town so take a taxi.

Getting Around

Local buses to nearby villages leave from the street intersections shown on the map. Just show up and wait until a bus appears: most routes have buses every few minutes. Cochas buses (from Giráldez and Huancas) are cream-brown and come every 15 minutes. Ask other passengers if you're unsure. The tourist office is a good source of local bus information.

RÍO MANTARO VALLEY

Two main road systems link Huancayo with the villages of the Río Mantaro valley, and are known simply as the left and right of the river. *Izquierda* (left) is the east and *derecha* (right) is the west side of the river, as you head into Huancayo from the north. It is best to confine your sightseeing on any given day to one side or the other; few bridges link the two sides.

Perhaps the most interesting excursion on the east side is a visit to the twin villages of **Cochas Grande** and **Cochas Chico**, about 11km from Huancayo. These villages are the major production centers for the incised gourds that have made the district famous. Oddly enough, the gourds are grown mainly on the coast, in the Chiclayo and Ica areas. Once transported into the highlands, they are dried and scorched, then decorated using woodworking tools. The house of **Señor Alejandro Cipriano** (☎ 064-76-6486; mateburilado@hotmail.com; Huancayo 733, Cochas Grande) is recommended for seeing the finished products.

On the west side, the town of **Chupaca** has an interesting livestock market. Starting early, you can visit and continue by bus to **Ahuac**, then hike a further 1km up to **Laguna Ñahuimpuquio**, which offers restaurants, boat rides and a cave to explore. From the east shore a path climbs to a ridge for great valley views and the ruins of **Arwaturo**, constructed to maximize illumination by the sun's rays.

Other villages known for their handicrafts include: **San Agustín de Cajas**, known for the manufacture of wicker furniture; **Hualhuas**, a manufacturing center for wool products, including ponchos and weavings; and **San Jerónimo de Tunán**, known for its filigree silverwork and also boasting a 17th-century church with fine wooden altars. While most trading is done in Huancayo, the villages are easily visited from the city. They have few facilities but there is no substitute for the experience of seeing the crafts in the villages themselves. The key is an ability to speak some Spanish and make friends with the locals.

IZCUCHACA
☎ 067

The main village between Huancayo and Huancavelica, Izcuchaca has a pottery center, hot (well, distinctly lukewarm) springs and a **historic bridge**. This, legend has it, was built by the Incas and defended by Huascar against the advance of Atahualpa's troops during the civil war that was raging in the Inca empire just before the Spaniards arrived. (To learn more on this period, see p35.)

The only reason to linger here is to make a connection for the Huancavelica train (when it's running, see p312) if coming from Ayacucho. As bus arrival times and train departure times don't match, this may require staying overnight; try blue-colored **Hospedaje La Pequeñita** (r without bathroom S10, d S25) near the train station. You *might* be lucky to find room in a Huancavelica-bound *colectivo* taxi, but a bus pickup is a more reliable option.

HUANCAVELICA
☎ 067 / pop 41,350 / elev 3690m

It's a mystery why more travelers don't visit this pretty colonial city: it's bursting with beautiful churches and charming plazas, boasts a museum and mineral springs and lies picturesquely nestled within craggy peaks. These days, it's even easily accessible, with a good road connecting it to Huancayo 147km to the north. Still, few people make it here and therein lies another attraction: Huancavelica is a safe, serene spot to take a break from the Gringo Trail and soak up life as the locals live it. This entails partying at one of the frequent fiestas, browsing the markets or, for the most part, strolling the streets and sitting watching the colorful cross-section of society pass by.

This historic city was a strategic Inca center and shortly after the conquest the Spanish discovered its mineral wealth. By 1564 the Spaniards were sending indigenous Peruvian slaves to Huancavelica to work in the mercury and silver mines. The present town was founded in 1571 under the name of Villa Rica de Oropesa (Rich Town of the Lord): somewhat ironic given that Huancavelica is today the poorest city in Peru. Bear in mind the city suffers from frequent bone-chilling winds and icy temperatures at night.

Information
More than a dozen central places provide internet access.

@Internet (Segura 166) On the Plaza de Armas.
BCP (☎ 45-2831; Toledo 384) Has a Visa ATM and changes money.
Dirección de Turismo (☎ 45-2938; dreceturhvc@ yahoo.es; V Garma 444, 2nd fl; 8am-1pm & 2-5pm Mon-Fri) Provides good directions (in Spanish) for local hikes such as the 6km hike to the ghostly deserted mine of Santa Barbara.

Lavandería Sam (Toledo 346) A reasonably modern place to get your gear washed.
Main post office (Pasaje Ferrua 105) Near Iglesia de Santa Ana.
Multired (Muñoz) A stand-alone ATM next to the Municipalidad; doesn't work with all cards.

Sights & Activities
INSTITUTO NACIONAL DE CULTURA
The **INC** (☎ 45-2544, 45-3420; Raimondi 205; admission free; 10am-1pm & 3-6pm Tue-Sun), in a colonial building on Plaza San Juan de Dios, has information and displays about the area; ask the helpful director if you have any questions. A small **museum** features Inca artifacts, fossils, displays of local costumes and paintings by Peruvian impressionist artists. You even have the option of taking a class in *folklórico* dancing.

CHURCHES
Huancavelica churches are noted for their silver-plated altars, unlike the altars in the rest of Peru's colonial churches, which are usually gold-plated. There are several churches of note here, although they are generally closed to tourism. However, you can go as a member of the congregation when they are open for services, usually early in the morning on weekdays, with longer morning hours on Sunday.

The oldest church in Huancavelica is **Santa Ana**, founded in the 16th century. The **cathedral**, built in 1673, has been restored and contains what some say is the best colonial altar in Peru, including *escuela cuzqueña* paintings.

Other 17th-century churches include **San Francisco**, renowned for its 11 intricately worked altars; **Santo Domingo**, with famous statues of Santo Domingo and La Virgen del Rosario, which were made in Italy; **San Sebastián**, which has been well restored; **San Cristóbal**; and **La Ascensión**.

SAN CRISTÓBAL MINERAL SPRINGS
These **mineral springs** (pool/private shower S1.50/3; 6am-3pm) are fed into two large, slightly murky swimming pools. The lukewarm water supposedly has curative properties. You can rent a towel, soap and a bathing suit if you've forgotten yours (though the selection is limited and unlovely). You can reach the springs via a steep flight of stairs – enjoy the view of the city as you climb.

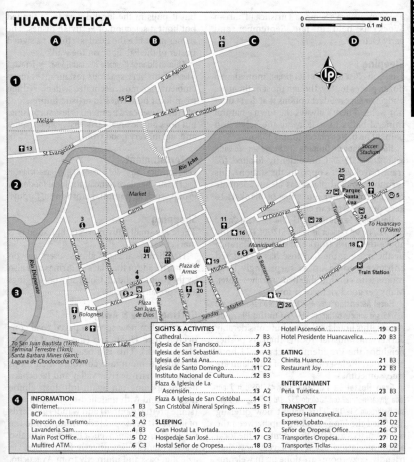

HUANCAVELICA

SIGHTS & ACTIVITIES
Cathedral	**7** B3
Iglesia de San Francisco	**8** A3
Iglesia de San Sebastián	**9** A3
Iglesia de Santa Ana	**10** D2
Iglesia de Santo Domingo	**11** C2
Instituto Nacional de Cultura	**12** B3
Plaza & Iglesia de La Ascensión	**13** A2
Plaza & Iglesia de San Cristóbal	**14** C1
San Cristóbal Mineral Springs	**15** B1

SLEEPING
Gran Hostal La Portada	**16** C2
Hospedaje San José	**17** C3
Hostal Señor de Oropesa	**18** D3
Hotel Ascensión	**19** C3
Hotel Presidente Huancavelica	**20** B3

EATING
Chinita Huanca	**21** B3
Restaurant Joy	**22** B3

ENTERTAINMENT
Peña Turística	**23** B3

TRANSPORT
Expreso Huancavelica	**24** D2
Expreso Lobato	**25** D2
Señor de Oropesa Office	**26** C3
Transportes Oropesa	**27** D2
Transportes Ticllas	**28** D2

INFORMATION
@Internet	**1** B3
BCP	**2** B3
Dirección de Turismo	**3** A2
Lavandería Sam	**4** B3
Main Post Office	**5** D2
Multired ATM	**6** C3

MARKETS
Market day in Huancavelica is Sunday and, although there are smaller daily markets, Sunday is the best day to see locals in traditional dress. The main Sunday market area snakes up Barranca then continues along Torre Tagle behind the cathedral.

LAGUNA DE CHOCLOCOCHA
One of many lakes adorning the Rumichaca road, this body of water, 70km south of Huancavelica, can be visited by taking the Rumichaca-bound bus at 4:30am. It's about two hours to Choclococha 'town' (then a 10-minute walk); the same bus can pick you up again on its return to Huancavelica at 2pm (check with the driver). This lake at 4700m is dazzling on a sunny day when the surrounding mountains are mirrored in its waters. Birdlife at the lake includes condors. There is good hiking and fishing, and lakeside restaurants.

Festivals & Events
Huancavelica's vibrant fiestas are renowned and, due to the mostly indigenous population, feel particularly authentic. Colorful traditional festivities occur on major Peruvian holidays, such as Carnaval, Semana Santa, Todos Santos and Christmas. Among the best is the Fiesta de las Cruces (Festival of the Crosses) held for six days during May: revelers bear crosses, local bands play music in the plazas and proceedings culminate in bull fights. Check with the INC for upcoming festivals.

Huancavelica's Semana Turística (Tourism Week) is held in late September and early October.

Sleeping

Huancavelica does in fact boast more than a dozen places to stay, though most of them are budget to superbudget options that don't offer hot water. There's always the town's natural mineral baths to soak away the aches and pains. The better places to stay follow.

Hostal Señor de Oropesa (Huancayo s/n; s/d without bathroom S12/20) Conveniently located for train-travelers (it's opposite the station), this turquoise-walled place has clean, adequate rooms, cold water and piles of blankets to keep out the Andean chill.

Hospedaje San José (☎ 45-1014; Huancayo s/n; s/d with S35/45, s/d without bathroom S12/20) Towering above the south (top) end of Calle Baranca by the market, the San José has a cluttered entrance leading up to surprisingly large rooms with comfortable beds and hot water. Many get good views over town.

Hotel Ascensión (☎ 45-3103; Manco Cápac 481; s/d S35/45, s/d without bathroom S15/25) On the Plaza de Armas, this hotel has larger, but considerably darker and mustier rooms than its posher neighbor the Presidente. It claims 24-hour hot water: the last two words of this claim is true, sometimes.

Gran Hostal La Portada (☎ 45-1050; h_laportada_hvca@hotmail.com; Toledo 252; s/d S45/65, s/d without bathroom S12/18) This bright new offering has filled the long-standing gap between the budget places and the Presidente in the local accommodation scene. It's very traveler-friendly: cozy rooms are done up in welcoming orange, have cable TV and hot water and center on a quiet courtyard.

Hotel Presidente Huancavelica (☎ /fax 45-2760; Plaza de Armas; s/d S100/145) The presentable old Hotel Presidente Huancavelica is, truth be told, a bit pricey for what you actually get. Rooms are plain but do benefit from guaranteed hot showers, telephone, cable TV and a laundry service – not to forget a handy restaurant.

Eating

There are no standout restaurants but plenty of chicken places and *chifas* (Chinese restaurants).

Restaurant Joy (☎ 45-2860; Toledo 230; mains S7-15; ☻ 9am-2pm & 5-10pm) For excellent grilled trout cast a line here. There's not a lot of room

but it pulls in the local diners for a limited but honest selection of Peruvian dishes. The owner must like the Beatles – there's a signed poster of the Fab Four on the wall.

Chinita Huanca (Gamarra 305; mains S4-8; ☻ breakfast & lunch) This very spacious restaurant is more ambient than most, decorated with everything from local butterflies to artistic impressions of Huancavelica. The menu is less surprising, but does ample breakfasts, tasty *chicharrones* and, again, very good trout.

Entertainment

Peña Turística (☎ 45-3623; Toledo 319; ☻ 6pm- midnight Thu, Fri, Sat) The place to head for local *folklórica* groups such as Rammi, Llantuy and Taipuy.

Shopping

There are small daily markets, but Sunday is market day.

Handicrafts are sold almost every day on the north side of the Plaza de Armas and also by the Municipalidad. Colorful wool leggings are especially popular.

Getting There & Away

Huancavelica now sports a paved road connecting it to Huancayo (the easiest means of approach). This is a beautiful route that ascends on mountain contours then loops down to a narrow river valley and Izcuchaca before opening out again into lush alpine meadowland with thatched-roof settlements (some prettily painted) and wandering herds of llamas. It then spirals downwards into the valley where Huancavelica lies. You can also reach Huancavelica directly from Pisco via a 4850m pass and indirectly from Ayacucho.

The most interesting way to Huancavelica always used to be by train from Huancayo (marginally faster than the buses and taking the circuitous route mostly along the river valley). However, at the time of writing, the line was closed (for more information, see p312). Buses are of the ponderous local variety – filled with locals and their goods and produce. Most but not all take the scenic alpine route.

If you are in a hurry, from Huancayo it's a good idea to take a *colectivo* taxi: these take two hours and ply the scenic route.

BUS

All major buses depart from the *terminal terrestre*, inconveniently located about 2km to the west of the town center. A taxi here costs S3. Buy your bus tickets in the downtown offices.

Companies serving Huancayo (S10, three hours) include **Transportes Ticllas** (☎ 45-1562; 0'Donovan 505) with six daily departures. Other companies go less often or at night, or may go via Huancayo en route to Lima.

For Lima (S30 to S40, 10 to 13 hours) companies go via Huancayo or via Pisco. The higher price tag is for more luxurious *bus camas*. Via Huancayo is usually a little faster but it depends on road conditions. The Pisco route is freezing at night: bring warm clothes. **Transportes Oropesa** (☎ 45-3181; 0'Donovan 599) departs for Lima at 6pm (12 hours) and also has buses to Pisco (S30, nine hours) and Ica (11 hours). **Expreso Lobato** (Muñoz 489) has comfortable overnight buses via Huancayo. Also try **Expreso Huancavelica** (Muñoz 516).

For Ayacucho things are a little trickier (see below). The 'easiest' option is to take a 4:30am (!) minibus to Rumichaca. In the west of town from Plaza Tupac Amaru, San Juan Bautista (S10, six hours) depart daily. Then wait for an Ayacucho-bound bus coming from the coast – usually from Lima. Most days buses from Lima don't get to Rumichaca until about 2pm so you might want to try your hitchhiking skills rather than waiting for several hours in this rather bleak spot. Ensure, however, that there are at least two of you, and remember that hitchhiking can always be risky. The other more adventurous option is to minibus it to Lircay, find another onward minibus passage to Julcamarca and finally seek yet another minibus from Julcamarca to Ayacucho. Allow a full day to execute this option: roads are abysmal.

You can get to Lircay by minibus from Huancavelica. Señor de Oropesa (S8, 3½ hours) has a 1pm departure.

TAXI
Colectivo taxis for Huancayo (S25, 2½ hours) leave when full (four-passenger minimum). They leave from the *terminal terrestre* but a better option is to wander east down Muñoz from the Plaza de Armas and you'll see various companies touting for your custom.

TRAIN
Trains were not running from Huancavelica at the time of research. Before track improvements, they used to depart at 6.30am from Monday to Saturday for Huancayo. See p312 for more details.

AYACUCHO
☎ 066 / pop 151,000 / elev 2750m
The name of this mesmerizing colonial city, originating from the Quechua *aya* (death, or soul) and *cuchu* (outback), offers a telling insight into its past. Ayacucho's status as isolated capital of a traditionally poor department meant it provided the perfect breeding ground for Professor Abimael Guzmán to nurture the Sendero Luminoso (Shining Path) Maoist revolutionary movement bent on overthrowing the government and causing thousands of deaths in the region during the 1980s and '90s. Yet

---

THE MISSING LINK

On the map, Huancavelica (see p314) looks tantalizingly close to Ayacucho. A shortish haul northwest across the Andes and you're there, right? The town is a convenient way station for travelers on a south–north loop towards Huancayo (see p307) and on through the central highlands. That's where plans almost meet a dead end.

There is no direct bus route from Ayacucho to Huancavelica but the journey *can* be done. The first option requires taking a local minibus at 4am from Ayacucho to Julcamarca, where you can take a short break while looking for an onward minibus to Lircay, famed as the production centre for Huancavelica department's traditional clothing. There are simple hotels here. Then seek out yet another local minibus to Huancavelica. Total traveling time: 10 hours.

Option two: take an early-morning Lima-bound bus as far as Rumichaca (2½ to three hours). Disembark here and hopefully catch a connecting minibus to Huancavelica. This is supposed to arrive from Huancavelica at 10:30am, but delays often occur. The Huancavelica-bound minibus doesn't 'connect' as such with the Lima buses; you just need to be at Rumichaca by 10:30am. Total traveling time: nine to 10 hours.

If all else fails, you can bus it to Huancayo and backtrack by road or rail (when functioning; at the time of research, the rail track was due to reopen in April 2010) to Huancavelica.

the city's historically poor links with the outside world have also helped foster a fiercely proud, independent spirit evident in everything, from the unique festivals to the booming cultural self-sufficiency.

The shadow of Ayacucho's dark past has long been lifted but travelers are only just rediscovering its treasures. Richly decorated churches dominate the vivid cityscape alongside peach- and pastel-colored colonial buildings hung with wooden balconies. Amongst the numerous city festivities, Ayacucho boasts Peru's premier Semana Santa celebrations while in the surrounding mountains lie some of the country's most significant archaeological attractions.

Perhaps Ayacucho's most alluring feature is the authenticity with which it pulls off its charms. Its development has been tasteful, its commercialization blissfully limited, and if you take to the pedestrianized, cobbled city central streets early enough, it is easy to imagine yourself transported back several centuries to its colonial heyday. That said, these days designer-clad students and businesspeople are increasingly in evidence and behind many colonial facades are plenty of sumptuous accommodation options, suave shops and restaurants. What is clear is that Peru's most enticing Andean city after Cuzco is experiencing a resurgence – and one well worth witnessing.

History

Some of the first signs of human habitation in Peru were allegedly discovered in the Pikimachay caves, near Ayacucho (there is nothing of interest to be seen there).

Five hundred years before the rise of the Incas, the Wari dominated the Peruvian highlands and established their capital 22km northeast of Ayacucho (see p326). The city's original name was San Juan de la Frontera de Huamanga and grew rapidly after its founding in 1540 as Spanish sought to defend it against attack from Manco Inca. Ayacucho played a major part in the battles for Peruvian independence and a huge nearby monument marks the site of the Battle of Ayacucho, fought in 1824, where 5800 patriots overcame 8200 Spanish to end colonial rule.

Ayacucho's first road link with the Peruvian coast was not finished until 1924; as late as 1960 there were only two buses and a few dozen vehicles in the city.

However, completion of a paved road link with Lima in 1999 has turned it to face the 21st century. Following Guzmán's capture in 1992, Ayacucho is once again a safe place to visit. The populace doesn't discuss the dark days of the 1980s much and welcomes travelers with enthusiasm and good cheer. (For more on this history, see p322.)

Orientation

The Plaza de Armas is also known as Plaza Mayor de Huamanga. The street names of the four sides of the plaza, clockwise from the east (with the cathedral), are Portal Municipal, Portal Independencia, Portal Constitución and Portal Unión.

Information

For good general information, try www.peru-ayacucho.com.

EMERGENCY
Police (☎ 31-2055, 31-6245; Jirón 28 de Julio 325; ☼ 24hr)
Policía de Turismo (☎ 31-7846; Jirón 2 de Mayo 100; ☼ 7:30am-8pm)

INTERNET ACCESS
There are many options.
Hueco Internet (☎ 31-5528; Portal Constitución 9) Among the better ones, it has newer machines and phone booths where you can make cheap calls overseas.

LAUNDRY
Lavandería Arco Iris (Bellido 322) Provides both wash-and-dry and dry-cleaning services.

MEDICAL SERVICES
Clínica de La Esperanza (☎ 31-7436; Independencia 355; ☼ 8am-8pm) English is spoken.
Hospital Central (☎ 31-2180/1; Independencia 335; ☼ 24hr) Provides basic services.
Inka Farma (☎ 31-8240, 83-6273; Jirón 28 de Julio 250; ☼ 7am-10:30pm) Pharmacy.

MONEY
BCP (☎ 31-4102; Portal Unión 28) Visa ATM.
Interbank (☎ 31-2480; Jirón 9 de Diciembre 183)
Money changers (Portal Constitución) On the southwest corner of the Plaza de Armas.

POST
Post office (☎ 31-2224; Asamblea 293; ☼ 8am-8pm Mon-Sat) It's 150m from the Plaza de Armas.

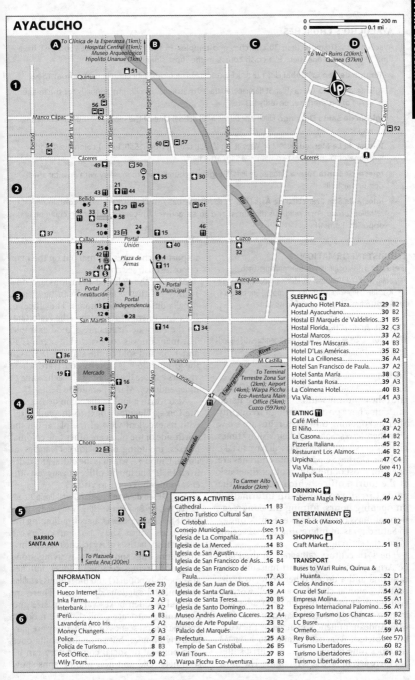

AYACUCHO

0   200 m
0   0.1 mi

To Clínica de la Esperanza (1km);
Hospital Central (1km);
Museo Arqueológico
Hipolito Unanue (1km)

To Wari Ruins (20km);
Quinua (37km)

To Terminal
Terrestre Zona Sur
(2km); Airport
(4km); Warpa Picchu
Eco-Aventura Main
Office (5km);
Cuzco (597km)

To Carmer Alto
Mirador (2km)

To Plazuela
Santa Ana (200m)

BARRIO
SANTA ANA

SLEEPING

Ayacucho Hotel Plaza	29 B2
Hostal Ayacuchano	30 B2
Hostal El Marqués de Valdelirios	31 B5
Hostal Florida	32 C3
Hostal Marcos	33 A2
Hostal Tres Máscaras	34 B3
Hotel D'Las Américas	35 B2
Hotel La Crillonesa	36 A4
Hotel San Francisco de Paula	37 A2
Hotel Santa María	38 C3
Hotel Santa Rosa	39 A3
La Colmena Hotel	40 B3
Via Via	41 A3

EATING

Café Miel	42 A3
El Niño	43 A2
La Casona	44 B2
Pizzería Italiana	45 B2
Restaurant Los Alamos	46 B2
Urpicha	47 C4
Via Via	(see 41)
Wallpa Sua	48 A2

DRINKING

Taberna Magía Negra	49 A2

ENTERTAINMENT

The Rock (Maxxo)	50 B2

SHOPPING

Craft Market	51 B1

TRANSPORT

Buses to Wari Ruins, Quinua & Huanta	52 D1
Cielos Andinos	53 A2
Cruz del Sur	54 A2
Empresa Molina	55 A1
Expreso Internacional Palomino	56 A1
Expreso Turismo Los Chancas	57 B2
LC Busre	58 B2
Ormeño	59 A4
Rey Bus	(see 57)
Turismo Libertadores	60 B2
Turismo Libertadores	61 B2
Turismo Libertadores	62 A1

SIGHTS & ACTIVITIES

Cathedral	11 B3
Centro Turístico Cultural San Cristobal	12 A3
Consejo Municipal	(see 11)
Iglesia de La Compañía	13 A3
Iglesia de La Merced	14 B3
Iglesia de San Agustín	15 B2
Iglesia de San Francisco de Asis	16 B4
Iglesia de San Francisco de Paula	17 A3
Iglesia de San Juan de Dios	18 A4
Iglesia de Santa Clara	19 A4
Iglesia de Santa Teresa	20 B5
Iglesia de Santo Domingo	21 B2
Museo Andrés Avelino Cáceres	22 A4
Museo de Arte Popular	23 B4
Palacio del Marqués	24 B2
Prefectura	25 A3
Templo de San Cristóbal	26 B5
Wari Tours	27 B3
Warpa Picchu Eco-Aventura	28 B3

INFORMATION

BCP	(see 23)
Hueco Internet	1 A3
Inka Farma	2 A3
Interbank	3 A2
iPerú	4 B3
Lavandería Arco Iris	5 A2
Money Changers	6 A3
Police	7 B4
Policía de Turismo	8 B3
Post Office	9 B2
Wily Tours	10 A2

AYACUCHO'S CHURCHES

Ayacucho boasts more than 30 churches and temples. In the likely event that you don't have time to visit each one, here is a crash course in the most significant.

- **Templo de San Cristóbal** (Jirón 28 de Julio, cuadra 6) The oldest city church, dating from 1540.
- **Iglesia de Santa Clara** (Grau at Nazareno) Attracts thousands of pilgrims annually for the image of Jesus of Nazareth supposedly inside.
- **Iglesia de Santa Domingo** (Jirón 9 de Diciembre at Bellido) One of the most photogenic churches, dating from 1548.
- **Iglesia de La Merced** (Jirón 2 de Mayo at San Martín) Dating from 1550, full of colonial art and with one of Peru's oldest convents (1540) attached.
- **Iglesia de Santa Teresa** (Jirón 28 de Julio) Gorgeous church-cum-monastery with an altar studded in seashells.
- **Iglesia de San Francisco de Asis** (Jirón 28 de Julio) Visually striking stone church containing *retablos* (ornamental religious dioramas) and an attractive 17th-century adjoining convent. It's opposite the market.

TOURIST INFORMATION

iPerú (☎ 31-8305; iperuayacucho@promperu.gob.pe; Plaza Mayor, Portal Municipal 48, Municipalidad Huamanga; ☒ 8:30am-7:30pm Mon-Sat, to 2:30pm Sun) One of Peru's best tourist offices. Helpful advice; English spoken.

TRAVEL AGENCIES

Wily Tours (☎ 31-4075; Jirón 9 de Diciembre 107) Good for flight and bus reservations.

Sights

Sights in Ayacucho consist primarily of churches and museums. While the listed museums have posted (although frequently altering) opening times, churches are a law unto themselves. Some list their visiting times on the doors; with others you will have to take potluck. During Semana Santa churches are open for most of the day; at other times ask at the tourist office, which publishes the guide *Circuito religioso* with information on opening hours. Joining the congregation for mass (usually 6am to 8am Monday to Saturday) is an interesting way of seeing inside the churches.

The 17th-century **cathedral**, on the Plaza de Armas, has a religious-art museum. The cathedral and a dozen other 16th- to 18th-century colonial churches are well worth a visit for their incredibly ornate facades and interiors, mainly Spanish baroque but often with Andean influences evinced by the wildlife depicted. Ayacucho claims to have 33 churches (one for each year of Christ's life) but there are, in fact, several more. The most

important churches are marked on the map, opposite (also see above).

Most of the colonial mansions are now mainly political offices and can be visited, usually during business hours. The offices of the department of Ayacucho (the **Prefectura**) on the Plaza de Armas are a good example. The mansion was constructed between 1740 and 1755 and sold to the state in 1937. On the ground floor is a pretty courtyard where visitors can see the cell of the local heroine of independence, María Parado de Bellido.

Also worth a look is the Salón de Actas in the **Consejo Municipal**, next to the cathedral, with its excellent view of the plaza. On the north side of the plaza are other fine colonial houses, including the **Palacio del Marqués**, at Portal Unión 37, which is the oldest and dates from 1550. The tourist office can suggest others around the center to visit.

The **Museo de Arte Popular** (Portal Unión 28; admission free; ☒ 8am-1pm & 1.30-3.15pm Mon-Fri) is in the 18th-century Casa Chacón, adjoining the Banco de Crédito. The popular art covers the *ayacucheño* (natives of Ayacucho) spectrum – silverwork, rug- and tapestry-weaving, stone and woodcarvings, ceramics (model churches are especially popular) and the famous **retablos** (ornamental religious dioramas). These are colorful wooden boxes varying in size and containing intricate papier-mâché models; Peruvian rural scenes or the nativity are particularly popular, but some interesting ones with political or social commentary can be seen here. Old and new photographs show

how Ayacucho changed during the 20th century. Opening hours here change frequently: go in the morning to maximize your chances of admission.

The **Museo Andrés Avelino Cáceres** (Jirón 28 de Julio 508-512; admission S4; ☺ 8am-12pm/9am-1pm & 2-6pm Mon-Sat) is housed in the Casona Vivanco, a gorgeous 16th-century mansion. Cáceres was a local man who commanded Peruvian troops during the War of the Pacific (1879–83) against Chile. Accordingly, the museum houses maps and military paraphernalia from that period, as well as colonial art: check the painting of the Last Supper – with *cuy*!

The **Museo Arqueológico Hipólito Unanue** (Museo INC; ☎ 31-2056; admission S4; ☺ 9am-1pm & 3-5pm Mon-Sat, to 1pm Sun) is in the Centro Cultural Simón Bolívar at the university, located more than 1km from the town center along Independencia – you can't miss it. Wari ceramics make up most of the small exhibition, along with relics from the region's other various civilizations. While there, check out the university library for a free exhibition of mummies, skulls and other niceties. The buildings are set in a botanical garden. The best time to visit the museum is in the morning: afternoon hours sometimes aren't adhered to.

Centro Turístico Cultural San Cristóbal (Jirón 28 de Julio 178) is a remodeled colonial building transformed into a hip little mall. Here you'll find bars, restaurants and coffee shops, along with art galleries and craft stores and flower stands. A nice place to hang during the day.

The **mirador** in the Carmen Alto district, one of the city's most traditional areas, offers fabulous views of Ayacucho, as well as decent restaurants: taxis here charge S5, otherwise catch a bus from the Mercado Central or walk (one hour).

Tours & Guides
Several agencies arrange local tours; most cater to Peruvian tourists and guides mainly speak Spanish. Ask about tours in other languages.

Wari Tours (☎ 31-3115; Lima 148)

Warpa Picchu Eco-Aventura (☎ 31-9483, 966-90-1941; pverbistperu@gmail.com; Carretera Cuzco Km 5) Experienced, multilingual guide Pierre Verbist offers adventure tours in the area, including by 4WD. Contact Pierre in advance to arrange tours; his central office is at San Martín 425.

Courses
Via Via (☎ 31-2834; ayacucho.peru@viaviacafe.com; Portal Constitucion 4) runs Quechua courses. Fees are S30 per lesson for private tuition and significantly less for groups.

Festivals & Events
Ayacucho's **Semana Santa** celebration, held the week before Easter, is Peru's finest religious festival and attracts visitors from all over the country. Rooms in most hotels fill well in advance. The tourist office has lists of local families who provide accommodations for the overflow.

Each year, iPerú prints a free brochure describing the Semana Santa events with street maps showing the main processions. Visitors are advised to use this detailed information. The celebrations begin on the Friday before Palm Sunday and continue for 10 days until Easter Sunday. The Friday before Palm Sunday is marked by a procession in honor of La Virgen de los Dolores (Our Lady of Sorrows), during which it is customary to inflict 'sorrows' on bystanders by firing pebbles out of slingshots. Gringos have been recent targets, so be warned.

Each succeeding day sees solemn yet colorful processions and religious rites, which reach a fever pitch of Catholic tradition. They culminate on the Saturday before Easter Sunday with a huge all-night party including dawn fireworks to celebrate the resurrection of Christ. If you want to party too, stay on your guard, as proceedings are notoriously wild. Crime in the city escalates dramatically during festivities: robbery and rape are not unheard of.

In addition to the religious services, Ayacucho's Semana Santa celebrations include art shows, folk-dancing competitions, local music concerts, street events, sporting events (especially equestrian ones), agricultural fairs and the preparation of traditional meals.

The tourist office here is a good source of information about the large number of minor fiestas held throughout the department.

Sleeping
The revival of tourism in the late 1990s has resulted in a boom of hotels and *hospedajes* (small, family-owned inns). In addition to the myriad small affairs with generally limited facilities, there is an ever-growing number of plusher (yet still reasonably priced) options with creature comforts like round-the-clock

A NOT-SO-SHINING PATH

The Sendero Luminoso's (Shining Path) activities in the 1980s focused on deadly political, economic and social upheaval. In remote towns and villages, mayors were murdered, uncooperative villagers massacred, police stations and power plants bombed and government and church-sponsored aid projects destroyed. The government responded by sending in armed forces, who were often equally brutal, and in the ensuing civil war almost 70,000 people died or disappeared, most of them in the central Andes. Ayacucho was almost completely off-limits to travelers during the 1980s. Things finally changed when the Sendero Luminoso's founder, Guzmán, was captured and imprisoned for life in 1992, followed quickly by his top lieutenants, leading to an eventual halt in activities that has lasted for some 12 years. In recent years the fragmented group has been only sporadically active, with its political idealism giving way to pragmatism – drug trafficking has been its most notable activity in recent times. A major exception to this was in April 2009, when Shining Path rebels killed 13 army officers in the Ayacucho region. That said, the threat to tourists is still minor and all of the listings in this chapter can be visited as safely as anywhere else in Peru.

For more on Peru's Internal Conflict, see p45.

hot water. During Semana Santa prices rise markedly – by 25% to even 75%.

BUDGET

Hotel La Crillonesa (☎ 31-2350; Nazareno 165; s/d S30/45, s/d without bathroom S15/25) A popular and helpful hotel, it offers a rooftop terrace with photogenic views, a cafe, TV room, tour information and 24-hour hot water. Its rather small, clean rooms have comfy beds; those with shower may have cable TV. The best rooms are right at the top.

La Colmena Hotel (☎ 31-1318; Cuzco 140; s/d S35/50, s without bathroom S15) This popular hotel is often full by early afternoon, partly because it's one of the longest-standing places in town and partly because it's only steps from the plaza. It's a great building that has rather been resting on its laurels – many bathrooms are run-down. The drop in rates now makes this a good budget option. It also has a locally popular restaurant and a courtyard with balconies.

Hostal Tres Máscaras (☎ 31-2921, 31-4107; Tres Máscaras 194; s/d with S30/45, s/d without bathroom S18/30) The pleasing walled garden and friendly staff make this an enjoyable place to stay. Hot water is on in the morning and later on request. A room with TV is S5 extra. Continental/American breakfast is available for S6/7.

Hostal Ayacuchano (☎ 31-9891; Tres Máscaras 588; s/d S20/35) Amply sized, inoffensively decorated well-furnished rooms get cable TV and, in some cases, even balconies. Not all singles have private bathrooms, but the bathrooms in some of the doubles are the sanitary surprises

of Ayacucho: spacious, with actual baths and hot water to boot.

Hotel D'Las Américas (☎ 31-3903; Asamblea 258; s/d S30/45) The rooms here are not quite as impressive as the bright, spacious, plant-filled entrance and the surprisingly pleasant communal areas but for the price you can't complain: they're clean, with hot water and cable TV. Street-facing rooms are noisy, although overlooking the bustling thoroughfare outside is visually agreeable.

Hostal Florida (☎ 31-2565; fax 31-6029; Cuzco 310; s/d S35/50) This traveler-friendly *hostal* (guest house) has a relaxing courtyard garden and clean rooms (those on the upper level are better) with bathrooms and TV, hot water in the morning and later on request. There is a basic cafeteria too.

our pick **Via Via** (☎ 31-2834; ayacucho.peru@viavia cafe.com; Portal Constitucion 4; dm S35, s/d/ste S60/95/145) The most imaginative sleeping option is brand-new Via Via, with an enviable plaza location and cool, vibrantly decorated rooms themed around different continents. There is a sun roof and hammock room and it's all centered on a plant-filled courtyard. Backpackers will appreciate the two-level, six-bed Ayacucho room: the city's very first, most traveler-oriented dormitory-style accommodation.

Hostal El Marqués de Valdelirios (☎ 31-8944; fax 31-7040; Bolognesi 720; s/d S40/60) This lovely, unsign-posted colonial building is about 700m from the center. While it is in a quiet location, the walk back at night involves passing through some dark neighborhoods. There is a restaurant, bar and a grassy garden where food can be served. Rooms vary in size and in amenities (views, balconies, telephone) but all have beautiful furniture, cable TV and hot showers.

Hostal Marcos (☎ 31-6867; Jirón 9 de Diciembre 143; s/d incl breakfast S45/70) Twelve spotless rooms in a little place somewhat sequestered away at the end of an alley, which is clearly signposted off Jirón 9 de Diciembre. This place is often full, so call ahead if you can. Rooms offer 24-hour hot water and cable TV; a light breakfast is included.

MIDRANGE

Hotel San Francisco de Paula (☎ 31-2353; www.hotel sanfranciscodepaula.com; Callao 290; s/d incl breakfast S70/90) This rather rambling, oldish hotel isn't flash, but it is presentable. It has a restaurant and bar and decent-sized, tiled rooms get the usual midrange facilities. Outside doubles are better as the inside singles can be very poky. There is also laundry and internet.

Hotel Santa María (☎ /fax 31-4988; Arequipa 320; s/d S95/125) Of the places opened during the hotel rush of the late '90s, this one seems to have got it right. It looks impressive from the outside and despite a slightly sterile interior, the rooms are very comfortable, quite spacious and tastefully decorated. There's a bar and cafe-restaurant, too.

Hotel Santa Rosa (☎ 31-4614; Lima 166; www.hotel -santarosa.com; s/d incl breakfast S75/130) Less than a block from the Plaza de Armas, this capacious hotel with its twin courtyards has spacious, airy and cosily furnished rooms. Some come with a fridge (a luxury in the Central Andes) and all have TV, DVD player and phone. The bathrooms are large and the showers have oodles of hot water. There's also a decent and well-priced on-site restaurant for meals.

Ayacucho Hotel Plaza (☎ 31-2202; fax 31-2314; Jirón 9 de Diciembre 184; s/d S200/240; ▣) Once considered the best in town, it's an impressive-looking colonial building and the interior does admittedly exude a certain kind of colonial charm. However, for what you pay, the rooms are oh-so-plain and in reality no more than adequate. The better rooms have balconies (request one) and some have plaza views.

Eating

Restaurants within two blocks of the Plaza de Armas may be more expensive than places further out but it's a fair trade-off for the added ambience and convenience. Regional special-

ties include *puca picante*, a potato and beef stew in a spicy red peanut and pepper sauce, served over rice; *patachi*, a wheat soup with various beans, dried potatoes and lamb or beef; and *mondongo*, a corn soup cooked with pork or beef, red peppers and fresh mint. *Chicharrones* and *cuy* are also popular. Vegetarians may accordingly be challenged to find meatless fare: *chifas* (Chinese restaurants) are often the best bet. For cheap eats try *cuadra* 4 of San Martín. Within the Centro Turístico San Cristóbal, some upbeat eats provide quality food and atmospheric, if slightly touristy, dining.

Café Miel (☎ 31-7183; Portal Constitución 4; snacks from S2; ☼ 10am-10pm) Breakfast is the best time to visit this reader-recommended place with its chirpy atmosphere and checkered tablecloths – we're talking great fruit salads and Ayacucho's best (freshly brewed) coffee. It serves hearty lunches and great chocolate cake too.

Wallpa Sua (☎ 31-2006; Calle de la Vega 240; mains S6-20; ☼ 6-11pm Mon-Sat) This is an upscale, locally popular and ever-busy chicken restaurant, with a quarter-chicken and fries starting at S6 and various other meat plates (like beef-heart brochettes) available. *Wallpa sua* is Quechua for 'chicken thief' – makes you wonder where it gets its poultry supplies.

La Casona (☎ 31-2733; Bellido 463; mains S5-20; ☼ 7am-10:30pm) This popular, ambient restaurant has been recommended by several travelers for its big portions. It focuses on Peruvian food like the excellent *lomo saltado* and often has regional specialties but seems to have difficulty serving even slightly chilled beer.

Restaurant Los Alamos (☎ 31-2782; Cuzco 215; mains average S10; ☼ 7am-10pm) In an attractive patio within the hotel of the same name, this restaurant has good service and a long menu of Peruvian selections and a few vegetarian plates; it may have musicians in the evening.

El Niño (☎ 31-4537, 31-9030; Jirón 9 de Diciembre 205; mains S10-18; ☼ 11am-2pm & 5-11pm) In a colonial mansion with a sheltered patio containing tables overlooking a garden, El Niño specializes in grills yet dishes up a variety of Peruvian food. The individual *parrillada* is good, although in practice sufficient for two modest eaters. This is one of the city's best restaurants.

Via Via (☎ 31-2834; Portal Constitucion 4; mains S15-30; ☼ 10am-10pm Mon-Thu, to midnight Fri/Sat, to 3pm Sun) With its upstairs plaza-facing balcony, Via Via has the best views (and steepest prices) with which to accompany your meal in Ayacucho. It's ethically sourced, organic food – the spicy *albondigas* (meatballs) are tempting – but this is Peruvian-European fusion cuisine, so you'll find something to sate you and some crisp South American wine (from S30) to wash it down.

ourpick Urpicha (☎ 31-3905; Londres 272; mains S10-25; ✆ 11am-8pm) This is a homey place, with tables in a flower-filled patio and an authentic menu including the dishes listed in the Eating introduction. Order the house special: the chef's mix of the top dishes of the day. It has a bit of a local cult following and few outsiders make it down here. However, the neighborhood isn't great, so take a taxi after dark.

Pizzería Italiana (☎ 31-7574; Bellido 490; pizzas S12-25; ✆ 4:30-11:30pm) The wood-burning oven makes this a very cozy place on cold nights; musicians may wander in and the pizza is excellent.

Drinking & Entertainment

Outside of Semana Santa this is a quiet town, but there is a university so you'll find a few bar-clubs to dance or hang out in, mostly favored by students. Ask at the tourist office about the latest *peña* (bar or club featuring live folkloric music) scene: at last report there were no stand-out choices.

Taberna Magía Negra (Jirón 9 de Diciembre 293; ✆ 4pm-midnight Mon-Sat) A bar-gallery with good local art, beer and pizza – plus great music.

The Rock (Cáceres 1035; ✆ to 2am Wed-Sat) is the liveliest local disco, known locally as Maxxo, where gringos, as well as locals, go to strut their stuff. There is another disco on the same block playing mostly salsa.

Shopping

Ayacucho is a renowned handicraft center: a visit to the Museo de Arte Popular will give you an idea of local products. The tourist office can recommend local artisans who will welcome you to their workshops. The Santa Ana *barrio* (neighborhood) is particularly well known for its crafts: there are various workshops around Plazuela Santa Ana. Such work costs considerably less when bought directly from the artist rather than from shops in Lima.

A **craft market** (Independencia & Quinua) is open during the day.

Getting There & Around

AIR

The airport is 4km from the town center. Taxis charge S7. Flight times and airlines can change without warning, so check airline websites for the latest schedules.

Cielos Andinos (☎ 31-3060; Jirón 9 de Diciembre 123) has flights from Lima at 7am on Tuesdays, Fridays and Sundays, with the Tuesday flight continuing to Andahuaylas. Flights to Lima are on the same days, departing Ayacucho at 8.30am. The Andahuaylas leg may be cancelled if there are not enough passengers.

LC Busre (☎ 31-6012; Jirón 9 de Diciembre 160) has three daily flights to Lima: two morning departures and one afternoon departure.

Departure tax for domestic flights is S12.

BUS

Buses arrive at and depart from a bewildering array of individual company terminals scattered throughout town, but all are relatively near one another. The new Terminal Terrestre Zona Sur handles all departures to regional destinations south of Ayacucho.

Most transport connections are with Lima via the relatively fast and spectacular Hwy 24 that traverses the Andes via Rumichaca to Pisco. Night departures outnumber day departures, but day trips are naturally more interesting for the wild scenery en route. Choose your bus and company carefully. Ticket prices to/from Lima range from S30 for a regular seat to S60 for a reclining armchair that you can sleep in. The trip takes around nine hours. Take warm clothing if traveling by night.

For Lima, **Empresa Molina** (☎ 31-9989; Jirón 9 de Diciembre 459-73) is probably the best option (and has the nicest terminal to wait in). There are two daily departures and no less than seven night departures with the 'special' *cama* service being best for comfort. **Expreso Internacional Palomino** (☎ 31-3899; Manco Cápac 255) also offers an evening *cama* service. **Cruz del Sur** (☎ 31-2813; Cáceres 1264) and **Ormeño** (☎ 31-2495; Libertad 257) offer executive-style services with comfortable seats, but not fully reclinable. Other cheaper options include **Turismo Libertadores** (☎ 31-3614) at Tres Máscaras 493, on Pasaje Cáceres and on Manco Cápac, and **Rey Bus** (☎ 31-9413; Pasaje Cáceres 166).

Traveling north or south to other Andean towns presents some challenges. Many roads are unpaved and subject to washouts in the rainy season. Destinations in this category include Abancay, Andahuaylas and Cuzco to the south and southeast and Huancayo to the north. Be prepared for delays. For Cuzco (S50, 22 hours) and Andahuaylas (S30, 10 hours), seek out **Expreso Turismo Los Chancas** (☎ 31-2391; Pasaje Cáceres 150), which has four departures daily. It's a long, rough trip: the journey can be broken at Andahuaylas.

For Huancayo (S30, nine to 10 hours), Empresa Molina is the preferred choice, with one daily and five night departures. Take note: this is a tough 250km trip and not for the faint-hearted. Around 200 of those kilometers take you along a narrow, potholed, unpaved road between Huanta and Mariscal Cáceres through the wild Río Mantaro valley. The road runs at times high along unguarded cliff faces with nothing but space between your bus window and the foaming river below. Sit on the right side of the bus if you don't like vertiginous drops.

Huancavelica to the northwest is notoriously hard to get to from Ayacucho (see p317).

Change in Huancayo for onward services to Huánuco, Tingo María, Pucallpa and Satipo.

The new Terminal Terrestre Zona Sur has at least brought order to regional southbound departures. Buses to Julcamarca and Vischongo (S10, four hours) leave from here. Departures are normally in the morning. There are also buses to Vilcashuamán (S14, five hours) about hourly from 5am to 9am. A taxi to the terminal costs S4.

Pickup trucks and buses go to many local villages, including Quinua (S3, one hour), and to the Wari ruins, departing from the Paradero Magdalena at the traffic circle at the east end of Cáceres.

WARI RUINS & QUINUA

An attractive 37km road climbs about 550m to Quinua, 20km along which you will pass the extensive **Wari ruins** (admission incl small museum S3; ☽ 8am-5:30pm) sprawling for several kilometers by the roadside. The five main sectors of the ruins are marked by road signs; the upper sites are in rather bizarre forests of *Opuntia* cacti. If you visit, don't leave the site too late to look for onward or return transport – vehicles can get hopelessly full in the afternoon. Note that you have to pay the full fare to Quinua and remind the driver to drop you off at the ruins.

The ruins have not been well restored but a knowledgeable site attendant is on hand to inform. You can also visit with a guide from Ayacucho as part of a tour combined with Quinua (you need to speak Spanish and may well end up shelling out for a guide that knows no more than the site attendant). It's more magical to go solo.

The road climbs beyond Wari, yielding great views, until it reaches the pretty village of Quinua; buses usually stop at the plaza. Steps from the left-hand side of the plaza, as you arrive from Ayacucho, lead up to the village church on an old-fashioned cobblestone plaza. A small **museum** (admission S5) nearby with erratic hours displays various relics from the major independence battle fought in this area. Beside the museum is the room where the Spanish royalist troops signed their surrender, leading to the end of colonialism in Peru.

To reach the battlefield, turn left behind the church and head up out of the village along Jirón Sucre, which, after 10 minutes' walk rejoins the main road. As you walk, notice the red-tiled roofs elaborately decorated with ceramic model churches. Quinua is famous as a handicraft center and these model churches are typical of the area. Local stores sell these and other crafts.

The **white obelisk**, intermittently visible for several kilometers as you approach Quinua, now lies five minutes' walk above you up clearly marked steps. The impressive monument is 40m high and features carvings commemorating the Battle of Ayacucho, fought here on December 9, 1824. You can climb the obelisk (S1) and continue half an hour by horseback (S8 there and back) to waterfalls where swimming is possible. The whole area is protected as the 300-hectare **Santuario Histórico Pampas de Ayacucho**.

Accommodations in Quinua are limited but you'll pass a couple of places en route to the obelisk from the museum charging S15 per person for beds in basic rooms. There is a small market on Sunday.

VILCASHUAMÁN & VISCHONGO

Vilcashuamán (Sacred Falcon) was considered the geographical center of the Inca empire. Here the Inca road between Cuzco and the coast crossed the road running the length of the Andes. Little remains of the city's earlier magnificence; Vilcashuamán has fallen prey to looters, and many of its blocks have been

CENTRAL HIGHLANDS

THE WARI

Before the Incas ruled the roost in the Peruvian Highlands, the Wari were top dogs. Their empire extended north beyond Chiclayo and south as far Lake Titicaca, with its capital on the pampa above Ayacucho. The heyday was from AD 600 to AD 1100, during which time the Wari took control over many settlements previously occupied by the Moche people in northern Peru, had dealings with the Tiwanaku culture to the south and established a power base in Cuzco.

The Wari rose to dominance through developing a series of key administrative centers in topographically contrasting regions: Moquegua on Peru's southern coast, Pikllaqta near Cuzco and Viracochapampa in the northern highlands. This maximized trade in resources including coca, cotton and corn. At its zenith, the empire enjoyed wealth then-unprecedented in Peruvian civilizations.

The capital, now a swathe of ruins 22km northeast of Ayacucho, once housed some 50,000 people and was well-organized into sectors for agriculture, workshops and a grandiose area reserved for burial of dignitaries (the Cheqowasi sector of the site shows this). The Wari certainly had grand plans. Their architectural style placed an emphasis on a display of power with public spaces, possibly for nobles to interact in, and platforms to promote rank seniority, as well as distinctive ceramics which indicate sophisticated trade interaction with neighboring cultures like the Tiwanaku.

However, by AD 1000, for unknown reasons, the empire had entered a period of decline. It has been speculated that because defense had never been a priority, Wari buildings were vulnerable to attack. Significantly, however, the civilization left behind a legacy of roads and settlements so important that they were still in use by the Inca empire almost 500 years later.

used to build modern buildings. The once-magnificent Temple of the Sun now has a church on top of it! The only Inca structure still reasonably in tact is a five-tiered pyramid called an *usnu*, topped by a huge stone-carved double throne.

Several direct daily buses for the rough, scenic 115km run to Vilcashuamán (S14, five hours), leave from Ayacucho's Terminal Terrestre del Sur. At a crossroads 2km before Vischongo, a road branches off for the final 22km to Vilcashuamán where there is a tourist office and basic accommodations like **Hostal Fortaleza** (s/d without bathroom S10/15). You'll also find an Inca pyramid here with the same name, which you can climb (S2) for spectacular surrounding views, particularly at sunrise.

To reach Vischongo, backtrack to the crossroads (Ayacucho-bound buses leave from Vilcashuamán's plaza several times daily, taking about one hour). Locals here refer to Ayacucho city as Huamanga: buses will be marked accordingly. From the crossroads, marked by a handy green sign, it's 2km to Vischongo. It's quicker to walk from here than wait for a bus.

In Vischongo, no-frills rooms at places like Albergue Ecoturistico de Vischongo, a block from the plaza, cost S10 per person. Ask at the Albergue about renting horses to surrounding

sights. You can hike 1½ hours from here up to a *Puya raimondii* **forest** (see p72). Largely redundant as the Sendero Luminoso is these days, their power base is reportedly in this area. You're unlikely to experience problems, but proceed with caution.

From the crossroads you can also hike on a well-defined path to an **Intihuatana ruin** (admission S1). If returning by bus to Ayacucho from the crossroads, you may wait some time for a vehicle with space: check times beforehand.

You can do a day tour with agencies in Ayacucho for about S60 per person.

NORTH OF TARMA

North of Tarma the highway passes through some of the more visually stark and tropically lush scenery in Peru in relatively short succession. Climbing high on to the altiplano, you pass through Junín, perched on the southern edge of the eponymous lake, before lurching upwards to Peru's highest town, the breath-sapping mining town of Cerro de Pasco. The road then plunges downwards in a series of twists and turns towards thriving Huánuco before dipping down again to the *ceja de la selva* in lush, tropical Tingo María.

JUNÍN & AROUND

☎ 064 / elev 4125m

An important independence battle was fought at the nearby pampa of Junín, 55km due north of La Oroya. This is now preserved as the 2500-hectare **Santuario Histórico Chacamarca**, where there is a monument 2km off the main road.

In Junín village, basic cold-water *hospedajes* charge around S15 for basic rooms; there are simple restaurants around the Plaza de Libertad.

About 10km beyond the village is the interesting **Lago de Junín**, which, at about 30km long and 14km wide, is Peru's largest lake after Titicaca. More than 4000m above sea level, it is the highest lake of its size in the Americas and is known for its birdlife. Some authorities claim that one million birds live on and around the lake at any one time. These include one of the western world's rarest species, the Junín Grebe and, among the nonwinged inhabitants, wild *cuy*. It's a little-visited area and recommended for anyone interested in seeing water and shorebirds of the high Andes. The lake and its immediate surroundings are part of the 53,000-hectare **Reserva Nacional Junín**. Visit by taking a *colectivo* 5km north to the hamlet of **Huayre**, from where a 1.5km path leads to the lake. Otherwise it can be quite hard to actually visit or even see the lake as it is mostly surrounded by swampy marshlands and no main highway gets within eyeshot of the lake itself.

The wide, high plain in this area is bleak, windswept and very cold, so be prepared with warm, windproof clothing. Buses ply the route via Junín quite often: watch for intermittent herds of llama, alpaca and sheep.

CERRO DE PASCO (CERRO)

☎ 063 / pop 66,860 / elev 4333m

With its *soroche*- (altitude sickness) inducing height above sea level and its icy, rain-prone climate, this dizzyingly high altiplano mining settlement is never going to be a favorite traveler destination. First impressions however are still striking: houses and streets spread haphazardly around a gaping artificial hole in the bare hills several kilometers wide. The Spanish discovered silver here in the 17th century and this, along with other mineral wealth, has made Cerro a lucrative Peruvian asset. It has also worked hard at image improvement in recent years and boasts decent hotels and pleasing plazas to take your mind off the cold and industrial clamor. Besides being the highest place of its size in the world, Cerro attracts the odd traveler through its self-proclaimed status as the gateway for visiting some of Peru's most spectacular rock formations. If you are traveling by *colectivo* taxi around the altiplano it is also handy for picking up a connecting ride. The high, oxygen-poor altitude makes the town bitterly cold at night: *soroche* sufferers will really feel its effects.

Change your money at **BCP** (Arenales 162), which has an ATM. It's below Hotel Arenales. Emergency health care is available at **Clínica Gonzales** (☎ 42-1515; Carrión 99).

On the Plaza, **Hostal Santa Rosa** (☎ 42-2120; Libertad 269; s/d without bathroom S14/20) has basic, spacious rooms sharing three bathrooms and one highly prized hot shower. There's a self-catering kitchen; the owner is a guide with information on how to visit the rock formations at Santuario Nacional Huayllay (see below).

Hotel Yaban (☎ 42-1964; jose18_95@hotmail.com; Circumvalación Mza D-Lote 1; s/d S35/50) is the tall red-colored building by the bus terminal entrance. This spick-and-span hotel boasts a restaurant and 41 rooms with 24-hour hot water and cable TV. Nearby, long-standing **Hostal Arenales** (☎ 42-3088; Arenales 162; s/d S25/35) has hot water in the mornings. Opposite the bus terminal.

In the suburb of San Juan, Cerro's best digs are at **Hotel Señorial Class** (☎ 42-1026; hotel senorial@hotmail.com; San Martín; s/d S50/80), where smart rooms are on the smallish side but have the standard hot water and cable TV. The city's best (practically only) restaurant is here.

The bus terminal five blocks south of the Plaza de Armas has buses to Huánuco (S10, three hours), Huancayo (S15, four hours), Lima (S15, eight hours), La Oroya (S10, 2½ hours) and Tarma. There are also minibuses to Tarma (S6, three hours). Faster *colectivos* from the bus terminal charge S20 to either Huánuco or Tarma: however you might have to change up to three times.

SOUTHWEST OF CERRO DE PASCO

An infrequently used road runs southwest of Cerro de Pasco to Lima, passing west of Lago de Junín and close to Huayllay, a village near the 6815-hectare **Santuario Nacional Huayllay** or *bosque de piedras* (forest of stones). It's the world's largest and highest rock forest: a fascinating place with rock formations looming out of the desolate pampa in such shapes as an elephant, a king's crown and an uncannily lifelike grazing alpaca. The area is highly rated for rock-climbing. The sanctuary also has thermal baths and prehistoric cave paintings: you might need a guide to find these. Señor Raul Rojas of Hostal Santa Rosa (p327) in Cerro de Pasco is a recommended guide. You can get here independently (the sanctuary entrance is just before Huayllay village, a 25km run from the Cerro–Lima road) by taking a *colectivo* from Parque Minero in Cerro de Pasco, near the bus terminal (S6, 1½ hours).

Five hours further southwest the road descends into the lushly rolling Chillón valley and the town of **Canta**, with basic hotels. The area around Canta was the hotbed of the pre-Columbian Atavillos culture: remains of the civilization can be seen at **Cantamarca**, a three-hour hike from town. Two kilometers north of Canta, **Obrajillo** is another scenic small town oozing faded colonial charm with camping, horseback riding and hiking op-

portunities along the shady river banks and hills nearby. The area is a popular weekend getaway for *limeños* but otherwise rarely visited. From Canta it's 105km to Lima: buses leave three times daily (S8, three hours). Canta-bound buses leave around 6am from opposite the Universidad de Ingeniera in the San Martín de Porras district of Lima.

HUÁNUCO
☎ 062 / pop 170,000 / elev 1894m

Huánuco lay on the important Inca route from Cuzco to Cajamarca, the key settlement in the north of the empire, and developed as a major way station accordingly. The Incas chose Huánuco Viejo, 150km west, as their regional stronghold but the exposed location prompted the Spanish to move the city to its current scenic setting on the banks of the Río Huallaga in 1541. Little is left of its colonial past but the profusion of archaeological remains in the surrounding mountains is the main reason to linger in this busy little place. Locals also boast Huánuco's perfect elevation gives it the best climate in Peru: indeed, after the wild climes of the altiplano,

HUÁNUCO

INFORMATION		
Banco Continental	1	C2
BCP	2	B3
Locutorio Público	3	C3
Tourist Office	4	C3

SIGHTS & ACTIVITIES		
Iglesia San Francisco	5	B2
Mya Tours	6	C3

SLEEPING		
Grand Hotel Huánuco	7	C2
Hostal Huánuco	8	C3
Hotel Caribe	9	B2
Hotel Imperial	10	B2
Hotel Real	11	C2
Hotel Trapiche Suites	12	C2
Sosa	13	C3

EATING		
Chifa Khon Wa	14	C3
Govinda	15	B2
Lookcos Burger Grill	16	C2
Piazolla	17	C2
Shorton Grill	18	C2

ENTERTAINMENT		
Adamique	19	C2
Cheers Karaoke	20	C2

TRANSPORT		
Bahía Continental	21	C3
Cars & buses to Tingo María & Pucallpa	22	D3
Comité Autos No 5	23	C3
LC Busre	24	C2
León de Huánuco	25	C3
Transportes Chasqui	26	A3
Transportes Rey	27	C2
Turismo Central	28	B3
Turismo Unión	29	A3

it seems positively balmy. With several good accommodation options it certainly makes for a convenient and tempting stopover on the Lima–Pucallpa jungle route. Nearby is one of Peru's oldest Andean archaeological sites, the Temple of Kotosh (aka the Temple of the Crossed Hands), while further up in the hills lie the still more impressive ancient ruins of Huánuco Viejo and Tantamayo.

Orientation

Huánuco is easy enough to find your way around on foot. Most transport options arrive and depart from within 200m of the main square: hotels and restaurants are all within three blocks of here too.

Information

Almost identical sets of internet *cabinas* grace most blocks.

Banco Continental (☎ 51-3348; Jirón 2 de Mayo 1137) Has a pair of ATMs.

BCP (☎ 51-2213; Jirón 2 de Mayo 1005) With a Visa ATM.

Locutorio Público (Jirón 28 de Julio 810) Make cheap overseas phone calls here.

Tourist office (☎ 51-2980; Jirón 28 de Julio 940; 🕙 8am-1:30pm & 4-6pm Mon-Fri) Pretty useless.

Sights & Activities

The archaeological site of the **Temple of Kotosh** (admission incl guided tour S5; 🕙 8am-6pm) is also known as the Temple of the Crossed Hands because of the life-sized mud molding of a pair of crossed hands, which is the site's highlight. The molding dates to about 2000 BC and is now at Lima's Museo Nacional de Antropología, Arqueología e Historía del Perú (p97); a replica remains. Little is known about Kotosh, one of the most ancient of Andean cultures. The temple site is not in great shape, but is easily visited by taxi (S12, including a 30-minute wait and return) or the bus to La Unión. In the hills 2km above the site, **Quillaromi** cave has impressive prehistoric paintings. Kotosh is about 5km west of town off the La Unión road.

About 25km south of Huánuco is **Ambo**, noted for its distilleries producing *aguardiente*, a locally popular sugarcane liquor. You might be able to try/buy some.

The **Iglesia San Francisco** (cnr Huallayco & Beraún) is Huánuco's most appealing church, with lavish baroque-style altars and interesting *escuela cuzqueña* paintings.

Mya Tours (☎ 962-60-4331; General Prado 815) arranges regional excursions.

Festivals & Events

Huánuco's most unusual festival is the **Dance of the Blacks**, held each January 1st, 6th and 18th. Revelers remember the slaves brought to work in the area's mines by donning black masks, dressing up brightly and drinking until the early hours.

Sleeping

BUDGET

On the southeast side of the plaza is a glut of uninspiring options offering basic accommodation with a plaza price tag.

ourpick Hostal Huánuco (☎ 51-2050; Huánuco 777; s/d S25/35, s without bathroom S15) This traditional mansion simply exudes character, with old-fashioned tiled floors, a 2nd-floor terrace overlooking a garden and hall walls covered with art and old newspaper clippings. Delightful rooms contain characterful old furniture and have comfortable beds. Showers are hot but can take an age to warm up, so ask in advance.

Hotel Caribe (☎ 51-9708; fax 51-3753; Huánuco 546; s/d S16/20, s/d without bathroom S13/15) Service is surly, showers are hot, cable TV is included in the price of the doubles and there's a karaoke cafe downstairs.

Sosa (☎ 51-5803; hotelsosa@hotmail.com; General Prado 872; s/d S30/40) The main draw at this new five-story hotel are the huge, tiled hot-water bath/showers that most of the clean, tastefully decorated rooms come with. One room has a Jacuzzi; there's a small restaurant below.

Hotel Imperial (☎ 51-4758; hotelimperial_hco@hotmail.com; Huánuco 581; s/d S35/40) Near the market, this Huánuco newcomer offers little out of the ordinary but has decent-sized pastel-colored rooms, dependable hot water, cable TV and a pleasing cafe, all within clean, secure environs.

MIDRANGE

Hotel Trapiche Suites (☎ 51-7091; hoteltrapiche huanuco@hotmail.com; General Prado 636; s/d S70/90; 🖳) It's official: boutique hotels have reached Huánuco. Rooms at this snazzy new place have funky artwork on the walls, huge, comfy, colorful beds, copiously stocked mini-fridges and telephones. It's clearly aiming at well-to-do business types (who, if they exist in the

CENTRAL H

city right now are keeping a low profile) and offers a viable luxury alternative to the city's other more staid top hotels.

Hotel Real (☎ 51-1777; real_hotel@hotmail.com; Jirón 2 de Mayo 1125; s/d S90/120; ☎) On the Plaza de Armas, this fairly comfortable, modern hotel has large rooms with good beds, cable TV and phone. It has a sauna, restaurant and a handy 24-hour cafe.

Grand Hotel Huánuco (☎ 51-4222; www.grand hotelhuanuco.com; Beraún 775; s/d S132/185; ☎) Also on the Plaza de Armas is this grande dame of Huánuco hotels. Its public areas are airy and pleasant, high-ceilinged rooms have solid parquet floors as well as a phone and a fuzzy, mainly Spanish-language cable-TV service. A sauna, billiard room, Jacuzzi, pretty good restaurant and bar are on the premises.

Eating

The 24-hour cafe at the Hotel Real is an excellent choice for midnight munchies or predawn breakfasts. For more formal dining try the stately dining room at the Grand Hotel Huánuco.

Govinda (☎ 52 5683; General Prado 608; menú S5; ☉ 7am-7:30pm Mon-Sat, to 3pm Sun) This Hare Krishna-run restaurant serves excellent vegetarian set meals with all the predictable permutations of tofu, veggies, rice and noodles in a somewhat gloomy setting.

Lookcos Burger Grill (☎ 51-2460; Castillo 471; meals S7.50-12; ☉ 6pm-midnight) This large, squeaky-clean restaurant serves mean burgers and sandwiches. Popular with a young student crowd, the upstairs sports a balcony and a hip bar blares out Peruvian rock (and sometimes karaoke) come nightfall.

Chifa Khon Wa (☎ 51-3609; General Prado 816; mains US$2-3; ☉ 10:30am-11pm) Khon Wa is the largest and most popular Chinese eatery in town. With two cooking areas, a children's play park and fast, attentive service, dining here is a pleasure. The chicken fried rice (with very hot chilies) is a good option at lunchtime.

Shorton Grill (☎ 51-2829; Beraún 685; mains about S10; ☉ 11am-midnight) Just off the plaza, this grilled-chicken restaurant is thinly disguised as a grill; chicken, chips and beer is where this place is at, and it's good.

Piazolla (☎ 51-2941; Beraún 847; meals S12-28; ☉ 6-11pm Mon-Sat) This upscale restaurant does quality Italian food including tasty pizzas: service is prompt and there is a good range of Chilean and Argentine wines.

Entertainment

Adamique (Beraún 636; ☉ 6pm-late) A suave, mellow kind of place with a small dance floor downstairs and a cozy upstairs area for drinks: the house sangria is what most of the clientele choose to knock back.

Cheers Karaoke (☎ 51-4666; Jirón 2 de Mayo 1201) Stop by this restaurant on a Friday or Saturday night to catch a could-be Peruvian singing star.

Getting There & Away

AIR

LC Busre (☎ 51-8113; www.lcbusre.com.pe; Jirón 2 de Mayo 1357) flies to and from Lima daily. The airport is 5km north of town. Take a cab (S10) to get there.

BUS & TAXI

Buses go to Lima (S20 to S30, eight hours), Pucallpa (S30, 11 hours), La Merced (S20, six hours), Huancayo (S20, six hours) and La Unión (S15, five hours), with companies all over town. The following are among the best:

Bahía Continental (☎ 51-9999; Valdizán 718) One of the more luxury options. Regular bus to Lima at 10am plus *bus-camas* at 10pm and 10:15pm.

León de Huánuco (☎ 51-1489, 51-2996; Robles 821) Lima at 10am, 8:30pm and 9:30pm, La Merced at 8pm, Pucallpa at 7pm.

Transportes Rey (☎ 51-3623; Jirón 28 de Julio 1215) Lima 9am and 10:15pm, Huancayo 8:30pm.

Turismo Central (Tarapaca 552) Pucallpa 7pm and 8pm, Huancayo 9.30pm.

Transportes Chasqui (Mayro 570) Tantamayo at 6:30am.

Turismo Unión (☎ 52-6308; Tarapaca 449) La Unión at 7:15am.

Other companies near Turismo Unión also go west toward villages on the eastern side of the Cordillera Blanca: rough roads, poor buses.

For Tingo María (S10, 3½ hours), take a Pucallpa-bound bus or a *colectivo* taxi (S18) with **Comité Autos No 5** (☎ 51-8346; General Prado 1085) near the river. There are more *colectivo* taxis for Tingo María on the other side of the river such as Trans Milagros, or wait here for a passing bus.

For Cerro de Pasco, minibuses (S6, three hours) or *colectivo* taxis (S20, two hours) leave from Paradero de Cayhuayna, a 1km *mototaxi* ride from the center.

LA UNIÓN

This tiny town is the first significant community on the rocky road from Huánuco to Huaraz: from here you can hike to the extensive Inca ruins of **Huánuco Viejo** (admission S4; ☺ 8am-6pm) on a swathe of barren pampa at 3700m. It's a two-hour trek on a steep path from behind the market heading toward a cross on a hill. Minivans leaving from the market place at 5am, as well as other vehicles, can take you to within a 30-minute walk of the site. There are 2 sq km of ruins and supposedly more than 1000 buildings and storehouses in total here. Most impressive is the *usnu*, a huge 4m-high ceremonial platform with engravings of animals (monkeys with lion faces) adorning the entrance. A key figure in the Inca resistance against the Spanish, Illa Tupac defended Huánuco Viejo until 1543, significantly after many Inca settlements had fallen.

La Unión has public but no listed phones and a handy **Banco de la Nación** (Jirón 2 de Mayo 798) with what is surely Peru's remotest Visa ATM. Just a block from here you'll also find **Hostal Picaflor** (Jirón 2 de Mayo 840; s/d without bathroom S10/20). Basic but agreeable rooms cluster around a bright courtyard. **Restaurant Recreo** (Jirón 2 de Mayo 971; mains S10-15) is the best of a basic bunch of eateries (Commercio has others) with relaxed courtyard dining.

All transport arrives/departs from the well-ordered bus terminal on Commercio at the west end of town. Several companies leave around 6pm for Lima (S20, 10 hours) while two or three buses daily ply the route east to Huánuco (S15, five hours). (For more information on the back route from Lima see below.) La Unión Huánuco has a service to Huaraz that departs at the ungodly hour of 3:45am, taking five hours.

TANTAMAYO
elev 3400m

Tantamayo is connected only by a rough track to the outside world. The first sign you are approaching is the green-brown patchwork of fields standing out from the stark, precipitous sides of the Upper Marañon valley. From this serene, chilly village flows a river that will, hundreds of kilometers downstream, morph into the Amazon itself. Tantamayo was capital of the pre-Columbian Yarowilca culture, remains of which are scattered throughout the nearby hills. The most impressive ruins are those at **Piruro** and **Susupillo**. This culture was one of the oldest known in Peru and very architecturally advanced. Buildings were constructed with up to six floors connected via internal spiral staircases, giving them a different appearance to the constructions of the Incas, whom many believe were unable to emulate Yarowilca style.

Piruro is easiest to visit: it's a 1½-hour walk down from Tantamayo village and up the other side of the valley. Vehicles can take you as far as Coyllabamba; then it's a 20-minute uphill walk. The path is hard to find: be sure to ask. The most photogenic ruins as seen in the pictures adorning the walls of almost every house in Huánuco are towards the top of the complex. For Susupillo, vehicles can take you to the village of Florida, a 20-minute drive from

---

ROAD TO THE RUINS

Heading to the highlands from Lima? Fascinated by ancient Peruvian civilizations and off-the-beaten-path attractions? Listen up: an adventurous back route between Huánuco and the capital exists, taking in tantalizing scenery and a glut of the country's best archaeological sites to boot.

The swathe of the central highlands between Huánuco and the Cordillera Blanca hides the important Inca settlement of Huánuco Viejo and the remains of the mysterious Yarowilca culture at Tantamayo. You'll need three days to do this route – which links both sites – justice.

Starting from Huánuco, you first need to catch the bumpy Tantamayo bus at 6:30am, arriving between 2pm and 4pm, depending on weather conditions. The Yarowilca ruins of Piruro and Susupillo lie nearby: you could see one in a morning or both in a full day. Minivans leave Tantamayo around 11:30am for the small town of La Unión daily, taking three hours. Once here, you can hire a vehicle or hike up to Huánuco Viejo. Buses leave La Unión for Lima at 6:30pm daily, taking 10 hours. There is also the option of skipping Tantamayo and traveling direct between La Unión and Huánuco.

The roads are rough and the accommodation basic but this is the Andes at its rawest, most archaeologically rich and genuine.

Tantamayo, from where you can hike to the site.

The basic lodgings in Tantamayo include hospitable **Albergue Ocaña Althuas** (Capitán Espinosa s/n; s/d without bathroom S10/20) beyond the Plaza on the main street into town. The folks here provide meals. Tantamayo has public phones (these can't dial internationally) but no listed ones, no cell phone reception and no banks. Buses from Huánuco take eight hours. Tantamayo can also be visited as part of a little-plied route from Huánuco to Lima (see p331).

TINGO MARÍA

☎ 062 / pop 55,000 / elev 649m

This languid, humid and warm university and market town lies in the *ceja de la selva*:

its back may rest against the mountains – as the conical, forested hills that flank it testify – but its feet are firmly fixed in the lush vegetation of the Amazonas region and its sticky, tropical embrace. Tingo María, or Tingo for short, is popular as a weekend destination for holidaying *limeños*, while travelers pause here en route to the Amazon.

Tingo used to get bad press (and still often does) courtesy of the *narcotraficantes* (drug traffickers) who control the production and processing of coca plants, hidden in the wild Huallaga valley to the north. As a result, guidebooks have recently tried to reverse this negative coverage and sing the town's praises, but the truth is that there is precious little to do in Tingo itself.

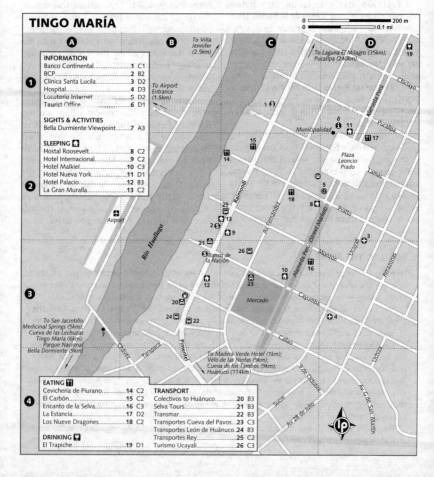

TINGO MARÍA

To Villa Jennifer (2.5km)
To Airport Entrance (1.5km)
To Laguna El Milagro (35km); Pucallpa (240km)
Municipalidad
Plaza Leoncio Prado
Airport
Río Huallaga
Banco de la Nación
Mercado
To San Jacintillo Medicinal Springs (5km); Cueva de las Lechuzas Tingo María (6km); Parque Nacional Bella Durmiente (9km)
To Madera Verde Hotel (1km); Velo de las Ninfas (9km); Cueva de los Tambos (9km); Huánuco (114km)

The highlight here is a visit to Parque Nacional Tingo María to the south: a dazzling forested network of valleys festooned with caves, lakes, waterfalls and sufficient adventures to warrant several days' exploration.

Caution is strongly advised when heading either to the park or eastwards on the lonely road into the *selva* to Pucallpa (see p488).

Orientation & Information

Tingo María is airy, spacious and easily navigated on foot. Arrivals tend to happen at the southwest corner of town. There are internet places on most blocks.

Banco Continental (☎ 56-2141; Raimondi 543) US dollars can be changed and there's a US dollar and nuevo sole ATM machine.

BCP (☎ 56-2111; Raimondi 249) Also changes US cash. It has a Visa ATM and may change traveler's checks.

Clínica Santa Lucila (☎ 56-1020; Ucayali 637) A private, better option than the hospital.

Hospital (☎ 56-2018/9; Ucayali 114) A block east of Alameda Perú.

Locutorio Internet (cnr Pratto & Alameda Perú)

Main post office (Plaza Leoncio Prado)

Tourist office (☎ 56-2351 ext116; Alameda Perú 525) On Plaza Leoncio Prado: publishes useful information on sights in Parque Nacional Tingo María.

Sights & Activities

For a tour guide (strongly advised if exploring the surrounding countryside), ask at the tourist office, or try **Jesús Oncoy Montes** (☎ 96-296-3991) who knows the area well and has his own *mototaxi*. The area around town is not without its dangers (see right).

PARQUE NACIONAL TINGO MARÍA

This 18,000-hectare park lies on the south side of town, around the mouth of the Río Monzón, a tributary of the Río Huallaga. The most distinguishing feature is the **Bella Durmiente** (Sleeping Beauty), a hill overlooking the town, which, from some angles, looks like a recumbent woman wearing an Inca crown.

Also in the park is **La Cueva de las Lechuzas** (the Cave of the Owls), which, despite its name, is known for the colony of oilbirds that lives inside. In addition, there are stalactites and stalagmites, bats, parrots and other birds around the cave entrance, but the oilbirds are the main attraction.

The caves are about 6km away from Tingo María; taxis can take you there. There is a S5

national-park fee and guides can show you around. The best times to visit the park are in the morning, when sunlight shines into the cave mouth, or dusk, when the oilbirds emerge. Don't be tempted to use your flashlight to see the birds, as it disturbs their sleeping and breeding patterns.

There is a myriad of great **bathing spots** in and around the park. Recommended are the **San Jacintillo Medicinal Springs**, 1km before the Cave of the Owls, **Velo de las Ninfas** and **Cueva de los Tambos**, 9km south of Tingo and the **Laguna el Milagro**, 35km north of town. There is a nominal entrance fee of S3 to S5 at each spot.

Sleeping

Showers are cold unless stated otherwise.

BUDGET

Hostal Roosevelt (☎ 56-2685; Pratto 399; s/d S20/30, s/d without bathroom S10/20) This neat little hostelry has a cool black-and-white-tiled floor leading to a series of smallish but very clean rooms. The color scheme here really is odd (kitsch purples and yellows) but you won't go wrong for the price. Rooms with cable TV are S10 extra.

Hostal Palacio (☎ 56-2319; www.hostal-palacio.com; Raimondi 158; s with/without bathroom S25/10, d S30/20) Now sporting four floors of rooms, the Palacio is a good budget choice. Staff are helpful and decent-sized rooms surround a plant-filled courtyard and cafe: those with bathrooms get cable TV, fans and phones. Guests staying up top can enjoy great views of Tingo.

Hotel Nueva York (☎ /fax 56-2406; Alameda Perú 553; s/d from S25/40) Spacious rooms have fans and showers hooked up to rooftop tanks so water gets warm come afternoon. Cable TV

DANGERS NEAR TINGO MARÍA

Unfortunately for a town in need of an image boost, the area around Tingo María is not without its dangers. There have been recent reports of travelers being robbed and raped at gunpoint en route to destinations in the Tingo María National Park. It is strongly recommended that you do not venture into the countryside around Tingo without a guide and ensure you return before dark. The Cave of the Owls has police protection, but the road there is still risky, as are more remote destinations.

is extra. There is also laundry service and cafeteria, where you can breakfast for another S5. Rooms are set back from the road and quiet.

Hotel Malkiel (☎ 56-2877; hotel_malkiel@hotmail .com; Alameda Perú 223; s/d S25/40) Four floors of large, neutrally decorated, solid rooms with fan, cable TV and reading lights in each. Some of the doubles have Jacuzzis (S60).

La Gran Muralla (☎ 56-2934; www.hotel-lagran muralla.com; Raimondi 277; s/d S35/60) This relatively new, breezy riverside complex has a light, bright feel to it, exemplified by its welcoming lobby painted with jungle scenes. Its modern, pleasantly furnished rooms are of a decent size and have cable TV, fans and phones. From the 2nd-floor terrace you can gaze over the river to the airport and the jungle beyond.

Hotel Internacional (☎ 56-3035; hinternacional_ TM2@hotmail.com; Raimondi 232; s/d S40/60) Close to the bus stations, this is unquestionably a pleasant choice and beckons the jaded *viajero* (traveler) with its cool, tiled interior and well-designed rooms. Though a tad dark, these have 24-hour hot water, cable TV and phone.

MIDRANGE

our pick **Villa Jennifer** (☎ 962-69-5059, 79-4/14; www .villajennifer.net; Castillo Grande Km 3.4; s/d S70/90; ☙) Located north of the airport, and handy now that flights have recommenced, is this peaceful tropical hacienda and lodge, run by a Danish-Peruvian couple. They have done wonders out of a lush expanse of tropical bushland bounded by rivers on two sides. Suave rustic accommodations range from simple rooms with shared bathrooms to airy mini-homes that can sleep up to 10 people. You can also

play table tennis, darts or table soccer, catch a movie in the DVD lounge or go see the resident animals, including crocodiles, tortoises, a sloth and some monkeys. There's also camping space (per person S20), backpackers rooms (per person S35), an excellent restaurant (the local fruit, including *anonas* – or custard apples – is delectable), two swimming pools and minigolf.

Madera Verde Hotel (☎ 56-2047; www.geocities .com/maverde_pe; Universitaria; s/d incl breakfast S125/165; ☙) Just over 1km south of town and set in leafy gardens, the 40 rooms here are a good size, with bathrooms, hot water, TV and minibar. Walk-in rates can be discounted. Three quadruple bungalows are available, too. You'll also find a pleasant restaurant and bar, a playground, a pool and a butterfly park.

Eating

Eating out in Tingo is a bit of a hit-or-miss experience: just as one good restaurant opens, another closes. The best bakery is Panadería Dulce Tentación, below the Hotel Nueva York. Villa Jennifer's restaurant is recommended, comes with complimentary pool use and is open to nonresidents on weekends. The following eateries also stand out against the proliferation of other OK hole-in-the-wall options.

Los Nueve Dragones (Av Fernández 394; mains S7-15; ☙ lunch & dinner) The 'Nine Dragons' *chifa* has put some effort into making its restaurant a pleasant and cheery eating environment and serves a predictable range of Peruvian-Chinese fusion plates.

LA RUTA DE COCA

Growing the coca plant itself is not illegal. Its leaves are used for chewing, making infusions of *mate de coca* (coca-leaf tea) and for other medicinal purposes.

However it is the mashing of coca leaves into *pasta básica* (basic paste) that gets people into trouble. This is the stuff that has hitherto been surreptitiously ghosted out of the region to processing centers – notably in Colombia – where the refined drug cocaine is produced. Coca grows in profusion in the hidden corners of the long Huallaga valley that runs from Tingo María to Tarapoto in the north. Close to Tingo, Monzón and its valley is a particularly troublesome area where police rarely tread. This is primary army territory.

But the battle against cocaine is a tough one. Farmers who make a pittance out of growing fruit or coffee can earn a viable living out of coca. It is a perverse logic played out equally in other South American nations with coca, or in Afghanistan with its poppies. *Narcotraficantes* (drug traffickers) have now established hidden processing centers within the Huallaga region instead of exporting the *pasta básica*. Pure cocaine now flows out of the region via various routes and methods. While the police and army try hard to stem the flow, it is ultimately a losing battle.

La Estancia (☎ 79-5703; Alameda Perú 554; mains S8-15; ☺ to midnight daily) You won't munch your chicken or *lomo saltado* in a better setting in Tingo: La Estancia has about the only pavement dining in town plus a 2nd-floor eating area. Dishes are unsurprising, but it's lively enough.

Encanto de la Selva (☎ 40-6440; Alameda Perú 288; mains S8-15; ☺ breakfast & lunch) For local jungle specialties this bright, two-floor establishment ticks all the boxes. Try *tacacho con cecina* (a bed of barbecued banana pummeled into rice-sized grains with dried, smoked meat on top) and wash it down with some cool coconut juice. It's simple, satisfying food.

Cevichería de Piurano (☎ 56-1822; Pratto 100; menú S8-15; ☺ lunch only) Service is slow here but you'll see why when you see the lovingly prepared ceviche platters: besides, it's no hardship to spend that bit longer with a cool beer on the flower-festooned outside terrace, watching the Rio Huallaga flow lazily alongside.

El Carbón (Raimondi 345; mains S15-25; ☺ lunch & dinner) One of the best restaurants in town these days, doing good grilled chicken, fish and steak.

Drinking

El Trapiche (Alameda Perú & San Alejandro; ☺ 11am-3am) A stylishly rustic venue, El Trapiche is stacked to the gills with bottles and serves a dangerously extensive array of aphrodisiac cocktails.

Getting There & Away

AIR

The airport is 1.5km from town: as of July 2009 **Cielos Andinos** (☎ 01-348-6405; contacto@cielosandinos.com.pe) has begun operating flights to/from Lima on Tuesday and Fridays (US$99).

BUS & TAXI

Transport here mostly serves Lima and destinations in between like Huánuco, as well as local villages and Pucallpa. The road between Tingo and Pucallpa can be risky; see p333.

Buses to Lima (S40 to S60, 12 hours) are operated by **Transportes León de Huánuco** (☎ 56-2030, 962-56-2030; Pimentel 164), **Transmar** (☎ 56-3076; Pimentel 145) and **Transportes Rey** (☎ 56-2565; Raimondi 297). Buses usually leave at 7am or 7pm. Some operators go to Pucallpa (S20, nine hours). Faster service to Pucallpa is with **Turismo Ucayali** (cnr Tito Jaime Fernández s/n, cuadra 2) which has *colectivo* taxis (S45, six hours).

From around the gas station on Av Raimondi near the León de Huánuco bus terminal, *colectivos* depart to Huánuco (S18, two hours) and other destinations.

Selva Tours (☎ 56-1137; Raimondi 207) has cars to Tocache (S40, four hours) from where other vehicles continue another five hours to Juanjui and a further three to Tarapoto (S65). They'll go direct if there's the demand.

Transportes Cueva del Pavos is a signed stop with *mototaxis* to the Cave of the Owls in Parque Nacional Tingo María. It's about S20 for the round trip, including a wait at the cave.

North Coast

Southern Peru can keep its Machu Picchu. The unruly northern coast is flush with enough ancient chronicles to fill a library of memoirs, and boasts beaches and surf that are the envy of Peru. Here, the coastal desert spreads out from Lima all the way to Ecuador as the Pan-American Hwy heroically divides restless sand dunes and burly cliffs from the Pacific Ocean's belligerent waves.

This heaving coastline is scattered with more antediluvian ruins than you can poke a pre-Inca civilization at. The few travelers who manage to slip the familiar clutches of the Gringo Trail and venture this far north scratch their collective heads at the 5000-year-old remnants of the Americas' oldest civilization. They drool at the gold-laden million-dollar treasures buried in long-forgotten pyramids and tombs, and listen to tall tales of modern-day treasure hunters clashing wits with archaeologists in a race to uncover the untold wealth of the region.

Occasional oases of bottle-green farmland lie scattered along the coastline, and animated colonial towns will doff their collective *campesino* (peasant) hats to all who make the effort to visit. Meanwhile, the graceful surf that continually pounds the coast has had surfers board-waxing lyrical for years, while the enduring sunny months and frisky seaside resorts beckon modern-day sun worshippers to the coast's sandy shores.

HIGHLIGHTS

- Take a day trip from Trujillo to visit the ruins of **Chan Chan** (p349) and the beautifully preserved friezes of **Huacas del Sol y de la Luna** (p351)

- Indulge in sun, surf and sand at **Máncora** (p376), Peru's premier beachside hot spot

- Drool over a vast wealth of once-buried treasure around **Chiclayo** (p364)

- Drag your board up the coast in search of that elusive perfect swell at **Huanchaco** (p352), **Puerto Chicama** (p357), **Pacasmayo** (p357) and around **Máncora** (p376)

- Seek out **shamans** (p373) for the perfect cure – or curse – in the mountain wilds of Huancabamba

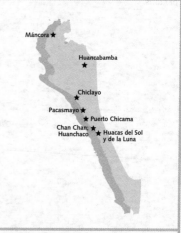

★ Máncora

★ Huancabamba

★ Chiclayo

★ Pacasmayo ★ Puerto Chicama

Chan Chan; ★ ★ Huacas del Sol
Huanchaco   y de la Luna

- BIGGEST CITY: TRUJILLO, POPULATION 291,400

- AVERAGE TEMPERATURE: January 10°C to 20°C, July 10°C to 21°C

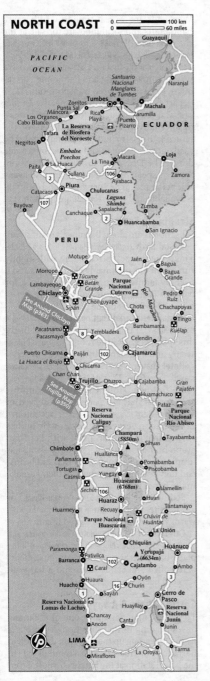

NORTH COAST

LIMA TO BARRANCA

The Carretera Panamericana (Pan-American Hwy) winds its way north out of chaotic Lima through nonstop desert all the way to Ecuador. At Km 105, a marked dirt road heads 4km east to **Reserva Nacional Lomas de Lachay** (admission S6; ☼ dawn-dusk), a 5070-hectare natural reserve where moisture from coastal mists has created a unique microenvironment of dwarf forest, which conceals a plethora of small animals and birds. The park has campsites and picnicking areas, pit toilets and trails, but there are no buses – you will have to hire a vehicle or hike from the Pan-American Hwy to get here.

Further north, the village of **Huaura**, opposite **Huacho**, is where José de San Martín proclaimed Peru's independence. Ask for someone to show you the building where it occurred. There is an inconsequential **museum** (admission S2.50; ☼ 9am-5pm) and a Spanish-speaking guide who'll show you the balcony from where the desire for self-rule was decreed.

BARRANCA

☎ 01 / pop 54,000

Barranca, located 195km north of Lima, has a relaxed, fountain-spouting plaza and a cacophony of traffic plowing through on the Carretera Panamericana, which dissects the town. Neighboring Pativilca, located 10km further north, is where the road branches off to Huaraz and the Cordillera Blanca. This spectacular route climbs inland through cactus-laden cliff faces, and you can watch the cathedrals of sheer rock slowly turn into a carpet of greenery as the road climbs up to Huaraz.

Sights
PARAMONGA

The adobe temple of **Paramonga** (admission S3) is situated 4km beyond the turnoff for the Huaraz road and was built by the Chimú culture, which was the ruling power on the north coast before it was conquered by the Incas (see p355). The fine details of the massive temple have long been eroded, yet the multi-tiered construction is nonetheless impressive and affords fantastic panoramas of the lush valley. Local buses from Barranca (S3, 25 minutes) will drop you off at a spot 3km from the entrance, or a taxi here will cost about S10.

CARAL

About 25km inland from Barranca lie the monumental ruins of **Caral** (adult S11; 9am-5pm), which confounded Peruvian archaeologists when they proved to be part of the oldest civilization in all of South America. Before Caral's discovery, the city of Chavín de Huántar near Huaraz, built around 900 BC, held that particular title. Caral culture arose in the Supe valley between an incredible 4500 and 5000 years ago, making it one of the earliest large cities, alongside those in Mesopotamia, Egypt, India and China. This ancient culture was a conglomeration of 18 city-states and controlled the three valleys of Supe, Pativilca and Fortaleza, with the main seat of government at Caral. At the site, six stone-built pyramids (most of which have been excavated) were found alongside amphitheaters, ceremonial rooms, altars, adobe complexes and several sunken circular plazas. Most of the pyramids have stairways leading to their peaks, where offerings were once made; the stairs can be climbed for great views of the lush Supe River valley.

The people of Caral Supe were experts in agriculture, construction, public administration and making calendars and musical instruments. Evidence of elaborate religious ceremonies among elites suggests a highly stratified culture in which classes were organized according to their labor in society; archaeologists at Caral believe that men and women may have enjoyed considerable equality. Among the many artifacts you'll see at the sites are millennia-old bone flutes and Peru's oldest *quipus* (a system among Andean cultures of tying cords and knots to convey information). A large geoglyph – a design carved into earth – called Chupacigaro attests to the Caral people's sophisticated measurements of the movements of the stars. Unesco declared the Sacred City of Caral a World Heritage site in 2009.

Considering how few people visit Caral, and how even fewer know about it, the site is well set out for visitors. There are plaques in both Spanish and English illustrating points of interest. **Proyecto Especial Arqueológico Caral** (www .caralperu.gob.pe) is in charge here, and its **Lima office** (205-2500, 495-1516; Av Las Lomas de La Molina 327, Lima 12) has tons of information and also does informative full-day tours – often including Chupacigaro – on weekends for S90 per person (see the website for a calendar).

Weekends are a great time to visit because handicrafts and local food are for sale at the site. **Lima Tours** (Map pp88-9; 01-619-6900; www.lima tours.com.pe; Jr Belén 1040, Central Lima; 9:30am-6pm Mon-Fri, to 1pm Sat) in Lima arranges expensive private tours to Caral and Paramonga on request. *Colectivo* (shared transportation) taxis depart from Barranca to the nearby hamlet of Caral fairly regularly for S5 (two hours), or alternatively a taxi will cost S90 for the return journey (including waiting time). The road out here is rough and may be impassable during the December to March wet season. Spanish-speaking local guides are also available at the site for S25 per group, and camping is available at the site for S20 per person.

Sleeping & Eating

Most hotels are along Barranca's main street.

Hostal Birch (Pedro Reyes Barbosa 159; s/d S15/24) This is the cheapest place to stay, with slightly run-down but reasonably clean rooms and a friendly family running the show – look for colorful jungle murals lining the entryway. It's one block east of the plaza.

Hostal Residencial Continental (235-2458; A Ugarte 190; s/d S30/45) A step up from Hostal Birch, this spot has great little rooms that are clean, secure and brightened by loud bedspreads.

Hotel Chavín (235-2358, 235-2253; www.hotel chavin.com.pe; Gálvez 222; s/d S75/110;) The best place in town, Hotel Chavín has comfortable rooms that are perfectly preserved in a resplendent '70s style. Their restaurant, El Liberador, serves Las Vegas–style buffets (with a free pisco sour, made with Peruvian grape brandy, between 1pm and 4pm) has heaping *tacu tacu* (pan-fried rice and beans) and they couldn't be prouder of their karaoke in the bar at nights.

Sech (A Ugarte 190; snacks S3-8; 8am-10pm) For a tasty bite, visit this busy modern cafe with warm yellow walls and a varied menu.

Cafetería El Parador (Hotel Chavín, Gálvez 222; breakfasts S6-9, sandwiches S4-8; 7am-11pm) This place has several breakfast combos, mediocre coffee and sandwiches and a bar with ice-cold beers.

Getting There & Away

To get to Lima, flag down one of the many buses heading in that direction. Most buses from Lima going up the coast can drop you in Barranca. For Huaraz, catch a minibus (S1) to the petrol station at the Huaraz turnoff. From there, infrequent buses stop to pick up passengers (S15, five hours) or you can catch a much faster *colectivo* taxi (S25, 3½ hours).

CASMA

☎ 043 / pop 24,700

A small and unflustered Peruvian coastal town, Casma has little to do except watch the whirring of passing buses. The big draw here is the archaeological site of Sechín, about 5km away. Casma's once-important colonial port (11km from town) was sacked by various pirates during the 17th century and the town today is merely a friendly blip on the historical radar.

From here, the Pan-American Hwy branches off for Huaraz via the Callán Pass (4225m). This route is tough on your backside but offers excellent panoramic views of the Cordillera Blanca. Most points of interest in town lie along the Pan-American Hwy, between the Plaza de Armas in the west and the petrol station in the east.

Information

There's no tourist office, but **Sechín Tours** (☎ 41-1421; Hostal Monte Carlo, Nepeña 16; ☯ 8am-1pm & 3-8pm) has a small office in the Hostal Monte Carlo that dishes out tourist information and travelers' assistance, and also arranges local tours. There's a branch of **BCP** (☎ 71 1314, 71 1471; Bolívar 111) here and several internet cafes line the plaza.

Sights

Sechín (adult S6; ☯ 8am-5pm), 5km southeast of Casma, is one of Peru's granddaddy archaeological sites, dating from about 1600 BC. It is among the more important and well-preserved ruins along this coast, though it has suffered some damage from grave robbers and natural disasters.

The warlike people who built this temple remain shrouded in mystery. The site consists of three outside walls of the main temple, which are completely covered in gruesome 4m-high bas-relief carvings of warriors and captives being vividly eviscerated in a grisly fashion. Ouch. Inside the main temple are earlier mud structures that are still being excavated: you can't go in, but there is a model in the small on-site **museum**. If you visit the museum first, you may be able to pick up a Spanish-speaking guide (ie one of the caretakers) for around S12.

To get here, a *mototaxi* (three-wheeled motorcycle rickshaw taxi) from Casma costs around S5. You can also visit on a tour organized by Sechín Tours in Casma, or by using pedal power if you rent one of the company's bicycles. The route is well signposted.

Other early sites in the Sechín area have not been excavated due to a lack of funds. From the museum, you can see the large, flat-topped hill of **Sechín Alto** in the distance. The nearby fortress of **Chanquillo** consists of several towers surrounded by concentric walls, but it is best appreciated from the air. Aerial photographs are on display at the museum.

The entry ticket to Sechín also allows you to visit the Mochica ruins of **Pañamarca**, 10km inland from the Panamericana on the road to Nepeña. These ruins are badly weathered, but you can see some of the covered murals if you ask the guard.

Tours & Guides

The friendly folks at **Sechín Tours** (☎ 41-1421; Hostal Monte Carlo, Nepeña 16; ☯ 8am-1pm & 3-8pm) arrange full-day trips to Sechín and Tortugas, including entrance fees, lunch and a Spanish-speaking guide, for S45 per person (minimum two people). You can rent mountain bikes here to explore the ruins under your own steam (for three hours S15, per day S30). They also rent sandboards (per day S5) for plummeting down the nearby **Manchan** dunes, a S10 *mototaxi* ride away. They also have a branch (p394) in Huaraz if you want to set up a tour from there.

Sleeping & Eating

Hostal Gregori (☎ 9-631-4291; Ormeño 579; s/d S30/38, s/d without bathroom S15/24) Probably the best and most popular budget pick. This funky white hotel has random potted plants in specially designed crevices, architecturally rakish wall angles and very comfortable, fresh rooms. Hot water and TVs are available on request and the whole place has radiantly airy feng shui.

Hostal Monte Carlo (☎ 41-1421; Nepeña 16; s/d S20/48) The big rooms here couldn't be any cleaner if your mother had scrubbed them herself. All come with TV. Sechín tours operates out of the reception, and there's a neat little cafe serving cheap snacks (S1.50 to S4) and breakfasts (S3 to S6). It's just east of the plaza.

Hotel El Farol (☎ 41-1064, in Lima 01-424 0517; Túpac Amaru 450; s/d S65/95; ☒) One of the fanciest places to bed down in Casma, El Farol curves around a fetching garden, complete with a dainty gazebo and a bamboo-lined restaurant and bar. The walled-in compound supplies an oasis of calm from the street clamor and has great rooms. There are useful maps and photographs in the lobby if you plan to explore surrounding ruins.

Hotel Los Poncianos (☎ 41-1599, ☎ /fax 41 2123; Panamericana Norte Km 376; s/d S65/95; ▣ ▤) Just a block off the main highway and six blocks from the Plaza de Armas, this place is in a hushed spot and has both an Olympic-sized pool and a children's pool in its grounds. The restaurant will feed you, hot showers will bathe you, cable TV will entertain you and a ceiling fan will keep you cool.

There are no fancy restaurants in town, but for a passable coffee and early, bready breakfast try the bakery **Sol Caribeño** (Ormeño 544; snacks S2-5; ☯ 7am-6pm). **La Careta** (Peru 895; mains around S10; ☯ 7-11pm) is a popular meatery serving sizzling grills nightly – though be warned that the only 'greens' you'll come across here are the indoor potted plants. **Chifa Tío Sam** (☎ 71-1447; Huarmey 138; mains around S10; ☯ 7am-9pm) is also a good place to grab a bite.

Getting There & Away

Colectivo taxis to Chimbote (S5, 45 minutes) leave frequently from the Plaza de Armas.

Several bus companies, including Cruz del Norte, Movil and Turismo Paraiso, have a communal **booking office** (☎ 41-2116; Ormeño 145) in front of the petrol station at the eastern end of town. Most buses stop here to pick up extra passengers. There are frequent buses to Lima (S18 to S35, six hours), to Trujillo (S15, three hours) and buses to Huaraz (check which route they take; Yungay Express and Transport Huandoy have buses that take the scenic route via the Callán Pass) at 6:30am, 10:30am and 10:30pm (S18 to S22.50, five to six hours). Nearby **Tepsa** (☎ 41-2658; Ormeño 546) has comfortable buses to Lima (S28 to S45), a direct 8:30pm bus all the way to Tumbes (S64, 11 hours) and a 10:15pm bus to Cajamarca (S60, seven hours).

TORTUGAS

This small beach resort hugs a diminutive, calm bay about 22km northwest of Casma, off the Panamericana at Km 392. There's a decent, pebbly beach with clean water, and pleasant swimming in the bay. It's a popular weekending spot, and a visit can be combined with an all-day Sechín tour from Casma. Stay at the **Hotel Farol Beach Inn** (☎ 968-2540; s/d S40/65), which has big rooms with hot water and top vistas from its airy communal areas. *Colectivo* taxis to Tortugas (S2, 20 minutes) leave frequently from the Plaza de Armas in Casma.

CHIMBOTE
☎ 043 / pop 204,000

Chimbote is Peru's largest fishing port – and with fish-processing factories lining the roads in and out of Chimbote you'll probably smell it before you see it. The odor of fermenting fish may take a while to get used to, but the quiet, open plaza in the town's heart is less overwhelming. The fishing industry has declined from its 1960s glory days due to overfishing, but you'll still see flotillas moored offshore every evening. This roguish port town is not a tourist destination and there's little to do, but you may have to stay overnight if you're catching an early morning bus to Huaraz via the hair-raising Cañón del Pato route.

Information

Internet cabins are found on Aguirre to the south of Pardo. Tourist information is impossible to come by.

Banco Continental (Bolognesi)
BCP (Bolognesi)
Oficina de migraciónes (immigration office; ☎ 32-2481; Centro Cívico Comercial de Chimbote, 2nd fl) Does visa extensions.
Police (☎ 32 4485; cnr Palacios & Prado)
Post office (☎ 32-2943; cnr Tumbes & Prado; ☯ 9am-7pm Mon-Fri, to 1pm Sat)
Scotiabank (Bolognesi)

Sleeping

There are lots of hotels in Chimbote, though nothing in the top-end range.

BUDGET
Hostal Chimbote (☎ 34-4721; Pardo 205; s/d S18/24) The cell-like rooms here have windows onto the corridor, but it's an acceptable cheapie that boasts cold-water showers and TV. There are cheaper rooms without showers or the aforementioned TV.

Hostal Residencial el Parque (☎ 34-1552, 34-5572; Palacios 309; s/d S30/45) With Spartan, windowless rooms, this friendly, secure venture is right on the Plaza de Armas and continues to be a popular spot for passing *extranjeros* (foreigners). Hot showers and cable TV come as standard.

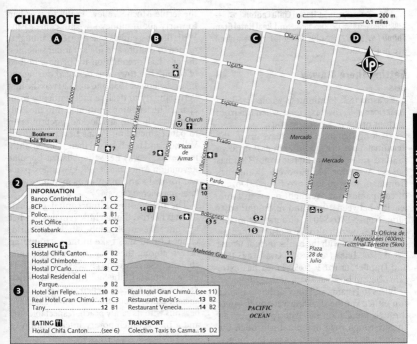

CHIMBOTE

0 ——— 200 m
0 ——— 0.1 miles

NORTH COAST

INFORMATION
Banco Continental............1 C2
BCP......................2 C2
Police....................3 B1
Post Office................4 D2
Scotiabank................5 C2

SLEEPING
Hostal Chifa Canton.........6 B2
Hostal Chimbote...........7 B2
Hostal D'Carlo.............8 C2
Hostal Residencial el
Parque..................9 B2
Hotel San Felipe..........10 B2
Real Hotel Gran Chimú....11 C3
Tany....................12 B1

EATING
Hostal Chifa Canton.......(see 6)

Real Hotel Gran Chimú...(see 11)
Restaurant Paola's.........13 B2
Restaurant Venecia........14 B2

TRANSPORT
Colectivo Taxis to Casma..15 D2

Tany (☎ 32-3441; Palacios 553; s/d with breakfast S39/65) Though it's a little spendier than most budget options, Tany has massive and immaculately kept rooms with polished floorboards, a quiet location and a free breakfast, giving it a decent bang-for-buck ratio.

Hotel San Felipe (☎ 32-3401; Pardo 514; s/d with breakfast S38/56) The clean rooms here are reached by elevator and have strong hot showers and cable TV. Be sure to take your continental breakfast on the 5th-floor terrace with plaza views. A glitzy downstairs casino will help you live out your Las Vegas card-shark fantasies.

MIDRANGE
Hostal D'Carlo (☎ 34-4044, ☎/fax 32-1047; Villavicencio 376; s/d with breakfast S75/98) Cheerfully painted walls, nice bedspreads, fans and cable TV welcome you here. Rooms are spacious but the bathrooms (with hot water) can be Lilliputian. There's room service from the hotel cafe between 7am to 10pm, and some rooms overlook the plaza.

Hostal Chifa Canton (☎ 34-4388; Bolognesi 498; s/d with breakfast S84/98) The town's best hotel – remember, we're talking about Chimbote here – Hostal Chifa Canton has large, carpeted rooms with modern amenities. Some rooms look onto the sea. It has a good *chifa* (Chinese restaurant) with lackluster service and a pool hall on the premises.

Real Hotel Gran Chimú (☎ 32-3721, 32-8104; Gálvez 109; s/d S98/118; ⚡) This charming and dignified old building is roomy and aloof, lazing by the sea and espousing a laissez-faire life philosophy that's a welcome reprieve from Chimbote's buzzing streets. Upstairs, 76 rooms and three suites supply either fans or air-con, cable TV and phone, and some come with a view over the trawler-filled bay. It has a decent restaurant and bar.

Eating
Restaurant Paola's (☎ 34-5428; Bolognesi 401; sandwiches S2-4; ⏲ 1-10pm) Try this place for sandwiches, snacks and ice creams.

Restaurant Venecia (☎ 32-5490; Bolognesi 386; mains from S12; ⏲ 6am-1am) This is a popular place for chunks of grilled meaty goodies, seafood and breakfasts.

The restaurants at **Hostal Chifa Canton** (☎ 34-4388; Bolognesi 498; 🕓 8am-10pm) and **Real Hotel Gran Chimú** (☎ 32-3721, 32-8104; Gálvez 109; 🕓 8am-10pm) are both good.

Getting There & Away

BUS

For Casma (S2, 45 minutes), whale-sized old American *colectivo* taxis leave when full from in front of the *mercado* (market).

All long-distance buses leave from the Terminal Terrestre, about 5km east of town (S5 taxi ride). **America Express** (☎ 35-3468) has buses leaving for Trujillo every 15 minutes from 6am to 9pm (S5, two hours). Dozens of companies run overnight buses to Lima, leaving between 10pm and midnight; costs range from S27 to S70 (six hours). Reputable companies, which also have offices lined up along Bolognesi with the banks, include **Oltursa** (☎ 35-3586), **Línea** (☎ 35-4041), **Civa** (☎ 35-1808) and **Cruz Del Sur** (☎ 35-5665). Línea has extra Lima-bound buses at 10am and 12:30pm.

Buses to Huaraz and the Cordillera Blanca run either via the dazzling yet rough route through the Cañón del Pato (p417), via an equally rough road that climbs through the mountains from Casma, or via the longer, comfortably paved route through Pativilca. Travel times on these routes range from seven to nine hours. **Transport Huandoy** (☎ 35-3086) has an 11:15am bus to Caraz (S20, eight to nine hours) through the *cañón* (canyon) and 6am, 10am and 1pm buses to Huaraz (S20, six to eight) through Casma. **Yungay Express** (☎ 35-1304, 35-2850) has an 8:30am Caraz bus (S20) through the Cañón del Pato and a 9pm bus to Huaraz (S21) via Casma. Ritzy **Movil Tours** (☎ 35-3616) has a 10:15pm and 11pm bus to Huaraz (S30 to S45) via Trujillo that also goes onto Caraz. It pays to book Huaraz buses a day in advance.

TRUJILLO

☎ 044 / pop 291,400

Stand in the right spot and the glamorously colonial streets of old Trujillo look like they've barely changed in hundreds of years. Well, OK, there are more honking taxis now – but the city still manages to put on a dashing show with its flamboyant buildings and profusion of churches. Francisco Pizarro founded Trujillo in 1534, and he thought so highly of this patch of desert he named it after his birthplace in Spain's Estremadura. Spoiled by the fruits of the fertile Moche Valley, Trujillo never had to worry about money – wealth came easily. With life's essentials taken care of, thoughts turned to politics and life's grander schemes; the city has a reputation for being a hotbed of revolt. The town was besieged during the Inca rebellion of 1536 and in 1820 was the first Peruvian city to declare independence from Spain. The tradition continued into the 20th century, as bohemians flocked, poets put pen to paper (including Peru's best poet, César Vallejo), and rebels raised their fists defiantly in the air. It was here the Alianza Popular Revolution Americana (APRA) workers' party was formed – and many of its members were later massacred (see p42).

The behemoth Chimú capital of Chan Chan is nearby, though little remains of what was once the largest adobe city in the world. Other Chimú sites bake in the surrounding desert, among them the immense and suitably impressive Moche Huacas del Sol y de la Luna (Temples of the Sun and Moon), which date back 1500 years. When you get yourself ancient-cultured out, the village of Huanchaco beckons with its sandy beach, respectable surf and a more contemporary interpretation of sun worship.

Information

EMERGENCY

Policía de Turismo (Tourist Police, Poltur; ☎ 29-1705, 20-4025; Independencia 630)

IMMIGRATION

Oficina de Migraciónes (☎ 28-2217; Larco, cuadra 12) Does visa extensions.

INTERNET ACCESS

InterWeb (Pizarro 721; per hr S2; 🕓 8:30am-11pm) One of many internet places, this spot offers a decent connection.

LAUNDRY

Most midrange hotels supply laundry services at reasonable rates.

Lavanderías Unidas (☎ 20-0505; Pizarro 683; per kg S2.50; 🕓 8am-9pm)

MEDICAL SERVICES

Clínica Americano-Peruano (☎ 23-1261; Mansiche 702) The best general medical care in town, with English-speaking doctors. It charges according to your means, so let the clinic know if you don't have medical insurance.

Hospital Regional (☎ 23-1581, Napoles 795) For more rudimentary care.

MONEY

Changing money in Trujillo is a distinct pleasure; some of the banks are housed in well-preserved colonial buildings, and all have ATMs that accept Visa and MasterCard. If lines are long, visit the *casas de cambio* (foreign-exchange bureaus) near Gamarra and Bolívar, which give good rates for cash.

Banco Continental (Pizarro 620) Housed in the handsome Casa de la Emancipación. Good rates for cash.

BCP (Gamarra 562) Has the lowest commission for changing traveler's checks.

Interbank (Gamarra at Pizarro) Reasonably fast service.

Scotiabank (Pizarro 314) Has an ATM.

POST

Post office (Independencia 286; ☼ 9am-7pm Mon-Fri, to 1pm Sat)

TOURIST INFORMATION

Local tour companies can also provide you with some basic information on the area.

iPerú (☎ 29-4561; cnr Almagro & Independencia, Municipalidad de Trujillo, mezzanine level; ☼ 8am-7pm Mon-Sat, to 2pm Sun) Provides tourist information and a list of certified guides and travel agencies.

Dangers & Annoyances

Single women tend to receive a lot of attention from males in Trujillo – to exasperating, even harassing, levels. If untoward advances are made, firmly state that you aren't interested. Inventing a boyfriend or husband sometimes helps get the message across. See p527 for more advice for women travelers.

Like many other cities, the noise pollution levels in Trujillo are high. Civic groups have attempted to protest the constant bleating of taxi horns.

Sights

Trujillo's colonial mansions and churches, most of which are near the Plaza de Armas, are worth seeing, though they don't keep very regular opening hours.

Hiring a good local guide is recommended if you are seriously interested in history. The churches often are open for early morning and evening masses, but visitors at those times should respect worshippers and not wander around.

The creamy pastel shades and beautiful wrought-iron grillwork fronting almost every colonial building are unique Trujillo touches.

PLAZA DE ARMAS

Trujillo's spacious and fetching main square hosts an impressive statue dedicated to work, the arts and liberty. The plaza is fronted by the **cathedral**, begun in 1647, destroyed in 1759, and rebuilt soon afterward. The cathedral has a famous basilica and a museum of religious and colonial art.

One elegant colonial mansion now houses the **Hotel Libertador** (Independencia 485). Another, **Casa de Urquiaga** (Pizarro 446; admission free; ☼ 9:30am-3:15pm Mon-Fri, 10am-1:30pm Sat), belongs to the Banco Central de la Reserva del Perú.

At 8am on Sunday there is a **flag-raising ceremony** on the Plaza de Armas, complete with a parade. On some Sundays there are also *caballos de paso* (pacing horses) and performances of the *marinera* (a typical coastal Peruvian dance involving much romantic waving of handkerchiefs).

EAST OF PLAZA DE ARMAS

The **Iglesia de la Merced**, built in the 17th century, has a striking organ and cupola. Uniquely, an altar here is painted on the wall, an economical shortcut when funds ran out for a more traditional gold or carved-wood alternative.

Now the Banco Continental building, the **Casa de la Emancipación** (Pizarro 620; ☼ 9am-1 & 4-8pm Mon-Sat) is where Trujillo's independence from colonial rule was formally declared on December 29, 1820. Nearby, the canary yellow 19th-century mansion **Palacio Iturregui** (Pizarro 688; ☼ 8am-10:30pm) is unmistakable and impossible to ignore unless you're color-blind. Built in neoclassical style, it has beautiful window gratings, slender interior columns and gold moldings on the ceilings. General Juan Manuel Iturregui lived here after he famously proclaimed independence.

Colonial art enthusiasts will not want to miss the Carmelite museum in the **Iglesia del Carmen** (cnr Colón & Bolívar; museum admission S2.50; ☼ 9am-1pm Mon-Sat).

The **Museo de Arqueología** (☎ 24-9322; Junín 682; adult S5; ☼ 9am-3pm Mon-Fri, to 1pm Sat) displays a rundown of Peruvian history from 12,000 BC to the present day. There's also a small but interesting collection of artifacts from the Huaca de la Luna. The museum is housed in La Casa Risco, a restored 17th-century mansion.

Casona Orbegoso (Orbegoso 553; ☼ 9:30am-1pm & 4:30-7pm Tue-Sun), named after a former president of Peru, is a beautiful 18th-century manor

NORTH COAST

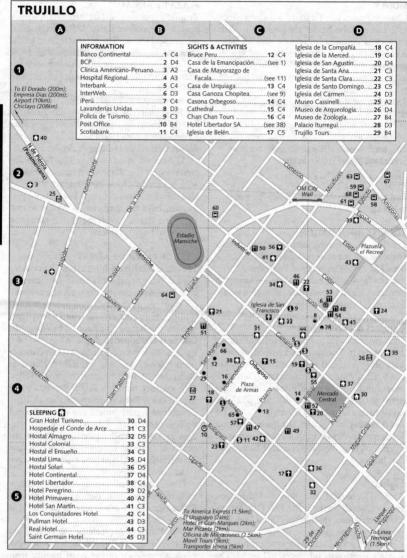

TRUJILLO

To El Dorado (200m);
Empresa Días (200m);
Airport (10km);
Chiclayo (208km)

To America Express (1.5km);
El Uruguayo (2km);
Hotel el Gran Marques (2km);
Mar Picante (2km);
Oficina de Migraciones (2.5km);
Movil Tours (5km);
Transportes Horna (5km)

To Línea
Terminal
(1.5km)

with a collection of well-worn art and period furnishings. On the opposite side of Bolívar, **Iglesia de San Agustín** has a finely gilded high altar and dates from 1558. Further southwest is **Iglesia de Belén** and north of here is another mansion, **Casa de Mayorazgo de Facala** (Pizarro 314; ☻ 9:30am-1pm & 4-7 Mon-Fri), which houses Scotiabank.

NORTH & WEST OF PLAZA DE ARMAS

Northeast of the cathedral is **Casa Ganoza Chopitea** (Independencia 630), also known as Casa de los Léones, which is considered to be the best mansion of the colonial period in Trujillo. The tourist police are housed here. Good contemporary Peruvian art is sometimes shown here, as are some rather arcane

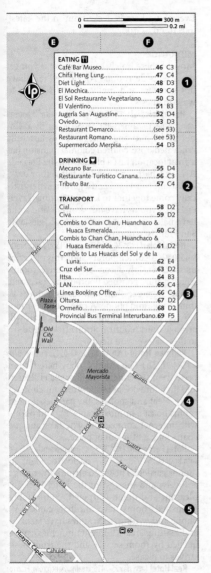

certainly don't belong under a gritty petrol dispensary. Have a look at the bird-shaped whistling pots, which produce clear notes when air is blown into them (ask the curator to show you). Superficially the pots are very similar, but when they are blown each produces a completely different note that corresponds to the calls of the male and female birds.

Museo de Zoología (San Martín 368; admission S2; 8am-7pm Mon-Fri, to 1pm Sat), just west of the Plaza de Armas, is mainly a taxidermic collection of Peruvian animals (many so artificially stuffed they look like nightmarish caricatures of their former selves).

There are three other interesting churches near the Plaza de Armas; **Iglesia de la Compañia** (Independencia), **Iglesia de Santa Ana** (cnr Mansiche & Zepita) and **Iglesia de Santo Domingo** (Larco).

Activities

The aid organization **Bruce Peru** (☎ 23-2664; www.volunteertrujillo.com; San Martín 444) helps kids that are unable to attend school. Volunteer opportunities are best arranged beforehand, though short-term, walk-in volunteers are sometimes needed.

Tours & Guides

There are dozens of tour agencies. Some agencies supply guides who speak English but don't know much about the area, or vice versa. Entrance fees are *not* included in the tours prices listed below. Friendly and recommended **Trujillo Tours** (☎ 23-3091; Almagro 301; 7:30am-1pm & 4-8pm) has three- to four-hour tours to Chan Chan and Huanchaco (S20), and to Huacas del Sol y de la Luna (S20), as well as city tours (S18). Some English, French and German is spoken. Established **Chan Chan Tours** (☎ 24-3016; Independencia 431; 7am-1:30pm & 4-8pm), right on the square, organizes similar trips for S20 to S50 per person (two-person minimum). Its guides speak some English.

If you prefer your own guide, it's best to go with a certified official guide who knows the area well. Ask at **iPerú** (☎ 29 4561; Almagro & Independencia; 8am-7pm Mon-Sat, to 2pm Sun) for a list of certified guides and contact details.

Festivals & Events

Fiesta de la Marinera This is the national *marinera* contest; held in the last week in January.
El Festival Internacional de la Primavera (International Spring Festival) Trujillo's major festival is celebrated

pieces that you may never have a chance to see elsewhere. Hours vary. Further north of the mansion is **Iglesia de Santa Clara**.

The **Museo Cassinelli** (N de Piérola 601; admission S8; 9am-1pm & 4-7pm Mon-Fri, to 1pm Sun) is a private archaeological collection housed in the basement of a gas station. The museum is fascinating, with hundreds of pieces that

with parades, national dancing competitions (including, of course, the *marinera*), *caballos de paso* displays, sports, international beauty contests and other cultural activities. It all happens in the last week in September, and better hotels are booked out well in advance.

Sleeping

Decent budget places are thin on the ground in Trujillo, but pay a little extra and you'll be soaking up colonial ambience. Some travelers prefer to stay in the nearby beach town of Huanchaco.

BUDGET

Hostal Lima (☎ 23-2499; Ayacucho 718; s/d S10/15) If you've been on a tour of Alcatraz and thought 'I could live here,' this is your chance. The prison-bare, cell-like rooms in this secure building are sometimes used by super-shoestring gringos.

Hospedaje el Conde de Arce (☎ 29-1607; Independencia 577; r per person S20) With a giant, cluttered patio, this is a simple, safe and budget lodging right in the center. The rooms are weathered, but it's not a bad deal by Trujillo standards.

Hostal el Ensueño (☎ 20 7/44; Junín 336; s/d S22/32) After navigating the narrow and dark hallways here, you will find clean rooms with giant bathrooms. The owners also run Hostal El Encanto (Junín 319), located across the street with cheaper but danker rooms.

Hotel Primavera (☎ /fax 23-1915; N de Piérola 872; s/d S22/40; ☒) You can't miss the pseudo-modern, semicircular blue flourishes lining the side of this '70s relic. It's only slightly shabby, fairly clean and convenient to several northbound bus stations. The invigorating concrete pool may help you overlook the general mustiness.

Hotel San Martín (☎ /fax 25-2311; San Martín 745; s/d S36/56) Although characterless, this massive hotel (furnished with faux-wood floor tiles for insta-charm) is fair value for rooms with cable TV and phone. It has a restaurant and bar.

Hostal Almagro (☎ 22-3845; Almagro 748; s/d/tr S45/60/70) No pretensions of a colonial past here, just modern, well-maintained, sparse rooms with TVs and glistening bathrooms. There's a cafe downstairs.

Gran Hotel Turismo (☎ 24-4181; Gamarra 747; s/d S45/69; ☒) Live out your swinging Austin Powers fantasies at this hotel, which has its original hip decor, hallways the length of football fields and spotless, cozy rooms.

Everything here is decked out in the 'latest' '60s trends. Groovy.

MIDRANGE

Most of these hotels can be noisy if you get the streetside rooms. All hotels here have hot showers and many offer discounts to walk-in guests.

Hostal Colonial (☎ 25-8261; hostcolonialtruji@hotmail.com; Independencia 618; s/d/tr S55/85/110) Easily a winner in the midrange category, this tastefully renovated, rose-colored colonial mansion has a great location just a block from the Plaza de Armas. Chatty and helpful staff, a tour desk, a pleasant courtyard and a garden synergistically come together to keep attracting travelers. Cozy rooms have hot showers, and some have balconies and great views of Iglesia de San Francisco opposite.

Hostal Solari (☎ 24-3909; Almagro 715; s/d with breakfast S60/92) A contemporary spot, this place has massive, sensibly decorated 'executive' rooms, which feature polished floorboards, a separate sitting area, excellent mattresses, cable TV, mini-fridge and phone. A cafe provides room service, and the helpful front-desk staff will arrange tours, confirm airline tickets and try to do whatever you need.

Pullman Hotel (☎ 47-1645, 47-0517; Pizarro 879; s/d S74/92; ☐) The swanky lobby here faces a pedestrian street near the Plazuela el Recreo and therefore doesn't suffer from much street noise. Neat and spotless, the parquet-floored rooms boast a minibar, cable TV and phone with internet connection. The fake antique chairs look a little out of place.

Hotel Peregrino (☎ 20-3990; Independencia 978; s/d with breakfast S75/90; ☐) No backyard? Plant an indoor garden! The green atrium downstairs is lovely, and the rest of the hotel is clean, pleasant and quiet. Carpeted, comfortably furnished rooms have minibar, cable TV, phone and writing desk. Suites have Jacuzzis and a sitting area. Midnight munchies can be quelled by room service and the front desk strives to please.

Real Hotel (☎ /fax 25-7416; crealh@viabcp.com; Pizarro 651; s/d with breakfast S75/108; ☒) In the middle of Trujillo's busy shopping district, Real Hotel is crisp, bright and splashy. It has good, airy rooms with all the conveniences, but it sits over a casino and disco so it can get noisy at night.

Hotel Continental (☎ 31-0046; www.hotelcontinental trujillo.com; Gamarra 663; s/d S75/120) High on professionalism, low on inspirational decor, this place has shipshape rooms, some of which look onto a concrete garden light well. There's a restaurant downstairs and airport pick-up for S15.

Saint Germain Hotel (☎ 25-0574; www.perunorte .com/saintgermain; Junín 585; s/d S90/159) The boutiquey Saint Germain has great rooms to get comfortable in and the usual slew of modern conveniences, as well as immaculate bathrooms. The rooms facing inward are quieter than most and have windows onto a bright light well. There's a bar and cafe here.

Los Conquistadores Hotel (☎ 24-4505; www.los conquistadoreshotel.com; Almagro 586; s/d S150/180, ste from S330, all incl breakfast; ❄ 🖵 🖳) Courteous doormen will eagerly greet you at the entrance of this contemporary venture, a few steps away from the Plaza de Armas. The relaxing rooms here are carpeted and come with cable TV, phone, mini-bar and 24-hour room service. Suites have Jacuzzis. The swanky downstairs restaurant and bar is a good place to unwind over a pisco sour. Rates include airport transfers, wall-to-wall wi-fi, a travel service and the use of exercise rooms.

TOP END

Hotel el Gran Marqués (☎ 24-9161, 24-9366; Díaz de Cienfuegos 145; s/d S250/330, ste from S330; ❄ 🖳) A couple of kilometers southwest of the city center, this hotel offers a sauna, gym, restaurant and bar. Unfortunately, it has to be content playing second fiddle in the top-end stakes to Hotel Libertador.

Hotel Libertador (☎ 23-2741; www.libertador.com.pe; Independencia 485; d S270, ste S375-600, both incl breakfast; 🖳) The classy dame of the city's hotels, the Libertador is in a beautiful building that's the Audrey Hepburn of Trujillo – it wears its age with refined grace. It earns its four stars with a sauna, good restaurant, amiable bar, airport pick-up and comfortable rooms with all the conveniences you might expect. Try to avoid the streetside rooms unless you want to watch the goings-on, as they tend to be noisy.

Eating

The 700 block of Pizarro is where Trujillo's power brokers hang out and families go out, and they're kept well fed by a row of trendy yet reasonably priced cafes and restaurants. Some of the best eateries in Trujillo are found a short taxi ride outside the town center.

Jugería San Augustín (Bolívar 526; juice S2; ❄ 8am-10pm) You can spot this place by the near-constant lines snaking around the corner

in summer as locals queue for the drool-inducing juices.

Diet Light (Pizarro 724; snacks S2-7; ❄ 9:30am-10pm) This perennially busy place serves not-very-diet, but yummy nonetheless, ice cream (S2 to S5) and whopping servings of mixed fruit (S3) – with ice cream.

El Sol Restaurante Vegetariano (cnr Industrial & Zepita; meals S3-8; ❄ 8am-10pm) Recently moved to a new location, 'The Sun' maintains a short but surprising list of meat-imitating dishes and always has a daily lunch *menú* for about S3. Plenty of nonvegetarians eat here, attesting to its hearty and delicious offerings.

Oviedo (☎ 22-3305; Pizarro 737; breakfast & sandwiches S4-12; ❄ 7am-midnight) If you're sick of the tiny plate of eggs your hotel is throwing at you in the morning, check out Oviedo's long list of breakfasts – from a simple Continental to a hearty *criollo* (spicy Peruvian fare with Spanish and African influences) that comes with a steak.

Mar Picante (☎ 22-1544; América Sur 2199; meals S8-25; ❄ 11am-10pm). This large, bamboo-lined seafood palace specializes in some of Trujillo's best and freshest ceviche (raw seafood marinated in lime juice) and is packed daily with hundreds of savvy locals. Try the heaped *ceviche mixto*, which has various kinds of fish and crustaceans (S10 to S12). The restaurant is a S3 taxi ride south of town.

Chifa Heng Lung (☎ 24-3351; Pizarro 352; mains S10-18; ❄ noon-10pm) Owned by a Chinese family that has been cooking Cantonese food in Trujillo for more than a decade, Heng Lung is slightly upscale, with big booths and tablecloths. The menu is a predictable list of southern Chinese dishes, but very long on options and flavors.

Café Bar Museo (☎ 29-7200; cnr Junín & Independencia; mains S10-21; ❄ 7:30am-midnight) This locals' favorite shouldn't be a secret. The tall, wood-paneled walls covered in artsy posters and classic marble-top bar feels like a cross between an English pub and a Left Bank cafe. A big drinks and dessert menu make this a great place to sit with friends and share something sweet.

Restaurant Romano (☎ 25-2251; Pizarro 747; mains S10-25; ❄ 7am-midnight) This place has been around since 1951, so you know these guys have been doing something right. Whipping up a decent espresso, as well as breakfast, snacks and meals all day, the Romano is one of the most popular eateries in town. Expect meaty and meatless sandwiches, desserts and a mainly Peruvian menu.

our pick **Restaurant Demarco** (☎ 23-4251; Pizarro 725; mains S10-25; ⏰ 7:30am-11pm) Although this small bistro specializes in Italian food and crispy crust pizzas – if you read Italian, so much the better for deciphering the extensive menu – they have mouth-watering *chupe de camarones*, a seafood stew of jumbo shrimp simmering in a buttery broth with hints of garlic, cumin and oregano. The desserts are excellent, from classic tiramisu to mile-high *tres leches* (a spongy cake made with evaporated milk).

El Mochica (☎ 29-3441; Bolívar 462; mains S10-28; ⏰ noon-10pm) Industrially hygienic and scattered with bits of art to take the edge off, this place has a variety of midpriced steaks and seafood, as well as cheaper local dishes. There's a snug *salón de té* (tea room) next door.

El Valentino (☎ 24-6643, 29-5339; Orbegoso 224; mains S15-30; ⏰ 5pm-1am) This popular place is currently the best Italian restaurant in town. Pasta and meat dishes are on the menu.

El Uruguayo (☎ 28-3369; América Sur 2219; meals S15-30; ⏰ 6:30pm-1am) Vegetarians might want to make a wide berth around this place. Located a S3 taxi ride south of town, little El Uruguayo serves up delicious barbecued meat to a nightly crowd of salivating in-the-know patrons. A massive sizzling plate of mixed meats (Argentinean steak, chicken, chorizo, beef heart, plus a few surprises), salad and fries – enough for two to three people – will set you back S30. Dig in.

Supermercado Merpisa (Pizarro 700; ⏰ 9:15am-1:15pm & 4:30-9pm) is good for self-catering.

Drinking & Entertainment

Trujillo's local newspaper *La Industria* is the best source for information about local entertainment, cultural exhibitions and other events.

Mecano Bar (☎ 20-1652; www.mecanobarperu .com; Gamarra 574; admission S20; ⏰ 9pm-late) This is the current top spot to see and be seen in Trujillo. Sway your hips to salsa, reggae and techno alongside a mix of well-to-do Peruvians and expats. It's very busy on weekends.

Restaurante Turístico Canana (☎ 23-2503, 23 1482; San Martín 791; admission S10; ⏰ 5pm-late) Although this place is open every night and serves good Peruvian coastal food (mains S15 to S35), late Thursday to Saturday is the time to go. Local

musicians and dancers perform, starting at around 11pm, and the audience joins in.

Tributo Bar (☎ 29-4546; cnr Pizarro & Almagro; ⏰ 9pm-late) This pleasant bar on the corner of the plaza is great for a quiet tipple and a chat with your friends. It attracts a younger, livelier crowd on weekends, when there is live music.

Getting There & Away

AIR

The **airport** (code TRU; ☎ 46-4013) is 10km northwest of town. There's a departure tax of S11.

LAN (☎ 80-11-1234; Almagro 490) has three daily flights leaving Lima for Trujillo – at 7am, 3pm and 8:35pm – and returning from Trujillo to Lima– at 6:45am, 6:45pm, and 10:15pm.

BUS

Buses often leave Trujillo full, so booking a little earlier is advised. Several companies that go to southern destinations have terminals on the Panamericana Sur, the southern extension of Moche, and Ejercito; check where your bus actually leaves from when buying a ticket.

Línea has services to most destinations of interest to travelers and is one of the more comfortable bus lines. The company's **booking office** (☎ 24-5181; cnr San Martin & Orbegoso; ⏰ 8am-8pm Mon-Fri) is conveniently located in the historical center, although all buses leave from the **terminal** (☎ 24-3271; Panamericana Sur 2857) on Panamericana Sur, a S3 taxi ride away. Línea goes to Lima (S40 to S100, eight hours) 10 times daily, with many departures going overnight; to Piura (S15 to S45, six hours) at 2:15pm and 11pm; to Otuzco (S5, two hours) five times a day, to Cajamarca (S15 to S45, six hours) at 10:30am, 10pm and 10:30pm; to Chiclayo (S11, three hours) hourly from 6am to 6pm, stopping at Pacasmayo (S5, 1¾ hours) and Guadalupe (S7, two hours); to Chimbote (S5, two hours) five times a day; and to Huaraz (S35 to S60, nine hours) at 9pm and 9:15pm.

There's an enclave of bus companies around España and Amazonas offering Lima-bound night buses (eight hours). **Cruz del Sur** (☎ 26-1801; Amazonas 237), one of the biggest and priciest bus companies in Peru, goes to Lima five times a day for S35 to S85. **Ormeño** (☎ 25-9782; Ejército 233) has three night buses to Lima for between S31 and S63, leaving between 9pm and 10pm, as well as two night buses to Tumbes (S45 to S63, 10 hours) that continue on to Guayaquil, on the Ecuadorean coast.

Cial (☎ 20-1760; Amazonas 395), **Oltursa** (☎ 26-3055; Ejército 342) and **Civa** (☎ 25-1402; Ejército 285) all have at least one night bus to Lima leaving between 9:30pm and 10:30pm, with prices between S45 and S65.

For Chimbote, **America Express** (☎ 26-1906; La Marina 315) is a S2 taxi ride south of town and has buses every 15 minutes between 5am and 9pm (S9, two hours).

If you're heading north, **El Dorado** (☎ 29-1778; N de Piérola 1070) has rudimentary buses to Piura and Sullana (S18 to S21, six hours) at 12:30 and 10pm, as well as buses to Tumbes (S22 to S27, 10 hours), with a stop in Máncora at 7pm, 8pm and 9:30pm. **Empresa Días** (☎ 20-1237; N de Piérola 1079), opposite El Dorado, has an 11:30am bus to Cajamarca (S14, six hours). **Ittsa** (☎ 25-1415; Mansiche 145) has buses for Piura (S10 to S27, six hours) leaving at 1:30pm, 11:30pm and 11:45pm, as well as Lima-bound buses (S50 to S63) at 1pm, 10pm and 10:30pm. **Transportes Horna** (☎ 25-7605; America Sur 1368) has an 8:30am and 10:30am bus to Huamachuco (S14, seven hours) and several morning buses to Cajamarca (S14, six hours).

Movil Tours (☎ 28-6538; Panamericana Sur 3959) specializes in very comfortable long-haul tourist services. It has a 10pm service to Lima (S58, eight hours), an 8pm and a 9pm overnight bus to Huaraz (S45 to S60, eight hours), a bus at 3:30pm bus to Chachapoyas (S60, 13 hours) and a 2:30pm bus to Tarapoto (S68, 18 hours). If you want to travel to Huaraz by day, you'll need to go to Chimbote and catch a bus from there. For more frequent buses to Cajamarca and the northern highlands, head to Chiclayo.

White-yellow-and-orange B *combis* to Huaca Esmeralda, Chan Chan and Huanchaco pass the corners of España and Ejército, and España and Industrial every few minutes. Buses for La Esperanza go northwest along the Panamericana and can drop you off at La Huaca Arco Iris. *Combis* leave every half hour from Suarez for the Huacas del Sol y de la Luna. Fares are generally S2 on these routes. Note that these buses are worked by professional thieves; keep valuables hidden and watch your bags carefully. A taxi to most of these sites will cost S9 to S14.

El Complejo Arqueológico la Huaca el Brujo, about 60km northwest of Trujillo, is harder to reach. Start at the Provincial Bus Terminal Interurbano off Atahualpa, and head to Chocope (S2, 1½ hours). Ask there for *combis* going toward the site (S2).

Getting Around

The **airport** (☎ 46-4013), 10km northwest of Trujillo, is reached cheaply on the Huanchaco *combi*, though you'll have to walk the last kilometer. It will cost S2 and take around 30 minutes. A taxi from the city center costs S9 to S14.

A short taxi ride around town costs about S2. For sightseeing, taxis charge about S23 to S27 per hour, depending on distance.

AROUND TRUJILLO

The Moche and Chimú cultures left the greatest marks on the Trujillo area, but they were by no means the only cultures in the region. In a March 1973 *National Geographic* article, Drs ME Moseley and CJ Mackey claimed knowledge of more than 2000 sites in the Río Moche valley and many more have been discovered since.

Five major archaeological sites can be easily reached from Trujillo by local bus or taxi. Two of these are principally Moche, dating from about 200 BC to AD 850. The other three, from the Chimú culture, date from about AD 850 to 1500. The recently excavated Moche ruin of La Huaca el Brujo (60km from Trujillo) can also be visited, but it's not as convenient.

Joining a tour to the archaeological sites isn't a bad idea, even for budget travelers. The ruins will be more interesting and meaningful with a good guide. Alternately, you could hire an on-site guide.

The entrance ticket for Chan Chan is also valid for the Chimú sites of La Huaca Esmeralda and La Huaca Arco Iris, as well as the Chan Chan museum, but it must be used within two days. All sites are open from 9am to 4:30pm and tickets are sold at every site, except La Huaca Esmeralda.

Chan Chan

Built around AD 1300 and covering 36 sq km, **Chan Chan** (adult S11; ◷ 9am-4:30pm) is the largest pre-Columbian city in the Americas, and the largest adobe city in the world. At the height of the Chimú empire, it housed an estimated 60,000 inhabitants and contained a vast wealth of gold, silver and ceramics. The wealth remained more or less undisturbed after the city was conquered by the Incas, but once the Spaniards hit the stage the looting began. Within a few decades little but gold dust remained. Remnants of

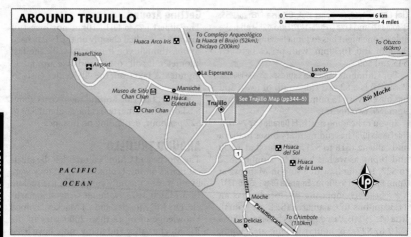

AROUND TRUJILLO

what was found can be seen in museums nearby. Although Chan Chan must have been a dazzling sight at one time, devastating El Niño floods and heavy rainfall have severely eroded the mud walls of the city. Today the most impressive aspect of the site is its sheer size; you'll need an active imagination to fill in the details.

The Chimú capital consisted of nine major cities, also called royal compounds. Each contained a royal burial mound filled with vast quantities of funerary offerings, including dozens of sacrificed young women and chambers full of ceramics, weavings and jewelry. The Tschudi complex, named after a Swiss naturalist, is the only section of Chan Chan that's partially restored. It is possible that other areas will open in the future, but until they are properly policed and signed, you run the risk of being mugged if you visit them.

At the Tschudi complex you'll find an entrance area with tickets, snacks, souvenirs, bathrooms, the small **Museo de Sitio Chan Chan** (admission free with Chan Chan ticket) with information in English and Spanish and guides (S18). The complex is well marked by fish-shaped pointers, so you can see everything without a guide if you prefer. Your entry ticket for Chan Chan is also valid for the Chimú sites of La Huaca Esmeralda and La Huaca Arco Iris.

Combis to Chan Chan leave Trujillo every few minutes, passing the corners of España and Ejército, and España and Industrial.

TSCHUDI COMPLEX

Also called the Palacio Nik-An, the complex's centerpiece is a massive restored **Ceremonial Courtyard**, whose 4m-thick interior walls are mostly decorated with recreated geometric designs. The ground-level designs closest to the door, representing three or four sea otters, are the only originals left and are slightly rougher looking than the modern work. A ramp at the far side of the high-walled plaza enters the second level (early wheelchair access?). Though all the Chan Chan walls have crumbled with time, parts of Tschudi's walls once stood more than 10m high.

Head out of the Ceremonial Courtyard and walk along the **outside wall**, one of the most highly decorated and best restored of Tschudi's walls. The adobe friezes show waves of fish rippling along the entire length of the wall above a line of seabirds. Despite their time-worn appearance, the few rougher-looking originals retain a fluidity and character somehow lacking in the contemporary version.

At the end of this wall, the marked path goes through the labyrinthine **Audience Rooms**. Their function is unclear, but their importance is evident in both the quantity and quality of the decorations – the rooms have the most interesting friezes in Tschudi. Living so close to the ocean, the Chimú based much of their diet on seafood, and the importance of the sea reached venerable proportions. Fish, waves, seabirds and sea mammals are represented throughout the city, and in the Audience Rooms you'll find all of them in the one place. For the Chimú, both the moon and the sea were of religious importance (unlike the Incas, who worshipped the sun and venerated the earth).

Further on, the **Second Ceremonial Courtyard** also has a ramp to the second level. From behind this plaza, you can see a huge rectangular depression that was once a **walk-in well** supplying the daily water needs of the royal compound.

To the left is an area of several dozen small, crumbling cells that has been called the **Military Sector**. Perhaps soldiers lived here, or the cells may have been used for storage. Next is the **Mausoleum**, where a king was buried along with human sacrifices and ceremonial objects. To the left of the main tomb, a pyramid containing the bodies of dozens of young women was found.

The final area is the **Assembly Room**. This large rectangular room has 24 seats set into niches in the walls, and its amazing acoustic properties are such that speakers sitting in any one of the niches can be clearly heard all over the room.

MUSEO DE SITIO CHAN CHAN
The site museum contains exhibits explaining Chan Chan and the Chimú culture. It is on the main road, about 500m before the Chan Chan turnoff. The museum has a few signs in Spanish and English but a guide is still useful. A sound-and-light show plays in Spanish every 30 minutes. The aerial photos and maps showing the huge extension of Chan Chan are fascinating, as tourists can only visit a tiny portion of the site.

Huaca Esmeralda
Halfway between Trujillo and Chan Chan, this Chimú **temple** (admission free with Chan Chan ticket) is to the south of the main road, four blocks behind the Mansiche Church. Thieves reportedly prey on unwary tourists wandering around, so go with a large group or a guide and keep your eyes open.

Huaca Esmeralda was buried by sand and was accidentally discovered by a local landowner in 1923. He attempted to uncover the ruins, but El Niño of 1925 began the process of erosion, which was exacerbated by the floods and rains of 1983. Although little restoration work has been done on the adobe friezes, it is still possible to make out the characteristic Chimú designs of fish, seabirds, waves and fishing nets.

White-yellow-and-orange B *combis* to Huaca Esmeralda leave Trujillo every few minutes; they pass the corners of España and Ejército, and España and Industrial.

Huaca Arco Iris
Also known locally as Huaca del Dragón, **Huaca Arco Iris** (Rainbow Temple; admission free with Chan Chan ticket) is in the suburb of La Esperanza, about 4km northwest of Trujillo.

Dating from the 12th century, Huaca Arco Iris is one of the best preserved of the Chimú temples – simply because it was buried under sand until the 1960s. Its location was known to a handful of archaeologists and *huaqueros* (grave robbers), but excavation did not begin until 1963. Unfortunately, the 1983 El Niño caused damage to the friezes.

The *huaca* used to be painted, but these days only faint traces of yellow hues remain. It consists of a defensive wall more than 2m thick enclosing an area of about 3000 sq meters, which houses the temple itself. The building covers about 800 sq meters in two levels, with a combined height of about 7.5m. The walls are slightly pyramidal and covered with repeated rainbow designs, most of which have been restored. Ramps lead the visitor to the very top of the temple, from where a series of large bins, found to contain the bones of infants – possibly human sacrifices – can be seen. This may have been a fertility temple since in many ancient cultures the rainbow represents rain, considered to be the bringer of life.

There is a tiny on-site **museum**, and local guides are available to show you around.

Buses for La Esperanza go northwest along the Panamericana and can drop you off at La Huaca Arco Iris.

Huacas del Sol y de la Luna
The **Temples of the Sun and the Moon** (adult S11; ☯ 9am-4pm) are more than 700 years older than Chan Chan and are attributed to the Moche period. They are on the south bank of the Río Moche, about 10km southeast of Trujillo by a rough road. The entrance price includes a guide.

The Huaca del Sol is the largest single pre-Columbian structure in Peru, although about a third of it has been washed away. The structure was built with an estimated 140 million adobe bricks, many of them marked with symbols representing the workers who made them.

At one time the pyramid consisted of several different levels connected by steep flights of stairs, huge ramps and walls sloping at 77 degrees. The last 1500 years have wrought their inevitable damage, and today the pyramid looks like a giant pile of crude bricks partially covered with sand. The few graves within the structure suggest it may have been a huge ceremonial site. Certainly, its size alone makes the pyramid an awesome sight, and the views from the top are excellent.

Size isn't everything, however. The smaller but more interesting Huaca de la Luna is about 500m away across the open desert. This structure is riddled with rooms that contain ceramics, precious metals and some of the beautiful polychrome friezes for which the Moche were famous. The *huaca* (tomb or grave) was built over six centuries to AD 600, with six succeeding generations expanding on it and completely covering the previous structure. Archaeologists are currently onion-skinning selected parts of the *huaca* and have discovered that there are friezes of stylized figures on every level, some of which have been perfectly preserved by the later levels built around them. It's well worth a visit; you'll see newly excavated friezes every year. Reproductions of some of the murals are displayed in the Museo de Arqueología in Trujillo (p343).

As you leave, check out the souvenir stands, some of which sell pots made using the original molds found at the site. Also look around for one of the *biringos,* the native Peruvian hairless dogs that hang out here; their body temperature is higher than the normal dog, and they have traditionally been used as body warmers for people with arthritis.

Combis leave for the Huacas del Sol y de la Luna every half hour from Suárez in Trujillo. It's also possible to take a taxi.

Complejo Arqueológico la Huaca el Brujo

This **archaeological complex** (admission negotiable; ⏲ 9am-5pm) consists of the Huaca Prieta site, the recently excavated Moche site of Huaca Cao Viejo with its brilliant mural reliefs and Huaca el Brujo, which is only starting to be excavated. The complex is 60km from Trujillo on the coast and is hard to find without a guide. It's technically not open to the public as there is little to see of the excavations so far, but tour agencies in Trujillo can arrange a visit to the area on request.

To get to the complex, take a bus from the Provincial Bus Terminal Interurbano in Trujillo to Chocope (S2, 1½ hours), then jump on a *combi* going toward the site (S2).

HUACA CAO VIEJO

The main section of Huaca Cao Viejo is a 27m truncated pyramid with some of the best friezes in the area. They show magnificently multicolored reliefs – much more color than you see at the *huacas* closer to Chiclayo – with stylized life-sized warriors, prisoners, priests and human sacrifices. There are also many burial sites from the Lambayeque culture, which followed the Moche. The people who live near this *huaca* insist that it has positive energy and ceremonies are occasionally performed here when someone needs to soak up a bit of this positive vibration.

HUACA PRIETA

Huaca Prieta has been one of the most intensively studied early Peruvian sites. However, for non-archaeologists, it's generally more interesting to read about than to tour. Although it's simply a prehistoric pile of refuse, it does afford extensive vistas over the coastal area and can be visited along with the other *huacas* in the archaeological complex.

HUANCHACO

☎ 044 / pop 41,900

This once-tranquil fishing hamlet, 12km outside Trujillo, woke up one morning to find itself a brightly highlighted paragraph on Peru's Gringo Trail. Managing to retain much of its villagey appeal, Huanchaco has cottoned onto its own popularity and today is happy to dish up a long menu of sleeping and dining options to tourists. Come summertime, legions of local and foreign tourists descend on its lapping shores, and this fast-growing resort town makes a great alternative base for exploring the ruins surrounding Trujillo.

Orientation & Information

Larco is the main drag running the length of the bay and there's a small pier in the middle of Huanchaco, often filled with hobbyist fishermen. There's a S0.50 entry charged to the pier on the weekends. Building numbering can be a bit confusing as the local council changed all the building numbers in 2003, and many places still use the old ones.

See www.huanchaco.com for lots of useful tourist information. There's a Banco Continental next to the *municipalidad* (town hall) with an ATM that accepts Visa cards. Next door is **Internet K.M.E.K** (La Riviera 269A; per hr S2; ☽ 8am-11pm), which moonlights as a Western Union office and can change US dollars. **Mr Phil's Lavandería** (Los Helechos 619; per wash or dry S5; ☽ 9am-7pm) has self-service laundry. There's a small **post office** (Manco Cápac 220; ☽ 9am-7pm Mon-Fri, to 1pm Sat) a block back from the pier.

Dangers & Annoyances
Be careful walking the streets late at night, as robberies are not uncommon.

Sights & Activities
Things change slowly here. So slowly that local fisherman are still using the very same narrow reed boats depicted on 2000-year-old Moche pottery. The fishermen paddle and surf these neatly crafted boats like seafaring cowboys, with their legs dangling on either side – which explains the nickname given to these elegantly curving steeds, *caballitos de tortora* (little horses). The inhabitants of Huanchaco are among the few remaining people on the coast who remember how to construct and use the boats, each one only lasting a few months before becoming waterlogged. You'll see rows of these iconic craft extending their long fingers to the sun as they dry along the beach of Huanchaco. At the northern end you can see the reeds that are gown to manufacture the boats. To try surfing the 2000-year-old way, ask the fishermen on the beach to show you how to use their *caballitos*. Just S5 will get you paddled out and surfed back in Huanchaco style. If that whets your appetite, you can ask one of the locals to take you out fishing with them for a few hours: the price is highly negotiable.

The curving, grey-sand beach here is fine for swimming during the December to April summer, but expect serious teeth chatter during the rest of the year. The good surf here, perfect for beginners, draws its fair share of followers and you'll see armies of bleached-blond surfer types ambling the streets with boards in hand. You can rent surfing gear (S15 to S30 per day for a wetsuit and surfboard) from several places along the main drag, including **Wave** (☎ 58-7005; Victor Larco 525).

For surfing lessons, visit **Un Lugar** (☎ 957-7170; www.otracosa.info; cnr Bolognesi & Atahualpa), two blocks back from the main beach road. This place is run by the super-friendly and highly skilled Juan Carlos and provides private two-hour lessons for S45. It also rents boards and suits, organizes surfing safaris to Puerto Chicama and, best of all, runs a volunteer program helping local street children. Travelers are welcome to volunteer.

Otra Cosa (☎ 46-1346; www.otracosa.info; Victor Larco 921; ☽ 9am-8pm Wed-Sun), a Middle Eastern restaurant, also organizes several volunteer projects in the area; see its website for more information.

The church above town, **Santuario de la Virgen del Socorro** (☽ dawn-dusk), is worth a visit. Built between 1535 and 1540, it is said to be the second-oldest church in Peru. There are sweeping views from the restored belfry.

Festivals & Events
Carnaval A big event in Huanchaco; February/March.
Festival del Mar This festival re-enacts the legendary arrival of Takayamo, founder of Chan Chan. Expect surfing and dance competitions, cultural conferences, food, music and much merrymaking. Held every other year (even years) during the first week in May.

Sleeping
BUDGET
You can find Naylamp, Huanchaco's Garden and Las Brisas Hostal in the northern part of Huanchaco, while at the southern end of town there are a few guesthouses in the small streets running perpendicular to the beach.

our pick Naylamp (☎ 46-1022; www.hostalnaylamp .com; Larco 1420; campsites/dm S10/15, s S30-40, d S50-60) Top of the pops in the budget stakes, Naylamp has one building on the waterfront and a second, larger building up a hill behind the hotel. Great budget rooms share a spacious seaview patio, and the lush camping area has perfect sunset views and hammocks for everyone! Kitchen and laundry facilities, hot showers and a cafe are all thrown in.

My Friend Hospedaje (☎ 46-1080; myfriend_huan chaco@hotmail.com; Los Pinos 533; dm/d S11/30) It's a wonder why the hot and dark rooms are full most nights, but this hole-in-the-wall attracts droves of backpackers and surfers with only a few nuevo soles left in their pockets. The little cafe downstairs serves breakfast and you can get hooked up with surf lessons here, if that's your game.

PRE-COLUMBIAN PEOPLES OF THE NORTH COAST

Northern Peru has played host to a series of civilizations stretching as far back as 5000 years ago. Listed below are the major cultures that waxed and waned in Peru's coastal desert areas over the millennia.

Huaca Prieta

One of first peoples on the desert scene, the Huaca Prieta lived at the site of the same name (p352) from around 3500 BC to 2300 BC. These hunters and gatherers grew cotton and varieties of beans and peppers and subsisted mainly on seafood. They were preceramic people who didn't use jewelry, but had developed netting and weaving. At their most artistic, they decorated dried gourds with simple carvings. Homes were single-room shacks half buried in the ground, and most of what is known about these people has been deduced from their middens.

Chavín

Based around Huaraz in Peru's central Andes, the Chavín also had a significant cultural and artistic influence on coastal Peru, particularly between the years 800 BC and 400 BC. For more information on the Chavín culture, see p422.

Moche

Evolving from around AD 100 BC to AD 800, the Moche created ceramics, textiles and metalwork, developed the architectural skills to construct massive pyramids and still had enough time for art and a highly organized religion.

Among all their expert productions, it's the ceramics that earn the Moche a ranking in Peru's pre-Inca civilization hall of fame. Considered the most artistically sensitive and technically developed of any ceramics found in Peru, Moche pots are realistically decorated with figures and scenes that leave us with a very descriptive look at everyday life. Pots were modeled into lifelike representations of people, crops, domestic and wild animals, marine life and monumental architecture. Other pots were painted with scenes of both ceremonial activities and everyday objects.

Some facets of Moche life illustrated on pots include punishments, surgical procedures (such as amputation and the setting of broken limbs) and copulation. One room in Lima's Museo Larco (p95) is devoted to pots depicting a cornucopia of sexual practices, some the products of very fertile imaginations. Museo Cassinelli in Trujillo (p345) also has a fine collection.

A few kilometers south of Trujillo, there are two main Moche sites: Huaca del Sol and Huaca de la Luna (p351).

The Moche period declined around AD 700, and the next few centuries are somewhat confusing. The Wari culture, based in the Ayacucho area of the central Peruvian Andes, began to expand after this time, and its influence was reflected in both the Sicán and Chimú cultures.

La Casa Suiza (☎ 46-1285; www.casasuiza.com; Los Pinos 451/310; r per person from S20; ☐) Under new ownership and with plenty of fresh paint to show for it, the Swiss House's spacious rooms have Peru-themed, airbrushed murals, and good mattresses for your sleeping pleasure. The little cafe downstairs prepares crunchy crust pizzas, and the patio upstairs hosts a nice view and the occasional barbecue. Good-quality bikes are also available for rent (per half-day S15). French American owner Philippe Faucon and staff offer a friendly welcome.

Huanchaco's Garden (☎ 46-1194; huanchacosgarden@yahoo.es; Av Circumvalación 440; s/d S40/60; ☒) Back from the beach, the clinically clean rooms here are in low white adobe buildings surrounding the promised shady garden. There are a couple of small swimming pools and lots of grass in the walled-in compound. The friendly family that runs the place will try their best to make your stay enjoyable.

Huanchaco Hostal (☎ 46-1688; Plaza de Armas; s/d/tr S50/70/95; ☒) This neat red building looks cute enough to have housed the three little pigs in a past life. On the town's small Plaza de Armas, this little place has Spartan white rooms and a handsome backyard concealing a secluded pool and garden. There's plenty of arty touches to make it feel homey.

Sicán

The Sicán were probably descendants of the Moche and flourished in the same region from about AD 750 to 1375. Avid agriculturalists, the Sicán were also infatuated with metallurgy and all that glitters. The Sicán are known to many archaeologists for their lost-wax (mold-cast) gold ornaments and the manufacture of arsenical copper, which is the closest material to bronze found in pre-Columbian New World archaeology. These great smiths produced alloys of gold, silver and arsenic copper in vast quantities, using little more than hearths fired by *algarrobo* (carob tree) wood and pipe-blown air to achieve the incredible 1000°C temperatures needed for such work.

Artifacts found at Sicán archaeological sites suggested that this culture loved to shop, or at least trade. They were actively engaged in long-distance trade with peoples along the length and breadth of the continent, acquiring shells and snails from Ecuador, emeralds and diamonds from Colombia, bluestone from Chile, and gold from the Peruvian highlands.

With a structured and religiously controlled social organization, the Sicán engaged in bizarre and elaborate funerary practices, examples of which can be seen at the Museo Nacional Sicán in Ferreñafe (p365).

Unfortunately, as was the case with many pre-Inca societies, the weather was the ultimate undoing of the Sicán. Originally building their main city at Batán Grande (p366), northeast of Trujillo, they were forced to move to Túcume (p366) when El Niño rains devastated that area in the 13th century.

Chimú

The Chimú were contemporaries of the Sicán and lasted from about AD 850 to 1470. They were responsible for the huge capital at Chan Chan (p349), just north of Trujillo. The artwork of the Chimú was less exciting than that of the Moche, tending more to functional mass production than artistic achievement. Gone, for the most part, was the technique of painting pots. Instead, they were fired by a simpler method than that used by the Moche, producing the typical black-ware seen in many Chimú pottery collections. While the quality of the ceramics declined, skills in metallurgy developed, with gold and various alloys being worked.

The Chimú are best remembered as an urban society. Their huge capital contained about 10,000 dwellings of varying quality and importance. Buildings were decorated with friezes, the designs molded into mud walls and important areas were layered with precious metals. There were storage bins for food and other products from across the empire, which stretched along the coast from Chancay to the Gulf of Guayaquil (southern Ecuador). There were huge walk-in wells, canals, workshops and temples. The royal dead were buried in mounds with a wealth of offerings.

The Chimú were conquered by the Incas in 1471 and heavy rainfall has severely damaged the adobe moldings of this once vast metropolis.

MIDRANGE

All these hotels have hot showers and TVs. You can get discounts of up to 50% outside festival and holiday times, so don't be shy about asking for it.

Hostal Caballito de Totora (☎ 46-1154; caballito detotora.tripod.com; La Rivera 219; s/d S54/81, d/tr with ocean view S108/135; ⚲) Although there are lots of different rooms at Caballito de Tortora, it's the suites that take the cake, each with perfect sea views and private patios. There's also lots of greenery and the white walls with blue flourishes give it a truly Mediterranean feel. The regular rooms can be a little stuffy.

Las Brisas Hostal (☎ 46-1186; www.lasbrisasperu.com; Raimondi 146; s/d S60/85) This recently renovated white multistory monolith seems to have gotten lost on its way to the Greek Islands. It has decent rooms, many with views of the sea and a pleasant patio area. If you want to burn some calories, it's one of the few hotels in town with a gym.

Las Palmeras (☎ 46-1199; www.laspalmerasde huanchaco.com; Larco 1150; s S100, d S130-170; ⚇ 🖳 ⚲) Probably the nicest place to stay in town, this well-trimmed, mellow-yellow resort hotel has spotless rooms (some with sea views), a secluded green lawn, a lovely pool, spots of shade and a restaurant to boot. It's in an enclosed compound right near the beach and is a great place for travelers with kiddies.

Hostal el Malecón (☎ 46-1275; www.hostalelmalecon .com; La Rivera 212/233; s/d S105/150) This 'highly qualified lodging company' features a cafe, a terrace with views of surfers and a pub that plays videos on demand. English and German are spoken.

Hostal Bracamonte (☎ 46-1162; www.hostal bracamonte.com; Los Olivos 503; s/d S110/132, bungalows per person from S40; ☐ ☒) Popular, friendly, welcoming and secure behind high walls and a locked gate, the Bracamonte has nice gardens, a games room, video room, barbecue, restaurant, bar, and toddlers' playground. The rooms include cable TVs, fans and phone. This is the oldest of Huanchaco's good hotels and it remains among the best choices.

Huankarute Restaurant & Hospedaje (☎ 46-1705; www.hostalhuankarute.com; La Rivera 233; s/d S120/140; ☒) A small place with bright rooms that have fan and cable TV. The top-floor doubles afford great vistas as well as a real treat – bathtubs!

Eating

Not surprisingly, Huanchaco has oodles of seafood restaurants, especially near the *caballitos de tortora* stacked at the north end of the beach.

Otra Cosa (☎ 46-1346; www.otracosa.info; Larco 921; dishes S3-9; ☒ 9am-8pm Wed-Sun) Decorated with Middle Eastern flair, this cozy, hammock-filled beachside pad serves up yummy vegetarian victuals like falafel and hummus.

Grill A Bordo (☎ 937-4026; Los Pinos 491; dishes S3-18; ☒ 6-11pm Mon-Sat, 11am-11pm Sun) The ships-ahoy theme, complete with waiters dressed as sailors, may be unnecessary as this *parrillada* (grill house) serves only one fish dish – but there are plenty of scrumptiously grilled meats on offer. Located a few blocks back from the beach, it's a cozy little place that also houses a small ceramics gallery.

El Caribe (Larco at Atahualpa; dishes S9-14; ☒ 10am-7pm) Recommended for its seafood, particularly the reasonably priced ceviche.

Mamma Mía (☎ 997-3635; Larco at Independencia; pasta S15, pizza S25; ☒ 6-11pm) Come here for delicious concoct-your-own pizzas prepared with the freshest ingredients. The pastas are also great, but for a real treat you should check to see if the Peruvian owner, Fernando, is making any of his famous secret-recipe crab lasagna. Yum.

Club Colonial (☎ 461-015; Grau 142; meals S15-28; ☒ noon-11pm) On the plaza, this Belgian-run place is in a striking, candle-lit colonial mansion and serves up finely prepared Peruvian and French dishes. It also doubles as a gallery for quality local artists and is the best place in town for a romantic rendezvous. Hours can be erratic.

Restaurant Big Ben (☎ 46-1378; Larco 836; mains S18-25; ☒ 11am-11pm) At the far north end of Huanchaco, Big Ben specializes in lunchtime ceviches and has a reputation for top-notch seafood.

our pick **Restaurante Mococho** (☎ 46-1350; Bolognesi 535; 3-course meals about S45; ☒ 1-3pm) This tiny place sits secluded in a walled garden where patrons wait to see what amazing seafood concoctions the skilled don Victor will serve up that day. It's not cheap, but ceviche and seafood does not get any better than this.

Getting There & Away

Combis to Huanchaco frequently leave from Trujillo (S2). To return, just wait on the beachfront road for the bus as it returns from the north end. A taxi from Trujillo is S9 to S14.

OTUZCO

☎ 044 / pop 11,400 / elev 2627m

The small town of Otuzco is only two hours away from Trujillo, making it the only place in Peru where you can go coast-to-Andean peaks in such a short amount of time. The cobblestone streets, cool weather and relaxed pace of life make this a great day trip or stopover on the mountain route to Cajamarca. The modern church here houses the Virgen de la Puerta (Virgin of the Door), the object of a popular Peruvian pilgrimage on December 15.

The trip itself is worthwhile, as you'll be greeted by excellent scenery while your fillings jitter on the rough journey through coastal subtropical crops and into the highland agricultural regions.

There are some modest places to stay, the best being the cheap **Hostal Los Portales** (Santa Rosa 680; s/d S12/20). A few inexpensive restaurants serve Peruvian food, but none are outstanding.

Línea has buses from Otuzco and Trujillo (S5, two hours). *Colectivos* to Huamachuco leave regularly from the southern part of town (S6.50, four hours).

PUERTO CHICAMA
☎ 044

The small fishing outpost of Puerto Chicama might not look like much, but it's the offshore action that draws a dedicated following. Puerto Chicama, also called Malabrigo, lays claim to one of the longest left-hand point breaks in the world. Originally a busy port for the sugar and cotton grown on nearby haciendas, Puerto Chicama now draws adrenaline-seeking surfers who try their luck catching that rare, long ride. Peru's National Surfing Championship is usually held here in March.

The lengthy break is caused by a shallow, flat beach and on a good day waves can reach up to 2m and travel for an incredible 2km. Good waves can be found year-round, but the marathon breaks only come about when the conditions are just so, usually between March and June. There is some gear available for hire at El Hombre, though it's best to bring your own. The water is very cold for much of the year, except for December through March.

The aid organization **Bruce Peru** (☎ in Trujillo 94-992-4445; www.bruceperu.com/malabrigo; San Martín 444, Trujillo) helps kids who are unable to attend school. Volunteer opportunities are best arranged beforehand – contact the Trujillo office – although short-term, walk-in volunteers are sometimes needed.

El Hombre (☎ 57-6077; s/d from S15/25) is the original surfers' hostel and is run by local legend 'El Hombre,' a surfer guru who's been at it for more than 40 years. Facing the ocean, the hostel has comfy beds, good simple meals, kitchen privileges and a communal TV often seen flickering with surf videos. Next door, the French-owned **El Inti** (☎ 57-6138; s/d S30/45) has a sea-view restaurant where Peru doffs its hat to French influences. There are a few garden bungalows here, a barbecue and a pool table. A few doors down, **Hostal los Delfines** (☎ 57-6103; losdelfineschicama@hotmail.com; s/d/ste S60/80/120; 🏊) is the midrange choice, with more ocean views, a heart-shaped pool and Jacuzzis in the suites.

Some surf shops in Huanchaco, including Un Lugar (p353), arrange surfing safaris to Puerto Chicama. Buses leave frequently from Trujillo's Provincial Bus Terminal Interurbano to the town of Paiján, 40km further north on the Panamericana (S5, 1½ hours). From here you can catch *colectivos* for the 16km to Puerto Chicama (S1, 20 minutes).

PACASMAYO
☎ 044 / pop 25,700

This lively, mostly forgotten beach town is crammed with colonial buildings in various states of disrepair and blessed with a pretty stretch of beach. Check out the pier here; it's one of the largest in Peru. Dedicated surfers often drop in, particularly from May to August, when there is a decent offshore break. It's also a great place to spend some time away from the more popular resort towns and get swept up in the ageing nostalgia of the whole place.

The **Balin Surf Shop** (Junín 84) rents boards and does repairs. There's a **BCP** (Ayacucho 20) bank on the small plaza near the beach with a Visa ATM. Internet access is available all over town.

A few kilometers north, just before the village of Guadalupe, a track leads toward the ocean and the little-visited ruins of **Pacatnamú**, a large site that was inhabited by the Gallinazo, Moche and Chimú cultures.

There are several cheap, basic-but-clean hotels in town and some swisher converted colonial mansions and new constructions along the beach. **Hotel San Francisco** (☎ 52-2021; Prado 21; s/d S20/30, s/d without bathroom S15/20) is on the main commercial strip and has clean, bare-bones rooms. The good-value **Hospedaje El Mirador** (☎ 52-1883; www.pacasmayoperu.com; Aurelio Herrera 10; d S30-60, tr S40-75) is all brick and tile, but the rooms, varying from *económico* (basic) to *de lujo* (luxury) all have cable TV, hot water and balconies; the nicest rooms have kitchens and DVD players. **Hotel Pakatnamú** (☎ 52-3255; www.actiweb.es/hotelpakatnamu; Malecón Grau 103; s/d/ste S75/105/125; 🏊) is in a freshly painted colonial building along the waterfront. The plush rooms here come with TV, fridge and even a mounted car stereo with 'surround sound.' A few doors down, **La Estación Pacasmayo Hotel** (☎ 52-1515; www.hotellaestacion.com.pe; Malecón Grau 69; s/d S80/120; 🏊) is a similarly majestic, restored Republican-era building with a lovely terrace restaurant; all the rooms have balconies. The best place in town to eat is the seafood-centric restaurant at **Hospedaje El Mirador** (mains & breakfasts S4.50-18; 🕑 7am-11pm).

In Guadalupe village, try **Hotel el Bosque** (☎ 56-6490; s/d S50/75).

Frequent buses to and from Trujillo (two hours), Chiclayo (two hours) and Cajamarca (four hours) pass through the northern end of town.

CHICLAYO

☎ 074 / pop 256,900

Spanish missionaries founded a small rural community on this site in the 16th century. Either by chance, or through help from above, Chiclayo has prospered ever since. In one of the first sharp moves in Peruvian real estate, the missionaries chose a spot that sits at the hub of vital trade routes connecting the coast, the highlands and the deep jungle. Chiclayo's role as the commercial heart of the district has allowed it to overtake other once-vital organs of the region, such as the nearby city of Lambayeque, and this bustling metropolis shows few signs of slowing down.

La Ciudad de la Amistad (the City of Friendship) holds a friendly, outstretched hand to the wayward venturer. While it's shaking hands hello, it will probably slip in a bold mix of unique regional dishes to tickle your taste buds. Known for its *brujos* (witch doctors), the fascinating market here is a Wal-Mart of shamanistic herbs, elixirs and other sagely curiosities. While the town itself is pretty light on tourist attractions, the dozens of tombs with Moche and Chimú archaeological booty surrounding the area should not be missed.

Information

EMERGENCY
Policía de Turismo (☎ 23-6700; Saenz Peña 830) Useful for reporting problems.

IMMIGRATION
Oficina de Migraciónes (☎ 20 -6838; La Plata 70) Near Paseo de Las Museos; does visa extensions.

INTERNET ACCESS
Internet abounds.
Ciber C@fe (Izaga 716; per hr S2; ☼ 8am-11pm) Has a cozier feeling than most.

LAUNDRY
Biolav (☎ 23-3159; Saenz Peña btwn Izaga & Cabrera; per kg S5; ☼ 8am-9pm)

MEDICAL SERVICES
Clínica del Pacífico (☎ 23-6378; Ortiz 420) The best medical assistance in town.

MONEY
There are several banks on *cuadra* (block) 6 of Balta. Money changers outside the banks change cash quickly at good rates.

Banco Continental (☎ 23-9110; Balta 643)
BCP (☎ 23-7291; Balta 630) Has a 24-hour Visa and MasterCard ATM.
Interbank (☎ 23-8361; cnr Colón & Aguirre)
Scotiabank (☎ 22-4724; Balta 609)

POST
Post office (Aguirre 140; ☼ 9am-7pm Mon-Fri, to 1pm Sat) West of Plaza Aguirre.

TOURIST INFORMATION
Centro de Informacíon Turístico (☎ 23-3132; Sáenz Peña 838) Has lots of information.
Information booth (Plaza de Armas) Hours are irregular.

Sights & Activities

In 1987 a royal Moche tomb at **Sipán**, 30km southeast of Chiclayo, was located by researchers. This find proved to be extraordinary, as archaeologists recovered hundreds of dazzling and priceless artifacts from the site. Excavation continues. Partly because of these rare treasures, the Chiclayo area has single-handedly cornered the Peruvian market for exceptionally well-designed museums; a case in point is the excellent museum in **Lambayeque**, 11km north of Chiclayo. Other sites worth visiting are the ruins at **Túcume**, another great museum in **Ferreñafe**, as well as a number of coastal villages.

Make sure not to miss a visit to **Mercado Modelo** (☼ 9am-5pm), one of Peru's most interesting markets. This place sprawls for several blocks and is a thick maze of fresh fruits and vegetables, woven goods, handicrafts, live animals, fish, meats and, most interestingly, the *mercado de brujos* (witch doctors' market) in the southwest corner. This area is a one-stop shop for medicine men and has everything you might need for a potent brew: whale bones, amulets, snake skins, vials of indeterminate tonics, hallucinogenic cacti and piles of aromatic herbs. If you'd like to make contact with a *brujo* for a healing session, this is a good place to start, but be wary of sham shamans. It's best to go with a recommendation (see also p374).

Chiclayo's **cathedral** was built in the late 19th century, and the Plaza de Armas (Parque Principal) wasn't inaugurated until 1916, which gives an idea of how new the city is by Peruvian standards. The **Paseo de las Musas** showcases classical-style statues of mythological figures. The **Plaza de Armas** is a great place to amble as it fills nightly with sauntering

CHICLAYO

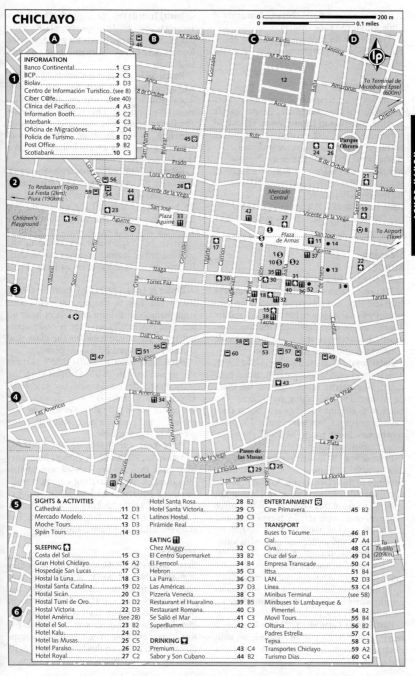

0 — 200 m
0 — 0.1 miles

INFORMATION
Banco Continental.....................**1** C3
BCP..**2** C3
Biolav.......................................**3** D3
Centro de Información Turístico..(see 8)
Ciber C@fe..............................(see 40)
Clínica del Pacífico....................**4** A3
Information Booth.......................**5** C2
Interbank..................................**6** C3
Oficina de Migraciónes...............**7** D4
Policía de Turismo......................**8** D2
Post Office................................**9** B2
Scotiabank...............................**10** C3

SIGHTS & ACTIVITIES
Cathedral.................................**11** D3
Mercado Modelo.......................**12** C1
Moche Tours.............................**13** D3
Sipán Tours..............................**14** D3

SLEEPING
Costa del Sol............................**15** C3
Gran Hotel Chiclayo...................**16** A2
Hospedaje San Lucas..................**17** C3
Hostal la Luna..........................**18** C3
Hostal Santa Catalina.................**19** D2
Hostal Sicán.............................**20** C3
Hostal Tumi de Oro....................**21** D2
Hostal Victoria..........................**22** C3
Hotel América........................(see 28)
Hotel el Sol..............................**23** B2
Hotel Kalu...............................**24** D2
Hotel las Musas.........................**25** C5
Hotel Paraíso............................**26** D2
Hotel Royal..............................**27** C2

Hotel Santa Rosa.......................**28** B2
Hotel Santa Victoria....................**29** C5
Latinos Hostal...........................**30** C3
Pirámide Real............................**31** C3

EATING
Chez Maggy.............................**32** C5
El Centro Supermarket.................**33** B2
El Ferrocol...............................**34** B4
Hebron....................................**35** C3
La Parra...................................**36** C3
Las Américas............................**37** D3
Pizzería Venecia........................**38** C3
Restaurant el Huaralino...............**39** B5
Restaurant Romana....................**40** C3
Se Salió el Mar..........................**41** C3
SuperBumm..............................**42** C2

DRINKING
Premium..................................**43** C4
Sabor y Son Cubano...................**44** B2

ENTERTAINMENT
Cine Primavera.........................**45** B2

TRANSPORT
Buses to Túcume.......................**46** B1
Cial..**47** A4
Civa..**48** C4
Cruz del Sur.............................**49** D4
Empresa Transcade....................**50** C4
Ittsa.......................................**51** B4
LAN..**52** D3
Línea......................................**53** C4
Minibus Terminal....................(see 58)
Minibuses to Lambayeque &
  Pimentel...............................**54** B2
Movil Tours..............................**55** B4
Oltursa....................................**56** B2
Padres Estrella..........................**57** C4
Tepsa......................................**58** C3
Transportes Chiclayo...................**59** A2
Turismo Dias............................**60** C4

couples, evangelical preachers and an army of underemployed shoe shiners.

Travelers with kids might want to check out the **children's playground** at the west end of Aguirre.

Tours & Guides

Agencies offer frequent inexpensive tours of Sipán, Túcume, Ferreñafe, Batán Grande and the museums in Lambayeque. Tours cost between S30 and S50, depending on whether entrance fees to museums are included.

Moche Tours (☎ 22-4637; mochetours_chiclayo@ hotmail.com; Calle 7 de Enero; ☷ 8am-2pm & 5-8pm) This new tour office has cheap daily tours with Spanish- and English-speaking guides.

Sipán Tours (☎ 22-9053, sipantours@terra.com.pe; Calle 7 de Enero 772; ☷ 8am-1pm & 4-8pm) Has guided tours in Spanish.

Sleeping

BUDGET

Hospedaje San Lucas (☎ 49-9269; Aguirre 412; s/d S20/30, s without bathroom S10) Elementary, but kept trim and tidy, this shoestringer steps up successfully to its 'Welcome Backpackers' motto. There's a nice city view from the top floor, mostly hot showers and some locally made handicrafts for sale at the reception.

Hotel Royal (☎ 23-3421; San José 787; s/d S25/40) This is the choice for aficionados of old, run-down, characterful hotels right on the Plaza de Armas. The only thing royal about this hotel is its elegant visiting card, but it does have large rooms, hot water and a TV room downstairs. Some rooms overlook the plaza, which is fun but noisy.

Pirámide Real (☎ 22-4036; piramidereal@hotmail.com; Izaga 726; s/d S30/40) Blink and you'll miss the tiny entrance of this place. If you do find it, inside you'll see tidy rooms with cable TV and hot water – a reasonably good deal at this price range. Romanesque statues fill the halls and add some kind of personality to the hotel – though we're still undecided as to what kind.

Hostal Victoria (☎ 22-5642; Izaga 933; s/d/tr S30/45/55) This is a great find just east of the main plaza. It's quiet, sanitary and has colorful rooms spruced up by nice bits of furniture. Lots of potted plants breathe some life into the indoors and there's a friendly family vibe to the whole place.

Hostal Santa Catalina (☎ 27-2119; Vicente de la Vega 1127; s/d S35/42.50) The 10 rooms here, with electric hot showers and cable TV, are clean and quiet.

Hostal Tumi de Oro (☎ 22-7108; fax 23-7767; Prado 1145; s/d/tr S35/55/65) This Spartan place almost has all the midrange goods for a budget price. Rooms have hot showers and there's a lobby with cable TV.

Hostal Sicán (☎ 23-7618; Izaga 356; s/d S40/55) An appealing pick with lots of polished wood and wrought iron creating an illusion of grandeur. The rooms are small, comfortable and cool. All have more wood paneling, as well as some tasteful bits of art and a TV. This great choice also has a laundry service.

Hotel el Sol (☎ 23-2120; www.hotelelsoltresestrellas .com; Aguirre 119; s/d S45/63; ☒) This fastidiously maintained and professionally run deal has tip-top rooms with all the mod cons – a steal at this price. The varied rooms have TV, fans and phones, though we wouldn't want to be responsible for cleaning the spotless white leather couches downstairs. It's run by the same owners as Hotel Vicus in Piura.

Hostal la Luna (☎ 20-5945; Torres Paz 688; s/d S50/70) The airy rooms here are OK, with some bamboo furniture and lots of hush on tap. The downstairs frontage is easily spotted from the street; look for the glass wall completely covered by indoor plants.

Hotel Santa Victoria (☎ /fax 22-5074; La Florida 586; s/d with breakfast S50/70) Overlooking the leafy Paseo de las Musas, the laid-back Hotel Santa Victoria is a longish walk from the center but is top value. Rooms have fan, cable TV and phone; a restaurant with room service is also available.

Hotel Kalu (☎ 22-9293, 22-8767; hotelkalu@ hotmail.com; Ruiz 1038; s/d S56/70) Almost boutique-like, these quarters are dressed with stylish '80s pizzazz. With dazzling colors, a wall-mounted aquarium and an attentive door-man, it's a spiffy-looking hotel all-round. Carpeted rooms have fan, cable TV and hot showers, and some have a minifridge.

MIDRANGE

Hotel Paraíso (☎ 22-8161, 22-2070; www.hotelesparaiso .com.pe; Ruiz 1064; s/d S65/75; ☐) Brighter and cheerier than its immediate neighbors, the value equation falls in Hotel Paraíso's favor. Spotless and modern tiled rooms boast decent furniture, a hot shower and cable TV. Breakfast is available in its cafe. It's the cheapest of several hotels on this block, but holds its head up in comparisons with any of them.

Hotel América (☎ 22-9305, 27-0664; Gonzáles 943; s/d S65/98; 🖳) Part underground beatnik club, part '70s casino, the América is dark and moody, with lots of velvet, plush carpeting and kitsch gold trimmings (gold deer statues, anyone?). The good-sized rooms are nicely appointed and have fans, cable TV and minifridges.

Hotel Santa Rosa (☎ 22-4411, fax 23-6242; Gonzáles 927; s/d with breakfast S70/85) This quiet, clean and pleasant hotel has comfortable rooms with fan, cable TV and phones. The size of the bathrooms varies from unit to unit, so look around. There's a good restaurant.

Latinos Hostal (☎ 23-5437; Igaza 600; s/d S70/100) An excellent choice, this new-looking hotel is thoroughly maintained with perfect little rooms; some of the corner rooms have giant curving floor-to-ceiling windows for great street views and plenty of light. The staff is very helpful.

Hotel las Musas (☎ 23-9884-86; nazih@viabpc .com; Faiques 101; s/d with breakfast S105/140; 🖂 🖳) Overlooking the peaceful Paseo de las Musas, this hotel has modern, spacious rooms with cable TV, phone and minifridge. There's a cascading 'waterfall' backed by a mossy green wall in the foyer and the bathrooms all have bathtubs as well as showers – a rarity in Peru. Some rooms have good views of the Paseo de las Musas. A restaurant is open 7am to 11pm, and room service is available 24 hours. There is a karaoke-disco, small casino and tourist information, plus tours are available.

TOP END

Gran Hotel Chiclayo (☎ 23-4911; www.granhotelchiclayo .com.pe; Villarreal 115; s/d S252/296; 🖂 🖳 🍴) The top end of Chiclayo living, it's all superswanky here, with everything you'd expect, including room service, laundry, travel agency, car rental, cappuccino bar, karaoke and casino. Serious-looking businessmen flock here in droves.

Costa Del Sol (☎ 22-7272; www.costadelsolperu .com; Balta 399; s/d/ste S268/329/503; 🖂 🖳 🍴) Part of a northern Peru chain, this establishment has all the creature comforts, including pool, gym, sauna, Jacuzzi and impeccable service. The tastefully and simply designed rooms have cable TV, minibar, safe, and direct-dial phone.

Eating

Chiclayo is one of the best places to eat on the North Coast. *Arroz con pato a la chiclayana* (duck and rice cooked in cilantro and beer) and *tortilla de manta raya* (Spanish omelet made from stingray) are endless sources of culinary pride. For dessert, try the local street sweet called a King Kong, a large cookie filled with a sweet caramel cream made of milk and sugar; it's available everywhere.

SuperBumm (☎ 27-0549; San José 677; meals S5-14; 🕑 7am-late) This buzzing, neon-lit young thing whips out local dishes, sandwiches, pizzas and cakes faster than you can blink and is filled every night with hungry diners. The upstairs seating is a little quieter. The portions here are elephantine.

Las Américas (☎ 20-9381; Aguirre 824; sandwiches S4, mains S5-25; 🕑 7:30am-11:30pm) This bright, popular place off the southeast corner of the plaza is a perennial favorite. With '60s-style red-and-white booths, Las Américas has a varied menu of soups, meats and fish dishes – try the fish in a savory onion and spicy tomato sauce. This place can be a little hygienically challenged.

Se Salió el Mar (cnr Colón & Torres Paz; mains S6-12; 🕑 8am-8pm) The warm-hearted owner here whips up fresh-from-the-sea grills and ceviche in a tiny family-owned shop with plastic tablecloths. It's a gem.

La Parra (☎ 22-7471, 22-5198; Izaga 752; mains S6-14; 🕑 11:30am-midnight) There are two restaurants side by side here; one is a *chifa* and the other is a grill, but they share an entrance and a kitchen. Go figure.

Restaurant Romana (☎ 22-3598; Balta 512; breakfasts S7, mains S9-18; 🕑 7am-late) This locally popular place serves a bunch of different dishes, all of them local favorites. If you're feeling brave, try the *chirimpico* for breakfast: it's stewed goat tripe and organs and is guaranteed to either cure a hangover or give you one. Otherwise, you can have pastas, steaks, seafood, chicken or pork *chicharrones* (breaded and fried pieces of meat) with yucca.

Chez Maggy (☎ 20-9253; Balta 413; pizzas S8-10; 🕑 6-11pm) It's not how Papa Giuseppe used to make it, but the wood-fired pizzas at this restaurant have a pretty darn good crispy crust and fresh toppings. They have convenient personal-size pizzas for solo diners.

El Ferrocol (Las Américas 168; meals S9-21; 🕑 11am-7pm) This hole-in-the-wall, a little out of the center, is well worth the trip, as chef Lucho prepares some of the best ceviche in all of Chiclayo. Treat yourself.

Hebron (☎ 22-2709; Balta 605; mains from S12; 🕑 24hr) This flashy, contemporary and bright two-story restaurant is a luxury *pollería* (restaurant specializing in roast chicken) on steroids. Lots of windows, impeccable service and a giant children's playground that would put McDonalds to shame keep this restaurant marked on the calendars of most Chiclayans. Hebron may have the only kids menu in town.

Pizzería Venecia (☎ 23-3384; Balta 413; half-pizza S12; ◷ 6:30pm-late) This rip-roaring pizzeria attracts a young crowd that listens to rock and Latin favorites while they chug beer with their food.

Restaurant el Huaralino (☎ 27-0330; Libertad 155; mains S15-30; ◷ noon-11pm Mon-Sat, to 5pm Sun) One of Chiclayo's most upscale restaurants, this place serves good Chiclayan specialties, *criollo* dishes and international cuisine. Bonus brownie points for some of the cleanest bathrooms in Peru.

ourpick Restaurant Típico La Fiesta (☎ 20-1970; Salaverry 1820; mains S28-38; ◷ noon-11pm) Another quality top-end choice, La Fiesta is in the Residencial 3 de Octubre suburb, about 2km west of central Chiclayo. If you want to experience the best of this region's world-famous cuisine, Fiesta is the place to splurge. The pisco sours constructed tableside and elegant meat dishes, such as rack of lamb with risotto and sirloin with poached quail egg, are worth every nuevo sol. Or try the farm-raised duck, which must be a black-feathered quacker not a day over three months old. There is a sister restaurant in Lima (p114).

El Centro Supermarket (cnr Gonzáles & Aguirre; ◷ 8am-10pm) is good for self-catering.

Drinking

Premium (☎ 22-6689; Balta 100; ◷ 9pm-late) Turns into a popular place for a tipple and a dance after hours, with loud international music, a mixed crowd, free entry and a boisterous vibe.

Sabor y Son Cubano (☎ 27-2555; San José 155; ◷ 9pm-late Fri-Sun) This spot gives the over-35 crowd somewhere to shake their rumps on the weekends, with jazz, classic salsa and Cuban music setting the pace.

Entertainment

Cine Primavera (☎ 20-7471; Gonzáles 1235) This place has five screens, often showing some Hollywood flicks.

Getting There & Away

AIR

The **airport** (code CIX; ☎ 23-3192) is 1.5km east of town; a taxi ride there is a S3 and departure

tax is S11. **LAN** (☎ 27-4875; Izaga 770) has the monopoly on flights here, arriving from Lima to Chiclayo daily at 4am and 8:10pm, and returning to Lima at 5:50am, 6:15pm and 10pm.

BUS

Cruz del Sur, Movil Tours and Línea usually have the most comfortable buses.

Cial (☎ 20 -5587; Bolognesi 15) Has a 9pm Lima bus (S59 to S76, 10 hours) and a 6pm bus to Tarapoto (S36, 12 hours).

Civa (☎ 22-3434; Bolognesi 714) Lima buses at 8pm and 8:30pm (S45 to S72, 10 hours), Jaén buses at 10am and 9:30pm (S14, six hours), a Tarapoto bus at 6pm (S36, 12 hours) and a Chachapoyas bus at 5:30pm (S18, 10 to 11 hours).

Cruz del Sur (☎ 22-5508; Bolognesi 888) Has six departures to Lima (S41 to S81, 10 hours) between 8am and 10:30pm.

Empresa Transcade (☎ 23-2552; Balta 110) Has buses to Jaén (S14) at 8:30am and 8:30pm.

Ittsa (☎ 23-3612; Bolognesi 155) *Bus-cama* (bed bus) to Lima (S45 to S72, 10 hours) at 8pm.

Línea (☎ 23-3497; Bolognesi 638) Has a comfortable Lima service (S50 to S100, 10 hours) at 7:30pm and 8pm and regular hourly services to Trujillo (S11, two hours) and Piura (S12, three hours). Also has buses to Chimbote at 9:15am and 3:15pm (S18, four hours), buses to Cajamarca at 10pm and 10:45pm (S22 to S45, six hours) and buses to Jaén at 10:15am and 11pm (S15 to S25).

Movil Tours (☎ 27-1940; Bolognesi 199) Has a Lima bus (S67.50, 10 hours) at 8:30pm, a Tarapoto bus (S63, 12 hours) at 6:30pm and a Chachapoyas bus (S45, 10 to 11 hours) at 7:30pm.

Oltursa (☎ 23-7789; Vicente de la Vega 101) Three *bus-cama* services to Lima (S63 to S75, 10 hours) between 7:30pm and 9pm.

Padres Estrella (☎ 20-4879; Balta 178) Has Tarapoto-bound buses (S36, 12 to 14 hours) at 5am, 7am and 4pm, with the 4pm bus going onto Yurimaguas (S63, 20 to 24 hours).

Tepsa (☎ 23-6981; Bolognesi 504) *Bus-cama* services to Lima (S60.50, 10 hours) at 7:30pm, 8:15pm and 9:15pm.

Transportes Chiclayo (☎ 23-7984; Ortíz) Has buses to Piura (S11, three hours) every hour from 6am to 9:30pm, with the last bus going on to Tumbes (S18, eight hours).

Turismo Dias (☎ 23-3538; Cuglievan 190) Has a cheaper bus to Lima (S36 to S45, 10 hours) at 7pm as well as departures to Cajamarca (S18, six hours) at 6:45am, 5pm and 10:30pm.

Behind Tepsa there is a minibus terminal where a dozen small companies have at least six buses throughout the day to Cajamarca (S14 to S18), a night bus to Tumbes at 8:30pm (S20), buses at 7:30pm, noon and 8:30pm to Chachapoyas (S35), 9am and

3pm buses to Tarapoto (S18), a 5pm bus
to Yurimaguas (S50) and frequent services
to Jaén (S14). These times tend to change
with the setting of each moon, so check the
schedule ahead of time.

The minibus terminal at the corner of San
José and Lora y Lora has regular buses to
Lambayeque (S2, 20 minutes) and Pimentel
(S, 25 minutes).

Buses for Ferreñafe (S2), Sipán (S2),
Monsefú (S1), Zaña (S2.50) and Chongoyape
(S2) leave frequently from **Terminal de
Microbuses Epsel** (Nicolás de Píerola at Oriente).

Buses to Túcume (S2) leave from the intersection of Angamos and Manuel Pardo.

AROUND CHICLAYO
Pimentel & Santa Rosa
☎ 074

Two coastal municipalities, Pimentel (pop
27,000) and Santa Rosa (pop 10,800), can
be conveniently visited from Chiclayo on
day trips.

Pimentel, 14km from Chiclayo, has a
long, sandy beach with a huge, decaying jetty
curving out well into the sea. There are some
gracefully aging colonial buildings around the
Plaza Diego Ferre and at the south end of the
beach you can sometimes see fishermen building *caballitos*. The surf here is also good. This
place gets very crowded on summer weekends
(January to March), as Chiclayans flock to the
dozens of low-rise summer apartments lining
the oceanfront. Other times of the year it can
be practically deserted and visitors should be
alert and avoid walking along empty streets
and beaches.

Stay at **Hostal Garuda** (☎ 45-2964; Quiñones 109;
s/d S35/60). In a well-preserved colonial house,
this *hostal* has excellent rooms sporting some
refined aesthetics and enormous bathrooms.
It's a block back from the coast.

At Playa las Rocas, a 20-minute walk
south, sprawls **Katuwira Lodge** (☎ 97-972-3360,
97-973-7961; www.katuwira.com; campsites/r without bathroom per person S15/30, both incl full board), a funky,
hippyish beachside hangout made of bam-
boo and sporting vibes and art in equal
measures. Katuwira has distinctive pyramid
bungalows sleeping five to seven people,
complete with beautifully finished bamboo
lounges downstairs and bedrooms with awesome sea views upstairs. There are a few
smaller double rooms and some rudimentary
lean-to singles (think castaway style). This is

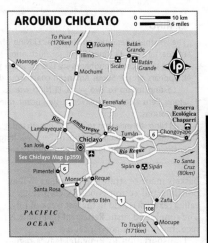

the place to arrange fishing trips with local
fishermen in their *caballitos*, to learn handicrafts from local artisans and to eat some
sensationally prepared meals. It's run by the
helpful Mario, who speaks English, Japanese
and French, and who also organizes occasional cultural shows, beach bonfires and
surf lessons in nearby Pimentel.

A few kilometers south of Pimentel is
Santa Rosa, a busy fishing village where *caballitos* can also be seen among the brightly
colored modern fishing fleet. It's famed
for its *chicha* (fermented corn beer), and
with 28 different types of *chicha* to sample, you're bound to find one to your liking (unless, of course, you pass out before
you do). The local delicacy *tortilla de raya*
(stingray tortilla) is worth sampling. There's
great surfing just south of here at **El Faro**.
You can walk from Pimentel to Santa Rosa
in less than an hour, but walking along the
empty beach here is not recommended for
security reasons; it's best to take a *colectivo*
taxi (S2).

Colectivos from Santa Rosa head south to
the small port of **Puerto Etén**, once an important commercial center. Legend has it that
Jesus himself appeared here in 1649; the small
Capilla del Milagro (Chapel of the Miracle) now
stands in that spot. Check out the 19th-century
train engine in the (disused) **train station**.

You can return to Chiclayo via the village
of **Monsefú**, 15km south of Chiclayo. Monsefú
is known for its flowers and handicrafts, and
has an artisanal market selling hats, bags and

EL NIÑO

The weather phenomenon known as El Niño (the Baby) has played a ferocious role in the history of coastal Peru. El Niño is a major fluctuation in the surface temperature of the eastern Pacific Ocean that occurs roughly every two to seven years. The phenomenon was called El Niño since it appears on the South American coast around Christmastime.

Lasting for up to two years, El Niño wreaks havoc with heavy, unremitting rains and floods along Peru's coast. It played a significant role in the collapse of both the Sicán and Moche civilizations.

El Niño still manages to mess things up today; as recently as 1998, and to a lesser extent in 2003, months of rain deluged northern Peru, washing away much of the infrastructure of that region (including roads, bridges and entire towns) and destroying nearly all of the coast's crops.

---

baskets made of straw and rattan, as well as ponchos and cotton goods. A craft festival called **Fexticum** is held in the last week of July. The simple and rustic **Restaurant Tradiciones** is recommended for good local fare.

Transportation to Pimentel leaves regularly from Chiclayo's minibus terminal (S2, 25 minutes); during summer (January to March), they continue from Pimentel along the so-called *circuito de playas* (beach circuit) through Santa Rosa, Puerto Etén and Monsefú before returning to Chiclayo.

Sipán

The story of Sipán reads like an Indiana Jones movie script: buried treasure, *huaqueros,* police, archaeologists and at least one killing. The archaeological **site** (☎ 80-0048; adult S8; ☯ 9am-5pm), also known as Huaca Rayada, was discovered by *huaqueros* (see p366) from the nearby hamlet of Sipán. When local archaeologist Dr Walter Alva saw a huge influx of intricate objects on the black market in early 1987, he realized that an incredible burial site was being ransacked in the Chiclayo area. Careful questioning led Dr Alva to the Sipán mounds. To the untrained eye the mounds look like earthen hills, but in AD 300 these were huge truncated pyramids constructed from millions of adobe bricks.

At least one major tomb had already been pillaged by looters, but fast protective action by local archaeologists and police stopped further plundering. Luckily several other, even better, tombs that the grave robbers had missed were unearthed, including an exceptional royal Moche burial which became known as the Lord of Sipán. One *huaquero* was shot and killed by police in the early, tense days of the struggle over the graves. The Sipán locals were not too happy at losing what they considered their treasure trove. To solve this

problem, the locals were invited to train to become excavators, researchers and guards at the site, which now provides steady employment to many of them. The full story has been detailed by Dr Alva in the October 1988 and June 1990 issues of *National Geographic,* and the May 1994 issue of *Natural History.*

The Lord of Sipán turned out to be a major leader of the Moche people, indicated by his elaborate burial in a wooden coffin surrounded by hundreds of gold, ceramic and semi-precious mineral objects, as well as an entourage consisting of his wife, two girls, a boy, a military chief, a flag-bearer, two guards, two dogs and a llama. Another important tomb held the *sacerdote* (priest), who was accompanied into the afterlife with an equally impressive quantity of treasures, as well as a few children, a guardian whose feet were cut off and a headless llama. Archaeologists don't understand why the body parts were removed, but they believe that important members of the Moche upper class took with them in death those who composed their retinues in life.

Some of the tombs have been restored with replicas to show what they looked like just before being closed up more than 1500 years ago. Opposite the entrance is a new **Museo de Sitio Sipán** (admission S8; entrance included in site ticket; ☯ 9am-5pm Mon-Fri), opened in January 2009, which is worth a visit – but note that the most impressive artifacts, such as the Lord of Sipán and the Sacerdote, were placed in the Museo Tumbas Reales de Sipán in Lambayeque, after going on world tour. Spanish- and English-speaking guides can be hired (S15).

Daily guided tours are available from tour agencies (p360) in Chiclayo for around S50. Alternately, buses for Sipán (S2.50) leave frequently from Chiclayo's Terminal de Microbuses Epsel.

Lambayeque

☎ 074 / pop 47,900

About 11km north of Chiclayo, Lambayeque was once the main town in the area but now plays second fiddle to Chiclayo.

SIGHTS

The town's museums are its best feature. **La Casa de Logia**, a block south of the main plaza, has a 67m-long, 400-year-old balcony, said to be the longest balcony in Peru. The two museums in Lambayeque are both within a 15-minute walk of the plaza.

Museo Tumbas Reales de Sipán

Opened in November 2002, the **Museum of the Royal Tombs of Sipán** (☎ 28-3977, 28-3988; admission adult/child S10/3; ☺ 9am-5pm Tue-Sun, last admission 4pm) is the pride of northern Peru – as well it should be. With its burgundy pyramid construction rising gently out of the earth, it's a world-class facility specifically designed to showcase the marvelous finds from Sipán. Photography is not permitted and all bags must be checked.

Visitors are guided through the museum from the top down and are shown some of the numerous discoveries from the tomb in the same order that the archaeologists found them. The first hall contains detailed ceramics representing gods, people, plants, llamas and other animals. Descending to the 2nd floor there are delicate objects like impossibly fine turquoise-and-gold ear ornaments showing ducks, deer and the Lord of Sipán himself. The painstaking and advanced techniques necessary to create this jewelry place them among the most beautiful and important objects of pre-Columbian America. Finally, the ground floor features exact reproductions of how the tombs were found. Numerous dazzling objects are displayed, the most remarkable of which are the gold pectoral plates representing sea creatures such as the octopus and crab. Even the sandals of the Lord of Sipán were made of precious metals, as he was carried everywhere and never had to walk. Interestingly, since nobility were seen as part-animal god, they used the *nariguera* (a distinctive nose shield) to conceal their very human teeth – and the fact that they were no different from everyone else.

The lighting and layout is exceptional, especially a large, moving diorama of the Lord of Sipán and his retinue – down to the barking Peruvian hairless dogs. The signage is all in Spanish, but English-speaking guides are available for S20.

Bruning Museum

This **museum** (☎ 28-2110, 28-3440; adult S8; ☺ 9am-5pm), once a regional archaeological showcase, is now greatly overshadowed by the Museo Tumbas Reales de Sipán; however, it still houses a good collection of artifacts from the Chimú, Moche, Chavín and Vicus cultures. Budding archaeologists will enjoy the displays showing the development of ceramics from different cultures and the exhibits explaining how ceramics and metalwork were made. Architecture and sculpture lovers may find some interest in the Corbusier-inspired building, bronze statues and tile murals adorning the property. Models of several important sites are genuinely valuable for putting the archaeology of the region into perspective. English-speaking guides charge S15.

EATING

El Rincón del Pato (☎ 28-2751; Leguía 270; meals S6-16; ☺ 11am-3pm) This place also gets the thumbs-up from people who are authorized to give such ratings for good ceviches, grills and local specialties.

El Cantaro (☎ 28-2196; Calle 2 de Mayo 180; mains S10-18; ☺ 10am-6pm) Continue past La Casa de Logia to this popular local restaurant with typical food and good service. When we were there one guest said that the *sudado de pescado* (whole fish stew) was the best dish he'd had in all of South America.

GETTING THERE & AWAY

The minibus terminal at the corner of San José and Lora y Lora in Chiclayo has regular buses to Lambayeque (S1.50, 20 minutes), which will drop you off a block from Bruning Museum.

Ferreñafe

☎ 074 / pop 34,500

This old town, 18km northeast of Chiclayo, is worth visiting for the excellent **Museo Nacional Sicán** (☎ 28-6469; www.sican.perucultural.org.pe; adult S8; ☺ 9am-5pm Tue-Sun). Sicán culture thrived in the Lambayeque area between AD 750 and 1375 (see p355), around the same time as the Chimú. The main Sicán site at Batán Grande lies in remote country to the north and is best visited on a tour from Chiclayo (p360) or Pacora (p366). This splendid museum dis-

HUAQUEROS

The word *huaquero* is heard frequently on the north coast of Peru and literally means 'robber of *huacas*.' *Huacas* are pyramids, temples, shrines and burial sites of archaeologial significance.

Since the Spanish conquest, *huaqueros* have worked the ancient graves of Peru, selling valuables to anybody prepared to pay. To a certain extent, one can sympathize with a poor *campesino* (peasant) hoping to strike it rich, but the *huaquero* is one of the archaeologist's greatest enemies. The *huaqueros'* efforts have been so thorough that archaeologists rarely find an unplundered grave.

plays replicas of the 12m-deep tombs found there, among the largest tombs found in South America. Enigmatic burials were discovered within – the Lord of Sicán was buried upside down, in a fetal position with his head separated from his body. Beside him were the bodies of two women and two adolescents, as well a sophisticated security system to ward off grave robbers: the red-colored *sinabrio* dust, which is toxic if inhaled. Another important tomb contained a nobleman sitting in a cross-legged position and wearing a mask and headdress of gold and feathers, surrounded by smaller tombs and niches containing the bodies of one man and 22 young women. The museum is worth the ride out and it's never crowded. Guided tours from Chiclayo to Ferreñafe and Túcume cost around S50 per person, or buses for Ferreñafe (S1.50) leave frequently from Chiclayo's Terminal de Microbuses Epsel.

Túcume
☎ 074 / pop 7900

This is a little-known **site** (☎ 80-0052; adult S8; ☯ 8am-4:30pm Tue-Sun), which lies around 30km to the north of Lambayeque on the Panamericana. A vast area – with more than 200 hectares of crumbling walls, plazas and no fewer than 26 pyramids – it was the final capital of the Sicán culture (see p355), who moved their city from nearby Batán Grande around AD 1050 after that area was devastated by the effects of El Niño. The pyramids you see today are a composite of structures made by several civilizations; the lower levels belonged to the Sicán while the next two levels, along

with the distinctive surrounding walls, were added by the Chimú. While little excavation has been done and no spectacular tombs have been found, it's the sheer size of the site that makes it a memorable visit.

The site can be surveyed from a stunning *mirador* (lookout) atop Cerro Purgatorio (Purgatory Hill). The hill was originally called Cerro la Raya (Stingray Hill), but the name was changed after the Spaniards tried to convert local pagans to Christianity by dressing as demons atop the hill and throwing non-believers to their deaths. There is a small but attractive on-site **museum** (admission free with site ticket) with some interesting tidbits. Guides are available for S15.

Buses from Chiclayo (S2) and Lambayeque (ask at the Bruning Museum) go here. Guided tours cost around S45 per person (p360).

Reserva Ecológica Chaparrí

This 34,000-hectare private **reserve** (☎ 43-3194; www.chaparri.org; admission S12), located 75km east of Chiclayo, was established in 2000 by the community of Santa Catalina and the famous Peruvian wildlife photographer Heinz Plenge. This is one of the few places in the world where you can spot the rare spectacled bear in its natural habitat. This area is an ornithologist's dream, with more than 140 species of birds, including rare white-winged guans, Andean condors, king vultures and several species of eagle. A large number of threatened species are also found here, including pumas, collared anteaters, and Andean weasels. Nearly a third of these vertebrates are not found anywhere else in the world.

You can visit the reserve on your own by catching a bus from Chiclayo's Terminal de Microbuses Epsel to Chongoyape (S4.50), from where you can hire a local guide and car for about S160 to tour the reserve. Alternatively, Moche Tours (p360) in Chiclayo arranges day tours, including transportation and guide, for S78 per person (minimum four people).

Batán Grande & Chota

About halfway from Chiclayo to Chongoyape a minor road on your left leads to the Sicán ruins of **Batán Grande**. This is a major archaeological site where about 50 pyramids have been identified and several burials have been excavated. With the urging of Dr Walter Alva, among others, the site was transformed into the **Santuario Histórico Bosque de Pomac**, but there is no tourist infrastructure. The more-or-less protected reserve lies within one of the largest dry tropical forests in the world and hosts more than 30 species of birds; healthy stands of *algarrobo* (carob tree) offer beautiful shade along the way. As there is almost no public transportation to Batán Grande, you will have to find a taxi or tour to take you.

One of the best ways to visit this area is on horseback from **Rancho Santana** (☎ 97-971-2145, 97-968-7560; www.cabalgatasperu.com; r per person S45) in Pacora, about 45km northeast of Chiclayo. Readers rave about their experiences riding typical Peruvian pacing horses at this Swiss-owned ranch, which also has a comfortable whitewashed villa with a big swimming pool; a real treat is fresh milk and sweet mangos and other tropical fruits always on hand. The owners are highly knowledgeable of Lambayeque cultures and will pick you up in Chiclayo for half-day to five-day *cabalgatas* (horse rides) through the Pomac Forest, Batán Grande and the pyramids at Túcume. The owners care for their horses exceptionally well and can make even the most inexperienced rider feel comfortable. The tours are a great value at S45 for a half-day to S360 for five days. You can also camp for free (with cooking and washing facilities) at the ranch.

A rough but scenic road climbs east from Chongoyape into the Andes until it reaches **Chota** (at an altitude of around 2400m), a 170km journey that takes about eight hours. Two or three buses a day from Chiclayo travel there, from where a daily bus makes the rough journey via Bambamarca and Hualgayoc to Cajamarca (five hours).

Zaña
☎ 074

The old site of this town is a ghost town about 50km southeast of Chiclayo. Founded in 1563, Zaña was once an opulent city that controlled the shipping lanes between Panama and Lima from the nearby Cherrepe port. It was even slated to become the viceroyalty's capital at one stage, but the excessive wealth and rich churches and monasteries soon attracted the eye of robbers and pirates. During the 17th century it was sacked by pirates, including the famous Edward Davis, and survived several slave uprisings, only to be destroyed by the great flood of 1720. Today, great walls and the arches of four churches poke eerily out of the desert sands. Nearby, the present-day village of Zaña houses about 1000 people and is famous for its *brujos*. Stay at the **Centro Vacacional Santa Ana** (☎ 43-1052; Calle de La Torre 102; s/d S26/36). Buses go to the new town from Chiclayo's Terminal de Microbuses Epsel (S2.50).

PIURA
☎ 073 / pop 252,200

After several hours of crossing the vast emptiness of the Sechura Desert, Piura materializes like a mirage on the horizon, enveloped in quivering waves of heat. It's hard to ignore the sense of physical isolation forced on you by this unforgiving environment; the self-sufficiency imposed upon early settlers may explain why they identify as Piuran rather than Peruvian. Being so far inland, the scorching summer months will have you honing your radar for air-conditioning, as you seek out chilled venues in which to soothe your sweltering skin. But the lovely narrow cobbled streets and charismatic colonial houses of central Piura make up for the fact that there's little else for tourists to do here. Its role as a hub for the spokes of the northern towns means that you'll probably end up spending some time here sighing in the relief of the occasional afternoon breeze.

Francisco Pizarro settled the first city in this district in 1532 as he whirred past on his way to trounce the Incas. It was originally located in Sullana, which was not the smartest move, given that the oppressive heat and disease-ridden river there meant that settlers had a rather unpleasant time of it. Fed up, they moved the city around a few times before resettling in Paita on the coast. The run of bad luck continued as Paita was sacked by English pirates in 1577. The very miffed settlers finally moved their city for the last time to its current spot.

Intense irrigation of the desert has made Piura a major agricultural center that feeds the masses, while rich coastal oil fields near Talara run overtime fueling the machinery of development. The department was hard hit by the El Niño floods of 1983, which destroyed almost 90% of the rice, cotton and plantain crops, and also caused serious damage to roads, bridges, buildings and oil wells in the area.

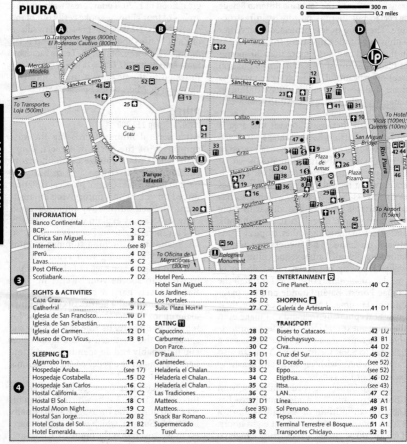

PIURA

0 — 300 m
0 — 0.2 miles

Information

Casas de cambio are at the Ica and Arequipa intersection.

Banco Continental (☎ 33-1702; Tacna 598)

Scotiabank (☎ 32-8200; cnr Huancavelica & Libertad)

BCP (☎ 33-6822; Grau 133)

Clínica San Miguel (☎ 30-9300, 33-5913; Los Cocos 111; ☯ 24hr) The best medical attention in Piura.

Internet (Tacna 630; per hr S2; ☯ 8am-11pm) Plenty of interneting to do here.

iPerú (☎ 32-0249; Ayacucho 377; ☯ 8:30am-7pm Mon- Sat, to 2pm Sun) Has tourist information; the airport also has an iPerú counter.

Lavas (☎ 30-4741; Callao 602; per kg S5) For some reason, laundry services are fiendishly difficult to come by; thankfully, Lavas will wash your *ropas* (clothes).

Oficina de Migraciónes (☎ 33-5536; cnr Sullana & Circunvalación) Does visa extensions.

Post office (☎ 30-9595; cnr Ayacucho & Libertad; ☯ 9am-7pm Mon-Fri, to 1pm Sat) Also on the plaza.

Sights

Jirón Lima, a block east of the Plaza de Armas, has preserved its colonial character more than most areas in Piura.

MUSEUMS

The small **Museo de Oro Vicus** (Museo Municipal; ☎ 30-9267; Huánuco 893; admission S2.50; ☯ 9am-5pm Tue-Sun) has an underground museum with gold from nearby Vicus culture sites. Some excellent pieces are displayed, including a gold belt decorated with a life-sized gold cat head that puts today's belt buckles to shame. The hours here can vary with unexpected closures.

Casa Grau (☎ 32-6541; Tacna 662; admission by donation; ◷ 8am-noon & 3-6pm Mon-Fri, to noon Sat & Sun) is the house where Admiral Miguel Grau was born on July 27, 1834. The house was restored by the Peruvian navy and is now a naval museum. Admiral Grau was a hero of the War of the Pacific against Chile (1879–83), and the captain of the British-built warship *Huáscar*, a model of which can be seen in the museum.

CHURCHES

The **cathedral** on the Plaza de Armas was originally constructed in 1588, when Piura was finally built in its current location. The impressive gold-covered side altar of the Virgin of Fatima, built in the early 17th century, was once the main altar in the church. Famed local artist Ignacio Merino painted the canvas of San Martín de Porres in the mid-19th century.

Other churches worth seeing are the **Iglesia de San Francisco** (Jirón Lima), where Piura's independence was declared on January 4, 1821, and the colonial **Iglesia de San Sebastián** (cnr Moquegua & Tacna) and **Iglesia del Carmen** (Sánchez Cerro), which has a religious art museum and the chair used by the pope in 1985.

Sleeping
BUDGET

Hospedaje Aruba (☎ 30-3067; Junín 851; s/d without bathroom S20/35) All white and bright, the small, Spartan rooms here all share bathrooms. This *hospedaje* (small family-owned inn) has a few random decorations that give it a slight edge over your run-of-the-mill cheapie.

Hostal California (☎ 32-8789; Junín 835; s/d without bathroom S20/35) Popular with shoestring travelers, this clean hotel has small, slightly stuffy rooms with fans and cold showers. Walls are thin, however, so pray for unamorous neighbors.

Hostal Moon Night (☎ 33-6174; Junín 899; s with/without bathroom S26/15, d S38/15) Five floors of passable, faux-wood-lined abodes with evening hot water and cable TV. Grab a top-floor room for some quiet and city views.

Hospedaje San Carlos (☎ 30-6447; Ayacucho 627; s/d S26.50/34) Winning the budget stakes by a nose, this brand-spanking-new little *hospedaje* has immaculate and trim rooms, each with TV. The back rooms are best for light sleepers.

The smiles here are broader and more genuine than anywhere else in town.

Suite Plaza Hostal (☎ 30-6397; www.suiteplazahostal.queydonde.info; Apurímac 420; s/d S40/62; ◻) Although none of the rooms are actually suites, the Suite Plaza has cable TV and wi-fi throughout. The bright hallways and hyper-hygienic rooms make up for the abundance of unimaginative tile and pleather couches.

Los Jardines (☎ 32-6590; Los Cocos 436; s/d S45/70) Located in a smart, quiet residential area around Club Grau, the rooms here are enormous and all have TV. The friendly family who runs the joint offers laundry facilities and shares its small communal garden area.

Hotel San Miguel (☎ 30-5122; Apurímac 1007; s/d S45/75) Modern, sterile and overlooking a quiet park, this place dishes out standard but spotless rooms with cable TV and fans. There's a cafe and the staff is helpful.

Hostal San Jorge (☎ 32-7514; fax 32 2928; Loreto 960; s/d S50/75) This is a cookie-cutter standard-issue hotel with hot showers. There's a pool and all rooms have table fans.

Hotel Perú (☎ 33-3421, fax 33 1530; Arequipa 476; s/d S49/89; ◷) This place has the goods: a pleasant bamboo lounging area, an elegant restaurant (with lots of gold fixtures, unfortunately) and neat, spacious rooms with hot water and TV. Worth its weight in nuevos soles.

Algarrobo Inn (☎ 30-7450; Los Cocos 389; s/d S50/75, d with air-con S75, all with breakfast; ◷) The walled-in compound here has both grass and shade in spades, both at a premium in Piura. Rooms are just OK, but there's a decent restaurant and – this may well be the deal clincher – you get free use of the Club Grau pool next door!

MIDRANGE

Hotel Vicus (☎ 34-3201; Guardia Civil B-3; s/d S70/80; ◲) The well-appointed rooms here are spaced out around a drive-in, motel-style layout and have everything you might crave, except air-con. They're neat and spotless nonetheless, with lots of splashy color; there's also room service.

Hostal El Sol (☎ 32-4461, 32-6307; mailservitucoral@terra.com.pe; Sánchez Cerro 455; s/d S80/120; ◲) An elegant lobby leads to rooms that are good-sized and reasonable value, with a ceiling fan and cable TV. A restaurant is available for breakfast and a S4 to S6 *menú* (set meal).

Hotel Esmeralda (☎ 33-1205, 33-1782; www.hotelesmeralda.com.pe; Loreto 235; s/d with air-con S115/170, all with breakfast; ◷ ◻) This place is a shining white-and-bright cocktail of glass, gold and tiles. The carpeted rooms look like they were decorated by your grandmother, but are comfy and have cable TV, phone and mini-fridge. There is an elevator, restaurant and room service, and the staff is efficient and helpful.

Hotel Costa del Sol (☎ /fax 30-2864; www.costadel solperu.com; Loreto 649; s/d S212/289; ✿ 🖳 🖭) This attractive old-fashioned hotel has a well-stocked bar, elegant restaurant with room service, Jacuzzi, small gym and a casino (naturally). Well-kept and comfortably furnished rooms offer cable TV, a direct-dial phone and minibar. Ask about airport transfers.

TOP END

Los Portales (☎ 32-3072, 32-1161; losportales@cpi.udep .edu.pe; Libertad 875; s/d/ste with breakfast S270/340/410; ✿ 🖳 🖭) Live out dreams of conquistador grandeur in this beautiful and fully refurbished colonial building on the Plaza de Armas. Handsome public areas with iron grillwork and black-and-white checkered floor lead to a poolside restaurant and rooms with large cable TV, minibar and great beds. Unfortunately, the conquistador doesn't sleep well here – the downstairs bar blares music on the weekends and there's odd elevator music playing throughout the building at all hours.

Eating

To tuck into some regional delicacies, a lunchtime trip to the nearby town of Catacaos is a must. Vegetarians will be pleased by Piura's wealth of non-meat options.

D'Pauli (Jirón Lima 451; cakes from S1; ✿ 9am-1pm & 4-10pm) Leave room for dessert after your meal and visit here – it's a great cake shop.

Heladería el Chalán (Tacna 520; snacks S1.50-8; ✿ 7:30am-10pm) This fast-food joint has multiple outlets whipping up burgers and sandwiches, but our money's on the excellent selection of juices and the dozens of flavors of cool, cool ice cream. There are also branches at Grau 173 and 453.

Ganimedes (☎ 32-9176; Jirón Lima 440; menús S6, mains S6-8; ✿ 7am-10pm Mon-Sat, 11am-9pm Sun) No goat-head soups here, but plenty of refreshing fruit juices, yummy yogurts, wholegrain biscuits and lots and lots of salads. Ganimedes doubles as a whole-grain bakery, making it a great place to stock your picnic basket or to try their signature focaccia.

Las Tradiciones (☎ 32-2683; Ayacucho 579; menús S5, mains S6-18; ✿ 10am-10pm) With wicker chairs spread throughout a gently crumbling colonial building, this is another decent place to sample cheap local fare.

Snack Bar Romano (☎ 32-3399; Ayacucho 580; menús S6, mains S9-21; ✿ 7am-11pm, closed Sun) With an excellent *menú*, this local favorite has been around as long as its middle-aged waiters. It gets the double thumbs-up for ceviches and local specialties.

Matteos (☎ 30-8096; Libertad 487; meals S6-12; ✿ 7am-10pm) With two central locations, Matteos serves as an antidote to the hills of *parrillada* found all over Peru. The all-veggie menu has lots of I-can't-believe-it's-not-meat versions of local dishes, salads and heaped plates of fruit and yogurt. The second branch is at Tacna 532.

Don Parce (Tacna 642; ☎ 30-0842; mains S6-18; ✿ 7am-11pm) Serving a long list of Peruvian standards as well as daily specials, Don Parce is an inviting lunch and dinner spot in a convenient location off the Plaza de Armas. The best deal is a three-course lunch *menú*, always with a hearty, meaty main dish.

Carburmer (☎ 30-9475; Libertad 1014; mains S12-27; ✿ 6-11pm; ✿) This cozy and romantic place is the best Italian restaurant in town. Dripping with moodily lit ambience (check out the wacky pulley system that opens the door), this is the ideal place for that special night out. It has an excellently executed menu where Italian dishes vie for your attention with Peruvian specialties.

our pick Capuccino (☎ 30-1111; www.capuccino -piura.com; Tacna 786; meals S12-28; ✿ 10am-11pm Mon-Sat) Recently relocated into a beautiful dining room with modern decor, Capuccino serves upscale salads, fresh seafood, sandwiches and desserts that work great for both light lunches or full dinners with a bottle of wine. Try the elegant and simple appetizer of grilled squid with olive oil. For caffeine freaks, Capuccino is the only place in town serving real-deal espressos and coffee drinks.

Supermercado Tusol (Plaza Grau; ✿ 8:30am-10:30pm) is good for self-catering.

Drinking

Queens (cnr Guardia Civil & Cayeta; admission S20; ✿ 9pm-late Thu-Sun) If you really need to shake your rump, head down to Queens, which is not in New York, but just east of town. On rowdy weekend nights the place is filled with gringos and well-heeled Peruvians shakin' their money-makers to an eclectic international music mix.

Entertainment

Cine Planet (☎ 30-3714; Huancavelica 537; admission S6-9) In a brand-spanking-new shopping complex, this cinema shows Hollywood flicks in blissful air-conditioned comfort.

Shopping

The **Galería de Artesanía** (☎ 78-3247; cnr Huánuco & Libertád; ☽ 9:30am-1:30pm & 4-8pm Mon-Sat) is actually a tiny mall of about a dozen different craft shops featuring regional specialties from baskets to weavings to Chulucanas pottery. With fair and negotiable prices, it's a great stop if you don't have time to go to the outlying craft towns.

Getting There & Away

AIR

The **airport** (PIU; ☎ 34-4505) is on the southeastern bank of the Río Piura, 2km from the city center. Schedules change often. The usual S11 airport tax is charged.

LAN (☎ 30-2145; Grau 140) flies from Lima to Piura at 4am, noon, 4pm, and 7pm daily, returning to Lima at 6:15am, 2:15pm, 6:15pm and 9:15pm. LAN also has at least two flights per day to Chiclayo, leaving between 4pm and 10pm; the planes immediately turn around to return to Lima.

BUS
International
The standard route to Ecuador goes along the Panamericana via Tumbes to Machala. Alternatively, **Transportes Loja** (☎ 30-9407; Sánchez Cerro 228) goes via La Tina to Macará (S12, four hours) and Loja (S28, eight hours) at 9:30am, 8:45pm and 9:30pm. These buses stop for border formalities, then continue. For warnings about the Ecuador–Peru border, see the boxed text, p382.

Domestic
Services to Lima take 12 to 16 hours. Several companies have offices on the 1100 block of Sánchez Cerro, though for Cajamarca and across the northern Andes, it's best to go to Chiclayo and get a connection there.

Chinchaysuyo (☎ 30-4651; Sánchez Cerro 1156) Has been known to run direct buses to Huaraz (S52, 12 to 14 hours) at 10:30pm.

Civa (☎ 34 5451; Tacna 101) Has a 5pm and a 6pm bus to Lima (S45 to S62.50, 15 hours), frequent buses to Chulucanas (S2.50, 45 minutes), and a bus to Huancabamba (S24, eight to 10 hours) at 8:30am. On the east side of the river.

Cruz del Sur (☎ 33-7094; Bolognesi at Jirón Lima) has a Lima bus (S89 to S129) at 6pm.

El Dorado (☎ 32-5875, 33-6952; Sánchez Cerro 1119) Buses for Tumbes (S14, five hours) every two hours, and six buses a day to Máncora (S18, 2½ hours).

El Poderoso Cautivo (☎ 30-9888; Sullana Norte 7) Buses for Ayabaca (S18, six hours) at 8:30am and 3pm.

Eppo (☎ 30-4543, Sánchez Cerro 1141) Has buses to Sullana (S2, 45 minutes) and Talara (S8, two hours) every 30 minutes. Also fast services to Máncora (S11, 3½ hours) hourly.

Etipthsa (☎ 34-5174; Tacna 277) Buses to Huancabamba (S23, eight to 10 hours) leaving at 7:30am and 5:30pm.

Ittsa (☎ 33-3982; Sánchez Cerro 1142) Has a bus to Trujillo (S10 to S28, six hours) and Chimbote (S23, seven hours) at 11pm, and a *bus-cama* to Lima at 6:30pm (S90).

Línea (☎ 32-7821; Sánchez Cerro 1215) Hourly buses to Chiclayo (S12, three hours) between 5am and 8pm, and a 2pm and 11pm bus to Trujillo (S15 to S45, six hours).

Sol Peruano (☎ 41-8143; Sánchez Cerro 1112) Goes direct to Tarapoto at 1pm (S45, 18 hours).

Tepsa (☎ 30-6345, Loreto 1198) Lima buses (S78) at 5pm and 7:30pm.

Transportes Chiclayo (☎ 30-8455; Sánchez Cerro 1121) Hourly buses to Chiclayo (S11, three hours) and a bus to Tumbes (S20, five hours) at 10am.

Transportes Vegas (☎ 30 -8729; Panamericana C1, Lot 10) Has buses leaving for Ayabaca (S21, six hours) at 7:15am and 3pm.

East of the San Miguel pedestrian bridge, buses and *combis* leave for Catacaos (S1, 15 minutes). Sullana (S2, 45 minutes) and Paita (S2.50, one hour) buses leave from **Terminal Terrestre el Bosque** (Sánchez Cerro, cuadra 12).

TAXI
If you are heading to Tumbes, you can catch a much faster *colectivo* taxi (S18 to S20, 3½ hours).

CATACAOS
☎ 073 / pop 64,200
Catacaos, a bustling small town 12km southwest of Piura, is the self-proclaimed capital of *artesanía* (handicrafts) in the region. And justifiably so: its **arts market** (☽ 10am-4pm) is the best in northern Peru. Sprawling for several

blocks near the Plaza de Armas, here you will find excellent weavings, gold and silver filigree jewelry, wood carvings, ceramics (including lots of pieces from Chulucanas), leather goods and more. The weekends are the best and busiest times to visit.

Not satisfied with the *artesanía* crown, Catacaos is also shooting for the culinary medal, with dozens of *picanterías* (local restaurants) open for lunch daily. You can get local specialties like *chicha, seco de chabelo* (a thick plantain and beef stew), *seco de cabrito* (kid goat), *tamales verdes* (green corn dumplings), *copus* (dried goat heads cured in vinegar and then stewed) and loads of other dishes, not all of them that adventurous. Several good *picanterías* advertising their specialities are located on Jirón Zepita off the Plaza de Armas.

Catacaos is famous for its elaborate **Semana Santa** (Holy Week) processions and celebrations. Reach it by *colectivo* on the east side of the San Miguel pedestrian bridge in Piura (S1, 15 minutes).

PAITA

☎ 073 / pop 72,000

The main port of the department of Piura is the historic town of Paita, 50km due west of Piura by paved road. This dusty, crumbling colonial port town looks like it sprouted organically from the desert that surrounds it and has a roguish, Wild West feel to it – understandable when you look at its history.

In 1527, Pizarro became the first European to land here, and Paita has been attracting seafaring conquistadors ever since. It became a Spanish colonial port and was frequently sacked by pirates and swashbuckling buccaneers such as Sir Francis Drake. Raids continued, and in the 18th century Protestant adventurer George Anson attempted to decapitate the wooden statue of Our Lady of Mercy. The statue, complete with slashed neck, can still be seen in the church of La Merced. The only flotilla you're likely to see nowadays is a scrappy Technicolor shipping fleet bobbing offshore.

Information

There are several banks here and a basic hospital.

Sights & Activities

Manuela Sáenz, the influential Ecuadorean mistress of Simón Bolívar, arrived here upon Bolívar's death in 1850. Her **house** still stands

(and people live there), and a plaque commemorates its history. Across the street is **La Figura**, a wooden figurehead from a pirate ship.

To the north and south of the port are good beaches popular with summer holidaymakers. About 13km north (by road) is the good beach of **Colán**, home to the oldest colonial church in Peru. This whitesand beach is a trendy summer destination for the Peruvian jet set, but is practically deserted the rest of the year. The curving bay has a shallow beach that's excellent for swimming.

The beach of **Yasila**, some 12km to the south, is also popular.

Sleeping & Eating
PAITA

Despite the town's historic interest and beaches, Paita has only a few hotels, and most visitors stay in Piura.

our pick Hostal Miramar (☎ 21-1083; Jorge Chávez 418; d S40) Our pick of the bunch is this place, housed in a funky, weathered colonial building standing at bright orange alert on the waterfront. There are bright pastel colors throughout and the massive rooms have tall ceilings and large windows.

Hostal Las Brisas (☎ 21-2175; fax 61-2175; Ayurura 201 at Ugarte; s/d from S45/90) This place has small, carpeted rooms with phones, cable TV, hot-water bathrooms and a hospital-white restaurant.

Hotel El Faro (☎ 32-0322; Junín 320; s/d S60/85) This hotel has bigger rooms near the waterfront, though they're tattered and vary from downright stuffy to bright and airy.

Tiny fresh-seafood stands line the waterway near the main pier. The best place to eat is **Club Liberal** (☎ 61-1173; Jorge Chávez 162; meals S10-18; ☺ 7am-10pm), which has creaky wooden floors and lots of rickety charm in its 2ndfloor pier location; the breezy, sweeping vistas are excellent.

COLÁN

Hospedaje Frente del Mar (☎ 9-66-6914; d S22) Run by the ever-helpful Alfredo, this *hospedaje* has a good seaside restaurant and rents out a couple of 'rustic' rooms at the back.

Bahía del Sol (☎ 9-97-6488; bahiadelsol_colan@hotmail.com; r S78 per person) On the south part of the beach, this spot has clean, austere, modern rooms sleeping up to four people.

Playa Colán Lodge (☎ 32-6778; 2-/4-/5-person cabin S195/225/255; ⚑)) Further south, this has to be the best place to stay. Built from a combination of natural materials it has an upmarket Robinson Crusoe feel and hosts cute, pastel-colored bungalows along the beach. There are lots of hammocks, shady palm trees, a tennis court, plus restaurant and bar. In the low season ask for a S50 discount.

Getting There & Away

There are buses every 10 minutes to Paita from the Terminal Terrestre el Bosque in Piura (S2.50, one hour). *Colectivos* leave from the main terminal in Paita, near the market, to Colán (S2, 20 minutes) and Sullana (S3.20, 1¼ hours).

SULLANA

☎ 073 / pop 144,800 / elev 90m

Abandoned as a location for modern-day Piura, Sullana today is a hot and dusty little city with several parks and more shops than you can poke a S20 bill at. It's also a transportation hub for destinations north of Piura.

There's little to see here except the hustle and bustle of a commercial Peruvian market town. Still, you'll meet a lot of folks in this region who hail from Sullana, and it can be a good conversation-starter to mention that you've passed through.

Be wary of personal safety outside central areas and take *mototaxis* to and from the outskirts of town.

Decent budget hotels include the **Hostal Lion's Palace** (☎ 50-2587; Grau 1030; s/d S25/60), with large, dark and cool rooms with bathrooms, and the slightly more spiffy **Hostal El Churre** (☎ 50-7006; Tarapacá 501; s/d S35/54), which has contemporary rooms that get a bit of noise due to its corner location. The best is **Hostal La Siesta** (☎ /fax 50-2264; Av La Panamericana 404; s/d from S85/120; ▨ ⚑)), on the outskirts of town, with hot water (but do you really need it?), cable TV and a restaurant.

Restaurant Park Plaza (☎ 50-9904; Plaza de Armas; menús S5; ☽ 8am-10pm) is owned by a fanatical fan of Hollywood (the walls are covered with pictures of stars) and has a good Peruvian menu.

Buses to Piura leave from the **Terminal Terrestre** (José de Lama 481) every few minutes (S2, 45 minutes). There are also buses to Máncora (S9, 2½ hours).

CHULUCANAS

☎ 073 / pop 55,000 / elev 95m

This village is about 55km east of Piura, just before the Sechura Desert starts rising into the Andean slopes. It's known Peru-wide for its distinctive ceramics – rounded, glazed, earth-colored pots that depict humans. Chulucanas' ceramics have officially been declared a part of Peru's cultural heritage and are becoming famous outside Peru.

The best place to buy ceramics around here is in La Encantada, a quiet rural outpost just outside of Chulucanas, whose inhabitants work almost exclusively in *artesanía*. La Encantada was home to the late Max Inga, a local legend who studied ceramic artifacts from the ancient Tallan and Vicus cultures and sparked a resurgence in the art form. The friendly artisans are often happy to demonstrate the production process, from the 'harvesting' of the clay to the application of mango-leaf smoke to get that distinctive black-and-white design. The village is reached from Chulucanas by a 10-minute *mototaxi* ride (around S5).

There are a few basic hotels in Chulucanas, including **Hostal Chulucanas Soler** (☎ 37-8576; Ica 209; s/d S20/36), two blocks from the plaza.

Civa has frequent buses to and from Piura (S2, 45 minutes).

HUANCABAMBA

☎ 073 / pop 8000 / elev 1957m

For the daring adventurer, Huancabamba, deep in the eastern mountains, is well worth the rough 10-hour journey from Piura. This region is famed in Peru for the powerful *brujos* and *curanderos* (healers) who live and work at the nearby lakes of Huaringas. Peruvians from all over the country flock to partake in these ancient healing techniques (see p374). Many locals (but few gringos) visit the area, so finding information and guides is not difficult.

The mystical town of Huancabamba is surrounded by mountains shrouded in mist and lies at the head of the long, narrow Río Huancabamba. The banks of the Huancabamba are unstable and constantly eroding and the town is subject to frequent subsidence and slippage. It has earned itself the nickname *La Ciudad que Camina* (the Town that Walks). Spooky.

There's a small **tourist information office** (☎ 47-3321; ☽ 8am-6pm) at the bus station that has an elementary map of the area and a list

SHOPPING FOR SHAMANS

When people from the West think of witchcraft, visions of pointed hats, broomsticks and bubbling brews are rarely far away. In Peru, consulting *brujos* (witch doctors) and *curanderos* (healers) is widely accepted and has a long tradition predating Spanish colonization.

Peruvians from all walks of life visit *brujos* and *curanderos* and often pay sizable amounts of money for their services. These shamans are used to cure an endless list of ailments, from headaches to cancer to chronic bad luck, and are particularly popular in matters of love – whether it's love lost, love found, love desired or love scorned.

The **Huaringas** lake area near Huancabamba (p373), almost 4000m above sea level, is said to have potent curative powers and attracts a steady stream of visitors from all corners of the continent. The most famous lake in the area is **Laguna Shimbe**, though the nearby **Laguna Negra** is the one most frequently used by the *curanderos*.

Ceremonies can last all night and entail hallucinogenic plants (such as the San Pedro cactus), singing, chanting, dancing and a dip in the lakes' painfully freezing waters. Some ceremonies involve more powerful substances like *ayahuasca* (Quechua for 'vine of the soul'), a potent and vile mix of jungle vines used to induce strong hallucinations. Vomiting is a common side effect. The *curanderos* will also use *ícaros*, which are mystical songs and chants used to direct and influence the spiritual experience. Serious *curanderos* will spend many years studying the art, striving for the hard-earned title of *maestro curandero*.

If you are interested in visiting a *curandero* while in Huancabamba, be warned that this tradition is taken very seriously and gawkers or skeptics will get a hostile reception. *Curanderos* with the best reputation are found closer to the lake district. The information booth at the bus station has a list of registered *curanderos*. In Salala, closer to the lakes, you will be approached by *curanderos* or their 'agents', but be wary of scam artists – try to get a reference before you arrive. Know also that there are some *brujos* who are said to work *en el lado oscuro* (on the dark side). Expect to pay around S200 for a visit.

These days, busy Peruvian professionals can get online and consult savvy, business-minded shamans via instant messenger. Not quite the same thing as midnight chants and icy dunks in the remote lakes of the Andes.

of accredited *brujos* and *curanderos*. You can also change US dollars at the bus station. There's a basic **hospital** (☎ 47-3024).

Hotels are all rudimentary and most share cold-water bathrooms. **Hostal-El Dorado** (☎ 47-3016; Medina 116; s/d without bathroom S12/18) is on the Plaza de Armas, and has one of the best restaurants in town, and a helpful owner. **Hospedaje Tres Estrellas** (☎ 47-3077; San Martín 115; s/d without bathroom S20/27) is another bare-bones budget deal in an old building on the plaza; it also has ludicrously friendly staff. **Hostal Danubio** (☎ 47-3200; Grau 206; s/d S25/30, without bathroom S15/25), on the corner of the plaza, has the most solid rooms in town, all with TVs.

Restaurants to try include the busy **Casa Blanca** (Unión 304; menús S3.50, meals S4-6; ☑ 7am-11pm), which serves Peruvian food and has a cheap *menú*. The local beverage is *rompope*, a concoction of sugarcane alcohol with raw egg, honey, lemon and spices – a pauper's pisco sour.

At the Huancabamba bus terminal, **Etipthsa** (☎ 47-3000), **Civa** (☎ 47-3488) and **Turismo Express** (☎ 47-3320) each have a morning service between 7am and 9am to Piura (S23 to S24, 10 to 11 hours). Two afternoon buses also depart for Piura at 4:30pm and 5pm. To visit the lakes, catch the 5am *combi* from this terminal to the town of Salala (S9, two hours), from where you can arrange treks to the lakes (S20 return).

AYABACA
☎ 073 / pop 5500 / elev 2715m

For the final three hours of the journey between Piura and Ayabaca (sometimes spelled Ayavaca), the bumpy road starts to climb through cultivated fields and dense clouds and doesn't stop until it reaches the pretty town of Ayabaca.

This aged colonial highland hamlet is surrounded by green valleys and cloud forest peaks darting out of the fog. Ayabaca's Plaza de Armas is graced by a 17th-century cathedral with a gold-plated altar and some religious paintings from the Quito school of art, while almost every little house in town seems to adhere to the whitewash neocolonial style with adobe brick walls and wooden balconies. This is small-town highland life at its tranquil best.

Information

You can change US dollars at the **Banco de la Nación** (Grau 448). Limited tourist information is available at the **municipalidad** (☎ 47 1003; Cáceres 578), on the Plaza de Armas.

Sights & Activities

The overgrown Inca site of **Aypate** (admission free) contains walls, flights of stairs, terraces (some still in use), ceremonial baths and a central plaza. This territory here is stunning and you will see hazy mountains full of orchids, bromeliads, birds, white-tailed deer and other species. It's about five hours by truck on a rough road, then a very short hike to the center of the ruins.

There are other, unexplored Inca and pre-Inca sites in the area. Some utterly fascinating and understudied petroglyphs are scattered around the tile-roofed hamlets of Yanchala, El Toldo and Espíndola near the Ecuadorean border, and mysterious caves, lakes and mountains – some of which are said to be bewitched – are explorable.

Ornithologists report outstanding **birdwatching** habitats. All in all, the Ayabaca region offers weeks of adventures rarely undertaken by gringos.

Visit the area in the May to November dry season when the trails are passable. **Raul Bardales** (☎ 47-1043; Piura 331) guides tourists to Aypate (S150 to S200 per person per day). **Segundo Celso Acuña Calle** (☎ 47-1209; Cáceres 257) is very knowledgeable on the area, and will talk your ear off if you go with him on one of his five-day treks S150 per person per day, guiding only), which take in Inca ruins and trails, pre-Inca sites and lagoons. You might also find him at the town's little museum, which houses some local archeological pieces, on the Plaza de Armas.

Festivals & Events

Held from October 12 to 15, the gaudy religious festival of **El Señor Cautivo**, rarely seen by tourists, packs every hotel in town. Pilgrims pour in from all over the country to pay tribute to the statue of the Señor Cautivo, which sits in the town's cathedral throughout the year; some have walked continuously for months from and Ecuador and crawl their last few miles on hands and knees. It's an unforgettable sight.

Sleeping & Eating

Hostal Alex (☎ 47-1101; Bolívar 112; s/d without bathroom S10/15) One of the cheapest choices in town.

Hostal Oro Verde (☎ 41-1056; Salaverry 381; r per person without bathroom S10, s/d S30/40) Just off the plaza, this place has the usual budget barebones rooms as well as much nicer, newer rooms with TV, bathroom and steaming hot water.

Hotel Samanga Municipal (☎ /fax 47-1049; s/d S28/40) On the Plaza de Armas, Hotel Samanga Municipal is the pick of the bunch, with friendly staff, a decent restaurant and rooms with TV and hot showers.

For meals, there are *pollerías* aplenty, but the best restaurant is **Flor de Milan** (☎ 47-1093; Tacna 111; meals S3-9; ◷ 7am-10pm), with fancy checkered tablecloths and a small menu serving local dishes. **Oasis** (☎ 47-1095; Arequipa 215; ◷ 9am-5pm) specializes in ceviches and *chicharrones* (deep-fried chunks of pork).

Getting There & Away

Transportes Vegas (☎ 47-1080) and **El Poderoso Cautivo** (☎ 47-1478) on the plaza both have buses to Piura (S18, six hours); Vegas goes at 8:15am and 6pm; El Poderoso Cautivo goes at 8:30am, 9:30am and 6pm.

TALARA
☎ 073 / pop 100,400

Once a small fishing village, Talara today is the site of Peru's largest oil refinery, producing 60,000 barrels of petroleum a day. Although there are some good beaches near Talara, the town has little to interest the tourist. It's a good idea for women travelers to stay alert.

Negritos, 11km south of Talara by road, is on Punta Pariñas and is the most westerly point of the South American continent.

Some 20 hotels house oil workers, but water supply is an ongoing problem. **Hostal Grau** (☎ 38-2841; Grau 77A; s/d S20/35) is clean and friendly and has hot water for part of the day. **Gran Hotel Pacífico** (☎ 38-5449; s/d S72/127; ▨ ▨) is the best place in town and has a bar, cafe and restaurant.

Star Perú flies from Lima to Talara with a stop in Cajamarca. The flight leaves the capital at 12:30pm and returns at 3:30pm.

Buses leave for Piura (S7, two hours) and Tumbes (S7, two hours), stopping in Máncora (S3, 40 minutes) at least every hour.

CABO BLANCO
☎ 073

The Pan-American Hwy runs parallel to the ocean north of Talara, with frequent glimpses of the coast. This area is one of Peru's main oil fields, and pumps are often seen scarring both the land and the sea with offshore oil rigs.

About 40km north of Talara is the sleepy town of Cabo Blanco, one of the world's most famous fishing spots. Set on a gently curving bay strewn with rocks, the town has a flotilla of fishing vessels floating offshore where the confluence of warm Humboldt currents and El Niño waters creates a unique microcosm filled with marine life. Ernest Hemingway was supposedly inspired to write his famous tale *The Old Man and the Sea* after fishing here in the early 1950s. The largest fish ever landed on a rod here was a 710kg black marlin, caught in 1953 by Alfred Glassell Jr. The angling is still good, though 20kg tuna are a more likely catch than black marlin, which have declined and are now rarely over 100kg. Fishing competitions are held here and 300kg specimens are still occasionally caught. From November to January, magnificent 3m-high pipeline waves attract hard-core surfers.

La Cristina is a 32ft deep-sea fishing boat, with high-quality Penn tackle, which can be rented through Hostal Merlin and other hotels in the area for US$350 per six-hour day, including drinks and lunch. January, February and September are considered the best fishing months.

Hostal Merlin (☎ 25-6188; s/d with breakfast S69/99) has 12 massive rooms with handsome stone-flagged floors, private cold showers and balconies with ocean views. This cavernous hotel doesn't get many visitors.

Cabo Blanco is several kilometers down a winding road from the Pan-American Hwy town of Las Olas. Catch a ride in one of the regular pickup trucks that ply the route (S2, 20 minutes).

MÁNCORA
☎ 073 / pop 9700

Peru's worst-kept secret, Máncora is *the* place to see and be seen along the Peruvian coast – in the summer months foreigners flock here to rub sunburned shoulders with the frothy cream of the Peruvian jet set. It's not hard to see why – Peru's best sandy beach stretches for several kilometers in the sunniest region of the country, while dozens of plush resorts and their budget-conscious brethren offer up rooms within meters of the lapping waves. On shore, a plethora of restaurants provides fresh seafood straight off the boat as fuel for the long, lazy days. The consistently good surf draws a sun-bleached, board-toting bunch and raucous nightlife keeps visitors busy after the sun dips into the sea in a ball of fiery flames. However, even though it has seen recent explosive growth, Máncora has somehow managed to cling to its fishing community roots.

Located about halfway between Talara and Tumbes, Máncora has the Pan-American

---

BORDER CROSSING: ECUADOR VIA LA TINA

The border post of La Tina lacks hotels, but the Ecuadorean town of Macará (3km from the border) has adequate facilities. La Tina is reached by *colectivo* (shared transportations) taxis (S18, two hours) leaving Sullana throughout the day. **Transportes Loja** (☎ 073-30-9407; Sánchez Cerro 228, Piura) buses from Piura conveniently go straight through here and on to Loja (S32, eight hours).

The border is the international bridge over the Río Calvas and is open 24 hours. Formalities are relaxed as long as your documents are all in order. There are no banks, though you'll find money changers at the border or in Macará. The Peruvian immigration office is on the left, before the international office.

Travelers entering Ecuador will find taxis (US$1) and *colectivos* (US$0.25) to take them to Macará, where the Ecuadorean immigration building is found on the second floor of the *municipalidad* (town hall), on the plaza. Most nationalities are simply given a T3 tourist card, which must be surrendered when leaving, and granted 90 days' stay in Ecuador. There is a Peruvian consulate in Macará. See Lonely Planet's *Ecuador & the Galápagos Islands* for further information on Ecuador.

Hwy passing right through its middle, within 100m of the surf. During the December to March summer period, the scene can get rowdy and accommodation prices tend to double. But year-round sun means that this is one of the few resort towns on the coast that doesn't turn into a ghost town at less popular times.

Orientation

The Pan-American Hwy, called Calle Piura at the south end of town and Calle Grau at the north, is the main drag, with businesses lining both sides. From the bridge at the south end, the Antigua (Old) Panamericana is a dirt road following the coast and sprinkled with remote, upscale hotels. The Antigua rejoins the Pan-American Hwy about 12km further south near Los Organos.

Addresses are not used much here – just look for signs in the center.

Information

There is no information office, but the website www.vivamancora.com has tons of useful information. Two ATMs (no bank) accept Visa and MasterCard.

Banco de la Nación (☎ 25-8193; Piura 625; ⏰ 8:30am-2:30pm Mon-Fri) Change US dollars here.

Costa Norte Lavandería (Piura 212; per kg S5) Hours vary at the laundry; knock even if they look closed.

Emergency 24 Hrs (☎ 25-8713; Piura 306; ⏰ 24 hr) If you get stung by a ray or break a bone, head to this full-service clinic.

Internet Marlon (☎ 25-2437; Piura 520; per hr S2; ⏰ 9am-midnight) Attached to Marlon; has the newest computers and the most reliable service.

Marlon (☎ 25-2437; Piura 520) The best general store; it sells phonecards and has several telephone booths.

Activities

There are remote, deserted beaches around Máncora; ask your hotel to arrange a taxi or give you directions by bus and foot, but be prepared to walk several kilometers.

SURFING & KITESURFING

Surf here is best from November to February, although good waves are found year-round and always draw dedicated surfers. In addition to Máncora, Los Organos, Lobitos, Talara and Cabo Blanco are popular surfing spots for experienced surfers. You can rent surfboards from several places at the southern end of the beach in Máncora (per

day S15 to S20). **Soledad** (☎ 929-1356; Piura 316) sells boards, surf clothing and organizes lessons for about S60 per hour (including board rental). The friendly Pilar, at **Laguna Camp** (☎ 9-401-5628; www.vivamancora.com/lagunacamp), also does surf lessons for S60 for 90 minutes of instruction (including board rental). For something a little more extreme, you can get lessons in kitesurfing (per hour S120); ask about it at **Del Wawa** (☎ 25-8427; www.delwawa.com).

MUD BATHS

About 11km east of town, up the wooded Fernández valley, a natural **hot spring** (admission S2) has bubbling water and powder-fine mud – perfect for a face pack. The slightly sulfurous water and mud is said to have curative properties. The hot spring can be reached by *mototaxi* (S35 including waiting time).

TREKKING

To see some of the interior of this desert coast, hire a pickup (around S75, including waiting time) to take you up the Fernández valley, past the mud baths and on until the road ends (about 1½ hours). Continue for two hours on foot through mixed woodlands with unique birdlife to reach Los Pilares, which has pools ideal for swimming. You can also visit these areas as part of a tour.

OTHER ACTIVITIES

Máncora Rent (Hospedaje Las Terrazas; ☎ 25-8351; Piura 496) rents off-road motorbikes (per hour/24 hours S18/95) as well as small quad bikes for teens (per hour S60) and jet skis (per 30 minutes S100). For transportation with a mind of its own, **horses** are available for hire along the beach for S18 per hour.

Tours & Guides

Ursula Behr from **Iguana's** (☎ 9-853-5099; www.vivamancora.com/iguanastrips; Piura 245) organizes full-day trips to the Los Pilares dry forest, which include wading through sparkling waterfalls, swimming, horseback riding and a soak in the mud baths, for S90 per person. She's also a professional rafting guide (she earned her stripes in Cuzco) and has set up a two-day class III river-running trip through the tropical forest at Rica Playa (per person about S300). Sea kayaking trips, ideal for bird-spotting, cost S110 per person for the day.

Sleeping

Rates for accommodations in Máncora are seasonal, with the January to mid-March high season commanding prices up to 50% higher than the rest of the year, especially at weekends. During the three major holiday periods (Christmas to New Year, Semana Santa and Fiestas Patrias) accommodations can cost triple the low-season rate, require multinight stays and be very crowded; this time is generally best avoided. High-season rates are given here. Many pricier hotels accept payment in US dollars.

BUDGET

Budget rooms are spendier here than other parts of the coast, but there are cheap beds in *hospedajes* in the center of town and the southern part of the beach. Most places offer triples and quad rooms for slightly less per person.

Hospedaje Don Carlos (☎ 25-8007; Piura 641; s/d S16/32) Of the many cheap places in the center of Máncora, this is among the best run, with helpful owners. Barely passable concrete rooms sleep two to six and have cold water showers and fans.

Laguna Camp (☎ 9-401-5628; www.vivamancora .com/lagunacamp; r per person S18) This laid-back pad is a hidden gem, sandwiched between the town's lagoon and the ocean. Indonesian-style bamboo bungalows sit around a pleasant sandy garden right near the water and lots of swinging, shady hammocks will provide days of entertainment. There's a small communal kitchen and the whole vibe is chilled and friendly. The cheery owner, Pilar, is also a surf instructor.

HI La Posada (☎ 25-8328; Panamericana Km 1164; campsites per person S5, dm/s/d S18/23/35) La Posada is a hushed compound close to the beach and perennially popular with backpackers. Safe, with a pleasant garden, hammocks and basic kitchen facilities, this HI-affiliated *hostal* has recently added a restaurant and has improved, more comfortable rooms. Owner-manager Luisa goes out of her way to make guests feel comfortable. It's by the bridge at the southern end of town.

Hospedaje Crillón (☎ 25-8017; Paita 168; r per person with/without bathroom S24/18) One quiet block back from the beach, this place has cubbylike cells with four walls, four beds and no room for anything else – though surfers manage to get their boards in here. It is surprisingly busy.

Hostal Sausalito (☎ 25-8058, in Lima 01-479 0779; jcvigoe@terra.com.pe; Piura, cuadra 4; s/d S30/45) If the intense colors of the walls here don't keep you up at night, the traffic noise might. The tiny rooms are acceptably clean and well kept, plus they have TVs and ceiling fans. Be careful with your valuables though.

El Pirata (☎ 25-8459; www.vivamancora.com/elpirata; Panamericana Km 1164; s/d S32/48, s/d without bathroom S22.50/29) A mishmash of austere, split-bamboo rooms, some with more gaps in the walls than bamboo. Other, slightly more solid rooms have attached bathrooms. There's a kitchen, a few hammocks to laze in and little else. It's very relaxed and the owners have a laissez-faire attitude to the whole endeavor.

Casa Palmera (☎ 9825-8793; r per person S45) Behind Las Olas, the new rooms here are in a bright lemon-colored building and face a small patch of vibrant grass. The abodes are immaculate and quiet, but lack any view. It's one row of houses back from the beach.

ourpick Del Wawa (☎ 25-8427; www.delwawa.com; s/d S45/75) This surfer's mecca has a great set-up right on the beach with warm-colored adobe rooms all facing the ocean. There are lots of hammocks, a chill space with great views of the best breaks on the beach, and surfboard rental. Del Wawa also organizes kitesurfing lessons for S120 per hour.

Hostal las Olas (☎ 25-8099; lasolasmancora@yahoo .com; r per person with breakfast S70) Rooms here are minimalist white and some come with ocean views, though they're all the same price. The small, cozy restaurant looks onto the beach's best breaks and is a surf-spotter's dream. You can rent boards here for S18.

MIDRANGE

South of Máncora, along Antigua Panamericana, are multiple tranquil resorts spread out over several kilometers of beaches, including Las Pocitas and Vichayito beach. All have restaurants and can be reached by *mototaxi* (S5 to S10). The places further south are the quietest and are more likely to have individual bungalow accommodation. The following places are listed in the order you will reach them when traveling from Máncora.

Punta Ballenas Inn (☎ 25-8136; www.punta ballenas.com; Panamericana Km 1164; d S150; 🏊) At the southern end of town where the Antigua Panamericana branches off, this hotel is far enough away from town to be silent but still close enough to allow frequent visits. White brick all round, this laid-back place has a great restaurant, an inviting pool, a colorful bar, foosball tables and lots of art gracing the walls. The rooms are comfortable but possibly overpriced.

Casa de Playa (☎ 25-8005; www.vivamancora.com/casadeplaya; s/d S110/175; 🐾) About a kilometer further along the Antigua Panamericana, this large place offers up modern, slick dwellings colored in warm orange and yellow tones and constructed with lots of gently curving lines. All the large rooms have hot water, arty bits and a balcony with a hammock and fine sea views. The restaurant here is good and a lovely two-story lounge hangs out over the sea.

Sunset Hotel (☎ 25-8111; www.hotelsunset.com.pe; d S186-234, q S297-475; 🐾) Another smooth and showy resort, the ultrahip, boutique-styled Sunset wouldn't be out of place on the cover of a glossy travel mag. It has beautifully furnished interiors and great aqua-themed rock sculptures, plus good-sized rooms supply solid mattresses, hot showers, balconies and views of the seascape. The pool is tiny and ocean access is rocky, though a short walk brings you to a sandy beach. The hotel's Italian restaurant is excellent.

Las Pocitas (☎ 25-8432; www.laspocitasmancora.com; d S195/225; 🐾) Las Pocitas' rooms have whitestone walls timbered with bamboo, that are cool, inviting and bespeckled with shell decorations (in case you'd forgotten you were at the beach). Patios with a hammock and sea views are standard and a children's playground, table tennis, foosball, *sapo* (a game in which brass disks are tossed into a table with holes in it) and a grassy lawn are featured.

Balcones de Máncora (☎ 76-2617; 8-person bungalows S360) If you have money to burn, let this be your pyre: this place easily wins the 'most beautiful bungalows' plaudit. Set on a cliff overlooking the beach, these three deluxe bamboo-and-thatch dwellings have giant overhanging roofs, a full kitchen (complete with microwave), two bedrooms, a living space and lots of glass frontage for an unimpeded panorama of the coast. Inside, they're elegantly decorated and have all the creature comforts needed for extended stays. The upstairs double bedroom is completely open to the ocean and has its own bathroom. At the time of writing, plans were afoot to build smaller, cheaper, double bungalows.

Los Corales (☎ 25-8309, 969-9170; s/d incl breakfast S110/165; 🐾) The alluring little rooms here are filled with seashell decorations and painted in cheery colors. All have balconies, cable TVs and hammocks, though only some have sea views. There is a tiny pool and a small children's playground and the beachfront is rocky.

Las Arenas (☎ 25-8240; www.lasarenasdemancora.com; d S360-420; 🔅 🐾) A 5km *mototaxi* ride from Máncora brings you to this spruced-up resort with a slick, angular pool. Enshrined amid a fastidiously trimmed lawn, the Mediterranean-style white-and-blue bungalows are scattered along the beachfront and come with air-con and DVD players (with a free movie library). The staff is very professional and there's a kiddy playground to keep the tots entertained. Sea kayaks, bicycles and horse rides are available.

Vichayito (☎ 436-4173, in Piura 99-410-4582; www.vichayito.com; d S243, 6-person bungalows S447; 🐾) About 8km south of Máncora, this is an attractively constructed hotel with lovely cane, bamboo-and-wood bungalows, all finished in soothing white tones and sporting soaring roofs. Isolated and quiet, the minimalist styling here makes it a great place to unwind. Travelers with cars can reach the hotel by turning off the Pan-American Hwy at Km 1155 (2km north of the village of Los Organos), and following the Antigua Panamericana for 3km to the hotel.

Eating

Seafood rules the culinary roost in Máncora, while other ingredients tend to be pricier due to transportation costs. There is all manner of ceviches, *majariscos* (a mix of seafood nibbles), *chicharrones, sudados* (seafood soup or stew) and just plain *pescado* (fish) on offer. It's good and always fresh. Most midrange hotels have their own restaurants, but in town there are loads of other eating choices.

Juguería Mi Janett (Piura 250; juices S1-3; ⏰ 7am-2:30pm & 5:30-10pm Mon-Sat, 7:15am-3pm Sun) The best juice place in town – come here for massive jugs of your favorite tropical fruit juice.

La Bajadita (☎ 25-8385; Piura 424; dishes S3-8; ⏰ 10am-10pm Tue-Sun) This is the place to sink your sweet tooth into some great cakes, including tiramisú, pecan pie, brownies and the ever-popular apple pie. They also do small meals and all-day breakfasts here.

Angela's Place (☎ 25-8603, Piura 396; breakfasts S4-14, mains S5-12; ⏰ 7am-8pm) Angela the Austrian bread wizard started selling her delicious sweet potato, yuca and wheat breads from her bicycle years ago. Now you can get them at her cheery cafe on the main drag, along with creative and substantial vegetarian (and vegan!) dishes, energizing breakfast combos and sweet pastries.

El Faro Lounge (☎ 9745-2928; Piura 233; meals S6-14; ✆ 6-11pm) Packed to the rafters nightly with salivating gringos, this budget eatery is a Pandora's box of gastronomical specimens, with everything from grilled meats to fish to *wantans* (wontons) to sandwiches on the varied menu.

Punto Pollo (☎ 9662-6647; Piura 609; ¼ chicken S8; ✆ 6pm-midnight) Arguably the best *pollería* in town – and who are we to argue?

ourpick Hnos Lama (☎ 25-8215; Grau 503; meals S10-15; ✆ 8am-8pm) The best of three Lama restaurants, all owned by different family members, this one is owned by Orlando and has a reputation for some of the best ceviche (what else?) in town. It's opposite the Eppo terminal.

Las Gemelitas (☎ 51-6115; Bastidas 154; mains S10-22; ✆ 11am-9pm) Three blocks off the Pan-American Hwy, behind the Cruz del Sur office, this cane-walled restaurant does great seafood and nothing else. Ceviches and *chicharrones* are the specialty, and the portions are ginormous.

Chan Chan (☎ 25-8146; Piura 384; meals S15-24; ✆ 6:30-11pm Wed-Mon) Run by Italian chef Udo, this Italian eatery has a cozy atmosphere and lots of bright, white, curving adobe walls smartly decorated with tasteful art. The food here is great, the pizzas look like the real, thin-crust deal and the service is very attentive – it's well worth the splurge. Get here early for a breezy patio seat. To find it, look out for the palm-frond-concealed frontage.

Sunset (☎ 25-8111; mains S15-35; ✆ 8am-11pm) With a short menu of excellent Italian food, this is the most gourmet restaurant in town when the Italian chef is on, but disappointing when he isn't. It's in the hotel of the same name.

El Espada (☎ 25-8338; Piura, cuadra 5; mains S18-29; ✆ 11am-8pm) This place, with two locations close to one another, is among the most tourist-oriented seafood eateries in the center. Similar places are nearby.

Getting There & Away

AIR

LAN flies from Talara, a 40-minute bus ride south of Máncora, to Lima with a stop in Cajamarca. The flight leaves the capital at 12:30pm and returns from Talara at 3:30pm.

BUS

Many bus offices are in the center, though most southbound trips originate in Tumbes. *Combis* leave for Tumbes (S5.50, two hours) regularly; they drive along the main drag until full. *Bus-camas* from Máncora go direct to Lima (14 hours); other services can drop you in intermediate cities on the way to Lima (16 hours). Regular minibuses run between Máncora and Punta Sal (30 minutes).

Cial (☎ 25-8558; Piura 654) Has Lima-bound buses at 3pm (S45), 7pm (S90 to S108) and 8pm (S63 to S72).

Civa (☎ 01-9805-5131; Piura 688) Has an economical 3:30pm service to Lima (S45), as well as a nicer bus at 5:30pm (S81).

Cruz del Sur (☎ 25-8232; Grau 208) Has a *bus-cama* service to Lima at 6:30pm (S100 to S145).

El Dorado (☎ 25-8582; Grau 111) Six buses a day to Piura (S18, 2½ hours) with fast transfers to Chiclayo (S29, six hours) and Trujillo (S28, nine hours).

Eppo (☎ 25-8027; Grau 470) Fast and regular hourly buses to Talara (S5.50, 1½ hours), Sullana (S9, 2½ hours) and Piura (S11, 3½ hours) between 4am and 7pm.

Oltursa (☎ 25-8267; Piura 509) Lima *bus-cama* (S100 to S150) at 6pm.

Ormeño (☎ 25-8334; Piura 611) Lima buses (S75 to S108) at 2:30pm and 7:30pm. Also has buses direct to Quito (S100, 16 hours) at 6am on Wednesdays and Fridays, and direct service to Guayaquil (S35, seven to nine hours).

Tepsa (☎ 25-8043; Grau 113) Lima bus (S85) at 4pm.

PUNTA SAL
☎ 072 / pop 3300

The long, curvy bay at Punta Sal, 25km north of Máncora, has fine sand and is dotted with rocky bits – but it's still great for a dip in the ocean. The sea here is calm and the lack of surfer types means that this tranquil oasis of resorts is particularly popular with families.

One of the few budget options on this beach, **Las Terrazas** (☎ 54-0001; lasterrazaspuntasal@ yahoo.com; r per person S25) has solid rooms inside the main house, as well as some poky small bamboo rooms at the back, all for the same price – choose wisely! The terrace restaurant here has awesome sunset views.

A wooden sundeck nearly hangs out over the sea at **Sunset Punta Sal** (☎ 54-0004; www.hotel sunsetpuntasal.com; r per person with breakfast/full board S45/70) and is indeed a great place to admire the setting sun. The bright white adobe is reminiscent of a Greek isle and fishing paraphernalia adorns the walls. The rooms themselves are plain but come with some fine wooden

---

THE NORTH COAST'S TOP FIVE SURF BREAKS

Dedicated surfers will find plenty of action on Peru's North Coast, from the longest break in the world at Puerto Chicama to consistently good surf at Máncora. Most spots have reliable swell from April to October. For the inside scoop on surfing throughout Peru, see p178.

- **Los Organos** (p377) A rocky break with well-formed tubular waves reaching up to 2m; it's for experienced surfers only.
- **Cabo Blanco** (p376) A perfect pipeline ranging between 1m and 3m in height and breaking on rocks; again, experienced surfers only.
- **Puerto Chicama** (p357) On a good day, this is the longest break in the world (up to 2km!); it has good year-round surfing for all skill levels.
- **Máncora** (p377) Popular and easily accessible, with consistently decent surf up to 2m high; it's appropriate for all skill levels.
- **Huanchaco** (p352) Long and well-formed waves with a pipeline; it's suitable for all skill levels.

---

touches, balconies and sea views. The staff can arrange inexpensive fishing trips.

Hotel Bucanero (☎ 54-0118; www.elbucaneropuntasal .com; s/d with breakfast S66/99; ☎) Has 14 rooms by the beach, each with cold shower, fan and patio or balcony. The hotel has a game room, TV room, restaurant, two bars, a grassy garden and a lookout with an ocean seascape. Rates include a welcome drink.

The 23 ocean-view rooms at **Hotel Caballito de Mar** (☎ 54-0048, in Lima 01-446-3122; www.hotelcaballito demar.com; r per person incl full board S225-285; ☐ ☎) literally climb up the sea cliff and have pretty bamboo accents and private patios. Hit the restaurant, bar, Jacuzzi, TV room, games room and the gorgeous pool that practically dips its toe into the sea. Activities such as fishing, boating, horseback riding, waterskiing and surfing can be arranged.

Off the Pan-American Hwy at Km 1192, the seaside **Punta Sal Club Hotel** (☎ 54-0088; www.puntasal .com.pe; s/d per person incl full board S252/420; ☒ ☐ ☎) has the full-service deal. Perfect for families, it has mini-golf, laundry facilities, banana-boat rides, waterskiing, tennis, volleyball, table tennis, billiards and a wooden-decked pool – and what resort would be complete without a near-life-size replica of a conquistador galleon? It also offers deep-sea fishing trips for US$600 per day in a boat that will take up to six anglers.

Regular minibuses run between Máncora and Punta Sal (30 minutes).

ZORRITOS

☎ 072 / pop 9400
About 35km south of Tumbes, Zorritos is the biggest fishing village along this section of coast. While the thin beach here isn't as nice as beaches further south, it is home to interesting coastal **birdlife**. Look for frigate birds, pelicans, egrets and other migratory birds.

A few kilometers south of central Zorritos is **Hostel Casa Grillo** (☎ 9-764-2836; www.casagrillo .net; Pan-American Hwy, Km 1236; r per person with/without bathroom S21/15), which has basic rooms and a seaside camping set-up. It has a restaurant with vegetarian specials (sandwiches S3 to S6, mains S8 to S25) and information about tours to nearby national reserves. Horseback riding and hiking to nearby mud baths can also be arranged. The hostel runs popular five-day *hostal*-and-camping tours that take in beaches, trekking, lagoons and mud baths and cost only S525 per person – including everything! Longer trips are also available.

At Km 1235 is **Tres Puntas Ecological Tourist Center** (☎ 9764-2836; campsites S15, r with/without bathroom per person S55/40). Constructed (mainly by volunteers) from natural materials such as bamboo and cane, everything here, including water, is recycled. Breezy, rustic cabins with balconies and hammocks sit on the beach, and campsites have electricity and a shade roof. All rooms share interesting outdoor communal bathrooms covered in mosaic tiles and seashells. Dog-lovers should ask the owner to show you his 14 Peruvian hairless dogs – he breeds them.

Right in Zorritos, **Puerta del Sol** (☎ 54-4294; hosppuertadelsol@hotmail.com; s/d S29/41) is a skinny little *hospedaje* that is just too lovely for words. It has a miniature garden dissected by a winding, yellow-brick path and patches of vibrant lawn. The only accessory missing is a garden gnome. The rooms are simple and neat and beach access is available, but there are no views.

Midrange choices include the beachfront **Hotel Los Cocos** (☎ 9867-1259; www.hotelloscocos.com; Panamericana Km 1242; s/d/t incl full board S90/120/180; 🏊), with big rooms filled with bamboo furniture, a few arty bits, and sporting balconies with hammocks and sea vistas. The pool has rock features and a separate children's section. There's also a small kids' play area, a trampoline and a beach-volleyball court here.

Costa Azul (☎ 54-4268; www.costaazulperu.com; s/d/t S225/255/390) is a huge sprawling complex of various-sized Spartan bungalows, all with TV. Some sleep up to six people and sit right on the beach.

Combis to Zorritos leave regularly from Tumbes (S2, about one hour). Coming from the south, just catch any bus heading toward Tumbes.

TUMBES

☎ 072 / pop 128,600

Only 30km from the Ecuadorean border, Tumbes is in a uniquely green part of coastal Peru, where dry deserts magically turn into mangroves and an expanse of ecological reserves stretches in all directions. It's also the springboard for trips to the excellent and popular beaches of Máncora, two hours further south.

A flashpoint for conflict during the 1940–41 border war between Ecuador and Peru, Tumbes remains a garrison town with a strong military presence. It's hot and (depending on the season) dusty or buggy, and most travelers don't stay long. The nearby national reserves are distinctive and a boon for nature buffs.

Tumbes was an Inca town when it was first sighted by Pizarro in 1528. Pizarro invited an Inca noble to dine aboard his ship and sent ashore two of his men, who reported the existence of an obviously well-organized and fabulously rich civilization. Based on those accounts Pizarro returned a few years later to begin his conquest of Peru. Present-day Tumbes is about 5km northeast of the old Inca city, which is marked on maps as San Pedro de los Incas. The Panamericana passes through the site, but there is little to see.

Despite its interesting history, Tumbes's only real appeal is its convenient access to

---

WARNING: BORDER-CROSSING BLUES

Shady practices at the border crossing between Ecuador and Peru at Aguas Verdes have earned it the dubious title of 'the worst border crossing in South America.' Whether it deserves to wear that crown is hard to prove empirically, but it pays to be wary.

Try not to change dollars into soles here as 'fixed' calculators are common and many bills offered to foreigners are fake (see p523). If you must change money, find out the exchange rate before you arrive and change just enough to get you to the nearest bank in Tumbes. Ignore 'helpful' advice along the lines of 'you can't change dollars in Tumbes,' 'the banks are closed,' 'there's a strike,' or 'Tumbes is flooded.'

Taxi drivers will use similarly persuasive methods to convince you that *combis* and *colectivo* taxis aren't running. Overcharging here can be audacious. *Combis* run from the border to Tumbes all day and charge S1.50, and a *colectivo* costs around S2.50 per person or about S14 for the whole taxi. Establish a price before you get into the vehicle and make sure it covers the fare all the way to Tumbes, not just to the immigration post 3km away.

A rule of thumb for getting across this border without being scammed is to take a direct bus across the border; jump off at immigration to get stamped in or out and get back on the bus immediately. If you must make a connection, however, use only *combis* and *colectivos* and stay out of situations where you are the only passenger, even in a marked taxi. An extremely common scheme, originating in both Tumbes and at the border, involves travelers ending up in taxis at the end of a dirt road, where they must pay upwards of US$50 or hundreds of soles for the privilege of being returned to civilization.

Many people will offer their services as porters or guides. Most are annoyingly insistent, so unless you really need help, they are best avoided.

Remember that there are no entry fees into either country. If the border guards say otherwise, always be polite but insistent in your refusal to pay.

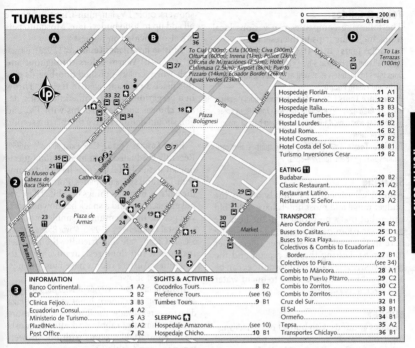

the ecological reserves. If you're headed to beaches south of here, keep going and avoid this unpleasant pit stop if you can.

Information
Apart from offering tours to local sights, Tumbes tour companies can also provide some tourist information.

Banco Continental (☎ 52-3914; Bolívar 129)

BCP (☎ 52-5060; Bolívar 261) Changes traveler's checks and has an ATM.

Clinica Feijoo (☎ 52-5341; Castilla 305) One of the better medical clinics in Tumbes.

Ecuadorean consul (☎ 52-5949; Bolívar 129, 3rd fl; ☼ 9am-1pm & 4-6pm Mon-Fri) On the Plaza de Armas.

Ministerio de Turismo (☎ 52-3699, 52 4940; Bolognesi 194, 2nd fl) Provides useful tourist information, especially for the nearby ecological reserves.

Oficina de Migraciones (☎ 52-3422; Tumbes 1751) Along the Pan-American Hwy, 2km north of town. Does visa extensions.

Plaz@Net (Bolívar 161; per hr S1; ☼ 8am-11pm) Internet access.

Police (☎ 52-5250; Tumbes 1742) Located north of town.

Post office (☎ 52-3866; San Martín 208; ☼ 9am-7pm Mon-Fri, to 1pm Sat) On the block south of Plaza Bolognesi.

Dangers & Annoyances
The border crossing has a bad reputation. For detailed warnings, see the boxed text, opposite.

Sights
There are several **old houses** dating from the early 19th century on Grau, east of the Plaza de Armas. These rickety abodes are made of split-bamboo and wood and it seems like they are defying gravity by sheer will. The plaza has several outdoor restaurants and is a nice place to relax. The **pedestrian streets** north of the plaza (especially Bolívar) have several large, modern monuments and are favorite hangouts for young and old alike.

About 5km south of town, off the Pan-American Hwy, is an overgrown archaeological site that was the home of the Tumpis people and, later, the site of the Inca fort visited by Pizarro. The story is told in the tiny site museum, **Museo de Cabeza de Baca** (adult S2; ☼ 9am-2pm Mon-Sat), which also displays some 1500-year-old ceramic vessels.

Tours & Guides

The following companies run various local tours, including trips to the reserves.

Cocodrilos Tours (☎ 52-4133; cocodrilostours@ terramail.com.pe; Huáscar 309; ⏱ 8am-1pm & 4-8pm) Does tours to the reserves as well as to local beaches, mud baths and Puerto Pizarro.

Preference Tours (☎ 52-4757; turismomundial@terra .com.pe; Grau 427; ⏱ 8:30am-1pm & 5-7pm) Runs some of the most economical tours in town if you have a group of three or more.

Tumbes Tours (☎ 52-6086; www.tumbestours.com; Tumbes 341; ⏱ 8am-1pm & 4-8pm)

Sleeping

Almost all of Tumbes' hotels are in the budget range and most hotels have only cold water, but that's no problem in the heat. Be sure your room has a working fan if you're here in the sweltering summer (December to March). During the wet season and the twice-yearly rice harvests, mosquitoes can be a big problem, and there are frequent water and electricity outages.

BUDGET

Tumbes abounds with budget options, ranging from barely acceptable to pretty good value. In the lower end of the budget range, watch your valuables carefully.

Hospedaje Franco (☎ 52-5295; San Martín 107; s/d S18/28) Clean enough and quieter than most, this place made some tile vendor very wealthy – they cover nearly every surface. TV costs S5 extra.

Hospedaje Tumbes (☎ 52-2203; Grau 614; s/d S20/32) Dark but welcoming, the good-sized rooms here have fans. The walls are decorated with oh-so-hip '80s posters; a few plants help spruce the place up. TV costs S5 extra.

Hospedaje Italia (☎ 52-3396; Grau 733; d S25) The Italia is a good deal for double rooms, each of which has plenty of natural light and space, tiled floors and TVs as standard.

Hospedaje Florián (☎ 52-2464; Piura 414; s/d S28/40) Has warm showers and fans, plus cable TV for S4 extra. It's a little hygienically challenged though.

Hospedaje Amazonas (☎ 52-5266; Tumbes 317; s/d S28/42) Aged but well maintained, the huge rooms here have fans, and a communal TV lounge offers some entertainment.

Hospedaje Chicho (☎ 52-2282, ☎ /fax 52 3696; Tumbes 327; s/d S35/38) Very clean rooms in a central location, helpful and friendly staff, hot showers, cable TV, fan, mini-fridge and phone all add up to solid budget fare. Mosquito nets are also provided on request.

Turismo Inversiones César (☎ 52-2883; Huáscar 311; s/d S26/45) Warm colors throughout and well-worn, creaky polished floorboards give this place a pleasant lived-in feeling. Throw in a gregarious owner, some interesting design choices and clean rooms with TV, and you should definitely give this place a second look.

Hotel Cosmos (☎ 52-4366; Piura 900; s/d S36/60) Recently graduated from mere *hostal* (guesthouse) status, Hotel Cosmos has solid rooms with TVs and space in spades. Potted plants in the hallway brighten things up a bit. There are poker machines and a snack bar downstairs if you get the urge to munch, gamble or both.

Hostal Lourdes (☎ 52-2966; Mayor Bodero 118; s/d S40/62) Clean, safe and friendly, the Lourdes includes a top-floor restaurant among its amenities. Austere rooms have fans, phones, TV and hot showers.

Hostal Roma (☎ 52-4137, 52-2494, 52-5879; Bolognesi 425; s/d S55/70) A modern hotel with top Plaza de Armas real estate, the Roma is a little more upscale than the rabble and affords guests clean, comfortable rooms with hot shower, fan, phone and cable TV.

MIDRANGE

Hotel Chilimasa (☎ 52-4555; Pan-American Hwy North, Km 1172, Manzana 2A; s/d S78/108; ⚑) About 2km north of town en route to the airport, this hotel supplies comfortable rooms and a restaurant, but it's the pool that will probably get your attention.

Hotel Costa del Sol (☎ 52-3991; www.costadelsolperu .com; San Martín 275; s/d/ste with breakfast S215/280/325; ⚑ ⚑) This is by far the best hotel in town, providing a decent restaurant, a pleasant bar and a garden, plus a Jacuzzi, adult and children's swimming pools, a small casino and a gym. The comfortable rooms have cable TV, direct-dial phone, fan, mini-fridge, and bathroom, hot shower and blow dryer. A cold cocktail is included – and is most welcome.

Eating

There are several bars and restaurants on the Plaza de Armas, many with shaded tables and chairs outside – a real boon in hot weather. It's a pleasant place to sit and watch the world go by as you drink a cold beer and wait for your bus.

our pick Restaurant Sí Señor (☎ 52-1937; Bolívar 115; menús S4-5, meals S9-18; ✆ 7:30am-2am) With pleasant streetside tables outside and quixotic, slow-turning fans inside, Sí Señor serves delicious seafood dishes – any kind of a grilled fish is a great bet here – and is a cheaper version of the nearby Restaurant Latino.

Las Terrazas (☎ 52-1575; Araujo 549; meals S8-18; ✆ 9am-8pm) A little bit out of the town center, this popular place is well worth the S1 moto-taxi ride. Packed with hungry diners daily, it serves up heaped plates of seafood, and will ceviche or cook anything from fish to lobster to octopus. It's all prepared in the northern coastal style and they have live folk music on the weekends. It's on a classy 3rd-floor terrace and has flowing tablecloths, lots of decorations and a festive mood.

Classic Restaurant (☎ 52-4301; Tumbes 185; mains S11-16; ✆ 8am-5pm; ✇) Small, quiet and dignified, Classic Restaurant is a wonderful place to escape torrid Tumbes and relax with a long lunch, as many of the town's better-connected locals do. The food is good and mainly coastal, but secretly we like this place for its air-con.

Budabar (☎ 50-4216; Grau 309; meals S11-18; ✆ 8am-2am) Occupying a huge cavernous space and with streetside tables, this place has a full bar and serves typical Peruvian fare, including the usual chicken, fish and beef suspects. As you might have guessed from the name, this joint serves shots and cold beers until the wee hours.

Restaurant Latino (☎ 52-3198; Bolívar 163; mains S12-21; ✆ 7am-11pm) This popular place serves from a long menu of Peruvian food, especially seafood. You can eat inside, or outside on the shaded pavement.

Getting There & Away

AIR

The **airport** (code TBP; ☎ 52-5102) is 8km north of town; the usual S11 airport departure tax is charged. **Aero Condor Perú** (☎ 52-4835; Grau 454) has a daily flight from Lima to Tumbes leaving at 5:30pm and returning to Lima at 7:30pm.

BUS

You can usually find a bus to Lima within 24 hours of your arrival in Tumbes, but they're sometimes (especially major holidays) sold out a few days in advance. You can take a bus south to another major city and try again from there.

Buses to Lima take 16 to 18 hours. Some companies offer a limited-stop special service, with air-con, bathrooms and very loud video; some have deluxe, nonstop bus-cama services.

Slower services stop at Piura (five hours), Chiclayo (seven to eight hours) and Trujillo (nine to 10 hours). If you are heading to Piura, you can catch a much faster colectivo taxi (S20, 3½ hours).

If you're going to Ecuador, it's easiest to go with Cifa, an Ecuadorean company, or Oremeño. Both stop at the border for you to complete passport formalities.

Cial (☎ 52-6350; Tumbes 572) Slower services to Lima at 1pm and 6pm (S45), and a bus-cama at 6pm (S84 to S108).

Cifa (☎ 52-7120; Tumbes 572) Heads to Machala (S6, two hours) and Guayaquil (S15, five to seven hours), both in Ecuador, about every two hours.

Civa (☎ 52-5120; Tumbes 518) Lima services at 1:30pm (S45), 4pm (bus-cama S78 to S108) and 6:15pm (S45).

Cruz del Sur (☎ 52-6200; Tumbes 319) To Lima (bus-cama S100 to S145) at 4pm and 10pm.

El Sol (☎ 50-9252; Piura 403) Economy buses to Chiclayo (S26) at 8:15am and 9:30am. Also a service to Lima (S55) via Chiclayo (S20) and Trujillo (S28) at 8:20pm.

Oltursa (☎ 52-6524; Tumbes 946) Bus-cama service to Lima (S100 to S145) at 4pm.

Ormeño (☎ 52-2288, 52-2228; Tumbes 314) Two classes of bus to Lima (S65 to S100) via Chiclayo (S25 to S42) and Trujillo (S42 to S58), the cheaper one leaving at 1pm and the pricier one at 5:30pm. Also has direct buses to Guayaquil (S18) at 9am, 3pm and 5pm.

Tepsa (☎ 52-2428; Tumbes 199) To Lima (S86) at 2:30pm.

Transportes Chiclayo (☎ 52-5260; Tumbes 464) Daily bus to Chiclayo (S26) at 2:30pm via Piura (S20).

If you're heading for Puerto Pizarro (S1, 15 minutes), Zorritos (S2, about one hour) or Máncora (S4, two hours), there are combi stops in Tumbes near the market area. Ask locals, as the stops aren't marked. Buses to Casitas leave at 1pm (S10, five hours), while the Rica Playa bus leaves at noon (S2.50, two hours).

Getting Around

A taxi to the airport is about S18, depending on your bargaining abilities. There are no combis to the airport.

BORDER CROSSING: ECUADOR VIA TUMBES

Colectivo (shared transportation) taxis (per person S2.50, 25 minutes) and *combis* (minibuses; S1.50, 40 minutes) for Aguas Verdes on the Peru–Ecuador border leave from the corner of Puell and Tumbes. It's S18 for the whole taxi. Unless you have a real love for loitering at dirty border towns, it's far better to take a **Cifa International** (☎ 072-52-7120; Tumbes 572) bus straight through to Machala (S10, two to four hours) or Guayaquil (S33, five to seven hours) in Ecuador.

The Peruvian **immigration office** (El Complejo; ☎ 072-56-1178; ☺ 24hr) is in the middle of the desert at Aguas Verdes, about 3km from the border. Travelers leaving Peru obtain exit stamps here – if you're catching public transportation make sure you stop to complete these border formalities. If you're entering Peru you'll receive a Tourist Card (actually a piece a paper) that you will need to present when leaving Peru; don't lose it. If you require a visa, ensure you obtain it before reaching the border; otherwise, you'll have to go back to the Peruvian consulate in Machala to get one. Although a ticket out of Peru is officially required to enter the country, gringo travelers are rarely asked for one unless they look thoroughly disreputable. A bus office in Aguas Verdes sells (non-refundable) tickets out of Peru, and the immigration official can tell you where it is.

From the immigration office, *mototaxis* can take you to the border town of Aguas Verdes (S2).

Aguas Verdes is basically a long, dusty street full of vendors that continues into the near-identical Ecuadorean border town of Huaquillas via the international bridge across the Río Zarumilla. If you are forced to stay the night at the border, there are a few basic hotels in Aguas Verdes, but they're all noisy and pretty sketchy. You're better off catching a S2 *mototaxi* to the quiet Peruvian town of Zarumilla, 5km away. Here, **Hostal Prisalex** (☎ 072-56 5601; www.prisalex.mbperu. com; Calle del Ejército 112; s/d S20/30) offers immaculate, large and recently painted rooms for bargain prices in their quiet, blue *hostal* (guesthouse).

The Ecuadorean Immigration office, about 4km to the north of the bridge, is also open 24 hours. Taxis from the bridge charge about US$1. Very few nationalities need a visa for Ecuador, but everyone needs a T3 embarkation card, available for free at the immigration office. You must surrender your T3 when you leave Ecuador, so don't lose it. Exit tickets out of Ecuador and sufficient funds (US$20 per day) are legally required, but rarely asked for. Tourists are allowed only 90 days per year in Ecuador without officially extending their stay at a consulate – if you have stayed more, you may fined between US$200 and US$2000 when you leave.

There are a few basic hotels in Huaquillas, but most people make the two-hour bus trip to the city of Machala, where there are much better facilities. See Lonely Planet's *Ecuador & the Galápagos Islands* for more information.

AROUND TUMBES
Puerto Pizarro
☎ 072

About 14km north of Tumbes, the character of the oceanfront changes from the coastal desert, which stretches more than 2000km north from central Chile to northern Peru, to the mangrove swamps that dominate much of the Ecuadorean and Colombian coastlines. There's an explosion of **birdlife** here, with up to 200 different migrating species visiting these areas. Boats can be hired to tour the mangroves; one tour goes to a **crocodile sanctuary** where you can see Peru's only crocodiles being nursed back from near extinction. The nearby **Isla de Aves** can be visited (but not landed on) to see the many nesting seabirds, especially between 5pm to 6pm, when huge flocks of birds return to roost for the night. **Isla del Amor** has lunch restaurants and attractive swimming beaches. Boats line the waterfront of Puerto Pizarro and cost S35 to S40 per hour per boat; you can do a tour of the mangroves and the above-mentioned sites for S80. Tour companies in Tumbes also provide guided tours to the area.

Most visitors stay in Tumbes and visit Puerto Pizarro on a day trip; however, accommodation is available at **Bayside Hotel** (☎ 54-3045; s/d S45/65; ☒) on the waterfront. The Bayside has a faded Palm Springs attitude and its yellow concrete bungalows are large and weathered, but supply plenty of character. It's a good place to chill, with a pleasant thatch-roofed restaurant and seaside hammocks to watch the world float by. The hotel also rents kayaks for S5 per hour and jet skis for S60 per hour – though you won't see much wildlife zooming around on one of those.

There are regular *combis* between Puerto Pizarro and Tumbes (S1, 15 minutes).

Reserva de Biosfera del Noroeste

The Northwestern Biosphere Reserve consists of four protected areas that cover 2344 sq km in the department of Tumbes and northern Piura. A lack of government funding means that there is little infrastructure or tourist facilities – much of what exists was funded by organizations such as the Fundación Peruana para la Conservación de la Naturaleza (FPCN; also called ProNaturaleza), with assistance from international bodies such as the WWF.

Information about all four areas is available from the Tumbes office of **Inrena** (☎ 972-52-6489; www.inrena.gob.pe; Tarapacá 427, Ministerio de Agricultura; ☒ 9am-5:30pm), the government department in charge of administering this region. The biologist in charge is Oscar García Tello and this office has lots of pamphlets and information on the area, some maps, and may be able to give you a lift to one of the reservations if it has people heading there that day. It's here you will need to get permission papers to visit any of the protected areas on your own; these are free and take minutes to organize.

Tour companies in Tumbes can arrange tours, as can Hostel Casa Grillo (p381) in Zorritos. There are few roads into these areas and visiting during the wet months of December to April can prove very difficult.

PARQUE NACIONAL CERROS DE AMOTAPE

The tropical dry forest ecosystem of Cerros de Amotape is protected by this 913-sq-km national park, which is home to flora and fauna including jaguars, condors and anteaters, though parrots, deer and peccaries are more commonly sighted. Large-scale logging, illegal hunting and overgrazing are some of the threats facing this habitat, of which there is very little left anywhere in Peru. **Guides** are essential for spotting wildlife and can be arranged in the town of **Rica Playa**, a small, friendly village located just within the park. Although there are no hotels here, you can camp and local families will sell you meals.

During the dry season, a bus leaves for Rica Playa from the Tumbes market (S2.50, two hours) at noon. Most of the route, bar the last 18km, is paved.

Another way to visit the park is to go to the village of **Casitas** (pop 350) near Caña Veral; buses leave from the Tumbes market at 1pm (S10, five hours).

Agencies in Tumbes also organize tours for S30 to S90 per person, depending on the number of people.

ZONA RESERVADA DE TUMBES

This reserve is probably the best place to spot a wide range of wild animals. The forest is similar to the tropical dry forest of Cerros de Amotape, but because it lies more on the easterly side of the hills, it is wetter and has slightly different flora and fauna, including crocodiles, howler monkeys and nutria. You can also see various orchids and a wide variety of birds. There is no public transportation here, so you'll need to either have your own wheels or come on a tour, which can cost anywhere between S30 to S90 per person.

COTO DE CAZA EL ANGOLO

This 650-sq-km extension at the southwest border of Cerros de Amotape is the most remote section of the tropical dry forest. It's a hunting preserve.

SANTUARIO NACIONAL LOS MANGLARES DE TUMBES

This national sanctuary was established in 1988 and lies on the coast, separated from the other three dry-forest areas. Only about 30 sq km in size, it plays an essential role in conserving Peru's only region of mangroves.

You can travel here by going to Puerto Pizarro and taking a dirt road northeast to the tiny community of **El Bendito**. From here, ask around for someone to guide you by canoe. Guided tours are available from Puerto Pizarro as well, though the mangroves here are not technically within the protection of the sanctuary. Another way to visit is to go to **Zarumilla** (pop 17,200), 5km before the Ecuador border, and seek out **Oriol Cedillo Ruiz** (☎ 50-7816; Independencia 690). He can arrange two- to three-hour kayak tours (per kayak S35). Access depends on the tides. Agencies in Tumbes also arrange tours for S45 to S90 per person.

Huaraz & the Cordilleras

The mountainous region of the Cordillera Blanca is where superlatives crash and burn in a brave attempt to capture the beauty of the place. A South American mecca for worshippers of outdoor adventure, this is one of the pre-eminent hiking, trekking and backpacking spots on the continent. Every which way you throw your gaze, perennially glaciered white peaks razor their way through expansive mantles of lime-green valleys. In the recesses of these prodigious giants huddle scores of pristine jade lakes, ice caves and torrid springs. This is the highest mountain range in the world outside the Himalayas, and its 22 ostentatious summits of more than 6000m will not let you forget it for a second.

Huaraz is a fast-beating heart linking the trekking trails and roads that serve as the mountains' arteries. It's here that plans of daring ice climbs, mountain-biking exploits and rock-climbing safaris are hatched over ice-cold beers in fireplace-warmed bars. Meanwhile, in the eastern valley, the enigmatic 3000-year-old ruins of Chavín de Huántar await daily rediscovery, while further north picture-perfect villages, steeped in pre-Inca traditions, dispense affectionate smiles like they're going out of style.

HIGHLIGHTS

- Traipse for weeks around the magnificent peaks of the **Cordillera Blanca** (p404) and **Cordillera Huayhuash** (p410)

- Tunnel through the mysterious millennia-old ruins of **Chavín de Huántar** (p422)

- Plummet down precipitous mountain-bike trails and clamber up vertical rock-climbing cliffs around **Huaraz** (opposite)

- Wind your way through the 1000m sheer rock walls of the staggering **Cañón del Pato** (p417)

- Chill out on the tranquil shores of the **Lagunas Llanganuco** (p417) or dozens of other emerald mountain lakes

Cañón del Pato ★   Lagunas ★ Llanganuco

Cordillera ★ Blanca

Huaraz ★   ★ Chavín de Huántar

Cordillera Huayhuash ★

■ BIGGEST CITY: HUARAZ, POPULATION 48,500

■ AVERAGE TEMPERATURE: JANUARY 10°C TO 16°C, JULY 12°C TO 17°C

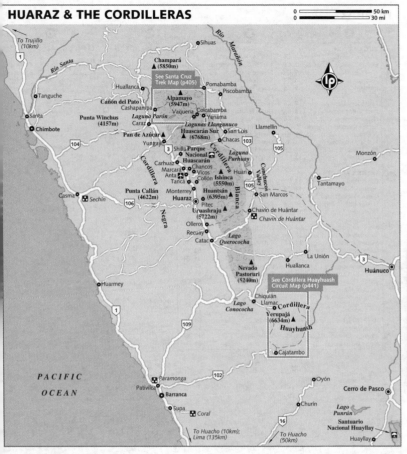

HUARAZ & THE CORDILLERAS

See Santa Cruz
Trek Map (p405)

See Cordillera Huayhuash
Circuit Map (p441)

HUARAZ

☎ 043 / pop 48,500 / elev 3091m

Huaraz is the restless capital of this Andean adventure kingdom and its rooftops command exhaustive panoramas of the city's dominion: one of the most impressive mountain ranges in the world. Nearly wiped out by the earthquake of 1970, Huaraz isn't going to win any Andean-village beauty contests anytime soon, but it does have personality – and personality goes a long way.

This is first and foremost a trekking metropolis. During the high season the streets buzz with hundreds of backpackers and adventurers freshly returned from arduous hikes or planning their next expedition as they huddle in one of the town's many fine watering holes. Dozens of outfits help plan trips, rent equipment and organize a list of adventure sports as long as your arm. An endless lineup of quality restaurants and hopping bars keep the belly full and the place lively till long after the tents have been put away to dry. Mountain adventures in the off-season can be equally rewarding, but the vibe is more subdued and some places go into hibernation over the rainy season.

INFORMATION
Emergency

Casa de Guías (☎ 42-1811; www.casadeguias.com.pe; Plaza Ginebra 28G; ⏲ 7-11am & 2-11pm) It offers safety and rescue courses and it will save your life if you get into

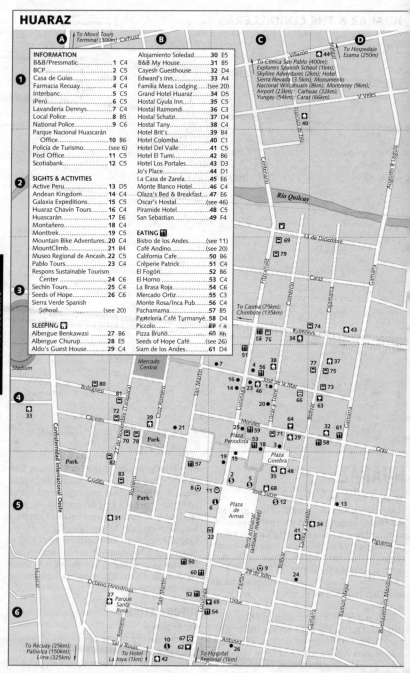

HUARAZ

INFORMATION
B&B/Pressmatic..................1 C4
BCP.....................................2 C5
Casa de Guías....................3 C4
Farmacia Recuay................4 C5
Interbanc..........................5 C5
iPerú..................................6 C5
Lavandería Dennys.............7 C4
Local Police.......................8 B5
National Police..................9 C6
Parque Nacional Huascarán
  Office.............................10 B6
Policía de Turismo...........(see 6)
Post Office.......................11 C5
Scotiabank.......................12 C5

SIGHTS & ACTIVITIES
Active Peru......................13 D5
Andean Kingdom..............14 C4
Galaxia Expeditions..........15 C5
Huaraz Chavín Tours.........16 C4
Huascarán........................17 E6
Montañero........................18 C4
Monttrek..........................19 C5
Mountain Bike Adventures.20 C4
MountClimb......................21 B4
Museo Regional de Ancash.22 C5
Pablo Tours......................23 C4
Respons Sustainable Tourism
  Center............................24 C6
Sechín Tours.....................25 C4
Seeds of Hope..................26 C6
Sierra Verde Spanish
  School.........................(see 20)

SLEEPING
Albergue Benkawasi..........27 B6
Albergue Churup...............28 E5
Aldo's Guest House...........29 C4

Alojamiento Soledad..........30 E5
B&B My House...................31 B5
Cayesh Guesthouse............32 D4
Edward's Inn.....................33 A4
Familia Meza Lodging.....(see 20)
Grand Hotel Huaraz...........34 D5
Hostal Gyula Inn...............35 C5
Hostal Raimondi................36 C3
Hostal Schatzi...................37 D4
Hostal Tany......................38 C4
Hotel Brit's.......................39 B4
Hotel Colomba..................40 C1
Hotel Del Valle.................41 C5
Hotel El Tumi....................42 B6
Hotel Los Portales.............43 D3
Jo's Place..........................44 D1
La Casa de Zarela..............45 E6
Monte Blanco Hotel...........46 C4
Olaza's Bed & Breakfast.....47 E6
Oscar's Hostal................(see 46)
Piramide Hotel..................48 C5
San Sebastian...................49 F4

EATING
Bistro de los Andes.........(see 11)
Café Andino..................(see 20)
California Cafe..................50 B6
Crêperie Patrick................51 C4
El Fogón..........................52 B6
El Horno..........................53 C6
La Brasa Roja....................54 C6
Mercado Ortiz..................55 C3
Monte Rosa/Inca Pub........56 C4
Pachamama.....................57 B5
Pastelería Café Turmanyé...58 D4
Piccolo.............................59 C4
Pizza Bruno......................60 B6
Seeds of Hope Café........(see 26)
Siam de los Andes.............61 D4

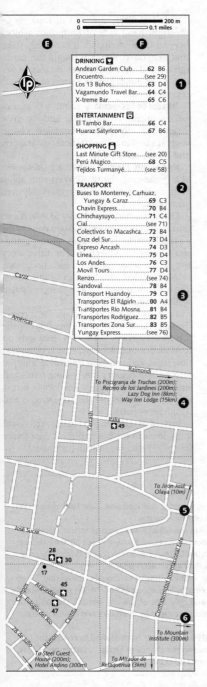

trouble in the mountains – but only if you're trekking or climbing with one of its guides certified by the Mountain Guide Association (AGM). Ask for a list of guides or see the website. Register here before heading out on a trek or climb.

Local Police (☎ 42-1221, 42-1331; José Sucre near San Martín)

National Police (☎ 42-6343; Calle 28 de Julio 701)

Policía de Turismo (☎ 42-1341; Plaza de Armas; ⏲ 8am-1pm Mon-Sat & 5-8pm Mon-Fri) On an alley on the west side of the Plaza de Armas, above iPerú. Some officers speak limited English.

Internet Access

There are literally dozens of places on Plaza Ginebra and the corresponding block of Luzuriaga.

Laundry

Both of the laundries listed below are good for washing down gear and dry cleaning.

B&B/Pressmatic (☎ 42-1719; José de la Mar 674; per kg S2.50)

Lavandería Dennys (☎ 42-9232; José de la Mar 561; per kg S2.50)

Medical Services

Clínica San Pablo (☎ 42-8811; Huaylas 172; ⏲ 24hr) North of town, this is the best medical care in Huaraz. Some doctors speak English.

Farmacia Recuay (☎ 42-1391; Luzuriaga 497) Will restock expedition medical kits.

Hospital Regional (☎ 42-4146; Luzuriaga, cuadra 13) At the south end of town; for rudimentary medical care.

Money

All of these banks have ATMs and will exchange US dollars and euros.

BCP (☎ 42-1692; Luzuriaga 691)

Interbanc (☎ 42-1502; José Sucre 687)

Scotiabank (☎ 42-1500; José Sucre 760)

Post

Post office (☎ 42-1031; Luzuriaga 702)

Tourist Information

The travel agencies mentioned on p394 and popular meeting points for tourists in Huaraz can be good sources of local and trekking information.

iPerú (☎ 42-8812; Plaza de Armas, Pasaje Atusparia, Oficina 1; ⏲ 9am-6pm Mon-Sat, to 2pm Sun) Has general tourist information but little in the way of trekking info.

Parque Nacional Huascarán Office (☎ 42-2086; www.areasprotegidasperu.com/pnh; Sal y Rosas 555) Staff have limited information about visiting the park.

DANGERS & ANNOYANCES

Time to acclimatize is important. Huaraz' altitude will make you feel breathless and may give you a headache during your first few days, so don't overexert yourself. The surrounding mountains will cause altitude sickness if you venture into them without spending a few days acclimatizing in Huaraz first. See p548 for more advice on altitude sickness.

Huaraz is a safe city that experiences little crime; unfortunately, robberies of trekkers and tourists do happen, especially in the area of the Mirador de Retaqeñua and the Wilkahuaín (sometimes also spelled Wilcawain) ruins, and to groggy backpackers arriving early in the morning on overnight buses. In these cases, stay alert and walk with a group or hire a taxi to avoid problems.

SIGHTS

The **Museo Regional de Ancash** (☎ 42-1551; Plaza de Armas; adult incl guided tour S6; ☻ 8am-6:30pm) houses the largest collection of ancient stone sculptures in South America. Small but interesting, it has a few mummies, some trepanned skulls and a garden of stone monoliths from the Recuay culture (400 BC to AD 600) and the Wari culture (AD 600 to 1100).

At the trout hatchery **Piscigranja de Truchas** (admission S1; ☻ 9am-1pm & 3-5pm), you can see the stages of the trout-hatching process from eggs to adults. By the entrance, the **Recreo de los Jardínes** serves trout for lunch. It's a half-hour walk from the center: walk east on Raimondi to Confraternidad Este, then turn left and cross the bridge over the Río Quilcay; the hatchery is just beyond.

Jirón José Olaya, also east of town, is on the right-hand side of Raimondi a block beyond Confraternidad. It's the only street that remained intact through the earthquakes and shows what old Huaraz looked like; go on Sunday when a street market sells regional foods.

Mirador de Retaqeñua is about a 45-minute walk southeast of the center and has great views of the city and its mountainous backdrop. It's best to take a taxi here (see Dangers and Annoyances, left).

Monumento Nacional Wilkahuaín (adult/student S4/2; ☻ 8am-5pm), the small Wari ruin about 8km north of Huaraz, is remarkably well preserved.

Dating from about AD 600 to 900, it's an imitation of the temple at Chavín done in the Tiwanaku style. Wilkahuaín means 'grandson's house' in Quechua. The three-story temple has seven rooms on each floor, each originally filled with bundles of mummies. The bodies were kept dry using a sophisticated system of ventilation ducts.

Taxis cost about S15, or ask for a *combi* (minibus; around S1) at the bus stops by the Río Quilcay in town. The two-hour walk up to Wilkahuaín is an easy, first acclimatization jaunt and can be a rewarding glimpse into Andean country life, passing farms and simple *pueblos* (villages). Ask locally if it is safe before you set off and see Dangers and Annoyances (left).

Instead of returning to Huaraz, you could walk down to the hot springs at Monterrey (see p413) along a footpath (one hour).

TREMORS & LANDSLIDES

Records of *aluviones*, a deadly mix of avalanche, waterfall and landslide, date back almost 300 years, but three recent ones have caused particular devastation.

The first occurred in 1941, when an avalanche in the Cojup Valley, west of Huaraz, caused the Laguna Palcacocha to break its banks and flow down onto Huaraz, killing about 5000 inhabitants and flattening the city. Then, in 1962, a huge avalanche from Huascarán roared down its western slopes and destroyed the town of Ranrahirca, killing about 4000 people.

The worst disaster occurred on May 31, 1970, when a massive earthquake, measuring 7.7 on the Richter scale, devastated much of central Peru, killing an estimated 70,000 people. About half of the 30,000 inhabitants of Huaraz died, and only 10% of the city was left standing. The town of Yungay was completely buried by the *aluvión* caused by the quake and almost its entire population of 18,000 was buried with the city.

Since these disasters, a government agency (Hidrandina) has been formed to control the lake levels by building dams and tunnels, thus minimizing the chance of similar catastrophes. Today, warning systems are in place, although false alarms do occur.

ACTIVITIES

Trekking & Mountaineering

Whether you're arranging a mountain expedition or going for a day hike, Huaraz is the place to start – it is the epicenter for planning and organizing local Andean adventures. Numerous outfits can prearrange entire trips so that all you need to do is show up at the right place at the right time. Many experienced backpackers go camping, hiking and climbing in the mountains without any local help and you can too if you have the experience. Just remember, though, that carrying a backpack full of gear over a 4800m pass requires much more effort than hiking at low altitudes. See Trekking & Mountaineering (p402) in the Cordilleras section for more information.

Rock Climbing

Rock climbing is one of the Cordillera Blanca's biggest pastimes. Avid climbers will find some gnarly bolted sport climbs, particularly at Chancos (p414), Recuay (p421) and Hatun Machay (p421). For some big-wall action that will keep you chalked up for days, head to the famous Torre de Parón, known locally as the Sphinx. Most trekking tour agencies (see p394) offer climbing trips, both for beginners and advanced, as part of their repertoire. Many also rent gear and with a bit of legwork and some information-gathering you can easily arrange your own do-it-yourself climbing expedition. Galaxia Expeditions (p395), Andean Kingdom (p395) and Monttrek (p395) all have indoor *rócodromos* (climbing or bouldering walls).

Ice Climbing

With enough glaciers to sink your ice axe into for the rest of your life, the Cordillera Blanca is a frozen heaven for folks who want to learn ice climbing or attack new peaks and heights. Since many summits require a degree of technical know-how, ice climbing is a big activity in the Cordillera, and many tour and trekking operators can arrange excursions, equipment rental and lessons. The best trekking agencies, listed under Tours & Guides (p394) have years of experience with ice climbing and safe equipment. In Parque Nacional Huascarán a certified guide or proof of credentials from your local climbing club is required (see p404).

Mountain Biking

Mountain Bike Adventures (☎ 42-4259; www.chakinani peru.com; Lúcar y Torre 530, 2nd fl; ✆ 9am-1pm & 4-8pm Mon-Sat) has been in business for more than a decade and receives repeated visits by mountain-bikers for its decent selection of bikes, knowledgeable and friendly service, plus its good safety record. The owner is a lifelong resident of Huaraz who speaks English and has spent time mountain biking in the USA – he knows the region's single-track possibilities better than anyone. The company offers bike rentals for independent types or guided tours, ranging from an easy five-hour cruise to 12-day circuits around the Cordillera Blanca. Rates start at S60 per day for equipment rentals and S90 for one-day tours.

Volunteering

For the latest on volunteering opportunities, check out the community notice boards at popular gringo cafes and hangouts around Huaraz. **Seeds of Hope** (☎ 39-6305; www.peruseeds .org; Dámaso Antunez 782) is an aid organization that works with Huaraz's poorest children and provides accommodations and food to volunteers for a small fee. **Teach Huaraz Peru** (☎ 42-5303; www.teachhuarazperu.com) also works primarily with children and can arrange English-teaching and other kinds of experiences for volunteers; homestays with local families are available. Agencies specializing in community and sustainable tourism (below) may also be able to help you arrange different kinds of volunteer activities in the region. It's best to arrange service activities in advance, though agencies sometimes take short-term, walk-in volunteers.

Community Tourism

More than just a buzz word in travel these days, community tourism offers an alternative experience to the traditional low-interaction, look-from-a-distance travel characterized by holidays holed up in resorts or giant tour groups. It brings travelers into close contact with local people, who are major stakeholders and beneficiaries of tourism projects that they design themselves (often with help from outside organizations). Activities range from preparing traditional food to participating in farming and craft production and in many cases you can combine volunteer activities with a homestay. Community tourism is taking off in a big way in Huaraz and the

RESPONSIBLE TREKKING

The Andes are part of a sensitive ecological environment, so it's important to be conscious of the impact of mass tourism. Here are a few tips to keep your impact minimal.

■ Help prevent deforestation: avoid disturbing flora or fauna and do not cut down trees or live branches for fires or other use; open fires are illegal.

■ With the amount of traffic some trails see, litter is an ongoing problem – even in remote areas. If you carry it in, carry it out – and if you can pick up and carry out some extra garbage, all the better.

■ Respect the park guards and follow their recommendations.

■ Camp at least 60m from water sources to avoid contaminating them.

■ Avoid playing music or making noise that will disturb animals and other people.

■ Don't give children money, sweets or gifts. This encourages persistent begging, which has become a major problem on some busy routes. If you wish to help, consider donating directly to local schools, NGOs and other volunteer organizations (p393).

■ Keep a low profile: the gear you are carrying costs more than many locals earn in a month (or a year!). Stow everything inside your tent at night.

HUARAZ & THE CORDILLERAS

Cordilleras, and a number of local agencies (opposite) can help you set up an itinerary.

Other Activities

Skiers will not find ski lifts in the Cordillera Blanca, but there is limited mountain **skiing** for die-hards who want to climb with skis. Ask locally for current conditions. **River running** (whitewater rafting) is sometimes offered on the Río Santa, but it's a very polluted river (mine-tailings upstream and raw sewage certainly don't help things) and people have fallen ill doing it. It's not recommended.

Horseback riding is a possibility; although there is no dedicated outfit in Huaraz, horses can be arranged by many travel agencies. The Lazy Dog Inn outside Huaraz (p398) has its own horses and does treks to the surrounding mountains. **Parapenting** (hang gliding) and **parasailing** are increasing in popularity, though you will need to bring all your own equipment. Aparac, a precipice behind Taricá, and Pan de Azúcar near Yungay are popular launching spots. Ask at Monttrek (opposite) for the latest info.

COURSES

Both of the following schools have Spanish teachers who are native speakers.

The **Sierra Verde Spanish School** (☎ 42-7954; sierra verde_sp@hotmail.com; Lúcar y Torre 530) has Spanish lessons for S15 per hour. **Explorers Spanish School** (☎ 94327761; Candelaria Villar 461) offers flex-

ible hours and group (up to four)/individual lessons for S15/S20 per hour.

TOURS & GUIDES
Day Tours

Dozens of agencies along Luzuriaga can organize outings to local sites, including several day excursions. One popular tour visits the ruins at Chavín de Huántar (see p422); another passes through Yungay to the beautiful Lagunas Llanganuco (p417), where there are superb vistas of Huascarán and other mountains; a third takes you through Caraz to Laguna Parón (p417), which is ravishingly surrounded by glaciated peaks; and a fourth travels through Caraz to see the massive *Puya raimondii* plant (p418) and then continues on to Nevado Pastoruri, where you can view ice caves, glaciers and mineral springs.

Any of these trips cost between S25 and S35 each; prices may vary depending on the number of people going, but typically include transport (usually in minibuses) and a guide (who may or may not speak English). Admission fees and lunch are extra. Trips take a full day; bring a packed lunch, warm clothes, drinking water and sunblock. Tours depart daily during the high season, but at other times departures depend on demand.

Out of the throng of agencies in Huaraz, **Pablo Tours** (☎ 42-1145; pablotours@terra.com.pe; Luzuriaga 501), **Huaraz Chavín Tours** (☎ 42-1578; hct@chavintours.com.pe; Luzuriaga 502) and **Sechín Tours** (☎ 42-1419; www.sechintours.com; Morales 602), which also has a satellite office in Casma, have fairly solid reputations.

Trekking & Mountaineering

Mountaineers and trekkers should check out **Casa de Guías** (☎ 42-1811; www.casadeguias.com.pe; Plaza Ginebra 28G, Huaraz; ⏰ 7-11am & 5-11pm), the head-quarters of the **Mountain Guide Association of Peru**, for a list of certified guides. All of the agencies below arrange full trekking and climbing expeditions that include guides, equipment, food, cooks, porters and transport. Depending on the number of people, the length of your trip and what's included, expect to pay from under S50 to S150 per person per day. Try not to base your selection solely on price, as is often the case you get what you pay for. The list below is by no means exhaustive; things change, good places go bad and bad places get good. One of the best resources for guides in Huaraz is other travelers who have just come back from a trek and can recommend (or not recommend) their guides based on recent experience. The South American Explorers Club in Lima (p86) is also an excellent source of information and maps.

Also see p402 and the boxed text, p403.

Active Peru (☎ 42-3339; www.activeperu.com; Gamarra 699) Run by the Belgian Dennis, who has a good reputation.

Andean Kingdom (☎ 42-5555; www.andeankingdom .com; Luzuriaga 522) One of the cheapest and more popular agencies in town. Be sure to double-check the equipment here and confirm exactly what's included in your trip before you set off.

Galaxia Expeditions (☎ 42-5335; Parque Periodista) Peruvian-run agency with a fine reputation and good gear. Also does local tours, climbing trips and has an indoor climbing wall.

Huascarán (☎ 42-2523; Campos 711) Gets repeatedly good reviews from satisfied travelers; also does tours.

Montañero (☎ 42-6386; Parque Ginebra) This good agency also rents or sells gear.

Monttrek (☎ 42-1124; www.monttrek.com; Luzuriaga 646, 2nd fl) A reputable agency that has lots of local information and arranges rock climbing, mountain biking and parapenting trips.

Community Tourism

In addition to the mountain lodges, the following agencies are involved in community tourism and can help you set up trips to learn about traditional weaving, farming, cooking and most other aspects of indigenous life. Almost anything you do with these agencies will benefit local families and contribute to the growing community-tourism movement in the region.

Incaroca Travel (☎ 77-0843; www.incaroca.it, in Italian) A highly recommended trekking company that leads many European groups through tiny, high-altitude villages and engages indigenous youth in tourism projects. The eight brothers speak almost any language you can throw at them, including Quechua, English and most modern European idioms. They don't have an office, but contact them in town or ahead of your arrival to get information.

Mountain Institute (☎ 42-3446; mtorres@mountain .org; Ricardo Palma 100) Arranges excellent trips to the Inca Trail (p409).

Respons Sustainable Tourism Center (☎ 42-7949; Calle 28 de Julio 821; www.respons.org; ⏰ 9am-1pm & 3-7:30pm) Works as a clearinghouse for information about community tourism in the area: arranges homestays, sells locally made woven goods and shares information free of charge.

FESTIVALS & EVENTS

Semana Santa (Holy Week) is very busy, with Peruvian tourists flooding to town. On the Tuesday before Easter there's a day of intense water fights. (Stay inside your hotel if you don't want to get soaked.) **Ash Wednesday** is much more interesting and colorful, with funeral processions for *ño carnavalón* (king of carnival) converging on the Plaza de Armas. Here, his 'will' is read, giving the opportunity for many jabs at local politicians, police and other dignitaries, before the procession continues to the river where the coffin is thrown in. Participants dress in colorful costumes with papier-mâché heads, some of which are recognizable celebrities.

Huaraz pays homage to its patron, **El Señor de la Soledad** (The Christ of Solitude), beginning May 3. This weeklong festival involves fireworks, music, dancing, elaborately costumed processions and lots of drinking.

Semana de Andinismo is held annually in June. It attracts mountaineers from several countries and competitions and exhibitions are held.

SLEEPING

The prices given here are average high (dry) season rates. Hotel prices can double during holiday periods and rooms become very scarce. Perhaps because Huaraz is seen as a trekking, climbing and backpacking center, budget hotels predominate.

Budget

Especially during the high season, locals meet buses from Lima and offer inexpensive accommodations in their houses. Hostels also employ individuals to meet buses, but beware of scams or overpricing – don't pay anybody until you've seen the room.

Hospedaje Ezama (☎ 42-3490; ezama_623@yahoo.es; Melgar 623; dm/s/d S10/15/25) Going north of town on Centenario and then right on Melgar brings you to this quiet, friendly, seven-room place that has spacious rooms and good hard beds. Hot water and tourist information are available.

Oscar's Hostal (☎ 42-2720; José de La Mar 624; r per person S12-18) Centrally located, Oscar's offers passable rooms with TV – though noise from the outside can be an issue.

Jo's Place (☎ 42-5505; www.josplacehuaraz.com; Villazón 278; dm S15, s/d S30/45, s/d without bathroom S25/35) Bright splashes of color and a rambling grassy area mark this informal and slightly chaotic place. Popular with trekkers and climbers (camping is allowed and there's plenty of room to dry out your gear), it has four floors linked by spindly staircases that lead to a warren of basic rooms, only some with bathrooms. Owner Jo provides UK newspapers, makes bacon and eggs for breakfast and has free coffee on tap.

Familia Meza Lodging (☎ 42-6763; Lúcar y Torre 538; s/d S15/30) In the same building as Café Andino and Mountain Bike Adventures, this charming family guest house has cheery rooms and is decorated throughout with homey, frilly touches. What's more, the owners are friendly and helpful enough to cure the worst bout of homesickness. Hot showers are shared and there's a top-floor communal area with a small kitchen.

Cayesh Guesthouse (☎ 42-8821; www.cayesh.net; Morales 867; s/d from S25/40) The folks at Cayesh take backpackers' delights seriously, offering an extensive DVD library, free kitchen use and luggage storage. The rooms are simple but have comfortable beds from which you can gander at the views of magnificent peaks.

Albergue Churup (☎ 42-2584; www.churup.com; Figueroa 1257; dm S25 s/d incl breakfast S65/90) This immensely popular family-run hostel continues to win the top budget-choice accolade. Immaculate and comfortable rooms share cushy, colorful lounging areas on every floor. The building is topped by a massive, fireplace-warmed lounge space with magnificent 180-degree views of the Cordillera. If that isn't enough, the affable Quirós family has built a sauna, there's a cafe and bar, communal kitchen, a pretty garden, a book exchange, laundry facilities and a travel office that rents out trekking gear and arranges Spanish lessons. Reservations are advised.

Aldo's Guest House (☎ 42-5355; Morales 650; r per person S30) Budget travelers love little Aldo's, a cheery, homey place decorated with bright colors and located right in the center of town. All rooms have cable TV and private bathrooms with hot showers, and you can use the kitchen or order breakfast and lunches.

Albergue Benkawasi (☎ 42-3159; www.huaraz benkawasi.com; Parque Santa Rosa 928; s/d S30/50) With coke-bottle glass windows, plaid bedspreads and brick walls, the Benkawasi has a kind of '70s mountain chalet feel to it. Plop yourself down in front of the main room's fireplace or chill out in the quiet rooms in this reader-recommended option.

Hostal Tany (☎ 42-7680; Lúcar y Torre 648; s/d S32/45; 🖳) The big and bright rooms here have massive windows to help you appreciate the awesome mountain vistas around. There's an internet cafe downstairs.

Edward's Inn (☎ 42-2692; www.edwardsinn.com; Bolognesi 121; r per person S35) Rooms in this popular place all have hot water, but are otherwise elementary. There is a nice grassy bit and the owner, Edward, speaks excellent English and is a knowledgeable guide.

Hostal Gyula Inn (☎ 42-1567; www.hostalgy.on.to; Plaza Ginebra 632; s/d S35/55) Set around a plaza in the middle of town, Gyula has good rooms with comfortable mattresses, 24-hour hot showers and some climbing- and trekking-gear rental.

Monte Blanco Hotel (☎ 42-6384; José de la Mar 620; s/d S35/60) Recently repainted blindingly pink, the digs here are Spartan, clean and shiny. Big cushioned couches await slumping in the hallways; this is a solid back-up choice.

Hostal Raimondi (☎ 42-1082; Raimondi 820; s/d S40/45) Greeted by an immense antique foyer reminiscent of an echoing train station, inside you'll find dark, austere rooms painted in dizzying, bright patterns. All come with comfy beds and writing desks, and hot showers are provided in the morning. It's convenient for buses and has a small cafe for early breakfasts.

Hotel Del Valle (☎ 42-2399; Larrea y Loredo 780; s/d S42/55) Not a bad deal for this price range. It has nice communal sitting areas and the orderly rooms are rather presentable.

Hotel Brit's (☎ 42-6720; Cáceres 391-399; s/d S45/60)
A six-story monolith with good rooms for the price; each is clean, carpeted and comes with cable TV. It's a secure place and some of the top-floor rooms have good views.

La Casa de Zarela (☎ 42-1694; www.lacasadezarela.com; Arguedas 1263; s/d S50/70) Zarela's helpfulness is legendary. Double and triple rooms here have hot showers and kitchen facilities, as well as lots of neat little patio areas in which to relax with a book. The scenic black-and-white photos of the environs are worth perusing.

Hostal Schatzi (☎ /fax 42-3074; www.schatzihostal.com; Bolívar 419; s/d S50/70) Plenty of leafage in the pleasant courtyard here manages to keep the concrete at bay. Charismatic little rooms surround this garden and inside have exposed wood-beam ceilings and great top-floor views. This is a reliable bet.

B&B My House (☎ 42 3375; bmark@ddm.com.pe; Calle 27 de Novembre 773; s/d incl breakfast S50/70) A small, bright patio and six rooms decorated like a home away from home welcome you to this hospitable B&B. Rooms have a writing desk and hot shower and there's a cheery communal yard. English and French are spoken.

Midrange

Alojamiento Soledad (☎ 42-1196; www.lodgingsoledad.com; Figueroa 1267; s/d S65/90; 🖳) A cozy family house with eight rooms – six with bathrooms and hot showers. Its rooftop terrace has the prerequisite sweeping views and a BBQ for sunset cook-outs. Helpful owners speak English and German and there is a cable-TV room, kitchen and laundry facilities.

Hotel Sierra Nevada (☎ 44-9613; Monterrey Km 3.5; s/d S65/90) Laid out in a large V shape, this hotel sits perched on a hilltop 3.5km north of town and has sensational views of the valley below. The rooms are just comfortable enough and you can take your breakfast in the dainty garden gazebo while the pet alpaca roams the grounds aimlessly.

Hotel Los Portales (☎ 42-8184; Raimondi 903; s/d incl breakfast S65/110) A little swisher than most choices in Huaraz, the quiet, carpeted rooms here are clean and without fault. A games room (pool and table tennis) adds some attraction and there is a restaurant and sauna to boot. At night, the whole place is dimly lit with romantic mood lighting.

Olaza's Bed & Breakfast (☎ 42-2529; www.olazas.com; Arguedas 1242; s/d S70/90; 🖳) This smart little hotel has a boutique feel, spacious bathrooms and comfortable beds, but the best part is the big lounge area upstairs and great breakfasts (not included) on the terrace. The owner is an established figure in the Huaraz trekking and tourism scene and he can point you in the direction no matter where you want to go.

Grand Hotel Huaraz (☎ 42-2227; grandhotel@terra.com.pe; Larrea y Loredo 721; s/d S70/110; 🖳) The spiffy Grand Hotel Huaraz is a little short on personality, but the solid rooms have everything you'll need for a comfortable stay.

Hotel El Tumi (☎ 42-1784, 42-1852; www.hoteleltumi.com; San Martín 1121; s/d S85/150; 🖳) If serious businesspeople lodged in chalets, this large and comfortable establishment is where they would flock. The rooms are handsomely finished with dark wood, come with cable TV and many have great mountain views. It all has a cozy retreat feel. Downstairs there's a lounge, posh restaurant with room service and wi-fi for laptopping mountain-road warriors.

Piramide Hotel (☎ 42-8250, 42-5801; Plaza Ginebra U22; s/d/ste incl breakfast S105/136/180) This is a modern hotel with phones and TVs and some rooms have balconies looking out into the plaza or toward the mountains. There's a restaurant with room service and rates include an American breakfast.

Steel Guest House (☎ 42-9709; www.steelguest.com; Pasaje Maguina 1467; s/d S108/141; 🖳) Staying here is a little like landing at your grandma's house: the rooms are frilly and white-glove clean and the owner tends to dote on her guests. Loads of facilities round out the offerings, including cable TV, outdoor hammocks, billiards, sauna and a roof terrace.

Hotel La Joya (☎ 42-5527; www.hotellajoya.com; San Martín 1187; s/d S120/220; 🖳) With true, glittering '80s panache, this towering, mirror-lined monolith offers hotel-standard rooms, with TV and writing desk. There's a very cheesy but comfortable lounge downstairs with endless muzak on tap. The top-floor rooms come with views and for some reason a disturbing statue of a mountaineer guards the elevator.

San Sebastián (☎ 42-6960; Italia 1124; s/d incl breakfast S150/170) A fetching white-walled and red-roofed building with balconies and arches overlooking a grassy garden and an inner courtyard with a soothing fountain – this four-story hotel is a neocolonial architectural find. All rooms have a writing desk, good beds, hot shower and TV on request. A few rooms have balconies.

MOUNTAIN RETREATS

If trudging around the mountains for days at a time doesn't appeal to you, a good alternative is to make a home right among them. These mountain lodges let you explore deep in the stunning hills by day, and still come back to a comfortable bed every night.

Way Inn Lodge (☎ 42-8714; www.thewayinn.com/lodge.htm; camping S15, dm S32-35, bungalows S120-180, all incl breakfast) Extremely popular with travelers of all stripes for many years, the Way Inn Lodge's rooms range from bunks in one of their Flintstone-esque 'cave' rooms to deluxe, well-appointed bungalows with fireplaces. A hand-built sauna and hot tub round off the long list of facilities rather nicely. There's tons of information here about one-day and multiday treks and trails you can do right from the front door, plus hiking equipment is available for rent. All rates include breakfast and other meals are available. Call ahead or visit its website for directions.

ourpick Lazy Dog Inn (☎ 978-9330; www.thelazydoginn.com; s/d without bathroom S120/180, d inside main house S240, 2-person cabins S260, all incl breakfast & dinner) Run by rugged and proud Canadians Diana and Wayne, this deluxe ecolodge is at the mouth of the Quebrada Llaca, 8km east of Huaraz. It's made entirely of adobe and built by hand and you can stay in either comfortable double rooms in the main lodge or in fancier private cabins, which have fireplaces and bathtubs. Lots of trekking opportunities are available here, including numerous day hikes right around the lodge, plus you can rent horses for S60 for one to three hours. Call ahead or visit its website for directions.

See also the Llanganuco Mountain Lodge outside of Yungay (p416), and three modest and remote refuges under the boxed text The Italian Connection (p415).

Hotel Colomba (☎ 42-7106, 42-1501; www.huarazhotel .com; Francisco de Zela 278; s/d S150/200) One of the best picks in town, the bungalows here are speckled around a dense and compulsively trimmed hedge forest. Each bungalow has a relaxing veranda, TV and telephone and the sprawling gardens conceal a kids' playground, huge bird enclosures and a dainty restaurant.

Top End

Hotel Andino (☎ 42 1662; www.hotelandino.com; Pedro Cochachín 357; s/d S281/339, with balcony S314/388; 🖳) All the immaculate, carpeted rooms at this Swiss-run hotel have great views and such mod cons as cable TV and hair dryers. Splurge on a room with a balcony if you can. The on-site restaurant, Chalet Suisse, serves international and Peruvian food in addition to Swiss specialties. It's very popular with international trekking and climbing groups, and reservations can be hard to come by in high season.

EATING

Restaurant hours are flexible in Huaraz, with shorter opening times during low-season slow spells and longer hours at busy times.

Seeds of Hope Café (☎ 39-6305; www.peruseeds .org; breakfast from S4; Antunez 782; 🕑 7am-2pm) Who thought filling up on homemade granola and cakes would help a good cause? At this cafe, run by the aid organization Seeds of Hope (p393), profits go toward its efforts to help needy children in Huaraz – and the coffee, tea and delicious breakfasts are tasty and healthy.

Pastelería Café Turmanyé (Morales 828; sandwiches S5-8, pastries S3-5; 🕑 8am-6pm) Serving paella, sandwiches and rich Spanish-style pastries and cakes, this little eatery also has the distinction of benefiting the local Arco Iris Foundation, which helps children and young mothers.

El Fogón (☎ 42-1267; Luzuriaga 928, 2nd fl; mains S6-15; 🕑 noon-11pm) A bright, modern and slightly upscale twist on the traditional Peruvian grill house, this place will grill anything that moves – including the usual chicken, trout and rabbit and it does great *anticuchos* (shish kebabs). Everything is very tasty and the place gets packed nightly with Peruvians in on the secret. Vegetarians will go hungry though.

ourpick Café Andino (☎ 42-1203; www.cafeandino .com; Lúcar y Torre 530, 3rd fl; breakfast S6-20; 🕑 8am-8pm Tue-Sun; 🖳) This modern top-floor cafe has space and light in spades, comfy lounges, art, photos, books and groovy tunes – it's the ultimate all-day hangout and meeting spot. You can get breakfast anytime (Belgian waffles – yum!) and this place is serious about its coffee, roasting its own. Ask Chris, the US owner, about information on trekking in the area and check out the message board for local info.

Pachamama (☎ 42-1834; San Martín 687; snacks & mains S6-22; ◷ 5pm-11pm) This warm and delightful restaurant-bar features a glass roof, plant-filled interior garden, fireplace, pool table, table tennis, art on the walls and giant chessboard on the floor. It's a hip, fun and popular locale that may have live music and dancing at weekends (not *folklórico*!). The menu is Peruvian and international with a Swiss twist.

Piccolo (☎ 42-7306; Morales 632; mains S8-28; ◷ 7am-midnight) Very popular with gringos attracted to the outdoor pavement seating, friendly service and reasonable prices, the Piccolo is a cafe and pizzeria that moonlights as a restaurant. It has a good Italian and international menu, but make sure you see its Peruvian menu.

La Brasa Roja (☎ 42-7738; Luzuriaga 919; mains S9-21; ◷ noon-midnight Mon-Sat) This scrumptious *pollería* (restaurant specializing in roast chicken) is the ultimate budget refueling stop. The 'Red-Hot Coals' also serves up sandwiches, pastas and beef – but stick with the chicken, it's what it does best.

Encuentro (☎ 79-7802; Morales 650; mains S10-22; ◷ 8am-11pm) One of three Encuentro locations around Huaraz serving breakfasts, coffees, cocktails and Peruvians dishes – the trout *tiradito* (Japanese-influence version of ceviche, served in thin slices and without onions) is fresh and delicious.

California Café (☎ 42-8354; www.huaylas.com; Calle 28 de Julio 562; breakfast S12-18; ◷ 7:30am-7pm; 🖵) Run by Tim, from California no less, this hip pad does breakfasts at any time, plus light lunches and salads – it's a funky, chilled space to while away many hours. You can spend the day listening to the sublime world music collection or reading one of the hundreds of books available for exchange. Wi-fi is a godsend to laptop junkies and rich espressos and dozens of herbal teas will keep you sipping till closing time. Tim is active in the development of ecotourism in the Cordillera Huayhuash and is a goldmine of information on that area. He organizes 'ultimate Frisbee' games every Friday.

El Horno (☎ 42-4617; www.elhornopizzeria.com; Parque Periodista; pizzas S12-18, mains S12-26; ◷ 10am-11pm Mon-Sat) If you can cook it on a grill or in a wood oven, El Horno can make it sing. The different varieties of meat skewers and pizzas are the best picks here. The place often fills up with trekking groups, so arrive early or make a reservation.

Pizza Bruno (☎ 42-5689; Luzuriaga 834; pizza S12-28; ◷ 5-11pm) This French-owned pizzeria has nice pastas and big salads, but the pizzas taste like they are made by people who really know how to use a wood-fired oven and make a great sauce.

Siam de los Andes (☎ 40-9173; Gamarra 560; mains S12-38; ◷ 6-10pm) More expensive than many Huaraz restaurants, the authentic Thai fare is prepared by an infectiously cheery Thai chef and well worth the few extra soles. You'll find everything from aromatic veggie soups to chicken *satay* (skewers with peanut sauce) to Pad Thai noodles with jumbo shrimp.

Crêperie Patrick (☎ 42-3364; Luzuriaga 422; mains around S15; ◷ 8am-10pm) This French-influenced place is recommended for crêpes, ice cream and continental dinners (trout, fondue, pasta). It has a rooftop patio that's open in the mornings for enjoying breakfast under the sun.

Bistro de los Andes (☎ 42-6249; Plaza de Armas; mains from S18; ◷ 7:30am-11pm) This restaurant with a European air is owned by a multilingual Frenchman. It serves an international and Peruvian menu ranging from pancakes to pastas. Good coffees, delectable desserts, fabulous fish dishes – there's something for everyone at any time of day. The service is excellent, a happy-hour special is always on offer and the long rows of tables along the windows look out onto the Plaza de Armas.

Monte Rosa/Inca Pub (☎ 42-1447; José de la Mar 661; mains S18-30; ◷ 11am-11pm) This warm, snug Swiss-run restaurant has an Alpine vibe; it does an international menu that includes fondue and *raclette* (melted cheese over potatoes or bread) as well as pizzas and Peruvian plates. If it's full, service can be slow. The owner also sells Victorinox Swiss army knives.

Mercado Ortíz (cnr Luzuriaga & Raimondi; ◷ 8am-10pm) is a good supermarket to pick up goodies for trekking or self-catering.

DRINKING

Huaraz is the best place in this part of the Andes to take a load off and get pleasantly inebriated.

Los 13 Buhos (José de la Mar 812, 2nd fl; ◷ 5pm-late) Located upstairs from Makondos, the 13 Owls is a chilled-out bar that is the most popular place in town to kick back and chat in the early evening while listening to excellent, funky sounds. Warm lighting flickers over graffiti-covered walls and climbing paraphernalia clings to the rafters, while couches help you ease into the evening's frivolities over a cold Crystal.

Vagamundo Travel Bar (Morales 753; ☽ 10am-late) Opens late morning and has erratic hours. Come in for a beer, snack and a game of foosball. Enjoy rock and blues while perusing the many maps on the walls, or sit outside on the patio.

Andean Garden Club (Luzuriaga 1032; ☽ 11am-6pm, high season only) Owned by the same people as the X-treme Bar, this laid-back option has an outdoor garden setting and sells beer and snacks, plus it has a climbing wall for the perennially active. Just don't drink and climb.

X-treme Bar (☎ 42-3150; Luzuriaga 1044, 2nd fl; ☽ 7pm-late) This classic watering hole hasn't changed in years. Bizarre art, drunken graffiti, strong cocktails and good rock and blues keep things rambunctious well into the night as it fills to the brim with a steady stream of bodies.

ENTERTAINMENT

Discos and *peñas* (bars or clubs featuring folkloric music) abound around Huaraz, though names and levels of popularity change with the seasons.

El Tambo Bar (☎ 42-3417; José de la Mar 776; ☽ 9pm-4am) If you're hankerin' to shake your groove-thang, this is the most popular disco in town. Fashionable with both *extranjeros* (foreigners) and Peruvians, the music swings from techno-*cumbia* to Top 20, to salsa to reggae to most things in between – all in a space of 20 minutes. Occasional live bands also play. Although there's no cover charge, you may want to consult your accountant before buying a round of drinks: the prices are astronomical.

Huaraz Satyricon (☎ 955-7343; Luzuriaga 1036; admission S5) This place may just be the world's most perfect little cinema. A small and intimate space that has snug couches, fresh popcorn, snacks and espresso, it shows top-quality international and repertoire flicks (all with English subtitles) on a private projection screen. Look out for flyers around town advertising the changing schedule. Note that the theater may be shut for periods during low season.

SHOPPING

Inexpensive thick woolen sweaters, scarves, hats, socks, gloves, ponchos and blankets are available if you need to rug up for the mountains; many of these are sold at stalls on the pedestrian alleys off Luzuriaga or at the *feria*

artesanal (artisans' market) off the Plaza de Armas. Quality climbing gear and clothes are sold by several agencies that rent equipment and gear (p403).

High-quality, attractive T-shirts with appropriately mountainous designs are made by Andean Expressions and sold at gift shops in Olaza's Bed & Breakfast (p397) and the **Last Minute Gift Store** (Lucar & Torre 530; ☽ 10am-1pm, 4-8pm Mon-Sat) – watch out for lower-quality imitators. **Perú Magico** (José Sucre btwn Farfán & Bolívar; ☽ 9am-2pm & 3-9pm Mon-Sat) has an assortment of jewelry, textiles and pottery from around the country. **Tejidos Turmanyé** (Morales 828; ☽ 8am-5pm) sells handsome locally made weavings and knit garments to support a foundation that provides occupational training to young mothers, and Respons Sustainable Tourism Center (p395) hawks some pretty hip knits made by Huaraz-area artisans.

GETTING THERE & AWAY
Air

LC Busre operates flights from Lima to Huaraz everyday at 8:40am; the return journey leaves at 10:20am. The Huaraz **airport** (ATA; ☎ 44 3095) is actually at Anta, 23km north of town. A taxi will cost about S12.

Bus

Combis for Caraz (S5, 1½ hours) leave every few minutes during the day from near the petrol station on Calle 13 de Diciembre. These will drop you in any of the towns along the way. Minibuses south along the Callejón de Huaylas to Recuay, Catac and other villages leave from the Transportes Zona Sur terminal on Gridilla at Calle 27 de Novembre.

A plethora of companies have departures for Lima (six to eight hours), so shop around for the price/class/time you prefer. Most depart midmorning or late evening. Some buses begin in Caraz and stop in Huaraz to pick up passengers. During high season it is recommended that you book your seats at least a day in advance.

Three bus routes reach Chimbote on the north coast. Most buses take the paved road to Pativilca (the same route as Lima-bound buses, eight hours) and then head north on the Pan-American Hwy. A second, bumpier route follows the Callejón de Huaylas and passes through the narrow, thrilling Cañón del Pato (eight to nine hours, see p417) before descending to the coast. A third route – and the roughest – crosses the 4225m-high Punta Callán (seven hours) and provides spectacular views of the Cordillera Blanca before plummeting down to Casma and pushing north.

Many small companies with brave, beat-up buses cross the Cordillera to the towns east of Huaraz.

Of the following long-haul companies, the locally owned Movil Tours and Línea are recommended.

Chavín Express (☎ 42-4652; Cáceres 338) Has 4am, 8:30am, 11am and 2pm services to Chavín (S10, three hours), going on to San Marcos (S12, 3½ hours) and Huari (S12, six hours). Also has a bus to Llamellin at 9:30am (S15, eight hours).

Chinchaysuyo (☎ 42-6417; Morales 650B) Has a 9pm bus to Trujillo (S27, 10 hours) via Pativilca.

Cial (☎ 42-9253; Morales 650) Good, midpriced night buses to Lima (S35 to S45).

Cruz del Sur (☎ 42-8726; Bolívar 491) Has 11am and 10pm luxury nonstop services to Lima for S70 to S90.

Expreso Ancash (☎ 42-5371; Raimondi 835) Has cheap services to Lima at 1:45pm and 8:45pm (S25).

Línea (☎ 42-6666; Bolívar 450) Has excellent buses at 9pm and 9:15pm to Trujillo (S35 to S60, 10 hours) via Pativilca and Chimbote.

Los Andes (☎ 42-7362; Raimondi 744) Has a 6am bus to Pomabamba (S21, eight hours) via Piscobamba, Yanama, Colcabamba and Vaqueria.

Movil Tours (☎ 42-2555; Bolívar 452) Buses to Lima at 9am and 1pm and several night buses between 10pm and 11pm (S35 to S65). Has 9pm and 9:30pm buses to Chimbote via Pativilca (S25 to S35) and on to Trujillo (S45 to S55). The terminal is at Confraternidad Internacional Oeste.

Renzo (☎ 42-9673; Raimondi 835) Has a rambling 6am and 7pm service to Pomabamba (S21, nine hours) stopping at Piscobamba, Yanama, Colcabamba and Vaqueria. Another service leaves at 6:15am and 2:30pm for San Luis (S17, six hours) via Chacas (S14, five hours).

Sandoval (☎ 42-8069; Cáceres 338) Has buses to Huari (S14) via Chavín (S12) at 4am, 10am, 3pm and 8:30pm. Also has a bus to Huánuco at 8pm (S18, eight hours).

Transport Huandoy (☎ 42-7507; Fitzcarrald 261) There's a bus at 11am to Chimbote via Cañón del Pato (S21, eight hours), as well as 8am, 10am and 1pm Chimbote buses (S21, seven hours) via Casma.

Transportes El Rápido (☎ 42-2887; Bolognesi 261) Buses leave at 5:30am and 2pm to Chiquián via Recuay (S9, 2½ hours); 6am, 1pm and 3pm to Huallanca (S14, four hours); and 1pm to La Unión (S18, four hours).

Transportes Río Mosna (☎ 42-6632; Calle 27 de Noviembre) Has buses at 10am and 3pm to Chavín (S12, three hours) and Huari (S14, four hours).

Transportes Rodríguez (☎ 42-1353; Calle 27 de Noviembre 622) Night buses to Lima at 10:30pm (S23).

Yungay Express (☎ 42-4377; Raimondi 744) There's a morning bus at 7am to Chimbote via Cañón del Pato (S21, eight hours), and a night bus via Pativilca (S21, seven hours).

GETTING AROUND
A taxi ride around Huaraz costs about S3. A taxi ride to Caraz is at least S35. Look for taxis at the bridge on Fitzcarrald or along Luzuriaga.

THE CORDILLERAS

Huaraz lies sandwiched in a valley carved out by the Río Santa, flanked to the west by the brown Cordillera Negra and to the east by the frosted Cordillera Blanca. A paved road runs along the valley, more commonly known as the Callejón de Huaylas, and links a string of settlements while furnishing visitors with perfect views of lofty elevations.

The Cordillera Negra, though an attractive range in its own right, is snowless and often eclipsed by the stunning, snow-covered crown of the Cordillera Blanca.

The Cordillera Blanca, about 20km wide and 180km long, is an elaborate collection of toothed summits, razor-sharp ridges, pea-colored lakes and green valleys draped with crawling glaciers. More than 50 peaks of 5700m or higher grace this fairly small area. North America, in contrast, has only three mountains in excess of 5700m, and Europe has none. Huascarán, at 6768m, is Peru's highest mountain and the highest pinnacle in the tropics anywhere in the world.

South of the Cordillera Blanca is the smaller, more remote, but no less spectacular Cordillera Huayhuash. It contains Peru's second-highest mountain, the 6634m Yerupajá, and is a more rugged and less frequently visited range.

Where once pre-Columbian and Inca cultures used the high valleys as passageways to eastern settlements, backpackers and mountaineers now explore and marvel at the spectacle of Mother Nature blowing her own trumpet.

The main trekking areas of the Cordilleras include sections of the Cordillera Blanca, which is mostly encompassed by Parque Nacional Huascarán and the Cordillera Huayhuash, to the south of Huaraz. There's something here for scramblers of all skill and fitness levels: from short, easy hikes of a day or two, to multiweek adventures requiring technical mountain-climbing skills. Foreigners flock here yearly and favorite hikes like the Santa Cruz trek can see a lot of hiking-boot traffic in the high season. While the more remote 10-day Cordillera Huayhuash Circuit doesn't see half as many visitors as the Santa Cruz trek, savvy travelers are rapidly discovering its rugged beauty and appreciating the friendly highland culture. Dozens of shorter routes crisscross the Cordillera Blanca and can provide an appetizing taste of the province's vistas, or can be combined with longer treks to keep you walking in the hills for months on end.

See the boxed text, p394, for advice and information about responsible trekking in Peru.

Trekking & Mountaineering

INFORMATION

To get the lowdown on trekking and the latest conditions, your first port of call should be Casa de Guías (p395), which has information on weather, trail conditions, guides and mule hire. Some IGN and Alpenvereinskarte topographic maps are sold here.

Trekking and equipment-rental agencies are also good sources of local knowledge and can also advise on day hikes. For more impartial advice, be sure to visit popular Huaraz haunts such as California Café (p399) and Café Andino (p398), whose foreign owners keep abreast of local developments, sell hiking maps and guides and freely dole out advice alongside tasty treats. While you're there, be sure to check out their noticeboards and talk to other travelers and mountaineers – recently returned climbers will have the best advice on what to expect.

WHEN TO GO

People hike year-round, but the dry season of mid-May to mid-September is the most popular time to visit, with good weather and the clearest views. It's still advisable to check out the latest weather forecasts, however, as random heavy snowfalls, winds and electrical storms are not uncommon during this period. December to April is the wettest time, when it is often overcast and wet in the afternoons and trails become boggy. With the appropriate gear and some preparation, hiking is still possible and some trekkers find hiking then

more rewarding, as many of the most popular trails are empty. For serious mountaineering, climbers pretty much stick to the dry season.

TRAIL GUIDEBOOKS & MAPS

Lonely Planet's *Trekking in the Central Andes* covers the best hikes in the Cordillera Blanca and the Cordillera Huayhuash. A great resource for the Huayhuash region is the detailed *Climbs and Treks of the Cordillera Huayhuash of Peru* (2005) by Jeremy Frimer, though it's only available locally in Huaraz. The best overview of climbing in the Cordillera Blanca is Brad Johnson's *Classic Climbs of the Cordillera Blanca Peru* (2003).

Felipe Díaz's 1:286,000 *Cordilleras Blanca & Huayhuash* is a popular and excellent map for an overview of the land, with towns, major trails and town plans – though it's not detailed enough for remote treks. The Alpenvereinskarte (German Alpine Club) produces the most detailed and accurate maps of the region; look for the regularly updated 1:100,000 *Cordillera Blanca Nord* (sheet 0/3a) and *Cordillera Blanca Sur* (sheet 0/3b) maps. For the Cordillera Huayhuash, get the Alpine Mapping Guild's 1:50,000 *Cordillera Huayhuash* topographic map. These maps are available in Caraz, Huaraz and at South American Explorers' clubhouses.

IGN produces six 1:100,000 scale maps covering the Cordilleras, although they're somewhat dated and often use atypical place names.

TOURS & GUIDES

The Casa de Guías and agencies (see p395), in Huaraz, and Pony Expeditions (p418), in Caraz, are good places to start your search for qualified mountain guides, *arrieros* (mule drivers) and cooks. If you wish to put together a support team for your own expedition, trekking agencies can also arrange individual guides, cooks or pack animals.

If your Spanish is up to it and you're not in a great hurry, you can hire *arrieros* (mule drivers) and mules in trailhead villages, particularly Cashapampa, Colcabamba and Vaqueria, among others. Horses, donkeys and mules are used as pack animals, and while llamas are occasionally provided, they cannot carry as much weight. Try to get a reference for a good *arriero* and establish your trekking goals (ie pace, routes) before you depart. Check the state of the pack animals before you hire them – some *arrieros* overwork their beasts of burden or use sick or injured animals.

Prices are generally set by the Dirección de Turismo and the guides' union. Expect to pay around S15 per day for a horse, donkey or mule and S30 per day for an *arriero*. Official rates for guides are S90 to S150 per day for a trekking guide, S150 to S225 for a climbing guide and S300 to S360 for a technical climbing guide.

Qualified guides and *arrieros* are issued with photo identification by the tourism authority – ask for credentials. Even experienced mountaineers would do well to add a local guide, who knows exactly what has been happening in the mountains, to their group. Prices do not include food and you may have to provide your *arriero* with a tent and pay for their return journey. Confirm what's included before you set off.

EQUIPMENT & RENTALS

If you lack the experience or equipment required to mountain it, fear not, as dozens of 'savoir faire' businesses offer guides, gear rental and organize entire adventures for you, right down to the *burros* (donkeys). If you go on a tour, trekking agencies (see p393) will supply everything from tents to ice axes. Some of them also rent out gear independently. **Skyline Adventures** (☎ 64-9480; www.skyline-adventures .com; Pasaje Industrial 137, Huaraz), based just outside of Huaraz, comes highly recommended and has some of the best-quality rental equipment in the area. It also provides guides for treks and mountain climbs and leads two- and three-day mountaineering courses. Another reliable rental agency is **MountClimb** (☎ 42-6060; www.mountclimb.com; Cáceres 421, Huaraz), which has top-end climbing gear. **Monte Rosa/Inca Pub** (☎ 42-1447; José de la Mar 661, Huaraz) sells and buys good-quality climbing gear and skis and is an official Swiss army knife outlet.

HUARAZ & THE CORDILLERAS

WHAT TO ASK BEFORE PAYING FOR A GUIDED TREK

Before you lay out your cold, hard cash for a guided trek make sure you know what you're getting. Ask the company or guide to list the services, products and price they're offering on your contract. In the event that they don't live up to their promises you may or may not be able to do anything about it, but a list ensures that the company understands exactly what you expect.

On your end, it is critical that you are crystal clear with your guides about your experience and fitness level. Also important is that you are properly acclimatized before setting out on a trek. All too often, parties set out for big treks and climbs just after arriving in Huaraz, with the predictable result of altitude sickness and having to turn back. Take the time to adjust in Huaraz, do a couple of acclimatization hikes, and *then* enjoy a trouble-free, multiday trek.

Below are some suggested questions to ask before choosing your guide; keep in mind that the answers will make a difference in the price.

■ Can I meet our guide ahead of time? This is an opportunity to meet the person you'll spend a lot of time with for multiple days and nights, and if necessary, to confirm ahead of time that he speaks English.

■ Will we use public or private transportation?

■ Will there be a cook and an *arriero* (mule driver)?

■ Will there be a separate cooking tent and a separate bathroom tent?

■ How many meals and snacks will we get every day? Many trekkers complain about inadequate breakfasts and too few energizing noshes.

■ Do we have to provide equipment and food for the guides, cooks and *arrieros*? Remember that prepackaged dehydrated meals are not staples in the Cordillera Blanca. You will almost certainly be eating whole, local foods that weigh more and require more effort to carry.

■ How many people will be on our trek? Larger numbers mean lower prices, but make sure you're comfortable trekking with a dozen strangers.

■ Can I check the equipment before we set off? If you don't have your own sleeping bag, make sure that the one provided is long enough and warm enough (good to -15°C), and inspect the tents for holes and rain resistance.

It often freezes at night, so make sure you have an adequately warm sleeping bag, wet-weather gear (needed year-round), and a brimmed hat and sunglasses. It's best to bring strong sunblock and good insect repellant from home, as they're difficult to find in Huaraz.

CORDILLERA BLANCA

One of the most breathtaking parts of the continent, the Cordillera Blanca is the world's highest tropical mountain range and encompasses some of South America's highest mountains. Andean leviathans include the majestic Nevado Alpamayo (5947m), once termed 'the most beautiful mountain in the world' by the German Alpine Club. Others include Nevado Huascarán (at 6768m, Peru's highest), Pucajirca Oeste (6039m), Nevado Quitaraju (6036m) and Nevado Santa Cruz (Nevado Pucaraju; 6241m).

Situated in the tropical zone, the Cordillera Blanca stands to be affected greatly as global warming increases; there exists significant evidence that the glaciers of the Cordillera Blanca show a measurable decrease in their volume and that the snow line has receded in recent decades. Other threats to the park include litter and high-altitude grazing on endangered qeñua (Polylepis) trees. For more information about these threats, contact the Mountain Institute (p393) in Huaraz.

Parque Nacional Huascarán

Peruvian mountaineer César Morales Arnao first suggested protecting the flora, fauna and archaeological sites of the Cordillera Blanca in the early 1960s, but it didn't become a reality until 1975, when the national park was established. This 3400-sq-km park encompasses practically the entire area of the Cordillera Blanca above 4000m, including more than 600 glaciers and nearly 300 lakes, and protects such extraordinary and endangered species as the giant Puya raimondii plant, the spectacled bear and the Andean Condor.

Visitors to the park should bring their passports to register at the park office in Huaraz (p391) and pay the park fee. This is S5 per person for a day visit or S60 for a one-month pass. You can also register and pay your fee at one of the control stations.

Money from fees is used to help maintain trails, pay park rangers and offset the effects of the legions of visitors to the area. It makes sense that as foreign visitors are among those frequenting the area and causing the greatest change, they should contribute to the financing of the national park with their user fees. Although it's sometimes possible to dodge paying the park fee – because control station hours and locations vary – remember that the cheapest option isn't always the correct one; you can always pay your fee at the office in Huaraz.

Santa Cruz Trek

This trek ascends the spectacular Quebrada Santa Cruz valley and crosses the Punta Union pass (4760m) before tumbling into Quebrada Harípampa on the other side. Head-turning sights along the way include emerald lakes, sensational views of many of the Cordillera's peaks, beds of brightly colored alpine wildflowers and stands of red qeñua trees. Another less thrilling sight here, as in many trekking areas, is the constant sight of cow patties dimpling the valleys and meadows. Watch your step!

The Santa Cruz is one of the most popular routes in Peru for international trekkers and it is clearly signposted for much of its length. Each day requires about 13km of hiking (between five and eight hours of hiking) and ascents ranging from 500m to 700m; the third day requires a knee-busting 900m descent.

The first and second days are the toughest, but probably the most rewarding, as they take you past many small waterfalls and a series of lakes and interconnecting marshy areas. The first, smaller lake is **Laguna Ichiccocha** (also referred to as Laguna Chica), closely followed by the much larger **Laguna Jatuncocha** (or Laguna Grande). You'll camp at Taullipampa (4250m) in a gorgeous meadow at the foot of the majestic **Nevado Taulliraju** (5830m). The glacial icefall on the flanks of Taulliraju is very active and large chunks regularly break off, especially under the influence of the afternoon sun. To the south, Nevado Artesonraju (6025m) and Nevado Parón (5600m) dominate the skyline.

> **FAST FACTS**
>
> Duration: 4 days
> Distance: 50km
> Difficulty: easy-moderate
> Start: Cashapampa (2900m)
> Finish: Vaqueria (3700m)

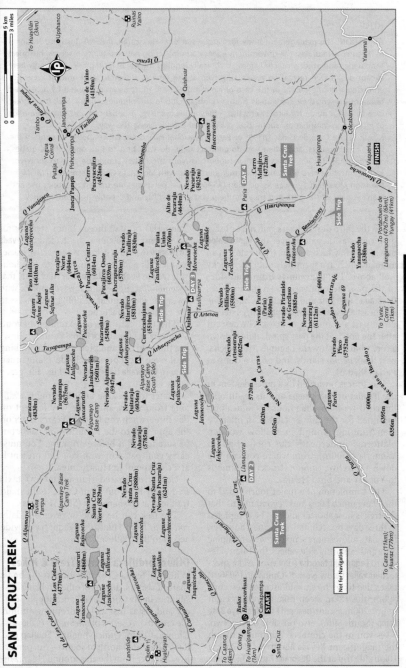

SANTA CRUZ TREK

Not for Navigation

HUARAZ & THE
CORDILLERAS

¡OJO!

ATTENTION! The management body for Parque Nacional Huascarán, INRENA (Instituto Nacional de Recursos Naturales; the government agency administering national parks, reserves, historical sanctuaries and other protected areas), technically requires the use of local guides for everywhere except designated recreation zones. However, at the time of research, local officials were not enforcing this rule except in the case of ice climbers, who must be accompanied by a certified guide or present their credentials from a climbing club in their home country. Still, it's a great idea to hire a guide for almost any trip – they're inexpensive, experienced and can share a lot of interesting information about local culture and wildlife along the way.

Ask at the Casa de Guías (p395) or Parque Nacional Huascarán Office (p391) to confirm the latest requirements, and when you do contract help, do your best to hire only official guides, *arrieros* (mule drivers), cooks or other support for your trip – they should be able to show you an identification card indicating their membership to with Mountain Guide Association (AGM) or the High Mountain Services Association (ASAM). These personnel are trained in proper use and management of the park and they can help you most swiftly and capably in an emergency.

On the third day, trekkers gain major bragging rights as they push over the **Punta Unión pass** (4760m), which appears from below at an angular notch in a seemingly unbroken rocky wall above. The panoramas from both sides of the pass are captivating. To the west lies **Quebrada Santa Cruz** and its lakes, while to the southeast, **Quebrada Huarípampa** plunges steeply down past a scattering of lakes. The descent after the notch at the pass tightly down a rocky buttress toward Lagunas Morococha, past thick *qeñua* stands, and on to a camp at Paria (3850m).

Day four is rewarded by a quick descent in the hamlet of **Huarípampa** and its traditional thatched-roof Quechua houses. Guinea pigs (destined for the dinner table) can often be seen running around in shallow wooden platforms underneath the roofs. End in Vaqueria (3700m), from where you can flag down a *colectivo, camión* (truck) or minibus to Yungay and onto Huaraz.

The completion of a major tourist road to the Llanganuco lakes and beyond means that the trek is now shorter and can be completed in three days by acclimatized parties; however, four days allows more scope for viewing alpine flora and exploring side valleys: the 14km side-trip to **Laguna Quitacocha** (day two) and a spectacular **valley** below Nevado Quitaraju (6036m) takes five to six hours and ascends/descends 800m; the 12km steep hike (seven to eight hours, 700m ascent/descent) to **Alpamayo Base Camp** (South Side), also possible on day two, takes you to the climbers' camp underneath the magnificent **Nevado Alpamayo** (5947m); a 10km side trip at the **Quebrada Paria** (Quebrada Vaqueria) on day three climbs steadily for three hours and 600m in the shadow of **Nevado Chacraraju** (6112m), below its very active glacier and icefall; and an 11km, four- to five-hour side trek to **Quebrada Ranincuray** (day four) that ascends/descends 800m rewards hikers with awesome views, great camping and access to the Lagunas Tintacocha.

The trek can also be extended beyond Vaqueria (as for the original route), following the road out and picking up the walking trail over the Portachuelo de Llanganuco pass to **Quebrada Llanganuco** and its jade-green lakes.

Water for cooking and drinking is available from rivers along the way (except on day three, when you'll need to carry water on the approach to the Punta Unión pass), but be sure to boil it before drinking. You must carry your passport with you and present it at a checkpoint in Huarípampa.

Colectivo (shared transportation) taxis frequently head out from Caraz to the main trailhead at Cashapampa (S5, 1½ hours).

The trek can be done in reverse – daily *colectivos* from Huaraz to Vaqueria provide access to the trailhead.

Other Cordillera Blanca Treks & Hikes

While the Santa Cruz trek attracts the lion's share of visitors, dozens of other trekking possibilities in the Cordillera Blanca supply scenery and vistas just as jaw-dropping (minus the crowds). A series of *quebradas* (valleys) – Ishinca, Cojup, Quilcayhuanca, Shallap and Rajucolta (listed north to south) – run parallel to each other from the area around Huaraz up into the heart of the Cordillera Blanca, and most of them have a high-altitude lake (or two) somewhere along the way; they each offer trekking opportunities ranging from one day to several, and some of the many possibilities are described below. Interested trekkers can inquire with local agencies about connecting these valley treks with high-altitude traverses, but they are generally explored individually.

Some – but not all – trails on the multi-day treks listed here aren't clearly marked yet, so it's best to either go with a guide or have excellent reference maps on hand (see p402). Getting to some trailheads requires travel to nearby towns or along the rugged and beautiful Conchucos valley (east of the Cordillera Blanca), where a handful of ludicrously friendly indigenous towns provide basic facilities and vivid cultural experiences for the intrepid explorer (see p409). For less ambitious hikers who aren't keen on camping or refuges, consider making a day hike out of some of the longer trips by starting early and turning back with enough time to transfer back to your hotel. You'll need to pay the park entrance (S5) to do these hikes.

HUARAZ–WILKAHUAÍN–LAGUNA AHUAC (ONE DAY)

You can start this relatively easy and well-marked day hike to Laguna Ahuac (4560m) in Huaraz or at the Wilkahuaín Ruins (p392). From the latter (a S15 taxi ride), it takes about four hours and makes an excellent early acclimatization trip or pleasant day trip; starting in Huaraz adds about two hours. On the ground you'll notice furry rabbit-like *vizcachas* sniffing around. Looking up, you can't miss the big mountain views of the southern end of the Cordillera Blanca.

LAGUNA CHURUP (ONE DAY)

The hamlet of **Pitec** (3850m), just above Huaraz is the best place to start this six-hour hike to the beautiful Laguna Churup (4450m) at the base of Nevado Churup. You can select from approaching along either the left-hand or right-hand side of the valley; most folks opt for the left approach. This day hike is often chosen as an acclimatization hike, but note the altitudes and the 600m ascent – make sure you're ready before charging this one. A taxi from Huaraz to Pitec will cost about

---

PICK YOUR PEAK

With 25 glaciated summits over 6000m and more than 50 over 5500m, the Cordillera Blanca is one of the most important ranges in the world for high-altitude climbers. Add to that the sheer multitude of options, generally short approaches and almost no red tape or summit fees (although you have to pay your park fee) and the appeal is obvious. While Huascarán Sur is the undisputed grandddaddy and Alpamayo voted 'most beautiful' by climbers and photographers the world over, Pisco is certainly the most popular climb for its straightforward accessibility and moderate technical requirements.

But that may change. Among many consequences of global warming and contemporary climate change in the Cordillera Blanca, glaciers are retreating and undergoing significant transformations, and well-plied routes have altered dramatically in recent years.

Here are 10 popular climbs and 10 major summits of the Cordillera Blanca, just a few of many peak possibilities offering relatively easy to hard-core ice climbing.

- Huascarán Sur (6768m)
- Chopicalqui (6354m)
- Copa Sur (6188m)
- Quitaraju (6036m)
- Tocllaraju (6035m)
- Alpamayo (5947m)
- Pisco (5752m)
- Ishinca (5550m)
- Maparaju (5326m)
- Urus (5497m)

S30; *combis* for Llupa (S3, 30 minutes) leave Huaraz from the corner of Raimondi and Luzuriaga about every 30 minutes (ask to be dropped off at the path to Pitec); from there it's a two-hour walk to Pitec.

LAGUNA SHALLAP (ONE DAY)
No one is going to argue that this valley is prettier than the neighboring ones and you won't be lonely for bovine company, but it's a relatively easy five-hour hike rewarded by waterfalls and a giant icefall from Nevado San Juan (5843m) that seems headed straight into the narrow Laguna Shallap (4300m). Instead of heading left/northwest out of Pitec for Laguna Churup or up the Quilcayhuanca Valley trek (opposite), a right/southwest trail will lead you to the Quilcayhuanca Bridge. Cross the bridge and advance toward the hamlet of Cahuide and up the Quebrada Shallap. About 200m beyond Cahuide, you'll see some corrals and a park entrance sign; another 400m on you'll have to cross the Shallap Bridge and negotiate a locked cattle gate. From there, the route is easy to discern and smooth going, passing an old mining camp near the lake.

LAGUNA PARÓN (1 DAY)
Laguna Parón (4200m) was probably more picturesque before its water levels were lowered from 75m to 15m to prevent a collapse of Huandoy's moraine; still, it is a fantastically beautiful site with views of Pirámide de Garcilaso (5885m), Huandoy (6395m), Chacraraju (6112m) and several 1000m granite rock walls. Hikers typically hire a truck or taxi to take them 25km to the Electroperú station at Laguna Parón and ask the taxi to wait for the day (S90). The walk rambles around the lake on flat terrain for about two hours and then up the valley for about 4km to a campsite at 4200m. This day hike can be extended into an overnight trip if you want to step onto the Parón glacier (4900m) at the foot of Artesonraju. See p417 for more information about starting this hike in Caraz.

LAGUNA RAJUCOLTA (TWO DAYS)
Having been compared to Zion National Park in Utah, this favorite trek is best known for its unparalleled views of Huantsán (6395m). Catch a *colectivo* to Macashca, for the start of the trek, from the corner of Cáceres and Calle 27 de Noviembre in Huaraz. From there, a well-defined path works its way up the Quebrada Rajucolta toward Laguna Rajucolta (4250m), passing through meadows overshadowed by skyscraper-tall granite walls, some marshy stretches and a massive boulder field created during the 1970 earthquake. Along the way, you can sleep at many makeshift campsites along the valley streams before backtracking toward Macashca the next day.

COJUP–ISHINCA VALLEY (TWO DAYS)
This 12km route climbs from the village of Collón (3400m) and up a beautiful Ishinca valley for six hours toward the Refugio Ishinca (4350m, p415), where you can spend the night. To get to Collón, you have to take a north-bound *colectivo* from Huaraz and ask to get off at the Collón junction; you might be able get on a passing truck or walk the 2½ hours to Collón, joining the trek from there. This is the approach that climbers use to tackle Ulus (5497m), so you may see parties headed that way along the trip. After the *refugio*, parties soon see Laguna Ishinca (4950m) and hike toward a difficult high-altitude traverse over the glaciated Ishinca pass (5350m), which connects the Ishinca Valley with the Cojup Valley and makes for a spectacular two-day circuit. Leave by way of Llupa, from which you can catch a *combi* to Huaraz. You can also bypass the Cojup Valley and keep heading south toward the Quilcayhuanca Valley (opposite) to descend toward Pitec and return to Huaraz by hired truck.

LAGUNA 69 (TWO DAYS)
This is a beautiful, short overnight trek through backdrops dripping with marvelous views. The campsite on the way to the laguna is a true highlight, where you can wake up to a crystal morning vision of Chopicalqui (6354m), Huascarán Sur (6768m) and Norte (6655m). In the morning you scramble up to Laguna 69, which sits right at the base of Chacraraju (6112m), and then hike down past the famous Llanganuco lakes. That's a lot of impressive lakes crammed into just two days. The trails to Laguna 69 commence near the Yurac Corral (3800m), on the northern tip of a big bend in the Llanganuco road.

PISCO (TWO TO THREE DAYS)

Pisco (5750m) is one of the most sought-after summits in the Cordillera Blanca, with hundreds of climbers bagging it every summer. Fortunately the approximately 5km trek to the Refugio Perú (4765m, see p415) at the base of the mountain is just as popular and brings you into stone-throwing distance of this thrilling peak (or at least it looks that way). The trek is a short but very challenging hike that starts in Cebollapampa and gains altitude quickly; navigation is a no-brainer on this well-marked trail.

QUILCAYHUANCA VALLEY (THREE TO FOUR DAYS)

This hike, also from Pitec, is only moderately difficult, although you'll need to be well acclimatized to tackle it. It winds up the Quilcayhuanca valley through *qeñua* trees and grassy meadows until reaching the Laguna Cuchillacocha and Tullpacocha. Along the way, you pass breathtaking views of Nevado Cayesh (5721m), Maparaju (5326m), Tumarinaraju (5668m) and a half-dozen other peaks over 5700m. Because this trek is not well marked, it's best to go with a guide (or have top navigations skills and a topo map). You can descend back down the Quilcayhuanca valley or connect by a high-altitude trail to the Cojup–Ishinca trek (opposite).

INCA TRAIL (THREE TO SIX DAYS)

This three- to six-day hike along an Inca trail, between Huari and the city of Huánuco, is just starting to be developed. Hikers cross well-preserved parts of the old Inca trail and end up in Huánuco Viejo, which was one of the most important military sites of the Incas in northern Peru. This route is being organized in conjunction with the Inka Naani project. It aims to encourage tourism that respects the cultural heritage of the region and ties together several independent grassroots tourism initiatives. All guides are local (and English-speaking if requested) and porters and adobe shelters called *tambos* (the Quechua word for resting place) are available if you want to sleep out of the elements. Contact the Mountain Institute or Respons Sustainable Tourism Center (p395) in Huaraz.

CALLEJÓN DE CONCHUCOS TREKS (THREE TO EIGHT DAYS)

If you're short on time but still want to cross the Cordillera and soak in some icy peak time, the relatively easy two- to three-day **Olleros to Chavín de Huántar trek** comes to the rescue. You can start the 40km trek in either town, though most people start in Olleros (population 1390) in the Callejón de Huáylas on the western side of the Cordillera Blanca, where you can arrange llamas as pack animals. Pretty villages and pre-Inca roads with great views of the Uruashraju (5722m), Rurec (5700m) and Cashan (5716m) mountains dot the landscape heading up to the 4700m Punta Yanashallash high pass. Where you end on the Callejón de Conchucos side is absolutely gorgeous. Best of all, in Chavín you can soak your weary bones in hot springs and get up early the next day to visit the ruins without the usual throng of tourists. Dedicated riders have mountain-biked this route. To get to Olleros, catch a south-heading *combi* from Huaraz, get off at the Bedoya bridge and hike the 30 minutes up to Olleros. A taxi there costs between S35 and S40.

If this trek whets your appetite for ambling, you can continue on to Huari by bus (see p425) or by walking along the road, and commence the equally impressive **Huari to Chacas trek**, making your way along the eastern flanks of the Cordillera Blanca. Be sure to make time to camp near the Laguna Purhuay – this picturesque spot deserves an overnight visit. The easy two- to three-day route passes several other lakes, reaches its zenith at a 4550m pass and finishes up through misty high-altitude tropical forests of the Parhua valley (3500m) to Chacas.

After a rest in the fetching town of Chacas, you can continue on to do the one- to two-day **Chacas to Yanama trek**. This is the shortest of the three hikes and has the lowest pass of the lot, at a 'mere' 4050m. From Chacas you hike through the municipalities of Sapcha and Potaca and can either finish the trek at Yanama or continue to the Keshu valley, which has several good places to camp. Colcabamba, a few hours further on from Yanama, is the end of the Santa Cruz trek and endurance hikers can tag this trek onto the end of their Herculean circuit before returning to Huaraz.

Incaroca Travel (p395) in Huaraz has lots of experience with these treks and offers community-tourism options along the way. Ask for César Roca.

HONDA–ULTA (SIX TO SEVEN DAYS)

This loop starting at Vicos and ending at the village of Shilla, near Carhuaz, is a moderate trek, with the exception of a couple of difficult high-altitude passes at Laguna Yanayacu (4850m) and Portachuelo Honda (4750m). Along the way, parties can stop into the tiny community of Juitush and the impossibly precious village of Chacas (p426) and linger on views of Yanaragra (5987m), Pucaranra (6156m), Palcaraju (6274m) and two remote lakes. This is a great hike if you want to experience a route done much less frequently than most and enjoy a few charismatic indigenous villages along the way.

LOS CEDROS–ALPAMAYO (SEVEN DAYS)

This is one of the more dazzling and demanding treks of the Cordillera. The 90km route involves very long ascents to high passes, incredible alpine scenery (including the regal north side of Nevado Alpamayo) and traditional Quechua communities with no road access. Starting in Cashapampa (same as the Santa Cruz trek) or Hualcayan and ending in Pomabamba, it is only recommended for experienced and acclimatized hikers who are familiar with navigation. The route is relatively straightforward, but not signposted. You can treat yourself to well-earned dips in hot mineral spring baths at both ends of this trek.

CORDILLERA HUAYHUASH

Often playing second fiddle to its limelight-stealing cousin, the Cordillera Blanca, Huayhuash hosts an equally impressive medley of glaciers, summits and lakes – all packed into a hardy area only 30km across. Increasing numbers of travelers are discovering this rugged and remote territory, where trails skirt around the outer edges of this stirring, peaked range. Several strenuous high-altitude passes of over 4500m throw down a gauntlet to the hardiest of trekkers. The feeling of utter wilderness, particularly along the unspoiled eastern edge, is the big draw and you are more likely to spot the graceful Andean condor here than dozens of *burro*-toting trekking groups.

In the waning moments of 2001, Peru's Ministry of Agriculture declared the Cordillera Huayhuash a 'reserved zone,' giving a transitory measure of protection to nearly 700 sq km of almost-pristine land. Since then, the ministry has backed away from official support as a unique, private and community-managed conservation effort has taken root. The six communities whose traditional territory lies at the heart of the Huayhuash range are becoming formally recognized as 'Private Conservation Areas.' Several districts along the circuit now charge user fees of S10 to S12 with costs for the entire circuit approaching S50. Part of the fees goes to improved security for hikers and part goes to continued conservation work – support this grassroots preservation attempt by paying your fees, carrying enough small change and by always asking for an official receipt.

Cordillera Huayhuash Circuit

Circling a tight cluster of high peaks, including Yerupajá (6634m), the world's second-highest tropical mountain, this stunning trek crosses multiple high-altitude passes with spine-tingling views. The dramatic lakes along the eastern flanks provide great campsites (and are good for trout fishing) and give hikers a wide choice of routes to make this trek as difficult as they choose to make it.

Daily ascents range from 500m to 1200m, but a couple of days in the middle and at the end of the trek involve major descents, which can be just as tough as going uphill. The average day involves about 12km on the trail, or anywhere from four to eight hours of hiking – although you may experience at least one 10- to 12-hour day. Most trekkers take extra rest days along the way, partly because the length and altitude make the entire circuit very demanding and partly to allow for the sensational sights to sink in. Others prefer a shorter version and can hike for as few as five days along the remote eastern side of the Huayhuash. Described here is the classic Huayhuash Circuit trek, but many side trips and alternate routes along the way can add a day or two to your trekking time.

The trek starts in **Llamac**, the last town for several days as the trail leaves 'civilization,' passing a small pre-Inca platform with excellent mountainscapes and 4m-high *cholla* cacti. The **Pampa Llamac pass** bursts out on a fabulous view of glaciated peaks: Rondoy (5870m), the

---

FAST FACTS

Duration: 10 days

Distance: 115km

Difficulty: demanding

Start/finish: Chiquián

Nearest towns: Chiquián, Llamac and Cajatambo

CORDILLERA HUAYHUASH CIRCUIT

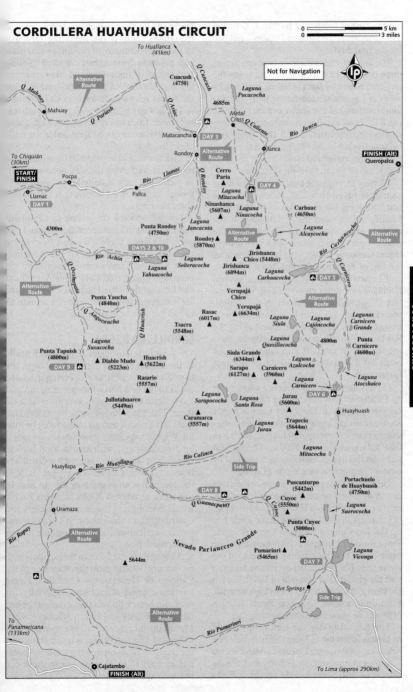

0 ————— 5 km
0 ————— 3 miles

Not for Navigation

To Huallanca
(41km)

Q Curcush

Cuncush
(4750)

Q Mahuay

Mahuay

Q Parash

Laguna
Pucacocha

4685m

Metal
Cross

Q Caliente

Rio Janca

To Chiquián
(30km)

Matacancha   **DAY 3**

Rondoy

Alternative
Route

Janca

FINISH (Alt)
Queropalca

**START/
FINISH**

Pocpa

Rio Llamac

Pallca

Q Rondoy

Cerro
Paria

Laguna
Mitucocha   **DAY 4**

Llamac
DAY 1

4300m

Q Oshpatia

Punta Rondoy
(4750m)

Ninashanca
(5607m)

Laguna
Ninacocha

Carhuac
(4650m)

Q Carhuacocha

Alternative
Route

Rio Achin   **DAYS 2 & 10**

Rondoy ▲
(5870m)

Laguna
Jancacuta

Laguna
Solteracocha

Jirishanca
Chico (5448m)

Jirishanca ▲
(6094m)

Laguna
Alcaycocha

Alternative
Route

Laguna
Yahuacocha

Laguna
Carhuacocha   **DAY 5**

Q Carnicero

Alternative
Route

Q Angocancha

Punta Yaucha
(4840m)

Q Huacrish

Yerupajá
Chico

Yerupajá ▲
(6634m)

Alternative
Route

Laguna
Susucocha

Rasac
(6017m)

Tsacra
(5548m)

Laguna
Siula

Laguna
Cajóncocha

Lagunas
Carnicero
Grande

Punta Tapuish
(4800m)   **DAY 9**

Diablo Mudo
(5223m)

Huacrish ▲
(5622m)

Siula Grande
(6344m)

Laguna
Quesillococha

4800m

Punta
Carnicero
(4600m)

Rasario
(5557m)

Sarapo ▲
(6127m)

Carnicero ▲
(5960m)

Laguna
Azulcocha

Laguna
Atocshaico

Jullutahuarco
(5449m)

Laguna
Sarapococha

Laguna
Santa Rosa

Laguna
Carnicero   **DAY 6**

Caramarca
(5557m)

Jurau
(5600m)

Huayhuash

Laguna
Jurau

Trapecio
(5644m)

Huayllapa

Rio Huayllapa

Rio Calinca

Side Trip

Laguna
Mitucocha

Portachuelo
de Huayhuash
(4750m)

Uramaza

DAY 8

Q Guanacpatay

Puscanturpo
(5442m)

Cuyoc
(5550m)

Laguna
Suerococha

Rio Rapay

Alternative
Route

Q Cuyoc

Punta Cuyoc
(5000m)

5644m

Nevado Pariaucco Grande

Pumarinri ▲
(5465m)   **DAY 7**

Laguna
Viconga

To
Panamericana
(133km)

Alternative
Route

Hot Springs

Side Trip

Rio Pumarinri

To Lima (approx 290km)

Cajatambo
FINISH (Alt)

HUARAZ & THE
CORDILLERAS

double-fanged Jirishanca (6094m), Yerupajá Chico, Yerupajá (6634m) and others – not bad for the first day!

The second and third days take you across three passes over 4500m until you reach the tiny community of **Janca** (4200m), getting nice views of Laguna Mitacocha (4230m). On day four, southeast of the Carhuac pass (4650m), you'll see more excellent mountain panoramas and eventually reach a cliff that overlooks Laguna Carhuacocha (4138m) and the glaciated mountains behind Siula Grande (6344m) and Yerupajá looming in the distance.

Midway through the trek parties hit a short section of paved Inca trail, about 1.5m wide and 50m long, the remnants of an Inca road heading south from the archaeological site of Huánuco Viejo near La Unión. Over the next couple of days work your way toward **Laguna Carnicero** (4430m), the **Laguna Mitucocha**, the top of **Portachuelo de Huayhuash** (4750m), and **Laguna Viconga** (4407m). After several glaciated mountain crowns come into view, including the double-peaked Cuyoc (5550m), you can either camp and continue the main circuit, or you can head southwest along the Río Pumarinri valley toward **Cajatambo**, leaving the circuit early. If you keep going, get ready for the challenging 5000m-plus Punta Cuyoc pass.

On day seven the trail crests a small ridge on Pumarinri (5465m), giving trekkers face-on views of **Cuyoc**. Look out for the hardy *Stangea henricii*, a grayish-green, flat, rosette-shaped plant of overlapping tongue-like leaves that only grows above 4700m. The highest point on the trek is soon reached, marked by a rather unglorious single pile of stones.

On the eighth day you can continue the direct circuit by hiking past the village of Huayllapa; exit the circuit through Huayllapa and the town of Uramaza to Cajatambo; or make a side trip up the Río Calinca valley to Lagunas Jurau, Santa Rosa and Sarapococha, where there are some of the best mountain panoramas of the entire trek. The traditional circuit will take you past the glacier-clad pyramid of Jullutahuarco (5449m) and a stupendous 100m-high **waterfall**. Push on to a small lake near Punta Tapuish (4800m) for good high-altitude camping.

The following day the trail drops gently to **Laguna Susucocha** (4750m) shortly before a junction (4400m) with Quebrada Angocancha. The trail skirts boggy meadows and climbs into rock and scree before reaching **Punta**

Yaucha (4840m), offering wonderful views c the range's major peaks, including Yerupajá to the east and many of the minor glaciatec high points to the southeast. Go fossil-hunting for imprints of ammonites and other creatures that once dwelled under the sea – and imagine the Andes relegated to the ocean's bottom.

The last day is short, with an early arriva in Llamac, from where transport to Chiquián and on to Huaraz can be arranged in the middle of the day.

Trekkers should be prepared for aggressively territorial dogs along the way; bending dowr to pick up a rock usually keeps them off – though refrain from throwing it unless you absolutely must.

For information on getting to Chiquián and transport to Llamac for the trailhead, see p421. In Llamac there is a soccer field where camping is permitted. Among the three *hospedajes* (small, family-owned inns) here the plain, four-room, cold-water Hotel Santa Rosa and the slightly better Hospedaje Huayhuash are both good. Both have rooms for around S5 to S10 per person and provide meals.

CORDILLERA NEGRA

The poor little Cordillera Negra lives literally in the shadows of its big brother range, the Cordillera Blanca, whose towering glaciated peaks to the east block the morning sun and loom dramatically over everything around them. The 'Black Range,' which gets its name from its obvious contrast to the more beautiful 'White Range,' will probably always look a bit dressed down – with its arid, mud-brown, merely hilly silhouette – against the Cordillera Blanca's stunning icy and craggy profile. Still, the Negra has an important role to play in the area's ecology as it blocks warm Pacific winds from hitting the Blanca's glaciers and contributing to their thaw. It's also an important agricultural and mining area for the local population.

Although second fiddle to the big-mountain recreational offerings on the other side of the Callejón de Huaylas, the Cordillera Negra has some great attractions, especially for rock climbers, who will find excellent bolted climbs in Recuay and Hatun Machay (p421). Mountain-bikers have access to seemingly unlimited kilometers of roads and trails over the rugged landscape; bike-guiding companies (p393) in Huaraz know these old byways well.

Day hikers can also explore these routes. Hire a truck to take you to Punta Callan (4225m) above Huaraz or to Curcuy (4520m) above Recuay and walk down to town. Another suggested hike is a three-hour ascent to the ruins of Quitabamba near Jangas. Take a *olectivo* towar Carhuaz, getting off at La Cruz de la Mina and look for signs to the ruins.

The villages over here don't see a lot of tourists, and you'll be interacting with indigenous people who in many cases live an untouched, traditional lifestyle. Of course, if none of the above activities appeal to you, you might find great photo opportunities of big brother Cordillera Blanca from this side of the Río Santa.

NORTH OF HUARAZ

As the Río Santa slices its way north through the Callejón de Huaylas, a road shadows its every curve past several subdued towns to Caraz, and on to the menacingly impressive Cañón del Pato. The Andean panorama of the Cordillera Blanca looms over the length of the valley like a wall of white-topped sentries, with the granddaddy of them all, Huascarán, barely 14km away from the road as the condor flies. Many hiking trailheads are accessible from towns along this route and two unsealed roads valiantly cross the Cordillera, one via Carhuaz and another via Yungay.

MONTERREY

☎ 043 / pop 1100 / elev 2800m

Huddled around a scattered spine of tourist facilities, this tiny *pueblo*, 9km north of Huaraz, earns a spot on the map for its natural **hot springs** (admission S3; ⏱ 6am-6pm). It also makes for a low-key sleeping alternative to Huaraz. The baths are run by the Real Hotel Baños Termales Monterrey next door, which fronts a popular rock-climbing wall. Buses terminate right in front.

The hot springs are divided into two sections; the lower pools are more crowded while the upper pools are nicer and have private rooms (S2.50 per person for 20 minutes). Before you wrinkle your nose at the brown color of the water, know that it's due to high iron content rather than questionable hygiene practices. It's best to visit in the morning as the baths are cleaned overnight. The pools get crowded on weekends and holidays.

Sleeping & Eating

All the hotels are within a five-minute walk of the springs. Some of the restaurants are a little further afield, but still within walking distance.

Apart from the hotel restaurants, several eateries are worth mentioning. On Sundays many serve a traditional Peruvian feast called *pachamanca* (*pacha* means 'earth' and *manca* means 'oven' in Quechua), a magnificent bounty of chicken, pork, lamb, guinea pig, corn, potatoes and other vegetables cooked for several hours over hot stones.

Hostal El Nogal (☎ 42-5929; s/d S32/64) The slightly dank rooms at Hostal El Nogal find redemption in its attractive, wood-lined building and flourishing rear garden.

Real Hotel Baños Termales Monterrey (☎ 42-7690; s/d S63/78, 2-/4-person bungalows S108/160; 🖳) Crowning the hill like a thermal-bath overlord, you can hear the history of this grand old structure through its creaky wooden floors. Old-world charm oozes from every crack in the wall. It is set in a motley garden, there's a simple restaurant with outdoor dining (overlooking the pool) and reasonably priced meals. Rather Spartan rooms have hot showers and a TV that shows local channels. The four bungalows sleep either two or four. Rates include access to the springs.

El Patio de Monterrey (☎ 42-4965; elpatio@terra .com.pe; s/d S145/180) The fanciest venture around, this has colonial-style architecture around a toothsome hacienda, complemented by the colonial-style furniture. Most of the ship-shape rooms are spacious and have bathtubs, phones and local TV. Some rooms (S330) sleep up to four and a few have a fireplace. Most rooms look out onto a bountiful garden that's strewn with wagon wheels and fountains; some have a balcony. Meals are available in the fireplace-heated restaurant-bar.

El Regimontano (meals S3-6; ⏱ 8am-7pm) Opposite the baths, this place is guarded by mannequins dressed in traditional mountain garb and opens into a secret garden. Local specialties – including *cuy* (guinea pig), *chicharrónes* (pork crackling) and trout – are the norm and the large benches, protected from the elements by thatch roofs, are popular with groups.

Recreo Mochica (☎ 42-9074; Km 2.5; mains S3-15; ⏱ 8am-8pm) This is a small but locally popular place serving roast chicken and trout.

Recreo Buongiorno (☎ 42-7145; Km 2.5; meals S9-18; ⏱ 11am-8pm) You can't miss the rock model of the Cordillera Blanca outside this joint. Local and national food is served, as well as yummy pastries. Outside is a nice garden with a play set for children that attracts families.

El Ollón de Barro (☎ 42-3364; Km 7; meals S9-27; ✆ 10am-7pm) This is surrounded by a near-impenetrable wall of hedge guarding a large, enticing garden with a fronton court, children's swings and trees. Typical plates such as *rocoto relleno* (spicy hot pepper stuffed with rice and pepper) and *ají de gallina* (chicken stewed with walnuts and chilis) are on offer, as well as the usual country grills.

El Cortijo (☎ 42-3813; mains S18-30; ✆ 10am-7pm) An excellent grill chars ostrich alongside *cuy* and other meats, as well as serving 'ordinary' food. Outdoor tables are arranged around a fountain (complete with little boy peeing) in a grassy flower-filled garden, with swings for children.

Getting There & Away

Local buses from Huaraz go north along Luzuriaga, west on Calle 28 de Julio, north on Calle 27 de Novembre, east on Raimondi and north on Fitzcarrald. Try to catch a bus early in the route, as they soon fill up. The fare for the 15 minute ride is S1. A taxi ride between Huaraz and Monterrey costs about S5.

MONTERREY TO CARHUAZ

About 5km north of Monterrey, the road goes through the little village of **Taricá** (population 1500) which earns its tourist stripes with locally made pottery. Stop at the friendly **Hostal Sterling** (☎ 49-1277, 49-0299; s/d S20/35), which has funky, concrete-block rooms with electric showers, a small restaurant and a bar that looks like it's barely been touched since the 1950s – the dust is piled high. Behind the hotel is an elevation called Aparac, which is used for hang-gliding.

About 18km north of Monterrey is minuscule Anta airport and 2km beyond is the hamlet of **Marcará** (population 1275). From here, minibuses and trucks leave regularly for the hot springs and natural saunas of **Chancos**, 4km to the east, where the waters supposedly harbor curative properties. The rustic Chancos **hot springs** are popular with weekending locals and tend to be crowded then. At some great 'steam baths' here in natural vapor caves (S5 for 15 minutes) you can buy herbs to aromatize and medicate your sauna experience. The smaller caves tend to be hotter so check out a few. The pools, on the other hand, are rather tepid; private pools cost S2 and the public pool S1 for a long as you like. There's a popular, prebolte **climbing wall** just before the hot pools.

Buses occasionally continue another 4km to **Vicos**, beyond which the Quebrada Honda tra (for hikers only) continues across the Cordiller Blanca and passes the **Laguna Lejíacocha**. I Vicos the community-based tourism project **Cuyaquiwayi** (Quechua for 'Beautiful House' maintains a rustic lodge with private bathroom and a fireplace right next to a local family' farm. The family invites guests to share in al aspects of their lives, including baking bread farming and interacting with the local children With prior notice they will also arrange a *pacha manca*. Prices start at S250 for the first day, bu rapidly decrease if you are traveling with other or plan to stay multiple days; contact Respons (p395) in Huaraz for more information.

Marcará serves as the base for a very active Italian nonprofit organization that's been helping disenfranchised local youth for decades (see opposite). The **Cooperative Artesanal Don Baso** (☎ 74-3061; Los Pinos 3A) has a large workshop here where you can see adolescents busy creating superior-quality carvings, ceramics sculptures, furniture and other crafts.

The **Hostal Los Jazmines** (r per person S15) on the main plaza is predictably austere and has shared bathrooms.

CARHUAZ

☎ 043 / pop 7100 / elev 2638m

Carhuaz, 35km north of Huaraz, lays claim to one of the prettiest Plazas de Armas in the valley, with a combination of rose gardens and towering palm that make lingering here a pleasure. The Sunday market is a kaleidoscopic treat as *campesinos* (peasants) descend from surrounding villages to sell a medley of fresh fruits, herbs and handicrafts. A road passes over the Cordillera Blanca from Carhuaz, via the beautiful Quebrada Ulta and Punta Olímpica pass, to Chacas and San Luis.

Carhuaz's annual **La Virgen de La Merced fiesta** is celebrated from September 14 to 24 with processions, fireworks, dancing, bullfights and plenty of drinking – so much that the town is often referred to as *Carhuaz borachera* (drunk Carhuaz)!

Sleeping & Eating

A number of rudimentary, family-run *hostales* have simple, clean rooms with hot-water bathrooms. **Hostal Río Santa** (☎ 39-4128; Calle 28 de ulio; s/d S15/20) and **Hostal Las Torrecitas** (☎ 39-4213; mazonas 412; s/d S20/30) provide little to differenti-te between them. One of the oldest running ~entures, **Hotel La Merced** (☎ 39-4241; Ucayali 724; s/d 20/30) has lots of windows for Cordillera adu-ation and plenty of religious posters for inter-al speculation. Rooms are clean and have hot showers. The haughtiest place to stay in town s **Hostal El Abuelo** (☎ 39-4456; hostalelabuelo@terra com.pe; Calle 9 de Diciembre 257; s/d incl breakfast S90/120; 🖳), which has immaculately neat rooms with good mattresses and hot showers in a large, older-styled house. There's a lovely restaurant on the premises.

On the plaza, **La Punta Olímpica** (☎ 39-4022; meals S4-6; ☺ 8am-10pm) slaps together cheap local dishes and *menús* (set meals) for an ap-preciative local crowd. **Café Heladería El Abuelo** (☎ /fax 39-4149; meals S5-15; ☺ 8am-9pm), also on the plaza, is owned by local cartographer Felipe Díaz (you probably have his map; everyone does). It serves breakfast, snacks and ice cream made from local fruits, and provides local in-formation. Don't miss the town's ubiquitous treat, *raspadilla*, a slurpee of Cordillera Blanca glacier ice slathered in fruity syrup.

El Mirador (☎ 49-4244; meals S10-18), about 2km south of Carhuaz on the south of a hill, is a lunchtime restaurant with typical food. It delivers on its promise of great views.

Getting There & Away

The Plaza de Armas is where you can pick up passing minibuses to Huaraz (S5, 50 minutes), Yungay (S2.50, 30 minutes) and Caraz (S5, 45 minutes). Morning and afternoon buses from Huaraz to Chacas and San Luis also pass by the plaza. Buses between Caraz and Lima, and Huaraz and Chimbote, pass by here also.

YUNGAY

☎ 043 / pop 12,600 / elev 2458m

Light on overnight visitors, serene little Yungay has relatively few tourist services. It has the best access for the popular Lagunas Llanganuco, via a dirt road that continues over the Cordillera to Yanama and beyond. Surrounded on all sides by lush hills wafting brisk mountain air, it's difficult to believe the heartrending history of this little junction in the road.

The original village of Yungay is now a rubble-strewn zone about 2km south of the new town and marks the site of the single worst natural disaster in the Andes. The earth-quake of May 31, 1970 loosened 15 million cu meters of granite and ice from the west wall of Huascarán Norte. The resulting *aluvión* reached a speed of 300km/h as it dropped over three vertical kilometers on its way to Yungay, 14km away. The town and almost all of its 18,000 inhabitants were buried (see p392).

THE ITALIAN CONNECTION

Established by the pioneering Father Ugo de Censi, a priest of the Salesian order, the Italian nonprofit organization **Don Bosco**, based in Marcará, has a long and active history in South America, particularly the eastern Cordillera Blanca.

Since 1976, enterprising and well-meaning Italians have been working overtime to help in-digenous youth of the region. They've established the School and Workshop of Carpentry and Woodcarving, where orphans and street children can accumulate free hands-on experience and training in carpentry and woodcarving. The Italians have also been busy founding schools and artisan cooperatives in the area and organizing reforestation and agricultural programs. In Chacas, the best hospital in the eastern Cordillera was built and staffed by this organization and many churches have had extensive renovations paid for through its funding efforts. Oh, and we can't forget the too-large-to-ignore statue of Christ blessing your journey as you approach Chavín – these guys also had a hand in that.

Three **refuges** (☎ 44-3061; www.rifugi-omg.org) have also been constructed by this organization, all deep within the belly of the Cordillera. Each refuge is heated and has a radio, basic medical supplies, 60 beds, and charges S105 per night for bed, breakfast and dinner (S150 with lunch). Profits go to local aid projects. Refuges include **Refugio Perú** (4765m), a two-hour walk from Llanganuco and a base for climbing Pisco; **Refugio Ishinca** (4350m), a three-hour walk from Collón village in the Ishinca valley; and **Refugio Huascarán** (4670m), a four-hour walk from Musho. Trekkers, mountaineers and sightseers are all welcomed.

The founder of this Andean mission, Father Ugo de Censi, continues to be actively involved at the sprightly old age of 85. He is the parish priest in Chacas.

Information

Policía de Montaña (USAM; ☎ 79-3327, 79-3333, 79-3291; usam@pnp.gob.pe) has two helicopters, search-and-rescue dogs and police officers who have taken mountaineering courses. They often work with experts from the Mountain Guide Association at the Casa de Guías (see p395) in Huaraz. It's located behind Hostal Gledel.

Sights & Activities

The site of old Yungay (Yungay Viejo), **Campo Santo** (admission S2; ☺ 8am-6pm) is marked by a towering white statue of Christ standing on a knoll and overlooking the path of the *aluvión*. Flower-filled gardens top the hill, with occasional gravestones and monuments commemorating the thousands of people who lie buried beneath the 8m to 12m of soil. At the old Plaza de Armas, you can just see the very top of the cathedral tower and a few palm-tree tips (one of them remarkably still alive). A replica of the cathedral's facade has been built in honor of the dead.

If you're interested in DIY mountain-biking adventures, visit **Cycle World** (☎ 30-3109; Arias Graciani; ☺ 9am-6pm). It rents mountain bikes for S30 per day, including a helmet, puncture repair kit and simple map. You can do several trails in the area, but the most popular one involves catching a *colectivo* to Portachuelo (S10) and cycling back downhill over three to four hours. A park entry fee of S5 applies.

Sleeping & Eating

Hostal Gledel (☎ 39-3048; Aries Graziani; s/d S10-15) The gregarious and generous Señora Gamboa rents out 13 impossibly cute and Spartan rooms. Expect at least one hug and a sample of her cooking during your stay. Showers are shared and you can get breakfast here. This is both the cheapest and best place to stay in town – it's deservedly popular.

Hostal Yungay (☎ 39-3053; Santo Domingo 1; s/d S15/20) Also decent, this place has 25 simple rooms with electric showers and they'll scrub your laundry for S2 per kilogram.

Hostal Sol de Oro (☎ 39-3116; Santo Domingo 7; s/d S15/25) Another good pick – it has bright, clean rooms with solid mattresses and hot showers.

Yungay's market, next to the plaza, has several cheap and rustic places to eat. Surrounded by gardens, **Restaurant Turístico Alpamayo** (☎ 39-3090; meals S9-15; ☺ 7am-7pm), off the main highway at the north end of town, is the best restaurant.

OUTSIDE OF TOWN

Llanganuco Mountain Lodge (☎ 94-366-9580; www.llanganucolodge.com; dm S38, s/d from S140/180) About 45 minutes by taxi from Yungay toward the Llanganuco Lakes, this recommended lodge run by Brit Charlie Good is in a prime position for exploring the lakes area or charging the Santa Cruz trek. Choose camping with hot-water showers and breathtaking views or lodge rooms with down-feather beds and balconies. Mountain biking, volleyball and even crossbow are just some the lodge's activities in addition to the usual trekking and mountaineering circuits. All meals are available. Call ahead or see the website for directions.

Humacchuco community tourism project (☎ 42-7949; www.respons.org; per person incl meals from S108) Six members of the Humacchuco community maintain a comfortable guest house as part of an established sustainable-tourism program. Here visitors can learn about the local culture and natural-resource management, savor a *pachamanca* and go on guided hikes, including a day hike of Laguna 69. You can tailor your own program through Response (p408) in Huaraz; call ahead for reservations and discounts for larger groups.

Getting There & Away

Minibuses run from the Plaza de Armas to Caraz (S2, 15 minutes) and Huaraz (S5, 1¼ hours). Buses from Caraz to Lima and from

Huaraz to Chimbote pick up passengers at the Plaza de Armas.

Departures on beat-up buses from Huaraz to Pomabamba via Lagunas Llanganuco pass by daily.

LAGUNAS LLANGANUCO

A dirt road climbs the Llanganuco valley to reach its two stunning Llanganuco lakes, which are also known as Laguna Chinancocha and Laguna Orconcocha, 28km east of Yungay. Nestled in a glacial valley just 1000m below the snow line, these pristine lagoons practically glow in their bright turquoise and emerald hues. There's a 1½-hour trail hugging Chinancocha and passing by rare *Polylepis* trees, and you can rent boats at this lake, which is a popular day-tripping spot. This location gets killer views of the mountain giants of Huascarán (6768m), Chopicalqui (6354m), Chacraraju (6112m), Huandoy (6395m) and others, particularly if you drive a few kilometers beyond the lakes. The road continues over the pass beyond the lakes to Yanama on the other side of the Cordillera Blanca; several early-morning vehicles go from Huaraz going to Yanama and beyond.

To reach the Lagunas Llanganuco, you can take a tour from Huaraz or use buses or taxis from Yungay. During the June to August high season, frequent minibuses leave from Yungay's Plaza de Armas (S15), allowing about two hours in the lake area. A national-park admission fee of S5 is charged. During the rest of the year, minibuses do the trip if there's enough demand. *Colectivo* taxis are available for S15 per person each way. Go in the early morning for the clearest views.

CARAZ

☎ 043 / pop 13,100 / elev 2270m

With an extra helping of superb panoramas of the surrounding mountains and a more kick-back attitude than its rambunctious brother Huaraz, Caraz makes for an excellent alternate base of operations. Trekking and hiking trails meander in all directions – some of the short, day-trip variety, some much longer sojourns. One of the few places in the valley spared total destruction by earthquake or *aluvión*, the town still has a gentle whiff of colonial air. Its lazy Plaza de Armas wouldn't be out of place in a much smaller *pueblo*.

Caraz is both the end point of the time-honored Llanganuco–Santa Cruz trek (which can also be done in reverse, starting here) and the point of departure for rugged treks into the remote northern parts of the Cordillera Blanca. The north side of Alpamayo (5947m), once enthusiastically labeled the most beautiful mountain in the world for its knife-edged, perfectly pyramidal northern silhouette, is easily accessible from here.

Information

The **Cámara de Turismo** (San Martín 1129; ☽ 8am-noon & 3-7 Mon-Fri), on the Plaza de Armas, has irregular hours and limited tourist information.

BCP (☎ 39-1010; cnr Daniel Villar & San Martín) changes cash and traveler's checks but lacks an ATM. Pony Expeditions (see p418) can change US cash and euros and arrange Visa advances. The **post office** (San Martín 909; ☽ 8am-8pm Mon-Fri) is north of the cathedral.

Sights & Activities

The partially excavated Chavín ruins of **Tumshukaiko** are about 2km on a dirt road north of Caraz. There is no sign or fee. The extensive walls (now in poor condition) and buried underground chambers indicate this was once an important Chavín site. A *moto-taxi* to get here costs S3, while a taxi is S5.

The pastel-blue **Laguna Parón** (4200m), 25km east of Caraz, is surrounded by spectacular snow-covered peaks, of which Pirámide de Garcilaso (5885m), at the end of the lake, looks particularly brilliant. The challenging rock-climbing wall of Torre de Parón, known as the **Sphinx**, is also found here. The road to the lake goes through a canyon with 1000m-high granite walls – this drive is as spectacular as the better-known Llanganuco trip. Fit and acclimatized hikers can trek to the lake in one long day, but it's easier to catch local transport to Pueblo Parón and hike the remaining four hours.

If you continue north from Caraz along the Callejón de Huaylas, you will wind your way through the outstanding **Cañón del Pato**. It's here that the Cordillera Blanca and the Cordillera Negra come to within kissing distance for a battle of bedrock wills, separated in parts by only 15m and plummeting to vertigo-inducing depths of up to 1000m. The road snakes along a path hewn out of sheer rock, over a precipitous gorge and passes through 35 tunnels, hand-cut through solid

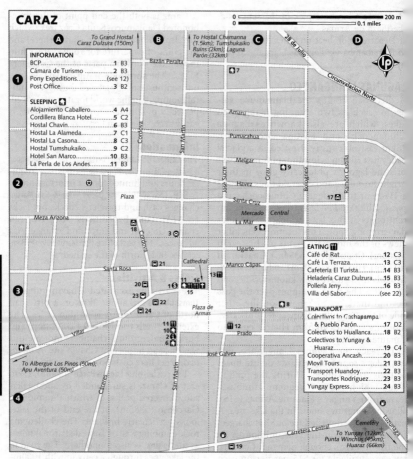

CARAZ

INFORMATION
BCP..1 B3
Cámara de Turismo 2 B3
Pony Expeditions...............(see 12)
Post Office....................................3 B2

SLEEPING
Alojamiento Caballero.............4 A4
Cordillera Blanca Hotel............5 C2
Hostal Chavín.............................6 B3
Hostal La Alameda....................7 C1
Hostal La Casona........................8 C3
Hostal Tumshukaiko..................9 C2
Hotel San Marco.......................10 B3
La Perla de Los Andes...............11 B3

EATING
Café de Rat................................12 C3
Café La Terraza.........................13 C3
Cafetería El Turista...................14 B3
Heladería Caraz Dulzura...........15 B3
Pollería Jeny.............................16 B3
Villa del Sabor..................(see 22)

TRANSPORT
Colectivos to Cashapampa
  & Pueblo Parón...................17 D2
Colectivos to Huallanca...........18 B2
Colectivos to Yungay &
  Huaraz...................................19 C4
Cooperativa Ancash.................20 B3
Movil Tours...............................21 B3
Transport Huandoy..................22 B3
Transportes Rodríguez.............23 B3
Yungay Express.........................24 B3

stone. Gargantuan, crude walls tower above the road on all sides, and as the valley's hydroelectric plant comes into sight you realize that it's dramatic enough to house the secret lair of a James Bond arch-villain. Sit so you're looking out of the right-hand side of the bus (as you face the driver) for the best views along the way.

Punta Winchus, a remote 4157m pass in the Cordillera Negra 45km west of Caraz and reached by tour vehicles, is the center of a huge stand of 5000 rare *Puya raimondii* plants. This is the biggest-known stand of these 10m-tall members of the pineapple family, which take 100 years to mature and in full bloom flaunt up to 20,000 flowers each! On a clear day you have an astounding 145km panorama from the Cordillera Blanca all the way to the Pacific Ocean.

For detailed trekking information you can visit one of the two main trekking outfits in Caraz. Alberto Cafferata at **Pony Expeditions** (☎ /fax 39-1642; www.ponyexpeditions.com; José Sucre 1266; ☺ 8am-10pm Mon-Sat) speaks English, French and Spanish and provides equipment rental (including bicycles), transport, guides, *arrieros* and various excursions. Books, maps, fuel and other items are for sale at the shop. You can also visit Luis at **Apu Aventura** (☎ 96832740; www.apuaventura.com), based at Albergue Los Pinos (see opposite). Luis is an experienced guide who can also help arrange treks, horse riding, climbing and equipment rental.

leeping

Caraz has yet to see the tourist development of Huaraz and offers straightforward facilities and budget sleeping options. Prices remain quite stable throughout the year.

Hostal La Casona (☎ 39-1334; Raimondi 319; s/d 15/28, s/d without bathroom S10/15) Although many of the large rooms here are dark and window-ess, the attractive patio still makes this place a budget fave.

Albergue Los Pinos (☎ 39-1130; Parque San Martín 03; campsites per person S10; s/d S45/65, s/d without bath-oom S20/35; 💻) This popular, HI-affiliated place offers outstanding rooms in a massive, multicolored mansion that is thoughtfully decorated inside and out. There are several great garden courtyards and a funky restaurant that serves breakfast and snacks. The owner, Luis, organizes trekking and tours of the area.

Hotel San Marco (☎ 39-1558; San Martín 1133; s/d 25/35, s/d without bathroom S10/15) You wouldn't think that exposed concrete could look inviting, yet somehow this place manages to exude a certain bucolic appeal. This large, rambling brick building has modest rooms that are kept reasonably clean by the friendly owners.

Alojamiento Caballero (☎ 39-1637; Villar 485; s/d 15/30) It's a small, simple, clean, friendly, family-run place with views and shared hot showers.

Cordillera Blanca Hotel (☎ 39-1435; Grau 903; s/ d S25/35) This multistory hotel opposite the market is decidedly lacking in anything that might resemble character, but the immaculate pink rooms and gleaming bathrooms are without fault and good value for money. The restaurant downstairs, Chifa El Dragón Rojo, offers a Chinese twist on the traditional *pollería*.

Grand Hostal Caraz Dulzura (☎ 39-1523; www .huaraz.com/carazdulzura; Sáenz Peña 212; s/d S25/35) About 10 blocks north of town along San Martín, this is a clinically clean and modern rural retreat that provides good bang for your buck. Rooms are bright and have hot showers and comfortable beds. There's a patio backed by a rocky hill and covered in lots of greenery, a TV room, book exchange and restaurant for doing breakfast (S6) and dinner (mains S8 to S12).

Hostal Chavín (☎ 39-1171; hostalchavin@latinmail .com; San Martín 1135; s/d S30/40) The friendly owner, who is involved with the local tourism authority, knows the area and provides information,

tours and local transportation. Rooms are simple, but all have TV and hot showers.

Hostal La Alameda (☎ 39-1177; www.hotellaalameda .com; Bazán Peralta 262; s/d S40-65, s without bathroom S30-60) Lots of places to sit and relax adorn the flourishing garden here, and although the cheaper rooms are a little cell-like, the better rooms are relatively good value. The ladies running this show are ridiculously friendly. Hot showers and breakfasts are available here.

La Perla de Los Andes (☎ /fax 39-2007; Plaza de Armas 179; s/d S35/55) A swish place that wears its multiple layers of polished wood with pride, La Perla has a great location right on Caraz' quiet plaza. Although rooms are a mite small, they all have cable TV, solid mattresses, hot showers and some have balconies with an ideal plaza view. A restaurant serves breakfast and the staff is helpful.

Hostal Chamanna (☎ 9691645; Nueva Victoria 185; r with/without bathroom per person S45/30) It's less than 2km from the center on the road to Cashapampa (ask locals for directions and take a taxi at night). The Chamanna has six pleasant cabins, all with hot showers, set in a bucolic garden. Recently, however, there's been a change of management and the bungalows are starting to dabble with the 'abandoned' look – call ahead to make sure that it's still open.

Hostal Tumshukaiko (☎ 39-2212; Melgar 114; s/d S60/80) Located five blocks north of town is this hotel with fine, modern 2nd-floor rooms decorated in a rustic theme and featuring excellent mattresses and hot showers. Downstairs is a cactus garden and a Spanish-influenced restaurant that serves bonza buffet breakfasts (S9). There's a small discount in the off-season.

Eating

Heladería Caraz Dulzura (Plaza de Armas; ice cream S2; 🕑 8am-9:30pm) This popular ice-cream place gets packed on hot days. It also serves some local meals, but the ice cream is what it's really all about.

Pollería Jeny (☎ 39-1101; Plaza de Armas; meals S5-10; 🕑 7am-10:30pm) Good set lunches and the best chicken in town attract the indigent; slightly pricier à la carte items include steak and trout. Breakfast, snacks and sandwiches are also available.

Cafetería El Turista (☎ 30-1518; San Martín 1127; breakfast S5-10; 🕑 7am-noon & 5-8pm) A great place to grab an early breakfast, this tiny little cafe is a one-woman show run by the exuberant Maria. It's filled with a warren of crafts and knickknacks – all for sale.

Café La Terraza (☎ 30-1226; José Sucre 1107; dishes S5-15; ☺ 7am-11pm) Does some of the best coffee in town and has lots of breakfast options (pancakes!), pizzas and pastas – all in a cavernous but cheerful art-covered space.

Café de Rat (☎ /fax 39-1642; José Sucre 1266; meals S7-15, large pizzas S18-25; ☺ 7am-11pm Mon-Sat) Don't mind the name, the menu has been cleared of rodents. This atmospheric wood-beamed restaurant and cafe serves sandwiches, pastas, coffees and drinks throughout the day, as well as a massive buffet breakfast (S12). It also has a book exchange, darts, a bar and music; it's a top spot to hang out. There's a fireplace and you can gaze onto the plaza from its upstairs balcony. Find it above Pony Expeditions.

Villa del Sabor (☎ 39-1273; Villar 224; meals S10-18; ☺ 7am-7pm) Right off the Plaza de Armas, the flower-filled 'House of Flavor' serves *ají de gallina* and trout almost any way you can think of. The best day to come is Sunday, when *pachamanca* is served for S18.

Getting There & Around

Caraz is often the final destination for buses heading from the coast to the Callejón de Huaylas. Most coastal buses go via Huaraz.

BUS
Long Distance

Transportes Rodríguez (☎ 39-1184; Cordova 141) has a Lima via Pativilca bus at 8pm (S30, 10 hours), while **Cooperativa Ancash** (☎ 39-1126; Cordova 139) has a service at 11am, 7pm and 8pm (S30). **Movil Tours** (☎ 39-1922; cnr Cordova & Santa Rosa) has comfortable Lima buses at 8am and 8:30pm (S24 to S30), as well as a *semi-cama* (semi-sleeper) Trujillo bus via Pativilca at 7:30pm (S45, 12 hours).

Yungay Express (☎ 39-1693; Villar 316) has three buses a day to Chimbote via the Cañón del Pato leaving at 9am (S20, eight to nine hours) and via Casma (S21, six to eight hours) at 7pm and 8pm. **Transport Huandoy** (☎ 39-1236; Villar 224) also has a 12:30pm Chimbote bus through the Cañón (S20) and Casma bus (S20) at noon, 4pm and 8pm.

Caraz Area

Minibuses to Yungay (S2, 30 minutes) and Huaraz (S5, 1½ hours) leave from the station on the Carretera Central.

TAXI

Colectivo taxis for Cashapampa (S5, 1½ hours) for the northern end of th Llanganuco–Santa Cruz trek leave when fu from the corner of Ramón Castilla at Sant Cruz. *Colectivos* to Huallanca, for the Cañó del Pato and onwards, leave from the corne of Cordova and La Mar when full (S5, 1½ hours). From the corner of Ramón Castill at Santa Cruz are 4am, 7am, 11am and 1pm *colectivos* to Pueblo Parón (S4, 45 minute for the famous Laguna Parón, which is abou 9km further on foot or by truck.

Taxis (S2 to S3) and *mototaxis* (S1) trundl around town.

SOUTH OF HUARAZ

Covering the southern extent of th Cordillera Blanca and the majestic Cordiller Huayhuash, this part of the Andes refuse to be outdone in the 'breathtaking mountain scenery' stakes. Several peaks here alse pass the 6000m mark, huddling to form a near-continuous, saw toothed ridge of precipitous summits. **Yerupajá** (6634m), Peru's second-highest mountain, is the icing on the Cordillera cake and is followed in height by its second lieutenant **Siulá Grande** (6356m), where climber Joe Simpson fell down a crevice to his near death and lived to tell the tale in the book and movie *Touching the Void*.

The rugged and rewarding 10-day Cordillera Huayhuash Circuit (see p410), accessed through the town of Chiquián, is the glittering star attraction. This fairly strenuous hike is less accessible and receives fewer visitors than its Cordillera Blanca counterpart, but rewards those who make the effort with stunning and remote azure lakes, snow-covered peaks and green-carpeted valleys.

The Puente Bedoya bridge, about 18km south of Huaraz, marks the beginning of a 2km dirt road to the community of **Olleros**, the starting point for the three-day trek across the Cordillera Blanca to Chavín de Huántar (see p422). Respons Sustainable Tourism Center (p395) in Huaraz arranges a colorful day trip (S90 for two people, less per person for larger groups) to the village of **Huarípampa**, just a few minutes south of Huaraz, to see two local women dye and weave wool with plants from their own gardens and on their own hand looms.

Recuay (population 2900), a town 25km from Huaraz, is one of the few municipalities to have survived the 1970 earthquake largely unscathed. Catac (population 2300), 10km south of Recuay, is an even smaller hamlet and the starting point for trips to see the remarkable *Puya raimondii* plant.

Further south, about 70km from Huaraz on the road to Lima and in the vicinity of the village of Pampas Chico, **Hatun Machay** (www.andean kingdom.com/hatunmachay; dm incl all meals, equipment & transport from Huaraz S150) is a rock-climber's paradise. The folks at Andean Kingdom have developed dozens of climbing routes throughout this 'rock forest' nestled high in the Cordillera Negra. The whole complex, including the climbing routes and a large rustic refuge with kitchen facilities is at your service for beginning rock-climbing instruction, as well as hard-core ascents. If that weren't enough, two treks around the area take you past archaeological remains of rock carvings and a view of the Pacific Ocean (on a clear day), and make for great half-day acclimatization hikes.

CHIQUIÁN
☎ 043 / pop 3700 / elev 3400m

A subdued hill town, Chiquián was traditionally the base of operations for folk trekking the Cordillera Huayhuash Circuit. Now, however, it can be bypassed using the new road that extends to a trailhead at Llamac. Great views of the Huayhuash come into view as you drive into the village.

Trekking services can be arranged through a couple of small agencies in town. Andes Top, based at Hotel Los Nogales, arranges trekking and climbing excursions departing from Chiquián. Daily rates are roughly the same as in Huaraz.

The annual festival in Chiquián is in honor of **Santa Rosa de Lima**, held in late August and celebrated with dances, parades, music and bullfights. **Club Esperanza** (☎ 44-7161; Comercio 310) sells good-quality alpaca products handknitted by local artisans.

Sleeping & Eating
Hotel Los Nogales (☎ 44-7121; Comercio 1301; s/d S20/35, without bathroom S10/15) Clean and attractive, this place is about three blocks from the central plaza. Rooms surround a comely, colonial-style courtyard and meals are available on request. There is hot water.

Hostal Chavín (San Martín, cuadra 1; d S15) An adequate pick for shoestring travelers trying to squeeze value out of their nuevo soles.

Gran Hotel Huayhuash (☎ 42-5661; www.hotel huayhuash.com; Calle 28 de Julio 400; s/d S45/60) Some rooms at this more contemporary place have cable TV and afford good vistas; hot water is available and the hotel has the town's best restaurant. The hotel owner here is a good source of information.

Chifa Huaycayinita (☎ 58-8604; Sáenz Peña; meals S5-10; ☺ noon-4pm & 7-10pm) A decent hole-in-the-wall restaurant that serves Chinese and Peruvian fare.

Getting There & Away
If you're interested in heading straight to Chiquián and the Cordillera Huayhuash, you'll find direct buses from Lima. However, as you'll probably need a few days to acclimatize, note that Huaraz offers a wider selection of distractions. **Turismo Cavassa** (☎ 44-7036; Bolognesi 421) has buses to and from Lima, leaving at 9am daily from either city (S20, nine hours).

El Rápido (☎ 42-2887) and **Virgen Del Carmen** (☎ 44-7003) have buses that leave from Chiquián's Plaza de Armas to Huaraz at 5am and 2pm (S8 to S10, 2½ hours).

If you're starting the Huayhuash Circuit, catch a 9am *combi* to Llamac or Pocpa (S6, three hours). There is also a 9am *combi* to Quero (S5, 2½ hours), from where you can hike to Mahuay and Matacancha for the trek's alternate start. It's possible to get from Chiquián to Huallanca, although service is erratic at best. Ask locally. Huallanca (population 1950) has a basic hotel, and transport continues on from here to La Unión and Huánuco.

CAJATAMBO
☎ 01 / pop 3000 / elev 3380m

This small market town on the far side of the Cordillera Huayhuash is reached by trekking, or by snaking up a hair-raising dirt road from Lima. The plaza, topped by the standard colonial-style church, is rather nice. Because it is at the north end of the department of Lima, it has Lima-style seven-digit phone numbers.

Hostal Huayhuash (☎ 244-2016; Plaza de Armas 215; s/d S14/30) has private bathrooms with hot water and a good restaurant. **Tambomachay** (☎ 244-2046; Bolognesi 140; s/d S30/45) supplies better service, hot water and arranges local bus tickets.

The top of the price range in Huayhuash, though probably not really worth the money, is **International Inn** (☎ 244-2071; international.inn@hostal.net; Benavides, cuadra 4; s/d S120/150). The small rooms have comfortable beds, hot water and TV. Bargain hard for a discount. There's an expensive restaurant here as well. Cheap *pollerías* encircle the Plaza de Armas if you're in need of sustenance.

Empresa Andina (Plaza de Armas) has 6am buses to Lima (S25, nine hours).

EAST OF THE CORDILLERA BLANCA

The Conchucos Valley (locally called the Callejón de Conchucos) runs parallel to the Callejón de Huaylas on the eastern side of the Cordillera. Sprinkled liberally with remote and rarely visited gems, this captivating dale is steeped in history and blessed with isolated, postcard-perfect Andean villages so tranquil that they'd fall into comas if they were any sleepier. Interlaced with excellent yet rarely visited hiking trails, this untapped region begs for exploration. Tourist infrastructure is still in its infancy, with a handful of welcoming but modest hotels and erratic transport along rough, unpaved roads that can be impassable in the wet season. If you do make the effort to get here, the highland hospitality of Quechua *campesinos* and awe-inspiring scenery will more than make up for the butt-smacking, time-consuming bumps in the road.

Chavín de Huántar, at the south end of the valley, is the most accessible area of the lot and lays claim to some of the most important and mysterious pre-Inca ruins on the continent. From Huari, just north of Chavín, you can either catch rides on pseudo-regular buses north to Pomabamba, or hike your way north, skirting the eastern peaks of the Cordillera Blanca to Chacas and Yanama (see p426).

CHAVÍN DE HUÁNTAR
☎ 043 / pop 2000 / elev 3250m

The unhurried town of Chavín abuts the northern end of the ruins and is too often whizzed through by visitors on popular day trips from Huaraz. A shame really, as this attractive Andean township has excellent tourist infrastructure, a slew of nature-centered activities and some of the best-value accommodations in the Cordilleras. If you decide to overnight it here, you get to visit the impressive archaeological site in the early morning and have it all to yourself.

The main drag of Chavín town is Calle 17 de Enero, which leaves the peaceful Plaza de Armas southbound, passing rows of restaurants, internet cafes and the entrance to the archaeological site. The **Banco de la Nación** (☯ 7am-5:30pm Mon-Fri, 9am-1pm Sat), on the Plaza de Armas, doesn't have an ATM but will change US dollars.

Sights
CHAVÍN DE HUÁNTAR RUINS

This **archaeological site** (adult/student S11/5; ☯ 8am-5pm), a Unesco World Heritage site since 1985, is thought to be the only large structure left behind by the Chavín culture, one of the oldest wide-ranging civilizations on the continent. Quite possibly a major ceremonial center, it's a stupendous achievement of ancient construction, with large temple-like structures above ground and labyrinthine (electronically lit) underground tunnels. Although squatters built on top of the ruins or carried away stone treasures and a large portion of the area was covered by a huge landslide during an earthquake in 1945, this site is still intact enough to provide a full-bodied glimpse into one of Peru's oldest cultures.

Chavín is a series of older and newer temple arrangements built between 1200 BC and 800 BC. In the middle is a massive central square, slightly sunken below ground level, with an intricate and well-engineered system of channels for drainage. From the square, a broad staircase leads up to the single entrance of the largest and most important building, the Castillo, which has withstood some mighty earthquakes over the years. Built on three different levels of dry stone masonry the walls here were at one time embellished with *tenons* (keystones of large projecting blocks carved to resemble human heads with animal or perhaps hallucinogen-induced characteristics). Only one of these remains in its original place, although the others may be seen in the local museum related to the site.

A series of tunnels underneath the Castillo are an exceptional feat of engineering, comprising a maze of complex alleys, ducts and chambers. In the heart of this complex is an exquisitely carved, 4.5m rock of white granite known as the **Lanzón de Chavín**. In typical terrifying Chavín fashion, the low-relief carvings on the Lanzón represent a person with snakes radiating from his head and a ferocious set of fangs, most likely feline. The Lanzón, almost certainly an object of worship given its prominent, central placement in this ceremonial center, is sometimes referred to as the Smiling God – but its aura feels anything but friendly.

Several beguiling construction quirks, such as the strange positioning of water channels and the use of highly polished minerals to reflect light, led Stanford archaeologists to believe that the complex was used as an instrument of shock and awe. To instill fear in nonbelievers, priests manipulated sights and sounds. They blew on echoing Strombus trumpets, amplified the sounds of water running through specially designed channels and reflected sunlight through ventilation shafts. The disoriented were probably given hallucinogens like San Pedro cactus shortly before entering the darkened maze. These tactics endowed the priests with awe-inspiring power.

The new, outstanding **Museo Nacional de Chavín** (☎ 45-4011; admission free; ☻ 9am-5pm Tue-Sun), funded jointly by the Peruvian and Japanese governments, houses most of the intricate and horrifyingly carved *tenons*, as well as the magnificent Tello Obelisk, another stone object of worship with low relief carvings of a caiman and other fierce animals. The obelisk had been housed in a Lima museum since the 1945 earthquake that destroyed much of the original museum, and was only returned to Chavín in 2009.

To get the most from your visit, it's worth hiring a guide to show you around (S25) or go on a guided day trip (including transportation) from Huaraz; this latter option is by far the most budget-friendly way to see these ruins, especially since it can be difficult to get a bus back to Huaraz from Chavín late in the day – you may get stuck in a high-priced *colectivo* (S20).

CENTRO ARTESANAL CEO CHAVÍN

A few hundred meters along the road to Huari, **Centro Artesanal CEO Chavín** (Tello Sur 350; ☻ dawn-dusk) sells locally made textiles, alpaca weavings and stone carvings – visit in the afternoon to see weavers weaving wildly.

Activities

Relaxing sulfur **thermal baths** (admission S2), a 30-minute walk south of town, house four private baths and one larger pool. Keep your eyes peeled for a small, signed path that leads down to the river. **Horse riding** on Peruvian pacing horses can be arranged through the Cafetería Renato (p424) for S20 per hour (including a guide).

From Chavín you can hike for a few hours into a lofty valley, in the direction of Olleros, to a high pass with stirring views of Huantsán (6395m) – the highest mountain in the southern Cordillera Blanca. If you're interested in longer treks originating here, **Don Donato** (☎ 45-4136; Tello Sur 275) of the Asociación de Servicios de Alta Montaña, offers a four-day trek that circles the back side of the Cordillera Blanca, passes by several alpine lakes and exits through the Carhuascancha valley.

Sleeping & Eating

Chavín has a surprisingly good selection of accommodations. Camping by the ruins is also possible with permission of the guard.

La Casona (☎ 45-9004; Plaza de Armas 130; s/d S25/50) Nestled in an old house, the well-kept rooms here are a little on the dark side, but the beautiful courtyard, dripping with plants, is an excellent place to hang out and soak up the ambience. The hot water here can be erratic, however. Some rooms have a TV or a plaza balcony and there's a restaurant.

Hotel Chavín (☎ 45-4055; Inca Roca 141; s/d S27/45) This hotel is modern, has hot water and a TV in all rooms and a restaurant. Around the corner is the affiliated but cheaper and more basic Hostal Chavín. Between the two of them you'll find a room to suit; guests bargain for the best deal.

Hostal Inca (☎ 45-4092; Plaza de Armas; s/d S30/40) The reputation of this secure, popular place is as solid as its hot showers and it boasts very respectable rooms. There's a small garden and the family that runs it is super-friendly and helpful. Hostal Inca also houses the lab for the ongoing excavation project of the ruins.

Gran Hotel Rickay (☎ 45-4068; Calle 17 de Enero 600; s/d S45/85) With slightly pricier digs, this grandiose neocolonial option has top rooms, is newly renovated and has a patio, restaurant (serving pizzas and pastas) and modern rooms with hot showers and a TV.

Most of the town's eateries can be found along Calle 17 de Enero and in hotels.

CHAVÍN CULTURE

Named after the site at Chavín de Huántar, this is considered one of the oldest major cultures in Peru, strutting its stuff on the pre-Inca stage from 1000 BC to 300 BC. The Chavín wielded their influence with great success, particularly between the formative years of 800 BC to 400 BC when they excelled in agricultural production of potatoes and other highland crops, animal husbandry, ceramic and metal production and engineering of buildings and canals. Chavín archaeologists have formerly referred to this cultural expansion as the Chavín Horizon, though Early Horizon is also used.

The principal Chavín deity was feline (jaguar or puma), although lesser condor, eagle and snake deities were also worshipped. Representations of these deities are highly stylized and cover many Chavín sites and many extraordinary objects, such the Tello Obelisk in the Museo Nacional de Chavín (p423), the *Lanzón,* often referred to as the Smiling God, which stands in mystical glory in the tunnels underneath the Chavín site, and the Raimondi Stone at the Museo Nacional de Antropología, Arqueología e Historia del Perú in Lima (p97). The Raimondi Stone (which is currently considered too fragile to move to Chavín) has carvings of a human figure, sometimes called the Staff God, with a jaguar face and large staffs in each hand – an image that has shown up at archaeological sites along the northern and southern coasts of Peru and which suggests the long reach of Chavín influence. The images on all of these massive stone pillars are believed to indicate a belief in a tripartite universe consisting of the heavens, earth and a netherworld, or as an alternative theory goes, a cosmos consisting of air, earth and water.

As a major ceremonial center, the most powerful players in Chavín were its priests, who reigned with terrifying authority over castes of artisans and ordinary workers. The priests relied on sophisticated observation and understanding of seasonal changes, rain and drought cycles, and the movement of the sun, moon, and stars to create calendars that helped the Chavín reign as agriculturalists. Some archeologists have argued that women also served as priests and played a powerful role in Chavín culture.

Restaurants have a reputation for closing soon after sunset, so dig in early.

Cafetería Renato (☎ 50-4279; Plaza de Armas; breakfast & snacks S7-14; ☼ 7am-4pm) On the casual Plaza de Armas, this cozy place serves yummy local and international breakfasts alongside homemade yogurt, cheese and *manjar blanco* (homemade caramel spread). There's a lovely garden you can laze in while waiting for your bus and the owners organize horse trekking from here.

Chavín Turístico (☎ 45-4051; Calle 17 de Enero 439; meals S7-15; ☼ 11am-9pm) A good lunch option, this place has a chalkboard of traditional plates and rickety tables around a tiny courtyard. The food is tasty and popular with tour groups.

Buongiorno (☎ 45-4112; Calle 17 de Enero 439; meals S10-15; ☼ 10am-9pm) Probably the best restaurant in town, Buongiorno serves well-executed local dishes and a few gringo regulars in a cordial garden backdrop. The *lomo a la pimienta,* a Peruvian fave of grilled steak in wine, cream and cracked-pepper sauce (S13), is excellent. Keep an eye out for the unnatural-looking stuffed deer guarding the entrance.

Getting There & Away

The scenic drive across the Cordillera Blanca via Catac passes the Laguna Querococha at 3980m. From here, there are views of the peaks of Pucaraju (5322m) and Yanamarey (5237m). Along the way it passes through the Kahuish tunnel, at 4516m above sea level, which cuts through the Kahuish pass. As you exit the tunnel and descend toward Chavín, look out for the massive statue of Christ, built by Italian missionaries (see p415), blessing your journey.

Tour buses make day trips from Huaraz. See p400 for details of Chavín Express and other companies that have multiple daily departures to Chavín (S10, three hours). Either Chavín Express or Sandoval leave from the Plaza de Armas for the return trip to Huaraz – ask about departure times at the Plaza de Armas – but seats are limited and you may be forced to take a *colectivo* (S20, two hours).

Continuing north along the east side of the Cordillera Blanca involves asking around. Most of the buses originating in Huaraz continue on to Huari (S5, two hours), from where you can catch onward transport on some of the infrequent buses that pass through from Lima. Frequent minibuses to San Marcos depart from the plaza (S1, 20 minutes).

Hikers can walk to Chavín from Olleros in about three days; it's a popular but uncrowded hike (see p409).

NORTH OF CHAVÍN

The road north of Chavín goes through the villages of San Marcos (after 8km), Huari (40km, two hours), San Luis (100km, five hours), Pomabamba and eventually Sihuas (population 4000). The further north you go, the more inconsistent transport becomes, and it may stop altogether during the wet season.

From Sihuas, it is possible to continue on to Huallanca (at the end of Cañón del Pato) via Tres Cruces and thus return to the Callejón de Huaylas (see Do-It-Yourself Andean Exploration, p416). This round-trip is scenic, remote and rarely made by travelers.

There are two roads that offer picturesque crossings back to El Callejón de Huaylas. The road from Chacas to Carhuaz, via the Punta Olímpica pass (4890m), is spectacular. A road from Yanama to Yungay takes passengers over yet another breathtaking pass (4767m) and into the valley made famous by the Llanganuco lakes, with top views of the towering Huascarán, Chopicalqui and Huandoy (6356m).

Huari

☎ 043 / pop 4700 / elev 3150m

A small Quechua town barely clinging to the mountainside, Huari has nearly 360-degree mountain panoramas from its steep, cobbled streets. Market day here is Sunday, when *campesinos* from surrounding towns descend on Huari to hawk fruits and vegetables. The annual town **fiesta**, Señora del Rosario, is held in early October and has a strange tradition of cat consumption (see below). The town has a small and modern Plaza de Armas and a larger Plaza Vigil (known as El Parque) one block away. All buses leave from Plaza Vigil. You should be able to change US dollars into soles at the Banco de la Nación near the market; there is no ATM.

For sweeping panoramas of the valley, keep walking uphill from the El Dorado hotel until you come to a *mirador* (lookout). A good day hike is to **Laguna Purhuay**, a beautiful lake about 5km away. An excellent two- or three-day backpacking trip continues past the lake to emerge at the village of Chacas. Another three- to four-day trek trails along the old Inca highway to Huánuco (see p409).

There are several cheap hotels in town, but **El Dorado** (☎ 45-3028; Simon Bolívar 353; r per person with/ without bathroom S25/15; 🖳) is the pick of the bunch with hot water, the cleanest rooms, smiling staff and internet on tap. **Hostal Paraíso** (☎ 45-3029; Simón Bolívar 263; s/d S15/25) is up the hill from El Dorado and has more modest rooms and a courtyard with some greenery. For breakfast, try **Restaurant Turístico El Milagro** (San Martín 589; dishes S3-12; 🕑 7am-8:30pm), which also does local food and ceviche (raw seafood marinated in lime juice). For a real treat, look behind the market for **Chifa Dragón Andino** (☎ 45-4110; Magisterial 300; dishes S5-10; 🕑 10am-11pm), which serves some of the best Chinese food in the Cordillera.

Buses for Huaraz and Lima leave most days from Plaza Vigil. Sandoval, Chavín Express and Rio Mosna all have 9am, 3pm and 8:30pm buses to Huaraz (S12, four hours). Turismo Andino has daily buses to Lima at 9am (S35) – although you'll have more options if you got to Huaraz first – and daily buses to Chacas via San Luis (8:30am on Saturday and Tuesday, S10, four hours) as well as buses to Pomabamba (S18, seven hours) at around 10pm on Wednesday and Sunday only. For Laguna Purhuay you can hire a taxi to take you for about S30 return, including waiting time.

HUARI CATS

The annual fiesta of La Virgen del Rosario (Virgin of the Rosary) in Huari is also known locally as the *Fiesta de los Gatos* (Festival of the Cats). It's held in October and the people of Huari have an odd tradition of cooking up *miche broaster* – roasted cat. Though no one's quite sure how this all began, it probably arose when an alternative source of protein was needed during a particularly tough growing season and thus a tradition was formed. Locals get quite excited by this fried feline fetish. So much so that one year there was no cat on the menu – too many felines were consumed at a previous fiesta to sustain the cat population. Check out the fountain in the Plaza de Armas, it has eight cat statues pawing and peeing into a central pool.

San Luis

☎ 043 / elev 3130m

This simple municipality is little more than a crossroad blip on the tourist radar. It's reached by daily buses from Huaraz, via Yungay and Yanama, or by buses between Huari and Pomabamba (you get some super views coming from Huari). The best of several basic hotels here is **Hostal San Lucho** (☎ 83-3435; Calle 28 de Julio 250; r per person with/without bathroom S20/15), with passable rooms around a typical Andean courtyard open to the mountain air.

Regular *combis* leave for Chacas when full (S2.50) and several buses depart for Huaraz (S18, five hours) throughout the day.

Chacas

☎ 043 / pop 2000 / elev 3360m

This ornate mountain town sits atop a hill crest, surrounded by fertile hills and with guest appearances by the occasional snow-capped Cordillera peak. The charismatic main plaza is dominated by a brilliant church built by a religious Italian aid organization (see p415), many of whom use Chacas as their base for helping operations.

White-walled houses around the plaza look idyllic against the mountain backdrop and many have intricate wooden balconies and brightly colored doors and window shutters just screaming to have their picture taken. Best of all, the town is whisper-quiet as there's no traffic to speak of. Look out for the impossibly petite, smiling Andean ladies who sit meditatively spinning wool on every second corner. This is an excellent place to while away a few days. The whole town has only five fixed-line phones, yet surprisingly there's internet access across from the church (S2 per hour). The Chacas **fiesta** is held on August 15.

You can do great two- to three-day treks from here to Huari or Yanama, from where energetic hikers can continue on to do the Santa Cruz trek (p404).

The friendly and very simple **Hostal Saragoza** (Bolognesi; 370; r per person with/without bathroom S15/10) is on the Plaza de Armas – a couple of rooms have windows onto the plaza and the place manages to scrap together a certain bucolic appeal. **Hospedaje Alameda** (Lima 305; r per person with/without bathroom S30/10) has some similarly modest rooms as well as much nicer, newer abodes with attached bathrooms. Both places have hot water. Pilar Ames (the owner of El Cortijo restaurant in Monterrey, p413) has

the most comfortable digs in town at **Hostal Pilar** (☎ in Monterrey 42-3813; Ancash 110; d S115), with decent modern facilities. This place is used a part of a local tour and is open only to those with prior reservations. There are a few hole-in-the-wall restaurants and *pollerías* around all serving similar local dishes.

Copa and Transporte Renzo run buses to Huaraz (via Punto Olímpica and Carhuaz) a 7am and 2pm (S14, four hours). *Combis* leave for San Luis from in front of the cathedra when full (S2.50) and from San Luis you car catch passing buses to Pomabamba or Huari

Yanama

☎ 043 / pop 500 / elev 3400m

Yanama is a tiny, mountain-enveloped *pueblo*, where the most exciting thing to happen this decade is a connection to the electricity grid in 2005. The town is about 1½ hours' walk (or a 20-minute drive) from the end of the popular Santa Cruz trek (see p404) and makes a good stopover point, where trekkers and mountain-bikers can refuel and recharge. The town **festival of Santa Rosa** is held here in August.

A daily morning bus links Yungay with Yanama, passing the famed Lagunas Llanganuco and traveling within 1km of the village of **Colcabamba** (population 360), the starting point for the Llanganuco–Santa Cruz trekking circuit. Facilities are rudimentary in Yanama and showers can be as frosty as the mountain air. A couple of *hospedajes* supply austere rooms for around S10 per person, but the best option in town is **Hospedaje El Pino** (☎ 83 3449; r per person without bathroom S10), behind the church with a huge pine tree outside. Exceptionally friendly, it's basic but has comfortable beds and the owners will heat up hot water on request for a 'bucket' shower. You'll also find the best restaurant in town here – misty views of the mountains come standard.

ourpick **Andes Lodge Peru** (☎ 84-7423; www.andes lodgeperu.com; Jirón Gran Chavín s/n; s/d without bathroom S45/90, s/d S60/110), although pricier, is just a couple of blocks from the Plaza de Armas, and one of the best mountain lodges in the Callejón de Huaylas. Readers rave about the home-cooked meals, blazing hot showers, snug beds with down comforters and the ever-helpful Peruvian owners ready to escort their guests into the homes of local weavers and farmers. All rooms come with breakfast, and other meals are available.

In Colcabamba you'll find several home-tays that offer beds with dinner for S15 to $20 per person.

Colectivos leave for Yungay from the plaza around midday (S10, 3½ hours) or you can catch one of the buses originating n Pomabamba.

Pomabamba

☎ 043 / pop 4400 / elev 2950m

Known as the City of Cedars (check out the specimen on the plaza), Pomabamba is a great place to spend some time between trekking trips. Soak in a lung-full of the crisp mountain troposphere and the small-town ambience. Several cross-Cordillera treks begin and end at this township and you'd be forgiven for failing to notice that this is supposed to be the 'largest' settlement north of Huari.

A small **museum** by the plaza and several sets of natural private **hot springs** (admission S1) lie in wait for weary hikers on the outskirts of town. These may make up for the fact that the town has no hot showers. It's sometimes possible to arrange trekking guides from here – ask at your hotel. Internet cafes abound near the plaza.

The next town along toward San Luis or Huari, **Piscobamba**, has decent views of the mountains and that's about it.

Pomabamba single-handedly dominates the Cordillera Blanca's SBC (simple, basic, clean) *hostal* market. **Hostal Pomabamba** (☎ 45-1276; Huamachuco 338; r per person with/without bathroom S15/8), on the main plaza, is one of the more economical rudimentary alternatives. The genial **Alojamiento Estrada** (☎ 50-4615; Huaraz 209; r per person S10), by the church, has a small courtyard and just trumps the competition in the charm stakes. **Albergue Turístico Via** (☎ 44-1052; Primavera 323; r per person from S10) has typical shared-bathroom basics as well as nicer, newer rooms with bathrooms attached.

If you are a *pollería* connoisseur, as we have become on our travels in Peru, check out **Mikey's Pollería** (Huamachuco 330; meals S5-10) on the plaza for some of the best darn grilled chicken south of the equator. **Davis David** (Huaraz 269; menús S5) has local regulars and a respectable daytime *menú*.

All buses to Huaraz and Lima leave from near the Plaza de Armas. **Turismo Andino** (☎ 45-1290) has buses to Huaraz at 7am and 7pm (S24, eight hours) via Yanama (S10, four hours), a 6am bus to Lima (S35, 18 hours) on Monday and Thursday via Huari (S11 four hours), and occasional buses to Sihuas (S9, three hours). **Transporte Renzo** (☎ 45-1088) has an early Huaraz bus at 5:30am on Monday, Wednesday and Saturday, as well as regular daily buses at noon and 7pm (S21). **El Solitario** (☎ 45-1133) has a 6:30am Lima bus (S41) via Huari (S9) on Sunday, Monday and Wednesday. *Combis* go to Sihuas and Piscobamba daily from the town center.

HUARAZ & THE CORDILLERAS

Northern Highlands

Vast tracts of unexplored jungle and mist-shrouded mountain ranges guard the secrets of the northern highlands like a suspicious custodian. Here, Andean peaks and a blanket of luxuriant forests stretch from the coast all the way to the deepest, darkest jungles of the Amazon. Interspersed with the relics of Inca kings and the jungle-encrusted ruins of cloud-forest-dwelling warriors, these outposts of Peru remain barely connected by disheveled and circuitous roads.

The cobbled streets of Cajamarca testify to the beginning of the end of the once-powerful Inca empire, and remnants of the work of these famed Andean masons still line the sur-rounding countryside. Meanwhile, the delicate colonial structures lining Cajamarca's heart attest to the final outcome of the 16th-century battle of swords and wills.

The hazy forests of Chachapoyas have only recently revealed their archaeological bounty: the rarely seen yet staggering stone fortress of Kuélap, which clings for dear life to a craggy limestone peak. Hundreds of misplaced archaeological remnants from this mysterious alli-ance of city-states can be visited on a trek or by horse while meandering through pristine forgotten countryside. At Tarapoto, where the paved road reaches its conclusion, the jungle waits patiently, as it has for centuries, endowed with a cornucopia of wildlife and exquisite good looks.

NORTHERN HIGHLANDS

HIGHLIGHTS

- ◾ Scramble through **Kuélap** (p448), an im-mense citadel that rivals Machu Picchu in grandeur, but lacks its crowds

- ◾ Hike through cloud forests to boldly (re)discover long-forgotten cities, Indiana Jones–style, in the region of **Gran Vilaya** (p446) near Chachapoyas

- ◾ Follow Inca footsteps to soak in **Los Baños del Inca** (p438), outside Cajamarca, the steaming baths once used by kings

- ◾ Get to within a hairbreadth of the fracas of the jungle at **Tarapoto** (p453) without leav-ing the comfort of the paved highway

- ◾ Get close-up looks at hundreds of recently discovered mummies and the strange Marvelous Spatuletail Hummingbird, near **Leimebamba** (p449)

Gran Vilaya

Kuélap ★   Tarapoto ★
        ★ Leimebamba

★ Los Baños
del Inca

◾ BIGGEST CITY: CAJAMARCA, POPULATION 146,000

◾ AVERAGE TEMPERATURE: JANUARY 18°C TO 28°C, JULY 16°C TO 25°C

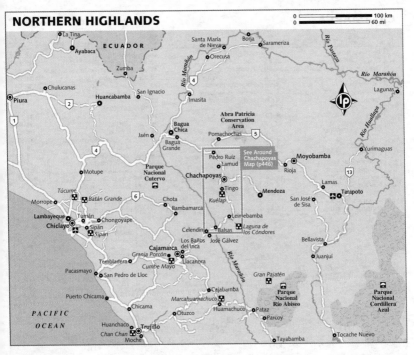

NORTHERN HIGHLANDS

| 0 | 100 km |
| 0 | 60 mi |

CAJAMARCA

☎ 076 / pop 146,000 / elev 2750m

The most important town in the northern highlands, Cajamarca is a dainty colonial metropolis cradled in a languid valley and stonewalled by brawny mountains in every direction. Descending into the vale by road, Cajamarca's mushroom field of red-tile-roofed abodes surely confesses a secret desire to cling to its village roots. Fertile farmland carpets the entire valley and Cajamarca's streets belong as much to the wide-brimmed-hat-wielding *campesinos* (peasants) bundled in brightly colored scarves, as the young city slickers who frequent the boutique restaurants and bars. In the colonial center, the capacious Plaza de Armas is bordered by majestic churches. From here, once-decadent baroque mansions spread out in concentric circles along the cobbled streets, many enclosing ethereal hotels and fine restaurants.

Things have changed slowly here. Only recently has the Yanacocha gold mine (see the boxed text on p432) injected Cajamarca with an avalanche of cash and a steady stream of moneyed engineers. Not many tourists pass through this way, but dozens of sights from the town's pivotal past, including the famous Baños del Inca, will keep those that make it here absorbed for days.

History

In about 1460, the Incas conquered the local Cajamarca populace and Cajamarca evolved into a major city on the Inca Andean highway linking Cuzco and Quito.

After the death of the Inca Huayna Capac in 1525, the remaining Inca empire, which then stretched from southern Colombia to central Chile, was pragmatically divided between his sons, with Atahualpa ruling the north and Huascar the south. Obviously not everyone was in concord, as civil war soon broke out and in 1532 Atahualpa and his victorious troops marched southward toward Cuzco to take complete control of the empire. Parked at Cajamarca to rest for a few days, the Inca emperor was camped at the natural thermal springs, known today as Los Baños del Inca, when he heard the news that the Spanish were nearby.

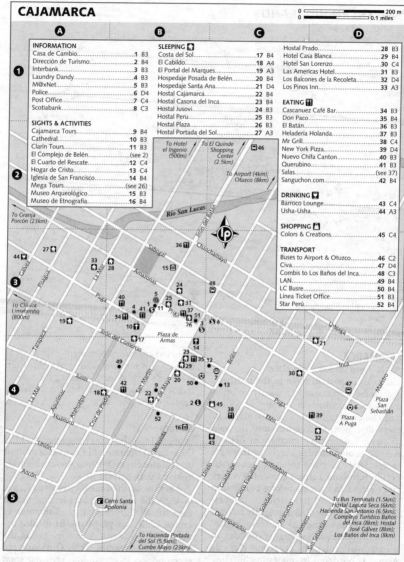

CAJAMARCA

Francisco Pizarro and his force of 168 Spaniards arrived in Cajamarca on November 15, 1532, to a deserted city; most of its 2000 inhabitants were with Atahualpa at his hot-springs encampment. The Spaniards spent an anxious night, fully aware that they were severely outnumbered by the nearby Inca troops, who were estimated to be between 40,000 and 80,000. The Spaniards plotted to entice Atahualpa into the plaza and, at a pre-arranged signal, capture the Inca should the opportunity present itself.

Upon Atahualpa's arrival, he ordered most of his troops to stay outside while he entered the plaza with a retinue of nobles and about 6000 men armed with slings and hand axes.

He was met by the Spanish friar Vicente de Valverde, who attempted to explain his position as a man of God and presented the Inca with a Bible. Reputedly, Atahualpa angrily threw the book to the ground and Valverde needed little more justification to sound the attack.

Cannons were fired and the Spanish cavalry attacked Atahualpa and his troops. The indigenous people were terrified and bewildered by the fearsome onslaught of never-before-seen cannons and horses. Their small hand axes and slings were no match for the well-armored Spaniards, who swung razor-sharp swords from the advantageous height of horseback to slaughter 7000 indigenous people and capture Atahualpa. The small band of Spaniards was now literally conquistadors (conquerors).

Atahualpa soon became aware of the Spaniards' lust for gold and offered to fill a large room in the town once with gold and twice with silver in return for his freedom. The Spanish agreed and slowly the gold and silver began pouring into Cajamarca. Nearly a year later the ransom was complete – about 6000kg of gold and 12,000kg of silver had been melted down into gold and silver bullion. At today's prices, this ransom would be worth almost $180 million, but the artistic value of the ornaments and implements that were melted down to create the bullion is impossible to estimate.

Atahualpa, suspecting he was not going to be released, sent desperate messages to his followers in Quito to come to Cajamarca and rescue him. The Spaniards, panic-stricken by these messages, sentenced Atahualpa to death. On July 26, 1533, Atahualpa was led out to the center of the Cajamarca plaza to be burned at the stake. At the last hour, Atahualpa 'accepted' baptism and, as a reward, his sentence was changed to a quicker death by strangulation.

Most of the great stone Inca buildings in Cajamarca were torn down and the stones used in the construction of Spanish homes and churches. The great plaza where Atahualpa was captured and later killed was in roughly the same location as today's Plaza de Armas, though in Atahualpa's time it was much larger. The Ransom Chamber, or El Cuarto del Rescate, where Atahualpa was imprisoned, is the only Inca building still standing.

Information

Money changers linger on the Plaza de Armas; take the usual precautions (p523). There's internet access practically on every block.

Casa de Cambio (Jirón del Batán) Changes US dollars quickly.

Clínica Limatambo (☎ 36-4241; Puno 265; ⊗ 8am-5pm) Has the best medical service; west of town.

Dirección de Turismo (☎ 36-2903; El Complejo de Belén; ⊗ 7:30am-1pm & 2:30-5pm Mon-Fri) Tourist information and local map for sale (S1).

Interbank (☎ 36-2460; Calle 2 de Mayo 546) Changes traveler's checks and has an ATM accepting Visa and MasterCard.

Laundry Dandy (☎ 36-3454; Puga 545; per kg S5)

M@xNet (☎ 36-5385; Jirón del Batán 177; ⊗ 8am-midnight) Internet access.

Police (☎ 36-2165; cnr Puga & Ayacucho) Toward the eastern part of town.

Post office (☎ 36-4065; Puga 668; ⊗ 9am-7pm Mon-Fri, to 1pm Sat) Behind the Iglesia de San Francisco.

Scotiabank (☎ Amazonas 750) Changes traveler's checks and has an ATM accepting Visa and MasterCard. Another outlet is located at El Quinde Shopping Center (p436).

Sights

All the following sights are officially open 9am to 1pm and 3pm to 6pm daily – most of the time. They don't have addresses but are in the center of town. The S5 ticket to El Cuarto del Rescate includes El Complejo de Belén and Museo de Etnografía if they are all visited on the same day.

EL COMPLEJO DE BELÉN

Construction of this sprawling colonial complex, church and hospital of Belén, made entirely from volcanic rock, occurred between 1627 and 1774. The hospital was run by nuns and 31 tiny, cell-like bedrooms line the walls of the T-shaped building. In what used to be the women's hospital is a small archaeology museum. The facade here has a fascinating statue of a woman with four breasts – it was carved by local artisans and supposedly represents an affliction (supernumerary nipples, that is) commonly found in one of the nearby towns. The kitchen and dispensary of the hospital now houses an unimpressive art museum.

The baroque church next door is one of Cajamarca's finest and has a prominent cupola and a well-carved pulpit. Among several interesting wood carvings, one extremely tired-looking Christ sits cross-legged

---

THERE'S GOLD IN THEM THERE HILLS

The hills outside Cajamarca are laced with gold. Tons of it – but don't reach for your shovel and pan just yet, as this gold is not found in the kind of golden nuggets that set prospectors' eyes ablaze. It's 'invisible gold,' vast quantities of minuscule specks that require advanced and noxious mining techniques to be pried out of its earthly ore.

The American-run Yanacocha mine has quarried open pits in the countryside surrounding Cajamarca, becoming one of the most productive gold mines in the world. Over US$7 billion worth of the shiny stuff has been extracted so far. That, combined with plenty of new jobs and an influx of international engineers into Cajamarca, has meant a surge in wealth for the region – but locals are starting to question the environmental and social costs.

According to a joint investigation by the *New York Times* and the PBS program *Frontline World* (a US news-magazine on public TV), the history of the mine is clouded by charges of corruption.

In 2000, a large spill of toxic mercury raised doubts about Yanacocha's priorities: gold over safety seemed to be the predictable marching cry. The mine makes its profits by washing vast quantities of mountainside with cyanide solution, a hazardous technique that utilizes masses of water – the very stuff farmers' lives depend on. An internal environmental audit carried out by the company in 2004 verified villagers' observations that water supplies were being contaminated and fish stocks were disappearing.

In the autumn of 2004, disillusioned *campesinos* (peasants) rallied against the opening of a new mine in the area of Quilish, and clashed violently with the police employed to protect the mine's interests. After weeks of conflict, the company eventually gave in and has since re-evaluated its priorities. It currently pumps millions of dollars back into the community and is starting to pay more than lip service to the need for community consent. Several environmental concerns have been addressed and the company's safety record has indeed improved. What remains to be seen, however, is whether Yanacocha can keep its promises once the profits run dry; the millions of tons of acid-contaminated earth left behind will require treatment for decades to come.

---

on his throne, propping up his chin with a double-jointed wrist and looking as though he could do with a pisco sour after a hard day's miracle working. Look out for the oversized cherubs supporting the elaborate centerpiece, which represents the weight of heaven. The outside walls of the church are lavishly decorated. The tourist office is housed in one of the interior complex rooms.

EL CUARTO DEL RESCATE

The Ransom Chamber is the only Inca building still standing in Cajamarca. Although it's called the Ransom Chamber, the room shown to visitors is actually where Atahualpa was imprisoned, not where the ransom was stored. The small room has three trapezoidal doorways and a few similarly shaped niches in the inner walls – signature Inca construction. Although well built, the chamber does not compare with the Inca buildings in the Cuzco area. In the entrance to the site are a couple of modern paintings depicting Atahualpa's capture and imprisonment. The stone of the building is weathered and has only recently been covered by a large protective dome.

MUSEO DE ETNOGRAFÍA

This small, sparsely filled museum, just a few meters from El Complejo de Belén, has limited exhibits of local costumes and clothing, domestic and agricultural implements, musical instruments and crafts made from wood, bone, leather and stone, as well as other examples of Cajamarca culture. Large-scale photographs and modern art interpretations illustrate traditional lives of the district's farmers.

MUSEO ARQUEOLÓGICO

This small, university-run **museum** (Jirón del Batán 289; admission free; 🕙 8am-2:30pm Mon-Fri) is worth visiting; just knock on the door to enter. Its varied ceramics collection includes a few examples of pots from the Cajamarca culture and an unusual collection of ceremonial spears, also from the same period. The Cajamarca culture, which existed here before the Incas conquered the region, is little studied and relatively unknown. The Museo Arqueológico also has black-and-white photographs of historic and prehistoric sites in the Cajamarca area; its director is knowledgeable and willing to talk to visitors about the museum's exhibits.

PLAZA DE ARMAS

The genial plaza has a well-kept topiary garden with hedges trimmed into the shape of llamas and other Andean animals. The fine central **fountain** dates from 1692 and commemorates the bicentenary of Columbus' landing in the Americas. Come evening, the town's inhabitants congregate in the plaza to stroll and mull over the important events of the day – a popular pastime in this area of northern Peru.

Two churches face the Plaza de Armas: the **cathedral** (admission free; ⓨ hours vary) and the **Iglesia de San Francisco** (admission S3; ⓨ 9am-noon & 4-6pm Mon-Fri). Both are often imaginatively illuminated in the evenings, especially on weekends. The cathedral is a squat building that was begun in the late 17th century and only recently finished. Like most of Cajamarca's churches, this cathedral has no belfry. This is because the Spanish Crown levied a tax on finished churches and so the belfries were not built, leaving the church unfinished and thereby avoiding the tax.

Iglesia de San Francisco's belfries were finished in the 20th century – too late for the Spanish Crown to collect its tax. Inside are elaborate stone carvings and decadent altars, and at the entrance is an interesting collection of dangling silver sacred hearts. Visit the church's small **Museo de Arte Religioso** (Religious Art Museum) to see 17th-century religious paintings done by indigenous artists and the creepy **catacombs**, where many monks lie buried. The intricately sculpted **Capilla de la Dolorosa** to the right of the nave is considered one of the finest chapels in the city.

CERRO SANTA APOLONIA

This garden-covered **viewpoint** (admission S1; ⓨ 9am-1pm & 3-5pm) overlooks the city from the southwest and is a prominent Cajamarca landmark. It is easily reached by climbing the stairs at the end of Calle 2 de Mayo, and walking paths spiral around the whole hilltop, making this a nice spot to take a stroll. The pre-Hispanic carved rocks at the summit are mainly from the Inca period, but some are thought to originally date back to the Chavín period. One of the rocks, which is known as the Seat of the Inca, has a shape that suggests a throne, and the Inca (king) is said to have reviewed his troops from this point.

Activities

Hogar de Cristo (☎ 36-5778; Belén 676; ⓨ 8am-6pm) is a charity that is always looking for volunteers to help with its various programs for street children.

Tours & Guides

Tour companies provide information and inexpensive guided tours of the city and its surroundings. The companies claim to have English-speaking guides, but only a few really pass muster. Tours to Cumbe Mayo (S15), Baños del Inca (S20), Granja Porcón (S20) and Ventanillas de Otuzco (S20) are the most popular. The companies will often pool tours. The following companies have received recommendations:

Cajamarca Tours (☎ 36-5674; Calle 2 de Mayo 311)
Clarín Tours (☎ 36-6829; clarintours@hotmail.com; Jirón del Batán 161)
Mega Tours (☎ 35-7793; jpilcon@yahoo.es; Puga 691)

CARNAVAL CAJAMARCA

The Peru-wide pageantry of Carnaval is celebrated at the beginning of Lent, usually in February. Not all Carnavals are created equal, however. Ask any Peruvian where the wildest celebrations are at, and Cajamarca will invariably come out trumps.

Preparations begin months in advance; sometimes, no sooner have Carnaval celebrations wound down than planning for the following year begins. Cajamarcans take their celebrations seriously. The festival is nine days of dancing, eating, singing, partying, costumes, parades and general rowdy mayhem. It's also a particularly wet affair and water fights here are worse (or better, depending on your point of view) than you'd encounter elsewhere. Local teenagers don't necessarily limit themselves to soaking one another with water – paint, oil and other unsightly liquids have all been reported.

Hotels fill up weeks beforehand, prices skyrocket and hundreds of people end up sleeping in the plaza. Considering it's one of the most rambunctious festivals in Peru, it certainly seems worth it.

Festivals & Events

Carnaval The Carnaval festivities here are reputed to be one of the most popular and rowdy events in the country (see p433). It's held in the last few days before Lent.

Corpus Christi A popular feast day in Cajamarca; it's held on the ninth Thursday after Easter.

Fiestas Patrias Celebrations marking National Independence Days (July 28 and 29) may include a bullfight.

Sleeping

Hotel rates (and other prices) rise during festivals and special events and are also usually slightly higher in the dry season (May to September). Prices given here are for May to September.

BUDGET

Most of the budget options in Cajamarca have hot-water showers, though often for only a few hours each day.

Hostal Plaza (☎ 36-2058; Puga 669; s/d S25/40, s/d without bathroom S15/25) There's hot water in the mornings and evenings, and while the communal bathrooms can be on the smelly side of things, the eight rooms with bathrooms are great value. Try to snag a room with a balcony and plaza views.

Hospedaje Santa Ana (☎ 34-0427; Sabogal 1130; s/d S25/40) A great budget pick, this brightly colored shoebox of a place has neat modern rooms, complete with gently curving yellow walls and cable TV. At the entrance you'll be greeted by both a statue of the Virgin Mary and smiling, helpful staff.

Hotel San Lorenzo (☎ 36-2909; Amazonas 1070; s/d/tr S25/45/70) Helpful, friendly owners provide dark but good-sized rooms (though the street-side ones can be noisy), cable TV, hot showers and a cafe.

Hostal Jusovi (☎ 36-2920; Amazonas 637; s/d S30/40) Boasting what must be the smallest rooms in town, Hostal Jusovi's abodes are kept perfectly clean and manage to squeeze in private showers with morning hot water. Some rooms have cable TV and the rooftop terrace with views of the cathedral spire is a welcome addition.

Hostal Perú (☎ 36-4030; Puga 605; s/d S30/60) This hotel on the plaza has private bathrooms with hot showers all day, but is a little more worn than most and is exposed to dinnertime noise from a downstairs restaurant.

Hostal Prado (☎ 36-6093; La Mar 582; s/d S40/70, s/d without bathroom S21/35) This well-kept, clean property has a cafe and hot water all day. Rooms have TVs, but you'll have to

fork out extra for cable. Some of the staff speak English.

MIDRANGE

All hotels in this range have 24-hour hot water and many throw in a free breakfast.

Hostal Casona del Inca (☎ 36-7524; www.casonadelincaperu.com; Calle 2 de Mayo 458-460; s/d S60/90) You might begin questioning your sobriety when you notice that all the brightly painted walls of this plaza-side colonial seem to be on a slight angle. Don't worry – they are. The aged carnival fun-house appearance just adds to the charm, however. The rooms follow in the footsteps of this slightly wonky theme and are clean and cozy. This place is justifiably popular with gringos.

Hospedaje Posada del Belén (☎ 83-0681; Jirón del Comercio 1008; s/d S60/95) A newcomer on the corner of the Plaza de Armas, the Belen is proud of its two floors of balconies offering views of the colonial street and main square; otherwise, it's a fairly straightforward choice with solid beds, hot water and cable TV.

Complejo Turístico Baños del Inca (☎ /fax 34-8385; www.ctbinca.com.pe; bungalows/albergue S60/120) Right behind Los Baños del Inca are eight spacious bungalows, each with sitting room, bedroom, mini-fridge and cable TV. Too bad they don't have a kitchenette. There are views of reservoirs of scalding 78°C water, steaming Dante-esquely – the water must be mixed with cold water before it flows into the spa complex.

Los Balcones de la Recoleta (☎ /fax 36-3302, 36-4446; Puga 1050; s/d S65/90; 🖳) Polished wood glistens throughout this 19th-century building. The 12 rickety rooms ooze charisma and encircle a lovely plant-filled courtyard. It's a relaxing place and with hot showers all day, cable TV, wi-fi and good beds, what more do you need? OK, throw in a small restaurant, crafts on most of the walls and friendly staff and you're onto a real winner.

Hostal Portada del Sol (☎ 36-3395; portasol@amet.com.pe; Pisagua 731; s/d incl breakfast S68/90; 🖳) The bright colors in this cozy colonial are as warm as the staff. Inside you will find thoughtfully decorated spaces with polished floorboards and exposed wooden beams, as well as a skylight-protected courtyard to while away the time in. The owners also have a rammed-earth hacienda (☎ 36-3395; Pisagua 731), 5.5km away in the countryside on the unpaved road to Cumbe Mayo. The 15 rooms here are tranquil, private and many have countryside vistas. A tree house and playground make this a top getaway for families and groups.

Hostal José Gálvez (☎ 34-8396; s/d S70/80) Near Los Baños del Inca, this clean hotel has a bar and is popular with large groups. The rooms all have hot thermal showers.

Hotel Casa Blanca (☎ 36-2141; www.hotelcasablanca .migueb.com; Calle 2 de Mayo 446; s S75, d S90-130, all incl breakfast) This dignified old structure on the Plaza de Armas exudes plenty of character while also providing a few mod cons in the medley of rooms. Quarters range from poky to good-sized and come with cable TV, direct-dial telephone and mini-fridge. The hotel cafe provides room service and the staff can also arrange car rental and free airport transfers. Some of the larger rooms have bathtubs, while a family room with five beds costs S170.

El Cabildo (☎ 36-7025; www.cabildoh.com; Junín 1062; s/d incl breakfast S80/105) One of the town's best-value sleeping options, this huge historic mansion conceals an eclectic collection of well-maintained and graceful older rooms. Some of the rooms come with split levels and all are filled with plenty of gleaming wood and tasteful decorations. At the mansion's heart, a gorgeous courtyard area is filled with greenery, a fountain and a cacophony of sculptures and statues.

Hostal Cajamarca (☎ 36-2532; fax 36 2813; Calle 2 de Mayo 311; s/d S86/110) A presentable, spacious hotel in a colonial house, with a courtyard and a recommended restaurant that occasionally hosts live music. You'll find a full-service tour agency in the lobby.

Los Pinos Inn (☎ 36-5992/5991; pinoshostal@yahoo .com; La Mar 521; s/d incl breakfast S95/130) This majestic and drafty colonial building, dripping in marble staircases, intricate tile work and strewn with antiques looks like a museum yet manages to refrain from being ostentatious. Hallways with enormous gilded mirrors lead to 21 large and varied rooms, all with solid beds. Continental breakfast is served in a pleasing courtyard cafe covered with a stained-glass roof. The hotel was undergoing remodeling at the time of research, so visitors may see higher prices in the future.

Las Americas Hotel (☎ 82-3951; Amazonas 618; s/d incl breakfast S125/175) Breaking away from the 'cozy colonial hotel' pack, this contemporary property is all business. It has a central atrium filled with plenty of plants and a rooftop terrace giving plaza and church views. The 28 rooms are all carpeted and have direct-dial phones, mini-fridges, cable TVs and excellent mattresses; five of them have Jacuzzi tubs and three have balconies, so it pays to check around. A restaurant provides room service.

Hotel el Ingenio (☎ 36-7121; www.elingenio.com; Vía de Evitamiento 1611-1709; s/d/ste incl breakfast S125/165/235) Built in the style of an attractive colonial hacienda, this modern and relaxing alternative has charisma in spades. Stone archways lead to plenty of garden areas to loll around in and the warm-colored rooms are large, comfortable and classically decorated. Cable TV, direct-dial telephones, mini-fridges and tubs in the bathrooms are standard, while some rooms have patios or balconies. The six minisuites each have a Jacuzzi. The staff is very attentive. It's a 20-minute walk into town.

our pick El Portal del Marques (☎ 36-8464; www .portaldelmarques.com; Jirón del Comercio 644; s/d/ste incl breakfast S150/183/300; ☐) Set around an immaculately groomed garden, this restored colonial mansion has standard carpeted rooms with TVs and mini-fridges. There's a fancy-looking restaurant that provides room service and, if bathing in Baños del Inca doesn't do it for you, you can splurge on the hotel's suite, which comes with a Jacuzzi. The mood lighting in the garden makes it a romantic evening hangout. Make reservations, as this one fills up fast.

TOP END

Costa del Sol (☎ 36-2472; www.costadelsolperu.com; Cruz de Piedra 707; s/d S188/283; ☐ ⧖) Costa del Sol is part of a chain of Peruvian luxury hotels and has recently taken over the southwest corner of the Plaza de Armas. No colonial bent here, just uncluttered, slick rooms filled with all the mod cons and catering to the Peruvian jet set. A stylish restaurant and a top-floor pool, gym and sauna round off an extensive list of amenities.

Hostal Laguna Seca (☎ 59-4600; www.lagunaseca .com.pe; s/d S288/354; ⧖ ⧖) Situated 6km from Cajamarca near Los Baños del Inca, this Swiss-owned resort runs, not surprisingly, like clockwork. It features a huge, heated swimming pool, Jacuzzi and Turkish bath and the hot water in all rooms is fed by the natural thermal springs nearby. Rooms have large bathrooms with deep tubs for soaking, direct-dial phones, cable TVs, mini-fridges and radios. Horseback riding (S30 per hour) and bicycle rental (S8 per hour) are available and massages and spa health treatments pamper the hedonists among you. There's also a pleasant garden with children's playground and a decent restaurant. Call ahead for free transfers from Cajamarca's airport.

Eating

Heladería Holanda (☎ 34-0113; Puga 657; ice creams S3; ☻ 9am-7pm) Don't miss the tiny entrance on the town's Plaza de Armas; it opens into a large, bright cafe selling what might be the best ice cream in northern Peru. The cafe has about 20 changing flavors, including Italian classics like *stracciatella* (vanilla with chocolate chips) and others made with local and seasonal fruit. Excellent espressos, cappuccinos with giant foam and homemade pies round out the menu.

New York Pizza (☎ 50-6215; Puga 1045; pizzas S3-9; ☻ 4-11pm) OK, it's not real New York pizza, but then again nothing else is. They still make a great pie though, as the yummy smells wafting down the street will verify. They get double bonus points for their delivery service.

Cascanuez Café Bar (☎ 36-6089; Puga 554; desserts S3-10; ☻ 7am-11pm) This cafe sells snacks and meals but people flock here for the good choice of fine desserts and respectable coffee.

ourpick Don Paco (☎ 36-2655; Puga 726; meals S8-20; ☻ 8:30am-11pm) Tucked away near the plaza, Don Paco has a big following among both residents and expats. There's something for everyone here, including typical breakfasts and great renditions of Peruvian favorites, as well as a whole bunch of veggie options. The lentil burgers and quinoa (an Andean grain) salad are particularly good.

Sanguchon.com (Junín 1137; mains from S9; ☻ 6pm-late) This popular hamburger and sandwich joint with an excellent bar often remains rowdy till the wee hours.

Salas (☎ 36-2867; Puga 637; mains S10-20; ☻ 7am-10pm) This barn of a restaurant on the Plaza de Armas has been a local favorite since 1947 – and some of the diners look like they have been patronizing the joint since the very beginning. Knowledgeable elderly staff in white suits will help you navigate the extensive menu, which lists local specialties such as goat, tamales (corn dough stuffed with meat, beans or chilis) and even *sesos* (cow brains). More-standard plates are also available.

Nuevo Chifa Canton (☎ 34-4517; Puga 519; mains from S12; ☻ noon-4pm & 6-11pm) A step up from the usual Chinese restaurants that abound in Peru, the menu here is filled with hundreds of options great for everyone, from vegetarians to the most daring meat eaters. The chef hails from Canton and boasts more than 15 years of cooking experience.

Querubino (☎ 34-0900; Puga 589; mains S12-18; ☻ noon-midnight) Modern and stylish, warm and busy, and generally full of tourist groups, this place has a ponderous menu of Peruvian and international dishes and is renowned for its great pastas. It also has a solid wine selection.

El Batán (☎ 36-6025; Jirón del Batán 369; menús S15-30, mains S12-24; ☻ 10am-11pm) One of the town's best places to eat, this is a mix of gallery-restaurant, *peña* (bar or club featuring live folkloric music) and cultural center, and serves varied Peruvian and international dishes with has a decent wine list. The *menú* (set meal) is an excellent deal. On Friday and Saturday nights, El Batán has live shows of local music, anything from folk songs to traditional Andean music to Afro-Peruvian dance rhythms. There is a full bar and an upstairs art gallery.

Mr Grill (☎ 36-8341; Urrelo 849; mains S15-30; ☻ 7-10pm) It only takes a step into this low-key dining room to be seduced by the smell of roast chicken and choice cuts of meat. A table for five could easily get stuffed on their *parrillada* (selection of grilled meats) for S75.

El Quinde Shopping Center (Av Hoyos Rubio, cuadra 7; www.elquinde.com; ☻ 7am-9pm) has the closest supermarket to town, about 2.5km north of the Plaza de Armas.

Drinking

Barroco Lounge (☎ 36-5647; Santisteban 168-172; ☻ 7pm-late) Although they also serve good sushi, the all-white, ultra-hip Barroco is all about martinis, boat-sized couches and mile-high bar stools. For all this gloss, the staff is surprisingly down to earth.

Usha-Usha (Puga 142; admission S5; ☻ 9pm-late) For something a little more intimate, this place is a graffiti-covered, hole-in-the-wall bar run by an eccentric local musician. It serves strong mixed drinks and hosts live jazz music most nights of the week. It's definitely worth searching out.

Shopping

Small shops selling local and Peruvian crafts line the stairwells along Calle 2 de Mayo south of Junín.

Colors & Creations (☎ 34-3875; Belén 628; ☻ 9:30am-1:30pm & 2:30-7pm Mon-Sat, 10am-6pm Sun) An artisan-owned-and-run cooperative selling excellent-quality crafts.

Getting There & Away

AIR

Schedules are subject to change, as well as occasional cancellations and delays, so reconfirm and arrive early at the **airport** (CJA; ☎ 36-2523), about 4km outside town. The airport departure tax is S11.

Star Perú (☎ 36-7423; Junín 1300) flies from Cajamarca to Talara, near Máncora, at 2pm and returns at 3:30pm. They also have a Lima–Cajamarca flight that leaves the capital at 12:30pm and leaves Cajamarca at 4:30pm on Tuesdays, Thursdays and Sundays; on Mondays, Tuesdays, Fridays and Saturdays, this flight leaves Lima at 7:15am and leaves Cajamarca at 8:50am.

LC Busre (☎ 36-1098; Jirón del Comercio) also plies this route, with two daily flights leaving Lima for Cajamarca at 3:30pm and 3:45pm and returning at 5:30pm and 5:45pm.

LAN (☎ in Lima 213-8200; Cruz de Piedra 657) has a daily flight between Lima and Cajamarca, leaving the capital at 8:10am and Cajamarca at 10am.

BUS

Cajamarca continues its ancient role as a crossroads, with buses heading to all four points of the compass. Most bus terminals are close to *cuadra* (block) 3 of Atahualpa, about 1.5km southeast of the center (not to be confused with the Atahualpa in the town center), on the road to Los Baños del Inca.

The major route is westbound to the Panamericana near Pacasmayo on the coast, then north to Chiclayo (eight hours) or south to Trujillo (eight hours) and Lima (14 hours).

The southbound road is the old route to Trujillo (at least 15 hours) via Cajabamba (4½ hours) and Huamachuco (7½ hours). For Huamachuco and on to Trujillo, change at Cajabamba. The trip to Trujillo takes two or three times longer on this rough dirt road than it does along the newer paved road via Pacasmayo, although the old route is only 60km longer. The scenery is prettier on the longer route, but most buses are less comfortable and less frequent beyond Cajabamba.

The rough northbound road to Chota (five hours) passes through wild and attractive countryside via Bambamarca, which has a busy market on Sunday morning. Buses run from Chota to Chiclayo along a knobby, rough road.

The staggeringly scenic eastbound road winds to Celendín (four hours), then bumps its way across the Andes, past Chachapoyas and down into the Amazon lowlands. The road between Celendín and Chachapoyas is beautiful but in bad condition and transport can be sporadic; if you're going to Chachapoyas, consider traveling via Chiclayo and Bagua Grande, unless you have plenty of time and patience.

Cial (☎ 36-8701; Independencia 288) Has buses to Lima at 7pm (S54 to S74).

Civa (☎ 36-1460; Ayacucho 753) Good buses to Lima (S72) at 7pm.

Cruz del Sur (☎ 36-1737; Vía de Evitamiento 750) Luxury *bus-cama* (bed bus) to Lima (S76.50) at 7pm. This terminal is several kilometers further along the road to Los Baños del Inca.

El Cumbe (☎ 36-3088; Atahualpa 300) Cheap buses to Chiclay (S14 to S17) at 7am, 11:30am, 3pm and 9pm.

Flores (☎ 34-1294; Atahualpa 248) Cheap bus to Lima (S36 to S63) at 5pm.

Línea (☎ 36-3956; Atahualpa 318) Good-quality buses go to Lima (S81) at 7pm, Chiclayo (S14 to S27) at 11am, 10:45pm and 11pm and Trujillo (S14 to S32) at 10:30am, 1:30pm, 10pm and 10:30pm. They also have a ticket office on the Plaza de Armas

Ormeño (☎ 36-9885; Independencia 304) Good buses to Lima (S40.50) at 8pm.

Royal Palace's (☎ 34-3063; Atahualpa 337) Services to Celendín (S9) at 9am and cheap buses to Trujillo (S14) at 11am and Lima (S27) at 7:30pm.

Tepsa (☎ 36-3306; Atahualpa 300) Comfortable *semi-cama* (half-bed) Lima service (S80) at 6pm.

Transportes Atahualpa (☎ 36-3060; Atahualpa 299) Buses to Cajabamba (S27) at noon, Celendín (S9) at 7am and 1pm and Chota (S14) via Bambamarca at 11am.

Transportes Horna (☎ 36-7671; Atahualpa 313) Buses to Lima (S27) at 6pm, Trujillo (S14) at 8am and 10pm and Cajabamba (S27) at 2am and 5pm.

Transportes Rojas (☎ 34-0548; Atahualpa 405) Services to Cajabamba (S27) at 2am, 9am, 11am, 2pm and 4pm.

Turismo Nacional (☎ 34-0357; Atahualpa 309) Services to Celendín (S9) at 7am and 1pm and Chota (S27) via Bambamarca at 11am.

Several minibuses go to Cajamarca (S14 to S18), also leaving from *cuadra* 3 of Atahualpa.

Buses for Ventanillas de Otuzco (S2, 20 minutes) leave from 500m north of the plaza. These pass the airport (S1), though taking a taxi is much faster (S4.50).

Combis (minibuses) for Los Baños del Inca (S1, 25 minutes) leave frequently along Sabogal, near Calle 2 de Mayo.

NORTHERN HIGHLANDS

AROUND CAJAMARCA

Places of interest around Cajamarca can be reached by public transport, on foot, by taxi or with a guided tour. Tour agencies pool their clients to form a group for any trip, although more expensive individual outings can be arranged.

Los Baños del Inca

Atahualpa was camped by these natural **hot springs** (4:30am-8pm) when Pizarro arrived, hence the name. Now you can take a dip in the same pools that an Inca king used to bathe his war wounds – though the pools have probably been cleaned since then. Set around flourishing grounds with sculpted shrubbery, this attractive compound has hot water channeled into private cubicles (S.80 to S5 per hour), some large enough for up to six people at a time. Dip into the public pool (S2), which is cleaned on Monday and Friday; sauna rooms and massages are available for S27 each. This place gets hundreds of visitors daily, so it's best to come in the morning to avoid the rush. There's a **Complejo Recreativo** (admission S2; 8am-8pm) opposite the main bath complex that has swimming pools, a children's playground and 'waterslides of the Incas,' which are a big hit with kids. The *baños* (baths) are 6km from Cajamarca and have a few hotel possibilities (p434). *Combis* for Los Baños del Inca (S1, 25 minutes) leave from Sabogal in Cajamarca.

Cumbe Mayo

About 20km southwest of Cajamarca, Cumbe Mayo (derived from the Quechua *kumpi mayo,* meaning 'well-made water channel') is an astounding feat of pre-Inca engineering. These perfectly smooth aqueducts were carved around 2000 years ago and zigzag at right angles for 9km, all for a purpose that is as yet unclear, since Cajamarca has an abundant water supply. Other rock formations are carved to look like altars and thrones. Nearby caves contain **petroglyphs**, including some that resemble wooly mammoths. The countryside is high, windswept and slightly eerie. Superstitious stories are told about the area's eroded rock formations, which look like groups of shrouded mountain climbers.

The site can be reached on foot via a signed road from Cerro Santa Apolonia in Cajamarca. The walk takes about four hours if you take the obvious shortcuts and ask every passerby for directions. Guided bus tours (around S15) are offered by tour companies in Cajamarca; these can be a good idea as public transport to Cumbe Mayo is sporadic at the best of times.

Ventanillas de Otuzco & Combayo

These pre-Inca necropolises have scores of funerary niches built into the hillside, hence the name Ventanillas (Windows). Ventanillas de Otuzco is in alluring countryside, 8km northeast of Cajamarca and is easily walkable from either Cajamarca or Los Baños del Inca (ask for directions). The larger and better-preserved Ventanillas de Combayo are 30km away and are best visited on a S30 tour from Cajamarca. Buses to Ventanillas de Otuzco leave frequently from north of the Plaza de Armas in Cajamarca (S2, 20 minutes), or tours cost around S25.

Granja Porcón

Located about 23km by road from Cajamarca, this is a successful evangelical cooperative that began in 1975 and is still going strong. The community has its own Plaza de Armas, plus two *pueblos* (towns or villages), Tinte and Huaquin. Overlooked by 'God loves you' billboards in Spanish and Quechua, about 1200 residents work in fields, a dairy, trout hatchery, wood mill, looms, craft shops and simple restaurants. You can stay overnight in the simple but attractive **lodge** (36-5631; granjaporcon@yahoo.com; s/d S60/85) that boast fireplaces in each of its 10 rooms. There's even a small zoo here, housing a condor, jaguars, Spectacled Bears (the only type of bear found in South America), ostriches and monkeys. It's an interesting ongoing project and is visited by daily tours (S15). A highlight is the herd of vicuñas (threatened, wild relatives of alpacas) running free among deer and alpaca herds.

CAJABAMBA

076 / pop 14,400 / elev 2655m

The old route from Cajamarca to Trujillo takes at least 15 hours along 360km of mostly dirt road via Cajabamba and Huamachuco. Although this route passes through more interesting scenery and towns than the road via Pacasmayo, the bus trip is very rough and few tourists come through.

The friendly town of Cajabamba sits on a natural ledge overlooking swaths of farms and plantations. Whitewashed houses and red-tiled roofs lend the place a colonial aesthetic.

The **feast of La Virgen del Rosario** is celebrated around the first Sunday in October with bullfights, processions, dances and general bucolic carousing and an interesting cattle market springs up on Mondays. Several sights are within an hour's walk of Cajabamba, including the caverns of **Chivato** and the fetching mountain lagoons of **Ponte** and **Quengococha**. Ask at **Hostal La Casona** (☎ 35 8285; Bolognesi 720) for information on visiting these sights.

Most of the town's simple hotels line the Plaza de Armas and can fill up fast before the feast of La Virgen del Rosario. They also suffer from periodic water shortages and dim lighting. **Hostal Ramal** (☎ 50-5539; Cárdenas 784; s/d without bathroom S10/27) has basic rooms with cold-water bathrooms. **Hostal Flores** (☎ 55-1086; Prado 137; s/d without bathroom S15/24) has rooms with a balcony onto the plaza. **Hostal La Casona** (☎ 35-8285; Bolognesi 720; s/d S20/29) gets the ribbon for the top place to stay in town, with DVD players in the rooms, a DVD library (S1), hot showers and several rooms with balconies and plaza views.

La Casona Restaurant (☎ 35-8285; Bolognesi 720; meals S5-10; ☺ 7am-10pm), below the hotel of the same name, is one of the better places to grab a bite in town. It serves the usual Peruvian victuals.

Transportes Rojas (☎ 55-1399; Bolognesi 700) has buses to Cajamarca (S9, 4½ hours) at 4am, 8:30am and 2pm. **Transportes Horna** (☎ 55-1397; Prado 153) has daily Cajamarca buses (S3, 4½ hours) at noon, 4:30pm and 8:30pm and buses to Huamachuco (S4.50, three hours) at 4am and 3:30pm. **Los Andes** (☎ 80-5594; Grau 1170) also goes to Huamachuco at 4am, 8:30am and 4pm (S4.50).

HUAMACHUCO
☎ 044 / pop 29,400 / elev 3160m
This small colonial town is located between Cajabamba and Trujillo. It has an impressive Plaza de Armas, said to be Peru's largest, and a large contemporary church.

The massive ruins of the pre-Inca mountain fort of **Marcahuamachuco** (admission free) lie 10km away via a track passable only by 4WD or truck. This 2.5km-long site dates from around 400 BC and has tall defensive perimeter walls and interesting circular structures of varying sizes. Marcahuamachuco culture seems to have developed independently of surrounding civilizations of the time. A taxi can reach within 5km of the site in the dry season (S12),

but you'll have to hike along the dirt road the rest of the way. Bring all necessary food and drink with you.

Transport east to the mining town of **Pataz** runs during the dry season, from where expeditions can be mounted to the little-explored ruins of various jungle cities. The largest of these are the vast Chachapoyas ruins of **Gran Pajatén**. The ruins are north of the recently formed Parque Nacional Río Abiseo, which has no infrastructure for travelers at this time and is very hard to get to. This is an undertaking for determined explorers, archaeologists or Indiana Jones.

Basic and clean, **Hostal San José** (Bolívar 361; s/d S10/17) has cold water and offers little else in the way of amenities. The better **Hostal Huamachuco** (☎ 44-1393; Castilla 354; s/d S29/34 s/d without bathroom S18/25) is on the plaza and has hot water and TV. **Hostal Colonial** (☎ 51-1101, 44-1334; Castilla 347; s/d/tr S30/40/60), in a pleasant colonial-style house (no surprises there), is similar and has a good restaurant downstairs.

Several minivans leave from the Plaza de Armas throughout the day bound for Cajabamba (S4.80, three hours). Transportes Horna and Los Andes both have several early morning and evening buses to Cajamarca (S7 to S9, seven hours) and Trujillo (S14, six hours). *Colectivo* (shared) buses to Otuzco leave when full from near the plaza (S7, four hours).

CELENDÍN
☎ 076 / pop 16,600 / elev 2625m
Easily reached by an unpaved road from Cajamarca, Celendín itself is a delightfully sleepy little town that receives few travelers except for those taking the wild and scenic route to Chachapoyas. Celendín is particularly known for high-quality straw hats, which can be bought at its interesting Sunday market. It's an ideal place to observe traditional highland life and interact with local indigenous people, who will certainly take an interest in your unexpected visit.

There's a **Banco de la Nación** (Calle 2 de Mayo 530) here that can change US dollars and has an ATM. The annual **fiesta** (July 29 to August 3) coincides with Fiestas Patrias and features bullfighting with matadors from Mexico and Spain. The fiesta of **La Virgen del Carmen** is celebrated on July 16.

A BRIEF HISTORY OF THE GUINEA PIG

Love it or loathe it, *cuy*, or guinea pig (or *Cavia porcellus* if you really must know), is an Andean favorite that's been part of the local culinary repertoire since pre-Inca times. And before you dredge up childhood memories of cuddly mascots in protest, know that these rascally rodents were gracing Andean dinner plates long before anyone in the West considered them worthy pet material.

Pinpointing the gastronomic history of the *cuy*, a native of the New World, is harder than trying to catch one with your bare hands. It's believed that *cuy* may have been domesticated as early as 7000 years ago in the mountains of southern Peru, where wild populations of *cuy* still roam today. Direct evidence from Chavín de Huántar shows that they were certainly cultivated across the Andes by 900 BC. Arrival of the Spanish in the 18th century led to the European debut of *cuy*, where they rode a wave of popularity as the must-have exotic pet of the season (Queen Elizabeth I of England supposedly kept one).

How they earned the name guinea pig is also in doubt. Guinea may be a corruption of the South American colony of Guiana, or it may refer to Guinea, the African country that *cuy* would have passed through on their voyage to Europe. Their squeals probably account for the latter half of their name.

Cuy are practical animals to raise and have adapted well over the centuries to survive in environments ranging from the high Andean plains to the barren coastal deserts. Many Andean households today raise *cuy* as part of their animal stock and you'll often see them scampering around the kitchen in true free-range style. *Cuy* are the ideal livestock alternative: they're high in protein, feed on kitchen scraps, breed profusely and require much less room and maintenance than traditional domesticated animals.

Cuy is seen as a true delicacy, so much so that in many indigenous interpretations of *The Last Supper*, Jesus and his disciples are sitting down to a hearty final feast of roast *cuy*.

An integral part of Andean culture, even beyond the kitchen table, *cuy* are also used by *curanderos* (healers) in ceremonial healing rituals. *Cuy* can be passed over a patient's body and used to sense out a source of illness and *cuy* meat is sometimes ingested in place of hallucinogenic plants during shamanistic ceremonies.

If you can overcome your sentimental inhibitions, sample this furry treat. The rich flavors are a cross between rabbit and quail, and correctly prepared *cuy* can be an exceptional 7000-year-old feast.

Hot springs (admission free) and mud baths will help soothe aching bones and can be found at Llanguat, reached by a 30-minute drive. You can also take a 7am *combi* from the Plaza de Armas (S2.50, 45 minutes) on Mondays, Wednesdays, Fridays and Saturdays. It returns around noon.

The Dutch-run organization **Proyecto Yannick** (☎ 77-0590; www.celendinperu.com; Jirón Unión 333) offers volunteer opportunities working with children with Down's Syndrome, and the English-, German-, and Dutch-speaking manager, Susan, also arranges private transportation and tours to the hot springs and local caves. Visit the project office for a map and excellent information about hotels, local sites and transport.

Hostal Raymi Wasi (☎ 97-855-1133; José Gálvez 420; s/d S20/30, s without bathroom S10) is a small space with dark but acceptable rooms; you can still see the cock-fighting ring in the middle of the courtyard (it was recently shut down because guests found it too noisy to sleep). Pay only a little more at **Hostal Loyers** (☎ 55-5210; José Gálvez 440; s/d S15/25, s/d without bathroom S10/17) and you'll get colorful rooms, a fetching courtyard and hot(ish) electric showers. Right on the Plaza de Armas, **Hostal Celendín** (☎ 55-5041; Unión 305; s/d S24/34.50; 💻) has reliable hot water and worn but inviting rooms, many with balconies and grand plaza views. The new kid on the block, **Hostal Imperial** (☎ 55-5492; 2 de Mayo 568; s/d S25/35 s/d without bathroom S15/25) has the best rooms of this bunch, though the singles with shared bathrooms are poky. The town's disco is held here on Saturday nights (bring earplugs). Susan at Proyecto Yannick was constructing a budget hostel in the center of town at the time of research; inquire at the office for more information.

Snack Cafe (José Gálvez 512; meals S4-7; 6-10pm) makes a valiant attempt at pizza. **Hostal Celendín** (Plaza de Armas; meals S5-12; 8am-11pm), serves pizzas and lots of local specialties, including the tasty *cuy típico* – fried guinea pig with mashed sweet potato and spring-onion-and-lemon sauce (S12). **La Reserva** (50-5817; José Gálvez 420; meals S4-10; 7pm-midnight) is another popular eating choice, with multilevel seating and a warm ambience. **Carbon & Leña** (80-5736; Calle 2 de Mayo 416; meals S3-8; 10am-10pm) uses, as it name indicates, charcoal and wood fires to roast every kind of meat, from beef to goat.

The rough road from Cajamarca is far better than the one from Chachapoyas. Most bus companies are found around the Plaza de Armas.

Transportes Rojas (José Gálvez 418) has daily buses to Cajamarca (S10, four hours) at 5:30am, 2:30pm and 4:30pm, and **Royal Palace's** (55-5322; Unión 504) also has departures to Cajamarca (S10) at 2pm and 4:30pm. **Virgen del Carmen** (55-5238; Cáceres 110), located behind the market, goes to Chachapoyas (S30, 10 to 11 hours) via Leimebamba (S20, seven to eight hours) at 9am on Mondays, Wednesdays, Thursdays, Fridays and Sundays. *Colectivos* for Chachapoyas (S30) depart from the intersection of Cáceres and Marcelino González at 2pm. If you hang out at the intersection called El Monumento, you may be able to flag down a ride with a passing truck or private vehicle as a paying passenger; bring enough food and snacks for the long journey.

CELENDÍN TO CHACHAPOYAS

Although this rough but beautiful road may still be temporarily impassable during the wet season, it has improved immeasurably in the last few years. It has been upgraded to *afirmada* (packed and leveled dirt), cutting travel time down three to four hours and making it considerably easier on passengers' backsides. Maintenance crews keep the surface in good shape. Heading north, the left side of the bus affords the most scenic viewing time, but the right side is less nauseating for those who fear great heights.

The road climbs over a 3085m pass before plummeting steeply to the Río Marañón at the shabby and infernally hot village of **Balsas** (975m), 55km from Celendín. A scruffy guesthouse here rents a barely passable room for S5 per night,

but camping should be possible if you ask locals for a good spot (and offer them a few nuevo soles). The road climbs again, through gorgeous cloud forests and countryside swathed in a lush quilt a million shades of green. It emerges 57km later at **Abra de Barro Negro** (Black Mud Pass, 3678m), which offers the highest viewing point of the drive, over the Río Marañon, more than 3.5 vertical kilometers below. Ghostly low-level clouds and mists hug the dispersed communities in this part of the trip and creep eerily amongst the hills. The road then drops for 32km to Leimebamba at the head of the Río Utcubamba valley and follows the river as it descends past Tingo and on to Chachapoyas. The final 20km approach into Chachapoyas is freshly paved. Travelers should carry water and food, as the few restaurants en route are poor and unhygienic.

The normal route to Chachapoyas is from Chiclayo via Bagua Grande; it's a faster, but considerably less spectacular, route.

CHICLAYO TO CHACHAPOYAS

This is the usual route for travelers to Chachapoyas. From the old Panamericana 100km north of Chiclayo, a paved road heads east over the Andes via the 2145m Porculla Pass, the lowest Peruvian pass going over the Andean continental divide. The route then tumbles to the Río Marañón valley. About 190km from the Panamericana turnoff, you reach the town of **Jaén**, the beginning of a newly opened route to Ecuador (p442). Continuing east, a short side road reaches the town of **Bagua Chica** in a low, enclosed valley (elevation about 500m), which Peruvians claim is the hottest town in the country. The bus usually goes through **Bagua Grande** (population 28,830) on the main road, and follows the Río Utcubamba valley to the crossroads town of Pedro Ruíz, about 90 minutes from Bagua Grande. From here, a newly paved southbound road branches to Chachapoyas, 54km and about 1¼ hours away.

CHACHAPOYAS

041 / pop 22,900 / elev 2335 m

Also known as Chachas, Chachapoyas is a laid-back town insulated by a buffer of rough unpaved roads and high-altitude cloud forests. The town was an important junction on jungle-coast trade routes until a paved road

BORDER CROSSING: ECUADOR VIA JAÉN

If your next port of call is Ecuador, remember that you don't have to spend days on winding roads to get back to the Peruvian coast. From Jaén, a good northbound road heads 107km to San Ignacio (population 10,720) near the Ecuadorian border. Since the peace treaty was signed with Ecuador in late 1998, it has become possible to cross into Ecuador at this remote outpost.

Begin at the fast-growing agricultural center of **Jaén** (population 70,690), which has a couple of banks and more than a dozen hotels. Good ones include the budget **Hostal Jaén** (☎ 076-43-1333; San Martín 1528; s/d S14/7.50), with friendly staff and cold showers, and the family-run **Hostal Diana Gris** (☎ 076-43-2127; Urreta 1136, 2nd fl; s/d S25/35), which has hot showers, fans, cable TVs and a restaurant. Also try the recommended **Prim's Hotel** (☎ 076-43-2970; Palomino 1353; s/d S45/75; 🗨), which has a *chifa* (Chinese restaurant), or the town's best option, **Hotel El Bosque** (☎ 076-43-492; Muro 632; s/d S75/95; 🖵 🗨), with bungalows set in gardens.

From Jaén, *colectivo* (shared) buses leave for **San Ignacio** (S15, 2½ hours), where there's a simple hotel and places to eat. Change here for another *colectivo* for the rough road to **La Balsa** (S15, 2½ hours) on the Río Blanco dividing Peru from Ecuador. There used to be a *balsa* (ferry) here (hence the name), but there's now a new international bridge linking the countries. Border formalities are straightforward if you have your papers in order, although the immigration officers don't get to see many gringos coming through.

Once in Ecuador, curious yet typical *rancheras* (trucks with rows of wooden seats) await to take you on the uncomfortable and unpredictable (because of the weather) 10km drive to Zumba (US$2, 1½ to 2½ hours). From here, buses go to the famed 'valley of longevity' of Vilcabamba (US$4, four hours) where you'll be ready to relax in one of the comfortable hotels and read Lonely Planet's *Ecuador & the Galápagos Islands* book. If you leave Jaén at dawn, you should be able to make it to Vilcabamba in one day.

was built in the 1940s through nearby Pedro Ruíz, bypassing Chachapoyas altogether. The unlikely capital of the department of Amazonas, this pleasant colonial settlement is now a busy market town and makes an excellent base for exploring the awesome ancient ruins left behind by the fierce civilization of the Chachapoyas ('People of the Clouds').

Vast zones of little-explored cloud forest surround the city of Chachapoyas, concealing some of Peru's most fascinating and least-known archaeological treasures. Although the ravages of weather and time, as well as more recent attentions of grave robbers and treasure seekers, have caused damage to many of the ruins, some have survived remarkably well. Kuélap is by far the most famous of these archaeological sites, though dozens of other ruins lie besieged by jungle and make for tempestuous exploration.

More than a dozen tour agencies in Chachapoyas will vie for your custom and help you arrange trekking trips that include guides, horses, accommodations and all food. Some hikes will require at least sleeping bags; check what you will need ahead of time. The driest months (May to September) are the best time to go hiking and to organize a group to share costs. October to December isn't too wet, but January to April can be soggy.

The traditional evening pastime of strolling around the Plaza de Armas provides the town's main form of entertainment, relaxation and socializing.

History

The Chachapoyas culture was conquered – but never fully subdued – by the Incas a few decades before the Spaniards arrived (see p448). When the Europeans showed up, local chief Curaca Huamán supposedly aided them in their conquest to defeat the Inca. Because of the relative lack of Inca influence, the people didn't learn to speak Quechua and today Spanish is spoken almost exclusively. Local historians claim that San Juan de la Frontera de las Chachapoyas was the third town founded by the Spaniards in Peru (after Piura and Lima) and it was, at one time, the seventh-largest town in the country.

Information

Several stores on the plaza will change US dollars at reasonable rates.

BCP (Ortiz Arrieta) Changes US dollars and traveler's checks and has an ATM.

I@NNET (cnr Ayacucho & Grau; per hr S2; ⏰ 8am-midnight) Try internetting here.

International Language Center (Ayacucho 1045; ⏰ 8am-1pm, 4-7pm) In addition to Spanish lessons for S15 per hour, the friendly owners here (who speak perfect English) freely dole out tourist information and often have paid positions for English teachers. They have luggage storage if you need to stow your bags for a day or two.

iPerú (☎ 47-7292; Ortíz Arrieta 588; ⏰ 8am-7pm) Excellent maps, transportation information and recommendations.

Laundry (Chincha Alta 417; per kg S2.50; ⏰ 7am-9pm) The lovely family here will turn around clothes in their machines or by hand in about one day. Knock if the door is closed.

Post office (☎ 47-7019; Ortíz Arrieta; ⏰ 9am-7pm Mon-Fri, to 1pm Sat) Just south of the plaza.

Sights & Activities

The **Instituto Nacional de Cultura Museo** (INC; Ayacucho 904; admission free; ⏰ 9am-noon & 3-5pm Mon-Sat) houses a half a dozen mummies and ceramics from several pre-Columbian periods.

A 10-minute stroll northwest along Salamanca brings you to **Mirador Guayamil**, a lookout with a city panorama. A S10 taxi ride will take you to **Mirador Huancas**, which has soaring views of the Utcumbamba valley; hike back 1½ hours along the road or ask at the small **artisanal gift shop** (⏰ 8am-4pm) for directions for the shortcut back to Chachapoyas through the fields.

Trekking to the numerous impressive sights and ruins around Chachapoyas (p446) is becoming increasingly popular and is easy to arrange in town. The most popular trek is the four- or five-day Gran Vilaya trek, from Choctámal to the Marañón canyon, through pristine cloud forest and past several ruins and the heavenly Valle de Belén. Another popular adventure heads out to the Laguna de los Cóndores (p450), a three-day trip on foot and horseback from Leimebamba. Both are for walkers in good shape and with stamina. Treks to any of the other ruins in the district can be arranged and tailored to suit your needs – though there's so much to see here that several weeks would not be enough.

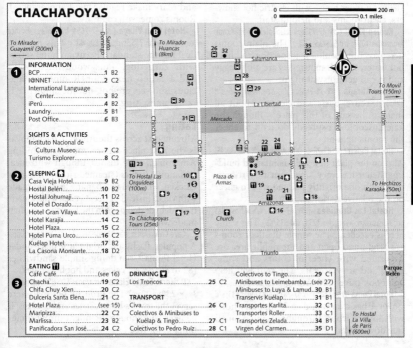

Tours & Guides

All the tour agencies are found near the Plaza de Armas. Ask around for other travelers' experiences before you choose an agency. Expect to pay S100 to S150 per person for multiday treks (a little more for groups of less than four) and around S50 for day tours.

Chachapoyas Tours (☎ 47-8078; www.kuelapperu .com; Santo Domingo 432) These guys get rave reviews for their day tours of the area. The company also organizes multiday treks and has some English-speaking guides.

Turismo Explorer (☎ 47-8162; www.turismoexplorer peru.com; Grau 509) This company also has a great reputation and specializes in multiday treks. It has guides who speak excellent English.

Sleeping

Most places in Chachapoyas fall squarely in the budget category.

Hostal Johumaji (☎ 47-7279; olvacha@terra.com .pe; Ayacucho 711; s S14, dS20-35) The better of the town's super-cheap hotels, Johumaji has small, Spartan and tidy rooms that are well lit and have electric hot showers. Laundry service for S4 per kilogram is available, as is a TV for S5 extra per night.

Hotel el Dorado (☎ 47-7047; Ayacucho 1062; s/d S18/30) An older house with electric hot showers, clean rooms and helpful staff.

Kuélap Hotel (☎ 47-7136; kuelaphotel@hotmail.com; Amazonas 1057; s/d S25/35; 🖳) The plain rooms here pass the cleanliness inspection and have hot water, though mattresses are a bit saggy and it can get noisy at night.

Hotel Karajía (☎ 31-2606; Calle 2 de Mayo 546; s/d S25/35) Secure, basic and clean is about all that can be said of this place – though the kaleidoscopic bedspreads do tend to cheer the rooms up a bit.

Hostal Belén (☎ 47-7830; Ortiz Arrieta 540; s/d S30/45) Also on the plaza in a well-maintained building, Belén has very small but tidy rooms, each with one brightly painted wall to cheer up the relative darkness.

Hostal Las Orquídeas (☎ 47-8271, www.hostallas orquideas.com; Ayacucho 1231; s/d S35/65) The value here is excellent. The simple tile-floor rooms are bright and open and the public area are decorated with cheerful colors and some wood and artsy accents. The staff will help you book travel and arrange excursions.

Hotel Puma Urco (☎ /fax 47-7871; Amazonas 833; s/d S50/80) A basic, new and contemporary hotel with lots of wood throughout and a small cafe downstairs.

Hostal La Villa de Paris (☎ 79-2332; www.hostalvilla paris.com; entrance to Chachapoyas; s/d S65/95, bungalow S180-250; 🖳) Only 1.5km from the main square, this lovely colonial-style hotel furnished with lots of wood and antiques has the feel of a much more expensive hotel. Large windows and balconies bring in the light and all rooms have cable TV. The restaurant here is also worth a visit.

Casa Vieja Hostal (☎ /fax 47-7353; www.casaviejaperu .com; Chincha Alta 569; s/d S60/90; 🖳) Very comfortable quarters in a classy converted mansion make Casa Vieja Hostal a very special choice. All of the rooms have handcrafted wood accents, decorative or working fireplaces and big windows facing onto the verdant garden. A touch of the modern is provided by flat-screen TVs with cable and body-friendly mattresses. The showers are hot and breakfast is available.

La Casona Monsante (☎ 47-7702; www.lacasona monsante.com; Amazonas 746; s/d/tr S60/90/130) This lovely colonial mansion is one of the town's top picks. Walk in to find a large, plant-filled stone courtyard and unwind in the inviting and super-comfy rooms decorated with photos of the region and paintings (in which Jesus and Mary make regular guest appearances). Rooms come with cable TV.

Hotel Gran Vilaya (☎ 47-7664; hotelvilaya@viabcp .com; Ayacucho 755; s/d S70/80; 🖳) This modern deal has the standard Peruvian hotel setup, with carpeting, faux-wood-lined walls and a casino next door. Rooms are spacious, showers are hot, but the ambience is rather unexciting.

Eating

Moving east across the Andes, Chachapoyas is the first place where you begin finding Amazonian-style dishes, though with local variations. *Juanes* (steamed rice with fish or chicken, wrapped in a banana leaf) are made with yucca instead of rice. *Cecina*, a dish made from dehydrated pork in the lowlands, is often made with beef.

Café Café (Amazonas 829; desserts S1-3; 🕑 7am-10pm) A popular, flashy and bright little place under Hotel Puma Urco doing simple sandwiches (S2 to S6), sweet cakes and hot beverages.

Dulcería Santa Elena (Amazonas 800-804; mains S1-3; 🕑 7:30am-10pm) The grouchy old man here serves the town's best pastries and cookies; if he likes you, though, he might throw something in for free.

Panificadora San José (Ayacucho 816; breakfasts S2-5; ⏰ 6:30am-10pm) This bakery features a few tables where you can enjoy a tamal, *humita* (mashed corn dumpling filled with spiced beef, vegetables and potatoes) or sandwich with coffee for breakfast, and snacks and desserts all day. Be sure to try their rich hot chocolate (S2).

Chifa Chuy Xien (☎ 47-8587; Amazonas 840; mains S4-10; ⏰ 12-4pm & 6-10pm) Behold, the town's best (only?) Chinese restaurant.

Hotel Plaza (☎ 47-7554; Grau 534, 2nd fl; menús S5) It's ambience galore at this plaza-view restaurant, though unfortunately it only has a few tables by the window. Recommended for its set lunches; the service can be slow, though.

Chacha (☎ 47-7107; Grau 545; menús S5, mains S6-12; ⏰ 7am-10pm) This is an old standby on the plaza – service is slooooow, but the meals are reliable.

Maripizza (☎ 47-8876; Ayacucho 832; pizzas S12-30; ⏰ noon-late) This pizzeria dedicates itself to homemade pasta and pies, served in a casual dining room that is popular with locals as well as gringos.

our pick **Marlissa** (☎ 47-7118; Ayacucho 1139; meals S20-60; ⏰ noon-10pm) Specializing in *parrilladas* (meats cooked on an open flame), Marlissa's grill experts will deliver a sizzling platter of beef, chicken and sausage to your table. They also specialized in *cuy* (guinea pig) cooked in several ways – with *maní* (peanut) sauce is one local specialty – and host a disco night on the weekends.

Drinking & Entertainment

Los Troncos (☎ 47-7239; Calle 2 de Mayo 561; ⏰ 7pm-5am) The top spot to get your boogie on at the moment is this place, which fills up by 10pm on weekends and blasts international music to a gyrating crowd.

Hechizos Karaoke (Recreo btw Ayacucho & Amazonas; ⏰ 7pm-late) Come here if you feel like belting out your own unique rendition of Céline Dion.

Getting There & Away

AIR

Although Chachapoyas has an airport, at the time of writing no carriers flew in or out of it. This may change, though probably not soon.

BUS & TAXI

The frequently traveled route to Chiclayo (10 to 11 hours) and on to Lima (20 to 23 hours) starts along the vista-lined route to Pedro

Ruíz along the Río Utcubamba. **Transervis Kuélap** (☎ 47-8128; Ortíz Arrieta 412) has a daily bus to Chiclayo (S27) at 7pm. **Civa** (☎ 47-8048; Salamanca 956) has a daily 6pm bus to Chiclayo (S30) and buses bound for Lima on Monday at noon and Wednesday and Friday at 4pm (S80). **Transportes Zelada** (☎ 37-8066; Ortíz Arrieta 310) goes to Lima (S60) at 11:30am, stopping at Chiclayo (S22.50). It also has a direct bus to Chiclayo only at 8pm. The very comfortable **Movil Tours** (☎ 47-8545; La Libertad 464) has an express bus to Lima (S15, 22 hours) at 4pm, as well as a 7:30pm bus to Trujillo (S60, 12 hours) via Chiclayo (S45, nine hours).

Virgen del Carmen (☎ 79-3558; Salamanca, cuadra 8) departs for Celendín (S30, 10 to 11 hours) on Mondays at 6pm, Wednesdays, Thursdays and Fridays at 4am, and on Sundays at 6am, stopping at Leimebamba (S10, three to four hours). **Transportes Karlita** (Salamanca, cuadra 9) also goes to Leimebamba at noon and 4pm for S10.

Transportes Roller (Grau 302) has two buses to Kuélap (S10, 3½ hours), via Tingo, Choctámal and María, at 4pm. These return from Kuélap at 6am and 8am.

Colectivo taxis to Kuélap (S14, three hours) depart throughout the day when full from Grau, but be warned that safety is a low priority for these drivers, who sometimes take unnecessary risks and proceed at excessive speeds to save time. It sometimes helps to ask drivers what their maximum driving speed is and if anyone says that can get you there in a ridiculously short amount of time, move on. This block also has frequent minibuses (S5, 1½ hours) and *colectivo* taxis for Tingo (S5.20, 1½ hours); the taxis may continue on to María (S10, three hours). Minibuses to Leimebamba leave at noon and 4pm (S9, three to four hours).

To continue further into the Amazon Basin, take a *colectivo* taxi to the crossroads at Pedro Ruíz (S10, 1½ hours) and wait for an eastbound bus. Ask around for trucks and minibuses to other destinations.

If you start early and have plenty of time on your hands, you can see some of the attractions around Chachapoyas by public minibus. For Karajía, you can take a minibus to Luya (S7, 50 minutes), from where regular minibuses go to the nearby village of Cruz Pata (S5, 50 minutes).

A taxi for the day to Kuélap or to sites around Chachapoyas and Leimebamba costs S150.

AROUND CHACHAPOYAS

Relics of Chachapoyas and Inca civilizations and daring, rugged scenery speckle the mountains surrounding Chachapoyas. Scores of archaeological sites dot this area, most of them unexcavated and many reclaimed by vivacious jungle. Below is a list of some of the main points of interest, though there are many others – and even more await discovery.

Catarata de Gocta

This 771m **waterfall** somehow escaped the notice of the Peruvian government, international explorers and prying satellite images until 2005, when German Stefan Ziemendorff and a group of locals put together an expedition to map the falls and record their height. Various claims ranging from the third-loftiest waterfall on earth to the fifteenth resulted in an international firestorm in the always-exciting contest to rank the world's highest cascades, Gocta's current measurement is probably correct, give or take a few meters, putting it solidly after Norway's 773m Mongefossen Falls. Whether you're hung up on numbers or not, the falls are impressive and accessible, although it's better to go with a tour company from Chachapoyas for about S50. They provide transport and a local guide for the two-hour hike to the falls, which are dripping in lore about a mermaid who guards a lost treasure (who knew there were mermaids so far inland?). With luck you might see the bizarre, orange bird called the Andean Cock-of-the-Rock or the rare and endemic Yellow-tailed Woolly Monkey.

Gran Vilaya

The name Gran Vilaya refers to the bountiful valleys that spread out west of Chachapoyas, reaching toward the rushing Río Marañón. Abutting the humid Amazon, this region sits in a unique microcosm of perennially moist high-altitude tropics and cloud forests – an ecological anomaly that gave rise to the Chachapoyas culture's moniker, People of the Clouds. The fertility of this lush area was never a big secret – the valley successfully supported the huge populations of the Chachapoyas and Inca cultures, and to date more than 30 archaeological sites have been found dotting the mountains. Important sites like **Paxamarca**, **Pueblo Alto**, **Pueblo Nuevo** and **Pirquilla** lie connected by winding goat-tracks as they did hundreds of years ago, completely unexcavated, and can be visited on multi-

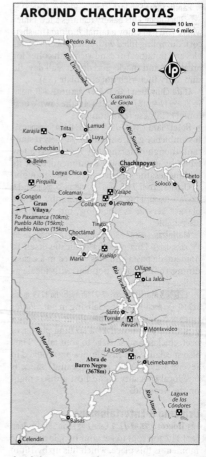

day hikes. Immaculately constructed Inca roads weave up and around the hills, past many ruined cities camouflaged by centuries of jungle.

The breathtaking, impossibly green and silt-filled **Valle de Belén** lies at the entrance of Gran Vilaya. The flat valley floor here is dissected by the mouth of the widely meandering Río Huaylla, coiled like a languid serpent. Filled with grazing cattle, horses and surrounded on all sides by mist-covered hills, the vistas here are mesmerizing.

Roads barely make a dint into this terrain, so the only way to really explore it is on foot or by horse. If your Spanish is up to it and you have the gear, it is possible to hike independently – but trails are not always marked and the overgrown ruins are difficult to find. Most travel agencies in Chachapoyas offer trekking tours of this region.

Karajía

This extraordinary funerary site hosts **six sarcophagi** perched high up a sheer cliff face. Each long-faced tomb is constructed from wood, clay and straw and is uniquely shaped like a stylized forlorn individual. The characters stare intently over the valley below, where a Chachapoyas village once stood; you can see stone ruins scattered among the fields of today. Originally there were eight coupled sarcophagi, but the third and eighth (from the left) collapsed, opening up the adjoining coffins – which were found to contain mummies, plus various crafts and artifacts related to the deceased. Look out for scattered bones below the coffins. Only important individuals were buried with such reverence: shamans, warriors and chieftains. The skulls above the tombs are thought to have been trophies of enemies or possibly human sacrifices. Locals charge a S3 admission fee.

Karajía is a 45-minute walk from the tiny outpost of Cruz Pata. Minibuses from Chachapoyas travel to Luya (S5.50, 50 minutes), from where minibuses go to Cruz Pata (S4.50, 50 minutes).

Levanto

A great day trip from Chachas is Levanto, a small village three to four hours' walk south along an Inca road, or 1½ hours by minibus (S5), which leave from near the market in Chachapoyas in the early morning.

our pick **Levanto Lodge** (s/d S45/75) is a much-recommended hostal built in the style of a traditional round Chachapoyas house. The attractive rooms have hot water and handsome wood furnishing and there are views of the Kuélap site and good opportunities to see the Marvelous Spatuletail Hummingbird (p452). Twenty minutes' walk outside of Levanto, at **Colla Cruz**, sits another reconstructed Inca building with round Chachapoyas walls, meticulous Inca stone foundations and a three-story thatch roof. Ask around for directions.

Revash

Near the town of Santo Tomás, Revash is the site of several brightly colored funerary buildings tucked into limestone cliff ledges.

Looking a bit like attractive-yet-inaccessible summer cottages, these *chullpas* are made of small, mud-set stones that were plastered over and embellished with red and cream paints. This bright taste in decor is still clearly visible today. While much of the site was looted long ago, the skeletons of 11 adults and one child, along with a wealth of artifacts such as musical instruments and tools made from bones, were found inside by archaeologists. A number of pictographs decorate the walls of the cliff behind the tombs, and a funerary cave, originally containing over 200 funerary bundles, lies 1km from the main set of tombs.

The ruins are a steep 3½-hour walk from the turnoff for Santo Tomás, which can be reached by Leimebamba-bound *combis* from Chachapoyas, which leave at noon and 4pm.

La Jalca (Jalca Grande)

This lovely little mountain town, also known as Jalca Grande, is a small, cobblestoned municipality that has managed to retain much of its historical roots, though modernization is slowly creeping its way in. Quechua is still spoken throughout much of the town and traditional, Chachapoyas-influenced round-walled houses with thatch roofs hide around the corners. Look for **Choza Redonda**, a tall-roofed traditional Chachapoyas house that was supposedly continually inhabited until 1964. It is still in excellent condition and was used as a model for the re-creation of Chachapoyas houses in Kuélap and Levanto. At the ruins of **Ollape**, half an hour's walk west of La Jalca, you can see several house platforms and circular balconies decorated with complex designs. To get here, catch a Chachapoyas–Leimebamba bus and ask to be let off at the La Jalca turnoff, from where it's a one-hour walk up a dirt road.

Yalape

On the road between Chachapoyas and Levanto, these ruins of limestone residential buildings make an easy day trip from Chachas. With good views of Levanto below, Yalape has some decent defense walls with some frieze patterns, all impressed with lots of forest growth. Yalape is four hours' hike from Chachapoyas or half an hour's walk from Levanto. Occasional *combis* head to Levanto early in the morning from near the market in Chachapoyas; they can let you off at Yalape.

KUÉLAP

elev 3100m

Matched in grandeur only by the ruins of Machu Picchu, this fabulous, ruined citadel city in the mountains southeast of Chachapoyas is the best preserved and most accessible of the district's extraordinary archaeological sites. This monumental stone-fortified city crowns a craggy limestone mountain and affords exceptional panoramas of a land once inhabited by the Chachapoyas. The site receives remarkably few visitors, but those who make it get to witness one of the most significant and impressive pre-Columbian ruins in all of South America.

Sights & Activities

Constructed between AD 900 and 1100, and rediscovered in 1843, **Kuélap** (adult/child S12/1; ☉ 8am-noon & 1-5pm) is made up of millions of cubic feet of remarkably preserved stone. Some say more stone was used in its construction than for the Great Pyramid of Egypt. Though the stonework is not as elaborate as that of the Incas, the 700m-long oval fortress is surrounded by an imposing, near-impenetrable wall that towers 6m to 12m high. Entrance into this stronghold is via three deep, lean gates – an ingenious security system that forced attacking parties into easily defeated single files.

Inside are three levels scattered with the remnants of more than 400 circular dwellings. Some are decorated with zigzag and rhomboid friezes, and all were once topped by soaring thatched roofs. One dwelling has been reconstructed by Canadian archaeologist Morgan Davis. In its heyday, Kuélap housed up to 3500 people and, surrounded by wispy cloud, must have been a breathtaking sight. The most impressive and enigmatic structure, named **El Tintero** (Inkpot), is in the shape of a large inverted cone. Inside, an underground chamber houses the remains of animal sacrifices, leading archaeologists to believe that it was a religious building of some kind. Recent evidence suggests it may have also been a solar calendar. Another building is a lookout tower with excellent 360-degree vistas. The mountain summit on which the whole city sits is surrounded by abundant greenery, towering bromeliad-covered trees and exotic orchids.

Tours & Guides

The guardians at Kuélap are very friendly and helpful; one is almost always on hand to show visitors around and answer questions. Don José Gabriel Portocarrero Chávez has been there for years; he can guide you and

---

THE CHACHAPOYAS

The Chachapoyas, or 'People of the Clouds,' controlled the vast swath of land around present-day Chachapoyas from AD 800 to the 1470s, when they were conquered by the Incas. Very little is known about this civilization, whose inhabitants were thought to be great warriors, powerful shamans and prolific builders who were responsible for one of the most advanced civilizations of Peru's tropical jungles. Today, among the many dozens of cliff tombs and hamlets of circular structures left behind, archaeologists match wits with grave robbers in a race for a deeper understanding of the Chachapoyas.

The Chachapoyas were heavily engaged in trade with other parts of Peru. However, isolated in their cloud-forest realm, they developed independently of these surrounding civilizations. The Chachapoyas cultivated a fierce warrior cult; the heads of enemies were often displayed as war trophies. The eventual expansion of the Inca empire in the 15th century was met with fierce resistance and sporadic fighting continued well after the initial conquest.

Environmentalists long before Greenpeace members got into rubber dinghies, the Chachapoyas built structures that were in perfect harmony with their surroundings and that took advantage of nature's aesthetic and practical contributions. The Chachapoyas religion is believed to have venerated some of the salient natural features of these territories; the serpent, the condor and the puma were worshipped as powerful representatives of the natural world.

The unique use of circular construction was complemented by intricate masonry friezes, which used zigzags and rhomboids. The buildings were covered by thatch roofs, which were tall and steep to facilitate the runoff of the area's frequent rains. Hundreds of ruins illustrate Chachapoyas architecture, but none stand out as much as the impressive fortified city of Kuélap, surrounded by a colossal 20m-high wall and encompassing hundreds of dwellings and temples.

is a good source of information on this and other ruins in the area. Other local guides congregate at the car park under the ruins – tip accordingly.

Sleeping & Eating

Kuélap itself has limited sleeping options, although nearby towns provide a good range of accommodations and can be used as a base for exploring the area.

Hospedaje El Bebedero (r per person S12) sits just beneath the Kuélap ruins and has very basic rooms without electricity or running water; bringing your own sleeping bag is recommended. The nearby INC Hostel has free camping, but the rooms are permanently occupied by the Kuélap excavation team. The caretaker of the ruins is happy to cook up a basic dinner for you if you ask and you can buy drinks and some snacks near the ticket office. Alternatively, for truly local fare, go to the second house down the road from the Kuélap car park; it has an unsigned home **kitchen** (meals S2-5; ☾ 8am-4pm). Try the free range *cuy* (you can hear them scampering around the kitchen) or egg soup with *mote* (corn dumplings).

The next closest sleeping choices are in the hamlet of María, two hours' walk from Kuélap and connected to Chachapoyas by daily minibuses. Here you will find a cottage industry of half a dozen charming and near-identical **hospedajes** (r per person S9) – they all go to the same sign-maker for their signs. All offer clean, modest rooms with electric hot water and will cook up hearty meals for guests for about S5. Try Hospedaje el Torreón or Hospedaje Lirio. One hour further down the road from María and 3km above the village of Choctámal, the pleasant **Choctámal Lodge** (☎ in Chachapoyas 47-8838; s/d S90/120) sits perched on a hillcrest with stunning 360-degree panoramas of the valley and Kuélap. The lodge has seven rustic but comfortable rooms here, all with some arty decorations and electric hot water. The caretakers are a wonderful local couple. Meals are available for S18 to S24.

In Tingo (elevation 1900m), at the far base of Kuélap, there's the bare-bones **Albergue León** (r without bathroom per person S27), with tiny, bucolic rooms and electric hot water. On the outskirts, the inviting **Valle Kuélap Hotel Inn** (☎ 041-81-3025, in Chachapoyas 041-47-8258; vallekuelap@hotmail.com; s/d S9/18) is a great deal for furnished and comfortable duplex bungalows, all with smart decorations. You can get hot showers here and the restaurant has agreeable river views. **Estancia Chillo** (☎ 041-83-0108; www.estanciachillo.com; r per person incl meals S275), 5km south of Tingo, is one of the nicest places to stay in the area. The beautiful hacienda-style compound has rustic and well-designed rooms, complete with ranch props, wagon wheels and brightly colored pet parrots wandering the grounds. All the fixtures you see were handmade by the owner Oscar Arce Cáceres. You can organize guides from here (S36 per day) as well as horses or donkeys (S25 per day) to go out and explore nearby ruins.

Getting There & Around

A 9.8km trail climbs from the south end of Tingo to the ruins, situated about 1200m above the town. Signposts on the way make the trail easy to follow, but it is an exhausting, often hot, climb; allow five to six hours. Remember to bring water as none is available along the trail. During the rainy season (October to April), especially the latter half, the trail can become very muddy and travel can be difficult. You can hike to Kuélap from Choctámal Lodge in about three hours and from María in about two hours.

Colectivo taxis to Kuélap (S14, three hours) depart from Chachapoyas throughout the day. **Transportes Roller** (Grau 302) has buses to Kuélap (S27.60, 3½ hours), via Tingo, Choctámal and María, leaving Chachapoyas at 4pm and returning from Kuélap at 6am and 8am the next morning. Alternatively, at Kuélap you can ask about getting a ride back to Chachapoyas with returning private *colectivos* or *combis*. Frequent *combis* (S5, 1½ hours) and *colectivo* taxis (S8, 1½ hours) run between Tingo and Chachapoyas. Tour agencies arrange day trips from Chachapoyas.

LEIMEBAMBA
pop 1100 / elev 2050m

This convivial cobblestoned town – often spelled 'Leymembamba' – lies at the head of the Río Utcubamba. It has an endearingly laid-back allure that is maintained by its relative isolation: the nearest big city is many hours away by dirt roads. Horses are still a popular form of transport around town and the friendliness of the townsfolk is legendary in the region. Surrounded by a multitude of archaeological sites from the Chachapoyas era, this is a great place to base yourself while exploring the province.

Information

Two phone offices, an internet cafe and a police station are on the plaza. Leimebamba doesn't have an ATM; bring cash.

Sights & Activities

In Leimebamba a small **tourist center & museum** opens erratically on the main plaza. A new **tomb**, three day's walk south from Leimebamba, was discovered in 1999.

LAGUNA DE LOS CÓNDORES

This part of Peru hit the spotlight in 1996 when a group of farmers found six *chullpas* (ancient Andean funerary towers) on a ledge 100m above a cloud-forest lake. This burial site was a windfall for archaeologists, and its 219 mummies and more than 2000 artifacts have given researchers a glimpse past the heavy curtain of history that conceals the details of the Chachapoyas civilization. So spectacular was the find that a Discovery Channel film was made about it and a museum was built in Leimebamba to house the mummies and cultural treasures.

Some of the tombs, plastered and painted in white or red-and-yellow ochre, are decorated with signature Chachapoyas zigzag friezes. All lie huddled against the cliff on a natural ledge overlooking the stunning Laguna de los Cóndores. Don't get too excited about spotting any of the wide-winged Andean wonders though – this lake was renamed after the find to make it more 'tourist friendly.'

The only way to get to the Laguna is by a strenuous 10- to 12-hour hike on foot and horseback from Leimebamba. The return journey takes three days; horses and guides can be arranged either in Leimebamba or at travel agencies in Chachapoyas.

LA CONGONA

The most captivating of the many ancient ruins strewn around Leimebamba, La Congona is definitely worth the three-hour hike needed to get here. The flora-covered site contains several well-preserved circular houses that, oddly for Chachapoyas culture, sit on square bases. Inside, the houses are adorned with intricate niches, and outside wide circular terraces surround each house. This archaeological site is renowned for the intricate decoration on the buildings and particularly for the numerous sophisticated masonry friezes. A tall tower can be climbed by a remarkable set of curving steps for wide-angle panoramas of the surrounding valley. Based on the location of this site, it's believed that it may have been a military bunker.

The site is reached in three hours from Leimebamba along a path beginning at the lower end of Calle 16 de Julio. A guide is recommended; expect to pay around S20 to S30.

MUSEO LEIMEBAMBA

The mummies found at Laguna de los Cóndores are now being studied in the **Museo Leimebamba** (www.museoleymebamba.org; adult S10; 9:30am-4:30pm Tue-Sun), located 3km south of town. The museum is in a wonderfully constructed complex with multi-tiered roofs, all generously funded by the Austrian Archaeological Society. Most of the mummies are wrapped in bundles and can be seen in glass cases; some have been unwrapped for your gruesome viewing pleasure. Well-presented artifacts on display include ceramics, textiles, wood figures and photos of Laguna de los Cóndores.

Kentikafé (www.museoleymebamba.org/kentikafe.htm; admission S10; 9:30am-4:30pm Tue-Sun), just a short stroll across the street and up the hill, is owned by an Austrian member of the team that built the museum. Perched on a hill with views of the museum and valley below, Kentikafé maintains about a dozen feeders visited by the Marvelous Spatuletail Hummingbird (p452) and 16 other hummingbird species – they drink some 5kg of sugar per day! You can lie in wait for glimpses of the Spatuletail while sipping super-fresh gourmet coffee and homemade cakes.

Tours & Guides

Local guides (inquire at the museums) will arrange trips to the tombs and various other sites; some are easily visited on a day trip, while others require several days. Homer Ullilen, the son of the owner of the **Albergue Turístico de la Laguna de los Cóndores** (Amazonas 320), can guide you to sites near their land. Expect to pay around S30 per day for a guide (not including food) and S18 to S30 for horses.

Sleeping & Eating

One of the better cheapies in town, **Hotel Escobedo** (Calle 16 de Julio 514; s/d without bathroom S9/27) has rickety wooden rooms. Further along the same street, **Albergue Turístico de la Laguna de los Cóndores** (Amazonas 320; s S40/66, s/d without bathroom S15/30), located half a block from the plaza, is a family-run affair with a verdant courtyard and lots of comfortable sitting areas draped in thick, colorful blankets. They have hot showers, cozy rooms and tours of the area can be arranged from here. **La Casona** (☎ 83-0106; Amazonas 221, s/d S18/12) has polished floors in its neat rooms and new bathrooms with electric hot water. Some rooms have little balconies looking onto the quiet, cobblestoned street below. There's also a small restaurant at La Casona.

On the plaza, **LucyBell** (menús S4-6; ☺ 7am-10pm) does one of the better *menús* in town and attracts roast-chicken lovers. **Cely's Pizza** (La Verdad 530; pizzas S6-14; ☺ 6:30am-10:30pm) does perfectly respectable pizza, as well as a bunch of Peruvian dishes.

Shopping
AMAL (San Augustine 429; ☺ 9am-6pm) Located on the plaza, AMAL is a women's artisan cooperative selling top-grade handicrafts and local weavings.

Getting There & Away
Minibuses for Chachapoyas leave frightfully early – at 3am and 5am (S27, three to four hours) – from a signed areas on the plaza. Reserve a seat the night before. A taxi to Chachapoyas costs S80. The two weekly buses to Chachapoyas (S27, three to four hours) from Celendín pass through at about 5pm on Mondays, Wednesdays, Thursdays, Fridays and Sundays. In the reverse direction, heading toward Celendín (S18, seven to nine hours), they pass at about 10pm on Mondays, 7am on Wednesdays, Thursdays and Fridays, and about 9am on Sundays. Occasional trucks and private vehicles pick up paying passengers to Chachapoyas and Celendín.

PEDRO RUÍZ
☎ 041 / elev 1400m
This dusty transit town sits at the junction of the Chiclayo–Tarapoto road and the turnoff to Chachapoyas. When traveling from Chachapoyas, you can board east- or westbound buses here. The pick of the sorry hotels in Pedro Ruíz is the **Casablanca Hotel** (☎ 83-0135; s/d S9/13.50), by the road junction, but try to get a room away from the noisy highway. Hostal

Amazonense is cheaper, simpler and, more often than not, closed.

Buses from the coast pick up passengers heading to Rioja or Moyobamba (S18 to S24, five hours) and Tarapoto (S22 to S27, seven hours). Several come through daily, but they may be crowded. The road is paved to Tarapoto.

Buses bound for Chiclayo pass by mostly in the late afternoon and cost S23 to S32 (eight hours). If coming from Tarapoto, you'll find plenty of *colectivo* taxis for Chachapoyas (S10, 1½ hours) leaving from the junction.

The journey east from Pedro Ruíz is spectacular, climbing over two high passes, traveling by a beautiful lake, and dropping into fantastic high-jungle vegetation in between.

POMACOCHAS
☎ 041 / pop 4500 / elev 2300
The dead giveaway that you have arrived in Pomacochas is the large **lake** known by the same name ('puma lake' in Quechua). A tranquil village nestled in a fetching agricultural valley, Pomacochas is one of the best places to try to see the Marvelous Spatuletail (see p452), arguably the world's most beautiful and strange hummingbird.

Fifteen minutes west on the road to Pedro Ruíz, the San Lucas de Pomacochas **interpretation center** (☺ 7:30am-6pm; admission S15) maintains feeders on a 31-acre private reserve that attracts this and many other hummingbirds; the views over the valley and the plunging road from here are also spectacular. The center's administrator, Santos Montenegro, may also show you the Spatuletail at the breeding ground on his poverty, on the west edge of town and fifteen minutes hike up into the scrub forest; his family does not formally charge for this excursion, but a donation would only be appropriate. Inquire at the center, about a S5 per person *mototaxi* ride away.

A few small hostals, including the Hostal Cajamarquino and the Hostal Oro Verde on the main strip through town charge about S30 for a room. La Colina on the east end of town has set meals for S6 to S10. The best place to stay is **Puerto Pumas** (☎ 712-0550/0551; www.puerto palmeras.com.pe/pumas.htm; Bolognesi 125, ste 1403; s/d S155/215) overlooking the lake. Surrounded by a lush flower- and bird-filled garden, the hotel is covered in original art and has a real mummy

DAHLING, YOU LOOK MARVELOUS!

You don't have to be a big-time bird-watcher to get turned on by the Marvelous Spatuletail (*Loddigesia mirabilis*), a rare and exquisitely beautiful hummingbird that lives in limited habitats of scrubby forest between 2000m and 2900m in northern Peru's Utcubamba valley. As with most bird species, the males get the prize in the looks category, and the Marvelous male is no exception, with his shimmering blue crown and green throat and a sexy set of curved and freakishly long quills that splay out from his backside and end in wide, feather 'rackets' or 'spatules.' He can independently maneuver these long plumes into extravagant mating displays, crossing the two spatuletail feathers over each other or swinging them in front of his head as he hovers in front of a female.

As bewitching and beautiful as the Spatuletail is, scientists have wondered why the male would evolve such large, showy feathers at the expense of so much energy: as much as 50% of the bird's calories go to working the spatuletails, which seem to get in the way when the handsome fellow is trying to navigate through the thickets or battle his notoriously competitive fellow-hummingbirds. Most ornithologists agree, however, that the tails are features of sexual selection, used to court the female Spatuletail.

According to some Peruvians in the Utcubamba valley, the Spatuletail's most spectacular anatomical feature is its heart, which is considered an aphrodisiac when eaten. The hunting of the birds for this purpose has probably contributed to keeping its numbers low – perhaps less than 1000 pairs remain – although conservation efforts in the region have led to increased awareness about the precarious status of the bird, whose habitat is quickly diminishing due to deforestation and agricultural development, and the need to protect it. Some conservation centers – at KentiKafé (p450) and the San Lucas de Pomacochas Interpretation Center (p451) – offer great chances of seeing the Marvelous Spatuletail in all his glory.

in the lobby (how it got there no one knows). It's a tranquil place to unwind and certainly a better place to stop over than Pedro Ruíz.

Heading east from Pomacochas, many travelers pass through one of northern Peru's most successful private reserves without noticing it. The 2960-hectare **Abra Patricia conservation area** (☎ 81-6814; www.ecoan.org; r per person with 3 meals S1350), about 40 minutes east of Pedro Ruíz on the road to Moyobamba, is managed by the Association of Andean Ecosystems (ECOAN) and offers large and exceptionally clean, quiet rooms for nature lovers and anyone who just wants to get away from the noise of civilization. The gourmet meals are served in a dining room with views of mountainous forest that has never seen the swipe of a chainsaw. Although a favorite of bird-watching tour groups – who come to see such endemic species as Yellow-scarved Tanager, Lulu's Tody-tyrant and the extremely rare Long-whiskered Owlet – it's also the best place to see the Yellow-tailed Woolly Monkey.

MOYOBAMBA
☎ 042 / pop 41,800 / elev 860m

Moyobamba, the capital of the department of San Martín, was founded in 1542, but earthquakes (most recently in 1990 and 1991)

have contributed to the demise of any historic buildings. Nevertheless, Moyobamba is a pleasant enough town to spend a few days in and local tourist authorities are slowly drumming up sites of interest to visit.

Information
Alt@ntin Internet (Calle de Alvarado 863; per hr $0.90) Email your folks here.
BCP (☎ 56-2572; Calle de Alvarado 903) Changes money and has an ATM.
Dirección Regional de Industria y Turismo (☎ 56-2043; www.turismosanmartin.com; San Martín 301) Has limited tourism information.

Sights & Activities
The well-maintained hot springs of **Baños Termales de San Mateo** (admission S1.50; 🕑 6am-8pm) with temperatures of around 40°C are 4km south of town. Taxis cost S5, or catch a *colectivo* (S1) at Jirón Varacadillo, cuadra 1, in Moyobamba. On weekends the baths get crowded with locals, who know the waters are curative; travelers rarely make it here. The Cascadas Paccha and Lahuarpía are impressive **waterfalls**, each 30 minutes away by car. The region is famed for its orchids; there's an orchid festival held in October and a giant orchid statue guards the town's entrance. You

can see these and other exotic plants in a giant geodesic-domed hothouse at the **Jardín Botánico San Francisco** (admission S1; ☉ 8am-5pm). It's 2km from town, a S4 *mototaxi* ride away. For more orchids in a natural setting, visit **Waqanki Orchid Center** (www.waqanki.com; Carretera a Los Baños Termales de San Mateo), about 3km outside of town. They have some 150 species of orchids growing along two-, four- and six-hour trail circuits winding through beautiful forest.

The **Instituto Nacional de Cultura** (INC; ☎ 56-2281; Benavides 352; admission S1; ☉ 9am-noon & 2-5pm Mon-Fri) is a small museum and has some information as well.

Tours & Guides

Tingana Magic (☎ 56-1436; www.tinganaperu.com; Reyes Guerra 422; ☉ 10am-6pm) can arrange tours around the area to waterfalls, caves and ecological reserves.

Sleeping & Eating

Hospedaje Santa Rosa (☎ 80-9890; Canga 478; s/d S12/24) A great shoestring pick with a few rudimentary, newly painted rooms set around a brick patio. The occasional potted plant helps liven up the concrete-jungle feel.

Hostal Royal (☎ 56-2662; Calle de Alvarado 784; s/d S18/27) With cubby-sized rooms and friendly service, this cheap option also has a basic restaurant downstairs.

Country Club Hostal (☎ 56-2110; www.moyabamba .net/countryclub; Calle de Aguila 667; s/d S25/35; ☒) Spartan tiled rooms have hot showers and sit around a green lawn lined with scraggly bushes. There's a tiny pool, though it was empty when we last visited.

Atlanta Hotel (☎ 56-2063; Calle de Alvaro 865; s/d S27/45) With a Motel 6-inspired setup around a tiled courtyard, this place has good, clean rooms with hot water and smiles all round.

Hostal Marcoantonio (☎ 56-2045; Canga 488; s/d S65/90) This is the place to come for a touch of comfort in Moyobamba. The spotless rooms have the necessary mod cons, such as TV and hot water, but lack flair or any distinguishing features. The downstairs restaurant has room service and staff can arrange local tours.

Hotel Puerto Mirador (☎ /fax 56-2050; www.hotel puertomirador.com; Jirón Sucre; s/d S120/150, bungalows incl breakfast S168; ☒) Located 1km northeast of town, this fine hotel with relaxing views over the Río Mayo has oodles of luxuriant lawn, a great pool and lots of sitting areas made from natural materials. A restaurant provides room service.

Chifa Shanghai (☎ 9-62-7436; Calle de Avaro; meals S6-9) Packed nightly with more diners than you can poke a *wantan* (wonton) at, this is the place to go for a taste of the Middle Kingdom.

La Olla de Barro (☎ 56-3450; Canga at Filomeno; mains S6-18; ☉ 8am-11pm) This local institution is set up like a tiki lounge, complete with faux flames licking around a 'bubbling' pot, lots of bamboo and jungle knickknacks. This is the best place in town to sample local jungle dishes – don't miss it.

Hospedaje Ecológico Rumipata (☎ 79-5291; www .rumipata.com; Carretera a Los Baños Termales de San Mateo; bungalows S30) A five-minute walk from the San Mateo hot springs and Waqanki Orchid Center, Rumipata is situated in a verdant and idyllic setting outside of Moyobamba. Rooms are in thatched-roof bungalows with rustic interiors, and the on-site restaurant is delicious.

Getting There & Away

Colectivos to Rioja (S3, 30 minutes) and Tarapoto (S18, two hours) leave frequently from the corner of Benavides and Filomeno, three blocks east of the Plaza de Armas.

The bus terminal is on Grau, about 1km from the center. Most buses between Tarapoto and Chiclayo stop here to pick up passengers.

TARAPOTO

☎ 042 / pop 65,900 / elev 356m

Tarapoto straddles the base of the Andean foothills and the edge of the vast jungles of eastern Peru. A sweltering rainforest metropolis, it dips its toe into the Amazon Basin while managing to cling to the rest of Peru by the umbilical cord of a long paved road back to civilization. From here you can take the plunge deeper into the Amazon, or just enjoy the easily accessible jungle lite, with plenty of places to stay and eat and reliable connections to the coast. There's a bunch of natural sights to explore nearby, from waterfalls to lagoons, and river-running opportunities will entertain the adventure-seeking contingent.

The largest and busiest town in the department of San Martín, Tarapoto's recent growth can be accounted for by coca-growing enterprises in the middle and upper Río Huallaga valley to the south. Tourists don't usually encounter problems and

the situation has been improving since the government crackdown on Sendero Luminoso (Shining Path) guerillas in the 1990s. The exception is the Saposoa region; the trip through there to Tingo María is not recommended. The route from Moyobamba through Tarapoto and on to Yurimaguas is safe, but be sure to check the latest conditions.

Information

Internet cafes hide around every corner.

BCP (Maynas 130; 8am-5pm Mon-Fri) Cashes traveler's checks and has an ATM.

Clínica San Martín (52-3680, 52-7860; San Martín 274; 24hr) The best medical care in town.

Interbank (89-5092; Grau 119)

Post office (50-3450; San Martín 482; 9am-7pm Mon-Fri, to 1pm Sat) Tarapoto's main post office.

Puerto Net (cnr Hurtado & Bolognesi; per hr S2; 8am-midnight) Has new computers with big screens.

Scotiabank (Hurtado 215; 8am-5pm Mon-Fri, 9am-1pm Sat) Cashes traveler's checks and has an ATM.

Tarapoto Express Lavanderia (52 -6367; Manco Cápac; per kg S5; 8am-9pm) With another location for you laundry pleasure on Calle de Moray.

Sights & Activities

Tarapoto itself has little to do, apart from just hanging out in the town's Plaza de Armas or visiting the tiny **Museo Regional** (Maynas 174; admission S1; 8am-noon & 12:30-8pm Mon-Fri), but you can make several excursions to nearby towns, waterfalls and lakes.

Lamas is an indigenous village that unfortunately lost many of its colonial buildings in a 2005 earthquake; however, it's a standard tour destination for its small museum and crafts. The large indigenous population here has an annual **Feast of Santa Rosa de Lima** in the last week of August. Although minibuses (S7, 45 minutes) and *colectivos* go to Lamas, it's easiest to visit with a guided tour (S30 to S50 per person, four to six hours), which usually includes a visit to Ahuashiyacu waterfalls.

The town of **Chazuta**, a two-hour drive away, boasts the impressive 40m, three-level **Tununtunumba** waterfalls, another small museum showcasing pre-Inca funerary urns, artisanal crafts and a port on the Río Huallaga with great fishing. Agencies in Tarapoto are starting to promote 'mystical tourism' here, where trips include a visit to local *bru-*

jos (witch doctors). Really the only way to get to Chazuta is on a day tour (S80) or by private transport.

Several lakes lie tucked away in the surrounding mountains. **Laguna Azul** (also called Laguna de Sauce) is a popular local spot reached by crossing the Río Huallaga, 45km away, on a vehicle raft ferry and continuing by car for another 45 minutes. Day tours (S65 to S80 per person, minimum three people) and overnight excursions are available. You'll find good swimming, boating and fishing here, and accommodations, ranging from camping to upscale bungalows, are available. Several *combis* a day go to nearby Sauce (S14, four hours) from a bus stop in the Banda de Shilcayo district, east of the town. Taxi drivers know it. Meanwhile, **Laguna Venecia** and the nearby 40m waterfalls, **Cataratas de Ahuashiyacu,** are about 45 minutes toward Yurimaguas. There's a small restaurant nearby and a locally favored swimming spot. Five-hour tours cost S40 per person. Also popular is a similarly priced trip to the **Cataratas de Huacamaillo,** which involves two hours of hiking and wading across the river several times. These places can be reached by public transport and then on foot, but go with a guide or get detailed information to avoid getting lost.

River running (whitewater rafting) on the Río Mayo, 30km from Tarapoto, and on the lower Río Huallaga, is offered from June to November. The shorter trips (half- and full-day trips, from S63 per person) are mainly class II and III whitewater, while longer trips (up to six days, from July to October only) ride out class III and class IV rapids. Rafting trips to the class III rapids of the upper Mayo, 100km from Tarapoto, are possible. Inflatable kayaks are available for rent for S45/75 for a half-/full day. Check with **Los Chancas Expeditions** (☎ 52 2616; www.geocities.com/amazonrainforest; Rioja 357), the local river-running specialists.

Brujos play a pivotal role in the *pueblos* of the jungle. A few kilometers north of Tarapoto, you'll find the **Takiwasi Center** (☎ 52-2818; www .takiwasi.com; Prolongación Alerta 466). Started in the early 1990s by French physician Jacques Mabit, this rehabilitation and detox center combines traditional Amazonian medicines and plants, as used by *brujos* or *curanderos* (healers), with a combination of psychotherapy. This treatment is not for the fainthearted: intense 'vomit therapy' and *ayahuasca* (hallucinogenic brew made from jungle vines) are used as part of the healing process. Rehabilitation programs for all kinds of ailments run for nine months and cost around US$500, though no one is turned away for lack of funds. Information and introductory sessions can be organized.

Tours & Guides
All of these licensed agencies have several years' experience in local tourism.

Quiquiriqui Tours (☎ 52-4016; www.quiquiriquitours .com; Pimentel 309; ☻ 8am-7pm Mon-Fri, to 6pm Sat, 9am-noon Sun) A full-service travel and tour agency that books flights, offers information on and arranges tours to local sites.

Selva Mayo (☎ 53-1489; www.selvamayoperu.com; Grau 233; ☻ 8am-8pm Mon-Sat, 9am-1pm Sun) Books day tours and longer excursions to local lakes and waterfalls and cultural trips to experience *ayahuasca* rituals and medicinal plant demonstrations.

Turismo Selva (☎ 52-7419; San Pablo de la Cruz 233; ☻ 8am-6pm Mon-Sat, 9am-noon Sun) Smiley staff here can book numerous local tours and flights.

Festivals & Events
Patronato de Tarapoto A festival in mid-July that celebrates the town's indigenous heritage.

Aniversario de Tarapoto The anniversary of the town is the city's biggest fiesta, with music, dancing and frivolities in the streets. *Uvachado,* made by steeping macerated grapes in cane liquor, keeps the party fueled. The fiesta lasts for an entire week around the anniversary (August 20).

Sleeping
BUDGET
Hostal Pasquelandia (☎ 52-2290; Pimentel 341; s/d without bathroom S10/15) It's a dirt-cheap, beat-up, wooden affair with cold water.

   El Paso Texas II (☎ 52-3799; Calle de Morey 115; s/d/tr S20/25/30) Don't ask us where Paso Texas I is. All we know is this place has basic digs with private bathrooms and a few cheesy paintings that liven things up. The front rooms are noisy, while the rear rooms are a little dark.

   Alojamiento Grau (☎ 52-3777; Grau 243; s/d S20/25) Family-run and friendly, this place has quiet, clean, elementary rooms, all with exposed brick walls and windows to the inside. A very solid budget option.

   Hospedaje Misti (☎ 52-2439; Prado 341; s/d S20/25) The typically modest rooms here are redeemed by the skinny, leafy courtyard and a laid-back cafe. Tiny bathrooms with cold water leave little maneuvering room, but you get a TV and ceiling fan – good shoestring value. Discounts are available for groups and monthly rentals.

Alojamiento Arevalo (☎ 52-5265, 52-7467; Moyobamba 223; s/d S27/45) The best thing about this quiet hotel is the large rooms – there's space enough to swing a couple of cats. Each has a cold shower, cable TV, fan and mini-fridge. A large public area with tables adjoins a lush courtyard.

Alojamiento July (☎ 52-2087; Calle de Morey 205; s/d/tr 30/40/60) Cheerfully painted rooms with electric shower, cable TV, mini-fridge and fan are OK for the price. Every wall here is covered with jungle murals, endless rows of beads and knickknacks clank in the hallways, and the whole place is run by a gregarious Imelda Marcos type. Ask for a room on the top floor.

El Mirador (☎ 52-2177; San Pedro de la Cruz 517; s/d S45/60) This spic-and-span hotel has 13 rooms, all with big fans and great mattresses. Some of the rooms have hot showers and doors have linen curtains that can be left open for a cool breeze (but little privacy). Being a few blocks away from the center cuts down most of the *mototaxi* noise. You can take breakfast on the rooftop terrace with views of the city one way and treetops the other.

Hostal Luna Azul (☎ 52-5787, lunaazulhotel@hotmail .com; Manco Cápac 262; s/d S45/65, s/d with air-con S54/74; ✗ ⌨) So clinically clean you could eat off the floors, the Luna Azul is a modern hotel with comfortable, small rooms, some with air-con. Hot water, direct-dial phones, grinning staff and cable TV put it close to the midrange class. It has a snack bar.

La Patarashca (☎ 52-3899, 52-7554; www.la patarashca.com; Lamas 261; s S50, d S60-75, all incl breakfast) Don't miss this little gem of a *hospedaje* (family inn). Tucked away between a couple of restaurants, some rooms have hot-water showers and cable TVs, while nice bits of furniture and crafty lamps make them feel homey and welcoming. There's a green lounging area under a giant thatched roof, hammocks, couches and some English-speaking staff. Look out for the bilingual talking parrots, which, while cute initially, can be a little annoying at 6am. Best of all, you can get room service at a discount from the identically named restaurant next door.

Hostal la Cumbre (☎ 52-9987; Circunvalación 2040; s/d incl breakfast S54/74) This friendly family-run affair, 3km (an S2 *mototaxi* ride) northwest of town, gets good reviews from readers. It's in a modern building and good-sized rooms come with TV and mini-fridges. The garden area with great views of the surrounding misty mountains is good spot to relax. The best thing is the Amazonian breakfast.

MIDRANGE

Tarapoto has fewer midrange hotels than most cities its size but every option in this range has cable TV and hot water.

La Posada Inn (☎ 52-5557, 52-2234; laposadainn@latin mail.com; San Martín 146; s/d incl breakfast S45/79; s/d with air-con S55/80; ✗) This quaint hotel has beamed ceilings, traditional ironwork and an inviting wooden staircase. The classy rooms are an eclectic mix: some have balconies, some have air-con and some have electric showers. Even though it's right in the town center, La Posada manages to remain quiet. Breakfast menus rotates between eggs and local treats like tamales.

Hotel Monte Azul (☎ 52-2443, 52-3145; www.hotel monteazul.com.pe; Morey 156; s/d S75/109, s/d with air-con S109/159; ✗) Adorned with some nice flopping areas, it's cozy, orderly and bright and at this price is pretty good bang for your buck. The staff is always switched on and friendly, and the rooms all have quality mattresses, direct-dial phones and mini-fridges.

Hotel Lily (☎ 52-3154; Pimentel 407; s/d incl breakfast S100/145; ✗ ⌨) Unpretentious but secure and restful, this business-oriented hotel features a sauna and a breakfast room by the pool. Rooms are spacious, with writing desks, mini-fridges, phones and vivid colors (think blue carpet and lime green blankets). Streetside rooms have balconies but can be noisy.

Hotel Nilas (☎ 52-7331/2; nilas-tpto@terra.com.pe; Moyobamba 173; s/d S120/160; ✗ ⌨ ⌨) A canary yellow hotel like this would not be out of place swaying over a Miami beach – and the palm-fringed 3rd-floor pool rounds off the illusion nicely. The good-sized rooms have the all the necessary mod cons and you'll find a gym, restaurant and conference center tucked away among the maze of cheery floors.

Hotel Río Shilcayo (☎ 52-2225, ☎ /fax 52-4236; www.rioshilcayo.com; Pasaje La Flores 224; s/d/bungalows incl breakfast S189/229/259; ✗ ⌨) Almost 2km east of town, this hotel is quiet and cool and has a sauna, good restaurant, bar and rooms with good amenities – and a tropical bird enclosure thrown in for good measure. Rates include airport transfer.

TOP END

Puerto Palmeras (☎ 52-3978, 52-4100; www.puerto palmeras.com; Presidente FB Terry Km 614; s/d S199/289, ste S389-559; 🛏 🍴) This resort, 6km east of town, has the whole kit and caboodle. Set on sprawling green grounds, the decked-out rooms are spread out in hacienda-style complexes constructed with white adobe walls and decorated with loads of attractive pieces of art. The resort grounds have a large fishing pond, a beautiful pool, artfully decorated restaurant and sitting areas, billiard tables, horses, a fleet of 4WDs for hire and more. It's a S4 taxi ride from town or you can call for a pickup.

Eating

Don't leave Tarapoto without trying *inchicapi* (chicken soup with peanuts, cilantro and yucca) or *juanes* (steamed rice with fish or chicken, wrapped in a banana leaf).

Banana's Burgers (☎ 52-3260; Calle de Morey 102; S3-6; 🕐 24hr) A good burger joint, this place is always open and there's a bar on the 2nd floor.

Chifa Tai Pai (☎ 52-4393; Prado 250; meals S5-18; 🕐 12-3pm & 6-11pm) Modern and shiny, this *chifa* serves up good Chinese fare to eager locals and families.

Real Grill (☎ 52-2183; Moyobamba 131; mains S8-27; 🕐 8am-midnight) An institution right on the Plaza de Armas, this place has (noisy) outdoor tables and serves pastas, Chinese meals, local dishes, meat, seafood, burgers and so on. The food is middle of the road.

Café d' Mundo (☎ 50-3223; Calle de Morey 157; meals S9-21; 🕐 7pm-midnight) A funky establishment illuminated nightly by moody candlelight, this hip restaurant and bar has outdoor seating and snug indoor lounges. Good pizzas, pastas and other tidbits adorn a small menu and a full bar will help you pass the rest of the evening away comfortably. The continually roaring *mototaxis* tend to detract from the mood a little, however.

El Brassero (☎ 52-2700; Lamas 231; mains S9-21; 🕐 noon-late) Carnivores congregate at this great grill. Choose your cut; pork ribs are the specialty, funky acid-jazz tunes are a bonus. The owners love to chat – they only close when the coals die down and people leave.

ourpick La Patarashca (☎ 52-3899; Lamas 261; mains S9-32; 🕐 8am-11pm) Regional Amazon cuisine is on tap in Patarashca's casual 2nd-floor dining room. With street views and a tropical ambience, it's a popular weekend place to see and be seen. Don't miss the *paiche* (a freshwater fish) and salad made of *chonta*, thin strips of a local palm plant doused in vinaigrette, or the namesake *patarashcas*, heaping platters of giant shrimp or fish grilled with garlic and cilantro.

La Collpa (☎ 52-2644; Circunvalación 164; mains S13-32; 🕐 10am-11pm) You can practically taste the jungle air at this stilt restaurant, with a bamboo balcony over a river and a patch of rainforest. The menu offers up everything imaginable, from ceviche (raw seafood marinated in lime juice) to typical jungle food to grills to Chinese food to pastas. It's best to come for lunch to appreciate the views, though candlelit dinners are also a treat.

El Rincón Sureño (☎ 52-2785; Leguia 458; meals S14-35; 🕐 noon-11pm) One of the best grills in town, this swish-looking establishment has intimate wood-lined rooms as well as a bustling outdoor seating area. The grilled meats here are delicious and El Rincón Sureño boasts what must be one of the largest wine collections in all of South America.

Supermercado la Inmaculada (☎ 52-7598; Calle de Compagnon 126; 🕐 8:30am-10pm) This supermarket has everything you might need for self-catering.

Drinking

Stonewasi Taberna (☎ 52-4681; Lamas 222; 🕐 6pm-late) This is the place to see and be seen in Tarapoto. The whole intersection of Lamas and La Cruz transforms each evening into a cruising scene, with several good people-watching restaurants and bars. Stonewasi is the pick of the bunch and lays out streetside tables where punters and *mototaxi* drivers throng nightly to the sound of international rock and house music. Check out the path leading to one of the entryways – it's made entirely of conch-shell fossils.

La Alternativa (☎ 52-7898; Grau 401; 🕐 9am-8pm) This 'alternative' hole-in-the-wall bar is more like a medieval pharmacy than a bar – shelves are stacked with dusty bottles containing *uvachado* and various homemade natural concoctions based on soaking roots, lianas etc in cane liquor. All the potent Amazonian tonics and brews are for the tasting – but not for the faint-hearted.

Entertainment

Papillón (☎ 52-2574; Peru 209; admission S9; 🕐 evening Fri & Sat) This nightclub has live salsa bands or DJ-fuelled dancing. Popular with young locals and travelers, it's in the Morales district, by the Río Cumbaza about 3km west of the center. *Mototaxis* go there for under S3.

NORTHERN HIGHLANDS

Getting There & Away

AIR

The **airport** (TTP; ☎ 52-2278), 3km southwest of the center, charges S11 departure tax.

Star Perú (☎ 52-8765; San Pablo de la Cruz 100) has daily flights from Lima to Tarapoto (S278) at 1:30pm, returning at 3pm. This flight continues on to Iquitos (S254) at 5pm. A daily **LAN** (☎ 52 9318; Hurtado 184) flight leaves Lima (S399) at noon and 9:30pm, returning to Lima at 2pm and 11:30pm.

BUS & TAXI

Several companies head west on the paved road to Lima (24 to 28 hours) via Moyobamba (two hours), Chiclayo (14 to 16 hours) and Trujillo (18 to 20 hours), generally leaving between 8am and 4pm. All these companies can be found along the same block of Salaverry in the Morales district, an S2 *mototaxi* ride from the town center. If you're heading to Chachapoyas, you'll need to change in Pedro Ruíz (seven hours).

Cial (☎ 52-7629; Salaverry) Has a noon express bus to Lima (S102) and a 4:30pm Chiclayo bus (S45).

Civa (☎ 52-2269, Salaverry) Has a comfortable 7pm bus to Lima (S102) stopping at Chiclayo (S45) and Trujillo (S72). Also has a 6pm bus to Chiclayo.

Ejetur (☎ 52-6827; Salaverry) Has a bus to Lima (S72) at 11:15am via Chiclayo (S41.50) and Trujillo (S50). Also has direct Trujillo buses at 7:30am, 8:30am and 1:30pm. A bus leaves for San Ignacio (S36, 18 hours) at 7:30am for the alternative Ecuador border crossing (see p442).

Expreso Huamanga (☎ 52-7272; Salaverry) Slower buses to Chiclayo (S36, 16 hours) via Jaén (S27, nine hours) at 8:30am, Chiclayo direct at 11:30am (S36), Lima at 2:30pm (S72) and Yurimaguas at 8am (S11, six to eight hours).

Movil Tours (☎ 52 -9193; Salaverry) Top-end express buses to Lima (S102, 24 hours) leave at 8am and 1pm, with a 3pm departure to Trujillo (S67) and a 4pm bus to Chiclayo (S59).

Paredes Estrella (☎ 52-1202; Salaverry) Has a cheaper 11am service to Lima (S72) stopping at Chiclayo (S36) and Trujillo (S45), as well as a 2:30pm bus to Trujillo, a 3pm bus to Chiclayo and a 7am bus to Yurimaguas (S27, six to eight hours).

Turismo Tarapoto (☎ 52 -5240; Salaverry) A cheaper 3pm bus to Trujillo (S41) via Chiclayo (S45) as well as an 11am bus to Piura (S45, 18 hours).

Minibuses, trucks and *colectivo* taxis for Yurimaguas (S14 to S22) leave when full from the *mercado* (market) in the eastern suburb of Banda de Shilcayo and take five to six hours in the dry season, more in the wet. The rough (especially in wet season) 130km road climbs over the final foothills of the Andes and emerges on the Amazonian plains.

Colectivo taxis to Moyobamba (S25) leave when full from Salaverry in the Morales district. Minibuses to Lamas (S5, 45 minutes) can also be found along this road.

The southbound journey via Bellavista to Juanjuí (145km) and on to Tocache Nuevo and Tingo María (485km), though safer than it once was, is still dangerous and not recommended because of drug-running and problems with bandits (see p333). If you go, avoid traveling at night, and see if any flights are available. Bellavista, Juanjuí and Tocache Nuevo all have basic hotels. Tingo María is safe enough.

Getting Around

Mototaxis cruise the streets like circling sharks. A short ride in town is around S1, to the bus stations S2 and to the airport S3.

Amazon Basin

The sheer vastness and impenetrability of the Amazon Basin has protected its diverse flora, fauna and indigenous communities from the outside world for time immemorial. Tribes exist in its depths that have never had contact with outside civilization. As the 21st century slowly dawns on this enticing expanse of jungle territory, the abundance of natural resources contained within it – ranging from oil to ranch land – is set to threaten and possibly forever change it. The jungle here comprises 50% of the nation, yet only 5% of Peruvians live in it. Stretching away from beneath the eastern flank of the Andes for thousands of kilometers to the Atlantic Ocean, this wilderness has long been synonymous with the word 'adventure,' and Peru's portion of it has been judiciously preserved. More plant types flourish in a single rainforest hectare here than in any European country. Some of the world's most diverse nature reserves beckon, making this one of the continent's premier wildlife-watching spots.

Divided into three primary areas, the Peruvian Amazonas not only offers a mixture of birding and animal-spotting, jungle trekking and river life but also a dash of raucous rainforest city living. There are only three towns of any size: Pucallpa can be reached by a paved road, Puerto Maldonado is accessible mostly by dirt track and Iquitos is connected to the rest of Peru by river and air alone. This lush region begs for the attention of adventure seekers but it also begs for protection. Its natural wealth also attracts loggers, energy companies, slash-and-burn farmers and developers. This is frontier country. Travel is tough but rewards are unlimited: forging your way by rough road, raging river and overgrown path, you'll feel like the explorers who first brought outside attention to this region.

HIGHLIGHTS

- Travel overland through mountains, cloud forest and jungle to **Parque Nacional Manu** (p477)
- Spot Amazonian animals and birds at the **upper Río Tambopata** (p471) and **Reserva Nacional Pacaya-Samiria** (p493)
- Visit the Asháninka people from **Puerto Bermúdez** (p484)
- Swing in a hammock on a riverboat heading to **Iquitos** (p488 and p497)

■ BIGGEST CITY: IQUITOS, POPULATION 371,000

■ AVERAGE TEMPERATURE: JANUARY 22° C TO 32° C, JULY 21° C TO 30° C

AMAZON BASIN

Geography & Climate

Three key jungle areas of Peru are accessible to the traveler. In the southeast, near the Bolivian border, there's Puerto Maldonado (right), a port at the junction of the Ríos Tambopata and Madre de Dios reached by air from Lima via Cuzco or by a slowly improving road from Cuzco. South of Puerto Maldonado lie numerous lodges and campsites in the Reserva Nacional Tambopata (p471) and in the Parque Nacional Bahuaja-Sonene (p471).

Northeast of Cuzco, and fairly easily accessible from there, is Parque Nacional Manu (p477), one of the best-protected areas of Amazon rainforest.

In central Peru, east of Lima, the Chanchamayo area (p480) consists of the two small towns of San Ramón and La Merced, both easily accessed by road from Lima, and several nearby villages, including Puerto Bermúdez and Oxapampa. From La Merced a paved road continues to the boomtown of Satipo, a major coffee-growing area.

A rough jungle road goes north from La Merced, via Puerto Bermúdez, to the river port of Pucallpa (p484), capital of the department of Ucayali. Most Pucallpa-bound travelers, however, take the better roads from Lima via Tingo María, or fly.

Further north, in the department of Loreto, is the small port of Yurimaguas (p491), reached from the north coast by road. Sequestered far in the northeast, and accessible only by riverboat from Pucallpa or Yurimaguas, or by air, is Peru's major jungle port, Iquitos (p494).

Wherever you go in the Amazon Basin, you can be sure of two things: there will be rainforest and it's going to rain. Even in the drier months of June to September, the area gets more rain than the mountains do in their wettest months. When it's not wet, it's scorchingly hot and, whatever the weather, humid.

SOUTHERN AMAZON

Abutting the neighboring nations of Bolivia and Brazil, the vast tract of the southern Amazon Basin is one of the Peru's remotest territories. Ecosystems here have been less disturbed than in any other part of the Amazon, yet there are also some of the best-developed facilities for ecotravelers.

Travel here is challenging, but the benefits are clear: visitors will be rewarded with a vibrant treasure trove of unforgettable close encounters of the wild kind.

PUERTO MALDONADO

☎ 082 / pop 56,450 / elev 250m

At first sight a mayhem of mud streets and manically tooting *mototaxis* (three-wheeled motorcycle rickshaw taxis), Puerto Maldonado soon endears itself to you. Its money-spinning proximity to some of the most easily visited animal-rich jungle in the entire Amazon Basin is its blessing but also its curse: travelers arrive yet all too quickly leave again en route to the lodges and wildlife on the nearby rivers.

Yet the town's languid, laid-back ambience invites you to linger. Whether you arrive by air or by road, Puerto Maldonado will certainly be a shock to the system. Unlike Peru's larger Amazon cities further north, this is a rawer, untidier jungle town with a mercilessly sweltering climate and a fair quantity of mosquitoes. But its beautiful plaza and burgeoning accommodation options will, together with a lively nightlife, provide plenty of reason to hang around here for a couple of days.

The town itself has been important over the years for rubber, logging and even for gold and oil prospecting, and its role as a crossroads is about to take on greater dimensions as the Interoceanic Hwy (p76), linking the Atlantic and Pacific Oceans via Brazil and Peru, takes shape. For the moment, though, it's of foremost importance to travelers as the jumping-off point for a voyage on the Ríos Tambopata and Madre de Dios, converging here. These watery wildernesses offer the most unspoilt yet accessible jungle locales in the country, yet are served by some excellent accommodation options for travelers who want that touch of luxury. Undisputedly, Puerto Maldonado gives the traveler the chance to see, feel and hear the Amazonian jungle like nowhere else in Peru.

ORIENTATION

The town is fairly compact. The small airport is 7km north of the town center, while buses arrive and depart from individual offices on Tambopata, some twelve blocks north of the center. Small river ports on both the Ríos Tambopata and Madre de Dios close to the town center serve the closer jungle lodges; more distant lodges are served by a jetty at Infierno, a 45-minute bus ride away.

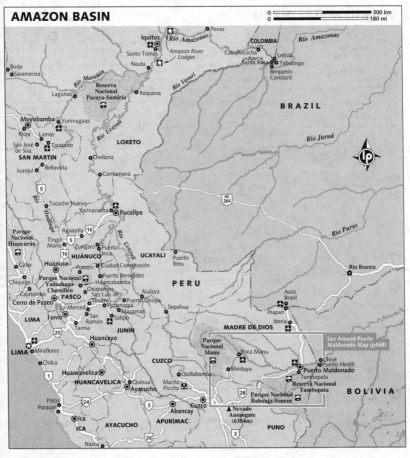

AMAZON BASIN

Information

IMMIGRATION

The border town of Iñapari (see p466) has regular border-crossing facilities to enter Brazil.

Oficina de migraciónes (immigration office; ☎ 57-1069; Av 28 de Julio 467; ☀ 8am-1pm Mon-Fri) To leave Peru via Puerto Heath for Bolivia (see p467), get your passport stamped here. Travelers can also extend their visas or tourist cards here.

INTERNET ACCESS

Internet is slower here than in other Peruvian cities, and costs about S2 per hour.

UnAMad (Av 2 de Mayo 287) Best of several places downtown.

ZonaVirtual.com (Velarde) Near Plaza de Armas.

LAUNDRY

Lavandería (Velarde 898) Wash your repulsive jungle rags here.

MEDICAL SERVICES

Hospital Santa Rosa (☎ 57-1019, 57-1046; Cajamarca 171) Provides basic services.

Social Seguro Hospital (☎ 57-1711) A newer option at Km 3 on the Cuzco road.

MONEY

Brazilian reais and Bolivian bolivianos used to be hard to exchange here. There is now a growing presence of Brazilian visitors since the opening of new bridge link at Iñapari, and Brazilian reais are becoming more commonplace.

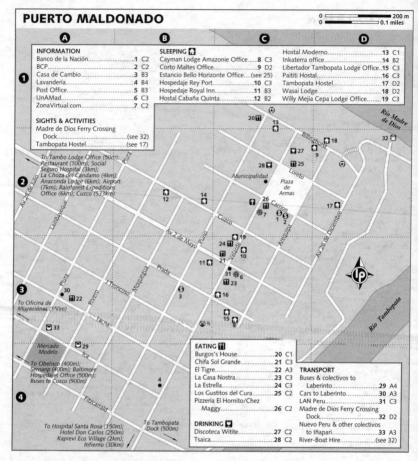

PUERTO MALDONADO

0 ——————— 200 m
0 ——————— 0.1 miles

INFORMATION
Banco de la Nación....................1 C2
BCP...2 C2
Casa de Cambio.........................3 B3
Lavandería.................................4 B4
Post Office.................................5 B3
UnAMad....................................6 C3
ZonaVirtual.com........................7 C2

SIGHTS & ACTIVITIES
Madre de Dios Ferry Crossing
    Dock..................................(see 32)
Tambopata Hostel.................(see 17)

SLEEPING
Cayman Lodge Amazonie Office......8 C3
Corto Maltes Office.....................9 D2
Estancio Bello Horizonte Office....(see 25)
Hospedaje Rey Port...................10 C3
Hospedaje Royal Inn..................11 B3
Hostal Cabaña Quinta................12 B2

Hostal Moderno.......................13 C1
Inkaterra office.........................14 B2
Libertador Tambopata Lodge Office..15 C3
Paititi Hostal...........................16 C3
Tambopata Hostel....................17 D2
Wasai Lodge...........................18 D2
Willy Mejia Cepa Lodge Office....19 C3

To Tambo Lodge Office (50m);
Restaurant (100m); Social
Seguro Hospital (3km);
La Choza del Candamo (4km);
Anaconda Lodge (6km); Airport
(7km); Rainforest Expeditions
Office (6km); Cuzco (533km)

Municipalidad

Plaza
de
Armas

To Oficina de
Migraciónes (150m)

Mercado
Modelo

To Obelisco (400m);
Sernanp (400m); Baltimore
Hospedajes Office (500m);
Buses to Cuzco (900m)

Río Madre
de Dios

Río Tambopata

EATING
Burgos's House......................20 C1
Chifa Sol Grande....................21 C3
El Tigre.................................22 A3
La Casa Nostra......................23 C3
La Estrella.............................24 C3
Los Gustitos del Cura.............25 C2
Pizzería El Hornito/Chez
    Maggy..............................26 C2

DRINKING
Discoteca Witite....................27 C1
Tsaica...................................28 C2

TRANSPORT
Buses & colectivos to
    Laberinto..........................29 A4
Cars to Laberinto..................30 A3
LAN Peru..............................31 C3
Madre de Dios Ferry Crossing
    Dock...............................32 D2
Nuevo Peru & other colectivos
    to Iñapari.........................33 A3
River-Boat Hire..................(see 32)

To Hospital Santa Rosa (150m);
Hotel Don Carlos (250m);
Kapievi Eco Village (2km);
Infierno (30km)

To Tambopata
Dock (500m)

Banco de la Nación (Plaza de Armas) Limited facilities; has a Multired ATM that does not take all cards.

BCP (formerly Banco de Crédito; Carrión 201) On Plaza de Armas; changes US cash or traveler's checks and has a Visa ATM.

Casa de Cambio (Puno at Prada) Standard rates for US dollars.

POST

Post office (Velarde) Southwest of the Plaza de Armas.

TOURIST INFORMATION

Sernanp (☎ 57-3278; rn_tambopata@sernanp.gob .pe; Av 28 de Julio, cuadra 8) The national-park office gives information and collects entrance fees (if you're going with a tour, guides sort this out); standard entrance to the

Tambopata reserve zone is S30 but increases to S65 for visiting areas away from the riverside lodges.

Tourist Booth (airport) Run by the Ministerio de Industria y Turismo; provides limited information on tours and jungle lodges.

Sights & Activities

Although the strangely cosmic, blue **Obelisco** (Fitzcarrald & Madre de Dios; admission S2; 🕙 10am-4pm) was designed as a modern *mirador* (lookout tower), its 30m height unfortunately does not rise high enough above the city for viewers to glimpse the rivers. The view is still fantastic: a distant glimmer of jungle and plenty of corrugated-metal roofs can be admired! Photos displayed on the way up document such historic moments as when the first *mototaxi* arrived in town. The tower is often closed during rainstorms: water from the roof drains down the stairwells, making them impassable.

The **Madre de Dios ferry** (per person S1; ⏱ dawn-dusk), at Puerto Capetania close to the Plaza de Armas, is a cheap way of seeing a little of this major Peruvian jungle river, which is about 500m wide at this point. The river traffic is colorfully ramshackle: *peki-pekis* (canoes powered by two-stroke motorcycle engines with outlandishly long propeller shafts) leave from the dock regularly, tracking at an almost impossible angle of 45 degrees to counter the strong river current. Brazil-bound drivers can ferry their vehicles across on wooden or metal catamarans to a rather desultory-looking ferry 'terminal' on the opposite side. Commit the sight to memory – when the Interoceanic Hwy comes to town, a huge bridge will span the river here, making all this chaos a thing of the past.

About an hour southeast of Puerto Maldonado is **Infierno** (Hell!), home and hub of activity for the Ese'eja tribespeople. It's a lively, spread-out settlement, which is establishing a reputation for its *ayahuasca* rituals, conducted by local shamans. *Ayahuasca* is the derivative of a hallucinogenic jungle vine, used to attain a purgative trancelike state by witch doctors for centuries and now increasingly popular with Westerners. Be wary of taking *ayahuasca*: it can have serious side effects, including severe convulsions and dramatic rises in blood pressure. If mixed with the wrong substances, it has even been known to be fatal. Arrange your own transport here via car or motorbike: *mototaxis* won't make the rough journey.

Courses

Tambopata Hostel (☎ 57-4201; www.tambopatahostel .com; Av 26 de Diciembre 234) can arrange fun salsa classes, basic Spanish lessons and Peruvian cookery classes for very reasonable prices.

Tours & Guides

Most visitors arrive with prearranged tours and stay at a jungle lodge – which is convenient but by no means the only possibility. You can arrange a tour upon arrival, either by going to the lodge offices, where you might get a small discount on a tour that would cost more in Lima or Cuzco, or by looking for a guide.

Choosing a guide is a lottery: they'll offer you tours for less, but stories of bad independent guides are not uncommon. Beware of guides at the airport, who often take you to a 'recommended' hotel (and collect a commission) and then hound you throughout your stay. There are crooked operators out there, too: shop around, don't prepay for any tour and, if paying an advance deposit, insist on a signed receipt. If you agree to a boat driver's price, make sure it includes the return trip.

There are about 30 guides with official licenses granted by the local Ministerio de Industria y Turismo. Many of the best ones work full time for one of the local jungle lodges. Having a licensed guide gives you some recourse in the unlikely event of a disastrous trip. Note that tours require boat rides to leave from Puerto Maldonado: boats use a lot of gas and are notoriously expensive to run. Guides charge from S75 to S150 per person per day, depending on the destination and number of people. Ask if quoted prices include park fees. Going with more people reduces the cost; in fact, some guides will only take tours with a three-person minimum.

The following are recommended:

Hernán Llavé Cortéz (☎ 57-3306, 982-61-0065) Speaks some English. If he's not on a tour, you'll find him in the baggage reception area of the airport, waiting for incoming flights.

Gerson Medina Valera (☎ 57-4201; gerson_bw@ hotmail.com) Formerly a guide for Rainforest Expeditions, Gerson has lots of experience in bird-watching tours and speaks fluent English. His one- to three-day Lago Sandoval tours (around S150 per person per day) are inclusive of all costs. You can also contact him at Tambopata Hostel (p464).

Victor Yohamona Dumay (☎ 982-68-6279; victor guideperu@hotmail.com) A well-known, experienced guide, also reachable through Hostal Cabaña Quinta (p464).

Sleeping

Options have markedly improved in the last few years. Besides the plethora of basic budget places, you can now choose from pleasant backpacker accommodation or comfortable lodges and hotels. Note that not all lodges have reservations offices in Puerto Maldonado; some only have offices in Cuzco, Lima or the USA.

BUDGET

Hospedaje Rey Port (☎ 57-1177; Velarde 457; s/d without bathroom 10/20, s/d S30/50) Rooms are mostly clean and have fans, but aren't remarkable. Bargain

---

WACKY AMAZON

You may know about off-the-beaten-track, but how about off-the-wall? Try one of these less-conventional Amazon experiences.

- Ditch the big names in the Tambopata lodge scene and stay with the locals at **Baltimore** (p473), where you can help out with community tasks and shower in waterfalls.

- Buy fresh coffee straight from the plantation at **Chanchamayo Highland Coffee** (p482) in La Merced.

- Experience an unexpected smattering of German culture and customs in **Oxapampa** (p483).

- Watch out for piranhas at the Amazon's only **golf club** (p497), in Iquitos.

- Swim off the **creeks and beaches** (p503) most Amazon travelers cruise straight past, on the road to Nauta, near Iquitos.

- Travel hours down the Amazon and step out of the wilderness at the art gallery of **Francisco Grippa** (p507) in Pevas, near Iquitos.

---

hunters: ground-floor courtyard rooms with shared bathrooms may be cheapest, but the top floor has large rooms with private bathrooms for S15 per person. They're grubbier but have good views (the hotel's best feature).

Hostal Moderno (☎ 30-0043; Billinghurst 359; s/d/tr without bathroom S15/22/30) Despite the up-to-date name, this family-run place has been around for decades. Rooms are simple but clean, although you'll feel like you're sleeping in a cargo crate. Occasional new licks of paint keep this quiet budget choice presentable.

Tambopata Hostel (☎ 57-4201; www.tambopatahostel .com; 26 de Diciembre 234; dm S20, s/d S35/65, s/d without bathroom S25/50; 💻) Puerto Maldonado finally has the backpacker accommodation it desperately needed. This clean, relaxing hostel has a mix of dorm and private rooms abutting a garden courtyard with hammocks, and a huge breakfast is included in the price. There are secure lockers and the owner is one of the town's best jungle guides.

Kapievi Eco Village (☎ 901-99-686, katherinapz@ hotmail.com; Carretera Tambopata Km 1.5, bungalows per person without bathroom S30) This rustic, reader-recommended retreat, 2km southwest of town, lets backpackers experience a taste of lodge life without the price tag, in several basic bungalows (for one, two or four people) enclosed within a wild plot of jungle scrub. The laid-back owners offer vegetarian food, *ayahuasca* ceremonies and yoga classes. Food and drink is an additional S15 per person per day.

Hospedaje Royal Inn (☎ 57-1048; 2 de Mayo 333; s/d S30/40) A good choice for travelers, sporting lots of large, clean rooms with fans around a courtyard that has seen better days. Cable TV

comes with each. Some rooms are quite dark; get a courtyard-facing room as street-facing rooms are noisy.

MIDRANGE

our pick Anaconda Lodge (☎ 79-276; Av Aeropuerto Km 6; www.anacondajunglelodge.com; bungalow s/d/tr S100/160/280, bungalow without bathroom s/d S50/80; 🛒) Cocooned in its own tropical garden on the edge of town, Anaconda has a decidedly more remote feel than its location would suggest. There are eight double-room bungalows with shared bathroom and four luxury bungalows with private facilities; all are mosquito netted. There's also camping space (per person S20), a small pool and a spacious two-floor restaurant-bar serving great Thai food and pancake breakfasts. Maldonado's quiet airport is only a few hundred meters away but once inside the gates, you'll feel a universe apart.

Paititi Hostal (☎ 57-4667; fax 57-2567; Prada 290; s/d incl breakfast S70/90) A new, relatively flash, central place, the Paititi has a series of spacious, airy rooms, many full of attractive old wooden furniture, along with telephones and cable TV. A continental breakfast is included, and there's even hot water at night – very un-Amazon.

Hostal Cabaña Quinta (☎ 57-1045; fax 57-3336; cabanaquinta_reservas@hotmail.com; Cuzco 535; s/d standard S70/120, s/d superior S120/160; 🛒 🛒) This is the hotel of choice for folks wanting economical comfort in the town center. Standard rooms have cold showers, fans and TV; superior rooms boast air-con, minifridges and hot showers as well. There is a restaurant, room service for superior rooms, and a decent pool.

AMAZON BASIN

Wasai Lodge (☎ 57-2290; www.wasai.com; Billinghurst at Arequipa; s/d S120/160; 🈁 🈁) This small lodge consists of comfortable wooden bungalows overlooking the Madre de Dios. A few rooms offer air-con for an extra S30. Minifridges, hot showers, cable TV and river views, however, are standard. The room lighting is pretty abysmal, so bring a flashlight for good measure. There is a good restaurant (mains S15 to S20), room service, a bar and a small pool. The lodge arranges various trips in the local area.

Hotel Don Carlos (☎ 57-1323, 57-1029; reservas maldonado@hoteldoncarlos.com; León Velarde 1271; s/d incl breakfast S150/180) The decent-sized, wood-paneled rooms here have hot showers, mini-fridges and TVs. The location – about 1km southwest of the center – is quiet, and the Río Tambopata can be seen from the grounds. A little restaurant, which opens on demand, has an outdoor dining balcony and room service. Airport transfer is included in the rates. The promotional lower rates are for walk-in guests or in the low season.

Outside Puerto Maldonado are a dozen jungle lodges (see p469 and p471).

Eating

There are no fancy restaurants in town, although several down-to-earth, excellent-value places serve up good Peruvian food. Regional specialties include *juanes* (rice steamed with fish or chicken in a banana leaf), *chilcano* (a broth of fish chunks flavored with the native cilantro herb) and *parrillada de la selva* (a barbecue of marinated meat, often game, in a Brazil-nut sauce). A *plátano* (plantain) is served boiled or fried as an accompaniment to many meals.

La Casa Nostra (☎ 57-2647; Av 2 de Mayo 287a; snacks S3-8; 🕑 7am-1pm & 5-11pm) This convivial joint used to serve as a local hangout for guides; it has now moved to smaller premises and lost its hangout status but remains the top cafe in town. It serves varied breakfasts, tamales, great juices, snacks, desserts and Puerto Maldonado's best coffee.

Los Gustitos del Cura (☎ 57-3107; Loreto 258; snacks S3-8; 🕑 11am-10pm) For a sweet treat or the best ice cream in town, drop in to this French-owned patisserie with a pleasant courtyard at the rear. Sandwiches, cakes and drinks are dished up, and local *objets d'arte* are on sale.

Chifa Sol Grande (Av 2 de Mayo 306; menú S5-8; 🕑 lunch & dinner) The Peruvian Amazon version of Chinese food is actually quite tasty. This place is the most locally popular joint to try it out. Closing time is officially 11pm, though the place often stays open much later.

La Estrella (☎ 57-3107; Velarde 474; menú from S6; 🕑 5pm-10pm) This chicken restaurant looks like a US fast-food outlet. Its clean, bright decor attracts locals happy to wolf down the quarter-chicken, fries and chicken broth – the standard and most popular menu item.

Restaurant (cnr Av 2 de Mayo & Madre de Dios; mains S8-15; 🕑 dinner) It may have no name, street number or phone number but this place is far from unknown by the locals, who flock here for great fish with rice and *plátano*. Food is prepared on a grill outside and tables fill up fast.

Burgos's House (☎ 57-3653; Puno 106; mains S13-22; 🕑 10am-10pm) There has long been need of a restaurant like this in the town center: large, airy, courteous and serving up regional goodies with an emphasis on fish. Burgos's also provides *juanes* and a mixed platter of jungle dishes for S22.

El Tigre (☎ 57-2286; Tacna 456; menú S10-15; 🕑 lunch) This place is popular at lunch for its ceviche (seafood marinated in lime juice). Other local fish dishes are also offered.

Pizzería El Hornito/Chez Maggy (☎ 57-2082; Carrión 271; pizzas S15-25; 🕑 6pm-late) This popular but dimly lit hangout on the Plaza de Armas serves pasta and amply sized, wood-fired pizzas – the best in town. There's no lunch: the oven makes it too hot during the day!

Also consider the ambient restaurant at Wasai Lodge (opposite).

Drinking

A handful of nightclubs sputter into life late on weekend nights, usually with recorded and occasionally live music. Loreto has most of the good bars.

Discoteca Witite (☎ 57-2419, 57-3861; Velarde 151) Brightly painted Witite has stood the test of time. The crowd is mixed and at weekends the partying here goes on all night.

Tsaica (Loreto 327) With funky indigenous art on the walls, this is Puerto's liveliest bar. Recommended.

La Choza del Candamo (☎ 57-2872; 🕑 7pm-late) Outside of town, this relaxed *peña* (bar/club featuring live folkloric music) has a restaurant where you can sample food from all three regions of Peru – coast, mountain and jungle – and listen to the latest live musical offerings. You'll find it 4km along the airport road.

BORDER CROSSING: BRAZIL VIA PUERTO MALDONADO

A reasonable, mostly paved road, part of the future Interoceanic Hwy, goes from Puerto Maldonado to Iberia and on to Iñapari, on the Brazilian border. Along the road are small settlements of people involved in the Brazil nut farming, cattle ranching and logging industries. After 170km you reach **Iberia**, which has very basic hotels. The village of **Iñapari** is another 70km beyond Iberia.

Peruvian border formalities can be carried out in Iñapari. Stores around the main plaza accept and change both Peruvian and Brazilian currency; if leaving Peru, it's best to get rid of any nuevos soles here. Small denominations of US cash are negotiable, and hotels and buses often quote rates in US dollars. A block north of the plaza, **Hostal Milagritos** (☎ 082-57-4274; s/d US$8/13) has the best rooms. From Iñapari, you can cross over the new bridge to **Assis Brasil**, which has better hotels (starting from around US$10 per person).

US citizens need to get a Brazilian visa beforehand, either in the USA or Lima. It's about 100km (four hours) by bus from here to Brasiléia, then another 244km (4½ hours) by paved road to the important Brazilian city of Rio Branco.

For detailed coverage beyond this point, pick up Lonely Planet's *Brazil*, or get *The Amazon Travel Guide* from the **Lonely Planet online shop** (http://shop.lonelyplanet.com).

Shopping

Proximity to local tribes means many of the lodges around town, such as Posadas Amazonas on the Rio Tambopata, are far better for purchasing local handicrafts than in the town itself.

Getting There & Away

Most travelers fly here from Lima or Cuzco. The long road or river trips are only for travelers prepared to put up with discomfort and delay. A new highway is slowly being established to link western Brazil with the Andes; when complete, road travel from Cuzco to Puerto Maldonado will be a viable option.

AIR

The airport is 7km out of town. Scheduled flights leave every day to and from Lima via Cuzco with **LAN Peru** (☎ 57-3677; www.lan .com; Velarde 503) and **Star Perú** (☎ 01-705-9000; www .starperu.com; airport). Schedules and airlines can change from one year to the next, but numerous travel agents in the town center have the latest details.

Light aircraft to any destination can be chartered as long as you pay for five seats and the return trip. Ask at the airport.

BOAT

Hire boats at the Río Madre de Dios ferry dock for local excursions or to take you downriver to the Bolivian border. It's difficult to find boats going up the Madre de Dios (against the current) to Manu; Cuzco is a better departure point for Manu. Occasionally, people reach Puerto Maldonado by boat from Manu (with the current) or from the Bolivian border (against the current). If you're set on the former option, Amazon Trails Peru of Cuzco (p475) can arrange boat/bus options with a Manu package. Transportation is infrequent: be prepared for waits of several days.

At the Tambopata dock, 2km south of town and reached by *mototaxis*, there are public boats up the Tambopata as far as the community of Baltimore. The *Tiburón* leaves twice a week (currently Monday and Thursday) and can drop you off at lodges between Puerto Maldonado and Baltimore. The fare is S20 or less, depending how far you go. All passengers must stop at La Torre Puesto de Control (checkpoint), where passports and Sernanp permits (S30) are needed. (For details on Sernanp permits, see p462).

When transporting visitors upriver, some Río Tambopata lodges avoid two hours of river travel by taking the bumpy track to Infierno (about one hour), and continuing by boat from there. Travel to Infierno needs to be arranged in advance: there is nowhere to stay there and no boats await passengers.

BUS & TAXI

Laberinto-bound trucks, minibuses and *colectivos* (shared taxis) leave Puerto Maldonado for Laberinto (1½ hours), passing the turnoff to Baltimore at Km 37 on the Cuzco road. They leave frequently during the morning and less often in the afternoon from the corner of Ica and Rivero. *Colectivos* to Iñapari (S40, three hours), near the borders with Brazil and Bolivia, leave from **Nuevo Peru** (☎ 57-4235; cnr Piura & Ica) when they have four passengers. Other companies on the same block also advertise this trip.

The 500km road to Cuzco has improved rapidly in the last few years, and long sections were already paved when this book was researched. That said, it was dubbed Peru's worst road before improvements began, and while there are now fewer potholes, roadworks are still causing two- or three-hour delays. The journey currently takes 17 to 20 hours, sometimes more in the wet season. When complete, this road will form part of the Interoceanic Hwy. Completion is still some time off but several brave bus companies already ply the route, including **Expreso Los Chankas** (☎ 83-72-2441, S50), and leave around 1:30pm from offices on Tambopata, 12 blocks north of the town center. It's an incredibly scenic journey and the adventurous, airplane loathing or budget minded might wish to give it a go even now. When paved, the route should take under eight hours.

GETTING AROUND

Mototaxis take two or three passengers (and light luggage) to the airport for S5 to S7, depending on your powers of negotiation.

Short rides around town cost S2 or less. There are also *mototaxi* Honda 90s that will take one passenger around town for about S1.

You can rent motorcycles if you want to see some of the surrounding countryside; go in pairs in case of breakdowns or accident. There are several motorcycle-rental places, mainly on Prada between Velarde and Puno. They charge about S7 per hour and have mainly small, 100cc bikes. Driving one is fun but crazed local drivers and awful road conditions can make this option intimidating. Bargain for all-day discounts.

AROUND PUERTO MALDONADO
Río Madre de Dios

This important river flows eastwards past Puerto Maldonado, heading into Bolivia and Brazil, and the Amazon proper. In the wet season it is brown colored, flows swiftly and looks very impressive, carrying huge logs and other jungle flotsam and jetsam downstream. The main reason people come here is to stay for a few days in one of several jungle lodges, all of which are to be found between one and two hours upstream from Puerto Maldonado itself.

Additionally, travelers can partake in fishing and nature trips, and visit beaches and

---

BORDER CROSSING: BOLIVIA VIA PUERTO MALDONADO

There are two ways of reaching Bolivia from the Puerto Maldonado area. One is to go to Brasiléia in Brazil (see opposite) and cross the Río Acre by ferry or bridge to **Cobija** in Bolivia, where there are hotels, banks, an airstrip with erratically scheduled flights further into Bolivia, and a gravel road to the city of **Riberalta** (12 hours in the dry season).

Alternatively, hire a boat at Puerto Maldonado's Madre de Dios dock to take you to the Peru–Bolivia border at **Puerto Pardo**. A few minutes from Puerto Pardo by boat is **Puerto Heath**, a military camp on the Bolivian side. The trip takes half a day and costs about US$100 (but is negotiable) – the boat will carry several people. With time and luck, you may also be able to find a cargo boat that's going there anyway and will take passengers more cheaply.

It's possible to continue down the river on the Bolivian side, but this can take days (even weeks) to arrange and isn't cheap. Travel in a group to share costs, and avoid the dry months of July to September, when the river is too low. From Puerto Heath, continue down the Río Madre de Dios as far as Riberalta (at the confluence of the Madre de Dios and Beni, far into northern Bolivia), where road and air connections can be made. Basic food and shelter (bring a hammock) can be found en route. When river levels allow, a cargo and passenger boat runs from Puerto Maldonado to Riberalta and back about twice a month, but this trip is rarely done by foreigners. From Puerto Heath, a dirt road goes to **Chivé** (1½ hours by bus), from where you can continue to Cobija (six hours).

Get your Peruvian exit stamp in Puerto Maldonado. Bolivian entry stamps can be gotten in Puerto Heath or Cobija. Visas are not available, however, so get one ahead of time in Lima or your home country if you need it. Formalities are generally slow and relaxed.

AMAZON BASIN

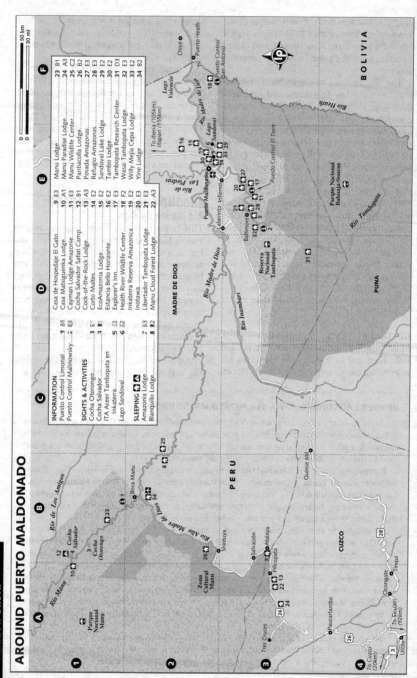

AROUND PUERTO MALDONADO

INFORMATION
Puesto Control Limonal	**1** B1
Puesto Control Malinowsky	**2** E3

SIGHTS & ACTIVITIES
Cocha Otorongo	**3** E7
Cocha Salvador	**4** B1
ITA Aceer Tambopata en Inkaterra	**5** E2
Lago Sandoval	**6** E2

SLEEPING
Amazonia Lodge	**7** B3
Blanquillo Lodge	**8** B2
Casa de Hospedaje El Gato	**9** E3
Casa Matsiguenka Lodge	**10** A1
Cayman Lodge Amazonie	**11** E3
Cocha Salvador Safari Camp	**12** B1
Cock-of-the-Rock Lodge	**13** A3
Corto Maltes	**14** E2
EcoAmazonia Lodge	**15** E2
Estancia Bello Horizonte	**16** E2
Explorer's Inn	**17** E2
Heath River Wildlife Center	**18** F2
Inkaterra Reserva Amazonica	**19** E2
Inotawa	**20** E3
Libertador Tambopata Lodge	**21** E3
Manu Cloud Forest Lodge	**22** A3
Manu Lodge	**23** B1
Manu Paradise Lodge	**24** A3
Manu Wildlife Center	**25** C2
Pantiacolla Lodge	**26** B2
Posada Amazonas	**27** E3
Refugio Amazonas	**28** E2
Sandoval Lake Lodge	**29** E2
Tambo Lodge	**30** E2
Tambopata Research Center	**31** D3
Wasai Tambopata Lodge	**32** E3
Willy Mejia Cepal Lodge	**33** E3
Yine Lodge	**34** B2

indigenous communities. Some excursions involve camping or staying in simple thatched shelters. Lodges often provide rubber boots for the muddy jungle paths. (For advice on kit to bring with you, see p472).

Madre de Dios and Tambopata lodges quote their prices in US dollars, which include transportation unless stated. Luggage per person is often limited but can be stored in lodge offices in Puerto Maldonado.

SIGHTS & ACTIVITIES

The **ITA Aceer Tambopata en Inkaterra** (www.wcupa .edu/aceer) is an important research center that was built on the site of a 19th-century house formerly occupied by one of the first doctors to practice in this part of the Amazon. ITA retains parts of the original house while providing modern research facilities in the new construction. Although the modern accommodations are mainly for researchers, ecotourists can visit to attend lectures and examine the small exhibit about local conservation issues. The Inkaterra Reserva Amazonica Lodge is 7km away.

You can reach Lago Sandoval (p470) from some of the lodges here.

SLEEPING

Most lodge-style accommodations are based along the rivers. Riverside lodges are listed as you travel away from Puerto Maldonado, irrespective of price.

Corto Maltes (☎ 082-57-3831; www.cortomaltes -amazonia.com; s 3 days & 2 nights US$240); Puerto Maldonado (Map p462; Billinghurst, cuadra 2) The closest lodge to Puerto Maldonado is traveler-friendly and upbeat. Only 5km from town, this lodge offers 15 comfortable, fully screened, high-ceilinged bungalows with solid mattresses, eye-catching Shipibo indigenous wall art, patios with two hammocks, and cheerful decorative touches in the public areas. Electricity is available from dusk until 10:30pm, and showers have hot water. The French owners pride themselves on the excellent European-Peruvian fusion cuisine.

Tambo Lodge (☎ 082-57-2227; tambojunglelodge@ hotmail.com; per person 3 days/2 nights US$210) Puerto Maldonado (Map p462; Ancash 250) Just beyond Corto Maltes, this pleasant lodge offers 14 large, airy bungalows, each furnished with hot-water showers and copious supplies of fresh drinking water, around a clearing in secondary jungle. The main restaurant-bar area is con-

vivial, with lots of board games. Included are trips to Sandoval Lake, a 5km walk away, and Monkey Island (supposedly containing each of the Amazon's monkey species).

Inkaterra Reserva Amazonica (www.inkaterra.com; 3 days & 2 nights s/d US$673/1082, ste per person double occupancy US$739); Cuzco (Map pp224-5; ☎ 084-24-5314, Plaza Nazarenas 167); Lima (☎ 01-610-0400, Andalucía 174, Miraflores) Further down the Madre de Dios, almost 16km from Puerto Maldonado, this option is exceptionally luxurious, and offers a better look at the jungle. Tours here include 10km of private hiking trails, and a series of swaying, narrow, jungle canopy walkways up to 35m above the jungle floor for flora and fauna observation.

A huge, traditionally thatched, cone-shaped, two-story reception, restaurant, bar, library and relaxation area greets the arriving traveler. Some of the Southern Amazon's best meals are served here; travelers with special dietary needs can be accommodated. There are occasional alfresco barbecues, where guests stuff their own choice of food into bamboo tubes and leave them on hot coals to roast. A resident kinkajou – an odd, raccoon-like creature – sometimes darts among the tables, startling diners.

Upstairs, four separate sitting areas come complete with couches and balconies for imbibing the views and spotting the birdlife outside. A separate building houses an interpretation center (with maps, photos, casts of mammal footprints – ask about making your own – and occasional slide shows). Guides speak English, French or Italian. About 40 rustic individual cabins have bathrooms and porches with two hammocks. Six suites boast huge bathrooms, writing desks and two queen beds each.

EcoAmazonia Lodge (www.ecoamazonia.com.pe; per person 3 days & 2 nights US$210, per person 4 days & 3 nights US$280); Cuzco (Map pp224-5; ☎ 084-23-6159, Garcilaso 210, Office 206); Lima (☎ 01-242-2708, Palacios 292, Miraflores); Puerto Maldonado (☎ 082-57-3491) Roughly 30km from Puerto Maldonado is another lodge boasting a huge, thatch-roofed restaurant and bar, with fine river views from the 2nd floor. Guides speak English, French and Italian; the knowledgeable manager also speaks Japanese. Forty-seven rustic, completely screened bungalows each have a bathroom and a small sitting room. There are several trails from this lodge, including a tough 14km hike to a lake, and several shorter walks. Boat tours to local

AMAZON BASIN

lakes and along the rivers are also offered, and *ayahuasca* ceremonies can be arranged by advance request.

There is one superb getaway located away from the rivers in the jungle itself. For a touch of Franco-Swiss style and comfort, you won't go far wrong at the relaxing hideaway resort of **Estancia Bello Horizonte** (☎ 082-57-2748, 982-60-2356; estancia@estanciabellohorizonte.com; JM Grain 105, Puerto Maldonado; per person 4 days & 3 nights US$320), which is built all in local wood and situated in a large open clearing on a ridge overlooking the rainforest. Located 20km from Puerto Maldonado on the east side of the Río Madre de Dios, the final approach to the Estancia is along a 6km private road through dense jungle. The wooden accommodation bungalows contain smallish, comfortable rooms with bathrooms; each has a hammock and reclining chairs for lounging in. The main building contains a relaxing dining, reading, drinking and chill-out space where you can enjoy impressive views over the virgin rainforest. The child-friendly grounds include a soccer pitch, a volleyball court, a swimming pool and sign-posted jungle walks.

Lago Sandoval

An attractive jungle lake, Lago Sandoval is surrounded by different types of rainforest and is about two hours from Puerto Maldonado down the Madre de Dios. The best way to see wildlife is to stay overnight and take a boat ride on the lake, though day trips to the lake are offered. Half the trip is done by boat and the other half on foot. Bring your own food and water. For about S75 to S125 (bargain – several people can travel for this price), a boat

from Puerto Maldonado will drop you at the beginning of the trail and pick you up later. The boat driver will also guide you to the lake on request. With luck, you might see caiman, turtles, exotic birds, monkeys and maybe the endangered giant river otters that live in the lake.

You can also reach the lake by hiking along a 3km trail from the jungle lodges here, located between Reserva Amazonica Lodge and EcoAmazonia Lodge but on the opposite (south) side of the river. The flat trail has boardwalks and gravel, and is easily passable year-round. From the end of this trail, you can continue 2km on a narrower, less-maintained trail to the inexpensive Willy Mejía Cepa Lodge, or take a boat ride across the lake to Sandoval Lake Lodge, the best lodge in this area.

Family-run **Willy Mejía Cepa Lodge** (r per person US$15-25) has been offering basic accommodations to budget travelers for two decades. Willy's father, Don César Mejía Zaballos, homesteaded the lake 50 years ago. The lodge can sleep 20 people in bungalow-style rooms with shared bathrooms. Bottled drinks are sold. Prices include simple family meals, accommodation and excursions (in Spanish). Book first in Puerto Maldonado at Velarde 187 and ask about discounts, which are frequently given according to group size.

Sandoval Lake Lodge (per 3 days/2 nights s/d US$348/596) is on the other side of the lake to Willy Mejía. Getting there is half the fun. After hiking the 3km to the lake (bicycle rickshaws are available for luggage and for people with walking difficulties), you board canoes to negotiate narrow canals through a flooded

---

PUNK CHICKENS

Listen carefully as your boat passes the banks of the Río Tambopata. If you hear lots of hissing, grunting and sounds of breaking vegetation, it is likely that you have stumbled upon the elaborate mating ritual of one of the Amazon's weirdest birds, the hoatzin. This is an oversized wild chicken with a blue face and a large crest on its head (hence the nickname 'punk chicken'). Scientists have been unable to classify this bird as a member of any other avian family, mainly due to the two claws the young have on each wing. To evade predators, hoatzin chicks will fall out of the nest to the river and use their claws to help them scramble back up the muddy banks. The clawed wing is a feature no other airborne creature since the pterodactyl has possessed. The hoatzin's appearance is outdone by its terrible smell (caused by an exclusively leaf-based diet, which necessitates their having multiple microorganisms in their stomachs to aid digestion), which may well be the first indication they are nearby. Good news for the hoatzin: their odd odor makes their flesh taste bad, so they are rarely hunted. In this age of rainforest depletion, they are one of the few native birds with a flourishing population.

AMAZON BASIN

palm-tree forest inhabited by red-bellied ma-caws, then silently paddle across the beautiful lake to the lodge. With luck, you may spot the endangered giant river otter, several pairs of which live in the lake (early morning is best). Various monkey species and a host of birds and reptiles can also be seen. Hikes into the forest are offered, and the knowledgeable guides are multilingual.

The spacious lodge is built on a hilltop about 30m above the lake and surrounded by primary forest. The lodge was built from salvaged driftwood; the owners pride them-selves on the fact that no primary forest was cut during construction (this is also true of some other lodges, though not always men-tioned). The rooms, with heated showers and ceiling fans, are the best in the area. The restaurant-bar area is huge, airy and con-ducive to relaxing and chatting. Book with **InkaNatura** (www.inkanatura.com); Cuzco (Map pp224-5; ☎ 084-23-1138; Ricardo Palma J1 Urb Santa Mónica & Plateros 361); Lima (☎ 01-440-2022; Manuel Bañón 461, San Isidro).

Lago Valencia
Just off the Río Madre de Dios and near the Bolivian border, Lago Valencia is about 60km from Puerto Maldonado. At least two days are needed for a visit here, though three or four days are recommended. This lake report-edly offers the region's best **fishing**, as well as good **bird-watching** and **wildlife-watching** (bring your binoculars). There are trails into the jungle around the lake. Lodges nearer Puerto Maldonado can arrange tours, as can independent guides.

Río Heath
About two hours south of the Río Madre de Dios and along the Río Heath (the latter forming the Peru–Bolivia border), the **Parque Nacional Bahuaja-Sonene** (admission S30) has some of the best wildlife in Peru's Amazon region, including such rarities as the maned wolf and the spider monkey, although these are hard to see. Infrastructure in the park, one of the nation's largest, is limited, and wildlife-watching trips are in their infancy here. The park entrance fee should be paid at Sernanp (p462) in Puerto Maldonado, because check-points along the way don't sell tickets.

The simple, 10-room **Heath River Wildlife Center** (s/d 5 days & 4 nights US$915/1430) is owned by the Ese'eja indigenous people of Sonene, who pro-vide guiding and cultural services. Trails into

the recently created Parque Nacional Bahuaja-Sonene are available, and field biologists have assessed this area as one of the most bio-diverse in southeastern Peru. Capybaras are frequently seen, and guided tours to a nearby *colpa* (clay lick), a popular attraction for ma-caws and parrots, are arranged. Hot water is provided and park entrance fees are included. The first and last nights of tours are spent at Sandoval Lake Lodge (opposite). Contact **InkaNatura** (www.inkanatura.com); Cuzco (Map pp224-5; ☎ 084-23-1138; Ricardo Palma J1 Urb Santa Mónica & Plateros 361); Lima (☎ 01-440-2022; Manuel Bañón 461, San Isidro).

Río Tambopata
The Río Tambopata is a major tributary of the Río Madre de Dios, joining it at Puerto Maldonado. Boats go up the river, past sev-eral good lodges, and into the **Reserva Nacional Tambopata** (admission S30), an important protected area divided into the reserve itself and the **zona de amortiguamiento** (buffer zone). The park entrance fee needs to be paid at the Sernanp office in Puerto Maldonado (p462), unless you are on a guided tour, in which case you will pay at the relevant lodge office. An additional fee is required if you are head-ing into the reserve proper (such as to the Tambopata Research Center) rather than just the buffer zone.

Travelers heading up the Río Tambopata must register their passport numbers at the Puesto Control (Guard Post) next to the Explorer's Inn and show their national-park entrance permits obtained in Puerto Maldonado. Visiting the reserve is only re-ally possible if you book a guided stay at one of the lodges within it. One of the reserve's highlights is the Colpa de Guacamayos (Macaw Clay Lick), one of the largest natu-ral clay licks in the country. It attracts hun-dreds of birds and is a spectacular sight (see the January 1994 *National Geographic* for a photographic story).

Lodges are listed in the order in which you would arrive at them if traveling from Puerto Maldonado.

our pick **Posada Amazonas** (s/d 3 days & 2 nights US$385/590) is about two hours from Puerto Maldonado along Río Tambopata, followed by a 10-minute uphill walk. The *posada* is on the land of the Ese'eja community of Infierno, and tribal members, as well as local *mestizos* (persons of mixed indigenous and Spanish descent), are among the guides. (Several other

AMAZON BASIN

JUNGLE CHECKLIST

If this is your first voyage into the jungle, you'll find it far more pleasant and relaxing than the movies make out. The jungle, you'll see, has largely been packaged to protect delicate tourists. With lodge facilities and the below kit list, you should be ready for most eventualities.

■ Two pairs of shoes, one for jungle traipsing and one for wearing at camp.

■ Spare clothes – because of the humidity, clothes get wet quickly; take a spare towel, too.

■ Binoculars and a camera with a zoom lens, to catch wildlife at close quarters.

■ Flashlight for night walks and when the electricity cuts out.

■ Mosquito repellent with DEET – bugs are everywhere. Mosquitoes can bite without you knowing it; ants bite, too – hard.

■ Sunblock and sunglasses – you'll be in the sun a lot.

■ First-aid kit for basics such as bites, stings or diarrhea.

■ Plastic bags to waterproof your gear and pack nonbiodegradable litter to take back with you.

■ Lightweight rainproof jacket, because it will rain – lots.

■ Sleeping bag, mat or hammock if you'll be sleeping outside.

■ Books – cell phones don't work and neither do TVs; electricity is limited to a few hours per day.

For tips on viewing wildlife, see p68.

---

lodges use 'native' guides, but these are often *mestizos* rather than tribe members) There are excellent chances of seeing macaws and parrots on a small salt lick nearby, and giant river otters are often found swimming in lakes close to the lodge. Guides at the lodge are mainly English-speaking Peruvian naturalists with varying interests. Your assigned guide stays with you throughout the duration of your stay. Visits are also made to the Centro Ñape ethnobotanical center, where medicine is produced for members of the Ese'eja community. There is a medicinal-plant trail and, a short hike from the lodge, a 30m-high observation platform giving superb views of the rainforest canopy. The lodge has 30 large double rooms with private showers and open (unglazed) windows overlooking the rainforest. Mosquito nets are provided. Electricity is available at lunchtime and from 5:30pm to 9pm. Book with **Rainforest Expeditions** (www.perunature.com) Cuzco (☎ 084-24-6243, cusco@rainforest.com.pe, Portal de Carnes 236); Lima (☎ 01-421-8347; postmaster@rainforest.com.pe; Aramburu 166, Miraflores); Puerto Maldonado (☎ 082-57-2575; pem@rainforest.com.pe; Av Aeropuerto Km 6, CPM La Joya).

Inotawa (☎ in Puerto Maldonado 082-57-2511, in Lima 01-479-9247; www.inotawaexpeditions.com; per person 3 days & 2 nights US$240) lies a few kilometers beyond Posada Amazonas and is a good budget option, although guides here don't have the repu-

tation that those of other nearby lodges do. It's a 200m walk up from the river. Rates include transport, meals, guided walks and boat rides. The lodge features a high roof with a transparent window at the ceiling apex, allowing more light than most other lodges. Electricity is available from 6pm to 10pm. Most of the 10 rooms have shared bathrooms, but there are also a couple of rooms with their own. A large, cool hammock room invites relaxation, and the Swiss-Peruvian owners deliver excellent food with a European flair. Campers can pitch their tent on the grounds for a small fee. On advance request, guides speaking German, French and English are available. Extra nights cost US$45 per person.

Explorer's Inn (www.explorersinn.com; s/d 3 days & 2 nights US$238/396) Cuzco (☎ 084-23-5342, Plateros 365); Lima (☎ 01-447-8888, 01-447-4761; sales@explorersinn.com; Alcanfores 459, Miraflores) Puerto Maldonado (☎ 082-57-2078) is 58km from Puerto Maldonado (three to four hours of river travel) and features 15 rustic double and 15 triple rooms, all with bathrooms and screened windows. Around since the '70s, it's a more open lodge than the others previously mentioned, in a pleasant grassy clearing. The central lodge room has a restaurant, a bar and a small museum. Outside is a soccer pitch, and you can also browse through an assortment of plants in the medicinal garden. The lodge is located in the former

55-sq-km Zona Preservada Tambopata (itself now surrounded by the much larger Reserva Nacional Tambopata). More than 600 species of bird have been recorded in this preserved zone, which is a world record for bird species sighted in one area. Despite such (scientifically documented) records, the average tourist won't see much more here than at any of the other Río Tambopata lodges during the standard two-night visit. The 38km of trails around the lodge can be explored independently or with naturalist Peruvian guides. German, English and French are spoken. Rates include meals and guided tours. Four-night tours include a visit to the macaw clay lick (single US$530, double US$900).

Next up is the new **Cayman Lodge Amazonie** (☎ 082-57-1970; www.cayman-lodge-amazonie.com; s/d 2 days & 3 nights US$400/560); Puerto Maldonado (Map p462; Arequipa 655), some 70km from Puerto Maldonado. Run by the effervescent French Anny and her English-speaking Peruvian partner, Daniel, this lodge boasts an open, relaxing environment with banana, *cocona* (peach tomato) and mango trees in a lush tropical garden. Activities include visits to the oxbow Lagunas Sachavacayoc and Condenado, and there is also a five- to seven-day shamanism program, where you can learn about tropical medicine and even be treated for ailments. There is a large bar and restaurant area. The rooms are a little on the small side, but are more than comfortable; windows have mosquito meshes. One of its more arresting features is the hammock house, from where you can watch the sun set over the Río Tambopata.

Further along is the **Libertador Tambopata Lodge** (☎ 082-57-1726, 082-968-0022; www.tambopatalodge.com; s/d 3 days & 2 nights US$379/614); Puerto Maldonado (Map p462; Prada 269). Set mainly near secondary forest, this considerably more luxurious lodge is still within the Reserva Tambopata. A short boat ride from here will get you into primary forest. Tours to nearby lakes and to the salt lick are included on tours of four days or longer (single from US$688, double from US$1160), and naturalist guides are available. There are 12km of well-marked trails, which you can wander at will without a guide. The lodge consists of a series of spacious individual bungalows, some of which have solar-generated hot water. Each enjoys a tiled patio with a table and chairs, and all look out onto a lush tropical garden. There is the mandatory

restaurant and a cozy separate bar complex: the overall effect is like a set from the TV series *Lost*.

New in 2006, the latest addition to the jungle accommodations scene is the rather impressive **Refugio Amazonas** (4 days & 3 nights s/d US$565/860). This lodge is better for a longer stay, as it is a fairly lengthy boat ride up the river to get here. It is built on a 20-sq-km private reserve in the buffer zone of the Tambopata National Reserve. While it feels just that little more isolated, the lodge is not lacking in creature comforts, with a large reception, dining and drinking area. Rooms are comfortable and similar in style to those of its sister lodge, the Posada Amazonas. Activities include a Brazil-nut trail and camp and, for children, a dedicated rainforest trail. The increased remoteness usually means better opportunities for spotting wildlife. Book with **Rainforest Expeditions** (www.perunature.com); Cuzco (☎ 084-24-6243; cusco@rainforest.com.pe; Portal de Carnes 236); Lima (☎ 01-421-8347; postmaster@rainforest .com.pe; fax 01-421-8347; Aramburu 166, Miraflores); Puerto Maldonado (☎ 082-57-2575; pem@rainforest.com.pe; Av Aeropuerto Km 6, CPM La Joya).

A little further up the Tambopata, near the community of **Baltimore**, are several *hospedajes* (small, family-owned inns), now part of a project to get tourists to experience local life on the river for a fraction of the prices lodges charge. Inquire at the **office** (Off Map p462; ☎ 57-2380; informes@baltimoreperu.org.pe; Ancash 950) in Puerto Maldonado about these, or just show up (maybe bring some food and water). One magical option is **Casa de Hospedaje El Gato**, across the river from Baltimore. Owned by the Ramírez family, it has basic beds, showers at waterfalls in the river, and includes meals and forest walks. Prices for this and other lodgings here are not fixed but start at daily rates per person of US$10 for volunteer programs to more than US$100 for a three-day, two-night stay.

Baltimore is reached by a twice-weekly passenger boat from Puerto Maldonado (see p466), or by bus and foot. Take any vehicle from Puerto Maldonado heading to Laberinto, and ask to get off at Km 37. From there, a footpath goes to Baltimore (two to three hours).

Shortly past Baltimore is the small **Wasai Tambopata Lodge** (www.wasai.com; s/d per day US$80/160). This is the penultimate lodge on the river and, unlike the others, it does not feature programmed ecoactivities. So if you just want to relax, read a book, enjoy a beer or just amble around the 20km of well-signed trails yourself, this is the place to do it. Fishing and canoe paddling are other options. The lodge consists of four large bungalows and two smaller ones, and can accommodate a maximum of 40 guests. There is a tall observation tower from where you get good views of the surrounding jungle. Transportation is not included in the price. Contact **Wasai Lodge** (Map p462; ☎ 082-57-2290; www.wasai.com; Billinghurst at Arequipa, Puerto Maldonado).

Finally, about seven hours' river travel from Puerto Maldonado, the **Tambopata Research Center** (s/d 5 days & 4 nights US$945/1490) is known for a famous salt lick nearby that attracts four to 10 species of parrots and macaws on most mornings. Research here focuses on why macaws eat clay, their migration patterns, their diet, nesting macaws and techniques for building artificial nests. The lodge itself is fairly simple, with 18 double rooms sharing four showers and four toilets, but because of the distances involved, rates are higher than the other places. If you're interested in seeing more macaws than you ever thought possible, it's worth the expense, although the owners point out that occasionally, due to poor weather or other factors, macaws aren't found at the lick. Still, about 75% of visitors get a good look at macaws. Travel time to the lodge varies, depending on river levels and the size of your boat motor: a stopover is usually made at Refugio Amazonas on the first and last nights. The last section of the ride is through remote country, with excellent chances of seeing capybaras and maybe more unusual animals. Have your passport ready at the Puesto Control Malinowsky. Book with **Rainforest Expeditions** (www.perunature.com) Cuzco (☎ 084-24-6243; cusco@rainforest.com.pe; Portal de Carnes 236); Lima (☎ 01-421-8347; postmaster@rainforest.com.pe; Aramburu 166, Miraflores); Puerto Maldonado (☎ 082-57-2575; pem@rainforest.com.pe; Av Aeropuerto Km 6, CPM La Joya).

MANU AREA

The Manu area encompasses the Parque Nacional Manu and much of the surrounding area. Covering almost 20,000 sq km (about the size of Wales), the park is one of the best places in South America to see a wide variety of tropical wildlife. The park is divided into three zones. The largest sector is the *zona natural,* comprising 80% of the total park area and closed to unauthorized visitors. Entry to this sector is restricted to a few indigenous groups, mainly the Matsiguenka (also spelled Machiguenga), some of whom continue to live here as they have for generations; some groups have had almost no contact with outsiders and do not seem to want any. Fortunately, this wish is respected. A handful of researchers with permits are also allowed in to study the wildlife. The second sector, still within the park proper, is the *zona reservada,* where controlled research and tourism activities are permitted. There are only a couple of official accommodation options here. This is the northeastern sector and comprises about 10% of the park area. The third sector, covering the southeastern area, is the *zona cultural,* where most other visitor activity is concentrated. The area around the park still provides great wildlife-watching opportunities, and is recommended for the spectacular macaw and tapir licks southeast of Boca Manu, as well as the bird-watching at the Manu Wildlife Center (p479).

Tours to the Manu Area

It's important to check exactly where the tours are going: Manu is a catchall word that includes the national park and much of the surrounding area. Some tours, such as to the Manu Wildlife Center, don't actually enter Parque Nacional Manu at all (although the wildlife center is recommended for wildlife-watching, nonetheless). Some companies aren't allowed to enter the park, but offer what they call 'Manu tours' either outside the park or acting as agents for other operators. Other companies work together and share resources such as lodges, guides and transportation services. This can mean the agency in whose office you sign up for the tour isn't the agency you end up going with. Most will combine a Manu experience with a full Peru tour on request. Confusing? You bet!

The companies listed in this section are all authorized to operate within Manu by the national park service and maintain some level of conservation and low-impact practices. The number of permits to operate tours into Parque Nacional Manu is limited; only about 3000 visitors are allowed in annually. Intending visitors must book well in advance. Be flexible with onward travel plans as delays are common. Entering by bus and boat and returning by flight is the best means of seeing Manu.

Tour costs depend on whether you camp or stay in a lodge, whether you arrive and depart overland or by air and whether you enter the *zona reservada*. A tour inside the zone won't necessarily get you better wildlife viewing – although, since it's virgin jungle here, chances of seeing larger animals are greater. If your budget allows, the more expensive companies really are worth considering. They offer more reliable and trained multilingual guides, better equipment, a wider variety of food, suitable insurance and emergency procedures. Perhaps most importantly, there are more guarantees that your money is going partly towards preserving Manu, as many of these companies fund conservation costs.

All companies provide transportation, food, purified drinking water, guides, permits and camping equipment or screens in lodge rooms. Personal items such as a sleeping bag (unless staying in a lodge), insect repellent, sunblock, flashlight with spare batteries, suitable clothing and bottled drinks are the traveler's responsibility. Binoculars and a camera with a zoom lens are highly recommended.

All lodges and tour operators in the big-money business of Manu excursions quote prices in US dollars.

Manu Expeditions (Map pp224-5; ☎ 084-22-5990, 084-22-4235; www.manuexpeditions.com; Clorinda Matto de Turner 330, Urb Magisterial, Cuzco), owners of the only tented camp within the national park, and co-owners of the Manu Wildlife Center, comes highly recommended, with more than two decades of Manu experience. Its guides are excellent, experienced and highly knowledgeable, but if you are lucky enough to go with the owner, British ornithologist and long-time Cuzco resident, Barry Walker, you will really be in excellent hands, particularly if birding is your main interest. The most popular trip leaves Cuzco every Sunday (except January, February and March, when it's the first Sunday of the month only) and lasts nine days, including overland transportation to Manu with two nights of camping at the company's Cocha Salvador Tented Camp, three nights at the Manu Wildlife Center, three nights at other lodges and a flight back to Cuzco. This costs US$1895. The overland section can include a mountain-biking descent if arranged in advance. Shorter, longer and customized trips are offered.

Manu Nature Tours (Map pp224-5; ☎ 084-25-2721; www.manuperu.com; Pardo 1046, Cuzco) operates the respected Manu Lodge, the only fully appointed lodge within the reserve and open year-round. The lodge has 12 double rooms (score one of the two above the main dining area for prime views) plus a bar-cum–dining room next to a lake that's home to a breeding family of giant otters. A 20km network of trails and guided visits to lakes and observation towers are also provided. A five-day tour, flying in or out, is US$1628 per person, double occupancy, with fixed departures every Thursday. Three-day tours are from US$1109/1618 for one/two people. The trip has a bilingual naturalist guide and all meals are provided. For an extra fee, mountain biking or river running (whitewater rafting) can be incorporated into the road descent. Longer tours are also available. This company also has departures to its Manu Cloud Forest Lodge (p476).

Pantiacolla Tours (Map pp224-5; ☎ 084-23-8323; www.pantiacolla.com; Saphi 554, Cuzco) owns three lodges in the Manu region and is frequently recommended by a variety of travelers for its knowledgeable and responsibly executed tours, helped by the fact that its staff members were raised in the area. It offers a variety of tours, including the opportunity to study Spanish at its jungle lodge. It also helps fund conservation of Manu, so ecologically, there's no better bet. Trips start at US$1135 per person for five days, flying out, or US$1035 per person for nine days, all overland, and include a mixture of camping and lodge accommodations. Pantiacolla Tours also works with local indigenous groups in its Yine Project, which is outlined on its website.

Amazon Trails Peru (☎ 084-43-7499, 084-23-6770; www.amazontrailsperu.com; Tandapata 660, Cuzco) comes reader-recommended and has a growing reputation for providing the best service amongst the cheaper tour operators. It's a husband-and-wife run outfit: tours provide a great deal of quirky insider information on places en route. Less obvious itineraries, such as one of the supposed sites of the legendary Inca city El Dorado, can be accommodated, and if you're heading on to Puerto Maldonado, onward boat/bus transport can be arranged to save backtracking to Cuzco. High-power binoculars are also provided, increasing chances of decent wildlife sightings. Six-day tours to the *zona reservada* start from US$1195, including flight out.

AMAZON BASIN

InkaNatura (www.inkanatura.com) Cuzco (Map pp224-5; ☎ 084-25-5255; Ricardo Palma J1 Urb Santa Mónica & Plateros 361) Lima (☎ 01-440-2022; Manuel Bañón 461, San Isidro) USA (Tropical Nature Travel; ☎ 1-877-888-1770, 1-352-376-3377; POB 5276, Gainesville FL 32627-5276) is a highly respected international agency and co-owner of the Manu Wildlife Center. The operators can combine a visit here with trips to other parts of the southern Peruvian rainforest, including Pampas del Heath near Puerto Maldonado, where they also have a lodge.

Another highly recommended budget option is **Bonanza Tours** (☎ 084-50-7871; www.bonanza-toursperu.com; Suecia 343, Cuzco), a family-operated company run by Ryse Choquepuma and his brothers, who grew up in Manu and know it better than most. Tours are arranged to the family home, which has been converted into a well-appointed lodge – with a hummingbird garden! The land here virtually backs onto the park proper and there are trails as well as a clay lick that attracts plenty of wildlife. The two-day and three-night option at the family lodge is US$300. Bonanza also runs longer tours into the *zona reservada*.

CUZCO TO MANU

This spectacular journey provides opportunities for some excellent **bird-watching** at the lodges en route, as well as some of Peru's most dramatic scenery changes. The route runs from bare Andean mountains into cloud forest before dropping into a steamy tangle of lowland jungle. You can get as far as Boca Manu, an hour before the entrance point for the *zona reservada*, independently. This is challenging but possible, although to either enter the *zona reservada* or maximize your chances of seeing wildlife, you will need a guide and therefore a tour. Most lodges en route will let you stay but giving them advance notice is advised.

If traveling overland, the first stage of the journey involves taking a bus or truck from Cuzco via Paucartambo (see p293) to Shintuya. Buses run by **Gallito de las Rocas** (Off Map pp224-5; Av Diagonal Angamos 1952, Cuzco) leave at 6am, 10am and 1pm for Pilcopata (S20, 10 to12 hours in good weather) daily. Get a taxi to the departure point – it's extremely difficult to find independently. Cheaper trucks also leave sporadically from the Coliseo Cerrado in Cuzco for Shintuya (about 24 hrs in dry season). Breakdowns, extreme overcrowding and delays are common, and during the rainy season (even during the

dry) vehicles slide off the road. It's safer, more comfortable and more reliable to take the costlier tourist buses (often heavy-duty trucks) offered by Cuzco tour operators. Many tour companies in Cuzco offer trips to Manu (see p474).

There are several lodges between Paucartambo and Pilcopata. Around six hours from Cuzco and overlooking the Kosñipata River valley, **Manu Paradise Lodge** (☎ 084-22-4156; www.manuparadiselodge.com; r per person incl meals US$70) Cuzco (Urb Magisterio 2da etapa) sleeps 16 people in spacious rooms with private hot-water bathrooms. It looks quite modern, unlike the more rustic lodges further into the park. Among its assets are an attractive dining room–bar with a fireplace and telescopes for wildlife viewing. Rafting and mountain-biking tours can be arranged, but the primary attraction is bird-watching.

Cock-of-the-Rock Lodge (s/d 3 days & 2 nights US$725/1150) is just a few minutes' walk from a *lek* (mating ground) for cocks-of-the-rock (brightly colored rainforest birds that live on rock cliffs and outcrops), where they conduct elaborate communal mating 'dances'. This lodge offers exceptional cloud forest bird-watching at a pleasant 1600m elevation. The owners claim you can get photos of male cocks-of-the-rock displaying about 7m from your camera. The lodge has a restaurant and 12 rustic double cabins with private bathrooms and hot water. Normally, visitors overnight here en route to Manu, but the lodge can be used as a destination in itself for cloud-forest birding. Rates include meals and round-trip transportation from Cuzco, which takes on average eight hours. Discounts are available for longer stays and larger groups. Contact **InkaNatura** (www.inka natura.com) Cuzco (Map pp224-5; ☎ 084-25-5255; Ricardo Palma J1 Urb Santa Mónica & Plateros 361) Lima (Map p96; ☎ 01-440-2022; Manuel Bañón 461, San Isidro).

Nearby, **Manu Cloud Forest Lodge** (Map pp224-5; ☎ 084-25-2721; www.manuperu.com; Pardo 1046, Cuzco; per person s/d 3 days/2 nights US$748/1046) is by the same stretch of road. The 16- to 20-bed lodge provides six rooms with hot showers, a restaurant and bird-watching opportunities in the high cloud forest. Transportation and use of the sauna cost extra.

The truck trip to these lodges is often broken at **Pilcopata**, which is the biggest village along the road. It's currently the end of the public bus route and indeed contact with the outside world of all kinds: the last public phone before Manu is located here. There are a couple of basic hotels and a few stores in town. A bed costs about S15: floor or hammock space is less. Pickup trucks leave early every morning for Atalaya and Shintuya (about five hours).

About 40km before Shintuya is the village of **Atalaya**, on the Río Alto Madre de Dios (not to be confused with the village of the same name on the Río Ucayali; see p483). Ten minutes by boat on the other side of the river is the gorgeous **Amazonia Lodge** (☎ 084-23-1370; www.amazonialodge.com; r per person US$70) Cuzco (Map pp224-5; Matará 334), in an old hacienda in the foothills of the Andes. Expect clean, comfortable beds and communal hot showers; simple but satisfactory meals are also included. The lodge has forest trails, excellent bird-watching (guided tours are offered), blissfully few mosquitoes and no electricity. The lodge can make transportation arrangements, or tour agencies in Cuzco can make reservations.

The village of **Salvación**, about 10km closer to Shintuya, has a national park office and some basic hotels. Ask here for boats continuing down the river but note that park entry is restricted to tour groups and there are very few other boats available.

Shintuya is the end of the road at this time and is the closest village to the park, but it has only a few places to stay. You may be able to camp at the mission station by talking to the priest.

The Ecuadorian-Dutch Moscoso family lives 30 minutes downriver from Shintuya and operates **Pantiacolla Lodge** (s/d US$95/130). There are 14 double rooms here, 11 with shared bathrooms and three with private ones. Rates include meals but not transportation or tours, though right near the lodge are forest trails, a parrot lick and hot springs. Various transportation and guided-tour options are available. As with all Manu lodges mentioned above, you can get here independently by bus/truck. It is necessary to give advance notice for the boat to the lodge, which is on the fringe of the national park. Good wildlife sightings have been reported. Contact **Pantiacolla Tours** (Map pp224-5; ☎ 084-23-8323; www.pantiacolla.com; Saphy 554, Cuzco).

Boats can travel from Pilcopata, Atalaya, Salvación or Shintuya toward Manu. People on tours often start river travel from Atalaya after a night in a lodge. The boat journey down the Alto Madre de Dios to the Río Manu takes

almost a day. At the junction is the village of **Boca Manu**, which has basic facilities. This village is known for building the best riverboats in the area, and it is interesting to see them in various stages of construction. A few minutes from the village by the air strip is **Yine Lodge** (s/d US$95/130), which has six double rooms sharing showers and toilets, run by the Yine people in conjunction with **Pantiacolla Tours** (Map pp224-5; ☎ 084-23 8323; www.pantiacolla.com; Saphy 554, Cuzco). The Boca Manu airstrip is often the start or exit point for commercial trips into the park. Companies including **Servicios Aereos de Los Andes** (☎ 098-481-7103; Cuzco airport) fly small aircraft here from Cuzco several times per week for US$195 one way. Most seats are taken up with tour groups, but empty seats are often available. A steep US$30 airport fee is charged at Boca Manu.

PARQUE NACIONAL MANU

This national park starts in the eastern slopes of the Andes and plunges down into the lowlands, hosting great diversity over a wide range of cloud forest and rainforest habitats. The most progressive aspect of the park is the fact that so much of it is very carefully protected – a rarity anywhere in the world.

After Peru introduced protection laws in 1973, Unesco declared Manu a Biosphere Reserve in 1977 and a World Natural Heritage Site in 1987. One reason the park is so successful in preserving such a large tract of virgin jungle and its wildlife is that it is remote and relatively inaccessible to people, and therefore has not been exploited by rubber tappers, hunters and the like.

It is illegal to enter the park without a guide. Going with an organized group can be arranged in Cuzco (see p474 and p239) or with international tour operators. It's an expensive trip; budget travelers should arrange their trip in Cuzco and be very flexible with travel plans. Travelers often report returning from Manu three or four days late. Don't plan an international airline connection the day after a Manu trip!

Permits, which are necessary to enter the park, are arranged by tour agencies. Transportation, accommodations, food and guides are also part of tour packages. Most visits are for a week, although three-night stays at a lodge can be arranged.

The best time to go is during the dry season (June to November); Manu may be inaccessible or closed during the rainy

FUEL FOR FEUDS

In June 2009, a clash between protesters and police in Bagua, near Chachapoyas in northern Peru, resulted in 33 deaths and a further 200 people injured – Peru's worst crisis since the demise of the Sendero Luminoso (Shining Path) guerrillas. The indigenous communities were protesting the Peruvian government's forest and wildlife law granting hydrocarbon companies access to their traditional lands. Continued protests during June and roadblocks by communities resulted in President Alan García's government suspending (temporarily) the forest and wildlife law that started the controversy.

Manu, Peru's most prized and protected area of jungle, is an apt illustration of the problem García faces. In 2006 his administration granted concessions for hydrocarbon extraction to Hunt Oil in the east of Manu's cultural zone. This included the Reserva Comunidad Amarakaeri (RCA), designated a protected zone four years earlier as a biological corridor set aside for sustainable use by tribespeople, stretching to the Brazil–Bolivia border. Local communities reluctantly approved the project management plan provided that the area surrounding the headwaters of the rivers on which they subsisted remained uncontaminated. Yet this was a key area identified for hydrocarbon extraction. A lack of cross-cultural communication resulted in the project getting the green light from four of the eight community leaders, despite their claim to have had little understanding of the implications of signing. Protesters against the legitimacy of the management plan that gave Hunt Oil the go-ahead cite that the meeting was held on December 27th (2007), a distracting time for these people due to the important community celebrations held over this period.

Many organizations are fighting to have this decision overruled. There's a precedent of foreign companies gaining access to the lands of indigenous communities worldwide when multibillion-dollar contracts are at stake. In neighboring Ecuador, for instance, the Yana Curi Report (1999) cited increased health risks to villages near some of Chevron Oil's oil fields.) This time, however, the economically regenerative interests of multinationals are being pitted against the popular environmental cause of the stewardship of the world's largest rainforest. A solution appears a long way off.

months (January to April), except to visitors staying at the two lodges within the park boundaries.

Virgin jungle lies up the Río Manu northwest of Boca Manu. At the Puesto Control Limonal (guard post), about an hour from Boca Manu, a park entrance fee of S150 per person is payable (usually included in your tour). Continuing beyond is only possible with a guide and a permit. Near Limonal are a few trails.

Six hours upstream is **Cocha Salvador**, one of the park's largest and most beautiful lakes, with guided camping and hiking possibilities. Half an hour's boat ride away is **Cocha Otorongo**, another oxbow lake with a wildlife-viewing observation tower. These are not wide-open habitats like the African plains. Thick vegetation will obscure many animals, and a skilled guide is very useful in helping you to see them.

During a one-week trip, you can reasonably expect to see scores of different bird species, several monkey species and possibly a few other mammals. Jaguars, tapirs, giant anteaters, tamanduas, capybaras, peccaries and giant river otters are among the common large Manu mammals. But they are elusive, and you can consider a trip very successful if you see two or three large mammals during a week's visit. Smaller mammals you might see include kinkajous, pacas, agoutis, squirrels, brocket deer, ocelots and armadillos. Other animals include river turtles and caiman (which are frequently seen), snakes (which are less often spotted) and a variety of other reptiles and amphibians. Colorful butterflies and less pleasing insects also abound.

There are two lodges within the park.

At **Manu Lodge**, a row of 14 simple double rooms is screened and has comfortable beds; a separate building has cold showers and toilets. The lodge is on Cocha Juarez, a 2km-long oxbow lake, and is about 1km from the Río Manu. A breeding family of giant river otters is often encountered. For an extra fee, you can climb up to a canopy platform; river running can also be arranged. A 20km network of trails from the lodge around the lake and beyond provides ample opportunities for spotting monkeys and birds. Contact **Manu Nature Tours** (☎ 084-25-2721; www.manuperu .com; Pardo 1046, Cuzco).

Cocha Salvador Safari Camp lies beyond Manu Lodge. This camp has raised platforms supporting large walk-in screened tents containing cots and bedding. Modern showers, toilets and meals are available. Manu Expeditions occasionally uses the more rustic **Casa Matsiguenka Lodge**, built in traditional style by the Matsiguenka tribespeople in 1998. Contact **Manu Expeditions** (☎ 084-22-5990, 084-22-4235, fax 084-23-6706; www.manuexpeditions.com; Clorinda Matto de Turner 330, Urb Magisterial, Cuzco).

More primitive camping, usually on the sandy beaches of the Río Manu or on the foreshore of a few of the lakes, is another possibility. Tour operators can provide all necessary equipment. During the rainy season (January to April) these beaches are flooded and the park is closed to camping. Campers should come prepared with plenty of insect repellent.

MANU WILDLIFE CENTER & AROUND

A two-hour boat ride southeast of Boca Manu on the Río Madre de Dios takes you to **Manu Wildlife Center** (s/d 4 days & 3 nights US$1550/2700). The center is a jungle lodge owned by **InkaNatura Travel** (www.inkanatura.com) Cuzco (☎ 084-25-5255; Ricardo Palma J1 Urb Santa Mónica & Plateros 361) Lima (☎ 01-440-2022; Manuel Bañón 461, San Isidro) and **Manu Expeditions** (☎ 084-22-5990, 084-22-4235; www.manuexpeditions.com; Clorinda Matto de Turner 330, Urb Magisterial, Cuzco), both of which take reservations. Although the lodge is not in the Manu Biosphere Reserve, it is recommended for its exceptional wildlife-watching and birding opportunities. There are 22 screened double cabins with hot showers, a dining room and a bar-hammock room. The lodge is set in tropical gardens.

There are 48km of trails around the wildlife center, where 12 species of monkey, as well as other wildlife, can be seen. Two canopy platforms are a short walk away, and one is always available for guests wishing to view the top of the rainforest and look for birds that frequent the canopy.

A 3km walk through the forest brings you to a natural salt lick, where there is a raised platform with mosquito nets for viewing the nightly activities of the tapirs. This hike is for visitors who can negotiate forest trails by flashlight. Chances to see animals are excellent if you have the patience, although visitors may wait for hours. Note that there isn't much happening at the lick during the day.

A short boat ride along the Madre de Dios brings visitors to another well-known salt lick that attracts various species of parrot and macaw. Most mornings you can see flocks in the hundreds. The largest flocks are seen from late July to September. As the rainy season kicks in, the numbers diminish. There are usually some birds all year, except for June, when birds don't visit the salt lick at all. May and early July aren't reliable either, though ornithologists report the presence of the birds in other nearby areas during these months, and birders will usually see them.

The macaw lick is visited on a floating catamaran blind, with the blind providing a concealed enclosure from which 20 people can view the wildlife. The catamaran is stable enough to allow the use a tripod and scope or a telephoto lens, and gets about halfway across the river. Boat drivers won't bring the blind too close to avoid disturbing the birds.

In addition to the trails and salt licks, there are a couple of nearby lakes accessible by catamaran where giant otters may be seen (as well as other wildlife). If you wish to see the macaw and tapir lick, the lakes and the canopy, and hike the trails in search of wildlife, you should plan on a three-night stay at the Manu Wildlife Center. Shorter and longer stays are workable.

Near the Manu Wildlife Center, the rustic **Tambo Blanquillo Lodge** has rooms with shared bathrooms. Expansion plans, including bungalows with private rooms, were being completed at the time of research. Some companies in Cuzco combine this cheaper option with a tour including other lodges in the Manu area, but prices vary. Staying just at Blanquillo isn't possible. Tour operators include **Pantiacolla Tours** (Map pp224-5; ☎ 084-23-8323; www.pantiacolla .com; Saphy 554, Cuzco).

If you continue down the Madre de Dios past gold-panning areas to Puerto Maldonado, you won't see much wildlife. This takes 14 hours to two days and may cost as little as S50. Amazon Trails Peru (p475) can also organize onward boat/bus transportation, but transportation to Puerto Maldonado is infrequent; almost all visitors return to Cuzco.

CENTRAL AMAZON

For a quick Amazon fix on long weekends and holidays, *limeños* (inhabitants of Lima) usually head for this relatively accessible Amazon region, reachable in eight hours by bus. The tropical Chanchamayo province is as different to the coastal desert strip or the Andean mountains as can be. The last hour of the journey here is particularly remarkable for the rapid change in vegetation and climate as you slip down from the rugged Andes into the vibrant green of La Selva Central, as it is known in Spanish. Comprising the two main towns of San Ramón and La Merced, plus a scattering of remoter communities, the area is noted for coffee and fruit production. Despite its popularity with Peruvian holidaymakers, the region offers the traveler a good insight into Amazon life, and better transport links mean there are more opportunities here for interacting with rainforest tribes than elsewhere in the Amazonas. Two rough, adventurous back routes also await, forging via Satipo

and Puerto Bermúdez through Peru's central belt of Amazon to the port city of Pucallpa, jumping-off point for river trips deeper into the jungle.

SAN RAMÓN & LA MERCED
☎ 064 / pop 40,000 / elev 800m

San Ramón is 295km east of Lima and La Merced is 11km further along. Chanchamayo's two key settlements are quite likable in a languid sort of way. Resistance to colonists by the local Asháninka people meant that these towns were not founded until the 19th century. Today they are popular Peruvian holiday destinations and great bases for exploring the luxuriant countryside nearby, characterized by photogenic forested hills and waterfalls that tumble into the Chanchamayo River valley. Accommodation bookings are recommended at busy periods, when room rates are also more expensive.

Orientation

San Ramón is the quieter of the two towns, but it does own the regional airstrip. The town has a pleasant plaza but is otherwise uninterest-

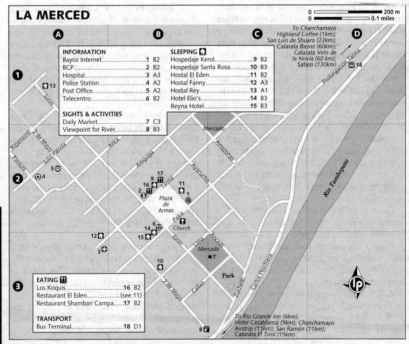

LA MERCED

0 ————— 200 m
0 ————— 0.1 miles

To Chanchamayo
Highland Coffee (1km);
San Luis de Shuaro (22km);
Catarata Bayoz (60km);
Cataratá Velo de
la Novia (60km);
Satipo (130km)

INFORMATION		
Bayoz Internet	1	B2
BCP	2	B2
Hospital	3	A3
Police Station	4	A2
Post Office	5	A2
Telecentro	6	B2

SIGHTS & ACTIVITIES		
Daily Market	7	C3
Viewpoint for River	8	B3

SLEEPING		
Hospedaje Kerol	9	B2
Hospedaje Santa Rosa	10	B3
Hostal El Eden	11	B2
Hostal Fanny	12	A3
Hostal Rey	13	A1
Hotel Elio's	14	B3
Reyna Hotel	15	B3

EATING		
Los Koquis	16	B2
Restaurant El Eden	(see 11)	
Restaurant Shambari Campa	17	B2

TRANSPORT		
Bus Terminal	18	D1

Mercado

Plaza
de
Armas

Church

Mercado

Park

To Rio Grande Inn (6km);
Hotel Casablanca (9km); Chanchamayo
Airstrip (11km); San Ramón (11km);
Catarata El Tirol (15km)

AMAZON BASIN

ing. Across the bridge is the main road to La Merced (the Carretera Central), which has decent top-end hotels.

La Merced is a bustling kind of place with squadrons of buzzing *mototaxis* careening down the streets. It's compact, too, with most traveler facilities within a coconut's throw of the main plaza. La Merced is also the main transport center, with buses, minibuses and *colectivo*s departing from here to all parts of the Selva Central.

Information

Both towns have a **BCP** with an ATM, and plenty of public telephones. La Merced has the better facilities.

Bayoz Internet (Plaza de Armas, La Merced) Internet access.

Hospital (☎ 53-1002; Tarma, cuadra 1; La Merced) Small.

Police station (Julio Piérola at Passuni, La Merced)

Post office (Av 2 de Mayo, La Merced)

Telecentro (Palca 12, La Merced) Make cheap calls here.

Sights & Activities

Both towns are more for strolling around to take in the local color.

The stairs at the northwest end of **Av 2 de Mayo** afford a good view of La Merced, and from the balcony at the southwest end there's a photogenic river view.

Around San Ramón are many impressive **waterfalls**. A much-visited 35m cascade, **Catarata El Tirol**, lies 5km east of San Ramon off the La Merced road. You can take a taxi the first 2km; the last 3km is along shady forest paths and streams. Off the Pichanaqui road at Puente Yurinaki are the higher waterfalls of **Catarata Velo de la Novia** and **Catarata Bayoz**, a dramatic series of cascades. Agencies in La Merced or Tarma arrange tours.

There is a colorful **daily market** in La Merced. An interesting **weekend market** visited by local *indígenas* (people of indigenous descent) is held at San Luis de Shuaro, 22km beyond La Merced. Asháninka tribespeople occasionally come into La Merced to sell handicrafts.

Sleeping

La Merced has most of the decent digs; San Ramón sports some luxury hotels.

LA MERCED

Hospedaje Santa Rosa (☎ 53-1012; Av 2 de Mayo 447; s/d S20/60) The cleanest of the cheapest hotels, the Santa Rosa boasts light rooms. Doubles get cable TV and large windows. Showers are cold. There are cheaper rooms with shared showers.

Hostal Fanny (☎ 77-5530, 95-448-4183; Tarma, cuadra 1; s/d S35/50) Clean, pleasant option with sizeable, well-decorated, airy rooms and a restaurant.

Hotel Elio's (☎ 53-1229; Palca 281; s/d S35/60) Just off the plaza, this is a good bargain. Spacious rooms make the beds look almost lost. There are writing desks, fans, cable TV and spotless bathrooms. Street-facing rooms are very noisy.

Hospedaje Kerol (☎ 33-5187; Tarma 373; s/d S40/50) Opposite Los Koquis restaurant, and set back from the plaza, this place offers clean, comfortable, plain rooms with cable TV. It's secure, too. The owner is as sunny as an Amazonian summer. Rooms at the back are quietest.

Hostal Rey (☎ 53-1185; www.hotelrey.net; Junín 103; s/d S45/55) Bright, inviting hallways lead to attractive rooms with fans, cable TV and hot showers. A restaurant on the top floor serves decent breakfasts, lunches and dinners while offering good views of the town. This place will do your laundry, too.

Hostal El Eden (☎ 53-1183; eleden@hotmail.com; Ancash 347; s/d S45/60) You pay for the plaza location, but the well-decorated rooms are OK, with TVs, fans and cold showers. Not all rooms have windows.

Reyna Hotel (☎ 53-1780, 53-2196; www.hotelreyna .com; Palca 259; s/d S60/80) You can't go wrong with this modern, brightly tiled hotel and its sparkling cafeteria. Rooms feature direct-dial phones, fans, cable TV, excellent beds and hot showers. A nice, comfy choice.

SAN RAMÓN

The town itself is unexceptional. However, the best places to stay in this region lie outside, on the La Merced road.

Hotel Casablanca (☎ 33-1295; www.hotelcasablanca .com.pe; Carretera Central Km 100.2; s/d S80/100) One of the better hotels on the San Ramon–La Merced strip, the Casablanca has spacious rooms tucked away down long, tiled corridors. The decor is old fashioned but rooms have minifridges, fans, cable TV and sizeable hot-water bathrooms. Most overlook the hotel pool, and there's also a pleasant restaurant serving regional specialties such as *tacacho* (pork and plantain).

ourpick Rio Grande Inn (☎ 33-2193, 95-71-3316; www.riograndebungalows.com; Carretera Central Km 97; d S160) This smart and well-appointed hotel is set in verdant grounds by the Río Chanchamayo. Rooms have wood paneling and minifridges along with the usual top-end hotel facilities. Breakfast is included in the price, as is use of the gorgeous pool. A restaurant serves light meals and refreshments.

Eating

LA MERCED

Consider any one of many chicken restaurants around the corner of Tarma and Ayacucho: a quarter-chicken with fries here sets you back S5. The *mercado* at Tarma and Amazonas has plenty of stalls selling juice and cake – for travel-hardened stomachs.

Los Koquis (☎ 53-1536; Tarma 376; mains S10-20; � 11am-11pm) On the plaza, set back down a leafy passageway, this place advertises its jungle specialties to lure punters in. Its *pachamanca* chicken (cooked in an earthen 'oven' of hot rocks) and ceviche are also well regarded.

Restaurant El Eden (☎ 53-1183; Anchas 347, mains S12-20; � breakfast from 8am, lunch & dinner) Spot where all the gringos in town are eating. There is a reason: this is a laid-back hangout right on the plaza, a recommended breakfast stop and a cracking *heladería* (ice-cream parlor). There are a smattering of North American faves alongside the more standard Peruvian meals available. Given what the region is renowned for, a real coffee wouldn't go amiss.

Restaurant Shambari Campa (☎ 53-2842; Tarma 389; mains about S15; � 6:30am-12:30am) Also on the plaza, this famous hole-in-the-wall restaurant has been serving good local food for decades. The menu, including the set lunches, is so extensive you can be literally lost for choice. Service is quick and attentive.

SAN RAMÓN

The hotel restaurants are worth a visit.

Chifa Felipe Siu (☎ 33-1078; Progreso 440; � 11am-2pm & 6:30-11pm) Locals say this is the best place to eat Chinese food in the Amazon – it's certainly a bit of an establishment here.

Shopping

Chanchamayo Highland Coffee (☎ 53-1198) is the only place around where you can sample and buy the coffee for which Chanchamayo is famous. (Peru is one of the world's largest coffee

producers but nearly all of it is exported.) It's gimmicky but enjoyable, and besides the shop, you can browse displays on coffee production and check out old coffee-producing machinery. It's 1km northeast of the bus terminal on the Satipo road.

Getting There & Away

AIR

The Chanchamayo airstrip is a 30-minute walk from San Ramón. *Mototaxis* will take you there (around S3). Small planes can theoretically be chartered to almost anywhere in the region but the strip is virtually deserted most of the time.

BUS

The bus terminal is a 1km downhill walk east of the center of La Merced. Most buses arrive and leave from here. Schedules are haphazard – go down there as early as you can and ask around.

Direct buses go from Lima to Chanchamayo, though many travelers break the journey at Tarma. Try to travel the 70km stretch from Tarma to San Ramón in daylight for the views during the spectacular 2200m descent. Companies going to Lima (S20 to S30, eight hours) include **Junín** (☎ 53-1256), which has two day buses and two luxury night sleeping buses daily to Lima (S70) – and is considered the most reliable service.

Other companies such as Transportes Salazaar also go to Lima, with several daily and nightly departures. Their offices are all located at the terminal or across the road on Prolongación Tarma. **Empresa de Transportes San Juan** (☎ 53-1522) has an office in the terminal and charges S15 for the five-hour journey to Huancayo (with stops at Tarma and Jauja), departing every two to three hours throughout the day. Frequent buses from various companies go to Tarma (around S10, 2½ hours).

Transportation into the jungle is by large minibus or pickup truck. *Colectivos* ply some routes for a slightly higher price. Minibuses leave for Pichanaqui (S5, on hour) about every half-hour; change here for services to Satipo. **Empresa Santa Rosa** has frequent minibuses to Oxapampa (S10, three hours), where you can change for services to Pozuzo (four hours further on). Pickup trucks to Puerto Bermúdez (S25, eight to 10 hours) leave from outside the terminal when full: be there ready for 4am. Journey time depends on road conditions but this is always an arduous trip, especially if you travel on top (in which case bring sunglasses, a waterproof jacket and gloves to prevent blisters caused by clinging on).

TAXI
Colectivos seating four passengers go to Tarma (S15), Oxapampa (S15, two hours) and Pichanaqui (S10). Ask at the bus terminal.

Getting Around
Minibuses linking La Merced with San Ramón and the hotels in between leave every few minutes (S1.50, 15 minutes) from outside the bus terminal. Drivers try charging more if they think you're staying at one of these hotels. *Mototaxis* charge S1 to drive you from the terminal up into La Merced center or anywhere round town.

SATIPO
☎ 064 / pop 15,700 / elev 630m
This jungle town is the center of a coffee- and fruit-producing region lying about 130km by road southeast of La Merced. This road was paved in 2000 to provide an outlet for produce, and accordingly Satipo is growing quickly. It is also linked by a poor road to the highlands of Huancayo.

The attractive main plaza has an extremely helpful **tourist office** (☎ 76-1244; 8am-1pm & 3pm-5pm Mon-Sat), which can arrange tours to nearby sites including waterfalls and petroglyphs (ancient rock carvings), as well as a BCP (ATM).

The pick of Satipo's mushrooming accommodation scene is **Hostal San Luis** (☎ 54-5319; cnr Grau 173 & Leguía; s/d S40/60), which has huge rooms with cable TV, phones, fans and reading lights as well as nicely tiled bathrooms, although water isn't always hot. There's a cafeteria downstairs.

On the Central Plaza, there is also **Hotel Majestic** (☎ /fax 54-5762; Colonos Fundadores Principal 408; s/d S40/55), a clean choice with private cold showers and cable TV in surrounds of decrepit colonial splendor.

Satipo has surprisingly good eateries, including **El Bosque** (☎ 54-5236; Manuel Prado 554; mains around S10), a lovely courtyard restaurant (food served from 8am to 5pm) also good for a drink of an evening.

The nearby airport has light aircraft for charter. Flights to Atalaya and other jungle towns leave irregularly, when there are enough passengers.

Minibuses and *colectivos* leave regularly for Pichanaqui, where you can change for La Merced. Larger buses leave every morning and evening for La Merced, some continuing on to Lima, including **Turismo Central** (☎ 54-6016; Los Incas 359), which has Lima and Huancayo buses. **Selva Tours** (☎ in Huancayo 21-8427) was running buses to Huancayo (S18, eight to nine hours) via the spectacular but difficult direct road through Comas, but at the time of research, security issues meant that only *colectivo* taxis were using this route. Phone ahead to check: the road is often impassable in bad weather anyway.

EAST OF SATIPO
Continuing east into the jungle, a decent unpaved road goes through **Mazamari**, 20km away. Here you'll find **Hospedaje Divina Montaña** (☎ 064-33-8767; r from S25) offering hot showers, a sauna and a popular restaurant. Rooms with fans are extra. Another 40km further is **Puerto Ocopa**, reached by *colectivo* from Satipo in two hours. Beyond Puerto Ocopa, a rough road continues to **Atalaya**, at the intersection of the Ríos Urubamba, Tambo and Ucayali. If the road is impassable, take a boat along the Río Tambo to Atalaya, which takes one day.

In Atalaya, a real jungle frontier village, there are basic hotels and an airstrip with connections to Satipo. Irregular boats can be found to Pucallpa, about 450km downstream (one to three days). Use your bargaining powers to negotiate a rate (it shouldn't be above S50 per person per day). Eight indigenous tribes inhabit the remote jungle beyond Atalaya. Travel here is not without dangers, one of which is armed plantation saboteurs. It's a trip for the travel hardened.

OXAPAMPA
☎ 063 / pop 7800 / elev 1800m
There is a distinctly alpine feel to this pretty ranching and coffee center, 75km north of La Merced. Perhaps this was why during the mid-19th century it attracted some 200 German settlers, the descendants of which (many still blonde haired and blue eyed) inhabit Oxapampa and smaller, lower **Pozuzo** (four hours north of Oxapampa by daily minibus; longer in the wet season), and have preserved many Germanic customs. Buildings have a Tyrolean look, Austrian-German food is prepared and an old-fashioned form of German is still spoken by some families.

North of Oxapampa rear the cloud-capped hills of little-visited **Parque Nacional Yanachaga-Chemillén**. The park preserves some spectacular cloud forest and diverse flora and fauna, including the rare spectacled bear. Visiting the park is complicated. First, get permission from the **INRENA Office** (☎ 46-2544; San Martín, cuadra 2). Then take a Pozuzo-bound minibus for 60km to Yuritunqui, where there is a *guardabosque* (park-ranger booth). Pay the park entrance fee of S30 here. There are basic bungalows to stay in nearby. Bring your own bedroll and provisions. Get the Oxapampa office to radio ahead so that the guards know you're coming.

Oxapampa has a BCP on the main plaza and decent accommodation options.

The new **Hostal Papaquëll** (☎ 33-7070; Bolognesi 288; s/d S25/50) fronts the plaza. Large, comfortable rooms have chunky wooden furniture and lovely hot-water bathrooms.

D'Palma Lodge (☎ 46-2123; www.depalmalodge.com; Thomas Schaus; lodge per person S100) is extremely conducive to relaxation, set into lush hillside above town. There are several Swiss-style lodges (including three for self-caterers) and a stylishly rustic restaurant-bar. New for 2010; a swimming pool. It's located at the end of Thomas Schaus.

Pozuzo buses run at 6am, 10am and 1pm from Oxapampa's Plaza de Armas along a rough road. In Pozuzo, accommodation includes **El Tirol**, at about S30 per person including meals. Oxapampa's pleasant bus station is eight blocks from the center on the mostly paved La Merced road. La Merced transport leaves from here, and there are also direct Lima buses in the evenings.

PUERTO BERMÚDEZ
☎ 063 / pop 1000 / elev 500m

Looking at the huddle of dugout canoes tied up to the mud bank of the Río Pachitea flowing past sleepy Puerto Bermúdez, it is difficult to imagine that one could embark on a river journey here that would eventually lead down the Amazon to the Atlantic.

Times were not always so peaceful. The area southeast of Puerto Bermúdez is home to the Asháninka tribespeople, Peru's largest indigenous Amazon group. In the late 1980s and early '90s, Sendero Luminoso (Shining Path) guerrillas attempted to indoctrinate the Asháninka to become fighters. When this didn't succeed, they tried intimidation

by massacring dozens. Today it's possible to visit the Asháninka from Puerto Bermúdez: in fact this is one of the best places in the Amazon to interact with indigenous tribes. Contact Albergue Humboldt to arrange Asháninka visits.

Located near the river, **Albergue Humboldt** (☎ 83-0020, 963-72-2363; www.alberguehumboldt.com; r without bathroom S15) is the best place to stay in the region. There are small rustic rooms with shared cold showers, hammocks or camping in the secure, secluded garden. There is no electricity in the mornings. Three meals, plus tea and coffee, can be had for an extra S8 to S20 per day. Chilled beer is available, as is a well-stocked book and DVD library. Hospitable Basque-born owner Jesús López de Dicastillo will arrange all manner of trekking and cultural expeditions deep into Asháninka territory with local guides from S90 per person per day, depending on group size and distance traveled and including food, boats and accommodation in simple shelters. Sometimes, you can help tribes with day-to-day activities such as boat-building. Highly recommended for budget adventurers!

The town's main street has simple eateries and even an internet cafe.

Trucks to La Merced leave for the arduous journey daily around 6am. Continuing north the road deteriorates: erratic transportation via Ciudad Constitución, Zungaro and Puerto Inca to Pucallpa is often by truck. This trip is very rough and takes one to two days. Boats go north to Ciudad Constitución and Puerto Inca, but do not have particular schedules. Puerto Inca is the best journey breaker, with basic accommodation such as **Hospedaje Brisas**. During the dry season, the river may be too low for passage, and the road is the better bet. During the wet months, the road can be barely passable, and boats are better. There are no flights to Puerto Bermúdez any more – the mayor is building a town hall on the air strip instead.

PUCALLPA
☎ 061 / pop 205,000 / elev 154m

The busy port of Pucallpa, Peru's only jungle settlement to be connected by paved road to the rest of the country, has a distinctly less jungle-like appearance than other Amazonian towns. Although this is an important distribution center for goods along the broad, brown Río Ucayali, which sweeps past the city en route to join the

Río Amazonas, the rainforest feels far away. After all those miles of tropical travel to get here, Pucallpa seems underwhelming.

Flocks of ominous-looking vultures hover over the town and bland, hasty modern development in the center barely disguises the shantytown simplicity a few blocks further out. Still, it's a lively enough place come sundown and most importantly, a starting point for a spectacular river adventure north to Iquitos and, if time and inclination allow, on to Brazil and the Atlantic.

Beyond the city sprawl, there are reasons for the traveler to linger: interesting indigenous communities to visit and river lodges to relax at.

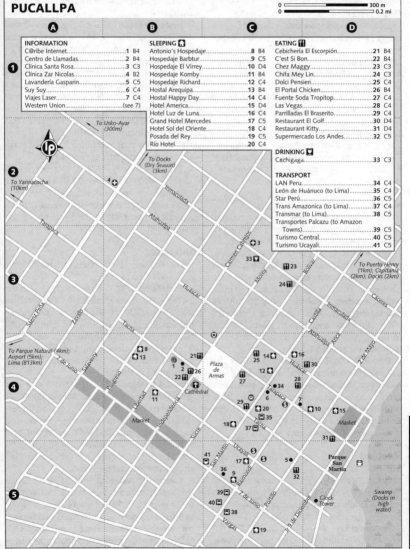

PUCALLPA

INFORMATION	
C@ribe Internet	**1** B4
Centro de Llamadas	**2** B4
Clínica Santa Rosa	**3** C3
Clínica Zar Nicolas	**4** B2
Lavandería Gasparin	**5** C5
Suy Suy	**6** C4
Viajes Laser	**7** C4
Western Union	(see 7)

SLEEPING ⌂	
Antonio's Hospedaje	**8** B4
Hospedaje Barbtur	**9** C5
Hospedaje El Virrey	**10** D4
Hospedaje Komby	**11** B4
Hospedaje Richard	**12** C4
Hostal Arequipa	**13** B4
Hostal Happy Day	**14** C4
Hotel America	**15** C4
Hotel Luz de Luna	**16** C4
Grand Hotel Mercedes	**17** C5
Hotel Sol del Oriente	**18** C4
Posada del Rey	**19** C5
Río Hotel	**20** C4

EATING ⌶	
Cebichería El Escorpión	**21** B4
C'est Si Bon	**22** B4
Chez Maggy	**23** C3
Chifa Mey Lin	**24** C3
Dolci Pensieri	**25** C4
El Portal Chicken	**26** B4
Fuente Soda Tropitop	**27** C4
Las Vegas	**28** C4
Parrilladas El Braserito	**29** C4
Restaurant El Golf	**30** D4
Restaurant Kitty	**31** D4
Supermercado Los Andes	**32** C5

DRINKING ⌑	
Cachigaga	**33** C3

TRANSPORT	
LAN Peru	**34** C4
León de Huánuco (to Lima)	**35** C4
Star Perú	**36** C5
Trans Amazonica (to Lima)	**37** C4
Transmar (to Lima)	**38** C5
Transportes Palcazu (to Amazon Towns)	**39** C5
Turismo Central	**40** C5
Turismo Ucayali	**41** C5

AMAZON BASIN

Information

Internet *cabinas* abound on every block. Several banks have ATMs and change money and traveler's checks. Foreign-exchange bureaus are found along the fourth, fifth and sixth *cuadras* (blocks) of Raimondi. For jungle guides, go to Yarinacocha.

C@ribe Internet (Tacna 326) Nice and central.

Centro de Llamadas (Tacna 388) Call center that's even more central. International calls possible.

Clínica Santa Rosa (☎ 57-1689; Inmaculada 529; ☽ 24hr) Quite good for stool, urine or blood tests.

Clínica Zar Nicolás (☎ 57-2854; Sáenz Peña 166) Also good.

Lavandería Gasparin (Portillo 526; ☽ 9am-1pm & 4-8pm Mon-Sat) Provides both self-service and drop-off laundry services.

Suy Suy (☎ 57-8223; Tarapaca 810) A travel agency with long opening hours: good for purchasing last-minute flight tickets.

Tourist booth (☎ 57-1303; 2 de Mayo 111) At the airport; a small booth that is more often than not unattended.

Viajes Laser (☎ 57-1120; fax 57-3776; Raimondi 399) Western Union is here, at one of Pucallpa's better travel agencies.

Sights

Many travelers visit nearby Yarinacocha, which is more interesting than Pucallpa and has some good accommodation options.

About 4km from the center of Pucallpa, off the airport road, is **Parque Natural** (adult/child 5-14 S3/1; www.parquenaturalpucallpa.com; ☽ 9am-5pm). This is an Amazon zoo set in lush grounds, with a museum displaying Shipibo pottery and a few other objects, a small children's playground and a snack bar. Buses heading to the airport can drop you here, or take a *mototaxi* for about S4.

Usko-Ayar (☎ 57-3088; Sánchez Cerro 465) is the gallery of the visionary local artist Pablo César Amaringo Shuna, whose work and biography can be accessed at www.egallery.com. Other promising Amazonian artists study, work and display here – it's well worth a visit. Tell drivers it's near the Iglesia Fray Marcos.

Sleeping

BUDGET

Hospedaje Barbtur (☎ 57-2532; Raimondi 670; s/d without bathroom S13/18, s/d S25/35) This family-run hotel is small, friendly and well maintained, with cold showers. En suite rooms have cable TV.

Posada del Rey (☎ 57-5815; Portillo 753; s/d S17/22) The 18 high-ceilinged rooms here are compact, clean, pleasant for the price and – if you score one with a street-facing balcony – light. Cold showers and fans keep you cool; a TV can be added for S5.

Hospedaje Richard (☎ 57-6477; San Martín 350; s/d with air-con S45/70, s/d without air-con S25/50; ☒) The mixed bag of rooms at this centrally located place are all quite small. Note that the better ones with air-con are on the lower floor, while up top are bare-bones affairs with fans.

Hospedaje Komby (☎ 57-1562; hostalkomby@hotmail .com; Ucayali 360; s/d S35/45; ☒) Clearly in a quandary about whether to aim for budget or luxury, Komby has rooms that veer between the two brackets. Accommodation overall is clean but basic, though the small pool and a restaurant compensate for this.

Hostal Happy Day (☎ 57-2067; fax 57-3263; Huáscar 440; s S35-60, d S45-70; ☒) You can't miss this orange-and-ochre-colored building. Rooms are small but neat and quiet. Breakfast is included; the top tariffs are for air-con.

Hospedaje El Virrey (☎ 57-5611; hotelvirrey@speedy .com.pe; Tarapaca 945; s/d from 45/70; ☒) Rooms are neat, well kept and quiet, although quite small. Some more expensive rooms have air con. An American breakfast in the hotel restaurant is included.

MIDRANGE

All the following have rooms with bathrooms, fans and cable TV.

Hotel América (☎ 57-5989; hamericapcl@speedy.com .pe; Portillo 357; s/d with air-con S80100, s/d without air-con S45/60, mini ste S130; ☒ ☒) Rooms are modern but small and amenities vary; minifridges, telephones and hot showers are available. There is also a cafeteria and a small restaurant here. A continental or American breakfast is included in the rate.

Hostal Arequipa (☎ 57-3171, 57-1348; www.hostal -arequipa.com; Progreso 573; s/d with air-con S80/100, s/d without air-con S50/65; ☒) This is a popular, professional and often full midrange choice, and has hot water, minifridges, a restaurant, and attractive public areas decorated with Shipibo art. The pricier rooms with air-con also include a continental breakfast.

Antonio's Hospedaje (☎ 57-3721, 57-4721; antonions _hs@hotmail.com; Progreso 545; s/d with air-con S90/100, s/d without air-con 80/70; ☒ ☒) Rooms here are huge and have hot showers, nice tiled bathrooms, comfortable mattresses and minifridges. One of Pucallpa's best swimming pools now awaits in the garden. Higher rates cover airport pickup and air-con.

Río Hotel (☎ 57-1280, 57-2771; www.riohotelcasino .com.pe; San Martín 475; s/d incl breakfast S90/135; 🟦) An odd-looking hotel-cum-casino with only three of its six stories completed, it nonetheless takes guests. Rooms are Spartan but bigger than average, and have phones, warm showers, cable TV and minifridges.

our pick **Grand Hotel Mercedes** (☎ 57-5120; www .grandhotelmercedes.com; Raimondi 610; s S90-115, d S135-175; 🟦 🟦) Pucallpa's first good hotel has recently had a sprucing up. All rooms now have air-con and minifridges. There is a dated elegance to this clean, comfortable place, with its echoing tiled corridors, beige room decor and gorgeous garden courtyard with swimming pool (also open to nonguests, S3).

Hotel Luz de Luna (☎ 57-1729, 57-1206; www .hotelluzdelunaeirl.com; San Martín 283; s/d/ste incl breakfast S110/130/300; 🟦) A brand new addition to the top-end hotel scene, this offering sports ample rooms with plump beds, minifridges, telephones, 21-inch TVs with DVD players and free internet. The top-floor restaurant boasts great views; there is also a roof terrace and a cafe. Several suites with Jacuzzis are available.

TOP END

Hotel Sol del Oriente (☎ 57-5510; hsoloriente@qnet .com.pe; San Martín 552; s/d/ste S230/285/460, s/d with Jacuzzi S285/320; 🟦 🟦) This is about the best you'll get in Pucallpa proper. It's not that flash but it's comfortable. The rooms are of a decent size, have air-con, TV, minifridges and good, always-hot showers. Within, the hotel boasts a pool and a palm-shaded garden: you get a welcome cocktail on arrival.

Eating

Pucallpa does cafes and ice-cream parlors well, but has few noteworthy restaurants. The heat in the middle of the day means that restaurants tend to open by 7am for breakfast. Many are closed Sunday.

C'est Si Bon (Independencia 560; snacks from S3) This bright spot does Pucallpa's best coffee. Also head here for breakfasts, good ice cream, sandwiches and other snacks.

Restaurant Kitty (☎ 57-4764; Tarapaca 1062; menús S5-15; 🕙 7am-11pm Mon-Sat, to 5pm Sun) The Kitty is clean and popular, and brings in local lunch crowds for a wide variety of Peruvian culinary classics. Join 'em!

Dolci Pensieri (☎ 59-1263; Sucre 331, mains S6-20; 🕙 11am-11pm) This well-designed, attractive *heladería*-cum-restaurant does great cakes and juices, plus a line in pizzas and Mexican food in the evenings.

El Portal Chicken (☎ 57-1771; Independencia 510; mains about S10; 🕙 5pm-midnight) This three-story restaurant, with its open-air plaza views and the brightest neon lights in town, is Pucallpa's best chicken restaurant.

Cebichería El Escorpión (☎ 57-4516; Independencia 430; meals S10-20) This option has a prime plaza location, with (noisy) sidewalk tables, and serves good seafood (tender and fresh despite Pucallpa's distance from the coast) for breakfast and lunch.

Restaurant El Golf (☎ 57-632; Huáscar 545; mains S15-25; 🕙 10am-5pm Tue-Sun; 🟦) This more upscale seafood restaurant has a variety of ceviche made with freshwater fish – try the local *doncella* instead of the endangered *paiche*.

Parrilladas El Braserito (San Martín 498; mains S16-28; 🕙 11:30am-4pm daily, 6-11pm Mon-Sat) For good grills (steak, fish and venison) in a refined but somewhat bland atmosphere, this is a good choice.

Chifa Mey Lin (☎ 57-4687; Immaculada 698; mains S17-24; 🕙 closed Sun) This place gets the gong for being the best of Pucallpa's *chifas* (Chinese restaurants). A spacious, convivial eating environment.

Chez Maggy (☎ 57-4958; Inmaculada 643; medium pizza S22) Maggy serves up pizzas nothing short of superb, and from a wood-burning oven. The interior is modern and not plasticized like some neighboring restaurants. The unusual, tropical-tasting sangria goes down well with all dishes.

Mean cakes and ice cream can be found at other good cafes such as **Fuente Soda Tropitop** (☎ 57-2860; Sucre 401) and **Las Vegas** (☎ 57-1936; Raimondi 332).

For long trips, stock up at **Supermercado Los Andes** (Portillo 545).

Drinking

A few half-decent bars can be found along Inmaculada on the endearingly named 'pizza strip,' of which **Cachigaga** (Inmaculada 552) seems the liveliest.

Shopping

The local Shipibo tribespeople wander the streets of town selling souvenirs. More of their work is seen near Yarinacocha. For details on their handicrafts, see p490.

Getting There & Away

AIR

Pucallpa's decent-sized airport is 5km north-west of town. **LAN Peru** (☎ 1-213-8200, ext 3; Tarapaca 805) has two flights daily to/from Lima, leaving the capital at the inconvenient times of 3:55am and 8:35pm and returning from Pucallpa at 5:35am and 10:15pm. **Star Perú** (☎ 59-0586; 7 de Junio 865) has an alternative similarly priced direct flight leaving from/to Lima at 9:30am and 2:25pm. Take up to 8kg luggage in the cabin or 25kg in the hold. The morning flight from Lima usefully continues to Iquitos at 11:10am. Departure tax is S11.46, payable at the bank in the concourse lounge before check-in.

Other towns and settlements (including Atalaya, Contamaná, Juanjuí, Puerto Breu, Sepahua, Tarapoto and Yurimaguas) are served by small local airlines using light aircraft. **North American** (☎ 57-2351; fax 57-3168; airport) flies to Contamaná daily and also to Tarapoto. Luggage on these flights is limited to 10kg per passenger.

BOAT

Pucallpa's port moves depending on water levels. During high water (January to April) boats dock at the town itself, abutting Parque San Martín. As water levels drop, the port falls back to several spots along the banks, including **Puerto Henry** (Manco Cápac s/n) and eventually to about 3km northeast of the town center, reached by *mototaxi* (S3). The town port stretches some way: different boats for different destinations depart from different areas, usually referred to by the name of the nearest intersecting road.

Wherever the port is, riverboats sail the Río Ucayali from Pucallpa to Iquitos (p501) (S100, slinging your own hammock and with basic meals, three to five days). Cabins with two or four bunks come with better food service and cost about S180.

Boats announce their departure dates and destinations on chalkboards on the boats themselves, but these can be unreliable. Talk to the captain or the cargo loadmaster for greater dependability. They must present boat documents on the morning of their departure day at the **Capitanía** (☎ 59-0193; M Castilla 860) – come here to check for the latest reliable sailing information. Many people work here, but only the official in charge of documents knows the real scoop and can give you accurate sailing information. Passages are daily when the river is high, but in the dry season low water levels result in slower, less frequent passages.

The quality of the boats varies greatly both in size and comfort. Choose a boat that looks good. The *Henry V,* when it is in port, is one of the better-equipped outfits, with a 250-passenger capacity.

This is not a trip for everyone; see p537 for more details on boat travel. Come prepared – the market in Pucallpa sells hammocks, but the mosquito repellent may be of poor quality. Bottled drinks are sold on board, but it's worth bringing some large bottles of water or juice.

When negotiating prices for a riverboat passage, ask at any likely boat, but don't pay until you and your luggage are aboard your boat of choice, then pay the captain and no one else. Always get to the port well in advance of when you want to leave: it can take hours hunting for a suitable vessel. Most boats leave either at first light, or in late afternoon/evening.

The river journey to Iquitos (two to four days from Pucallpa; about S100) can be broken at various villages, including Contamaná (S30, 15 to 20 hours) and Requena, and continued on the next vessel coming through. Alternatively, ask around for speedboats to Contamaná (about S100, five hours), which depart at 6am most days. The return trip (six to seven hours) goes against the current.

WARNING

The long, lonely section of road between Pucallpa and Tingo María (see p332), the only paved link between Peru's Amazon region and the rest of the country, can be a risky road to travel. Armed robberies during daylight (around 6pm, to be precise), as well as at night, have been occurring and travelers have been caught up in hold ups. This includes passages by bus, car and truck. Holidays and feast days seem to be the worst times. Robbers take valuables then, assuming no one resists, allow onward passage. The posting of police at various intervals in the vicinity (they usually ask for a nominal 'protection' fee – best to pay it) has improved matters, but this is a journey you take at your own risk. Buses do make the daily trip from Tingo to Pucallpa but flying to Pucallpa from Lima is a safer option.

Smaller boats occasionally head upriver towards Atalaya; ask at the Capitanía or the town port.

Jungle 'guides' approaching you on the Pucallpa waterfront are not recommended. For jungle excursions, look for a reliable service in Yarinacocha.

BUS

A direct bus to/from Lima (S70 to S90) takes 20 hours in the dry season; the journey can be broken in Tingo María (S20, nine hours) or Huánuco (12 hours). The road is paved but vulnerable to flooding and erosion. Also see opposite.

León de Huánuco (☎ 57-2411, 57-9751; Tacna 655) serves Lima at 1pm (*bus-cama*, bed bus) and 5:30pm. Another good company is **Turismo Central** (☎ 59-1009; Raimondi 768), which has one morning departure and two afternoon departures. Less luxurious buses going to Lima include **Transmar** (☎ 57-4900, 57-9778; Raimondi 793), at 1pm and 4:30pm; and **Trans Amazonica** (Tacna 628), at 5pm daily.

Turismo Ucayali (☎ 59-3002; 7 de Junio 799) has cars to Tingo María (S45, six hours) via Aguaytía leaving about every hour all day and night. Other companies nearby serve the same destinations for similar prices.

Transportes Palcazu (☎ 961-93-3136; Raimondi 730) has trucks and buses to more remote Amazonian destinations such as Puerto Bermúdez and Puerto Inca via the rough, rough road to La Merced.

Getting Around

Mototaxis to the airport or Yarinacocha are about S6; taxis are S10. *Colectivos* to Yarinacocha (S1) leave from Jirón 9 de Diciembre near the market, San Martín at Ucayali, and other places.

YARINACOCHA

About 10km northwest of central Pucallpa, Yarinacocha is a lovely oxbow lake where you can go canoeing, observe wildlife, and visit indigenous communities and purchase their handicrafts. The lake, once part of the Río Ucayali, is now entirely landlocked, though a small canal links the two bodies of water during the rainy season. Boat services are provided here in a casual atmosphere. It's well worth spending a couple of days here.

A part of the lake has been set aside as a reserve. There is also a **botanical garden** (ad-mission S2; ⏰ 8am-4pm), which is reached by a 45-minute boat ride followed by a 30-minute walk. Go early in the morning to watch birds on the walk there.

The lakeside village of **Puerto Callao** is a welcome relief from the chaos of downtown Pucallpa's streets. It's still a ramshackle kind of place with only a dirt road skirting the busy waterfront. Buzzards amble among pedestrians, and *peki-peki* boats come and go to their various destinations all day.

Here you'll find a limited choice of generally good accommodations, as well as some decent food. You can also hire **boats** here – in fact, you'll be nabbed as soon as you turn up by boat touts seeking to lure you to their vessel. Choose your boat carefully: make sure it has new-looking life jackets and enough petrol for the voyage, and pay at the end of the tour. Wildlife to watch out for includes freshwater pink dolphins, sloths and meter-long green iguanas, as well as exotic birds such as the curiously long-toed wattled jacana (which walks on lily pads) and the metallic-green Amazon kingfisher. If you like **fishing**, the dry season is apparently the best time.

Internet is available at three or four places, most near or on the main square up the hill.

Tours & Guides

Lots of *peki-peki* boat owners offer tours. Take your time in choosing; the first offer is unlikely to be the best. Guides are also available for walking trips into the surrounding forest, including some overnight hikes.

A recommended guide is **Gilber Reategui Sangama** (☎ message 57-9018, 061-962-7607; jungle secrets@yahoo.com), who owns the boat *La Normita* in Yarinacocha. He has expedition supplies (sleeping pads, mosquito nets, drinking water) and is both knowledgeable and environmentally aware. He speaks some English, is safe and reliable, and will cook meals for you. He charges about S125 per person per day, or S25 per hour, with a minimum of two people, for an average of three to five days. Gilber lives at the lakeside village of Nueva Luz de Fátima, and offers tours to stay with his family: his father is a shaman with 50 years' experience. Gilber works with Arcesio Morales and Roberto 'Jungle Man' Tamani, who don't speak English. He also recommends his uncle and nephew, Nemecio and Daniel Sangama, with their boat *El Rayito*.

AMAZON BASIN

SHIPIBO TRIBESPEOPLE

The matriarchal Shipibo tribespeople live along the Río Ucayali and its tributaries in small loose villages of simple, thatched platform houses. Often visited settlements are **San Francisco**, at the northwest end of Yarinacocha and accessible by dirt road from Pucallpa, and the village of **Santa Clara**, accessible only by boat. San Francisco even has simple lodgings (about S10 per person).

Shipibo women craft delicate pots and textiles, decorated with highly distinctive, geometric designs. Shops in Puerto Callao and Yarinacocha sell these products but it is best to go the villages and look for crafts there. Around 40 Shipibo villages produce crafts; pieces are handmade so though patterns are similar, each one is unique. They range from inexpensive small pots and animal figurines to huge urns valued at hundreds of dollars (and more, internationally).

Another good guide is **Pedro Tello** (☎ 961-94-5611), with his boat *Tiburón*.

Other guides, however, will claim the above are unavailable or no longer work there. Don't believe all you hear: a good boat driver will float slowly along, so that you can look for birdlife at the water's edge, or *perezosos* (sloths) in the trees. Sunset is a good time to be on the lake.

Boat trips to the Shipibo villages of either **San Francisco** (also now reached by road) or, better, **Santa Clara** (reached only by boat,) are also popular. For short trips, boat drivers charge S15 to S20 an hour for the boat; these can carry several people. Bargaining over the price is acceptable.

Sleeping & Eating
PUERTO CALLAO

La Maloka Ecolodge (☎ 59-6900; lamaloka@gmail .com; s/d S120/180; ❄) is the only decent place to stay in the port. It is worth forking out the extra cash for the comfort. La Maloka Ecolodge is located at the right-hand end of the waterfront, this lodge is built right out on the water, with the amply sized but un-adorned rooms sitting on stilts over the lake. There is a relaxing outdoor restaurant and bar area overlooking the lake; pink dolphins regularly flash their flippers for guests. The only downside is a small menagerie of sad-looking caged animals.

Several inexpensive restaurants and lively bars line the Puerto Callao waterfront. The better ones are toward the right-hand side as you face the lake, where you'll find La Maloka and the **Anaconda**, a floating restaurant, among other choices.

LAKESIDE

La Jungla (☎ 57-1460; www.thejungleecolodge.com; bungalows per person S75) This enthusiastically run place currently only has two rustic bungalows open to guests, each sleeping up to four people. There is a zoo, a resident tapir, a spacious bar-restaurant and a swimming pool on a floating platform on the lake. The owner's father can guide you in the surrounding jungle. La Jungla is within an hours' walk of the botanical garden.

Pandisho Albergue (☎ 57-5041, 961-65-9596; www .amazon-ecolodge.com; 2 days & 1 night incl meals per person S285) About 40 minutes from Puerto Callao, this place has eight rooms with bath-rooms, and electricity for three hours in the evening. Its bar is popular with locals on weekends when there's music, but it's quiet otherwise. Tours include transporta-tion from the airport to the lake, a welcome cocktail and a full program of walks to visit wildlife and indigenous communities, as well as piranha fishing! Ask about cheaper, room-only options.

CONTAMANÁ TO REQUENA

Contamaná has a colorful waterfront mar-ket, a frontier-town atmosphere and is settled mainly by *mestizo* descendents of colonists. It also boasts an airstrip, 24-hour electricity and some internet cafes, as well as a couple of OK accommodation options near the plaza for around S30 a room such as **Hostal Augustus**. The next major port is **Orellana**, which has electricity from 6:30pm to 10:30pm and half a dozen basic hotels charging up to S10 for single rooms and S15 for doubles with shared bathroom. Further on again, **Juancito** has some very basic rooms.

In the town of **Requena** (two to four days from Pucallpa), with 24-hour electricity, the nicest sleep is tiny, cute **Hostal Jicely** (☎ 065-41-2493; Manaos 292; d S30). There are other more basic *hostales*. Boats to Iquitos leave on most days, taking 12 to 15 hours.

NORTHERN AMAZON

Raw, vast and encapsulating the real spirit of the Amazon, the northern Amazon Basin is home to the eponymous river that wells up from the depths of the Peruvian jungle before making its long, languorous passage through Brazil to the distant Atlantic Ocean. Settlements are scarce in this remote region: Yurimaguas in the west and Iquitos in the northeast are the only two of any size.

YURIMAGUAS

☎ 065 / pop 45,000 / elev 181m

This sleepy, unspectacular port is one of the Peruvian Amazon's best-connected towns and the gateway to the northern tract of the Amazonas. It's visited by travelers looking for boats down the Río Huallaga to Iquitos and the Amazon proper or by those wanting to experience one of Peru's most animal-rich paradises, the Pacaya-Samiria reserve, which is accessible from here. There is little to detain visitors from continuing their Amazon adventure. A paved road now connects Yurimaguas with Tarapoto to the south.

Orientation & Information

Yurimaguas is a compact town, easily negotiable on foot. The Plaza de Armas abuts the Río Huallaga, and buses and taxis arrive and depart from offices 2km southwest of the center. Go to Lagunas for a jungle guide, although touts will approach you in Yurimaguas.

The **Consejo Regional** (Plaza de Armas) can give information, as can **Kumpanamá Tours** (☎ 50-2472; Jáuregui 934). It is better to arrange Pacaya-Samiria tours in Lagunas. **Banco Continental** (with a Visa ATM) and **BCP** will change US cash and traveler's checks. Internet and phone booths come and go frequently but there are a few around the plaza.

Sleeping

Few hotels have hot water. Other budget hotels flank *cuadra* 3 of Arica and *cuadra* 4 of Jáuregui.

Yacuruña (☎ 965-735-767; Malecón Shanusi 200; s/d without bathroom S15/25) This is a great rustic retreat right by the river. Four simple, nicely decorated rooms share a bathroom. Tours are offered both to local sites and the Pacaya-Samiria reserve. Access it via steps from the Plaza.

Leo's Palace (☎ 35-3008, ☎ /fax 35-2213; Lores 108; s/d S25/45) The oldest of the better hotels and now a bit run-down, Leo's has simple but spacious rooms with fans and a balcony overlooking the Plaza de Armas. TV is available on request and there is a restaurant serving decent cheap lunches.

our pick **Hostal El Naranjo** (☎ 35-2650, 35-1560; www.hostalelnaranjo.com.pe; Arica 318; s/d S40/60; ❖ 🖥 🐾) This clean, quiet hotel has rooms with ceiling fans and cable TV. Some more expensive rooms have air-con. Internal courtyard rooms face the tiny, pleasant pool. There's hot water and internet access (S2 per hour), plus it has a good restaurant.

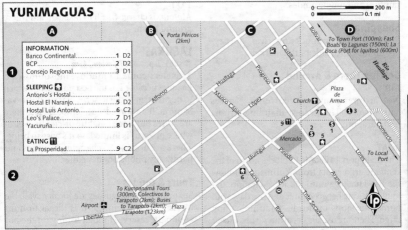

YURIMAGUAS

0   200 m
0   0.1 mi

INFORMATION	
Banco Continental.....................1	D2
BCP...2	D2
Consejo Regional......................3	D1

SLEEPING	
Antonio's Hostal.......................4	C1
Hostal El Naranjo......................5	D2
Hostal Luis Antonio...................6	C2
Leo's Palace.............................7	D1
Yacuruña.................................8	D1

EATING	
La Prosperidad.........................9	C2

Porta Péricos (2km)

To Town Port (100m); Fast Boats to Lagunas (150m); La Boca (Port for Iquitos) (600m)

Plaza de Armas

Church

Río Huallaga

Mercado

To Local Port

To Kumpanamá Tours (300m); Colectivos to Tarapoto (2km); Buses to Tarapoto (2km); Plaza Tarapoto (123km)

Airport

Libertad

AMAZON BASIN

Antonio's Hostal (☎ 35-1033; López 338; s/d S35/55) Despite the somewhat clueless staff, this smart new hostel is clearly aiming at the top end of the sleeping scene. The rooms are sizeable, light, tastefully decorated and adjoin very good bathrooms. Try to get one of the sumptuous street-corner-facing rooms with huge curved windows.

Hostal Luis Antonio (☎ 35-2065; antonio@viabcp .com; Jáuregui 407; s S50-70, d S60-100; 🖳 🖳) Prices here vary depending on whether you want cable TV, air-con or both. All standard rooms have a fan and are well maintained. There is also a small pool.

Porta Péricos (☎ 35-3462; San Miguel 720; s/d incl breakfast from S125-155; 🖳) On the northern outskirts, overlooking the Río Paranapura; the staff claim this hotel's breezy location negates the necessity for air-con. Renovations in 2009 included adding 20 separate bungalows and giving the pool that essential Jacuzzi, as well as building the hotel's own river port. Come reopening in 2010, it promises to be the gorgeous, peaceful and pricey establishment it always has been.

Eating

There are few good places to eat. Many restaurants close between meals. The hotel restaurants, especially El Naranjo, are among the best, but aren't anything special. Market stalls along Progresso sell great cakes and other snacks.

La Prosperidad (☎ 35-2057; Progreso 107; menú S3-8; 🕑 Tue-Sun) has tropical juices, burgers and chicken. It's popular as a hangout for young families and jungle guides.

Shopping

Stores selling hammocks for river journeys are on the north side of the market.

Getting There & Around
AIR

No airline company currently serves Yurimaguas. The nearest mainline airport is at Tarapoto.

BOAT

The main port 'La Boca' is 13 blocks north of the center. Cargo boats from Yurimaguas follow the Río Huallaga onto the Río Marañón and Iquitos, taking between three and five days with numerous stops for loading and unloading cargo. There are usually departures daily, except

Sunday. Passages cost about S100 on deck (sling your own hammock and receive basic food) or S180 for a bunk in double or quadruple cabins on the top deck, where the food is better and your gear safer. Bottled water, soft drinks and snacks are sold onboard. Bring insect repellent and a hat. Boat information is available from the **Bodega Dávila store** (☎ 35-2477) by the dock. The Eduardo boats (of which there are five) are considered the best, (although readers have reported graphic animal cruelty on these). The journey can be broken at Lagunas (S20 to S30, 10 to 12 hours), just before the Río Huallaga meets the Marañón.

Smaller slow boats and fast boats to Lagunas (S100, 3½ hrs) leave from the more convenient town port 200m northwest of the Plaza de Armas.

Cruise ships sometimes dock at Yurimaguas, bound for Iquitos. Ask around at 'La Boca' to see about scheduled departures.

BUS

The new paved road makes Yurimaguas easily accessible by Amazon standards. For Tarapoto (S15, 2½ hours), several companies leave from offices on the Tarapoto road including **Trans Gilmer Tours** (☎ 942-627-415, Victor Sifuentes s/n), which has departures every two hours. Likewise, there are multiple companies nearby with *colectivos* to Tarapoto (S25; two hours) from *cuadras* 5 and 6 of Sifuentes. There is nothing to choose between them: it's just a matter of which one leaves first, which will happen only when they've touted four passengers.

TAXI

Mototaxis charge S1.50 to take you anywhere around town.

LAGUNAS
☎ 065 / pop 4500 / elev 148m

Travelers come to muddy, mosquito-rich Lagunas because it is the best point from which to begin a trip to the Reserva Nacional Pacaya-Samiria. It's a spread-out, remote place: there are stores but stock (slightly pricier than elsewhere in Peru) is limited, so it's wise to bring. There are no money-changing facilities and hardly any public phones either.

Tours & Guides

Spanish-speaking guides are locally available to visit Pacaya-Samiria. It is illegal to hunt within the reserve (though fishing for the pot is OK). The going rate is a rather steep S100 per person per day for a guide, a boat and accommodations in huts, tents and ranger stations. Food and park fees are extra, although the guides can cook for you.

Several years ago, there was such a plethora of guides in Lagunas that to avoid harassment and price cutting, an official guides association was formed. Of course, this being Peru, things weren't so straightforward. The head of the organization left and set up a second 'official' guides association; there are currently two guides associations but watch this space. **Estypel** (☎ 40-1080; estypel@gmail.com; Jr Padre Lucero 1345) is the original organization and generally considered the best. Located near the market, it's headed by the reputable guide Juan Manuel Rojas Arévalo. Confusingly, many Estypel guides will tell you they work for Acestur but this is an affiliated agency. To muddy the waters further, former Estypel boss Gamaniel Valles has now set up **Etascel** (☎ 40-1007; etascel@hotmail.com; Fiscarral 530), found down a side street near the market. Both organizations give guides jobs in turn, so it is harder to get a particular guide. Juan Guerro, working for Estypel, and Etascel's Kleber Saldaña are experienced guides getting good reports from travelers. However, you don't know whom you will get until you arrive.

Sleeping & Eating

Accommodation is improving, but still very basic. Hostels provide cheap meals; if you like chicken and fried banana, try the basic restaurant on the plaza.

Hostal Eco (☎ 50-3703; hospeco@hotmail.com; s/d S15/20) Seven simple, clean rooms here flank a small courtyard. All have private bathrooms and nightlights for when the power cuts out.

Hostal Samiria (☎ 40-1061; Fitzcarrald; s/d/tr S15/20/30) This is probably the best option in town. Rooms are smallish but clean enough, with Spanish-language TV and OK bathrooms. The best feature is the secluded central courtyard that the rooms face onto, which includes an elevated area with hammocks. Situated near the market.

Getting There & Away

Boats downriver from Yurimaguas to Lagunas take about 10 hours and leave Yurimaguas between 7am and 8am most days. Times are posted on boards at the port in both Yurimaguas and Lagunas for a day in advance. To continue to Iquitos or return to Yurimaguas, ask which radio station is in contact with the boat captains in case of problems. Fast boats to Yurimaguas arrive in Lagunas between 12pm and 2pm for the four-to five-hour trip against the current.

RESERVA NACIONAL PACAYA-SAMIRIA

At 20,800 sq km, this is the largest of Peru's parks and reserves. **Pacaya-Samiria** (www.pacaya-samiria.com) provides local people with food and a home, and protects ecologically important habitats. An estimated 42,000 people live on and around the reserve; juggling the needs of human inhabitants while protecting wildlife is the responsibility of 20 to 30 rangers. Staff also teach inhabitants how to best harvest the natural renewable resources to benefit the local people and to maintain thriving populations of plants and animals. Three rangers were murdered by poachers in late 1998.

The reserve is the home of aquatic animals such as Amazon manatees, pink and grey river dolphins, two species of caiman, giant South American river turtles and many other bird and animal species. The area close to Lagunas has suffered from depletion: allow several days to get deep into the least-disturbed areas. With 15 days, you can reach **Lago Cocha Pasto**, where there are reasonable chances of seeing jaguars and larger mammals. Other noteworthy points in the reserve include **Quebrada Yanayacu**, where the river water is black from dissolved plants; **Lago Pantean**, where you can check out caimans and go medicinal-plant collecting, and **Tipischa de Huana**, where you can see the giant *Victoria regia* waterlilies, big enough for a small child to sleep upon without sinking. Official information is available at the reserve office in Iquitos.

The best way to visit the reserve is to go by dugout canoe with a guide from Lagunas (see opposite) and spend several days camping and exploring. Alternatively, comfortable ships visit from Iquitos (see p497). The nearest lodge is the Pacaya-Samiria Amazon Lodge (p505).

If coming from Lagunas, Santa Rosa is the main entry point, where you pay the park entrance fee (per person S60 for one to three days, S120 for four to seven days, additional days S20 each).

The best time to go is during the dry season, when you are more likely to see animals along the riverbanks. Rains ease off in late May; it then takes a month for water levels to drop, making July and August the best months to visit (with excellent fishing). September to November isn't too bad, and the heaviest rains begin in January The months of February to May are the worst times to go. February to June tend to be the hottest months.

Travelers should bring plenty of insect repellent and plastic bags (to cover luggage), and be prepared to camp out.

IQUITOS

☎ 065 / pop 430,000 / elev 130m

Linked to the outside world by air and by river, Iquitos is the world's largest city that cannot be reached by road. It's a prosperous, vibrant jungle metropolis teeming with the usual, inexplicably addictive Amazonian anomalies. Unadulterated jungle encroaches beyond town in full view of the air-conditioned, elegant bars and restaurants that flank the riverside; motorized tricycles whiz manically through the streets yet locals mill around the central plazas eating ice cream like there is all the time in the world. Mud huts mingle with magnificent tiled mansions; tiny dugout canoes ply the water alongside colossal cruise ships. You may well arrive in Iquitos for the greater adventure of a boat trip down the Amazon but whether it's sampling rainforest cuisine, checking out the buzzing nightlife or exploring one of Peru's most fascinating markets in the floating shantytown of Belén, this thriving city will entice you to stay awhile.

History

Iquitos was founded in the 1750s as a Jesuit mission, fending off attacks from indigenous tribes that didn't want to be converted. The tiny settlement survived and by the 1870s boasted 1500 inhabitants. Then came the great rubber boom, and by the 1880s the population had increased 16-fold. For the next 30 years, Iquitos was at once the scene of ostentatious wealth and abject poverty. The rubber barons became fabulously rich, while rubber tappers (mainly local tribespeople and poor *mestizos*) suffered virtual enslavement and sometimes death from disease or harsh treatment. Signs of the opulence of those days are seen in some of the mansions and tiled walls of Iquitos.

By WWI, the bottom fell out of the rubber boom as suddenly as it had begun. A British entrepreneur smuggled some rubber-tree seeds out of Brazil, and plantations were seeded in the Malay Peninsula. It was much cheaper and easier to collect the rubber from orderly rows of rubber trees in plantations than from wild trees scattered in the Amazon Basin.

Iquitos suffered economic decline during the decades after WWI, supporting itself with a combination of logging, agriculture (Brazil nuts, tobacco, bananas and *barbasco* – a poisonous vine used by indigenous peoples to hunt fish and now exported for use in insecticides) and the export of wild animals to zoos. Then, in the 1960s, a second boom revitalized the area. This time the resource was oil, and its discovery made Iquitos a prosperous modern town. In recent years tourism has also played an important part in the area's economy.

Orientation

Downtown Iquitos is 7km from its airport – most visitors arrive by air. If you choose to arrive by river, you'll end up at one of two ports, which are between 2km and 3km north of the city center.

Information

Because everything must be 'imported,' costs are higher than in other cities.

EMERGENCY

National police (☎ 23-3330; Morona 126)
Tourism police (☎ 24-2081, 965-93-5932; Lores 834)

IMMIGRATION

Brazil has a consul in Leticia, Colombia. If arriving/leaving from Brazil or Colombia, get your entry/exit stamp at the border.
Colombian Consulate (☎ 23-6246; Araujo 431; ☽ 9am-12:30pm & 2-4:30pm Mon-Fri)
Oficina de migraciónes (☎ 23-5371; Cáceres, cuadra 18)
Spanish Consulate (☎ 23-1608; Putumayo 567)

INTERNET ACCESS

Places charge about S3 per hour.
CQC Cyber Coffee (Raimondi 143) Quite fancy.
Sured Internet (Morona 213; 🖭) Lots of machines.

LAUNDRY

Other laundries can be found in town.
Lavandería Imperial (☎ 23-1768; Putumayo 150; ☽ 8am-8pm Mon-Sat) Coin-operated.

MEDICAL SERVICES

Clínica Ana Stahl (☎ 25-2535; Av La Marina 285; ☽ 24 hr) Good private clinic.

IQUITOS

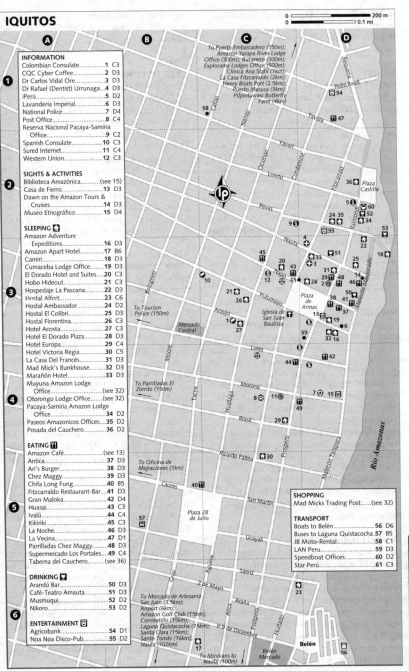

INFORMATION

Colombian Consulate	**1** C3
CQC Cyber Coffee	**2** D3
Dr Carlos Vidal Ore	**3** D3
Dr Rafael (Dentist) Urrunaga	**4** D3
iPerú	**5** D2
Lavandería Imperial	**6** D3
National Police	**7** D4
Post Office	**8** C4
Reserva Nacional Pacaya-Samiria Office	**9** C2
Spanish Consulate	**10** C3
Sured Internet	**11** C4
Western Union	**12** C3

SIGHTS & ACTIVITIES

Biblioteca Amazónica	(see 15)
Casa de Fierro	**13** D3
Dawn on the Amazon Tours & Cruises	**14** D3
Museo Etnográfico	**15** D4

SLEEPING

Amazon Adventure Expeditions	**16** D3
Amazon Apart Hotel	**17** B6
Camiri	**18** D3
Cumaceba Lodge Office	**19** D3
El Dorado Hotel and Suites	**20** C3
Hobo Hideout	**21** C3
Hospedaje La Pascana	**22** D3
Hostal Alfert	**23** C6
Hostal Ambassador	**24** D3
Hostal El Colibrí	**25** D3
Hostal Florentina	**26** C3
Hotel Acosta	**27** C3
Hotel El Dorado Plaza	**28** D3
Hotel Europa	**29** C4
Hotel Victoria Regia	**30** C5
La Casa Del Francés	**31** D3
Mad Mick's Bunkhouse	**32** D3
Marañón Hotel	**33** D3
Muyuna Amazon Lodge Office	(see 32)
Otorongo Lodge Office	(see 32)
Pacaya-Samiria Amazon Lodge Office	**34** D2
Paseos Amazonicos Offices	**35** D2
Posada del Cauchero	**36** D2

EATING

Amazon Café	(see 13)
Antica	**37** D3
Ari's Burger	**38** D3
Chez Maggy	**39** D3
Chifa Long Fung	**40** B5
Fitzcarraldo Restaurant-Bar	**41** D3
Gran Maloka	**42** D4
Huasai	**43** C3
Ivalú	**44** C4
Kikiriki	**45** C3
La Noche	**46** D3
La Vecina	**47** D1
Parrilladas Chez Maggy	**48** D3
Supermercado Los Portales	**49** C4
Taberna del Cauchero	(see 36)

DRINKING

Arandú Bar	**50** D3
Café-Teatro Amauta	**51** D3
Musmuqui	**52** D2
Nikoro	**53** D2

ENTERTAINMENT

Agricobank	**54** D1
Noa Noa Disco-Pub	**55** D2

SHOPPING

Mad Micks Trading Post	(see 32)

TRANSPORT

Boats to Belén	**56** D6
Buses to Laguna Quistacocha	**57** B5
JB Moto-Rental	**58** C1
LAN Peru	**59** D3
Speedboat Offices	**60** D2
Star Perú	**61** C3

0   200 m
0   0.1 mi

To Puerto Embarcadero (150m);
Amazon Yarapa River Lodge
Office (300m); Bucanero (300m);
Explorama Lodges Office (500m);
Clínica Ana Stahl (1km);
La Casa Fitzcarraldo (2km);
Henry Boats Port (2.5km);
Puerto Masusa (3km);
Pilpintuwasi Butterfly
Farm (4km)

To Tourism Police (150m)

To Parrilladas El Zorrito (150m)

To Oficina de Migraciones (1km)

To Mercado de Artesanía
San Juan (3.5km);
Airport (6km);
Amazon Golf Club (15km);
Corrientillo (15km);
Laguna Quistacocha (15km);
Santa Clara (15km);
Santo Tomás (16km);
Nauta (102km)

To Minivans to Nauta (100m)

Plaza Castilla

Plaza de Armas

Iglesia de San Juan Bautista

Mercado Central

Plaza 28 de Julio

Belén Mercado

Belén

Río Amazonas

AMAZON BASIN

Dr Rafael Urrunaga (☎ 23-5016, Fitzcarrald 201) Dentist.
Dr Carlos Vidal Ore (☎ 975-3346; Fitzcarrald 156) Central.

MONEY

Several banks change traveler's checks, give advances on credit cards or provide an ATM, including **BCP** (cnr Prospero & Putumayo), which has a secure ATM. All have competitive rates. For changing US cash quickly, street money changers are located on Próspero between Lores and Brasil. Most are OK, but a few run scams where they replace a S100 note with a S20 note. Exercise caution when changing money on the street. Also see p523 for further information on counterfeit money. Changing Brazilian or Colombian currency is best done at the border. Transfer money at **Western Union** (☎ 23-5182; Napo 359).

POST

Post office (☎ 23-1915; Arica 402; ⏲ 8am-6pm Mon-Fri, to 4:30pm Sat) Near the town center.

TOURIST INFORMATION

Apart from the places listed here, various jungle guides and jungle lodges give tourist information, obviously promoting their services, which is fine if you are looking for them but otherwise rarely helpful.
iPerú Airport (☎ 26-0251; Main Hall, Francisco Secada Vignetta Airport; ⏲ 8am-1pm & 4-8pm); City Center (☎ 23-6144; Loreto 201; ⏲ 8:30am-7:30pm) English spoken at the airport branch.
Iquitos Times (www.iquitostimes.com) A free monthly newspaper in English, aimed at tourists, is delivered to all hotels and restaurants. For the latest on what's going down, ask editor 'Mad' Mick Collis at his office at Putumayo 163.
Reserva Nacional Pacaya-Samiria Office (☎ 22-3460, Pevas 339; ⏲ 8am-4pm Mon-Fri) Entry to the reserve for three days costs S60, payable at Banco de la Nación around the corner.

Dangers & Annoyances

Street touts and self-styled jungle guides tend to be aggressive, and many are both irritatingly insistent and dishonest. They are working for commissions, and often for bog-standard establishments. There have been reports of these guides robbing tourists. It is best to make your own decisions by contacting hotels, lodges and tour companies directly. Petty thieving is common by opportunist young children who roam the streets looking for easy prey. Exercise particular caution around Belén, which is very poor. That said, violent crime is almost unknown in Iquitos.

Sights

CASA DE FIERRO

Every guidebook tells of the 'majestic' Casa de Fierro (Iron House), designed by Gustave Eiffel (of Eiffel Tower fame). It was made in Paris in 1860 and imported piece by piece into Iquitos around 1890, during the opulent rubber-boom days, to beautify the city. Although three different iron houses were imported, only one, at the southeast corner of the Plaza de Armas, survives. It looks like a bunch of scrap-metal sheets bolted together and was once a store and the Iquitos Club. There is now a store on the ground floor and a decent restaurant up top.

AZULEJOS

Other remnants of those rubber-boom days include *azulejos*, handmade tiles imported from Portugal to decorate the mansions of the rubber barons. Many buildings along Raimondi and Malecón Tarapaca are lavishly decorated with *azulejos*. Some of the best are various government buildings along or near the Malecón.

LIBRARY & MUSEUM

On the Malecón, at the corner with Morona, is an old building housing the **Biblioteca Amazónica** (the largest collection of historical documents in the Amazon Basin) and the small **Museo Etnográfico**. Both are open on weekdays (admission for both S3). The museum includes life-sized fiberglass casts of members of various Amazon tribes.

BELÉN

At the southeast end of town is the floating shantytown of Belén, consisting of scores of huts, built on rafts, which rise and fall with the river. During the low-water months, these rafts sit on the river mud and are dirty and unhealthy, but for most of the year they float on the river – a colorful and exotic sight. Seven thousand people live here, and canoes float from hut to hut selling and trading jungle produce. The best time to visit the shantytown is at 7am, when people from the jungle villages arrive to sell their produce. To get here, take a cab to 'Los Chinos,' walk to the port and rent a canoe to take you around.

AMAZON BASIN

Belén mercado, located within the city blocks in front of Belén, is the raucous, crowded affair common to most Peruvian towns. All kinds of strange and exotic products are sold here among the more mundane bags of rice, sugar, flour and cheap household goods. Look for the bark of the *chuchuhuasi* tree, which is soaked in rum for weeks and used as a tonic (it's served in many of the local bars). *Chuchuhuasi* and other Amazon plants are common ingredients in herbal pain-reducing and arthritis formulas manufactured in Europe and the USA. The market makes for exciting shopping and sightseeing, but do remember to watch your wallet.

Activities

AMAZON GOLF CLUB

Amazing as it may seem, you can play a round or two on the nine holes of the wonderful **Amazon Golf Club** (☎ 963-1333, 975-4976; Quistacocha; admission per day incl golf-club rental S60; ☺ 6am-6pm), the only course in the entire Amazon. Founded in 2004 by a bunch of nostalgic expats, the 2140m course was built on virgin bushland and it boasts, apart from its nine greens, a wooden clubhouse. Hole 4 is a beauty: you tee onto an island surrounded by piranha-infested waters. Don't go fishing for lost balls! When fully completed the clubhouse will also include a bar (it already has a fridge full of beer) and the grounds will feature a swimming pool and a tennis court. Meantime see cofounder Bill Grimes (below) at the course city office for information on how to get some swinging action.

RIVER CRUISES

Cruising the Amazon is an expensive business: the shortest trips can cost more than US$1000. It's a popular pastime, too, and advance reservations are often necessary. Cruises naturally focus on the Río Amazonas, both downriver (northeast) towards the Brazil–Colombia border and upriver to Nauta, where the Ríos Marañon and Ucayali converge. Beyond Nauta, trips continue up these two rivers to the Pacaya-Samiria reserve. Trips can also be arranged on the three rivers surrounding Iquitos: the Itaya, the Amazonas and the Nanay. Operators quote prices in US dollars.

Dawn on the Amazon Tours & Cruises (☎ 23-3730, 993-9190, 994-3267; www.dawnontheamazon.com; Malecón Maldonado 185, Iquitos; day trips incl lunch per person US$65, multiday cruises per person US$150 per day) This small outfit offers the best deal for independent travelers. The *Amazon I* is a beautiful 33ft wooden craft with modern furnishings, available for either day trips or longer river cruises up to two weeks. Included are a bilingual guide, all meals and transfers. You can travel with host Bill Grimes and his experienced crew along the Amazon, or along its quieter tributaries (larger cruise ships will necessarily stick to the main waterways). Dawn on the Amazon has exclusive permission to go twice as far into Pacaya-Samiria reserve as any other tour company. The beauty of these cruises is in their flexibility: many cruise operators have fixed departures and itineraries but Bill's can be adapted to accommodate individual needs. The tri-river cruise is a favorite local trip.

Amazon Cruises (☎ in the USA 800-747-0567; www.amazoncruise.net; 3-night Marañon & Ucayali cruise per person US$1401, 6-day Marañon & Ucayali cruise per person US$2261) Amazon Cruises operates the charming riverboat *MV Amazon Journey (El Arca)*, which has twice-weekly departures into the Pacaya-Samiria reserve. The vessel has 13 cabins with air-con that have upper and lower bunks, and three cabins with three- and four-bed configurations. There is also a dorm bunkroom. All cabins have private showers. The ship has an air-conditioned restaurant seating 22. Cruises last three or six days.

The company can also arrange passage on other cruise ships sailing downriver to the tri-border with Colombia (Leticia) and Brazil (Tabatinga). Cruises normally last six days (three there, three back).

Cruise boats come with plenty of deck space for river-watching, a full crew and bilingual guides. Meals are included and small launches are carried for side trips. Activities can involve visiting indigenous communities (for dancing and craft sales), hikes, and bird- and pink dolphin–watching (on big ships, don't expect to see too much rare wildlife). Excursions are three or six days.

Green Tracks Amazon Tours & Cruises (☎ in the USA 970-884-6107, 800-892-1035; www.amazontours.net; 7 days & 6 nights s/d US2700/5000) With three luxury ships plying the Peruvian Amazon, Green Tracks offers four- to seven-day excursions into the Pacaya-Samiria reserve. The *Ayapua* is a 20-passenger, rubber-boom-era boat used for seven-day/six-night voyages, with air-conditioned rooms, a bar and even a library. *Delfín I* and *Delfín II* are more modern vessels accommodating 12 and 28 passengers,

AMAZON BASIN

respectively, and operate four- and five-day cruises to the reserve. Contact the company in the USA for details.

International Expeditions (☎ in the USA 205-428-1700, 800-633-4734; www.ietravel.com; 10 days & 9 nights per person US$3298) This well-organized company operates three boats, generally using the 15-cabin *MV Amatista*, as well as the 14-cabin *MV Turmalina* and the larger 23-cabin *MV Turquesa*. Their relaxing and pampering nine-day river cruises take in the Ríos Amazon and Ucayali, passing through Requena en route to the Pacaya-Samiria reserve. These are elegant boats with three decks, air-conditioned double cabins with private showers, excellent dining and viewing facilities and experienced guides. Contact the company in the USA for details; you need advance reservations.

Sleeping

There's a broad range of accommodation choices in Iquitos, from basic budget to five-star comfort. Mosquitoes are rarely a serious problem in town, so mosquito netting is not always provided.

The best hotels tend to be booked up on Friday and Saturday. The busiest season is from May to September, when prices may rise slightly.

BUDGET

All of these hotels have bathrooms and fans unless otherwise indicated.

Mad Mick's Bunkhouse (☎ 975-4976; michaelcollis@hotmail.com; Putumayo 163; dm S12) A stone's throw from the Plaza de Armas, this is the city's cheapest accommodation: a dark, eight-bed dorm (four bunks) with one bathroom (interesting graffiti) that attracts shoestringers in droves.

Hostal Alfert (☎ 23-4105; Sáenz 1; s/d S15/25/35) With a great view of the river and the floating neighborhood of Belén, the gaudy green-painted Alfert tends to attracts budget travelers. With sizeable rooms and warm showers, it emits a kind of laid-back charm, but its out-of-the-way location in a rather insalubrious neighborhood is a disadvantage.

Hobo Hideout (☎ 23-4099; hobohideout@yahoo.com; Putumayo 437; dm/s/d without bathroom S17.50/25, d with/without bathroom S35/50) Looking rather sorry for itself lately, this place nevertheless retains its cool travelers vibe. Kitchen privileges, a laundry area, a bar and a cable TV room draw

international hobos. One (pricier) room towers above the rest on jungle-style stilts; others are small and dark. A variety of interesting expeditions can be arranged.

La Casa Del Francés (☎ 965-92-6442; jessia_20@hotmail.com; Raimondi 183; s/d S25/40) A secure, hammock-strung courtyard leads back to this pleasant budget choice offering several large simple rooms with spotless tiled bathrooms.

Camiri (☎ 965-98-2854; marcelbendayan@hotmail.com; end of Pevas cuadra 1; r per person with/without bathroom S30/25) For a memorable dose of relaxed, rustic Iquitos living, come to crash at this floating hostel-bar, accessed by boardwalks over the river. Five cozy rooms are offered here, one with private and four with shared showers. River views are exquisite and owner Marcel Bendayan is a mine of intriguing information. There is no electricity but plenty of lively candle-lit conversation on the river terrace.

Hospedaje La Pascana (☎ 23-5581, 23-1418; www.pascana.com; Pevas 133; s/d/t S35/40/50) This safe and friendly place with a small, verdant garden is deservedly popular with travelers and often full. A book exchange and a charming cafe serving fresh-brewed coffee add to the attraction.

Hostal El Colibrí (☎ 24-1737; hostalelcolibri@hotmail.com; Nauta 172; s/d S40/50) A very good budget choice close to the river and the main square, with pleasant, airy rooms sporting fans and TVs. The traveler-friendly folk running this place added three more floors of rooms in 2009; a street-front restaurant is planned for 2010.

Hostal Florentina (☎ 23-3591; Huallaga 212; s/d S40/50) Rooms in this old colonial house are smallish but very quiet. They come with fans, cable TV, mosquito nets and sparkling bathrooms, and are tucked well back from the road with a lovely courtyard for hammocks at the rear.

MIDRANGE

All places listed here have air-con and private bathroom, normally with hot water. Walk-in rates for standard rooms are given here; holiday rates may be higher.

Hotel Europa (☎ 23-1123; hoteleuropasac@yahoo.es; Próspero 494; s S70-90, d S110-130; ⊠) One of the best midrange bargains, the canary-yellow Europa is a homely hotel and ticks all the boxes you could expect for the price range: air-con, minifridges, a good restaurant and laundry service.

Hostal Ambassador (☎ /fax 23-110; Pevas 260; s/d incl breakfast S76/107; ☒) For some reason this is the American tour group hangout of choice. Ample if musty rooms get writing desks, cable TV and air-con but very little light. Continental breakfast in the pleasant cafeteria and free airport transfers are provided.

Marañón Hotel (☎ 24-2673; www.hmaranon.k25.net; Nauta 285; s/d incl continental breakfast S99/130; ☒ ☎) One of the newer Iquitos hotels, this place has light tiles everywhere and a restaurant with room service. The rooms have good-sized bathrooms as well as the usual amenities. Good value.

Posada del Cauchero (☎ 23-1699; latabernadel cauchero@yahoo.es; Raimondi 449; s/d/ste S100/120/180; ☒ ☎) Above the restaurant of the same name lurk 12 classy, massive, chalet-style rooms (seven with air-con), some of which are suites. All are decorated with cool, modern, tribal-themed art. There is a pool and some of the best river views in Iquitos.

Amazon Apart Hotel (☎ 26-6262; reservas@ AmazonApartHotel.com; Aguirre 1151; s/d S120/144, ste S144 ??1; ☒ ☐ ☎) This bright, new, well-appointed hotel is a little out of the way – but this is its only disadvantage. There are several levels of vast colorful rooms here. Rooms all have air-con and minifridges; many also have their own kitchenettes, so that you can self-cater in style. Also has internet, a restaurant doing mean ceviche and an attractive swimming pool.

our pick **La Casa Fitzcarraldo** (☎ 60-1138/39; info@lacasafitzcarraldo.com; www.lacasafitzcarraldo.com, Av La Marina 2153; r S130-200; ☒ ☐ ☎) Sequestered within a serene walled garden away from the city chaos, this is the most interesting accommodation option. The house takes its title from Werner Herzog's film – Herzog and co stayed here during the filming of *Fitzcarraldo* (see p502). Stay in the mahogany-floored Mick Jagger room, the luxuriantly green Klaus Kinski suite or five other individually designed rooms. There is a tree house (with wi-fi!), a lovely swimming pool (nonresidents S5) and a huge breakfast included in the price, as well as a bar-restaurant and several four-legged residents to check out.

Hotel Acosta (☎ 23-1761; www.hotelacosta.com; cnr Araujo & Huallaga; s/d S150/180) Owned by the same people as the Victoria Regia; you can be sure you're in good hands at this smart hotel. Rooms are large and all come with mini-fridges, air-con, minisafes and writing desks. There is a ground-floor restaurant.

TOP END

These top-end hotels have limited rooms and fill fast: reservations aren't a bad idea.

Hotel Victoria Regia (☎ 23-1983; www.victoriaregia hotel.com; Ricardo Palma 252; s/d incl breakfast S210/240, ste S300-450; ☒ ☐ ☎) A blast of icy, air-conditioned air welcomes guests to this comfortable hostelry. It has excellent beds and size-able rooms that include fancy reading lights and minifridges, plus hairdryers and baths in the bathrooms. One of the suites has a Jacuzzi. The indoor pool and fine restaurant-bar attract upscale guests and businesspeople.

Hotel El Dorado Plaza (☎ 22-2555; iquitos@eldorado plazahotel.com; Napo 258; r incl breakfast from S726; ☒ ☎) With a prime plaza location, this modern hotel is the town's best, with 64 well-equipped, spa-cious rooms (some with plaza views, others overlooking the pool). Jacuzzi, sauna, gym, restaurant, several suites, 24-hour room service, two bars and attentive staff make this a five-star hotel. Rates for rooms are often discounted when the hotel is not busy. The same group runs the slightly cheaper El Dorado Hotel & Suites (☎ 23-2574) at Napo 362 (singles S230, doubles S273, suites from S410), where you can still use the plaza hotel facilities.

Eating

There are great eats at the various markets, particularly the Belén *mercado* (cnr Prospero with Jirón 9 de Diciembre) and Mercado Central (Lores cuadra 5). A set *menú* here, including *jugo especial* (jungle juice) is under S5; watch your valuables. The city has great restaurants but sadly many regional speciali-ties feature endangered animals, such as *chich-arrón de lagarto* (fried alligator), *paiche* (local river fish) and *sopa de tortuga* (turtle soup). More environmentally friendly dishes include ceviche made with river fish and *chupín de pollo*, a tasty soup of chicken, egg and rice.

For self-catering supplies, visit **Supermercado Los Portales** (Próspero at Morona).

Ivalú (Lores 215; snacks from S2; ☽ breakfast & lunch) One of the most popular local spots for juice and cake in the city, this place does a handy sideline in tamales (chicken or fish in corn dough, wrapped in jungle leaves). It normally opens at 8am; go sooner rather than later if you want a seat.

Parilladas El Zorrito (☎ 23-3662; Fanning 355; mains S5-10) Food is cooked outside on a grill at this lively, ambient, immensely popular local joint.

Juanes and river fish are the thing to go for here. Portions are huge. There is great live music at weekends.

Kikiriki (☎ 23-2020; Napo 159; quarter-chicken from S6; ☼ dinner only) How does a Peruvian cock crow? '*Kikiriki.*' This is the best place in town for grilled chicken. Have it served on a bed of fried banana, the jungle way, with a dash of the legendary hot green sauce. Delivery is possible.

Huasai (☎ 24-2222; Fitzcarrald 131; mains S7-12; ☼ breakfast & lunch) Efficient service, a variety of dependable tasty meat and fish lunch specials and great juices are the cornerstones of this good-value, centrally located restaurant.

La Vecina (Tavara West 352, small/large ceviche S8/15; ☼ lunch only) There's else nothing but ceviche on the menú at this homely place, but that doesn't disappoint.

our pick La Noche (☎ 22-2373; Malecón Maldonado 177; sandwiches S8-10; mains S15-25; ☼ 7am-late) The friendliest service in Iquitos, the best location, a cool sophisticated vibe and oodles of tasty food: no wonder La Noche is the number one traveler choice for a relaxed Malecón meal. There's real espresso, a host of gourmet sandwiches (the vegetarian triple can't be beaten) for lunch, and river fish and crisp salads grace the dinner menu. There is street-front or balcony dining and a chill-out lounge-bar upstairs with sofas.

Chifa Long Fung (☎ 23-3649; San Martín 454; mains S10-20; ☼ 12pm-2.30pm & 7pm-12am) There are several inexpensive *chifas* and other restaurants near the Plaza 28 de Julio, of which the Long Fung is a little more expensive but worth it.

Amazon Café (cnr Putumayo & Próspero; starters S10-14, mains S20-35; ☼ 7am-12am) You can sit here on the balcony at the top of the Casa de Fierro and enjoy premium plaza views and a varied if overpriced menu ranging from seafood to steak. There is a good selection of whiskies and cocktails.

Fitzcarraldo Restaurant-Bar (☎ 24-3434; Napo 100; mains S10-25; ☼ noon-late; ☒) The Fitzcarraldo anchors a whole block of riverside restaurants and is the most upscale of them, with good food and service. Dine indoors (the air-con can be extra chilly) or on the streetside patio. It does good pizzas (delivery available) and various local and international dishes.

Ari's Burger (☎ 23-1470; Próspero 127; meals S10-25; ☼ 7am-3am) On the corner of the Plaza de Armas, this clean, chirpy and brightly lit joint is known locally as '*gringolandia.*' Two walls are open to the street, allowing great plaza- and people- watching. It's almost always open, serves American-style food as well as local plates and ice creams, changes US dollars and is popular with tourists and locals alike. Desserts in Iquitos don't get gooier.

Chez Maggy (☎ 24-1816; Raimondi 181; pastas around S12, pizzas S20-30; ☼ 6-11:30pm) A wood-burning oven produces fresh pizzas, just like its sister restaurants in Cuzco and other Amazon cities. Across the street, they've now opened a second, yet more ambient venue, Parilladas Chez Maggy, for those preferring grills.

Taberna del Cauchero (☎ 23-1699; latabernadelcauchero@yahoo.es; Raimondi 449; mains S15-30; ☼ 8am-10pm) This place pays homage to the city's rubber-boom days with intriguing memorabilia on the walls. The only Cordon Bleu chef in Iquitos serves up innovative modern takes on Amazon cuisine (such as river langostinos with chorizo and avocado stuffed into a Mexican-style tortilla) in a spacious, stylishly rustic eating area. It even does sushi, and there's a pool. A traveler hangout in the making.

Antica (☎ 24-1672; Napo 159; breakfasts S7-10, mains S18-30; ☼ 7am-midnight) New in 2006, the Antica is the best Italian restaurant in town. Primarily a pizza place – there's an impressive wood-fired pizza oven – pasta also takes a predominant spot on the menu with the lasagna being an excellent choice. Chow down at solid wooden tables and choose from the range of fine imported Italian wines; unparalleled for the Amazon.

Bucanero (Av Marina 124; mains S20-30; ☼ 11am-5pm; ☒) For great river views in civilized air-conditioned environs, this restaurant with a fish-dominated menu is a great lunch stop. *Pescado a la plancha* (grilled river fish) with *chicharrones* (fried chunks of pork) goes down remarkably well with an icy Iquiteña (Iquitos beer).

Gran Maloka (☎ 23-3126; Lores 170; menú S15, mains S25-40; ☼ noon-10pm; ☒) Enter the by-gone world of the rubber-boom glory days at this atmospheric Amazonian restaurant. It's an elegant tiled mansion with silk table-cloths, wall-length mirrors and imaginative regional delicacies such as *chupín de pollo*, Amazon venison with toasted coconut and the scrumptious Loretan omelet with jungle leaves. Locals consider this to be the town's best restaurant.

Drinking

Iquitos is a party city. The Malecón is the cornerstone of the lively nightlife scene.

Arandú Bar (☎ 24-3434; Malecón Maldonado 113) Next to the Fitzcarraldo, this is the liveliest of several thumping Malecón bars, great for people-watching and always churning out loud rock-and-roll classics.

Musmuqui (Raimondi 382; ☽ to midnight Sun-Thu, to 3am Fri & Sat) Locally popular lively bar with two floors and an extensive range of aphrodisiac cocktails concocted from wondrous Amazon plants.

Café-Teatro Amauta (☎ 23-3109; Nauta 250) Hosts live Peruvian music on most nights and has a well-stocked bar with local drinks, as well as a cafe.

Nikoro (☎ 50-8973; end of Pevas cuadra 1) A chic bar that goes through spates of being really popular or really dead. If it's lively, there's nowhere better for a beer to watch sunset on the river. Go down the left-hand set of steps from Pevas to get there.

Entertainment

Agricobank (Condamine at Pablo Rosell; admission around S5) For dancing, the most locally popular venue is this, a huge outdoor place where hundreds of locals gather for drinking, dancing and socializing. It's only open at weekends.

Noa Noa Disco-Pub (☎ 23-2902; cnr Fitzcarrald & Pevas; admission around S15) More upscale; a very trendy disco with salsa rhythms predominating. If gringos go out dancing, it's usually here.

Shopping

There are a few shops on the first block of Napo selling jungle crafts, some of high quality and pricey. A good place for crafts is **Mercado de Artesanía San Juan**, on the road to the airport – bus and taxi drivers know it. Don't buy items made from animal bones and skins, as they are made from jungle wildlife. It's illegal to import many such items into the US and Europe.

You can buy, rent or trade almost anything needed for a jungle expedition at **Mad Mick's Trading Post** (☎ 965-75-4976; michaelcollis@hotmail .com; Putumayo 163; ☽ 8am-8pm). Don't need it afterwards? Mick will buy anything back (if it's in good nick) for half-price.

Getting There & Away

AIR

Iquitos' small but busy airport currently receives flights from Lima and Pucallpa.

LAN Peru (☎ 23-2421; Próspero 232) operates the best and most expensive flights, with two morning and two afternoon flights to Lima. **Star Perú** (☎ 23-6208; Napo 256) also operates flights to and from Lima via Tarapoto or Pucallpa, all leaving in the afternoon. Fares are about US$130 to Lima and US$86 to Pucallpa or Tarapoto.

Charter companies at the airport have five-passenger planes to almost anywhere in the Amazon. Rates are around US$300 an hour. Other small airlines may have offices at the airport.

Airport domestic departure tax is S13.81.

The airport is about 7km from the center of Iquitos. A taxi costs around S7 for a *mototaxi* and S15 for a cab.

BOAT

Iquitos is Peru's largest, best-organized river port. You can theoretically travel all the way from Iquitos to the Atlantic Ocean, but most boats out of Iquitos today ply only Peruvian waters, and voyagers necessarily change boats at the Colombian–Brazilian border (see p506).

Three main ports are of interest to travelers.

Puerto Masusa on Av La Marina, about 3km north of the town center, is where cargo boats to Yurimaguas (upriver; three to six days) and Pucallpa (upriver; four to seven days) leave from. Fares cost S100 for hammock space up to S180 for a tiny (often cell-like) cabin. Boats leave most days for both ports: there are more frequent departures for the closer intermediate ports. The Eduardo boats to Yurimaguas are quite comfortable, although there have been reports from readers of them mistreating transported animals.

Downriver boats to the Peruvian border with Brazil and Colombia leave from Puerto Masusa too. There are about two or three departures weekly for the two-day journey (per person S50 to S80). Boats will stop at Pevas (hammock space S20; about 15 hours) and other ports en route. Boats may dock closer to the center if the water is very high (from May to July).

The Henry Boats ply the Iquitos–Pucallpa route and have their own more organized **port** (☎ 965-67-8630; ☽ 7am-7pm) on Av La Marina, closer to the center.

AMAZON BASIN

At both ports chalkboards tell you which boats are leaving when, for where, and whether they are accepting passengers. Although there are agencies in town, it's usually best to go to the dock and look around; don't trust anyone except the captain for an estimate of departure time. Be wary: the chalkboards have a habit of changing dates overnight! Boats often leave hours or even days late.

You can often sleep aboard the boat while waiting for departure, and this enables you to get the best hammock space. Never leave gear unattended – ask to have your bags locked up when you sleep.

Finally, there is tiny **Puerto Embarcadero**, for speedboats to the tri-border. These depart at 6am daily except Monday. You'll need to purchase your ticket in advance. Speedboat offices are bunched together on Raimondi near the Plaza Castilla. Standard fares are S150 to Pevas or S180 for the 10- to 12-hour trip to Santa Rosa, including meals.

You might also be able to book a berth on a Leticia-bound cruise ship (see p497) if space is available.

Getting Around

Taxis are relatively few and are pricier than in other Peruvian cities, but squadrons of busy *mototaxis* can oblige with lifts. The ubiquitous *mototaxis* cost less than taxis and are fun to ride, though they don't provide much protection in an accident. Always enter *mototaxis* from the sidewalk side – passing traffic pays scant heed to embarking passengers – and keep your limbs inside at all times. Scrapes and fender bending are common. Most rides around Iquitos cost a standard S1.50.

Buses and trucks for several nearby destinations, including the airport, leave from near Plaza 28 de Julio. Airport buses are marked Nanay-Belén-Aeropuerto: they'll head south down Arica to the airport.

A paved road now extends 102km through the jungle as far as Nauta on the Río Marañón, near its confluence with the Río Ucayali. Riverboat passengers from Yurimaguas can now alight at Nauta and pick up a local bus to Iquitos, thus making the journey shorter by some six hours. Boats from Pucallpa do not stop at Nauta. Minivans to Nauta take two

---

HERZOG'S AMAZON

Eccentric German director Werner Herzog, often seen as obsessive and bent on filming 'reality itself,' shot two movies in Peru's jungle: *Aguirre, the Wrath of God* (1972) and *Fitzcarraldo* (1987). Herzog's accomplishments in getting these movies made at all – during havoc-fraught filming conditions – are in some ways more remarkable than the finished products.

Klaus Kinski, the lead actor in *Aguirre*, was a volatile man prone to extreme fits of rage. Herzog's documentary *My Best Fiend* depicts details such incidents as Kinski beating a conquistador extra so severely that his helmet, donned for the part, was all that saved him from being killed. (To tell both sides of the story, however, *My Best Fiend* also reveals that Herzog admitted to once trying to firebomb Kinski in his house. Kinski's biography, *Kinski Uncut* (albeit partly ghostwritten by Herzog) paints a picture of the director as a buffoon who had no idea how to make movies.) Near the end of shooting, after altercations with a cameraman on the Río Nanay, Kinski prepared to desert the film crew on a speedboat. Herzog had to threaten to shoot him with a rifle to make him stay.

Filming *Fitzcarraldo*, the first choice for the lead fell ill and the second, Mick Jagger, abandoned the set to do a Rolling Stones tour. With a year's filming already wasted, Herzog was obliged to call upon Kinski once more. Kinski soon antagonized the Matsiguenka tribespeople being used as extras: one even offered to murder him for Herzog. While filming near the Peru–Ecuador frontier, a war between the two nations erupted and soldiers destroyed the film set. Then there was the weather: droughts so dire that the rivers dried and stranded the film's steamship for weeks, followed by flash floods that wrecked the boat entirely. (Some of these are chronicled in *Conquest of the Useless: Reflections from the Making of Fitzcarraldo*, Herzog's film diaries, translated into English in 2009.)

Herzog could be a hard man to work with, filming many on-set catastrophes and using them as footage in the final cut. The director once said he saw filming in the Amazon as 'challenging nature itself.' The fact that he completed two films in the Peruvian jungle against such odds is evidence that in some ways, Herzog did challenge nature – and triumphed.

hours and depart from the corner of Próspero and José Gálvez. There are swimming opportunities at the creeks and beaches en route.

JB Moto-Rental (☎ 22-2389; Yavari 702) rents motorcycles.

AROUND IQUITOS
Nearby Villages & Lakes
About 16km from town, past the airport, **Santo Tomás** is famous for its pottery and mask making, and has a few bars overlooking Mapacocha, a lake formed by an arm of the Río Nanay. You can rent boats by asking around (motorboat with driver about S30). **Santa Clara** is about 15km away, on the banks of the Río Nanay. There are white-sand beaches during low water (July to October), and boats are available for rent. Both villages can be reached by *mototaxi* (about S15) or a S2 minivan ride from the Nauta van stop.

Corrientillo is a lake near the Río Nanay. There are a few bars around the lake, which is locally popular for swimming on weekends and has good sunsets. It's about 15km from town; a *mototaxi* will charge about S15.

Pilpintuwasi Butterfly Farm
A visit to the fascinating **Pilpintuwasi Butterfly Farm** (☎ 065-23-2665; www.amazonanimalorphanage.org; Padra Cocha; admission S15; ✆ 9am-4pm Tue-Sun) is highly recommended. Ostensibly this is a conservatorium and breeding center for Amazonian butterflies. Butterflies aplenty there certainly are, including the striking blue morpho (*Morpho menelaus*) and the fearsome-looking owl butterfly (*Caligo eurilochus*), which has a big owl-like eye on its wing. But it's the farm's exotic animals that steal the show. Raised as orphans and protected within the property are several mischievous monkeys, Lolita the tapir and Pedro Bello, a majestic orphaned jaguar, who has his own enclosure. You'll also meet capricious Rosa, a giant anteater who wanders around freely looking for ants. To get there, take a small boat from Bellavista-Nanay, a small port 2km north of Iquitos, to the village of Padre Cocha. Boats run all day. The farm is signposted and is a 15-minute walk through the village from the Padre Cocha boat dock.

Laguna Quistacocha
This lake, 15km south of Iquitos, is served by minibuses several times an hour from near Plaza 28 de Julio (cnr Bermúdez with Moore; S2), as well as *mototaxis* (S12). There

is a small **zoo** of local fauna here, much improved of recent years, and an adjoining **fish hatchery**, which has 2m-long *paiche*, now an endangered river fish due to loss of habitat and its popularity as a food. An attempt to rectify the situation is being made with the breeding program here. A pedestrian walk circles the lake, swimming is possible and paddleboats are available for hire. There are several restaurants and a hiking trail to the Itaya River. It's fairly crowded with locals on the weekend but not midweek. Admission is S10.

Jungle Lodges & Expeditions
Jungle 'guides' will approach you everywhere in Iquitos. Some will be independent operators, and many will be working on behalf of a lodge. Travelers have had mixed experiences with private guides; none are especially recommended. All guides should have a permit or license – if they don't, check with the tourist office. Get references for any guide, and proceed with caution (also see Dangers & Annoyances, p496). The better lodges snap up the best guides quickly and can arrange wilderness trips.

There are numerous lodges both up- and downriver from Iquitos. Take your time choosing: a bewildering variety of programs and activities are available and quality varies considerably. There is the usual mix of luxury options, where relaxation plays a key part, and more rustic lodges offering camping, hiking, fishing (July to September are the best months) and other adventurous side trips. Most lodges have offices in Iquitos.

A wide range of options at varying prices can be booked from abroad or in Lima, but if you show up in Iquitos without a reservation you can certainly book a lodge or tour and it'll cost you less. Bargaining is not out of the question, even though operators show you fixed price lists. If the lodge has space and you have the cash, they'll nearly always give you a discount. If planning on booking after you arrive, avoid the major Peruvian holidays, when places fill with local holidaymakers. June to September (the dry months and the summer vacation for North American and European visitors) is also quite busy.

The lodges are some distance from Iquitos, so river transport is included in the price. Most of the area within 50km of the city is not virgin jungle. Chances of seeing big mammals here is remote, and tribespeople will be and interaction with local tribespeople is likely to be geared towards tourists. Nevertheless, much can be seen of the jungle way of life, and birds, insects and small mammals can be observed. The more remote lodges have more wildlife.

A typical two-day trip involves a river journey of two or three hours to a jungle lodge with reasonable comforts and meals, a jungle lunch, a guided visit to an indigenous village to buy crafts and to see dances (where tourists often outnumber tribespeople), an evening meal at the lodge, maybe an after-dark canoe trip to look for caiman by searchlight, and jungle walks to search for other wildlife. A trip like this will set you back about US$300, depending on the operator, the distance traveled and the comfort of the lodge. On longer trips you'll get further away from Iquitos and see more of the jungle, and the cost per night drops.

There are many good lodges in the Iquitos area that will give you a rewarding rainforest experience. All prices quoted here are approximate; bargaining is often acceptable, and meals, tours and transportation from Iquitos should be included. Lodges will provide containers of purified water for you to fill your own bottle, as well as 24-hour hot water with instant coffee and tea bags, but bring extra water for the journey. Meals normally include juice. Also see p472 for advice on items to bring with you. The following lodges are listed in order of distance from Iquitos.

Paseos Amazonicos (www.paseosamazonicos.com; 3 days & 2 nights per person US$130-180); Iquitos (☎ 065-23-1618; Pevas 246) Lima (☎ 01-241-7576; Office 4, Bajada Balta 131, Miraflores) This company runs three lodges. One of the oldest and best established is Amazonas Sinchicuy Lodge, on a small tributary of the Amazon 30km northeast of Iquitos. The 32 rooms, which can sleep up to four, have private cold showers and are lantern-lit. Some rooms are wheelchair accessible. This lodge can be visited on a day trip from Iquitos. The palm-thatched Tambo Yanayacu Lodge, 60km northeast of Iquitos, has 10 rustic rooms with private bathrooms. The staff here can supply tents for jungle expeditions. Stays at these two lodges can be combined into one trip, including visits to local Yagua communities. Finally, the Tambo Amazonico Lodge is about 160km upriver on the Río Yarapa. It is less a lodge and more of a camping place, with two open-air dormitories sleeping up to 20 people, with beds and mosquito nets.

Camping trips can be arranged, including into the Pacaya-Samiria reserve.

Cumaceba Lodges (☎ 065-22-1456; www.cumaceba .com; Putumayo 184, Iquitos; 3 days & 2 nights US$180-222) This company has been in business since 1995 and operates three lower-end lodges. Guides speak English, French and even Japanese. The lodges are all aimed at providing budget travelers with an Amazon experience, and also operate day-trips within the Iquitos area for US$65.

First up, Cumaceba Lodge is about 35km downriver from Iquitos. This popular budget option has 15 screened rooms with private showers, and can arrange more adventurous trips where accommodations are in simple, open-sided shelters. At 90km downstream from Iquitos, Amazonas Botanical Lodge places an emphasis on studying rainforest plants, in addition to wildlife-watching. Rustic en suite bungalows are right near primary jungle and there's a botanical garden. *Ayahuasca* ceremonies and a trip to a *paiche* farm are also offered. Finally, about 180km upstream past Nauta is Piranha Ecoexplorer Lodge (www .peruamazon.com), offering a variety of adventurous activities. The five-day program includes fishing with spears, camping and a trip to see stupendously sized *Victoria regia* lilies. Accommodation is rustic, much like other Cumaceba lodges.

ourpick Otorongo Lodge (☎ 065-22-4192, 965-75-6131; www.otorongoexpeditions.com; Departamento 203, Putumayo 163, Iquitos; 5 day & 4 nights US$590) Travelers have been giving great feedback about this relatively new, rustic-style lodge, 100km from Iquitos. It's a down-to-earth place, with 12 rooms with private bathrooms and a relaxing common area, surrounded by walkways to maximize appreciation of the surrounding wildlife. Otorongo is run by a former falconer who can imitate an incredible number of bird sounds and get you up close and personal to a huge variety of wildlife. This lodge comes recommended for a magical, personal experience of the Amazonian wilderness. The five-day option can include lots of off-the-beaten-path visits to nearby communities, and camping trips deeper in the jungle. Otorongo offer passersby (!) en route to the Colombian border a daily rate of US$50; backpackers have the option of a separate simple lodge with hammock space in nearby Oran village (15km away) for US$10. A separate lodge in Pevas is due to open late in 2009.

Amazon Yarapa River Lodge (☎ 065-993-1172; www.yarapa.com; Av La Marina 124, Iquitos; 4 days & 3 nights s/d US$1020/1840, s/d without bathroom 940/1680; 🖳)) Approximately 130km upriver from Iquitos on the Río Yarapa, this lodge is simply stunning. It has a huge and well-designed tropical biology laboratory, regularly used by Cornell University (USA) for research and postgraduate classes. The lab is powered by an expansive solar-panel system, which provides electric power throughout the lodge; there are also satellite phone connections. Facilities are beautifully maintained: elaborate woodcarvings in the restaurant-bar and even on the bed heads were made by local artists, and fully screened rooms are linked by screened walkways. Eight huge bedrooms with oversized private bathrooms are available (professors stay here when Cornell is in residence) and 16 comfortable rooms share a multitude of well-equipped bathrooms. With its scientific agenda, the lodge offers top-notch guides for its jungle tours, which visit remote areas. The boats take about three to four hours from Iquitos but have a bathroom aboard. Recommended.

Tahuayo Lodge (www.perujungle.com; 8 days per person US$1295); USA (Amazonia Expeditions; ☎ 813-907-8475, 800-262-9669) Iquitos (Av La Marina 100) You'll hear the phrase 'Pacaya-Samiria' bandied around a lot in these parts but this is only one of several reserves in the northern jungle. This lodge, 140km from Iquitos, has exclusive access to the 2500-sq-km Tamshiyacu-Tahuayo reserve, an area of pristine jungle where a record 93 species of mammal have been recorded. The 15 lodge cabins are located 65km up an Amazon tributary, built on high stilts and connected by walkways; half have private bathrooms. There is a laboratory with a library here, too. Wildlife viewing opportunities are among the best of any lodge listed: they usually include a peek at the pygmy marmosets that nest near the lodge. Visitors can also stay at the nearby Tahuayo River Research Center, which boasts an extensive trail network.

Muyuna Amazon Lodge (☎ office 065-24-2858, 065-993-4424; www.muyuna.com; ground fl, Putumayo 163, Iquitos; 3 days & 2 nights s/d US$385/640) About 140km upriver from Iquitos on the Río Yanayacu, this intimate lodge is surrounded by 10 well-conserved lakes in a remote area less colonized than jungle downriver, which makes for a great rainforest experience. Ten stilted, thatched bungalows here each sleep between

two and six people and get a private cold shower and a balcony with a hammock. All are fully screened. The helpful owners live in Iquitos and have a very hands-on approach to maintaining their lodge, ensuring that recycling occurs, staff set an ecofriendly example to visitors, and guests are happy. During high water, the river rises up to the bungalows, which are connected to the lodge's dining building with covered, raised walkways. Lighting is by kerosene lanterns. The bilingual guides are excellent and they guarantee observation of monkeys, sloths and dolphins, as well as rich avian fauna typical of the nearby Amazonian *varzea* (flooded forest), including the *piuri* – the wattled curassow *(crax globulosa)*, a critically endangered bird restricted to western Amazonia, which can only be seen in Peru at Muyuna.

Pacaya-Samiria Amazon Lodge (☎ 065-23-4128; www.pacayasamiria.com.pe; Raimondi 378, Iquitos; per 1/2 people 3 days & 2 nights US$765/940, per 1/2 people 6 days & 5 nights US$1600/1960). About 190km upriver on the Marañón, this excellent lodge is past Nauta on the outskirts of the Pacaya-Samiria reserve, four hours from Iquitos. It can arrange overnight stays within the reserve. Rooms feature private showers and porches with river views, and the lodge has electricity in the evening. There are special bird-watching programs.

Explorama Lodges (☎ 065-25-2530; www.explorama .com; Av La Marina 340, Iquitos) This well-established and recommended company owns and operates lodges and is an involved supporter of the Amazon Conservatory of Tropical Studies (ACTS). It has a lab at the famed canopy walkway, which is suspended 35m above the forest floor to give visitors a bird's-eye view of the rainforest canopy and its wildlife. You could arrange a trip to visit one or more lodges (each of which is very different) combined with a visit to the walkway. Sample rates are given; contact Explorama for other options and combinations. Explorama serves all-you-can-eat lunch and dinner buffets, has fast boats (50km/h) and half-price rates for under-12s. Ask about group discounts. The well-trained, friendly and knowledgeable guides are locals who speak English (other languages on request). The following are lodges operated by Explorama:

ACTS Field Station (srmadigosky@widener.edu; per person US$115) Near the Canopy Walkway, the 20 rooms here are in buildings similar to those at Explorama Lodge. Book ahead, because accommodations are often used by researchers and workshop groups. Scientists and researchers wishing to use the accommodations here should contact head of scientific research Dr S Madigosky at the email address above. The station is nearly always visited as part of a program including nights at other lodges.

Ceiba Tops (2 days & 1 night per person US$270, 3 days & 2 nights per person US$380; ✗ ☐ ☙) Forty kilometers northeast of Iquitos on the Amazon, this is Explorama's and the area's most modern lodge and resort. There are 75 luxurious rooms and suites, all featuring comfortable beds and furniture, fans, screened windows, porches and spacious bathrooms with hot showers. Landscaped grounds surround the pool complex, complete with hydromassage, waterslide and hammock house. The restaurant (with better meals than at Explorama's other lodges) adjoins a bar with live Amazon music daily. Short guided walks and boat rides are available for a taste of the jungle; there is primary forest nearby containing *Victoria regias* (giant Amazon waterlilies). This lodge is a recommended option for people who really *don't* want to rough it. It even hosts business incentive meetings.

Explorama Lodge (3 days & 2 nights per person US$365) Eighty kilometers away on the Amazon, near its junction with the Río Napo, this was one of the first lodges constructed in the Iquitos area (1964) and remains attractively rustic. The lodge has several large, palm-thatched buildings; the 55 rooms have private cold-water bathrooms. Covered walkways join the buildings and lighting is by kerosene lantern. Guides accompany visitors on several trails that go deeper into the forest.

ExplorNapo Lodge (5 days & 4 nights per person US$950) On the Río Napo, 157km from Iquitos, this simple lodge has 30 rooms with shared cold-shower facilities. The highlights are guided trail hikes in remote primary forest, bird-watching, an ethnobotanical garden of useful plants (curated by a local shaman) and a visit to the nearby Canopy Walkway (half-hour walk). Because of the distance involved, you spend the first and last night of a five-day/four-night package at the Explorama Lodge.

ExplorTambos Camp (5 days & 4 nights per person US$1070) This lodge is a two-hour walk from ExplorNapo. It's a self-declared 'primitive' camp and creature comforts get short shrift. Guests (16 maximum) sleep on mattresses

---

BORDER CROSSING: THE PERU-COLOMBIA-BRAZIL BORDER ZONE

Even in the middle of the Amazon, border officials adhere to formalities and will refuse passage if documents are not in order. With a valid passport and visa or tourist card, border crossing is not a problem.

When leaving Peru for Brazil or Colombia, you'll get an exit stamp at a Peruvian guard post just before the border (boats stop there long enough for this; ask the captain).

The ports at the three-way border are several kilometers apart, connected by public ferries. They are reached by air or boat, but not by road. The biggest, nicest border town, **Leticia**, in Colombia, boasts by far the best hotels and restaurants, and a hospital. You can fly from Leticia to Bogotá on almost-daily commercial flights. Otherwise, infrequent boats go to **Puerto Asis** on the Río Putumayo; the trip takes up to 12 days. From Puerto Asis, buses go further into Colombia. (See p516 for more on safety issues in this area.)

The two small ports in Brazil are **Tabatinga** and **Benjamin Constant**; both have basic hotels. Tabatinga has an airport with flights to Manaus. Get your official Brazilian entry stamp from the Tabatinga police station if flying into Manaus. Tabatinga is a continuation of Leticia, and you can walk or take a taxi between the two with no immigration hassles, unless you are planning on traveling further into Brazil or Colombia. Boats leave from Tabatinga downriver, usually stopping in Benjamin Constant for a night, then continuing on to Manaus, a week away. It takes about an hour to reach Benjamin Constant by public ferry. US citizens need a visa to enter Brazil. Make sure you apply in good time – either in the USA or in Lima.

Peru is on the south side of the river, where currents create a constantly shifting bank. Most boats from Iquitos will drop you at the small village of Santa Rosa, which has Peruvian immigration facilities. Motor canoes reach Leticia in about 15 minutes. For travelers to Colombia or Brazil, Lonely Planet has guidebooks for both countries.

If you are arriving from Colombia or Brazil, you'll find boats in Tabatinga and Leticia for Iquitos. You should pay US$20 or less for the two-day trip on a cargo riverboat, or US$60 for a *mas rápido* (fast boat; 12 to 14 hours), which leave daily. Cruise ships leave Wednesday and arrive in Iquitos on Saturday morning.

Remember that however disorganized things may appear, you can always get meals, money changed, beds and boats simply by asking around.

on open-sided sleeping platforms covered with a mosquito net; don't plan a passionate honeymoon here! Basic toilets and washing facilities are provided, and wildlife-watching opportunities here are better than at the lodges. A Canopy Walkway visit is included. One night is spent at ExplorNapo because of the distance.

Amazon Adventure Expeditions (☎ 065-24-1228; www.amazonadventureexpeditions.com; Putumayo 155, Iquitos; 14-day wilderness adventure per person US$750) is a recommended outfit for providing lengthy excursions into the jungle. These are true (guided) adventures where you can catch your own food and survive in the wild for up to two weeks. The operator has a basic lodge, the Yarapa, 220km from Iquitos, a starting point for trips out to its wilderness camp, 450km from Iquitos on the Aucayacu tributary. Prices are tailored according to distances traveled and time spent. Based out of the same office is independent guide **José López Pérez** (lopez .jose87@yahoo.es), who can take travelers upriver on tributaries toward the Ecuador border. He charges US$100 per person per day for about 10 days. Contact with the outside world really is severed on these trips, provisions are limited and transportation is by dugout canoe.

PEVAS

Pevas, about 145km downriver from Iquitos, is Peru's oldest town on the Amazon. Founded by missionaries in 1735, Pevas boasts about 5000 inhabitants but no cars, post office or banks (or attorneys!); the first telephone was installed in 1998. Most residents are *mestizos* or indigenous people from one of four tribes, and are friendly and easygoing. Pevas is the most interesting town between Iquitos and the border and is visited regularly (if briefly) by the cruise boats traveling to Leticia. Independent travelers, however, are a rarity.

The main attraction in Pevas is the studio-gallery of one of Peru's best-known living artists, **Francisco Grippa**. Grippa handmakes his canvases from local bark, similar to that formerly used by local tribespeople for cloth. The paintings on view are the outcome of Grippa's 23 years' observation of Amazonian people, places and customs. You can't miss the huge house with its red-roofed lookout tower on the hill immediately above the port.

The best 'accommodation' in the conventional sense is at **Hospedaje Rodríguez** (☎ 83-0296; Brasil 30; s/d with shared shower S15/20), just down from the Pevas Plaza. Rooms face onto a pleasant courtyard.

The rustic but attractive **Casa de la Loma** on a hill in the Pevas outskirts offers Amazon views and activities including night walks, piranha fishing and visiting nearby indigenous communities (mostly part-acculturated). Reservations are notoriously problematic; the owner is contactable only by rarely functioning cell phone. Prices are not fixed, but start at around S15 for a bed in one of five dark, screened rooms sharing shower facilities. This is a place to get to know the town and the inhabitants by joining in a fiesta or shopping at the market. Be adventurous and show up: heading down from the plaza to the river, take the first left down to a bridge. On the bridge, a path leads up through woods to the entrance.

Francisco Grippa also has basic rooms in his house at the top of town that are sometimes offered to visitors.

Meals are available at **Hospedaje Rodríguez** and the more popular pool hall–restaurant **El Amigo** (☽ lunch).

Leticia-bound cargo boats make request stops at Pevas, as do daily (except Monday) fast boats to the tri-border (the same applies if you are coming from Leticia). These slow cargo boats (S20, around 15 hours) or fast boats (S150, 3½ hours downriver, five hours upriver) also connect Pevas with Iquitos. Tour operators can also incorporate a Pevas trip into packages. Arriving independently, there's an element of risk – you might get stuck here for a while – but a boat *will* eventually turn up.

Directory

CONTENTS

ACCOMMODATIONS

Accommodations in Peru range from basic crash pads and cozy Spanish-style B&Bs to luxury lodges that offer bath butlers and turn-down service. In touristy areas, you'll find plenty of accommodations, and in every imaginable guise; choices in small villages are usually limited. In well-trodden destinations, hotel staff will generally speak some English (in addition to other languages), but in rural areas, you'll need a grasp of Spanish basics. Many places will store your luggage for free if you have a late bus or flight to catch after checkout; some spots may charge for storage of more than one day. When storing bags, it is always a good idea to lock them and get a receipt.

Hotels are the most standard type of accommodations and will normally include private hot showers, telephone, TV and other facilities, such as a café or restaurant. Smaller than a hotel, an *hostal* is like a guesthouse, offering private rooms with en suite bathrooms and fairly reliable hot water. In some cases, these will include a very simple continental breakfast. Better *hostales* offer hot breakfasts and many of the same services as small hotels, while cheaper ones may have shared bathrooms. *Hospedajes* and *albergues* are generally small, family-owned inns. Expect basic rooms, including dormitory-style accommodations, and, in some cases, a shared kitchen. In remote settings, don't count on *hospedajes* and *albergues* to have hot showers, private bathrooms or too many other amenities. Popular traveler destinations such as Cuzco and Lima are cluttered with modern hostels offering everything from communal lounges to free wi-fi. Street noise can be an issue in hotels at all budget levels, so choose your room accordingly.

Within most types of accommodations, *habitación simple* refers to a single room, *habitación doble* to a double room with two twin beds, and *habitación matrimonial* to a double room with a double or queen-sized bed. If you're traveling as a couple, be sure to ask for the latter, or you'll find yourself sleeping in separate beds. Shared rooms or dormitory-style lodging is generally referred to as *un habitación compartida*. Prices in these might be listed *por cama* (by bed).

BOOK YOUR STAY ONLINE

For more accommodation reviews and recommendations by Lonely Planet authors, check out the online booking service at www.lonelyplanet.com/hotels. You'll find the true, insider low-down on the best places to stay. Reviews are thorough and independent. Best of all, you can book online.

PRACTICALITIES

■ **Electricity:** Electrical current is 220V, 60Hz AC. Standard outlets accept round prongs, but many places will have dual-voltage outlets which take flat prongs. Even so, you may need an adapter with a built-in surge protector.

■ **Magazines:** The most well-known political and cultural weekly is *Caretas* (www.caretas.com .pe), while *Etiqueta Negra* (etiquetanegra.com.pe) focuses exclusively on culture. For alternative travel journalism in Spanish and English, pick up the monthly *Rumbos* (www.rumbos delperu.com).

■ **Newspapers:** The government-leaning daily *El Comercio* (www.elcomercioperu.com.pe) is dry, but it's the leading daily. For opposing viewpoints, see the slightly left-of-center *La República* (www.larepublica.com.pe). A number of small, tabloid papers – known colloquially as *diarios chicha* – report on sensational crime stories and celebrity capers. In English, look for the long-running *Peruvian Times* (www.peruviantimes.com).

■ **TV:** Cable and satellite TV are widely available for a fix of CNN or even Japanese news. Local stations have a mix of news, variety shows, talk shows and *telenovelas,* Spanish-language soap operas. Ask if your hotel has cable or you'll be watching the latter.

■ **Video:** Buy or watch videos on the NTSC system (compatible with North America).

■ **Websites:** Two helpful online resources in English are expatperu.com and www.theperu guide.com.

■ **Weights & Measures:** Peruvians use the metric system except for gas (petrol), which is meas ured in US gallons.

Homestays are sometimes offered to people taking Spanish courses, but are an infrequent option. Lima, Cuzco and the area around Lake Titicaca tend to be the places where you are most likely to find these.

There aren't many camping grounds, except around trekking and river-running sites.

There are many more places to stay than we're able to list in this book. We've focused on including the best and most convenient spots. If you try any new spots, be sure to let us know how it goes!

Rates

Costs for accommodations vary greatly in Peru, depending on the season and the region. Rates in this book are generally for the high season, but note that prices can often fluctuate from one year to the next.

Cuzco is the most expensive town for hotels, despite being stuffed full of them. During the high season (June to August) demand is very high; the busiest times are Inti Raymi, Semana Santa and Fiestas Patrias (see p517), when advance reservations are a must.

Other cities that are pricier than average include Lima, Iquitos, Huaraz and Trujillo. In Lima, prices generally remain steady throughout the year, although many midrange and top-end places will feature last-minute specials online. In other cities, at off-peak times, you can get good deals with a little bit of negotiation. Walk-in guests should ask for the 'best price' *(mejor precio)*. Paying cash always helps; and be sure to ask for discounts if you're staying somewhere for more than five nights.

Many places will add a surcharge of 7% or more to all credit-card transactions, not including the foreign-currency exchange fee that your own bank may add. When paying cash, either *nuevos soles* (local currency) or US dollars (US$) are often accepted. Note that the exchange rate featured at hotels may be different from that being offered at local banks or *casas de cambio* (foreign-exchange bureaus); you can count on it being less favorable.

In the remote jungle lodges of the Amazon and in popular beach destinations such as Máncora, all-inclusive resort-style pricing may be the norm.

Apartments

Midrange and high-end travelers can find a limited number of furnished homes and apartments available for short-term rentals (primarily in Lima). Check www.vrbo.com and www.cyberrentals.com for listings.

DIRECTORY

Hostels

There are a number of Hostelling International (www.hihostels.com) hostels in the country's main tourist areas, including Lima, Cuzco and Arequipa. Beyond that, there is a wide gamut of backpacker-geared hostels in the principal tourist towns (especially Lima), from mellow bunk-spaces to rowdy, all-night party spots – choose carefully. Many places come equipped with all manner of backpacker goodies, including wi-fi, book exchanges, lockers for gear (bring a lock), hot water, TV rooms with DVD libraries and shared kitchens. Rates on these vary, from S14 to S35 per person, per night.

Hotels
BUDGET

All budget spots listed in this book have rates of less than S75 per night. Basic one- and two-star hotels, *hostales, hospedajes* and *albergues* are Peru's cheapest accommodations and are generally very basic, simply furnished spots. In this price range, expect to find small rooms, with decent beds and a shared or private bathroom. In the major cities, these options will generally include hot showers; in more rural and remote areas, they likely will not. Soundproofed walls in this price range are rare, and soundproofed windows are even rarer. Some budget inns will include a very simple breakfast in the rate, such as instant coffee with toast.

Rooms vary remarkably in quality and facilities, even within the same establishment, so always ask to see a room before accepting it. Avoid rooms overlooking noisy streets (unless you're a very sound sleeper), lacking windows or appearing insecure (test the locks on doors and windows). Shopping around can yield a much more suitable room for about the same rate.

Many areas around bus stations, are chockfull of cheap places to sleep. Proceed with caution; theft is a frequent problem.

MIDRANGE

Mid-priced *hostales* and hotels range from S75 to S240 for a double room. Again, these accommodations can include everything from small, no-frills business hotels to cozy B&Bs with trickling fountains and Peruvian art. Many midrange places will accept credit cards, sometimes for an additional fee.

At this level, rooms generally have private bathrooms with hot-water showers and small

HOT SHOWERS

The cheapest places to stay in Peru don't always have hot water, or it may be turned on only at certain hours of the day. Early birds often use up all the hot water, so if you're a late riser be mentally prepared for a chilly wake-up call.

Be careful with those electronic showerheads – a single cold-water showerhead hooked up to an electric heating element that is switched on when you want a hot shower. These work best when you keep the water pressure low. Don't fiddle with the heating unit while the water is on or you may get a shock. It won't be strong enough to throw you across the room, but it will be unpleasant nonetheless. Tall travelers: keep your eyes peeled.

portable heaters or fans may be provided for climate control. Some newer spots are also equipped with air conditioning. (The Amazon is an exception; accommodations in this area tend to be more rustic, even in the higher price ranges.) Rooms tend to have more amenities than their budget counterparts, such as cable TV and in-room telephones and, in some cases, in-room safes. These phones usually only connect to the reception desk and can only receive incoming calls. To make outgoing calls, guests give the outside number to reception, hang up, then wait to be called back. See p524 for more information about making calls.

These types of hotels are often equipped with a small lounge or an on-site café that serves breakfast and snacks. Many midrange hotels include a continental breakfast in the rate; in some cases, an American-style breakfast with eggs is offered as well.

As is the case with budget offerings, ask to see a room before committing. Styles and quality can vary widely from one room to the next and from one hotel to the next.

TOP END

Hotels in this category cost upwards of S240. Like high-end hotels everywhere, these run the gamut from design-conscious boutique spaces to international chains to atmospheric spots bearing all manner of baroque detailing.

Top-end hotel rates frequently include a 19% tax in the room rate (a fee which can be refunded to non-Peruvian travelers if the hotel can retain a photocopy of your passport). When booking, ask whether these taxes are included in the rate and whether the hotel refunds them. Many high-end places also tack on a nonrefundable 'service charge' of 10%.

Peru's top hotels are generally equipped with en suite bathrooms with bathtubs, international direct dial phones, handy dual-voltage outlets, central heating or air-conditioning, hairdryers, in-room safes, cable TV and internet access (either through high-speed cable or wi-fi); some may come with minifridges, microwaves or coffee makers. A large high-end spot may also feature a bar, café or restaurant (or several), as well as room service, concierge services and an obliging, multilingual staff. Expect the biggest places (particularly in Lima) to come with business centers, spas and beauty salons.

Reservations

In the principal tourist destinations, most hotels at all levels accept reservations. If you are flying into Lima, a reservation for your first night is a good idea since a lot of places can arrange airport pickup, and because many flights arrive late at night, this is an inadvisable time to begin searching for a place to sleep. Around the country, reservations are absolutely a necessity if you are going to be in a town during a major festival day (such as Inti Raymi in Cuzco) or a holiday such as Semana Santa (Easter Week), when all of Peru is on vacation. In the Amazon, reservations are needed at remote lodges, which aren't always equipped to handle walk-in clients. In smaller villages and areas off the beaten path, service tends to be on a first-come, first-served basis.

Cheap, budget places may not honor a reservation if you arrive late. Even if you've made a reservation in advance, it is best to confirm things a day or two before your arrival, as wires can get crossed and reservations lost. Late check-in is not a problem at many midrange and top-end hotels, in which case a deposit may be required. Some lodges, especially in the Amazon, may also require all or part of the payment up front. Make sure your travel plans are firm if you are paying in advance, as securing refunds from some Peruvian hotels can be a challenge.

Making reservations online is convenient, but if you are traveling in the off-season, walk-in rates off the street may be lower. At top-end hotels, however, last-minute online deals are the norm, so always check a hotel's website for discounts and special promotional packages.

ACTIVITIES

From scaling icy peaks to paddling remote patches of lush Amazon rainforest, Peru offers a plethora of adrenaline-pumping activities. You'll find a broad overview of these in the Peru Outdoors chapter (p173), which covers all the basics on hiking, trekking, mountain and rock climbing, river running, surfing, sandboarding, mountain biking, swimming, scuba diving, horseback riding and even paragliding.

Wildlife-watching is another top activity in this neck of the Andes. The Environment chapter (p67) details the country's rugged landscape and gives a detailed summary of what types of animal and plant species you might expect to ogle during your time in Peru (see p68). There is a handy guide to the country's top national parks and wilderness areas along with a list of what there is to see and do in each of them (see boxed text, p74), in addition to some pointers on how to make the best of your wildlife-watching excursions (boxed text, p68). If you're headed into the Amazon, make sure you've reviewed our Jungle Checklist (boxed text, p472).

One of the top activities is touring some of the country's incredible ancient sites. From a 1700-year-old temple site in Lima (p97) and one of the continent's oldest cities in Caral (p338) to the heart of the old Inca empire in Cuzco (p228), there is a profusion of historic places to visit, many of which are situated in extraordinary natural locales. A

RECYCLING

Wondering what to do with your accumulated plastic bottles and dead batteries? Recycle them! Though recycling is still in its infancy in much of Peru, you can easily recycle or appropriately dispose of items in a conscientious way. In Lima, you can dispose of batteries in special containers at many **Wong** (www.ewong.com), Metro (owned by Wong) and **Plaza Vea** (www.plazavea.com.pe) supermarkets. Likewise, Wong and Metro take plastic bottles and paper. Most supermarkets, including the upscale **Vivanda** (www.vivanda.com.pe), recycle glass.

DIRECTORY

comprehensive guide to these top pre-Columbian wonders is covered in the Ancient Peru chapter (p269).

Peak season for most outdoor activities is during the cooler dry season (June to August). Avoid trekking during the wet season (December to March), when some areas become impassable because of the rain. These hotter summer months, however, are the best time of year for surfing along the Pacific coast. For more information on climate, see opposite.

The fledgling status of many outdoor activities in Peru is both an advantage and a pitfall. While you may dream about having a surf break or a mountain-bike trail all to yourself, there are drawbacks. Equipment rental can be expensive and hard to find. Organized tour agencies may not be very organized and some may be downright reckless – with your safety and the environment. Likewise, many local guides are unregulated and untrained. To assure the greatest safety, and the best experience, seek out recommended operators and travel agencies and avoid the cheapest, cut-rate agencies, especially when it comes to activities such as rafting, trekking and mountain climbing. For these specialized sports, bring your own gear whenever possible. Shell out a little more for a well-trained guide and organized trips by a reputable outfitter. It will be worth the extra expense.

BUSINESS HOURS

Hours are variable and liable to change, especially in small towns, where regular hours are rarely regular. Posted hours are a guideline, not gospel, and services can be slow. Be patient, and forget about getting anything done on a Sunday, when most businesses (other than restaurants) are closed.

Most cities, however, are equipped with 24-hour ATMs. In addition, Lima has pharmacies, bookstores and electronics supply shops that are open every day of the week. There are also a few 24-hour supermarkets. In other major cities, taxi drivers often know where the late-night stores and pharmacies are.

Many shops and offices close for a lunch break (usually from 1pm until around 4pm), but some banks and post offices stay open. In addition, many restaurants open only for lunch, or breakfast and lunch, especially in small towns. Reviews in this book won't list opening hours unless they vary from the standard. Typically, opening hours are as follows:

Banks 9am-6pm Mon-Fri, some 9am-1pm Sat
Bars and clubs 5:30pm-midnight, some until 2am
Restaurants 10am-10pm, some closed 3-6pm
Shops 9am-6pm Mon-Fri, some 9am-6pm Sat

CHILDREN

In a country that holds the family dear, traveling families are welcome in Peru, and will even excite friendly, well-intentioned interest (expect your children to be patted on the head – a lot).

Children who are under the age of 12 receive discounts of 25% to 50% for airline travel, while infants under two pay only 10% of the fare provided they sit on their parent's lap. On buses, children pay full fare if they occupy a seat, but aren't normally charged if they sit on their parent's lap. Often, someone will give up a seat on public transportation for a parent traveling with a small child, or they'll offer to put your child on their lap (don't be put off by this – it's normal).

Most midrange and top-end hotels will have reduced rates for children under 12 years of age, provided the child shares a room with parents. Cots are not normally available, except at the most exclusive hotels. In addition, 'kids' meals' are not offered in most restaurants, but many eateries will happily accommodate special requests (see p62). Adult portions are generally massive, so children can share an order with each other or with parents. High chairs are rarely available.

If you're traveling with an infant, bring disposable diapers (nappies) and creams from home, or stock up in Lima or other major cities before heading to the countryside. In rural areas, supplies may be harder to find. Other things to pack: infant medicines, a thermometer and, of course, a favorite toy.

Breastfeeding in public is not uncommon, but most women discreetly cover themselves. Poorly maintained public bathrooms may be a concern for parents. Always carry toilet paper, tissues and wet wipes. While a woman may take a young boy into the ladies' bathroom, it is socially unacceptable for a man to take a girl of any age into the men's room.

For more advice, see Lonely Planet's *Travel with Children*.

CLIMATE CHARTS

Peru has three main climatic zones: the tropical Amazon jungle to the east; the arid coastal desert to the west; and the Andean mountains and highlands in between. In the Andes, which have altitudes over 3500m, average daily temperatures fall below 10°C (50°F) and overnight temperatures can dip well below freezing. Travelers flying straight to Cuzco (3326m), or other high-altitude cities, should allow several days to acclimatize since altitude sickness, or *soroche,* can be a problem (see p548).

June to August is the dry season in the mountains and altiplano (Andean plateau); the wettest months are from December to March. It rains all the time in the hot and humid rainforest, but the driest months there are from June to September. However, even during the wettest months, from December to May, it rarely rains for more than a few hours at a time. Along the arid coastal strip, the hot summer months are from December through March. Some parts of the coastal strip see rain rarely, if at all. From April to November, Lima and other areas by the Pacific Ocean are enclosed in *garúa* (coastal fog, mist or drizzle) as warmer air masses off the desert and drifts over the ocean where the cold Humboldt Current hits. (For more information on Lima's fog, see boxed text, p95.)

The El Niño effect, which occurs on average every seven years, is when large-scale changes in ocean currents and rising sea-surface water temperatures bring heavy rains and floods to coastal areas, plunging tropical areas into drought and disrupting weather patterns worldwide. The name El Niño (literally 'the Child') refers to the fact that this phenomenon usually appears around Christmas. El Niño is usually followed the next year by La Niña, when ocean currents that cool abnormally create even more havoc and destruction.

For more information on when to go to Peru, see p19.

COURSES

Peru is not as well known for its Spanish-language courses than some other Latin American countries are. However, there are schools in Lima (p102), Cuzco (p239), Arequipa (p170), Huaraz (p394), Puerto

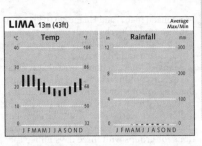

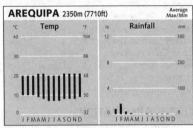

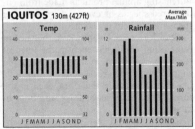

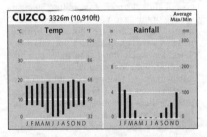

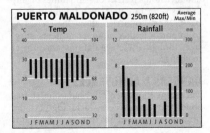

Maldonado (p463) and Huancayo (p307). You can also study Quechua with private teachers or at one of the various language institutes in Lima, Cuzco and Huancayo.

Many of these schools organize regular Peruvian cooking classes as well as salsa dancing lessons for their enrolled students. In the town of Urubamba, in the Sacred Valley, Tres Keros Restaurant Grill & Bar (p262) will do Peruvian cooking demonstrations for groups with three days notice (per person US$40).

If you're interested in studying Peruvian instruments or learning traditional folk dances such as the *marinera,* try the Museo de la Cultura Peruana in Lima (p93). These courses, however, aren't geared toward short-term travelers – most run over several weeks and Spanish is a must.

CUSTOMS REGULATIONS

Peru allows duty-free importation of 3L of alcohol and 20 packs of cigarettes, 50 cigars or 250g of tobacco. You can import US$300 of gifts. Legally, you are allowed to bring in such items as a laptop, camera, portable music player, kayak, climbing gear, mountain bike or similar items for personal use.

It is illegal to take pre-Columbian or colonial artifacts out of Peru, and it is illegal to bring them into most countries. If purchasing reproductions, buy only from a reputable dealer and ask for a detailed receipt. Purchasing animal products made from endangered species or even just transporting them around Peru is also illegal.

Coca leaves are legal in Peru, but not in most other countries, even in the form of tea bags, which are available in Peruvian shops. People subject to random drug testing should be aware that coca, even in the form of tea, may leave trace amounts in their urine.

Check with your own home government about customs restrictions and duties on any expensive or rare items you intend to bring back. Most countries allow their citizens to import a limited number of items duty-free, though these regulations are subject to change.

DANGERS & ANNOYANCES

There is no shortage of wild and wooly stories about traveling in Peru, including periodic protests, thefts, and bus drivers who act as if

every bend in the road should be assaulted at Autobahn speeds. Certainly, the country is not for the faint of heart. Buses are filled to overflowing – and then some. Violent political protests and roadblocks can shut down arterial highways for days, even weeks. And Peru's grinding poverty – more than half of the country lives under the poverty line, with a fifth of the population surviving on less than US$2 a day – means that petty crime is rampant. The biggest annoyance most travelers will experience, however, is a case of the runs, so don't let paranoia ruin your holiday.

As with every other place on earth, a little common sense goes a very long way.

Thefts, Muggings & Other Crime

The situation has improved significantly since the 1980s, especially in Lima, where muggings used to be par for the course even in the well-touristed parts of town. Nonetheless, Peru's widespread poverty means that street crimes such as pickpocketing, bag-snatching and muggings are all too common. Sneak theft is by far the most widespread type of crime, while muggings and 'choke and grab' attacks happen with less regularity. Even so, they do happen, and every year we hear from travelers who have been robbed in one way or another.

A few basic precautions and a reasonable amount of awareness, however, and you probably won't be robbed. Some tips:

- crowded places such as bus terminals, train stations, markets and fiestas are the haunts of pickpockets; wear your day pack in front of you or carry a bag that fits snugly under your arm
- thieves look for easy targets, such as a bulging wallet in a back pocket or a cam-

era held out in the open; keep spending money in your front pocket and your camera stowed when it's not in use

- passports, traveler's checks and larger sums of cash are best carried in a money belt or an inside pocket that can be zipped or closed – or better yet, stowed in a safe at your hotel
- snatch theft can occur if you place a bag on the ground (even for a few seconds), or while you're asleep on an overnight bus; never leave a bag with your wallet and passport in the overhead rack of a bus
- don't keep valuables in bags that will be unattended
- blending in helps: walking around town with oodles of brand-new hiking gear or a shiny leather jacket will draw attention; stick to muted colors and simple clothing
- leave jewelry and fancy watches at home
- hotels – especially cheap ones – aren't always trustworthy; lock valuables inside your luggage, or use safety deposit services
- walk purposefully wherever you are going, even if you are lost; if you need to examine your map, duck into a shop or restaurant to do it

Some thieves work in pairs or groups. One person creates a distraction as another robs. This can take the form of a bunch of kids fighting in front of you, an elderly person 'accidentally' bumping into you or someone spilling something on your clothes. In these cases, hold your bag tightly. Most thieves don't want the public hassle of having to wrestle anyone for a pocketbook. Some razorblade artists may slit open your bag, whether it's on your back or on the luggage rack of a bus.

In some cases, there have been robberies and armed muggings of trekkers on popular hiking trails, especially around Huaraz (p392), in the Cordilleras Blanca and Huayhuash. Going as part of a group with a local guide may help prevent this. In addition, the area around Tingo María (see boxed text, p333), on the eastern edge of the central highlands, is a renowned bandit area, with armed robberies and other crimes a regular occurrence. Keep any activities in the area, including bus rides, to daylight hours.

In recent years, 'express' kidnappings have been recorded, particularly in some of the unsavory neighborhoods that surround the airport in Lima. An armed attacker (or attackers) grabs someone out of a taxi or abducts them off the street, then forces them to go to the nearest bank to withdraw cash using their ATM cards. Victims who do not resist their attackers generally don't suffer serious physical harm.

The *policía de turismo* (tourist police, aka Poltur) can be found in major cities and tourist areas and can be helpful with criminal matters. If you are unsure how to locate them, contact the main office in Lima (p81). If you are the victim of a crime, file a report with the tourist police immediately. At some point, inform your country's embassy about what has happened. They won't be able to do much, but embassies do keep track of crime geared at foreigners as a way of alerting other travelers to potential dangers.

If you have taken out travel insurance (p520) and need to make a claim, Poltur will provide you with a police report. Airlines may reissue a lost ticket for a fee (though this is increasingly unnecessary, since most airlines use electronic tickets). Stolen passports can be reissued at your embassy (p517), though you may be asked for an alternative form of identification first. After receiving your new passport, go to the nearest Peruvian immigration office (p526) to get a new tourist card. For more on legal issues, see p520.

For issues of safety affecting female travelers, turn to p527.

Corruption & Scams

The military and police (even sometimes the tourist police) have a reputation for being corrupt. While a foreigner may experience petty harassment (usually to procure payment of a bribe), most police officers are quite courteous to tourists, or just leave them alone.

Perhaps the most pernicious thing travelers face are the persistent touts that gather

---

IMPORTANT DOCUMENTS

All important documents (passport, credit cards, travel insurance policy, driver license etc) should be photocopied before you leave home. Leave one copy at home and keep another with you, separate from the originals.

at bus stations, train stations, airports and other tourist spots to offer everything from discounted hotel rooms to local tours. Many touts – among them, many taxi drivers – will say just about anything to steer you to places they represent. They will tell you the establishment you've chosen is a notorious drug den, it's closed down or is overbooked. Do not believe everything you hear. If you have doubts about a place you've decided to stay at, ask to see a room before paying up.

Moreover, it is not advisable to book hotels, travel arrangements or transport through these independent agents. Often, they will demand cash up-front for services that never materialize. Stick to reputable, well-recommended agencies and you'll be assured a good time.

Transport Issues

When taking buses, choose operators carefully. The cheapest companies will be the most likely to employ reckless drivers and have roadside breakdowns. Overnight travel by bus can get brutally cold in the highlands (take a blanket or a sleeping bag). In some parts, nighttime trips are also subject to the vagaries of roadside bandits, who create impromptu road blocks, then relieve passengers of their valuables. For more on overland transport in Peru, see p538.

Environmental Hazards

Some of the natural hazards you might encounter in Peru include earthquakes and avalanches. Rescues in remote regions are often done on foot because of the inability of helicopters to reach some of the country's more challenging topography. Perhaps the most common hazard is travelers' diarrhea (p548), which comes from consuming contaminated food or water. Other problems include altitude sickness, animal and insect bites, sunburn, heat exhaustion and even hypothermia. You can take precautions for most of these. See p548 for medical advice.

Protests & Other Conflict

During the Internal Conflict, through the 1980s and into the 1990s, terrorism, civil strife and kidnappings meant that entire regions were off limits to both foreign and domestic travelers. Thankfully, the situation has improved dramatically and travelers visit much of the country without ever

> **WARNING!**
>
> Be wary when traveling on overnight buses. Even on the well-traveled Pan-American Hwy route between Arequipa and Lima, buses have been hijacked (including by criminals posing as fellow passengers) and foreign tourists have been robbed and assaulted – even raped. Military checkpoints can appear anywhere, as can road blockades by protestors.

encountering problems. Even so, Peru remains a politically volatile place and public protests are a familiar sight. Generally speaking, these have little effects on tourists, other than blocking roads, but on some occasions they do turn violent and people are killed (see p478). It is worth staying aware of current events while in the country; and if a road is blocked or an area cut off, respect the situation. Being a foreigner will not grant you immunity from violence.

Moreover, while Sendero Luminoso (Shining Path) guerrillas have been quelled, there are isolated incidents of violence in rural areas in the provinces of Ayacucho, Huancavelica, Huánuco, Junín and San Martín. These are generally directed at the Peruvian military or the police. Even so, it is worth exercising caution: avoid transit through isolated areas in these regions at night.

Likewise, the country's drug trafficking areas can be dangerous, especially at night. Travelers should avoid the upper Río Huallaga valley between Tingo María and Juanjui and the Río Apurímac valley near Ayacucho, where the majority of Peru's illegal drug-growing takes place (see also boxed text, p334). Exercise similar caution near the Colombian border, where trafficking also goes on. For more information on drug-related legal matters, see p520.

Landmines

A half century of armed conflict over the Cordillera del Condor region on Peru's northeastern border with Ecuador was finally resolved in 1998. However, unexploded ordinance (UXO) in the area has not been completely cleaned up. Only use official border crossings and don't stray from the beaten path when traveling in this region.

DISCOUNT CARDS

An official International Student Identity Card (ISIC), with a photograph, can get you a 50% discount at some museums and attractions and for organized tours. Senior discount cards are not recognized.

EMBASSIES & CONSULATES

Most foreign embassies are in Lima, with some consular services in major tourist centers such as Cuzco (p223).

It is important to realize what your embassy can and can't do if you get into trouble in Peru. Generally speaking, it won't be much help if the trouble you're in is even remotely your own fault. Your embassy will not be sympathetic if you end up in jail after committing a crime locally, even if such actions are legal in your own country. In genuine emergencies, you might get some assistance, but only if other channels have been exhausted. If you need to get home urgently, a free ticket is exceedingly unlikely – the embassy would expect you to have travel insurance (p520). If all your money and documents are stolen, they will assist you with getting a new passport, but a loan for onward travel is out of the question.

It pays to call in advance to double-check operating hours or schedule an appointment. While many consulates and embassies are staffed during regular business hours, attention to the public is often more limited. Public operating hours are listed below. For after-hours and emergency contact numbers, check individual websites.

Australia Lima (Map p96; ☎ 01-222-8281; www
.australia.org.pe; Ste 1301, Torre Real 3, Av Victor A
Belaúnde 147, San Isidro; 🕓 9am-noon Mon-Fri)
Belgium Lima (Map p98; ☎ 01-241-7566; www
.diplomatie.be/lima; Av Angamos Oeste 380, Miraflores;
🕓 9-11am)
Bolivia Lima (Map p96; ☎ 01-422-8231; fax 01-222-
4594; Los Castaños 235, San Isidro; 🕓 8am-4pm); Puno
(Map p200; ☎ /fax 051-35 1251; 2nd fl, Jirón Arequipa
136, Puno; 🕓 8am-2pm Mon-Fri)
Brazil Lima (Map p98; ☎ 01-512-0830; www.embajada
brasil.org.pe; Av José Pardo 850, Miraflores; 🕓 9:30am-
noon & 4-5pm Mon-Fri)
Canada Lima (Map p98; ☎ 01-319-3200; www.canada
international.gc.ca/peru-perou/; Bolognesi 228, Miraflores;
🕓 8am-12:30pm & 1:15-5pm Mon-Thu, 8am-1pm Fri)
Chile Lima (Map p96; ☎ 01-710-2211; chileabroad.gov
.cl/peru; Av Javier Prado Oeste 790, San Isidro; 🕓 9am-
5pm Mon-Thu, to 2pm Fri)

Colombia Lima (Map p96; ☎ 01-441-0954; www
.embajadacolombia.org.pe; Av Jorge Basadre 1580, San
Isidro; 🕓 8:30am-1pm & 2:30-6pm Mon-Fri); Iquitos (Map
p495; ☎ 065-23-6246; Araujo 431, Iquitos; 🕓 9am-
12:30pm & 2-4:30pm Mon-Fri)
Ecuador Lima (Map p96; ☎ 01-421-7050; www
.mecuadorperu.org.pe; Las Palmeras 356, San Isidro;
🕓 9am-1pm Mon-Fri); Tumbes (Map p383; ☎ 072-
52-5949; 3rd fl, Jirón Bolívar 129, Plaza de Armas, Tumbes;
🕓 9am-1pm & 4-6pm Mon-Fri)
France Lima (Map p96; ☎ 01-215-8400; www
.ambafrance-pe.org; Av Arequipa 3415, San Isidro;
🕓 9am-noon)
Germany Lima (Map p96; ☎ 01-212-5016; www.lima
.diplo.de; Av Arequipa 4210, Miraflores; 🕓 8:30-11:30am
Mon-Fri)
Ireland Lima (Map p96; ☎ 01-449-6289; irish
consulperu@yahoo.ca; Miguel Alegre Rodríquez 182,
Miraflores) The main consul for Latin America is in Mexico
City (☎ 52-55-5520-5803). Lima has only an honorary
consul with limited services.
Israel Lima (Map pp88-9; ☎ 01-418-0509; lima
.mfa.gov.il; 6th fl, Natalio Sánchez 125, Santa Beatriz;
🕓 10am-1pm Mon-Thu, to noon Fri)
Italy Lima (Map pp82-3; ☎ 01-463-2727; www
.amblima.esteri.it; Av Giuseppe Garibaldi, ex Gregorio
Escobedo 298, Jesús María; 🕓 8:30am-11pm Mon-Fri)
Netherlands Lima (Map p98; ☎ 01-213-9800; www
.nlgovlim.com; 13th fl, Torre Parque Mar, Ave José Larco 1301,
Miraflores; 🕓 9am-noon Mon-Fri) By appointment only.
Spain Lima (Map p96; ☎ 01-513-7930; www.mae.es/
consulados/lima; Calle Los Pinos, San Isidro; 🕓 8:30am-
1pm Mon-Fri)
Switzerland Lima (Map pp82-3; ☎ 01-264-0305;
www.eda.admin.ch/lima; Av Salaverry 3240, San Isidro;
🕓 8am-noon Mon-Fri)
UK Lima (Map p98; ☎ 01-617-3000; ukinperu.fco.gov
.uk; 22nd fl, Torre Parque Mar, Av José Larco 1301, Miraflores; 🕓 8am-1pm & 2-5pm Mon-Thu, 8am-1pm Fri)
USA Lima (Map pp82-3; ☎ 01-618-2000; lima
.usembassy.gov; Av La Encalada s/n, cuadra 17, Monterrico;
🕓 7:30am-5:30pm Mon-Thu, to 12:30pm Fri) This place is
a fortress – call before showing up in person.

For up-to-date visa information on travel to Peru, visit www.lonely planet.com.

If you need to extend your stay in Peru, receive an exit stamp or secure a new entry card, see p526 for *oficinas de migraciónes* (immigration offices).

FESTIVALS & EVENTS

Many Peruvian festivals echo the Roman Catholic liturgical calendar and are celebrated with great pageantry, especially in indigenous highland villages, where Catholic feast days are often linked with traditional agricultural festivals, such as the harvest. These days provide an excuse for a fiesta, and include plenty of drinking, dancing, rituals and processions. Other holidays are of historical or political interest, such as Fiestas Patrias (National Independence Days). Local fiestas and festivals are held somewhere almost every week. Many are described under the individual towns where they are held. See opposite for public holidays that are observed nationally.

January
Año Nuevo (New Year's Day) This holiday, held on January 1, is particularly important in Huancayo, where a fiesta continues until Epiphany (January 6; see boxed text, p308).
Fiesta de la Marinera (last week in January) National dance festival in Trujillo (p345).

February
La Virgen de la Candelaria (Candlemas) Held on February 2, this highland fiesta is particularly colorful around Puno, where folkloric music and dance celebrations last for two weeks (see boxed text, p201).
Carnaval Held on the last few days before Lent (February/March), this holiday is often 'celebrated' with weeks of water fights, so be warned. It's popular in the highlands, with the fiesta in Cajamarca being one of the biggest (see boxed text, p433). It's also busy in the beach towns.

March & April
Fiesta de la Vendimia (Wine Festival) Sample local wine in Ica (p138). Held in the second week of March.
Semana Santa (Holy Week) The week before Easter Sunday is celebrated with spectacular religious processions almost daily, with Ayacucho (p321) being recognized as having the best in Peru. Arequipa (p171), Huancayo (p308) and Huaraz (p395) are also good for Easter processions.

May
Festival of the Crosses This festival is held on May 3 in Lima, Apurímac, Ayacucho, Junín, Ica and Cuzco.
Q'oyoriti At the foot of Ausangate, outside of Cuzco, in May/June (see boxed text, p295).

June
Corpus Christi Processions in Cuzco (p240) are especially dramatic. Held on the ninth Thursday after Easter.
Inti Raymi (Festival of the Sun; also the Feast of St John the Baptist and Peasant's Day) The greatest of the Inca festivals celebrates the winter solstice on June 24. It's certainly the spectacle of the year in Cuzco (p240), attracting thousands of Peruvian and foreign visitors. It's also a big holiday in many jungle towns.

San Pedro y San Pablo (Feasts of Sts Peter & Paul) More fiestas on June 29, especially around Lima and in the highlands.

July
La Virgen del Carmen Held on July 16, this holiday is mainly celebrated in the southern sierra, with Paucartambo (p293) and Pisac near Cuzco, and Pucará near Lake Titicaca being especially important.
Fiestas Patrias (National Independence Days) Celebrated nationwide on July 28 and 29, with festivities in the southern sierra beginning with the Feast of St James on July 25.

August
Feast of Santa Rosa de Lima This involves major processions on August 30 and is held in Lima (p103), Arequipa and Junín to honor the patron saint of Lima and of the Americas.

September
El Festival Internacional de la Primavera (International Spring Festival) Supreme displays of horsemanship, dancing and cultural celebrations in Trujillo during the last week of September (p345).

October
La Virgen del Rosario Held on October 4 in Lima, Ancash, Apurímac, Arequipa and Cuzco.
El Señor de los Milagros (Lord of the Miracles) A major religious festival in Lima (p103) on October 18, around which time the bullfighting season starts.

November
Todos Santos (All Saints' Day) Held on November 1, this is a religious precursor to the following day.
Día de los Muertos (All Souls' Day) Celebrated on November 2 with gifts of food, drink and flowers taken to family graves; especially colorful in the Andes. Some of the 'gift' food and drink is consumed, and the atmosphere is festive rather than somber.
Puno Week Starting November 5, this weeklong festival involves several days of spectacular costumes and street dancing to celebrate the legendary emergence of the first Inca, Manco Cápac; see boxed text, p201.

December
Fiesta de la Purísima Concepción (Feast of the Immaculate Conception) This national holiday, held on December 8, is celebrated with religious processions in honor of the Virgin Mary.
Christmas Day Held on December 25, Christmas is less secular and more religious, especially in the Andean highlands.
La Virgen del Carmen de Chincha Frenzied dancing and all-night music in the *peñas* (bars or clubs featuring live folkloric music) of El Carmen on December 27 (p128).

FOOD

Reviews listed under Eating sections in this book are arranged by price, from cheapest to most expensive. Budget eateries generally serve meals (appetizer, main dish and dessert, not including beverages or alcohol) costing S24 or less, while meals at midrange spots typically cost from S24 to S45. Top-end restaurants cost over S45 for a three-course meal. This latter category generally also charges a 10% service fee and a 19% tax. The greatest variety of restaurants, especially at the high end, are in Lima (p109), while Cuzco (p246), Arequipa (p182) and, to a lesser extent, Chiclayo (p361), also serve as culinary destinations. Prices in Lima and in the major tourist centers will generally be more expensive.

See p58 for more on Peruvian cuisine.

GAY & LESBIAN TRAVELERS

Peru is a strongly conservative, Catholic country. While many Peruvians will tolerate homosexuality on a 'Don't ask; don't tell' level when dealing with foreign travelers, gay rights in a political or legal context does not exist as an issue. When it does arise in public, hostility is most often the response. As a result, many gays in Peru don't publicly identify as homosexual, and some men, in keeping with the macho nature of Peruvian culture, will identify as straight, even if they have sex with other men or transvestite prostitutes. Effeminate men, even if they are straight, may be called *maricón* (which roughly translates as 'faggot'), although this word has come to be a catch-all insult that is also used in jest.

Public displays of affection among homosexual couples is rarely seen. Outside gay clubs, it is advisable to keep a low profile. HIV/AIDS transmission, both homosexual and heterosexual, is a growing problem in Peru, so use condoms. Lima is the most accepting of gay people, but this is on a relative scale. Beyond that, the tourist towns of Cuzco, Arequipa and Trujillo tend to be more tolerant than the norm.

FYI: the rainbow flag seen around Cuzco and in the Andes is *not* a gay pride flag – it's the flag of the Inca empire.

There are several organizations that provide resources for gay and lesbian travelers:

Deambiente.com (www.deambiente.com, www.intro spektivo.com) Spanish-language online magazine about politics and pop culture, plus nightlife listings.

Gay Lima (lima.queercity.info) A handy guide to the latest gay and gay-friendly spots in the capital, along with plenty of links.

Gayperu.com (www.gayperu.com) A modern, Spanish-language online guide that lists everything from bars to bathhouses; also runs a multilingual travel agency (www.gayperutravel.com).

Global Gayz (www.globalgayz.com) Excellent, country-specific information about Peru's gay scene and politics, with links to international resources.

Lima Tours (Map pp88-9; ☎ 01-619-6901; www.limatours.com.pe; Jirón Belén 1040, Central Lima) A travel agency that is not exclusively gay, but that organizes gay-friendly group trips around the country.

Movimiento Homosexual de Lima (Map pp82-3; ☎ 01-332-2945; www.mhol.org.pe; Mariscal Miller 822, Jesús María) Peru's best-known gay and lesbian activist organization.

Purpleroofs.com (www.purpleroofs.com) Massive GLBT portal with links to a few tour operators and gay-friendly accommodations in Peru.

Rainbow Peruvian Tours (Map p96; ☎ 01-215-6000; www.perurainbow.com; Río de Janeiro 216, San Isidro, Lima) Gay-owned tour agency based in Lima, with a multilingual website.

HOLIDAYS

On major holidays, banks, offices and other services are closed, hotel rates can triple and transportation tends to be very crowded, so book ahead. If an official public holiday falls on a weekend, offices close on the following Monday. If an official holiday falls midweek, it may or may not be moved to the nearest Monday to create a long weekend. Major holidays may be celebrated for days around the official date.

Fiestas Patrias (National Independence Days) is the biggest national holiday, when the entire nation seems to be on the move. Major national, regional and religious holidays include the following:

New Year's Day January 1
Good Friday March/April
Labor Day May 1
Inti Raymi June 24
Feast of Sts Peter & Paul June 29
National Independence Days July 28-29
Feast of Santa Rosa de Lima August 30
Battle of Angamos Day October 8
All Saints Day November 1
Feast of the Immaculate Conception December 8
Christmas December 25

See also p517.

DIRECTORY

INSURANCE

Having a travel-insurance policy to cover theft, loss, accidents and illness is highly recommended. Many policies include a card with toll-free or collect-call hotlines for 24-hour assistance (carry it with you). Not all policies compensate travelers for misrouted or lost luggage. Some policies specifically exclude 'dangerous activities,' which can include scuba diving, motorcycling and even trekking. Also check if the policy coverage includes worst-case scenarios, such as evacuations and flights home. A variety of travel-insurance policies are available. Those handled by STA Travel (www.statravel.com) and other budget travel organizations are usually good value.

Always read the fine print carefully. You may prefer a policy that pays doctors or hospitals directly rather than you having to pay on the spot and make a claim later. If your bags are lost or stolen, the insurance company may demand a receipt as proof that you bought the goods in the first place. You must usually report any loss or theft to local police (or airport authorities) within 24 hours. Make sure you keep all documentation to make any claim.

INTERNET ACCESS

Accessing the internet is a snap in Peru. Wi-fi is becoming increasingly common in big cities, where internet cafés are also plentiful. Even tiny towns will usually have at least one internet café. Many McDonald's fast-food outlets in big cities offer free wi-fi (provided you don't mind the smell).

Rates for high-speed connections at internet cafés average less than S2 per hour, and it's only in remote places that you will pay more for slower connection speeds. Most internet cafés are open from the early morning till late and also offer cheap phone calls (see p524). Hotel business centers are generally overpriced, with some charging up to US$6 per hour. Many top-end establishments now offer wi-fi or high-speed cables in your room.

Before plugging in your laptop, ensure that your power source adheres to Peru's 220V, 60Hz AC electricity supply. You may need a portable converter with a built-in surge protector. Your PC-card modem may not work, but you won't know until you try. The easiest option is to buy a 'global' modem before you leave home. Dial-up internet access is generally a hassle because few ISPs have local access numbers in Peru, forcing you to make an international call. Likewise, only top-end hotel rooms tend to have international direct-dial (IDD) phones. Peruvian telephone sockets use a North American RJ-11 jack.

A few internet cafés allow you to hook up your laptop to a cable connection at the same rates charged for using one of their terminals. Consider bringing along a portable USB flash drive, which will enable you to seamlessly transfer files between your laptop and any other computer equipped with a high-speed USB port, and can also be used to store photo files uploaded from your digital camera memory cards.

See p22 for useful Peruvian websites.

LAUNDRY

Self-service laundry machines are available in only a few major cities. This means that you will likely have to pay someone to wash your clothes, or wash them yourself in the sink – a practice that's forbidden at many accommodations. The best hotels offer on-site laundry services and dry cleaning, but these can be expensive. Most towns are equipped with plenty of *lavanderías* (laundries) where you can leave your clothes overnight, or drop them off in the morning and pick them up later the same day. Some *lavanderías* charge per item (which can be expensive); others, by weight (a better deal). Rates average S6 per kilogram.

LEGAL MATTERS

Your own embassy is of limited help if you get into trouble with the law in Peru, where you are presumed guilty until proven innocent. If you are the victim, the *policía de turismo* (tourist police; Poltur) can help, and usually have someone on hand who speaks at least a little English. There are Poltur stations in more than a dozen cities, with the main headquarters situated in Lima (p81).

Be aware that some police officers (even tourist police) are corrupt, but that bribery is illegal. Since most travelers won't have to deal with traffic police, the most likely place you'll be expected to pay officials a little extra is (sometimes) at land borders. This too is illegal, and if you have the time and fortitude to stick to your guns, you'll eventually be allowed in without paying a fee.

Definitely avoid having any conversation with someone who offers you drugs. In fact, talking to any stranger on the street can hold risks. There have been reports of travelers being stopped soon after by plain-clothes police officers and accused of talking to a drug dealer. Should you be stopped by a plainclothes officer, don't hand over any documents or money. Never get into a vehicle with someone claiming to a police officer, but insist on going to a bona fide police station on foot. Peru has draconian penalties for possessing even a small amount of drugs; minimum sentences are several years in jail.

If you are imprisoned for any reason, make sure that someone else knows about it as soon as possible. (If you are a member of the South American Explorers Club, they can be helpful in this regard. See boxed text, p86.) Being detained in prison for extended periods of time before a trial begins is not uncommon. Peruvians bring food and clothing to family members who are in prison, where conditions are extremely harsh.

If you think that you were ripped off by a hotel or tour operator, register your complaint with the **National Institute for the Defense of Competition and the Protection of Intellectual Property** (Indecopi; ☎ 01-224-7800; www.indecopi.gob .pe, in Spanish) in Lima.

MAPS

The maps in this book will take you almost everywhere you want to go. The best road map of Peru is the 1:2,000,000 *Mapa Vial* published by Lima 2000 and available in better bookstores. The 1:1,500,000 *Peru South and Lima* country map, published by International Travel Maps, covers the country in good detail south of a line drawn east to west through Tingo María, and has a good street map of Lima, San Isidro, Miraflores and Barranco on the reverse side.

For topographical maps, go to the **Instituto Geográfico Nacional** (IGN; Map pp82-3; ☎ 01-475-3030, ext 119; www.ign.gob.pe; Aramburu 1190-98, Surquillo; ◷ 8am-6pm Mon-Fri, to 1pm Sat). In January, the IGN closes early, so call ahead. Its maps are for sale or for reference on the premises. Its good road map of Peru (1:2,000,000) is S51, and a four-sheet 1:1,000,000 topographical map of Peru costs S120. Departmental maps at various scales are available from S19. High-scale topographic maps for trekking are available, though sheets of border areas might be hard to get. Geological and demographic maps and CD-ROMs are also sold.

The **Servicio Aerofotográfico Nacional** (Map pp82-3; ☎ 01-467-1341; ◷ 9am-5pm Mon-Fri), at Las Palmeras Air Force base in Surco, sells aerial photographs. Don't wear shorts when you go there, take a passport and expect a two-week waiting period for prints. Some aerial photos are also available from the IGN. The best way to find the base is to take a taxi.

Topographic, city and road maps are also at the South American Explorers' clubhouses in Lima (see boxed text, p86) and Cuzco (p222).

Up-to-date topo maps are often available from outdoor outfitters in major trekking centers such as Cuzco, Huaraz and Arequipa. If you are bringing along a GPS unit, ensure that your power source adheres to Peru's 220V, 60Hz AC standard and always carry a compass.

MONEY

Peru uses the *nuevo sol* (S), which has traded at S3 to S5.50 per US dollar (US$) for several years, although you should keep an eye on current events. Prices in this book are generally quotes in *nuevos soles,* though some are listed in US dollars. For more exchange rates, see the Quick Reference page inside the front cover.

Carrying cash, an ATM card or traveler's checks, as well as a credit card that can be used for cash advances in case of emergency, is advisable. When receiving local currency, always ask for *billetes pequeños* (small bills), as S100 bills are hard to change in small towns or for small purchases. Carry as much spare change as possible, especially in small towns. Public bathrooms often charge a small fee for use and getting change for paper money can be darn near impossible.

The best places to exchange money are normally *casas de cambio* (foreign-exchange bureaus), which are fast, have longer hours and often give slightly better rates than banks. Many places accept US dollars. Do not accept torn money as it will likely not be accepted by Peruvians. It is best not to change money on the street as counterfeits are a problem. See boxed text, p523, for more.

See also p20 for information on costs and money.

ATMs

Cajeros automáticos (ATMs) are found in nearly every city and town in Peru, as well as at major airports, bus terminals and shopping areas. ATMs are linked to the international Plus (Visa), Cirrus (Maestro/MasterCard) systems, American Express and other networks. They will accept your bank or credit card as long as you have a four-digit PIN. To avoid problems, notify your bank that you'll be using your ATM card abroad. Even better, leave your bank card at home and buy a traveler's check card instead.

ATMs are a convenient way of obtaining cash, but rates are usually lower than at *casas de cambio*. Both US dollars and *nuevos soles* are readily available from Peruvian ATMs. Your home bank may charge an additional fee for each foreign ATM transaction. Surcharges for cash advances from credit cards vary, but are generally expensive, so check with your credit-card provider before you leave home.

ATMs are normally open 24 hours. For safety reasons, use ATMs inside banks with security guards, preferably during daylight hours.

Cash

The *nuevo sol* ('new sun') comes in bills of S10, S20, S50, S100 and (rarely) S200. It is divided into 100 *céntimos*, with copper-colored coins of S0.05, S0.10 and S0.20, and silver-colored S0.50 and S1 coins. In addition, there are bimetallic S2 and S5 coins with a copper-colored center inside a silver-colored ring.

US dollars are accepted by many tourist-oriented businesses, though you'll need *nuevos soles* to pay for local transportation, meals and other incidentals. For specific advice on paying for accommodations, see p509.

A NOTE ABOUT PRICES

Prices in this guidebook are generally listed in Peruvian *nuevos soles*. However, many higher-end hotels will only quote prices in US dollars; likewise for many travel agencies and tour operators. Therefore, prices in this book are generally listed in *soles*, except in cases where a business quotes its costs in dollars.

Both currencies have experienced fluctuations in recent years, so expect many figures to be different from what may be printed in the book.

Changing Money

Carrying cash enables you to get the top exchange rates quickly. The best currency for exchange is the US dollar, although the euro is increasingly accepted in major tourist centers. Other hard currencies can be exchanged, but usually with difficulty and only in major cities. All foreign currencies must be in flawless condition.

Cambistas (money-changers) hang out on street corners near banks and *casas de cambio* and give competitive rates (there's only a little flexibility for bargaining), but are not always honest. Officially, they should wear a vest and badge identifying themselves as legal. They're useful after regular business hours or at borders where there aren't any other options.

Credit Cards

Many top-end hotels and shops accept *tarjetas de crédito* (credit cards) but usually charge you a 7% (or greater) fee for using them. The amount you'll eventually pay is not based on the point-of-sale exchange rate, but the rate your bank chooses to use when the transaction posts to your account, sometimes weeks later. Your bank may also tack on a surcharge and additional fees for each foreign-currency transaction.

The most widely accepted cards in Peru are Visa and MasterCard, although American Express and a few others are valid in some establishments, as well as for cash advances at ATMs. Before you leave home, notify your bank that you'll be using your credit card abroad.

Taxes, Tipping & Refunds

At Peruvian airports, international (boxed text, p531) and domestic (boxed text, p535) departure taxes are payable in US dollars or *nuevos soles* (cash only). Expensive hotels will add a 19% sales tax and 10% service charge; the latter is generally not included in quoted rates. Non-Peruvians may be eligible for a refund of the sales tax only (see p510). A few restaurants charge combined taxes of more than 19%, plus a service charge (*servicio* or *propina*) of 10%. At restaurants that don't do this, you may tip 10% for good service. Taxi drivers do not generally expect tips (unless they've assisted with heavy luggage), but porters and tour guides do. There is no system of sales-tax refunds for shoppers.

FUNNY MONEY *Rafael Wlodarski*

Counterfeiting of both US and local-currency bills has become a serious problem in Peru. Merchants are extremely careful about accepting large-denomination notes; you should be, too. Everyone has their own technique for spotting a fake – some can feel the difference in paper quality, while others will sniff out counterfeit ink. You should look for a combination of signs; new forgeries simulate some security features, but never all of them. Politely refuse to accept *any* worn, torn or damaged bills, even small-denomination notes, since many businesses will not accept these.

Watch out for the following issues:

- Check the watermark – most fake bills have these, but real bills will have a section where the mark is made by discernibly thinner paper.

- The writing along the top of the bill should be embossed – run your finger to see that it is raised from the paper and test the back for an impression.

- The line underneath this writing is made up of tiny words – if it's a solid line, then it's a fake.

- The value of the bill written on the side should appear metallic and be slightly green, blue, and pink at different angles – fake bills are only pink and have no hologram.

- The metal strip running through the note has the word 'Peru' repeatedly written along its length in tiny letters when held up to the light – fake bills also have this, but the letters are messier and difficult to read.

- The tiny pieces of colored thread and holographic dots scattered on the bill should be embedded in the paper, not glued on.

Traveler's Checks

If you carry some of your money as *cheques de viajero* (traveler's checks), these can be refunded if lost or stolen. Bear in mind that exchange rates for traveler's checks are quite a bit lower than for US dollars. With the commissions that are sometimes charged, you can lose more than 10% of the checks' value when you exchange them, and they may be impossible to change in small towns. Almost all businesses and some *casas de cambio* refuse to deal with them, so you will need to queue at a bank to change them. American Express checks are the most widely accepted, followed by Visa and Thomas Cook.

Reloadable traveler's check cards work just like ATM cards, but are not linked to your home bank account. These cards enjoy some of the same protections as traveler's checks, and can be replaced more easily than a bank ATM card. During your trip, you can add more funds to a traveler's check card either online or by making an international collect call, or you can authorize someone else at home to do this for you, which eliminates the need for emergency wire transfers. **American Express** (www.americanexpress.com) offers traveler's check cards, as do many **Visa providers** (www.cashpassportcard.com).

PHOTOGRAPHY & VIDEO

Indigenous people in remote areas may regard your camera with suspicion. There will be a few who regard the lens as an 'evil eye' that can bring bad luck, but there will be many others who are just tired of being photographically exploited for the purpose of a million tourist photo albums. Always ask permission before pointing and shooting. In touristy locations, locals dressed in their finest traditional clothes stand beside their most photogenic llamas and expect a small payment for any photos you may take. Negotiate a price in advance. At markets, you may be able to photograph a vendor and/or their wares after making a purchase.

Print and slide film and replacement camera batteries are available in major cities and tourist centers. Digital memory cards and sticks may be harder to find, so stock up at home or in Lima (p119). Many internet cafés and photo shops offer cheap CD-burning services that let you download and save files from your digital camera's memory. If your camera uses rechargeable batteries, be sure that your charger adheres to Peru's 220V 60Hz AC electricity standard before plugging it in. If you're traveling to remote areas where electricity is questionable, carry extra batteries.

It's best to carry film and digital memory cards with you onto airplanes. It's not advisable

DIRECTORY

to put them into checked luggage because the scanners used for those bags are much stronger and can damage your film or erase digital memory cards. If you place all your film into a clear plastic bag, you may be able to get it hand-checked at security checkpoints.

POST

The privatized postal system is run by **Serpost** (www.serpost.com.pe). Its service is fairly efficient and reliable, but surprisingly expensive. Airmail *postales* (postcards) and *cartas* (letters) cost about S6 to the US, S7 to Europe and S8 to Asia. Most mail will take about two weeks to arrive from Lima; longer from the provinces.

Lista de correos (general delivery or poste restante) can be sent to any major post office. Bring your passport when picking up mail and ask the post-office clerk to check alphabetically under the initial letter of each of your first, last and middle names, as well as under 'M' (for Mr, Ms et al). Ask your correspondents to make sure that your name is clearly printed and to capitalize and underline your last name to avoid confusion. For example:

Margarita SILVA
Lista de Correos
Correo Central
Lima
Peru

For express mail and packages, international couriers such as **Federal Express** (www.fedex.com .pe) and **DHL** (www.dhl.com.pe) are more reliable than post offices, but may only have drop-off centers in Lima or other major cities. They are also more expensive than Serpost.

SHOPPING

Arts and crafts are inevitably sold wherever tourists gather. Popular souvenirs include alpaca wool sweaters and scarves, woven textiles, ceramics, masks, gold and silver jewelry and the backpacker favorite: Inca Kola T-shirts. While Lima offers a wealth of crafts, highly specialized regional items may be difficult to find.

Expensive foreign-language books are stocked at better bookstores, especially in Lima (p80) and Cuzco (p222).

Bargaining is the norm at street stalls and markets, where it's cash only. Prices are fixed in upscale stores, which may add a surcharge for credit card transactions.

SOLO TRAVELERS

Peru's top tourist spots are good places for solo travelers. Inexpensive hostels with communal kitchens encourage social exchange, while a large number of language schools, tours and volunteer organizations provide every traveler with plenty of opportunities to meet others.

Outside popular areas, this type of infrastructure may be limited, in which case you might be spending a lot more time by yourself. It is not recommended to undertake long treks in the wilderness on your own.

Traveling alone as a woman is riskier than for a man – but still do-able. For more specific advice for women travelers, see p527.

TELEPHONE

Public pay phones operated by **Telefónica-Perú** (www.telefonica.com.pe) are available on the street even in small towns. Most pay phones work with phonecards which can be purchased at supermarkets and groceries. Often internet cafés have private phone booths with 'net to-phone' and 'net-to-net' capabilities (such as Skype), where you can talk for pennies or even for free.

When calling Peru from abroad, dial the international access code for the country you're in, then Peru's country code (51), then the area code *without the 0* and finally, the local number. When making international calls from Peru, dial the international access code (00), then the country code of where you're calling to, then the area code and finally, the local phone number.

PERUVIAN ADDRESSES

A post-office box is known as an *apartado postal* (abbreviated 'Apartado,' 'Apto' or 'AP') or a *casilla postal* ('Casilla' or 'CP'). Some addresses have *s/n* (short for *sin numero,* or 'without a number') or *cuadra* ('block,' eg Block 4) after the street name.

Only addresses in Lima and neighboring Callao require postal codes. Those used most often by travelers are Lima 1 (Central Lima), Lima 4 (Barranco), Lima 18 (Miraflores) and Lima 27 (San Isidro). Note that the word 'Lima' is essential to these postal codes.

In Peru, any telephone number beginning with a 9 is a cell-phone number. Numbers beginning with 0800 are often toll-free only when dialed from private phones, not from public pay phones. See the inside front cover of this book for more useful dialing codes, including how to contact an operator or directory assistance. To make a credit card or collect call using AT&T, dial ☎ 0800-50288. There's an online telephone directory at www.paginasama rillas.com.pe.

Cell Phones

It's possible to use a tri-band GSM world phone in Peru (GSM 1900). Other systems in use are CDMA and TDMA. This is a fast-changing field, so check the current situation before you travel: just do a web search and browse the myriad products on the market. In Lima and other larger cities, you can buy cell phones that use SIM cards for about US$65, then pop in a SIM card that costs from US$6.50. Claro is a popular pay-as-you-go plan. Cell-phone rentals may be available in major cities and tourist centers. Expect cell-phone reception to fade the further you go into the mountains or jungle.

Phonecards

Called *tarjetas telefónicas,* these cards are widely available and are made by many companies in many price ranges. Some are designed specifically for international calls. Some have an electronic chip that keeps track of your balance when the card is inserted into an appropriate phone. Other cards use a code system whereby you dial your own personal code to obtain balances and access; these can be used from almost any phone. The most common are Telefónica-Perú's 147 cards; you dial 147, then enter your personal code (which is on the back of the card), listen to a message telling you how much money you have left on the card, dial the number, and listen to a message telling you how much time you have left for this call. The drawback is it's in Spanish. The 147 card is best used for long-distance calls. For local calls, the Holá Perú card is cheaper, and works the same way except that you begin by dialing 0800. There are numerous other cards – ask around for which ones offer the best deal.

TIME

Peru is five hours behind Greenwich Mean Time (GMT). It's the same as Eastern Standard Time (EST) in North America. At noon in Lima, it's 9am in Los Angeles, 11am in Mexico City, noon in New York, 5pm in London, 4am (following day) in Sydney.

Daylight Saving Time (DST) isn't used in Peru, so add an hour to all of these times between the first Sunday in April and the last Sunday in October.

Punctuality is not one of the things that Latin America is famous for, so be prepared to wait around. Buses rarely depart or arrive on time. Savvy travelers should allow some flexibility in their itineraries. Bring your own travel alarm clock – tours and long-distance buses often depart before 6am.

TOILETS

Peruvian plumbing leaves something to be desired. There's always a chance that flushing a toilet will cause it to overflow, so you should avoid putting anything other than human waste into the toilet. Even a small amount of toilet paper can muck up the entire system – that's why a small, plastic bin is routinely provided for disposing of the paper. This may not seem sanitary, but it is definitely better than the alternative of clogged toilets and flooded floors. A well-run hotel or restaurant, even a cheap one, will empty the bin and clean the toilet every day. In rural areas, don't expect much more than simply a rickety wooden outhouse built around a hole in the ground.

Public toilets are rare outside of transportation terminals, restaurants and museums, but restaurants will generally let travelers use a restroom (sometimes for a charge). Those in terminals usually have an attendant who will charge you about S0.50 to enter and then give you a miserly few sheets of toilet paper. Public restrooms frequently run out of toilet paper, so always carry an extra roll with you.

TOURIST INFORMATION

The government's official tourist agency, **PromPerú** (www.peru.info), doesn't have any international offices, but its website – in Spanish, English, French, German, Italian and Portuguese – is an easy way to obtain information before you depart. In the USA and Canada, you can call its toll-free **hotline** (☎ 866-661-7378). Some Peruvian embassies in foreign countries (see p517) supply tourist information as well.

PromPerú runs tourist information offices, called iPerú, in the following cities:

Arequipa Airport (☎ 054-44-4564; 1st fl, Main Hall, Rodríguez Ballón Airport; ☽ 10am-7:30pm); Plaza de Armas (☎ 054-22-3265; Portal de la Municipalidad 110; ☽ 8:30am-7:30pm)

Ayacucho (☎ 066-31-8305; Municipalidad Huamanga, Plaza Mayor, Portal Municipal 48; ☽ 8:30am-7:30pm Mon-Sat, to 2:30pm Sun)

Chachapoyas (☎ 041-47-7292; Plaza de Armas, Ortiz Arrieta 588; ☽ 8am-7pm)

Cuzco Airport (☎ 084-23-7364; Main Hall, Velasco Astete Airport; ☽ 6am-4pm); City Center (☎ 084-23-4498; Office 102, Galerías Turísticas, Av Sol 103; ☽ 8:30am-7:30pm); Machu Picchu (☎ 084-21-1104; Edificio del Instituto Nacional de Cultura, Pachacútec, cuadra 1; ☽ 9am-1pm & 2-8pm)

Huaraz (☎ 043-42-8812; Oficina 1, Pasaje Atusparia, Plaza de Armas; ☽ 9am-6pm Mon-Sat, to 2pm Sun)

Iquitos Airport (☎ 065-26-0251; Main Hall, Francisco Secada Vignetta Airport; ☽ 8am-1pm & 4-8pm); City Center (☎ 065-23-6144; Loreto 201; ☽ 8:30am-7:30pm)

Lima Airport (☎ 01-574-8000; Main Hall, Jorge Chavez International Airport; ☽ 24hr); Miraflores (Map p98; ☎ 01-445-9400; Module 14, by movie theater box office, LarcoMar Center; ☽ noon-8pm); San Isidro (Map p96; ☎ 01-421-1627; Jorge Basadre 610; ☽ 9am-6pm Mon-Fri)

Puno (☎ 051-36-5088; Plaza de Armas, cnr Lima & Destua; ☽ 8:30am-7:30pm)

Trujillo (☎ 044-29-4561; mezzanine level, Municipalidad de Trujillo, Plaza Mayor, Jirón Pizarro 412; ☽ 8am-7pm Mon-Sat, to 2pm Sun)

There is a 24-hour **iPerú hotline** (☎ 01-574-8000), which can provide general information and nonemergency assistance. Municipal tourist offices are listed under the relevant cities earlier in this book.

TRAVELERS WITH DISABILITIES

Peru offers few conveniences for travelers with disabilities. Features such as signs in Braille or phones for the hearing-impaired are virtually nonexistent, while wheelchair ramps and lifts are few and far between, and the pavement is often badly potholed and cracked. Most hotels do not have wheelchair-accessible rooms, at least not rooms specially designated as such. Bathrooms are often barely large enough for an able-bodied

person to walk into, so few are accessible to wheelchairs. Toilets in rural areas may be of the squat variety.

Nevertheless, there are Peruvians with disabilities who get around, mainly through the help of others. It is not particularly unusual to see mobility-impaired people being carried bodily to a seat on a bus, for example. If you need assistance, be polite and good-natured. Speaking Spanish will help immeasurably. If possible, bring along an able-bodied traveling companion.

Organizations that provide information for travelers with disabilities:

Access-Able Travel Source (www.access-able.com) Partial listings of accessible transportation and tours, accommodations, attractions and restaurants.

Apumayo Expediciones (Map pp224-5; ☎ /fax 084-24-6018; www.apumayo.com; Interior 3, Calle Garcilaso 265, Cuzco) An adventure-tour company that takes disabled travelers to Machu Picchu and other historic sites in the Sacred Valley.

Conadis (Map pp88-9; ☎ 01-332-0808; www.conadisperu.gob.pe; Av Arequipa 375, Santa Beatriz) Governmental agency for Spanish-language information and advocacy for people with disabilities.

Emerging Horizons (www.emerginghorizons.com) Travel magazine for the mobility impaired, with handy advice columns and news articles.

Mobility International USA (MIUSA; ☎ /TTY 541-343-1284; www.miusa.org; Ste 343, 132 E Broadway, Eugene, OR 97401, USA) International development and exchange programs for people with disabilities.

Society for Accessible Travel & Hospitality (SATH; ☎ 212-447-7284; www.sath.org; Ste 610, 347 Fifth Ave, New York, NY 10016, USA) A good resource for general travel information.

VISAS

With a few exceptions (notably some Asian, African and communist countries), visas are not required for travelers entering Peru. Tourists are permitted a 30- to 90-day stay, which is stamped into their passports and onto a tourist card, called a Tarjeta Andina de Migración (Andean Immigration Card), that you must return upon leaving the country. The actual length of stay is determined by the immigration officer at the point of entry. Be careful not to lose your tourist card, or you will have to queue up an *oficina de migraciónes* (immigration office), also simply known as *migraciónes*, for a replacement card. It's a good idea to carry your passport and tourist card on your person at all times, especially when traveling in remote areas (it's required by law on the Inca Trail). For security, make a photocopy of both documents and keep them in a separate place from the originals.

Thirty-day extensions cost about US$50 and can be obtained at immigration offices in major cities, with Lima (p81) being the most painless place to do this (see the Lima section for how to download necessary paperwork ahead of time). There are also immigration offices in Arequipa, Cuzco, Iquitos, Puerto Maldonado, Puno and Trujillo, as well as near the Chilean and Ecuadorian borders. Although extensions are a bureaucratic hassle, you can keep extending your stay up to 180 days total. When your time is up, you can leave the country overland and return a day later to begin the process again.

Anyone who plans to work, attend school or reside in Peru for any length of time must obtain a visa in advance. Do this through the Peruvian embassy or consulate in your home country.

VOLUNTEERING

General advice for finding volunteer work is to ask at language schools; they usually know of several programs suitable for their students. South American Explorers (SAE) has an online volunteer database and also folders with reports left by foreign volunteers at the SAE clubhouses in Lima (see boxed text, p86) and Cuzco (p222).

Both nonprofit and for-profit organizations can arrange volunteer opportunities, if you contact them in advance. These include the following:

Action Without Borders (www.idealist.org) Online database of social work-oriented jobs, internships and volunteer opportunities.

ADRA Perú (Map p98; ☎ 01-712-7700; www.adra.org .pe; Av Angamos Oeste 770, Miraflores, Lima) A development and relief agency with countrywide projects in health, education and agriculture.

Cross-Cultural Solutions (☎ in USA 800-380-4777, in UK 0845-458-2781; www.crossculturalsolutions .org) Educational and social-service projects in Lima and Ayacucho; program fees include professional in-country support.

Earthwatch Institute (☎ in USA 800-776-0188; www.earthwatch.org) Pay to help scientists on archaeological, ecological and other real-life expeditions in the Amazon Basin and the Andes.

Global Crossroad (☎ in USA 866-387-7816, in UK 0800-310-1821; www.globalcrossroad.com) Volunteer, internship and job programs in the Andes. Summer cultural immersion programs for 18- to 29-year-olds include language instruction, homestays, volunteer work and sightseeing.

Global Volunteers (☎ in USA 800-487-1074; www .globalvolunteers.org; 375 E Little Canada Rd, St Paul, MN 55117, USA) Offers short-term volunteer opportunities helping orphans in Lima.

HoPe Foundation (☎ 084-24-9885, in the Netherlands 0413-47-3666; www.stichtinghope.org; Casilla 59, Correo Central, Cuzco) Provides educational and healthcare support in the Andes.

Kiya Survivors/Peru Positive Action (☎ 1273-721902; www.kiyasurvivors.org; 1 Sussex Rd, Hove BN3 2WD, UK) Organizes two- to six-month volunteer placements for assistant teachers and therapists to work with special-needs children in Cuzco, Urubamba in the Sacred Valley and Máncora on the north coast.

ProWorld Service Corps (☎ in USA 877-429-6754, in UK 018-6559-6289; www.myproworld.org) This highly recommended organization offers two- to 26-week cultural, service and academic experiences, including in the Sacred Valley and the Amazon. It has links with affiliated NGOs throughout Peru and can organize placements for individuals or groups.

Teaching & Projects Abroad (☎ 01903-708300; www.teaching-abroad.co.uk; Aldsworth Pde, Goring, Sussex BN12 4TX, UK) For summer, gap-year and career breaks, this UK-based organization has opportunities for community care and English teaching in the Sacred Valley and conservation in the Amazon jungle.

Volunteers for Peace (VFP; ☎ 802-259-2759; www .vfp.org; 1034 Tiffany Rd, Belmont, VT 05730, USA) Places volunteers in short-term work-camp programs, usually in Lima or Ayacucho. Program fees are more than reasonable and may be partially paid directly to local communities.

Working Abroad (www.workingabroad.com) Online network of grassroots volunteer opportunities (eg social development, environmental restoration, indigenous rights, traditional art and music) with trip reports from the field.

WOMEN TRAVELERS

Machismo is alive and well in Latin America. Most female travelers to Peru will experience little more than shouts of *mi amor* (my love) or an appreciative hiss. If you are fair-skinned with blond hair, however, be prepared to be the center of attention. Peruvian men consider foreign women to have looser morals and be easier sexual conquests than Peruvian women and will often make flirtatious comments to single women.

Staring, whistling, hissing and catcalls in the streets are run-of-the-mill – and should be treated as such. Many men make a pastime of dropping *piropos* (cheeky, flirtatious or even vulgar 'compliments'). However, these are generally not meant to be insulting. Most men rarely, if ever, follow up on the idle chatter (unless they feel you've insulted their manhood). Ignoring all provocation and staring ahead is generally the best response. If someone is particularly persistent, roll your eyes or try a potentially ardor-smothering phrase such as *soy casada* (I'm married). If you appeal directly to locals, you'll find most Peruvians to be protective of lone women, expressing surprise and concern if you tell them you're traveling without your family or husband.

It's not uncommon for fast-talking charmers, especially in tourist towns such as Cuzco, to attach themselves to gringas and be surprisingly oblivious to a lack of interest from their quarry. Many of these young Casanovas are looking for a meal ticket (see boxed text, p252), so approach any professions of undying love with extreme skepticism.

Use common sense when meeting men in public places. In Peru, outside of a few big cities, it is rare for a woman to belly up to a bar for a beer, and the ones that do tend to be prostitutes. If you feel the need for an evening cocktail, opt for a restaurant instead. Likewise, heavy drinking by women might be misinterpreted by some men as a sign of promiscuity. When meeting someone, make it very clear if only friendship is intended. This goes double for tour and activity guides. When meeting someone for the first time, it is also wise not to divulge where you are staying until you feel sure that you are with someone you can trust.

In highland towns, dress is generally fairly conservative and women rarely wear shorts, opting instead for long skirts. Slacks are fine, but note that shorts, miniskirts and revealing blouses may draw unwanted attention.

As in any part of the world, the possibilities of rape and assault do exist. Use your big city smarts (even in small towns). A few tips:

- skip the hitchhiking
- do not take unlicensed taxis, especially at night (licensed taxis have an authorization sticker on the windshield)
- avoid walking alone in unfamiliar places at night
- if a stranger approaches you on the street and asks a question, answer it if you feel comfortable – but *don't* stop walking as

it could allow potential attackers to surround you
- avoid overnight buses through bandit-ridden areas, since women have been known to be raped during robberies (see p514 for more on this and other personal safety issues)
- be aware of your surroundings; attacks have occurred in broad daylight around well-touristed sites and popular trekking trails
- when hiring a private tour or activity guide, seek someone who comes from a recommended or reliable agency
- choose your hotel wisely; there have been reports of women being sexually harassed at cheap hotels

Travelers who are sexually assaulted can report it to the nearest police station or to the tourist police. However, Peruvian attitudes toward sexual assaults favor the attackers, not the survivors. Rape is often seen as a disgrace, and it is difficult to prosecute. Until recently, a rapist could avoid punishment by marrying the woman he attacked, something survivors were often pressured into doing by their own families. Because the police tend to be unhelpful, we recommend calling your own embassy or consulate (p517) to ask for advice, including on where to seek medical treatment, which should be an immediate priority.

On a far more mundane note: tampons are difficult to find in smaller towns, so stock up in major cities, or investigate purchasing **The Keeper** (www.thekeeper.com), which could change your traveling life. Birth-control pills and other contraceptives (even condoms) are scarce outside metropolitan areas and not always reliable, so bring your own supply from home. Rates of HIV infection are on the rise, especially among young women. Abortions are illegal, except to save the life of the mother.

These organizations provide useful information for female travelers:

Centro de La Mujer Peruana Flora Tristán (Map pp88-9; ☎ 01-433-1457; www.flora.org.pe; Parque Hernán Velarde 14, Lima; ⏰ 1-5pm Mon-Fri) Feminist social and political advocacy group for women's and human rights in Peru, with a Spanish-language website and a library in Lima.

Instituto Peruano de Paternidad Responsable (Inppares; ☎ 01-640-2000; www.inppares.org.pe) Planned Parenthood-affiliated organization that runs a dozen sexual and reproductive health clinics for both women and men around the country, including in Lima.

WORK

Short-term business travelers can normally enter Peru on a tourist visa (p526). Many top-end hotels have fully equipped business centers and international direct dialing (IDD) telephones in guest rooms; ask about these when making reservations. Better hotels will provide dual-voltage outlets and electricity converters upon request, while luxury hotels have concierge staff to arrange everything from taxis to translators. Smaller hotels and guesthouses often have capable front desk staff who can assist business travelers. See p520 for more information on internet access.

If you want to live and work in Peru, you will need a work visa. However, you might be able to get a part-time job teaching English in language schools without one. This is illegal, however, and such jobs are increasingly difficult to get without a proper work visa. Occasionally, schools advertise for teachers in the newspapers, but more often, jobs are found by word of mouth. Schools expect you to be a native English speaker, and the pay is low. If you have teaching credentials, so much the better. Average pay is US$200 per week.

American and British schools in Lima sometimes hire teachers of math, biology and other subjects, but usually only if you apply in advance. They pay much better than the language schools, and might possibly be able to help you get a work visa if you want to stay. In Lima, the South American Explorers clubhouse (see boxed text, p86) and international cultural centers (p81) may have contacts with schools that are looking for teachers.

Most other jobs are obtained by word of mouth (eg bartenders, hostel staff, jungle guides), but the possibilities are limited. For internships and short-term job opportunities through volunteer organizations, see p527.

Transportation

GETTING THERE & AWAY

ENTERING THE COUNTRY

Arriving in Peru is typically straightforward, as long as your passport is valid for at least six months beyond your departure date. When arriving by air, US citizens must show a return ticket or open-jaw onward ticket – don't show up with just a one-way ticket to South America. Immigration officials at airports are efficient, while those at overland border crossings may take their time scrutinizing your passport before they stamp it. For information on Peruvian visas, see p526.

When arriving by air or overland, immigration officials may only stamp 30 days into your passport (though 90 days is standard); if this happens, explain how many more days you need, supported by an exit ticket for onward or return travel.

Bribery is illegal, but some officials may try to procure extra 'fees' (known colloquially as *coima*) at land borders.

AIR

Peru (mainly Lima) has direct flights to and from cities all over the Americas, as well as continental Europe. Other locations require a connection.

Note: if you're headed to Cuzco, but are flying into Peru from another continent, your flight will likely land in Lima late in the evening or at night. This will require an overnight stay there since domestic flights to Cuzco generally depart only in the morning and early afternoon.

Airports & Airlines

Located in the port city of Callao, Lima's **Aeropuerto Internacional Jorge Chávez** (airline code LIM; ☎ 01-517-3100; www.lap.com.pe; Callao) completed a four-year remodel in 2009 that has left the main terminals sparkling (and chock-full of services). It is a major hub, serviced by flights from North, Central and South America, and two regular direct flights from Europe (Madrid and Amsterdam). Check the airport website or call ☎ 01-511-6055 for updated departure and arrival schedules for domestic and international flights. See p119 for details of airport services and p121 for transportation options to/from the airport. Cuzco (p253) has the only other airport with international service, to La Paz, Bolivia.

AIRLINES FLYING TO/FROM PERU

The phone numbers and addresses listed here are for airline offices in Lima; add ☎ 01 if calling from outside the capital.

If you plan to visit an office, call before you go or check a phone directory under 'Líneas Aéreas,' as they change addresses frequently. **Aerolineas Argentinas** (airline code ARG; ☎ 513-6565; www.aerolineas.com.ar/ar/pe/)

THINGS CHANGE...

The information in this chapter is particularly vulnerable to change. Check directly with the airline or a travel agent to make sure you understand how a fare (and ticket you may buy) works and be aware of the security requirements for international travel. Shop carefully. The details given in this chapter should be regarded as pointers and are not a substitute for your own careful, up-to-date research.

INTERNATIONAL DEPARTURE TAX

Lima's departure tax for international flights is US$31. Pay the tax in cash (dollars or *nuevos soles*) at the check-in counter before proceeding to departure gates. Note: some airlines include this fee in your ticket price.

Aeroméxico (airline code AMX; ☎ 705-1111; www
.aeromexico.com)
Aeropostal (airline code LAV; ☎ 444-1199; www
.aeropostal.com)
Air Canada (airline code ACA; ☎ 626-0900; www
.aircanada.com)
Air France (airline code AFR; ☎ 213-0200; www
.airfrance.com)
Alitalia (airline code AZA; ☎ 241-1026; www.alitalia.it)
American Airlines (airline code AAL; ☎ 211-7000;
www.aa.com)
Avianca (airline code AVA; ☎ 440-4104; www.avianca
.com)
British Airways (airline code BAW; ☎ 411-7801; www
.britishairways.com)
Continental Airlines (airline code COA; ☎ 712-9230;
www.continental.com)
Copa Airlines (airline code CMP; ☎ 610-0808; www
.copaair.com)
Delta Airlines (airline code DAL; ☎ 211-9211; www
.delta.com)
Iberia (airline code IBE; ☎ 411-7800; www.iberia
.com.pe)
KLM (airline code KLM; ☎ 213-0200; www.klm.com)
LAN (airline code LPE; ☎ 213-8200; www.lan.com)
TACA (airline code TAI; ☎ 511-8222; www.taca.com)

Tickets

From most places in the world, South America can be a relatively costly destination. The high season for air travel to and within Peru is late May to early September, as well as around major holidays (p519). Lower fares may sometimes be offered outside peak periods.

Contacting a travel agent that specializes in Latin American destinations and shopping around for competing online fares can turn up cheaper tickets. Students with international student ID cards (ISIC is one widely recognized card) and anyone aged under 26 can often get discounts with budget or specialty travel agencies. A good option to check out

is **STA Travel** (www.statravel.com), which has offices around the globe. (Bonus points: it's also a supporter of the Planeterra foundation's project for street kids in Cuzco.)

Tickets bought in Peru are subject to a 19% tax. It is essential that you reconfirm all flights 72 hours in advance, either on the telephone or online, or you may get bumped off the flight. If you are traveling in remote areas, have a reputable travel agent do this for you.

INTERCONTINENTAL FLIGHTS

Some of the best deals for travelers visiting many countries on different continents are round-the-world tickets. Itineraries from the USA, Europe or Australasia typically require at least five stopovers, possibly including unusual destinations such as Tahiti. Fares vary widely, but check **Air Treks** (www.airtreks.com) and **Air Brokers** (www.airbrokers.com). These types of tickets have restrictions, so read the fine print carefully.

Africa

A combination of international air carriers and at least one connection is needed to fly from any point in Africa to Peru. If flying from northern Africa, a stop in Europe will generally be required (usually in Amsterdam or Paris). Flights from southern Africa are most likely to connect in South American gateway cities such as São Paulo or Buenos Aires.

Asia

Flights from Asia require at least one connection in the US; expect to travel on multiple international carriers. Some of the most common transfer points are Atlanta, Detroit, Houston, Los Angeles, New York, Newark and San Francisco. Flights from India generally travel through various European capitals.

Australia & New Zealand

Santiago, Chile tends to be the most common gateway city from Australia and New Zealand, though some carriers connect through the US as well.

In Australia, **Destination Holidays** (☎ 03-9725-4655, 800-337-050; www.south-america.com.au) and **South American Travel Centre** (☎ 03-9642-5353; www.satc.com.au) are agencies specializing in travel to Latin America.

Canada

There are direct flights to Lima from Toronto, but most trips require a connection in the US (see right) or Mexico City.

Continental Europe

There are direct flights from Amsterdam and Madrid, but connections through the USA, Central America or Colombia are often cheaper.

Latin America

There are direct flights from a large number of Latin American cities to Peru, including Bogotá, Buenos Aires, Caracas, Guayaquil, La Paz, Mexico City, Panama City, Quito, Rio de Janeiro, San José (Costa Rica), Santiago (Chile) and São Paulo. LAN, Copa and TACA are the principal Latin American airlines that fly to Lima.

Recommended agencies in Latin America:

ASATEJ Viajes (www.asatej.com, in Spanish) In Mexico, Argentina and Uruguay.

IVI Venezuela (☎ 0212-993-6082; www.ivivenezuela .com) In Venezuela.

Latin America for Less (☎ 11-5199-2517 ext 25; latinamericaforless.com) In Argentina.

Student Travel Bureau (STB; ☎ 11-3038-1555; www .stb.com.br) In Brazil.

UK & Ireland

Flights from the UK or Ireland connect through gateway cities in continental Europe, North America and Brazil.

In the UK, the following agencies specialize in travel to Latin America:

Austral Tours (☎ 020-7233-5384; www.latinamerica .co.uk)

Journey Latin America (JLA; ☎ 020-8747-3108; www.journeylatinamerica.co.uk)

North-South Travel (☎ 0125-608-291; www.north southtravel.co.uk) Donates a portion of its profits to projects all over the developing world.

South American Experience (☎ 0845-277-3366; www.southamericanexperience.co.uk)

USA

There are direct (nonstop) flights to Lima from Atlanta, Dallas-Fort Worth, Houston, Los Angeles, Miami and New York. In other cases, flights will connect either in the US or in Latin American gateway cities such as Mexico City and Bogota.

US travel agencies that specialize in travel to Latin America:

Ana Travel (☎ 800-643-6606; www.anatravel.com)

Exito Travel (☎ 800-655-4053; www.exitotravel.com)

Latin America for Less (☎ 877-269-0309; latinamericaforless.com)

CLIMATE CHANGE & TRAVEL

Climate change is a serious threat to the ecosystems that humans rely upon, and air travel is the fastest-growing contributor to the problem. Lonely Planet regards travel, overall, as a global benefit, but believes we all have a responsibility to limit our personal impact on global warming.

Flying & Climate Change

Pretty much every form of motor travel generates CO_2 (the main cause of human-induced climate change) but planes are far and away the worst offenders, not just because of the sheer distances they allow us to travel, but because they release greenhouse gases high into the atmosphere. The statistics are frightening: two people taking a return flight between Europe and the US will contribute as much to climate change as an average household's gas and electricity consumption over a whole year.

Carbon Offset Schemes

Climatecare.org and other websites use 'carbon calculators' that allow jetsetters to offset the greenhouse gases they are responsible for with contributions to energy-saving projects and other climate-friendly initiatives in the developing world – including projects in India, Honduras, Kazakhstan and Uganda.

Lonely Planet, together with Rough Guides and other concerned partners in the travel industry, supports the carbon offset scheme run by climatecare.org. Lonely Planet offsets all of its staff and author travel.

For more information check out our website: lonelyplanet.com.

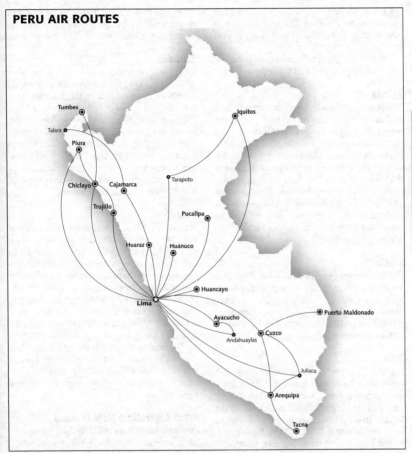

PERU AIR ROUTES

LAND & RIVER

Because no roads bridge the Darien Gap, it is not possible to travel to South America by land from the north (unless you spend a week making your way through swampy, drug-dealer-infested jungle), so bringing your own vehicle from North America is a costly undertaking.

Overland travel from neighboring Bolivia, Brazil, Chile, Colombia and Ecuador tends not to be as safe or as straightforward as you might like. See p526 for important information on visas, immigration offices and other border-crossing formalities.

Ormeño (☎ 01-472-1710; www.grupo-ormeno.com .pe) is the main bus company offering international travel, and goes to Chile, Ecuador, Colombia, Bolivia and Argentina. Many other smaller, regional companies do cross-border travel, but on a far more limited basis. The only rail service that crosses the Peru border is the train between Arica, Chile, and Tacna on Peru's south coast.

Whatever form of transport you choose, keep in mind that while it may be a bit cheaper to buy tickets to the border, cross over and then buy onward tickets on the other side, it's usually much easier, faster and safer to buy a cross-border through ticket. When traveling by bus, check carefully with the company about what is included in the price of the ticket, and whether the service is direct or involves a transfer, and possibly a long wait, at the border.

Getting to Peru by boat is possible from points on the Amazon River in Brazil and from Leticia, Colombia, as well as to the port cities on Peru's Pacific coast.

The following sections outline the principal points of entry to and exit from Peru.

Bolivia

Peru is normally reached overland from Bolivia via Lake Titicaca (see boxed text, p214); the border crossing at Yunguyo is much safer and a lot less chaotic than the one at Desaguadero. There are many transportation options for both of these routes, most of which involve changing buses at the Peru–Bolivia border before reaching Puno. For the adventurous, it is possible to cross into Bolivia along the north shore. It's also possible, but quite difficult, to cross into Bolivia from Puerto Maldonado (see boxed text, p467).

Brazil

You can travel overland between Peru and Brazil via Iñapari (see boxed text, p466). Traveling from Iquitos, it's more straightforward to go along the Amazon to Tabatinga in Brazil via Leticia, Colombia. For more information on boat trips, see boxed text, p506.

Chile

Traveling on the Pan-American Hwy, the major crossing point is between Arica, Chile, and Tacna on Peru's south coast (see boxed text, p158). Long-distance buses to Tacna depart from Lima, Arequipa and Puno. *Colectivo* (shared) taxis are the fastest and most reliable way to travel between Tacna and Arica. It's also possible to make the crossing, albeit much more slowly, by train; border formalities are done at the respective stations. Flights to Tacna from Arequipa are cheap but book up quickly. Alternatively, Ormeño runs through buses from Lima all the way to Santiago, Chile. From Arequipa, Ormeño goes to Santiago, Chile, and Buenos Aires.

Colombia

It is easiest to travel between Peru and Colombia via Ecuador. Ormeño has through buses between Lima and Bogota via Ecuador. This long-haul trip is better done in stages, though.

If you are in the rainforest, it is more straightforward to voyage along the Amazon by boat between Iquitos and Leticia, Colombia,

from where there are flights to Bogota. For more details on border formalities there, see boxed text, p506.

Ecuador

The most common way to get to or from Ecuador is along the Pan-American Hwy via Tumbes (see boxed text, p386). Another route is via La Tina to Loja in Ecuador (see boxed text, p376). A third way is via Jaén (see boxed text, p442). **Cifa** (☎ 072-52-7120) runs buses between Tumbes in Peru and Machala or Guayaquil in Ecuador. **Transportes Loja** (☎ 073-30-9407) runs buses between Piura in Peru and Machala or Loja in Ecuador. Ormeño has weekly through buses between Lima and Quito.

TOURS

Scores of overseas companies offer tours of Peru for travelers who prefer not to travel on their own, or who have a limited amount of time and want to maximize their Peruvian experience, perhaps combining it with other South American countries. Usually, groups travel with knowledgeable guides, but you will pay a great deal extra for this privilege – it's worth it for highly specialized outdoor activities (eg river running, mountaineering, bird-watching, mountain biking). Otherwise, it's just as convenient and much cheaper to travel to Peru independently, then take organized day trips and overnight tours along the way (see p540).

From Australia & New Zealand

Peregrine Adventures (☎ 03-8601-4444; www .peregrine.net.au; 380 Lonsdale St, Melbourne, VIC 3000) Hotel-based and trekking trips in Peru.

Tucan Travel (☎ 1300-769-249, in Cuzco 084-24-8691; www.tucantravel.com; 217 Alison Rd, Randwick, NSW 2031) Long-running tour operator specializing in Latin America provides a wide variety of options in Peru; also has an office in Cuzco.

From Canada & the USA

With easy flight connections, the USA has more companies offering tours of Peru than the rest of the world.

Adventure Center (☎ 510-654-1879, 800-228-8747; www.adventurecenter.com; Ste 200, 1311 63rd St, Emeryville, CA 94608) A clearinghouse for tour operators offering various trips.

Adventure Life (☎ 406-541-2677, 800-344-6118; www.adventure-life.com; Suite 1, 1655 S 3rd St W, Missoula, MT 5980) Andean trekking, Amazon exploring and multi-sport itineraries; reputable agency that uses bilingual guides, family-run hotels and local transportation.

Exodus (☎ 510-654-1879, 800-343-4272; www.exodus .co.uk; Ste 200, 1311 63rd St, Emeryville, CA 94608) Award-winning responsible-travel operator offering long-distance overland trips and shorter cultural and trekking adventures.

Explorations (☎ 239-992-9660, 800-446-9660; www .explorationsinc.com; 27655 Kent Rd, Bonita Springs, FL 34135) Amazon trips include biologist-escorted cruises, lodge-based expeditions and fishing trips in the Reserva Nacional Pacaya-Samiria.

GAP Adventures (☎ 800-708-7761; www.gap.ca; 19 Charlotte St, Toronto, ON M5V 2H5) The premier Canadian agency with offices in Vancouver, Boston, USA, and London, UK. Budget-priced tours include hotel-based, trekking, Amazon and cultural trips.

International Expeditions (☎ 205-428-1700, 800-633-4734; www.ietravel.com; One Environs Park, Helena, AL 35080) Offers Amazon tours, staying in jungle lodges or on river boats, with an emphasis on natural history and bird-watching.

Mountain Travel Sobek (☎ 510-594-6000, 888-831-7526; www.mtsobek.com; 1266 66th St, Emeryville, CA 94608) Luxury trekking tours along the Inca Trail or in the Cordillera Blanca, and occasional rafting trips on the Río Tambopata.

Sacred Rides (☎ 647-999-7955, 888-423-7849; sacredrides.com; 261 Markham St, Toronto, ON M6J 2G7) A mountain biking specialist that organizes various multi-day bike tours throughout the Peruvian Andes.

Southwind Adventures (☎ 303-972-0701, 800-377-9463; www.southwindadventures.com; PO Box 621057, Littleton, CO 80162) Peruvian-American tour operator with trekking, cycling, rafting and boat-cruise itineraries in the Andes, the Amazon and the Galapagos Islands.

Tropical Nature Travel (☎ 352-376-3377, 877-888-1770; www.tropicalnaturetravel.com; PO Box 5276, Gainesville, FL 32627) Organizes multiday itineraries in the Amazon, as well as trekking, river rafting and archaeological and cultural tours.

Wilderness Travel (☎ 510-558-2488, 800-368-2794; www.wildernesstravel.com; 1102 Ninth St, Berkeley, CA 94710) Offers luxury treks, from four nights to two weeks, throughout the highlands and the Amazon.

Wildland Adventures (☎ 206-365-0686, 800-345-4453; www.wildland.com; 3516 NE 155th St, Seattle, WA 98155) Environmentally sound, culturally sensitive treks around the Sacred Valley and the Cordillera Blanca, as well as Amazon tours.

From the UK & Continental Europe

Amazonas Explorer (☎ 01437-891-743; www .amazonas-explorer.com) Rafting, mountain-biking, trekking and multi-activity trips in the Amazon and the Andes, plus custom itineraries.

Andean Trails (☎ 0131-467-7086; www.andeantrails .co.uk; The Clockhouse, Bonnington Mill Business Centre, 72 Newhaven Rd, Edinburgh, Scotland EH6 5QG) Mountain-biking, climbing, trekking and rafting tours in some unusual spots.

clubaventure (☎ 08-26-88-20-80; www.clubaventure .fr; 18 rue Séguier, 75006 Paris, France) A reputable French company organizing treks and tours.

Guerba Adventure & Discovery Holidays (☎ 01373-826-611; www.guerba.co.uk; Wessex House, 40 Station Rd, Westbury, Wiltshire BA13 3JN, UK) Trekking, activity and family-focused tours of the Andes and the Amazon.

Hauser Exkursionen (☎ 89-235-0060; www.hauser -exkursionen.de, in German; Spiegelstrasse 9, D-81241 Munich, Germany) Among the best German companies offering Andean treks.

Journey Latin America (☎ 020-8747-8315; www .journeylatinamerica.co.uk; 12 & 13 Heathfield Tce, Chiswick, London W4 4JE, UK) Cultural trips and treks in the Cordilleras Blanca and Huayhuash and to Machu Picchu.

GETTING AROUND

AIR

Domestic-flight schedules and prices change frequently. New airlines open every year, as those with poor safety records close. Most big cities are served by modern jets, while smaller towns are served by propeller aircraft.

Airlines in Peru

Most airlines fly from Lima to regional capitals, but service between provincial cities is limited. The following domestic airlines are the most established and reliable.:

LAN (airline code LPE; ☎ 01-213-8200; www.lan.com) Peru's major domestic carrier flies to Arequipa, Chiclayo, Cuzco, Iquitos, Juliaca, Piura, Puerto Maldonado, Tacna, Tarapoto and Trujillo. Additionally it offers link services between Arequipa and Cuzco, Arequipa and Juliaca,

---

DOMESTIC DEPARTURE TAX

At most airports, the departure tax for domestic flights will generally be about US$6, though the fee does vary (ever so slightly) from department to department. In most cases, you will pay the tax in cash (dollars or *nuevos soles*) at the check-in counter before proceeding to departure gates.

Arequipa and Tacna, Cuzco and Juliaca, and Cuzco and Puerto Maldonado.

LC Busre (airline code LCB; ☎ 01-619-1313; www .lcbusre.com.pe) A small airline with small, turbo-prop aircraft; flies to Andahuaylas, Ayacucho, Cajamarca, Huancayo, Huánuco, Huaraz, Iquitos, Pucallpa and Tarapoto.

Star Perú (airline code SRU; ☎ 01-705-9000; www .starperu.com) Another domestic carrier, flying to Ayacucho, Cajamarca, Cuzco, Iquitos, Pucallpa, Puerto Maldonado, Talara and Tarapoto; with link service between Tarapoto and Iquitos.

TACA (airline code TAI; ☎ 01-511-8222; www.taca.com) Central American airline that offers service between Lima and Cuzco.

Most domestic airlines have offices in Lima (p119). Smaller carriers and charters are listed under destinations throughout this book. The most remote towns may require connecting flights, and smaller towns are not served every day. Many airports for these places are often no more than a dirt strip.

Be at the airport at least 60 minutes before your flight departs (at least 90 minutes early in Cuzco, and two hours in Lima). This is a precaution as your flight may be overbooked, baggage handling and check-in procedures tend to be chaotic, and it's not unknown for flights to leave *before* their official departure time because of predicted bad weather. More likely, however, your flight will be late, so pack plenty of reading material.

Tickets

Two one-way tickets typically cost the same as a round-trip ticket. Most travelers travel in one direction overland and save time returning by air. The peak season for air travel within Peru is late May to early September, as well as around major holidays. Buy tickets for less popular destinations (anywhere other than Lima, Cuzco and Arequipa) as far in advance as possible, as these infrequent flights book up quickly.

Buying tickets and reconfirming flights is best done at airline offices in remote areas; otherwise, you can do so online or via a recommended travel agent. You can sometimes buy tickets at the airport on a space-available basis, but don't count on it. It's almost impossible to buy tickets for just before major holidays (p519), notably Semana Santa (the week leading up to Easter) and Fiestas Patrias (the last week in July). Overbooking is the norm.

Ensure all flight reservations are *confirmed and reconfirmed* 72 and 24 hours in advance; airlines are notorious for overbooking and flights are changed or canceled with surprising frequency, so it's even worth calling the airport or the airline just before leaving for the airport. Many midrange and top-end hotels will do this free of charge if you ask. Confirmation is especially essential during the peak travel season, particularly during the busy months of June, July and August.

If you're planning to travel around the country only by air, the air passes currently available offer no substantial savings compared with buying individual one-way tickets. Instead, they inconveniently lock you into a preplanned itinerary, with fees charged for making any changes. You'll enjoy more flexibility and a greater choice of airlines by *not* buying an air pass.

BICYCLE

The major drawback to cycling in Peru is the country's bounty of kamikaze motorists. On narrow, two-lane highways, drivers can be a serious hazard to cyclists. Cycling is more enjoyable and safer, though very challenging, off paved roads. Mountain bikes are recommended, as road bikes won't stand up to the rough conditions. See p179 for more about mountain biking and cycling in Peru.

Reasonably priced rentals (mostly mountain bikes) are available in popular tourist destinations, including Cuzco (p235), Arequipa (p170), Huaraz (p393) and Huancayo (p308). These bikes are rented to travelers for local excursions, not to make trips all over the country. For long-distance touring, bring your own bike from home. See p534 for organized tours.

Airline policies on carrying bicycles vary, so shop around. Some airlines will fly your bike as checked baggage if it's boxed. However, boxing the bike gives baggage handlers little clue to the contents, and the box may be roughly handled. If it's OK with the airline, try wrapping it in heavy-duty plastic, so baggage handlers can see the contents. Domestic airlines will charge you extra for this service – and that's if they even allow a checked bike.

BOAT

There are no passenger services along the Peruvian coast. In the Andean highlands, there are boat services on Lake Titicaca. Small

ROAD DISTANCES (KM)

	Arequipa	Ayacucho	Cajamarca	Chachapoyas	Chiclayo	Cuzco	Huancayo	Huaraz	Lima	Puno	Tacna	Trujillo	Tumbes
Arequipa	---												
Ayacucho	1135	---											
Cajamarca	1865	1439	---										
Chachapoyas	2132	1808	336	---									
Chiclayo	1677	1353	260	455	---								
Cuzco	518	582	1958	2337	1872	---							
Huancayo	705	318	1154	1523	1068	900	---						
Huaraz	1326	678	631	1000	545	1521	717	---					
Lima	907	1009	856	1225	770	1102	298	419	---				
Puno	584	323	2188	2557	2102	389	1289	1751	1332	---			
Tacna	963	368	2149	2518	2063	768	1477	1712	1293	419	---		
Trujillo	1468	1570	295	664	209	1663	859	336	561	1893	1854	---	
Tumbes	759	2329	810	805	550	2422	1618	1095	1320	2652	2613	759	---

TRANSPORTATION

motorized vessels take passengers from the port in Puno to visit various islands on the lake (p207), while catamarans zip over to Bolivia (p205).

In Peru's Amazon Basin, boat travel is of major importance. Larger vessels ply the wider rivers. Dugout canoes powered by outboard engines act as water taxis on smaller rivers. Some of the latter are powered by a strange arrangement that looks like a two-stroke motorcycle engine attached to a tiny propeller by a 3m-long propeller shaft. Called *peki-pekis*, these canoes are a slow and rather noisy method of transportation. In some places, modern aluminum launches are used.

The classic way to travel down the Amazon is while swinging in your hammock aboard a banana boat. You can travel from Pucallpa or Yurimaguas to Iquitos and on into Brazil this way (see p501). The lower deck of these boats is for cargo, and the upper deck (or decks) for passengers and crew.

At ports, there are chalkboards with ships' names, destinations and departure times displayed; these are usually optimistic. The captain has to clear documents with the *capi-tanía* (harbor master's office) on the day of departure, so asking the person in charge at the *capitanía* can yield information, but asking the captain is best. Nobody else really knows. Departure time often depends on a full cargo, and *mañana* (tomorrow) may go on for several days if the hold isn't full. Usually, you can sleep on the boat while waiting if you want to save on hotel bills. Never leave your luggage unattended.

Bring your own hammock, or rent a cabin for the journey. If using a hammock, hang it away from the noisy engine room and not directly under a light, as these are often lit late at night, precluding sleep and attracting insects. Cabins are often hot, airless boxes, but are lockable (for your luggage). Sanitary facilities are basic but adequate, and there's usually a pump shower on board.

Basic food is usually included in the price of the passage, and may be marginally better on the bigger ships, or if you are in cabin class. Finicky eaters or people with dietary restrictions should bring their own food. Bottled soft drinks are usually available and priced very reasonably.

TRANSPORTATION

BUS

Buses are the usual form of transport for most Peruvians and many travelers. Fares are cheap and services are frequent on the major long-distance routes, but buses are of varying quality. Less-traveled and remote rural routes are often served by older, more uncomfortable vehicles, many with inadequate legroom for taller travelers. Try to avoid seats at the back of the bus, because the ride is bumpier.

The scores of competing Peruvian bus companies have their own offices, and no one company covers the entire country. In some towns, the companies have their offices in one main bus terminal. In many cities, bus companies are clustered around a few city blocks, while elsewhere the terminals may be scattered all over town. For a rundown of major companies with offices in Lima, see p120.

Buses rarely arrive or depart on time, so the average trip times quoted throughout this book or by the operators themselves are almost certainly best-case scenarios. Buses can be significantly delayed during the rainy season, particularly in the high lands and the jungle. Especially from January through to April, quoted journey times can double or buses can even be delayed indefinitely because of landslides and bad road conditions.

Local and long-distance buses alike can be a risk to your personal safety, as fatal accidents are not unusual in Peru. Avoid overnight buses, on which muggings and assaults are more likely to occur. For important information on this, see p514.

Classes

The bigger companies often have luxury buses (called Imperial, Royal, Business, Executive or something similar), for which they charge up to 10 times more than *económico* buses. The former are express services with toilets, snacks, videos and air-conditioning. Some companies offer *bus-camas* (bed buses), on which the seats recline halfway or almost fully – you can sleep quite well on them. But for trips under six hours, you may have no choice but to take an *económico* bus, and these are usually pretty beaten up.

Better long-distance buses stop for bathroom breaks and meals (except on luxury buses, which serve paltry snacks and don't stop). Many companies have their own special rest areas, sometimes in the middle of nowhere, so you'll have no choice but to eat there. The food is fairly inexpensive, but not particularly appetizing, so many travelers bring their own food. Almost every bus terminal has a few convenience shops where you can stock up. Be aware that *económico* services don't stop for meals, although snack vendors will board the bus, and men and women alike have to answer nature's call in the open at the side of the road – women may want to wear a skirt or tie a jacket around their waist.

Costs & Reservations

Schedules and fares change frequently and vary from company to company; therefore, the prices quoted in this book are only approximations. You can check schedules online (but not make reservations, at least

---

MEMORABLE BUS MOMENTS *Rafael Wlodarski*

Love it or hate it, chances are you'll be spending time on the buses that brave the winding, potholed routes of the Andes and curving coastal highways of the deserts. We feel like we've spent half our lives on them – here's a hit list of memorable moments:

- Seatside shopping as armies of mobile vendors hawk fruits, vegetables and mysterious yet tasty snacks-on-a-stick. Look out for *choclo con queso* (grilled corn with cheese).

- Peruvian panpipe pop tunes that initially provide a rich, auditory tapestry to your trip, but manage to lose their luster somewhere around the 14th replaying.

- The unfortunate realization that Jean-Claude Van Damme has made more movies than all of the world's martial-art-less actors combined.

- When the bus leaves on time, the air-conditioning works and is not set to arctic, the radio and TV are silent and the seat-back actually reclines – you realize you have stumbled upon the long-lost bus-trip nirvana.

not yet) for the major players, including **Cruz del Sur** (www.cruzdelsur.com.pe), **Ormeño** (www.grupo-ormeno.com), **Transportes Línea** (www.transporteslinea.com.pe, in Spanish) and **Oltursa** (www.oltursa.com.pe, in Spanish).

There's no bus-pass system. During off-peak travel periods, some companies offer discounted fares. Conversely, fares can double around major holidays (see p519), especially for Christmas, Semana Santa (the week leading up to Easter) or Fiestas Patrias at the end of July, when tickets sell out days ahead of time.

At other times, reservations for short journeys aren't usually necessary. Just go to the terminal and buy a ticket for the next bus to your destination. For long-distance or overnight journeys, or if you're headed someplace remote with only limited services, buy your ticket at least the day before. Most travel agencies will make reservations for you, but shockingly overcharge you for the ticket. Except in Lima, it's cheaper to take a taxi to the bus terminal and buy the tickets yourself.

Luggage

When waiting in bus terminals, watch your luggage very carefully. Some terminals have left-luggage facilities. If not, the bus company may agree to keep your bags behind the desk, especially if you have an onward ticket later that same day. If you do this, don't leave any valuables in your bag.

During the journey, your luggage will travel in the luggage compartment unless it is small enough to carry on board. This is reasonably safe. You are given a baggage tag in exchange for your bag, which should be securely closed or locked. Watch to be sure that your bag actually gets onto, and stays on, the bus.

Your hand luggage is a different matter. If you're asleep with a camera around your neck, you might wake up with a neatly razored strap and no camera. Hide all valuables! Some travelers bring their rucksack on the bus with them, because of the reports of theft from luggage compartments. This only works if your pack is small enough to shove between your legs or keep on your lap. Never place any bags on the overhead luggage racks, which are unsecured.

For more advice on theft, see p514.

CAR & MOTORCYCLE

It's a long way from Lima to most destinations, so it's better to take a bus or fly to wherever you want to go and rent a car from there.

Given all the headaches and potential hazards of driving yourself around, consider hiring a taxi instead (p540), which is often cheaper and easier.

At roadside checkpoints, where the police or military conduct meticulous document checks, you'll occasionally see Peruvian drivers slipping an officer some money to smooth things along. The idea here is *not* to offer an (illegal) bribe, but simply a 'gift' or 'on-the-spot fine' so that you can get on your way. If you are driving and are involved in an accident that results in injury, know that drivers are routinely imprisoned for several days or weeks until innocence has been established. For more advice on legal matters, see p520.

Driver's License

A driver's license from your own home country is sufficient for renting a car. An International Driving Permit (IDP) is only required if you'll be driving in Peru for more than 30 days.

Rental

Major rental companies have offices in Lima (p120) and a few other large cities. Renting a motorcycle is an option mainly in jungle towns, where you can go for short runs around town on dirt bikes, but not much further.

Economy car rental starts at US$50 a day. But that doesn't include sales tax of 19%, 'super' collision-damage waiver, personal accident insurance and so on, which together can climb to more than US$100 per day, not including excess mileage. Vehicles with 4WD are more expensive.

Make sure you completely understand the rental agreement before you sign. A credit card is required, and renters normally need to be over 25 years of age.

Road Rules & Hazards

Bear in mind that the condition of rental cars is often poor, roads are potholed (even the paved Pan-American Hwy), gas is expensive, and drivers are aggressive, regarding speed limits, road signs and traffic signals as mere guides, not the law. Moreover, road signs are often small and unclear.

Driving is on the right-hand side of the road. Driving at night is not recommended because of poor conditions, speeding buses and slow-moving, poorly lit trucks. At night, and even during the day, bandits can also be a problem on some roadways (see p514).

Theft is all too common, so you should not leave your vehicle parked on the street. When stopping overnight, park the car in a guarded lot (the better hotels have them).

Gasoline or petrol stations (called *grifos*) are few and far between. At the time of research, the average cost of *gasolina* in Peru was about S16 to S17 (more than US$5 to US$6) per US gallon.

HITCHHIKING

Hitchhiking is never entirely safe in any country in the world and is not recommended. Travelers who decide to hitchhike should understand that they are taking a serious risk. Hitchhikers will be safer if they travel in pairs and let someone know where they are planning to go. In Peru hitchhiking is not very practical, as there are few private cars, buses are so cheap and trucks are often used as paid public transportation in remote areas.

LOCAL TRANSPORTATION

In most towns and cities, it's easy to walk everywhere or take a taxi. Using local buses, *micros* and *combis* can be tricky, but is very inexpensive.

Bus

Local buses are slow and crowded, but startlingly cheap. Ask locally for help, as there aren't any obvious bus lines in most towns.

A faster, more hair-raising alternative is to take *micros* or *combis,* sometimes called *colectivos* (though that term usually refers to taxis). Typically, *micros* and *combis* are, respectively, minibuses or minivans stuffed full of passengers. They can be identified by stickers along the outside panels and destination placards in the front windows. You can flag one down or get off anywhere on the route. A conductor usually leans out of the vehicle, shouting out destinations. Once inside, you must quickly squeeze into any available seat, or be prepared to stand up or crouch down. The conductor will come around and collect the fare, or you can pay when getting off. Be aware that safety is not a high priority for *combi* drivers. The only place for a passenger to safely buckle up is the front seat, but in the event of a head-on collision (not an unusual occurrence), that's the last place you'd want to be.

Taxi

Taxis seem to be everywhere. Private cars that have a small taxi sticker in the windshield aren't necessarily regulated. Safer, regulated taxis usually have a lit company number on the roof and are called for by telephone. These are more expensive than taxis flagged down on the street, but are more reliable. Solo women travelers should stick to regulated taxis, especially at night (see p527). For more tips on safety, see p514.

Always ask the fare in advance, as there are no meters. It's acceptable to haggle over a fare; try to find out what the going rate is before taking a cab, especially for long trips. The standard fare for short runs in most cities is around S5. Tipping is not the norm, unless you have hired a driver for a long period or he has helped you with luggage or other lifting.

TAXI

Hiring a private taxi for long-distance trips costs less than renting a car and takes care of many of the problems outlined earlier (see p539). Not all taxi drivers will agree to drive long distances, but if one does, you should carefully check the driver's credentials and vehicle before hiring.

Colectivo (shared) taxis for longer trips wait on busy corners and at major roundabouts, often by a signposted taxi stand.

TOURS

Major tourist towns have dozens of travel agencies offering group tours of the surrounding area. Whether you want to visit archaeological ruins, watch wildlife or be whisked around the city's sights in a private air-con minibus, there's a tour guide waiting for you.

In fact, the local tourism industry makes it *too* easy to join a tour, especially since doing it yourself can often be more rewarding. Keep in mind that group tours rarely give you enough time to enjoy the places you want to visit. The major exception is trekking the Inca Trail (p283), for which you're legally required to sign up for a group tour in advance.

Lima, Cuzco, Arequipa, Puno, Trujillo, Huaraz, Puerto Maldonado and Iquitos have the most travel agencies offering organized tours; for details, see the Tours sections listed under these and many other destinations in this book. For all-inclusive package tours from abroad, see p534.

For more specialized, individual or small-group tours, you can generally hire a bilingual guide for about US$15 an hour or US$50 a day plus expenses; tours in other languages may be more expensive. Some students or unregistered guides are cheaper, but the usual caveat applies – some are good, others aren't. A few local guides are listed in this book, but it's always good to ask other travelers for up-to-date recommendations.

TRAIN

The privatized rail system, **PeruRail** (☎ 084-58-1414; www.perurail.com), has daily services between Cuzco and Aguas Calientes, aka Machu Picchu Pueblo, and services between Cuzco and Puno on the shores of Lake Titicaca three times a week; see p255 for details of both services. Passenger services between Puno and Arequipa have been suspended indefinitely, but will run as a charter for groups.

Train buffs won't want to miss the lovely **Ferrocarril Central Andino** (☎ 01-226-6363; www.ferrocarrilcentral.com.pe), which reaches a head-spinning altitude of 4829m. It usually runs between Lima (p120) and Huancayo weekly from mid-April through October. In Huancayo, cheaper trains to Huancavelica leave daily from a different station. See p312 for details of both services. Another charmingly historic railway makes inexpensive daily runs between Tacna on Peru's south coast and Arica, Chile (see p158).

Health

CONTENTS

Prevention is the key to staying healthy while abroad. Travelers who receive the recommended vaccines and follow common-sense precautions usually come down with nothing more than a little diarrhea.

Medically speaking, Peru is part of tropical South America, which includes most of the continent except for the southernmost portion. The diseases found in this area are comparable to those found in tropical areas in Africa and Asia. Particularly important are mosquito-borne infections, including malaria, yellow fever and dengue fever, although these are not a significant concern in the temperate regions of the country.

BEFORE YOU GO

Since most vaccines don't provide immunity until at least two weeks after they're given, visit a doctor four to eight weeks before departure. Don't forget to take your vaccination certificate with you (aka the yellow booklet); it's mandatory for countries that require proof of yellow-fever vaccination on entry.

Bring medications in their original, clearly labeled containers. A signed and dated letter from your physician describing your medical conditions and medications, including generic names, is also a good idea. If carrying syringes or needles, be sure to have a physician's letter documenting their medical necessity.

If your health insurance doesn't cover you for medical expenses abroad, get extra travel insurance – check p520 for more information. Find out in advance if your travel insurance will make payments directly to providers or reimburse you later for overseas health expenditures. (Many doctors in Peru, though, expect payment in cash.)

H1N1

The H1N1 virus (commonly referred to as swine flu) was given a Phase 6 rating by the World Health Organization in June 2009. A Phase 6 alert means the virus is now considered a global pandemic. Like most countries, Peru has been affected. As of October 2009, the virus was widespread geographically in Peru but the number of cases were relatively low, as was their severity.

At press time, airport staff in some countries were screening arriving passengers for symptoms of the H1N1 flu. Check with the Peruvian embassy to get up-to-date information about travel restrictions. It's best not to travel if you have flulike symptoms of any sort.

For the latest information, check with the **World Health Organization** (www.who.intl).

ONLINE RESOURCES

There is a wealth of travel-health advice on the internet. For further information, the website of **Lonely Planet** (www.lonelyplanet.com) is a good place to start. The **World Health Organization** (www.who.int/ith/) publishes a superb book called *International Travel and Health*, which is revised annually and is available online at no cost. Another website of general interest is **MD Travel Health** (www.mdtravelhealth .com), which provides complete travel-health recommendations and is updated daily.

It's usually a good idea to consult your government's travel-health website before departure, if one is available:

Australia (www.smartraveller.gov.au/tips/travelwell.html)
Canada (www.travelhealth.gc.ca)
UK (www.nhs.uk/livewell/travelhealth/)
USA (www.cdc.gov/travel/)

FURTHER READING

For further information, see *Healthy Travel Central & South America,* also from Lonely Planet. If you're traveling with children, Lonely Planet's *Travel with Children* may be useful.

IN TRANSIT

DEEP VEIN THROMBOSIS (DVT)

Blood clots may form in the legs during plane flights, chiefly because of prolonged immobility. The longer the flight, the greater the risk. Though most blood clots are reabsorbed uneventfully, some may break off and travel through the blood vessels to the lungs, where they could cause life-threatening complications.

MEDICAL CHECKLIST

- antibiotics
- antidiarrheal drugs (eg loperamide)
- acetaminophen (Tylenol) or aspirin
- anti-inflammatory drugs (eg ibuprofen)
- antihistamines (for hay fever and allergic reactions)
- antibacterial ointment (eg Bactroban; for cuts and abrasions)
- steroid cream or cortisone (for poison ivy and other allergic rashes)
- bandages, gauze, gauze rolls
- adhesive or paper tape
- scissors, safety pins, tweezers
- thermometer
- pocketknife
- insect repellent containing DEET (for the skin)
- insect spray containing permethrin (for clothing, tents and bed nets)
- sunblock
- oral rehydration salts
- iodine tablets (for water purification)
- syringes and sterile needles
- acetazolamide (Diamox; for altitude sickness)

The chief symptom of DVT is swelling or pain of the foot, ankle or calf, usually – but not always – on just one side. When a blood clot travels to the lungs, it may cause chest pain and difficulty breathing. Travelers with any of these symptoms should immediately seek medical attention.

To prevent the development of DVT on long airplane flights, you should walk about the cabin, flex the leg muscles while sitting, drink plenty of fluids and avoid alcohol and tobacco.

JET LAG

The onset of jet lag is common when crossing more than five time zones, resulting in insomnia, fatigue, malaise or nausea. To minimize jet lag, try drinking plenty of (nonalcoholic) fluids and eating light meals. Upon arrival, get exposure to natural sunlight and readjust your schedule (for meals, sleep etc) as soon as possible.

IN PERU

AVAILABILITY OF HEALTH CARE

There are several high-quality medical clinics in Lima open 24 hours for medical emergencies (for details see p84). They also function as hospitals and offer subspecialty consultations. For a guide to clinics in Lima, check out the website for the **US embassy** (lima .usembassy.gov/acs_peru.html). There are also many English-speaking physicians and dentists in private practice in Lima, which are listed on the same website. Good medical care may be more difficult to find in other cities and impossible to locate in rural areas.

Many doctors expect payment in cash, regardless of whether you have travel insurance. If you develop a life-threatening medical problem, you'll probably want to be evacuated to a country with state-of-the-art medical care. Since this may cost tens of thousands of dollars, be sure you have insurance to cover this before you depart. You can find a list of medical evacuation and travel insurance companies on the website of the **US State Department** (travel.state.gov/travel/tips/brochures/brochures_1215.html).

The pharmacies in Peru are known as *farmacias* or *boticas,* and are identified by a green or red cross in the window. They're

HEALTH

IMMUNIZATIONS

The only required vaccine for Peru is yellow fever, and that's only if you're arriving from a yellow-fever-infected country in Africa or the Americas. A number of vaccines are recommended.

Vaccine	Recommended for	Dosage	Side effects
chickenpox	travelers who have never had chickenpox	two doses, one month apart	fever, mild case of chickenpox
hepatitis A	all travelers	one dose before trip; booster six to 12 months later	soreness at injection site, headaches, body aches
hepatitis B	travelers who will have long-term contact with the local population	three doses over six months	soreness at injection site, long-term fever
measles	travelers born after 1956 who've never had measles and who've had only one measles vaccination	one dose	fever, rash, joint pains, allergic reactions
rabies	travelers who will have contact with animals or won't have access to medical assistance	three doses over a four-week period	soreness at injection site, headaches, body aches
tetanus/ diphtheria	all travelers who haven't had a booster in 10 years	one dose every 10 years	soreness at injection site
typhoid	all travelers	four capsules by mouth, one taken every other day	abdominal pain, nausea, rash
yellow fever	travelers to jungle areas at altitudes below 2300m	one dose every 10 years	headaches, body aches, severe reactions are rare

generally reliable and offer most of the medications available in other countries. InkaFarma and Botica Fasa are two well-known pharmacy chains.

INFECTIOUS DISEASES

Of the diseases listed below, malaria, yellow fever and dengue fever are spread by mosquitoes. For information about protecting yourself from mosquito bites, see p549.

Cholera

An intestinal infection, cholera is acquired through ingestion of contaminated food or water. The main symptom is profuse, watery diarrhea, which may cause life-threatening dehydration. The key treatment is drinking oral rehydration solution. Antibiotics are also given, usually tetracycline or doxycycline, but quinolone antibiotics (eg ciprofloxacin and levofloxacin) are also effective.

Cholera occurs regularly in Peru, but it's rare among travelers. Cholera vaccine is no longer required to enter Peru, and is in fact no longer available in some countries, including the USA, because the old vaccine was relatively ineffective and caused side effects. There are new vaccines that are safer

and more effective, but they're not available in many countries and are only recommended for those at particularly high risk.

Dengue Fever

This is a viral infection found throughout South America. Dengue is transmitted by aedes mosquitoes, which usually bite during the daytime and are often found close to human habitations. They breed primarily in artificial water containers, such as cans, cisterns, metal drums, plastic containers and discarded tires. As a result, dengue is especially common in densely populated, urban environments, including Lima and Cuzco.

Dengue usually causes flulike symptoms, including fever, muscle aches, joint pains, headaches, nausea and vomiting, often followed by a rash. The body aches may be quite uncomfortable, but most cases resolve uneventfully in a few days. Severe cases usually occur in children aged under 15 who are experiencing their second dengue infection.

There is no treatment for dengue fever except to take analgesics such as acetaminophen/ paracetamol (Tylenol) and drink plenty of fluids. Severe cases may require hospitalization for intravenous fluids and supportive care.

Hepatitis A

A viral infection of the liver, hepatitis A is usually acquired by ingestion of contaminated water, food or ice, though it may also be acquired by direct contact with infected persons. Hepatitis A is the second most common travel-related infection (after travelers' diarrhea). The illness occurs throughout the world, but the incidence is higher in developing nations. Symptoms may include fever, malaise, jaundice, nausea, vomiting and abdominal pain. Most cases resolve without complications, though hepatitis A occasionally causes severe liver damage. There is no treatment; to aid recovery, avoid alcohol and eat simple, nonfatty foods.

The vaccine for hepatitis A is extremely safe and highly effective. If you get a booster six to 12 months later, it lasts for at least 10 years. You really should get it before you go to Peru or any other developing nation. Because the safety of hepatitis A vaccine has not been established for pregnant women or children under the age of two; they should instead be given a gamma globulin injection.

Hepatitis B

Like hepatitis A, hepatitis B is a liver infection that occurs worldwide but is more common in developing nations. Unlike hepatitis A, the disease is usually acquired by sexual contact or by exposure to infected blood, generally through blood transfusions or contaminated needles. The vaccine is recommended only for long-term travelers (on the road more than six months) who expect to live in rural areas or have close physical contact with the local population. Additionally, the vaccine is recommended for anyone who anticipates sexual contact with the local inhabitants or a possible need for medical, dental or other treatments while abroad, including transfusions or vaccinations.

Hepatitis B vaccine is safe and highly effective. However, a total of three injections is necessary to establish full immunity. Several countries added hepatitis B vaccine to the list of routine childhood immunizations in the 1980s, so many young adults are already protected.

HIV/AIDS

The Human Immunodeficiency Virus (HIV) may develop into Acquired Immune Deficiency Syndrome (AIDS; SIDA in Spanish). HIV/AIDS has been reported in all South American countries. Exposure to blood or blood products and bodily fluids may put an individual at risk. Be sure to use condoms for all sexual encounters. Fear of HIV infection should never preclude treatment of serious medical conditions as the risk of infection remains very small.

Malaria

Cases of malaria occur in every South American country except Chile, Uruguay and the Falkland Islands. It's transmitted by mosquito bites, usually between dusk and dawn. The main symptom is high spiking fevers, which may be accompanied by chills, sweats, headache, body aches, weakness, vomiting or diarrhea. Severe cases may affect the central nervous system and lead to seizures, confusion, coma and death.

Taking malaria pills is strongly recommended for all areas in Peru except Lima and its vicinity, the coastal areas south of Lima, and the highland areas (including around Cuzco, Machu Picchu, Lake Titicaca and Arequipa). The number of cases of malaria has risen sharply in recent years. Most cases in Peru occur in Loreto in the country's northeast, where malaria transmission has reached epidemic levels.

There is a choice of three malaria pills, all of which work about equally well. Mefloquine (Lariam) is taken once weekly in a dosage of 250mg, starting one to two weeks before arrival in an area where malaria is endemic, and continuing through the trip and for four weeks after returning. The problem is that some people develop neuropsychiatric side effects, which may range from mild to severe. Atovaquone/proguanil (Malarone) is a newly approved combination pill taken once daily with food starting two days before arrival, and continuing through the trip and for seven days after departure. Side effects are typically mild. Doxycycline is a third alternative, but may cause an exaggerated sunburn reaction.

In general, Malarone seems to cause fewer side effects than mefloquine and is becoming more popular. The chief disadvantage is that it has to be taken daily. For longer trips, it's probably worth trying mefloquine; for shorter trips, Malarone will be the drug of choice for most people. None of the pills is 100% effective.

HEALTH

If you may not have access to medical care while traveling, you should bring along additional pills for emergency self-treatment, which you should take if you can't reach a doctor and you develop symptoms that suggest malaria, such as high spiking fevers. One option is to take four tablets of Malarone once daily for three days. However, Malarone should not be used for treatment if you're already taking it for prevention. If taking Malarone, take 650mg of quinine three times daily and 100mg doxycycline twice daily for one week. If you start self-medication, see a doctor at the earliest possible opportunity. If you develop a fever after returning home, see a physician, as malaria symptoms may not occur for months.

Ensure that you take precautions to minimize your chances of being bitten by mosquitoes (p549).

Rabies

A viral infection of the brain and spinal cord, rabies is almost always fatal unless treated promptly. The rabies virus is carried in the saliva of infected animals and is typically transmitted through an animal bite, though contamination of any break in the skin with infected saliva may result in rabies. Rabies occurs in all South American countries. In Peru, most cases are related to bites from dogs or vampire bats.

The rabies vaccine is safe, but a full series requires three injections and is quite expensive. Those at high risk for rabies, such as animal handlers and spelunkers (cave explorers), should certainly get the vaccine. In addition, those at lower risk for animal bites should also consider asking for the vaccine if they might be traveling to remote areas and might not have access to appropriate medical care if needed. The treatment for a possibly rabid bite consists of rabies vaccine with rabies immune globulin. It's effective, but must be given promptly.

All animal bites and scratches must immediately be thoroughly cleansed with large amounts of soap and water, and local health authorities should be contacted to determine whether further treatment is necessary (see p548 for more details).

Tetanus

This potentially fatal disease is found in undeveloped tropical areas. It is difficult to treat, but it is preventable with immuniza-

tion. Tetanus occurs when a wound becomes infected by a germ that lives in the feces of animals or people, so clean all cuts, punctures or animal bites. Tetanus is also known as lockjaw, and the first symptom may be discomfort in swallowing, or stiffening of the jaw and neck; this is followed by painful convulsions of the jaw and whole body.

Typhoid Fever

This fever is caused by ingestion of food or water contaminated by a species of salmonella known as *Salmonella typhi*. Fever occurs in virtually all cases. Other symptoms may include headache, malaise, muscle aches, dizziness, loss of appetite, nausea and abdominal pain. Either diarrhea or constipation may occur. Possible complications include intestinal perforation or bleeding, confusion, delirium or, rarely, coma.

Unless you expect to take all your meals in major hotels and restaurants, getting typhoid vaccine is a good idea. It's usually given orally, but is also available as an injection. Neither vaccine is approved for use in children under two.

The drug of choice for typhoid fever is usually a quinolone antibiotic such as ciprofloxacin (Cipro) or levofloxacin (Levaquin), which many travelers carry for treatment of travelers' diarrhea. However, if you self-treat for typhoid fever, you may also need to self-treat for malaria, since the symptoms of the two diseases may be indistinguishable.

Yellow Fever

A life-threatening viral infection, yellow fever is transmitted by mosquitoes in forested areas. The illness begins with flulike symptoms, which may include fever, chills, headache, muscle aches, backache, loss of appetite, nausea and vomiting. These symptoms usually subside in a few days, but one person in six enters a second, toxic phase characterized by recurrent fever, vomiting, listlessness, jaundice, kidney failure and hemorrhage, leading to death in up to half of the cases. There is no treatment except for supportive care.

Yellow-fever vaccine is strongly recommended for all those who visit any jungle areas of Peru at altitudes less than 2300m (7546ft). Most cases occur in the departments in the central jungle. Proof of vaccination is required from all travelers arriving in Peru from an area where yellow fever is endemic in Africa or the Americas.

Yellow-fever vaccine is given only in approved yellow-fever vaccination centers, which provide validated vaccination certificates. The vaccine should be given at least 10 days before any potential exposure to yellow fever and remains effective for about 10 years. Reactions to the vaccine are generally mild, though some people may experience severe side effects. While you may not be required to have proof of a yellow-fever vaccination to enter Peru, after visiting a region where yellow fever occurs, you'll need to have the vaccination to get to most other countries – even your home country. So you're better off getting your jab before you leave home.

Other Infections

Bartonellosis (Oroya fever) is carried by sand flies in the arid river valleys on the western slopes of the Andes in Peru, Colombia and Ecuador between altitudes of 800m and 3000m. The chief symptoms are fever and severe bone pains. Complications may include marked anemia, enlargement of the liver and spleen, and sometimes death. The drug of choice is chloramphenicol, though doxycycline is also effective.

Chagas' disease is a parasitic infection that is transmitted by triatomine insects (reduviid bugs), which inhabit crevices in the walls and roofs of substandard housing in South and Central America. In Peru, most cases occur in the southern part of the country. The triatomine insect drops its feces on human skin as it bites, usually at night. A person becomes infected when he or she unknowingly rubs the feces into the bite wound or any other open sore. Chagas' disease is extremely rare in travelers. However, if you sleep in a poorly constructed house, especially one made of mud, adobe or thatch, you should be sure to protect yourself with a bed net and a good insecticide (see p549).

Leishmaniasis occurs in the mountains and jungles of all South American countries. The infection is transmitted by sand flies, which are about a third of the size of mosquitoes. In Peru, more cases have been seen recently in children aged under 15, due to the increasing use of child labor for brush clearing and preparation of farmlands on mountain slopes of the Andes. Most adult cases occur in men who have migrated into jungle areas for farming, working or hunting. Leishmaniasis may be limited to the skin, causing slowly grow-

TRADITIONAL MEDICINE	
Some common traditional remedies:	
Problem	**Treatment**
altitude sickness	ginkgo
jet lag	melatonin
mosquito-bite prevention	oil of eucalyptus, soybean oil
motion sickness	ginger

ing ulcers over exposed parts of the body, or less commonly may disseminate to the bone marrow, liver and spleen. There is no vaccine. To protect yourself from sand flies, follow the same precautions as for mosquito bites (p549), except that netting must be made of finer mesh (at least 18 holes to the linear inch).

Leptospirosis is acquired by exposure to water contaminated by the urine of infected animals. Outbreaks often occur at times of flooding, when sewage overflow may contaminate water sources. The initial symptoms, which resemble a mild flu, usually subside uneventfully in a few days, with or without treatment, but a minority of cases are complicated by jaundice or meningitis. There is no vaccine. You can minimize your risk by staying out of bodies of fresh water that may be contaminated by animal urine. If you're visiting an area where an outbreak is in progress, as occurred in Peru after flooding in 1998, you can take 200mg of doxycycline once weekly as a preventative measure. If you actually develop leptospirosis, the treatment is 100mg of doxycycline twice daily.

Gnathostomiasis is an intestinal parasite acquired by eating raw or undercooked freshwater fish, including ceviche. Note, though, that ceviche eaten on the coast will be almost certainly made from seafood.

Plague is usually transmitted to humans by the bite of rodent fleas, typically when rodents die. Symptoms include fever, chills, muscle aches and malaise, associated with the development of an acutely swollen, exquisitely painful lymph node, known as a bubo, most often in the groin. Cases of the plague are reported from Peru nearly every year, chiefly from the departments of Cajamarca, La Libertad, Piura and Lambayeque in the northern part of the country. Most travelers are at extremely low risk for this disease. If you might have contact with rodents or their fleas, however, especially

HEALTH

in the above areas, you should bring along a bottle of doxycycline, to be taken prophylactically during periods of exposure. Those less than eight years old or allergic to doxycycline should take trimethoprim-sulfamethoxazole instead. In addition, you should avoid areas containing rodent burrows or nests, never handle sick or dead animals, and follow the guidelines for protecting yourself from mosquito bites (opposite).

Taeniasis and the more serious **cysticercosis** are both caused by pork tapeworm *(Taenia solium)*. Humans become hosts to the nasty parasite by eating infected or undercooked pork. Although pork tapeworm is rare, it does turn up in Peru, so be careful when eating pork.

TRAVELERS' DIARRHEA

You get diarrhea from taking contaminated food or water. See opposite and p550 for ideas for reducing the risk of getting diarrhea. If you develop diarrhea, be sure to drink plenty of fluids, preferably an oral rehydration solution containing lots of salt and sugar. A few loose stools don't require treatment but if you start having more than four or five stools a day, you should start taking an antibiotic (usually a quinolone drug) and an antidiarrheal agent (such as loperamide). If diarrhea is bloody, persists for more than 72 hours or is accompanied by fever, shaking chills or severe abdominal pain you should seek medical attention.

ENVIRONMENTAL HAZARDS
Altitude Sickness

Those who ascend rapidly to altitudes greater than 2500m (8100ft) may develop altitude sickness. In Peru, this includes Cuzco (3326m), Machu Picchu (2410m) and Lake Titicaca (3820m). Being physically fit offers no protection. Those who have experienced altitude sickness in the past are prone to future episodes. The risk increases with faster ascents, higher altitudes and greater exertion. Symptoms may include headaches, nausea, vomiting, dizziness, malaise, insomnia and loss of appetite. Severe cases may be complicated by fluid in the lungs (high-altitude pulmonary edema) or swelling of the brain (high-altitude cerebral edema). If symptoms are more than mild or persist for more than 24 hours (far less at high altitudes), descend immediately by at least 500m and see a doctor.

To help prevent altitude sickness, the best measure is to spend two nights or more at each rise of 1000m. Alternatively, take 125mg or 250mg of acetazolamide (Diamox) twice or three times daily starting 24 hours before ascent and continuing for 48 hours after arrival at altitude. Possible side effects include increased urinary volume, numbness, tingling, nausea, drowsiness, myopia and temporary impotence. Acetazolamide should not be given to pregnant women or anyone with a history of sulfa allergy. For those who cannot tolerate acetazolamide, the next best option is 4mg of dexamethasone taken four times daily. Unlike acetazolamide, dexamethasone must be tapered gradually upon arrival at altitude, since there is a risk that altitude sickness will occur as the dosage is reduced. Dexamethasone is a steroid, so it should not be given to diabetics or anyone for whom taking steroids is not advised. A natural alternative is ginkgo, which some people find quite helpful.

When traveling to high altitudes, it's also important to avoid overexertion, eat light meals and abstain from alcohol. Altitude sickness should be taken seriously; it can be life threatening when severe.

Animal Bites

Do not attempt to pet, handle or feed any animal, with the exception of domestic animals known to be free of any infectious disease. Most animal injuries are directly related to a person's attempt to touch or feed the animal.

Any bite or scratch by a mammal, including bats, should be promptly and thoroughly cleansed with large amounts of soap and water, followed by application of an antiseptic such as iodine or alcohol. The local health authorities should be contacted immediately for possible postexposure rabies treatment, whether or not you've been immunized against rabies. It may also be advisable to start an antibiotic, since wounds caused by animal bites and scratches frequently become infected. One of the newer quinolones, such as levofloxacin (Levaquin), which many travelers carry in case of diarrhea, would be an appropriate choice.

Snakes and leeches are a hazard in some areas of South America. In the event of a venomous snake bite, place the victim at rest, keep the bitten area immobilized and move the victim immediately to the nearest medical facility. Avoid tourniquets, which are no longer recommended.

Earthquakes & Avalanches

Peru is in an earthquake zone, and small tremors are frequent. Every few years, a large earthquake results in loss of life and property damage. Should you be caught in an earthquake, the best advice is to take shelter under a solid object, such as a desk or door frame. Do not stand near windows or heavy objects, and do not run out of the building. If you are outside, attempt to stay clear of falling wires, bricks, telephone poles and other hazards. Avoid crowds in the aftermath.

There's not much you can do when caught in an avalanche. Be aware that the main danger times are after heavy rains, when high ground may subside.

Food

Salads and fruit should be washed with purified water or peeled when possible. Ice cream is usually safe if it is a reputable brand name, but beware of street vendors and of ice cream that has melted and been refrozen. Thoroughly cooked food is safest, but not if it has been left to cool or if it has been reheated. Shellfish such as mussels, oysters and clams should be avoided, as should undercooked meat, particularly in the form of minced or ground beef. Steaming does not make bad shellfish safe for eating. Having said that, it is difficult to resist Peruvian seafood dishes such as ceviche, which is marinated but not cooked. This is rarely a problem, as long as it is served fresh in a reputable restaurant.

If a place looks clean and well run, and if the vendor also looks clean and healthy, then the food is probably safe. In general, places that are packed with travelers or locals will be fine, while empty restaurants are questionable.

Hypothermia

Too much cold is just as dangerous as too much heat, as it may cause hypothermia. If you are trekking at high altitudes, particularly in wet or windy conditions, or simply taking a long bus trip over mountains, mostly at night, be prepared.

It is surprisingly easy to progress from very cold to dangerously cold due to a combination of wind, wet clothing, fatigue and hunger, even if the air temperature is above freezing. It is best to dress in layers; silk, wool and some of the new artificial fibers are all good insulating materials. A hat is important, as a lot of heat is lost through the head. A strong, waterproof outer layer is essential, because keeping dry is vital. Carry basic supplies, including food containing simple sugars to generate heat quickly, and lots of fluid to drink. A space blanket – an extremely thin, lightweight emergency blanket made of a reflective material that keeps heat in – is something all travelers in cold environments should carry.

Symptoms of hypothermia are exhaustion, numb skin (particularly toes and fingers), shivering, slurred speech, irrational or violent behavior, lethargy, stumbling, dizzy spells, muscle cramps and violent bursts of energy. Irrationality may take the form of sufferers claiming they are warm and trying to take off their clothes.

To treat mild hypothermia, first get the person out of the wind or rain, remove their clothing if it's wet and replace it with dry, warm clothing. Give them hot liquids – no alcohol – and some high-calorie, easily digestible food. Do not rub victims, as rough handling may cause cardiac arrest.

Mosquito Bites

To prevent mosquito bites, wear long sleeves, long pants, hats and shoes (rather than sandals). Bring along a good insect repellent, preferably one containing DEET, which should be applied to exposed skin and clothing, but not to eyes, mouth, cuts, wounds or irritated skin. Products containing lower concentrations of DEET are as effective, but for shorter periods of time. In general, adults and children aged over 12 should use preparations containing 25% to 35% DEET, which usually lasts about six hours. Children aged between two and 12 should use preparations containing no more than 10% DEET, applied sparingly, which will usually last about three hours. Neurologic toxicity has been reported from DEET, especially in children, but appears to be extremely uncommon and generally related to overuse. Compounds containing DEET should not be used on children under the age of two.

Insect repellents containing certain botanical products, including oil of eucalyptus and soybean oil, are effective but last only 1½ to two hours. DEET-containing repellents are preferable for areas where there is a high risk of malaria or yellow fever. Products based on citronella are not effective.

HEALTH

For additional protection, you can apply permethrin to clothing, shoes, tents, and mosquito nets. Permethrin treatments are safe and remain effective for at least two weeks, even when items are laundered. Permethrin should not be applied directly to skin.

Don't sleep with the window open unless there is a screen. If sleeping outdoors or in an accommodation where mosquitoes can enter, use a mosquito net, preferably treated with permethrin, with edges tucked in under the mattress. The mesh size should be less than 1.5mm. If the sleeping area is not otherwise protected, use a mosquito coil, which will fill the room with insecticide through the night. Repellent-impregnated wristbands are not effective.

Sunburn & Heat Exhaustion

To protect yourself from excessive sun exposure, you should stay out of the midday sun, wear sunglasses and a wide-brimmed sun hat, and apply sunblock with SPF 15 or higher and UVA and UVB protection, before exposure to the sun. Sunblock should be reapplied after swimming or vigorous activity. Be aware that the sun is more intense at higher altitudes, even though you may feel cooler.

Dehydration or salt deficiency can cause heat exhaustion. You should drink plenty of fluids and avoid excessive alcohol or strenuous activity when you first arrive in a hot climate. Long, continuous periods of exposure to high temperatures can leave you vulnerable to heatstroke, when body temperature rises to dangerous levels.

Water

Tap water in Peru is not safe to drink. Vigorous boiling of water for one minute is the most effective means of water purification. At altitudes greater than 2000m (6500ft), boil for three minutes.

Another option is to disinfect water with iodine or water-purification pills. You can add 2% tincture of iodine to one quart or liter of water (five drops to clear water, 10 drops to cloudy water) and let stand for 30 minutes. If the water is cold, longer times may be required. Otherwise you can buy iodine pills, available at most pharmacies in your home country. The instructions for use should be carefully followed. The taste of iodinated water may be improved by adding vitamin C (ascorbic acid). Iodinated water should not be consumed for more than a few weeks. Pregnant women, those with a history of thyroid disease, and those allergic to iodine should not drink iodinated water.

A number of water filters are on the market. Those with smaller pores (reverse osmosis filters) provide the broadest protection, but they are relatively large and are readily plugged by debris. Those with somewhat larger pores (microstrainer filters) are ineffective against viruses, although they remove other organisms. Manufacturers' instructions must be carefully followed.

TRAVELING WITH CHILDREN

It's safer not to take children aged under three to high altitudes. Also, children under nine months should not be brought to jungle areas at lower altitudes because yellow-fever vaccine is not safe for this age group.

When traveling with young children, be particularly careful about what you allow them to eat and drink, because diarrhea can be especially dangerous to them and because the vaccines for the prevention of hepatitis A and typhoid fever are not approved for use in children aged under two.

The two main malaria medications, Lariam and Malarone, may be given to children, but insect repellents must be applied in lower concentrations (see p549).

WOMEN'S HEALTH

Although travel to Lima is reasonably safe if you're pregnant, there are risks in visiting many other parts of the country. First, it may be difficult to find quality obstetric care, if needed, outside Lima, especially away from the main tourist areas. Second, it isn't advisable for pregnant women to spend time at high altitudes where the air is thin, which precludes travel to many of the most popular destinations, including Cuzco, Machu Picchu and Lake Titicaca. (If you are still determined to visit these places regardless, then ascend more slowly than normally recommended; see p548 for details.) Lastly, yellow-fever vaccine, strongly recommended for travel to jungle areas at altitudes less than 2300m, should not be given during pregnancy because the vaccine contains a live virus that may infect the fetus.

Language

CONTENTS

Spanish is the main language the traveler will need in Peru. Even though English is understood in the best hotels, airline offices and tourist agencies, it's of little use elsewhere. In the highlands, most indigenous people are bilingual, with Spanish as a second tongue. Quechua is the main indigenous language in most areas, except around Lake Titicaca, where Aymara is spoken. Outside Peru's very remote areas, where indigenous languages may be the only tongue, it's unlikely that travelers will encounter indigenous people with no Spanish at all.

SPANISH

If you don't speak Spanish, don't despair. It's easy enough to pick up the basics and for those who want to learn the language in greater depth, courses are available in Lima (see p102) and Cuzco (p239). Alternatively, you can study with books, CDs and other resources while you're still at home and planning your trip, or you might consider taking a course. With the basics under your belt, you'll be able to talk with people from all parts of Latin America (except Brazil, where Portuguese is the predominant language).

For a more comprehensive guide to the Spanish of Peru, pick up a copy of Lonely Planet's *Latin American Spanish* phrasebook. If you're planning on heading into more remote areas, Lonely Planet's *Quechua* phrasebook would also be a very handy addition to your luggage. Another useful resource is the compact and comprehensive University of Chicago *Spanish-English, English-Spanish Dictionary*.

PRONUNCIATION

Spanish pronunciation is easy, as most of the sounds are also found in English. If you follow our pronunciation guides (included alongside the Spanish phrases), you'll have no problems being understood.

Peruvian Spanish is considered one of the language's 'cleanest' dialects – enunciation is relatively clear, pronunciation is very similar to Castilian Spanish (the official language of Spain), and slang is a lot less common than in other parts of Latin America.

Vowels

There are four sounds that roughly correspond to diphthongs (vowel sound combinations) in English.

a	as the 'a' in 'father'
ai	as in 'aisle'
ay	as in 'say'
e	as the 'e' in 'met'
ee	as the 'ee' in 'meet'
o	as the 'o' in 'more' (without the 'r')
oo	as the 'oo' in 'zoo'
ow	as in 'how'
oy	as in 'boy'

Consonants

Pronunciation of Spanish consonants is similar to their English counterparts. The exceptions are given in the following list.

kh	as the throaty 'ch' in the Scottish *loch*
ny	as the 'ny' in 'canyon'
r	as in 'run' but stronger and rolled, especially at the beginning of a word and in all words with *rr*
s	not lisped (unlike in Spain)

LANGUAGE

The letter 'h' is invariably silent (ie never pronounced) in Spanish.

Note also that the Spanish **b** and **v** sounds are very similar – they are both pronounced as a very soft 'v' in English (somewhere between 'b' and 'v').

You may also hear some variations in spoken Spanish as part of the regional accents across Peru (and Latin America in general). The most notable of these variations is the pronunciation of the letter *ll*. In some parts of Peru (and the continent) it's pronounced as the 'lli' in 'million,' however in most areas it's pronounced as 'y' (eg as in 'yes'), and this is how it's represented in our pronunciation guides, so you won't have problems being understood.

Word Stress

In general, words ending in vowels or the letters **n** or **s** have stress on the next-to-last syllable, while those with other endings have stress on the last syllable. Thus *vaca* (cow) and *caballos* (horses) both carry stress on the next-to-last syllable, while *ciudad* (city) and *infeliz* (unhappy) are both stressed on the last syllable.

Written accents will almost always appear in words that don't follow the rules above, eg *sótano* (basement), *América* and *porción* (portion). When counting syllables, be sure to remember that diphthongs (vowel combinations, such as the **ue** in *puede*) constitute only one. When a word with a written accent appears in capital letters, the accent is often not written, but is still pronounced.

GENDER & PLURALS

Spanish nouns are either masculine or feminine, and there are rules to help determine gender (with the obligatory exceptions). Feminine nouns generally end with **-a** or with the groups **-ción**, **-sión** or **-dad**. Other endings typically signify a masculine noun. Endings for adjectives also change to agree with the gender of the noun they modify (masculine/feminine **-o**/**-a**). Where both masculine and feminine forms are included in this language guide, they are separated by a slash, with the masculine form first, eg *perdido/a*.

If a noun or adjective ends in a vowel, the plural is formed by adding **s** to the end. If it ends in a consonant, the plural is formed by adding **es** to the end.

ACCOMMODATIONS

I'm looking for ...	Estoy buscando ...	e-stoy boos-kan-do ...
Where is ...?	¿Dónde hay ...?	don-de ai ...
a hotel	un hotel	oon o-tel
a boarding house	una pensión/ residencial/ un hospedaje	oo-na pen-syon/ re-see-den-syal/ oon os-pe-da-khe
a youth hostel	un albergue juvenil	oon al-ber-ge khoo-ve-neel

I'd like a ... room.	Quisiera una habitación ...	kee-sye-ra oo-na a-bee-ta-syon ...
single	simple	seem-ple
double (with one bed)	matrimonial (con una cama)	ma-tree-mo-nyal (kon oo-na ka-ma)
twin (with two beds)	doble (con dos camas)	do-ble (kon dos ka-mas)

How much is it per ...?	¿Cuánto cuesta por ...?	kwan-to kwes-ta por ...
night	noche	no-che
person	persona	per-so-na
week	semana	se-ma-na

Does it include breakfast?
¿Incluye el desayuno? een-kloo-ye el de-sa-yoo-no

May I see the room?
¿Puedo ver la habitación? pwe-do ver la a-bee-ta-syon

I don't like it.
No me gusta. no me goos-ta

It's fine. I'll take it.
OK. La alquilo. o-kay la al-kee-lo

I'm leaving now.
Me voy ahora. me voy a-o-ra

MAKING A RESERVATION

To ...	A ...
From ...	De ...
Date	Fecha

I'd like to book ...	Quisiera reservar ...
in the name of ...	en nombre de ...
for the nights of ...	para las noches del ...

credit card ...	tarjeta de crédito ...
number	número
expiry date	fecha de vencimiento

Please confirm ...	Puede confirmar ...
availability	la disponibilidad
price	el precio

full board	pensión completa	pen·syon kom·ple·ta
private/shared bathroom	baño privado/ compartido	ba·nyo pree·va·do/ kom·par·tee·do
too expensive	demasiado caro	de·ma·sya·do ka·ro
cheaper	más económico	mas e·ko·no·mee·ko
discount	descuento	des·kwen·to

CONVERSATION & ESSENTIALS

In their public behavior, Peruvians are very conscious of civilities, sometimes to the point of ceremoniousness. Never approach a stranger for information without extending a greeting, and use only the polite form of address, especially with the police and public officials. Young people may be less likely to expect this, but it's best to stick to the polite form unless you're quite sure you won't offend by using the informal mode. The polite form is used in all cases in this guide; where options are given, the form is indicated by the abbreviations 'pol' and 'inf.'

Hello.	Hola.	o·la
Good morning.	Buenos días.	bwe·nos dee·as
Good afternoon.	Buenas tardes.	bwe·nas tar·des
Good evening/ night.	Buenas noches.	bwe·nas no·ches
Goodbye.	Adiós.	a·dyos
See you soon.	Hasta luego.	as·ta lwe·go
Yes./No.	Sí./No.	see/no
Please.	Por favor.	por fa·vor
Thank you.	Gracias.	gra·syas
Many thanks.	Muchas gracias.	moo·chas gra·syas
You're welcome.	De nada.	de na·da
Pardon me.	Perdón.	per·don
Excuse me.	Permiso.	per·mee·so
(used when asking permission)		
Forgive me.	Disculpe.	dees·kool·pe
(used when apologizing)		

How are things?
¿Qué tal?   ke tal
What's your name?
¿Cómo se llama?   ko·mo se ya·ma (pol)
¿Cómo te llamas?   ko·mo te ya·mas (inf)
My name is ...
Me llamo ...   me ya·mo ...
It's a pleasure to meet you.
Mucho gusto.   moo·cho goos·to
The pleasure is mine.
El gusto es mío.   el goos·to es mee·o
Where are you from?
¿De dónde es/eres?   de don·de es/e·res (pol/inf)

I'm from ...
Soy de ...   soy de ...
Where are you staying?
¿Dónde está alojado?   don·de es·ta a·lo·kha·do (pol)
¿Dónde estás alojado?   don·de es·tas a·lo·kha·do (inf)
May I take a photo?
¿Puedo sacar una foto?   pwe·do sa·kar oo·na fo·to

DIRECTIONS

How do I get to ...?
¿Cómo puedo llegar a ...?   ko·mo pwe·do ye·gar a ...
Is it far?
¿Está lejos?   es·ta le·khos
Go straight ahead.
Siga/Vaya derecho.   see·ga/va·ya de·re·cho
Turn left.
Voltée a la izquierda.   vol·te·e a la ees·kyer·da
Turn right.
Voltée a la derecha.   vol·te·e a la de·re·cha
I'm lost.
Estoy perdido/a.   es·toy per·dee·do/a
Can you show me (on the map)?
¿Me lo podría indicar   me lo po·dree·a een·dee·kar
(en el mapa)?   (en el ma·pa)

north	norte	nor·te
south	sur	soor
east	este/oriente	es·te/o·ryen·te
west	oeste/occidente	o·es·te/ok·see·den·te
here	aquí	a·kee
there	allí	a·yee
avenue	avenida	a·ve·nee·da
block	cuadra	kwa·dra
street	calle/paseo	ka·ye/pa·se·o

EATING OUT

I'd like ...
Quisiera ...   kee·sye·ra ...
I'd like the set lunch, please.
Quisiera el menú,   kee·sye·ra el me·noo
por favor.   por fa·vor

LANGUAGE

EMERGENCIES

Help!
  ¡Socorro! — so·ko·ro
It's an emergency.
  Es una emergencia. — es oo·na e·mer·khen·sya
Fire!
  ¡Incendio! — een·sen·dyo
Could you help me, please?
  ¿Me puede ayudar, — me pwe·de a·yoo·dar
  por favor? — por fa·vor
Where are the toilets?
  ¿Dónde están los baños? — don·de es·tan los ba·nyos
I'm lost.
  Estoy perdido/a. — es·toy per·dee·do/a
I've been robbed.
  Me robaron. — me ro·ba·ron
Go away!
  ¡Déjeme! — de·khe·me
Get lost!
  ¡Váyase! — va·ya·se

Call ...!
  ¡Llame a ...! — ya·me a ...
  the police
  la policía — la po·lee·see·a
  a doctor
  un médico — oon me·dee·ko
  an ambulance
  una ambulancia — oo·na am·boo·lan·sya

I'm a vegetarian.
  Soy vegetariano/a. (m/f) — soy ve·khe·ta·rya·no/a
The menu/bill, please.
  La carta/cuenta, — la kar·ta/kwen·ta
  por favor. — por fa·vor
Is service included in the bill?
  ¿El servicio está — el ser·vee·syo es·ta
  incluido en la cuenta? — een·klwee·do en la kwen·ta
Thank you, that was delicious.
  Muchas gracias, estaba — moo·chas gra·syas es·ta·ba
  buenísimo. — bwe·nee·see·mo

breakfast	*desayuno*	de·sa·yoo·no
lunch	*almuerzo*	al·mwer·so
dinner	*cena*	se·na
(cheap)	*restaurante*	re·stow·ran·te
restaurant	*(barato)*	(ba·ra·to)
set meal	*el menú*	el me·noo

HEALTH

I'm sick.
  Estoy enfermo/a. — es·toy en·fer·mo/a
I need a doctor.
  Necesito un médico. — ne·se·see·to oon me·dee·ko

Where's the hospital?
  ¿Dónde está el hospital? — don·de es·ta el os·pee·tal
I'm pregnant.
  Estoy embarazada. — es·toy em·ba·ra·sa·da
I've been vaccinated.
  Estoy vacunado/a. — es·toy va·koo·na·do/a

I'm allergic to ...	*Soy alérgico/a a ...*	soy a·ler·khee·ko/a a ...
antibiotics	*los antibióticos*	los an·tee·byo·tee·kos
penicillin	*la penicilina*	la pe·nee·see·lee·na
peanuts	*los maníes*	los ma·nee·es

I'm ...	*Soy ...*	soy ...
asthmatic	*asmático/a*	as·ma·tee·ko/a
diabetic	*diabético/a*	dya·be·tee·ko/a
epileptic	*epiléptico/a*	e·pee·lep·tee·ko/a

I have ...	*Tengo ...*	ten·go ...
altitude sickness	*soroche*	so·ro·che
diarrhea	*diarrea*	dya·re·a
nausea	*náusea*	now·se·a
a headache	*un dolor de cabeza*	oon do·lor de ka·be·sa
a cough	*tos*	tos

LANGUAGE DIFFICULTIES

Do you speak (English)?
  ¿Habla/Hablas (inglés)? — a·bla/a·blas (een·gles) (pol/inf)
Does anyone here speak English?
  ¿Hay alguien que hable — ai al·gyen ke a·ble
  inglés? — een·gles
I (don't) understand.
  (No) Entiendo. — (no) en·tyen·do
How do you say ...?
  ¿Cómo se dice ...? — ko·mo se dee·se ...
What does ... mean?
  ¿Qué quiere decir ...? — ke kye·re de·seer ...

Could you please ...?	*¿Puede ..., por favor?*	pwe·de ... por fa·vor
repeat that	*repetirlo*	re·pe·teer·lo
speak more slowly	*hablar más despacio*	a·blar mas des·pa·syo
write it down	*escribirlo*	es·kree·beer·lo

NUMBERS

1	*uno*	oo·no
2	*dos*	dos
3	*tres*	tres
4	*cuatro*	kwa·tro

5	cinco	seen·ko
6	seis	says
7	siete	sye·te
8	ocho	o·cho
9	nueve	nwe·ve
10	diez	dyes
11	once	on·se
12	doce	do·se
13	trece	tre·se
14	catorce	ka·tor·se
15	quince	keen·se
16	dieciséis	dye·see·says
17	diecisiete	dye·see·sye·te
18	dieciocho	dye·see·o·cho
19	diecinueve	dye·see·nwe·ve
20	veinte	vayn·te
21	veintiuno	vayn·tee·oo·no
30	treinta	trayn·ta
31	treinta y uno	trayn·ta ee oo·no
40	cuarenta	kwa·ren·ta
50	cincuenta	seen·kwen·ta
60	sesenta	se·sen·ta
70	setenta	se·ten·ta
80	ochenta	o·chen·ta
90	noventa	no·ven·ta
100	cien	syen
101	ciento uno	syen·to oo·no
200	doscientos	do·syen·tos
1000	mil	meel
5000	cinco mil	seen·ko meel
10,000	diez mil	dyes meel
50,000	cincuenta mil	seen·kwen·ta meel
100,000	cien mil	syen meel
1,000,000	un millón	oon mee·yon

SHOPPING & SERVICES

I'd like to buy ...
Quisiera comprar ...   kee·sye·ra kom·prar ...

I'm just looking.
Sólo estoy mirando.   so·lo es·toy mee·ran·do

May I look at it?
¿Puedo mirar(lo/la)?   pwe·do mee·rar(·lo/la)

How much is it?
¿Cuánto cuesta?   kwan·to kwes·ta

That's too expensive for me.
Es demasiado caro   es de·ma·sya·do ka·ro
para mí.   pa·ra mee

Could you lower the price?
¿Podría bajar un poco   po·dree·a ba·khar oon po·ko
el precio?   el pre·syo

I don't like it.
No me gusta.   no me goos·ta

I'll take it.
Lo llevo.   lo ye·vo

Do you take ...?	¿Aceptan ...?	a·sep·tan ...
American dollars	dólares americanos	do·la·res a·me·ree·ka·nos
credit cards	tarjetas de crédito	tar·khe·tas de kre·dee·to
traveler's checks	cheques de viajero	che·kes de vya·khe·ro
small bills	billetes pequeñas	bee·ye·tes pe·ken·yas
less/more	menos/más	me·nos/mas
large	grande	gran·de
small	pequeño/a	pe·ke·nyo/a
I'm looking for (the) ...	Estoy buscando ...	es·toy boos·kan·do ...
ATM	el cajero automático	el ka·khe·ro ow·to·ma·tee·ko
bank	el banco	el ban·ko
bookstore	la librería	la lee·bre·ree·a
embassy	la embajada	la em·ba·kha·da
foreign exchange bureau	la casa de cambio	la ka·sa de kam·byo
general store	la tienda	la tyen·da
laundry	la lavandería	la la·van·de·ree·a
market	el mercado	el mer·ka·do
pharmacy/ chemist	la farmacia/ la botica	la far·ma·sya/ la bo·tee·ka
post office	el correo	el ko·re·o
tourist office	la oficina de turismo	la o·fee·see·na de too·rees·mo

What time does it open/close?
¿A qué hora abre/cierra?   a ke o·ra a·bre/sye·ra

I want to change some money/traveler's checks.
Quiero cambiar dinero/   kye·ro kam·byar dee·ne·ro/
cheques de viajero.   che·kes de vya·khe·ro

What is the exchange rate?
¿Cuál es el tipo   kwal es el tee·po
de cambio?   de kam·byo

I want to call ...
Quiero llamar a ...   kye·ro ya·mar a ...

airmail	correo aéreo	ko·re·o a·e·re·o
black market	mercado negro/ paralelo	mer·ka·do ne·gro/ pa·ra·le·lo
letter	carta	kar·ta
phonecard	tarjeta telefónica	tar·khe·ta te·le·fo·nee·ka
postcards	postales	pos·ta·les
poste restante	lista de correos	lee·sta de ko·re·os
registered (mail)	certificado	ser·tee·fee·ka·do
stamps	estampillas	es·tam·pee·yas

TIME & DATES

What time is it?	¿Qué hora es?	ke o·ra es
It's one o'clock.	Es la una.	es la oo·na
It's two o'clock.	Son las dos.	son las dos
midnight	medianoche	me·dya·no·che
noon	mediodía	me·dyo·dee·a
half past two	dos y media	dos ee me·dya
now	ahora	a·o·ra
today	hoy	oy
tonight	esta noche	es·ta no·che
tomorrow	mañana	ma·nya·na
yesterday	ayer	a·yer
Monday	lunes	loo·nes
Tuesday	martes	mar·tes
Wednesday	miércoles	myer·ko·les
Thursday	jueves	khwe·ves
Friday	viernes	vyer·nes
Saturday	sábado	sa·ba·do
Sunday	domingo	do·meen·go
January	enero	e·ne·ro
February	febrero	fe·bre·ro
March	marzo	mar·so
April	abril	a·breel
May	mayo	ma·yo
June	junio	khoo·nyo
July	julio	khool·yo
August	agosto	a·gos·to
September	septiembre	sep·tyem·bre
October	octubre	ok·too·bre
November	noviembre	no·vyem·bre
December	diciembre	dee·syem·bre

TRANSPORTATION

Public Transportation

What time does	¿A qué hora	a ke o·ra
... leave/arrive?	sale/llega ...?	sa·le/ye·ga ...
the bus	el autobus	el ow·to·boos
the plane	el avión	el a·vyon
the ship	el barco/buque	el bar·ko/boo·ke
the train	el tren	el tren
airport	el aeropuerto	el a·e·ro·pwer·to
train station	la estación de ferrocarril	la es·ta·syon de fe·ro·ka·reel
bus station	la estación de autobuses	la es·ta·syon de ow·to·boo·ses
bus stop	la parada de autobuses	la pa·ra·da de ow·to·boo·ses
luggage check room	guardería/ equipaje	gwar·de·ree·a/ e·kee·pa·khe
ticket office	la boletería	la bo·le·te·ree·a

I'd like a ticket to ...		
	Quiero un boleto a ...	kye·ro oon bo·le·to a ...
What's the fare to ...?		
	¿Cuánto cuesta hasta ...?	kwan·to kwes·ta a·sta ...
student's	de estudiante	de es·too·dyan·te
1st class	primera clase	pree·me·ra kla·se
2nd class	segunda clase	se·goon·da kla·se
single/one-way	ida	ee·da
return/round trip	ida y vuelta	ee·da ee vwel·ta
taxi	taxi	tak·see

Private Transportation

I'd like to hire ...	Quisiera alquilar ...	kee·sye·ra al·kee·lar ...
a 4WD	un todo terreno	oon to·do te·re·no
a bicycle	una bicicleta	oo·na bee·see·kle·ta
a car	un auto	oon ow·to
a motorbike	una moto	oo·na mo·to
pickup (truck)	camioneta	ka·myo·ne·ta
truck	camión	ka·myon
hitchhike	hacer dedo	a·ser de·do
diesel	diesel	dee·sel
gas (petrol)	gasolina	ga·so·lee·na

Where's a gas station?		
	¿Dónde hay una gasolinera/un grifo?	don·de ai oo·na ga·so·lee·ne·ra/oon gree·fo
Please fill it up.		
	Lleno, por favor.	ye·no por fa·vor
I'd like (20) liters.		
	Quiero (veinte) litros.	kye·ro (vayn·te) lee·tros
Is this the road to ...?		
	¿Se va a ... por esta carretera?	se va a ... por es·ta ka·re·te·ra
(How long) Can I park here?		
	¿(Por cuánto tiempo) Puedo aparcar aquí?	(por kwan·to tyem·po) pwe·do a·par·kar a·kee
Where do I pay?		
	¿Dónde se paga?	don·de se pa·ga
I need a mechanic.		
	Necesito un mecánico.	ne·se·see·to oon me·ka·nee·ko
The car has broken down (in ...).		
	El carro se ha averiado (en ...).	el ka·ro se a a·ve·rya·do (en ...)
The motorbike won't start.		
	No arranca la moto.	no a·ran·ka la mo·to
I have a flat tire.		
	Tengo un pinchazo.	ten·go oon peen·cha·so

LANGUAGE

I've run out of gas.
Me quedé sin gasolina. me ke-*de* seen ga-so-*lee*-na
I've had an accident.
Tuve un accidente. *too*-ve oon ak-see-*den*-te

AYMARA & QUECHUA

The few Aymara and Quechua words and phrases included here will be useful for those travelling in the Andes. Aymara is spoken by the Aymara people, who inhabit the area around Lake Titicaca. While the Quechua included here is from the Cuzco dialect, it should prove helpful wherever you travel in the highlands too.

In the following lists, Aymara is the first entry, Quechua the second. The principles of pronunciation for both languages are similar to those found in Spanish (see the Spanish pronunciation guide, p551). An apostrophe (') represents a glottal stop, which is the 'nonsound' that occurs in the middle of 'uh-oh.'

Hello.
Kamisaraki. *Napaykullayki.*
Please.
Mirá. *Allichu.*
Thank you.
Yuspagara. *Yusulipayki.*

Yes.
Jisa. *Ari.*
No.
Janiwa. *Mana.*
How do you say …?
Cun sañasauca'ha …? *Imainata nincha chaita …?*
It is called …
Ucan sutipa'h … *Chaipa'g sutin'ha …*
Please repeat.
Uastata sita. *Ua'manta niway.*
How much?
K'gauka? *Maik'ata'g?*

father	auqui	tayta
food	manka	mikiuy
mother	taica	mama
river	jawira	mayu
snowy peak	kollu	riti-orko
water	uma	yacu

1	maya	u'
2	paya	iskai
3	quimsa	quinsa
4	pusi	tahua
5	pesca	phiska
6	zo'hta	so'gta
7	pakalko	khanchis
8	quimsakalko	pusa'g
9	yatunca	iskon
10	tunca	chunca

LANGUAGE

Also available from Lonely Planet:
Latin American Spanish phrasebook and
Quechua phrasebook

Glossary

See p63 for useful words and phrases about cooking and cuisine. See p551 for more useful words and phrases.

albergue – family-owned inn
altiplano – literally, a high plateau or plain; specifically, it refers to the vast, desolate Andean flatlands of southern Peru, Bolivia, northern Chile and northern Argentina
aluvión – fast-moving flood of ice, water, rocks, mud and debris caused by an earthquake or the bursting of a dam in a mountainous region
apu – mountain deity
arequipeño – inhabitant of Arequipa
arriero – animal driver, usually of *burros* or *mulas* (mules)
avenida – avenue (abbreviated Av)
ayahuasca – potent hallucinogenic brew made from jungle vines and used by shamans and traditional healers

barrio – neighborhood
bodega – winery, wine shop, wine cellar or tasting bar
boleto turístico – tourism ticket
bruja/brujo – shaman, witch doctor, or medicine woman or man
burro – donkey
bus-cama – long-distance, double-decker buses with seats reclining almost into beds; toilets, videos and snacks are provided on board

caballito – high-ended, cigar-shaped boat; found near Huanchaco
calle – street
campesino – peasant, farmer or rural inhabitant
cañón – canyon
carretera – highway
casa – home, house
casa de cambio – foreign-exchange bureau
cerro – hill, mountain
chullpa – ancient Andean burial tower, found around Lake Titicaca
cocha – lake, from the indigenous Quechua language; often appended to many lake names, eg Conococha
colectivo – shared transportation; usually taxis, but sometimes minibuses, minivans or even boats
combi – minivan or minibus (usually with tiny seats, cramming in as many passengers as possible)
cordillera – mountain chain

criolla/criollo – Creole or native of Peru; also applies to coastal Peruvians, music and dance; *criollo* food refers to spicy Peruvian fare with Spanish, Asian and African influences
cuadra – city block
curandera/curandero – traditional healer
cuzqueño – inhabitant of Cuzco (also spelled Cusco or Qosq'o)

escuela cuzqueña – Cuzco school; colonial art movement that combined Spanish and Andean artistic styles

feria – street market with vendor booths

garúa – coastal fog, mist or drizzle
grifo – gas (petrol) station
gringa/gringo – generally refers to all foreigners who are not from South or Central America and Mexico
guanaco – large, wild camelid that ranges throughout South America, now an endangered species in Peru

hospedaje – small, family-owned inn
hostal – guesthouse, smaller than a hotel and with fewer amenities
huaca – sacred pyramid, temple or burial site
huaquero – grave robber
huayno – traditional Andean music using instrumentation with roots in pre-Columbian times

iglesia – church
inca – king
indígena – indigenous person (male or female)
Inrena – Insituto Nacional de Recursos Naturales (National Institute for Natural Resources); government agency that administers national parks, reserves, historical sanctuaries and other protected areas
Inti – ancient Peruvian sun god; husband of the earth goddess Pachamama
isla – island, isle

jirón – road (abbreviated Jr)

lavandería – laundry
limeño – inhabitant of Lima
locutorio – calling center

marinera – a typical coastal Peruvian dance involving the flirtatious waving of handkerchiefs
mestizo – person of mixed indigenous and Spanish descent
micro – a small bus used as public transport
mirador – watchtower, observatory, viewpoint

mototaxi – three-wheeled motorcycle rickshaw taxi; also called *motocarro* or *taximoto*

museo – museum

nevado – glaciated or snow-covered mountain peak

nuevo sol – the national currency of Peru

oficina de migraciónes – immigration office

Pachamama – ancient Peruvian earth goddess; wife of the sun god Inti

pampa – large, flat area, usually of grasslands

Panamericana – Pan-American Highway (aka Interamericana); main route joining Latin American countries

parque – park

peña – bar or club featuring live folkloric music

playa – beach

pongo – narrow, steep-walled, rocky, jungle river canyon that can be a dangerous maelstrom during high water

pueblo – town, village

puna – high Andean grasslands of the *altiplano*

puya – spiky-leafed plant of the bromeliad family

quebrada – literally, a break; often refers to a steep ravine or gulch

quero – ceremonial Inca wooden drinking vessel

río – river

selva – jungle, tropical rainforest

sillar – off-white volcanic rock, often used for buildings around Arequipa

soroche – altitude sickness

taximoto – see *mototaxi*

terminal terrestre – bus station

totora – reed of the papyrus family; used to build the 'floating islands' and traditional boats of Lake Titicaca

turismo vivencial – homestay tourism

vals peruano – Peruvian waltz, an upbeat, guitar-driven waltz played and danced to in coastal areas

vicuña – threatened wild relative of the alpaca; smallest living member of the camelid family

The Authors

CAROLINA A MIRANDA
Coordinating Author, Lima

Born of a Peruvian father from Chiclayo (an area – FYI – that has a reputation for producing very fierce people), Carolina has spent her life making regular sojourns to Peru to kiss her aunts, wrestle her cousins and eat as much ceviche as is humanly possible. When not experimenting with pisco sour ratios (three parts pisco, one part lime juice, simple syrup to taste), she makes her living as a freelance writer in New York City. She has contributed stories to *Time, Budget Travel, Travel + Leisure* and public radio station WNYC – and is the author of the uncouth and saucy arts blog *C-Monster.net*.

AIMÉE DOWL
**North Coast, Huaraz &
the Cordilleras, Northern Highlands**

Whether spotting condors in the *páramo* (high-altitude Andean grasslands) or chasing hummingbirds in the cloud forest, prancing around glaciers or trekking up jungle volcanoes, Aimée feels right at home in the high altitudes and ancient cultures of the Andes. Holding no hard feelings toward destinations at sea level, however, she also finds that the Peruvian Amazon is one her favorite places on earth. Aimée lives at a cool 2850m in Quito, Ecuador, where she is a freelance travel and culture writer, and has worked as a secondary educator. Her work has appeared in the *New York Times, Viajes, Ms.* magazine, *BBC History* and four Lonely Planet books.

KATY SHORTHOUSE
Lake Titicaca, Cuzco & the Sacred Valley

Katy's career highlights include walking the Inca Trail 13 times and Australia's Overland Track seven times, guiding multisport tours in Ecuador and Patagonia, and running an adventure business in New Zealand. Lowlights include writing junk mail, telemarketing and cleaning toilets. Katy aspires to travel but she keeps stopping and putting down roots, with the result that she now divides her time between Peru, New Zealand and Australia (and lives in dread of finding somewhere else she likes). If you know of a place that combines Melbourne's culture, Cuzco's food and fiestas, and the multisport hills of Queenstown, please let her know via www.aspiringadventures.com or drop in to her bar in Cuzco, La Chupitería.

LONELY PLANET AUTHORS

Why is our travel information the best in the world? It's simple: our authors are passionate, dedicated travelers. They don't take freebies in exchange for positive coverage so you can be sure the advice you're given is impartial. They travel widely to all the popular spots, and off the beaten track. They don't research using just the internet or phone. They discover new places not included in any other guidebook. They personally visit thousands of hotels, restaurants, palaces, trails, galleries, temples and more. They speak with dozens of locals every day to make sure you get the kind of insider knowledge only a local could tell you. They take pride in getting all the details right, and in telling it how it is. Think you can do it? Find out how at **lonelyplanet.com**.

LUKE WATERSON
Central Highlands, Amazon Basin
Raised in the remote Somerset countryside in southwest England, Luke quickly became addicted to exploring out-of-the-way places. Having completed a creative-writing degree at the University of East Anglia in Norwich, he shouldered his backpack and vowed to see as much of the world as was humanly possible. He has spent almost two years backpacking South America and writes for various publications including the *Guardian*. When not wolfing down a plate of *lomo saltado* (strips of beef stir-fried with onions, tomatoes, potatoes and chili) or hiking through the Andes, he can be found living on a rather smaller hill outside London, concocting further travel plans.

BETH WILLIAMS
South Coast, Arequipa & Canyon Country
While earning a degree in Latin American studies, Beth spent summers traveling and serving pisco sours at a Peruvian restaurant in her hometown of Portland, Oregon, in the USA. She then followed an interest in women's health to a village nestled at 3000m in the Peruvian Andes. There she spent a year building 'vertical' birthing facilities for Quechua women to give birth in the traditional fashion – standing up. Beth then retreated to sea level to work for a Peruvian nonprofit in the slums of Lima, during which time she added four stamps to her passport and traveled the Peruvian Pan-American Hwy at least five times. What's next? A master's at New York's Columbia University.

CONTRIBUTING AUTHORS
Dr David Goldberg MD wrote the Health chapter. David completed his training in internal medicine and infectious diseases at Columbia-Presbyterian Medical Center in New York City, where he has also served as voluntary faculty. At present he is an infectious-diseases specialist in Scarsdale, New York State, and the editor-in-chief of the website MDTravelHealth.com.

Behind the Scenes

THIS BOOK

This is the 7th edition of *Peru*. Carolina A Miranda served as coordinating author, writing all of the front and back chapters as well as researching and writing the Lima chapter. Aimée Dowl researched and wrote the North Coast, Huaraz & the Cordilleras and Northern Highlands chapters. Katy Shorthouse researched and wrote the Lake Titicaca and Cuzco & the Sacred Valley chapters. Luke Waterson researched and wrote the Central Highlands and Amazon Basin chapters, and Beth Williams researched and wrote the South Coast and Arequipa & Canyon Country chapters. Dr David Goldberg MD contributed the Health chapter. The 6th edition was written by Sara Benson, Paul Hellander, Carolina A Miranda and Rafael Wlodarski. This guidebook was commissioned in Lonely Planet's Oakland office, and produced by the following:

Commissioning Editor Kathleen Munnelly
Coordinating Editor Penelope Goodes
Coordinating Cartographers Joelene Kowalski, Andy Rojas
Coordinating Layout Designer Aomi Hongo
Managing Editor Laura Stansfeld
Managing Cartographers Shahara Ahmed, Alison Lyall
Managing Layout Designer Sally Darmody
Assisting Editors Kate Evans, Melissa Faulkner, Helen Koehne, Anne Mulvaney, Sally O'Brien

Assisting Cartographers Mark Griffiths, Chris Love, Joanne Luke, Jolyon Philcox, Andrew Smith
Cover Naomi Parker, lonelyplanetimages.com
Internal image research Sabrina Dalbesio, lonelyplanetimages.com
Project Manager Anna Metcalfe
Language Content Laura Crawford

Thanks to Lucy Birchley, Helen Christinis, Chris Girdler, Indra Kilfoyle, Ali Lemer, Robyn Loughnane, Wayne Murphy, Raphael Richards, Saralinda Turner, Branislava Vladisavljevic

THANKS
CAROLINA A MIRANDA

To the readers who submitted tips on divine ceviche, to the friends who shared their secret eats, to the Lonely Planet team – especially Kathleen Munnelly! – and to this guide's writers, who endured my endless emails: you kick ass. Special *gracias* to Elvira Miranda Arbulú, for making me *anguitas* when my belly hurt; Arturo Rojas and Vera Lauer, for foodie wisdom; Camille Ulmer at SAE, for so many tips; Howard Chua-Eoan, for sharing his tasting notes; Robin Cembalest, for the library; Rosa Lowinger, for being Rosa; the Miranda Silvas, for being great cooks. Bear hugs to Ed Tahaney, who tolerates my wandering. For Felipe, who woulda been proud of this book.

THE LONELY PLANET STORY

Fresh from an epic journey across Europe, Asia and Australia in 1972, Tony and Maureen Wheeler sat at their kitchen table stapling together notes. The first Lonely Planet guidebook, *Across Asia on the Cheap,* was born.

Travelers snapped up the guides. Inspired by their success, the Wheelers began publishing books to Southeast Asia, India and beyond. Demand was prodigious, and the Wheelers expanded the business rapidly to keep up. Over the years, Lonely Planet extended its coverage to every country and into the virtual world via lonelyplanet.com and the Thorn Tree message board.

As Lonely Planet became a globally loved brand, Tony and Maureen received several offers for the company. But it wasn't until 2007 that they found a partner whom they trusted to remain true to the company's principles of traveling widely, treading lightly and giving sustainably. In October of that year, BBC Worldwide acquired a 75% share in the company, pledging to uphold Lonely Planet's commitment to independent travel, trustworthy advice and editorial independence.

Today, Lonely Planet has offices in Melbourne, London and Oakland, with over 500 staff members and 300 authors. Tony and Maureen are still actively involved with Lonely Planet. They're traveling more often than ever, and they're devoting their spare time to charitable projects. And the company is still driven by the philosophy of *Across Asia on the Cheap*: 'All you've got to do is decide to go and the hardest part is over. So go!'

AIMÉE DOWL

Now on my third guide, I must offer my headlining thanks to Kathleen Munnelly, who makes these long-haul projects sweeter and lighter. Second only is Carolina Miranda, our team's supportive, ever-Peru-loving coordinating author. In Huaraz, Chris Benway and Diana Morris kept me in the know, as did Fidel, Vanessa and Turismo Explorer in Chachapoyas. In Lima the crew at South American Explorers and Inka Frog are the best friends a Lonely Planet author could have. As ever, the strongest appreciation is reserved for last, for my dear friend and partner, Derek Kverno, whose patience is unbounded, whether looking for the Marvelous Spatuletail or waiting for me to finally come home.

KATY SHORTHOUSE

In Cuzco: Paul Cripps, Dougie Stewart, Robyn Quintana, Juan Ccama Arias, Rocsana Soto, Fernando Astete, Paolo Greer and Klever Marca Coronel. In Puno: Juan Salamanca de Dircetur, Angel Canales, Briseida Paoro Pino, Ulises Mamani Apaza, y Nancy *en el terminal, ¡por el mapa! Los que me hacen querer vivir aquí*: Vane, Lucho, Manu, Arturo, Crisanto, Claire, Fiona, Ximena, Sally, Yohn, Monica, Maka y Cynthia. Kerryn; all the Kathies, boys and Melissa. Yve, Lu, Sal, Liz, Anna, Mum, Dad, Dom and Carrie. Colleen, and inspirational walking ladies. Ned Myopus, the Brownedy-Hemingway clan, and all chunky seagulls. Paul, for being lovely. Jarrod, wish you were here. Andrew, Steve, Kelly, Phil, for teaching me everything I know.

LUKE WATERSON

A book could be filled with everyone that deserves a mention here. A special *muchas gracias* to Marianne Van Vlaardingen of Pantiacolla Tours for her advice on Manu, to Gerson Medina for ferrying me around the Río Tambopata and yet again to Huancayo's ever-informative Lucho Hurtado. In Ayacucho I'm indebted to Txema and Zigi; in Iquitos to Marcel Bendayan and Bill Grimes; and in Pevas to Francisco Grippa. Thanks also to Cath Lanigan, to my fellow authors, to Kathleen Munnelly and the rest of the Lonely Planet team. Finally, thanks to Poppy, the best muse any author could wish for.

BETH WILLIAMS

A special thanks to Edwin Junco Cabrera of Pablo Tour, Vlado Soto of Colca Trek and Manuel Zuñiga Cheáux, three sources of incomparable knowledge about Arequipa and all the region has to offer. Thanks to my parents, to whom I owe my wandering spirit and route-finding ability. I also could not have done it without the moral support and encouragement of Beto Arambulo Vinatea and Alison Koler. Lastly, thanks to the entire Lonely Planet crew, my fellow authors, and all those who contributed bits and pieces along the way.

OUR READERS

Many thanks to the travelers who used the last edition and wrote to us with helpful hints, useful advice and interesting anecdotes:

A Nelleke Aben, Kylee Abrahamson, Kate Adlam, Rian Adrichem, Mustafa Akcay, Nick Aldridge, Isabel Allen, Debbie Amos, Edwin Anarcaya Roca, Sidsel Angelo-Pérez, Anonymous Anon, Suzie Anon Y Garcia, Pete Appleyard, Sarah Arblaster, Daniel Armyr, Johnny Atkin, Christian Avila **B** Stelios Bafaloukos, Ian Baker, Elizabeth Ballon, Paul Bamford, Barbara Bansemer, Ryan Barber, Gary Barberan, Jared Barnes, Russ Barnes, Alejandro Barrios, Marlene Beard, Sebastien Beauchamps, Lucy Beaumont, Alex Beesley, Rinat Ben Avraham, Yolanda Benavente Carla, Kaja Beton, Matthew Bianchi, Sandra Bickel, Arjan Biemond, Ulrik Bjerre Holm, Maree Blackburn, Jane Blackmore, Joanna Blint, Arris Blom, Jozanne Bolduc, Siegfried Bolek, Anika Bolle, Julie Booth, Rikard Borjesson, Todd Born, Joyce Bosman, Raf Bossaerts, Miranda Böttcher, Babs Boumans, Grégory Boyer, James Bradley, Edmund Breen, Louis Brescia, Krista Brewer, Joseph Bright, Benjamin Brooking, Chelsea Brothers, Caroline Brouwer, Bianca Brouwer, Mink Bruijninckx, Van Eerdenbrugh Bruno, Mirka Bulinova, Neil Bulman-Fleming, Erin Burger, Ondrej Burkert, James Burn, Ron Buttenshaw, Tammie Buxton, Allegra Buyer, Inge Bynens **C** Christian Caceres, Lincoln Calixto, Paul Callcutt, Jesse Calm, Caroline Lodging Huaraz Peru Caroline Lodging Huaraz Peru, Fabrizio Castillo, Saul Ceron, Alex Chaikin, Paul Chamberlain, Enoch Chang, Linda Chesnut, Fermin Chimatani Tayori, Karen Chiu, Louise Choquette, Janey Christoffersen, Angle Cina, Chantal Cirusse, Matt Clapp, Acacia Clark, Acacia Clark, Bryan Clark, Liz Clasen, Michele Cloghesy, Maggie And John Coaton, Simon Cole, Jared Collingwood, Elmer Conde Mescco, Chiara Conrado, Patricio Corzo, Helena Costa, Lydia Costello, Brian Coulter, Cynthia Cox, Craig, Benjamin Craigen, Martha Croft, Joel Cross, Marion Curry **D** Maggie D'Aversa, Catherine Dagenais, Gunder Dahl, Jan Dale, Anthea Dare, Richard Davies, John Davies, Robyn Davis, Ruud De Dood, Sanna De Graaff, Johan De Ridder, Kirk Dearden, Erika Debenedictis, Jeff Deblieu, Inge Deeks, Angela Defelice, Jane Dent, Sharon Depauw, Jane Desborough, Valerie Destrooper, Sonia Dewhurst, Dana Diamant, Andrew Dier, Rene Dimetman, Shelly Dolev, Susie Donaldson, Leitner Doris & Markus, Janine Dorschu, Colin Dow, Tamia And Rowshan Dowlatabadi, Justin Downer, Caroline Driver, Pierre Duboux, Aisling Duff **E** Andrea Edelmueller, Sinead Edney, Ariadna I Eduard, John Edwards, John Elliott, Lars Emonts, Donna Englund Pacho, Monica Esgueva, Elizabeth Essex, Mervyn Evans, Anton Evers, Ann Evers **F** Daniel Farber, Tom Farr, Alexandra Farr, Mathieu Faucher, Joshua Faulkner, Parel Feddema, Joos Feenstra, Jordyn

BEHIND THE SCENES

Feiger, Diane Ferchel, Inga Ferm, Margot Fernandez, Denise Fernandez Mendez, Louis Ferrand, Matthew Fielding, Luca Finotti, Frauke Finster, Khaliah Fleming, Julio Flores, David Ford, Robert Forstag, Valerie Frey, Charlotte Frey, Martina Freyenmuth, Jessica Friedman, Richard From **G** Luciano Gallotti, Lourdes Galvez, Rafael Garay, Romina Gatti, Judy Gayne, Breeze Geier, Herbert Geiges, Heather Gelmi, Sven Gentner, Marie-Amelie George, Milton Gerverdinck, Helene Giacometti, Linda Glenn, Michelle Godwin, Dawn Gold, Erica Gomez, Angel Gonzales, Michelle Graham, Abby Grayzel, Michaela Grill, Eric Gritz, Walter Grossenbacher, Vladimir Gudilin, Thiago Guedes, Ayre Gysella **H** Tim Hadlow, Samuel Hagler, Kathie Hagwell, Tamsin Hannah, Isabelle Harbrecht, Abigail Harper, Paul Harries, Jason Harris, Justin Harris, Matt Harrison, David Harrison, Bill Hatfield, Frauke Heesing, Sofie Hendrikx, Laura Henning, Peter Herd, Sharon Herkes, Lyle Herman, Joel Hextall, Alex Higgins, Brent Hill, Stuart Holder, Layton Holsinger, Terry Hoops, Frederic Horta, Joanne Houck, Diandra Howard, Gretta Howard, Grace Huang, Alicia Huarca, Marc Huckle, Edward Hudson, Osmar Huidobro, Whitney Huston, Ann Huston, Kay Hutchings, Ortwin Hutten **I** Marco Ianniruberto, Natalie Imrisek, Mike Isbister, Marni And Nathan Ison, Karen Itow **J** Kim Jae Moon, Cameron James, Lisa Jean, Andrea Johnson, Tobin Jones, Lora Jones, Matyj Jones **K** Ellen Kahan, Markus Kaim, William Kaiser, Alicia Kamm, Christian Kanne, Bernhard Karshagen, Margriet Katoen, Melissa Katzman, Kathleen Keefe, Jessica Kelso, Aud Kennedy, Paul Kennedy, Arlene Kerr, Sjaan Kerr, Andrew Kersten, Heather Keys, Markus Kielkopf, Jo Kilner, Justine Kirby, Meghan Kizulk, Kathleen Klein, Lisa Knappich, Angela Kociolek, Robert Kolek, Heath Kondro, Kristy And Lane Krahl, Johanna Kramer, Egor Krementsov, Jay Krishnan, Clarice Kuhling, John Kulczycki, Hannah Davina Küßner **L** Chris Labozzetta, Tom Lambers, Roberto Lamonica, Jerome Landry, Jennifer Landry, Sarah Lane, Nina Lange, Jack Last, Sivy Laura, Cedric Laval, Niamh Lawlor, Teresa Lee, Bert Leffers, Dave Lehmann, Richard Leon, Julien Leroy, Clifford Lewis, Sabrina Libralon, Zach Linder, Morgan Lloyd, Bethan Lloyd Lewis, René Loli Alva, Isabelle Long, Ben Lough, Cinzia Luce, Sam Lüscher, Aidan Lynn-Klimenko **M** Thomas Mace, Eduardo Machuca, Tony Madsen, Catherine Mahoney, Jason Malinowski, René Mally, Veronica Mamani, Ellen Mannion, Annemieke Maquiné, Elizabeth Marden, Nikolas Marggraf, Janan Markee, Debs Marriage, Marie-Pierre Martel, Hamish Martin, Debby Matheny, Diana Matt, Midori McDaniel, Matthew McGuffin, Line McKein, Penny McMullin, Kristel Meijers, Mindy Melemed, Liv Mertens, Michele Micheli, Jane Miller, Jamie Miller, Anouk Minnebach, Rahel Minola, Jenny Miro Quesada, Lindsey Mitchell, James Mohler, Loana Monetta, Nicolas Mongilardi, Anamaria Montealegre, Walter Montorsi, Lauren Moore, Shaun Morris, Andy Morrison, Graeme Mount, Andrea Mueller, Rafael Mukmenov, Katrina Munir, Aideen Murphy, Harold Murphy, Jessica Murray, Lesley Myburgh **N** Farid Naepflin, Elciario Naranjo, Megan Nedzinski, Matthew Neuner, Seagan Ngai, Jo Nicel, Mette Bech Nielsen, Niki Niens, Jan Tijs Nijssen, Irene Noceti, Elisha Novak, Marco Nueesch **O** Rebecca O'Donovan, Lyndsey O Connell, Louise Obermayer, Louis-Phillppe Ostiguy, Roberto Otárola, Yunus Emre Ozigci **P** Marea Palmer-Loh, Jacinta Pam, Max Parknas, Supaya Pasbo, Nestor Paz, Henry Pederse Tor, Montse Pejuan, Drew Pekarek, Matt Pepe, Adelio Pornes, Chistian Peters, Michael Peters, John Pether, Nicky Phillips, Cuong Pho, Paul Piales, Vanessa Pilares, Laura Pinar Pesquera, Rochelle Pincini, Carisa Piraino, Vikki Playforth, Jack Plotkin, Kate Plyler, Andrea Poehner-Manger, Christa Polkinhorn, Stephanie Pool, Maria Ester Porta **R** Carol Radford, Stephen Radnedge, Peter Raeside, Guy Raven, Henry Raymond, Richard Reid, Lex Reis, Maria Reyes, Sarah Rhodes, Isabel Ribe, Christoph Richter, Ariana Rickard, Graciela Rios, William Ritchie, Kim Ritter, Elliot Roberts, William Robertson, Angelika Robillard, Frederick Robinson, Paul Robinson, Allan Roed, Rik Roelofs, Anna Roffey, Willi Rögels, Hilary Rollen, Agustina Romero, Paul Rondeau, Gustavo Rosas, Alyssa Rosemartin, Andrew Rosenblatt, Alejandro Rubio, Javier Ruiz, Jens Ruprecht, Kathrin Russell, Priska Rutishauser **S** Anu S, Aurora Salazar, Aurora Salazar, Claire Salisbury, Vicki Salkin, Emile Salkind, Mathilde Salmon, Ricardo Sanchez Uychoco, Hilary Sanders, Adolfo Sanguinetti, Tal Sapir, Nicole Schierberl, Marta Schlemayer, Natasja Schlicht, Tobias Schmid, Angela Schmitzberger, Nina Schroeder, Theodore Scott, Alexander Semenov, Nitzan Shadmi, Yaron Shaposhnik, Akbar Sharfi, Shariff Baker, Stephen Shaw, Tassos Shialis, Mairlou Siau, Betty Siemaszko, Timothy Silvers, Sheree Silvey, Izidora Skracic, Anna Smith, Darren Smith, Ariel Smith, Bret Snape, Robert Sommers, William Song, Joceline Sosa, Finn Speijer, Kelly Spencer, Donny Spoel, Eva Spunkt, S J Srinivas, Gunnar Staniczek, Cherry Steyn, Sarah Strachan, Alessio Strada, Charlie Strader, Clem Strain, David Strathy, Anna Strub, Liz Struble, Kim Strudwick, Timm Stuetz, Martin Stump, Sandman Sudamerika, Tom Sukanen, Elisabeth Summers, Susan D Fry Susan D Fry, Elizabeth Susman, Helga Svendsen, Paulina Szewczyk **T** Anthony Taieb, Laura Takacs,

Esteban Tamayo, Amandine Tatry, Maryann Taylor, Paul Taylor, Lars Tebruegge, Renee Teernstra, Filiz Telek, Uwe Thiel, Lieve Thienpont, Rachel Thomas, Michael Thomas, David Thompson, Richard Thorpe, Tom Thulin, Ria & Karlijn Tibbe, Peter Tipping, Melissa Tola, Annelies And Sjoerd Ton And Hartman, Vannesa Tong, Joey Tonis, Laura Torres, Joan Tripp, Jacopo Truzzi, Patricia Tuck-Lee, John Tuckwell, Liz Turner, Jon Tydeman **U** Takehiro Uno **V** Lydia Van De Fliert, Leander Van De Visse, Noortje Van Den Berg, Marc Van Der Heijde, Roy Van Der Meys, Eveline Van Drielen, Katia Van Eeckhoudt, Wilko Van Erp, Marc Van Lierop, Monique Van Meegeren, Arie Van Oosterwijk, Maarten Van Vliet, Christophe Vandendries, Vaidya Venkateswaran, Maria Laura Vergara, Sally Vernon, Kathryn Victor, Victor Vignale, Constanze Voelkel-Hutchison, Martin Von Hohnhorst, Marieke Vrolix **W** Emily Walker, Barry Walker, Paul Ward, Kathryn Elizabeth Ward, Paul Ward, Charly Warren, Ray Warren, Edith Watson, Leejo Weldontaylor, Thomas Weller, Anna-Julia Welsch, Sherri Wendorff, Anne Werfl, David Westenberg, Tony White, Jennifer White, Lisa Whitworth, Carsten Wiuff, Van Wong, Sarah Wood, Beth Woolley, Beat Wuersch, Victoria Wymark **Y** Benny And Yael Yalon, Peter Young, Johanna Yuen **Z** Yvonne Zbinden, Josef Zeyer, Mihael Znidersic, Teja Hlacer, Abigail Zoltie, Jullie Zotou, Jean Zuber, Mauricio Zylberman

ACKNOWLEDGMENTS

Many thanks to the following for the use of their content:

Globe on title page ©Mountain High Maps 1993 Digital Wisdom, Inc.

Index

000 Map pages
000 Photograph pages

INDEX

INDEX

000 Map pages
000 Photograph pages

000 Map pages
000 Photograph pages

INDEX

GreenDex

It seems like everyone's going 'green' these days, but it can sometimes be difficult to tell who is truly sustainable. The following sights, tour operators, accommodations, shops and restaurants have all been chosen because they meet our criteria for sustainable tourism: either because of sound environmental practices or because they promote local tradition and otherwise support community development at a grassroots level.

For tips on responsible trekking, see the boxed text on p394. For up-to-date information on how to pick an Inca Trail operator that treats its porters ethically, see p286. For a comprehensive listing of Peru's national parks and wilderness areas, see p74.

We want to keep developing our sustainable-travel content. If you think we've omitted someone who should be listed here, or if you disagree with our choices, contact us at www.lonelyplanet .com/contact. For more information about sustainable tourism and Lonely Planet, see www .lonelyplanet.com/responsibletravel.

GREENDEX

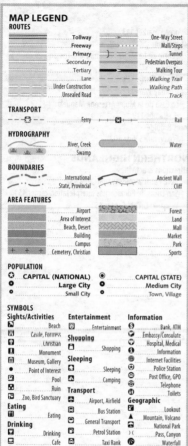

MAP LEGEND

ROUTES

Tollway
Freeway
Primary
Secondary
Tertiary
Lane
Under Construction
Unsealed Road
One-Way Street
Mall/Steps
Tunnel
Pedestrian Overpass
Walking Tour
Walking Trail
Walking Path
Track

TRANSPORT

Ferry
Rail

HYDROGRAPHY

River, Creek
Swamp
Water

BOUNDARIES

International
State, Provincial
Ancient Wall
Cliff

AREA FEATURES

Airport
Area of Interest
Beach, Desert
Building
Campus
Cemetery, Christian
Forest
Land
Mall
Market
Park
Sports

POPULATION

⊛ CAPITAL (NATIONAL)
⊙ CAPITAL (STATE)
● Large City
● Medium City
● Small City
● Town, Village

SYMBOLS

Sights/Activities
Beach
Castle, Fortress
Christian
Monument
Museum, Gallery
Point of Interest
Pool
Ruin
Zoo, Bird Sanctuary

Eating
Eating

Drinking
Drinking
Cafe

Entertainment
Entertainment

Shopping
Shopping

Sleeping
Sleeping
Camping

Transport
Airport, Airfield
Bus Station
General Transport
Petrol Station
Taxi Rank

Information
Bank, ATM
Embassy/Consulate
Hospital, Medical
Information
Internet Facilities
Police Station
Post Office, GPO
Telephone
Toilets

Geographic
Lookout
Mountain, Volcano
National Park
Pass, Canyon
Waterfall

LONELY PLANET OFFICES

Australia (Head Office)
Locked Bag 1, Footscray, Victoria 3011
☎ 03 8379 8000, fax 03 8379 8111
talk2us@lonelyplanet.com.au

USA
150 Linden St, Oakland, CA 94607
☎ 510 250 6400, toll free 800 275 8555
fax 510 893 8572
info@lonelyplanet.com

UK
2nd fl, 186 City Rd,
London EC1V 2NT
☎ 020 7106 2100, fax 020 7106 2101
go@lonelyplanet.co.uk

Published by Lonely Planet
ABN 36 005 607 983

© Lonely Planet 2010

© photographers as indicated 2010

Cover photograph: Inca ruins of Machu Picchu, Design Pics Inc/Photo library. Many of the images in this guide are available for licensing from Lonely Planet Images: lonelyplanetimages.com.

Printed by Hang Tai Printing Company, Hong Kong
Printed in China

Mixed Sources
Product group from well-managed forests and other controlled sources
www.fsc.org Cert no. SGS-COC-005002
© 1996 Forest Stewardship Council
FSC